W. E. B. GRIFFIN

Three Complete Novels

Also By W. E. B. Griffin

BROTHERHOOD OF WAR

Book I: The Lieutenants
Book II: The Captains
Book III: The Majors
Book IV: The Colonels
Book V: The Berets
Book VI: The Generals
Book VII: The New Breed
Book VIII: The Aviators

THE CORPS

Book IV: Battleground
Book V: Line of Fire
Book VI: Close Combat

BADGE OF HONOR

Book I: Men in Blue
Book II: Special Operations
Book III: The Victim
Book IV: The Witness
Book V: The Assassin

Honor Bound

W.E.B. GRIFFIN

THREE COMPLETE NOVELS

THE CORPS:

SEMPER FI
CALL TO ARMS
COUNTERATTACK

G. P. PUTNAM'S SONS NEW YORK

G. P. Putnam's Sons
Publishers Since 1838
200 Madison Avenue
New York, NY 10016

Map illustration by Lisa Amoroso

Published simultaneously in Canada

Library of Congress Cataloging-in-Publication Data

Griffin, W. E. B.
[Selections. 1994]
Three complete novels / W.E.B. Griffin
p. cm.
Contents: Semper fi—Call to arms—Counterattack.
ISBN 0-399-13913-3
1. United States. Marine Corps—History—Fiction. 2. United States—History, Military—20th century—Fiction. 3. World War, 1939–1945—Fiction. 4. War stories, American. I. Title.
PS3557.R489137A6 1994 93-31937 CIP
813'.54–dc20

Printed in the United States of America
1 2 3 4 5 6 7 8 9 10

THE CORPS *is respectfully dedicated to the memory of*
Second Lieutenant Drew James Barrett III, USMC
Company K, 3d Battalion, 26th Marines.
Born Denver, Colorado, 3 January 1945,
Died Quang Nam Province,
Republic of Vietnam, 27 February 1969
and
Major Alfred Lee Butler III, USMC
Headquarters 22nd Marine Amphibious Unit.
Born Washington, D.C., 4 September 1950,
Died Beirut, Lebanon, 8 February 1984

"Semper Fi!"

And to the memory of Donald L. Schomp
A Marine Fighter Pilot who became a legendary
U.S. Army Master Aviator
RIP 9 April 1989.

CONTENTS

SEMPER FI

PREFACE

In 1900, with the approval of the Dowager Empress of China, a Chinese militia, the I Ho Chuan, (or "Righteous Harmony Fists," hence "Boxer") began, under the motto "Protect the country, destroy the foreigner!" to kill both Westerners and Chinese Christians. The German ambassador in Peking was murdered, as were thousands of Chinese Christians throughout China, and the Boxers laid siege to the Legation Quarter at Peking.

The ninety-day siege of Peking was relieved on August 14, 1900, by an international force made up of Russian, French, Italian, German, English, and American troops.

The Imperial Court fled to Sian. Although war had not been declared against China, the "Foreign Powers" nevertheless demanded a formal settlement. The Protocol of 1901 provided, among other things, for the punishment of those responsible for the Boxer Rebellion; the fortification of the Legation Quarter at Peking, to be manned by "Powers" troops; and the maintenance by foreign troops of communication between Peking and the sea.

As far as the Americans were concerned, this initially meant the stationing of U.S. Army troops and U.S. Marines in Shanghai, Peking, and elsewhere; and the formation of the U.S. Navy Yangtze River Patrol. The Navy acquired shallow draft steamers, armed them, designated them "Gun Boats," and ran them up and down the Yangtze River.

The Russians, following their resounding defeat in the Russian-Japanese War of 1905, had for all practical purposes turned over their interests in China to Japan. Furthermore, the Versailles Treaty, which had set the terms of the peace between the Western Allies and the Germans and Austro-Hungarians at the end of The World War of 1914–1918, had also given the Japanese rights over the Shantung Province of China.

The reality of the situation in China in 1941 was that the lines had already been drawn for World War II. It was no secret that Japan's ultimate ambition was to take as much of China as it could, into the "Greater Japanese Co-Prosperity Sphere." It was also no secret that they intended to expel the British, the French, and the Americans when the time was ripe. And they most likely wanted the Italians out, too, although the Italians and the Japanese were on much better terms than either was with the French, the English, or the Americans.

The official hypocrisy was that all were still allies, in very much the same way they had been since the Boxer Rebellion in 1900.

It had been agreed then, when the international military force was formed to relieve Peking, that they were not waging war upon China, but rather simply suppressing the Boxers and protecting their own nationals from the savagery of the Chinese.

Thus the Japanese view in 1941, which no one challenged, was that their actions in China were nothing but extensions of what the "allies" started in 1900.

The Japanese were prepared to protect all foreigners from Chinese savagery, and they expected the French, the Italians, and the Americans to do likewise.

But because the Imperial Japanese Army's tanks and artillery were doing nothing more than protecting their own, and other foreign nationals, they could logically raise no objection to the Americans or others protecting their nationals with token military forces.

The Japanese carefully restrained themselves, with several notable exceptions, from becoming involved in incidents involving an exchange of gunfire between themselves and troops of the neutral powers. They still paid lip service to international convention, because international convention condoned their occupation of Shantung Province. If an incident came before the League of Nations, it was likely to go off at a tangent into such things as the behavior of the Imperial Japanese Army.

Everyone understood that the Japanese prefer not to openly tell the League of Nations to go to hell. If necessary, of course, they would. But as long as they could avoid doing so, they would.

In January 1941, the American military presence in China consisted of the U.S. Navy Yangtze River Patrol; the U.S. Navy Submarine Force, China and the 4th Regiment USMC (both based in Shanghai); and the U.S. Marine Detachment, Peking.

I

(ONE)
Company "D," 4th Marines
Shanghai, China
2 January 1941

PFC Kenneth J. McCoy, USMC, stood with his hands on his hips staring at the footlocker at the end of his bed. He'd been that way for quite some time; he was trying to make up his mind. McCoy was twenty-one years old, five feet ten and one-half inches tall, and he weighed 156 pounds. He was well built, but lithe rather than muscular. He had even features and fair skin and wore his light brown hair in a crew cut. His eyes were hazel, and bright; and when he was thinking hard, as he was now, one eyebrow lifted and his lip curled as if the problem he faced amused him. He had once been an altar boy at Saint Rose of Lima Church in Norristown, Pennsylvania, and there were traces of that still in him: There was now, as then, a suggestion that just beneath the clean-cut, innocent surface, was an alter ego with horns itching for the chance to jump out and do something forbidden.

It was the day after New Year's, and PFC McCoy had liberty. And it was two days after payday, and he had his "new gambling money" in his pocket. So he wanted to go try his luck. But what he couldn't quite make up his mind about was whether or not he should leave the compound armed, and if so, how.

What had happened was that on Christmas Eve at a dance hall called the "Little Club," there had been a not entirely unexpected altercation between United States Marines and marines assigned to the International Military Force in Shanghai by His Majesty, Victor Emmanuel III, King of the Italians. It wasn't the first time the Americans and the Italians had gotten into it, but this time it had gotten out of hand.

McCoy had heard that as many as eighteen Italians were dead, and there were eight Marines in sick bay, two of them in very serious condition. Rumor had it—and McCoy tended to believe it—that there were bands of Italian marines roaming town looking for U.S. Marines. The officers certainly didn't doubt it. They'd granted permission for Marines to wear cartridge belts (with first-aid pouches) and bayonets. A sheathed bayonet made a pretty good club; a drawn bayonet was an even better personal defense weapon. But sending the men out with bayonets, sheathed or unsheathed, was far short of sending them out with rifles, loaded or otherwise.

McCoy had not been at the Little Club on Christmas Eve, partly because a Marine who wanted to celebrate Christmas Eve by getting drunk had offered him three dollars (McCoy had negotiated the offer upward to five) to take the duty. But even without the offer, McCoy wouldn't have gone to the Little Club on Christmas Eve. He had known from experience that the place would either be depressing as hell, and/or that there would be a fight between the Marines and the

Italians. Or between the Marines and the Seaforth Highlanders. Or between the Marines and the French Foreign Legion.

Getting into a brawl on Christmas Eve was not McCoy's idea of good clean fun. And getting into any kind of a brawl right now was worse than a bad idea.

McCoy's blue Marine blouse had two new adornments, the single chevron of a private first class and a diagonal stripe above the cuff signifying the completion of four years' honorable service. He had just shipped over for another four years, with the understanding that once he had shipped over he would be promoted to PFC. With the promotion came the right to take the examination for corporal.

It had also been understood, unofficially, that he would get a high rating when he went before the promotion board for the oral examination. They were willing to give him that, he knew, because no one thought he would stand a chance, first time out, of getting a score on the written exam that would be anywhere close to the kind of score needed to actually get promoted.

Well, they were wrong about that. He wanted to be a corporal very much, and he had prepared for the examination. The tough part of it was "military engineering," which mostly meant math questions. He had a flair for math, and he thought it was likely that he hadn't missed a single question. But McCoy had more going for him. When the promotion board sat down at Marine Barracks in Washington to establish the corporal's promotion list, they paid special attention to something called "additional qualifications."

McCoy had found out, by carefully reading the regulations, that there was more to this than the sort of skills you might expect, skills like making Expert with the .45 and the Springfield. You got points for that, of course, and he would get them, because he was a pretty good shot.

But you also got points if you could type sixty words per minute or better. When he took the test, he had been rated at seventy-five words a minute. He had kept that ability a secret before reenlisting, because he hadn't joined the Marine Corps to be a clerk. But even that wasn't his real ace in the hole. What that was, was "foreign language skills."

"Foreign language skills," he was convinced, was going to make him a corporal long before anyone else in the 4th Marines thought he had a chance. His mother had been French, and he'd learned that from her as a baby. Then he'd taken Latin at Saint Rose of Lima High School because they made him, and French because he thought that would be easy.

When he'd come to Shanghai, he had not been surprised that he could talk French with the French Foreign Legionnaires, but he *had* been surprised that he could also make himself understood in Italian, and that he could read Italian documents and even newspapers. And that still wasn't all of it.

Like every other Marine who came to the 4th, he had soon found himself exchanging half his pay for a small apartment and a Chinese girl to share the bed, do the laundry, and otherwise make herself useful. Mai Sing could also read and write, which wasn't always the case with Chinese girls. Before he had decided that he really didn't want a wife just yet—not even a temporary one—and sent Mai Sing back wherever the hell she had come from with two hundred dollars to buy herself a husband, she had taught him not only to speak the Shanghai version of Cantonese, but how to read and write a fair amount of the ideograms as well.

There was a standard U.S. Government language exam, and he'd gone to the U.S. Consulate and taken it. So far as the U.S. Government was concerned, he was "completely fluent" in spoken and written French, which was as high a rating as they gave; "nearly fluent" in spoken and written Italian; "nearly fluent" in spoken Cantonese; and had a 75/55 grade in written Cantonese, which meant that he could read seventy-five percent of the ideograms on the exam, and could come up with the ideogram for a specific word more than half the time.

The guy at the consulate had been so impressed with McCoy's Chinese that he tried to talk him into taking a job with the Marine guard detachment. He could get him transferred, the guy said, and he wouldn't have to pull guard once he got to the consulate. They always needed clerks who could read and write Chinese.

McCoy had turned that down, too. He hadn't joined the Corps to be a clerk in a consulate, either.

The promotion list would be out any day now. He was sure that his name was going to be near the top of it, and he didn't want anything to fuck that up. Like getting in a brawl with a bunch of Italian marines would fuck it up.

They wouldn't make him a corporal if he was dead, either, and the way this brawl was going, getting meaner and meaner by the day, that was a real possibility.

There were two things wrong with going out wearing a cartridge belt and bayonet, he decided in the end. For one thing, he would look pretty silly walking into the poker game at the Cathay Mansions Hotel with that shit. And if he did run into some Italian marines, they would take his possession of a bayonet as a sure sign he was looking for a fight.

McCoy finally bent over the footlocker and took his "Baby Fairbairn" from beneath a stack of neatly folded skivvy shirts. He had won it from a Shanghai Municipal cop after a poker game. He'd bet a hundred yuan against it, one cut of the deck.

There was an officer named Bruce Fairbairn on the Shanghai Municipal Police, and he had invented a really terrific knife, sort of a dagger, and was trying to get everybody to buy them. He had made quite a sales pitch to General Smedley Butler, who commanded all the Marines in China. And Butler, so the story went, had wanted to buy enough to issue them, but the Marine Corps wouldn't give him the money.

McCoy's knife was made exactly like the original Fairbairn, except that it wasn't quite as long, or quite as big. It was just long enough to be concealed in the sleeve, with the tip of the scabbard up against the joint of the elbow, and the handle just inside the cuff.

McCoy took off his blouse, strapped the Baby Fairbairn to his left arm, put the blouse back on over it, looked at himself in the full-length mirror mounted on the door, and left his room.

Their billets had once been two-story brick civilian houses that the 4th Marines had bought when they came to China way back in 1927—blocks of them, enough houses to hold a battalion. Cyclone fences had been erected around these blocks. And the fences were topped with coils of barbed wire, called concertina. At the gate was a sandbagged guardhouse, manned around the clock by a two-man guard detail.

As McCoy walked through, the PFC on guard told him he had heard that the Wops had ganged up on some Marines and put another two guys in the hospital. If he were McCoy, he went on, he would go back and get his bayonet.

"I'm not going anywhere near the Little Club," McCoy said. "And I'm not looking for a fight."

The faster of two rickshaw boys near the gate trotted up and lowered the poles.

"Take me to the Cathay Mansions Hotel," McCoy ordered in Chinese as he climbed onto the rickshaw.

The guard understood "Cathay Mansions Hotel."

"What the fuck are you going to do there, McCoy?" he asked.

"They're having a tea dance," McCoy said, as the rickshaw boy picked up the poles and started to trot down Ferry Road in the direction of the Bund.

As they approached the hotel, McCoy called out to the rickshaw boy to pull to the curb at the corner. He paid him and then walked down the sidewalk past the marquee, and then into an alley, which led to the rear of the building. He went down a flight of stairs to a steel basement door and knocked on it.

A small window opened in the door, and Chinese eyes became visible. McCoy was examined, and then the door opened. He walked down a long corridor, ducking his head from time to time to miss water and sewer pipes, until he came to another steel door, this one identified as "Store Room B-6." He knocked, and it opened for him.

United States Marines were not welcome upstairs in the deeply carpeted, finely paneled lobby and corridors of the Cathay Mansions Hotel. The often-expressed gratitude of the Europeans of the International Settlement for the protection offered by the United States Marines against both the Japanese and Chiang Kai-shek's Kuomintang did not go quite as far as accepting enlisted Marines as social equals.

PFC Ken McCoy was welcome here, however, in a basement storeroom that had been taken over with the tacit permission of Sir Victor Sassoon, owner of the hotel, by its doorman, a six-foot-six White Russian. The storeroom was equipped with an octagonal, green baize-covered table and chairs. A rather ornate light fixture had been carefully hung so as to bathe the table in a light that made the cards and the hands that manipulated them fully visible without causing undue glare.

McCoy was welcome because he always brought to the table fifty dollars American—sometimes a good deal more—which he was prepared to lose with a certain grace and without whining.

In the nearly four years that he had been in China, McCoy had evolved a gambling system that had resulted in a balance of nearly two thousand dollars at Barclays Bank. He thought of this as his retirement program.

He began each month's gambling with fifty dollars, twenty-five of which came from his pay (by the time they had made the deductions, this now came to about forty-nine dollars) and twenty-five of which came from the retirement fund in Barclays Bank.

He played until he either went broke or felt like quitting. If he was ahead of his original fifty dollars when he quit, he put exactly half of the excess over fifty dollars away, to be deposited to his account at Barclays. The rest was his stash for the next game.

Almost always, he went broke sometime during the month, and he never played again until after the next payday. But again, he had almost always put a lot more into Barclays Bank during the month than the twenty-five dollars he would take out after the next payday. And sometimes—not often—the cards went well, and post-game deposits were sixty, seventy dollars. Once there had been a post-game deposit of $140.90.

As he approached the group, the bright light illuminating the table made everything but the lower arms and hands of the players seem to disappear for a moment into the darkness, but gradually his eyes became adjusted, and he could see faces to go with the hands.

The White Russian, who claimed to have been a colonel of cavalry in his Imperial Majesty's 7th Petrograd Cavalry, was at the table. Piotr Petrovich Muller (he had a German surname, he once told McCoy, because he was a descendant of the Viennese who had been imported into Moscow to build the Kremlin) was a very large man with a very closely shaven face.

He bowed his head solemnly when he saw McCoy and then gestured for him to take an empty chair.

There was another Russian who had found post-revolution employment with the French Foreign Legion, and a Sikh, a uniformed sergeant of the Shanghai Municipal Police. There was also Detective Sergeant Lester Chatworth of the Shanghai Municipal Police, who looked up at McCoy and spoke.

"I thought you'd be out bashing Eye-talians."

Except for a thick, perfectly trimmed mustache, Chatworth looked not unlike McCoy, but he spoke with the flat, nasal accent of Liverpool.

"I thought I'd rather come here and take your money," McCoy said.

"Why not? Everybody else is," Detective Sergeant Chatworth said, grinning.

The men at the table had nothing at all in common except that they met Piotr Muller's rigid standard of a decent poker player: Each could play the game well enough and each, at one time or another, had lost a good deal of money gracefully. PFC Kenneth McCoy was younger than any of them by at least a decade, and a quarter of a century younger than Muller. Neither he nor any of the others associated when they were not playing cards, nor were they friendly with any of the perhaps forty other more or less temporary residents of Shanghai who were welcome at Muller's table in the basement of the Cathay Mansions.

There were no raised eyebrows when McCoy took off his blue blouse and revealed the Baby Fairbairn strapped to his arm. It was prudent, if technically illegal, to arm oneself when going out for a night on the town in Shanghai.

McCoy hung his blouse on the back of his chair, unstrapped the knife and tucked it in a pocket of the blouse, then sat down and laid his gambling money on the table. Fifty dollars American that month had converted to just over four hundred yuan. He had before him four one-hundred-yuan notes, which were printed lavender and white in England and were each the size of a British five-pound banknote. He also had some change, including an American dollar bill.

He made himself comfortable in the chair, and then watched as the hand in play was completed. When it was over, Muller nodded at him, and he reached for a fresh deck of cards, broke the seal, and went through them, finding and discarding the extra jokers. He then spread the cards out for the others to examine.

Afterward, he gathered the cards together, shuffled, announced, "Straight poker," and dealt.

Three hours later, there were twenty-odd lavender-and-white one-hundred-yuan notes in front of McCoy; the Sikh and the Foreign Legionnaire had gone bust; and it was between McCoy, Piotr Petrovich Muller, and Detective Sergeant Chatworth. A half hour after that, Muller examined the two cards he had drawn, threw his hand on the table, and pushed himself away from it.

That left only McCoy and Detective Sergeant Chatworth.

"I don't play two-handed poker," McCoy announced.

"I'm willing to quit," Chatworth said, and tossed the just-collected deck into the wastebasket, where it joined a dozen other decks of cards.

Stiff from three hours of little movement, McCoy stood up and stretched his arms over his head. He then strapped the Baby Fairbairn to his left arm, put his blouse on, and followed the others out of the storeroom.

When he was back out on the street, McCoy considered having his ashes hauled. It had been about a week, and it was time to take care of the urge. But he decided against it. For one thing, he had too much money with him. He hadn't counted it out to the last yuan, but he'd won a bunch—say at twelve dollars to the hundred-yuan note, a little better than $250. That was too much money to have in your pocket when visiting a whorehouse.

Even if the Italian marines weren't on the warpath.

The smart thing to do was go back to the billet. He put his hand up and flagged a rickshaw, and told the driver to take him down Ferry Road.

Three blocks from the compound, he saw the Italian marines, hiding in an alley. There were four of them, in uniform. The uniforms were a mixture of army and navy—army breeches and navy middie blouses.

I am minding my own business, McCoy told himself, *and I am not carrying a bayonet, and I was not at the Little Club when this whole business started. With a little bit of luck, they will let me pass.*

They didn't say anything to him as the rickshaw pulled past the alley and there could no longer be any question that the rickshaw passenger was a Marine. So for a moment he thought they'd decided to wait for Marines who were looking for a fight.

And then the rickshaw was turned over on its side. The rickshaw boy started to howl with fear and rage even before McCoy hit the ground, striking the elbow of his blouse on the filth of the street.

McCoy sat up and looked around to see if there was someplace he could run. But the Italian marines had picked their spot well. There was no place to run to.

Maybe I can talk to them, McCoy thought, *tell them the fucking truth, I wasn't at the Little Club, I have no quarrel with them.*

Then he saw the Italian marine advancing on him with a length of bicycle chain swinging in his hand. McCoy felt a little faint, and then tasted something foul in the back of his mouth.

"I don't know who you're looking for," he said in Italian. "But it isn't me."

The Italian marine replied that his mother fucked pigs and that he was going to mash his balls.

The bicycle chain missed McCoy's leg, but before it struck the pavement with a frightening whistle, it came close enough to catch his trouser's leg and leave the imprint of the chain there. McCoy quickly slid sideward, taking the Baby Fairbairn from his sleeve as he got to his feet.

The Italian marine told him his sister sucked Greek cocks and that he was going to take the knife away and stick it up his ass.

McCoy sensed, rather than saw, that two other Italian marines were making their way behind him.

The idea was that the two would grab him and hold him while the other one used the bicycle chain. The thing to do was to get past the Italian marine with the bicycle chain.

He made a feinting motion with the knife, and the Italian marine backed up.

It looked like it might work. And there was nothing else to do.

He made another feinting move, a savage leap accompanied by as ferocious a roar as he could muster, at the exact moment that the Italian marine lunged at where McCoy's Baby Fairbairn had been.

The tip of the Baby Fairbairn punctured the Italian marine's chest at the lower extremity of the ribs. McCoy felt it grate over a bone, and then immediately sink to the handguard. The knife was snatched from his hand as the Italian marine continued his plunge.

The man grunted, fell, dropped the bicycle chain, rolled over, sat up, and started to pull the Baby Fairbairn from his abdomen. He gave it a hearty tug and it came out. A moment later, a stream of bright red blood as thick as the handle of a baseball bat erupted from his mouth. The Italian marine looked puzzled for a moment, and then fell to one side.

Jesus Christ, I killed him!

One of the three remaining Italian marines crossed himself and ran away. The other two advanced on McCoy, one of them frantically trying to work the action of a tiny automatic pistol.

I can't run from that!

McCoy picked up the Baby Fairbairn and advanced on the two Italian marines.

He made it to the one with the gun and started to try to take it away from him, or at least to knock it out of his hand. The other one tried to help his friend. McCoy lashed out with the Baby Fairbairn again. The blade slashed the Italian's face, but that didn't discourage him. He got his arms around McCoy's arms and held him in a bear hug.

The other one managed to work the action of his tiny pistol.

McCoy remembered hearing that a .22 or a .25 will kill you just as dead as a .45, it just takes a little longer—say a week—to do it.

With a strength that surprised him, he got his right arm free and swung it backward at the man who had been holding him. He felt it cut and strike something, something not anywhere as hard as the ribcage, but something. And it went in far enough so that he couldn't hang on to it when the man fell down.

Then, free, he jumped at the man with the pistol. The pistol went off with a sharp crack, and he felt something strike his leg hard, like a kick from a very hard boot. And then he knocked the pistol from the Italian marine's hand and, when it clattered onto the cobblestones, dived after it.

He picked it up and aimed it at the Italian marine. Then he followed his eyes. What he had done when he had swung his knife hand backward was stick it in the man's groin. The man was now holding his groin with both hands. The handle of the Baby Fairbairn was sticking out between his fingers. The man was whimpering, and tears were on his face.

Down the street, McCoy could hear the growl of the hand-cranked siren at the compound.

This is going to fuck up my promotion, he thought. *Goddamn these Italians.*

(TWO)

Captain Edward J. Banning, USMC, was S-2, the staff Intelligence Officer, of the 4th Marines. He was thirty-six years old, tall, thin, and starting to bald. And he had been a Marine since his graduation from the Citadel, the Military College of South Carolina: a second lieutenant for three years, a first lieutenant for eight years, and he'd worn the twin silver railroad tracks of a captain for four years.

There were four staff officers. The S-1 (Personnel) and S-4 (Supply) were majors. The S-3 (Plans and Training) was a lieutenant colonel. As a captain, Banning was the junior staff officer. But he was a staff officer, and as such normally excused from most of the duties assigned to non-staff officers.

He took his turn, of course, as Officer of the Day, but that was about it. He was, for instance, never assigned as Inventory Officer to audit the accounts of the Officers' or NCO clubs or as Investigating Officer when there was an allegation of misbehavior involving the possibility of a court-martial of one of the enlisted men. Or any other detail of that sort. He was the S-2, and the colonel was very much aware that taking him from that duty to do something else did not make very good sense.

So Banning had been surprised at first when he was summoned by the colonel and told that he would serve as Defense Counsel in the case of the United States of America versus PFC Kenneth J. McCoy, USMC. But he was a Marine officer, and when Marine officers are given an assignment, they say "aye, aye, sir" and set about doing what they have been ordered to do.

"This one can't be swept under the table, Banning," the colonel said. "It's gone too far for that. It has to go by the book, with every 't' crossed and every 'i' dotted."

"I understand, sir."

"Major DeLaney will prosecute. I have ordered him to do his best to secure a conviction. I am now ordering you to do your best to secure an acquittal. The Italian Consul General has told us that he and Colonel Maggiani of the Italian marines will attend the court-martial. Do you get the picture?"

"Yes, sir."

The picture Banning got was that he was going to have to spend Christ alone knew how many hours preparing for this court-martial, participating in the court-martial itself, and then Christ alone knew how many hours after the trial, going through the appeal process.

About half of the total would have to come from the time Banning would have normally spent with his hobby. His hobby was Ludmilla Zhivkov, whom he called 'Milla.'

Milla was twenty-seven, raven-haired, long-legged and a White Russian. And he had recently begun to consider the possibility that he was in love with her.

Banning was a Marine officer—even worse, a Marine intelligence officer—and Marine intelligence officers were not supposed to become emotionally involved with White Russian women. It had not been his intention to become emotionally involved with her. He had met her, more or less, on duty. There had been an advertisement in the *Shanghai Post:* "Russian Lady Offers Instruction in Russian Conversation." It had coincided with an unexpected bonus in his operating funds: two hundred dollars for Foreign Language Training.

There were supposed to be fifteen thousand White Russian refugee women in Shanghai. They made their living as best they could, some successfully and some reduced to making it on their backs. He had somewhat cynically suspected that the Russian Lady offering Russian Conversation was doing so only because she was too old, or too ugly, to make it on her back.

Milla had surprised him. She was a real beauty, and she was the first White Russian he'd met who was not at least a duchess. She was also devoutly religious, which meant that she was not going to become a whore unless it got down to that. Milla told him her father had operated, of all things, the Victor Phonograph store in St. Petersburg. They had come from Russia in 1921 with some American dollars, and it had been enough, with what jobs he had been able to find, to keep them while they waited for their names to work their way up the immigration waiting list for the United States.

And then he had died, and she hadn't been able to make as much money as she had hoped, even working as a billing clerk in the Cathay Mansions Hotel and teaching Russian conversation. When he met her she was down to living in one room. The next step was to become somebody's mistress. After that she'd have to turn into a whore. Becoming a whore would keep her from going to the States.

The first thing Banning had done was pay her the whole two hundred dollars up front. Then one thing had led to another, and they had gone to bed. Soon he had helped her get a larger place to live.

But the ground rules established between them were clear: It was a friendly business relationship and never could be anything more. When he went home, that would be the end of it. She understood that. She had lived up to her end of the bargain. And she would, he believed, stick to it.

Her powerful character, he sometimes thought, was one of the reasons he was afraid he was in love with her. And sometimes he wondered if she wasn't playing him like a fish (she was also the most intelligent woman he had ever known) and nobly living up to her end of the bargain because she had figured that was the one way to get *him* to break it.

But what he nevertheless knew for sure was that if he married her, he could kiss his Marine career good-bye; and that he could not imagine life outside the Corps; and that he could not imagine life without Milla.

For the first time in his life, Ed Banning did not know what the hell to do.

Banning went by the orderly room of "D" Company, First Battalion and read through PFC Kenneth J. McCoy's records slowly and thoroughly. He talked to his company commander, his platoon leader, his platoon sergeant, his section leader and his bunk mate.

The picture they painted of McCoy was the one reflected by his records. He had joined the Corps right out of high school (in fact, several months before; his high school diploma had come to him while he was at Parris Island and was entered into his record then), had served for three months with the Fleet Marine Force at San Diego, and then been shipped to the 4th Marines in Shanghai, where they'd made him an assistant gunner on a water-cooled .30-caliber Browning machine gun.

He had by and large kept out of trouble since arriving in China. And he got along all right with his corporal and his sergeant, who both described him as "a good man."

But there were several things out of the ordinary: He didn't have a Chinese girl, for one thing. But he had had a Chinese girl, so there didn't seem to be reason to suspect he was queer. He didn't have a buddy, either, which was unusual. But some men were by nature loners, himself included, and this McCoy seemed to be another of them. There was nothing wrong with that, it was just a little unusual.

What was most unusual, though, was his skill as a typist and his language ability. Banning was a little chagrined to discover that Dog Company had a natural linguist who could type seventy-five words a minute assigned to a machine gun. If he had known that, PFC McCoy would have found himself assigned to headquarters company. Skilled typists were in short supply, but not nearly as short supply as people who could read and write French and Italian and Chinese.

Banning decided that McCoy, more than likely with the connivance of his first and gunnery sergeants, had wanted these skills kept a secret. Gunnery sergeants were concerned with having good men on the machine guns and cared very little for the personnel problems of the chairwarmers at regimental headquarters. And McCoy himself was probably one of those kids who did not want to be a clerk.

When he was convinced he had learned all he could about PFC Kenneth J. McCoy from his service records and those around him, Captain Banning went to the infirmary to see the accused face-to-face.

McCoy's medical records showed that he had been admitted to the dispensary at 2310 hours 2 January 1941 suffering cuts and abrasions and a penetrating wound of the upper right thigh possibly caused by a small-caliber bullet. A surgical procedure at 0930 hours 3 January 1941 had removed a lead-and-brass object, tentatively identified as a .25-caliber bullet, from the thigh. The prognosis was complete recovery, with return to full duty status in ten to fifteen days.

Captain Banning found PFC McCoy in a two-bed infirmary room. He was sitting in a chair by the window, using the windowsill as a desk while he worked the crossword puzzle in the *Shanghai Post.* An issue cane was hanging from the windowsill.

"As you were!" Banning barked, when McCoy saw him and started to rise. "Keep your seat!"

Banning could not remember ever having seen McCoy before, which was not that unusual. There were a number of young privates and PFCs in the 4th Marines who looked very much like PFC McCoy.

Captain Banning introduced himself and told McCoy he had been appointed his defense counsel. Then he made sure that McCoy understood his predicament. He told it as he saw it, that he didn't think there was any chance that McCoy would be found guilty of first-degree murder, which required serious elements such as previous intent, but that it was very likely that he would be found guilty of what was known as a "lesser included offense."

There was no question that there were two dead Italian marines or that McCoy had killed them. Neither was there any question that they had been killed with his knife. Banning then explained that while authority might—and did—look away at the illegal carrying of a concealed deadly weapon so long as nothing happened, when something did happen, the offense could no longer be ignored.

There were two lesser included offenses, Banning continued: "Manslaughter," which was the illegal taking of human life, and "Negligent Homicide," which meant killing somebody by carelessness.

"I haven't discussed this with Major DeLaney, who will serve as prosecutor, McCoy," Captain Banning said. "Because I wanted to talk to you first. But this possibility exists: When you come to trial, you have the option of pleading guilty to a lesser included offense. I feel reasonably sure that Major DeLaney would have no objection if you pleaded guilty to manslaughter, and perhaps I could persuade him to accept a plea of guilty to involuntary manslaughter."

PFC McCoy did not respond.

"If you did plead guilty to either of the lesser included offenses," Banning said, "the court-martial board would then decide on the punishment. No matter what they decided, the sentence would be reviewed both by the colonel and by General Butler, both of whom have the authority to reduce it."

"Sir, it was self-defense," McCoy said.

"Let me try to explain this to you," Banning said. "You would be better off if you had knifed two American Marines. But you killed two Italian marines, and they have to do something about it. The Italian Consul General and the Italian marine colonel are going to be at your court-martial. They want to be able to report that the U.S. Marine who killed two of their marines was found guilty and will be punished. Am I getting through to you?"

"Sir, it was self-defense," McCoy repeated doggedly.

"You don't have any witnesses," Banning said.

"There was the rickshaw boy and twenty, thirty Chinese that saw it."

"How do you plan to find them?" Banning asked.

McCoy shrugged his shoulders. "Ask around, I suppose."

There was no sense arguing with him, Banning decided. He just didn't understand the situation.

"Let me tell you what I think is going to happen," he said. "I think I can get Major DeLaney to accept a plea of guilty to a charge of manslaughter. You will be sentenced, and you might as well understand this, the sentence will be stiff. Maybe twenty years to life."

"Jesus Christ!" McCoy said.

"That will satisfy the Italians," Banning said. "You understand that's necessary?"

McCoy gave him a cold look but said nothing.

"The sentence is then subject to review by the colonel," Banning said. "He will take his time reviewing it, I think, to let things cool off a little. Then, he will decide that you're not really guilty of manslaughter, but of the lesser included offense of involuntary manslaughter, and he will reduce the punishment accordingly."

"To what?"

" 'To what, *sir,*' " Banning corrected him.

"To what, sir?" McCoy repeated, dutifully.

"The maximum punishment for involuntary manslaughter is five years."

"I've heard about Mare Island and Portsmouth," McCoy said, grim faced.

He had not appended "sir" as military courtesy required, but Banning did not correct him. It was Banning's personal opinion that the Naval Prisons at Mare Island, California, and Portsmouth, New Hampshire, where the brutality under Marine guards was legendary, were a disgrace to the Marine Corps.

"The next step in the process," Banning went on, "is the review of the sentence by General Butler. I think it's very possible that General Butler would reduce the sentence even further, say to one year's confinement. And then, by the time you got to the states, the Navy Department would review the sentence still again, and I'm sure they would pay attention both to your previous service and to the letter recommending clemency that your company and battalion commanders tell me they will write in your behalf. Your sentence could then be reduced again to time already served."

"In other words, sir," McCoy said, with a "sir" that bordered on silent insubordination, "I could count on being a busted Marine looking for a new home?"

"For Christ's sake, McCoy, you killed two people! You can't expect to get off scot-free!"

"Sir," PFC McCoy said, "no disrespect intended, but they gave me the court-martial manual to read, and in there it says I can have the defense counsel of my choice."

Banning felt his temper rise. The sonofabitch was a guardhouse lawyer on top of everything else.

"That is your right," he said, stiffly. "Who would you like to have defend you?"

"My company commander, sir."

"You can't have him, because he is your company commander. Neither can you have your platoon leader."

"Then Lieutenant Kaye, sir, the assistant supply officer."

With a massive effort, Captain Banning kept his temper under control.

"McCoy," he said. "I'm going to give you twenty-four hours to think this over. I want you to carefully consider your position."

"Yes, sir," PFC McCoy said.

(THREE)

On the way to his office from the infirmary, Captain Banning's anger rose. Among other things, he was going to look like a goddamned fool in front of the colonel when he had to go to him and tell him this knife-wielding PFC had refused his services as defense counsel. It was of course the kid's right, but Banning could not remember ever hearing of anything like this happening.

And PFC McCoy was not doing himself any good. If he went to trial and pleaded not guilty, he was digging his own grave. He was not being tried for stabbing the two Italians, but to make the point to the other Marines that they couldn't go around killing people.

If he went along with that, in three months he would be a free man at San Diego or Quantico, with only the loss of a stripe to show for having killed two men.

If he annoyed the court-martial board, they would very likely conclude that he was somebody who needed to be taught a lesson and sock him with a heavy sentence. If the colonel was annoyed, he would find nothing wrong with the sentence when it was reviewed. And if General Butler smelled that McCoy was a troublemaker, he wouldn't find anything wrong with the sentence, either.

PFC McCoy stood a very good chance of finding himself locked up in the Portsmouth Naval Prison for thirty years to life.

Captain Banning's rage lasted through lunch. And then he considered the situation from McCoy's point of view. The kid actually believed—since it was the truth—that he had acted in self-defense. It was therefore his own duty, Banning decided, to at least pursue that as far as it would go.

To prove self-defense he would need witnesses. The only witnesses right now were two Italian marines. *They* were prepared to testify that they were minding their own business when McCoy drew a knife on them, whereupon one of their number drew a pistol in self-defense.

When he went back to his office after lunch, Banning told his clerk to see if he could get a car from the motor pool. He had to go into town.

Banning hoped to find Bruce Fairbairn at the headquarters of the Shanghai Municipal Police. He knew him, and could explain the problem to him. But when he got to police headquarters, Fairbairn was not available, and neither was Chief Inspector Thwaite, who was the only other Shanghai Police officer he knew well enough to speak to with complete frankness.

He wound up talking to a Detective Sergeant Chatworth.

Chatworth sat at an old wooden desk covered with papers. As Banning approached, he shuffled angrily through them, searching for something he had apparently mislaid.

Banning introduced himself and told him what he had come for.

"Right," Chatworth said, looking at Banning with a screwed-up face. He seemed surprised to hear Banning's story. "You Yanks always seem to have to wear white," he said after a moment while searching through his pocket for a near-empty package of vile Chinese cigarettes. "Fag?" he offered, holding one out.

"Thanks, no," Banning said.

"I mean, Christ," he went on, lighting up. "Don't you have any loyalty towards your own? For the sake of Italians? Really!" He inhaled deep, savoring it. Then blew out. "And besides, I know the boy. McCoy is a good one. Protect him. You don't find his class all that often."

"That may be." Banning shrugged, stiffening. He did not like Chatworth very much. "But Italian pride has been badly hurt. They've gone to the foreign service boys at the consulate. One thing has led to the other. And the consequence is that there is nothing we can do but court-martial PFC McCoy.

"And then on top of that," Banning continued, "McCoy is being difficult. He thinks he did it all in self-defense; and he simply refuses to understand that without witnesses, he can't possibly get away with that plea."

"So?" Chatworth said, beginning to understand.

"And so, Sergeant, I'm desperate. Could you people possibly help us and see if you can find some Chinese who (a) saw the fight and (b) would be willing to testify in McCoy's behalf at his court-martial?"

Rather abruptly, Detective Sergeant Chatworth turned his attention back to his papers.

"I'll look into the matter," he said, dropping the now-dead cigarette on the floor and snuffing it out with his heel. "And I'll be in touch with you in due course."

Banning saw that Chatworth did not like him any more than he liked Chatworth. And Banning also realized that Chatworth knew even better than he did that there was virtually no chance of finding a Chinese who would be willing to testify that he had seen the fight between the Big Noses. And it would matter to the Chinese not at all that the U.S. Marine Big Nose had clearly been the aggrieved party. Detective Sergeant Chatworth had abruptly dismissed him because he was wasting Detective Sergeant Chatworth's valuable time.

Banning did not go back to the office. He went to the apartment. Milla was there, giving a Chinese woman hell because she had not ironed several of Banning's shirts to what Milla thought were Marine sartorial standards. She was acting wifely, and that upset him, too, and he got drunk.

And he told Milla about McCoy.

She was sympathetic. To *him.* She felt sorry for him that he had a problem with McCoy.

Later she consoled him in bed, which was usually enough to make him happy as hell. But not this time.

As he watched her get dressed to go to work, he tormented himself with fantasies of other men watching her naked, as she was now. And touching her naked flesh, as he had just done . . . which was sure as hell going to happen if he didn't marry her and get himself booted out of the Corps.

After she left, he hit the whiskey again, and ended up with some drunken ideas. He could go to trial and try to play on the sympathy of the court-martial board, paint PFC McCoy as a saint in uniform who was the innocent party in this whole mess. He could try to convince the court-martial that the reason PFC McCoy went around with a Fairbairn dagger in his sleeve was that he collected butterflies. He'd throw the fucking knife at them and pin their wings. The poor fucking Wops had fallen onto the blade of the knife when they slipped on a banana peel.

(FOUR)

At eight-fifteen the next morning, as Captain Banning drank his third Coca-Cola of the day in a vain attempt to extinguish the fire in his stomach, his clerk came into his office with the first batch of the day's official correspondence from the message center.

Among the items which required his initials was a communication from Headquarters, United States Marine Corps: A promotion board having been convened to consider candidates for promotion to the grade of corporal had reached the end of its deliberations. There were thirty names on the list and there were twelve vacancies within the Marine Corps for corporals. Therefore, commanding officers of the first twelve names on the list were herewith directed to issue promotion orders for the individuals concerned. As additional vacancies occurred, authority would be granted to promote individuals on the list numbers 13 through 30.

The second name on the list was PFC Kenneth J. McCoy, Company "D," 4th Marines.

The Navy, and thus the Marine Corps, was governed by common law of the United States, and a pillar of that code of justice was that an accused was presumed innocent until proven guilty.

The colonel had just been directed by Hq, USMC, to promote PFC McCoy to Corporal McCoy, an action that would be very difficult to explain to the colonel commanding the Italian marines and to the Consul General of the King of Italy at Shanghai. It would look as if the punishment for stabbing to death two Italians was promotion to corporal.

Captain Banning wondered whether it was his duty to bring the problem to the colonel's attention himself, or whether the S-1 would consider it part of his duty as personnel officer. Most likely, the problem would skip the G-1's attention, Banning decided. The Colonel was going to be furious when he found out about this, and the S-1 knew it, too.

He was still considering the problem, and half expecting his telephone to ring with a call from either the S-1 or the colonel's sergeant-major, when his clerk knocked at the door, put his head in, and announced that Detective Sergeant Chatworth and two Chinese were in the outer office.

As incredible as it sounded, had Chatworth turned up two witnesses? In so short a time?

"Ask him to come in, please," Banning said.

Chatworth came in with two coolies. Banning's heart sank again. The court-martial would not take the word of two coolies over that of two Italian marines.

"Good morning, Captain," Detective Sergeant Chatworth said. "May I present Constable Hang Chee and Senior Patrolman Kin Tong?"

The two coolies bowed their heads.

"Constable Hang and Patrolman Kin were fortunately in a position to see the McCoy incident from start to finish. Tell the captain what you saw, Hang."

Constable Hang spoke English very softly, but well. He reported that PFC McCoy had just stepped out of his rickshaw near the compound gate when he was beset by the five Italians and had no choice but to defend himself.

"He was three blocks from the compound," Banning said, "when four Italian marines overturned the rickshaw."

"Now that you mention it," Constable Hang said, "that's right. There were four

Italian marines and the assault took place several blocks from the compound entrance."

It was clear to Banning that they had no more seen the fight than he had.

"What's going on, Sergeant Chatworth?" Banning asked.

"You wanted witnesses, I found them," Chatworth said. "Will a sworn statement suffice, do you think, or will these officers have to testify in court?"

I don't want McCoy to go to Portsmouth, either. But I am a Marine officer, and I can't close my eyes and pretend I believe Chatworth's Chinese.

"I could not put these men on the stand," Banning said, disliking Chatworth more than ever. "I think you misunderstood the purpose of my visit yesterday."

"You're a bloody fool, then, Banning," Chatworth said, coldly.

"Good day, Sergeant Chatworth," Banning said.

"I'll send the report of these officers concerning the incident they witnessed to you via the British Consulate," Chatworth said. "It'll take two, three days to get here, I'd suppose."

"I told you: as much as I might personally like to, I can't put these men on the stand."

"Why not?" Chatworth asked.

"Being very blunt, I'm not sure I believe your men. Goddamn it, I know I don't believe them."

"That's not really for you to decide, is it?" Chatworth said. "And, if you don't let these men testify, wouldn't that be 'suppression of evidence'?"

"Why the hell are you doing this?" Banning asked.

"We're just doing our duty as we see it," Chatworth said, sarcastically. "I can only hope that you're not one of those bloody fools who doesn't know he's in Shanghai and thinks he can go by the bloody book."

"How dare you talk to me that way?" Banning flared.

"What are you going to do about it?" Chatworth asked calmly.

"I tell you now, Sergeant Chatworth, that I intend to discuss this with Captain Fairbairn."

"Odd that you should mention his name," Chatworth said. "Constable Wang and Patrolman Kin are members of Captain Fairbairn's Flying Squad."

Banning's temper flared. He reached for the telephone, actually intending to call Fairbairn. But reason prevailed. He instead had the operator connect him with the colonel.

"Sir," he said. "There has been a rather startling development. When PFC McCoy was attacked by the Italian Marines, the whole incident was witnessed by two Chinese police officers of Captain Fairbairn's Flying Squad. They are prepared to testify that it was clearly a case of self-defense."

"That's bloody well more like it," Detective Sergeant Chatworth said.

II

(ONE)
4th Marine Infirmary
Shanghai, China
6 January 1941

PFC Kenneth J. McCoy, wearing issue pajamas and a bathrobe, was stretched out on his bed working at a crossword puzzle in the *Shanghai Post* when Captain Banning walked into his room. Banning saw that they had brought him his breakfast on a tray, and that he had eaten little of it.

"As you were," Banning said, as McCoy started to swing his legs out of the bed.

McCoy looked at him warily.

"I want a straight answer to this question, McCoy," Banning began. "How well do you know a Sergeant Chatworth of the Shanghai Municipal Police?"

McCoy, Banning noticed with annoyance, debated answering the question before replying, "I know him, sir."

"Good friend of yours, is he?" Banning pursued.

"I wouldn't say that, sir," McCoy said. "I know him."

"Sergeant Chatworth has come up with two witnesses to support your allegation of self-defense," Banning said. "They saw the six Italians attack you when you got out of the rickshaw at the compound gate."

McCoy's eyebrows went up, but he said nothing.

This is a very bright young man, Banning thought. Bright and tough, who knows when to keep his mouth shut.

"The two witnesses were Chinese police officers of Captain Fairbairn's Flying Squad," Banning went on. "They have appeared before the adjutant and made sworn statements. The statements bring the number of Italian marines down to four, and say that your rickshaw was turned over where you said it was."

McCoy looked at Captain Banning without expression.

"The statements are so much bullshit, of course," Banning said, "and you know it."

"Sir, so were the statements of the Italians."

"The first thing I thought, McCoy, was that you and Chatworth were involved in something dishonest, and it was a case of one crook helping another. But I just came from seeing Captain Fairbairn, and he tells me that Chatworth is a good man. Off the record, he told me that if Chatworth was getting you out of the mess you're in, that speaks highly for you, because he doesn't normally do things like that."

"I don't know, sir, what you expect me to say," McCoy said.

"You think I'm a sonofabitch, don't you?"

McCoy, his face expressionless, met Banning's eyes, but he said nothing.

"If I were in your shoes, and the officer appointed to defend me against a charge I was innocent of tried to talk me into pleading guilty, I'd think he was a sonofabitch," Banning said.

"You're an officer, sir," McCoy said.

The implication of that, Banning thought, is that all officers are sonsofbitches. Do all the enlisted men think that way, or only the ones smart enough, like this one, to know when somebody's been trying to fuck them?

"And in this case, I was a sonofabitch," Banning said. "I'm going to give you that, McCoy. It's the truth. I am not exactly proud of the way I handled this. It's pretty goddamned shaming, to put a point on it, for me to admit that it took an English policeman to remind me that a Marine officer's first duty is to his men. I'd like to apologize."

"Yes, sir," McCoy said.

"Does that mean you accept my apology? Or that you're just saying 'Yes, sir'?" Banning asked. "It's important that I know. I would like a straight answer. Man to man."

"I didn't expect anything else," McCoy said. "And I've never had an officer apologize to me before."

"I guess what I'm really asking," Banning said, "is whether you do accept my apology, or whether you're just going to bide your time waiting for an opportunity to stick it in me."

"Am I carrying a grudge, you mean? No, sir."

"I really hope you mean that, McCoy, because you are going to be in a position to stick it in me," Banning said.

"Sir?"

"When your friend Chatworth came up with witnesses to your innocence, the colonel decided that there was no reason to go ahead with your court-martial. It would have been a waste of time and money. In light of the new evidence, all charges against you have been dropped. As soon as the surgeon clears you, you'll go back to duty."

"Aye, aye, sir," McCoy said. "Thank you, sir."

"But not to Dog Company," Banning said. "The colonel has given you to me. You're being transferred to Headquarters Company."

"I don't understand," McCoy said.

"The colonel said that a man with your many talents, McCoy," Banning said, dryly, "the typing and the languages—not to mention your ability to make friends in the international community—was wasting his time, and the Corps' time and money, on a machine gun. A man like you, McCoy, the colonel said, should work somewhere where his talents could be better utilized. Like S-2."

"I don't want to be a clerk," McCoy said.

"What you want, McCoy, is not up for debate," Captain Banning said. "But for your general information, I don't have any more choice in the matter than you do. What went unsaid, I think, was that the colonel wants me to make sure you don't stick that knife of yours in anyone else."

"Aye, aye, sir."

"There's more. As soon as you feel up to making the trip, you're going to Peking for a while. A month, six weeks."

"Get me out of Shanghai?" McCoy asked, but it was more thinking out loud than a question.

Banning nodded.

"You're a problem, McCoy," Banning said. "The Italians want you punished. Now that we can't do that, we want to get you out of sight for a while."

"Captain," McCoy said, "the surgeon told me that if there was going to be infection, I would have it by now. There's no reason for me to be in here."

"Do you feel up to going that far in a truck?" Banning asked.

"I thought we moved people by water between here and Tientsin," McCoy said.

"From time to time, we send a truck convoy up there," Banning said. "One is leaving on Thursday. Didn't you hear that?"

"The word is," McCoy said, "that what the convoys really do is spy on the Japs."

"And that would bother you?"

"No, Sir," McCoy said. "That sounds interesting. I asked my Gunny[1] how I could get to go, and he told me to mind my own business."

"Military intelligence isn't what you might think it is from watching Errol Flynn or Robert Taylor in the movies," Banning said.

"I didn't think it was," McCoy said, evenly.

"Are you familiar with the term 'Order of Battle'?" Banning asked.

"No, sir."

"It is the composition of forces," Banning said. "What units are where and in what condition. By that I mean how they are armed, equipped, fed, whether or not they're up to strength, whether or not there are any signs of an impending move. You understand?"

"Yes, sir."

"One of my responsibilities is to keep up to date on the Japanese Order of Battle," Banning said. "One of the ways I do that is give the officer in charge of the Tientsin-Peking convoys a list of things to look for. That does not mean, I should add, breaking into a Japanese headquarters in the middle of the night to steal secret plans, the way Errol Flynn operates in the movies. My instructions to the officer are that his first duty is to not get caught being nosy."

"I guess the Japanese watch him pretty closely?"

"Of course they do," Banning said.

"They'd be less likely to pay attention to a PFC," McCoy said. "They judge our PFCs by the way they treat their own. And their PFCs can't spit without orders."

"The low regard the Japanese have for their own enlisted men works both ways," Banning said. "They would shoot one of our PFCs they caught snooping around, and then be genuinely surprised that we would be upset about it."

"Then the thing for our PFCs to do is not get caught," McCoy said.

"Didn't you ever hear that the smart thing to do is never volunteer for anything?" Banning asked.

"There's always an exception to that," McCoy said. "Like when you think it might do you some good to volunteer."

"Go on," Banning said.

"I think I'm going to be on the corporals' promotion list," McCoy said. "I also think what I did is liable to fuck me up with getting promoted. Maybe I could get off the shit-list by doing something like snooping around the Japs."

"You're on the corporals' list," Banning said. "The promotion orders will be cut today. A separate order, by the way, hoping the Italians won't find out about it and think that we're promoting you for cutting up their marines. You will be a very young corporal, McCoy."

"Then maybe, if I volunteer for this and do it right," McCoy said, "I can get to be a very young sergeant."

[1]Gunnery Sergeant. A senior noncommissioned officer.

"And maybe you'd fuck up and embarrass the colonel and give him an excuse to bust you," Banning said. "I don't think busting you would make him unhappy."

"And maybe I wouldn't," McCoy said. "I'll take that chance."

"Right now, McCoy, and understand me good, all you are to do when you go on the convoy is sit beside the driver. I don't want you snooping around the Japanese unless and until I tell you what to look for. Do you understand that?"

"Aye, aye, sir," McCoy said. "I'm not going to charge around like a headless chicken and get you in trouble, Captain."

"As long as we both understand that," Banning said.

"Yes, sir," McCoy said.

"Unless you have any questions, then, that seems to be about it. I want you to stay in here until Wednesday, when you can go to your billet and pack your gear for the trip. You are not to leave the compound. And I think it would be a good idea if you didn't sew on your corporal's chevrons until you are out of Shanghai."

"Aye, aye, sir," McCoy said.

"Any questions?"

"Do I get my knife back?"

"So you can slice somebody else up?" Banning flared.

"I wasn't looking for trouble with the Italians," McCoy said. "But when it found me, it was a damned good thing I had that knife."

"Tell me something, McCoy," Banning said. "Does it bother you at all to have killed those two men?"

"Straight answer?"

Banning nodded.

"I've been wondering if something's wrong with me," McCoy said. "I'm sorry I had to kill them. But you're supposed to be all upset when you kill somebody, and I just don't feel that way. I mean, I'm not having nightmares about it, or anything like that, the way I hear other people do."

"It says in the Bible, 'Thou shalt not kill,' " Banning said.

"And it also says, 'An eye for an eye and a tooth for a tooth,' " McCoy said. "And that 'he who lives by the sword shall die by the sword.' "

Banning looked at him for a long moment before he spoke.

"I'm not absolutely sure about this," he said finally. "Your knife was evidence in a court-martial. But now that there's not going to be a court-martial, maybe I can get it back for you."

"Thank you," McCoy said. "I'd hate to have to buy another one."

(TWO)

On the way back to his office, Captain Banning wondered why in their meeting PFC/Corporal McCoy had not said "Yes, sir" as often as he was expected to—using the phrase as sort of military verbal punctuation.

And he wondered why he himself, except that once, hadn't called him on it. The fact, he concluded after a while, was that McCoy was neither intentionally discourteous nor insolent; and that the discussion had been between them as men, not officer and PFC. In other words, the kid had understood—either from instinct or from smarts—what was the correct tone to take with him.

The more he saw of McCoy, the more he learned about him, the more impressed he became both with his intelligence (his score on the written promotion examination should have prepared him for that, but it hadn't) and with his toughness. He was a very tough young man. But not entirely. Within, there was a soft center of young boy, who wished to sneak off and be a spy—for the pure glamour of it, and the romance.

He could not, of course, permit him to snoop around the Japanese, both because he would get caught doing it (always an embarrassment with the Japanese) and because it was very likely that the Japanese would in fact "accidentally" kill him . . . or, if they wanted to send a message to the Americans, behead him with a sword, and then arrange for his head to be delivered in a box.

Before the convoy left for Tientsin and Peking, Banning took McCoy aside and made it as clear as he could that he was to leave what espionage there was to Lieutenant John Macklin, who was the officer charged with conducting it. He was to go nowhere and do nothing that the other enlisted men on the convoy did not do.

McCoy said, "Aye, aye, sir."

Banning felt a little sorry for him when he saw him climb into the cab of a Studebaker truck. While it was true that the danger of infection of the small-caliber wound was over, it was also true that the little slug had caused some muscle damage, and the operation to remove the slug much more. What muscle fibers weren't torn were severely bruised. It was going to be a very painful trip over a long and bumpy road.

Almost a month to the day later, the convoy returned.

Two days later Lieutenant Macklin furnished Banning with a neatly typed-up report—a report that exceedingly dissatisfied him. Because he had acted with much too much caution, Macklin had not found out what Banning had told him to find out. And he had, for all his caution, been caught snooping by the Japanese.

They hadn't actually caught Macklin in a situation where they could credibly claim espionage, they just found him somewhere that the officer in charge of a supply convoy should not have been.

There were a number of legalities and unwritten laws involving the relationship between the Japanese Imperial Army in China and the military forces of the French, the Italians, the English, and the Americans. Captain Banning had come to China briefed on many of them. And his years in China had taught him much more. He had a pretty good sense by now of the rules of the game.

What the Japanese had done when they caught Macklin was what they had done before.

They had, as brother officers, courteously invited him to visit their headquarters. They then took him on an exhausting inspection of the area, with particular emphasis on the garbage dumps, rifle ranges, and other fascinating aspects of their operation. Then they brought him to the mess, where several profusely apologetic Japanese officers spilled their drinks on him while they got him drunk. At dinner they managed to spill in his lap a large vessel of something greasy, sticky, and absolutely impervious to cleaning.

The idea was to make him lose face. As usual, they succeeded.

Corporal Kenneth J. McCoy came to the S-2 office just after noon the day Banning received Macklin's report. He apologized for taking so long. But he explained that his gunnery sergeant had run him over to S-1 to take care of the paperwork that went with his promotion to corporal. This had not been taken care of when he had been shipped off to Peking.

"How's your leg?" Banning asked. "Bother you on the trip?" He didn't seem bothered by McCoy's delay in reporting to him—or else he didn't believe the kid would have anything worth reporting.

"It was rough on the way up, sir," McCoy said.

"All right now, though?"

"Yes, sir," McCoy said.

"Well, whether or not you like it, McCoy," Banning said, "I'm going to have to use you as a clerk."

"I thought that was probably going to happen," McCoy said.

"I'm sorry you're not pleased," Banning said. "But that's the way it's going to have to be."

"Captain, I've got something to say, and I don't know how to go about saying it."

"Spit it out," Banning said.

"The 111th and 113th Regiments of the 22nd Infantry Division are going to be moved from Süchow to Nantung, where they are going to be mobilized."

"Mobilized?" Banning asked, confused.

"I mean they're going to get trucks to replace their horses."

"You mean motorized," Banning corrected, chuckling.

"Yeah, motorized," McCoy said. "Sorry, sir. And then," he went on, "the 119th Regiment is going to stay at Süchow, reinforced by a regiment, I don't know which one, of 41st Division. Then, when the 111th and 113th come back, the 119th'll go to Nantung and get their trucks, and the other regiment will go back where it came from. When the whole division has trucks, they're going to move to Tsinan."

"You're sure of this?" Banning said, sarcastically.

"A couple of whores told me," McCoy said. "And I checked it out."

"Now, Corporal McCoy, why do you suppose Lieutenant Macklin's report doesn't mention this?"

As he spoke, Banning almost kicked himself for coming to Macklin's defense. And yet he knew he couldn't really help himself: Macklin was an officer, and officers do not admit to enlisted men that any other officer is less than an officer should be. But more important, there was bad chemistry between himself and Macklin. And Banning felt guilty about it, guilty enough to protect the lieutenant when he really shouldn't be protected.

Banning just did not like Macklin. He was a tall, dark-haired, fine-featured man, who fairly could be called handsome, and whose face seemed as bright and intelligent as it was handsome. The problem was that he was not nearly as bright as he looked—much less than he thought he was. The first time Banning had laid eyes on him, he had pegged him as the sort of man who substituted charm for substance, someone who spoke very carefully, never causing offense, never in a position he couldn't escape from by claiming misunderstanding.

"Well, I told you I didn't know how to say it," McCoy said. "I told him what I heard, and he laughed at me. But he's wrong. Whores know."

The truth was, Banning knew, that whores did indeed know.

"You said you 'checked it out,' " Banning said.

"Yes, sir."

"How?"

"I checked it out, sir," McCoy replied.

"You said that, and I asked you how."

"Sir, you told me not to go snooping around the Japs, and I'm afraid you're going to think I did anyhow."

"Why would I think that?" Banning asked.

"Well," McCoy said uneasily, "I got pretty close to them." He paused and then blurted, "I went to Nantung, Captain."

"You're telling me you went to Nantung? Without orders?"

"There was a Texaco truck going in," McCoy said. "With a load of kerosene. I gave the driver fifty yuan to take me with him. And then bring me back."

"And what did you do, Corporal McCoy, when you were in Nantung?" Banning asked.

The question seemed to surprise McCoy.

"I told you," he said. "I went to a whorehouse. One that the Jap officers go to."

"And there were Japanese officers in this brothel?"

"Yes, sir."

"And what did the Japanese officers think when they found a Marine Corps corporal in their whorehouse?" Banning asked. But before McCoy could reply, he went on: "They obviously did not see you, or you wouldn't be here. Did it occur to you, McCoy, that if they did see you, and they didn't slice your head off at the Adam's apple, I would have your ass if and when you came back?"

"They saw me," McCoy said. "They thought I was an Italian that works for Texaco. One of them had been in Rome and thought he talked Italian."

"Goddamn you, McCoy," Banning said. "You were ordered to leave the snooping to Lieutenant Macklin."

"You said not to go near them," McCoy said. "I thought you meant I wasn't to get near the compound. I didn't. I went to a whorehouse. And you made it sound like finding out about the trucks was important."

"And you're sure they didn't suspect you were a Marine?" Banning asked.

Dumb fucking question, Banning. If they suspected he was a Marine, he wouldn't be here.

"They thought I was Angelo Salini, from *Napoli,*" McCoy said, both matter-of-factly and a little smugly. "I went to high school with a guy with that name."

"And they told you about the trucks?" Banning asked.

"No, sir," McCoy said. "We just had a couple of drinks and messed around with the whores. The *whores* told me about the trucks."

Do I bring him up on charges for disobeying what was a direct order? Or do I commend him for his initiative?

"And did the ladies tell you what kind of trucks?" Banning said. "Or how many?"

"Just 'army trucks,' " McCoy said. "And since I couldn't go near the compound, I couldn't find out," McCoy said.

"Why should I believe this whorehouse scuttlebutt?" Banning asked.

"I don't know if you should or not, Captain," McCoy said. "But that's what I found out, and since Lieutenant Macklin wasn't going to report it, I figured I should."

Which means, of course, that he first told this to Macklin. Which means that Macklin knew McCoy had done something he wasn't supposed to do, and which Macklin should have reported to me. But if Macklin did report him, his own failure would be even more conspicuous. Sonofabitch!

"And did your lady friends tell you when all this is going to happen?"

McCoy nodded.

"By the time the next convoy goes through Süchow, one or the other of the regiments will probably be gone," McCoy said. "Maybe on the way back, one of them will already be back, and you could count the trucks."

"If you were on the next convoy, do you suppose you could count the trucks?" Banning asked.

"Yes, sir."

"I'm going to rephrase the question," Banning said. "Being fully aware of the risks involved—which means that if the Japanese catch you, they will more than likely break every bone in your body with clubs, and then behead you—would you be willing to try to get some photographs of the trucks, of their motorpool, photographs close enough up so that the bumper markings could be read?"

"I don't have a camera, Captain."

"I'll get you a camera, McCoy," Banning said.

"Then, yes, sir," McCoy said.

The cold-blooded decision, Banning realized, was whether or not it was worth it to determine if the Japanese were motorizing one of their divisions. It would be more than embarrassing if the Japanese caught this corporal. What he'd told McCoy would happen to him if he were caught was not hyperbole.

"Take the rest of the day off, McCoy," Banning said. "I want to have another talk with Lieutenant Macklin, and I want to think about this."

"He's liable to be pissed I went over his head," McCoy said.

"Don't worry about that," Banning said. "You're assigned to S-2. You work for me."

"Thank you, sir," McCoy said.

The moment McCoy walked out of his office, Banning had further thoughts about what he had just said. There was no question in his mind that the Japanese knew his name, as well as the names of everybody who worked closely with S-2. If it came to their attention that a corporal of his was making another trip on the Tientsin-Peking run, they were liable to drag him out of a truck on general principles.

But, he realized, they'd believe they had an officer in a corporal's uniform. Japanese corporals were not dispatched on missions of espionage, and therefore they could not imagine that Americans would do it either.

He realized he had already decided to send McCoy back to Peking on the next convoy.

Very early the next morning, Banning was summoned to the colonel's office. The colonel was in a near-rage.

"Are you aware, Banning, that there was a 'Welcome Home, Killer McCoy' party at the club last night? Complete with a banner saying exactly that?"

The club was called the "Million-Dollar Club," because it had allegedly cost that much to build fourteen years earlier, before the 4th Marines had come to China. It was on Bubbling Well Road, on the way to Shanghai's elegant race track.

"No, sir," Banning said. "I was not."

"What it looks like to the Italians is that we promoted him for stabbing those people," the colonel said. "If they haven't heard about it yet, the Italians soon will. We're going to have to get that kid out of Shanghai again, and quickly."

"I'd planned to send him back to Peking with the next convoy, sir," Banning said.

"When does it go?"

"On Thursday, sir."

"Is there any way it can leave sooner, say tomorrow?"

"I'll have to check with the S-4, sir, to be absolutely sure, but offhand I can't think of any reason it can't."

"Check with him. If there's any problem, let me know."

"Aye, aye, sir."

"What about the last trip?" the colonel asked. "Anything interesting?"

"I have some fairly reliable information, sir, say seven on a scale of one to ten, that the 22nd Infantry at Süchow is being motorized."

"That is interesting," the colonel said. "Wonder what the hell that's all about? Do they have that many trucks?"

"I'll be able to make a better guess when I have more information, sir. I'm going to try to get some photographs."

"Make sure whoever you send is a good man," the colonel said.

"Aye, aye, sir," Banning said. "I think he is."

"And get that damned Killer McCoy out of here as soon as possible. I don't want him waved like a red flag in front of the Italians."

"Aye, aye, sir."

(THREE)
Headquarters, 4th Regiment, USMC
Shanghai, China
11 May 1941

When his sergeant opened the office door to tell him that Lieutenant Sessions had arrived, Captain Edward J. Banning, USMC, was looking out the window of his office at the trees just coming into bloom. He had been thinking about Milla. If it wasn't for this character Sessions he was waiting for, he could be with her in the apartment. He had forced the image of Milla in her underwear out of his mind by reminding himself that the price they were going to have to pay for the beauty of spring would be the smell that would shortly come from Shanghai's infamous sewers.

"Ask him to come in, please, Sergeant," Banning said.

He turned and hoisted himself onto the window ledge. He was high enough off the floor for his feet to dangle.

Lieutenant Edward Sessions, USMC, marched into the office. He was wearing civilian clothing, a seersucker suit and a straw hat with a stiff brim. He looked, Banning decided, like another Macklin, another handsome sonofabitch with a full head of hair and nice white teeth.

And Lieutenant Sessions was clearly a little surprised to find, on this momentous occasion, the Intelligence Staff Officer of the 4th Marines sitting with his feet dangling like a small boy rather than solemnly behind a desk.

Sessions was not only fresh off the boat from the States, but he was fresh from Headquarters, USMC, and he was on a secret mission. All of these, Banning decided, had perhaps naturally made him just a little bit impressed with his own role in the scheme of things.

Fuck him!

Captain Banning was not awed by Lieutenant Sessions (whom he now remembered having once met years ago at Quantico), nor by the fact that he was fresh from Hq, USMC, nor by his secret mission. And he believed, in fact, that the secret mission itself was a little insulting to him, personally. Not only had he been in China four years and earned, he thought, a reputation for doing his duty the way it should be done, but his own man had been the reason why this whole secret-mission business had started.

Killer McCoy not only returned undetected from his second trip by motor convoy to Peking, but he came back with six rolls of 35-mm film. The Japanese 22nd Division had then been in the process of exchanging its horse-drawn transport for three kinds of trucks—a small truck, smaller even than an American pickup truck; a Japanese copy of a Ford ton-and-a-half stake-body truck; and a larger Mitsubishi two-ton, which was capable of towing both field pieces and ammunition trailers.

Banning had had the film processed, and then sent the negatives and a set of prints by the fastest means available (via the *President Wilson* of U.S. Lines to Manila, where it had been loaded aboard one of Pan American Airways' Sikorsky seaplanes bound for Hawaii and San Francisco) to Headquarters, USMC.

The first response to that had been a cryptic radio message:

> HQ USMC WASHINGTON DC VIA MACKAY RADIO FOR COMMANDING OFFICER 4TH MARINES SHANGHAI FOR BANNING REFERENCE PHOTOS WELL DONE STOP THE MORE THE MERRIER STOP MORE FOLLOWS COURIER STOP FORREST BRIG GEN USMC

Brigadier General Horace W. T. Forrest, Assistant Chief of Staff, Intelligence, Headquarters, USMC, was not only so pleased with Killer McCoy's photographs that he wanted more, but he was sending additional information (which he was reluctant to send via Mackay Radio) by courier.

That communication had taken nine days to arrive:

> There are several possible ramifications to the Japanese motorization of divisional-strength units which should be self-evident to you. Among these is the possibility that, considering the road network of China, it is the intention of the Japanese to employ these units elsewhere. It is therefore considered of the greatest importance that you continue to furnish this headquarters with the latest information available concerning actual, or projected, motorization of Japanese formations.
>
> Additionally, intelligence gathered in this area will serve to reflect the Japanese industrial capability.
>
> It has been learned from other sources that Germany will furnish to the Japanese an unknown quantity of so far unidentified field artillery. It is considered of the highest importance that information regarding the specific type of such German field artillery, the quantity of such artillery and ammunition stocks, and the identity of troop units to which such German artillery has been assigned be developed as soon as possible.
>
> Lieutenant Edward Sessions has been detached from Hq, USMC to assist in the gathering of this intelligence. He will be traveling to, and within, China, bearing a passport identifying him as a missionary of the Christian & Missionary Alliance. He will bring with him an encryption code, which, after the intelligence he develops concerning German artillery in Japanese hands is compiled with information you will have generated concerning Japanese motorization of tactical and logistical units, you will use to transmit refined intelligence data to this headquarters. This encryption code will be used for no other purpose, and you will continue to transmit data you generate as in the past.
>
> You will furnish to Lieutenant Sessions such support as is within your capability. Disbursal of confidential funds in this connection is authorized. Although Lieutenant Sessions will be functioning as a staff officer of this headquarters, he will be under your orders while in China.

Why it was considered necessary for them to send an officer to China to see if any German artillery pieces were in Japanese hands was interesting. Finding out what equipment the Japanese had was something that Banning had been doing all along. So Sessions's arrival meant one of two things: Either they didn't like the way he was handling things, or Lieutenant Sessions had friends in high places, and a secret mission to China would look good on his record when the next promotion board sat.

When Lieutenant Sessions walked into the office, Captain Banning was not surprised to see on his finger the ring signifying graduation from the United States Naval Academy at Annapolis. The conclusion to be drawn was that Sessions indeed was well connected politically.

"Lieutenant Sessions, sir," Sessions said, standing to attention.

Banning pushed himself off the windowsill and offered his hand.

"We met, I think, at Quantico in 'thirty-five," he said. "Nice to see you again, Sessions. Nice voyage?"

"Yes, sir," Sessions said, "I remember meeting the captain. And the trip was first class, long, but with first-class food and service to make it bearable."

"I came out here on the *Shaumont,*" Banning said. "And I have good reason to believe that she'll be back here just in time to take me home."

Sessions was sure there was more to that statement than was on the surface. It was a dig at him for being ordered to China on a passenger ship rather than on the *Shaumont,* one of the two Navy Transports (the other was the *Henderson)* that cruised around the world, stopping at every Naval base or port with a sizable Navy or Marine detachment from Portsmouth, New Hampshire, to Shanghai.

If I were in his shoes, Sessions thought, *I would be more than a little pissed-off myself. If I were the S-2, and they sent a major to "help" do what I am supposed to, it would be insulting. And I'm a lieutenant.*

"The *President Madison* was part of the plan, sir," Sessions said, "so that no questions would be raised if I suddenly joined the Christian & Missionary Alliance people here."

"I thought it might be something like that," Banning said dryly.

"There are seven Christian & Missionary Alliance missions in China," Sessions explained. "Six of them are located between here and Peking. They are regularly resupplied twice a year with both stores and personnel. That will be the cover for this operation. We will visit each of the six missions on the route. We'll drop off supplies and replacement personnel and pick up some missionaries who are due for a vacation in the United States. It is believed that I can simply blend in with the other missionaries and not attract Japanese attention."

"Well, you could pass for a missionary, I'll say that," Banning said.

"Sir, do I detect some sarcasm?"

The people in Washington who dreamed up this operation, Banning thought, *have apparently spent a lot of time watching Humphrey Bogart and Robert Taylor spy movies.*

"The people who dreamed up this idea, Sessions," Banning said, "left one important factor out of the equation."

"Sir?"

"With your passport and in civilian clothing, I have no doubt that the Japanese will indeed believe you are an American missionary," Banning said. "The trouble with that is that so far as the Japanese are concerned, all Americans, including missionaries, are spies."

"I don't know what to say, sir," Sessions said.

"In my judgment, Lieutenant Sessions," Banning went on, "this brilliant Washington scheme is tantamount to hanging a sign from both sides of the missionaries' trucks, 'CAUTION!! SPIES AT WORK!' "

He gave Sessions a moment to let that sink in, and then went on.

"But you and I are Marine officers, Lieutenant," he said. "And when we are given an order, we carry it out."

"Aye, aye, sir," Sessions said, uncomfortably.

"There is one small loophole in the Japanese perception of Americans," Banning said, "that I have had some success in exploiting. The Japanese believe—and I'm not sure if this is their code of Bushido or whether they picked it up from the British—that enlisted men come from the peasant class, and therefore can be presumed to be too stupid to have anything to do with intelligence."

"I'm not sure I follow you, sir," Sessions said.

"Bear with me," Banning replied. "What I'm going to do is inform Major Akkaido, who is the Japanese liaison officer, that I have been directed by higher authority to provide an escort for the Christian & Missionary Alliance vehicles. I am going to try very hard to convince Major Akkaido, as one soldier to another, that I am annoyed by this, and that, whether or not it is convenient for the missionaries, I am going to send the missionaries along with one of our regular Peking truck convoys."

"I think I'm beginning to see," Sessions said.

"The regular supply convoy consists of four Studebaker trucks and a GMC pickup that we've rigged up as sort of a half-assed wrecker. It can drag a broken-down truck, presuming it hasn't lost a wheel or broken an axle. If the motor officer can spare another Studebaker, we'll send that too, empty, to take the load if one of the other trucks breaks down."

"Presumably, there will be mechanics along?" Sessions asked.

"Each truck carries two people," Banning said, "one of whom is allegedly a mechanic. They give the trucks a pretty good going-over before they leave. But most of the difficulty we experience is with tires. There's nothing that can be done about them until they go flat or blow out. We carry spare tires and wheels, as well as an air pump, on the pickup and hope they will cover whatever trouble we have on the road."

"You're thinking the Japanese will pay less attention to the missionary vehicles and me, if we are part of a regular convoy?" Sessions asked.

"The picture I hope to paint for the Japanese," Banning said, "one I devoutly hope they buy, is that the regular, routine, no-longer-very-auspicious supply convoy is carrying with it this time a handful of missionaries and their supplies."

"I think that's a good idea," Sessions said.

"The convoy is under the command of an officer. These we rotate, both to give them a chance to see the landscape between here and Peking and to keep the Japanese from becoming suspicious of any particular man."

"I understand," Sessions said. "And whoever this officer is, you intend to make him aware of the mission?"

"No, I don't think that will be necessary," Banning said. "But I will tell him what I'm now going to tell you. There will be a Corporal McCoy along on the convoy. They call him 'Killer.' And Killer McCoy works for me. And when Killer McCoy makes a suggestion about what route the convoy is to take or not to take, or what the personnel on the convoy are or are not to do, that suggestion is to be interpreted as being an order from me."

" 'Killer' McCoy? Why do they call him 'Killer'?"

"They call him 'Killer,' " Banning said, matter-of-factly, "because four Italian marines attacked him. He killed two of them with a Baby Fairbairn."

"Excuse me? With a what?"

"There's a rather interesting Englishman, Captain Bruce Fairbairn, on the Shanghai Municipal Police," Banning explained. "He knows more about hand-to-hand combat, jujitsu, and the other martial disciplines than anybody else. He invented a knife, a long, narrow, sharp-as-a-razor dagger—which incidentally General Butler tried to get the Corps to buy and issue. Anyway, there is a smaller, more concealable version. The big knife is called the 'Fairbairn,' and the smaller one the 'Baby Fairbairn.' "

"And your noncom killed two people with it?"

"Two Italian marines," Banning said.

"And there was no court-martial?" Sessions asked. Banning shook his head no. "He knifed two people to death, and that's it?"

"It was self-defense," Banning said. "There were witnesses, two plainclothes Chinese policemen. That was the end of it. The Italians are still—this happened right after the New Year—pretty upset about it. And McCoy is something of a celebrity among the troops. Including the Japanese, who admire that sort of thing. The Japanese don't know that he works for me, of course. Only a few people do. On paper, he's assigned to the motor pool."

"I can hardly wait to meet this man," Sessions said.

"I think, Lieutenant Sessions, that you will find Corporal McCoy very interesting, and perhaps even educational," Banning said. "He speaks Chinese and Japanese, and even reads a little bit of it. And he's been making this run twice a month for six months. He's a good man. He uncovered the whole motorization business; and he took the photographs I presume you've seen."

"I've seen the photographs," Sessions said.

"I'm a little worried about the reaction of the missionaries to Corporal McCoy," Banning said.

"Why do you say that?"

"As a general rule of thumb, Lieutenant Sessions," Banning said, "I have found that most missionaries consider the Marines the tools of Satan. Our enlisted men fornicate with Chinese women, and our officers support the sinful repression of the natives. Now the Japanese enlisted men rape the Chinese women, and Japanese officers order the heads sliced from Chinese they judge unenthusiastic about the Greater Japanese Co-Prosperity Sphere. But that doesn't bother the missionaries, for the Japanese are heathens, and that sort of thing is to be expected of them."

"The Reverend Feller does not quite fit that picture, Captain," Lieutenant Sessions said. "He really hates the Japanese."

"Oh?"

"During his previous service here, he saw enough of the Japanese to see them for what they are. He was present at the rape of Nanking, for example, and believes that the promise of China can only be realized after the Japanese are expelled. He recognizes that can only happen with our assistance."

"I presume he knows that we're neutral in this war?" Banning asked, dryly.

"Apparently, he believes we're going to get in it sooner or later," Sessions said. "And in the meantime is anxious to help, even when that means a personal sacrifice."

"What does that mean?"

"It would have been far more convenient for him to remain in the United States and simply send for Mrs. Feller."

"I have no idea what you're talking about," Banning said.

"The Reverend Feller was summoned home for conferences with his superiors. While he was there, his church decided that he would not be returning to China."

"You mean he got fired?"

"No. He was given a bigger job. His wife remained in China when he went to the United States. She could have returned to the United States by herself, which would have been far more convenient for all concerned. But he elected instead to make the voyage over here 'to settle his replacement in his job,' to help me in my mission, and to take Mrs. Feller back with him. This was all really unnecessary, but he did it anyway."

"A real self-sacrificing patriot, huh?" Banning said, wondering what the Reverend's real purpose was. There were stories of missionaries accumulating chests of valuable Chinese antiques, so many stories that all of them could not be discounted. And what better way to carry valuable antiques out of China than under protection of the U.S. Marine Corps?

"I don't think that's quite fair, sir," Sessions said.

Banning didn't want to get into a discussion of missionary antiques, and changed the subject.

"Christ, I hope both the Reverend and you are wrong about us getting into a war with the Japs," he said.

Sessions looked at him in surprise. It was not the sort of remark he expected from a Marine officer.

"Lieutenant," Banning said, patiently, "certainly you can understand what a logistic horror it would be to attempt to field one division over here. This isn't Nicaragua. China could swallow the entire World War I American Expeditionary Force without a burp."

"I've thought about that, sir," Sessions said.

Banning looked at Sessions with annoyance. *Another Always-Agree-with-the-Superior-Officer ass-kisser like Macklin.* Then he changed his mind. Sessions was just saying what he was really thinking.

"Have you?" Banning asked.

"Eventually, we may have to face that logistic horror," Sessions said. "I really thought we were going to take action when the Japanese sank the *Panay*[2]."

"Tell me more about the Reverend Feller," Banning said. There was no point in discussing whether a force large enough to do any good could be deployed in China with an officer who had just gotten off the boat.

"He is willing to help us in any way he can," Sessions said, "consistent, of course, with his religious principles."

Banning thought, but did not say, that there was very little then that the good Reverend would be able to do. The principles of religion seemed to disagree almost entirely with the principles and practice of gathering intelligence. The more he thought about it, the more he thought it was likely that the Reverend Feller's motive in returning to China had less to do with patriotism than it did with transporting a case, or cases, of Chinese antiques back to the States.

"As a practical matter, Lieutenant," Banning said, "I am more concerned with the Reverend Feller's reaction to Corporal McCoy."

"I don't think I follow you."

"For one thing, on the way back and forth to Peking, McCoy spends a lot of time drunk, usually in brothels. I don't want the Reverend, or anyone else, interfering with that. Or anything else that McCoy might do."

"I understand, sir," Sessions said immediately.

[2]The U.S.S. *Panay,* a gunboat of the Yangtze River Patrol, was attacked and sunk, with many Americans killed and wounded, by Japanese aircraft in 1937.

Banning looked at him and was somewhat surprised to see that he did, in fact, understand why McCoy spent a lot of time in brothels.

"Did the missionaries weather the trip well?" Banning asked. "How soon can they be ready to start?"

"They're in the Hotel Metropole," Sessions said. "They can leave just as soon as their vehicles have been serviced."

"I'll send McCoy over to the hotel in the morning," Banning said. "The Japanese will hear of it immediately, of course. But they won't think anything about it after I tell them that he will be taking your missionaries with him to Peking. What he'll do at the hotel is what he would be expected to do."

"Which is?"

"Get the missionary vehicles in condition to roll. Tell the Reverend Feller that it will be his responsibility to bring his vehicles here to be examined and to provide two extra wheels and four extra tires and tubes for each of them. That sort of thing."

"Where is Feller going to get wheels and tires?"

"You can buy anything you want in Shanghai," Banning said.

"Wouldn't it make more sense to have Corporal McCoy get the wheels and tires for him? I have some funds . . ."

"The only reason a corporal of Marines would go shopping for a missionary," Banning said, "would be if he were ordered to. And the Japanese would then wonder why the Marines were going out of their way to be nice to a couple of missionaries—why these missionaries were different from any of the others."

Sessions winced, and exhaled audibly.

"I've got a lot to learn, don't I?"

"I'm sure that Corporal McCoy will be happy to point out the more significant rocks and shoals to you," Banning said.

"The most dangerous shoal would be getting caught in a compromising position," Sessions said. "What would happen if the Japanese detain or arrest me and charge me with espionage?"

"The thing to do, of course, is not get yourself arrested. And the way to do that is to listen to Killer McCoy. If he says don't go somewhere, don't go somewhere."

III

(ONE)
The Metropole Hotel
Shanghai, China
12 May 1941

None of his peers was surprised when Corporal Kenneth J. "Killer" McCoy, USMC, took an off-the-compound apartment immediately after his return from the first "Get Him out Of Sight" trip to Peking.

He was now a corporal, and most of the noncommissioned officers of the 4th Regiment of Marines in Shanghai had both a billet and a place where they actually lived. McCoy's billet, appropriate to a corporal, was half of a small room (not unlike a cell) in one of the two-story brick buildings that served the Headquarters Company, First Battalion, as barracks. It was furnished with a steel cot (on which rested a mattress, two blankets, two sheets, a pillow and a pillow case), a wall locker and a footlocker filled with the uniforms and accoutrements prescribed for a corporal of Marines.

With the exception of an issue mirror mounted to the door, that was all. There was not even a folding chair.

McCoy shared his billet with a staff sergeant assigned to the office of the battalion S-4 officer.[1] The two of them split the cost of a Chinese room boy (actually a thirty-five-year-old man) who daily visited the room, polished the floor, washed the windows, tightened the blankets on the bunks, touched up the gloss of the boots and shoes, polished the brass, saw that the uniforms and accoutrements were shipshape, and in every way kept things shipshape.

Before inspections that Corporal McCoy and Staff Sergeant Patrick O'Dell were obliged to attend (and there was at least one such scheduled inspection every month, on payday) Chong Lee, the room boy, would remove from the wall locker and the footlocker those items of uniform and accoutrements that were required by Marine regulation and lay them out on the bunks precisely in the prescribed manner.

To prepare for the monthly inspection of personnel in billets, it was only necessary for Staff Sergeant O'Dell and Corporal McCoy to go to the arms room and draw their Springfield Model 1903 rifles and the bayonets for them, ensure they were clean, and proceed to their billet.

The gunnery sergeant of Headquarters Company, First Battalion, 4th Marines, was a salty old sonofabitch who drew the line at some fucking Chink having access to the weapons. His men would fucking well clean their own pieces.

The assignment of Staff Sergeant O'Dell and Corporal McCoy to the same room was a matter of convenience. They did not like each other. And sometimes the only time they spoke was when they met, once a month for the scheduled in-

[1]Supply.

spection. The only thing they had in common was that neither of them had responsibility for the company supervision of subordinates. The six other enlisted men assigned to battalion S-4 were supervised outside the office by the assistant S-4 corporal, Corporal Williamson.

After his promotion and return from the first "Get Him out of Sight" trip to Peking, Corporal McCoy had been officially transferred from Dog Company to Headquarters Company and assigned to the motor pool.

Whether—as some reasoned—it had been decided to continue to keep him out of sight of the Italians, or whether—as others reasoned—that to get right down to it McCoy didn't know his ass from left field about being a motor pool corporal, he had been given the more or less permanent assignment of riding the supply convoys to Peking.

That kept him out of town more than he was in Shanghai. The result was that since he didn't have a shack job and since he was gone so often, the first sergeant and the gunny had decided there was no sense in putting him on duty rosters if more often than not he wouldn't be around when the duty came up.

And then after sometimes three or four weeks spent bouncing his ass around in the cab of a Studebaker truck, it seemed only fair to give him liberty when he was in Shanghai.

For all practical purposes, then, he didn't have any company duties when he wasn't off with one of the supply convoys. And it was understandable that he didn't want to hang around the billet waiting for some odd job to come up. When he was in Shanghai he stood the reveille formation. After that nobody saw him until reveille the next morning. He *needed* an apartment. You couldn't spend all day in bars and whorehouses.

Most of his peers found nothing wrong with the way McCoy was playing the game. Most of them had themselves made one or more trips away from Shanghai in truck convoys. For the first couple of hours, maybe even the first couple of days, it was okay. But then it became nothing but a bumpy road going on for fucking ever, broken only by meals and piss calls. And the meals were either cold canned rations or something Chink, like fried chunks of fucking dog meat.

But there were a few—generally lower-ranking noncommissioned officers with eight or more years of service—who held contrary opinions: The Goddamned Corps was obviously going to hell in a handbasket if a candy-ass sonofabitch with Parris Island sand still in his boots gets to be a corporal just starting his second fucking hitch, for Christ's sake, instead of having his ass shipped in irons to Portsmouth for cutting up them Italian marines.

What his peers did not know—and what McCoy was under orders not to tell them—was that not only did he have an apartment with a telephone but that the Corps was paying for it. The less the other enlisted men knew about the real nature of McCoy's S-2 duty, the better. Getting him out of the billets would help. And there was another secret from the troops, shared only by the colonel (who had to sign the authorizations), Captain Banning, and the finance sergeant: McCoy had been given a one-time cash grant of $125 for "the purchase of suitable civilian clothing necessary in the performance of his military duty" and was drawing "rations and quarters allowance."

Corporal Kenneth J. McCoy's apartment was on the top floor of a three-story building in P'u-tung. It was not at all elaborate. And it was small, one large room with a bed in a curtained alcove, and a tiny bathroom (shower, no tub) in another. There was no kitchen, but he had installed an electric hot plate so that he could make coffee. And he had an icebox to cool his beer.

But there was a tiny balcony, shielded from view, large enough for just one chair, on which he could sit when he had the time and watch the boat traffic on Soochow Creek.

There was a restaurant in the adjacent building. If he wanted something to eat, all he had to do was put his head out the window and yell at the cook, and food would be delivered to him. He often got breakfast like that, yelling down for a couple of three-minute eggs and a pot of tea. And sometimes late at night, when he was hungry, he'd call down for some kind of Chinese version of a Western omelet, eggs scrambled with onions, bits of ham, and sweet pepper.

He rarely ate in the NCO mess of the 4th Marines, although the chow there was good. It was just that there were so many places in Shanghai to eat well, and so cheaply, that unless he just happened to be near the mess at chow time, it didn't seem worth the effort to take a meal there.

The building on the other side was a brothel, the "Golden Dragon Club," where he had run an account for nearly as long as he'd been stationed in Shanghai. It was through his friend Piotr Petrovich Muller he had found the apartment. Piotr had known the proprietor of the Golden Dragon in the good old days, back in Holy Mother Russia.

The man had an unpronounceable name, but that didn't matter, because he liked to be called "General." He claimed (McCoy was sure he was lying) that he had been a General in the Army of the Czar.

When he had first moved into the apartment, McCoy had played "Vingt-et-Un" with the General long enough for the both of them to recognize the other was not a pigeon to be plucked. They had become more or less friends afterwards, despite the differences in their age and "rank."

Most of the items on the monthly bill the General rendered were for services not connected with the twenty-odd girls in the General's employ. The General's people cleaned McCoy's apartment and did his laundry. And then there were bar charges and food charges. The girls themselves were more than okay. Mostly they were Chinese, who ranged from very pretty to very elegant (no peasant wenches in the General's establishment), but there were a few Indochinese and two White Russians as well.

McCoy actually believed that the General, who exhibited a certain officer-type arrogance, had most probably been an officer, if not officially a general, in the Czarist Army. Something like captain or maybe major was what he probably had been when, like so many other White Russian "generals," he had come penniless and stateless to Shanghai twenty years before. McCoy didn't like to think how the General had survived at first—probably as a pimp, possibly by strong-arm robbery—but he was now inarguably a success.

He had an elegant apartment in one of the newer buildings, to which he sometimes invited McCoy for a Russian dinner. He drove a new American Buick, and he had a number of successful business interests now (some of them perfectly legal) in addition to the Golden Dragon.

There were eight sets of khakis hanging in the wardrobe when McCoy, naked, and still dripping from his shower, walked across the room and opened it. They were not issue. His issue khakis hung in his wall locker at the barracks. These uniforms were tailor-made. The shirts had cost him sixty cents, American, and the trousers ninety. The field scarves[2] had been a nickel, and the belt (stitched layers of khaki) a dime. The belt was not regulation. Regulation was web. But McCoy

[2]Neckties.

knew that the only time anything would ever be said about it was at a formal inspection, and he hardly ever stood one of those anymore.

Neither were his chevrons regulation. Regulation chevrons were embroidered onto a piece of khaki and then sewn onto the shirt. McCoy's chevrons (and those of the gunnery sergeant) had been embroidered directly onto their shirts. If it was good enough for the gunny, McCoy had reasoned, it was good enough for him. And now that he had made corporal, he knew that the shirts would be worn out long before he would make sergeant.

The shirt and trousers were stiffly starched. They would not stay that way long. It was already getting humid. Shanghai was as far south as New Orleans, and every bit as muggy. Before long the starch would wilt, and it was more than likely that he would have to change uniforms when he went to the compound, which is where he had to go after he introduced himself to the Reverend Feller, who was staying at the Hotel Metropole. He did not wish to give the assholes in Motor Transport any opportunity to spread it around that Killer McCoy had shown up in a sweaty uniform looking like a fucking Chinaman.

When he was dressed, with his field scarf held in place with the prescribed USMC tie clasp, there was no longer any question that he would need another uniform before the day was over. He decided that it made more sense to take one with him than to use one of the issue uniforms in his billet. He could change in the motor pool head and avoid going to the barracks at all.

Carrying an extra uniform on a hanger, he left the apartment and trotted down the stairs. He did not lock the apartment. The way that worked was that there were some Westerners whose apartments were robbable, and some whose apartments were not. It had nothing to do with locks on doors and bars over windows. The trick was to get yourself on the list of those whose apartments were safe. One way to do this was to have it known that you were friendly with a Shanghai policeman, and the other was to be friendly with the chief of the tong whom the association had granted burglary privileges in your area.

McCoy's apartment was twice safe. When he was in town, he continued to gamble regularly with both Detective Sergeant Lester Chatworth of the Shanghai Police, and (not at the same time, of course, but when the local celebrity honored the Golden Dragon with his presence) with Lon Ci'iang, head of the Po'Ti Tong.

On the crowded street, he stopped first to buy a rice cake, and then flagged down a rickshaw.

He told the boy, a wiry, leather-skinned man of maybe twenty-five, to please take him to the Hotel Metropole, and the boy swung around to look at him in unabashed curiosity. It always shocked the Chinese to encounter a white face who spoke their language.

When the rickshaw delivered him in front of the Hotel Metropole, there were several Europeans (in Shanghai, that included Americans), among them a quartet of British officers, standing on the sidewalk there. The civilians looked at him with distaste, the officers with curiosity. When McCoy saluted crisply, one of the officers, as he returned the salute with a casual wave of his swagger stick, gave him a faint smile.

He is giving me the benefit of the doubt, McCoy thought, *deciding that I wouldn't be coming here unless I were on duty. The civilians just don't like a place like this under any circumstances fouled by the presence of a Marine enlisted man.*

He went to the desk and asked for the room number of the Reverend Mr. Feller. Captain Banning had been specific on the telephone about that. The missionary named Sessions was really a Marine lieutenant, but McCoy was to deal with a Reverend Feller and not the lieutenant.

As he crossed the lobby to the elevators, one of the bellboys offered to relieve him of the spare uniform, but McCoy waved him away.

The elevators were contained within an ornate metal framework, and the cage itself was glassed in. As it rose, it gave McCoy a view of the entire lobby: the potted palms, the leather couches and chairs, the hotel guests, the men already in linen and seersucker suits, and the women in their summer dresses. He could see the outlines of underwear beneath some of the dresses; and in the right light, some of the women—the younger ones mostly—showed ghostly, lovely legs.

McCoy saw few European women. He hadn't, he thought, spoken to a European woman in over six months, the only exceptions being the General's two Russian whores, and they didn't really count.

He walked down the wide, carpeted corridor to 514, and knocked at the door.

"Who is it?" an American female voice called after a moment.

"Corporal McCoy, ma'am," he called out. "Of the Fourth Marines. I'm here to see Reverend Feller."

"Oh, my!" she said. He heard in the tone of her voice either displeasure or fright that he was here. He wondered what the hell that was all about.

The door opened.

"I'm Mrs. Moore," she said. "Please come in. I'll have to fetch the Reverend. He's with Mr. Sessions."

She was a large woman, big boned, just on the wrong side of fat. She was, McCoy judged, maybe forty. With the well-scrubbed, makeup-free face of a woman who took religion seriously. She had light brown hair, braided and pinned to the side of her head. And she wore a cotton dress, with long sleeves and buttons fastened up to the throat. Hanging from her neck was a four-inch Christian cross, made of wood.

"Thank you," McCoy said.

"Are you the man who was originally supposed to come?" she asked.

"I don't think I understand you," McCoy said.

"It doesn't matter," she said. "I'll go fetch the Reverend Feller," she added, smiling uneasily at him. She slid past him to the door, as if she were afraid he would pick her up, carry her into the adjacent bedroom, throw her on the bed, and work his sinful ways on her. The thought amused him, and he smiled, which discomfited her further.

He decided he'd have a word with the people in the convoy to watch what they said and did with her around. If somebody said "fuck," she would faint. Then her husband would bitch to the lieutenant in civilian clothes, and he would make trouble.

A minute later, the Reverend Glen T. Feller entered the room. He wore a broad, toothy smile, and his hand was extended farther than McCoy believed was anatomically possible.

He was of average height, slim, with dark hair plastered carefully to his skull, and a pencil-line mustache. He was immaculately shaven, and McCoy could smell his after-shave cologne.

"I'm the Reverend Feller," he said. "I'm happy to meet you, Corporal, and I'm sorry I wasn't here when you came."

"No problem, sir," McCoy said. The Reverend Feller's hand was soft, clammy, and limp. McCoy was a little repelled, but not surprised. It was the sort of hand he expected to find on a missionary.

Mrs. Moore moved around them, so as to stand behind the Reverend and put him between herself and McCoy.

There was a rap at the door, and then "Mr." Sessions entered the room.

Even in the civilian clothes, McCoy decided, *this guy looks like he's an officer. But like a regular platoon leader, not a hotshot intelligence officer from Headquarters, USMC, in Washington.*

"You're Corporal McCoy?" Sessions asked, surprised. "The one they call 'Killer'?"

"Some people have called me that," McCoy said, uncomfortably.

"You're not quite what I expected, Corporal, from the way Captain Banning spoke of you," Sessions said.

Well, shit, Lieutenant, neither are you.

"Well, I'm McCoy," he said.

He was aware that Mrs. Moore was looking at him very strangely; he decided she had heard all about the Italian marines.

"How long have you been in the Corps, Corporal?" Lieutenant Sessions asked.

"About four years," McCoy said.

"There aren't very many men who make corporal in four years," Sessions said. "Or as young as you are."

McCoy looked at him, but said nothing.

"How old are you, Corporal?"

"Twenty-one, sir," Corporal Killer McCoy said.

"Presuming Captain Banning was not pulling your leg, Ed," the Reverend Feller said, laughing, "we must presume the Killer's bite is considerably worse than his bark."

I don't like this sonofabitch, McCoy thought.

"Killer," the Reverend Feller said, "we place ourselves in your capable hands."

"I said some people call me that, Reverend," McCoy said. "I didn't mean you could."

"Well, I'm very sorry, Corporal," the Reverend Feller said. He looked at Sessions, as if waiting for him to remind Corporal McCoy that he was speaking to a high-ranking missionary. When Sessions was silent, Feller said, "I don't want us to get off on the wrong foot. No hard feelings?"

"No," McCoy said.

(TWO)
Motor Pool, First Bn, 4th Marines
Shanghai, China
14 May 1941

The Christian & Missionary Alliance vehicles had been taken from the docks to the motor pool of the First Battalion, 4th Marines, where they were carefully examined by Sergeant Ernst Zimmerman, who was the assistant motor transport supervisor and would be the NCOIC[3] of the Peking convoy.

The vehicles were greased and their oil was changed. And just to be on the safe side, Ernie Zimmerman changed the points and condensers and cleaned and gapped the spark plugs. Zimmerman, at twenty-six, was already on his third hitch, and had been in China since 1935.

He was a phlegmatic man, stocky, tightly muscled, with short, stubby fingers on

[3]Noncommissioned Officer In Charge.

hands that were surprisingly immaculate considering that he spent most of his duty time bent over the fender of one vehicle or another doing himself what he did not trust the private and PFC mechanics to do.

He lived with a slight Chinese woman who had borne him three children. She and the children had learned to speak German. Though he understood much more Chinese than he let on, Zimmerman spoke little more than he had the day he'd carried his sea bag down the gangway of the Naval Transport U.S.S. *Henderson* more than six years before.

At 0700 hours, two hours before the convoy was to get underway, a meeting was held in the motor pool office, a small wooden building at the entrance to the motor pool. The motor pool itself was a barbed-wire-fenced enclosure within the First Battalion compound.

Present were Lieutenant John Macklin, who would again be the officer in charge of the convoy; Sergeant Zimmerman; Corporal McCoy; and the eight other enlisted men of the convoy detail. They had just spread maps out on the dispatcher's table when they were joined by Captain Edward Banning.

The usual route the convoy traveled could not be followed on this trip, because of the necessity to stop at the six Christian & Missionary Alliance missions. The first deviation would be to Nanking. Normally they turned off the Shanghai-Nanking highway onto a dirt road just past Wuhsi. Fifty miles down that road was the ferry across the Yangtze River between Chiangyin and Chen-chiang.

It would now be necessary to enter Nanking, drop off supplies for the Christian & Missionary Alliance there, and pick up the Reverend Feller's wife, her luggage, and their household goods. It was a hundred miles from where they normally turned off, a two-hundred-mile round trip, because it still made good sense to cross the Yangtze between Chiangyin and Chen-chiang.

"It has been suggested, sir," Lieutenant Macklin said to Captain Banning, "that at the turnoff point for Chiangyin we detach from the convoy one of the Studebaker automobiles, the wrecker, and the missionary truck with the Nanking supplies. The rest of the convoy would go on to Chiangyin and wait for the others to return from Nanking there. That would mean spending the night in Nanking."

There was no question in Sergeant Ernst Zimmerman's mind who had made the suggestion, and he was not at all surprised when Captain Banning said, "That seems to make more sense than having the whole convoy make the round trip." Banning continued, "Why don't you have McCoy drive the civilian car? That would make sort of a Marine detachment, with the wrecker, to accompany the missionary vehicles."

"Aye, aye, sir," Lieutenant Macklin said.

There was therefore, Sergeant Ernie Zimmerman concluded, some reason for McCoy to go to Nanking, as there was obviously some reason why McCoy had been given the convoy as kind of a primary duty. He had not been told what that reason was, and he had no intention of asking. If they wanted him to know, they would have told him. He believed the key to a successful career in the Corps was to do what you were told to do as well as you could and ask no questions. And to keep your eyes open so that you noticed strange little things, like the fact the regimental S-2 paid a lot of attention to a truck convoy that was really none of an intelligence officer's business, and that the real man in charge of the convoys was not whichever officer happened to be sent along, but Corporal "Killer" McCoy.

It took about an hour to decide—and mark on the three maps they would take with them—where the convoy would leave their normal route to visit the other five missions where they would be stopping.

Then Lieutenant Macklin sent the enlisted men to the arms room to draw their weapons. Each Marine drew a Colt Model 1911A1 .45 ACP pistol with three charged magazines. Two PFCs drew Browning Automatic Rifles, caliber .30–06, together with five charged twenty-round magazines. Sergeant Zimmerman and Corporal McCoy drew Thompson submachine guns, caliber .45 ACP with two fifty-round drum magazines. Everybody else took their assigned Springfield Model 1903 rifles from the arms room. There was also a prepacked ammo load, sealed cases of ammunition for all the weapons, plus a sealed case of fragmentation grenades.

There never had been any trouble on the Peking convoys. Sergeant Zimmerman, unaware that he was in complete agreement with the colonel, believed this was because the convoy detail was heavily armed.

There were nine vehicles in the convoy when it rolled out of the First Battalion compound: four Marine Corps Studebaker ton-and-a-half trucks, with canvas roofs suspended over the beds on wooden bows; two Christian & Missionary Alliance trucks, also Studebakers, differing from the Marine trucks only in that they did not have a steel protective grille mounted to the frame; two gray Studebaker "Captain" sedans, with the Christian & Missionary Alliance insignia (a burning cross) and a legend in Chinese ideograms painted on their doors; and bringing up the rear was the homemade pickup/wrecker, stacked high with spare tires and wheels.

Sergeant Zimmerman drove the wrecker. He usually rode in it as a passenger, but its normal driver was at the wheel of one of the missionary trucks. The second missionary truck was driven by a Marine who ordinarily would have been assistant driver on one of the trucks. Lieutenant Macklin drove one of the missionary Studebakers, and Corporal McCoy the other.

As the trucks made their way through heavy traffic toward the Nanking Highway, the passenger cars left the convoy and went to the Hotel Metropole to pick up the missionaries. Zimmerman was not surprised when they had to wait by the side of the Nanking Highway for more than an hour for the missionaries. Missionaries were fucking civilians, and fucking civilians were always late.

The first hundred miles went quickly. The Japanese Army kept the Nanking Highway and the rail line that ran parallel to it in good shape. Every twenty miles or so, near intersections, there were Japanese checkpoints, two or three soldiers under a corporal. But they just waved the convoy through. Long lines of Chinese, however, were backed up at every checkpoint.

It was less a search for contraband, McCoy thought, than a reminder of Japanese authority.

Just past Wuhsi, two and a half hours into the journey, the convoy rolled through another Japanese checkpoint, then turned off the highway onto a gravel road which led, fifty miles away, to the ferry between Chiangyin and Chen-chiang.

Once they had reached the ferry, the Reverend Feller, Mr. Sessions, and Mrs. Moore got in the back seat of the Studebaker McCoy was driving, and (trailed by one of the missionary trucks) headed down the highway for Nanking.

The rest of the convoy, led by Lieutenant Macklin in the other missionary Studebaker, started off toward Chiangyin. It was the rainy season, and, predictably, it began to rain buckets. The road turned slick and treacherous, and it took them nearly as long to make that fifty miles as it had to come from Shanghai to Wuhsi.

(THREE)
Christian & Missionary Alliance Mission
Nanking, China
1630 Hours 14 May 1941

Nanking was a curious mixture of East and West, ancient and modern. The tallest building in the city, for instance, was not a modern skyscraper but the Porcelain Tower, an octagon of white glazed bricks 260 feet tall, built five hundred years before by the Emperor Yung Lo to memorialize the virtues of his mother.

Recently, from 1928 until 1937, Nanking had been the capital of the Republic of China. But in 1937 the Japanese had captured it in a vicious battle followed by bloody carnage. Their victory was soon known as "The Rape of Nanking."

There had nevertheless still been time for Chiang Kai-shek's Kuomintang government to make their modern mark on it. Outside of town was the Sun Yat-sen mausoleum, honoring the founder of the Chinese Republic. And within the city half a dozen large, Western-style office buildings were built on wide avenues to house governmental ministries. There was also a modern railroad station and a large airport.

After "The Rape of Nanking," in the correct belief that representatives of the foreign press (whom they could not bar from China) would all immediately head for Nanking, the Japanese had made a point of keeping Nanking peaceful. Only a handful of military units were stationed there, and they were on their good behavior. When, in the interests of furthering the Greater Japanese Asian Co-Prosperity Sphere it became necessary to slice off some heads, the persons designated were first removed from Nanking.

The Christian & Missionary Alliance mission was in an ancient part of town, close to the Yangtze and within sight of the cranes on the docks. The mission covered a little more than two acres, which were enclosed by walls. Directly across from the gate a four-hundred-year-old granite-block building had been converted to a chapel. A wooden, gold-painted cross sat atop it.

There were two large wooden crates in the courtyard of the mission, obviously the household goods of the Fellers. Captain Banning had told McCoy of his suspicions about their contents, and now he wondered idly if the captain was right. Then, more practically, he wondered how they were going to load the crates onto the trucks. The damn things probably weighed a ton.

A woman who was almost certainly Mrs. Feller appeared in the courtyard as the truck and car drove through the gate. She was more or less what McCoy expected, a somewhat thinner, somewhat younger copy of Mrs. Moore—a well-scrubbed, makeup-free do-gooder. She even wore her hair the same way, braided and then pinned to the sides of her head. But unlike Mrs. Moore, McCoy noticed, she had good-looking legs, trim hips, and an interesting set of knockers.

She kissed her husband like a nun kisses a relative. On the cheek, as if a little uncomfortable with that little bit of passion.

When the Reverend Feller marched her over to the car and introduced her, McCoy was surprised that her hand was warm. He had expected it to be sort of clammy, like her husband's.

She had a boy show McCoy and PFC Everly (the tall, gangly hillbilly driving the missionary truck) where they were to sleep. Except for a Bible on a bedside table and a brightly colored framed lithograph of Jesus Christ gathering children around his knee, it was very much like McCoy's billet in the First Battalion compound in Shanghai. A steel cot, bedclothes, a chair, and nothing else.

Sessions came to the room shortly after the mission boy left them there.

"Could I have a word with you, Corporal McCoy?" he asked.

"Take a walk, why don't you, Everly?" McCoy ordered.

"Where am I supposed to go?"

"See if you can scout up a decent-looking place for us to eat. Come back in fifteen minutes."

When he was gone, Sessions said, "Mrs. Feller has asked you to supper, McCoy."

"Everly and I will get something," McCoy said.

"She meant the both of you, of course," Sessions said. "You're welcome, you understand? She's really a very nice person."

"Lieutenant, I didn't come here to eat supper with missionaries," McCoy said. "I'm going out on the town."

"In the line of duty, of course," Sessions said, sarcastically.

"The Corps's paying for it," McCoy said. "Why not?"

"Yes, of course," Sessions said. "Is there anything of interest here that I could credibly have a look at?"

"There's Kempei-Tai[4] watching this place. They're not going to think much if two Marines leave here to get their ashes hauled. They might get very curious if a newly arrived missionary did the same thing."

"I wasn't thinking of going to a brothel," Sessions replied, chuckling. "I was suggesting that it would be credible if the Fellers, while I was here, showed me the sights. And that while so doing, I might come across something of interest."

"If the Japs have German artillery, it's not going to be here in Nanking," McCoy said flatly. "And I think the less attention you call to yourself, the better it would be."

"McCoy, I am simply trying to do my job," Sessions said, annoyed at what he considered McCoy's condescension. He wondered what Captain Banning had told McCoy about him.

"That's all I'm trying to do, Lieutenant," McCoy said. "Captain Banning said I was to do what I could for you, and that's what I'm trying to do."

As the whores later confirmed, nothing was happening in Nanking. So at half past ten, McCoy decided that there wasn't anything more to be gained from spending the night in the whorehouse. He put on his clothes, paid off his girl, and went to the room Everly had taken.

"I'm heading back in," he told Everly, who was standing there in the doorway a little dazzled by the interruption. He had wrapped a towel around his middle. It threatened to fall.

"Do I have to?" he said.

"Just be at the mission at five o'clock," McCoy said, after a moment. Everly was a fucker, not a fighter; and he didn't drink dangerously. There was little chance that he would get in trouble. On the other hand, if he spent the night in the whorehouse, it would give the Kempei-Tai agents who had trailed them something to do. And the report they would write would state that a Marine had hired a whore for the night and stayed with her.

He returned to the mission and searched in vain through the small mission library for something that had nothing to do with Christianity. Then, disappointed,

[4]The Japanese Security Police.

he retreated to his room, undressed to his skivvies, and took from his musette bag one of the copies of the *Shanghai Post* that had accumulated during his last trip to Shanghai. After he'd read it, he started in on the crossword puzzle.

Someone knocked at the door. Certain that it was the boy, he called permission to enter in Chinese.

It was Mrs. Feller, a very different Mrs. Feller from the tight-assed lady he had met that afternoon. She was wearing a cotton bathrobe over a silk gown; and her hair was free now, hanging halfway down her back. It was glossy and soft, as though she had just brushed it. Then he noticed—more than noticed—the unrestrained breasts under her thin night clothes. . . . The Reverend was about to get a little, after what presumably was a long dry spell.

"Do you speak Chinese?" she asked, in Chinese.

"Some," McCoy said, in English.

"I just wanted to see if you or the other gentleman needed anything," she said.

"No, ma'am," McCoy said, chuckling. "We're fine, thank you."

"Why are you chuckling?" she asked, smiling.

"Hearing you call Everly 'the other gentleman,' " McCoy said.

"Where is he?" she asked.

When McCoy didn't reply, her face flushed.

"Mrs. Moore told me an incredible story about you," she said. "I can't believe it's true."

"What did she tell you?"

"Now I'm sorry I brought this up," she said. "I shouldn't have."

He nodded his acceptance of that.

"But do they call you 'Killer'? Or were they just teasing my husband and Mr. Sessions?"

"Some people call me that," McCoy said. "I don't like it much."

"But you're just a boy," she said, after deciding that the rest of the story was also probably—if incredibly—true.

"I don't like to be called a boy, either," McCoy said. "I'm a corporal in the Marine Corps."

"I'm really sorry I brought the whole thing up," she said.

McCoy nodded.

"Breakfast will be at six-thirty," she said. "My husband wants to get on the way early. Is that all right with you?"

"Yes, ma'am," he said. "We'll be there. Thank you."

"Then I'll say good night," she said.

He thought that he would really have liked to get a look at her teats. Chinese women, by and large, didn't have very big teats, and it had been a long time since he had seen an American woman's teats.

Come to think of it, he had seen very few American women's teats. Before he had come to China it had been a really big deal to get a look at a set of teats—not to mention actually getting laid. But getting laid in China was about as out-of-the-ordinary as blowing your nose. And in fact he had come to see there was no big difference between Chinese women and American (the story that their pussies ran sideward had turned out to be so much bullshit); but it would still be kind of nice to make it with a real American.

He would, come to think of it, really like to jump Mrs. Feller, though he immediately recognized that dream as the same kind of fantasy as wishing he would make sergeant next week . . . out of the goddamned question for two hundred different reasons.

He turned his attention back to the crossword puzzle.

(FOUR)
The Christian & Missionary Alliance Mission
Nanking, China
0830 Hours 15 May 1941

The Christians of the mission put on a little farewell ceremony for Mrs. Feller. After maybe fifty Chinese had manhandled the wooden crates onto the bed of the Studebaker, they went to one side of the courtyard and stood in some kind of a formation. McCoy settled into the front seat of the car, and watched.

Next came maybe fifty little Chinese kids dressed in middie-blouse uniforms (which reminded McCoy of the uniform of the Italian marines). They lined up in four ranks. Finally, the missionary equivalent of the officers appeared—all the white Christians and half a dozen suit-wearing Chinese Christians. They sat down on a row of chairs set up on a sort of platform against a wall. One of them rose and said a prayer. Then the Chinese kids sang a hymn in Chinese. McCoy recognized the melody but could not recall the words.

One of the Chinese Christians gave Mrs. Feller a present. She thanked him, and they sang another hymn, this time in English. The Reverend Feller then gave what was either a sermon or a very long prayer. Then came another hymn.

All this time, McCoy was looking up Mrs. Feller's dress. He hadn't started out to do that. But the way she was sitting up on the platform, and the way he was looking out the Studebaker window, that's where his eyes naturally fell. And then it got worse. He was originally looking at a lot of white thigh. But then she had uncrossed her knees, and put her feet flat on the little platform just far enough apart to show all the way up. And she wasn't wearing any pants.

He didn't believe what he saw at first. Ladies didn't go around without their underpants, and she was not only a lady, she was a lady missionary. But there was no question about it. She was sitting there with everything showing.

And then Lieutenant Sessions came over and sat beside McCoy. The minute he did, Mrs. Feller crossed her legs.

Did she suddenly remember how she was sitting? Or didn't it matter, since only an enlisted man was getting an eyeful? Or was she playing the cockteaser with me, and stopped only because Sessions showed up?

When the ceremony was finally over, and the officer-type Christians walked with Mrs. Feller to the Studebaker, McCoy did not get out from behind the wheel to open the door. He had a hard-on.

Mister/Lieutenant Sessions, obviously anxious to get the show on the road again, opened the door and motioned for Mrs. Feller to get in.

"If you don't mind, Mr. Sessions," Mrs. Feller said. "I'll sit with Corporal McCoy. I get woozy if I ride in backseats."

She got in beside McCoy and smiled at him.

"I'm sorry you had to wait," she said.

"No sweat," McCoy said, devoting all of his attention to starting the engine.

"I always wondered how you did that," she said.

"Did what?" he asked. In spite of his misgivings, curiosity forced him to look at her.

She was holding up his hat press.[5] He had put his campaign hat in it when

[5]A device that keeps the brim of the felt campaign hat from curling.

he'd got in the car. It was the rainy season, and humidity was hell on fur felt hats.

"Oh," McCoy said. "That."

She put the hat press back where it had been.

"Very clever," she said.

"Okay to go?" McCoy asked.

"Get the show on the road, McCoy," Sessions said.

Mrs. Feller waved to the Christians, and blew several of them a kiss.

For somebody who got screwed as much as she probably got screwed last night, having been away from the Reverend all that time, McCoy thought, *she don't look all that worn out.*

Then he realized he was wrong about that. The reason she was going around without any underpants was that she and the Reverend had screwed it sore.

She half turned on the seat, pulling her dress above her knees in the process, and started talking to Sessions. "Where are you from?" And "Where is your wife from?" And "How much do you like the Marine Corps?" That sort of thing.

McCoy kept his eyes off her knees as much as he could.

He had it made now, he told himself. It would be real dumb fucking that up by doing something dumb with this missionary woman. He had probably the best duty of any corporal in the Corps. For all practical purposes, he didn't have anybody telling him what to do. And the Corps was paying all his expenses, even what he spent getting laid. And it was even better than that:

When he filled out the "report of expenses" Captain Banning made him do about once a month, he put down on it usually twice (sometimes three times) what it really cost him. He wasn't greedy, and Captain Banning probably thought he was getting a bargain. But the prices McCoy listed on the report were what Marines would be expected to pay for a room, a meal, a whore, or whatever. Marines who spoke Chinese didn't pay half what Marines who didn't speak Chinese did. Not a month had passed since he'd gone to work for Banning that he hadn't been able to add a hundred dollars to his retirement-fund account at Barclays Bank. And that didn't include his gambling money.

They always spent two days in the Marine Compound at Tientsin on the way to Peking, then two days in Peking, and then another day at Tientsin on the way back to Shanghai. As regular as clockwork, he'd been taking ten, fifteen dollars a night from the Tientsin and Peking Marines. He hadn't been greedy, which wasn't easy, because there were Tientsin and Peking Marines who played poker so bad it was sometimes hard not to clean them out.

It was hard to believe how much money he had in Barclays Bank.

And he could fuck the whole thing up by doing something stupid with this missionary who went around without her underpants.

When they were out of Nanking, the humidity started to close in so bad that the outside of the windshield kept clouding over and he had to run the wipers every once in a while. It would be better whenever it started to rain. He wished it would start soon.

Mrs. Feller glanced at McCoy to make sure he had his eyes on the road. Then she took a little bottle of perfume or cologne from her purse and shook a tiny dab of it on a handkerchief. She touched her temples with it, and her ears, and her forehead, and then quickly opened a couple of buttons on her dress and rubbed a little in the crack between her breasts.

McCoy's erection was painful.

He was sure, to make it worse, that she had seen him looking.

Goddamn these missionaries anyway! If the Corps had wanted to find out if the

11th Jap Division had German artillery pieces, I could have found out, without dragging a bunch of fucking missionaries around with me.

It finally started to rain, a steady, soft rain that meant it would probably go on forever.

And now the inside of the windshield started to steam up. Mrs. Feller, trying to be helpful, kept wiping it with a handkerchief. Sometimes when she leaned over to wipe his window, her hand rested on his knee. And every time he could see her boobs straining against her brassiere and the thin cotton of her dress.

It was still raining when they reached the Yangtze ferry at Chiangyin. McCoy was not pleased with what he found. Not only was one of the two ferries that normally worked the crossing tied up at a wharf and out of service, but none of the other vehicles in the convoy had crossed over.

Several hundred Chinese were milling around. A few drove trucks, and half a dozen had oxcarts. But mostly there were hand-pulled carts, and people carrying huge bundles on their backs. That meant that they would have to post a guard on every truck. Otherwise, if they blinked, they would have an empty truck.

Zimmerman told McCoy that when he tried to load the vehicles the night before, Lieutenant Macklin wouldn't let him. Macklin thought it would be better to wait on this side of the Yangtze for the car and truck from Nanking.

Officer-type thinking, McCoy decided. *You had to keep your eyes on the bastards all the time, or they would think of something smart like this.*

The remaining ferry was going to require three trips to transport all of the vehicles, so it was going to be at least an hour, probably closer to an hour and a half, before they were all across the river, which was at least four miles across at that point.

McCoy went to Lieutenant Macklin and told him he thought it would probably be a good idea if he took one of the cars, two Marine trucks, and one missionary truck on the first trip. Two of the three remaining trucks could cross on the second trip. And the remaining truck, the pickup/wrecker, and the other car could cross on the third . . . if that was all right with Lieutenant Macklin.

There was a nice little restaurant in Chen-chiang on the far shore, and McCoy could see no reason to remain on the near shore hungry, while there was a commissioned officer and gentleman (two, if you counted Sessions) available to supervise the loading of the rear echelon.

And if he was just a little lucky, he'd be able to overhear a conversation (or perhaps even join in one) in the restaurant that might tell him something about Japanese activity farther up the road.

Lieutenant Macklin thought that was as good a way to do it as any.

"Sergeant Zimmerman can handle it by himself, sir," McCoy said, "if you'd rather cross with the first load."

"I'll bring up the rear, McCoy," Lieutenant Macklin said, as McCoy had been eighty percent sure he would. "You and Sergeant Zimmerman go over and see what you can do to get the men something to eat."

"Aye, aye, sir."

Might as well let Zimmerman feed his face first, too. McCoy liked Zimmerman. He was a placid, quiet German who had found a home in the Corps, started a family with a Chinese girl, and did not resent McCoy's unofficial—if unmistakable—authority on the convoys the way some other senior noncoms did.

Ernie had some kind of rice bowl going on the Peking trips, McCoy was sure, but whatever it was, he did it quietly. And he didn't get fall-down drunk in a whorehouse as soon as there was the chance. Ernie understood Chinese, too, although for some strange reason, he pretended he didn't.

He was also faster on the pickup than you'd expect. For instance, he caught on right away to what McCoy wanted when McCoy suggested that he eat at a different restaurant from the big one McCoy was going to. Ernie would pick up whatever he could learn about any Japanese activity farther up the road while he sipped slowly on a beer. Too bad Lieutenant Macklin wasn't as sharp, McCoy thought.

The other two drivers McCoy took on the first ferry were PFCs, and they were on their best behavior because making the trips got them out from under the harassment of the motor pool. McCoy gave them his ritual "one beer, no more, or I'll have your ass" speech, confident that he'd be obeyed.

When Ernie came into the big restaurant (six tables, plus a low counter), McCoy was gnawing on a nearly crystallized piece of duck skin. Ernie took off his wide-brimmed campaign hat, gave it several violent shakes to knock the water loose from the rain cover, and then looked for and found McCoy.

Ernie was a man of few words: "The other Studebaker car's on the ferry."

McCoy nodded, and Ernie left. McCoy shoved the rest of the crisp duck skin in his mouth, daintily dipped his fingers into a bowl of warm water, dried them, and reached for his hat. He put it on at the prescribed angle, twisted his head around to seat the leather strap against the back of his head, and started out of the restaurant.

Then he changed his mind.

Fuck him. So Macklin and/or Sessions sees me eating and having a beer, so what?

He gave the proprietor a large bill and told him he would be back for his change after he'd returned the empty beer bottle and the napkin he was taking with him.

Then he walked quickly to the ferry, keeping himself (more importantly, the campaign hat) out of the rain as much as possible.

He didn't know why Lieutenant Macklin had decided to come in the second car rather than the third ferry trip, but it didn't matter: It was a to-be-expected thing for an officer—any officer—to do. No matter what an enlisted man decided, it could be improved upon by any officer. That's why they were officers.

McCoy paid little attention to the Studebaker until it was off the ferry and, with its wheels slipping and skidding, had made it up the road from the ferry slip. Then he stepped out from beneath the overhang of a building where he had been sheltered from the rain, went into the middle of the road, and made more or the less official Corps hand signals to tell Lieutenant Macklin where the car should be parked.

But Macklin wasn't driving the Studebaker. The lady missionary, Ol' No Underpants, Perfume on the Teats herself, was at the wheel. And she was alone.

What the hell's going on?

McCoy reclaimed the beer bottle he had been prepared to discard for either of the officers and walked nimbly—avoiding puddles where possible—to where Ol' No Underpants had parked.

She saw him coming and opened the door for him as he approached. The way she leaned over the seat to reach the door, he could see down her dress, down where she'd wiped perfume between her teats.

"I hope I'm not interfering with anything, Corporal McCoy," she said. "Lieutenant Macklin said it would be all right if I came now."

"Yes, ma'am," McCoy said.

"I also thought," she said, "that since there was no restaurant on that side, maybe there would be one on this one. I'm hungry."

"Yes, ma'am," McCoy said. "There's a restaurant here."

"Could you take me there?"

"Yes, ma'am."

"I've got an umbrella," she said, and reached into the backseat for it. He noticed that her breasts got in the way.

When she had it, she handed it to him.

"No, ma'am," McCoy said. "Thank you just the same."

"You mean you'd get wet?"

"I mean that Marines don't use umbrellas," McCoy said.

"It's against the rules, you mean?"

"Yes, ma'am."

"Don't you ever break the rules, Corporal?" she asked.

"Sometimes," he said.

"Everybody breaks them sometime," she said. "And this seems to be a good time for you to break this one."

He thought that sounded a little strange coming from a missionary, but decided to share the umbrella with her. There was no one here to see him who counted, and it was raining steadily.

Accepting the umbrella from her, McCoy got out of the car, opened the umbrella, and walked around to the driver's side. She slid out of the Studebaker, stepped under the umbrella, closed the door, and then took his arm. Her arm pressed against his, and he could feel the heaviness of her breast.

He marched with her back to the restaurant, shifting course to avoid the larger puddles.

The eyes of the proprietor widened without embarrassment when he saw the woman. Blond hair simply fascinated Orientals.

He came to the table for their order.

"What do you recommend?" she asked.

"I had the duck," McCoy said, almost blurted, "the way they fix it in Peking. I don't like the duck much, but the skin's first rate."

"Then I'll have that," she said. "Are you going to have anything?"

"I've had mine, thank you," McCoy said.

"Not even another beer?"

"I told the men they could have one beer," McCoy said. "It wouldn't be right if I had two."

"I'm sorry to hear that," she said.

"Why?" he asked, surprised.

"Because I would like a beer," she said. "But I can't have one. My husband doesn't like me to drink."

"What you mean is, you could have had a sip of mine?"

She nodded her head conspiratorially.

There was something perversely pleasant in frustrating the morality of a missionary, McCoy thought. He told the proprietor to put a bottle of beer in a tea pot and to bring the lady a cup to go with it.

When it was delivered she said, "I thought that you were telling him something like this."

"You did?" he asked.

"Your eyes lit up like a naughty boy's," she said.

He didn't know what to make of this missionary lady. She was being much too friendly. And he was well aware of the kind of relationship possible between American women and Marines in China: none. American women, probably because there were so few of them, were on a sort of pedestal. They were presumed to be ladies. They wore gloves and hats and did no work. And they did not speak to enlisted Marines, who were at the opposite end of the American social structure—only a half step above the Chinese. Most American women in China pretended that Marines were invisible. They did not walk arm in arm with them under umbrellas, or sit at tables with them in restaurants, or look directly—almost provocatively—into their eyes.

He could only come up with two explanations for Mrs. Reverend Feller's behavior. She could simply be acting according to her private idea of what it meant to be Christian; in other words, treating him as a social equal out of some strange notion that everybody was really equal in the sight of God. Or else maybe she was in fact flirting with him, or at least pretending to.

There were a couple of reasons that she might be doing just that. One was that she had caught him looking at her when she was putting perfume on her teats and thought it was funny. If that was the way it was, then she knew she could tease him and have her fun in perfect safety, because she knew that only a goddamned fool of a Marine would make a pass at an American lady missionary. And might even be hoping that he would say or do something out of line, so that she could run and tell the Reverend about it.

He'd heard about that happening. Not with a missionary lady, but with the wives of American businessmen. They'd catch their husband with a Chinese girl and decide to make it look like they were paying him back by getting some Marine to start hanging around and panting with his tongue hanging out. They had no intention of giving the poor fucker any; they just wanted to let their old man know there was a Marine with the hots for them. And then if the old man went to the colonel and the Marine wound up on the shit list, that was his problem.

Whatever Mrs. Reverend Feller was up to—even if she was just being Christian—it made him uncomfortable, and he wanted nothing to do with it. He changed the subject.

"There's one good thing about the bad road," McCoy said. "We can stay at Chiehshom tonight. It's going to be too dark to go any farther today."

"What's at Chiehshom?" she asked, looking at him over the edge of her teacup of beer.

"A nice hotel," he said, "built by a German. The plumbing works, in other words, and the kitchen's clean. It's on a hill over the lake."

"You always stay there?" she asked.

"Normally we get a lot farther than this," he said.

"When you don't have to carry missionaries with you, you mean?"

"I didn't say that," McCoy said.

"No, but that's what you meant," she said.

McCoy stood up and put his campaign hat on. "I'll go down to the ferry and see what's up," he said. "You can stay here. You'll be all right."

IV

(ONE)
Chen-chiang, China
1500 Hours 15 May 1941

While the Reverend Feller, Lieutenant Macklin, and "Mr." Sessions ate in the "big" restaurant, and the Marine drivers at one of the tiny stalls, Ernie Zimmerman took the opportunity once again to carefully check the vehicles, paying particular attention to the tires. Changing a tire on a muddy road was bad enough, but changing one in the rain, at night, was a royal fucking pain in the ass.

Zimmerman found a couple of tires that looked as if they might blow, one on a truck, the other on one of the Studebaker sedans, and ordered them changed. McCoy and Zimmerman were watching a PFC remove the wheel of the car when Lieutenant Macklin and Sessions walked up to them.

"We about ready to roll, Sergeant?" Lieutenant Macklin asked.

"Aye, aye, sir," Zimmerman said.

"Well, get everyone loaded up, please," Macklin said. "We'd like a word with Corporal McCoy."

"Aye, aye, sir," Zimmerman said, and walked off toward the food stalls where the drivers were eating. Macklin and Sessions walked out of earshot of the driver changing the tire, and McCoy followed them.

"Under the circumstances, McCoy," Sessions said, "I decided that it was necessary to make Lieutenant Macklin aware of my real purpose in being here."

"Yes, sir," McCoy said.

He was not annoyed, but neither was he surprised. Sessions was more than a little pissed about their conversation in Nanking; and it was clear that Sessions was about to put him in his place. As missionaries have no authority to order Marine corporals around, it was necessary to let Macklin know who he actually was. He had thus told Macklin that he was an officer on a secret mission, and now they were both thrilled about their importance in the scheme of things—and prepared to deal with a lowly corporal who was standing in the way of their doing their duty. Captain Banning had warned him this was likely to happen.

"And we've been looking at the map," Sessions said. "Lieutenant Macklin thinks we can make it to Chiehshom before it gets dark. Do you agree with that?"

"Yes, sir," McCoy said. "It's a good place to spend the night. There's a good hotel there."

"So Lieutenant Macklin tells me," Sessions said. "More importantly, McCoy, it's not too far from Yenchi'eng, is it?"

McCoy's eyebrows went up as he looked at him. The Japanese 11th Infantry Division was at Yenchi'eng.

"No, sir," he said, "it's not."

"Have you ever been to Yenchi'eng, McCoy?" Sessions asked.

"Yes, sir," McCoy said.

"Do you know how the divisional artillery of the 11th Japanese Infantry is equipped?"

"Yes, sir," McCoy said. "They've got four batteries, they call it a regiment, of Model 94s. That's a 37-mm antitank cannon, but the Japs use it as regular artillery because they can throw so much fire. And the Chinese have damned little to use for counterfire."

"I want to check that out, McCoy," Lieutenant Sessions said.

"Sir?"

"I want to find out if the 11th Division has been equipped with German PAK38[1] cannon."

"They haven't," McCoy said. "What they've got, Lieutenant, is maybe thirty-five Model 94s. Eight to a battery, plus spares."

"You seem very sure of that, McCoy," Lieutenant Macklin said.

"Yes, sir, I am."

"You know the difference between the two cannon?" Macklin pursued, more than a little sarcastic.

"The PAK38 is bigger, with a larger shield and larger wheels than the Model 94," McCoy said, on the edge of insolence, Lieutenant Macklin thought. "And it has a muzzle brake. They're not hard to tell apart."

"And you're absolutely sure the 11th Division doesn't have any of those cannon?" Sessions asked.

"I took some pictures of their artillery park a couple of weeks ago," McCoy said. "That's what they've got, Lieutenant. Thirty, maybe thirty-five 94s. Captain Banning sent the pictures to Washington."

"But we have no way of knowing, do we, Corporal McCoy, whether or not the Japanese have received German cannon since your last visit? Without having another look?" Macklin asked sarcastically.

"We have people watching the docks, and the railroad, and the roads. If the 11th Division had gotten any new artillery, we'd have heard about it."

" 'We'?" Macklin asked sarcastically.

"Captain Banning," McCoy said, accepting the rebuke, "has people watching the docks and the railroads and the roads."

"Under the circumstances—and after all, we are so close—I'm afraid I can't just accept that," Lieutenant Sessions said. "How long would you say it is by car from Chiehshom to Yenchi'eng?"

"If you drive down there, Lieutenant," McCoy said, "they're going to catch you, and you'll find yourself being entertained by the Japs for a couple of days."

"What do you mean by 'entertained'?"

"They'll take you on maneuvers," McCoy said. "Walk you around in the swamps all night, feed you raw fish, that sort of thing." He stopped, and then his mouth ran away with him: "Some of them have got a pretty good sense of humor. They had Lieutenant Macklin three days one time."

"That's quite enough, McCoy!" Macklin flared.

"Well then, we'll just have to make sure they don't catch us, won't we?" Lieutenant Sessions said.

"Lieutenant, I'm not going to Yenchi'eng with you," McCoy said. "I'm sorry."

"How long did you say it will take us to drive from Chiehshom to Yenchi'eng, Corporal?" Sessions asked.

"It's about a two-hour drive, maybe two and a half, with the roads like this."

"And you presumably can manage the road at night?"

[1]PAK38: *Panzerabwehrkanone,* caliber 5cm, Model 1938.

"Sir, I'm sorry, but I'm not going to Yenchi'eng with you," McCoy said.

"I didn't ask you if you had volunteered, Corporal," Lieutenant Sessions said reasonably. "The decision to go has been made by Lieutenant Macklin and myself. Your presence will lend your knowledge of the terrain to our enterprise. I don't have to remind you, do I, that despite your special relationship with Captain Banning, you still remain subject to the orders of your superiors?"

"Lieutenant," McCoy said, "you're putting me on a spot."

"The only spot you'll be on," Macklin flared, "is if you persist in your defiance."

McCoy looked at him, shrugged, and took an envelope from his hip pocket. He extended it toward Sessions.

"I think you better take a look at this, Lieutenant," he said.

"What is that?" Sessions asked.

"My orders, sir, in writing," McCoy said. "Captain Banning said I wasn't to give them to you unless I had to. I think I have to."

Sessions took the envelope, tore it open, and unfolded the sheet of paper inside. He glanced at the sheet and then shook his head.

"What is it?" Lieutenant Macklin asked.

"It's a set of letter orders," Sessions said, and then read it aloud: " 'Headquarters, 4th Marines, Shanghai, 13 May 1941. Subject, Letter Orders. To Corporal Kenneth J. McCoy, Headquarters Company, First Battalion, 4th Marines. Your confidential orders concerning the period 14 May 1941 to 14 June 1941 have been issued to you verbally by Captain Edward Banning, USMC. You are reminded herewith that no officer or noncommissioned officer assigned or attached to the 4th Regiment, USMC, is authorized to amend or countermand your orders in any way,' " Sessions looked at Macklin. "Corporal McCoy's letter orders are signed by the colonel."

"Well, I'll be damned," Macklin said. "I never heard of such a thing."

"Lieutenant," McCoy said to Macklin. "I wish you'd read those orders."

"Just what the hell do you mean by that?" Macklin snapped.

"With respect, sir," McCoy said. "I'd like to burn them."

"Go ahead and burn them," Macklin said coldly.

Sessions handed the orders back to McCoy, who ripped the single sheet of paper into long strips, which he then carefully burned, one at a time, letting the wind blow the ashes and unburned stub from his fingers.

"I presume your 'confidential verbal orders' forbid you to go to Yenchi'eng?" Macklin asked, when he had finished.

"No, sir, except that Captain Banning said I was to use my own judgment if you wanted me to do something like that."

"Then you have not been forbidden to go to Yenchi'eng? You've taken that decision yourself?" Sessions asked.

"That's about the size of it, sir," McCoy said.

A very self-confident young man, Sessions thought. *Highly intelligent. He almost certainly believes in what he's doing. So where does that leave us?*

"I presume you have considered, Corporal," Macklin said, icily, "that Lieutenant Sessions's interest in the cannon of the 11th Division is not idle curiosity? That he has been sent here by Headquarters, USMC?"

"Yes, sir," McCoy said. "Captain Banning told me all about that."

"And you are apparently unimpressed by my decision that knowing that for sure is worth whatever risk is entailed in going to Yenchi'eng?" Macklin asked, coldly furious.

"I'm convinced there's no way you could go there without getting caught," Mc-

Coy said. "You have to go by road. The first checkpoint you pass, they'll phone ahead to the Kempei-Tai, and that will be it."

"There are ways of getting around checkposts and the Kempei-Tai," Macklin said. "You have done so."

"That was different," McCoy said.

"That was different, *sir,*" Macklin corrected him.

"That was different, sir," McCoy parroted.

"Well, then, perhaps you'd be good enough to tell Mr. Sessions and myself how you would go to Yenchi'eng."

"If I told you that, it would look like I thought you could get away with it, Lieutenant," McCoy said.

"So you refuse even to help us?" Macklin said, incredulously.

McCoy pretended he hadn't heard the question.

"And I don't see any point in taking the risk of going myself," he said. "If they had any German cannon, I'd know about it."

"Corporal," Lieutenant Macklin said, icily sarcastic, "I stand in awe of your self-confidence."

"Yes, sir," McCoy said.

"You will, I hope, tell us what you can about the location of the artillery park?" Lieutenant Sessions asked conversationally. "How we can find it?"

"Aye, aye, sir," McCoy said. "I hope you'll make it clear to Captain Banning, sir, that I told you you're going to get caught?"

"Oh, yes, Corporal McCoy," Lieutenant Macklin said. "You can count on our relating this incident to Captain Banning in detail."

(TWO)
Chiehshom, Shantung Province, China
15 May 1941

The three classes of accommodation at the Hotel am See at Chiehshom had (in descending order) been originally intended for Europeans, European servants, and Chinese servants. On McCoy's first couple of trips to and from Peking, all the enlisted Marines had been put up in the rooms set aside for European servants. But on the last couple of trips, like this one, the management had made quite a show of giving the noncoms "European" rooms—small ones, to be sure—in the main wing of the hotel.

McCoy realized that the proprietor had figured out that the sergeant, rather than the officer-in-charge, was the man who really decided (by speeding up or slowing down) where the convoy and its ten-man detail would stop for the night. That meant the sale of ten beds and twenty meals, plus whatever they all had to drink. There wasn't all that much business anyway.

McCoy really liked to stay at the Hotel am See. The food was good and the place was spotless. And even the small rooms they gave the noncoms had enormous bathtubs with apparently limitless clean hot water. He would take a bath at night, a long soak, and then a shower in the morning. It was the only shower he'd had in China that made his skin sting with the pressure. All the others were like being rained on.

After settling into his room, McCoy had hoped to have dinner with Ernie

Zimmerman and be gone from the dining room before the officers and the Fellers came down for dinner. That would give him a chance both to avoid Lieutenants Macklin and Sessions and to steel himself for another meeting with them that was scheduled for after dinner. They wanted him to go over their route to and from Yenchi'eng. As pissed as the both of them were with him, that was going to be bad enough without having dinner in the same room (where they didn't think enlisted Marines had any right to be anyway) with them.

But Ernie Zimmerman got hung up somehow getting the other Marines bedded down and was ten minutes late. Zimmerman and McCoy had no sooner sat down in the dining room than the officers and the Fellers showed up. Mrs. Feller said something to the Reverend, and he came over and insisted that they all have dinner together.

McCoy thought the officers would be pissed. Eating in the same room with enlisted Marines was bad enough, but not as bad as having to share a table with them. But they weren't. They were playing spy again, McCoy saw, and the dinner table gave them a stage for the playacting they thought was necessary.

"Mr." Sessions announced that he had asked Lieutenant Macklin if it would be all right if they spent two nights in Chiehshom, instead of the one originally planned. The Christian & Missionary Alliance was considering opening another mission in Yenchi'eng, and they wanted to take advantage of being close to it to have a good look at it.

He's a goddamned fool, McCoy thought. *They're all goddamned fools. They think they will look more innocent brazening it out, two missionaries and a Marine officer in full uniform simply out for a ride looking for a new place to save souls. It will take the Japs about ten minutes to learn they've left here, and there will be a greeting party waiting for them long before they get anywhere near Yenchi'eng.*

The only thing more dangerous than an officer convinced he's doing what duty requires is two officers doing the same thing. Two officers and a missionary.

They would be back in Chiehshom by nightfall, Sessions said, and spending the extra day would give Sergeant Zimmerman and his men the chance to go over the vehicles and make sure everything was shipshape.

"You're not going with them, Corporal McCoy," Mrs. Feller asked, "to drive the car?"

"No, ma'am," McCoy said. "I'm not going along."

Ernie Zimmerman, uncomfortable in the presence of the officers, and fully aware there was some friction between them and McCoy, bolted down his food and pushed himself wordlessly away from the table.

McCoy went after him.

"Ernie, jack up one of the trucks and drop the drive shaft," McCoy said.

"What the hell for?" Zimmerman demanded.

"Just do it, Ernie, please," McCoy said.

"What are they up to?" Zimmerman asked.

"You heard it," McCoy said.

"What was that bullshit anyway?"

"Just get somebody to drop a drive shaft, Ernie. And make sure one of the cars is gassed and ready to go," McCoy said. Then he went to his room to mark the route the damned fools should take to Yenchi'eng.

When McCoy met with the three of them in Sessions's room, they made no further attempt to get him to take them to Yenchi'eng. This surprised him until he realized they'd concluded that their brilliant inspiration of brazening it out was going to work, and they didn't need him.

After they came back from successfully spying on the Japs, they'd be in a position to rack his ass with Banning for refusing to go with them. They would have been right all along, and he would have been nothing but an insolent enlisted man with the gall to challenge the wise judgment of his betters.

There was nothing he could do to stop them, of course, and (except for having one of the missionary trucks jacked up and the drive shaft dropped so that it might fool the Kempei-Tai watching the hotel) there was nothing he could do to help them either.

But he set his portable alarm clock for half-past four and went down to the courtyard to see them off. Mrs. Feller was there too, the nipples to her teats sticking up under her bathrobe and her blond hair, now unbraided, hanging down her back.

Jesus Christ, without her hair glued to her head, she's a hell of a good-looking woman. I would give my left nut to get in the sack with her.

The officers and the missionary were a little carried away with the situation. They saw themselves, McCoy thought contemptuously, as patriots about to embark on a great espionage mission. McCoy had to temper his scorn, however, when Sessions took him aside and told him, dead serious, that no matter what happened today he wanted him to understand that he understood his position.

"This is one of those situations, Corporal, where we both must do what we believe is right. And I want you to know that I believe you thought long and hard about your obligations before you decided you couldn't go with me."

He's not so much of a prick as a virgin.

"Good luck, Lieutenant," McCoy said, and offered his hand.

What the hell, it didn't cost anything to say that. And if Sessions means what he said, then on the off chance they don't get bagged and Macklin tries to get me in trouble, maybe it'll help.

As they walked back to the hotel, Mrs. Feller's leg kept coming out of the flap of her bathrobe, and she kept trying to hold the robe closed. He remembered that all through dinner she had kept bumping her knee "accidentally" against his.

McCoy was now convinced she was just fucking around with him, getting some kind of sick kick out of trying to make him uncomfortable, the way some people get a sick kick out of teasing a dog. He intended to stay as far away from her as he could.

"Is there any interesting way you can think of to kill the time until they get back?" she asked, when they were inside the hotel.

She goddamned well knows there are two or three meanings I could put on that.

"Until it starts to rain, which should be about noon, you could fish, I suppose," McCoy said. "They've got tackle. I've got to work on the trucks."

"That doesn't sound very exciting," she said.

"I guess not," he said, turning and walking away from her down the corridor to his room.

He didn't see her at breakfast, and he ate with the Marines at lunch. They asked him where the officers and the Christer had gone, and how long that would keep them all in Chiehshom. Zimmerman had already told them he didn't know, they said, or else he wouldn't tell them. McCoy told them he didn't know, either.

At half-past three, a boy came to his room and told him that Sergeant Zimmerman wanted to see him in the lobby. When McCoy went down, there were two Japanese soldiers with Zimmerman, a sergeant and a corporal. They were both large for Japanese, and they were wearing leather jackets and puttees. Goggles hung loosely from leather helmets. Motorcycle messengers.

They bowed to McCoy and then saluted, and he bowed back and returned the salute. Then Zimmerman gave him two envelopes, one addressed to him and the other to Mrs. Feller.

"This is addressed to you," McCoy said.

"I can read," Zimmerman said. "And they want me to sign for it. I thought I better ask you."

One of the Japanese soldiers then handed McCoy some kind of a form to sign. He saw that it was just a message receipt form.

"Sign it," he said to Zimmerman.

"What is it?"

"A confession that you eat babies for breakfast," McCoy said.

Zimmerman, with obvious reluctance, carefully wrote his name on the form. He gave it to the Japanese sergeant, who bowed and saluted again, then marched out of the lobby with the other Japanese hopping along after him.

As he tore open the envelope and took out the message, McCoy heard their motorcycle engines start.

From what his note said, Lieutenant Macklin had obviously decided that the Japanese were going to read it before they delivered it:

> Yenchi'eng
> Sergeant Zimmerman:
> The Reverend Mr. Feller, Mr. Sessions and I have accepted the kind invitation of the commanding general of the 11th Division of the Imperial Japanese Army to inspect the division.
> I will send further orders as necessary.
> R.B. Macklin 1/Lt. USMC

McCoy realized there was absolutely no "I Told You So" pleasure in his reaction. He felt sorry for them, and he felt a little sorry for himself. Sooner (if he could get through on the telephone now) or later, Captain Banning was going to eat his ass out for letting them get their asses in a crack.

"Well, what the hell does it say?" Zimmerman asked.

McCoy handed him the note.

"I figured it was something like that," Zimmerman said. "How come you didn't go? You knew they was going to get caught?"

McCoy shrugged.

"You figure the Japs'll find out Sessions is an officer?"

"What makes you think he's an officer?"

"Come on, McCoy," Zimmerman said.

"Christ, for his sake, I hope not."

"What do we do now?"

"We wait twenty-four, maybe forty-eight hours to see what the Japs do."

"Then what?"

"Then I don't know," McCoy said. "There's reason the guys have to hang around here, but I don't want them getting shitfaced in case we need them."

"Okay," Zimmerman said. He walked out of the hotel lobby, and McCoy went up the wide stairs to the second floor and knocked on Mrs. Feller's door.

When she opened it, her hair was up in braids again, and she was wearing a pale yellow dress just about covered with tiny little holes.

He handed her the letter addressed to her. She raised her eyebrows questioningly and then tore open the envelope.

Even with her hair up again, she still looks pretty good. And Christ, what teats!

When she had read the letter, she raised her eyes and looked at him, obviously expecting some comment from him.

"Nothing to be worried about," he said. "They'll show them marching troops and barracks, and feed them food they know they won't like; and tonight they'll probably try hard to get them drunk. But there's no danger or anything like that. If there was, they wouldn't have let them send the letters."

"My husband doesn't drink," she said.

"He probably will tonight," McCoy said.

She seemed to find that amusing, he saw.

"His letter says that you will look after me," she said. "Are you going to look after me?"

"Yes, ma'am," he said.

"Starting at dinner? I missed you at lunch."

"I had something to do over lunch," he said. "And I'm afraid I'll be busy for dinner, too. If you'd like, I can ask Sergeant Zimmerman to have dinner with you."

"That won't be necessary," she said coldly.

Fuck you, too, lady!

"Are you going to do anything about this?" she asked. "Notify someone what's happened?"

"If I can get through on the phone," McCoy said.

It turned out he couldn't get through to Captain Banning in Shanghai, which didn't surprise him—and was actually a relief. Getting your ass chewed out was one of those things the longer you put off, the better.

And then he realized there was a way he could avoid it entirely. He thought it over a minute and went looking for Ernie Zimmerman.

(THREE)
The Hotel am See
Chiehshom, Shantung Province
0815 Hours 17 May 1941

McCoy had just finished a hard day and night in the country and was now lowering himself all the way into a full tub of hot clean water when there was a knock at his door.

"Come back later," he yelled in Chinese.

"It's Ellen Feller," she said.

"I'm in the bathtub."

Her response to this was a heavy, angry-sounding pounding on the door.

"Wait a minute, wait a minute," he called. "I'm coming."

McCoy hoisted himself out of the tub, wrapped a towel around his waist, and walked dripping to the door.

The moment it was opened a crack, she pushed past him into the room. She was wearing her robe, and her hair was again unbraided and hanging nearly to her waist. When he came back she must have seen him from her window talking to Ernie Zimmerman in the courtyard, he decided.

She walked to his small window, turned, and glared at him.

"Close the door, or someone will see us in here," she ordered.

In his junior year in St. Rose of Lima High, there had been a course in Musical Appreciation. They had studied *Die Walküre* then. That was what Mrs. Ellen Feller looked like now, McCoy thought, smiling. Obviously pissed off, she stood stiff and strident-looking, with her long hair flowing, her cheeks red, and her teats awesome even under her bathrobe—a goddamned Valkyrie.

"What are you smiling about?" she demanded furiously. Then, without waiting, demanded even more angrily, "And where have you been?"

"I don't think that's any of your business," McCoy said.

"You've been laying up with some almond-eyed whore in the village," she accused furiously. "You've been gone all night!"

"Don't hand me any of your missionary crap," McCoy said angrily. "Where I have been all night is none of your goddamned business. What did you do, come looking for me?"

He could tell from the look in her eyes that she had, indeed, come to his room looking for him.

"Why?" he asked. "What's happened?"

She shook her head. "Nothing," she said. "I just wondered where you were," she added awkwardly.

McCoy was still angry. "So you could start playing games with me again?" he asked.

"I don't know what you're talking about," she said automatically.

"You know goddamned well what I'm talking about," he said.

"So that's what you thought," she said, after a moment.

"Go find some clown in the mission," he said, warming to his subject, "if you get your kicks that way. Just leave people like me out of it."

"How can you be so sure it was a game?" she asked.

"Huh!" McCoy snorted righteously.

"Maybe you should have considered the possibility that it wasn't a game and that you didn't have to go buy a woman," she said. "Maybe what you need, Corporal McCoy, is a little more self-confidence."

"Jesus Christ!" he said.

"What's your given name?" she asked.

"Ken, Kenneth," he said without thinking. Then, "Why?"

"Because if I'm going to get in that bathtub with you and scrub the smell of your whore off you, I thought it would be nice to know your name."

"There was no whore," he said.

She looked intently at him and almost visibly decided he was telling the truth. She nodded her head.

"Then the bath can wait till later," she said. "Lock the door."

(FOUR)
Room 23
The Hotel Am See
Chiehshom, Shantung Province
1015 Hours 18 May 1941

"This is very nice," Ellen Feller said, picking the camera up from the chest of drawers and turning to look at him. She was naked. "Very expensive." That was a question.

"It's a Leica," he said. "It belongs to the Corps."

She held it up and pretended to aim it.

"Pity we can't use it," she said. "I would like to have a memento of this. Of us."

"For your husband to find," he said.

She laughed and put the camera down. It had been practically nonstop screwing (with breaks only for meals and trips to make sure none of the Marines had gone off on a drunk someplace); but this was the first time either of them had mentioned her husband.

"It's possible he could walk in any minute," McCoy said. "And catch us like this."

"You don't have to worry about him," she said. "But I wouldn't want to get you in trouble with your officers. Are they really likely to come back soon?"

"Can't tell. Why wouldn't I have to worry about him?"

"You mean you couldn't tell? Not even from the way he looked at you?"

"What are you saying, that he's a fairy?"

She shrugged.

"Then why do you stay married to him?" he asked. "Why did you marry him in the first place?"

"That's none of your business," she said. She leaned against the chest of drawers and arched her back.

She inhaled and ran her fingers across the flat of her belly. And then she told him.

"When I was fourteen, my father had a religious experience," she said. "Do you know what that means?"

"No," he admitted.

"He accepted the Lord Jesus Christ as his personal saviour," Ellen Feller said, evenly. "And brought his family, my mother and me, into the fold with him. She didn't mind, I don't suppose, although I suspect she's a little uncomfortable with some of the brothers and sisters of the Christian & Missionary Alliance. And I just went along. Girls at that age are a little frightened of life anyway; and when the hellfire of eternity is presented as a reality, it's not hard to accept the notion of being washed in the blood of the lamb."

"Jesus Christ," McCoy said.

"Yes," Ellen said wryly. "Jesus Christ."

She pushed herself off the chest of drawers and walked to the bed. Then she leaned over him and ran the balls of her fingers over his chest.

"So I passed through my high school years convinced that when I had nice thoughts about boys, it was Satan at work trying to get my soul."

"I was a Catholic," McCoy said. "They tried to tell us the same thing."

"Did you believe it?" she asked.

"I wasn't sure," he said.

"I was," she said. "And I went through college that way. It wasn't hard. I was surrounded with them. Whenever anyone confessed any doubts, the others closed ranks around her. Or him. We prayed a lot, and avoided temptation. No drinking, no dancing, no smoking. No touching."

She moved her hand to his groin and repeated, "No touching."

"So how come you married him? Where did you meet him?"

"I was a senior in college," she said. "The Christian & Missionary Alliance is, as you can imagine, big on missionaries; and he came looking for missionary recruits. Came from here, I mean. With slides of China and all the souls the Alliance was saving for Jesus. He told us all about the heathens and how they hungered for the Lord. Very impressive stuff.

"And then that summer, right after I graduated, he came to our church in Baltimore . . . I'm from Baltimore . . . to give his report to our church. My father is a pillar of our church, and he was important to my husband, because my father is pretty well off. He stayed with us while he was in Baltimore."

"And made a play for you," McCoy said. "Jesus, that feels good!"

She chuckled deep in her throat and bent over him and nipped his nipple with her teeth. He put his hand on her breast and dragged her down on top of him.

"Do you want to hear this, or not?" she asked.

"Yeah," he said.

"It's all right with me if you don't," she said.

"Finish it," he said.

"What I thought I was getting was a life toiling in the Lord's Vineyard," Ellen went on. "With a man of God. Saving the heathen Chinese from eternal damnation. What he knew he was getting was a wife, and a wife who would not only put to rest unpleasant suspicions that had begun to crop up, but a wife whose father would more than likely be very generous to his mission . . . he had the mission in Wang-Tua, then . . . but probably to him personally."

"When did you find out he was a faggot?" McCoy asked.

"We were married at nine o'clock in the morning," she said. "At noon, we took the train to New York. And then from New York, we took the train to San Francisco. I decided that it was wrong of me to think that anything would happen on a railroad train. And we boarded the *President Jefferson* for Tientsin the same day we arrived in San Francisco."

"And nothing happened on the ship?"

"*Something* happened on the ship," Ellen said. "I was not surprised that I didn't like it very much, and that it didn't happen very often."

"Then he can get it up?" McCoy asked.

"Not like this," she said, squeezing him so hard that he yelped. "But he can, yes. I suspect he closes his eyes and pretends I'm a boy."

"So why the hell did you stay married to him?"

"You just don't understand. I just didn't know. I was innocent. Ignorant."

He snorted.

"Meaning I'm not innocent now?" she asked.

"No complaints," McCoy said.

"There was somebody else, obviously."

"Who?"

"None of your business," she said, but then she told him: A newly ordained bachelor missionary with whom she'd been left alone a good deal when the Reverend Feller had been promoted to Assistant District Superintendent. They had been caught together. They had begged forgiveness. After prayerful consideration, the Reverend Feller had decided the way to handle the situation was to send the young missionary home, as "unsuited for missionary service," which happened often. A church would be found for him at home. As a guarantee of impeccable Christian behavior in the future, there was a written confession of his sinful misbehavior left behind in the Reverend Feller's safe.

McCoy was sure there'd been more than one "somebody else." She had done things to him he hadn't thought American women even knew about. Things that one missionary minister wouldn't have taught her. But he could hardly expect her to provide him with a list of the guys she had screwed. She wasn't like that. He was somewhat surprised to realize that he had come to like Ellen Feller.

"After that," Ellen went on, "he never came near me. I thought he was either disgusted with me or was punishing me."

"You still didn't know he was queer?"

"I didn't find out about that, believe it or not, until just before the Alliance called him home for consultation. That was the reason I didn't go home with him."

"How'd you find out?"

"I walked in on him," she said, matter-of-factly.

He was aware that she'd stopped manipulating him and he had gone down. She still had her hand on him, though, possessively, and he liked that.

"What did he say?" McCoy asked.

"Nothing," she said. "He didn't even stop. So I just closed the door and left. Very civilized."

"Why didn't you leave him?" McCoy asked.

"It's not that simple, my darling," Ellen said.

McCoy liked when she called him "my darling," even though it embarrassed him a little. He couldn't remember anyone ever saying that to him before. It was a lot different from a whore calling him "honey" or "sweetheart" or "big boy."

"Why not?" he asked.

"Well, there's Jerry's detailed, written confession, for one thing," she said, as if explaining something that should have been self-evident.

"So what?"

"He would show it to my father."

"So what? Tell your father he's queer."

"I wouldn't be believed," she said. "He's a man of God. My father is very impressed with him. He would think I made the accusation in desperation, to excuse my own behavior."

"Then fuck your father," McCoy said.

Her eyebrows went up. "I know how you meant that," she said.

"Jesus!" he said.

"I'm thirty years old," she said. "I have no money. I can play every hymn in the hymnal from memory on the piano. I speak Chinese. Unless I could find a job as a Chinese-speaking piano player, I don't know how I could support myself."

Thirty years old? At first I thought she was older than that. Then I thought she was younger. Thirty is too old for me. What the hell am I thinking about? In a week, she'll get on a ship, and that will be the last I'll ever see her.

"Can you type?" McCoy asked. She nodded. "Then get a job as a typist, for Christ's sake."

"For my own sake, you mean," she said. Then she added, mysteriously, "I have something else that might turn out. I won't know until I get to the States."

"Like a couple of thousand-year-old vases, for example?" McCoy asked. "Or some jade?"

Her face clouded, and she took her hand from his crotch and covered her mouth with it. "What did you do, look in the crates?"

"No. A stab in the dark," McCoy said.

"My God, does anybody else know?"

"My officer thinks that's the real reason your husband came back to China," McCoy said. "He doesn't believe the selfless patriot business."

"I have three Ming dynasty vases and some jade my husband doesn't know about," Ellen said. "I thought I could sell them and use the money to get a start."

"You probably can, if you can get them through customs," McCoy said.

"Your . . . officer . . . isn't going to say anything?"

"It's none of his business," he said.

"And the other officers? Do they know?"

"You've just seen how smart they are," McCoy said.

"It left us alone, my darling," she said.

"I like it when you say that," McCoy said. She looked into his eyes and it made him uncomfortable. "And I like it when you put your hand on my balls."

She stiffened. She didn't like him to talk that way, he thought. But she shifted on the bed and cupped her hand on him again.

"I would like it, too, if you said that to me," she whispered.

"Said what?"

"My darling."

"My darling," McCoy said, and flushed. It made him uncomfortable. "And I like to suck your teats," he added almost defiantly.

She stiffened again, and he wondered why he said that, knowing it would piss her off.

"I like the thought but not the vocabulary," she sighed. "Cows have teats, ladies have breasts."

"Pardon me," McCoy said.

"You're forgiven," she said.

"Move closer, so I can play with them," McCoy said.

"Why, you wicked little boy, you," she said, but she pushed herself closer to him, so that his hands and his mouth could reach her breast.

The "my darling" business was over, McCoy realized. First with relief, then with sadness.

She took her nipple from his mouth a moment later and kissed him lasciviously, then moved her head down his body. She was just straddling him when there was a knock at the door.

"Come back later," McCoy called in Chinese.

"It's Lieutenant Sessions, McCoy, open the door!"

Breathing heavily, Ellen reluctantly hauled herself off him and scurried around the room, picking up her clothing. McCoy watched her moves—lovely and graceful. She was the best-looking piece of ass he'd ever had, he had realized sometime during the last twenty-four hours. And the best.

He wondered how she was going to handle Sessions. She was not going to be able to holler rape, which was what usually happened when an American woman got caught fucking a Marine. Not only wouldn't she be able to get away with it (how could she explain being in his room?); but she had called him 'my darling' and he knew somehow that she meant it. He meant more to her than a stiff prick. She was not going to cause him any trouble, and he knew he didn't want to cause her any.

"Come on, Corporal, I have business with you!" Sessions called.

McCoy waited until she'd gone into the bathroom, then pushed himself out of the bed and went to the door, pulling on his shorts en route.

Lieutenant Sessions wore two days' growth of beard, and his seersucker suit was badly soiled. The Japanese knew that it embarrassed Americans not to be clean-shaven, so razors were not made available. And there was evidence of an "accident" at a meal. McCoy was amused at the Japanese skill in embarrassing their unwanted guests (and so was Captain Banning), but it was apparent that Lieutenant Sessions was not.

"Sergeant Zimmerman said he had no idea where you were," Sessions accused as he pushed past McCoy into the room.

McCoy didn't reply.

"I presume that you have reported our detention by the Japanese to Shanghai?" Sessions asked.

"No, sir," McCoy said.

"Why not, Corporal?" Sessions asked angrily.

"I thought I'd wait to see what the Japs decided to do," McCoy said.

"You 'thought you'd wait'?" Sessions quoted incredulously. "Good God! And it's pretty clear, isn't it, how you passed your time while you were waiting? What the hell have you been doing in here, McCoy? Conducting an orgy?"

McCoy didn't reply.

"A round-the-clock orgy," Sessions went on, looking at the debris, food trays, bottles of beer, and towels on the floor. He sniffed the air. "It smells like a whorehouse in here. Is she still here, for Christ's sake?"

McCoy nodded.

"Goddamn it, Corporal, in my absence you were supposed to take charge, not conduct yourself like a PFC on payday. You are prepared to offer no excuse at all for not getting in touch with Shanghai and reporting what had happened to us?"

"I was trying not to make waves," McCoy said.

"And what the hell is that supposed to mean?"

The bathroom door opened and Ellen Feller came into the room. She was in her bathrobe, and her hair fanned down her shoulders.

She looked directly at Lieutenant Sessions as she walked through the room and out the door.

"Well, that really does it," Sessions said coldly, almost calmly, when she had gone. "Instead of doing your duty . . . Jesus Christ! I'm going to have your stripes for this, McCoy. I'd like to have you court-martialed!"

McCoy walked across the room to the chest of drawers and picked up the Leica camera.

"Goddamnit, Corporal, don't you turn your back on me when I'm talking to you!" Sessions said furiously.

McCoy rewound the film, opened the camera, and slipped the film out. He held the small can of film between his thumb and index finger and turned to face Lieutenant Sessions.

"I hope you didn't lose your temper like that in Yenchi'eng," McCoy said. "So far as the Japs are concerned, you lose a lot of face when you lose your temper."

"How dare you talk to me that way?" Sessions barked, both incredulous and furious.

"Lieutenant, as I see it, you have two choices," McCoy said. "You can make a by-the-book report of what happened: That against my advice, you went to Yenchi'eng and got yourself caught, and that when you came back here, you found out that I hadn't even reported that the Japs had you . . ."

" 'Had completely abandoned your obvious obligations' would be a better way to put it," Sessions interrupted.

"And had 'completely abandoned my obvious obligations,' " McCoy parroted.

"That's Silent Insolence[2] on top of everything else!" Sessions snapped.

"And that you found Mrs. Feller in my room," McCoy said.

"What the hell were you thinking about in that connection?" Sessions fumed. "Good God, man, her husband is a missionary!"

"Who will say that his wife was in here reading the Bible to me," McCoy said calmly. "He's a faggot."

Surprise flashed over Sessions's face.

"She is a married woman, and you damned well knew she was," Sessions said, somewhat lamely. This confrontation was not going at all the way he had expected it would.

"The other choice you and Lieutenant Macklin have," McCoy said, "is to report that you have proof the Japs don't have any German PAK38 50-mm cannons, at least not in the 11th Division."

That caught Sessions by surprise.

"What are you talking about?" he asked. "What proof?"

"If they had German cannon, they would have turned in their Model 94s," McCoy said. "They didn't." He held up the can of film. "I took these at first light yesterday morning," he said. "I was lucky: The Japs were up before daylight lining them up and taking the covers off. Probably weekly maintenance, something like that."

It took Sessions a moment to frame his thoughts.

"So you went yourself. And of course didn't get caught. That was very resourceful of you, McCoy," he said.

McCoy shrugged.

"How the hell did you do it?" Sessions asked.

"The German's got a truck," he said.

"German? Oh, you mean the man who owns the hotel?"

McCoy nodded.

"You just borrowed his truck and drove into Yenchi'eng, that's it?"

"Not exactly," McCoy said. "I went into Yenchi'eng last night. On a bicycle. I told the boy who drives the German's truck there was a hundred yuan in it for him if he picked me up at a certain place on the road at half-past six yesterday morning."

"And then he just brought you back?"

"No, we had to go into town first. He picks up stuff—vegetables mostly, sometimes a pig and chickens. I had to go in with him."

"How did you keep from being seen?"

"I didn't," McCoy said. "When I'm around the Japs, I play like I'm an Italian."

"How do you do that? Do you speak Italian?"

McCoy nodded.

"Christ, you're amazing, McCoy!" Sessions said.

"It was stupid, me going in there like that," McCoy said. "I should have known better."

"Why did you go?" Sessions asked.

"You acted like it was important," McCoy said. "Anyway, it's done. And if you were to tell Captain Banning that you and Macklin and the Reverend were making

[2]Prior to 1948 the Universal Code of Military Justice included the offense "Silent Insolence." Among the offenses therein embraced was a "mocking attitude" to military superiors.

a diversion, that you knew I was going to Yenchi'eng, I wouldn't say anything," McCoy said.

"You're not, I hope, suggesting, McCoy, that I submit a patently dishonest report," Sessions said.

"Rule one, doing what we're doing," McCoy said, "is don't make waves. Either with the Corps or with the people you're watching. You tell them what really happened, you're going to look like a . . ."

The next word in that sentence was clearly going to be "horse's ass," Sessions thought. He stopped himself just in time from saying, "How dare you talk to me that way?"

A small voice in the back of his skull told him quietly but surely that he had indeed made a horse's ass of himself already—in China ten days and already grabbed by the Japanese doing something he had been told not to do, and digging himself in still deeper every time he opened his mouth.

He had been a Marine eleven years. Never before had an enlisted man—not even a Master Gunnery Sergeant when he had been a wet-behind-the-ears shavetail—talked to him the way this twenty-one-year-old corporal was talking to him now.

And the small voice in the back of his skull told him McCoy was *not* insolent. Inferiors are insolent to superiors. McCoy was tolerantly contemptuous, as superiors are to inferiors. And the painful truth seemed to be that he had given him every right to do so.

He had been informed—and had pretended to understand—that he would have to learn to expect the unexpected. And he hadn't. Because he was a thirty-two-year-old officer, he had presumed that he knew more than a twenty-one-year-old enlisted man.

If he followed the book—the code of conduct expected of an officer and a gentleman, especially one who wore an Annapolis ring—he would immediately grab a telephone and formally report to Captain Banning that—against McCoy's advice—he had taken the Reverend Feller and Lieutenant Macklin to Yenchi'eng, been detained by the Japanese, had a pot of some greasy rice substance dumped in his lap, and then had returned to find that not only was Corporal McCoy fornicating with the missionary's wife (conduct prejudicial to good military order and discipline) but was silently insolent to boot. And that he just incidentally happened to have a roll of 35-mm film of the 11th Japanese Division's artillery park.

"I need a bath, a shave, and a clean uniform, Corporal," Lieutenant Sessions said. "We'll settle this later."

"Aye, aye, sir."

"I'd like to get started again first thing in the morning," Sessions went on. "Will there be any problems about that?"

"No, sir," McCoy said. "Now that you're back, we can move anytime you want to."

Sessions realized he was still making an ass of himself and that he had to do something about it.

"What I intend to do when we get somewhere with secure communications, Corporal McCoy," he said, "is advise Captain Banning that I went to Yenchi'eng against your advice and was detained by the Japanese. I will tell him of your commendable initiative in getting the film of the Japanese artillery park. I can see no point in discussing your personal life. I would be grateful, when you make your own report, if you would go easy on how I stormed in here and showed my ass."

"I hadn't planned to say anything about that, sir," McCoy said.

"And I'm sure," Sessions said, searching for some clever way to phrase it, "that . . . you will not permit your romantic affairs to in any way cast a shadow on the Corps' well-known reputation for chastity outside marriage."

"No, sir," McCoy said, chuckling. "I'll be very careful about that, sir." And then he added: "I'd be grateful if you didn't tell Lieutenant Macklin about Mrs. Feller."

Sessions nodded. "Thank you, McCoy," he said, then turned and walked out of the room.

V

(ONE)
The Hotel am See
Chiehshom, China
2215 Hours 18 May 1941

McCoy could not sleep. The smell of Ellen was inescapably on the sheets. And her image was no less indelibly printed on his mind.

Earlier, he found himself next to her at dinner. The moment he sat down, her knee moved against his.

There wasn't anything particularly sexy about her touch, and she didn't try to feel him up under the table—or he her—or anything like that. She just wanted to touch him. She didn't say two words to him either, except "please pass the salt." But she didn't take her knee away once.

All too soon, the Reverend Feller announced, "Well, we have a long day ahead of us." Ellen rose after him and followed him out . . . leaving McCoy with a terrible feeling of loss.

Later, McCoy and Zimmerman went to the European servants' quarters to make sure none of the drivers had shacked up in town. Afterward, Zimmerman asked matter-of-factly, "Sessions find out you're fucking the missionary lady?"

He had *not* been "fucking the missionary lady." It had started out that way, but it wasn't that way now. McCoy couldn't bring himself to admit he was in love, but it was more than an unexpected piece of ass, more than "fucking the missionary lady." And she had called him "my darling," and had meant it. And he had meant it, too, when she made him say it back.

"Yeah," McCoy said.

"And?"

"And what?"

"What's he going to do about it?"

"He's not going to do anything about it," McCoy said. "He's all right."

"You're lucky," Zimmerman said. "If that bastard Macklin finds out, McCoy, you're going to find yourself up on charges."

"One good way for him to find out, Ernie, is for you to keep talking about it."

"You better watch your ass, McCoy," Zimmerman said.

"Yeah," McCoy said. "I will."

Jesus Christ, what a fucking mess!

He turned the light back on and reached for the crossword puzzles from the *Shanghai Post.* He did three of them before he fell asleep sitting up. Then, carefully, so as not to rouse himself fully, he turned the light off, slipped under the sheet, and felt himself drifting off again.

When he felt her mouth on him, he thought he was having a wet dream—and that surprised him, considering all the fucking they had done. And then he realized that he wasn't dreaming.

"I thought that might wake you up, my darling," Ellen Feller said softly.

"What about your husband?"

"What about him? As you so obscenely put it," she said, "fuck him."

"You mean he knows?"

"I mean he sleeps in a separate bed, and when I left him, he was asleep."

"I had a hard time getting to sleep," McCoy said, "thinking about you."

"I'm glad," she said. She moved up next to him and put her face in his neck. "I would have come sooner," she said, "but he insisted on talking."

"About what?"

"That his being detained by the Japanese was a good thing, that it will probably make it easier to get the crates on the ship. Without having them inspected, I mean."

The thought saddened him. In nine days she would leave, and that would be the last he would ever see of her.

"You'd better set your alarm clock," she said practically. "I don't want to fall asleep in here."

He set the alarm clock, but it was unnecessary. They were wide awake at half-past four. Neither of them had slept for more than twenty minutes all through the night.

(TWO)
Huimin, Shantung Province
27 May 1941

It took them another nine days to reach Huimin, nine days without an opportunity for McCoy and Ellen to be together.

The days on the way to Huimin were pretty much alike. They would start out early and drive slowly and steadily until they found a place where they could buy lunch. Failing that they stopped by the side of the road and picnicked on rice balls, egg rolls, and fried chicken from the hoods and running boards of the trucks and cars.

The road meandered around endless rice paddies. The inclines and declines were shallow, but the curves were often sharp, thus making more than twenty miles an hour impossible. Sometimes there was nothing at all on the road to the horizon, and sometimes the road was packed with Chinese, walking alone or with their families or behind ox-drawn carts.

The Chinese were usually deaf to the sound of a horn. So when the road was narrow, as it most often was, it was necessary to crawl along in low gear until the road widened enough to let them pass the oxcarts. But sometimes at the blast of the horn, the slowly plodding pedestrians would jump to the side of the road and glower as the convoy passed.

When they had to picnic by the side of the road, McCoy tried to stop when there was no one else on the road. But most of the time, in spite of McCoy's intentions, they were surrounded by hordes of Chinese within five minutes. Some stared in frank curiosity, and others begged for the scraps.

Or for rides. And that was impossible, of course. If they allowed Chinese in the backs of the trucks, the beds would be stripped bare within a mile.

At Ssuyango, T'anch'eng, and Weifang, McCoy spent the hours of darkness trying to find out whether various Japanese units had indeed received German field artillery pieces. And at T'anch'eng, he somewhat reluctantly took Lieutenant Sessions with him.

Sessions skillfully sandbagged him into that. He came to McCoy's room after supper, while McCoy was dressing: black cotton peasant shirt, trousers, and rubber shoes, and a black handkerchief over his head. It was less a disguise than a solution to the problem of crawling through feces-fertilized rice paddies. A complete suit cost less than a dollar. He wore one and carried two more tightly rolled and tied with string that he looped and fastened around his neck.

When he came out of a rice paddy smelling like the bottom of a latrine pit, he would strip and put on a fresh costume. It didn't help much, but it was better than running around soaked in shit.

During the stopover at Ssuyango, McCoy made a deal with a merchant: five gallons of gasoline for eight sets of cotton jackets and trousers. When Sessions came to his room at T'anch'eng, he still had three left, not counting the one he was wearing.

Sessions was politely curious about exactly what McCoy intended to do, and McCoy told him. It wasn't that much of a big deal. All he was going to do was make his way down the dikes between the rice paddies until he was close to the Japanese compound. Then he would slip into the water and make his way close enough to the compound to photograph the artillery park and motor pool. Then he would make his way out of the rice paddie, change clothes, and come back.

"How do you keep the camera dry?" Sessions asked.

"Wrap it in a couple of rubbers," McCoy said.

Sessions laughed appreciatively.

"Do you go armed?"

"I have a knife I take with me," McCoy told him. "But the worst thing I could do is kill a Jap."

Sessions nodded his understanding. Then he said, "Tell me the truth, McCoy. There's no reason I couldn't go, is there? If you were willing to take me, I mean."

"Christ, Lieutenant, you don't want to go."

"Yes, I do, McCoy," Sessions had said. "If you'll take me, I'll go."

Then he walked to the bed and picked up the peasant suit.

"I'd like to have a picture of me in one of these," he said. "It would impress the hell out of my wife."

He looked at McCoy and smiled.

"I really would like to go with you, McCoy," he said. It was still a request.

"Officers are supposed to be in charge," McCoy said. "That wouldn't work."

"You don't have to worry about that," Sessions said. "You're the expert, and I know it. It's your show. I'd just like to tag along."

"Once you get your shoes in a rice paddy, they'll be ruined," McCoy said. It was his last argument.

"Okay," Sessions said. "So I wear old shoes."

So he took Sessions with him. It went as he thought it would, and the only trouble they had was close to the Jap compound. Sessions panicked a little when he hadn't heard McCoy for a couple of minutes and came looking for him, calling his name in a stage whisper.

They didn't find any German PAK38s, but neither did they get caught. And McCoy was by then convinced that the PAK38s existed only in the imagination of chairwarming sonsofbitches in Washington, bastards who didn't have to crawl around through rice paddies or fields fertilized with human shit.

Sessions was so excited by his adventure that when they got back to the Christian & Missionary Alliance Mission, he insisted on talking about it until it was way too late to even think of getting together with Ellen for a quickie before breakfast.

After it was light, they killed the roll of film in the camera by taking pictures of each other dressed up like Chinamen.

McCoy hoped that the pictures of Sessions dressed up that way might get the guy off the hook in Washington. They might decide to forget that the Japs had caught him if they saw that he had at least tried to do what they'd sent him to do.

The next night, however, McCoy refused to take Sessions with him when he went to see what he could find near the mission at Weifang. It was a different setup there, the Japs ran perimeter patrols, and he didn't want to run the risk of the both of them getting caught. Sessions didn't argue. Which made McCoy feel a little guilty, because the real reason he didn't want to take Sessions along was that he slowed McCoy down. If Sessions wasn't along, maybe he could get back to the mission in time for Ellen to come to his room.

That hadn't done any good. When he got back, Sessions was waiting for him. Sessions kept him talking (even though there hadn't been any German cannon at Weifang, either) until it was too late to do anything with Ellen. It was really a royal pain in the ass doing nothing with her during the day but hold hands on the front seat for a moment, or touch legs under a table, or something like that. Or he would catch her looking at him.

He decided to take Sessions with him to look at a motorized infantry regiment, the 403rd, near Huimin, because it was the last chance they would have on this trip. If there were some of these German cannons at Huimin, Sessions might as well be able to say he found them. Otherwise—having gotten himself caught by the Japanese—he was going to come off this big-time secret mission looking like an asshole. The pictures of him dressed up like a Chinaman weren't going to impress the big shots as much as his report that he had been caught.

McCoy was beginning to see that Sessions wasn't that much of your typical Headquarters, USMC, sonofabitch. What was really wrong with him was that he didn't know what he was doing. And he could hardly be blamed for that. They didn't teach "How to Spy on the Japs" at the Officer School in Quantico. It was a really dumb fucking thing for the Corps to do, sending him over here the way they had; but to be fair, that was the Corps' fault, not his.

And at Huimin, they found PAK38s. The 403rd Motorized Infantry Regiment (Separate) of His Imperial Majesty's Imperial Fucking Army had eight of them. And the eight had the wrong canvas covers. So they'd taken covers from the Model 94s and put them over the PAK38s.

They didn't fit. The muzzle of the PAK38s, with its distinctive and unmistakable muzzle brake, stuck three feet outside the two small canvas covers. And with the Model 94s parked right beside them—looking very small compared to the PAK38s—there was absolutely no question about what they were.

McCoy shot two thirty-six-exposure rolls of 35-mm black and white film in the Leica, and then a twenty-exposure roll of Kodacolor, although he suspected that one wouldn't turn out. Kodacolor had a tendency to fuck up when you used it at first light—McCoy had no idea why.

Sessions was naturally all excited, and had a hard time keeping himself under control. But he didn't order McCoy, he asked him whether it would be a good idea to send somebody—maybe him, maybe Zimmerman—right off to Tientsin with the film. Or to take the whole convoy to Tientsin instead of making the other stops.

And Sessions just accepted it when McCoy told him that if he or Zimmerman took off alone with the film, the Kempei-Tai, who had been following them around since they crossed the Yangtze River, would figure there was something special up, and that would be the last time he or Zimmerman would ever be seen.

"Chinese bandits, Lieutenant," McCoy said. "Since there really aren't any, the Japs have organized their own."

"And similarly, taking the whole convoy to Tientsin right away would make them think something was out of the ordinary?"

"Yes, it would," McCoy said. "They probably would leave the whole thing alone, but you couldn't be sure. If we do what we told them we're going to do . . ."

"That would be best, obviously," Sessions concluded the sentence for him.

"Aye, aye, sir."

And it will give us another night on the road, maybe more if I get lucky and one of the trucks breaks down. And maybe that will mean maybe more than one other night with Ellen. Christ knows, I've done all the crawling through rice paddies I'm going to do on this trip.

He had no such luck. They spent the next night in a Christian & Missionary Alliance mission, where he was given a small room to share with Sergeant Zimmerman. Since he was in a different building from the officers and missionaries, there was just nothing he could do about getting together with Ellen.

He wondered if he might get lucky in Tientsin. He hoped so. It would probably be the last time in his life he would ever have a woman like that.

It was about two hundred miles from Huimin to Tientsin. About halfway there, there was another ferry. This one crossed a branch of the Yun Ho River. It wasn't much of a river, maybe two hundred yards across, and the ferry was built to fit. He thought for a minute that he and Ellen were going to get to cross first, which meant they would be alone for a little while. There probably was no place where they could screw—except maybe the backseat of the Studebaker. But he would have willingly settled for that.

At the last minute, though, Sessions decided to go too, and climbed in the backseat. And then, as McCoy was about to drive down the bank onto the ferry, Sessions had another officer inspiration.

"Sergeant Zimmerman!" he called. "Would you come with us, please?"

A moment later, he leaned forward.

"I don't think it's a good idea for us to be all alone over there," he said, significantly. "Do you?"

"No, sir," McCoy said. "I guess not."

What does he think is going to happen over there? I shouldn't have told him about the Chinese/Japanese bandits. If I hadn't, he would have stayed behind, and I could have had fifteen, twenty minutes alone with Ellen.

When Ellen turned to smile at Ernie Zimmerman as he moved into the back beside Sessions, she caught McCoy's hand in both of hers, and held it for a moment in her lap. He could feel the heat of her belly.

On the other side of the river, he drove the Studebaker far enough up the road to make room for the convoy to re-form behind it as they came off the ferry.

And then Lieutenant Sessions did something very nice.

"McCoy, you stay here in the car with Mrs. Feller. Sergeant Zimmerman and I will walk back to the river to wait for the others."

"Aye, aye, sir," McCoy said.

He took Ellen's hand as soon as they were out of the car. She held it in both of hers and drew it against her breast.

McCoy watched the rearview mirror very carefully until Sessions and Zimmerman had disappeared around a bend. Then he turned to her and put his arms around her.

"What are we going to do?" Ellen asked against his ear.

"I don't know," he said. "At least I got to put my arms around you."

She kissed him, first tenderly, then lasciviously, and then she put her mouth to his ear as she applied her fingers to the buttons of his fly.

"I know what to do," she said. "Just make sure they don't suddenly come walking back."

After a moment, she sat up to let him reach down and open her dress. Then he slipped his hand behind her, unclasped her brassiere, and freed her breasts.

And then, all of a sudden, the hair on the back of his neck began to curl, and he felt a really weird sensation—of chill and excitement at once.

He was being a goddamned fool, he told himself. He was just scared that the two of them would be caught together doing what they were doing.

And with a strange certainty, he knew that wasn't it at all.

He lifted himself high enough on the seat to look in the backseat. Zimmerman's Thompson was on the floorboard. That left Zimmerman and Sessions with nothing but Zimmerman's pistol.

"What are you doing?" Ellen asked, taking her mouth off him.

"There's a Thompson in the backseat," McCoy said. "You grab it and run after me."

He pushed his thing back in his pants and took his Thompson from the floorboard.

"What's the matter?" Ellen asked.

"Goddamnit, just do what I tell you!" he snapped, and sprang out of the car. As he trotted down the road, he chambered a cartridge in the Thompson.

I'm going to race the hell down there and find the two of them sitting on a bench waiting for the ferry. And they are both going to think I've lost my fucking mind.

But they weren't sitting on a bench when he trotted around the bend.

They were up against a steep bank, and there were twenty, twenty-five Chinese, dressed as coolies, crowding them.

The convoy would be broken in pieces in only one place between Huimin and Tientsin. The only place, therefore, where it could credibly be reported that Chinese bandits had attacked it. And the Japanese had damned well figured that out.

And they had handed the Japs the opportunity on a silver platter. Sessions and Zimmerman were isolated and practically unarmed. After the 'bandits' finished with them, they would have come to the car.

Zimmerman had the flap on his .45 holster open, but hadn't drawn it.

"Take the fucking thing out, for Christ's sake," McCoy called out.

The Chinese looked over their shoulders at him. Several of them took several steps in his direction. Several others moved toward Zimmerman and Sessions.

McCoy was holding the Thompson by the pistol grip, the butt resting against the pit of his elbow, the muzzle elevated. He realized that he was reluctant to aim it at the mob.

Goddamnit, I'm scared! If I aim it at them, the shit will hit the fan!

He pulled the trigger. The submachine gun slammed against his arm, three, four, five times, as if somebody was punching him. He could smell the burned powder, and he saw the flashes coming from the slits in the Cutts Compensator on the muzzle.

Everybody froze for a moment, and then the Chinese who had been advancing on Zimmerman and Sessions started to run toward them. After that the shit did hit the fan. Pistols were drawn from wherever they had been concealed. McCoy saw that at least two of the pistols were Broomhandled Model 98 Mausers, which fire 9-mm cartridges full automatic.

McCoy put the Thompson to his shoulder, aimed very carefully, and tapped the trigger. The Thompson fired three times, and one of the Chinese with a Broomhandle Mauser went down with a look of surprise on his face. McCoy found another Chinese with a Broomhandle and touched the trigger again. This time the Thompson barked only twice, a dull blam-blam, and the second Chinese dropped like someone who'd been slugged in the stomach with a baseball bat.

As he methodically took two more Chinese down with two- and three-round bursts from the Thompson, he saw Zimmerman finally get around to drawing his pistol and working the action.

A movement beside him startled him, frightened him. He twisted and saw that Ellen was standing a foot behind him. Everything seemed to be in slow motion. He had time to notice that she had her breasts back inside her brassiere, but that there was something wrong with her dress. Then he figured out that she hadn't gotten the right button in the right hole.

She had Zimmerman's Thompson in her hands, holding it as if she was afraid of it. And around her shoulder was Zimmerman's musette bag. The bulges told him there were two spare drum magazines in it. Her eyes were wide with horror.

He returned his attention to the mob, and fired again.

"Shoot, for Christ's sake!" McCoy shouted. Zimmerman looked baffled.

Sessions finally did something. He snatched the Colt from Zimmerman's hand. Holding it with both hands he aimed at the ground in front of the Chinese. He fired, and then fired again. McCoy heard a slug ricochet over his head.

That dumb sonofabitch is actually trying to wound them in the legs!

He put the Thompson back to his shoulder and emptied the magazine in four- and five-shot bursts into the mob of Chinese. There was no longer time to aim. He sprayed the mob, aware that most of his shots were going wild. And then when he tugged at the trigger, nothing was happening. The fifty-round drum was empty.

Conditioned by Parris Island Drill Instructors to treat any weapon with something approaching reverence—abuse was *the* unpardonable sin—he very carefully laid the empty Thompson on the ground and only then took Zimmerman's Thompson from Ellen.

When he had raised it to his shoulder, he saw that the mob had broken and was running toward the ferry slip. For some reason that produced rage, not relief. Telling himself to take it easy, to get a decent sight picture before pulling the trigger, he fired at individual members of the now-fleeing mob. He was too excited to properly control the sensitive trigger, and the Thompson fired in four-, five-, and six-shot bursts until the magazine was empty. By then there were five more Chinese down, some of them sprawled flat on their faces, one of them on his knees, and another crawling for safety like a worm, his hands on the gaping wound in his leg.

McCoy ejected the magazine and went for the spares in the musette bag around Ellen's shoulders. He snared one on the first grab, but as he did so he dislodged the top cartridge from its proper position in the magazine. He put the magazine to his mouth and yanked the cartridge out with his teeth. Then he jammed the magazine into the Thompson and put it back in his shoulder. Two Chinese were rushing toward him, one with a knife, the other with what looked like a boat pole. He took both of them down with two bursts. One of the 230-grain .45 slugs caught the second one in the face and blew blood and brains all over the road.

And then it was all over. No Chinese were on their feet; and when he trained the Thompson on the ground, the ones down there seemed to be dead. Except one, who was doggedly trying to unjam his Broomhandle Mauser. McCoy took a good sight on him and put two rounds in his head.

There were more than a dozen dead and wounded Chinese on the ground. Some were screaming in agony.

Lieutenant Sessions ran over to McCoy, looking as if he was trying to find something to say. But nothing came out of his mouth for several moments.

"My God," he whispered finally.

McCoy felt faint and nauseous. But forced it down. Then Ellen slumped to her knees and threw up. That made McCoy do the same thing.

"What the hell was that all about?" Sessions finally asked.

"Shit!" McCoy said.

Ellen looked at him, white-faced, and he thought he saw disgust in her eyes.

"I guess the Japs decided you're not really a Christer, Lieutenant," McCoy said.

"Jesus Christ, the film!" Sessions said. "Where is it?"

"Goddamn it," McCoy said, and started to run back to the car.

He was halfway to the car when he heard shots and then a scream. He spun around. Zimmerman had finally got his shit together. He had put a fresh magazine in McCoy's Thompson and was walking among the downed Chinese, methodically firing a couple of rounds into each of them to make sure they were dead.

Ellen was doing the screaming, while Lieutenant Sessions held her, staring horrified at what Zimmerman was doing.

And McCoy saw the cavalry finally galloping to the rescue.

The ferry was in midstream. Lieutenant Macklin, who had found his steel helmet somewhere, stood at the bow with his pistol in his hand and a whistle in his mouth. Behind him were the two BAR men, and behind them the rest of the drivers, armed with Springfields. McCoy did not see the Reverend Mr. Feller.

He ran the rest of the way to the car. The film was where he had left it, in the crown of his campaign hat, concealed there by a skivvy shirt.

He got behind the wheel and backed up to where Ellen stood with Lieutenant Sessions. Sessions opened the back door, and she got in and slumped against the seat, white-faced and white-eyed.

The ferry finally touched the near shore, and Lieutenant Macklin, furiously blowing his whistle, led the cavalry up the road to them.

(THREE)

Lieutenant Sessions learned quick, McCoy decided. You had to give him that. He took charge, the way an officer was expected to. Lieutenant Macklin was running around like a fucking chicken with his head cut off. The first thing he was worried about was that the Chinese would "counterattack." They were a bunch of fucking bandits, more than half of them were dead. Military units counterattacked. What was left of the Chinese were still running.

The second thing that worried Macklin was what the colonel would think. His orders were to avoid a "confrontation" at all costs. There had obviously been a "confrontation."

"There's sure to be an official inquiry," Macklin said. "We're going to have to explain all these bodies. God, there must be a dozen of them! How are we going to explain all these dead Chinese?"

"There's eighteen," McCoy said helpfully. "I counted them. I guess we're just going to have to say we shot them."

Both Sessions and Macklin gave him dirty looks. Sessions still didn't like it that McCoy was contemptuous of Macklin, who was after all an officer. And Macklin thought that Killer McCoy was not only an insolent enlisted man, but was more than likely responsible for what had happened.

What bothered Macklin, McCoy understood, was not that they had almost gotten themselves killed, but that he himself was somehow going to be embarrassed before the colonel. He was, when it came down to it, the officer in command.

"Corporal," Macklin snapped. "I don't expect you to understand this, but what we have here is an International Incident."

"You weren't even involved, Lieutenant," McCoy said. "You were on the other side of the river. By the time you got here, it was all over."

"That's enough, McCoy!" Sessions snapped.

"I'm the officer in charge," Macklin flared. "Of course I'm involved!"

"Aye, aye, sir," McCoy said.

Macklin sucked in his breath, in preparation, McCoy sensed, to really putting him in his place.

Sessions stopped him by speaking first.

"The important thing, Macklin," he said, while Lieutenant Macklin paused to draw in a breath, "is to place the rolls of film McCoy took into the proper hands at Tientsin. That's the primary objective of this whole operation."

"Yes, of course," Macklin said impatiently, itching to launch into McCoy. "But—"

Sessions cut him off again.

"Next in importance is the physical safety of the Reverend and Mrs. Feller."

"Yes, of course," Macklin repeated.

"And as you point out, there is the problem of the bodies," Sessions said.

"Obviously," Macklin said. "McCoy's latest contribution to the death rate in China."

Sessions smiled at that.

"We can't just drive off and leave eighteen bodies in the road," Sessions said. "And I think McCoy and I should separate, in case something should happen to one or the other of us—"

Now Macklin interrupted him: "You do think there's a chance of a counterattack, then?"

"I think it's very unlikely," Sessions said, "but not impossible."

He's humoring the sonofabitch, McCoy thought.

"As I was saying," Sessions went on, "I think we should do whatever we have to, to make sure that either McCoy or I make it to Tientsin, to be a witness to the fact that there are German PAK38s in Japanese hands."

"I take your point," Macklin said solemnly. "What do you propose?"

Just as solemnly, Sessions proposed that McCoy, two Marine trucks, and all the extra drivers be left behind in a detachment commanded by Lieutenant Macklin, while he and Sergeant Zimmerman and everybody and everything else immediately left for Tientsin.

"I think that's the thing to do," Macklin solemnly judged.

McCoy was almost positive the Japanese would not try anything else. They would think the Americans had something else in mind—like an ambush—when they stayed behind with the bodies. The Japanese would have left the bodies where they fell, he knew, unless they felt ambitious enough to throw them into the river.

But just to be sure, he set up as good a perimeter guard as he could with the few men he had. Meanwhile Lieutenant Macklin relieved him of the Thompson submachine gun. He kept it with him where he spent the night in the cab of one of the trucks.

Early the next morning a mixed detachment of French Foreign Legionnaires, Italian marines, and Tientsin Marines showed up.

McCoy was a little uncomfortable when he saw the Italians, but if they knew who he was, there was no sign. Somewhat reluctantly, they set about loading the bodies on the trucks they had brought with them.

It was dark before they got to the International Settlement in Tientsin, and there was no way McCoy could get away to try to go see Ellen Feller in the Christian & Missionary Alliance mission. The Tientsin officers kept him up all night writing down what had happened at the ferry.

Some of their questions made him more than uncomfortable.

First, they went out of their way to persuade him to admit that he had been more than a little excited. If he hadn't been a little excited (We're not suggesting you were afraid, McCoy. Nobody's saying that. But weren't you *really* nervous?) the "confrontation" could have been avoided.

"Sir, there was no way what happened could have been avoided. I was scared and excited, but that had nothing to do with what happened."

When they realized they weren't going to get him to acknowledge—even obliquely—that the incident was his fault, they dropped another, more uncomfortable accusation on him:

"Mrs. Feller tells us that you and Sergeant Zimmerman went around shooting the wounded, McCoy," one of them asked. "Was that necessary?"

McCoy had been around officers long enough to know when they were up to something. They were trying to stick it in Zimmerman. Zimmerman had a Chinese wife and kids. He couldn't afford to be busted.

"Nobody shot any wounded, Captain. Not the way you make it sound."

"Then why do you suppose both Mrs. Feller and Lieutenant Macklin both say that's what happened?"

"I don't know," McCoy said. "Lieutenant Macklin didn't even show up there until it was all over. So far as I know, Sergeant Zimmerman didn't fire his weapon. Lieutenant Sessions and I had to shoot a couple of them after they were down."

"Why did you feel you had to do that?"

"Because there was three of us and fifty of them, and the rest of the convoy was still across the river. Those guys that were down were still trying to fire their weapons."

"You don't say 'sir' very often, do you, Corporal?"

"Sir, no disrespect intended, sir," McCoy said.

"You say both you and Lieutenant Sessions found it necessary to shoot wounded men again?"

"Yes, sir."

"Mrs. Feller obviously confused you with Sergeant Zimmerman," the officer said, and McCoy knew that was the last anybody was going to hear about making sure the Chinese were really dead.

The next morning, a runner came after him while he was having breakfast in the mess. Lieutenant Sessions was waiting for him in the orderly room.

Sessions told him there that since the Japanese would by now suspect he was not a missionary, he had decided there was no point to his staying in China for the several months he had originally planned. So he was now going to take the *President Wilson* home with the Fellers.

"I'd like to say good-bye to her, Lieutenant," McCoy said.

"I'm not sure that's wise," Sessions said then. But in the end Sessions changed his mind and decided to be a good guy and told the Tientsin officers he wanted to speak to McCoy aboard the ship before he left.

On the way, he handed McCoy a thick envelope.

"This is for Captain Banning," he said. "I want you to deliver it personally."

"Aye, aye, sir," McCoy said, wondering why he hadn't given whatever it was to Macklin to deliver—until he realized that whatever it was, Sessions didn't want Macklin to see it.

"It's a report of everything that happened on the trip, McCoy," Sessions said. When he saw McCoy's eyebrows go up, he chuckled and added: "Everything of a duty, as opposed to social, nature, that is."

"Thank you, sir," McCoy said.

"I was up all night writing it," Sessions said. "There just wasn't time for the other letter I want to write. But that's probably just as well. I'll have time to write it on the ship, and it would probably be better coming from someone more important than me."

"I don't know what you're talking about, Lieutenant," McCoy said.

"You're going to get an official Letter of Commendation, McCoy," Sessions said. "For your record jacket. I'm going to write it, and I'm going to try to get someone senior to sign it. If I can't, I'll sign it myself."

"Thank you," McCoy said.

"No thanks are necessary," Sessions said. "You performed superbly under stress, and that should be recorded in your official records."

What Sessions meant, McCoy knew, was that without the sixth sense—or whatever the hell it was—that something was wrong, he wouldn't have shown up when he had, and Sessions would probably be going back to the States in a coffin in the reefer compartment of the *President Wilson.*

Sessions meant well, McCoy decided, but he doubted if there would be a Letter of Commendation. Even if Sessions really remembered to write one, he doubted if Headquarters, USMC, would let him make it official. From the way the officers here were acting (and the higher-ranking the officer, the worse it was), what had happened at the ferry was his fault. In their view he had "overreacted to a situation" which a more senior and experienced noncom would have handled without loss of life.

The letter report he was carrying to Captain Banning was nevertheless important. He trusted Sessions now: The report would tell it like it happened, and Banning would understand why he had done what he had.

At the gangplank of the *President Wilson,* Sessions got him a Visitor's Boarding Pass, and then asked the steward at the gangplank for the number of the Fellers' cabin.

When they reached the corridor leading to the Fellers' cabin, Sessions offered his hand.

"I'll say good-bye here, McCoy," he said. "I want to thank you, for everything, and to say I think you're one hell of a Marine."

"Thank you, Lieutenant," McCoy said. He was more than a little embarrassed.

"We'll run into each other again, I'm sure," Sessions said. "Sooner or later. Good luck, McCoy."

"Good luck to you, too, sir," McCoy said.

As he looked for the Feller cabin, he felt pretty good. He was beginning to believe now that there might be a Letter of Commendation. It would be nice to have something like that in the official records when his name came up before the sergeant's promotion board.

The good feeling vanished the moment Ellen answered his knock at her cabin door. The look on her face instantly showed she'd hoped she'd seen the last of him. Being the fucking fool he was, though, he didn't want to believe what he saw on her face and in her eyes. He told himself that what it was was surprise.

He started out by asking her if maybe she would write him. "Maybe, you never can tell, we'll be able to see each other again sometime." He ended up telling her he loved her. "I think it's still possible for me to buy my way out of the Corps," he went on. "I'll look into it, I have the money. And I do really love you."

She got stiff when he started talking, the way she did when he talked crude to her; and by the time he was telling her he loved her, her face was rigid and her eyes cold.

"How dare you talk to me like that?" she said when he had finished, with a voice like a dagger.

So what she wanted after all was nothing but the stiff prick her fairy husband couldn't give her. The funny thing about it was that he wasn't mad. He was damned close to crying.

He turned and walked out of her cabin, vowing that he would never make a fucking mistake like that again. He'd never mistake some old bitch with hot pants for the real thing. He didn't give a shit if she fucked Lieutenant Sessions eight times a day all the way across the Pacific. If she couldn't get Sessions, she'd grab some other dumb fucker. And failing that, she'd get herself a broomhandle.

(FOUR)
Headquarters, 4th Marines
Shanghai, China
11 June 1941

Once given permission to enter the office of Captain Edward Banning, Lieutenant John Macklin marched in erectly, came to attention before Banning's desk, and said, "Reporting as directed, sir."

The formalities over, he stepped to the chair in front of Banning's desk, sat down in it, and crossed his legs.

"Getting hot already, isn't it?" he asked.

"I don't recall giving you permission to sit down, Lieutenant," Captain Banning said, almost conversationally, but with a touch of anger in his voice.

Macklin, surprised, took a quick look at Banning's face and then scrambled to his feet. When he was again at the position of attention, he said: "I beg your pardon, Captain."

"Lieutenant," Banning said, "I have carefully read your report of the Tientsin-Peking trip, paying particular attention to those parts dealing with your detention at Yenchi'eng and the incident at the ferry."

"Yes, sir?"

"I have read with equal care the report Lieutenant Sessions wrote on the same subjects," Banning said.

"Sir?" Macklin asked.

"There was a caveat in Lieutenant Sessions's report," Banning said. "He wrote that he was writing in the small hours of the morning because he hoped to finish it before he went home. Thus he was afraid there would be some small errors in it because of his haste."

"I wasn't aware that Lieutenant Sessions had made a report, sir," Lieutenant Macklin said. "May I suggest that it might be a good idea if I had a look at it, with a view to perhaps revising my own report?"

Banning's temper flared again when he recalled Macklin's report. It boggled his mind to think that the man blamed the detention at Yenchi'eng on McCoy's "cowardly refusal to do what duty clearly required"; and that the "tragic events" at the river crossing could have been avoided if only Lieutenant Sessions had heeded his warning that "Corporal McCoy clearly manifested paranoid tendencies of a homicidal nature and had to be carefully watched."

And then, in the presumption that Sessions was on the high seas and safely removed from rebuttal, he'd even gone after him:

"The possibility cannot be dismissed that Lieutenant Sessions acquiesced, if he did not actually participate, in the brutal slaughter of the wounded Chinese civilians."

Banning waited a moment for his temper to subside.

"You are a slimy creature, aren't you, Macklin?" Banning asked calmly. "How the hell have you managed to stay in the Corps this long?"

"I don't know what you mean, sir," Macklin said.

"You know what a slimy creature is, Macklin. In the Marine Corps, a slimy creature is an officer who tries to pass the blame for his own failures onto the shoulders of a brother officer. I don't know of a phrase obscene enough to describe an officer who tries to cover his own ass by trying to blame his failures on an enlisted man. And you probably would have gotten away with it, you slimy sonofabitch, if Sessions hadn't spotted you for what you are and sent his report back with McCoy."

"There may be, Captain, some minor differences of judgment between the two reports, but nothing of magnitude that would justify these insulting accusations—"

"Shut your face, Lieutenant!" Banning shouted. It was the first time he had raised his voice, and his loss of temper embarrassed him. Glaring contemptuously at Macklin, he took time to regain control before he went on.

"If I had my druthers, Lieutenant," Banning said, "I'd bring charges against you for conduct unbecoming an officer. Or for knowingly uttering a false official statement. But I can't. If I brought you before a court-martial, we would have to get into security matters. And we can't do that. What I can do, what I will do, is see that your next efficiency report contains a number of phrases which will suggest to the captain's promotion board that you should not be entrusted with a machine-gun crew, much less with command of a company. It will be a very long time before you are promoted, Lieutenant. You're a smart fellow. Perhaps you will conclude that it would be best if you resigned from the Marine Corps."

"Captain Banning," Macklin said after a moment. "There is obviously a misunderstanding between us."

"There's no misunderstanding, Macklin," Banning said, almost sadly. "What's happened here is that you have proved you're unfit to be a Marine officer. It's as simple as that. The one thing a Marine officer has to have going for him is integrity. And you just don't have any."

"I'm sure I'll be able to explain this misunderstanding to the colonel," Macklin said. "And that is my intention, sir."

Banning looked at him for a moment and then picked up his telephone and dialed a number."

"Captain Banning, sir," he said. "I have Macklin in here. I have just informed him of the contempt in which I hold him. He tells me that he believes he can explain the misunderstanding to you."

There was a hesitation before the colonel replied.

"I suppose he is entitled to hear it from me," the colonel said. "Send him over."

"Aye, aye, sir," Banning said, and replaced the telephone in its cradle.

"You're dismissed, Macklin," Banning said. "The colonel will see you, if you wish."

Macklin did an about-face and marched out of his office.

Banning knew what sort of a reception Macklin was going to get from the colonel. He had had to argue at length with him to talk him out of a court-martial. It was only Banning's invocation of the Good of the Corps that finally persuaded the colonel to reluctantly agree that the only way to deal with the problem was to immediately relieve Macklin of duty until such time as he could be sent home.

(FIVE)
Headquarters, First Battalion, 4th Marines
Shanghai, China
12 June 1941

The first sergeant sent a runner into town to McCoy's apartment by rickshaw. Liberty or no liberty, the first sergeant wanted to see him right away.

McCoy shaved and put on a fresh uniform and went to the compound.

"I hope you're packed, McCoy," the first sergeant said when he walked into the company office. Then he handed him maybe twenty copies of a special order, held together with a paper clip.

HEADQUARTERS
4th Regiment, USMC, Shanghai, China

10 June 1941
Subject: Letter Orders
To: Cpl Kenneth J. MCCOY 32875 USMC
Hq Co, 1st Bn, 4th Marines

1. Reference is made to cable message, Hq, USMC, Washington, D.C., subject, "McCoy, Kenneth J., Transfer Of", dated 4 June 1941.

2. You are detached effective this date from Hq Co 1st Bn, 4th Marines, and transferred in grade to 47th Motor Transport Platoon, USMC, U.S. Navy Yard, Philadelphia, Penna.

3. You will depart Shanghai aboard the first available vessel in the Naval service sailing for a port in the United States. On arrival in the United States you will report to nearest USMC or U.S. Navy base or facility, who will furnish you with the necessary transportation vouchers to your final destination.

4. You are authorized the shipment of 300 pounds of personal belongings. You are NOT authorized the shipment of household goods. You are NOT authorized delay en route leave. You will carry with you your service records, which will be sealed. Breaking the seal is forbidden.

5. You will present these orders to the officer commanding each USMC or USN station or vessel en route. Such officers are directed to transmit by the most expeditious means to Hq, USMC, Washington, D.C., ATTN Q3-03A, the date of your arrival, the date and means of your transportation on your departure, and your estimated date of arrival at your next destination.

BY DIRECTION:

J. James Gerber
Major, USMC
Adjutant

"What the hell is all this?"

"I guess the Corps wants to get you out of China, Killer, before they run out of people for you to cut up or shoot," the first sergeant said.

"Jesus Christ," McCoy said.

" 'The first available vessel in the service of the U.S.,' " the first sergeant quoted, "is the *Whaley.*[1] She sails Friday morning. You will be aboard. You know the *Whaley,* McCoy?"

"I know the *Whaley,"* McCoy said. "Fucking grease bucket."

"It's going to Pearl Harbor, not the States," the first sergeant said. "They'll put you aboard something else at Pearl. With a little bit of luck, you could spend two, three weeks in Pearl," the first sergeant said.

"Top, I don't want to go home," McCoy said.

The first sergeant's reaction to that was predictable: "You don't want to go home?"

"You know what I mean, Top," McCoy said. "I just shipped over to stay in China."

"McCoy, I don't know how you got to be a corporal without figuring this out for yourself . . . I don't know, come to think of it, how you got to be a corporal, period . . . but this is the Marine Corps. In the Marine Corps the way it works is the Marine Corps tells you where you go, and when."

There really wasn't any point in arguing with the first sergeant, and McCoy knew it, but he did so anyway, thinking that maybe he could get an extra few days, an extra two weeks.

If he had that much time, maybe he could think of something.

"For Christ's sake, Top, I got stuff to sell. I'll have to give it away if I have to get rid of everything by Friday. How about letting me miss the *Whaley* and catch whatever is next?"

[1]The U.S.S. *Charles E. Whaley* was a fleet oiler that regularly called at Shanghai to replenish the fuel supplies of the vessels of the Yangtze River Patrol and the half dozen small pigboats of SUBFORCHINA (U.S. Navy Submarine Force, China).

"Like what, for instance, do you have to get rid of cheap? I'm always on the lookout for a bargain."

"Come on, Top, you could fix it if you wanted to."

"Fuck you, McCoy," the first sergeant said. "A little time on a tanker'll be good for you."

"Can I tell Captain Banning about this?" McCoy asked.

"You go tell him, if you think it'll do you any good," the first sergeant said. "And then get your ass back here and start packing. When the Gunny tells me your gear is shipshape, then maybe I'll think about letting you go into town and see about selling your stuff."

Captain Banning waved him into his inner office as soon as he saw him coming through the door.

"I guess you've just got the word from your first sergeant?" he asked.

"Yes, sir."

"Before you start wasting your breath, McCoy, let me tell you that not only is the colonel overjoyed at your departure, but he has told me to make sure, personally, that you get on the *Whaley.*"

"I'm on his shit list, am I?"

"Let us say that you have been the subject of considerable cable traffic between here and Headquarters, Marine Corps, following the shoot-out at the O.K. Corral. If you plan to make a career of the Marine Corps, Killer, you're going to have to restrain your urge to cut people up and shoot them."

"That's unfair, Captain," McCoy said.

"Yeah," Captain Banning said. "I know it is, McCoy. You didn't start that fight, and according to Sessions, you handled yourself damned well once it started. For what it's worth, I argued with the colonel until he told me to shut my face. But he's still getting crap from the Italians, and the Consul General's been all over his ass about you. I was there when he asked whether you were just a homicidal maniac, or whether you were trying to start World War II all by yourself."

"So for doing what I was told to do, keep Sessions and Macklin alive, I get my ass shipped home in disgrace."

"That's about the sum of it," Banning said. "But you don't have everything straight. First of all, the colonel's not shipping you home in disgrace or otherwise. I think underneath, he sort of admires you. You were ordered home by the Corps. I suspect that the Consul General had something to do with it—raised hell about you through the State Department, or something like that—but the colonel didn't do it. And you're not going home in disgrace. Not only do you get to keep your stripes, but your company commander is going to give you an efficiency report that makes you sound like Lou Diamond, Jr.[2] I know, because I wrote it."

McCoy was obviously puzzled by that, and it showed on his face. "It doesn't say anything about your working for me, McCoy," Banning said. "You understand that you can't talk to anybody, in or out of the Corps, about that?"

"Aye, aye, sir."

"But it should impress the hell out of your new commanding officer," Banning said.

"I'm going to a truck company," McCoy said. "A goddamned truck company. I'm a machine-gunner."

"I'm going home in a couple of months myself," Banning said. "You keep your nose clean in the truck company, and when I get settled, I'll see what I can do for

[2]Master Gunnery Sergeant Diamond was a Corps-wide Marine legend, the perfect Marine.

you. Either working for me, or doing something else interesting. Or, if you really want to, getting you back in a heavy-weapons company."

"Thank you," McCoy said.

"What are you going to do about the stuff in the apartment?"

"As soon as my Gunny decides my gear is shipshape, the first sergeant said I could go into town."

"I'll call your first sergeant and tell him I'm sending you into town," Banning said. "Take whatever time you need to do what you have to do. And then go back to your company. I want to put you aboard the *Whaley* first thing Friday morning. If you're not on her, McCoy, the colonel will have my ass."

"I'll be aboard her, sir," McCoy said.

VI

(ONE)
U.S. Marine Corps Base
San Diego, California
9 July 1941

The U.S.S. *Charles E. Whaley* was as miserable a pile of rust and rivets as McCoy expected it would be. Since she was not a man-of-war, there was no Marine detachment aboard, which translated to mean that he had hardly anybody to talk to. Sailors don't like Marines anyway, and there were six pigboat swab jockeys from SUBFORCHINA being shipped to Pearl Harbor, and they really hated China Marines. The only swabbie who gave him the time of day was a bald, hairy machinist's mate second class who quickly let him know that he didn't mind spending a lot of time at sea far from women.

Reeking of diesel fuel, riding light in the water, the *Whaley* took seventeen days to make Pearl Harbor—swaying and pitching even in calm seas.

There was plenty of time to think things over and conclude that he'd been handed the shitty end of the stick. Again. Like always.

Starting with Ellen Goddamn-the-Bitch Feller.

And getting sent home from China was also getting the shitty end of the stick, too. Christ, he'd practically given away the furniture in the apartment. And despite the efficiency report that was supposed to make him sound like Lou Diamond, even a bunch of dumb fuckers in a fucking truck company would smell a rat about somebody who was sent home from China just after he shipped over for the 4th Marines and got promoted.

And the new assignment stank, too. A goddamned truck company at the Navy yard in Philly. Philly was the last fucking place he wanted to go. It was too close to Norristown, and he never wanted to go there again, period. And there was no question in his mind that he was going to walk into this fucking truck company in Philly and immediately be on everybody's shit list. There weren't that many corporal's billets in a Motor Transport platoon, and sure as Christ made little apples, the people in Philly had planned to give this billet to some deserving asshole of a PFC with hash marks[1] halfway to his elbow.

McCoy had been in the Corps long enough to know that Stateside Marines didn't like China Marines[2] and here would be a China Marine, a corporal three months into his second hitch, showing up to fuck good ol' PFC Whatsisname out of his promotion.

When the U.S.S. *Charles E. Whaley* finally tied up at Pearl Harbor, there was

[1]Oblong bars, one for each four years of satisfactory service, worn on the lower sleeve of outer garments.

[2]The tales—amplified in the retelling—of houseboys to clean billets, of custom-made uniforms, of exotic women available for the price of a beer, of extra retirement credit, et cetera, tended to cause some resentment toward China Marines among their Stateside peers.

a Master of Arms and two Shore Patrol guys waiting for him at the foot of the gangplank. He wasn't under arrest or anything, the Master at Arms told him (although he really should write him up for his illegal, embroidered to the sleeves chevrons). It was just that the U.S.S. *Fenton* was about to sail for Diego, and they didn't want him to miss it.

The U.S.S. *Fenton* turned out to be an old four-stacker destroyer that was tied up the other side of Pearl. Ten minutes after he was shown his bunk in the fo'c'sle, a loudspeaker six inches from where he was supposed to sleep came to life:

"Now Hear This, Now Hear this, Off-Duty Watch Stand to in Undress Whites to Man The Rail."

That fucking loudspeaker went off on the average of once every ten minutes all the way across the Pacific to Diego.

The only kind thing McCoy could think of to say about the U.S.S. *Fenton,* DD133, was that it made San Diego six days out of Pearl. She was carrying a rear admiral who didn't like to fly and knew that with his flag abroad nobody was going to ask questions about fuel consumed making twenty-two knots. It must have been great on the bridge, turning the tin can into a speedboat. But where he was, McCoy thought, he had trouble staying in his bunk. And his body was bruised black in half a dozen places from bumping into bulkheads and ladder rails when he misjudged where the tin can was going to bounce.

But Diego was next, and he would soon be on land again, and there was no reason he couldn't get a nice berth on the train from San Diego to Philly. The Corps probably wouldn't pay for it, but he could do that himself. In his money belt he had a little over three hundred dollars in cash: the hundred he'd started with, plus the hundred ninety he'd won—ten and twenty dollars at a time—from the pigboat sailors on the *Charles E. Whaley* and the ten he'd won in the only game there had been on the tin can.

Plus an ornately engraved "Officer's Guaranteed Checque" on Barclays Bank, Ltd., Shanghai, for $5,102.40. That came from the last crazy thing that had happened in Shanghai. When he'd gone to the apartment to sell his stuff, the "General" said he'd make it easy for him. He'd take everything off his hands for five hundred dollars American. McCoy had jumped at that. Then the General pushed a deck of cards at him and demanded, "Double or nothing."

McCoy cut the deck for the jack of clubs to the General's eight of hearts.

"Once more," the General demanded.

"Just so long as it's *once* more," McCoy said. "I'm not going to keep cutting the deck until you win and quit."

He got a dirty look for that.

"Once more," the General said. "That's it."

McCoy cut the five of clubs. The General smiled, showing his gold teeth . . . until he cut the three of hearts.

But he paid up, even though he had to go to the bank to get that kind of cash.

McCoy added the General's two thousand American to the money already in Barclays Bank and then asked for a cashier's check for the whole thing. After a moment they understood that what he wanted was what they called an "officer's checque."

He made them make it payable in dollars. The Limeys were in a war, and he didn't want to take the chance that they'd tell him to wait for his money until the war was over when he went to cash it.

He could goddamned well afford a Pullman berth from California to Philly, even if they wouldn't give him credit for the government rail voucher and he had to pay for the whole damned thing himself.

McCoy had taken boot camp at Parris Island, and he'd shipped to China out of Mare Island, in San Francisco. So this was his first time in Diego. His initial impression of the place—or anyway of the part that he saw, which was the Marine Corps Recruit Depot—was that it was a hell of a lot nicer-looking, at least, than Parris Island, although he supposed that that didn't make a hell of a lot of difference to boots. They probably had the same kind of semiliterate, sadistic assholes for DIs here that they did at Parris Island.

There was a bullshit legend in the Corps that after you finished boot camp, you would understand why the DIs treated you like they did, how it had been necessary to make a Marine out of you, and how you'd now respect them for it. As he watched a Diego DI jab his elbow in the gut of some kid who wasn't standing tall enough, or who had dared to look directly at the DI, or some other chickenshit offense, McCoy remembered his own Parris Island DI.

If I ever see Corporal Ellwood Doudt, that vicious shit-kicking hillbilly again, he thought, *I'll make him eat his teeth, even if I have to go after him with a two-by-four.*

McCoy found the Post Transportation Office without trouble in a Spanish-looking building with a tile roof. He set his seabags down and presented his orders to a sergeant behind a metal-grilled window, like a teller's station in a bank.

"You need a partial pay, Corporal?" the sergeant asked.

"Let it ride on the books," McCoy said. "I was a little lucky on the ship."

"Your luck just ran out," the sergeant said. "I hate to do this to you, Corporal, but you report to the brig sergeant."

"What?"

"They'll explain it over there," the sergeant said. "I just do what I'm told."

"All I want from you is a rail voucher to Philadelphia," McCoy said.

"You would have been smarter to pay your own way and put in for it when you got there. But you didn't. You came here, and my orders are to send the next three corporals who come in here over to the brig. There's a shipment of prisoners headed for Portsmouth. The guard detail needs a sergeant and three corporals. Now that you're here, they can go."

"Give me a break. Forget I came in."

"I can't," the sergeant said. "I got to send a TWX to Washington saying you're in the States. You read the orders."

The brig sergeant was a forty-year-old gunnery sergeant, a wiry, tight-lipped man with five hash marks and a face so badly scarred that McCoy wondered how the hell he managed to shave.

"What did you do, Corporal, fuck up in China?" he said, when McCoy gave him his orders.

"Not as far as I know, Gunny," McCoy said. "I'm being transferred in grade."

"Well, we got sixteen sailors headed for Portsmouth," he said. "Mostly repeat ship-jumpers, one deserter, one assault upon a commissioned officer, one thief, and three fags. You, plus a second lieutenant, a staff sergeant, and two other corporals are going to take them there. And all the time you thought the Corps didn't love you, right?"

"There's no way I can get out of this?"

"You're fucked, Corporal," the Gunny said. "You just lucked out."

In addition to the other corporals, the sergeant, and the lieutenant, the guard detail consisted of seven privates and PFCs. The other corporals and the sergeant were at least ten years older than McCoy. The lieutenant was McCoy's age, a muscular, crew-cut, tanned man who—to prove his own importance, McCoy thought—went right after McCoy.

"You're a little young to be a corporal, aren't you? Have you had any experience with a detail like this?"

"No, sir."

"You've qualified with the shotgun?"

"No, sir."

"Why not?"

"I don't know, sir."

"What's your skill?"

"Motor transport, sir."

"They must be pretty generous with motor transport promotions in China," the lieutenant said.

"I guess so, sir."

"Frankly, I'd hoped to have a more experienced noncom," the lieutenant said. "One at least who has qualified with the shotgun."

"I'm an Expert with the Springfield and the .45, sir. I think I can handle a shotgun."

"You can't handle a shotgun, Corporal, until you're qualified with the shotgun," the lieutenant said, as if explaining something to a backward and unpleasant child. "I'll have the gunnery sergeant arrange for you to be qualified."

"Aye, aye, sir."

A corporal drove McCoy to the range in a pickup truck. The same corporal watched him fire ten brass-cased rounds of 00-buckshot from a Winchester Model 1897 12-gauge trench gun at a silhouette target at fifteen yards. He then drove him back to the brig and told McCoy it was SOP to clean a riot gun whenever it had been fired. That meant it had to be detail stripped . . . McCoy couldn't just run a brass brush and then a couple of patches though the bore.

As careful as McCoy was, he managed to spot his shirt, tie, and trousers with bore cleaner, which meant that he might as well use them for rags or throw them away, because no matter how many times you washed them, you couldn't get bore cleaner out of khakis.

When he reported back to the lieutenant, the lieutenant told him that he had a soiled uniform.

"Aye, aye, sir, I'll change it."

"When you do change it, Corporal, make sure you have a shirt with regulation chevrons."

"Sir?"

"Get rid of those Tijuana stripes, Corporal."

McCoy decided to take a chance; he had nothing to lose anyway.

"Sir, embroidered-to-the-garment chevrons are regulation in China."

"You're no longer in China, Corporal," the lieutenant said. "And I don't want to debate this with you. I expect to see you here at 0730 tomorrow in the correct uniform."

"Aye, aye, sir."

"And, Corporal, I've inquired; and regulations state that at my discretion the noncoms may be armed with the pistol. Since you say you are an Expert with the pistol, I think you had better draw one rather than arm yourself with a trench gun."

"Aye, aye, sir."

The 47th Motor Transport Company at Philadelphia, McCoy thought, had to be an improvement over what he was doing now. Otherwise he was going to belt some chickenshit sonofabitch like this before his discharge came and get dragged to Portsmouth with a trench gun pointed at his back.

He went to the clothing store and bought three shirts and had regulation chevrons sewn to their sleeves. And then he fought down the temptation to get a hotel room in Diego. The way his luck was running lately, he'd get in a fight or something and get his ass in a crack.

The duty NCO at the brig found a cot for him, and he slept there.

In the morning, the lieutenant gave everybody detailed instructions and a little pep talk, then they went to the brig gate to take over the prisoners. The prisoners were in blue denim, with a foot-high "P" stenciled on the knee of the trousers and on the back of the jacket. They each carried a small cotton bag, which contained a change of underwear and socks, another set of "P"-marked denims, a toilet kit, less razor (since attempted suicide was a possibility, especially among the 'deviates,' they would shave themselves under the supervision of their guards), and their choice of either New Testament or Roman Catholic missal.

They were handcuffed: the right wrist of one man to the left wrist of the man beside him. And their ankles were chained, which made them walk in a shuffle.

On the brig bus, the lieutenant informed the guard detail that if a prisoner escaped, Marine Corps regulations stated that the guard responsible for that prisoner would be confined in his place.

McCoy knew that was bullshit. But he wondered if the lieutenant really believed it or whether it was just one more instance of an officer believing the troops in line were so stupid he could tell them anything he wanted.

The brig bus delivered them to the San Diego railroad station.

A U.S. Army Troop Car had been made available to the Marine Corps for the trip. It was attached to the train immediately behind the locomotive.

McCoy marched his guard detail—their riot guns at port arms—and the fourteen handcuffed and shackled prisoners through the crowded concourse and down the platform to the Army Troop Car.

He tried to tell himself that all he was doing was his duty, that these guys had fucked themselves up, that they had no one to blame but themselves for the mess they were in. But it didn't work. None of the fourteen prisoners was old enough to vote. Most of them looked not only frightened and humiliated but insignificant—like little boys. And so did most of their guards.

He was going to have to have a quiet word with the guards on his shift to make sure that one of the little boys didn't without goddamned good reason turn his shotgun on another of the little boys.

McCoy was relieved when they were all inside the Army car. He could not ever remember being so uncomfortable—so ashamed of himself was more like it—than when he had marched this pathetic little band through the station.

The sergeant showed up just before the train pulled out to show McCoy and the other corporals where he and the lieutenant would be sleeping and to explain the arrangements the lieutenant had come to with the conductor regarding chow. The dining car would make available "sandwich meals" for the prisoners, which would have to be picked up by the guard detail.

"When things settle down, maybe you corporals can get a meal in the dining car, but for now the lieutenant says he doesn't want you to leave the car."

The lieutenant made four ritual appearances every day, at 0600, 1200, 1800, and 2400 hours. He stayed about ten minutes, making sure that every prisoner had eaten, washed, and shaved, and had washed his previous day's uniform and underclothing.

McCoy managed to eat in the dining car only once. The waiters made it perfectly clear by lousy service and exaggerated courtesy what kind of shit they considered the guards to be. He didn't need any more reminding.

He took every other meal in the U.S. Army Troop Car, which meant that he ate nothing but sandwiches and coffee all the way across the North American continent.

It wasn't what he had dreamed about on the Pacific: a plush seat in a Pullman car and meals and drinks in the club car, as America the Beautiful rolls past the windows.

But that, of course, was fantasy. This was reality. This was the fucking United States Marine Corps.

(TWO)
Boston, Massachusetts
1630 Hours 16 July 1941

McCoy had to change trains at Boston for the Philadelphia train. He had plenty of time. The Boston & Maine from Portsmouth had put him into Boston at five minutes to three. By quarter after three, he had a reserved seat on the club car. They'd given him a train voucher to Philly and two meal tickets at the Portsmouth Naval Prison, but he'd torn them into tiny pieces and thrown the pieces into a trash bucket.

He didn't want a fucking thing to do with anything concerning the Portsmouth Naval Prison. Or, more importantly, with the Fucking United States Marine Corps. He had made that decision somewhere between Diego and Chicago and still wondered why he hadn't thought of it before. For his *own* sake. Not in connection with any dumb fucking ideas he had about doing something with Ellen Goddamn-the-Bitch Feller. He had five thousand fucking dollars. There was absolutely no reason he had to stay in the Marine Corps and put up with all the shit.

He could buy his way out of the Corps and get a job. Things were better now, and he had a high school diploma. Maybe even go back to Shanghai and see if he couldn't work something out with Piotr Petrovich Muller, or the "General."

Five thousand simoleons plus was a lot of money. Even if he spent whatever it cost for passage back to Shanghai, he would have enough left over not to worry about getting a job right that minute. He could look around, see what looked good, and move into that.

So it was really a good thing in the end that the fucking Corps had sent him home as a fuck-up for doing what he was supposed to do, and even a better thing that he had gotten involved in the prisoner-escort detail. It had convinced him to get the hell out of the fucking Corps. Otherwise, he would have stayed in China sticking his neck out, and sooner or later the Japs would have done to him what they tried to do to Sessions.

The prisoner-escort detail had gotten worse toward the end after they'd changed trains in Boston for New Hampshire, and really rough when they actually got to Portsmouth.

There had been another bus with bars over the windows waiting for them along with three Marines carrying pistols in white web gear and three-foot-long billy clubs they kept slapping in the palms of their hands.

All the prisoners were scared shitless, and two of them—one of the fairies and the great big guy who was going to do ten years before he was dishonorably discharged for slugging an officer—had actually cried.

There was a little ceremony when the prison signed for the prisoners. Then one of them tried to ask a question and got the end of a billy club in his gut for it. Hard enough to knock the wind out of him and knock him down.

And that fucking lieutenant just stood there and made believe nothing had happened. He knew goddamned well it was a violation of Rocks and Shoals[3] to hit somebody with a billy club like that, but the chickenshit sonofabitch didn't do a thing about it.

He was more concerned with important things like taking McCoy aside and telling him he was willing to admit a mistake about him and that he had probably been put off by McCoy's Tijuana chevrons. Anyhow, the lieutenant went on, he wanted to tell McCoy his deportment during the trip was all and more that could be expected of a good Marine noncom and that when he got back to San Diego he was going to write his commanding officer a letter of commendation.

What that was going to mean after he got to this fucking truck company in Philly (and McCoy believed the chickenshit sonofabitch was serious about writing the letter) was that whenever some poor sonofabitch had to be transported to Portsmouth, that shitty detail would go to Corporal McCoy since he was so good at it. But fuck that. The first thing he was going to do when he got to the 47th Motor Transport Platoon was ask the first sergeant for the forms to buy himself out of the Corps.

There was a bar in the station in Boston, and McCoy walked by it half a dozen times waiting for the Philly train without going in. He wanted a drink. He wanted lots of drinks, but he was going to wait until he was safe on the train—had left Portsmouth Naval Prison behind him for good—before he took one.

The first time he noticed the guy looking at him was on the platform. He was a regular candy-ass, about his age, wearing a regular candy-ass seersucker suit; and McCoy thought he was probably a kid going home from college, except that it was now the middle of July, and colleges were closed for the summer.

The candy-ass wasn't just looking at him, he was sort of smiling at him, as if goosing up his courage to talk to him. Christ, there were fairies all over. Goddamn-the-Bitch Ellen Feller's husband wasn't the only one. And he never would have guessed that hairy machinist's mate second on the *Whaley* was a cocksucker. And now here was this kid making eyes at him who looked like an Arrow Shirt Company advertisement for a choirboy Boy Scout.

On the train the club car steward put McCoy in a velvet plush chair by a little table and handed him a menu. Fifty cents (not counting tip) was a hell of a lot of money for one lousy drink of Scotch whiskey; but he didn't give a fuck what it cost, he was entitled. He'd been thinking about this drink practically from the moment he went aboard that fucking fleet oiler in Shanghai. Just as the waiter was about to take his order, the guy who had been making eyes at him on the platform walked up.

"This free?" he asked, putting his hand on the back of the velvet plush armchair on the other side of the table.

"Help yourself," McCoy said.

How am I going to get rid of this pansy without belting him?

"Scotch," McCoy said to the waiter. "Johnnie Walker. Soda on the side."

"Same for me, please," the pansy said.

McCoy gave him a dirty look.

"I'm about to be a Marine myself," the pansy said.

[3]The Disciplinary Code for the Governance of the Naval Service.

"You're what?" McCoy asked, incredulously.

"I'm about to join the Marine Corps," the pansy repeated.

"I'm about to get out of the Marine Corps," McCoy said.

"You are?" the pansy-who-said-he-was-about-to-enlist asked, surprised. "I thought all discharges were frozen."

"I'm getting out," McCoy said firmly. He remembered hearing rumors of a freeze, or a year's extension, or something like that, but he hadn't paid a hell of a lot of attention.

Jesus Christ! What if this candy-ass is right? Then what?

"You sound as if you're not happy in the Marine Corps," the young pansy said.

He doesn't talk like a pansy, and wave his hands like a woman, but then, neither did the machinist's mate second.

"Do I?" McCoy replied, unpleasantly.

"Then you're just the guy I want to talk to," the young man said. "The way the recruiters talk, it's paradise on earth. All the food you can eat, all the liquor you can drink, and all the prettiest girls throwing themselves at you."

"You're really going in the Corps?" McCoy asked, his curiosity aroused—and his suspicions diminished just a little by the pretty girls.

"I'm really going in the Corps," the young man said. He put out his hand. "Malcolm Pickering," he said.

McCoy took it.

"Ken McCoy," he said. Pickering's grip was firm, not like a pansy's.

The steward set their drinks on the table.

"Put that on my tab," Pickering said.

"I can buy my own drink," McCoy said.

"Put the next round on your tab," Pickering said reasonably.

McCoy nodded. He twisted the cap off the miniature bottle and wondered idly if putting it in its own little bottle was how they got away charging half a buck for one lousy drink. He picked it up and read the label. It held 1.6 ounces. That brought it down to 37.5 cents an ounce, which was still a hell of a lot more than he was used to paying for liquor.

"Can I ask you a question, Corporal McCoy?" Malcolm Pickering asked.

McCoy looked at him and nodded.

"I saw you in Chicago on the track with some strange-looking guys," Pickering said. "What was that all about?"

Chicago? What the hell does he mean by that?

And then he understood. There had been an hour's wait while the railroad switched locomotives. The lieutenant had the bright idea that the prisoners should exercise. Since they couldn't do calisthenics or close-order drill handcuffed and with their feet shackled, what the lieutenant had done was send them shuffling up and back down the track for half a mile or so. This Pickering guy had obviously seen that.

"We were exercising the prisoners," he said. "That what you mean?"

"What did they do?" Pickering asked.

"Three of them were fags," McCoy said. "One of them slugged an officer. The rest of them found out the hard way that once you enlist, you're in until they let you out."

"They were Marines?"

"Sailors," McCoy said. "The Marine Corps does the Navy's dirty work, like guarding and transporting prisoners."

"What happened to them?"

"We took them to the Naval Prison at Portsmouth, New Hampshire, to serve their sentences," McCoy said.

"Is that what you do in the Marine Corps?" Pickering asked.

"No," McCoy said. "I just got to San Diego when they needed a couple of corporals for the guard detail."

"What do you do?" Pickering asked.

"I'm a motor transport corporal," McCoy said. Though he didn't like the sound of it, that's what he was on paper. "I work in the motor pool."

"You like it?"

"No. I told you, I'm just waiting to get out of the Marine Corps."

"Then what will you do?"

McCoy didn't want to tell this nosy guy that he was going back to China. That would trigger a whole new line of questions. And aside from going back to China, he couldn't think of a thing he was likely to do. He had been in the Marine Corps since he was seventeen. It was the only thing he had ever done.

"What made you join the Corps?" McCoy asked.

"My father was a Marine," Pickering said. "In the World War."

"And he didn't warn you off?" McCoy said.

"He was a corporal," Pickering said. "What he warned me to do was get a commission."

Then he realized what he had said.

"I didn't mean to offend . . ." he began.

"Your father was right," McCoy said.

"So, with war coming, I figured I had better get one," Pickering said. "A commission, I mean."

"You seem sure that we're going to get into this war," McCoy said.

"You don't?"

"Christ, I hope not," McCoy said.

"We're probably going to have to do something about the Japanese," Pickering argued.

"The Japs are probably thinking the same thing about us," McCoy said. "And you wouldn't believe how many of the bastards there are."

"But they're not like Americans, are they?" Pickering asked.

"The ones I've seen are first-class soldiers," McCoy said. He saw the surprise on Pickering's face.

"The ones you've seen?" Pickering asked.

"I just came from China," McCoy said. "I was with the Fourth Marines in Shanghai."

Now why the fuck did I start in on that?

"I'd like to hear about that," Pickering said.

"I'd rather talk about something else," McCoy said.

"Like what?" Pickering said, agreeably.

"I'm going to be stationed in Philly," McCoy said. "For a while, I mean, say a month or six weeks, until I can get my discharge. If you know anything about it, why don't we talk about the best way to get laid in Philadelphia?"

"The best way, I've found," Pickering said, "is to use a bed. But there is a school of thought that says that turning them upside down in a shower is the way to go."

McCoy looked at him for a moment and then laughed out loud.

"You tell me about the Marines in China, McCoy," Pickering said. "And then I will tell you about getting laid in Philadelphia. Maybe with a little luck, when we get there—that's where I'm going, too, to the Navy Yard, to give them my college records—we could conduct what they call a 'practical experiment.' "

If I keep drinking with this guy and then start chasing whores with him, I am probably going to get my ass in deep trouble. But right now, I don't give a fuck.

He raised his hand above his head, snapped his fingers at the steward for another drink, and turned to Malcolm Pickering.

"You can buy a fourteen-year-old virgin in Shanghai for three dollars," he said. "What's the going rate these days in Philly?"

"There are no fourteen-year-old virgins in Philadelphia," Malcolm Pickering said solemnly.

I'll be goddamned if I don't really like this candy-ass civilian.

(THREE)
The Bellevue Stratford Hotel
Philadelphia, Pennsylvania
0905 Hours 17 July 1941

The first thing McCoy remembered when he woke up was that there had been a woman in bed with him, which meant he was likely to find his money and his watch gone.

The second thought was more frightening: The "Guaranteed Officer's Checque" from Barclays Bank, Ltd., Shanghai, had been in his money belt with the three hundred bucks. The whore probably wouldn't be able to cash it; but sure as Christ, she would have taken it, and it was going to be a real pain in the ass to get it replaced.

When he sat up, his head hurt like a toothache, as if his brain had shrunk and was banging around loose inside his skull. His lips were dry and cracked and the tip of his tongue felt like the sole of a boot.

How the hell am I going to get from wherever the hell I am to the Navy Yard without any fucking money? Or for that matter, out of the hotel? Jesus Christ, I hope at least they made me pay in advance!

He looked around the room, and that made it worse. This was no dollar-a-night hot-sheet joint. This was not only a real hotel, but a fancy-hotel hotel. Great big fucking room, drapes over the windows, a couch and a couple of armchairs, and Christ only knows what he had paid for the bottles sitting on a chest of drawers across the room. Before the whore got his money, he thought, at least he'd spent a hell of a lot of it.

And then he saw the money belt. It was on the little shelf over the wash basin in the bathroom. That figured. Just before she left, the whore had taken the money belt into the bathroom, just in case he should wake up and see her going through it. Once she'd emptied it, she hadn't given a damn where she left it.

He needed a glass of water, and desperately. Maybe, if he hadn't been rolled, too, he could borrow say, ten bucks, from Pickering. It wasn't the end of the fucking world. He had his pay record with him, and he had at least two months' back pay on the books. All he had to do was come up with enough money to get from here to the Philadelphia Navy Yard, and he could draw enough money to keep him going.

And he would go to some bank and ask them what you were supposed to do when you lost a 'Guaranteed Officer's Checque.' He would say he lost it. And since he hadn't signed it, they would have to sooner or later make it good.

He staggered across the room to the bathroom and saw that it was really a high-class place. There was a little button marked ICE WATER that operated a tiny little chrome water pipe. And when you pushed the button, it really produced ice water.

He drank one glass of ice water so quickly it made his teeth ache. He drank a second glass more slowly, from time to time looking at his reflection in the mirror over the sink. His eyes were bloodshot, and—he had to check twice to make sure what it was—his ears were red with lipstick.

He looked down at other parts of his body.

Well, I apparently had a very good time, even if I can't remember the details.

There was something under the empty money belt, making a bulge. Idly curious, he pushed the money belt off it. It was his watch.

"I'll be goddamned," McCoy said, then told himself that just because the whore hadn't stolen the watch, it didn't mean she hadn't helped herself to the cash and the "checque." It wasn't that good a watch, he knew. He had bought it primarily because it had a lot of radium paint on the hands, so that he could see them at night. He picked up the money belt and worked the zipper. There was money in it, $250, and the "checque."

"I'll be goddamned," he said again.

Now he had a cramp in his bladder, so he went to the toilet and relieved himself. He saw that the bathroom had two doors: one led in from his fancy bedroom, and one went out into some other room. When he was finished taking a leak (an incredibly long leak), he tried the knob. It was unlocked, and he pushed it open.

Malcolm Pickering (McCoy remembered at that moment that sometime during last night, Pickering had told him to call him "Pick") was on his back on a double bed, stark naked. His arms and legs were spread. And he was awake.

"Please piss a little more quietly," Pick Pickering said. "I woke up thinking our ship was going down."

"Shit." McCoy laughed.

"I have come to the conclusion, Corporal McCoy," Pick Pickering said, "that you are an evil character who rides on railroads leading innocent youth such as myself into sin."

"It looks like we had a good time," McCoy said.

"Yeah, doesn't it?" Pickering said. "What time is it?"

"A little after nine," McCoy said.

"I treat my hangovers with large breakfasts and a beer," Pickering said. "That sound all right to you?"

"I don't want to report smelling of beer," McCoy said.

"They have Sen-Sen," Pickering said, and suddenly sat up. "Jesus!" he said, and then he swung his feet to the floor and reached for the telephone. "Room service," he ordered, and then: "This is Malcolm Pickering, in 907. Large orange juice, breakfast steak, medium, corned-beef hash, eggs up, toast, two pots of coffee, and two bottles of Feigenspann ale. Do that twice, please, and the sooner the better."

Very classy, McCoy thought. *That'll probably cost three, four, maybe five dollars. But what the hell, I've still got most of my money.*

"What's this place costing us?" McCoy asked.

"I probably shouldn't tell you this, Killer," Pickering said. "It is only because I am an upstanding Christian that I do. We flipped for it last night, and you won. It's not costing you a dime, and I don't want to think about what it's costing me."

McCoy was surprised that Pickering called him "Killer." The only way he could have known that was if he had told him. And the only way he would have told him, as if he needed another proof, was that he was pretty drunk.

"I want to pay my share," McCoy said.

"Don't be a damned fool. If that quarter had landed on the other side, you would have paid," Pickering said. He got to his feet and walked across the room. "But since I am paying, I get first shot at the shower."

If anything, McCoy decided, Pickering's room was larger than his. And then he noticed that a door and not just the bathroom connected both rooms. He went back to his own room, found his seabags in a closet, and took out a clean uniform. It was clean but mussed. He hated to report in a mussed uniform, even if the first thing he was going to do when he reported in was ask for the buy-out papers.

"What the hell," he said aloud and picked up the telephone. He didn't give a damn what it cost, he was going to have it pressed. So far, he hadn't spent much money at all.

A waiter and a bellboy delivered the breakfast on a rolling table. By the time he'd eaten everything and put down both bottles of ale, he felt almost human again.

When he was dressed, Pick Pickering lifted up the telephone and told them to send up a boy for the luggage and to have a cab waiting.

The MP at the gate to the Navy Yard took one look at McCoy's campaign hat and went back in the guard shack for his pad of violation reports.

"Got to write you up, Corporal, sorry," the MP said. "Maybe they'll let it ride because you just got back."

The Officer Procurement Board was in a three-story red-brick building near the gate, and McCoy said good-bye to Pickering there.

"Well, maybe we'll bump into each other again," Pickering said.

"I hope by then I'm a civilian. Otherwise, I'll be standing at attention and calling you 'sir,' " McCoy said.

"So what?" Pickering said.

"It doesn't work that way, Pick," McCoy said, giving him his hand. "As you are about to find out, this is the U. Fucking S. Fucking Marine Corps. But it was fun, and I'm glad the quarter landed the way it did."

"Good luck," Pickering said, and squeezed McCoy's hand a little harder, then got out of the cab and walked up the sidewalk to the big red-brick building.

The 47th Motor Transport Platoon was in a red-brick barracks building not far from the river. Two Marines were very slowly raking the small patch of carefully tended lawn between the sidewalk and the building.

McCoy paid the cabdriver and then stood by the open truck.

"You guys want to give me a hand with my gear?" he called to the guys with the rakes.

He was still a corporal, a noncommissioned officer. Noncommissioned officers don't carry things if there are privates around to carry things. They looked at him curiously, not missing the out-of-uniform campaign hat and the illegal chevrons. Then they stepped over the chain guarding the lawn and shouldered his seabags and followed him into the barracks building.

The linoleum deck inside glistened, and the brass doorknobs and push plates were highly polished. This was the States, McCoy thought, where American Marines—not Chinese boys—waxed the decks and polished the brass. And Marine corporals watched them to make sure they did it right.

There was a sign on the orderly room door. KNOCK, REMOVE HEADGEAR, AND WAIT FOR PERMISSION TO ENTER.

McCoy checked his uniform to make sure it was shipshape, removed his campaign hat, knocked, and waited for permission to enter.

"Come!" a voice called, and he pushed the door open and walked in.

There was a company clerk, a PFC, behind his desk, and a first sergeant, a squeaky-clean guy of about thirty-five behind his. Behind the first sergeant was a door marked LT A.J. FOGARTY, USMC, COMMANDING.

"You must be McCoy," the first sergeant said. "You was due in day before yesterday."

"At Portsmouth they told me I had forty-eight hours to get here," McCoy said. "I'm not due in until noon tomorrow."

"What were you doing at Portsmouth?" the first sergeant said.

"I was in a squad of prisoner-chasers from Diego," McCoy said.

"Shit!" the first sergeant said. "Nobody told us anything about you going to Portsmouth. You went on the Morning Report as AWOL this morning. Now we'll have to do the whole fucking thing over."

Well, I'm stepping right off on the wrong foot. Not only did I have to take those poor bastards to Portsmouth, but it put me right on the first sergeant's shit list.

"We can submit an amended report," the company clerk said.

"When I want your advice, I'll ask for it," the first sergeant said. He looked at McCoy. "Sit," he said. "You know that campaign hat's nonregulation?"

"No, I didn't," McCoy said.

"Well, it is," the first sergeant said. "And so are them chevrons."

"I just got a violation written by the MP at the Main Gate," McCoy said. "For the hat. He didn't say anything about the stripes."

"It'll take a week, ten days, to come down through channels," the first sergeant said. "I don't know nothing about violations until the message center delivers them. And sometimes they get lost. You want a cup of coffee?"

I'll be a sonofabitch, he's not entirely a prick.

"Yes, please, thank you."

The first sergeant picked up the telephone in his desk and dialed a number.

Then, while it was ringing, he covered the mouthpiece with his hand and spoke to the PFC: "You heard the corporal," he said. "Get him a cup of coffee and if they got any, a doughnut."

The PFC scurried from the orderly room.

"Sergeant-Major, this is Quinn," the first sergeant said to the telephone. "Corporal McCoy wasn't AWOL. They stuck him with a prisoner-chaser detail to Portsmouth. He just reported in a day early. I got him on the Morning Report as AWOL. How do you want me to handle it?"

Whatever the sergeant-major replied it didn't take long, for the first sergeant broke the connection with his finger and dialed another number.

"First Sergeant Quinn," he announced. "Is Lieutenant Fogarty there?"

A moment later, Lieutenant Fogarty apparently came on the line, for Quinn delivered the report that McCoy had arrived, that he wasn't AWOL, and that he'd caught the Morning Report before it left for Washington and was going to make out a new one.

"The Old Man says wait," First Sergeant Quinn said when he hung up. "You want to read the newspaper?"

He pushed a neatly folded *Philadelphia Bulletin* across his desk toward McCoy.

"Top," McCoy said, "what I'd really like is to get buy-out papers filled out."

"What?"

"No offense, but I've had enough of the Corps."

The first sergeant laughed, not unpleasantly.

"All discharges have been frozen," he said. "Nobody's getting out of the Corps except on a medical discharge. Didn't they know that in China?"

"Shit," McCoy said.

"There's some people thinks there's going to be war," the first sergeant said.

"I didn't know discharges had been frozen," McCoy said lamely.

Half an hour later, a young PFC came into the orderly room (without knocking, McCoy noticed).

"If you're Corporal McCoy," he said, "the Old Man's outside in the staff car."

McCoy looked at the first sergeant, who jerked his thumb in a signal for him to go with the driver.

The Old Man was about twenty-four, McCoy judged, a well-set-up, ex-football player–type. He returned McCoy's salute, motioned him into the backseat of the staff car, and then, as it moved off, turned to face McCoy.

"I'm glad it turned out you weren't AWOL, Corporal McCoy," he said. "That really would have disappointed a lot of people."

"Sir, I didn't volunteer to go to Portsmouth," McCoy said.

"I didn't think you did." Lieutenant Fogarty laughed.

They went back to the building where Pick Pickering had gone to deliver his college records to the Officer Procurement Board. That seemed a lot longer ago than an hour before, McCoy thought.

He followed Fogarty into the building and up two flights of stairs to the third floor. Fogarty pushed open a door and went into an office, holding the door open for McCoy. Then he spoke to a staff sergeant behind a desk.

"The not-really-AWOL Corporal McCoy," he said.

"You go right in and report to the captain, Corporal," the staff sergeant said. "He's been waiting for you."

Since I'm not going to be able to get out of the Corps, I'd better do what Captain Banning told me to do: Keep my nose clean in this truck platoon and hope that when he comes home from Shanghai, he'll remember his promise to see about getting me out of it.

That meant reporting according to the book. McCoy went to the closed door, knocked, was told to enter, and marched erectly in. Carefully staring six inches above the back of the chair that was facing him, so that whenever the captain spun around in it, he would be looking, as custom required, six inches over the captain's head. He came to attention and barked: "Corporal McCoy reporting to the captain as directed, sir!"

The chair slowly spun around until the captain was facing him.

"With that China Marine hat, Killer," Captain Edward Sessions, USMC, said, "I'm surprised they didn't keep you in Portsmouth. Aside from that, how was the trip?"

McCoy was literally struck dumb.

"You seem just a little surprised, McCoy," Sessions said, chuckling. "Can I interpret that to mean Captain Banning didn't guess what we had in mind for you?"

"What's going on here?" McCoy said.

"For public consumption, we're part of the administrative staff of the Marine Detachment, Philadelphia Navy Yard. And you were assigned to the 47th Motor Transport Platoon because that was a good way to get you to Philadelphia without a lot of questions being asked. What this really is—not for public consumption—is the Philadelphia Detachment of the Office of the Assistant Chief of Staff, Intelligence, of the Marine Corps."

"I don't understand," McCoy said.

"I'm disappointed," Sessions said. "Two things, McCoy. The first is that my boss believes you know a lot about the Japanese in China that no one else knows, including Captain Banning; and we want to squeeze that information out of you. Secondly, he thought the Japanese would probably decide to do to you what you kept them from doing to me. Either reason would have been enough to order you home."

"So what happens to me here?"

"I hope you have a clear head," Sessions said. "Because there are two officers here who are about to pump it dry."

"And then what?"

"Then, there are several interesting possibilities," Sessions said. "We'll get into that later."

"When did you make Captain?" McCoy asked, and belatedly added, "Sir?"

"I was a captain all the time," Sessions said. "The orders were cut two days after I sailed for Shanghai." He leaned across his desk and offered McCoy his hand. "Welcome home, McCoy. Welcome aboard."

VII

(ONE)
Golden's Pre-Owned Motor Cars
North Broad Street
Philadelphia, Pennsylvania
1 August 1941

There was no doubt in Dickie Golden's mind that despite the seersucker suit, the kid looking at the 1939 LaSalle convertible coupe on the platform was a serviceman. For one thing, he had a crew cut. For another, he was deeply tanned. For another, he didn't look quite right in his clothing. He was wearing a seersucker suit, but he was obviously no college kid.

He was probably a Marine from the Navy Yard, Dickie Golden decided. They looked somehow different from sailors. He was too young to be more than a PFC; but maybe, just maybe, he was a lance corporal; and the finance company would sometimes write up a lance corporal if he could come up with the one-third down payment. There was of course no way this kid could come up with one-third down on the LaSalle convertible, even though it was really one hell of a bargain at $695.

Cadillac had stopped making LaSalles as of 1940, which really cut into their resale value. And the last couple of years Cadillac made them, they had practically given them away. But that hadn't worked, and LaSalles were orphans now. A 1939 Cadillac convertible like this one, with the same engine . . . about the only real difference between a little Cadillac and a LaSalle was the grille and the chrome . . . would sell for twelve, thirteen hundred.

The down payment on this would have to be at least $250, and the odds were the kid looking at it didn't have that kind of money. Dickie Golden did the rough figures in his head. Say he had the $250, that would leave $500 over two years plus a hundred a year for insurance. A $700 note over two years at 6% was right at $29 a month. They paid Marine privates $21 a month. He didn't know what they paid lance corporals, but it wasn't much more.

But, Dickie Golden decided, what the hell; it was an up. It was possible the kid had just come off a ship or something, with money burning a hole in his pocket from a crap game. He just might have $300 for a down payment. More likely, he could switch the kid over to something he could afford. If he wanted an open car, there was a '37 Pontiac convertible at $495 and a '33 Ford—a little rough, needed a new top—for $229.

He walked over to the kid.

"Good-looking car, isn't it?" Dickie Golden said. "I've been thinking of buying it myself for the little woman."

McCoy didn't reply to that.

"You got the keys?" he asked.

McCoy had just about decided to buy the LaSalle. Everything else was crazy, why not buy a crazy car?

McCoy had just come from dinner with an officer and his wife. That was why he was wearing a suit. Maybe an apartment in a tall building at 2601 Parkway wasn't like officer's quarters on a base, and maybe there was some difference between a regular officer and an intelligence officer, but he was a corporal, USMC, and Sessions was a captain, USMC; it was the first time he had ever heard of a captain's wife "insisting" that a corporal come to dinner.

More than that. Grabbing him by the arms, and hugging and kissing him on the cheeks . . . with her husband watching.

She was a good-looking woman. *Decent* looking. Wholesome. She looked a lot like Mickey Rooney's girl friend in the Andy Hardy movies.

"Ed told me what you did at the ferry, Ken," Mrs. Sessions said. "I can call you 'Ken,' can't I?"

"Yes, ma'am," he said.

"Well, you can't call me 'ma'am,' " she said. "I won't have that. You'll call me Jean."

He hadn't replied. On the wall was an eight-by-ten enlargement of the picture he'd taken of Sessions in the black cotton peasant clothes.

"I want to thank you for my husband's life," Mrs. Sessions said when she noticed him looking at it, and then when she saw how uncomfortable she had made him, she added: "I know he's not much, but he's the only one I have."

Then Captain Sessions put a drink in his hand, and soon afterward they fed him, first-class chow that McCoy had never had before: one great big steak for all of them served in slices. Mrs. Sessions (he was unable to bring himself to call a captain's wife by her first name) told him they called it a "London broil."

Since they were both being so nice to him, he had been very careful not to say or do anything out of line. He watched his table manners and went easy on the booze (there was wine with the London broil and cognac afterward). And as soon as he thought he could politely get out of there, he left.

Which had put him all dressed-up on North Broad Street at eight o'clock at night with no place to go but a bar; and he didn't want to go to a bar. Drinking at a bar and trying to pick up some dame and get his ashes hauled did not seem like the right thing to do after a respectable dinner with a Marine Corps officer and his lady in their home.

So he had figured he would walk up North Broad Street and maybe see if he could find a car in one of the used-car lots—at least get an idea of what they were asking for iron these days. And then he'd seen the LaSalle and decided, what the hell, why not see what he could do?

"The down payment on a car like this would be $300, maybe a little more," Dickie Golden said, not wanting to let the kid take the car for a ride if there was no way he could handle it, "and the payments, including insurance, about thirty bucks a month over two years. Could you handle that much?"

"Yeah," McCoy said. "I could handle that much."

"You're a Marine, aren't you?" Dickie Golden said. One more fact out of him, and he would go get the keys.

"Yeah," McCoy said.

"The finance company don't like to make loans on a car like this to anybody's not at least a lance corporal."

"I'm a corporal," McCoy said. "And I can make the down payment, okay? You want to let me hear the engine, take it for a ride?"

Dickie Golden put out his hand. "I'm Dickie Golden, Corporal . . . I didn't catch the name?"

"McCoy," McCoy said.

"Well, I'm pleased to meet you, Corporal McCoy," he said. "You really know how to spot a bargain, I'll tell you that."

You bet your candy-ass I do, you sonofabitch. I grew up on a goddamned used-car lot. You're about to be had, buster, presuming the engine isn't shot in this thing.

"Seven hundred dollars seems like a lot of money for an orphan like this," McCoy said.

"Well, maybe we can shave that a little, if you don't have a trade," Dickie Golden said.

The battery was almost dead, and went dead before the engine would crank. A colored man with a battery on a little wheeled truck was called. Dickie Golden said he would replace the battery.

"Maybe all it needs is a charge," McCoy offered helpfully.

You dumb sonofabitch, if you knew what you were doing, you'd not only make sure there was a hot battery in here, but you'd start it up every couple of days. These flat-head 322-cubic-inch V-8s are always hard to start.

"No," Dickie Golden said, grandly, "I want this car to be right." He told the colored man to replace the battery. And then "while they were waiting" he suggested they take the information for the finance company down on paper.

He was obviously pleased with the facts McCoy gave him: That he was a corporal, unmarried, and had no other "installment loans" outstanding. McCoy decided he was going to come down $100 from the $695 and make it back by slipping the paper to some finance company who would give him half of the fifty back and make it up by charging eight percent, maybe ten. That would make the car $595. Then he would sell him insurance through some shyster outfit that would charge twice what it was worth—making it part of the easy payments—and slip Dickie Golden another twenty-five bucks back under the table. Then there would be a credit-check charge, and Christ only knew what else.

After McCoy's first look at the LaSalle, he went to another used-car lot and gave the wash boy there a dollar to go in the office and borrow the Blue Book for him. The Blue Book told him the LaSalle was worth $475 wholesale, the average retail was $650, and the average loan value was $400. McCoy decided he would pay $525 for the car.

Dickie Golden wanted to ride along with him, of course, when he took the test drive. McCoy handled that by passing the salesman three hundred in cash—enough for the down payment—"to hold." And when Dickie Golden said he still thought he'd better go along, McCoy turned indignant and asked if Dickie Golden didn't think he could drive; and Dickie Golden backed down.

McCoy drove up Broad Street until the engine was warm and then pulled in a gas station on a side street and gave the guy running it a buck to let him put it up on the grease rack and lend him some tools.

He could find nothing wrong with the car and would have been surprised if he had. It needed points and a condenser, and an oil change, and the wheels aligned, but there was nothing seriously wrong with it. The heads had never been off, and the engine was just as dirty as it ought to be. If it had required work it would have showed.

He drove back to Golden's Pre-Owned Motor Cars.

Dickie Golden told him he had been getting worried.

McCoy told him he thought the clutch was going.

Dickie Golden said he didn't think so, but that it was not much to worry about anyway, since they had a thirty-day fifty-fifty fix-anything policy. That meant they would pay half of the cost of anything that needed fixing or replacing in the next thirty days. And besides he was going to knock $100 off the price because Corporal McCoy didn't have a trade-in.

He showed McCoy the papers, already made out. With everything included, after a $300 down payment, the payments would come out to $27.80 over thirty months.

"I talked them into going thirty months," Dickie Golden said, "to keep your payments down."

You just hung yourself, buster. You must really get kickbacks from every sonofabitch and his brother. So much that you won't mind going down another $70 on the basic price.

"I'll give you $500 for it," McCoy said.

"You got to be kidding," Dickie Golden said.

"That's all I can afford," McCoy said.

"Then I guess we don't have a deal," Dickie Golden said.

"I guess not," McCoy said. "You want to give me my $300 back?"

"I guess I could ask my partner," Dickie Golden said. "I don't think he'll go along with this, but I'd like to see you in the LaSalle, and I could ask him. If I can catch him at home . . ."

If you've got a partner, at home or anywhere else, I'll kiss your ass at high noon at Broad and Market.

"Why don't you ask him?" McCoy said.

Dickie Golden was gone twenty minutes. When he came back, he had a whole new set of papers all made out.

"My partner says $525 is as low as we can go," Dickie Golden said. "That's less than wholesale."

McCoy read the finance agreement with interest. Then he handed Dickie Golden $225.

"Deal," he said.

"What's this?" Golden said, looking at the money but not picking it up.

"I already gave you $300," McCoy said. "That's the other $225."

"No, this deal was to finance the car and for you to buy your insurance through us."

"What do you want me to do, call a cop? It's against the law in Pennsylvania to take kickbacks from finance companies and insurance companies."

"What are you, some kind of wise guy?"

"You just write on there, paid in full in cash," McCoy said. "Or we call the cops."

"Give me those papers back and get your ass off my lot!"

"I'll walk just as far as the pay-phone booth down the block," McCoy said. "With the papers."

"I ought to kick your ass!" Dickie Golden said, but when McCoy handed him the papers, he wrote "paid in full" on the Conditions of Sale.

McCoy was pleased with himself when he drove the LaSalle off the lot and onto North Broad Street. Not only was the LaSalle a nice car, but he had just screwed a used-car dealer. McCoy hated used-car dealers: Patrick J. McCoy of Norristown, Pennsylvania, Past Grand Exalted Commander of the Knights of Columbus, Good ol' Pat, everybody's pal at the bar of the 12th Street Bar & Grill, Corporal Kenneth J. "Killer" McCoy's father, was a used-car dealer.

(TWO)

The next morning was a Saturday, but there was no reveille bugle, at least not one the enlisted members of the Philadelphia Detachment of the Office of the Assistant Chief of Staff for Intelligence had to pay any attention to. Reveille sounded and ten minutes later first call; and the truck drivers and mechanics of the 47th Motor Transport Platoon went down and out on the street and lined up for roll call.

But the seven enlisted men in the three rooms on the attic floor set aside for the "Special Detachment" didn't even get out of bed until the bugler sounded mess call. In addition to McCoy, there were two gunnery sergeants, a staff sergeant, and three PFCs. The PFCs were clerks. The staff sergeant worked for Captain Sessions. McCoy didn't know where the gunnery sergeants worked. The only time one of the gunnery sergeants spoke to him since he reported in was when one of them told him he didn't have to stand any formations, but that he had to be in the red-brick office building every morning at oh-eight-hundred.

What happened there was that from the very first day they sat him down in an upholstered chair he suspected had been stolen from a Day Room and talked to him about what he knew about the Imperial Japanese Army in China.

There were usually three of them: Captain Sessions, another captain, and two lieutenants. The other captain was pretty old—and an old Marine—because the first thing he asked McCoy was whether he had known Major Lewis B. "Chesty" Puller in Shanghai.

"He commanded the Second Batallion, sir," McCoy said. "I knew who he was."

Puller was a real hard-ass. Fair, but a hard-ass. He acted as if he thought the Second Battalion was going to war the next day and trained them that way.

"He's pretty good with a Thompson himself," the old captain said. "I thought maybe you two had got together and compared techniques."

Aside from recognizing it as a reference to the incident at the ferry, McCoy didn't know what the old captain was driving at.

"No, sir," he said.

Sometimes it was all the officers at once, sometimes it was a couple of them, and sometimes it was just one of the young lieutenants by himself. Always there was one of the PFCs to take care of changing the tubular records on a Dictaphone.

However many of them there were, the interrogation went generally the same every day.

They came with folders, notebooks, and pencils. And they had thumbtacked maps of Kiangsu, Shantung, Honan, and Hopeh provinces to a cork board. The locations of Japanese units were marked on each map. The wall beside the cork board was painted white, and they used that as a screen for a slide projector. Sometimes there were photographs, including some he took himself. Some of these were blowups, and some had been converted to slides.

And they asked question after question about the Japanese forces. McCoy was surprised at how wrong their information was about the Jap order of battle. And he could tell they didn't like some of his answers about the Japanese. It was as if they hoped he was going to tell them the Japs were nothing but a bunch of fuck-ups who had done so well against the Chinese because the Chinese were fucked up even worse.

But he told them what he knew and what he thought: The Chinese were *not* lousy soldiers, but they just didn't give a damn because they knew they were getting screwed by their officers, who would sell the day's ration if they could find a buyer. The Jap officers, on the other hand, were generally honest. Mean as hell, they thought nothing of belting the enlisted men—sergeants, too—in the mouth. But they didn't sell the troops' rations, and the rest of the Jap system seemed to work well. If a Jap soldier was told to do something, he did it, period.

One of the young lieutenants had studied Japanese in college. When he was alone with McCoy, he spoke a few words of Japanese to him. He didn't speak it all that well, but he spoke better Japanese than the old captain (who had done eight years, 1927–1935, with the 4th Marines in Shanghai) spoke Chinese.

McCoy learned (they didn't tell him, but he learned) that none of the young lieutenants was a regular. They had all come into the Corps right after college. McCoy wondered what the hell they were doing sitting around asking an enlisted man questions. As young lieutenants without any experience, they should instead have been out with troops in the field.

Once, a couple of civilians, an old one and a young one, dropped in while he was standing in a skivvy shirt by a map of Honan Province (the room was right under the roof and was hot as hell). When they entered the room, McCoy stopped talking, not knowing who they were.

"Don't let me interrupt," the older civilian said.

"Carry on, McCoy," the old captain ordered. So he carried on.

That was the day he was straightening them out about how good the Japanese soldiers were, and he went on with that. From time to time the old civilian would snort, as if he didn't think McCoy knew what the hell he was talking about, but McCoy decided to let the old guy fuck himself. The civilians stuck around until he was finished. When they were gone, McCoy asked who they were. For some reason, the officers thought that was funny. They laughed at him, and he never got an answer.

McCoy had no idea how long the "interviews" were going to go on. At first, he'd hoped they would go on forever. But by the end of the second week, he knew he was just about talked-out. If there was something he knew about China they hadn't gotten out of him, he couldn't think of what it was.

When first call blew that Saturday morning, he got out of bed and took a shower. Standing under the shower, shaving, reminded him of China and made him a little homesick for it. The only time in China he'd had to shave himself was when he was on a convoy. The rest of the time there'd been Chinese boys to do it for him.

After he was dressed, he went down to the mess for breakfast, and then he walked to the gate. When he had tried to bring the LaSalle onto the Yard the night before, the guard at the gate wouldn't let him, because he didn't have either a Yard sticker, license plates, or proof of insurance. But the guard had let him park the LaSalle inside the gate and had explained to McCoy that he could get a sticker on Saturday morning from the provost marshal if he got there before noon with proof of insurance and license plates.

McCoy started the LaSalle and drove to an office of the Pennsylvania Motor Vehicle Bureau, where he registered the car and got a cardboard temporary license plate until they mailed him a real one from Harrisburg. Then he went to an insurance agency and bought insurance. It was still early, and he didn't like the way the wear on the tires looked, so he found a Cadillac dealer. While they were aligning the front end, he went to the parts department and bought a set of points and condensers and a set of spark plugs and a carburetor rebuild kit.

Finally, on the way back to the Navy Yard, he saw a Sears, Roebuck where he bought a small set of tools on sale. Later he got a sticker from the provost marshal and drove to the barracks.

He would spend the weekend rebuilding the carburetor and changing the points and the plugs, and maybe giving it a good shine with Simoniz. Dickie Golden for sure had used some quickie polish, which made it look good but wouldn't last more than a week.

What he was doing, he knew, was not what he should really be doing. Working on the car was a dodge, an escape: He should *really* be going back to Norristown, even if he had to ride there on the Interurban Rapid Transit.

But he didn't want to go home now or next week or maybe ever. So maybe he would get lucky between now and next weekend. Maybe something would happen that would keep him from going home then. Like a transfer to the West Coast. Or maybe getting run over by a truck.

(THREE)
United States Navy Yard
Philadelphia, Pennsylvania
0830 Hours 4 August 1941

"Close the door, Ken," Captain Sessions said, "and then help yourself to coffee if you'd like. I want to talk to you."

McCoy expected that Sessions was going to talk to him about the LaSalle. He knew there was scuttlebutt around about it: Where the hell did a corporal come up with enough money to buy a car like that? Scuttlebutt had a way of getting around—and that meant to the officers. So he thought it had finally become official.

He poured black coffee in a china cup. When he turned around, Sessions waved him into a chair.

"Have you given any thought, Ken, about what you'd liked to do next?"

That meant that the "interviews," as McCoy suspected, were now over.

"Yes, sir," McCoy said.

Sessions made a "come on" gesture with his hand.

"Captain Banning said that when he gets home, he would try to find a home for me," McCoy said. "He said I should keep my nose clean, and he would either get me to work for him again or send me back to heavy weapons."

"Have you ever considered becoming an officer?" Sessions asked.

McCoy thought that over a moment before answering.

There were a number of officers around the Corps who had been enlisted men. And a number of noncoms had at one time or another been officers. An even larger number of old noncoms had been officers in the Haitian Constabulary, where the troops they'd commanded had been Haitians. McCoy had sometimes imagined that there would probably be a chance somewhere down the road after he had more time in, for him to get to be a warrant officer, and maybe even a commissioned officer. But he sensed that Sessions wasn't talking about some time in the future.

"You're talking about now, sir?" McCoy asked.

Sessions nodded.

"The Corps is about to really expand, McCoy. Even if we don't get in the war, the Corps is going to be five times as big as it is now. We're going to need large numbers of officers. And many of them are going to come from the noncommissioned officer corps. People like yourself, in other words. Are you interested?"

"I don't know," McCoy said, more thinking aloud than a direct reply.

"There are a number of people, myself included, Ken, who believe that you have what it takes."

"I hadn't even thought about now," McCoy said. "Maybe later."

"The process is simple," Sessions said. "You apply. Sergeant Davis has your application all typed up. All you have to do is sign it. Then you appear before a board of officers. The purpose of that is to give them a chance to see how well you can think under pressure. The board then votes on you; and if they approve, you'll be ordered to Marine Corps Schools in Quantico and run through the final phase of the Platoon Leader's Course. If you get through that, you'd be commissioned a second lieutenant."

"I never heard of the Platoon Leader's Course," McCoy said.

"The primary source of officers will be young men who have spent their college summer vacations going through officer training courses. The first summer they go through what amounts to boot camp. And the rest of the time we give them everything from customs of the service to the platoon in the assault. If you went to Quantico, you would be sent through the final phase with a group of them."

"College boys?" McCoy said, thinking of Pick Pickering. That's how Pickering was going to become an officer.

"Going through college is not a disease, McCoy," Sessions said. "You'd be surprised how many people have gone to college. Nice people. Jean went to college. I met her there."

McCoy smiled at him.

"I meant, I'm not sure I could hack it in that kind of company," McCoy said. "All I've got is a high school diploma."

"And four years in the Corps," Sessions said. "Which I think would give you a hell of an advantage at Quantico."

"You think I could make it through?" McCoy asked.

"I do," Sessions said. "But the only way to find out for sure is for you to apply, pass the board, and go."

"It's worth a shot, I guess," McCoy said, thinking aloud. "What have I got to lose?"

"Sergeant Davis has your application all typed up," Sessions repeated. "I'll approve it, of course."

"Thank you," McCoy said, simply.

(FOUR)

After he signed his name to the applications Staff Sergeant Davis had typed up for him, he put the whole business from his mind, convinced that like all other paperwork he'd seen in the Corps, it would take forever and a day to work its way through the system. He had more important things on his mind than the possibility that the application might, some months down the pike, be favorably acted upon . . . or that some further months down the pike he would be facing a board of officers—which probably wouldn't approve him anyway. After a while, in fact, he'd come to the conclusion that the incident at the ferry had a lot more to do with the whole business than Sessions's brilliant insight that he would make an officer. Sessions was being nice to him. The officers he would face on the board, when and if he got to face it, wouldn't think they owed him a thing.

And besides, he had three much more immediate problems to face, all of them connected. The first was what was going to happen to him now that the "interviews" were over. He didn't want to go to the Motor Transport Platoon, but on the other hand that would be a good place to keep his nose clean until Captain Banning came home from Shanghai. And he didn't really want to go to a heavy weapons platoon as a machine-gunner either. Since he'd be transferring in grade, they would try to bust him on general principles; and that would fuck up going back to work for Captain Banning.

He could also ask Captain Sessions to keep him around the detachment. Sessions would probably do it—as a favor. But that would mean he'd have to work as a clerk and push a typewriter and he was still not anxious to do that. And more important, if he stayed in Philadelphia, he'd have to deal with his two other problems: He had made up his mind to go home and face that and get it the hell over with once and for all. But going home once was not the same thing as having home so close to where he was stationed . . . Christ, Norristown was only an hour away in the LaSalle.

These were the thoughts that were occupying his mind, not the remote, way-down-the pike possibility of being called before a board of officers who would make up their minds whether or not he stood a chance of keeping up with a bunch of college boys at Quantico.

On Monday morning, he signed the application papers. On Wednesday morning, Staff Sergeant Davis came to the barracks and told him to put on his best uniform and report to the board at 1330.

"Sit down, Corporal," a major, who was the president of the board, said. The five officers of the board were sitting behind two issue tables pushed together. One was a second lieutenant who was functioning as secretary. Two of them were first lieutenants (Lieutenant Fogarty, the 47th Motor Transport Platoon commander was one of them). Captain Sessions was the fourth. And the last was the major McCoy was seeing for the first time.

McCoy sat down at attention in a straight-backed wooden chair facing the tables.

"We have before us what is apparently a well-turned-out corporal of the regular Marine Corps," the president of the board said, "who, with his shady reputation, his illegal chevrons, and his equally illegal campaign hat, is just about what we expected of a China Marine so highly recommended by Captain Sessions. And others."

"Come on, Major." Captain Sessions chuckled. "The lieutenant's going to write that all down."

"Strike everything after—what did I say?—'well-turned-out corporal of the regular Marine Corps,' Lieutenant," the president ordered.

"Aye, aye, sir," the lieutenant said, and smiled at McCoy.

"Who comes to us not only recommended by Captain Sessions but by another member of this board, Lieutenant Fogarty, whose recommendation is based on his long-time evaluation—it must be three weeks now—as the corporal's platoon leader. The corporal's qualifications having, after due evaluation, been judged to be more than adequate, we now turn to the real question. In your own words, Corporal, would you tell this board why you feel yourself qualified, after proper training, to serve your country and the Marine Corps as a commissioned officer?"

"I'm not sure I do, sir," McCoy said.

"That's the wrong answer, Corporal," the president of the board said. "You want to try again?"

"Tell us why not, McCoy," Captain Sessions said.

This whole fucking thing is unreal. How am I supposed to answer that?

He paraphrased what was in his mind: "I'm not sure I know how to answer that question, sir," he said.

"You've known second lieutenants, McCoy," Sessions said. "Pick out any one of them except this one, and tell us why you doubt your ability to do anything he can do."

"Sir, all I've got is a high school education," McCoy said.

"You speak Chinese, I have been told?" the president asked. "And Japanese? And several European languages?"

"I don't speak Japanese as well as Chinese, sir. And I can hardly read it at all."

"Well, here's a given for you, Corporal. So far as the Marine Corps is concerned, fluency in almost any foreign language is worth more than a bachelor's degree. Anything else?"

"I wouldn't know how to behave as an officer, sir."

"They'll teach you that at Quantico," the president said. "Anything else?"

"Sir, Captain Sessions just sprung this whole idea on me."

"Answer this question. Think it over first—yes or no. No qualifications. Do you want to be an officer or don't you?"

McCoy thought it over. For what seemed to him like a very long time. The president of the board began to tap his fingertips impatiently on the table. Captain Sessions's left eyebrow was arched, a sign of impatience, often followed by an angry outburst.

"Yes, sir," McCoy said.

"You are temporarily dismissed, Corporal," the president said, "while this board discusses your application. There may be other questions for you. Please wait in the corridor."

"Aye, aye, sir," McCoy said. He stood up, did an about-face, and marched out of the room. He had just managed to close the door when he broke wind. It smelled like something had died.

"The board will offer comments in inverse order of rank," the president said. "Lieutenant?"

"Sir, I'm a little concerned about his attitude," the second lieutenant said. "He certainly took his time thinking it over when you asked him straight out if he wanted to become an officer."

"It has been my experience, Lieutenant," the major said, "that what's wrong with most junior officers is that they leap into action without thinking things over carefully."

"Yes, sir," the lieutenant said.

"Lieutenant Bruce?"

"So far as I'm concerned," Lieutenant Bruce said, "he's what we're supposed to be looking for. A noncom of proven ability who can handle a wartime commission."

"Lieutenant Fogarty?"

"I'm impressed with him," Fogarty said simply. "He's a little rough around the edges, maybe, but they can clean up his language and teach him which fork to use at Quantico."

"Ed?" the president asked, turning to Captain Sessions.

"I admit of course to a certain personal bias. He saved my life. One finds all sorts of previously unsuspected virtues in people who do that."

There was laughter along the table.

"But even if he hadn't saved my skin, and even if a certain unnamed very senior officer had not made his desires known, I would enthusiastically recommend McCoy for a commission," Sessions added.

"Does he know about the general?"

"I'm sure he doesn't. The general and his aide were in civilian clothing, and they weren't introduced," Sessions said. "Being as objective as I can, I believe the Corps needs officers like McCoy."

"Because he's a linguist, you mean?" the President asked.

"He'd be a linguist anyway," Sessions said. "But that would be a waste of his talents, even though people who speak Chinese and Japanese are damned hard to come by."

"We will now vote in the same order," the president said. "Unless someone wants to call him back and ask him something else?"

He looked up and down the table.

"Lieutenant?" he asked, when he saw that no one had any additional questions.

"I vote yes, sir," the lieutenant said.

One by one, the others said exactly the same thing.

"This board, whose president is not about to put his judgment in conflict with that of the Assistant Chief of Staff for Intelligence, USMC . . . ," the president said, and waited for the expected chuckles.

After they came, he went on: "Especially after he said—slowly, carefully, and with great emphasis—'I think we ought to put bars on that boy's shoulders, if for no other reason than he seems to be the only one in the Marine Corps beside me and Chesty Puller who doesn't think the Japs can be whipped with one hand tied behind us.' "

He waited again for the chuckles, then concluded: "This board has in secret session just unanimously approved the application of Corporal McCoy to attend the Platoon Leader's Course at Quantico. Lieutenant, you are directed to make the decision known to the appointing authority."

"Aye, aye, sir," the lieutenant said.

"Call him back in here, will you?" the president said.

The lieutenant went to the door, opened it, and motioned McCoy back into the room. McCoy marched in and stood to attention beside the straight-backed wooden chair.

"Corporal," the president said, "this board has considered your application carefully, and after review by the appointing authority, that decision will be made known to you through channels. In the meantime, you will continue to perform your regular duties. Do you have any questions?"

"No, sir."

The president rapped his knuckles on the table. "This board stands adjourned until recalled by me."

McCoy, thinking he had been dismissed again, started to do another about-face.

"Hold it, Corporal," the president said. "Sit down a minute."

McCoy sat down, more or less at attention.

"Corporal, unofficially, what that Platoon Leader's Course actually is is Parris Island for officers. What it's really all about is to make Marines—Marine *officers*—out of civilians. To do that, they're going to lean hard on the trainees. That might be harder for a Marine corporal to take than it would be for some kid straight from college. It would be a shame if some Marine corporal who a lot of people think would make a good officer were to say, 'I'm a corporal; I don't have to put up with this crap. They can stick their commission.' Do I make my point?"

"Yes, sir."

"Now, while I cannot tell you how this board has acted on your application, or whether or not the appointing authority will concur with its recommendation, I can mention in passing that the next Platoon Leader's Course begins at Quantico One September, and if I were you I wouldn't make any plans for the period following One September. Perhaps between now and One September, your platoon commander could see his way clear to putting you on leave."

"Yes, sir," Lieutenant Fogarty said. "No problem there, sir."

"Well, that's it then," the president said. "Unless anyone else has something?"

"I want to see the corporal a minute when this is over," Captain Sessions said. "Stick around, please, Killer."

" 'Killer'? " the president asked, wryly. "Is that what you call him? My curiosity is aroused."

"With respect, sir, that is a little private joke between the corporal and myself," Captain Sessions said.

(FIVE)
Norristown, Pennsylvania
10 August 1941

Norristown was dingier, dirtier, grayer, and greasier than McCoy remembered; and he had a terrible temptation just to say fuck it and turn the LaSalle around and go back to Philly.

In China, McCoy had told himself more than once that he would never go back home, because as far as he was concerned there was nothing left for him there. That had been all right in Shanghai, but it hadn't been all right once the Corps had sent him to Philly. He knew he was at least going to have to make an effort to go see his sister Anne-Marie, who was probably a regular nun by now, and his brother Tommy, who was now eighteen and probably almost a man, and maybe even the old man.

McCoy told himself that at least he was not going back to Norristown the way he left . . . on the Interurban Rapid Transit car to Philly with nothing in his pocket but the trolley transfer the Marine recruiter had given him to get from the Twelfth Street Station in Philly to the Navy Yard.

He was coming home in a LaSalle convertible automobile; he was wearing a candy-ass college boy seersucker suit like Pick Pickering wore; and he had a couple of hundred bucks in his pockets and a hell of a lot more than that in the Philadelphia Savings Fund Society bank.

At the convent, a pale-faced nun behind a grille told him that she was sorry she couldn't help him but she had never heard of anyone named Anne-Marie McCoy.

A moment later, the door over the grille was once more shut and locked. After that he went to the rectory at Saint Rose of Lima's.

A young priest opened the door. He was a dark-eyed, dark-haired guy, who looked like he could be either some kind of a Mexican or maybe a Hungarian. He was only wearing a T-shirt; but the black slacks and shoes gave him away. Besides, McCoy could have told you this one was a priest even if he was naked in a steambath. He had *that* look. Still, McCoy was a little let down that the guy wasn't wearing a white collar and a black front.

"Can I help you?" the young priest asked.

"Is Father Zoghby in?" McCoy asked.

Standing in exactly this spot, he recalled, he had asked that same question at least a couple of hundred times before: When he was an altar boy. Later when he was in some kind of trouble in school and the sisters or the brothers sent him to see "the Father." And later still on the night when the old man went apeshit and came after him with crazy eyes, swinging the bottom of the lamp. McCoy came here that night because he hadn't known where else to go or what else to do.

"I'm sorry," the young priest said. "Father Zoghby's no longer at Saint Rose's."

"Where is he?" McCoy asked.

"He's in Saint Francis's, I'm sorry to say," the young priest said, and repeated, "Can I help you?"

Saint Francis's was a hospital near Philadelphia. It was where they sent you if you were going to die, or if you went crazy.

"I'm looking for Anne-Marie McCoy," he said. "She used to be in this parish, and then I heard she was at the Sisters of the Holy Ghost as a novice. But when I asked at the convent, they told me she wasn't there. And they wouldn't tell me where she went."

"What's your interest in her?"

"She's my sister," McCoy said. "I've been away."

"I see," the priest said.

There was recognition now in his eyes. McCoy thought the young priest had probably heard all about the grief and pain the incorrigible son had inflicted on good ol' Pat McCoy before they ran the incorrigible off to the Marines. Nobody but his family would believe it, but when good ol' Pat wasn't glad-handing people at the used-car lot or the KC or the 12th Street Bar & Grill, good ol' Pat McCoy was pouring John Jamieson's into his brain. Only his wife and kids knew it, but good ol' glad-hand Pat was a mean, vicious drunk who got his kicks slapping his wife and his kids around. Sometimes he beat them because there was some kind of reason like not showing the proper respect, or for bad grades or a note from one of the Sisters or the Brothers, or for leaving polish showing when you'd waxed one of the cars on the lot. More often he beat them for no reason at all.

Kenneth J. McCoy would never forget the time when good ol' Pat had dragged him in front of the judge: "God knows, Your Honor," Pat McCoy told the judge, the Honorable Francis Mulvaney, a fellow knight at the KC, "I have tried to do my best for my family. God knows that. I sent them to parochial school when it was a genuine sacrifice to come up with the tuition. I made them take Mass regular. I tried to set an example."

He paused then to blow his nose and wipe his eyes.

"And now this," his father went on. "Maybe God is punishing me for something I done in my youth. I don't know, Your Honor."

"I'll hear your side of this," His Honor said to the incorrigible.

Who replied that good ol' Pat had slapped his eldest—just turned seventeen—

son one time too many. And his eldest son (otherwise known to this court as the accused, Kenneth J. McCoy) had seen red and given him a shove back. And good ol' Pat, the loving father who had sent the accused to parochial school even when that had been a genuine financial sacrifice, had been so drunk that he fell down and tore his cheek when he knocked over the coffee table.

And that had made ol' loving Father so pissed that he came after the accused with the base of the table lamp. After he'd demonstrated his willingness to use it by smashing the Philco radio and the glass in the bookcases and the plaster statue of the Sacred Heart of Jesus, the accused had fled the premises and sought refuge in the rectory of Saint Rose of Lima Roman Catholic Church. There he had remained until, accompanied by the good Father Zoghby, he surrendered himself to the Norristown Police to face charges. Good ol' loving Father Pat McCoy had accused his eldest son of assault with intent to do bodily harm as well as general all-around incorrigibility and heathenism and ungrateful sonism.

"I'm sorry he cut his face," the accused mumbled to the judge.

"That's all?"

"Yes, sir."

It had already been arranged, Father Zoghby had told him when he'd come to the jail. He'd had a word with the judge. To spare his family any further shame and humiliation, the judge would drop all charges on condition that the accused join the U.S. Marine Corps for four years.

Later he'd tried to send his civvies home in the box they gave you at Parris Island, but it had come back marked REFUSED. So had the letters he'd written at first to his mother and Anne-Marie and Tommy. Then there had been a letter from Father Zoghby: His father could not find it in his heart to forgive him, and had started telling people he had no son named Kenneth. It would be better, Father Zoghby continued, if Kenneth stopped writing until things had a time to settle. He would pray that his father would in time forgive him, and he would keep him posted if anything happened he should know.

While McCoy was still running the water-cooled .30-caliber Browning in Dog Company, First Battalion, 4th Marines, Father Zoghby had written him one more letter: His mother was dead; Anne-Marie had a vocation and was a novice at the Convent of the Sisters of the Holy Ghost; Tommy had gone to Bethlehem, where the steel mills had reopened and there was work; and his father had remarried.

"Anne-Marie left the convent at least two years ago, I'm sorry to say," the young priest said. "I'm sure your father would know where she is."

"I can't ask him," McCoy said.

The priest looked at him for a moment, and McCoy sensed that he was making up his mind. Then the priest stepped outside and closed the rectory door after him.

"Maybe I can help you," he said.

He led him past the church building, then down the cracked concrete walkway to the school buildings—the grammar school to the left and the larger, newer Saint Rose of Lima High School building to the right—and finally to the nuns' residence.

He spoke first to Sister Gregory, who recognized McCoy as she looked down at him from the steps of the residence, but acted as if she had never seen him before in her life. She went back inside, and a minute later Sister Paul appeared at the door and walked down the steps to where McCoy and the young priest stood.

"How are you, Kenneth?" Sister Paul said.

"I'm all right, Sister," McCoy said. "How are you?"

"Have you made things right between you and God, Kenneth?"

"I don't know, Sister," McCoy said.

"You're not going to make trouble, are you, Kenneth?" she asked.

"I just came home from China," McCoy said. "I want to see Anne-Marie."

"You were in China, were you?"

"Yes, Sister."

"Anne-Marie left the Sisters of the Holy Ghost," Sister Paul said, "and I'm sorry to tell you, she has also abandoned the Church."

"Do you know where she is?"

"Here in Norristown," Sister Paul said. "She's taken up with a Protestant."

"Excuse me?"

"She chose to marry a young man outside the Church. He's a Protestant whose name is Schulter. He has the Amoco station at Ninth and Walnut. They have two babies, a little girl and a little boy."

"Thank you, Sister Paul," McCoy said.

"I don't want you to do anything, Kenneth, that will cause your father more pain," she said. "I hope you've had time to grow up, to think things through."

VIII

(ONE)

The man who walked out to the pump island when McCoy drove in wore an Amoco uniform: a striped shirt and trousers with a matching billed cap. There was an Amoco insignia on the brow of the cap and a nameplate, "Dutch," was sewn to the shirt breast. The man was about thirty, McCoy judged, and already wearing a spare tire.

"Fill it with high-test, sir?" he asked.

McCoy nodded. After Dutch had opened the hood, McCoy got out of the car.

"You must have just had the oil changed," Dutch said, showing McCoy the dipstick. "Clean as a whistle and right to the top."

"Your name Schulter?" McCoy asked.

"That's right," Dutch said, warily curious.

"I'm Anne-Marie's brother," McCoy said.

Dutch hesitated a moment and then put out his hand. "Dutch Schulter," he said. "I heard—she told me—you was in the Marines."

"I am," McCoy said.

"You must be doing all right in the Marines," Dutch Schulter said, making a vague gesture first at the LaSalle, and then at McCoy himself.

"I do all right," McCoy said.

The gas pump made a chugging noise when the automatic filler nozzle was triggered. Dutch Schulter moved to the rear of the car, topped off the tank, then hung the hose up. McCoy looked at the pump. Eleven point seven gallons at 23.9 cents a gallon: $2.79. He took a wad of bills from his pocket and peeled off a ten-dollar bill.

Dutch Schulter handed the change to him, together with a Coca-Cola glass.

"They're free with a fill-up," he said.

"How do I get to see my sister?" McCoy said.

Schulter looked at him for a moment as if making up his mind, and then raised his voice: "Mickey!"

A kid in an Amoco uniform appeared at the door of the grease-rack bay.

"Hold the fort, Mickey," Dutch called. "I got to go home for a minute."

Home was a row house on North Elm, a little wooden porch in front of a fieldstone house that smelled of baby shit, sour milk, and cabbage.

Anne-Marie looked older than he expected. She was already getting fat and lumpy, and she had lost a couple of teeth. She cried when she saw him, and hugged him, and told him he had really growed up.

Dutch touched his shoulder, and when McCoy turned to look at him, handed him a bottle of beer.

"You're an uncle, Kenny," Anne-Marie said. "We got a boy and a girl, but I just got them to sleep, and you'll have to wait to see them. You can stay for supper?"

"I thought I'd take you and Dutch out for supper," McCoy said.

"You don't want to do that," she protested. "You won't believe what restaurants ask for food these days."

"Yeah, I do," McCoy said.

"What I should have done," Dutch said, "is had him follow me in the truck. You want to run me back by the station? Could you find your way back here again?"

"Why don't you take my car?" McCoy said. "I've got no place else to go."

"You got a car, Kenny?" Anne-Marie asked, surprised.

"He's got a goddamned LaSalle convertible, is what he's got," Dutch said.

She looked at him in surprise.

"You been doing all right for yourself, I guess," she said.

"I've been doing all right," McCoy said.

"I'll put it up on the rack, and grease it," Dutch said. "And then have the kid works for me, you saw him, Mickey, wash it."

"Thank you," McCoy said, and tossed him the keys.

Dutch Schulter returned a few minutes after six, as soon as the night man came on at the station. McCoy was glad to see him. Anne-Marie was getting on his nerves. She was a goddamned slob. He had to tell her to change the diaper on the older kid; he had shit running down his leg from under his diaper.

The sink was full of unwashed dishes. McCoy remembered that, come to think of it, his mother had been sort of a slob herself. Many of the times the old man had slapped her around, it had started with him bitching about something being dirty.

She told him she would really rather make his supper herself. When Dutch returned with his car, she said, he could take her down to the Acme and she would get steaks or something; but she didn't mean it, and McCoy didn't want to eat in her dirty kitchen, off her dirty plates.

She asked him if he had been to see "Daddy," and he told her no. And she told him she hadn't seen him either. He had been mad at her since she left the convent (and boy, could she tell him stories about what went on in that place!); and after she had married Dutch, outside the church and all, it had gotten worse.

Dutch was a good man, she said. She had met him when she was working in the Highway Diner on the Bethlehem Pike after she left the convent. He had been nice to her, and one thing had led to another, and they'd started going out. Then they got married and started their family.

McCoy did the arithmetic in his head, and decided she had the sequence wrong: She and Dutch started their family, and then got married. The old man could count, too, which might be one of the reasons he was pissed-off at her.

How dare she embarrass Past Grand Exalted Commander Pat McCoy of the KC? She not only leaves (or gets kicked out of?) the convent, but she gets herself knocked up by some Dutchy she meets slinging hash at the Highway Diner.

Dutch came home with the LaSalle all greased and polished, then took a bath and got dressed-up in a two-tone sports coat and slacks. Anne-Marie had on a too-tight spotted dress with a flowery print. They loaded the kids in the car and went looking for someplace to eat.

Anne-Marie said the food in the 12th Street Bar & Grill was always good, and they didn't ask an arm and a leg for it. McCoy knew she was less concerned with good food and saving his money than she was in going where the old man would be hanging out so he'd see them together all dressed-up, and him driving a LaSalle.

"I saw a place on the way into town, Norristown Tavern . . . Inn . . . that looked nice," McCoy said.

"They charge an arm and a leg in there," Anne-Marie said.

"Yeah, they do, Kenny," Dutch agreed. He did care, McCoy decided, what it was going to cost.

"What the hell, I don't get to come all that often," McCoy said.

When they were in the Norristown Inn, in a booth against the wall, Anne-Marie looked up from trying to force a spoonful of potatoes into the boy and whispered, "There's Daddy."

Good ol' Pat McCoy was at the bar, with a sharp-faced female, her hair piled high on top of her head, her lipstick a red gash across her pale face . . . obviously the second Mrs. Patrick J. McCoy.

McCoy thought it over, and when they were on their strawberry shortcake, he got up from the table without saying anything and walked to the bar.

"Hello," he said to his father.

His father nodded at him. The second Mrs. McCoy looked at him curiously.

He's not surprised to see me, which means that he saw me at the table with Anne-Marie and Dutch. And didn't come over.

"You're home, I see," McCoy's father said.

"About ten days ago."

McCoy's father moved his glass in little circles on the bar.

"Learn anything in the Marine Corps?" McCoy's father asked.

That told his new wife who I am. Now she doesn't like me either.

"I learned a little," McCoy said.

"So what are you doing now, looking for a job?"

"Not yet."

"Maybe the Dutchman'll give you one pumping gas," his father said. He laughed at his own wit and turned to his wife for an audience. She dutifully tittered.

"Maybe he will," McCoy said, and walked back to the table.

"What did he say?" Anne-Marie asked.

"Not much," McCoy said.

He told himself he was being a prick when the bill came and he got mad that Anne-Marie had ordered one of everything on the menu. He'd offered to take them to dinner; he shouldn't bitch about what it cost.

He told Anne-Marie and Dutch that he had to go back to Philadelphia, so he couldn't stay over on the foldaway bed. But he promised to write. Then he dropped them at their row house. Before he left, he asked for Tommy's address.

They were obviously pressed for dough, and he considered slipping Anne-Marie fifty bucks "to buy something for the kids," but decided against it. She'd already started moaning about how hard it was to make it with two kids on what Dutch brought home from the Amoco station. If he gave her money, she would be back for more.

He didn't return to Philly. He never intended to. Though he wasn't on leave, he didn't have to go back or make the reveille formation or anything. Lieutenant Fogarty had pointedly told him that no one was going to be looking for him around the platoon, and that if he didn't want to use up his leave time, he could sack out in the barracks whenever and check in with the first sergeant every couple of days.

He just wanted to get away from the row house and the stink of baby shit and cabbage.

He stopped outside of town, put the roof up, then drove to Bethlehem and checked into the Hotel Bethlehem. It wasn't the Bellevue Stratford, but it was nice, and when he went down to the dining room in the morning, they had breakfast steaks and corned beef hash on the menu. He ordered it up, fuck what it cost.

Tommy lived in a rooming house, a great big old rambling building built on the side of a hill. He wasn't there, of course; but the landlady, a big pink-cheeked Polack woman, told him he could probably catch him at the walk bridge over the railroad tracks when his shift was over, and that if he missed him there, he could find him at the Lithuanian Social Club.

He drove around town. He saw Lehigh University and, just for the hell of it, drove inside. There really wasn't much to see. He was disappointed, and wondered why. What had he expected?

He went back to the Hotel Bethlehem, and checked out. When the eight-to-four shift let out, he was standing at the end of the bridge over the railroad tracks hoping he would be able to spot Tommy.

Tommy spotted him first. Tommy had changed so much he had let him walk right by him. But Tommy saw him out of the corner of his eye, and came back—even though the last fucking person in the fucking world he expected to see was his fucking brother on the fucking bridge wearing a fucking suit.

They went to the Lithuanian Club, and drank a lot of beer. Once Tommy told the guys his fucking big brother was a fucking corporal in the fucking Marines, it was all right with them despite the fucking suit that made him look like a fucking fairy.

The Lithuanian Club reminded McCoy of the Million Dollar Club in Shanghai. Not in looks. The Lithuanian Club was a dump. It smelled of beer and piss. But the Million Dollar Club was the place where Marines went because they had nowhere else to go and nothing else to do but get drunk when the duty day was over. And that's all the Lithuanian Club was, too, a place where the enlisted men from the steel mill went because there was no place else to go when they came away from the open hearths, and nothing to do but get drunk.

Tommy reminded McCoy of a lot of Marines he knew, particularly in the line companies.

They wound up in a whorehouse by the railroad station. McCoy paid for the all-night services of a peroxide blonde not because he was really all that interested in screwing her, but because the alternative was worse: He was too shit-faced to get in his car and drive back to Tommy's rooming house or the Hotel Bethlehem.

The Corps was hell on drunk driving and/or speeding. He still hadn't accepted the possibility that he could become an officer. Which was the main reason why he hadn't said anything about Quantico to either Anne-Marie or Tommy. Besides, they probably wouldn't believe it. Which was easy to understand; he didn't quite believe it himself. But getting arrested for drunk driving or speeding would be the end of it. He wanted to give it a shot, anyway.

Tommy pulled him out of the whore's bed at half-past six in the morning and said he had to go to fucking work and needed a fucking ride and some fucking breakfast: He couldn't work eight fucking hours on the fucking open hearth with nothing in his fucking stomach.

They went to a greasy spoon and had eggs and home fries and coffee. He dropped Tommy off at the walk bridge over the railroad tracks and drove back to the Navy Yard.

(TWO)
The San Mateo Club
San Mateo, California
27 August 1941

The building that housed the San Mateo Club had been built, in 1895, as the country residence of Andrew Foster, Sr. It so remained until 1939, when Andrew Foster, Jr., seventy, on the death of his wife, moved into the penthouse atop the Andrew Foster Hotel in San Francisco and put the estate on the market.

It had been quickly snapped up by the board of directors of the San Mateo Club. Not only was the price right and the house large enough for the membership then rather crowded into the "old clubhouse," but the money was there. A very nice price had been offered for the "old club" by developers who wanted to turn its greens and fairways into a housing development.

The Foster Estate ("the new club") contained land enough to lay out twenty-seven holes (as opposed to eighteen at the old club), as well as gently rolling pastures right beside the polo field that could accommodate far more ponies than the old club could handle. And old Mr. Foster, Jr. had thrown in all of the furnishings, except for those in his private apartment, which had moved to the hotel penthouse with him.

The woman was lanky and fair-haired. She wore a wide-brimmed straw hat, a pale blue dress, and white gloves. From where she was standing, by the foot of the wide staircase leading to the second floor of the clubhouse, she could see the reserve supply of champagne. It was practically, if somewhat inelegantly, stored by the door to the passageway to the kitchen in ice-filled, galvanized-iron watering troughs for horses.

She took a delicate bite of her hors d'oeuvre, a very nice pâté on a crisp cracker, sipped at her champagne, and seriously considered just picking up one of the bottles and carrying it upstairs. He would probably find that amusing.

But it would be difficult to explain if she met someone coming down the stairs. Without the champagne, it would be presumed that she was going up to use the john. There were inadequate rest room facilities for ladies on the main floor of the San Mateo Club. The men had no similar problem. What had been a private study off the library had been equipped with the proper plumbing and that was it.

Which meant that when nature called, the men could conveniently take a leak not fifty feet from the bar. But the women, when faced with a similar requirement, more often than not would find their small downstairs facilities occupied and would have to seek release in an upstairs john. The silver lining in that cloud was that no one looked curiously at a woman making her way up the wide, curving staircase.

She put her empty champagne glass on the tray of a passing waiter, smilingly shook her head when he offered her a fresh glass, and started up the stairs.

No one was in the upstairs corridors, which she thought was fortuitous. But she hurried nevertheless, and quickly entered, without knocking, a door halfway down the right corridor. There was a brass number on the door, 14. The numbered rooms were an innovation of the House Committee; before they had been put up, people spending the night or the weekend in the "new clubhouse" had been unable to find their own rooms.

She closed the door and fastened the lock. She could hear the sound of the shower and of his voice, an entirely satisfactory tenor. She smiled at that, then walked to the bed, saw that he had tossed his clothing on it, sniffed, and wrinkled her nose. She delicately picked up the sweat-soaked blue polo shirt (a cloth letter "2" still safety-pinned to it) and an equally sweat-soaked pair of Jockey shorts and dropped them onto the floor beside a very dirty pair of breeches, a scarred and battered pair of riding boots, and a pair of heavy woolen socks.

Then she pulled the cover off the bed and turned it down. She looked toward the bathroom, wondering how long he had been in there, how soon he could come out to find her.

Surprise! Surprise!

Then she had an even better idea. She walked to a credenza and pulled her hat and gloves off and dropped them there. Then she took off her wedding and engagement rings. And, very quickly, the rest of her clothing. It would be amusing only if she was finished undressing.

But when she had finished that, he still hadn't come out. The last time she'd seen him, she remembered, he had really needed a bath. He had been reeking with sweat; and perspiration was literally dripping off his chin. But enough was enough.

She examined herself in a mirror and smiled wickedly at herself, walked to the bathroom door, opened it, and went inside. There was no shower stall. One corner had been tiled. The tiled area was so large that water from three shower heads aimed at the corner did not splash beyond it.

His head and face were covered with lather. Still singing cheerfully, he was rubbing the tips of his fingers vigorously on his scalp. She saw a shower cap on a hook and quickly stuffed her hair under it. Then she stepped into the tiled area, hunching her shoulders involuntarily as the water, colder than she expected, struck her. Then she dropped to her knees, reached out, and put it in her mouth.

"Jesus Christ!" Pick Pickering said. "Are you crazy?" And then he yelped. "Christ, I got soap in my eyes!"

He stepped away from her abruptly to turn his face to a shower stream. Slipping and almost falling, the woman rose to her feet. She went to him, pressed her body against him, and nipped his nipple.

"Where the hell is your husband?" Pick Pickering asked.

"In the bar, I suppose," the woman said. "I got bored."

She put her hand on it and pumped it just a few times until it filled her hand.

"You want to try doing it standing up?" she asked. "It would be sort of like doing it in the rain."

"Dorothy!" Pick said.

She tried to arrange herself so he could penetrate her, and failed.

"I don't think that's going to work," she said, matter-of-factly.

Pick Pickering picked her up and carried her to the bed. Penetration there proved simple.

Three minutes later, he jumped out of bed.

"Wham, bam, thank you, ma'am?" she said. "That's not very nice."

"You're out of your mind, Dorothy, do you know that?"

"Where are you going?"

"I am due in town right now," he said.

"Who is she? Anyone I know?"

He didn't reply.

"No goddamned underwear!" he cried as he pawed through a canvas overnight bag. "I didn't bring any underwear!"

"How sexy!" Dorothy said.

"What the hell am I going to do?"

"Do without," she said. "I do that all the time."

He looked at her and smiled.

"You would crack wise at the moment your husband shot us both with a shotgun," he said.

"That presumes his being sober enough to hold a shotgun," Dorothy said. "You really do have to go, don't you?"

"The only reason I played at all today is because Tommy Whitlock canceled at the last minute."

He pulled a fresh polo shirt over his head, and then started to pull on a pair of cotton trousers.

"How lucky for the both of us," she said.

He looked at her and smiled again.

"Be careful with the zipper," she said. "I wouldn't want anything to get damaged."

"Neither would I," he said.

"I'm not going to see you again, am I?" she asked.

"I don't see how," Pick said.

"I'll miss you, baby."

"I'll miss you too, Dorothy," he said. He found his wristwatch on the bedside table and strapped it on. "Christ, I am late!" he said.

He looked down at her, and she pushed herself onto her elbows. He leaned over and kissed her.

"I really am going to miss you," she said.

"Me, too," he said.

"Be careful, baby," she said.

He jumped up and, hopping, pushed his bare feet into a pair of loafers.

Then he left, without looking back at her.

Thirty minutes later he was in San Francisco by the entrance to the parking garage of the Andrew Foster Hotel. A sign had been placed on the sidewalk there: SORRY, BUT JUST NOW, WE NEED ALL OUR SPACE FOR OUR REGISTERED GUESTS!"

Like everything else connected with the Andrew Foster Hotel, it was not an ordinary sign. It was contained within a polished brass frame and lettered in gold. And the frame was mounted in an ornate cast-iron mounting. The Andrew Foster was one of the world's great hotels (the most prestigious as well as the most expensive hotel in San Francisco), the flagship of the forty-two-hotel Foster Hotel chain. Certain standards would have been expected of it even if Andrew Foster were not resident in the penthouse.

Andrew Foster was fond of quoting the "One Great Rule of Keeping a Decent Inn." It was not the sort of rule that could be written down, for it changed sometimes half a dozen times a day. It could be summarized (and was, behind his back) as immediately correcting whatever offended his eye at the moment.

What offended Andrew Foster could range from a smudge on a bellman's shoes ("The One Great Rule of Keeping a Decent Inn is that the staff must be impeccably turned out. If you do that, everything else will fall into place."); to an overdone medium-rare steak ("The One Great Rule of Keeping a Decent Inn is to give people at table what they ask for. If you do that, everything else will fall into place."); to fresh flowers starting to wilt ("The One Great Rule of Keeping a Decent Inn is to keep the place from looking like a rundown funeral home! If you can do that, everything else will fall into place!").

The gilt-lettered sign appeared on the sidewalk shortly after Mr. Andrew Foster spotted a simple GARAGE FULL sign. Everything else would fall into place if people were told (by means of a sign that didn't look as if it came off the midway of a second-rate carnival) why they couldn't do something they wanted to and were offered the inn's apologies for the inconvenience.

Ignoring the sign, Pick Pickering drove his car, a black Cadillac convertible, roof down, a brand-new one, into the parking garage. He quickly saw that the garage was indeed full; there was not sufficient room for the rear of the car to clear the sidewalk.

One of the neatly uniformed (after the fashion of the French Foreign Legion) parking attendants rushed to the car.

"May I park your car for you, sir?" the attendant asked, very politely.

Pick Pickering looked at him and grinned.

"Would you please, Tony?" he asked. "I'm really late."

"No!" the attendant said, in elaborate mock surprise. "Is that why everybody but the Coast Guard's looking for you?"

"Oh, Christ," Pickering said.

" 'The One Great Rule of Keeping a Decent Inn,' " Tony quoted.

" 'Is That People Are Where They Are Supposed to Be, When They Are Supposed to Be There,' " Pickering finished for him.

"You've heard that, Pick, have you?" Tony asked. "You want me to let him know you're here?"

"Please, Tony," Pickering said and walked quickly, almost ran, between the tightly packed cars to a door marked STAFF ONLY.

Behind it was a locker room. Pickering started pulling the polo shirt off his head as he pushed the door open. He had his pants off before he stopped before one of the battered lockers.

Two dinner jackets were hanging in the locker, and three dress shirts in cellophane bags fresh from the hotel laundry, but there was no underwear where there was supposed to be underwear. And not even any goddamned socks!

Moving with a speed that could come only of long practice, he put suspenders on the trousers, studs and cufflinks in the shirt; and as he hooked the cummerbund around his waist, slipped his bare feet into patent leather shoes.

Ninety seconds after he opened the locker door, Pick Pickering tied the knot in the bow tie as he waited impatiently for an elevator.

The elevator door opened. The operator, a middle-aged black woman, stared at him and said, "You've got lipstick on your ear, Pick, and the tie's crooked."

"Would you believe this?" he said, showing her his bare ankles as he stepped into the elevator and reached for a handkerchief to deal with the lipstick.

"Going to be dull around here without you," she said, laughing.

"I understand he's in a rage," Pickering said. "Is there any special reason, or is he just staying in practice?"

"You know why he's mad," she chided. "Where were you, anyway?"

"San Mateo," he said. "I was delayed."

"I could tell," she said, then added, "You may wish you called him and told him."

Most of the "passenger waiting" lights on the call board were lit up, but the elevator operator ignored them as she took him all the way up without stopping. Pick watched annoyed and angry faces as the car rose past people waiting.

"Your ears are clean, but don't give him a chance to look at your feet," the operator said, as she opened the door.

Pickering was surprised to see that the foyer outside the elevator was full of people. Normally the only thing to be found in it were room service or housekeeping carts. He should have known the old man had more in mind than a lamb chop when he said he wanted Pick to have supper with him before he went.

Someone recognized him and giggled, and then applauded. That seemed like a good ideà to the others, and the applause caught on like a brushfire. Pick clasped his hands over his head like a victorious prize fighter. That caused more laughter.

"I believe the Marine Corps has landed," Andrew Foster's voice boomed. "An hour later, and more than likely a dollar short."

"I'm sorry, Grandfather," Pick Pickering said.

"I assume that she was worth it," the old man said. "I can't believe you'd keep your mother and father, not to mention your guests and me, waiting solely because you were riding around on a horse."

(THREE)
Bethlehem, Pennsylvania
21 August 1941

Two cops came to the cell.

"Okay, Joe Louis, on your feet!" one of them said, as the other signaled for the remotely operated door to be opened.

One of the cops came in the cell and stood over Tommy McCoy as he put his feet in his work shoes. When Tommy finally stood up, the cop took handcuffs from a holder on his belt.

"Put your hands behind you," he said.

"Hey, I'm all right now," Tommy said.

"Put your hands behind you," the cop repeated.

As he felt the manacles snap in place around his wrist, Tommy asked, "What happens now?"

The cop ignored him. He took his arm and sort of shoved him out of the cell, then out of the cellblock. They stopped at the property room and picked up their revolvers, then ripped open a brown manila envelope. They tucked his wallet, handkerchief, cigarettes, matches and change in his pockets, and led him out of the building to a parking lot in the rear.

"When do I get something to eat?" Tommy asked.

The cops ignored that question too.

He wasn't so much hungry as thirsty, Tommy thought. He'd really put away the boilermakers the night before, and the only water in the cell had been warm, and brown, and smelled like horse-piss.

What he really needed was a couple of beers, maybe a couple of boilermakers, to straighten himself out.

They took him to the mill to the small brick building just inside the gate. It looked like a regular house but was the place where the mill security police had their office. In there was also a dispensary where they took people until the ambulance arrived.

They led him into the office of the chief of plant security. He wasn't surprised to see him, but he was surprised to see Denny Walkowicz, Assistant Business Manager of Local 3341, United Steel Workers of America, a big, shiny-faced Polack.

No one said hello to Tommy, or offered him a chair.

"What's all this?" Tommy asked.

"You broke his nose, you might like to know," the chief of plant security said. "He said you hit him with a beer bottle."

"Bullshit," Tommy said.

"What do they call that?" the plant security chief said.

"We got him charged with 'assault with a dangerous object,' " one of the cops said.

"That's all?"

"Public drunkenness, resisting arrest," the cop said. "There's more."

"Nobody's asked for his side of it," Denny Walkowicz said.

"His side don't mean a shit, Denny. Let's not start that bullshit all over again."

Another man came into the room. One of the fucking white-collar workers from Personnel. Little shit in a shiny blue suit.

He had an envelope in his hand, which he laid on the table.

"Denny Walkowicz stood up for you, McCoy, Christ only knows why," the plant security chief said. "Here's what we worked out. There's two weeks' severance pay, plus what you earned through last Friday. You take that."

"Or what?"

"Or they take you back to jail."

"You're facing ninety days in the can, kid," Denny Walkowicz said. "At least, maybe a lot more. And it ain't only the time, it's a criminal record."

"For getting in a fight?"

"You don't listen, do you, McCoy?" the plant security chief said. "You hit a guy with a beer bottle, it's not like punching him."

"I told you, I didn't use no bottle."

"Yeah, you said that, but other people say different."

"Well, fuck you!"

"I'm glad you were here and the cops are to hear that, Denny," the chief of plant security said. " 'Using profane or obscene language to a supervisor or member of management shall be grounds for dismissal for cause,' " he quoted.

"He's got you, McCoy," Denny Walkowicz said. "You gotta learn to watch your mouth."

"Take him back to jail," the chief of plant security said, and then picked up the brown envelope and handed it back to the white-collar guy from administration. "Do what you have to," he said. "No severance pay."

"Now wait a minute," Denny Walkowicz said. "We had a deal, we worked this out."

"Nobody tells me, 'fuck you,' " the plant security chief said.

Denny Walkowicz took the envelope back from the white-collar guy.

"You," he said to Tommy McCoy, "keep your fucking mouth shut!"

Then he led him out of the room, with the cops following.

The cops took the handcuffs off him.

"If it was up to me," the larger one said, "you'd do time."

"Yeah, well it ain't up to you, is it?" Denny Walkowicz said.

"If you're smart, McCoy, you won't hang around Bethlehem," the cop said. "You know what I mean?"

As Denny Walkowicz drove Tommy to the boardinghouse in his blue Buick Roadmaster, he said: "You better pay attention to what the cop said. They're after your ass. It took three of them to hold you down, and you kicked one of them in the balls. They're not going to take that."

"That was all the union could do for me?"

"You ungrateful sonofabitch!" Denny Walkowicz exploded. "We kept you from going to jail!"

Tommy went to bed the minute he got to his room. He slept the rest of the day, and except for going out for two beers and some spaghetti about ten that night, slept right around the clock.

At ten-thirty the next morning, he went down to the post office and talked to the recruiter. The guy was especially nice to him after he told him his brother was a Marine, too. He told Tommy that if he enlisted for the duration of the present emergency plus six months, he could fix it for him to be assigned to the same unit as his brother. And when Tommy said that he had always wanted to be a pilot, the recruiter said he could arrange for that, too.

Thomas Michael McCoy was sworn into the United States Marine Corps at 1645 hours that same afternoon. He was transported by bus to the U.S. Navy Yard, Philadelphia, Pennsylvania, the next morning. At Philadelphia, he learned that the recruiter had been something less than honest with him. He wasn't going to be trained as a pilot, but as an infantryman. And the corporal in Philadelphia told him he stood as much chance of being assigned with his brother as he did of being elected pope.

But the corporal felt that professional courtesy to a fellow corporal required that he inform Corporal McCoy that his little brother was on the base awaiting transport to Parris Island. He called Post Locator, and they told him that Corporal McCoy had been the day before transferred to Marine Corps Schools, Quantico, Virginia.

Then the corporal made the connection. This dumb Mick's brother was the China Marine in the campaign hat driving the LaSalle convertible, the one they were sending to officers' school. They sure as Christ made little apples were not two peas from the same pod, he thought.

(FOUR)
Office of the Deputy Chief of Staff for Personnel
Headquarters, United States Marine Corps
Washington, D.C.
29 August 1941

The wooden frame building—designed for no more than five years' usage—had been built during the Great War (1917–18). The Chief of Company-Grade Officer Assignments stood waiting in one of the doorways to catch the eye of the Deputy Chief, Assignments Branch. The doorway sagged.

The Chief of Company-Grade Officer Assignments, a balding, stocky man, had taken off the jacket of his cord suit and rolled up the sleeves of his sweat-soaked white shirt. Standing there with his suspenders exposed, he didn't look much like the captain of Marines he was. He held two documents at his side. One was that week's listing of actual and projected billet vacancies. The other was the service record of MACKLIN, John D., 1st Lt.

The Deputy Chief, Assignments Branch, had been reading with great interest an interoffice memorandum which compared projected Company-Grade Officer Requirements for Fiscal Year 1942 against projected officer recruitment for Fiscal Year 1942 and was wondering where the hell they were going to dig up the 2,195 bodies that represented the difference between what they needed and what they were likely to get. Finally he noticed the Chief of Company-Grade Officer Assignments standing in his door and motioned him inside with a wave of his hand.

The Deputy Chief, Assignments Branch, who had also removed his jacket, was a major—although he looked, and sometimes felt, more like a bureaucrat than a Marine officer.

"How would you like me to handle this, sir?" the Chief of Company-Grade officer assignments asked. He handed the major the documents in his hand.

The major opened the service-record jacket of MACKLIN, John D., 1st Lt.

There was a file of orders concerning the officer in question bound to the record jacket with a metal expanding clip. The order on top, which made it the most recent one, had been issued by the 4th Marines. Lieutenant Macklin, having been decreed excess to the needs of the command, was relieved of duty and would proceed to the United States of America aboard the U.S.S. *Shaumont,* reporting on arrival to Headquarters, USMC, Washington, D.C., for further assignment. A thirty-day delay en route leave was authorized.

Macklin was not really expected to physically report in Washington. His orders and his records would be sent to Washington. When Washington decided what to do with him, either a telegram or a registered letter would be sent to his leave address telling him where to go and when to be there.

In a manila folder were copies of Lieutenant Macklin's efficiency reports, mounted in the same manner as his orders.

"I wonder what he did?" the major asked, without expecting an answer, as he turned his attention to Lieutenant Macklin's most recent efficiency report. Officers were rarely decreed excess to the needs of a command. Commands, as a rule of thumb, generally sent a steady stream of justifications for the assignment of additional officer personnel to carry out their assigned missions.

A civilian, reading the efficiency report, would probably have concluded that it was a frank, confidential appraisal of the strengths and weaknesses of what a civilian would probably think was a typical Marine officer.

He was described as a "tall, lean, and fit" officer of "erect bearing" with "no disfiguring marks or scars." It said that Lieutenant Macklin was "slightly below" the average of his peers in professional knowledge; that he had "adequately discharged the duties assigned to him"; that there was "no indication of abuse of alcoholic beverages or other stimulants"; and that Lieutenant Macklin had "a tendency not to accept blame for his failures, but instead to attempt to shift the blame to subordinates." In this connection, it said that Lieutenant Macklin was prone to submit official reports that both omitted facts that might tend to make him look bad, and "to present other facts in such a manner as to magnify his own contribution to the accomplishment of the assigned mission." It said finally that Lieutenant Macklin "could not be honestly recommended for the command of a company or larger tactical unit at this time."

A civilian would doubtless think that here was a nice-looking erect young man, who was mostly competent, did what he was told to do, and had no problem with the bottle. If there was anything wrong with him at all, it was a perfectly understandable inclination to present only his best side to his superiors. If he could not be recommended to be a company commander at this time, well, he was young, and there would be a chance for that later. In the meantime, there were certainly other places where his "slightly below average professional knowledge" could be put to good use.

In the Corps, Macklin's efficiency report was lethal.

"Jesus, I wonder what the hell he did?" the major repeated.

"The endorsing officer is Chesty Puller," the captain said. "Puller's a hardnose, but he's fair. And you saw how he endorsed it."

" 'The undersigned concurs in this evaluation of this officer,' " the major quoted.

"So what do we do with him?" the captain asked.

"Maybe he got too friendly with some wife?" the major asked.

"I think he got caught writing a false report," the captain said.

"In which he tried to shaft somebody . . ."

"Somebody who worked with him, you saw that remark about 'shifting blame to subordinates'? "

"And got caught," the major agreed. "That would tee Chesty Puller off."

"So what do we do with him?"

"Six months ago, I would ask when he planned to resign," the major said. "But that's no longer an option, is it?"

"No, sir."

"What's open?" the major asked.

"I gave you the list, sir."

The major consulted the week's listing of actual and projected billet vacancies for company-grade officers.

"It says here there's a vacancy for a mess officer at the School Battalion at Quantico. I thought we sent that kid from the hotel school at Cornell down there? Ye Olde Round Peg in Ye Olde Round Hole?"

"He developed a hernia," the captain said. "They sent him to the Navy hospital at Norfolk. It'll be more than ninety days before he's fit for full duty, so they transferred him to the Detachment of Patients."

"I would hate to see someone who has graduated from the Cornell Hotel School assigned anywhere but a kitchen," the major said.

The captain chuckled.

"I've sort of penciled in when he's available for assignment, assigning him to the Marine Barracks here. He'd make a fine assistant officers' club officer."

"Don't let him get away," the major said. "And in the meantime, I think we should send Lieutenant Macklin to Quantico, at least for the time being. All a mess officer does anyway—Cornell Hotel School graduates excepted—is make sure nobody's selling the rations."

"Aye, aye, sir," the chief of company-grade officer assignments said. And then he thought of something else: "We've got another one, sir."

"Somebody else with an efficiency report like that?" the major asked, incredulously.

"No, sir. Another hotelier. Is that right?"

The major nodded.

"One of the kids starting the Platoon Leader's course listed his current occupation as resident manager of the Andrew Foster Hotel in San Francisco. That sounded a little odd for a twenty-one-year-old, so I checked on it."

"And he really was?"

"He really was. And not only because he's Andrew Foster's grandson."

"Our cup runneth over," the major said. "Don't let that one get away, either. Maybe something can be done about the quality of the chow after all."

"Aye, aye, sir," the captain repeated with a smile.

IX

(ONE)
U.S. Marine Corps Schools
Quantico, Virginia
29 August 1941

The man at the wheel of the spotless Chevrolet pickup truck was Master Gunnery Sergeant Jack (NMI)[1] Stecker, USMC. Stecker was a tall, muscular, tanned, erect man of forty-one who looked the way a master gunnery sergeant, USMC, with twenty-five years in the Corps, was supposed to look.

He was in stiffly starched, impeccably pressed khakis. A vertical crease ran precisely through the buttons of the shirt pockets to the shoulders seam on the front of the shirt. There were four creases on the rear: One ran horizontally across the back of his shoulders. The other three ran down the back, one on each side, and one down the middle. There were a total of six pockets on his khaki shirt and trousers. Two were in use. Stecker's left hip pocket held his wallet; and his right shirt pocket held a small, thin notebook and a silver-plated Parker pen-and-pencil set. The other pockets were sealed shut with starch, and would remain sealed shut.

The keys to his office, to his quarters, and to his personal automobile, a 1939 Packard Phaeton, as well as a Saint Christopher medal, were on a second dogtag cord worn around his neck.

Stecker did not think it fitting that the uniform of a master gunnery sergeant, USMC, should bulge in any way. There was a handkerchief in his left sock. Sometimes, not often, when he knew he would be away from another source of smoking material for a considerable period of time, he carried a package of Lucky Strike cigarettes and a book of matches in his right sock. Mostly, he kept his smoking material in various convenient places—the glove compartment of the pickup, his desk drawer, and sometimes (if he knew he was not going to have to remove his campaign hat) in the crown of the hat.

Master Gunnery Sergeant Jack Stecker, USMC, turned off the macadam Range Road and slowed the Chevrolet pickup as he approached the barrier, a weighted pole, barring access to the ranges.

As it often is in Virginia in late August, it was hot and muggy, and Jack Stecker had rolled the driver's-side window down. But as he approached the Known Distance Rifle Range close enough to hear the firing, he rolled the window up. The crack of .30-caliber rifle fire does more than make your ears ring; it permanently damages your hearing if you get enough of it.

A large red flag hung limply from a twenty-five-foot pole, signaling that the range was in use. A young Marine had been assigned to bar access to the range by unauthorized personnel, and to raise the barrier to pass authorized personnel. He was about twenty-one, his nose was sunburned, and he wore utilities, a World

[1]No Middle Initial.

War I–style helmet, a web cartridge belt (from which hung a canteen and a first-aid packet), and had a U.S. Rifle, Caliber .30, Model 1903A3, slung over his shoulder by its leather sling.

When Master Gunnery Sergeant Jack Stecker first saw him, the young man with the sunburned nose was standing five feet from the flagpole. And Jack Stecker had no doubt that the young man (who looked like a boot about to graduate from the Recruit Depot at Parris Island, but who was in fact an officer candidate about to graduate from the Platoon Leader's Course and become a commissioned officer, second lieutenant, in the Marines) had probably been leaning on the pole. He had also probably propped the Springfield against the flagpole.

Stecker was not offended. What was important was that he had not caught him failing in his duties as a guard. He would have burned him a new asshole if he had caught him doing what he damned well knew he had been doing, but he had not.

When the trainee, recognizing Master Gunnery Sergeant Stecker's Chevrolet pickup, had quickly raised the weighted pole barrier, he was rewarded for his efforts by a slight but unmistakable nod of Stecker's head. The trainee nodded back, and smiled shyly—and with some relief. He had been forced to make a decision, and it had turned out to be the right one.

When he first recognized the pickup as Master Gunnery Sergeant Stecker's, he hadn't been sure whether Stecker expected him to raise the barrier immediately, or to bar Stecker's path until he had satisfied himself that Master Gunnery Sergeant Stecker indeed had official business on the range.

He had decided in the end that the safest course was to presume that whatever Master Gunnery Sergeant Stecker wanted to do on the Quantico reservation was official business and that it was not his role to question him about it.

It had not been difficult to differentiate Master Gunnery Sergeant Stecker's pickup from the perhaps fifty identical 1940 Chevrolet pickups on the Quantico reservation. Stecker's personal pickup was very likely the cleanest, most highly polished pickup in the Marine Corps, perhaps in the world.

When Master Gunnery Sergeant Stecker telephoned the motor sergeant to announce that he was through for the day with his transport, a motor pool corporal went to Base Headquarters to fetch it. He then drove it to the motor pool, where he examined the odometer to see how many miles Stecker had driven that day. He then filled out the trip ticket with probable, if wholly imaginary, destinations to correspond with the miles driven. It was universally recognized that Master Gunnery Sergeant Stecker had more important things to do with his time than fill out forms like a fucking clerk.

With that done, the vehicle went through prescribed daily maintenance. The fuel tank was filled; the tire pressure checked; and the oil level and radiator water replenished. The vehicle was then turned over to whatever enlisted men had run afoul of Rocks and Shoals; had gone to Office Hours; and were now performing punitive extra duty in the motor pool.

They washed the vehicle with soap and water, every inch of it, inside and out—except for the glove compartment, which was off limits. When the vehicle was washed and dried, it was swept out with whisk brooms, making sure there was no dust or sand in the cracks of the rubber covering of the running board or between the wooden planks of the bed. The vehicle was then inspected by the motor transport corporal. If the wax polish seemed to need touching up, the pickup was waxed. When it was finally judged likely to meet Master Gunnery Sergeant Stecker's standards, it was parked overnight inside, in the hoist section of the garage.

In the morning, a motor transport corporal drove the pickup to Base Headquarters, where he parked it in a space marked FOR OFFICIAL VISITORS ONLY, so that it would be available should Master Gunnery Sergeant Stecker need transport.

When the first Trucks, one-quarter ton, four-by-four, General Purpose (called "Jeeps") had been issued to Quantico, it had been proposed to Master Gunnery Sergeant Stecker that one be assigned to him, with a driver, for his use. Stecker had somewhat icily informed the motor transport sergeant that even though he could doubtless spare someone to spend most of his duty day sitting around with his thumb up his ass waiting to drive somebody someplace, he certainly could find real work for him to do that would be of value to the Corps.

Master Gunnery Sergeant Stecker had other reasons to refuse the assignment of a jeep and driver. One of them was that a driver would come to know where he went, and why, and talk about it at night in the barracks. The less the men knew where he went and what he did, the better. Neither could Master Gunnery Sergeant Stecker see any reason why he should exchange a perfectly satisfactory vehicle, which came with nicely upholstered seats and roll-up windows, for a small open truck with thin canvas-covered pads to cushion his bottom.

There was absolutely nothing that Stecker could find wrong, which is to say unmilitary, in finding comfort wherever it might be found. In his twenty-five years of service, he had been acutely uncomfortable on more occasions than he liked to remember. And there was no question whatever in his mind that he would be made acutely uncomfortable again—possibly, the Corps being what it was, as soon as tomorrow.

It was not necessary to train to be uncomfortable. That came naturally, like taking a leak.

When Master Gunnery Sergeant Stecker reached the Known Distance rifle range itself, he put wax plugs in his ears to protect them from the damaging crack of riflefire, and then got out of his pickup and approached the Range Tower. Pretending not to see the range officer, a young lieutenant who was in the tower itself, he examined the firing records, checked over two weapons that had failed to function, and the general police of the area; then discreetly inquired of the range sergeant how the new range officer was working out.

"He's all right, Gunny," the range sergeant said. "Better than most second lieutenants, to tell you the truth."

Stecker nodded. Then, with hands folded against the small of his back and the range sergeant trailing him, he marched to one end of the firing line, pausing now and again when the targets were marked or to stand behind one prone rifleman and his coach. Then he reversed course and marched to the other end. He found nothing that required correction. He really hadn't expected to. Except for the general truth that the way to keep things running smoothly was to keep your eye on them, there had really been no reason for him to "have a look" at the range.

Then he returned to the pickup and drove back to his office.

There was a glistening LaSalle convertible in one of the "Official Visitor" parking spaces. Stecker had almost bought a LaSalle convertible. Although he considered his Packard Phaeton to be a fine piece of machinery, sometimes he wished he had gone to the LaSalle. It wouldn't have cost nearly so much money, and it was, under the skin, a Cadillac. And there would not have been so many eyebrows raised at a Master Gunnery Sergeant driving a LaSalle.

The question was how could an enlisted man, even one in the highest enlisted grade, afford the monthly payments on a Packard Phaeton? The answer was that there were no monthly payments. He had paid cash on the barrel head for it. And the reason cash was available to pay for it was that shortly after he had married, when he was a twenty-one-year-old sergeant, he had gone out on payday and got tanked and blown most of his pay in a poker game.

Elly gave him what he later came to call "her look." Then she put it to him simply: Not only was he a damned fool, but she was in the family way, and if the marriage wasn't going to work, it would be better if they faced it and called it off. Either she would handle the money from now on, or she was going home to Tatamy the next day.

She then put him on an allowance, like a little boy, and kept him on it even later, when he'd gotten more stripes. When the kids were big enough, she'd gotten her teacher's certificate and gone to work. And it wasn't just her making the buffalo on the nickels squeal before she parted with one; Elly put the money to work.

Right from the first, she had started buying and selling things. She would read the "Unofficial" section of the Daily Bulletin looking for bargains for sale. She didn't only buy things to use (like kids' clothes and from time to time a nice piece of furniture), she bought things to resell. And she was good at buying things and selling them. She told him once that she had a twenty-five percent rule: She wouldn't buy anything unless she could buy it for twenty-five percent less than what somebody was asking for it, and she wouldn't sell it for less than twenty-five percent more than she had paid for it.

So the boys' college fund kept growing. Elly was determined from the beginning that the boys would go to college. And then, as the fund grew, her determination changed to "the boys would go to a *good* college."

In '34, when the Depression was really bad (Jack Stecker was a staff sergeant then), the bank had foreclosed on her brother Fritz's house in Tatamy. Elly took a chance and put in a bid at the sheriff's auction. Most everybody else in Tatamy had been laid off from Bethlehem Steel, too, and not many people wanted an old three-family row house anyway. So she got it at a steal and without the down payment really making a big dent in the boys' college fund.

Fritz went on living in what had been his apartment, and his oldest son and his family in another—neither of them paying rent, because they were out of work—but the third was rented out for nearly enough money to make the mortgage payment.

Jack Stecker hadn't said anything to her, because he always considered the boys' college money to really be Elly's money, and if she wanted to help her family out when they were in a bind, he understood that, too.

He came later to understand that what Elly had really done was put the money to work, and that if it also made things a little easier for her brother and nephew, fine, but that wasn't the reason she had bought the house.

Neither Fritz nor his kid paid any rent until they got called back by Bethlehem Steel, Fritz in '37, his kid not until '39. When Fritz complained that paying back rent was a hell of a thing for a sister to ask of her own brother, Elly told him that she was charging him two percent less than the bank would have charged him, that he knew damned well that the bank would not have loaned a laid-off steel worker a dime, and that he and his family would have been put out on the street.

Then she offered to sell him the house back at what an appraiser called the "fair market value." And she would carry the mortgage herself. So they had the house appraised and added what Fritz and his son owed for back rent to that, and Fritz was paying it off by the month at six percent interest. Not to Elly anymore. Elly had sold the mortgage to the Easton Bank & Trust Company. And that money had gone into the boys' college fund.

And then, as it turned out, they didn't need the boys' college fund at all. He'd gone home one afternoon and saw her with "her look." But Elly waited until he had changed out of his uniform, taken his beer from the icebox, and listened to the "Burns & Allen" program on the radio. Then she made room for herself on the footstool and handed him a paperbound book.

"You ever see this?" she asked.

Sure, he'd seen it. It was the catalog of the United States Naval Academy.

"You ever read it?" she asked.

"I glanced through it," he said, somewhat defensively. It was difficult for a master gunnery sergeant, USMC, to admit to anyone, including his wife, that there was any aspect of the Naval Service of the United States with which he was not intimately familiar.

"God, Jack," Elly said, disgusted. "You sometimes are a really thick-headed Dutchman!"

She handed him the catalog, open, with a passage marked in red ink.

"Additionally, an unlimited number of appointments are available noncompetitively to sons of winners of the Medal of Honor."

Jack Stecker never wore the Medal, but it was in the strongbox, together with a copy of the citation, and a non-yellowing photograph of General "Black Jack" Pershing hanging it around his neck.

> In the name of the American people, the Congress of the United States awards the Medal of Honor to Sergeant Jack NMI Stecker, USMC, for valor in action above and beyond the call of duty in the vicinity of Belleau Wood, near Château-Thierry, France, during the period June 6 to June 9, 1918. CITATION: Sergeant (then Corporal) Stecker, in command of a squad of United States Marines participating in an assault upon German positions on June 6, was grievously wounded in the leg. When it became necessary for American forces to temporarily break off the attack and reform prior to a second attack, Sergeant Stecker refused evacuation and, despite his wounds, established himself in a position from which he could bring rifle fire to bear upon the enemy.
>
> During the nights of June 6 through June 8, without regard to either his wound or the great risk to his life posed by incessant small arms and artillery fire, Sergeant Stecker searched the area between the lines of the opposing forces (commonly referred to as "no-man's-land") for other U.S. Marines who had also been unable or unwilling to withdraw to safe positions.
>
> Not only did Sergeant Stecker save the lives of many of these wounded men by administering first aid to them, but, inspiring them by his personal example of valor in the face of overwhelming odds, formed them into a 24-man-strong fighting force and established a rifle and machine-gun position from which, when the second, successful assault was launched on June 9, he laid a withering fire on German positions which otherwise would have been able to bring fire to bear on attacking American Forces with a resultant great loss of life.
>
> During the fighting involved during the second assault, Sergeant Stecker was wounded twice more, and suffered great loss of blood and excruciating pain. Despite his wounds and pain, Sergeant Stecker remained in command, inspiring his subordinates with his courage and coolness under fire until he lost consciousness.
>
> Sergeant Stecker's valor and dedication to duty are in keeping with the highest traditions of the United States Marine Corps and the Naval Service.
>
> Entered the Naval Service from Pennsylvania.

So the boys had gone to service academies, Jack Jr. to Annapolis, and Richard to West Point. Jack was an ensign on the Battleship *Arizona* in the Pacific Fleet in Pearl Harbor, and Richard would graduate next June and take a commission as a second lieutenant of Marines.

Elly had waited until she was sure the boys were set, then she had used some—not much—of what was now "the retirement fund" to buy him the Packard Phaeton. He was entitled, she said, and you only live once.

Three people were waiting outside Master Gunnery Sergeant Jack Stecker's office when he reached it: a staff sergeant, a PFC, and a corporal. He nodded at them, said, "Be with you in a minute," and went inside. When his clerk delivered his coffee, he would tell Stecker what they wanted.

He knew the staff sergeant; he was from Post housing, and that was personal, so it could wait. And he supposed the PFC was carrying some kind of message, and that could wait too. But the corporal was completely unfamiliar to Stecker, and he was a little curious about him.

The coffee (black, brewed no more than thirty minutes before; Stecker could not stand stale coffee) was delivered in a white china mess-hall mug within sixty seconds of his sitting down behind his desk.

"Sergeant Quinn's here about your quarters," Stecker's clerk, a corporal, said. "The PFC was sent by the first sergeant of 'B' Company. Your wife called and said if you could come home early that would be nice. And the colonel says he'd like to see you when you have time, nothing important."

"And the China Marine?" Stecker asked.

"You mean the corporal?" the clerk asked. Stecker nodded, barely perceptibly. "How do you know he's a China Marine?"

"What does he want?" Stecker asked, deciding that he would not mention the young corporal's embroidered-to-his-shirt chevrons, one of the marks of a China Marine.

"Wouldn't say," the clerk said. "Wants to see you. I seen him drive up. You see that LaSalle convertible when you come in?"

"Send the corporal in," Stecker said.

(TWO)

Corporal Kenneth J. "Killer" McCoy walked into the room, looked at Stecker, and said, "Thank you, Gunny."

Stecker liked that. The kid hadn't tried to kiss his ass with "Good afternoon, Sergeant, I'm sorry to bother you" or some candy-ass remark like that. But he was polite, and recognized that Master Gunnery Sergeants were busy men, and that he appreciated this one giving him a little bit of his time.

Stecker liked what else he saw. Aside from the embroidered-to-the-garment chevrons and the khaki fore-and-aft cap this young corporal looked the way Stecker liked his young corporals to look. Neat, trim, and military. And as far as the China stripes were concerned, if he had his way everybody would wear them.

"When did you ship home from China?" Stecker asked.

"It shows, does it?" McCoy said, smiling.

"Yeah," Stecker said. "Could you use some coffee?"

"Sure could," McCoy said.

"Doan!" Stecker raised his voice. "One java!"

"Reporting in, are you?" Stecker guessed, and then guessed again: "With a problem?"

"I've got until midnight tomorrow," McCoy said.

"Between now and midnight tomorrow," Stecker said, "get yourself a campaign hat."

McCoy chuckled.

"That's funny?"

"I just came from the Navy Yard in Philly," McCoy said. "The first thing the first sergeant said to me there was 'get rid of the campaign hat.' "

"That was there, this is here," Stecker said. "What were you doing in Philly? You ship home the long way around?"

"I shipped home to Diego on a tincan," McCoy said. "Diego shipped me to Philly via Portsmouth."

"Prisoner-chasing?" Stecker asked, and when McCoy nodded, went on: "Then you must just have bought the LaSalle."

He enjoyed the look of surprise on the kid's face, but left him wondering until after Doan delivered the coffee and left. "My clerk doesn't miss much," he said.

"Just bought it," McCoy said.

"Like it?"

"Except that it drinks gas, I like it fine," McCoy said.

"What kind of a rice bowl did you have going for you in China?" Stecker asked, and again enjoyed the look of surprise on the kid's face. "To bring home enough money to buy a car like that?"

"I spent a lot of time on back roads, drawing ration money," McCoy said.

"Motor transport?"

"Sort of," McCoy said.

"What do you mean, 'sort of'?"

"That's my skill," McCoy said.

"And you made corporal on one hitch, driving a truck?"

"Yeah," McCoy said.

"Why don't I believe that?" Stecker asked.

"I don't know," McCoy said. "It's the truth."

"You must have got along pretty good with the motor officer," Stecker said. The translation of that was, "You must have had your nose pretty far up his ass."

"Most of the time, I worked for an officer at regiment," McCoy said.

"I did a hitch, '35–'37, with the Fourth Marines," Stecker said. "I guess I still know some of the officers. Who did you work for?"

"Captain Banning," McCoy said.

Stecker was very pleased to hear that. It reconfirmed his first judgment of the young corporal. (His second, more negative judgment sprang from questions about his making corporal in one hitch in motor transport.) Ed Banning was the China Marines' S-2. If this kid had been made a corporal by Banning, that was a whole hell of a lot different from making it as an ass-licker.

"Ed Banning and I were in Nicaragua together in '29," Stecker said. "He was a lieutenant then. He was a good officer."

"He is a good officer," McCoy agreed.

"Well, what can I do for you, Corporal?" Stecker asked.

"Got a problem, Gunny," McCoy said, and added wryly: "And when I was a young Marine, at Parris Island, they told me whenever I had a problem I couldn't deal with myself, I should take it to the gunny."

Stecker smiled at him. The kid had a sense of humor.

"Just think of me as your father, son, and tell Daddy all," Stecker said.

"I need to get that LaSalle registered on the post," McCoy said.

"What's the problem? Unsafe? Or inadequate insurance?"

"No, I'm sure it'll pass the safety inspection, and I'm insured up to my ass."

Those were two of the three problems with a corporal getting a POV (Privately Owned Vehicle) registered on the post. Stecker now asked about the third:

"You lost your driver's license. Speeding or drunk driving?"

"I'm in the Platoon Leader's Course," McCoy said. "And a fat-bellied PFC over in Vehicle Registration got his rocks off telling me that means I can't have a car on the post."

Now Stecker was surprised. The Platoon Leader's Course was designed to turn college kids, not China Marine corporals, into second lieutenants. But now that he thought about it, he'd heard that starting with this class, they were going to slip some young Marines in with college kids. It was sort of an experiment, to see if they could hack it. The Marines in the course would be like this one, on their first hitch, or maybe starting their second, kids without enough experience to get a direct commission, but who had been judged to be above average.

"He's right," Stecker said. "You can't. No cars, civilian clothes, personal weapons, or dirty books or pictures."

"What am I supposed to do with it?"

"You should have read the instructions, Corporal," Stecker said, "the part where it said, 'don't take no POV's, civvies, weapons or dirty pictures.' "

"I don't have any instructions," McCoy said. "I don't even have any orders. I'm traveling VOCO (Verbal Order Commanding Officer)."

"He must have been pretty sure you were selected," Stecker said.

"He was on the board," McCoy said. "And as fast as this has gone, I've been wondering if the Corps didn't ship me home from China for this officer shit."

"Officer shit?" Stecker parroted. "You don't want to be an officer?"

"I didn't mean that the way it sounded, Gunny," McCoy said. "But I walked over and had a look at the school before I came over here. It reminded me that I'm a China Marine, not a college boy."

"You better not tell anybody that when you start the course," Stecker said. "One of the things they expect is enthusiasm. You better act as if your one great desire in the whole world is to pin a gold bar on your shoulder, or you'll get shipped out so quick it'll take your asshole six weeks to catch up with you."

McCoy chuckled. "That's what I mean about being a Marine, and not a college boy. I *know* about second lieutenants. Would you want to be a second lieutenant, Gunny?" McCoy challenged.

Stecker thought, *No, I wouldn't want to be a second lieutenant. I really don't want to be an officer, period.*

"Then you shouldn't have applied," Stecker said.

"The ways were greased," McCoy said.

"What do you mean by that?"

"I mean that an officer I knew in China asked me at nine o'clock one morning if I had ever heard of the Platoon Leader Program. I was through with the selection board before lunch three days later," McCoy said.

"But if you don't want to be an officer, then I guess you've wasted his effort, and the Corps' money and time coming here at all," Stecker said.

"Don't get me wrong, Gunny," McCoy said. "I'm going to go through that course. The minute I report in, I'm going to be the eagerest sonofabitch to get a commission they ever saw."

"Why?"

"Well, I thought that over, driving down here," McCoy said. "Asked myself what the fuck I was doing, why I hadn't told them what they could do with a gold bar in Philly. The answer is, why not? I'm a good Marine. I'll probably make as good a temporary officer as most of the college kids, and probably better than some of them. And since they greased the ways like they have—at least a couple of officers think I would make a good second lieutenant—who the hell am I to argue with them?"

"You seem pretty sure you won't bilge out of the course," Stecker said.

"Gunny, I'm a good Marine. I'll get through that course. My problem is what do I do with my car when I'm over there being eager as hell?"

"Where you from?"

"Pennsylvania, Norristown."

"If you left now, you could drive there, leave the car, catch a train, and be back here by midnight tomorrow. If you were a little late, so long as it was before reveille on the second, I could take care of that."

"I got no place to leave it."

"I thought you said your home was in Norristown."

"I said 'I'm from Norristown,' " McCoy said. "My home is the Corps."

"Then I guess you'll have to park it outside the gate," Stecker said.

"Yeah, and have it either stolen or fucked up, the roof cut."

"Hey, you're a Marine corporal, wants to be a Marine officer, you don't know a regulation's a regulation?"

McCoy looked at him, and Stecker saw anger, regret, and resignation in his eyes. But he didn't say anything, and he didn't beg.

"Thanks for the coffee, Gunny," McCoy said. "And your time."

He got up and walked toward the door.

"McCoy," Stecker called, and McCoy stopped and turned around.

"Forget what I said about getting a campaign hat. That was before I knew you were going to be a student. Students wear cunt caps like that [a soft cap, sometimes called an "overseas" cap]. Makes them easy to tell from Marines."

"Thanks," McCoy said.

"Doan!" Stecker called, raising his voice. "Send in the sergeant from Post Housing."

The sergeant came into the office with all the paperwork involved in turning in one set of government quarters and their furnishings so as to draw another set of quarters and furnishings. Stecker was moving—moving up. Though he thought about *that* pretty much the way McCoy did. Stecker took his Parker pen from his shirt pocket and began to write his signature, in a neat, round hand, where the forms were marked with small penciled *x*s.

Then he suddenly sat up straight in his chair and spun it around so that he could look out the window. He saw Corporal McCoy unlocking the door of the pretty LaSalle convertible that sure as Christ made little apples was going to get all fucked up if he had to leave it parked outside the gate.

Master Gunnery Sergeant Stecker leaned out the window.

"Corporal McCoy!" he bellowed.

McCoy looked around for him.

"Hold it right there, Corporal McCoy!"

He sat down again and, as quickly as he could, signed the rest of the forms. Then he stood up and went in the outer office.

"I'm going," he said.

"You going to see the colonel first?" Doan asked.

"I have an appointment with the colonel at oh-eight-thirty the day after tomorrow. Whatever's on his mind will have to wait until then."

"You coming back?" Doan asked.

"No. Have the motor pool fetch the truck," Stecker ordered.

"Is there anything else I can do for you?" Doan asked.

"Not a goddamned thing, Corporal Doan," Stecker snapped. "Not a goddamned thing."

He glowered at him a moment, and then added: "But I'll tell you this, Doan. I told the colonel that it was possible that under all your baby fat, there just might be a Marine, and that he could probably do worse than making you a sergeant. You're on orders as of 1 September. Try, at least, to act like a sergeant, Doan."

Now why the hell did I tell him? It was supposed to be a surprise.

"What do I tell anybody who calls?" Doan asked.

The fat little fucker is so surprised at the promotion that he looks like he might bawl. Hell of a thing for a Marine sergeant to be doing.

"Tell them to take a flying fuck at a rolling doughnut," Stecker said and, pleased with himself, marched out of the office."

He walked up to Corporal McCoy, where he was waiting by his LaSalle.

"I have a black Packard Phaeton machine, Corporal McCoy," he said, and pointed to it. "You will get in your machine and follow me."

"Where we going?"

"Wherever the hell I decide to take you," Stecker said.

McCoy followed him six blocks, ending up at the rear of the red-brick single-story building that housed the provost marshal's office. Next to it was an area enclosed by an eight-foot-high cyclone fence, topped with barbed wire. Every ten feet along its length was a red sign reading, MILITARY POLICE IMPOUNDING AREA OFF LIMITS. Inside a fence were a dozen vehicles, mostly civilian, but with several Marine Corps trucks mingled among them.

There was no one near the gate to the fenced-in area, so Stecker blew his horn, a steady ten-second blast, and then another. He saw that he had attracted the attention of the people in the provost marshal's building. His Packard was as well known as his pickup truck.

He motioned for Corporal McCoy to get out of his LaSalle and come to the Packard.

A minute later, the provost sergeant came out of the building and walked quickly over to him.

"What can I do for you, Gunny?" he asked.

"This is Corporal McCoy," Stecker said. "After you register his car and issue him a sticker for it, he will place his vehicle in the Impound Yard. From time to time, he will require access to his vehicle, to run the engine, for example. Therefore, you will put him on the list of people who are authorized access to the Impound Yard. Any questions?"

"Whatever you say, Gunny," the provost sergeant said. "Can he take the car out if he wants?"

"It's his car," Stecker said. He turned to McCoy. "I think that's all the business we have, McCoy," he said.

"Thanks, Gunny," McCoy said.

"In the future, McCoy, be very careful when you tell somebody you don't think much of officers or that you have doubts about being one yourself. You just might run into some chickenshit sonofabitch with bars on his collar who will take offense."

"I will," McCoy said. "Thanks again, Gunny."

"It would be a damned shame to have a good-looking machine like your LaSalle fucked up," Stecker said, and got behind the wheel of his Packard and drove home.

(THREE)

Elly was home. Her Ford was in the drive. He wondered why she asked him to come home early. Probably because she knew him well enough to worry that otherwise he would head for the NCO Club, establish himself at the bar reserved for senior noncoms, and start drinking hard liquor. She knew him well enough, too, not to call the office and order him home, or call the office and start whining and begging for him to come home. What she'd said was that "if he could come that would be nice."

So he was home. That was nice.

The sign (MASTER GUNNERY SERGEANT J. STECKER, USMC) was still on the lawn, equidistant between the driveway and the walkway, as housing regulations required, a precise four feet off the sidewalk. He wouldn't need that sign anymore; there'd be a new sign on the new quarters. He would have to remember to take this one down first thing in the morning. Or maybe, so that he wouldn't forget it, after dark tonight.

He entered the small brick house (the new quarters would be just a little bigger, now that the boys were gone and they didn't need the room) by the kitchen door, opened the icebox and helped himself to a beer.

"I'm home," he called.

"I'm in the bedroom," Elly called.

He went into the living room and turned on the radio.

Jesus Christ, it's been a long time since I came home and she made that kind of announcement. But all she meant by it, obviously, was that she happened to be in the bedroom. That was all.

She came into the living room.

"Where were you, Jack?" Elly asked.

"What do you mean, 'where was I'?" he asked.

"Doan came by," she said. "He said you walked off without your orders, and he thought you might need them. He said you told him you were going home."

She had the orders in her hand. She extended them to him.

"I've read them," he said. "I know what they say."

She shrugged.

"It was nice of Doan, I thought," Elly said. "He told me you got him sergeant's stripes. That was nice of you, Jack."

"So you called the NCO Club and asked for me, and I wasn't there, right?" he said, unpleasantly.

"You know better than that, Jack," Elly said, and he knew he'd hurt her.

"A kid came into the office," Jack Stecker said. "A China Marine, a corporal."

"Oh?"

"He worked for Ed Banning over there," Stecker went on. "Banning got him sent to the Platoon Leader's Course."

"And he came in to say hello for Ed Banning?"

"He came in because he's got a LaSalle convertible machine, and the kids in the Platoon Leader Program aren't supposed to have cars with them, and the provost marshal wouldn't give him a post sticker for it."

"Oh," she said.

"At first, I thought he reminded me of Jack," Stecker said. "Nice kid. Good-looking. Smart. But then I realized that he reminded me of me."

"Good looking and smart?" she teased.

"Like I was when I was a corporal," he said.

"I remember when you were a corporal," she said.

"He doesn't want to be an officer," Stecker said. "At least not very much."

"Neither did you," she said. "They would have sent you to Annapolis, if you had wanted to go."

"I wanted to get married," he said.

"You didn't want to be an officer," she said.

"I still don't, Elly," he said.

She started to say something, then changed her mind.

"Could you help him about his car?" she asked.

"I fixed it so he could leave it in the MP impounding area," he said. "That's where I was."

"I knew if you could come home early, you would," Elly said.

"Why did you want me to?" he asked.

"I bought you a present," she said. "I was afraid it wouldn't come in time, but it did, and I wanted to give it to you."

"What kind of a present?" he asked. "You keep this up, there won't be anything left in the retirement fund."

"Come in the bedroom, and I'll give it to you," Elly said.

"You give me a present in the bedroom, and I'll come home early all the time," he said.

Elly ignored him and walked toward the bedroom.

He got up, put his beer bottle down, turned the radio off, and walked into their bedroom.

There was a complete uniform on the bed.

"What the hell is this?" he said. "What did you do, go by the clothing store?"

"This comes from Brooks Brothers in New York City," she said. "I asked Doris Means where I should buy them, and that's where Doris said to go."

"You're now calling the colonel's wife by her first name?"

"I've known her for twenty years, Jack," Elly said. "She said I was to call her by her first name."

He looked down at the uniform. Good-looking uniform, he thought. First-class material. It had certainly cost an arm and a leg.

"Well?" she said. "Nothing to say?"

"Looks a little bare," he said. "No chevrons, no hash marks."

"Attention to orders," Elly said. Stecker looked at her in surprise. She had the orders in her hand, and was reading from them:

"Headquarters, United States Marine Corps, Washington, D.C., General Orders Number 145, dated 15 August 1941. Paragraph 6. Master Gunnery Sergeant Jack NMI Stecker 38883, Hq Company, USMC Schools, Quantico, Virginia, is Honorably Discharged from the Naval Service for the convenience of the government effective 31 August 1941. Paragraph 7. Captain Jack NMI Stecker, 44003 USMC Reserve is ordered to active duty for a period of not less than three years with duty station USMC Schools, Quantico, Virginia, effective 1 September 1941. General Officer commanding Quantico is directed to insure compliance with applicable regulations involved with the discharge of an enlisted man for the purpose of accepting a commission as an officer. For the Commandant, USMC, James B. McArne, Brigadier General, USMC."

"Well," Stecker said, "now that you've read it out loud, I suppose that makes it official?"

"Aren't you going to try it on?" Elly asked, ignoring him.

"I'm not sure I'm supposed to," he said. "I'm not an officer yet."

"Put it on, Jack," Elly said. "You can't put it off any longer."

He reached for the blouse and started to put his arm in a sleeve.

"No!" Elly stopped him. "Do it right, Jack."

He stripped to his underwear, then put on the shirt and the trousers, and then tied the necktie. Then he put on the tunic, and the Sam Browne belt, and the sword, and even the hat.

"You look just fine, Jack," Elly said. She sounded funny, and when he looked at her, she was dabbing at her eyes with a handkerchief.

"What the hell are you crying about?" Stecker asked.

She shrugged and blew her nose, loudly.

He examined his reflection in the mirror. He looked very strange, he thought. Very strange indeed. He saw for the first time that there was something new in his array of medal and campaign ribbons, an inch-long blue one dotted with silver stars, the one he never wore, the ribbon representing the Medal of Honor.

"What did you do that for?" he challenged.

"Colonel Means said to," she said. "And he said when you asked about it, I should tell you that he said that he expects his officers to wear all of their decorations, and that includes you, too."

"You really like this, don't you? Me being an officer?"

"All these years, Jack," Elly said, "I wondered if I did right, marrying you."

"Thanks a lot," he said, purposefully misunderstanding her.

"Otherwise, you would have gone to Annapolis," she went on. "And you would have been a major, maybe a lieutenant colonel, by now."

"Or I would have bilged out of Annapolis and taken up with a bar girl in Diego," he said. "I don't have any regrets, Elly."

"I don't have any regrets, either," she said. "But you deserve those bars, Jack. You should have been an officer a long time ago."

He turned to look at his reflection again.

"Maybe," Elly said, "you should take it off now, so it'll be fresh when you get sworn in."

He looked at her again. She was unbuttoning her dress.

"Don't look so surprised," she said softly. "I probably shouldn't tell you this, but I've always wanted to go to bed with a Marine officer."

"I'm not a Marine officer yet," he said. "Not until oh-eight-thirty day after tomorrow."

"Then I guess you want to wait till then?" she asked.

"No, what the hell," Captain-designate Jack NMI Stecker, USMC, Reserve, said. "Take what you can whenever you can get it, I always say."

X

(ONE)
Quantico, Virginia
1 September 1941

The U.S. Rifle, Caliber .30, M1, was known as the Garand, after its inventor, John B. Garand, a civilian employee of the U.S. Army's Springfield Arsenal. The Garand fired the same cartridge as the U.S. Rifle, Model 1903, the U.S. Rifle, Model 1903A3, and the Browning light machine guns. This cartridge was known as the .30-06.

The 1903-series rifles, known as "Springfields," were five-shot rifles, operated by a bolt. This bolt was a variation of the action designed by the Mauserwerke in Germany in the late 1800s and had been adapted by the United States after the Spanish-American war. The Spanish Army's Mausers were clearly superior to the American rifles. And when Theodore Roosevelt, who had faced the Spanish Mausers on his march up Kettle and San Juan Hills in Cuba, became President, pretty nearly his first order as Commander in Chief was to provide the military services with a Mauser-type weapon. A royalty was paid to the Mauser Company, and the Springfield Arsenal began manufacture of a near-copy of the Mauser Model 1898, differing from it in caliber and some minor details.

The Spanish Mausers had 7-mm bores, and the German 7.92. The Springfield Rifles had .30-caliber (7.62-mm) bores. In 1906, an improved .30 caliber was developed, which became known as the .30-06. The Springfield rifles served in World War I, where they proved reliable, efficient, and extremely accurate.

Development of the Garand began in the early 1930's, when General Douglas MacArthur was Army Chief of Staff. It was accepted for service, and production began in 1937.

It had a magazine capacity of eight rounds, as opposed to the Springfield's five. Far more important, it was semiautomatic. Once a spring clip of eight rounds was loaded into the weapon and the bolt permitted to move forward, it would fire the eight rounds as rapidly as the marksman could pull the trigger. When the last shot was fired, the clip was ejected, the bolt remained in its rearward position, and another eight-round clip could be quickly loaded.

The Ordnance Corps of the United States Army (which is charged with providing every sort of weaponry, from pistols to artillery, to the United States Marine Corps) was convinced that it was the best infantry rifle in the world. In the opinion of most Marines, the U.S. Rifle Caliber .30, M1 "Garand" was a Buck Rogers piece of shit with which only the lucky could hit a barn door at ten paces.

Experience had taught the Corps that skilled marksmen were very often the key to victory in a battle. Experience had further taught the Corps that the key to skilled marksmanship—in addition to the basics of trigger squeeze sight picture, and the rest of the technique crap—was joining together a Marine and his rifle so that they became one. A Marine was thus taught that first he cleaned and oiled his piece, then he could think of maybe getting something to eat and a place out of the rain to sleep. The Marine Corps further believed that an officer should not order his men to do anything he could not do himself.

There were two schools of thought concerning the issue of the U.S. Rifle, Caliber .30, M1 to the students of the Platoon Leader's Course. The official reason was that nothing was too good for the young men who possibly would soon be leading Marines in a war. It therefore followed that the young gentlemen be issued the newest, finest item in the Marine Corps' small weapons inventory. In the opinion of most Marines, however, the reason it was being issued to the young gentlemen of the Platoon Leader's Course was that real rifles were needed for real Marines.

It was therefore not surprising that Item #2 on the Training Schedule for Day #1 of Platoon Leader's Course 23-41 (right after "#1 Welcoming Remarks, Major J.J. Hollenbeck, USMC") was the issuance of rifles—Garand rifles—to the young gentlemen.

Some of the young gentlemen were wearing Marine Corps dungarees (sometimes called "utilities") and work shoes. They had been issued these uniforms during previous summer training periods. It was the prescribed uniform of the day.

But some of the young gentlemen, including Malcolm Pickering, were still in civilian clothing. It was not that they didn't have dungarees, but that they had not considered that day #1 would begin at 0345 hours and that they would be given ninety seconds to get out of bed, dress, and fall in outside the barracks. They presumed that they would have a couple of minutes to take their dungarees from their luggage before they stood the first formation and were marched to breakfast. There were 112 members of Platoon Leader's Course 23-41, and about a dozen of them were in civilian clothing. Most were in shirts and slacks, but there were two, including Malcolm Pickering, who had at the last second grabbed their jackets. Pickering had even managed to grab his necktie.

He was standing in the rear rank tying his necktie when he came to the attention of the Assistant Drill Instructor, a barrel-chested corporal of twenty-nine years with a nearly shaven head and a voice made harsh by frequent vocal exertion. His name was Pleasant, which later became the subject of wry observation by the young gentlemen.

On seeing movement in the rear rank, Corporal Pleasant walked quickly and erectly between the ranks until he was standing before Pickering. He then put his hands on his hips and inclined his head forward, so that the stiff brim of his campaign hat just about touched Pickering's forehead, and so that Pickering could smell Corporal Pleasant's toothpaste when he shouted.

"What the fuck are you doing, asshole?"

"I was tying my tie, sir," Pickering said, coming to attention. He was not entirely a rookie. He had been to two previous summer training encampments and knew that as a trainee, he was expected to come at attention when addressed by an assistant drill instructor, and to call him "sir," although in the real Marine Corps only commissioned officers were entitled to such courtesy.

"Why are you wearing a tie, asshole?" Corporal Pleasant inquired.

Pickering could think of no good answer to that.

"I asked you a question, asshole!" Corporal Pleasant reminded him.

"No excuse, sir," Pickering said, another remembered lesson from previous summers. One did not offer excuses. There was no excuse for not doing what you were supposed to do, or for doing what you were not supposed to do. The proper response in a situation like that was the one he had just given.

Corporal Pleasant was more than a little disappointed. He had hoped to have the opportunity to make an example of this candy-ass would-be officer, not because he disliked him personally, but because it would get the others in the right frame of mind. But there was nothing to do now but return to the front of the formation, which he did.

The young gentlemen were marched from the company to battalion headquarters, where Major J.J. Hollenbeck, USMC, on behalf of the Commanding General, U.S. Marine Schools, welcomed them to Quantico and wished them well during their course of instruction.

They were next marched to the company supply room. There they were issued a U.S. Rifle, Caliber .30, M1; a Sling, leather; and a Kit, individual, for U.S. Rifle, Caliber .30, M1. This consisted of a chamber brush and a folding screwdriver (all of one piece); a waxed cord and a patch holder that could be used (by dropping it down the bore) if a Rod, Cleaning, for U.S. Rifles, Model 1903 and M1 was not available; and a small plastic vial of a yellow grease, known as Lubricant, solid, for U.S. Rifle, Caliber .30, M1.

The rifles came in individual heavy wrapping paper, which appeared greasy. The reason it was greasy was that the rifles themselves were thickly coated with Cosmoline to protect them from rust while in storage.

Corporal Pleasant gave the young gentlemen rudimentary instruction in the assembly of the Sling, leather, and its attachment to the U.S. Rifle, caliber .30, M1, and then informed them that by 0345 the next morning, he expected the rifles to be cleaned, and that each individual would be expected, by 1300 that very day, to be as familiar with the serial number of the weapon as he was with his beloved mother's face.

"Where's the serial number?" one baffled young gentleman asked. "This fucking thing's covered with grease!"

It was the opportunity Corporal Pleasant had been waiting for.

The first thing the baffled young gentleman was required to do, while double-timing in place with the rifle held above his head, was shout "This is not my fucking thing. My fucking thing is between my legs. This is my rifle. I will not forget the difference." When he had recited this litany ten times, he was ordered to run around the arms-room building, with his rifle at port arms, accompanied by two other young gentlemen who had the erroneous idea that his calling his rifle his fucking thing was amusing and had smiled.

The young gentlemen were then double-timed to the mess hall for breakfast.

And it was there that Platoon Leader Candidate Pickering first saw Platoon Leader Candidate McCoy. At first he didn't place him. The face looked familiar, but he thought it was a face from other summer training camps. Then he remembered who he was.

His first reaction was distaste. Breakfast was scrambled eggs and bacon and home-fried potatoes, two pieces of bread and a lump of butter. The only thing that Pickering considered safe to put in his mouth were the home-fried potatoes. The eggs were cold and lumpy, the bacon half-raw, and the bread dried-out. McCoy was wolfing down this garbage as if he hadn't had a decent meal in a week.

Pickering watched, fascinated, as McCoy ate everything on his stainless steel tray, even wiping it clean with a piece of the stale bread.

When he had finished, McCoy picked up his tray and walked toward the mess hall exit. Pickering picked up his near-full tray and followed him.

Corporal Pleasant was there, standing before garbage cans under signs reading "Edible Garbage" and "Non-Edible Garbage."

Corporal Pleasant examined McCoy's tray, and with a curt nod of his head, passed him outside.

When Pick Pickering reached Corporal Pleasant, Corporal Pleasant said, "Over there, asshole," indicating with a nod of his head a group of perhaps a dozen young gentlemen holding their trays, U.S. Rifles, Caliber .30, M1 slung over their shoulders, standing against the concrete-block wall.

Eventually there were nearly thirty young gentlemen who had not found their breakfast appetizing and had left much, in some cases most, of it on their trays.

Corporal Pleasant stood before them.

"Gentlemen," he said. "The Marine Corps loves you. Because the Marine Corps loves you, it has gone to considerable effort and expense to provide you with a healthy, nutritious breakfast. The Marine Corps expects you to eat the healthy, nutritious breakfast it has provided for you."

The young gentlemen looked at him in some confusion for a moment. Then one of them, delicately holding his stainless steel tray in one hand, tried to fork a lump of scrambled egg with the other hand while simultaneously going into contortions trying to keep his U.S. Rifle, Caliber .30, M1 from slipping off his shoulder.

Corporal Pleasant immediately stepped in front of him, put his hands on his hips, and inclined his head so that the stiff brim of his campaign cap almost touched the young gentleman's forehead.

"What the fuck are you doing, asshole?" Corporal Pleasant inquired.

"Sir," the young gentleman bellowed, "eating my breakfast, sir!"

"With a fork! Did you hear me say anything, asshole, about eating with a fork?"

"No, sir!"

The young gentleman looked at him in absolute confusion, not quite able to accept what Corporal Pleasant seemed to be suggesting.

Corporal Pleasant nodded his head.

"Eat, asshole!" he said. "Every last fucking crumb!"

The young gentleman raised the tray, and then lowered his face and began to gulp and lick the tray.

Corporal Pleasant looked at the others.

"On my command," he said, "slurp it up. Ready, slurp!"

Nearly thirty young gentlemen raised their stainless steel trays to their faces and slurped.

When Pickering went outside the mess hall, McCoy was waiting where the trainees would be formed in ranks. There was a barely perceptible smile on his face. Pickering went and stood beside him.

"Now I know why you ate everything on your tray," he said.

"I've been through this sort of shit before," McCoy said.

"What are you doing here?"

"What does it look like?"

"I thought you were going to get out of the Marine Corps?"

"You were right, there's a freeze on discharges," McCoy said.

"Well, we can buddy around," Pickering said. "That'll be nice."

"It would be a bad idea," McCoy said.

"Why?" Pickering asked, surprised, wondering why McCoy was rejecting him. "Why do you say that?"

"I know about Pleasant," McCoy said. "Or people like him. If there's one thing he hates more than a college boy who wants to be an officer, it's another corporal who wants to be an officer. As soon as he finds out that I'm a Marine, he'll start in on me."

"So we'll be even," Pickering said. "He's already started on me."

"Take my word for it, Pickering," McCoy said. "It would be worse if he knew we were buddies. For both of us."

"I don't understand," Pickering said.

"You don't have to understand," McCoy said. "Just take my word for it. Stay away from me."

"Well, fuck you," Pickering said, his feelings hurt.

McCoy smiled at him.

"That's the spirit," he said. "Pick, honest to God, I know what I'm talking about," McCoy said. "Sooner or later, they'll have to give us some time off. Then we can see if there are any fourteen-year-old virgins in Virginia. But what you have to do until we can get away from that prick, especially if you plan to get through the course, is make yourself invisible."

Pickering still didn't understand. But he realized he was enormously relieved that McCoy was not rejecting his friendship. Then he wondered why he was so relieved.

(TWO)
Company "C" Marine Corps School Battalion
Quantico, Virginia
1805 Hours 1 September 1941

Corporal Pleasant placed the platoon "at ease" and then announced that it was now his intention to show them how to disassemble the Cosmoline-covered rifles they had been carrying around all day.

When they had them apart, they would clean them, Corporal Pleasant said. He would return at 2100 hours and inspect the cleaned pieces, and then he would show them how to reassemble their rifles. He knew, he continued, that they all wished to begin Day #2 of their training with spotless rifles. Good Marines prided themselves on having clean pieces.

This was pure chickenshit, Platoon Leader Candidate McCoy decided. A little chickenshit was to be expected, and was probably even a good thing: Pleasant had to make it absolutely clear to these college boys that they were under his absolute control. The college boys who had slurped their breakfast from their trays would never again take more chow than they could eat from the mess line. There had been a point to that.

But there was no point to this rifle-cleaning idea except to make everybody miserable. Except, of course, that Pleasant wanted something on every last one of them that would give him an excuse to jump their ass. There was absolutely no way to remove all the Cosmoline from a rifle with rags. Cosmoline did what it was intended to do, preventing rust by filling every last nook, crevice, and pore in both the action and the stock. You could wipe for fucking ever, and there would still be Cosmoline oozing out someplace.

There were too good ways to clean Cosmoline from a weapon. The best (and most dangerous) was with five gallons of gasoline in the bottom of a garbage can. If you didn't strike a spark and blow your ass up, the gasoline would dissolve the Cosmoline.

The second way was with boiling water. You took a field mess water heater[1] and filled it with rifle actions and let the sonsofbitches boil like lobsters.

[1]A gasoline-fired water-heating device inserted into a fifty-five-gallon garbage can. Mess kits are sterilized by dipping them into the boiling water.

Pleasant was offering neither alternative. He was just being a prick, and McCoy decided there was a limit to the chickenshit he would take. He had promised himself he would keep his nose clean, stay out of sight, and do whatever was demanded of him. But that did not go so far as spending the next three hours in a futile attempt to rub a rifle free of Cosmoline.

He was standing one rank behind and three files to the left of Pick Pickering as Corporal Pleasant delivered his lecture on the disassembly of the U.S. Rifle Caliber .30, M1. He considered for a moment taking Pickering with him, but decided against it. For one thing, cleaning an uncleanable rifle was probably an essential part of training for a college boy. For another, Platoon Leader Candidate McCoy was about to go AWOL, which (as Corporal Pleasant had with some relish informed them during one of the lectures during the day) was frowned upon. Anyone caught AWOL (defined as not being in the proper place, at the proper place, at the proper time, in the properly appointed uniform) would instantly have his ass shipped to a rifle company and could forget pinning the gold bars of a second lieutenant on his shoulders.

When they were dismissed and double-timed into the barracks, McCoy went directly to the latrine and washed his hands as well as he could with GI soap. Then he grabbed his Garand with a rag, and went out the back door of the barracks.

As he made his way toward the provost marshal's Impound Yard, he considered that after successfully evading every Jap sentry in Shantung Province, it was entirely possible that he'd be nailed cold by some eager college boy guarding a barracks with an unloaded Garand.

But he wasn't challenged. He hid the Garand in a ditch, and then went into the provost marshal's office. Master Gunnery Sergeant Stecker's order was on file, and an MP corporal went and unlocked the compound for him.

McCoy drove to where he had hidden the Garand and reclaimed it. Then he opened the trunk, took out a dungaree shirt with corporal's stripes painted on the sleeves, put it on, and then took his campaign hat from the hat press and set it on his head at the approved jaunty angle.

The MP at the gate, spotting the enlisted man's sticker on the windshield and the stiff-brimmed campaign hat on the driver, waved the LaSalle convertible through, but McCoy slowed and stopped anyway.

The MP walked up to the car.

"Where's the nearest gas station, garage, whatever, with a steam cleaner?" McCoy asked.

The MP thought it over.

"There's a Sunoco station's got one," he said. "Turn left when you hit U.S. 1."

"Much obliged," McCoy said, and let the clutch out as he rolled up the window.

The Sunoco station's steam cleaner wasn't working, but they had something even better, a machine McCoy had never seen before. It was designed to clean dirt- and grease-encrusted parts. A nonexplosive solvent poured out of a flexible spout, like water from a faucet, over a sort of sink. Thirty minutes' work with a bristle brush and there was no Cosmoline left on either the action or the stock of the Garand, period.

An hour after he had gone out of the Main Gate, McCoy drove the LaSalle back through it and stopped.

"Found it," he called to the MP. "Thanks."

"Anytime," the MP said.

There was time before Corporal Pleasant reappeared in the barracks to take a shower. The water was cold. The college boys, McCoy decided, had tried hot water. All it had done was leave a layer of Cosmoline on the shower floor. Everyone was still furiously rubbing rifle parts with rags.

McCoy tied rags around his feet, showered, removed the rags, threw them in the pile, and put on clean dungarees.

Then he disassembled the Garand, laid the parts on his bunk, then crawled under the bunk and lay down to await Corporal Pleasant.

Five minutes later, someone called "attention," and McCoy started to roll out from under the bunk. He was halfway to his feet when Pleasant, storming purposefully down the aisle, spotted him getting up.

As he came to attention, Pleasant leaned the brim of his campaign hat into his face.

"Anyone tell you to get in the sack, asshole?" Corporal Pleasant inquired.

"No, sir!" McCoy said.

"Then what were you doing in the sack, asshole!"

"Sir, I wasn't in the sack, sir!"

Corporal Pleasant, seeing the disassembled Garand on the bunk, was forced to face the fact that there was not room for the asshole to have been in the bunk, too.

He leaned over the bunk and picked up the first part he touched, which happened to be the magazine follower.

"You call this clean, asshole?" he demanded, before he had a chance to examine it at all.

"Yes, sir," McCoy said. "I believe that's clean, sir!"

Corporal Pleasant shoved the magazine follower under McCoy's nose, and in the very moment he demanded, "You call that clean, asshole?" he thought: *I'll be a sonofabitch, it's clean!*

"Yes, sir!" McCoy shouted.

"What's the serial number of your piece, asshole?"

"Sir, 156331, sir!"

Corporal Pleasant stood eyeball to eyeball with Platoon Leader Candidate McCoy for a moment.

"Assembly your piece, and then get your ass outside, asshole!" he ordered. "There is a light on a pole outside the orderly room. Guard it until I relieve you!"

"Yes, sir!" McCoy said.

Ten minutes later, Corporal Pleasant marched up to the light pole outside the orderly room.

McCoy came to port arms.

"Halt! Who goes there?" he demanded.

"Who the fuck do you think?" Corporal Pleasant replied, and then ordered: "Follow me."

He walked to the rear of the building, and opened the door of a 1939 Ford coupe.

"Get in," he said.

McCoy got in the seat beside him. Pleasant reached over the back of the seat and came up with two beer cans.

"Church keys in the ashtray," he said.

"Thank you," McCoy said, and opened his beer.

"You're McCoy, right? 'Killer' McCoy?"

"I'm McCoy."

"There's three Marines in there with the assholes," Pleasant said. "I wasn't sure which was who."

McCoy didn't reply.

"You going to give me trouble, McCoy?" Pleasant asked.

Strange question. Why should he think I might give him trouble? And why the beer? This sonofabitch doesn't have the balls to be a universal prick. He's only going to be a prick to those he's sure won't fight back. And for some reason, he's a little bit afraid of me. He called me "Killer." Does this dumb sonofabitch think I'm going to stick a knife in him?

"No," McCoy said. "Why should I?"

"How did you get that rifle clean?" Pleasant asked.

There was a time for truth, McCoy decided, but this wasn't it.

"Lighter fluid," he said.

"You must have used a quart of it," Pleasant said. "What you really need is gasoline."

"Lighter fluid works better than a rag," McCoy said.

"It also made you stand out from the others," Pleasant said. "That's not smart."

"I wasn't trying to be smart," McCoy said.

Corporal Pleasant looked at him for a long moment, and then nodded his head, accepting that.

"That wasn't the first Cosmolined rifle you ever cleaned, was it?" he asked rhetorically. "I guess I would have done the same thing."

McCoy didn't reply.

"There's two stories going around about you, McCoy," Pleasant said. "The first is that you killed a bunch of Chinamen in China. The second is that you have friends in high places who got you into this course. Anything to them?"

"There was some shooting in China," McCoy said. "It was in the line of duty."

"And have you got a rabbi?"

"Have I got a what?"

"Somebody important, taking care of you?"

"Not that I know about," McCoy said. "I applied for this, and I got accepted."

Pleasant snorted, as if he didn't believe him.

"Let me spell things out for you, McCoy," he said. "You stay out of my hair, and I'll stay out of yours. But there's two things you better understand: I don't give a shit about any rabbi. And there's people who think you belong in Portsmouth, not here."

"I don't know what you're talking about, Pleasant," McCoy said.

"The hell you don't," Pleasant said.

He put his beer to his mouth, draining the can, and then squeezed it.

"Finish your beer, McCoy," he said. "And go back to the barracks." He got out of the Ford coupe and walked away.

McCoy finished his beer slowly. He was sorry, but not surprised, that what had happened in China was apparently common knowledge. The Corps was small, and Marines gossiped as bad as women, especially when it was interesting, like a Marine shooting a bunch of Chinese. He figured that some other China Marines had come home and gone to see Gunny Stecker, another old China Marine, and told him what had happened at the ferry. And Gunny Stecker had connected it with him, and that was how Pleasant had heard about it.

But he couldn't figure out who his "rabbi" was supposed to be, or who the people were who thought he belonged in Portsmouth, instead of in the Platoon Leader's Program.

Ten minutes after Corporal Pleasant left him, McCoy got out of the Ford, put the U.S. Rifle, Caliber .30, M1 in the position of right shoulder arms, and in a military fashion marched back to the barrack, took off his utilities and climbed in the sack.

(THREE)
Marine Corps School
Quantico, Virginia
12 October 1941

The six weeks passed quickly. As McCoy suspected, the training was a repeat of Parris Island boot camp. It was necessary to turn the college boys into Marines, before they could be turned into Marine officers. That meant they had to be taught immediate, unquestioning obedience in such a way that it would become a conditioned reflex.

Thus: If a Platoon Leader Candidate did not immediately and unquestioningly respond to whatever order Corporal Pleasant or another of the Drill Instructors issued, there was immediate punishment.

If, for example, the young gentlemen did not respond to an order to fall out on the company street with the proper speed and enthusiasm, they were required to fall out again and again and again until Corporal Pleasant was satisfied.

And Pleasant was a man of some imagination: He might suggest that the young gentlemen were slow to fall out because they were unduly burdened by their accoutrements. Instead of falling out in helmets, full marching pack and rifles, they could try it again wearing only undershorts, skivvy shirts, leggings, and steel helmets. Plus, of course, their rifles.

This required that they remove their leggings and their utilities. The utilities were then folded in the proper manner and placed in the proper place in their footlockers, and the leggings laced back on over bare calves.

If this increased their speed, Corporal Pleasant then experimented. They would next fall out in only raincoats, utility trousers, skivvy shirts, and cartridge belts. This required unlacing the leggings, storing them as prescribed, then detaching the canteen, first aid packet, and web harness from the web cartridge belt, and storing these items in their appointed places.

Next, perhaps, Corporal Pleasant would order that they again try falling out with the proper speed and enthusiasm in full marching gear. This meant of course reattaching the canteen, the first aid packet, and the harness to the cartridge belt; folding the raincoat and placing it in its prescribed location in the footlocker; and then relacing the leggings.

The possible variations were almost limitless, and Corporal Pleasant experimented with as many as he could think of.

Then there was punishment for sin:

The greatest sin of all was dropping the U.S. Rifle, Caliber .30, M1. Anyone who did this could expect to double-time around the parade ground with the rifle held at arm's length above his head, while shouting in a loud voice, "My rifle is my best friend, and I am a miserable sonofabitch because I abused it. God have mercy on my miserable soul."

Another sin was laughter, or giggling, or even a detected snicker. These sinners would double-time around the parade ground with their rifles at arm's length above their heads, while shouting at the top of their lungs, "I am a hyena. A hyena is an animal who laughs when there is nothing funny to laugh at. This is the sound a hyena makes. Ha Ha Ha Ha Ha Ha."

Another means of instilling discipline was calisthenics and close-order drill. This also served to cause the young gentlemen to shed civilian fat and tone their musculature. There were thirty minutes of calisthenics (later forty-five minutes and then an hour) before breakfast. And there was at least an hour of close-order drill every day.

Individual young gentlemen who came to Corporal Pleasant's attention during the duty day (which ran from 0345 until whenever Pleasant decided the day was over) were often required to perform additional calisthenics. Normally, this was in the form of pushups, but sometimes, when one of the young gentlemen displayed what Pleasant thought was ungainly, awkward movement (such as being out of step) it took the form of the "duck walk."

When one did the duck walk, one first squatted, then one placed the U.S. Rifle, Caliber .30, M1 in a horizontal position against the small of the neck, and then one waddled, while shouting, "This is the way a duck walks. Quack! Quack! Quack! I will try very hard to try to walk like a Marine in the future!"

McCoy had been through all this before in boot camp at Parris Island, but that didn't make things any easier. He had been genuinely surprised to learn (his feet became raw and blistered and his muscles ached) how badly out of shape he had become. In fact, the only real advantages he (and the other two Marine noncoms) had over the college boys was that responding to commands had already been drilled into them and was a reflex action. Similarly, they had experience in giving close-order drill, had already learned how to bark out commands from the pits of their stomachs, and, more importantly, had learned the cadence so that it too was automatic.

All three of the Marines in the platoon learned something else: Taking close-order drill from someone who doesn't know what he is doing, someone who doesn't understand the cadence and the timing, could turn the Marine Corps Drum and Bugle Corps at the Marine Barracks in Washington into a mob of blind men stumbling over their own feet.

In addition to the inspections Pleasant called whenever the whim struck him (and sometimes, if he woke early, the whim struck before the official rising hour of 0345), there was a regularly scheduled inspection each Saturday morning. The official inspection was conducted by the gunnery sergeant of the company and the company commander.

In order that he not be embarrassed by slovenly young gentlemen or equipment, Corporal Pleasant conducted both a preinspection and a pre-preinspection of the platoon. The latter was held on Friday evening after the barracks had been scrubbed and polished. It was necessary that the platoon pass the pre-preinspection before they were permitted to retire for the evening. Sometimes the pre-preinspection did not meet Corporal Pleasant's high standards until very late at night.

The preinspection was conducted the next morning, half an hour before first call. It was to determine if the assholes had fucked anything up in the three or four hours while they'd been in the sack after the pre-preinspection. If they had, it could be corrected in the time officially set aside for breakfast.

Scuttlebutt had it that today's inspection was going to be a real bitch. The company commander, who was rough enough, was not on the base. Thus the inspection would be conducted for him by another officer, the battalion mess officer; and the scuttlebutt on him was that he had a corn cob up his ass and was really a chickenshit sonofabitch.

McCoy was not particularly concerned. He knew that once you had prepared your gear and arranged it, the situation was out of your hands. If an inspecting officer decided to jump your ass, he would. He would find something wrong, even if he had to step on the toes of the boots under your bunk so that he could get you for unshined shoes. If you couldn't control the situation, there was no point in worrying about it.

When Pleasant barked, "Ten-hut on the deck!" McCoy came to attention, his toes at a forty-five-degree angle, the fingers of his left hand against the seam of his trousers, his right hand holding the Garand just below the bayonet lug.

He stared straight ahead and heard the clatter of the rifles as one by one the gentlemen came from attention to inspection arms. While this was going on, he had speculated—a little unkindly—that with just a little bit of luck, one of the young gentlemen would catch his thumb in the M1 action during the inspection. That produced a condition known as M1 thumb. If he howled in pain, that just might bring the inspection to a quick end.

But there was no such fortuitous happenstance. The sound of clattering rifles moved closer to him. Out of the corner of his eye, he saw the inspection party approaching.

He shifted the Garand to a diagonal position in front of him, slammed the action open, bobbed his head over the action to insure that it was unloaded, and then looked ahead, waiting for it to be snatched from his hand.

He found himself looking into the face of First Lieutenant John R. Macklin, USMC.

There was no smile on Macklin's face, not even a flicker of recognition.

"This man is unshaven," Lieutenant Macklin said.

The gunny trailing him dutifully wrote this down on his clipboard.

Macklin snatched the Garand from McCoy's hand, looked into the open action, and then raised the butt high in the air, so that he could look into the barrel.

"And this weapon is filthy," Lieutenant Macklin said, before he threw the Garand back at McCoy so hard that it stung his hands and he almost dropped it.

The gunny dutifully wrote "filthy weapon" on his clipboard.

Lieutenant Macklin moved down the aisle to the next man. McCoy closed the action of the Garand and returned it to his side.

The Garand had been clean before McCoy had disassembled it and cleaned it, and he had shaved no more than two hours before.

There didn't seem to be much question any longer who believed that Killer McCoy belonged in the U.S. Naval Prison, Portsmouth, rather than in the Platoon Leader's Course at U.S. Marine Corps Schools, Quantico.

Captain Banning, McCoy concluded, had probably eaten Macklin's ass out for letting the Japs catch him at Yenchi'eng.

McCoy was summoned to the orderly room half an hour later.

The gunny was there, and Pleasant.

"Mr. McCoy," the gunny said, "there is no excuse in the Marine Corps for a filthy weapon."

McCoy brought the Garand from the position of attention—that is to say, with its butt resting on the deck beside the right boot—to the position of port arms. And then he threw it, like a basketball, to the gunny.

"What the fuck do you think you're doing?" the gunny said, furiously. He had been so surprised he had almost failed to catch it.

"Look at it, Gunny," McCoy said.

"Who the fuck do you think you are, telling me what to do?" the gunny snapped, but he slammed the action open and looked into it, and then raised the butt so that he could look down the barrel.

"You want to feel my chin, Gunny?" McCoy asked.

"This weapon is filthy, Mr. McCoy," the gunny said, throwing the Garand back to him, "and you need a shave. Because Lieutenant Macklin says so. You get the picture?"

"I got the picture."

"Corporal Pleasant will now escort you to the barracks, where he will supervise your shave. Then he will supervise you while you clean your filthy weapon. When you have shaved, and your rifle is clean, he will bring you back here, and I will check the closeness of your shave, and the cleanliness of your rifle. That means I will have to stay here, instead of going to my quarters. That pisses me off, McCoy. My wife has plans for the weekend, and you have fucked them up."

McCoy knew enough to keep his mouth shut.

"And I'll tell you something else I agree with Lieutenant Macklin about, McCoy. I don't know how in the fuck a China Marine motor transport corporal with a reputation like yours got it in his head he should be an officer. Or how you managed to get yourself in here. Except that you had your nose so far up some officer's ass that your ears didn't show. I don't like brown noses, McCoy, and I especially don't like people with rabbis. You get the picture?"

"Yes, sir," McCoy said.

"Finally, Mr. McCoy, I would like to make sure you understand that participation in the Platoon Leader's Course is purely voluntary. You may resign at any time, and keep your stripes."

"I'm not about to quit, Gunny," McCoy said.

"If you bust out of here," the gunny said, "for misbehavior, or malingering, something like that, they ship your ass to some rifle company. It's something to think about, McCoy."

"Yes, sir," McCoy said.

"Corporal Pleasant," the gunny said. "I think the deck in the barrack could stand a sanding. Do you think it might help Mr. McCoy to remember to shave and to keep his piece clean if he spent the weekend doing that?"

Pleasant nodded his agreement. He looked a little embarrassed, McCoy thought, but he was going to go along with the gunny. He had no choice.

(FOUR)
Headquarters, 4th Marines
Shanghai, China
19 October 1941

Only a few people were made privy to all the details, actual and projected, of the removal from China of United States Military and Naval Forces. Among these was Captain Edward Banning, S-2 of the 4th Marines.

The Yangtze River Patrol, its gunboats and personnel, was to sail as soon as possible for the U.S. Naval Base at Cavite, on the tip of a narrow, four-mile-long peninsula sticking into Manila Bay. It was intended that the Yangtze River Patrol reinforce U.S. Naval Forces, Philippines. How much value the old, narrow-draft, lightly armed riverboats would be was open to question. There was even concern that should there be severe weather en route to Manila Bay the gunboats would founder and sink. They were designed to navigate a river, not the high seas in a typhoon.

Likewise, the small, old pigboats of SUBFORCHINA were as soon as possible to sail for Cavite, though they were subject to similar fears as to their seaworthiness, for they were old and small and designed primarily for coastal, rather than deep-sea, operations. But unlike the riverboats, if it came to it, the pigboats could submerge for maybe five, six hours at a time, and ride out a storm.

The two battalions making up the 4th Marines were something else. They were Marines, which was to say they were trained and equipped to fight anywhere. But what they would be in fact, if war broke out, was infantry. The official role of the Marines was to make amphibious assaults on hostile shores. Two battalions of Marines without landing craft and without larger forces to reinforce them once a landing was made weren't going to make much of an amphibious assault force.

The advance party of the 4th Marines would sail from Shanghai aboard the U.S.S. *Henderson,* a Navy transport, on 28 October. The *Henderson* would then continue on to the United States, to on-load Army reinforcements for the Philippines. The U.S.S. *Shaumont,* the other U.S. Navy transport that normally served China, would similarly be involved in moving U.S. Army troops from the West Coast of the United States to reinforce the Philippines. The Navy had also chartered space aboard two civilian passenger liners. On 28 November, the *President Madison* would embark the First Battalion and the *President Harrison* the Second Battalion. If nothing went wrong, the 4th Marines would arrive in Manila during the first week of December. Then, either the *Henderson* or the *Shaumont* would be free to sail to Tientsin and pick up the Peking and Tientsin Marine detachments.

U.S. Navy Forces, Philippines, was sending to Shanghai a Consolidated Catalina, a long-range amphibious reconnaissance aircraft, to pick up senior officers of the Yangtze River Patrol and SUBFORCHINA and carry them to Cavite to prepare for the arrival of their vessels.

At the last moment, the colonel learned of this, and prevailed upon his Naval counterpart to make space available for one of his officers.

The colonel did not anticipate any logistical problems when the regiment arrived in the Philippines. The Cavite Navy Base was enormous—capable of supporting the Far East Fleet. It would be able to house and feed two battalions of Marines without difficulty.

But the colonel *did* want to know how Douglas MacArthur, former Chief of Staff of the U.S. Army and most recently Marshal of the Philippine Army, intended to employ the 4th Marines. The obvious officer to find that out was his S-2, and Captain Edward Banning was given twenty-two hours' notice to pack his things, make arrangements for the personal property he would necessarily have to leave behind, and be aboard the Catalina when it took off for Manila.

The first thing Captain Ed Banning did when he heard that was get in his Pontiac and drive to the headquarters of the Shanghai Municipal Police Department. He found Sergeant Chatworth there and told them he needed a big favor.

"Like what?" Chatworth asked, suspicious.

"I want to marry a stateless person," Banning said. "To do that, I need a certificate from the Municipal Police stating there is no record of criminal activity."

Chatworth's bushy eyebrows rose.

"Or moral turpitude," Chatworth added.

Banning nodded.

"That isn't all you'll need," he said. "You better figure on two weeks, at least, pulling in all the favors anybody owes you."

Banning looked at his watch.

"I have nineteen hours and thirty minutes," he said.

"What's her name?" Chatworth asked.

* * *

When he got back to his apartment, Milla told him she didn't want to marry him: She knew what it would do to his career, and she understood how things were when they'd started, and she didn't want him to marry her out of pity. "I'll be all right," she said finally, obviously not meaning it.

Two hours later, she held his hand tightly during the brief ceremony at the Anglican cathedral, and when she kissed him afterward, her cheeks were wet with tears.

"Sir, I ask permission to discuss a personal matter," Banning, standing at attention, said to the colonel.

"Just as long as you get on that plane, Ed, you have my permission to discuss anything you want with me."

"Sir, I was married this afternoon," Banning said.

"I don't think I want to hear this, Ed," the colonel said.

"Sir, my wife is a stateless person, with a Nansen travel document."

"Jesus Christ, Ed! You know the regulations."

"Yes, sir, I know the regulations."

"I didn't hear a word you said, Captain Banning," the colonel said. "I don't wish to believe that an officer of your rank and experience would deliberately disobey regulations concerning marriage and get married without permission."

"If I asked for permission, sir, it would have been denied."

"Or make a gesture like this, throwing a fine career down the goddamned toilet," the colonel said, angrily. "Jesus Christ!"

Banning didn't reply.

"Do you realize what a spot you've put me on, Ed?" the colonel asked in exasperation.

"I regret any embarrassment this may cause you, sir," Banning said. "I am, of course, prepared to resign my commission."

The colonel stared at him coldly for a long moment.

"It's a good goddamned thing I know you well enough, Captain Banning, to understand that was an offer to pay the price, rather than an attempt to avoid your duty," he said, finally. "Mrs. Banning must be quite a lady."

Again, Banning could think of nothing to reply.

"Sergeant-Major!" the colonel bellowed.

The sergeant-major appeared. The colonel told him to close the door.

"Captain Banning," he said, "was today married to a stateless person. Captain Banning did not have permission to marry."

The sergeant-major looked at Banning in surprise.

"It will therefore be necessary for you, Sergeant-Major, to prepare—suitably back-dated—the application to marry, and whatever other documentation is necessary. That includes, I believe, a letter to the Assistant Chief of Staff for Intelligence, Headquarters, USMC, explaining my reasons for not pulling Captain Banning's security clearance once it came to my attention that he is emotionally involved with a foreign national."

"Aye, aye, sir," the sergeant-major said.

"My reasons are that I believe the Corps cannot at this time afford to lose Captain Banning's services, despite his actions in this matter, and that I believe the disciplinary action I have taken closes the matter."

"The disciplinary action, sir?" the sergeant-major asked.

"You will prepare a letter of reprimand as follows," the colonel said. "Quote. It has come to my attention that you have married without due attention to the applicable regulations. You will consider yourself reprimanded. Unquote."

"Aye, aye, sir," the sergeant-major said.

"Thank you, sir," Banning said.

"If that's all you have on your mind, Captain Banning," the colonel said, "I'm sure you have a number of things to do before you board the aircraft."

Despite the sergeant-major's claims about his busting his butt to get the Consulate to issue Milla a "non-quota, married to an American citizen" visa, when Banning turned over the keys to his Pontiac to her, he had a strange feeling that he would never see her again.

They both pretended, though, that everything was now coming up roses: She would promptly get her visa. His (now *their*) furniture and other belongings (including, ultimately, the Pontiac) would be turned in for shipment to the Philippines. If it proved impossible for Milla to get her visa in time for her to ship to the Philippines with the other dependents, she would travel on the first available transportation once the visa was issued.

What was more likely to happen was that his car and household goods were going to be placed in a godown (warehouse) on the docks and more than likely disappear forever. And that when the dependents sailed, Milla would be left behind with no visa.

And he could tell from the look in her eyes that she knew.

On the Catalina he forced Milla and the future from his mind. There was no sense bleeding to death over something he had no control over.

It occurred to him that nice guys, indeed, do finish last.

Macklin, that despicable sonofabitch, had had three weeks to arrange for the shipment of his car and household goods. They had gone on the ship with him. And he was in the States, not headed for the Philippines.

He was, he realized, of two minds about Macklin. On one hand, it was goddamned unfair that the sonofabitch should be safe in the States. On the other hand, if there was to be war, it was better that the sonofabitch should be someplace else.

There was no question in Banning's mind that the officer corps of the United States Marine Corps was about to start earning its pay, and in that case, a slimy sonofabitch like Macklin would do more harm than good.

And finally, before the roar of the engine put him to sleep, his thoughts turned to Corporal "Killer" McCoy. Poor McCoy, hating every minute of it, was probably greasing trucks and keeping his nose clean in Philadelphia, waiting for him to come home from China and arrange for his transfer. McCoy, the poor sonofabitch, was going to have a long wait.

XI

(ONE)
Known Distance Range #2
U.S. Marine Corps Schools
Quantico, Virginia
19 November 1941

Because he'd participated, back in '38, in the troop test of the Garand rifle at Fort Benning, Captain Jack NMI Stecker, USMCR, Assistant S-3 of the School Battalion, U.S. Marine Corps Schools, Quantico, did not share the generally held opinion that the Garand was a piece of shit. The Corps had sent to the Army's infantry school a platoon of Marines, under Master Gunnery Sergeant Jack NMI Stecker, to find out for themselves what this new rifle was all about.

He hadn't liked it at first. It was bulky and heavy, and didn't have the lean lines of the Springfield. And he had found it difficult to accept that as soon as the slam of the butt into the socket of the shoulder was over, the fired cartridge was ejected, another cartridge was chambered, the action was cocked, and the Garand was prepared to fire again.

As a young Marine, Stecker had spent long hours endlessly working his Springfield until the action was as smooth as butter. And he had learned to fire and work the bolt so fast and so smoothly that the Springfield seemed like a machine gun with a slow rate of fire.

He and the other Marines involved in the troop test had been proud of that skill. *Most of them.* So that the test would not be conducted by forty expert marksmen, the Corps had detailed a dozen kids fresh from Parris Island to the platoon. They weren't experts. It took years to really become an expert with a Springfield.

Stecker went to the infantry school at Benning prepared to dislike the Garand.

But that changed. For one thing, even if this came close to heresy, there was no question that the sights on the Garand were better than the sights on the Springfield. On the other hand, the trigger pull started out really godawful, must have been ten pounds when they gave him the new Garand. But he was able to fix that with a little careful stoning of the sear. And the action was stiff as hell too, but that wore itself in after a couple of hundred rounds. And it actually got pretty slick once he learned, by trial and error, just how much of the yellow lubricant to use, and where.

And then the Doggie armorer loaned him his own Garand. What the hell, even if he was a Doggie, they had things in common. The Doggie armorer was a master sergeant, the same rank as Stecker, and he'd done a hitch with the 15th "Can Do" U.S. Infantry in Tientsin, 1935-38. And they knew about rifles. Stecker and the Doggie armorer had more in common with each other than Stecker had with the kids fresh from Parris Island involved in the troop test.

So first they had a couple of beers together at the NCO Club, and then the Doggie invited him to his quarters for supper, and the next morning, the Doggie armorer handed him a Garand and told him he'd "done a little work on it." What he'd done was a really good job on the trigger, and the action was really smooth, and he'd taken chisels to the stock and cut away all the wood, so the barrel was free floating, and (he wasn't sure if Stecker would like this) he'd replaced the rear sight with one he'd rigged up with an aperture about half as big as issue.

The first time Stecker fired the Doggie's Garand—at two hundred yards—when they marked the target and hauled it up again, there was only one spotter[1] on it, a white one, but only one.

"Have them re-mark that goddamned target!" Stecker demanded, angry and embarrassed. He had fired two loose rounds and an eight-round clip at that target, and apparently hit it only once.

The Doggie corporal on the field phone to the pits ordered the target re-marked, and it disappeared into the pits. It came back up a minute later with just the one white spotter, and Stecker felt humiliation sweep through him.

"Two and a quarter," the Doggie corporal sang out.

"What the hell does that mean?" Stecker asked. There was no such terminology in the Corps.

"That means, Sarge," the corporal said tolerantly, "that you put them all into just over two inches. Not bad!"

Stecker was so pleased (and to tell the truth of it, so relieved) that he'd put ten rounds into an area smaller than a spotter—which was damned near minute of angle[2]—that he didn't even jump the Doggie corporal's ass for calling him "Sarge."

That would have been good shooting even with Stecker's own personal Springfield, which he privately believed was as accurate as any Springfield in the Corps.

That was when he began to change his evaluation of the Garand. Obviously, when properly tuned, the ugly sonofabitch would shoot. Which was the important thing. And being absolutely fair and objective about it, which is what he was supposed to be as the NCOIC of the Marine Troop Test, you could get back on target after the recoil faster than you could with a Springfield. Like it or not, the gas-operated mechanism of the Garand ejected a round and chambered another faster than even a master gunnery sergeant of the Marine Corps could work the bolt of a Springfield.

And there was more to think about. Not only were the Marine marksmen doing well with the Garand—the sergeants and corporals who knew something about shooting—but the kids from Parris Island, too. They didn't, he realized, have a hell of a lot to unlearn. They just took the Garand and learned how to use it.

He didn't easily give in to admitting that the Garand was actually a fine weapon, though. For instance, he surprised hell out of a squad of the kids by ordering them not to detail strip their pieces when the day's firing was over.

"Just run a couple of patches, first bore cleaner, then oil down the bore. Don't brush the bore. I want to see how much it will take to jam it."

It was three days of firing before the first Garand jammed.

That night, he ordered the squad to detail strip and clean their Garands but not to reassemble them. When all the parts were clean, he ordered the kids to put them all together in a pile on the deck of the barrack.

The kids thought he was really nuts then, and even more so when he stepped

[1]Bullet holes in rifle targets are marked with circular cardboard disks, white if the hole is in the black of the bull's-eye, and black for holes elsewhere on the target. A peg in the center of the disk is inserted in the bullet hole. The bullet strike is thus visible from the firing line.

[2]One inch at 100 yards. Two inches at 200 yards, etc.

up to the pile and stirred the parts around with his toe. One of the claimed merits of the Garand was interchangeability of parts. This was a good way to find out.

"Now put them together," he ordered. He stood watching as the kids assembled rifles.

"I don't want anybody exchanging parts after I'm gone," he said. "I'm trying something."

There was only one malfunction of the squad's Garands the next day, a stovepipe[3] he suspected was a freak. He proved this by firing three clips through the rifle as quickly as he could and without further failure to eject.

Master Gunnery Sergeant Stecker returned from Fort Benning one of the few people in the Corps who believed the Garand was the best infantry rifle to come down the pike in a long time. He was worried then not about whether the Garand would be good for the Corps, but when—or even whether—the Corps would get it. The Army would take care of itself first, of course. The Corps would probably wind up with the Army's worn-out Springfields rather than new Garands.

Captain Jack NMI Stecker, USMCR, was therefore pleased when the first Garands were issued to the Corps. There were not enough of them to go around, of course, but the door was open. For the moment, unfortunately, there were only enough of them to equip a few detached units, and for instructional purposes.

Captain Stecker read with interest the reports of scores fired with the new rifle by the students of the battalion; and he was not happy with the results from either the commissioned officers at their annual qualification at Quantico or of the kids in the Platoon Leader's Course. He decided first to see what was wrong with the training of the Platoon Leader candidates and fix that, and then he'd see that the same fix was applied to the abbreviated training course given the officers before they fired their annual qualification.

At 0805, which was late enough for the firing on the known distance range to be well under way, he got up from his desk and walked out of his office.

"Come with me, son," he said to the S-3's jeep driver, a small, very neat PFC trying to make himself inconspicuous on a chair in the outer office.

As he invariably did when he went for a ride in the jeep with a PFC at the wheel, he thought about how much he'd liked it better when he'd been a master gunnery sergeant with the pickup and didn't have to sit like a statue on an uncomfortable pad in the jeep.

In the center of the line of Known Distance Rifle Range #2 (where the Platoon Leader Candidates were firing for record), there was a small clutter of buildings surrounding the range master's tower. Next to the buildings, several vehicles were parked with their front wheels against yellow-painted logs half-buried in the sand. There were two jeeps (one assigned to range NCO and the other to the range officer), two pickups, and a three-quarter-ton Dodge weapons carrier, which had brought the ammo from the dump. Two ambulances (new ones, built on the Dodge three-quarter-ton weapons carrier chassis) were backed up against the logs.

Stecker told the driver to park the jeep beside the weapons carrier. When he stopped, Stecker removed his campaign hat and took from the crown a small glass bottle, which once contained Bayer Aspirin. He took from it four globs of what looked like wax at the end of short pieces of string and handed two of them to the PFC.

"Here," he said to the driver. "Stick these in your ears."

[3]When the action fails to eject a fired cartridge case properly and jams it in place with the open end erect, it is known as a "stovepipe."

"What is it, sir?" the PFC asked doubtfully.

"Genuine Haiti Marine earplugs," Stecker said. "Do what I tell you."

"Aye, aye, sir," the PFC said, and after he watched Stecker carefully push with his index finger one of the wax globs into each ear, he somewhat uneasily put the plugs into his own ears.

Unless someone looked very carefully at his ears (which was highly unlikely) the earplugs would go unnoticed.

The night before, when Stecker checked the jar where he kept his earplugs, he found only one pair left, so he decided he had to make some more.

So Captain Stecker spent an hour at his kitchen sink making six pairs of the earplugs. He knew that he would be spending several hours on the known distance range, and he had long ago learned that ear damage from the muzzle blast of rifle fire was permanent and cumulative. There were a lot of deaf gunnery sergeants in the Marine Corps as proof of that.

From the time he had been a PFC, Stecker had understood that the Boy Scouts were right. "Be Prepared" said it all. He didn't really need any more earplugs than the pair he had in the Bayer Aspirin bottle, not for tomorrow. But the day after tomorrow was something else. He had no spares, and therefore it was time to make some.

The Haiti Marine earplugs were a good deal more complicated than they looked: He first carefully cut the erasers from a dozen pencils. Then with an awl heated red on the stove, he burned a hole through the center of the eraser. He then knotted a length of strong thread through the holes of a small button, just a bit larger than the diameter of the eraser. The loose end of the thread was then fed through the hole in the eraser.

One at a time, the dozen erasers were carefully placed in holes bored through a piece of wood. Then, in a small pot reserved for this specific purpose, he melted paraffin and beef tallow and carefully poured it into the holes in the wood. When it had time to cool, he pushed each earplug out with a pencil. While the beef tallow/paraffin mixture would remain flexible enough to seal his ear canal, it would neither run from the heat of his body, nor harden to the point where removal would be difficult.

It was a trick Captain Stecker had learned when he was a corporal in Haiti in 1922. A staff sergeant named Jim Finch had taken a shine to him, shown him how to make the plugs, and warned him that if he was going to spend any time around ranges, he had goddamned well better get in the habit of using them.

Stecker put the Bayer Aspirin bottle back in the crown of his stiff-brimmed campaign hat, and then with a quick, smooth movement to keep the bottle from falling out flipped it onto his head.

Aside from his field shoes, the campaign hat was about the only part of his enlisted man's uniforms that he had been able to use as an officer. He had to change the insignia on the campaign hat, but it hadn't been necessary to put it up for sale in the thrift shop along with just about everything else.

When he was ten feet away, the range officer spotted him and saluted, raising his arm crisply until the fingers touched the stiff brim of his campaign hat.

"Good morning, sir," he barked.

"Good morning," Stecker said.

"Is there something special, sir?" the range officer asked.

"Just checking," Stecker said. "But how are the young gentlemen doing?"

"Not bad, sir," the range officer said. "I think we have two who are going to shoot High Expert."

"And the low end?"

"I think they're all going to qualify, sir," the range officer said.

"You think, Lieutenant?" Stecker asked. Out of the corner of his eye, he had just seen Maggie's Drawers[4].

"Yes, sir," the range officer said.

"Think won't cut it, Lieutenant," Stecker said. "If one of the young gentlemen fails to qualify first time out, that means his instructors haven't been doing their job."

"Aye, aye, sir," the range officer said.

"I'm going to have a look around," Stecker said. "I won't need any company, and I don't want the pit officer to know I'm here."

"Aye, aye, sir," the range officer repeated.

Stecker walked erectly to the end of the firing line. There were twenty firing points, each occupied by two platoon leader candidates, one firing and one serving as coach. For each two firing points, there was a training NCO, so-called even though most of them were PFCs and not noncommissioned officers. A half dozen NCOs, all three stripe buck sergeants, moved up and down the line keeping an eye on the training NCOs and the firers.

The firing was near the end of the prescribed course. The young gentlemen were about to fire slow fire prone at bull's-eye targets five hundred yards down range. The course of fire would be twenty shots, with sixty seconds allotted for each one. The targets would be pulled and marked after each string of ten shots.

What they were doing now was firing "sighters." They had changed range and were permitted trial shots to see how they had done changing their sights.

The target before which Maggie's Drawers had flown was down in the pits. As Stecker watched, it came up. There was a black marker high on the right side of the target outside the scoring rings.

This young gentleman, Stecker thought wryly, had probably never held a gun in his hands before he became associated with the Marine Corps. Some people learned easily, and some didn't.

"Bullshit!" the firer said when he saw the marker, more in anger than embarrassment.

"Watch your mouth, Mister!" the training NCO snapped.

The firer turned his head in annoyance. And then he recognized Stecker as an officer and looked down the range again.

He didn't recognize me. Except as an officer. But I recognize him. That's the China Marine with the LaSalle convertible. That's surprising. A Marine noncom ought to be at least able to get them inside the scoring rings.

He watched as McCoy single-loaded another round.

At least he knows enough not to mess with the sights, Stecker thought. That was probably a flier.

He watched as McCoy slapped the stock of the Garand into the socket of his arm and wiggled his feet to get in the correct position. And he thought he could detect the expelling of half a breath just before the Garand went off again.

The target dropped from sight. When it appeared again, there was another black marker, this time low and left—in other words on the opposite side of the target from the last spotter disk.

"Oh, bullshit!" McCoy said, furious.

His coach, another young gentleman, jabbed him with his elbow to remind him that he was being watched by an officer.

Stecker gave in to the impulse. He reached out and kicked the sole of the

[4]A red flag waved before a target to show a complete miss.

coach's boot. When the coach looked up at him in surprise, he gestured for him to get up.

Stecker lay down beside McCoy.

When McCoy looked at him, there was recognition in his eyes.

"All sorts of people get to be officers these days," Stecker said softly. "What seems to be your trouble?"

"Beats the shit out of me," McCoy said, still so angry—and perhaps surprised to see Stecker—that it was a moment before he appended, "Sir."

Stecker reached up and tried to wiggle the rear sight. Sometimes they came loose. But not there. And neither was the front sight when he tried it.

"Try it again," Stecker ordered, turning and holding his hand out for another loose round.

When McCoy reached for it, Stecker saw his hands. They were unhealthy white, and covered with open blisters.

"What did you do to your hands?"

"I've sanded a couple of decks[5] lately, Captain," McCoy said.

Stecker wondered what McCoy had done to deserve punishment. The boy probably had an automatic mouth.

Stecker watched carefully as McCoy fired another round. There was nothing in his firing technique that he could fault. And while they were waiting for the target to be marked, he saw that McCoy had wads of chewed-up paper in his ears. It wasn't as good as Haiti earplugs, but it was a hell of a lot better than nothing. And it reminded Stecker that this boy had been around a rifle range enough to know what he was doing. There was no explanation for his shooting all over the target, much less missing it completely, except that there was something really wrong with the rifle.

When the target appeared, the marker was black, just outside the bull's-eye.

"That's a little better," Stecker said.

"I should have split the peg with that one," McCoy said, furiously.

By that he meant that he was confident of his shot, knew where it had gone.

That's either bravado, or he means it. And there's only one way to find out.

"Get out of your sling," Stecker ordered. "And hand me the rifle."

As McCoy pulled the leather sling off his arm, Stecker turned to the training NCO and signaled that he wanted a clip of ammunition. When McCoy handed him the Garand, Stecker put the strap on his own arm and squirmed into the correct position.

"Call my shot," he said to McCoy. "I'm going to take out your two-hundred-yard target number."

McCoy looked at him in surprise. So there would be no confusion about which was the correct target, there were markers at each distance with four-inch-high numbers painted on short, flat pieces of wood. They were not designed as targets.

Stecker himself wondered why he was going to fire at the target number, then realized that he thought somebody might be fucking around with McCoy's target in the pits. If that was the case, which now seemed likely, he would have the ass of the pit officer.

You just don't fuck around in the pits. The Marine Corps does not think rifle marksmanship is an area for practical jokes.

Stecker lined up his sights and squeezed one off.

"You took a chip out of the upper-right corner, Captain," McCoy reported.

[5]Sanding decks (cleaning them with sand and a brick) went back to the days of wooden-decked sailing ships. Now it was used as a punishment.

Maggie's Drawers flew in front of McCoy's target.

Stecker fired again.

"You blew it away, Captain," McCoy reported.

Stecker snapped the safety in front of the trigger guard on, then slipped out of the sling.

"The piece is loaded," he said. "Be careful. Have a shot at the target marker. Number eighteen."

"Aye, aye, sir," McCoy said.

The target number disappeared with McCoy's first shot.

"Nineteen," Stecker ordered.

McCoy fired again. Half of the target number disappeared when the bullet split it.

"Do you think you can hit what's left?" Stecker asked.

He saw Maggie's Drawers being waved furiously in front of the target.

McCoy fired again, and the narrow half remaining of the target number disappeared.

"At targets of opportunity, fire at will," Stecker ordered, softly.

McCoy fired the remaining two rounds in the eight-round en bloc clip at other target numbers. He did not miss.

"Insure that your weapon is empty, and leave the firing line, bringing your weapon with you," Stecker said calmly, reciting the prescribed litany.

By the time they were both on their feet, the range officer and the range NCO were standing beside the training NCO. Having witnessed not only a captain blowing away the target numbers, but apparently encouraging a trainee to do likewise, they were more than a little uneasy.

"This young man has a faulty weapon," Captain Stecker announced. "I think he should be given the opportunity to refire for record."

"Aye, aye, sir," the range officer said.

The range sergeant took the Garand from McCoy and started to examine it.

"Don't you think I know a faulty weapon when I see one, Gunny?" Captain Stecker asked.

"Yes, sir, no offense, sir."

"I realize that tomorrow is the first day of Thanksgiving liberty," Captain Stecker said, "but as we want to give this young man every opportunity to make a decent score, I think we should have the pit officer back, too. Who is he?"

Stecker had decided that the pit officer, whoever he might be, would never forget that Marines don't fuck around the pits after he had spent the first day of Thanksgiving liberty personally hauling, marking, and pasting targets for a Platoon Leader Candidate. That made more sense than writing him an official letter of reprimand, or even turning him in to the battalion commander.

"Lieutenant Macklin, sir," the range officer said.

"I don't think I know him," Stecker said.

"He's the mess officer, Sir. He volunteered to help out in the pits," the range officer said.

And then Stecker saw understanding and then bitterness in McCoy's eyes.

"Do you know Lieutenant Macklin, McCoy?" Stecker asked.

"Yes, sir, I know him."

Stecker made a come-on motion of his hands.

"We were in the Fourth Marines together, sir," McCoy said.

"I see," Stecker said. *I'll find out what the hell that is all about.* "I think you can get on with the firing, Lieutenant," Stecker said.

"Aye, aye, sir," the lieutenant said. And then when Stecker was obviously going to walk away, he called attention and saluted.

Stecker went back to his jeep and was driven off.

Since there was no point in his firing anymore with a faulty weapon, Platoon Leader Candidate McCoy and Platoon Leader Candidate Pickering were put to work policing brass from the firing line until that relay had finished. Then Platoon Leader Candidate McCoy served as coach for Platoon Leader Candidate Pickering while he fired for record. Platoon Leader Candidate Pickering qualified as "Expert."

(TWO)

After leaving McCoy, Captain Stecker went to Battalion Headquarters, where he examined the personal record jacket of First Lieutenant John R. Macklin, USMC. The personnel sergeant was a little uneasy about that—personal records were supposed to be personal—but he wouldn't have dreamed of telling Master Gunnery Sergeant Stecker to mind his own business, and Gunny Stecker was now wearing the silver railroad tracks of a captain.

Then Captain Stecker got back in the jeep and had himself carried to the Platoon Leader Course orderly room.

Word had already gotten back that Captain Stecker had been out on the range, and that he had ordered the re-firing for record of one of the candidates. And that the pit officer be in the pits when he did so. The sergeant-major had been sort of a pal before Stecker took a commission, and he knew there was more to it than he had been told.

He came to his feet and stood at attention when Stecker walked in.

"Good morning, sir," he said.

"As you were," Stecker said.

"How may I help the captain, sir?" the sergeant-major said.

"You wouldn't happen to have a cup of coffee, Sergeant-Major?"

"Yes, sir," the sergeant-major said.

"And if you have a minute, Sergeant-Major, I'd like a word with you in private."

"We can use the commanding officer's office, sir," the sergeant-major said. "He went out to check on the range, sir."

A corporal followed the two of them into the commanding officer's office with two china mugs of coffee, and then left, closing the door behind him.

"Tell me about a kid named McCoy, Charley," Stecker said.

"That's the one was a China Marine?" Stecker nodded. "What do you want to know, Jack?"

"How come he's been sanding decks?"

"I don't know," the sergeant-major said. "He fucked up, I guess."

"What do you know about Lieutenant Macklin?"

"Not much, Jack," the sergeant-major said, after thinking it over. "The cooks hate his ass. But that always happens when there's a new broom. And he's an eager sonofabitch. The scuttlebutt is he's got a lousy efficiency report and is trying to make up for it."

"So he volunteered to be pit officer?"

"And he takes Saturday inspections for the officers. That kind of stuff."

"I want a look at McCoy's records," Stecker said.

"Anything in particular?"

"Just say I'm nosy," Stecker said.

The sergeant-major went into the outer office and returned with a handful of manila files.

"He's more of a fuck-up than I thought," the sergeant-major said. "Jesus, he's been on report at every fucking inspection. He's given lip to the DIs. Even Macklin wrote him up twice for failure to salute. He'll be scrubbing decks again over the Thanksgiving liberty. He's right on the edge of getting his ass shipped out of here. He's going before the elimination board[6] on Friday."

Stecker grunted.

He took McCoy's records from the sergeant-major and read them carefully.

"Very odd," he said. "His last efficiency report says his 'personal deportment and military bearing serves as an example to the command.' I wonder what turned him into a fuck-up here?"

The sergeant-major raised his eyebrows but said nothing.

"It says here that he's an Expert with the Springfield and the .45, and the light and water-cooled Brownings. I was on the range before . . ."

"So I heard," the sergeant-major said.

"He could barely get a round on the target, much less in the black," Stecker said. "I found out he had a faulty weapon. He could hit target numbers with it. It was just that he was all over the target when he fired at a bull's-eye."

"Jesus, was he fucking around on the rifle range, too?" the sergeant-major asked.

"He wasn't fucking around on the rifle range, Charley," Stecker said.

"And Macklin was the pit officer, right?" the sergeant-major said, finally putting things together.

"Was he?" Stecker asked, innocently.

"Jesus Christ!" the sergeant-major said.

"I'm sure you know as well as I do, sergeant-major," Stecker said, "that no Marine officer is capable of using his office and authority to settle personal grudges."

"Yes, sir," the sergeant-major said.

"And under the circumstances, Sergeant-Major, I can see no reason for Platoon Leader Candidate McCoy to refire for record. It would be an unnecessary expenditure of time and ammunition. If he had a properly functioning rifle, I'm sure that he would—since he has been drawing Expert marksman's pay since boot camp—qualify with the Garand."

"Got you," the sergeant-major said.

"Further, it would interfere with his Thanksgiving liberty. Platoon Leader Candidate McCoy is shortly going to be commissioned . . ."

"He'll have to get past the elimination board," the sergeant-major said. "With this record, he has to go before it."

"What record do you mean, Sergeant-Major?" Captain Stecker said, as calmly and deliberately he tore from the manila folder all the official records of misbehavior and unsatisfactory performance Platoon Leader Candidate McCoy had acquired since beginning the course. He shredded them and dropped them into the wastebasket.

"What do I tell the old man, Jack?" the sergeant-major asked.

[6]A board of officers charged with determining whether or not a platoon leader candidate had proved himself unfit or unworthy of being commissioned.

"Three things, Charley," Stecker said. "First, that if there is some reason McCoy can't have Thanksgiving liberty, I want to hear about it. Second, that the colonel has taken two evening meals in the mess and found them unsatisfactory. And third, that I politely and unofficially suggest that maybe the chow would be better if the mess officer stayed where he belongs, in the kitchen."

The sergeant-major nodded.

"I'm sorry about this, Jack," he said. "I feel like a damned fool."

Stecker did not let him off the hook.

"When I was the gunny, Charley," he said, "the colonel expected me to know what was going on in the ranks. I found the best way to do that was get off my ass and have a look at things."

And then he walked out of the office.

(THREE)

Inasmuch as ceremonies are an integral part of the life and duties of young officers, and because the Marine Corps Schools believed that "doing is the best means of learning," ceremonies of one kind or another were frequently on the training program of the Platoon Leader's Course.

One such ceremony was scheduled for 1700 hours, 19 November 1941. It was a formal retreat. The platoon leader candidates would be returned from the Known Distance Firing Range in plenty of time to clean their rifles, shave and wash, and change into greens. The training schedule allotted all of thirty-five minutes for this purpose.

Waiting for Corporal Pleasant to blow his whistle, McCoy was pretty well down in the dumps. At first, he had been almost thrilled that Macklin had been caught sticking it to him. He'd thought that luck was finally falling his way. It hadn't taken long for the old-gunny-now-a-captain to figure out that somebody was fucking him in the pits, or even that the sonofabitch sticking it in him was Lieutenant Macklin.

But the good feeling soon dissipated. For one thing, officers took care of one another, and the captain, if he said anything at all to Macklin, wasn't going to jump his ass. Stecker believed that Macklin was either sloppy in the pits, or that he thought what he was doing was funny. Stecker had no reason to think that Macklin was personally doing his best to get him booted out of the Platoon Leader's Course.

All the whole incident had meant was that he was going to get a chance to fire for record again. That was all. And Macklin was being taught not to "fool around" when he was pit officer by having to spend Thanksgiving morning on the range. It was possible that he would pull the same shit all over again. Why not? There would be nobody there to watch him.

When he came off the rifle range, the sand and the bricks would be waiting for him, and he would spend Thanksgiving afternoon on his knees scrubbing the decks. For "disrespectful attitude."

And on Friday morning, he would go before the elimination board. Pleasant had told him about that. He could get out of it, Pleasant said, and probably get the whole Thanksgiving weekend as liberty, if he would just face the fact that they weren't going to make him an officer and resign.

He had told Pleasant to go fuck himself. Which is why he would be sanding the deck.

McCoy didn't believe he was ever going to get a gold bar to put on his shoulder. Not really. Not inside. But he was going to take the one chance he saw: Sometimes the elimination board wouldn't bust people out, but would instead "drop them back," which meant that you went through part of the course again with a class that started later. That happened when somebody bilged academics. He had never heard of somebody being dropped back for "attitude" or "unsuitability," which is what they called it when they sent you before the elimination board for fucking up.

But that's what he was going to ask for. He had come this far, and he wasn't just going to belly up for the bastards. He probably wouldn't get it, and next Monday he would probably be on his way as Pvt. McCoy to Camp LeJeune, or maybe Diego, as a machine-gunner.

And it was a real pain in the ass to get all shined up for a retreat parade knowing that they were going to read your name off on two lists, one for "extra training" which is what they called the deck sanding, and the other to go before the elimination board. And when they had done that, knowing that while everybody else was getting beered up at the slop chute, he would be on his fucking hands and knees sanding the deck.

"If I helped you with the deck," Pick Pickering said, as if he was reading his mind, "maybe we could get done quicker."

"Pleasant would get you your own deck," McCoy said. "But thanks, Pick."

"Let's give it a shot," Pickering said.

"When they hold formation," McCoy said, "they're going to read off names of people going before the elimination board. Mine is on it."

"You don't believe that," Pickering said, loyally.

"I know," McCoy said. "It's not scuttlebutt."

"That's not right," Pickering said. "Christ, it's goddamned unfair."

"It's an unfair world," McCoy said. "This is the Marine Corps."

"There ought to be some way to register a complaint," Pickering said.

McCoy laughed at him, but then, touched by Pickering's loyalty, punched him affectionately on the arm.

Pickering was a good guy. Dumb, but a good guy. Even after McCoy had told him that he was on everybody's shit list, and that if he kept hanging around, some of the shit they were throwing was bound to splatter on him, he'd hung around anyway. Pickering was going to be a good officer.

"Turn around, asshole," McCoy said. "Let me check you out."

There was nothing wrong with Pickering's uniform or equipment. But a pin on one of McCoy's collar point "oxes"[7] had come off, and the ox was hanging loose. Pickering fixed it.

What the fuck difference does it make? McCoy thought bitterly. *This is the last time I'll wear it anyway. I'll go before the elimination board in dungarees.*

Corporal Pleasant blew his whistle and all the freshly bathed and shaved young gentlemen rushed out onto the company street, where they formed ranks. Corporal Pleasant then issued the appropriate order causing the young gentlemen to open ranks so that he could more conveniently inspect their shaves, the press of their green uniforms, and the cleanliness of their Garand rifles.

They would be inspected again, a few minutes later, by the company com-

[7]Platoon Leader Candidates wore brass insignia, the letters OC (hence "Ox"), standing for Officer Candidate, on shirt collar points and fore-and-aft hats in lieu of insignia of rank.

mander and gunnery sergeant, but Corporal Pleasant wanted to make sure they were all shipshape before that happened.

To McCoy's surprise, Pleasant not only found nothing wrong with his appearance, shave, or shine, he didn't even inspect his rifle when he stepped in front of him.

He probably figures he doesn't have to bother anymore.

The company commander and the gunnery sergeant made their appearance at the end of the company street, and one by one, the drill instructors of the four platoons of platoon leader candidates called their troops to order.

McCoy's company commander, a lieutenant, spoke to him as he inspected his rifle.

"I understand you had some trouble with this today, McCoy?"

"Yes, sir."

"And I also understand the stoppage has been cleared?"

What the fuck is he talking about? Stoppage?

"Yes, sir."

The company commander moved on. The sergeant-major looked right into McCoy's face, but said nothing, and there was no particular expression on his face.

When the four platoons had been inspected, the officers took their positions, and the gunny read the orders of the day.

The next day was Thanksgiving[8], the Gunny announced, as if no one had figured that out for himself. Liberty for all hands, with the exception of those individuals requiring extra training, would commence when the formation was dismissed. The next duty day, Friday, would be given over to the purchase of uniforms. Those individuals who were to appear before the elimination board would not, repeat, not, order any officer-type uniforms until the decisions of the elimination board were announced. Liberty would begin on Friday, until 0330 hours the following Monday, as soon as the platoon leader candidates had arranged for the purchase of officer-type uniforms. There would be no, repeat, no, liberty for anyone called before the elimination board.

The gunny then read the list of those who required extra training, and then the list of those to face the elimination board.

And then he did an about-face and saluted the company commander, who returned the salute, ordered him to dismiss the formation, and walked off.

The gunny barked, "Dis-miss!"

Pick Pickering punched McCoy's arm.

"See? I told you you weren't gonna get boarded!"

And neither, McCoy thought, *did I hear my name called for extra training. And they didn't say anything about refiring for record, either.*

What the fuck is going on?

He thought it was entirely likely that the gunny had "forgotten" to read his name, so that when he failed to show up to sand the deck, or to refire for record, or for the elimination board itself, they could add AWOL to everything else.

He saw Pleasant going behind the building to get into his Ford. He ran after him. Pleasant rolled down the window.

"Something I can do for you, Mr. McCoy?"

"What the fuck is going on, Pleasant? Why wasn't my name called for extra training and for the elimination board?"

"Because you're not on extra training, Mr. McCoy, and because you're not going before the elimination board. You are on liberty, Mr. McCoy."

"You going to tell me what's going on?"

[8]Until December 1941, Thanksgiving was celebrated on the third Thursday of November.

"Very well, Mr. McCoy. It's very simple. In ten days they are going to pin a gold bar on your shoulder. Between now and then, the gunny and I will do whatever we can to make things as painless as possible for you."

"I thought you wanted to bust me out of here."

"Oh, we do," Pleasant said. "Nothing would give us greater pleasure. But then, we know better than to fuck with a rabbi."

"What rabbi?"

"Is there anything else, Mr. McCoy?" Pleasant said. "If not, with your permission, sir, I would like to start my Thanksgiving liberty."

"Fuck you, Pleasant," McCoy said.

Pleasant rolled up the window and drove off.

Pick Pickering was waiting for McCoy in the barracks.

"Well?"

"I'm on liberty like everybody else," McCoy said. "And no elimination board."

"Great!" Pickering said, and punched his arm. "Let's go find a cab and get the hell out of here."

"Out of here, where?"

"In compliance with orders from the United States Marine Corps, I am going to buy some officer-type uniforms."

"What the hell are you talking about? We're not supposed to buy uniforms until Friday."

"Right," Pickering said.

"Well?"

"I'm learning," Pickering said. "You will recall that they didn't say anything about where we were to buy the uniforms. Just that we buy them on Friday."

"So?"

"On Friday, I am going to buy uniforms. In Brooks Brothers in New York."

"What's Brooks Brothers?"

"It's a place where they sell clothing, including uniforms."

"Jesus!" McCoy said.

"And when we're not buying our uniforms, we can be lifting some skirts," Pickering said. "The only problem is finding a cab to get us off this fucking base to someplace we can catch a train to New York."

"We don't need a cab," McCoy said. "I've got a car."

"You have a car? Here?" Pickering asked, surprised.

McCoy nodded.

"Mr. McCoy," Pickering said. "The first time I laid eyes on you, I said, 'Now, there is a man of many talents, the sort of chap it would be wise to cultivate in the furtherance of my military career.' "

McCoy smiled.

"And will this car of yours make it to New York? Without what I have recently learned to call 'mechanical breakdown'?"

"It's a LaSalle," McCoy said.

"In that case, if you pay for the gas," Pickering said, "I will take care of the room. Fair?"

"Fair," McCoy agreed.

XII

(ONE)
The Foster Park Hotel
Central Park South
New York City, New York
2320 Hours 19 November 1941

Pick Pickering was at the wheel of the LaSalle when it pulled up in front of the marquee of the Foster Park Hotel. They had gassed up just past Baltimore and changed places there.

McCoy had gone to sleep thinking about Ellen Feller, about her probably being somewhere in Baltimore, and about what had happened between them in China—memories that reminded him of the very long time since he'd had his ashes hauled.

The doorman stepped off the curb, walked out to the driver's side, opened the door, and said, "Welcome to the Foster Park Hotel, sir," before he realized that the driver was some kind of a soldier, a Marine, and an enlisted man, not even an officer.

"May I help you, sir?"

Pickering got out of the car.

"Take care of the car, please," he said. "We'll need it sometime Sunday afternoon."

"You'll be checking in, sir?"

The question seemed to amuse the Marine.

"I hope so," he said. "The luggage is in the trunk."

He turned back to the car.

"Off your ass and on your feet, McCoy," he said. "We're here."

McCoy sat up, startled, looked around, and as almost a reflex action, opened his door and got out.

"Where are we?" he asked, groggily.

"My grandfather calls it Sodom-on-Hudson," Pickering said, and took McCoy's arm and propelled him toward the revolving door.

The desk clerk was busy with someone else as Pickering and McCoy approached registration. Pickering pulled the Register in front of him, took the pen, and filled out one of the cards.

When the desk clerk turned his attention toward Pickering, he thrust the Registration card at him.

"We'd like a small suite," he said.

"I'm not sure that we'll be able to accommodate you, sir," the clerk said.

The clerk didn't know what the OC insignia on the collar points of the uniforms meant, but he knew a Marine private when he saw one, and Marine privates couldn't afford the prices of the Foster Park Hotel.

"House is full, is it?" the Marine asked.

"What I mean to suggest, sir," the desk clerk said, as tactfully as he could, "is that our prices are, well, a little stiff."

"That's all right," the Marine said. "I won't be paying for it anyway. Something with a view of the park, if one is available."

The desk clerk looked down at the card in his hand.

He didn't recognize the name, but in the block "Special Billing Instructions" the Marine had written: "Andrew Foster, S/F, Attn: Mrs. Delahanty."

"Just one moment, please, sir, I'll check," the desk clerk said.

He disappeared behind the rack of mail-and-key slots and handed the card to the night resident manager, who was having a cup of coffee and a Danish pastry at his desk. He handed him the registration card. The night resident manager glanced at it casually, and then jumped to his feet.

He approached the Marines standing at the desk with his hand extended.

"Welcome to the Park, Mr. Pickering," he said. "It's a pleasure to have you in the house."

"Thank you," Pick Pickering said, shaking his hand. "Is there some problem?"

"Absolutely no problem. Would Penthouse C be all right with you?"

"If you're sure we can't rent it," Pickering said.

"Not at this hour, Mr. Pickering," the night resident manager said, laughing appreciatively.

"Well, if somebody wants it, move us," Pickering said. "But otherwise, that's fine. We'll be here until Sunday afternoon."

The night resident manager took a key from the rack and came from behind the marble counter.

"If we had only known you were coming, Mr. Pickering . . ." he said. "I'm afraid there's not even a basket of fruit in the penthouse."

"At half-past four this afternoon, it was even money that we would be spending the weekend with a brick and a pile of sand," Pick Pickering said. "I don't much care about fruit, but I wish you would send up some liquor, peanuts, that sort of thing."

"Immediately, Mr. Pickering," the night resident manager said, as he bowed them onto the elevator.

Penthouse C of the Foster Park Hotel consisted of a large sitting room opening onto a patio overlooking Fifty-ninth Street and Central Park. To the right and left were bedrooms, and there was a butler's pantry and a bar with four stools.

When he went directly to answer nature's call, McCoy found himself in the largest bathroom he had ever seen.

By the time he came out, there were two room service waiters and a bellboy in the room. The bellboy was arranging cut flowers in vases. One waiter was organizing on the rack behind the bar enough liquor bottles to stock a saloon, and the other was moving through the room filling silver bowls from a two-pound can of cashews.

Pick Pickering was sitting on a couch talking on the telephone. He saw McCoy and made a gesture indicating he was thirsty.

"Scotch," he called, putting his hand over the mouthpiece.

By the time McCoy had crossed to the bar, the night resident manager had two drinks made.

"We're glad to have you with us, sir," the night resident manager said, as he put one drink in McCoy's hand and scurried across the room to deliver the other to Pickering.

When they were all finally gone and Pickering finished his telephone call, McCoy sat down beside him.

"What the hell is all this?" he asked.

Pickering leaned back against the couch and took a swallow of his drink.

"Christ, that tastes good," he said. "Incidentally, I have located the quarry."

"What quarry?"

"The females with liftable skirts," Pickering said. "There's a covey of them in a saloon called El Borracho . . . which, appropriately, means 'The Kiss,' I think."

"I asked you what's going on around here," McCoy said.

"We all have our dark secrets," Pickering said. "I, for example, know far more than I really want to about your lady missionary."

"Come on, Pick," McCoy said.

"This is the Foster Park Hotel," Pickering said. "Along with forty-one others, it is owned by a man named Andrew Foster. Andrew Foster has one child, a daughter. She married a man who owns ships. A lot of ship, Ken. They have one child. Me."

"Jesus Christ!" McCoy said.

"It is not the sort of thing I would wish our beloved Corporal Pleasant, or our sainted gunny, to know. So keep your fucking mouth shut about it, McCoy."

"Jesus Christ!" McCoy repeated.

"Yes?" Pickering asked, benignly, as befitting the Saviour. "What is it you wish, my son?"

(TWO)

They did not get laid. All the girls at the first night club had escorts. They smiled, especially at Pick Pickering, but it proved impossible to separate them from the young men they were with. The candy-asses were worried about leaving their girls alone with Pickering, McCoy thought, approvingly. He was sure they had learned from painful experience that if they blinked their eyes, Pickering and their girls would be gone.

Most of the time McCoy didn't know what the hell anyone was talking about. Only one of the girls showed any interest at all in him. She asked him if he had been at Harvard with "Malcolm." When he said no, she asked him where he had gone to school. When he said "Saint Rose of Lima," she gave him a funny smile and ignored him thereafter.

In the second place, which was called the "21" Club, McCoy thought they probably could have gotten laid: There were enough women around, but the son of the proprietor fucked that up. He wanted to hear all about the Platoon Leader's Course because he'd joined the Corps and was about to report for active duty.

Pick kept him fascinated with tales of Corporal Pleasant and slurping food from trays and doing the duck walk. When they left, he insisted on paying for their drinks and told McCoy that he was welcome any time. But that didn't get them laid either.

The third place McCoy remembered hearing about somewhere. It was called the "Stork Club." When they got there, he didn't think they were going to get in because there was a line of people waiting on the sidewalk. But Pick just walked to the head of the line, and a bouncer or whatever lowered a rope and called Pick "Mr. Pickering," and they walked in.

There was a table against the wall with a "reserved" sign on it, but a headwaiter snatched that away and sat them down there. Moments later a waiter with a bottle of champagne showed up, soon followed by the proprietor of the Stork Club. The proprietor asked about "Mr. Foster" and told Pick to make sure he carried his best regards to his parents.

Like the guy at "21," he picked up the bill. That meant they got a decent load on without spending a dime.

"Tomorrow, Ken, we will get laid," Pickering said as they got in a cab to return to the hotel. "Look on tonight as reconnaissance. The key to a successful assault, you will recall, is a good reconnaissance."

As they were having breakfast the next morning, Pick had an idea.

He called the Harvard Club and had the steward put a notice on the bulletin board: "Mr. Malcolm Pickering will entertain his friends and acquaintances at post–Thanksgiving Dinner cocktails from 2:30 P.M., Penthouse C, the Foster Park Hotel. Friends and acquaintances are expected to bring two girls."

McCoy had a good time in the morning. He made some remark about what a nice hotel it was, and Pickering then took him on a tour. This was fascinating to McCoy; and it was a complete tour, kitchens, laundry, even the little building up above the penthouses where the elevator machinery was.

McCoy saw that there was more to the tour than showing him around. Pickering looked inside garbage cans, even went into rooms with open doors. He was inspecting the place, looking for things that weren't as they were supposed to be. The other side of that was that he knew how things were supposed to be. He might be rich as shit, but he understood the hotel business.

He wondered if Pickering had learned that in school, and asked him. Pick laughed and told him that the first job he'd had in a Foster hotel was as a twelve-year-old busboy, cleaning tables.

"I can do anything in the hotel except French pastry," Pickering said. "I've never been able to handle egg white properly."

About one o'clock, as they sat in the sitting room in their shirts and trousers drinking Feigenspann XXX Ale from the necks of the bottles, the hotel started setting up for the cocktail party. There was an enormous turkey, and a whole ham, and a piece of roast beef. And all kinds of other stuff. Thinking of how much it was costing made McCoy uncomfortable. No matter how nice Pick was being, McCoy was beginning to feel like a mooch.

It got worse when the people started showing up for the party: It wasn't hard to figure that if all the guests weren't as rich as Pick, they were still rich. And he had nothing in common with them. The only thing he had in common with Pick was the Marine Corps. And then there was one particular girl. She really made him uncomfortable.

He had never seen a more beautiful girl in his life. She was fucking near-perfect. She had black hair, in a pageboy, with dark, glowing eyes that made her skin seem pure white.

She wasn't dressed as fancy as the others, just a sweater and a skirt, with a string of pearls hanging down around her neck.

His first thought was that he would happily swap his left nut to get her in the sack, and his second thought was that she wasn't that kind of female at all. She wasn't going to give any away until she had the gold ring on her finger—not because she was careful, but because that was the kind of woman she was. Once, when she caught him looking at her, she looked right back at him, as if she was asking, "What's a scumbag like you doing looking at me? I'm not like the rest of these people."

And for some reason, she kept him from putting the make on anybody else. Not all of Pick's "friends and acquaintances" had shown up with two girls, but a lot of them had. And a bunch of women had come by themselves. One of them, a sharp-featured woman with blond hair down to her shoulders, had even come on to him, smiling at him and touching his arm when she asked him if he was in the Marines with Pick.

But he saw the girl in the pageboy looking at them with her dark eyes and didn't do anything about the blonde. After a moment, she went away.

Ten or fifteen minutes later, the smoke in the place (there must have been a hundred people, and they were all smoking) got to him; and he realized he'd had more Scotch than he should have. He didn't want to get shit-faced and make an ass of himself and embarrass Pick in front of his friends. So he took another bottle of ale from the refrigerator, walked into "his" bedroom, where he interrupted a couple kissing and feeling each other up, and went out on the patio for a breath of cold, fresh air.

The sun had come up, there wasn't much wind, and it wasn't as cold as he thought it would be. It was nippy, but that's what he wanted anyhow. He sat on the wall, carefully, because they were twenty-two floors up, and looked down at Fifty-ninth Street. When that started to make him feel a little dizzy, he looked into Central Park.

He was pretty far gone from where he thought he would be on Thanksgiving afternoon, he thought, sanding the fucking deck. Then he remembered he was really far from where he had been last Thanksgiving, a PFC machine-gunner in Dog Company, First Battalion, 4th Marines, in Shanghai. He'd taken the noon meal in the mess hall. They always sent in frozen turkeys on Thanksgiving and Christmas, and that was the only time there was turkey in China. They even bent the rules for Thanksgiving and Christmas, and you could bring guests who weren't European. He remembered that Zimmerman had brought his Chinese wife and all their half-white kids to the mess.

"Don't go to sleep," a female voice said to him. "That's a long step if you walk in your sleep."

Startled, he stood up and then looked to see who was talking to him.

It was the perfect fucking female in the pageboy haircut.

"I wasn't about to go to sleep," he said.

"You could have fooled me," she said. "You looked like you were bored to death and about to doze off."

"I was thinking," McCoy said.

The string of pearls around her neck had looped around one of her breasts. It wasn't sexy. It was feminine.

"About what?"

"What?"

"What were you thinking about?" she pursued.

She sat down on the wall, and looked up at him.

Jesus Christ! Up close she's even more beautiful!

"Where I was last Thanksgiving," he said.

"And where you might be next Thanksgiving?"

"No," he said. "I wasn't thinking about that."

"I thought you might be," she said, and she smiled.

"Why?"

"Well, you're a Marine," she said. "Don't they wonder where they'll be moved next?"

"I don't," he replied without thinking. "Not any further than the Corps, I mean.

I know I'm going to be in the Corps. It doesn't matter where I'll be. It'll still be the Corps."

She looked as if she didn't understand him, but the question she asked was perfectly normal: "Where were you last Thanksgiving?" she asked.

"Shanghai," he said. And added, "China."

"So that's where Shanghai is," she said brightly. "I knew it was either there or in Australia."

I knew fucking well that I would show my ass if I tried to talk to somebody like this. What a dumb fucking thing to say!

She saw the hurt in his eyes.

"Sorry," she said.

"It's all right," McCoy said.

"No, it's not," she said. "There are extenuating circumstances, but I shouldn't have jumped on you."

"What are the extenuating circumstances?" McCoy asked.

"I'm an advertising copywriter," she said.

"I don't know what that is," McCoy confessed.

"I write the words in advertisements," she explained.

"Oh," he said.

"Our motto is brevity," she said.

"Oh," McCoy repeated.

"We try not to say anything redundant," she said. "It's okay to jump on somebody who does."

"Okay," he said.

"I had no right to do that to you," she said.

"I didn't mind," McCoy said.

"Yes, you did," she said, matter-of-factly.

When she looks into my eyes, my knees get weak.

"What did you do in China, last Thanksgiving?"

"I was in a water-cooled Browning .30 crew," he said.

"Browning machine gun, you mean?" she asked.

He was surprised that she knew. He nodded.

"I somehow didn't think you were up in Cambridge with our host," she said.

"I guess that's pretty obvious, isn't it?"

She understood his meaning.

"Different means different," she said. "Not better or worse."

The door to the sitting room opened, and six or seven people came onto the patio and headed for them.

They sure as hell don't know me, which means they're headed for her. Probably to take her out of here. And if she goes, that's the last I'll ever see of her.

"Prove it," McCoy said.

"Huh?"

"Go somewhere else with me," McCoy said.

"Where?" she asked, warily.

"I don't know," McCoy said. "Anywhere you want."

She was still looking at him thoughtfully when Pickering's friends came over to her.

"We wondered what had happened to you," one of the girls said. "We're going over to Marcy's. You about ready?"

"You go along," the most beautiful female McCoy had ever seen said. "I've other plans."

She looked into his eyes and smiled.

He realized that his heart was throbbing. Like the water hose on a Browning .30.

(THREE)

"Where are you taking me?" she asked, as they walked through the lobby of the Foster Park.

"I don't know anyplace to take you," he said. "I've never been in New York before."

"I have sort of a strange idea," she said. "Chinese food."

"Huh?"

"I guess your 'Thanksgiving in Shanghai' speech triggered it," she said. "Or maybe I'm over my ears in turkey."

"You'll have to show me," he said. "I don't know anything about this town," he said.

"I think we could find a Chinese restaurant in Chinatown," she said.

"Let's get a cab," he said.

"Let's take the subway," she said.

"I can afford a cab," McCoy said.

Which means, of course, that you can't.

"I like to watch the people on the subway," she said, took his arm, and headed him toward Sixth Avenue.

"Why?" he asked.

"You ever been . . . No, of course, you haven't," she said. "You'll see."

His eyes widened at the variations of the species *homo sapiens* displayed on the subway. And they smiled at each other, and somehow she wanted to touch him, and did, and put her arm in his, her hand against the rough fabric of his overcoat.

Maybe it is the uniform, she thought. *Men in uniform are supposed to get the girls.*

She let herself think about that. It was not her style to leave parties with men she had met there. Especially friends of people like Malcolm Pickering. What was there about this young man that made him different?

A drunk, a young one in a leather jacket and a knitted hat with a pom-pom, walked past them and examined her with approval.

And something happened to the eyes of the young man whose arm she was holding. *And, my God, whose name I don't even know!* His eyes narrowed, just a little, but visibly. And they brightened and turned alert. And menacing.

She was more than a little frightened.

My God, he is a Marine! And all I need is to have him get in a fist fight with a drunk on the subway.

She watched, fascinated, as the drunk sensed the menace, put on a smile, and walked farther down the car. McCoy's eyes followed him until he was sure the threat had passed. Then his eyes moved to her, and they changed again. The menace disappeared and was replaced by something much softer. It was almost as if he was now frightened.

My God, he's afraid of me!

"I don't know your name," she said.

"McCoy," he said.

"McCoy Smith? McCoy Jones?" she asked.

"Kenneth McCoy," he said.

She took her arm from under his and gave him her hand.

"Ernestine Sage," she said. "My parents obviously hoped for a boy. Please don't call me either 'Ernestine' or 'Ernie.' "

"What can I call you?" Kenneth McCoy asked.

Not "what do I call you," she thought, *but, "what can I call you." He's asking permission. He doesn't want to offend me. I don't have to be afraid of him.*

"Most people call me 'Sage,' " she said. "Sage means wise."

"I know," he said.

She slipped her hand back under his arm. And she saw the skin of his neck deepen in color.

They walked down Mott Street with her hand very much aware of the warmth of his body, even through the overcoat.

"There is a legend that young white women should not come here alone," Sage said. "That they will be snatched by white slavers."

He did not sense that she was teasing him.

"You'll be all right," he said.

When she looked into his face, he averted his eyes.

"They say the best food is in little places in the alleys," Sage said. "That the places on Mott Street are for tourists. The trouble is that they speak only Chinese in the little places."

"I speak Chinese," he said, and while she was still wondering whether or not he was trying to pull her leg, he led her into one of the alleys. Fifty feet down it, he stopped in front of a glass-covered sign and started to read it.

He's really very clever. If I didn't know better I'd almost believe he knew what he was looking at.

"See anything you think I'd like?" she asked, innocently.

"No," he said. "This is a Szechaun restaurant. Most Szechuan food is hotter than hell."

An old Chinese woman scampered toward them.

McCoy spoke to her. In Chinese. Sage looked at him in astonishment. But there was no question he was really speaking Chinese, because, chattering back at McCoy, the old woman reversed direction and led them farther down the street.

"Her nephew," McCoy explained, "runs a Cantonese restaurant. You'll like that better, I think."

The restaurant was on the fourth floor of an old building. There were no other white people inside, and the initial response to the two of them, Sage thought, was resentment, even hostility.

But then McCoy spoke to the man who walked up to them, and smiles appeared. They were bowed to a table, tea was produced, and a moment later an egg roll rich with shrimp.

"This is to give us an appetite," McCoy said. "Hell, I can make a meal of egg rolls." Then he heard what he had said. "Sorry," he said. "You have to remember, I'm a Marine. We get in the habit, without being around women, of talking a little rough."

"Hell," Sage said. "I don't give a damn. If it makes you feel any better, cuss as much as you goddamn well please."

He looked at her without comprehension, then he smiled. When he smiled like that, he looked like a little boy.

Their knees touched under the table. He withdrew his as if the contact had burned. With a mind of its own, seemingly, Sage's foot searched for his. When they touched, he withdrew again. She finally managed to pin his ankle against the table leg.

Now they didn't seem to be able to look at each other.

There was a steady stream of food. Very small portions.

"I told him to bring us one of everything," he said. "If you don't like something, give it to me."

"What does that OC mean on your collar?"

"They call it the oxes," he said. "I suppose it stands for officer candidate."

"You're going to be an officer?"

He nodded, wondering if that would surprise her, and then hoping it might impress her a little.

"When?"

"End of the month," he said.

"Then what?"

"What do you mean, 'then what'?"

"Where will you be stationed?"

"I don't know," he said.

"I remember. It's all the Corps, and therefore it doesn't make any difference, right?"

"Something like that."

We are both pretending, Sage thought. *He is pretending that I am not playing anklesy with him, and I am pretending that I am not doing it.*

"I can't eat another bite," she said, after a while.

"I don't even know what I've eaten," McCoy said.

"To hell with turkey anyway," Sage said. "This is what I'm going to do from now on on Thanksgiving."

For some reason, when they got to the street, Sage felt a little dizzy.

"This time a cab," she said.

"Where are we going?"

"West Third Street," she said.

"What's there?"

"Another Chinese restaurant I heard about, what else?"

She motioned him into her apartment and then closed the door and locked it. He roamed the apartment, and when he came back, she was still leaning on the door.

"I like your apartment," he said.

"I'm glad," she said. "My father calls it my hovel."

"I was afraid you were going to turn out rich, like Pick."

"Would that have bothered you?"

"Yes," he said, simply.

They looked at each other, their eyes locking for a long moment.

"I don't know what the hell I'm doing," McCoy said. "All I know is that I don't want to fuck this up."

He's so upset that he didn't hear himself. Otherwise I'd have got an apology for the "fuck," and he would have blushed like a tomato.

"Neither do I," Sage said. "I don't expect you to believe this under the circumstances, but neither do I."

"I think maybe I had better go."

She pushed herself off the door and walked so close to him that she could smell the wet wool odor of his overcoat.

"There's a time and a place for everything," she said. "And this is the time and place where I think you should kiss me. If that goes the way I think it will, then I think you should pick me up and carry me into the bedroom."

"Pick you up?" he asked, incredulously.

"I could crawl, I suppose," she said.

He laughed, and scooped her up, and carried her into the bedroom. He lowered her onto the bed and then stood up.

He still hasn't kissed me. All we've done is play anklesy. And the way he's standing there with that dumb look on his face, nothing is going to happen.

Very deliberately, she reached for the hem of her sweater and pulled it over her head. He stared at her in marvel. She reached behind her back and unhooked her brassiere, so that he could look at her, naked to the waist.

"Now you," she said, very softly.

She looked at him then as he ripped the uniform off.

He's good at that. Very fast. He's probably had a lot of experience taking his clothes off in a hurry in situations like this.

And then he was naked.

"You're the most beautiful thing I have ever seen," he said.

"So are you," Sage said.

As McCoy came to the bed and put his arms around her and with a great deal more tenderness than she expected held her tight against him, Sage thought, *I wonder if it's going to hurt as much as they say it hurts, and if there will be a lot of blood, and if that will embarrass him.*

(FOUR)

Pick was sitting in his underwear having breakfast in the sitting room of Penthouse C when McCoy returned.

"Been out spreading pollen, have you?" Pick said.

McCoy didn't reply.

"I wondered what the hell had happened to you," Pickering said. "I took a chance and ordered breakfast for both of us."

"I'm not hungry," McCoy said.

But he sat down for a cup of coffee and wound up eating a breakfast steak and a couple of eggs and the half dozen remaining rolls.

"I thought you might take just a little bite," Pickering said, "for restorative purposes."

"Fuck you," McCoy said.

"Then you didn't get any," Pickering said. "With your well-known incredible good luck, you fell into the clutches of one of our famous cockteasers."

"I got a goddamned cherry," McCoy said.

"I didn't know there were any left," Pickering said without thinking, before realizing that McCoy wasn't boasting; that quite to the contrary, he was ashamed.

"Who was she?" he asked.

"There were two poor people in here yesterday," McCoy said. "I found the other one."

"What has being poor got to do with getting laid?" Pickering asked. "Just looking around, I get the idea that poor people spend a lot of time screwing."

"She's a nice girl, Pick," McCoy said. "And I copped her cherry."

"Death," Pickering said, mocking the sonorous tones of the announcer in the March of Time newsreels, "and losing cherries comes inexorably in due time to all men. And virgins."

"Screw you," McCoy said, but he was smiling.

"Which one was it?" Pickering asked.

McCoy didn't want to tell Pickering her name.

"We're going to have lunch," he said.

"I will, of course, vacate the premises," Pickering said.

"Nothing like that, goddamn it," McCoy said. "She has to work this morning. She said she would meet me for a sandwich. Someplace called the Grand Central Oyster Bar. You know where it is?"

"Oddly enough, I do. The Grand Central Oyster Bar, despite the misleading name, is in Grand Central Station." He stopped himself from saying what popped into his mind, that McCoy's deflowered virgin had apparently heard of the aphrodisiacal virtues of oysters. "It's right around the corner from Brooks Brothers."

"She said twelve-thirty. Is that going to give us enough time?"

"Sure," Pickering said.

Platoon Leader Candidates Pickering and McCoy were not the first about-to-be-commissioned Marine officers the salesman at Brooks Brothers had seen. More than that, he was pleased to see them. Not only was it a sale of several hundred dollars (more if the customer wanted his uniforms custom made rather than off the rack), it was a quick sale. None of the salesman's time had to be spent smiling approval as the customer tried on one item after another. There were no choices to be made. The style was set.

"Uniforms, gentlemen?" the salesman said.

"Sure," one of the Marines said. "I thought it would be a good idea if you re-measured me. I have just gone through a rather interesting physical training course, and I think I ain't what I used to be."

"Oh, you have an account with us, sir?"

"Yes," Pickering said. "But I'm glad you brought that up. This is Mr. McCoy. He's just come from the Orient, and he doesn't have an account. I don't think he's even had time to open a bank account, have you, Ken?"

"I've got a bank account," McCoy said.

"In any event, you'll have to open an account for him," Pickering said.

"I'm sure that won't be a problem, sir," the salesman said. "I didn't catch the name?"

"Pickering, Malcolm Pickering."

"One moment, sir, and I'll get your measurements," the salesman said.

Pickering's measurements were filed together with his account. There were coded notations that payment was slow, but was always eventually made in full.

Brooks Brothers preferred to be paid promptly, but they were just as happy to have very large accounts (the last order from young Mr. Pickering had been for two dinner jackets, three lounge suits, one morning coat, a dozen shirts, a dozen sets of underwear, a dozen dress shirts and two pairs of patent leather evening slippers) paid whenever it was convenient for the affluent.

The fitter was summoned. Mr. Pickering was an inch and a half larger around the chest than he had been at his last fitting, and his across-the-shoulder measurement had increased by an inch.

"You know what we're supposed to have?" Mr. Pickering asked.

"Yes, sir."

"Well, measure him, then, and we can get out of here. Mr. McCoy has a pressing social engagement."

When McCoy signed the bill, he couldn't quite believe the amount. They were to be paid a $150 uniform allowance. The uniforms he had just ordered (Brooks Brothers guaranteed their delivery, if necessary by special messenger, in time for their commissioning) were going to cost him just under $900.

He had the money in the account at the Philadelphia Savings Fund Society, but it was absolutely unreal that he was going to pay nearly twice as much for uniforms as he had paid for the LaSalle.

When they were on the street, Pickering said: "I debated you getting your uniforms there," he said. "They're expensive, but you're going to need good uniforms. In the long run, they're just as cheap. If you don't have the dough, I'll lend it to you."

"I don't need your money."

"Hey, get off my back. Get two things straight. First, that you're my buddy. And second, that being rich is better than being poor, and I have no intention of apologizing to you because I was smart enough to get born to rich people."

"The last shirts I bought cost me sixty-five cents," McCoy said. "I just bought a dozen at six-ninety-five apiece. That's what they call 'unexpected.' "

"Then you had better be careful with them, hadn't you?" Pickering said. "Make a real effort not to spill mustard on them when you're eating a hot dog?"

McCoy smiled at him. He found it very difficult to stay sore at Pickering for very long.

"It's five minutes after twelve," McCoy said. "Where's Grand Central Station?"

"Yonder," Pickering said, pointing at it. "Do I get to meet your deflowered virgin?"

"That's going too fucking far!" McCoy flared.

Pickering saw icy fury in McCoy's eyes.

"For that I apologize," he said.

The ice in McCoy's eyes did not go away.

"I'm sorry, Ken," Pickering said. "You know my mouth."

"Well, lay off this subject!"

"Okay, okay," Pickering said. "I said I was sorry and I meant it. If you're free, I'll be either in the room, or '21.' Call me. If you're not otherwise occupied."

McCoy nodded and then turned and walked toward Grand Central Station. Pickering watched him. Halfway down the block, he looked over his shoulder as if to check if Pickering was following him.

Pickering pretended to be looking for a cab.

The poor sonofabitch has really got it bad for this broad. I wonder who she is?

A cab stopped, and Pickering got in.

"Grand Central," he said.

"It's right down the street, for Christ's sake!"

Pickering handed him five dollars.

"Take the long way around," he said. "I'm in no hurry."

Feeling something like a private detective shadowing a cheating husband, he stationed himself in the Oyster Bar where he felt sure he could see McCoy and the deflowered virgin, but they could not see him.

Pickering was twice surprised when the deflowered virgin showed up five minutes early, and after a moment's hesitation kissed McCoy, first impersonally and distantly, and then again on the lips, looking into his eyes, as a woman kisses her lover.

Pick Pickering had known Ernie Sage most of her life. He was surprised that she had been a virgin. And he was surprised that McCoy thought she was poor. There were some people who thought Ernie Sage had gotten her job with J. Walter Thompson, Advertising, Inc., because she had graduated summa cum laude from Sarah Lawrence. And there were those who thought it just might be because J. Walter Thompson had the account of American Personal Pharmaceutical, Inc., which spent fifteen or twenty million a year advertising its wide array of toothpastes, mouthwashes, and hair lotions. The chairman of the board of American Personal Pharmaceutical (and supposedly, its largest stockholder) was Ernest Sage.

XIII

(ONE)
U.S. 1 Near Washington, D.C.
2230 Hours, 23 November 1941

They stopped for gas and a hamburger, and when they started off again, Pickering took the wheel.

"What did you think of the Met?" Pickering asked.

"What?"

"Since I didn't see you from the time we walked out of Brooks Brothers until five-thirty this afternoon, I naturally presumed that you had been enriching your mind by visiting the cultural attractions of New York City. Like the Metropolitan Museum of Art."

McCoy snorted.

"We did take the Staten Island Ferry," he said. "She said it was the longest ride for a nickel in the world."

"It must have been thrilling!" Pickering said.

"Fuck you," McCoy said, cheerfully. "Since you're so fucking nosy, we spent most of the time in her apartment."

"We are now going sixty-eight miles per hour," Pickering said.

"So what? You're driving. You'll get the ticket, not me." Then he added, "But maybe you had better slow down a little. The Corps goes apeshit when people get speeding tickets. Especially in cars they're not supposed to have in the first place."

"If you were to slug me, I would probably lose control, and we would be killed in a flaming crash," Pickering said.

McCoy looked at him curiously.

"I mention that because I have something to say to you. Some things—plural, two; and I want you to understand the risk you would be running by taking a poke at me."

"You can say anything you want," McCoy said. "God is in his heaven, and all is right with the world."

"Ernie Sage really got to you, huh?"

"How do you know her name?" McCoy demanded, suspiciously.

"I followed you," Pickering said. "When you met her in Grand Central, I was lurking behind a pillar."

"You sonofabitch!" McCoy said. But he wasn't angry. "I hope you got an eyeful."

"Very touching," Pickering said. "Romeo and Juliet."

"She's really something," McCoy said.

"I realize this is none of my business—"

"Then don't say it," McCoy interrupted.

"—but since you seem to put such weight on such things, I feel obliged to tell you something about her."

"Be careful, Pick," McCoy said, and there was menace in his voice.

"Ernie is named after her father," Pickering said. "Ernest Sage. Ernest Sage is chairman of the board of American Personal Pharmaceutical."

"So what?" McCoy said. "I never even heard of it."

Pickering recited a dozen brand names of American Personal Pharmaceutical products.

"In other words," McCoy said, finally catching on, "she's like you. Rich."

"The rich say 'comfortable,' Ken," Pickering said.

"I don't care what they say," McCoy flared. "Rich is rich." There was a moment's silence, and then McCoy said, "Oh, goddamn!"

It was a wail of anguish.

"As I have tried to point out, being rich is not quite as bad as having leprosy," Pickering said. "I'm sure that if you put your heart in it, you could learn to like it."

"She lied to me, goddamnit. Why did she do that?" McCoy asked. Pickering knew he hadn't heard what he had told him.

"There is a remote possibility that the lady finds you attractive," Pickering said. "Marines have that reputation, I'm told."

"She made a fucking fool out of me!" McCoy said. "Goddamnit, she got me to tell her all about Norristown."

"Norristown?"

"About why I went in the Corps. About my father. Even about my slob of a sister."

"If she wanted to hear about that, then that means she's interested in everything you are. What's wrong with that?"

"Just butt out of this, all right?"

"Now I'm sorry I told you," Pickering said.

"If you hadn't, I would have made an even bigger fucking fool of myself!" McCoy said, adding a moment later, "Jesus!"

"As I said," Pickering said, "there is a remote possibility that Ernie likes you—"

"She doesn't like to be called Ernie," McCoy said.

"—for what you are. Warts and all," Pickering continued.

"Jesus, you just don't understand, do you? This isn't the first time this has happened to me. All she wanted was a stiff prick. Marines have a reputation for having stiff pricks."

"I think you're dead wrong," Pickering said.

"Fuck what you think, I know," McCoy said.

"You told me that you"—Pickering paused and then went on—"were the first."

"So what?"

"That means something to women, from what I've seen. They can only give it away once. Ernie chose to give it away to you."

"She decided to get it over with, and I was available."

"That's bullshit and you know it."

"She lied to me, you dumb fuck! A whole line of bullshit, about this being her first job, right out of school, and I thought she meant high school, and how they were paying her eighteen fifty a week, and that's why her apartment was such a dump."

"That's all true," Pickering said.

"You know what I mean," McCoy said.

"She had to lie to you, you dumb fuck," Pickering said. "You have this well-developed inferiority complex, and she was afraid you'd crawl back in your hole."

"Do me a favor, Pickering," McCoy said. "Just shut your fucking mouth!"

"Ken, I want to keep you from—"

"Shut your fucking mouth, I said! The subject is closed."

Pick Pickering decided that under the circumstances, the only thing to do was shut his fucking mouth.

(TWO)

The last week of training in Platoon Leader's Course 23–41 went just as rapidly as the previous weeks had, but far more pleasantly.

In the words of Pick Pickering: "It's as if the Corps, having spent all that time and effort turning us into savages, has considered the risks they'd run if they turned us loose on an unsuspecting civilian population and is now engaged in recivilizing us."

There were several lectures on the manners and deportment expected of Marine Corps officers, and lectures on "personal finance management" and the importance of preparing a last will and testament. There was a lecture on insurance, and another on the regulations involved in the travel and transfers of officers.

They were even taken to the Officers' Club, where the intricacies of officer club membership were explained in a hands-on demonstration. They were ushered into the dining room, allowed to order whatever struck their fancy from the menu (which Pickering and McCoy found somewhat disappointing), and then shown how to sign the chit. Commissioned officers and gentlemen do not pay cash in officers' clubs.

Afterward, before they marched back to the company area, a lance corporal at a table outside the dining room permitted them to redeem the chits for cash.

But they got the idea. And they had their first meal as gentlemen—if not quite yet officers-and-gentlemen—and were thus free, since they had paid for it, not to eat if they didn't like it. Corporal Pleasant had not even marched them over to the officers' club (Platoon Leader Candidate McCoy had been ordered to do that) and there was thus no risk that any of them would be ordered to slurp it up.

And they were given liberty at night during the last few days, from retreat to last call. Pickering and McCoy went to the slop chute, where a pitcher of beer and paper cups were available for a quarter. McCoy put away a lot of beer; but neither he nor Pick Pickering got drunk or reopened the subject of Miss Ernestine Sage.

On Wednesday afternoon, in time for the retreat formation, most of the officer uniforms were delivered. The uniform prescribed for the retreat formation was a mixture of officer and enlisted uniforms. They could not be permitted to wear officer's brimmed caps, of course, because they were not yet officers. But they wore officer's blouses and trousers, without officer-type insignia, because the primary purpose of the formation was really to see if the uniforms would fit on Friday, when they would be sworn in.

Platoon Leader Candidates Pickering and McCoy did not have their officer's uniforms on Wednesday afternoon. When this was discovered by Corporal Pleasant, it afforded him one last opportunity to offer his opinion of the intelligence, responsibility, and parentage of two of his charges. But even after that, they were not restricted to the barracks for the evening. They got the LaSalle one last time from the provost marshal's impounding lot and went off the base so that Platoon Leader Candidate Pickering could make inquiries of Brooks Brothers.

It was a lot of trouble to make a lousy phone call, but there were few pay phones available on the base, and these generally had long lines waiting to use them. And they had to get the car from the Impounding Compound rather than take a bus, because the MPs checked passes on buses. McCoy's properly stickered car and campaign hat got them past the MP at the gate without inspection.

On Thursday morning, as the platoon was preparing to march off to rehearse the graduation and swearing-in ceremony, a blue Ford station wagon drove into the company area. A large black man emerged from it, and addressed Corporal Pleasant.

"Hey, Mac!" he called out. "Brooks Brothers. I'm looking for Mr. Pickering and Mr. McCoy."

Even Pleasant seemed amused.

"The asshole with the guidon," he said, "is Mr. McCoy, and Mr. Pickering is the tall asshole in the rear rank. Wave at the nice man, Mr. Pickering."

The man from Brooks Brothers cheerfully waved back at Mr. Pickering, and then began to unload bag-wrapped uniforms, cartons of shirts, and oblong hat boxes from his station wagon. He stacked everything on the ground, and then sought out Mr. Pickering and Mr. McCoy to get his receipt signed.

After the rehearsal, as they were unpacking their uniforms and preparing their enlisted men's uniforms to be turned in, Corporal Pleasant entered the barracks.

"Attention on deck!" someone bellowed.

"Stand at ease," Corporal Pleasant said. And then he went to each man and handed him a quarter-inch-thick stack of mimeograph paper. It was their orders.

There were three different orders, or more precisely, three different paragraphs of the same general order. The first sent about half of Platoon Leader Class 23–41 to Camp LeJeune, North Carolina, "for such duty in the field as may be assigned." The second sent just about the rest of 23–41 to San Diego, California, "for such duty in the field as may be assigned."

There were only two names on the third paragraph of the General Order. It said that the following officers, having entered upon active duty at Quantico, Virginia for a period of three years, unless further extended by competent authority, were further assigned and would proceed to Headquarters, U.S. Marine Corps, Washington, D.C., "for such administrative duty as may be assigned."

"What the hell does this mean?" Pickering asked, when Pleasant had left.

McCoy had a very good idea what it meant so far as he was concerned, but he had no idea what the Corps had planned for Pickering.

"It means while the rest of these clowns are running around in the boondocks, you and I will be sitting behind desks," he said.

At 1245 hours, Friday, 28 November 1941, Platoon Leader Candidate Class 23–41 fell in for the last time. They were wearing the uniforms of second lieutenants, U.S. Marine Corps, but Corporal Pleasant took his customary position and marched them to the parade field.

The first order of business was to give them the legal right to wear the gold bars on their shoulders. They raised their right hands and swore to defend the Constitution of the United States against all enemies, foreign and domestic, and to obey the orders of such officers who were appointed over them, and that they would discharge the duties of the office upon which they were about to enter to the best of their ability, so help them God.

"Detail commander, front and center, harch!" Corporal Pleasant barked.

McCoy, to his surprise, had been appointed to this role. He marched from his position at the left of the rear rank up to Corporal Pleasant.

Pleasant saluted.

"Take the detail, sir," Pleasant said.

"Take your post, Corporal," McCoy ordered.

They exchanged salutes again. Pleasant did a right-face and marched off to take a position beside the gunny and the first sergeant, just to the right of the reviewing stand.

McCoy did an about-face.

"Right-face!" he ordered, and then, "Fow-ward, harch!"

He gave them a column right, and then another, and when they got to the proper position relative to the reviewing stand, bellowed, "Eyes, right!" and raised his hand to the brim of his new Brooks Brothers $38.75 Cap, Marine Officers, with the cord loops sewn to its crown.

At the moment he issued the command, the Quantico Band, which had been silent except for the tick-tick beat of its drummers to give them the proper marching cadence, burst into the Marine Corps Hymn.

And the moment Second Lieutenant Pickering, USMCR, snapped his head to the right, he saw two familiar faces on the reviewing stand. His father and mother.

On the goddamned reviewing stand; not with the other parents and wives and whoever had showed up for the graduation parade. On the goddamned reviewing stand!

The officers on the reviewing stand returned McCoy's hand salute.

"Eyes, front!" McCoy ordered when he judged the last file of the formation had passed the reviewing stand. He marched them back to where they had originally been.

The officers marched off the reviewing stand, in order of rank. When the colonel got to McCoy, McCoy saluted.

"Put your detail at rest, Lieutenant," the colonel ordered.

"Puh-rade, rest!"

They moved their feet the prescribed distance apart, and put their hands and arms rigidly in the small of their backs.

"Congratulations," the colonel said to McCoy. "Welcome to the officer corps of the U.S. Marine Corps."

He shook his hand and simultaneously handed him a rolled-up tube of paper, which contained his diploma and his commission. Then, leaving McCoy at parade rest, the colonel, trailed by his entourage, went down the ranks and repeated the process, exactly, for each man.

Finally, the entourage returned to the reviewing stand.

"Lieutenant," the colonel called. "You may dismiss these gentlemen."

McCoy saluted, did an about-face, and barked, "Atten-hut. Dis-missed."

23–41 just stood there for a moment, as if unwilling to believe that it was actually over and that they were now in law and fact commissioned officers and gentlemen of the United States Marine Corps.

And then one of them yelped, probably, McCoy thought, that flat-faced asshole from Texas A&M who was always making strange noises. That broke the trance, and they started shaking hands and pounding each other on the back.

Captain Jack NMI Stecker walked off the reviewing stand, and then across the field to McCoy. As he approached McCoy, Pickering started for the reviewing stand. McCoy wondered where the hell he was going, but with Stecker advancing on him, there was no chance to ask.

He saluted Stecker, who offered his hand.

"Despite what some people think of China Marines, Lieutenant," Stecker said, "every once in a while some of them make pretty good officers. I think you will."

"Thank you, sir," McCoy said.

"I thought you might need a ride to the Impounding Compound," Stecker said.

"I got the car last night, sir," he said.

"Then in that case, McCoy, just 'good luck.' "

He offered his hand, they exchanged salutes, and Stecker walked away.

McCoy saw that most of 23–41 had formed a line by the reviewing stand. Corporal Pleasant was saluting each one of them. They then handed him a dollar. It was a tradition.

Fuck him, McCoy decided. Pleasant had been entirely too willing to kick him when he was down. And he wasn't even that good a corporal.

I'm not going to give the sonofabitch a dollar to have him salute me. He'll head right for the NCO Club with it and sit around making everybody laugh with stories about the incompetent assholes the Corps had just made officers.

And then he saw that Pick Pickering was not in the line. He was standing with a couple, the man well dressed, the woman in a full-length fur coat. Obviously, Pick's folks had come to see their son graduate. McCoy started to walk back to the company area.

Pickering ran after him and caught up with him.

"I want you to meet my mother and dad," Pick said.

"Wouldn't I be in the way?"

"Don't be an asshole, asshole," Pick said, and grabbed McCoy's arm and propelled him in the direction of the reviewing stand.

"I didn't see you giving Pleasant his dollar," Pickering said.

"I didn't," McCoy said. "Just because we're now wearing bars doesn't make him any less of a vicious asshole."

"My, you do hold a grudge, don't you, Lieutenant?" Pickering said.

"You bet your ass, I do," McCoy said.

Fleming Pickering smiled and put his hand out as the walked up.

"I knew who you were, of course," he said.

"Sir?" McCoy asked, confused.

"One Marine corporal can always spot another, even in a sea of clowns," Fleming Pickering said, pleased with himself.

"Flem!" Mrs. Pickering protested. She smiled at McCoy and gave him her hand. "You'll have to excuse my husband, his being a Marine corporal was the one big thrill of his life. I'm pleased to finally meet you, Ken . . . I can call you 'Ken,' mayn't I? . . . Malcolm's written so much about you."

"Yes, ma'am," McCoy said.

"I would like nothing better," Fleming Pickering said, "than to sit over a long lunch and have you tell me how you shepherded the lieutenant here around the boondocks, but we have a plane to catch."

"I'd forgotten about that," Pick said.

"This time tomorrow, we will be high above the blue Pacific," Fleming Pickering said. "Bound for sunny Hawaii. I was originally going by myself, but then some scoundrel told my wife about the girls in the grass skirts."

"I wasn't worried abut the hula-hula girls," Pick's mother replied. "What concerned me was the way you behave on a ship. If they serve eight meals a day—and Pacific-Orient does—and I wasn't along, you'd eat all eight of them, and they'd have to take you off the ship in a wheelbarrow."

"You're coming back by ship?" Pick asked. "I thought you were flying both ways."

"No," Pick's father said. "I put off the meeting in San Francisco until the twentieth. That way, we can board ship in Honolulu on the tenth and still make it back in plenty of time."

Pick nodded his understanding.

McCoy finally figured out what they were talking about. He had been a little impressed that Pick's parents would come all the way to Virginia just to see him get sworn in. But, so far as they were concerned, that was like a trip to the corner drugstore for cigarettes. They were about to fly to Hawaii. The only thing that had surprised Pick about that was they weren't going to fly both ways.

Pick and his family were people from a different world.

A world like Ernestine Sage's. A world where I don't belong, even with a gold bar on my collar.

(THREE)
Washington, D.C.
1600 Hours, 28 November 1941

Before Pickering's parents had showed up, it had been understood between McCoy and Pickering that immediately after they were sworn in, they would drive to Washington. The LaSalle was already loaded with their luggage.

He had been sure that would change because of his parents. But that hadn't happened. Pick shook hands with his father, allowed himself to be kissed by his mother, and then the Pickerings left. Taking trips halfway around the world was obviously routine stuff for them.

Pick and McCoy, as originally planned, then simply backed from the parade field to where McCoy had parked the LaSalle by the barracks, got in, and drove off.

There were no farewell handshakes with the others in 23–41. Because he had been on Pleasant's and the gunny's shit list, the others had most of the time avoided McCoy as if he were a leper. And they had avoided Pickering, too, because he was McCoy's buddy. And there had been whispers at the end about the two of them getting "administrative duty" in Washington rather than "in the field" at LeJeune and San Diego.

Pickering thought about this as they got in the LaSalle: If somewhere down the pike, Class 23–41 sent him an invitation to its twentieth reunion, he would send his regrets.

This time, they were stopped by the MP at the gate. First the MP waved them through, then he saw the bars and saluted, and finally he stepped into the road in front of them with his hand up.

He saluted as McCoy rolled down the window.

"Excuse me, sir, is this your car?"

"Yes, it is," McCoy said.

"It's got an enlisted decal, sir."

"That's because, until about twenty minutes ago, I was enlisted," McCoy said.

The MP smiled broadly. "I thought that was you," he said, admiringly. "You been sneaking in and out of here all the time you was in the Platoon Leader Course, haven't you?"

"How could you even suspect such a thing?" McCoy asked.

The MP came to attention and saluted.

"You may pass out, sir," he said. "Thank you, sir."

A minute later, after they had left the base, McCoy said, "I guess I better stop someplace and scrape that sticker off."

"And then what?"

"What do you mean, then what?"

"What are we going to do when we get to Washington?"

"I thought you'd be taking some leave," McCoy said.

"No," Pickering said. "I'd rather report in. I want to find out what's planned for me. How, exactly, do we do that?"

"Today is a day of duty," McCoy explained, patiently. "We get a day's travel time to Washington. That carries us up through midnight tomorrow. So long as we report in by midnight on Sunday, that makes Sunday a day of duty. So about eleven o'clock Sunday night, we'll find out where it is."

"You're not going home?" Pickering asked, and when McCoy shook his head, went on, "Or to New York?"

"No," McCoy said, stiffly.

"I thought maybe you'd come to your senses about going to New York," Pickering said.

"You miss the point," McCoy said. "I have come to my senses. And that's the end of that particular subject."

"Okay, so we'll go to the Lafayette," Pickering said. "It's a little stuffy, but it has a very nice French restaurant."

"Another hotel you own?"

"Grandpa owns it, actually," Pickering said. "It's right across from the White House. Do you suppose you can find the White House without a map, Lieutenant?"

"No, I've never been in Washington before, and I don't have a map, and I'm not going to sponge again off you or your 'Grandpa,' " McCoy said.

"Very well," Pickering said. "I will stay in the Lafayette, and you can stay in whatever flea-bag with hot-and-cold running cockroaches strikes your fancy, just so long as I know where to find you when it is time for us to go to the Marine Barracks and sign in. I hate to tell you this, Lieutenant, you being an officer and a gentleman and all, but you have a great talent for being a horse's ass."

McCoy laughed.

"You're sure you want to sign in early?" he asked. "It may be a long time until they offer you any leave again."

"I need to know what this 'administrative' duty is all about," Pickering said. "I don't like the sound of it."

"What's the difference?" McCoy asked. "Whatever it is, they're not offering you a choice."

"Indulge me," Pickering said. "Take me along with you, so that you can explain things to me. And for Christ's sake, stop being an ass about being comped in one of our hotels."

"Being what?"

" 'Comped,' " Pickering explained. " 'Complimentary accommodations.' It's part of the business. If you work for Foster Hotels, you're entitled to stay in Foster Hotels when you're away from home."

"I don't work for Foster Hotels," McCoy argued.

"That's all right, you're with me," Pickering said. "And I am the apple of Grandpa's eye. Will you stop being an ass?"

"It makes me uncomfortable," McCoy said.

"So do you, when you pick your nose," Pickering said. "But if you agree to stay in Grandpa's hotel, you can pick your nose all you want, and I won't say a thing."

The doorman at the Lafayette knew Pickering by sight. He rushed around and opened the door with all the pomp shown a respected guest. But what he said, was, "Jesus, Pick, are you for real? Or is there a costume party?"

"You are speaking, sir, to an officer and a gentleman of the U.S. Marine Corps," Pickering said. "You will not have to prostrate yourself; kneeling will suffice." He turned to McCoy. "Ken, say hello to Jerry Toltz, another old pal of mine. We bellhopped here all through one hot, long, miserable summer."

"How long are you going to be here?" the doorman asked.

"I don't know. Probably some time."

"They know you're coming?"

"I don't think so," Pickering said.

"I thought I would have heard," Jerry Toltz said. "The house is full, Pick."

"We need someplace to stay," Pickering said.

"Well, if they don't have anything for you, you and your pal can stay with me. There's a convertible couch."

"Thank you," Pickering said.

"Will you be needing the car?"

"Yeah," Pickering said. "I'm glad you asked. Don't bury it. We have to go out."

"That's presuming you can get in," the doorman said, and motioned for a bellboy and told him to park the car in the alley.

The man behind the reception desk also knew Malcolm Pickering.

He gave him his hand.

"You will be professionally delighted to hear the house is full," he said. "Personally, that may not be such good news. How are you? It's good to see you. Your grand-dad told me you were in the Marines."

"Good to see you," Pickering said. "This is my friend Ken McCoy."

They shook hands.

"How long have you been an officer?" the manager asked.

"It must be four, five hours now," Pickering said.

"And I don't have a bed for you! All I can do is call around. The Sheraton owes me a couple of big favors."

"What about maid's room in the bridal suite?"

"There's only a single in there," the manager protested.

"Put in a cot, then," Pickering said. "I'll sleep on that."

"I'll probably be able to find something for you tomorrow," the manager said.

"Lieutenant McCoy and I are going to be here for some time," Pickering said. "What about one of the residential hotels? I really hate to comp if we can rent it."

"There's a waiting list for every residential room in Washington," the manager said. "If you don't want to sleep on a park bench, you'll have to stay here. I'll come up with a bed-sitter for you in a day or two. Unless you need two bedrooms?"

"Lieutenant McCoy and I will not know how to handle the luxury of a bed-sitter. We have been sharing one room with thirty others."

"You want to go up now?"

"No, what we want to do now is locate the Marine Barracks."

The manager drew them a map.

They arrived at the Marine Barracks, coincidentally, just as the regularly scheduled Friday evening formal retreat parade was beginning. The music was provided by the Marine Corps Band, in dress blues.

It's like a well-choreographed ballet, Pickering thought as he watched the ceremony (the intricacies of which were now familiar) progress with incredible precision.

I'll be damned, McCoy thought, *these guys are really as good as they're supposed to be.*

There were Marines in dress blues stationed at intervals around the manicured grass of the parade ground. Their primary purpose, McCoy saw, was more practical then decorative. From time to time, one or more of them had to restrain eager tourists from rushing out onto the field to take a snapshot of the marching and drilling troops, or just to get a better look.

When the Marine Band had finally marched off, the perimeter guard near them, a lance corporal, left his post.

When he came to Pickering and McCoy, he saluted snappily.

"Good evening, sir!" he barked.

"Good evening," McCoy heard himself say.

Something bothered him. After a moment, he realized what it was. When the kid had tossed him the highball, he had done so automatically. The kid had seen a couple of officers, and he had saluted them. There had been nothing in his eyes that suggested he suspected he was saluting a China Marine corporal in a lieutenant's uniform.

I really am an officer, McCoy thought. *Until right now, it was sort of play-acting. But now it's real. When that kid saluted me, I felt like an officer.*

Well, this is the place to have it happen, he thought. *At the Marine Barracks in Washington after a formal retreat parade, with the smell of the smoke from the retreat cannon still in my nose, and the tick-tick of the drums of the Marine Band fading as it marches away.*

(FOUR)

On Saturday, Pickering and McCoy drove around Washington. Pickering was at first amused at the notion of playing tourist, but then he realized it wasn't so bad after all. He saw more of Washington with McCoy than he'd seen during the entire summer he'd spent bellhopping at the Lafayette.

And he came to understand that McCoy was doing more than satisfying an idle curiosity: He was reconnoitering the terrain. He wasn't sure if it was intentional, but there was no question that's what it was. It occurred to him again, as it had several times at Quantico, that McCoy was really an odd duck in society, as for example a Jesuit priest is an odd duck. They weren't really like the other ducks swimming around on the lake. They swam with a purpose, answering commands not heard by other people. A Jesuit's course through the waters of life was guided by God; McCoy's by what he believed—consciously or subconsciously—was expected of him by the Marine Corps.

They spent most of Sunday at the Smithsonian Institution. And again, Pickering was pleased that they had come. He was surprised at the emotion he felt when he saw the tiny little airplane Charles Lindbergh had flown to Paris and when he was standing before the faded and torn flag that had flown "in the rockets' red glare" over Fort McHenry.

At half-past ten on Sunday night (Pickering was still not fully accustomed to thinking in military time and had to do the arithmetic in his head to come up with 2230), Second Lieutenants M. Pickering and K.J. McCoy presented their orders to the duty officer at the Marine Barracks and held themselves ready for duty.

"Your reporting in early is probably going to screw things up with personnel," the officer of the day said. "I'll send word over there that you're here, and they'll call you at the BOQ [Bachelor Officers' Quarters]."

"We're in a hotel in town," Pickering said.

"Okay. Probably even better. As you'll find out, the Corps is scattered all over town. What hotel?"

"The Lafayette," Pickering said.

"Very nice," the officer of the day said. "What's the room number?"

"I don't know," Pickering said and started to smile.

"Then how do you know where to sleep when you get there?" the officer of the day asked, sarcastically.

"Actually, we're in the bridal suite," Pickering said. And then, quickly, he added: "In the maid's room off the bridal suite."

At 0915 the next morning, the telephone in the maid's room of the bridal suite rang. It was a captain from personnel. Lieutenant Pickering was ordered to report, as soon as he could get there, to Brigadier General D.G. McInerny, whose officer was in Building F at the Anacostia Naval Air Station. Before McCoy's reconnoitering over the weekend, Pickering had only a vague idea where Anacostia Naval Air Station was. Now he knew. He even knew where to find Building F. He had seen the building numbers—or rather building letters—in front of the office buildings there.

Lieutenant McCoy was to report to a Major Almond, in Room 26, Building T-2032, one of the temporary buildings in front of the Smithsonian. They knew where that was, too, as a result of McCoy's day-long scoping of the terrain.

"You drop me there," McCoy said. "I can walk back here. Anacostia's to hell and gone."

Pickering found Building F without difficulty. It was one of several buildings immediately behind the row of hangars. Three minutes later, to his considerable surprise, he was standing at attention before the desk of Brigadier General D.G. McInerney, USMC. Unable to believe that a brigadier general of Marines would have thirty seconds to spare for a second lieutenant, he had simply presumed that whatever they were going to have him do here, his orders would come from a first lieutenant.

General McInerney looked like a general. There were three rows of ribbons on his tunic below the gold wings of a Naval Aviator. He didn't have much hair, and what there was of it was cut so close to the skull that the bumps and the freckles on the skin were clearly visible.

The general, Pickering decided as he stood at attention, was not very friendly, and he was unabashedly studying him with interest.

"So you're Malcolm Pickering," General McInerney said finally. "You must take after your mother. You don't look at all like your dad."

Pickering was so startled that for a moment his eyes flickered from their prescribed focus six inches over the general's head.

"You may sit, Mr. Pickering," General McInerney said. "Would you like some coffee?"

"Yes, sir," Pick Pickering said. "Thank you, sir."

A sergeant appeared, apparently in reply to the pushing of an unseen buzzer button.

"This is Lieutenant Pickering, Sergeant Wallace," General McInerney said. "He will probably be around here for a while."

The sergeant offered his hand.

"How do you do, sir?" he said.

"Lieutenant Pickering's father and I were in the war to end all wars together," General McInerney said, dryly.

"Is that so?" the sergeant said.

"And the lieutenant's father called me and, for auld lang syne, Sergeant Wallace, asked me to take care of his boy. And of course, I said I would."

"I understand, sir."

Pickering felt sick and furious.

"I think we can start off by getting the lieutenant a cup of coffee."

"Aye, aye, sir," Sergeant Wallace said. "How would you like your coffee, Lieutenant?"

"Black, please," Pickering said.

"Aye, aye, sir."

"You get fixed up all right with a BOQ?" General McInerney inquired. "Or are you perhaps staying in a hotel? A Foster hotel?"

"I'm in the Lafayette, sir."

"I thought you might be," General McInerney said. "I mean, what the hell, if your family owns hotels . . . how many hotels does your family own, Lieutenant?"

"There are forty-two, sir," Pick said.

"What the hell, if your family owns forty-two hotels, why not stay in one of them, right? There's certainly no room service in the BOQ, is there?"

"No, sir."

The coffee was delivered.

"Thank you, Sergeant," Pickering said.

"Certainly, sir," Sergeant Wallace said.

"I guess it took a little getting used to, not having someone to fetch coffee for you. At Quantico, I mean?" General McInerney asked.

"Yes, sir," Pickering said.

"Well, at least here, you'll have Sergeant Wallace and several other enlisted men around for that sort of thing. It won't be quite like home, but it will be a little better than running around in the boondocks with a rifle platoon."

"Yes, sir," Pickering said.

"It's not quite what the Corps had in mind for you," General McInerney said, "but I've arranged for you to be my junior aide-de-camp. How does that sound?"

"Permission to speak frankly, sir?" Pickering asked.

"Of course," General McInerney said.

"My father had no right to ask you to do anything for me," Pickering said. "I knew nothing about it. If I had any idea that he was even thinking about something like that, I would have told him to keep his nose out of my business."

"Is that so?" General McInerney said, doubtfully.

"Yes, Sir," Pickering said fervently, "that's so. And with respect, Sir, I do not want to be your aide-de-camp."

"I don't recall asking whether or not you wanted to be my aide. I presented that as a fact. I have gone to considerable trouble arranging for it."

"Sir, I feel that I would make you a lousy aide."

"You are now a Marine officer. When a Marine officer is told to do something, he is expected to reply 'Aye, aye, sir' and set about doing it to the best of his ability."

"I am aware of that, sir," Pick said. "But I didn't think it would ever be applied in a situation where the order was to pass canapés."

"You're telling me that you would prefer to be running around in the swamp at Camp LeJeune to being the aide of a general officer?" General McInerney asked, on the edge of indignation.

"Yes, sir, that's exactly my position," Pickering said. "I respectfully request that I not be assigned as your aide."

"I am sorry to tell you, Lieutenant," General McInerney said, "that I have no intention of going back to Headquarters, USMC, and tell them that I have not changed my mind and don't want you as my aide after all. As I said, arranging for your assignment as my aide wasn't easy." He waited until that had a moment to sink in, and then went on: "So where would you say that leaves us, Lieutenant?"

"It would appear, sir," Pick said, "that until I am able to convince the general that he has made an error, the general will have a very reluctant aide-de-camp."

General McInerney snorted, and then he chuckled.

"Lieutenant, you are a brand-new officer. Could you take a little advice from one who has been around the Corps a long time?"

"Yes, sir."

"Don't jump until you know where you're jumping from, and where you're going to land," General McInerney said. "In other words, until you have all the intelligence you can get your hands on, and have time to evaluate it carefully."

"Yes, sir," Pick said, annoyed that he was getting a lecture on top of everything else.

"In this case, the facts as I presented them to you seem to have misled you."

"Sir?"

"Your dad is indeed concerned about you, and he did in fact call me and ask me to look after you. But what he was concerned about was the possibility that some chairwarmer would review your records, see what you did as a civilian, and assign you appropriately. He said he didn't want you to spend your hitch in the Corps as a mess officer. Or a housing officer. And when I checked, that's exactly what those sonsofbitches had in mind for you. If I had not gone over there, Lieutenant, and had you assigned to me, you would have reported for duty this morning to the officers' club at the Barracks."

Pick's eyes widened.

"So, because your Dad and I are old buddies—we were corporals together at Belleau Wood—I am protecting your ass. I think you would make a lousy aide, too. You will be my junior aide only until such time as I decide what else the Corps can do with you."

"I seem to have made an ass of myself, sir," Pickering said.

"We sort of expect that from second lieutenants," General McInerney said, reasonably. "The only thing you really did wrong was underestimate your father. Did you really think he would try to grease the ways for you?"

"My father is married to my mother, sir," Pickering said.

"I take your point," General McInerney said. "I have the privilege of your mother's acquaintance."

"May I ask a question, sir?"

"Sure."

"Was my moving into the hotel a real blunder?"

"Not so far as I'm concerned," General McInerney said. "I understand your situation."

"I was thinking of . . . my best friend, I suppose is the best way to describe him. I sort of pressured him to move in with me."

"I see," McInerney said. "Another hotelier? Classmate at school?"

"No, sir. He was a China Marine, a corporal, before we went through the platoon leader's course."

McInerney thought that over a moment before he replied.

"I think it might be a good idea if he moved into the BOQ," he said. "There would certainly be curiosity. It could even turn into an Intelligence matter. Where would a second lieutenant, an ex–China Marine enlisted man, get the money to take a room in the Lafayette? It could be explained, of course, but the last thing a second lieutenant needs is to have it getting around that Intelligence is asking questions about his personal life."

"Thank you, sir," Pickering said. "I was afraid it might be something like that. May I ask another question?"

"Shoot."

"How long will I be assigned here? I mean, you said something about deciding what to do with me. How long will that take?"

"That depends on what you would like to do, and whether or not you're qualified to do it. Presumably, you learned at Quantico that leading a platoon of riflemen is not quite the fun and games the recruiter may have painted it."

"Yes, sir."

"Have you ever thought of going to flight school?" General McInerney asked.

"No, sir," Pickering confessed.

General McInerney was a little disappointed to hear that, but decided that Fleming Pickering's kid meant what he said: that he simply had not thought of going to flight school—not that he had considered the notion and discarded it because he didn't like the idea of flying.

"That's an option," General McInerney said. "But only if you could pass the flight physical. On your way out, have Sergeant Wallace set up an appointment for a flight physical. And then take the rest of the day off, son, and get yourself settled. I'm talking about your friend, too, of course."

"I'll check out of the hotel, too, of course," Pickering said.

"Don't do it on my account," General McInerney said. "So far as I'm concerned, I'd be delighted to have you in there, in case my wife and I wanted to make reservations for dinner."

General McInerney stood up and offered his hand.

"Welcome aboard," he said. "You're your father's son, and that's intended as a compliment."

XIV

(ONE)
Room 26, Temporary Building T-2032
Washington, D.C.
0945 Hours, 1 December 1941

McCoy had seen quite a few office doors during his time in the Corps. Most of them had a sign announcing in some detail not only what function was being carried out behind the door, but by whom.

The door to room 26 didn't even have a room number. McCoy had to find it by counting upward from room number 2, which had a sign: OFFICER'S HEAD.

He thought he'd gotten it wrong even then, for what he thought was room 26 had two sturdy locks on it—a storeroom, in other words, full of mimeograph paper and quart bottles of ink. But with no other option that he could think of, he knocked on it.

As soon as he knocked, however, he heard movement inside, then the sound of dead-bolt locks being operated, and a moment later the door opened just wide enough to reveal the face of a grim-looking man. He said nothing, but the expression on his face asked McCoy to state his business.

"I'm looking for room 26," McCoy said.

The man nodded, waiting for McCoy to go on.

"I was ordered to report to room 26," McCoy said.

"What's your name, please?" the man asked.

"McCoy."

"May I see your identification, please?" the man asked.

McCoy handed over his brand-new officer's identification card. The man looked at it carefully, then at McCoy's face, and then opened the door wide enough for McCoy to enter.

Inside was a small area, just enough for a desk. On the other side of the room there was another door, again with double dead-bolt locks.

When the man walked to the telephone on the desk, McCoy saw that he had a .45 Colt 1911A1 on his hip. On his tail, really, and not in a GI holster, but in sort of a skeleton holster through which the front part of the pistol stuck out.

If he was wearing a jacket, McCoy thought, *you'd never know he had a pistol.*

"I have Lieutenant McCoy here," the man said to the telephone. "He's not due in until 15 December."

There was a pause.

"Well, shit, I suppose everybody's been told but us. What does he get?"

There was obviously a reply, but McCoy couldn't hear it. The man put the telephone down, and then reached into his desk and came out with a clipboard and a small plastic card affixed to an alligator clip.

"Sign here, please," he said. "Just your signature. Not your rank."

McCoy signed his name.

The man handed him the plastic card.

"You use this until we get you your own," he said. "Pin it on your blouse jacket."

McCoy looked at it before he pinned it on. It was a simple piece of plastic-covered cardboard. It said "VISITOR" and there was the insignia of the Navy Department. It was overprinted with purple stripes.

"That's good anywhere in the building," the man said. "Or almost everywhere. But it's not good for ONI [Office of Naval Intelligence]. Until you get your credentials, you'd better avoid going over to ONI."

"Okay," McCoy said, wondering what was going on.

The man stuck out his hand.

"I'm Sergeant Ruttman," he said. "We didn't expect you until the fifteenth."

"So I heard you say," McCoy said.

"You just went through that course at Quantico, right?"

"That's right," McCoy said.

"Pain in the ass?"

"Yes, it was," McCoy said.

"They want to send me," Sergeant Ruttman said. "But I've been putting off going. I figure if they really want me to take a commission, they can give it to me. I already know about chickenshit."

"Good luck," McCoy said, wondering if Ruttman was just running off at the mouth, or whether he was telling the truth.

Ruttman replaced the clipboard in his desk, and then took keys from his pocket and unlocked both of the locks in the door.

"Follow me," he said.

Beyond the door was a strange assortment of machinery. There were typewriters and other standard office equipment. But there were also cameras; what McCoy guessed was a blueprint machine; a large photograph print dryer, a stainless-steel-drum affair larger than a desk; and a good deal of other equipment that looked expensive and complicated. McCoy couldn't even guess the purpose of some of it.

The equipment was being manned by a strange-looking assortment of people, all in civilian clothes, and all of them armed. Most of them had standard web belts and issue flapped holsters for the .45 1911A1s they carried, but some carried the pistols the way Ruttman carried his, and others were armed with snub-nosed Smith & Wesson revolvers.

"What is this place, Sergeant?"

"The thing you're going to have to keep in mind, Lieutenant, is that it's just like boot camp at Parris Island. If they think you should know something, they'll tell you. Otherwise it's none of your business."

He turned his attention from McCoy to the drawer of a desk. He took a loose-leaf notebook from it and two blank forms, one of them a card with purple stripes like his "VISITOR" badge, and the other a Navy identification card of some sort.

"Before I fuck things up," he called out, raising his voice, "has anybody made out any of these and not logged them in the book?"

There was no response to the inquiry, and he put both identification cards in a typewriter and typed briefly and rapidly on them.

"I need an officer to sign these!" he called out again, and one of the civilians, a slight, tall man, walked to the desk. Despite the Smith & Wesson .38 snub-nose revolver on his hip, he looked like a clerk. He waited until Ruttman finished typing, and then took the card from him and scrawled his name on it. Then he looked at McCoy.

"You're McCoy?" he asked.

"Yes, sir."

"Not that I'm not glad to see you, but you weren't due to report in until the fifteenth."

"I reported in early, sir."

"You'll regret that," the officer said. " 'Abandon hope, all ye who enter here!' "

He walked back where he had come from. McCoy saw that he was making notations on a large map. Next to the map were aerial photographs and a stack of teletype paper liberally stamped "SECRET" in large letters.

"You want to sign this, Lieutenant?" Sergeant Ruttman asked.

There was space for two signatures on the identification: the holder and the issuing officer. The tall skinny civilian had already signed it. According to the card, he was Lieutenant Colonel F.L. Rickabee, USMC. He sure as Christ didn't look like any lieutenant colonel McCoy had ever seen before. He didn't even look much like a Marine.

"Just your signature, again," Ruttman said. "No rank."

"You didn't give me back my ID card," McCoy said.

"You don't get it back," Ruttman said, and then apparently had doubts. He raised his voice. "Does he get his ID card back?"

"No," the tall thin man who looked like a clerk called back. "Not anymore. They changed the policy."

As if McCoy hadn't heard the exchange, Ruttman said, "You don't get it back, Lieutenant."

The tall skinny clerk-type had another thought and turned from his map and SECRET teletype messages.

"How long is it going to take to get him his credentials?"

"I'm just about to take his picture," Ruttman said.

"Today, you mean? He'll get his credentials today?"

"He'll have them by lunchtime," Ruttman said, confidently.

"Okay," the clerk-type said, and returned his attention to the map.

Based on the total absence of military courtesy (Ruttman had not once said "sir," much less "aye, aye, sir," to him, and the clerk-type hadn't seemed to care) McCoy decided that the clerk-type was not Lieutenant Colonel F.L. Rickabee, USMC. It was common practice for junior officers to sign senior officers' names to routine forms, sometimes initialing the signature and sometimes not. He went further with his theory: The tall skinny clerk was probably a warrant officer. Warrant officers were old-time noncoms, generally with some special skill. They wore officer's uniforms, could go to the Officers' Club, and were entitled to a salute, but the most senior chief warrant officer ranked below the most junior second lieutenant. And a warrant officer, particularly a new one, would probably not get all excited if an old-time noncom like Ruttman didn't treat him as if he was a lieutenant or a captain.

Ruttman stood McCoy against a backdrop, at which was pointed a Speed Graphic four-by-five-inch plate camera.

"Take off your blouse and your field scarf, and the bars," Ruttman ordered, "and put this on."

He handed McCoy a soiled, well-worn, striped necktie.

McCoy looked at him in disbelief.

"The way I'll shoot this," Ruttman explained, "that shirt'll look just like an Arrow."

He took McCoy's picture twice, "to make sure I get it," then led him to a table where he inked his fingers. He put his thumb print on both of the ID cards, and then took another full set on a standard fingerprint card.

Ruttman handed him a towel and bottle of alcohol to clean his hands, and then said, "That's it, here, Lieutenant. Now you go see Major Almond. He's in the last office down the passageway."

There was no sign hanging on Major J.J. Almond's door, either; but aside from that, he was what McCoy expected a Marine major to be. He was a short man, but muscular, and so erect he seemed taller than he was. And he was in uniform. His desk was shipshape, and two flags were on poles behind his desk, the Marine flag and the national colors.

And to the left of Major Almond's desk was a door with another sign: LT. COL. F.L. RICKABEE, USMC, COMMANDING. It was clear to McCoy now that he'd just gone through some sort of administrative service office where they made out ID cards and did that sort of thing, and that he was now about to face his new commanding officer.

"Let me say, McCoy," Major J.J. Almond said, "that I appreciate your appearance. You look and conduct yourself as a Marine officer should. As you may have noticed, there is a lamentable tendency around here to let things slip. Because of what we do here, we can't run this place like a line company. But we go too far, I think, far too often. I am going to rely on you, Lieutenant, to both set an example for the men and to correct, on the spot, whomever you see failing to live up to the standards of the Corps."

"Aye, aye, sir," McCoy said.

"Now, before we get started, you reported in early."

"Yes, sir."

"You are entitled to a fourteen-day leave. If it is your intention to apply for that leave now that you have reported aboard, I would like to know that now."

"No, sir."

"You're in the BOQ at the Barracks, I presume?"

"No, sir."

"Where are you?"

"In a hotel, sir."

"I don't want to go through this, McCoy, pulling one fact after another from you."

"I'm in the Hotel Lafayette, sir. Sharing a room with another officer, sir. Lieutenant Malcolm Pickering, sir."

"Well, that is fortuitous," Major Almond announced. "It is the policy of this command that both officer and enlisted personnel live off the base. You will draw pay in lieu of quarters. Will that pay be enough to pay for your hotel room?"

"Yes, sir."

"What's your room number?" Almond asked. "And I'll need the hotel telephone number."

"I don't know the phone number, sir," McCoy said. "We're living in the maid's room of the bridal suite, sir."

Major Almond smiled and nodded approvingly.

"Very enterprising," he said. "I wondered how you could afford to live in the Lafayette."

He reached into his desk drawer and came out with a three-inch-thick manila folder. He saw his name lettered on it, and that it was stamped "SECRET—COMPLETE BACKGROUND INVESTIGATION."

"This is the report of the FBI's investigation of you, Lieutenant," he said. "It is classified SECRET, and you are not authorized access to it. I show it to you to show how carefully they have gone into your background."

McCoy had no idea what was going on.

Major Almond then handed him a printed form.

"In normal circumstances, the procedure would have been for you to complete this form before the FBI did its complete background check. But the circumstances have not been normal. Time was important. The FBI had to, so to speak, start from scratch using existing records. So what has happened is that I have had our clerks prepare your background statement using existing records and the FBI report. Are you following me, Lieutenant?"

"Yes, sir," McCoy said. "I think so, sir."

"The standing operating procedure requires that your completed background statement be in the files," Major Almond said. "Now, while I am sure that the FBI has done their usual thorough job, I am nearly as sure that they have missed something. What I want you to do is take your background statement to the desk over there and go over it with great care. If there is anything on it that is not absolutely correct, I want you to mark it. We will then discuss it. More important, I want you to pay particular attention to omissions, particularly of a nonflattering nature."

"Sir?"

"I want you to make sure that all the blemishes on your record are visible," Major Almond said. "The next step in the administrative procedure is to evaluate your record and judge whether or not you are qualified to be granted a top secret, and other, security clearances. If it came out later that there are blemishes which do not appear on the record, that would cause trouble, do you understand?"

"Yes, sir."

"The sergeant will give you a lined pad and pencils," Major Almond said. "Make your notations on the lined pad, not on the form."

"Aye, aye, sir," McCoy said.

"Work steadily, but carefully," Major Almond said. "Time is of the essence."

"Aye, aye, sir."

McCoy wondered if they had found out that he'd been under charges in Shanghai about the Italian marines, and whether or not he should tell them if they weren't. The charges had been dropped. Did that mean they didn't count? Was getting charged with murder a "blemish" if they dropped the charges?

He sat down at the desk and looked at the form.

It was immediately apparent that they knew more about him than he knew himself. He didn't know his mother's date of birth, or his father's, but they were in the blocks on the form. And so were Anne-Marie's and Tommy's, and even Anne-Marie's husband's.

(TWO)

An hour later, he had worked his way through the six-page form to a section headed, "Arrests, Detentions, Indictments, Charges, et cetera."

They knew about the charges in China. (Not Prosecuted, initial facts in error.) And they knew about the old man signing the warrant for his arrest (Nol prossed on condition enlistment, USMC.) And they knew about speeding tickets, reckless driving, and even two charges of malicious mischief and being found in possession of a Daisy Red Ryder BB Gun in violation of the city ordinances of Norristown, Pa. (Nol prossed. BB Gun confiscated. Released in custody of parents.)

It was absolutely incredible how much they knew about him. He wondered what was going to happen when whoever reviewed his records came to the business about the Marines in China. Was that going to keep him from getting a security clearance?

The door opened and the tall skinny clerk-type walked in.

Without knocking, McCoy saw. In the same moment Major Almond rose to his feet.

He is about to get his ass eaten out.

The clerk-type walked toward the door of Lieutenant Colonel F.L. Rickabee and put his hand on the knob. For all intents and purposes he looked as if he was going to barge in there, too, without knocking. Then he stopped, turned to McCoy, and smiled.

"Come on in, McCoy," he said. "Whatever that is, it'll wait." Then he looked at Major Almond. "What the hell is that?" he demanded.

"Sir, it's Lieutenant McCoy's background statement."

"Isn't that a waste of his time?" Rickabee demanded sharply. "And ours? When I read the FBI report I had the feeling they knew everything there is to know about him."

Major Almond seemed to have difficulty framing a reply.

"I know, Jake," Colonel Rickabee said, more kindly. "It's regulation."

"Yes, sir."

"Come on in, McCoy, and you, too, Jake. It'll save time."

"Aye, aye, sir," Major Almond said.

Rickabee sat down behind his desk.

"For openers, McCoy, despite that inexcusable outburst of mine, let me make it clear that Major Almond is what keeps this lash-up of ours functioning. Without him, it would be complete, rather than seventy-five percent, chaos. I didn't mean to jump your ass, Jake. I've had a bad morning."

"Yes, sir. I know, sir," Major Almond said. "No apology is necessary, sir."

Colonel Rickabee turned to McCoy.

"With a three-inch-thick FBI report on you in Major Almond's safe, McCoy, we won't have to waste much time asking and answering questions about your background. And in addition to the official report, I have two personal reports on you. You made one hell of an impression on the boss in Philadelphia."

"Sir?" McCoy asked.

"You apparently delivered quite a lecture on the high state of discipline in the Imperial Japanese Army and how they were going to be formidable foes. Since the one true test of an intelligent man is how much he agrees with you, the boss thinks you're a genius."

" 'The boss,' sir?"

"The chief of intelligence," Rickabee said. "You don't know what I'm talking about, do you?"

"No, sir."

"Let it pass, then," Rickabee said, smiling. "Newly commissioned second lieutenants should not be praised. It tends to swell their heads. I had another personal report on you just a week ago. Ed Banning wrote me from Manila . . . you knew that the fourth has been shipped to the Philippines?"

"No, sir, I didn't."

"Banning said that he thought I should have you transferred to this lash-up and that I should consider, somewhere down the line, even sending you to officer candidate school."

McCoy didn't know how to respond.

In Japanese, Colonel Rickabee said, "I understand you're reasonably fluent in Japanese and Chinese."

"I wouldn't say fluent, sir—"

"Say it in Japanese," Rickabee interrupted.

"I can't read very much Japanese, sir," McCoy said, in Japanese. "And my Chinese isn't much better."

Rickabee nodded approvingly. "That's good enough," he continued in Japanese, and then switched to English. "We can use that talent. But there's a question of priorities. When we knew you were coming here, McCoy, what we planned to do with you was to have you replace Sergeant Ruttman. I want to run him through Quantico, too. He thinks he's been successfully evading it. The truth is that I needed somebody to take his place while he was gone. You seemed ideal to do that. You're a hardnose, and it would give you a chance to see how things are done here. But the best-laid plans, as they say. There are higher priorities. Specifically, the boss has levied on us—and I mean the boss personally, not one of his staff—for three officer couriers. We're moving a lot of paper back and forth between here and Pearl and here and Manila, especially now that the Fourth is in the Philippines. You're elected as one of the three, McCoy."

"Sir, I don't know what an officer courier is."

"There are some highly classified documents, and sometimes material, that have to pass from hand to hand, from a specific officer here to a specific officer someplace else—as opposed to headquarters to headquarters. That material has to be transported by an officer."

"Yes, sir," McCoy said.

"There's one other factor in the equation," Rickabee said. "The Pacific—especially Pearl Harbor, but Cavite too—has been playing dirty pool. We have sent officer couriers out there with the understanding that they would make one trip and then return to their primary duty. What Pearl has done twice, and Cavite once, is to keep our couriers and send the homeward-bound mail in the company of an officer they didn't particularly need. We have lost two cryptographic officers and one very good intercept officer that way."

McCoy knew that a cryptographic officer dealt with secret codes, but he had no ideas what an "intercept" officer was.

"I've complained, of course, and eventually we'll get them back, after everything has moved, slowly, through channels. But I can't afford to lose people for sixty, ninety days. Not now. So there had to be a solution, and Major Almond found it."

McCoy said nothing.

"Aren't you even curious, McCoy?" Rickabee asked.

"Yes, sir."

"Every officer in the Marine Corps is required to obey the orders of any officer superior to him, right?"

"Yes, sir."

"If the orders conflict, he is required to obey the orders given him by the most senior officer, right?"

"Yes, sir."

"Wrong," Rickabee said. "Or at least, there is an interesting variation. There is a small, generally unknown group of people in the Corps who don't have to obey the orders of superior officers, unless that officer happens to be the chief of intelligence. Their ranks aren't even known. Just their name and photo and thumbprint is on their ID cards. And the ID cards say that the bearer is a Special Agent of the Assistant Chief of Staff, Intelligence, USMC, and subject only to his orders."

"Yes, sir."

"Congratulations, Lieutenant McCoy, you are now—or you will be when Ruttman finishes your credentials—a Special Agent of the Assistant Chief of Staff for Intelligence. If anybody at Pearl or Cavite knows, or finds out, that you speak Japanese and decides they just can't afford to lose you, you will show them your identification and tell them you are sorry, but you are not subject to their orders."

Rickabee saw the confusion on McCoy's face.

"Question, McCoy?"

"Am I going to Pearl Harbor, sir?"

"And Cavite," Rickabee said. "More important, I think you will be coming back from Pearl and Cavite."

"And you can get away with giving me one of these cards?"

"For the time being," Rickabee said. "When they catch us, I'm sure Major Almond will think of something else clever."

"Let me make it clear, Lieutenant McCoy," Major Almond said, "that the identification, and the authority that goes with it, is perfectly legitimate. The personnel engaged in courterespionage activity who are issued such credentials are under this office."

"Major Almond pointed out to me, McCoy, that I had the discretionary authority to issue as many of them as I saw fit."

"Yes, sir."

"We don't wish to call attention to the fact that people like you will have them," Rickabee said. "For obvious reasons. You will travel in uniform on regular travel orders, and you will not show the identification unless you have to. You understand that?"

"Yes, sir."

"I don't know how long we'll have to keep you doing this, McCoy," Colonel Rickabee said. "We have a certain priority for personnel, but so do other people. And that FBI background check takes time. And the FBI is overloaded with them. You'll just have to take my word for it that as soon as I can get you off messenger-boy duty and put you to work doing something useful to us, I will."

"Yes, sir."

"What's his schedule, Jake?" Rickabee asked.

"Well, today of course there are administrative things to do. Get him a pistol, get his orders cut. That may run into tomorrow morning. He'll need some time to get his personal affairs in order. But there's no reason he can't leave here on Wednesday night, Thursday morning at the latest. Presuming there's not fifty people ahead of him in San Francisco also with AAA priority, that should put him in Pearl no later than Monday, December eighth, and into Manila on the tenth."

"Is that cutting it too close for you, McCoy?" Colonel Rickabee asked.

"No, sir," McCoy said, immediately.

Rickabee nodded.

"Take him to lunch at the Army-Navy Club, Jake," Colonel Rickabee ordered. "Sign my name to the chit."

"Aye, aye, sir," Major Almond said.

"I like to do that myself," Rickabee said, turning to McCoy. "We don't have time for many customs of the service around here; but when I can, I like to have a newly reported-aboard officer to dinner. Or at least take him to lunch. But I just don't have the time today. Won't have it before you go to Pearl. I'm really sorry."

Then he stood up and offered his hand.

"Welcome aboard, McCoy," he said. "I'm sorry your first assignment is such a lousy one. But it happens sometimes that way in the Corps."

He headed out of his office, and then stopped at the door.

"Get him out of the BOQ before he goes," he said. "If there's no time to find a place for him, have his gear brought here, and we'll stow it while he's gone, until we can find something."

"He's got a room in the Lafayette, sir."

"I'll be damned," Colonel Rickabee said. "But then Ed Banning did say I would find you extraordinary."

For some reason, McCoy thought, it was no longer hard to think of F.L. Rickabee as a lieutenant colonel of Marines.

(THREE)

Second Lieutenant Malcolm Pickering, USMCR, was sitting in the maid's room's sole armchair, his feet up on the cot. When Second Lieutenant Kenneth J. McCoy, USMCR, carrying a briefcase, entered the room, Pickering was in the act of replacing a bottle of ale in an ice-filled silver wine cooler he had borrowed from the bridal suite.

"What the hell are you doing with a briefcase?" Pick asked.

"That's not all," McCoy said. "Wait till I tell—"

Pickering shut him off by holding up his hand.

"Wait a minute," he said. "I've got if not bad then discomfitting news."

"Discomfit me, then," McCoy mocked him. "Fuck up what otherwise has been a glorious day."

"My general thinks you should move into the BOQ," Pickering said.

"Oh, shit!" McCoy said. "What the fuck business is it of his, anyway?"

"He's a nice guy," Pickering said. "He and my father were corporals together, and he stayed in the Corps. He's trying to be nice."

"Sure," McCoy said. "Just a friendly word of advice, my boy. An officer is judged by the company he keeps. Disassociate yourself from that former enlisted man."

"Jesus Christ," Pick said without thinking. "You do have a runaway social inferiority complex, don't you?"

"Fuck you," McCoy said.

"It's not like that at all, goddamn your thick head. What he's worried about is getting you in trouble with Intelligence."

"What?" McCoy asked.

"I don't know if you know this or not," Pickering said. "But the Corps has intelligence agents, counterintelligence agents. What they do is look for security risks."

"No shit?" McCoy asked.

"Listen to me, goddamn you!" Pickering said. "What these guys do is look for something unusual. Like second lieutenants living in hotels like the Lafayette. Expensive hotels. They would start asking where you got the money to pay for the bill."

"Special agents of the Deputy Chief of Staff for Intelligence, USMC, you mean?" McCoy asked, smiling broadly.

"You know about them, then? Goddamn it, Ken, it's not funny."

"It's the funniest thing I heard of all day," McCoy said. He took off his jacket, and then opened the briefcase.

"What the hell are you doing?" Pickering asked.

McCoy took a leather-and-rubber strap arrangement that only after a moment Pickering recognized as a shoulder holster. He slipped his arms in it, and then took a Colt 1911A1 from the briefcase and put it in the holster. Then he put his tunic back on.

"Goddamn you, you haven't listened to a word I've said," Pickering said.

"Well, I may be dumb," McCoy said. "But you're a Japanese spy if I ever saw one. Come with me, young man. If you cooperate, it will go easier on you."

It was some kind of joke, obviously, but Pickering didn't have any idea where the humor lay.

McCoy took a small leather folder from his hip pocket, opened it, and shoved it in Pickering's face.

"Special Agent McCoy," he announced triumphantly. "You're a dead man, you filthy Jap spy!"

"What the hell is that?" Pickering asked, snatching it out of his hand, and then looking at it carefully. "Is this for real? What is it?"

"It's for real," McCoy said. "And it's my ticket to sunny Hawaii and other spots in the romantic Orient."

"It's for real?" Pickering repeated, in disbelief.

"Well, not really real," McCoy said. "I mean it's genuine, but I'm not in counterintelligence. I'm an officer courier. They gave me that so no one will fuck with me on the swift completion of my appointed rounds."

Pickering demanded a more detailed explanation of what had gone on.

"But how did you get involved in intelligence in the first place?"

"That's what I did in China," McCoy said.

It was the first time he had ever told anyone that. He remembered just before he'd boarded the *Charles E. Whaley,* Captain Banning ordering him not to tell anyone in or out of the Corps about it. But that order had been superseded by his most recent order, from Major J.J. Almond:

"You'll have to tell your roommate something, McCoy. You can say where you work, advising him that it is classified information. And what you do, because that in itself is not classified."

And with the 4th Marines gone from Shanghai, there didn't seem to be any point in pretending that he hadn't done what he had done. And it was nice to have an appreciative audience, an audience that had previously believed he had been a truck driver.

"The important thing," he said finally, when he realized that he was tooting his own horn too much, "is that my colonel doesn't want me in the BOQ. So where does that leave us?"

Pickering reached for the telephone.

"This is Malcolm Pickering," he said. "Will you get the resident manager on here, please?"

When the resident manager came on the line, Pickering told him there had been "another change in plans."

"I will need that suite," he said. "Lieutenant McCoy and I will be here for the indefinite future."

They went down to dinner. There Pickering talked about flight school.

"I'm going to take a flight physical Thursday afternoon," he said. "If I pass it, I think I'm going to go for it."

And then they began a lengthy, and ultimately futile, search for a couple of skirts to lift.

It did not dampen their spirits at all. There was always tomorrow, and the day after tomorrow, and the week after that. There were supposed to be twice as many women as men in Washington. . . .

Despite the legend, McCoy said, it had been his experience that a Marine uniform was a bar to getting laid. When he came back from Hawaii and Manila, they would do their pussy-chasing in civilian clothes.

(FOUR)
Security Intelligence Section
U.S. Naval Communications
Washington, D.C.
1540 Hours, Wednesday, 3 December 1941

The sign on the door said OP-20-G, and there was a little window in it, like a speakeasy. When McCoy rang the bell, a face appeared in it.

"Lieutenant McCoy to see Commander Kramer," McCoy announced.

"I'll need to see your ID, Lieutenant," the face said.

McCoy held the little leather folder up to the window. The man took his sweet time examining it, but finally the door opened.

"The commander expected you five minutes ago," the face said. The face was now revealed as a chief radioman.

"The traffic was bad," McCoy said.

He followed the chief down a passageway, where the chief knocked at a door. When he announced who he was, there was the sound of a solenoid opening a bolt.

"Lieutenant McCoy, Commander," the chief said. "His ID checks."

"I'm sure he won't mind if I check it again," a somewhat nasal voice said.

Commander Kramer was a tall, thin officer with a pencil-line mustache. He looked at McCoy's credentials and then handed them back.

"I was about to say that we don't get many second lieutenants as couriers," Kramer said. "That is now changed to 'we don't get to see much identification like that.' "

"No, sir," McCoy said.

"Are you armed, Lieutenant?"

"Yes, sir."

"And you're leaving when?"

"At sixteen-thirty, sir."

"From Anacostia, you mean?"

"Yes, sir. Naval aircraft at least as far as San Francisco."

"You normally work for Colonel Rickabee, is that it?"

"Yes, sir."

"I heard that they had levied him for officer couriers," Kramer said. "I'm sorry you were caught in the net. But it wouldn't have been done if it wasn't necessary."

"I don't mind, sir," McCoy said, solemnly.

Instead of heading around the world by airplane, I would of course prefer to be here in Washington inventorying paper clips. Or better than that, at Camp LeJeune running around in the boondocks, practicing "the infantry platoon in the assault."

"Your briefcase is going to be stuffed," Kramer said. "She was sealing the envelopes just now. I'll have her bring them in."

He pushed a lever on an intercom.

"Mrs. Feller, the courier is here. Would you bring the material for Pearl Harbor in here, please?"

Mrs. Feller?

Ellen Feller backed into Commander Kramer's office with a ten-inch-thick stack of heavy manila envelopes held against her breast.

"Mrs. Feller, this is Lieutenant McCoy," Commander Kramer said.

"The lieutenant and I are old friends," Ellen said.

"Really?"

"We got to know one another rather well in China, didn't we, Ken?"

"You don't seem very surprised to see me," McCoy said.

"I knew you were here," she said. "I didn't expect to see you so soon, but I did hope to see you."

"May I suggest you get on with the document transfer?" Commander Kramer said, a tinge of annoyance in his voice. "Lieutenant McCoy has a sixteen-thirty plane to catch at Anacostia."

There were thirteen envelopes in the stack Ellen Feller laid on Commander Kramer's desk. There was a numbered receipt to be signed for each of them, and McCoy had to place his signature across the tape sealing the flap at the place where it would be broken if the envelope was opened.

It took some time to go through the paperwork and stuff the unyielding envelopes into the briefcase. Enough time for Commander Kramer to regret jumping on both of them.

"Ellen," he said. "If you wished to continue your reunion with the lieutenant, there's no reason you can't ride out to Anacostia with him."

"Oh, I'd like that," Ellen said.

McCoy took the handcuffs from his hip pocket and looped one cuff through the handle of the briefcase, then held out his wrist for Kramer to loop the other cuff around it.

"Have a good trip, Lieutenant," Commander Kramer said, offering his hand. He then held the door for both of them to pass through.

"My coat's just down the corridor," Ellen said.

A Navy gray Plymouth station wagon and a sailor driver waited for them at the entrance. McCoy had ridden over to OP-20-G in the front seat with him, but when the sailor saw Ellen Feller, he ran around and held the back door open for her. McCoy hesitated a moment before he got in beside her, holding the heavy briefcase on his lap.

"You were right," Ellen said, as they drove off.

"About what?"

"That I could probably find a job because I speak Chinese." She switched to Chinese. "The first place I applied was to the Navy, and they hired me right on. As a translator. But there's not that much to translate, so I've become sort of office manager. I'm a GS-6."

"I don't know what that means," McCoy said, relieved that they could speak Chinese and the driver wouldn't understand them. "Where's your husband?"

"He's in New York, busy with his work," she said.

"You manage to smuggle the vase in all right?" McCoy asked.

She raised her eyebrows at the question, but didn't answer it.

"I have a nice little apartment here," she said. "You'll have to come see it."

"The last time I saw you, you seemed damned glad to be getting rid of me."

"Well, my God, you remember what happened the day before," she said. "That was quite a shock."

"Yeah," he said, sarcastically. "Sure."

"I was upset, Ken," she said. "I'm sorry."

"Forget it," he said. "Those things happen."

"I understand why you're . . . angry," she said.

He didn't reply.

She turned on the seat and caught his hand in both of hers.

"I said, I'm sorry," she said.

"Nothing to be sorry about," he said.

"If you're still angry, then there is," she said.

"I'm not angry," he said.

She rubbed his hand against her cheek and then let him go.

"Not everything that happened the day before was unpleasant, of course," she said.

He didn't reply.

"Do you remember what happened just before?"

You were blowing me, that's what happened just before.

"No," he said.

"I often think about it," she said.

"I don't know what you're talking about," McCoy said.

Fuck you, lady. You get to screw old McCoy just once. I'm not about to start up anything with you again!

"Don't you really?" Ellen asked, and then sat forward on the seat to give the driver instructions: "Stay on Pennsylvania," she ordered. "It's faster this time of day."

"Yes, ma'am," the driver said.

When she slid back against the seat, her hand went under the skirt of McCoy's tunic and closed around his erection.

"Liar," she said softly.

"For God's sake," he said, pushing her hand away.

"Pity there's not more time, isn't it? But you won't be gone all that long, will you?"

At least with her, I know what she's after. It's not like with Pick's rich-bitch friend.

And thirty minutes in the sack with the old vacuum cleaner, and I won't even be able to remember Miss Ernestine Sage's name, much less remember what she looked like.

"No," he said. "A couple of weeks, is all. No more than three."

"That'll give us both something to look forward to, won't it?" Ellen Feller said.

McCoy reached out for her hand and put it back under the skirt of his blouse.

XV

(ONE)
The Madison Suite
The Lafayette Hotel, Washington, D.C.
1410 Hours, 7 December 1941

Until this week, airplanes for Second Lieutenant Malcolm Pickering, USMCR, had been something like taxi cabs. They were there. When you needed to go somewhere you got in one and it took you.

That changed. The Navy medico (more properly, flight surgeon, which Pickering thought had a nice aeronautical ring to it) told him that he met the physical standards laid down for Naval aviators. General McInerney's senior aide-de-camp, himself a dashing Naval aviator with wings of gold, then explained that while there might officially be, say, fifty would-be birdmen in any course of Primary Flight Instruction at the Pensacola Naval Air Station[1], that was something of a fiction. More than the prescribed number were routinely ordered to the shores of the Gulf of Mexico. Experience had taught that a number of students would quickly prove themselves incapable of learning how to fly. By sending extras, the Corps wound up with the desired number after the inept had bilged out.

General McInerney was in a position to have Pickering sent as a member of the supernumeraries. Pickering knew his mother would have a fit when she heard that he was to become an aviator, which was a problem that would be a bit difficult to handle. On the other hand, there was a positive appeal about the prospect of swapping the slush-filled streets of Washington for the white sandy beaches of Pensacola.

On the way home from Anacostia Naval Air Station in McCoy's LaSalle on Friday evening, he stopped at a bookstore, asked for books on aviation (starting with the theory of flight), and bought half a dozen that looked promising.

He was now reading one of them, one with a lot of drawings. The others, stacked up beside his chair, waited for his attention. A small table beside him held a silver pot of coffee. He was attired for a more primitive means of transportation than he was reading about: A tweed jacket with leather patches over the elbows; a plaid cotton shirt open at the collar; a pair of pink breeches; and a pair of Hailey & Smythe riding boots, which rested on a pillow (to preserve the furniture) on the coffee table before him.

He had spent the morning in Virginia aboard a horse. Sort of a fox hunt without either the fox or the ceremony that went with a hunt. Just half a dozen riders riding about the countryside, jumping fences of opportunity.

They were going to sit around in the afternoon and get smashed. Rather nobly,

[1]Flight training for Marine aviators is conducted by the U.S. Navy. Marine aviators wear the same gold wings as Naval aviators.

he thought, he had pleaded the press of duty and returned to the hotel to read the airplane books.

The telephone rang, and he looked around for it, a look of annoyance crossing his face as he spotted it, ten feet out of reach. It had taken him some effort to reach his present comfortable position, with his feet just so, and his back just so, and with *The Miracle of Flight* propped up just so on his belly.

He had just begun to grasp the notion that aircraft are lifted into the air because there is less pressure on the upper (curved, and thus longer) portion of a wing than there is on the bottom (flat, and thus shorter) portion of a wing. As the wing moves through the air, it simply follows the path of least resistance, upward, and hauls the airplane along with it. He wasn't entirely sure he fully understood this. He was sure, however, that he didn't want to chat just now with whomever was on the phone, especially since he had to get up to go answer it.

"Yes?" he snapped impatiently, "what is it?"

Oh, shit! It's probably General McInerney. And I was supposed to have answered that, "Lieutenant Pickering speaking."

"Pick?"

It was a female. And a half-second later, he knew which one.

"Hello, Ernie," he said.

"Are you alone? Can you talk?" Ernestine Sage said.

"You have interrupted a splendid orgy, but what's on your mind?"

"I want to talk to you," Ernie Sage said.

"Then talk," he said. "Just make it quick."

"I'll be right up," Ernie Sage said.

"You're here?" he asked, genuinely surprised. "In the hotel?"

"I just happened to be in the neighborhood and thought I'd just pop in," she said, and the phone went dead.

Between the time she hung up and the time he answered her knock at the door, he had considered the possibilities: Certainly this had to do with Ken McCoy. But what would bring Ernie all the way to Washington except true love? And the possibility, not as astonishing when there was time to think it over, that Ernie was in the family way. Could she be sure, so soon? To the best of his recollection, it took several months to be sure about that. It hadn't been that long since he had seen Juliet kissing Romeo in the Grand Central Oyster Bar.

"Hi," Ernie said, when he opened the door. "Don't you look horsey?"

For the first time in a long time, Pickering looked at her as a female, and not as part of the woodwork.

Damned good-looking, he judged. Marvelous knockers. They had obviously grown a good deal since (he now remembered with somewhat startling clarity) he had last seen them, looking down her bathing suit in Boca Raton. He and Ernie must have been thirteen or fourteen at the time.

"Come into my den, as the spider said to the fly."

"You're a hard man to find," she said. "I called your mother, or tried to, and they said she was in Hawaii. So I called your grandfather, and he told me where you were."

"Why do I suspect that you weren't suddenly overcome with an irresistible urge to see me?" Pickering asked.

She looked into his face.

"Where is he?" she asked.

"Where's who?"

"Come on, Pick," she said.

"Ken, you mean?"

"Where is he?"

"In Hawaii, too, come to think of it," Pick said.

"Oh, hell," she said.

"Not to worry," he said. "He will be back."

She looked at his face.

"That's important to you, isn't it?" Pickering asked.

"Don't be a shit about this, Pick, please," Ernie Sage said.

"Okay," he said. "It will be an effort, obviously."

"Do you have something I could have to drink?"

He gestured to the bar.

"Help yourself," he said.

She walked to the bar and made herself a Scotch.

"You want one?" she asked.

"I want one, but . . . oh, what the hell. Yes, please."

She made him a drink, handed it to him, and then sat down on a couch and stirred the ice cubes in her glass with her index finger.

"I never imagined myself doing this," she said, without looking at him.

"Doing what?"

"Running after a boy," she said, and corrected herself: "A man."

"I'm not surprised," Pick said.

She looked at him quickly.

"For one thing, McCoy's quite special," Pick said. "And for another, I saw the two of you in the Oyster Bar."

She did not seem at all embarrassed to hear that. Just curious.

"What were you doing there?"

"McCoy had led me safely through the wild jungles of Quantico," Pickering said, "protecting me from unfamiliar savage beasts. I thought it only fair that I return the favor."

"Protect him from me, you mean? Thanks a lot."

"I didn't know who it was until I saw you," Pickering said.

"Where did you meet him?"

"On a train from Boston," Pickering said. "He had just escorted prisoners to the Naval Prison at Portsmouth. And then he showed up, wholly unexpected, at Quantico."

"Why unexpected?"

"Because our peers were . . . our peers. McCoy was a noncom of the regular Marine Corps, just in from years in China."

"He told me about China," she said. "He took me to a tiny little Chinese restaurant off Mott Street, where he talked Chinese to them."

"As I say, he's something special."

"Isn't he?" she said. Then she looked up at him. "Four hours after I met him, I took him to bed."

"He told me," Pickering said.

"I don't know what you think of me, Pick," Ernie Sage said. "But that's not my style."

"He told me that, too," Pickering said, gently.

That surprised her. She looked into his face until she was sure that she had not misunderstood him.

"Pretty close, are you? Or did he proudly report it as another cherry copped?"

"Actually, he was pretty upset about it," Pickering said.

"But not too upset to tell you all about it?"

"We are pretty close," Pickering said. "I don't know. It's something like having a brother, I guess."

"You heard about his brother? The one who was offered the choice of the Marine Corps or jail?"

"I even know that was the choice they gave him, too," Pickering said. "Like I say, Ernie, we're close."

"Okay, so tell me what happened? I have six letters, all marked 'REFUSED.' "

"He found out you were rich," Pickering said.

"Oh, God!" she wailed. Then the accusation: "You told him. Why the hell did you have to do that?"

Pickering shrugged his shoulders helplessly and threw up his hands.

"Now I'm sorry that I did," he said.

She turned her face away from him. Then turned back, frowning.

"But I suppose I was thinking that the bad news better come gently, and from me. I didn't want that shocking revelation suddenly thrust upon him."

"If you came from a background like his, it would upset you, too," Ernie Sage said, loyally. "He has pride, for God's sake. I know he's a fool, but—"

"Did he tell you about the lady missionary?"

"What lady missionary?"

"There was a lady missionary in China who apparently gave him a bad time. Strung him along. Hurt him pretty badly."

"I'd like to kill her," Ernie Sage said, matter-of-factly.

"You've really got it pretty bad for him, don't you?"

"As incredible as it sounds," she said, "I'm in love with him. Okay? Can we proceed from that point?"

"Love, as in 'forsaking all others, until death do you part'?"

"I was disappointed when I found out I wasn't pregnant," she said. "How's that?"

"I hope you know what you're getting into," Pickering said.

"It doesn't matter, Pick," she said. "I have absolutely no control over how I feel about him. I thought that only happened in romantic novels. Obviously, it doesn't only happen in fiction."

"I'm jealous," Pickering said.

"What have you got to be jealous about?" Ernie asked, and then she understood. "You should be," she said. "But that's your problem. What do we do about mine?"

"I don't know," Pickering said. "If you're really sure about this, Ernie, Big Brother will think of something."

"I have never been so sure of anything in my life," she said. "It's either him and me, hand in hand, or to hell with it."

"For what it's worth, with the caveat that I am relatively inexperienced in matters of this kind, I would not say it's hopeless."

Ernestine Sage brightened visibly.

"Really?" she asked.

"Really," Pickering said. "For reasons I cannot imagine, Lieutenant McCoy seemed to be more than a little taken with your many charms."

"God, I hope so," she said, and then asked, "what's he doing in Hawaii?"

"They made him an officer courier," Pickering said. "He carries secrets in a briefcase."

"I never heard of that," she said. "How long did you say he'll be gone?"

"He's going to Hawaii. He got there today. Or will get there today. There is something called the International Dateline, and I've never figured it out. And from there, he's going to Manila, and then back to Hawaii, and then back here."

"And what are we going to do when he gets back here?"

"We'll arrange for him to find you in a black negligee in his bed," Pickering said. "As a Marine officer, he would be duty-bound to do his duty. You can play the ball from there."

"If I thought that would work," she said, "I'd do it."

"I think, Ernie," Pick Pickering said seriously, "that all it would take would be for him to find you sitting there, just like you are now."

She looked at him and smiled. Then she got up and walked to him and kissed him on the cheek.

"And I was really afraid that you'd be a shit about this," she said.

"My God! Me? Pick Pickering? Cupid's right-hand man?"

She chuckled and looked at her watch.

"I was so sure of it, that I reserved a compartment on the three-fifteen to New York. I've still got time to make it."

"Maybe," Pickering said, "you should get some practice riding coach."

She looked at him curiously for a moment until she took his meaning.

"If that's what it takes, that's what I'll do," she said. "But the next time. Not today."

He smiled at her and walked with her to the door, where she kissed him impulsively again.

He had just rearranged himself in the chair with his feet on the pillow and *The Miracle of Flight* propped up on his belly when there was another knock on his door.

"Jesus H. Christ!" he fumed as he went to answer it.

It was Ernie Sage, and he could tell from the look in her eyes that something was terribly wrong.

"A radio," Ernie said. "Have you got a radio?"

"There's one in here," he said. She pushed past him into the sitting room.

She had the radio on by the time he got there.

"Repeating the bulletin," the voice of the radio announcer said, "the White House has just announced that the Navy Base at Pearl Harbor, Hawaii, has been attacked by Japanese aircraft and that there has been substantial loss of life and material."

"Jesus Christ!" Pickering said.

"If he's dead," Ernestine Sage said melodramatically, "I'll kill myself."

"You don't mean that," Pickering said.

"Oh, my God, Pick! Your mother and father are there!"

He hadn't thought of that.

Somehow, he wound up holding her in his arms.

"Everything is going to be all right, Ernie."

"Bullshit!" she said against his chest.

And then it occurred to him that he was a Marine officer and that what he should be doing now was getting into uniform and reporting for duty.

(TWO)
Pearl Harbor, Hawaii
7 December 1941

The Japanese task force, which had sailed from Hitokappu Bay in the Kurile Islands, began to launch aircraft at 0600 hours. The task force was then approximately 305 nautical miles from Pearl Harbor. In relation to the task force, Pearl Harbor was on the far side of Oahu Island, the second largest island of the Hawaiian Chain.

Japanese Intelligence was aware that the attack could not be entirely as successful as was initially hoped. In the best possible scenario, essentially all of the United States Pacific Fleet would be in Pearl Harbor. The worst possible scenario was that essentially all of the Pacific Fleet would be at sea. The reality turned out to be between these extremes. All the battleships of the Pacific Fleet were in Pearl Harbor, as well as a number of other ships.

But the seven heavy cruisers and the two aircraft carriers the Japanese had also hoped to find at anchor were at sea. The Japanese knew the composition of the at-sea forces, but not their location.

Task Force 8—an aircraft carrier, three cruisers, and nine destroyers and destroyer minesweepers—was approximately 200 nautical miles from Pearl. Task Force 3—one cruiser and five destroyers and destroyer minesweepers—was 40 nautical miles off Johnson Island, about 750 nautical miles from Pearl Harbor. Task force 12—one carrier, three cruisers, and five destroyers—was about as far from Pearl Harbor as Task Force 3, operating approximately 400 nautical miles north of Task Force 3.

The decision was made to attack anyway. There was always the chance of detection; the destruction of harbor facilities and airfields was of high priority, and the destruction of one or more battleships would severely limit the capability of the American fleet.

The code command for the attack was "Climb Mount Niitaka 1208."

Approximately 125 nautical miles from Pearl Harbor, the stream of aircraft from the Japanese task force split into two streams. Fifty miles from Oahu, what was now the left stream began to split again, this time into three streams. The first two turned right and made for Pearl Harbor across the island. The third stream continued on course until it was past the tip of Oahu, and then turned toward the center of the island and made an approach to Pearl Harbor from the sea.

Meanwhile, the right stream had broken into two, with one crossing the coastline and making for Pearl Harbor across the island, and the second continuing on course past the island, then turning back to attack Pearl Harbor from the open sea.

The first wave of Japanese bombers struck at 0755 hours and the second at 0900. By then the task force had changed course and was making for the Japanese Inland Sea, hoping to avoid any encounter with carrier-based aircraft from Task Forces 12 and 8 or with land-based aircraft on Oahu. Intelligence reported that at least one squadron of long-range, four-engine B-17 bomber aircraft was en route from the continental United States.

Despite the risk of detection by radio direction finders, shortly after 1030 hours, a priority message from the Japanese task force was radioed to headquarters of the

Imperial Japanese Navy in Tokyo: "Tora[2], Tora, Tora." It was the prearranged code for the successful completion of the attack.

(THREE)

Although he tried to be very nonchalant about the whole thing, Second Lieutenant K.J. McCoy made his first aerial trip from Anacostia to the West Coast. All in all, once he got used to it, he found it very enjoyable. The airplane was a Navy transport, but so far as he could tell, identical to the Douglas DC-3s used by civilian airlines. The Navy called it an R4-D, yet it even had white napkins on the seats to keep your hair tonic from soiling the upholstery.

It was considerably more plush than the aircraft that carried him from California to Hawaii. As Major Almond had warned, there were a lot of people in California with an AAA priority waiting for air transportation to Hawaii. He could wait, the sergeant told him, until there was a space, but he should understand that when two people had AAA priority, the one who was senior in rank got the seat. As a second lieutenant, he was liable to wait a long time.

There was another way to get to Hawaii. The Army Air Corps was flying a squadron of B-17 bombers to Hickam Field. They had excess weight capacity because they would not carry bombs, and they were carrying passengers.

"Well, if that's the only way to get there, Sergeant," McCoy said, with feigned reluctance, "I suppose that'll have to be it."

The truth of the matter was that he was a little excited about the idea of flying on a bomber. And the flight started off on an ego-pleasing note, too. When he got to the airbase and presented his orders, a thoroughly pissed-off Air Corps major had to get out of the airplane so that Second Lieutenant McCoy of the Marines with his briefcase and AAA priority could get on.

They were supposed to land at Hickam Field about noon. An hour before that, the radio operator established contact with Hawaii. Moments later the pilot came back in the fuselage and told the crew and the four supercargo passengers (two Air Corps lieutenant colonels, an Army master sergeant, and McCoy) what had happened in Hawaii.

It was all over when the B-17 appeared over Oahu, but some dumb sonsofbitches didn't get the word and shot at the B-17, not just once but twice, the second time as they made their approach to Hickam Field.

The airfield was all shot up. There were burning and burned-out airplanes everywhere, and not one hangar seemed to be intact. An enormous cloud of dense black smoke rose where the Japs had managed to set off an aviation fuel dump.

They had no sooner landed than an Air Corps major appeared in a jeep and told the pilot to take off again for a landing field on a pineapple plantation on one of the other islands. He seemed thoroughly pissed-off when the pilot said he didn't have enough fuel aboard to take off for anywhere.

McCoy very politely asked the Air Corps major about transportation to the Navy Base at Pearl Harbor.

"Good Christ, Lieutenant!" the Air Corps major said, jumping all over his ass. "Are you blind? Pearl Harbor isn't there anymore!"

[2]Tiger.

There was no point arguing with him, so McCoy, the briefcase in one hand and his suitcase in the other, started walking.

There were a lot of other excited types at Hickam running around like chickens with their heads cut off, and even more who seemed to be moving around with strange blank looks in their eyes.

None of them were any help about getting him from Hickam to Pearl Harbor, even after he showed a couple of them his credentials. So McCoy decided that under the circumstances it would be all right to borrow transportation. He found a Ford pickup with nothing in the back and the keys in the ignition.

The MP at the gate held him at rifle point until an officer showed up. The officer took one look at the credentials and let him go.

As he approached the Navy Base, there was even more smoke than there'd been at Hickam Field. When he got to the gate, the Marine MP on duty wasn't any more impressed with the credentials than the Army MP at Hickam Field had been, and he had to wait for an officer to show up before he would let him inside.

While he was waiting for the officer to come to the gate, McCoy asked the MP if the Marine Barracks had been hit, and if so, how badly. The MP wouldn't tell him. That worried McCoy even more. Tommy was in the Marine Barracks, which meant in the middle of this shit. He didn't like to consider the possibility that Tommy had got himself blown up.

The officer who came to the gate passed him through and told him where he was supposed to go.

The Navy seemed a lot calmer than the Air Corps had been, but not a whole hell of a lot. Still, he found a classified-documents officer, a middle-aged, harassed-looking lieutenant commander, who relieved him of the contents of the briefcase. As McCoy was taking off the handcuff and the .45's shoulder holster so he could put them into the briefcase, he asked the lieutenant commander what he was expected to do now.

"Get yourself a couple of hours of sleep, Lieutenant," the lieutenant commander said. "And then report back here."

"Aye, aye, sir."

The lieutenant commander looked at him strangely.

"You got a wife, anything like that, Lieutenant," he said. "You might want to write a letter."

McCoy's eyebrows rose quizzically.

"You're going on to Cavite," he said. "With a little bit of luck, you might get there before the Japs do."

"The Japs hit Cavite, too?"

"And everything else in the Philippines," the lieutenant commander said. "But what I meant is 'before the Japs land in the Philippines.' "

"Is that what's going to happen?" McCoy asked.

The lieutenant commander nodded. Then he shrugged.

"There was a Secret Operational Immediate [the highest-priority communication] a couple of hours ago," the lieutenant commander said. "A Japanese invasion fleet was spotted headed for the Lingayen Gulf. Why the hell it was classified Secret, I don't know. The Japs must know where they are and where they're headed."

"And you think that once I get there, I'm stuck?" McCoy asked.

"I didn't say that," the lieutenant commander said. "But if I was going to fly into Cavite on a Catalina, I'd write my wife, or whatever, a letter."

"Thank you," McCoy said.

McCoy didn't even consider writing his sister. If anything happened to him, she would find out when they sent the insurance check to her kids. Briefly, the notion of writing Pick entered his mind, but he dismissed it. He wouldn't know what the hell to say. And he thought, for a moment, of writing Ernie.

Just for the hell of it, I thought you would like to know I love you.

Then he saw that for what it was, a damned-fool idea, and went looking for Tommy. It wouldn't be exactly what he had had in mind when he'd thought about seeing Tommy at Pearl Harbor. Tommy didn't even know he was an officer. He'd planned to surprise him with that, to see what he did when he saw him with the lieutenant's bars.

He got back in the borrowed pickup and drove to the Marine Barracks.

One of the barracks building had been set on fire, but the fire was out. There were bullet marks all over, and in the middle of the drill field was a huge unidentifiable, fire-scarred chunk of metal.

There weren't very many people around. A few noncoms, and some other people. But no troops. Nobody seemed to be running around looking for something to do.

He found the headquarters building and went inside. There was a guard in field gear and steel helmet at the door. He saluted.

And there was a first lieutenant and a PFC in the personnel office.

The lieutenant spotted him before the PFC, who belatedly jumped to his feet.

"Reporting in, Lieutenant?" the lieutenant asked.

"Passing through, sir," McCoy said. For a moment, he thought about dazzling the lieutenant with his special agent credentials, and then decided that wouldn't be right.

"What can I do for you?"

"My brother's assigned to the First Defense Battalion," McCoy said. "I've been wondering about him."

"No doubt," the lieutenant said. He handed McCoy a yellow lined pad.

"This is the first casualty report," he said. "My clerk's about to type it up. All the names on there are confirmed casualties, or KIA, but that's not saying all the casualties are on the list."

"Thank you, sir," McCoy said. He quickly scanned the names. Tommy's name wasn't on it.

"Well, he's not on it," McCoy said. "He's a private. McCoy, Thomas J."

The lieutenant started to consult a list, and then remembered just seeing that name. He consulted another list at the head of which he had penciled, "Cut orders transferring Wake Island."

One of the names on the list of those to be shipped out (as soon as transport could be found) as reinforcements for the small Marine Force under Major James Devereux on Wake Island was McCoy, Thomas J.

"He's in the beach defense force," he said. "I don't know where the hell to tell you to look for him."

"I don't have the time, anyway," McCoy said.

"You said you were passing through?"

"On my way to Manila," McCoy explained.

"To the Fourth Marines?"

McCoy nodded. There was no point in telling this guy he was a courier.

"You're going to have a hell of a time finding transport," the lieutenant said.

"Maybe, with a little bit of luck, I won't be able to," McCoy said.

"I did a hitch with the Second Battalion until '39. As an enlisted man. Good outfit."

"I used to be on a water-cooled .30 in Dog Company, First Battalion," McCoy said.

"Look," the lieutenant said. "They're not going to ship you out of here for a couple of days, at least. The odds are, your brother will be back in here. If he gets in, I'll pass the word you're here and send him over to the transient BOQ."

"Thanks," McCoy said.

"What the hell, a couple of old China Marines have to take care of each other, right?"

"Absolutely," McCoy said. "Thanks again."

When McCoy had gone, the lieutenant looked over the list of names of people to be transferred to Wake Island as soon as possible, erased Private Thomas J. McCoy's name from it, and penciled in another. He had no doubt that Wake Island would fall. And besides, no matter where he was, there would be enough war left for Private McCoy. And for his brother. The Philippines were probably going to go under, too, if what happened this morning was any indication. Christ, Hawaii might fall.

This would give them a chance to say hello. Or good-bye.

When McCoy drove back to COMPACFLEET, he parked the borrowed truck where no one could see him get out of it, and then went in search of something to eat.

The lieutenant commander found him in the cafeteria eating a bologna sandwich.

"I just looked all over the goddamn BOQ for you," he said. "That's where I told you to go."

McCoy, his mouth full, held up the bologna sandwich.

The lieutenant commander handed McCoy a briefcase and a pad of receipt forms. Then he took him to Ford Island, where a Catalina was being fueled by hand.

The airbase was a shambles, and the dense cloud of black smoke rising from Battleship Row was visible for a long time after they had taken off.

(FOUR)
Headquarters, 4th Regiment, USMC
Cavite Naval Base
Manila Bay, Territory of the Philippines
1300 Hours, 9 December 1941

The 4th Marines was just about clear of the area when McCoy finally found it. They had apparently moved out in haste. There was a large pile of packaging material, rough-cut lumber, cardboard, and wood shavings, on what had been the neatly trimmed lawn in front of Regimental Headquarters.

The buildings were deserted. Completely deserted, McCoy thought, until he was nearly run down by the colonel, trailed by the sergeant-major, as he turned a corner.

They were in khakis, no field scarves, wearing web belts with .45s dangling from them, and tin hats. Both of them had '03 Springfields slung over their shoulders.

McCoy was in greens, with a leather-brimmed cap.

The colonel's eyebrows rose when he saw McCoy.

"I know you. Who are you?" the colonel demanded.

McCoy popped to attention.

"Corporal McCoy, sir!" he barked.

"Shit," the sergeant-major said, and laughed out loud.

"Lieutenant McCoy, sir," McCoy said.

"I'll be damned," the colonel said. "What the hell is going on, McCoy? *Lieutenant?*"

"I just graduated from Platoon Leader's Course, sir."

"And they assigned you back here?" the colonel asked, incredulously.

"No, sir," McCoy said. "I'm an officer courier. I just got in. I thought I'd . . . come by and say hello to Captain Banning."

"Jesus H. Christ!" the colonel said, and shook his head and marched out of the building.

(FIVE)
Santos Bay, Lingayen Gulf
Luzon, Territory of the Philippines
0515 Hours, 10 December 1941

Captain Edward J. Banning lay behind a quickly erected sandbag barrier at the crest of the hill leading down to the beach.

The day was going to be cloudless. Cloudless and probably hot.

It was entirely likely that he would die here today, possibly even this morning. Behind a sandbag barrier on a hot, cloudless day.

The beach was being defended by two companies of Marines. They had not had time (or material) to mine the approaches to the beach. They had four water-cooled .30-caliber Brownings, six air-cooled .30-caliber Brownings, and half a dozen mortars. Somewhere en route, allegedly, were two 75-mm cannon from a Doggie-officered, Philippine Scout Field Artillery Battery.

A mile offshore were two dozen Japanese ships, half merchantmen converted to troop transports, half destroyers.

At first light, they were supposed to have been attacked by Army Air Corps bombers. Banning was not surprised that they had not been. The Japs had wiped out the Air Corps in the Philippines after it had been conveniently lined up on airfields for them. It had occurred to some Air Corps general that since there was a chance of sabotage if the planes were in widely dispersed revetments, they could be more "economically" guarded if they were gathered together in rows.

They had been all lined up for the Japs when they came in.

There would be no bombers to attack the Japanese invasion force, and the Japanese landing force would not be repelled by two companies of Marines and a handful of .30-caliber machine guns.

These two companies of the 4th Marines would die here today, in a futile defense of an indefensible beach.

And the rest of the regiment would die on other indefensible beaches.

He was resigned to it.

That's what he had been drawing all his pay for, for all those years, so he would be available for a situation like this.

He heard movement behind him and turned to see what it was, and had trouble believing what he saw.

It was Corporal "Killer" McCoy, without headgear, wearing a khaki shirt and green trousers, staggering under the load of a BAR (Browning Automatic Rifle, Caliber .30–06) and what looked like twenty or more magazines for it.

"What the hell are you doing here?" Banning asked.

With what looked like his last ounce of energy, McCoy set the BAR down carefully on the sandbags and then collapsed on his back, breathing heavily, still festooned with bandoliers of twenty-round magazines for the BAR.

It was only then that Banning saw the small gold bars pinned to McCoy's collar.

"I found the BAR and the Ammo at a checkpoint," McCoy breathed, still flat on his back. "Whoever was manning the checkpoint took off."

"What are you doing here?" Banning asked. "And wearing an officer's shirt?"

"I thought you knew," McCoy said. "I went to the Platoon Leader's Course."

"No, I didn't know," Banning said. "But what the hell are you doing here?"

"I came in as a courier," McCoy said. "Now that I am here, I guess I'm doing what you're doing."

He rolled onto his stomach and raised his head high enough to see over the sandbags.

"Jesus Christ, they're just sitting out there! Isn't there any artillery?"

"There's supposed to be, but there's not," Banning said. "There was also supposed to be bombers."

"Shit, we're going to get clobbered!"

"Did somebody order you up here, McCoy?" Banning asked.

"No," McCoy said simply. "But I figured this is where I belonged."

"Where are you supposed to be?"

"They told me to hang around the Navy Comm Center, in case there was a way to get me out of here. But that's not going to happen."

"You've got orders ordering you out of the Philippines?" Banning asked. McCoy nodded. "You goddamned fool! I'd give my left nut for orders like that."

McCoy looked at him curiously.

Perhaps even contemptuously, Banning thought.

"Get your ass out of here, McCoy," Banning said.

McCoy didn't respond. Instead he picked up Banning's binoculars and peered over the sandbags through them.

"Too late," he said. "They're putting boats over the side."

He handed Banning the binoculars.

Banning was looking through them when the tin cans started firing the preassault barrage. The first rounds were long, landing two, three hundred yards inland. The second rounds were short, setting up plumes of water fifty yards offshore.

The third rounds would be on target, he thought, as he saw the Japanese landing barges start for the beach.

The first rounds of the "fire for effect" barrage landed on the defense positions close to the beach.

The fucking Japs knew what they were doing!

When the first of the landing barges were five hundred yards offshore, maybe six hundred yards from where they were, McCoy brought it under fire.

The noise of the BAR going off so close to Banning's ear was painful as well as startling. He turned to look at McCoy. McCoy was firing, as he was supposed to, short three-, four-, five-round bursts, aimed bursts, giving the piece time to cool a little as he fired.

He's probably hitting what he's shooting at. But it's like trying to stamp out ants. There's just too many of them. And in a minute, some clever Jap is going to call in a couple of rounds on us. And that will be the end of us.

Captain Edward J. Banning's assessment of the tactical situation proved to be correct and precise. Two minutes later, the first round landed on their position, so close to him that the shock of the concussion caused him to lose control of his sphincter muscle. He didn't hear the sound of the round explode, although he heard it whistle on the way in.

It's true, he thought, surprised, just before he passed out, *you don't hear the one that gets you.*

Banning awoke in great pain, and in the dark, and he couldn't move his right arm. He sensed, rather than saw, that he was no longer on the crest overlooking the beach. Then he felt his body and learned that he was bandaged. He was chilled with panic at the thought that he was blind, but after a moment, he could make out vague shapes.

He lay immobile, wondering where he was and what he was expected to do. And then there was light.

One of the vague shapes moved to him and put a matter-of-fact hand on his neck to feel for a heartbeat.

"McCoy?"

"Yes, sir."

"Where the hell are we?"

"In the basement of some church," McCoy said.

"You brought me here?"

"The sonsofbitches dropped one right on us," McCoy said, without emotion. "I don't know what the hell happened to the BAR, but it was time we got the hell out of there."

"Did you get hit?"

"I took a little shrapnel in the side," he said. "They just pulled it out."

"Where are the Japanese?" Banning asked.

"Christ only knows," McCoy said. "They went by here like shit through a goose."

"We're behind their lines?"

"Yes, sir."

"This may sound like a dumb question, but what kind of shape am I in?"

"We got you pretty well doped up," McCoy said. "The Filipino—she's a nurse, the one that took the shrapnel out of me—says you shouldn't be moved for a couple of days."

"Then what happens?" Banning asked.

"They say we probably can't make it back through the Jap lines. So when you can move, they're going to take us up in the mountains, and maybe off this island onto another one. Mindo something."

"Mindinao," Banning furnished.

"That's right."

"What happened to the Marines on the beach?"

"They were going before we got hit," McCoy said.

God forgive me, I have absolutely no heroic regrets that I did not die with the regiment. I'm goddamned glad I'm alive, and that's all there is to it.

"Do you think you could make it through the Japanese lines?" Banning asked.

"You can't go anywhere for a while," McCoy replied.

"That's not what I asked," Banning said.

"What the hell is the point?" McCoy asked. "I think I'd much rather go in the hills for a while and see how I could fuck them up. If I go back, they'll just give me a platoon, and the same thing will happen to me as happened to those poor bastards on the beach yesterday."

"The point, Lieutenant McCoy, is that you are a Marine officer, and Marine officers obey their orders. You have two that currently affect you. The first is to leave the Philippines."

McCoy chuckled.

"Who's going to enforce that one? They'd have to come get me."

"I am," Banning said. "This is an order. You will make your way through Japanese lines and report to the proper authorities so that you may comply with your basic orders to leave the Philippines."

"You're serious, aren't you?" McCoy asked, genuinely surprised.

"You bet your ass I'm serious, Lieutenant. You better get it through your head that you'll fight this war the way the Corps tells you to fight it, not the way you think would be nicest."

"And what happens to you?"

"I am in compliance with my orders. I was ordered to resist the Japanese invasion. I'll continue to do that, as soon as I am physically able."

"This sounds like one of those dumb lectures at Quantico," McCoy said.

"Maybe you should have paid closer attention to those dumb lectures," Banning said.

"Shit," McCoy said.

"Has it ever occurred to you, goddamn you, that you can do a hell of a lot more for this war as an intelligence officer than you could running around in the boondocks ambushing an odd Jap here and there?"

"So could you, Captain."

"But I can't move, and you can."

McCoy, several minutes later, asked once more: "You really think I should go back and try to get back to the States?"

"Yes, goddamnit, I do."

"Aye, aye, sir," McCoy said. "As soon as it gets dark, I'll go."

(SIX)
Quarters 3201
U.S. Marine Corps Base, Quantico, Virginia
14 December 1941

Elly Stecker knew what was happening when she saw Doris Means at her door with her husband, but she pretended she didn't. Even after she saw the staff car parked behind the Meanses' Lincoln on the street.

"Is Jack home, Elly?" Doris asked.

"Jack!" Elly called brightly. "It's Colonel and Mrs. Means!" Then she turned and said, "Excuse me. Please come in."

Jack came to the door to the living room in his shirt sleeves.

He seemed to know, too, right off, Elly thought. But he didn't say anything out of the ordinary.

"Good evening, sir," he said.

"We've got a telegram, Jack," Colonel Means said.

"Yes, sir?"

Colonel Means took it from the crown of his cap and extended it to Stecker.

"Would you read it, please, sir?"

Means cleared his throat.

"The Secretary of the Navy deeply regrets to inform you that your son, Ensign Jack NMI Stecker, Jr., USN, was killed in action aboard the U.S.S. *Arizona* at Pearl Harbor, Hawaii, 7 December 1941. Frank Knox, Jr. Secretary of the Navy."

Captain Jack NMI Stecker, USMCR, stood there at attention a moment, rigidly; then his body seemed to tremble, and then the sobs got away from him. Making a noise much like a wail, he fled into his living room.

"Jesus Christ, Elly," Colonel Means said. "I'm sorry."

(SEVEN)
The Madison Suite, the Lafayette Hotel
Washington, D.C.
2215 Hours, 17 January 1942

McCoy pushed open the door and threw his suitcase in ahead of him.

"Pick? You here?"

There was no response. He went to Pick's bedroom and pushed the door open. The bed was made.

He shrugged and went to the bar and poured two inches of Scotch in a glass and drank it down. And then poured another two inches into the glass. He was so fucking tired he could barely stand, which meant he would not be able to get to sleep. He didn't know why the hell it was, but that's the way it was.

They'd sent him out of the Philippines on a submarine. The sub had gone to Pearl. Stopping only for fuel, he had flown directly from Pearl, via San Francisco, here. His clothes had not come off for sixty hours. And he was so fucking tired he hadn't gone to see Ellen Feller, although he was convinced that was the only way he was going to get Miss Rich Bitch out of his mind.

"Welcome home," Ernie Sage said.

She was standing in the door to his bedroom, wearing a bathrobe.

Jesus Christ, she's beautiful!

"What are you doing here?"

"You can't get a hotel room in Washington," she said. "Pick's letting me stay here."

"Oh," he said.

"When did you come back?"

"About an hour ago," he said.

"Is it as bad as they say?"

"It's pretty fucking bad, lady, I'll tell you that."

"I was worried about you," she said. Then she raised her eyes to his: "Goddamn you, we thought you were dead!"

"No," he said. "Why did you think that?"

"Because there was a cable that said, 'Missing and presumed dead,' that's why."

"I was behind the lines for a while," he said. "They must have sent another cable when I got to Corregidor."

"And you think that makes it right? *Goddamn* you, Ken!"

"Why should you give a damn, one way or the other?"

"Because I love you, goddamn you!"

"You don't know what you're saying," he said.

"You'll get used to it in time," she said.

"I said, you don't know what you're saying," McCoy said.

She ignored it. "What happens to you now?" she asked.

"I'll get sent back out there, sooner or later."

"So we have between now and sooner or later," she said. "That's better than nothing."

"Will you knock that off?"

"Meaning 'stop'?"

"You got it."

"You didn't feel a thing? I was just a piece of ass? One more cherry to hang on the wall?"

"Goddamnit, don't talk like that."

"I want to put my arms around you," she said.

"You wouldn't want to do that, I smell like a horse."

"Just as long as you don't smell of perfume," she said. "That I couldn't handle."

"I thought of you," he said. "I couldn't get you out of my mind."

"Me either," she said. "Then what the hell are we waiting for?"

"I don't know," he said. Then he said, "Jesus, when I saw you there I thought I was dreaming!"

She walked to him and took his hand and guided it inside her bathrobe.

"No dream," she said. "Flesh and blood."

After that he forgot that he smelled like a horse. And she didn't mind.

CALL TO ARMS

AUTHOR'S NOTE

The Marine "Raiders" of World War II were an elite force of a few thousand men formed soon after the war began. Like British Commandos, their role was to operate behind enemy lines, attacking him where he was most vulnerable. They accomplished this job with no little success, most conspicuously on Guadalcanal later on in the war. Success being no guarantee of permanence, however, the Raiders were disbanded during 1944. Nevertheless, for the short period of their existence these brave and daring men wrote yet another magnificent chapter in the proud history of the United States Marine Corps.

This novel deals in part with the birth and early growth of the Marine Raiders and, specifically, with their first combat operation, an attack shortly after the start of the war on a more or less out-of-the-way and insignificant piece of Pacific real estate called Makin Island.

A novel, of course, is fiction, but a novel based on historical events requires some research. Brigadier General E. L. Simmons, USMC, Retired, the distinguished historian who is Director of Marine Corps History and Museums, was most helpful, providing me with a wealth of material about the Raiders generally and the Makin Operation specifically.

And then, truth being stranger than fiction, I learned over a glass of beer in my kitchen that my crony of twenty years, Rudolph G. Rosenquist, had not only been a Raider but serves on the Board of Directors of the Marine Raiders Association. And from Rudy I learned that another crony of twenty years, Glenn Lewis, had been a Raider officer.

I knew, of course, that both of them had been Marines, but neither had ever talked of having been a Raider. Like most men who have seen extensive combat, Raiders are notoriously closemouthed about their exploits and generally unwilling to talk to writers.

In this case, twenty years of friendship made my friends abandon that Standing Operating Procedure.

Soon after my incredible good fortune in turning up in my (population 7,000) hometown two Raiders willing to give me details of Raider life I couldn't hope to get otherwise, I was talking to another Marine friend, this one a retired senior officer, who asked me what I had managed to dig up about "the politics behind the Raiders." When I confessed I had heard nothing about that, he suggested I should look into it; I would probably find it fascinating.

Shortly afterward, I received through the mail from a party or parties unknown, a thick stack of photocopies of once TOP SECRET and SECRET, now declassified, letters, documents, and memoranda prepared at the highest levels of the government, the Navy, and the Marine Corps during the opening days of World War II.

And these were indeed fascinating: the players; what they wrote; and what lies between the lines. The Marine Corps is itself an elite body of fighting men; and the Raiders were conceived as an elite within the elite. A number of very powerful people felt strongly that an elite within an elite was a logical contradiction and that one elite was all that was necessary. These people did what they could to make sure that their view prevailed.

Since it is germane to my story, it seemed to me that some of this factual material belonged in this book.

The first document in the stack, chronologically, was Memorandum No. 94, dated 6 PM, December 22, 1941, addressed to Franklin D. Roosevelt, President of the United States, from Colonel William J. Donovan, Coordinator of Information. It was originally classified TOP SECRET.

Donovan was a most interesting man. In World War I he had won the Medal of Honor as commander of the 169th "Fighting Irish" Infantry Regiment in France. And between the wars, he had been a successful—and highly paid—Wall Street lawyer and a very powerful political figure. Donovan's power was in no small way enhanced because he and Franklin Delano Roosevelt were friends. They had been Columbia Law School classmates together, and they had maintained and developed their relationship afterwards. In December 1941, for one dollar a year, Donovan was operating as "Coordinator of Information" out of offices in the National Institutes of Health Building in Washington, D.C. The job was not, as its title might suggest, about either public relations or public information; it was about spying.

Donovan had been appointed to the position by President Roosevelt, and answered only to him. Roosevelt, using "discretionary" funds, had established the COI to serve as a clearinghouse for intelligence gathered by all military and governmental agencies. COI was to evolve later into the Office of Strategic Services (OSS) and ultimately into the Central Intelligence Agency.

Donovan had unlimited private access to the President, and when he dealt with British intelligence authorities, he spoke with the authority of the President. Thus, when Donovan wrote his memorandum of December 22 to the President, he could be sure that the President would pay attention to it. The memorandum was a philosophical discussion of guerrilla warfare, a form of warfare very close to Donovan's heart; he adored anything that was clandestine.

"The principle laid down," he wrote, *"is that the whole art of guerrilla warfare lies in striking the enemy where he least expects it and yet where he is the most vulnerable."*

He made two specific suggestions for implementing this principle. The first dealt with the Azores and North Africa, where he recommended that *"the aid of native chiefs be obtained; the loyalty of the inhabitants be cultivated; Fifth columnists organized and placed, demolition material cached; and guerrilla bands of bold and daring men organized and installed."*

The second suggestion dealt with American military forces. He asked:

> *2. That there be organized now, in the United States, a guerrilla corps independent and separate from the Army and Navy, and imbued with a maximum of the offensive and imaginative spirit. This force should, of course, be created along disciplined military lines, analogous to the British Commando principle, a statement of which I sent you recently.*

Just over two weeks later, on January 8, 1942, Admiral Ernest J. King, the senior officer of the Navy, to which service the Marine Corps is subordinate, sent a SECRET memorandum to the Major General Commandant[1] of the Marine Corps, Major General Thomas Holcomb.

The subject was "Use of 'Commandos' in Pacific Fleet Area":

> *1. The Secretary, [the Secretary of the Navy, Frank Knox, a close and longtime friend of Colonel Donovan] told me that the President is much interested in the development and use of the equivalent of British 'commandos'.*
>
> *2. The Secretary told the President that you have such groups in training.*
>
> *3. The President proposed the use of 'commandos' as essential parts of raiding expeditions which attack (destroy) enemy advanced (seaplane) bases in the Pacific Fleet area.*
>
> *4. Please let me have your views—and proposals—as to such use.*

Five days after this, on 13 January 1942, a reserve captain of the Marine Corps stationed at Camp Elliott near San Diego, California, addressed a letter to the Major General Commandant of the Marine Corps. The subject of the letter was *"Development within the Marine Corps of a unit for purposes similar to the British Commandos and the Chinese Guerrillas."*

It was not common then, nor is it now, for lowly captains of the reserve to write letters to the Commandant of the Marine Corps setting out in detail how they think the Commandant should wage war.

This was an unusual captain, however. He had several things going for him: For one thing, until recently, he had been a military aide to Colonel William J. Donovan, the Coordinator of Information.

For another, he was known to be a close friend and disciple of a very interesting Marine, Lieutenant Colonel Evans F. Carlson, USMCR.

Carlson had begun his military career in 1912 by enlisting (under age, at sixteen) in the U.S. Army. He was discharged as a first sergeant in 1916, but almost immediately returned to uniform to join the Mexican Punitive Expeditionary Force under Brigadier General (later General of the Armies) John J. "Black Jack" Pershing.

Carlson later served in France with the American Expeditionary Force, where he was wounded. He was promoted to second lieutenant (May 1917), and to captain (December 1917). Though he resigned from the Army in 1919, in 1922 he applied for reinstatement of his Army commission, but was offered only second lieutenant.

Unwilling to be junior to his former subordinates, Carlson rejected the commission and instead enlisted in the USMC as a private. A year later, he was commissioned as second lieutenant, USMC.

Carlson began, but did not complete, flight training at the Naval Air Station, Pensacola, Florida, in 1925. And from 1927 to 1929, he was stationed in Shanghai, China, with the 4th Marines. In 1930, he was sent to Nicaragua, as a first lieutenant, for duty with the *Guardia Nacional.* For his valor in an engagement between twelve Marines and one hundred Nicaraguan bandits, Carlson was awarded the Navy Cross, second only to the Medal of Honor.

Carlson returned to China in 1933, where he learned to speak Chinese, and in 1935, following his promotion to captain, was assigned as executive officer of the Presidential Marine Detachment at Warm Springs, Georgia.

[1]The traditional title of the senior officer of the Marine Corps, Major General Commandant, was in its last days. Holcomb shortly became the first Lieutenant General of the Marine Corps, and assumed the simple title of Commandant.

Roosevelt, who was crippled by polio, often visited this polio treatment facility. In 1945, he died there.

There followed (1937–41) a number of private letters from Carlson to the President, in which Carlson offered his views of the situation in China, his assessment of the possibility of a war between the United States and Japan, and the implications thereof.

In 1936, Carlson was a student at the USMC Schools, Quantico, Virginia, and took courses in international law and politics at George Washington University. In 1937 he returned for a third time to China, ostensibly to perfect his Chinese. As an additional duty, he was assigned as an observer of Chinese Communist guerrilla forces then involved in actions against the Japanese.

For three months, Carlson was for all practical purposes a member of the Chinese Communist Eighth Route Army. During that time, he came to know and admire both Chou En-lai and Mao Tse-tung. His official reports to Headquarters, USMC, reflected not only that admiration but also his professional judgment that the tactics, the morale, and the discipline of the Chinese Communists were vastly superior to those of the forces of Chiang Kai-shek's Nationalist Chinese forces. In his judgment, the Communists would eventually triumph over the Nationalists, and American foreign policy should be changed accordingly.

In April 1939, frustrated by his conviction that he was being ignored by both the Marine Corps and the United States government, Major Carlson once more resigned his commission. He then spent part of the next two years in China as a private citizen, and there and in the United States wrote two books: *The Chinese Army,* which dealt with the Chinese Communists; and *Twin Stars of China,* which generously treated Mao Tse-tung and Chou En-lai.

He also carried on an extensive private correspondence, much of it unanswered, with prominent Americans, including Douglas MacArthur, as first Army Chief of Staff and then Marshal of the Philippine Army.

In early 1941, he reapplied for a Marine Corps commission. He was offered, and accepted in April 1941, a U.S. Marine Corps Reserve commission as major, was called to active duty, and shortly afterward was promoted to lieutenant colonel.

The lowly reserve captain who, in January 1942, dared to write to the Major General Commandant, wrote a document that was itself only two pages long, but it contained several appendices, including a newspaper editorial from the San Diego *Union Leader* of January 6, 1942, which approvingly described British Commando raids in Norway and Malaysia.

The Major General Commandant, after all, was a busy man. Perhaps he hadn't heard what the English were up to with their Commandos.

Appendix A to the captain's letter was four pages long. It was his proposed organization of *"Mobile Columns (Commandos). (To be called 'Rangers' or some other appropriate name.)"*

In the introduction to the proposed table of organization and equipment, the captain's letter called for *"a closer relationship between leaders and fighters than is customary in orthodox military organizations."*

He then went on to explain how this would be accomplished. First of all, the *"mobile columns"* would not be burdened with ordinary Marine Corps ranks. Each column, to be the size of a battalion, would be under the command of a "commander," instead of, say, a major or lieutenant colonel.

Everybody else in the "mobile column" (except, for example, medical officers and radio operators, who would be known by their specialties) would either be a "leader" or a "fighter." In other words, there would be no captains, lieutenants, sergeants, or corporals.

In the *"Qualifications of Personnel"* section, the captain wrote that all personnel should be prepared to *"subordinate self to harmonious team-work"* as well as to be capable of making thirty- to fifty-mile marches in twenty-four hours.

In the next paragraph, the captain touched on the subject of Rank Hath Its Privileges: *"Leaders must be men of recognized ability who lead by virtue of merit and who share without reservation all material conditions to which the group may be subjected, arrogating to themselves no privileges or perquisites."*

And in the next, on discipline: *"Discipline should be based on reason and designed to create and foster individual volition."*

The captain's letter was submitted on January 13, 1942.

The very next day, Major General Clayton B. Vogel, Commanding General of the 2nd Joint Training Force, Camp Elliott, forwarded it by endorsement to the Major General Commandant of the Marine Corps. The endorsement read, *"The thought expressed in the basic letter is concurred in, insofar as the value of such an organization is concerned. It is believed, however, that the Marine Divisions should complete their organization and train units now authorized prior to the formation of any such new organizations."*

It is possible, of course, that General Vogel, having nothing better to do with his time, sat right down and read the letter and the appendices straight through, and came to the conclusion that the captain's recommendations (even if they sounded like the organization and philosophy of the Chinese Communist Route Armies) were touched with genius and should be brought immediately to the attention of the Major General Commandant.

It is also possible that the signature on the letter had something to do with General Vogel's astonishingly rapid action in sending the letter on to the Major General Commandant, and his equally astonishing silence on the subject of throwing out the existing rank structure, and the privileges that went with it.

The letter was signed by James Roosevelt; Captain Roosevelt's father was President of the United States and Commander in Chief of its armed forces.

The very same day—January 14, 1942—Major General Commandant Holcomb, back in Washington, wrote two letters, classified CONFIDENTIAL, that were dispatched by officer couriers. The letters were essentially identical. One went to Major General H. M. Smith, USMC, commanding the Marine Barracks at Quantico, Virginia; and the other went to Major General Charles F. B. Price, USMC, in San Diego.

> *1. Suggestion has been made that Colonel William J. Donovan be appointed to the Marine Corps Reserve and promoted immediately to Brigadier General for the purpose of taking charge of the "Commando Project."*
>
> *2. It will be recalled that Colonel Donovan served with distinction in the 27th Division during World War I. He has since then observed practically all wars that have taken place and in particular has specialized in Commando Operations (amphibious raids).*
>
> *3. A frank expression of opinion is requested from you as to the advisability of accepting this suggestion. Replies will be Confidential and will be forwarded as promptly as possible to the Major General Commandant by air mail where appropriate.*

General Holcomb did not indicate—then or ever—who had suggested that Wild Bill Donovan be commissioned a general of Marines. To this day, in fact, the identity of the "very high" authority who wanted Donovan commissioned as a

Marine (and thus relieved of his COI responsibilities and authority) has never been revealed, but there are a number of credible possibilities.

The suggestion may have come from the President himself, and then been relayed through Frank Knox, Admiral King, or someone else. Roosevelt was known to be firmly behind the "American Commandos" idea, and he knew that the Marine Corps brass was at best lukewarm about the concept. That problem would be solved if Donovan were a Marine general with "commando" responsibility.

Another possibility was General George Catlett Marshall, the Chief of Staff, who was known to be unhappy with the carte blanche Donovan had been given by Roosevelt, and saw in Donovan an unacceptable challenge to his own authority.

Donovan was a thorn, too, in the side of J. Edgar Hoover, Director of the FBI (even though he held his post in large part because Donovan had recommended him for it), who had already lost to Donovan's COI authority to conduct intelligence operations overseas (except in South America). Hoover was known to be privately furious that he no longer had the President's ear exclusively on intelligence and counterintelligence matters.

The British intelligence establishment was also not happy with Donovan, who had already made it clear that he intended to see that the United States had an intelligence capability of its own, a capability that would not be under British authority. Their objections to Donovan reached Roosevelt via Winston S. Churchill.

But Donovan was not without his promoters; he had a legion of politically powerful fans, most prominent among them his good friend Colonel Frank Knox, Secretary of the Navy. It is equally credible to suggest that Knox, who had charged up Kettle Hill in Cuba as a sergeant with Teddy Roosevelt's Rough Riders, and who viewed the Marine Corps with an Army sergeant's somewhat critical eye, really believed he would be doing the Marine Corps a favor by sending them someone who had not only impeccable soldierly credentials, but the President's unlisted phone number as well.

Nothing has ever come out, it seems useful to note, to hint that Colonel Donovan himself was behind the suggestion, or that the nation's first super-spy ever heard about it until long after World War II was over.

On January 16, 1942, two days after it was dispatched (indicating that the officer courier bearing the letter was given an air priority to do so; he otherwise could not have arrived in California until January 17), Major General Price replied to the Major General Commandant's letter.

In this letter, he didn't appear to be especially opposed to Donovan's becoming a Marine general in charge of Marine Commandos. He wrote that Donovan was *"well qualified by natural bent and experience and probably more so than any General officer of the regular Marine Corps at present available for such assignment."*

General Price then turned to the whole idea of commando forces and the Marine Corps:

> *If the personnel to conduct this new activity can be recruited almost entirely from new resources it would be the judgment of the undersigned that the entire spirit and plan of employment of the Commando groups is directly in line with the aggressive spirit of the Marine Corps, that it will add immeasurably to the fame and prestige of the Corps, and must inevitably attract to our ranks the most adventurous and able spirits of America's manhood.*
>
> *If, on the other hand, our very limited resources in trained officers must be further disbursed and if the best of the adventurous spirits and "go-*

getters" among our men must be diverted from the Fleet Marine Force in meeting the requirements of this additional activity (Commando Project), then the undersigned would recommend seriously against assuming this additional commitment.

That was the official reply. The same day, General Price wrote a "Dear Tom" letter to the Major General Commandant of the Marine Corps. In it he wrote,

There is another thing in this connection which I could not put in my other letter and that is the grave danger that this sort of thing will develop into a tail which will wag the dog eventually. I know in what quarter the idea of foisting this scheme upon the Marines originated, and I opine that if it is developed along the lines of a hobby in the hands of personnel other than regular Marine officers it could very easily get far out of hand and out of control as well.

It appears pretty clear to me that you are in a position of having to comply and that nothing can be done about it so please accept my sympathy.

Major General H. M. Smith's reply to the Major General Commandant's letter, also dated January 16, 1942, was typically concise and to the point:

(a) All Amphibious Force Marines are considered as commandos and may be trained to high degree under their own officers in this form of training.

(b) The appointment of Colonel Donovan to brigadier general could be compared to that of Lord Mountbatten in Great Britain—both are "royal" and have easy access to the highest authority without reference to their own immediate superiors.

(c) The appointment would be considered by many senior officers of the Corps as political, unfair and a publicity stunt.

(d) An appointment as brigadier general, Marines, doubtless would indicate that he is to form commandos from Marine Amphibious Forces. The commandant would lose control of that number of Marines assigned as commandos. We have enough "by-products" now.

(e) No strictures are cast upon Colonel Donovan. He has a reputation for fearlessness but he has never been a Marine and his appointment would be accepted with resentment throughout the Corps. It would be stressed that the Marines had to go outside their own service for leaders.

(f) It is the unanimous opinion of the staff of this headquarters that commando raids by the British have been of little strategical value. We have not reached the stage where our men are so highly trained and restless for action that they must be employed in commando raids.

And then, as if he wasn't sure that the Major General Commandant would take his point, General Smith added,

(g) I recommend against the appointment.

Meanwhile, another brushfire had broken out. The senior U.S. Navy officer in England, Admiral H. R. Stark, had recommended to the Commander in Chief, U.S. Fleet (Admiral King), that seven Marine officers and one hundred enlisted men be sent to England for training by and with British Commandos, and that when they were trained, they participate in a commando raid somewhere in Europe, under British command.

Admiral King killed most of this idea on January 16. He wrote the Chief of Naval Operations, with a carbon copy to the Major General Commandant, authorizing a *"small group of selected officers and non-commissioned officers"* to be sent to England for about one month, *"such personnel to be used as instructors in the Fleet Marine Force on their return,"* and disapproved Marine participation in British Commando operations.

Three days later, Holcomb wrote to Samuel W. Meek, an executive of *Time-Life,* and a personal friend. After discussing an article someone planned to write for *Life* about the Marine Corps, and expressing the hope that "Mr. Luce[2] will be willing to suppress it," he turned to the subject of Donovan:

> *The Donovan affair is still uppermost in my mind. I am terrified that I may be forced to take this man. I feel that it will be the worst slap in the face that the Marine Corps was ever given because it involves bringing into the Marine Corps as a leader in our own specialty that is, amphibious operations. Because commander* [sic] *work is simply one form of amphibious operation. It will be bitterly resented by our personnel, both commissioned and enlisted, and I am afraid that it may serve to materially reduce my usefulness in this office, if any, because I am expected, and properly so, to protect the Marine Corps from intrusions of this kind.*

Five days after this, the Commander in Chief, United States Fleet (Admiral King), sent a priority, SECRET radio message to the Commander in Chief, Pacific Fleet, Admiral Chester W. Nimitz:

> DEVELOP ORGANIZATION AND TRAINING OF MARINE AND NAVAL UNITS OF "COMMANDO" TYPE FOR USE IN CONNECTION WITH EXPEDITIONS OF RAID CHARACTER FOR DEMOLITION AND OTHER DESTRUCTION OF SHORE INSTALLATIONS IN ENEMY HELD ISLANDS AND BASES X

Admiral Nimitz promptly ordered the Commanding General, Second Joint Training Force, San Diego, to form four company-sized commando units. He wrote that he had requested the transfer of destroyer-transports from the Atlantic Fleet to the Pacific Fleet, for use with the commando units. He also "authorized and directed" General Vogel to "request the services of any personnel who may be familiar with training, organization, and methods of foreign commando units."

Lieutenant Colonel Evans F. Carlson was shortly thereafter named commanding officer of the 2nd Separate Battalion, Camp Elliot, San Diego, California (which was to be shortly renamed the 2nd Raider Battalion), and Captain James Roosevelt was named as his deputy.

And on February 16, 1942, Major General Holcomb finally heard from Colonel William J. Donovan. It had nothing to do with Commandos, Raiders, or his becoming a Marine general. Navy personnel officers, desperate for officers, were scraping the bottom of the barrel and had informed Donovan that they intended to reassign some of the Navy and Marine officers assigned to COI.

Donovan made a reasoned, concise plea not to have the officers he was about to lose replaced by *"a random selection of reserve or retired officers who would I am sure fall far short of our needs."*

[2]Henry Luce, founder of *Time* and *Life,* was then functioning as the supreme editor of the *Time-Life* empire.

If Major General Holcomb replied to Donovan, that letter is still buried in a dusty file someplace. But for the rest of the war, the Marine Corps was far more cooperative than any other service when it came to furnishing personnel to Colonel (later Major General) Wild Bill Donovan's Office of Strategic Services. They included such people as Captain John Hamilton, USMCR, better known as actor Sterling Hayden, and screenwriter Peter Viertel, Captain, USMCR. . . .

But that's still another story. . . .

PREFACE

The first surrender of United States military forces in World War II—the first time, in fact, since the Civil War that American military forces went forward under a white flag to deliver American soil over to an enemy—took place on a tiny but militarily useful dot of volcanic rock in the Pacific Ocean, Wake Island, shortly after the Japanese struck the U.S. Pacific Fleet at Pearl Harbor, Hawaii.

In 1939, with war on the horizon, the U.S. Navy began to pay particular attention to the tiny atoll in the middle of the Pacific. This almost infinitesimal U.S. possession was 450 miles from the Bikini atoll; 620 miles from the Marshalls, which the Japanese would certainly use for military purposes; 1,023 miles from Midway Island; and 1,300 miles from Guam. The USS *Nitro* was ordered to Wake to make preliminary engineering studies with a view to turning the atoll into a base for land (which of course included carrier-based) aircraft and submarines, and to fortify the island against any Japanese assault.

In 1940, Congress appropriated the funds. On 19 August 1941, 6 officers and 173 enlisted men of the 1st Defense Battalion, USMC, were put ashore on Wake Island from the USS *Regulus.* The first of what would be about 1,200 construction workers landed a few days later, and in October, Major James P. S. Devereux, USMC, arrived from Hawaii to take command.

Devereux brought with him two five-inch Naval cannon (which had been removed from obsolescent and scrapped battleships); four three-inch antiaircraft cannon (only one of which had the required fire-control equipment); twenty-four .50-caliber machine guns; and a large number (probably about one hundred) of air- and water-cooled .30-caliber Browning machine guns. And, of course, a stock of ammunition for his ordnance.

Nine Marine officers and two hundred enlisted men from the Navy base at Pearl Harbor arrived on 2 November 1941, bringing the strength of the 1st Defense Battalion to approximately half of that provided for in the table of organization and equipment. On 28 November 1941, Commander Winfield Scott Cunningham, USN, was detached from the aircraft tender USS *Wright* (after the Wright Brothers) with nine Navy officers and fifty-eight sailors to Wake to take control of the air station already under construction.

As senior officer, Cunningham replaced Devereux as Commander of United States Forces, Wake Island.

A five-thousand-foot runway was completed, and U.S. Army B-17 aircraft began to use Wake Island as a refueling stop en route to Guam, although it was necessary to fill the aircraft tanks by hand-pumping avgas from fifty-five-gallon barrels.

On 3 December 1941, the USS *Enterprise* launched at sea twelve Grumman F4F fighters, of Marine Fighter Squadron VMF-211, under Major Paul Putnam, USMC. They landed on the Wake Island landing strip that afternoon, and steps were immediately taken to begin bulldozing revetments for the aircraft.

On Sunday, 7 December 1941 (Saturday, 6 December 1941 in Hawaii) Major

Devereux gave his command the day off. His Marines swam in the surf, played softball, and many of them—most of the young, recently recruited enlisted men—hurried to complete letters home. The letters would be carried to civilization aboard the Pan American *Philippine Clipper* moored in the lagoon, which would take off at first light for Guam.[1]

Reveille sounded at 0600, 8 December 1941. While the Marines had their breakfast, the Pan American crew prepared the *Philippine Clipper* for flight.

At 0650, the radio operator on duty at the air station communications section, attempting to establish contact with Hickam Field, Hawaii, began to receive uncoded messages, which did not follow established message-transmission procedures, to the effect that the island of Oahu was under attack. He informed the duty officer, who went to Major Devereux.

At 0655, the *Philippine Clipper* rose from the lagoon and gradually disappeared from sight in the bright blue morning sky.

When he was told of the "Oahu under attack" message, Major Devereux attempted to contact Commander Cunningham by telephone, but there was no answer.

When he hung up the telephone, it immediately rang again. It was the communications shack; there was an urgent message from Hawaii, now being decoded.

"Has the *Clipper* left?"

"Yes, sir."

"Call it back," Devereux ordered, and then sent for his field music—his bugler.

"Yes, sir?"

"Sound 'call to arms,' " Major Devereux ordered.

Admiral Husband Kimmel's Pacific Fleet, and the navy base at Pearl Harbor, had been grievously wounded by the Japanese attack on December 7, 1941, but that is not the same thing as destroyed. The battleship force of the Pacific Fleet had been essentially wiped out at its moorings ("Battleship Row") at Pearl Harbor, together with a number of other men-of-war and supply ships, and there had been great loss of aircraft and matériel.

But the Fleet was not totally lost, nor were its supplies.

There were three aircraft carriers available—the *Saratoga,* the *Enterprise,* and the *Lexington*—as well as a number of cruisers, plus a large number of smaller men-of-war.

On December 13, 1941, Admiral Kimmel (who expected to be relieved at any minute as the Navy, and indeed the nation, searched for somebody on whom to blame the Pearl Harbor disaster) ordered Rear Admiral Frank Jack Fletcher to reinforce Wake Island.

Fletcher put out the same day from Pearl Harbor with the aircraft carrier *Saratoga;* the cruisers *Minneapolis, Astoria,* and *San Francisco;* nine destroyers; a fleet oiler; and the transport *Tangier.*

Marine Fighter Squadron VMF-211, equipped with Grumman F4F-3 Wildcats, was aboard the *Saratoga* (in addition to *Saratoga*'s own aircraft), and the 4th Defense Battalion, USMC, was aboard the *Tangier.* The relief force carried with it nine thousand shells for Devereux's old five-inch battleship cannon, twelve thousand three-inch shells for his antiaircraft cannon, and three million rounds of belted .50-caliber machine-gun ammunition.

The aircraft carrier *Enterprise,* and its accompanying cruisers and destroyers, was ordered to make a diversionary raid on the Japanese-held Marshall Islands. The carrier *Lexington* and its accompanying vessels put to sea to repel, should it come, a second Japanese attack on the Hawaiian Islands.

[1]Pan American had been using Wake as a refueling stop.

At 2100 hours, 22 December 1941, a radio message was flashed from Pearl Harbor, ordering the *Saratoga* Wake Island relief force back to Hawaii. It had been decided at the highest echelons of command that Wake Island was not worth the risk of losing what was in fact one third of U.S. Naval strength in the Pacific. When the message was received, the *Saratoga* was five hundred miles (thirty-three hours steaming time) from Wake.

At shortly after one in the morning of December 23, 1941, Japanese troops landed on Wake, near the airstrip.

That afternoon, his ammunition gone, his heavy weapons out of commission, and greatly outnumbered, Major Devereux was forced to agree with Commander Cunningham that further resistance was futile and that surrender was necessary to avoid a useless bloodbath.

Major Devereux had to roam the island personally to order the last pockets of resistance to lay down their arms.

Four hundred seventy officers and men of the Marine Corps and Navy and 1,146 American civilian workmen entered Japanese captivity.

I

(ONE)
Wake Island
1200 Hours, 18 December 1941

Ensign E. H. Murphy, USN, had planned the flight of his Consolidated Aircraft PBY5 Catalina to Wake Island with great care. It wasn't a question only of finding the tiny atoll, which of course required great navigational skill, but of reaching Wake when there was the least chance of being intercepted by Japanese aircraft.

His Catalina was a seaplane (though the PBY5-A, fitted with retractable gear, was an amphibian) designed for long-range reconnaissance. Its most efficient cruising speed was about 160 MPH, so it had little chance of running away from an attacker. The high-winged, twin-engine Catalina had three gun ports, one on each side of the fuselage mounting a single .50-caliber machine gun, and one in the nose with a .30-caliber machine gun.

If Ensign Murphy's Catalina encountered one of the Japanese bombers that had been attacking Wake on an almost daily basis, all the Japanese would have to do was slow down to his speed, and, far out of range of his .50-caliber machine guns, shoot him down at his leisure with his 20-mm machine cannon.

It was a five-hour flight from Guam. Murphy took off at first light in the hope that he could be at Wake before the Japanese began their "scheduled" bombing attack.

Hitting Wake on the nose was skill; finding it covered with a morning haze was good luck. He landed in the lagoon and taxied to the Pan American area. Commander Cunningham's requisition of Pan American's *Philippine Clipper* had been almost immediately overridden by Pacific Fleet, which had plans for the use of the aircraft itself, and it had flown on to Guam, carrying hastily patched Japanese bullet holes in its fuselage.

Marine Fighter Squadron VMF-211 was down to two Wildcats, although Major Putnam told Ensign Murphy that he hoped to get a third Wildcat back in the air within hours with parts scavenged from wrecked airplanes.

Murphy carried with him official mail for Commander Cunningham and Major Devereux, including the last known position of the *Saratoga* relief force, but the Navy had not risked one of its precious few Catalinas solely to deliver messages. Many Catalinas had been destroyed on December 7, and what planes were left were in almost constant use.

But there was on Wake one of the Marine Corps' few highly skilled communications officers, Major Walter L. J. Bayler, USMC, who had previously been assigned to the USS *Wright* and had come to Wake with Commander Cunningham. Bayler's services were desperately needed on Midway Island and the decision had been made to send for him, even at the great risk of losing him, and the Catalina carrying him, in the attempt.

Bayler spent the afternoon of December 20 collecting official documents (including casualty lists) from Cunningham and Devereux, and then personal messages from the Marines of the garrison, for delivery, when it could be arranged, to their families.

The next morning, Ensign Murphy lifted the Catalina from the Wake lagoon and pointed the nose toward Pearl Harbor, eight hours and 1,225 miles distant. The Catalina was the last American aircraft to visit Wake Island until the war was over.

At Pearl Harbor, mechanics swarmed over the Catalina to ready it for another flight. Three hours after it landed, it was airborne again with another flight crew, this time bound for the Philippines, where the Japanese were approaching Manila, and demolition at the Cavite U.S. Navy Base had already begun.

The Catalina remained in the Philippines only long enough to drop off its passengers—a Navy petty officer who was a Japanese linguist, and an Army Ordnance Corps major, a demolitions expert—and its mail bags. It loaded aboard the outgoing cargo, mail bags, and its Pearl Harbor–bound passengers while it was taking on fuel. These were a U.S. Foreign Service officer, an Army colonel of Artillery, and a Marine Corps second lieutenant.

Manila Bay was choppy, and the Catalina smashed heavily into unyielding water several times before the pilot was finally able to get it into the air. When they'd reached cruising altitude, he went back into the fuselage to see if any damage had been done to the aircraft—in particular to the floats—and to the passengers. He found the Army colonel and the Foreign Service officer doing what they could to bandage the Marine Corps second lieutenant.

Although it had not been visible under the lieutenant's uniform when he boarded the Catalina, his body was bandaged. The bone-jarring bounces of the Catalina as it had taken off had ripped loose four or five of the two dozen or so stitches holding an eight-inch gash in the young Marine officer's side together. There was some bleeding, and he was obviously in pain, but he refused, rather abruptly, the pilot's offer of a syringe of morphine.

They rigged a sort of bed for him out of life preservers and blankets, but that was all that could be done for him until the seaplane reached Pearl Harbor.

An hour out of Pearl, the young Marine went forward to the cockpit. The pilot was surprised to see him.

"Feeling better?" he asked.

The young Marine nodded.

"In a couple of minutes, I'll radio ahead, and they'll have medics meet us," the pilot said.

"I thought maybe you'd do that," the young Marine said. "That's why I came up here. Don't."

"Why not?"

"Because, unless I get put in a hospital, my orders will carry me to Washington," he said. "I can get myself rebandaged there."

"You may not make it to Washington, in your shape."

"Then in San Francisco, or Diego, wherever they land me. Do me a favor, just don't say anything."

"Suit yourself," the pilot said, after a moment's thought.

"Thank you," the young Marine officer said and he went back into the fuselage.

Curious, the pilot took his flight manifest out and looked at it. It gave no identification beyond, "McCoy, Kenneth J. 2nd Lt. USMCR," but then the pilot noticed that Second Lieutenant McCoy was listed first on the manifest. Passengers were listed in order of their travel priority, which meant that McCoy had a higher priority than even the Foreign Service big shot.

The pilot was curious about that, and said so to the copilot.

"He's a courier," he said. "Didn't you see the briefcase?"

The pilot shook his head. "No."

"He had it when he came on board, chained—actually handcuffed—to his wrist."

"I didn't notice," the pilot said.

"And when he took off his jacket, he had a .45 stuck in his belt, and a knife strapped to his arm."

"I wonder what's in the briefcase?" the pilot said.

"I don't know," the copilot replied, adding, "but I don't think I'd want to try to take it away from him."

(TWO)
The Willard Hotel
Washington, D.C.
1215 Hours, 26 December 1941

"Peacock Alley," which ran through the Willard Hotel from Fourteenth Street to Pennsylvania Avenue, was where, since before the Civil War, the elegant ladies of the nation's capital (and, some said, the more expensive courtesans) and their elegant gentlemen had strutted . . . like peacocks.

It was ornately decorated, still with Victorian elegance, and along the alley were small alcoves, furnished with tables and chairs where conversations could be held in private. The cynics said that more politicians had been bought and sold in the alcoves of Peacock Alley than in all the smoke-filled rooms in the United States combined.

Thomas C. Wesley, a tall, fifty-year-old, portly, ruddy-faced full colonel of Marines, got out of a 1941 Chevrolet staff car on Pennsylvania Avenue and entered the building. He removed his overcoat and hat and put them in care of the cloakroom. He tugged at the skirt of his blouse and checked the position of his Sam Browne leather belt, and then walked slowly down Peacock Alley all the way to the stairs leading down into the lobby, obviously looking for someone. When he didn't find him, he stationed himself halfway along the corridor and waited.

At just about the same time, a tall, thin, somehow unhealthy-looking man entered the Willard from Fourteenth Street. He was wearing a gray snap-brim felt hat, which he removed (exposing his balding head) as he came through the revolving door. He headed across the old and battered, but still elegant, lobby toward Peacock Alley shrugging awkwardly out of his gray topcoat. By the time he saw Colonel Wesley, he had it draped none too neatly over his left arm.

Colonel Wesley nodded stiffly, perhaps even disapprovingly, when he saw the tall, thin, unhealthy-looking man in the badly fitting blue pinstripe suit.

"Rickabee," he said.

"Colonel," Rickabee said, then looked around Peacock Alley until he found an empty table and two chairs in one of the alcoves and made a gesture toward it. Lieutenant Colonel F. L. Rickabee was carried on the Table of Organization of Headquarters, USMC, as "special assistant to the Public Affairs Officer," although his real duties had nothing to do with public relations.

Colonel Wesley marched to the alcove and sat down, leaving to Rickabee the other chair, which faced the wall. Rickabee moved the chair so that he, too, could look out into Peacock Alley.

"It's been some time, Rickabee, hasn't it?" Colonel Wesley said, and then, before Rickabee had a chance to reply, said what was actually on his mind: "Are you people exempt from the uniform requirements?"

"It's left to General Forrest's discretion, sir, who wears the uniform and who doesn't. The general feels I'm more effective in mufti."

Brigadier General Horace W. T. Forrest, USMC, was Assistant Chief of Staff, Intelligence, USMC.

"General Forrest explained the situation to you?" Colonel Wesley asked.

"He said that you and General Lesterby had been handed a very delicate problem by the Major General Commandant, and that I was to do what I could to help. How can we help you, sir?"

"*He* thought you might be interested in this," Colonel Wesley said, taking an envelope from his lower blouse pocket and handing it to Rickabee.

There was no question in Lieutenant Colonel Rickabee's mind who "He" was. Colonel Thomas C. Wesley was one of a handful of officers at the absolute upper echelon of the Marine Corps. They were somewhat derisively known as "the Palace Guard," because of their reputation for doing the bidding of, and protecting from all enemies, foreign and domestic, the Commandant of the U.S. Marine Corps.

"Captain James Roosevelt has been good enough to offer some suggestions on how he believes the Marine Corps should organize its own version of a Communist Route Army," Colonel Wesley said dryly.

"I thought he was working for Colonel Wild Bill Donovan," Rickabee said.

"Not any longer," Wesley said. "He now works for Lieutenant Colonel Evans Carlson."

Rickabee took from the envelope a thin sheath of carbon sheets. They were the fifth or sixth carbon, he concluded. They were just barely readable.

A waiter appeared.

"Nothing for me, thank you," Colonel Wesley said.

"I'll have a Jack Daniel's," Lieutenant Colonel Rickabee said. "No ice, and water on the side."

He sensed Colonel Wesley's disapproval.

"The way I handle drinking on duty, Colonel," Rickabee said, "is that for the first twenty-four consecutive hours I have the duty, I don't touch alcohol. After that . . ."

"Do what you like, Rickabee," Colonel Wesley said.

Rickabee returned to reading, very carefully, the sheath of carbon copies Wesley had given him. Finally, he finished and looked at Wesley.

"Very interesting," he said. "Where did you get this?"

"I'm not at liberty to say," Wesley said.

"You think he's actually going to submit it?"

"Yes, I do."

"And apparently you don't think that General Vogel is going to call him in for a little chat and point out that it's just a touch pushy for a reserve captain to tell him, much less the Commandant, how the Corps should be run?"

"I believe the letter will be forwarded to the Commandant," Wesley said. "I'm interested in your reaction to it."

"You are, or He is? Does He know you're showing this to me?"

Colonel Wesley nodded his head, signifying, Rickabee decided, that Wesley was running an errand.

"I would really like to know where you got this, where He got it," Rickabee said.

"I can assure you, Colonel," Wesley said, "that it is authentic."

"I'd still like to know how it came into His hands," Rickabee insisted. "That could be very important."

"The document was typed, from a handwritten draft, by a clerk, a corporal, who thought the sergeant major should see it. He made six, instead of five carbons. The sergeant major sent it on to . . . sent it on here."

"To you or to Him?" Rickabee asked.

"To Him," Wesley said.

The waiter, an elderly black man, delivered Rickabee's bourbon on a silver tray.

"I believe I will have one," Colonel Wesley said. "The same, with ice. . . . This is obviously a very delicate situation," he continued, when the waiter had gone.

"Well, there's one way to handle it," Rickabee said. "I know several people at San Diego who would be happy to run Carlson over with a truck. Better yet, a tank."

Wesley was not amused; it showed on his face.

"Then you think that Colonel Carlson has a hand in this?" he asked.

"That seems pretty obvious," Rickabee said. "Have you read his reports, Colonel? Or his books?"

"As much as I could stomach," Colonel Wesley said.

"That 'leaders' and 'fighters' business," Lieutenant Colonel Rickabee said, "has appeared before. That's pure Carlson. So is the business about everybody being treated equally, officers, noncoms, and privates. He got all that from the Chinese Eighth Route Army . . . and the term 'column,' too, meaning 'battalion.' That's pure Chinese Red Army."

"Well then, let's get right to that," Wesley said. "Did he get himself infected by them when he was with them? Is he a Communist?"

Rickabee sipped at his bourbon, and then took a sip of water before replying.

"No, I don't think so," he said. "He's been investigated. When he applied to get his commission back, the FBI investigated him, and came up with nothing we didn't already know."

"You've seen the FBI reports?" Wesley asked.

"Of course not," Rickabee said, dryly. "FBI reports are confidential and never shown to outsiders. What agencies requesting an investigation get is a synopsis of what the FBI thinks it found out."

He clearly meant, Wesley decided, that he had indeed seen the FBI reports on Lieutenant Colonel Evans Carlson, USMCR.

"What's your personal opinion of him?" Wesley said.

"I think he's a good Marine gone off the deep end," Rickabee said. "That he's a zealot, quite eccentric, perhaps even unbalanced. He might have gotten Roosevelt to sign this, but the Major General Commandant will know he was behind it."

Wesley grunted his agreement.

"But on the other hand," Rickabee said after taking a sip of his drink, "they said very much the same things about Jesus Christ, you will recall. *'What's happened to that nice Nazarene carpenter? Why is he attacking the established order?'* "

"I don't think that's funny, Colonel," Wesley said, coldly.

"It wasn't intended to be, Colonel. There is even the parallel between Christ being able to talk to his heavenly, all-powerful father. . . ."

What could have been a faint smile crossed Wesley's lips.

"And what about Roosevelt . . . the son, I mean?" he asked.

"Everything I know about him is positive. He's smarter than hell, hard working, everything a good reserve officer should be. After seeing this, I would suggest that he's fallen in with evil companions . . . *an* evil companion."

"You know him, personally?"

Rickabee nodded. "Not well. Great big guy. Getting bald. Has to wear glasses. Nice guy, from the little I know him. What I would like to know is why they gave Carlson his commission back."

"Isn't that obvious, Colonel?" Colonel Wesley replied, sarcastically. "He came highly recommended. He has the Navy Cross. And, as they say, 'friends in high places.' "

"A little backbone then would have kept this from happening," Rickabee said, and raised the sheets of paper.

"*He* made that decision," Wesley said.

"That was the big mistake," Rickabee said, undaunted.

"You say your mind, Colonel, don't you?" Colonel Wesley said, coldly.

"That's what I'm paid for," Rickabee said. "I would prefer to be at Camp Elliott myself. Believe it or not, I'm qualified to command an infantry battalion."

"Obviously, the Corps feels that what you're doing now is of greater importance," Colonel Wesley said.

"What does the Corps want me to do about this?" Rickabee asked, holding up the sheaf of paper again. "How does my run-him-over-with-a-truck suggestion sound?"

"As if you don't understand the seriousness of the problem," Wesley said. "Otherwise you wouldn't be joking."

"You seem to be very sure that I *was* joking," Rickabee said.

Colonel Thomas C. Wesley was furious with himself when he realized that he did not in fact know for sure that Rickabee was being flip. He met Rickabee's eyes for a long moment, and learned nothing.

"What I was hoping—" he said, finally.

"Was that I could give you proof positive," Rickabee interrupted him, "proof that He could take to at least Frank Knox, and/or to the White House, that Evans Carlson is in fact a Communist and/or certifiably out of his mind. I can't do that, Colonel. I can't even manufacture any evidence to that effect. It wouldn't stand up in the light."

"But you do see the problem," Wesley said.

"Would you like to hear how I see it?" Rickabee asked.

"Of course," Wesley said, impatiently.

"The Corps is in a no-win situation," Rickabee said. "When this document reaches His desk, He's going to have to approve it, at least on a trial basis. Carlson's Eighth Communist Route Army, also known as the Marine Commandos or Rangers or whatever, will have to be employed. That will result in one of two things: They will get wiped out on the beach of some Pacific island, and He will find Himself explaining why He approved such a nutty idea, resulting in such a terrible waste of young American life. Or, Carlson's private army will do what Carlson says it will do, which, by the way, is very likely to happen. Carlson has proved that he's a skilled, courageous officer. If Carlson succeeds—and to repeat, he damned well may—the Commandant will find himself turning the Corps into the U.S. Commandos, with at least full Colonel Carlson—and possibly General Carlson—at his side while the rules are written."

"It could mean the end of the Corps," Wesley said.

"Yes, it could," Rickabee said. "After the war, when there was no need for

Commandos, or for more than a few of them, the Marine Corps could become an Army regiment. A lot of people would like to see that happen."

"If you were charged with stopping this, Rickabee," Colonel Wesley asked, "how would you go about it?"

"Is that what this little chat is all about, Colonel? He sent you here to order me to stop it?"

"I said nothing of the kind," Wesley said quickly. "Just answer the question, please."

"I would look for proof positive that Carlson is crazy or a Communist, or both," Rickabee said. "That's the only chance I see to scuttle this."

"And, how would you do that?"

"I would put someone close to him, telling him what to look for, and to make sure he had witnesses . . . unimpeachable witnesses."

"A spy, you mean."

"An *undercover operative,*" Rickabee said.

"Have you such a man available?" Wesley asked.

"Not off the top of my head," Rickabee said, then changed his mind. "I might. He's a bright young shavetail—"

Wesley interrupted him. "I don't want to know the details," he said. "Not yet."

"Then where are we?" Rickabee said.

"I want you to think this through," Wesley said. "Come up with a plan, including the name of the man you intend to employ, and a synopsis of his background. When you have that, as soon as you have it, call me."

"Yes, sir," Rickabee said. He motioned to someone standing in Peacock Alley to come to the table.

"What are you doing?" Colonel Wesley asked, confused.

A good-looking young man in a camel's hair sports coat and gray flannel trousers came to the table.

"Colonel Wesley, Lieutenant Frame," Rickabee said.

"How do you do, sir?" Lieutenant Frame asked politely.

"Lieutenant," Colonel Wesley said.

"Bill, take this to the office and have it photographed," Rickabee ordered, handing Frame the sheaf of carbon copies. "Stick around until you have the negatives, then bring this back here. I have just accepted Colonel Wesley's kind invitation to lunch, and we'll be in the dining room."

"Aye, aye, sir," Lieutenant Frame said. He looked at Colonel Wesley, said, "It was a pleasure to meet you, sir," and then walked down Peacock Alley toward Fourteenth Street.

"And what's his reason for being in mufti?" Colonel Wesley asked. He was annoyed that Rickabee had, without asking, turned the carbon of Captain James Roosevelt's proposal for Marine Commandos over to Frame to be photographed.

"He'd look a little strange following a civilian around in uniform, don't you think, Colonel?" Rickabee replied, smiling.

"And that's necessary? His following you around?"

"That was the general's idea, Colonel," Rickabee said, and stood up. "Shall we have our lunch? He won't be long, and I've got a busy afternoon."

From Colonel Wesley's silence during lunch, Lieutenant Colonel Rickabee decided that Wesley was displeased with him. He had probably been a little too flip for the colonel, failed to display the proper respect for a senior member of the Palace Guard. But there was nothing that could be done about that now.

He was wrong. When Colonel Wesley returned to Headquarters, USMC, and to the office of Major General Lesterby, he told Lesterby that Rickabee might just be the answer to "the Carlson problem."

"He had a specific suggestion?"

"Yes, sir, that he arrange to have Carlson run over with a truck."

"You think he was serious?"

"Sir, I don't know."

"It may come down to that, Tom."

(THREE)
The Brooklyn Navy Yard
Brooklyn, New York
0400 Hours, 6 January 1942

Two noncommissioned officers of the United States Marine Corps, Staff Sergeant C. (for Casimir) J. Koznowski and Sergeant Ernst W. "Ernie" Zimmerman, stood on the cobblestone street before an old brick barracks, shifting their feet and slapping their gloved hands against the cold. Koznowski was twenty-seven, tall, and slim. Zimmerman was stocky, muscular, round faced, and twenty-three. There were two "hash marks"—red embroidered diagonal bars each signifying the satisfactory completion of four years' service—on the sleeve of Koznowski's overcoat, and one hash mark on Zimmerman's.

Sergeant Zimmerman's face was pale, and his uniform seemed just a hair too large for him. Sergeant Zimmerman had two days before been released from the St. Albans Naval Hospital where he had been treated for malaria. He had been certified as fit for limited service and was being transferred to Parris Island for duty in his military specialty of motor transport sergeant.

Two corporals came around the corner of the brick barracks building, and when they saw Koznowski and Zimmerman, broke into a trot to join them.

"Where the fuck have you two been?" Staff Sergeant Koznowski demanded. It was not really a question, but rather an expression of disapproval, and no answer was expected or given.

"Go get 'em," Staff Sergeant Koznowski said to one of the corporals, and threw a clipboard at the other.

Both corporals ran into the building. There was the blast of a whistle, and lights were on, and the sound of muffled shouts.

Less than a minute later, encouraged by curt shouts of "Move it! Move it! Move it!" the first of 106 young men began to pour out of the building. They were in civilian clothing. The day before, or two days before, they had been civilians. They were now recruits of the United States Marine Corps. And they were about to be transported, under the command of Staff Sergeant Koznowski, Sergeant Zimmerman, and the two corporals, to the United States Marine Corps Recruit Depot, Parris Island, South Carolina, for basic training.

One of the corporals stood on the street. He grabbed the first four men to reach him by the shoulders and placed them one behind the other. Then he got the others to form ranks on them, sometimes by pointing, sometimes by shoving them into place.

Finally, they were all lined up in four ranks.

"Ah-ten-hut!" the corporal with the clipboard barked.

One hundred and five of the 106 young men stood as stiff as they knew how. The 106th young man continued to try to tie the laces of his right shoe.

Staff Sergeant Koznowski walked quickly to him, standing before him until the shoe was tied and the young man stood erect.

"Got it all tied now?" Koznowski asked.

"Uh-huh," the young man replied. He was now wearing a nervous smile.

"When you are in ranks, and someone calls 'ah-ten-hut,' you come to attention, right *then,"* Koznowski said. "Not when it's convenient for you. You think you can remember that?"

"My shoe—"

"I asked, can you remember that?" Koznowski snapped.

"Yeah, sure."

"And you never, never, never say 'yeah, sure' to a sergeant," Koznowski said.

The young man was clever enough to sense that whatever he said next was going to be the wrong thing, so he said nothing.

"Take off the shoe," Koznowski said, conversationally.

The young man looked at him in disbelief.

"Take off the fucking shoe!" Koznowski shouted, his face two inches from the young man's face, spraying him with spittle.

The young man did as he was ordered, and finally stood up again, holding the shoe in his hand.

"Call the roll, Corporal," Staff Sergeant Koznowski ordered.

"Listen up, you people," the corporal with the clipboard said. "I will call off your last name, and you will respond with your first."

The roll was called.

The corporal turned and saluted. "The recruit draft is formed, sir," he reported.

Koznowski returned the salute, and then barked, "At ease."

Next he delivered a short speech. He told them that there was clear proof that God did not love him, for he had been assigned the unpleasant task of moving their miserable asses from the Brooklyn Navy Yard to Parris Island, South Carolina, where an attempt would be made to turn their miserable asses into something resembling Marines.

Before they could leave the Navy Yard, Staff Sergeant Koznowski announced, four things had to be done. First, they would be fed. After which they would run, not walk, back to the barracks. Second, their blankets, sheets, pillow cases, and mattress covers would have to be turned in. Third, the barracks and the head which they had managed to turn into a fucking pig sty in a remarkably short time would have to be returned to the immaculate state in which they had found it. Finally, they would have to wash and shave and do whatever else they could to make themselves as presentable as possible for the walk between the buses at the entrance to Pennsylvania Station and the train itself.

It was going to be humiliating enough, Staff Sergeant Koznowski said, for himself and Sergeant Zimmerman and Corporals Hayworth and Cohn to be seen shepherding so many assholes around without the assholes looking like they had just crawled out of the fucking sewer.

They had, he informed them, precisely twenty-eight minutes and twenty seconds to accomplish breakfast and get back here.

"Are there any questions?" Staff Sergeant Koznowski asked.

A tall, rather thin young man in the rear rank had raised his hand above his shoulders.

Koznowski looked at him. "Anyone tell you to put your hand up? You want permission to leave the room so you can take a piss?"

"Sergeant," the tall thin young man said, nervously, "you asked if there were questions."

"I didn't mean it," Staff Sergeant Koznowski said, pleased with himself. "Sergeant Zimmerman, take over."

With that, Staff Sergeant Koznowski marched off in the direction of the mess hall, leaving Sergeant Zimmerman in charge.

Like many—perhaps most—Marines, Zimmerman was ambivalent about the hoary Marine Corps tradition of shitting all over recruits until they had passed through either the Parris Island or San Diego Recruit Depots. He understood the philosophy, which was to break a man down and then rebuild him as a Marine; and he knew that it worked. It had turned him into a Marine. But he was personally uncomfortable with shitting on people; he could not have been a drill instructor himself, and he had been made uncomfortable when he had learned that he would be taking a draft of recruits to Parris Island.

When Koznowski had turned the corner, Zimmerman said, "Finish buttoning your clothes."

The young man holding his shoe in his hand looked at him questioningly. Zimmerman shook his head no.

When they had time to tuck their trousers in their pants and button their jackets and overcoats, Zimmerman called them to attention and marched them into the mess hall.

He watched the line until the young man with his shoe tucked under his arm passed through it, and then told him he could now put his shoe on. Then he had his own breakfast.

Afterward, he walked back to the barracks as the recruits ran past him. And there he supervised the turning in of the bed clothes and the cleaning of the barracks. He did not find it necessary to jump anybody's ass while doing so.

When Staff Sergeant Koznowski returned from the staff NCO mess he found the draft of recruits lined up on the street before the barracks waiting to be loaded onto the chartered buses for the trip into Manhattan and Pennsylvania Station.

II

(ONE)
Rocky Fields Farm
Bernardsville, New Jersey
0605 Hours, 6 January 1942

Second Lieutenant Malcolm S. Pickering, USMCR, stood in the bay window of the breakfast room, holding a cup and saucer in his hand. Pickering was a tall, erect young man of twenty-two, ruggedly handsome, with sharp features, and eyes that appeared experienced beyond his years. In his superbly tailored uniform, he looked, Elaine (Mrs. Ernest) Sage thought, like an advertisement in *Town & Country* magazine. Or a Marine Corps recruiting poster.

Elaine Sage was a striking, trim, silver-haired woman in her middle forties. She was wearing a pleated plaid skirt, a simple white blouse, and a pink sweater. There was an antique gold watch hanging from a gold chain around her neck, and a three-carat emerald-cut diamond engagement ring next to her wedding ring. She crossed the room to Pickering, surprising but not startling him, and kissed him on the cheek.

"Good morning, Pick," she said, and then she put her arm around his waist and leaned her head against his arm.

It was a motherly gesture. Elaine Sage had known "Pick" Pickering all his life; she had been at Sarah Lawrence with his mother; and she had taken the Twentieth-Century Limited to California and waited in Doctor's Hospital with his father for Patricia Foster Pickering to deliver her first and only child.

Just over a year later, Patricia Pickering had come to Elaine's room at Presbyterian Hospital and cooed and oohed over precious little Ernestine.

"Well," Patricia had said then, "the next thing we have to do is get the two of them together." That had been a running joke over the years, but not wholly a joke or a preposterous idea. It would have been nice, but it wasn't going to happen.

What Pick Pickering had been looking at from the bay window of the breakfast room was Ernestine Sage standing by the duck pond at the far side of the wide lawn. She was standing with another Marine officer, and he had his arm around her. Twice, they had kissed.

"What rouses you from bed at this obscene hour?" Pick Pickering asked Ernie Sage's mother.

"You could say I am just being a gracious hostess," she replied.

Pick Pickering snorted.

"When I went to bed last night," Elaine Sage said, "I went to Ernie's room. I was going to tell her . . . following the hoary adage that the best way to get rid of your daughter's undesirable suitor is to praise him to the skies . . . how much I liked your friend out there." She bent her head in the direction of the Marine who was holding her daughter.

Pickering looked down at her, his eyebrows raised.

"She wasn't in her bed," Elaine Sage said.

"If she wasn't, Aunt Elaine," Pick Pickering said, "it was her idea, not his."

"Ken McCoy frightens me, Pick," Elaine Sage said. "He's not like us."

"That may be part of his attraction," Pickering said.

"I'm not sure he's good for Ernie," Elaine Sage said.

"I think he's very good for her," Pickering said. When she looked at him, he added: "Anyway, I think it's a moot point. *She* thinks he's good for her. She thinks the sun comes up because he wants it to."

Ernestine Pickering and Second Lieutenant Kenneth J. McCoy had turned from the duck pond and were walking back to the house. He had unbuttoned his overcoat and she was half inside it, resting her face on his chest.

"You will forgive me for not being able to forgive you for introducing them at your party," Elaine Sage said.

"I *didn't* introduce them," Pickering said. "Ernie picked him up. She saw in him someone who was as bored with my party as she was. She walked up to him, introduced herself, and shortly thereafter they disappeared. I found out the next morning that he'd taken her to a Chinese restaurant in Chinatown. Where, apparently, he dazzled her by speaking to the proprietor in Chinese, and then won her heart with his skill with chopsticks."

Elaine Sage chuckled.

"For what it's worth, Aunt Elaine," Pickering went on, "he didn't know she had a dime."

"Love at first sight?" she said. "Don't tell me you believe that's possible?"

"Take a look," he said. "You have a choice between love at first sight or irresistible lust. I'm willing to accept love at first sight."

"They have nothing in common," she protested.

"I don't have a hell of a lot in common with him, either," Pickering said. "But I realized some time ago he's the best friend I've ever had. If you've come looking for an ally in some Machiavellian plot of yours to separate the two of them, you're out of luck. *I* think they're good for each other. My basic reaction is jealousy. I wish someone like Ernie would look at me the way she looks at McCoy."

"I wish *Ernie* would look at you the way she looks at McCoy," Elaine Sage said.

There was a rattling sound behind them. They turned and saw a middle-aged, plump woman in a maid's uniform rolling a serving cart into the breakfast room.

"Do you suppose that she was looking out the window, too, for the return of Romeo and Juliet?" Pickering asked dryly. "Will it be safe for him to eat the scrambled eggs?"

"I am placing what hope I have left in the 'praise him to the skies' theory," Elaine Sage said. "Poison will be a last desperate resort."

Ernestine Sage and Second Lieutenant Kenneth J. McCoy, USMCR, walked onto the broad veranda of the house, disappeared from sight, and a moment later came into the breakfast room. Their faces were red from the cold. McCoy was not quite as large as Pickering, nor as heavily built. He had light brown hair, and intelligent eyes.

Ernie Sage was wearing a sweater and a skirt, and she wore her black hair in a pageboy. She was, both her mother and Pick Pickering thought, a truly beautiful young woman, healthy, and wholesome.

"Mother," Ernie Sage said, "you didn't have to get up."

"All I *have* to do is die and pay taxes," Elaine Sage said. "I'm up because I want to be up. Good morning, Ken. Sleep well?"

"Just fine, thank you," McCoy said. His intelligent eyes searched her face for a moment, as if seeking a reason behind the "sleep well?" question.

"I'm starved," Ernie Sage said. "What are we having?"

"The cold air'll do that to you every time," Pickering said dryly.

"We'd better start eating," Elaine Sage said. "I asked Tony to have the car ready at half-past six. The roads may be icy."

Ernestine Sage looked at McCoy.

"If we're really ahead of time at Newark," she said, "you can ride into Manhattan with us and catch the train there."

"What time is your plane?" Elaine Sage asked Pickering.

"Half-past eleven," he said. "I've plenty of time."

"He said he'll catch the bus at the airlines terminal," Ernie Sage said.

"Don't be silly," Elaine Sage said. "You might as well use the Bentley."

"The bus is easier," Pickering said, as he went to the serving cart and started lifting silver covers. "Thanks anyway." He lifted his eyes to Elaine Sage. "Take a look at these scrambled eggs," he said. "Don't they have a funny color?"

Both mother and daughter went to examine the eggs.

"There's nothing wrong with the eggs," Elaine Sage said.

"Well, if you're sure," Pickering said. "There's supposed to be a lot of poisoned eggs around."

"Honey," Ernie Sage said. "You just sit, and I'll serve you."

" 'Honey'?" her mother parroted. McCoy flushed.

"It's a sticky substance one spreads on bread," Pickering said.

"It's also what I call him," Ernie Sage said. "It's what they call a 'term of endearment.' "

"Gee, Aunt Elaine," Pickering said. "Ain't love grand?"

"Ginger-peachy," Elaine Sage said. "I understand it makes the world go round." She smiled at Ken McCoy. "We get the sausage from a farmer down the road," she said. "I hope you'll try it."

McCoy looked at her; their eyes met.

"Thank you," he said.

Intelligent eyes, she thought. And then she amended that: *Intelligent and wary, like an abused dog's.*

(TWO)
Pennsylvania Station
New York City
9025 Hours, 6 January 1942

When the buses from the Navy Yard reached Penn Station, the recruits had been formed into two platoon-sized groups and marched into the station and down to the platform by the corporals. Koznowski and Zimmerman walked to one side. Commuters coming off trains from the suburbs had watched the little procession with interest. Some had smiled. The nation was at war; these were the men who would fight the war.

Two coach cars had been attached to the Congressional Limited, immediately behind the blue-painted electric locomotive and in front of the baggage car and railway post office, so that they were effectively separated from the rest of the train.

On the platform there, Staff Sergeant Koznowski had delivered another little lecture, informing the group that under the Regulations for the Governance of the Naval Service, to which they were now subject, anyone who "got lost" between here and Parris Island could expect to be tried by court-martial not for AWOL (Absence Without Leave) but for "missing a troop movement," which was an even more severe offense.

They were to sit where they were told to sit, Staff Sergeant Koznowski said, and they were not to get out of that seat for any reason without specific permission from one of the corporals. He also said that there had been incidents embarrassing the Marine Corps where recruits had whistled at young civilian women. Any one of them doing that, Staff Sergeant Koznowski said, would answer to him personally.

He had then stood by the door and personally checked the names of the recruits off on a roster as they boarded the cars. When the last was aboard, he turned to Sergeant Zimmerman.

"Let's you and me take a walk," he said. "Fucking train ain't going anywhere soon."

It was more in the nature of an order than a suggestion, so Sergeant Zimmerman nodded his agreement, although he would have much preferred to get on the car and sit down and maybe put his feet up. The malaria had got to him, and while he no longer belonged in the hospital, he was still pretty weak.

What Koznowski wanted to do, it immediately became apparent, was look at the young women passing through the station. Zimmerman had nothing against young women, or against looking at them, but if you were about to get on a train, it seemed futile. And he was tired.

They had been standing just to the right of the gate to the platform on which the Congressional Limited of the Pennsylvania Railroad was boarding passengers for about twenty minutes when Koznowski jabbed Zimmerman, painfully, in the ribs with his elbow.

"Look at that candy-ass, will you?" he said softly, contemptuously, barely moving his lips.

A Marine officer, a second lieutenant, was approaching the gate to the Congressional Limited platform. He was very young, and there was a young woman hanging on to his right arm, a real looker, with her black hair cut in a pageboy.

The customs of the Naval Service proscribed any public display of affection. The second lieutenant was obviously unaware of this proscription, or was ignoring it. The good-looking dame in the pageboy was hanging on to him like he was a life preserver, and the second lieutenant was looking in her eyes, oblivious to anything else.

Zimmerman was uncomfortable. It was his experience that the less you had to do with officers, the better off you were. And what the hell, so he had a girl friend, so what? Good for him.

Staff Sergeant Koznowski waited until the second lieutenant was almost on them, if oblivious to them.

"Watch this," he said softly, his lips not moving. Then he raised his voice. "Ah-ten-hut!" he barked, and then saluted crisply. "Good morning, sir!"

He succeeded in his intention, which was to shake up the candy-ass second lieutenant. First, the second lieutenant was rudely brought back to the world that existed outside the eyes of the good-looking dame in the black pageboy. Then, his right arm moved in Pavlovian reflex to return Staff Sergeant Koznowski's gesture of courtesy between members of the profession of arms, knocking the girl on his arm to one side and causing her to lose her purse.

Staff Sergeant Koznowski coughed twice, very pleased with himself.

But the second lieutenant did not then, as Staff Sergeant Koznowski firmly expected him to do, continue through the gate mustering what little dignity he had left, and possibly even growing red with embarrassment.

"I'll be goddamned," the second lieutenant said, as he looked at Staff Sergeant Koznowski and Sergeant Zimmerman. And then he walked toward them.

"Oh, shit!" Staff Sergeant Koznowski said softly, assuming the position of "attention."

The second lieutenant had his hand extended.

"Hello, Ernie," he said. "How the hell are you?"

Sergeant Zimmerman shook the extended hand, but he was speechless.

The good-looking dame in the black pageboy, having reclaimed her purse, walked up, a hesitant smile on her face.

"Honey," the second lieutenant said, "this is Sergeant Ernie Zimmerman. I told you about him."

There was a moment's look of confusion on her face, and then she remembered.

"Of course," she said, and smiled at Zimmerman, offering her hand. "I'm Ernie, too, Ernie Sage. Ken's told me so much about you."

"Yes, ma'am," Zimmerman said, uncomfortably.

"Stand at ease, Sergeant," the second lieutenant said to Staff Sergeant Koznowski.

The conductor called, "Bo-aard!"

"You're on the train?" the second lieutenant asked.

"Yes, sir," Zimmerman said.

"Save me a seat," the second lieutenant said. "I'm going to be the last man aboard."

The good-looking dame chuckled.

"We had better get aboard, sir," Staff Sergeant Koznowski said.

"Go ahead," the second lieutenant said.

Staff Sergeant Koznowski saluted; the second lieutenant returned it. Then, with Zimmerman on his heels, Koznowski marched through the gate and to the train.

"Where'd you get so chummy with the candy-ass, Zimmerman?" Koznowski asked, contemptuously.

"You ever hear of Killer McCoy, Koznowski?" Zimmerman asked.

"Huh?" Staff Sergeant Koznowski asked, and then, "Who?"

"Forget it," Zimmerman said.

When they were on the train, and the train had rolled out of Pennsylvania Station and through the tunnel and was making its way across the wetlands between Jersey City and Newark, Staff Sergeant Koznowski jabbed Zimmerman in the ribs again.

"Hey," he said. "There was a story going around about some real hardass in the Fourth Marines in Shanghai. That the 'Killer McCoy' you were asking about?"

Zimmerman nodded.

"Story was that he cut up three Italian marines, killed two of them."

"Right."

"And then he shot up a fucking bunch of Chinks," Koznowski said.

Zimmerman nodded again.

"True story?" Koznowski asked, now fascinated.

"True story," Zimmerman said.

"What's that got to do with that candy-ass second lieutenant?" Koznowski asked.

"That's him," Zimmerman said.

"Bullshit," Koznowski said flatly.

"No bullshit," Zimmerman said. "That was Killer McCoy."

"Bullshit," Koznowski said, "How the hell do you know?"

"I was there when he shot the Chinks," Zimmerman said. "I shot a couple of them myself."

Koznowski looked at him for a moment, and finally decided he had been told the truth.

"I'll be goddamned," he said.

(THREE)

Tony, the Sages' chauffeur, had parked the Bentley on Thirty-fourth Street, in a NO PARKING zone across from Pennsylvania Station in front of George's Bar & Grill. Ten minutes after Ernestine Sage had gone into the station with Second Lieutenant Kenneth J. McCoy, a policeman walked up to the car, rapped on the window with his knuckles, and gestured with a jerk of his thumb for Tony to get moving.

On the second trip around the block, they saw Ernestine Sage standing on the curb. Tony tapped the horn twice, quickly, and she saw the car and ran to it and got in.

"Just so you won't feel left out," Ernie Sage said to Second Lieutenant Malcolm Pickering, "I will now put you on your airplane."

"Where to, Miss Ernie?" Tony asked, cocking his head to one side in the front seat.

"My apartment, please, Tony," Ernie Sage said, and turned to Pickering. "I'll make you a cup of coffee."

"The Foster Park, Tony," Pickering ordered. "She makes a lousy cup of coffee."

They were stopped in traffic. There was a chance for Tony to turn to look into the backseat. Ernestine Sage nodded her approval.

Tony made the next right turn and pointed the Bentley uptown.

"You're not going to work?" Pickering asked. When she shook her head no, he asked, "What happened to Nose to the Grindstone?"

"When we get there," Ernie Sage said, "I will call in. I will say that I have just put my boyfriend-the-Marine on a train, that I am consequently in a lousy mood, and will be in later this afternoon."

"Patriotism," Pickering said solemnly, "is the last refuge of the scoundrel."

She laughed, and took his arm.

"He's only going to Washington, Ernie," Pickering said.

"He ever tell you about a Marine named Zimmerman?" Ernie asked. "When he was in China?"

Pickering shook his head. "No."

"The one who had a Chinese wife and a bunch of children?"

"Yeah," Pickering said, remembering. "Why?"

"He was in the station, by the gate," Ernie said. "With another Marine. A sergeant. Another sergeant."

"Really?"

"They looked like Marines, Pick," she said. "I mean, they *were* Marines. And they saluted Ken and stood stiff . . . what do they call it?"

"At attention," he furnished. "And?"

"I can't really understand that he's really a Marine officer . . . or you either, for that matter."

"I'm not so sure about me," Pickering said, "but you better get used to the idea that that's what Ken is. Hell, he's already been in the war, and it's hardly a month old."

"He was shot *before* the war, when he was in China, with Zimmerman," she said. "He told me about it. It's not that I didn't believe him, but it wasn't *real* until just now, when I saw Zimmerman. It wasn't at all hard to imagine Zimmerman with a gun in his hands, shooting people."

"The fact of the matter, Ernie, is that your boyfriend is one tough cookie. He may look like he's up for the weekend from Princeton, but he's not. What are you doing, having second thoughts about the great romance? Are you just a little afraid of him?"

"For him," she said, and then corrected herself. "No. For me. Oh, God, Pick, I don't want to lose him!"

"For the moment, Ernie, you can relax," Pickering said. "He's only going to Washington."

"Yeah, but where does he go from Washington?" she replied.

The Bentley turned right again onto Fifty-ninth Street, and halfway down the block pulled to the curb before a canvas marquee with THE FOSTER PARK HOTEL lettered on it.

A tall, florid-faced doorman in a heavy overcoat festooned with gold braid scurried quickly across the sidewalk and opened the door.

"Oh, good morning, Mr. Pickering," he said, as Pickering got out. "Nice to see you again, sir."

"Nice to see you, too, Charley," Pickering said, shaking his hand, "but it's 'Lieutenant Pickering.' We second lieutenants are very fussy about that."

"I was glad to hear your folks are all right," the doorman said. "And you're Miss Sage, right?"

"Hello," Ernie Sage said.

Pickering opened the front door of the Bentley.

"No sense you hanging around, Tony," he said. "I'll catch a cab to the airlines terminal."

"I don't mind, Mr. Pick," the chauffeur said.

"You go ahead," Pickering insisted.

The chauffeur leaned across the seat and offered his hand.

"You take care of yourself, young fella," he said. "We want you back in one piece."

"Thank you, Tony," Pickering said. "And keep your eye on Whatsername for me, will you?"

The chauffeur chuckled, and then Pickering closed the door.

When the bellman spun the revolving glass door, passing first Ernie Sage and then Pickering into the lobby of the Foster Park Hotel, an assistant manager was waiting for them.

"Mr. Pickering, I'm Cannell, the assistant manager. How can I be of service?"

"I've got to be at the airlines terminal at half-past ten," Pickering said. "Will you make sure there's a cab outside at quarter-past?"

"Why don't we just run you out to the airport in the limousine, Mr. Pickering?"

"Because the limousine is for paying guests," Pickering said. "A cab will do fine."

Pickering took Ernie Sage's arm and steered her across the lobby of the luxury-class hotel to the coffee shop, and then to a red leather banquette in the rear.

"Just coffee, please," Pickering ordered when a waitress appeared.

His order was ignored. With the coffee came toast and biscuits and slices of melon and an array of preserves.

The Foster Park Hotel was one of forty-two hotels in the Foster chain. Mr. Andrew Foster, the Chairman of the Board of the closely held Foster Hotels Corporation, who made his home in the penthouse atop the Andrew Foster Hotel in San Francisco, had one child, a daughter; and his daughter had one child, a son; and his name was Malcolm Pickering.

"Oh, nice!" Ernie Sage said, pulling a slice of melon before her and picking up a spoon.

"Amazing, isn't it," Pickering said, "what romance does for the appetite?"

"Meaning what?" Sage asked.

"Meaning that your mother went to your room last night to have a little between-us-girls tête-à-tête," Pickering said.

"Oh, my God!" Ernie Sage said, and then challenged: "You're sure? How do you know?"

"She told me," Pickering said. "As we watched you and Ken billing and cooing down by the duck pond."

"Okay," Ernie Sage said. "So she knows. I don't care."

"And if she tells Daddy?" Pickering asked.

Ernie Sage thought that over.

"She won't tell him," she announced. "She knows how he would react."

"You being his precious little girl and such?"

"She knows it would change nothing," Ernie Sage said. She spread strawberry preserve on a slice of toast and handed it to him. "My mother is a very level-headed woman."

"Her tactic for the moment is to praise your boyfriend to the skies," Pickering said. "If that fails, she's considering poison."

"Your goddamned Marine Corps may solve the problem for her," Ernie Sage said.

"For the third time, Ernie, he's only going to Washington."

"Yeah, and for the third time, where's your damned Marine Corps going to send him from Washington?"

"I probably shouldn't tell you this, Ernie," Pickering said. "But I don't think there's much chance that the Corps is going to hand Ken a rifle and send him off to lead a platoon onto some exotic South Pacific beach."

"Tell me more about that," she said sarcastically.

"It's true. He's an intelligence officer," Pickering said. "He speaks and reads Chinese and Japanese. That's why they sent him to Quantico to officer candidate school. And that's why they're not going to hand him a rifle and tell him to go forth and do heroic things. There are very few Marines who speak Chinese or Japanese, much less both, and they are far too valuable to send off to get shot up."

"That's how come he got wounded in the Philippines, right?" she challenged.

"He wasn't supposed to be where he was when he was hit," Pickering said.

"You know that wound is still . . . what's the word? He's still bleeding."

"*Suppurating,*" Pickering furnished. "They'll take care of him, Ernie. Really."

"I got that speech, too," she said. "They give you a thirty-day convalescent leave, not chargeable against your regular leave. And then ten days later, they call you up, and say, 'Come back, otherwise we lose the war.' "

"On the other hand, there is an adequate supply of people like myself," Pickering said, "who are—in the hoary Naval Service phraseology—available to be *'put in harm's way.'* "

She looked at him for a moment, her face serious.

"You're afraid, aren't you, Pick?" she asked. When he didn't reply, she went on. "Did I make you mad by asking?"

"Shitless, Ernie," Pickering said. "In the quaint cant of the Marine Corps, I am scared shitless. Not only do I have a very active imagination, but I have been associated with your boyfriend long enough to understand from him that there is very little similarity between war movies and the real thing."

She reached across the table and took his hand.

"Oh, Pick!" she said sympathetically.

"I have volunteered for flight training," he went on, "not with any noble motive of sweeping the dirty Jap from the sky, but because, cold-bloodedly, I have decided it will be a shade safer than being a platoon leader. And because, presuming no one will see that I have been wetting my pants in the airplane, it will keep me out of the war, with any luck, for six months, maybe longer. Just about all the guys in our class in Quantico are getting ready to go overseas. Some of them have already gone."

"Then why the hell did you enlist?" she asked.

"Daddy was a Marine," he said, dryly. "Could I disappoint Daddy?"

She leaned forward and kissed him on the cheek.

"You're a nice guy, Pick," she said.

"I can't imagine why I told you this," he said.

"I'm glad . . . proud . . . you did," Ernie Sage said.

"Wasted effort," he said. "I should have saved it for some female who would be moved to inspire the coward in the time-honored way."

"You sonofabitch," Ernie Sage said, chuckling. And she freed her hand. But only after she had kissed his knuckles tenderly.

(FOUR)

When the Congressional Limited stopped at Newark, Second Lieutenant Kenneth J. McCoy, USMCR, got off and walked up to the platform to the two cars immediately behind the locomotive.

The doors to the cars had not been opened, and he had some trouble figuring out how to open them himself before he could get on.

The moment he stepped into the car itself, one of the corporals saw him, jumped to his feet, and bellowed, "Attention on deck!"

"As you were," McCoy said quickly. Fifty-odd curious faces were looking at him.

"Who's in charge?" McCoy asked.

"Staff Sergeant Koznowski, sir," the corporal said. "He's up in front."

It had been Lieutenant McCoy's intention to find the man in charge and "borrow" Ernie Zimmerman, to take him back to the dining car and buy him breakfast, or at least a cup of coffee. His motive was primarily personal; Ernie Zimmerman was an old buddy whom he had last seen in Peking. But there was, he realized, something official about it. He knew where the Corps could put Zimmerman to work, doing something more important than he was now, escorting boots to Parris Island: Zimmerman spoke Chinese.

But before he had made his way down the aisle of the first car, the Congressional Limited began to roll out of the station, and McCoy knew he would be stuck in these coaches until the train stopped again.

Zimmerman saw him passing between the cars, and by the time McCoy had entered the second car, the boots were standing up. Or most of them. There were half a dozen, McCoy saw, who were confused by the order, "Attention on deck!" and were looking around in some confusion.

"As you were!" McCoy said loudly, and smiled when he saw that that command, too, was not yet embedded in the minds of the boots.

A fleeting thought ran through his mind: He, too, had taken this train on his way to boot camp at Parris Island, but by himself, not with a hundred others to keep him company.

And then the staff sergeant he had seen with Zimmerman walked up to him.

"Staff Sergeant Koznowski, sir," he said.

"I wanted a word with Sergeant Zimmerman, Sergeant," McCoy said. "If that would be all right with you."

"Yes, sir," Koznowski said.

"Zimmerman and I were in the Fourth Marines," McCoy said, as Zimmerman walked up to them.

"Yes, sir," Koznowski said. "Zimmerman told me."

And then Staff Sergeant Koznowski took a good look at Second Lieutenant McCoy and decided that Zimmerman had been bullshitting him. There *was* a Killer McCoy in the Corps, a tough China Marine who had killed two Eye-talian Marines when they had gone after him during the riots and who had left dead slopeheads all over the Peking Highway when they had been foolish enough to try to rob a Marine truck convoy Killer McCoy had been put in charge of.

Stories like that moved quickly through the Corps. Koznowski had heard it several times. And Koznowski now recalled another detail. It had been *Corporal* Killer McCoy. And nobody got to make corporal with the 4th Marines in China on the first hitch. This pleasant-faced, boyish-looking second lieutenant wasn't old enough to have been a corporal in the China Marines, and he sure as hell didn't look tough enough to have taken on three Eye-talian marines by himself with a knife.

"Zimmerman was telling me, sir," Staff Sergeant Koznowski said, with a broad, I'm-now-in-on-the-joke smile, "that you was Killer McCoy."

Second Lieutenant McCoy's face tightened, and his eyes turned icy. "You never used to let your mouth run away with you, Zimmerman," he said, coldly furious.

Zimmerman's face flushed. "Sorry," he said. Then he raised his eyes to McCoy's. "I didn't expect to see you in an officer's uniform."

Very slowly, the ice melted in McCoy's eyes. "I didn't expect to see you on a train in New Jersey," he said. "How'd you get out of the Philippines?"

"Never got there," Zimmerman said. "I come down with malaria and was in sick bay, and they never put me off the ship. It went on to Diego after Manila, and I was in the hospital there for a while. Then they shipped me here."

"You all right now?" McCoy asked.

"Yeah, I'm on limited duty. They're shipping me to the motor transport company at Parris Island."

"The story I heard," Koznowski said, "was that Killer McCoy was a corporal."

The ice returned to McCoy's eyes. He met Koznowski's eyes for a long moment until Koznowski, cowed, came to a position of attention.

Then he turned to Zimmerman and said something to him in Chinese. Zimmerman chuckled and then replied in Chinese. Koznowski sensed they were talking about him.

McCoy looked at Koznowski again. "I was a corporal in the Fourth Marines, Sergeant," he said. "Any other questions?"

"No, sir."

"In that case, why don't you go check on your men?" McCoy said.

"Aye, aye, sir," Staff Sergeant Koznowski said. *Fuck you!* he thought. He walked down the aisle. Then he thought, *I'll be a sonofabitch. He really is Killer McCoy. I'll be goddamned!*

"What about your family, Ernie?" McCoy asked, still speaking Chinese.

"Had to leave them in Shanghai," Zimmerman said. "I gave her money. She said she was going home."

"I'm sorry," McCoy said.

"I wasn't the only one," Zimmerman said. "Christ, even Captain Banning couldn't get his wife out. You heard he married that White Russian?"

McCoy nodded.

Captain Edward J. Banning had been the Intelligence officer of the 4th Marines in Shanghai. Corporal Kenneth J. McCoy had worked for him. McCoy thought that Banning was everything a good Marine officer should be.

And he had heard from Captain Banning himself that Banning had married his longtime mistress just before the 4th Marines had sailed from Shanghai to reinforce the Philippines, and that she hadn't gotten out before the war started. He had heard that from Banning as they lay on a bluff overlooking the Lingayen Gulf watching the Japanese put landing barges over the sides of transports. But this was not the time to tell Ernie Zimmerman about that.

"How'd you get to be an officer?" Zimmerman asked.

"They got what they call a platoon leader's course at Quantico," McCoy said. "It's like boot camp all over again. You go through it, and you come out the other end a second lieutenant."

"You look like an officer," Zimmerman said. It was more of an observation than a compliment, and there was also a suggestion of surprise.

"With what I had to pay for these uniforms," McCoy said, "I damned well better."

Zimmerman chuckled. "It got you a good-looking woman, at least," he said.

McCoy smiled and nodded. But he did not wish to discuss Miss Ernestine Sage with Sergeant Ernie Zimmerman.

"Ernie," he said. "If you like, I think I can get you a billet as a translator."

"What I want to do is figure out some way to get back to China," Zimmerman said.

"It'll be a long time before there are any Marines in China again," McCoy said.

"I have to try," Zimmerman said. "That what they got you doing, McCoy? Working as a translator?"

"Yeah, something like that."

"I'm a motor transport sergeant, McCoy," Zimmerman said.

"The Corps got a lot of those," McCoy said. "But not many people speak two kinds of Chinese."

Zimmerman paused thoughtfully.

"What the hell," he said finally. "If you can fix it, why not? I'd be working for you?"

"I don't know about that," McCoy said. "But it would be a better billet than fixing carburetors at Parris Island would be."

(ONE)
Corregidor Island
Manila Bay, Island of Luzon
Commonwealth of the Philippines
2115 Hours, 5 January 1942

The United States submarine *Pickerel,* a 298-foot, fifteen-hundred-ton submersible of the Porpoise class, lay two hundred yards off the fortress island of Corregidor. There was a whaleboat tied alongside, from which small and heavy wooden crates were being unloaded and then taken aboard through the fore and aft torpedo-loading hatches. A second whaleboat could just be made out alongside a narrow pier on the island itself, where it was being loaded with more of the small, heavy wooden crates.

Lieutenant Commander Edgar F. "Red" MacGregor, USN, commander of the *Pickerel,* was on the sea bridge of her conning tower. MacGregor was a stocky, plump-faced, redheaded thirty-five-year-old graduate of the United States Naval Academy at Annapolis, and he was wearing khaki shirt and trousers, a khaki fore-and-aft cap bearing the shield-and-fouled-anchor insignia of the U.S. Navy, and a small golden oak leaf indicating his rank.

When the last of the crates had been removed from the whaleboat alongside, and it had headed for the pier again, Commander MacGregor bent over a small table on which he had laid out two charts. One of them was a chart of Manila Bay itself, with the minefields marked, and the other was a chart of the South China Sea, which included portions of the islands of Luzon and Mindoro. On the "Luzon" chart was marked with grease pencil the current positions of the Japanese forces that had landed on the beaches of Lingayen Gulf on the morning of December 10, 1941, and were now advancing down the Bataan Peninsula.

To prevent its destruction, Manila had been declared an open city on December 26, 1941. Japanese troops had entered the city, unopposed, on January 2, 1942.

Meanwhile, General Douglas MacArthur had moved his troops, Philippine and American, to Bataan, where it was his announced intention to fight a delaying action until help reached the Philippines from the United States.

As Commander MacGregor observed the loading of his vessel, it was necessary again and again to force from his mind the thoughts that inevitably came to him. As a professional Naval officer, of course, he was obliged to view the situation with dispassionate eyes.

The Japanese had, almost a month before, destroyed the United States' battleship fleet. The only reason the Japs hadn't sent the aircraft carriers to the bottom of Pearl Harbor as well was that the aircraft carriers had been at sea when they had attacked.

The professional conclusion he was forced in honesty to draw was that the U.S. Pacific Fleet had taken a hell of a blow, one that very easily could prove fatal, and that the "help" MacArthur expected—the reinforcement of the Philippine garrison—was wishful thinking. The United States was very close to losing the Philippines, including the "impregnable, unsinkable 'Battleship' Corregidor."

The proof was that if anyone in a senior position of authority really believed that Corregidor could hold out indefinitely until "help" arrived, the *Pickerel* would at this moment be out in the South China Sea trying to put her torpedos into Japanese bottoms.

Instead, she was sitting here, for all intents and purposes an unarmed submersible merchantman, taking aboard as much of the gold reserves of the Philippine Commonwealth as she could carry, to keep them from falling into Japanese hands when Corregidor fell.

Commander MacGregor once again reminded himself that there was good reason for what the U.S. Navy had ordered him to do. And that he was a professional Naval officer. And that when he was given an order, he was obliged to carry it out, not to question it, or to entertain doubts about the ability of senior Naval officers. *They* had to bear the responsibility for getting the Navy into the kind of goddamned mess where a submarine was stripped of its torpedos and turned into a merchantman because control of the seas was in the hands of the enemy.

He did not take his eyes from the chart of Manila Bay again until the second whaleboat had tied up alongside again. Then he looked down from the conning tower.

"Christ!" he muttered. "Now what?"

"Sir?" his exec asked politely.

Commander MacGregor gestured impatiently downward.

Two ladders, lashed edge to edge, had been put over the side. The wooden crates carrying the gold reserves of the Philippine Commonwealth were heavy, too heavy to be carried aboard by one man. They had been taken from sailors in the whaleboat by two husky sailors, each grasping one rope handle, who had then together climbed the slanting ladders, carefully, grunting with the effort, one rung at a time.

What was coming aboard now was not a crateful of gold bars but a man in khaki uniform. He was being helped up the side-by-side ladders by another man in khaki uniform. He needed the help. His left shirt sleeve was empty. Commander MacGregor could not see whether the man had lost his arm or whether it was in a sling under his shirt. He could see that the man had bandages on his head, bandages covering his eyes.

When the one-armed man with the bandaged head reached the deck, he was helped to his feet. After having received the necessary permission to come aboard, he tried to observe the Naval custom of saluting the officer of the deck and then the national colors.

A Naval officer, Commander MacGregor decided.

The attempt to adhere to Naval tradition failed. The blinded man's salute of the officer of the deck and the colors was directed into the bay.

Commander MacGregor went quickly down from the conning tower to the deck. He could now see that the officer with the blinded man wore the silver eagle of a Navy captain. The blinded officer (MacGregor could not see that his arm was strapped against his chest, under his khaki shirt) was also a captain, but a captain of the United States Marine Corps, the equivalent of a U.S. Navy full lieutenant.

MacGregor saluted the Navy captain.

"Commander MacGregor, sir," he said. "I'm the skipper."

The Navy captain returned the salute. "Captain," he replied, acknowledging

Commander MacGregor's role as captain of his vessel, "this is Captain Banning. He will be sailing with you. Captain Banning, this is Captain MacGregor."

The blinded Marine officer put out his hand.

"How do you do, sir?" he said. "Sorry to inflict myself on you."

"Happy to have you aboard, Captain," MacGregor said, aware that it was both inane and a lie. He certainly felt sorry for the poor bastard, but the *Pickerel* was not a hospital ship, it was a crowded submarine, with only a pharmacist's mate aboard. No place for a man who was not only wounded but incapable of feeding himself—or of seeing.

"Captain Banning," the Navy captain said, "*will* sail with you. I now ask you how many other men in his condition you are prepared to take aboard."

"Sir, I have only a pharmacist's mate aboard," MacGregor replied.

The Navy captain said, "There are nine others suffering from temporary or permanent loss of sight. They will require no special medical attention beyond the changing of their bandages."

"I'll have to bed them down on the deck," Commander MacGregor said.

"You can, without jeopardizing your mission, take all of them?" the Navy captain asked.

"Yes, sir."

"They will come out with the next whaleboat," the Navy captain said. "Thank you, Captain. Have a good voyage."

"Thank you, sir," MacGregor said.

"Permission to leave the ship, sir?" the Navy captain asked.

"Granted," MacGregor said.

The Navy captain saluted MacGregor, then the colors, and then backed down the ladder into the whaleboat.

"Chief!" Commander MacGregor called.

"Yes, sir?" the chief of the boat, the senior noncommissioned officer aboard, said. He had been standing only a few feet away, invisible in the darkness.

"Take this officer to the wardroom," MacGregor said. "See that he's comfortable, and then tell Doc to prepare to take aboard nine other wounded. Tell him they are . . . in the same condition as Captain Banning."

"The 'same condition' is blind, Chief," Captain Banning said matter-of-factly. "Once you face it, you get used to it in a hurry."

"Aye, aye, sir," the chief of the boat said to MacGregor, then put his hand on Captain Banning's good arm. "Will you come this way, please, sir?"

MacGregor noticed for the first time that Captain Banning was wearing a web belt, and that a holstered Colt .45 automatic pistol was hanging from the belt.

A blind man doesn't need a pistol, MacGregor thought. *He* shouldn't *have one. But that guy's a Marine officer, blind or not, and I'm not going to kick him when he's down by taking it away from him.*

The chief torpedoman, who had been supervising the storage of the gold crates in the fore and aft torpedo rooms, came onto the deck.

"All the crates are aboard and secure, sir," he said.

"Let's have a look, Chief," MacGregor said, and walked toward the hatch in the conning tower.

The substitution of gold for torpedos had been on the basis of weight rather than volume. The equivalent weight of gold in the forward torpedo rooms was a small line of wooden boxes chained in place down the center line. The torpedo room looked empty with the torpedoes gone.

"We're taking nine blinded men with us, Chief," Commander MacGregor said.

"Ten, counting that Marine captain. I said they would have to bed down on the deck. But we can do better than that, with all this room, can't we?"

"I'll do what I can, Skipper," the chief torpedoman said.

"Let's have a look aft," MacGregor said.

Ten minutes later, the *Pickerel* got underway, her diesels throbbing powerfully.

Launched at the Electric Boat Works in Connecticut in 1936, the *Pickerel* had been designed for Pacific Service; that is, for long patrols. Since she was headed directly for the Hawaiian Islands, fuel consumption was not a problem. With at least freedom from the concern, Commander MacGregor ordered turns made for seventeen knots. Although this greatly increased fuel consumption, he believed it was justified under the circumstances. The farther he moved away from the island of Luzon into the South China Sea, the less were the chances he would be spotted by the Japanese.

There was time, until dawn—too much time—for Commander MacGregor to consider that he was now what he trained all his adult life to be, master of a United States warship at sea, in a war; but that, instead of going in harm's way, searching out the enemy, to close with them, to send them to the bottom, what he was doing was sailing through enemy-controlled waters, doing his very best to make sure the enemy didn't see him.

The one thing he could not do was fight.

He hated to see night begin to turn into day. He had been running at seventeen knots for seven hours. And he had thus made—a rough calculation, not taking into consideration the current—about 120 nautical miles. But as he had been on a north-northwest course, heading into the South China Sea as well as up the western shore of Luzon, he wasn't nearly as far north as he would have liked to be.

He was, in fact, very near the route the Japanese were using to bring supplies and reinforcements to the Lingayen Gulf, where they had made their first amphibious landing in the Phillipines three days after they had taken out almost all of the Pacific Fleet at Pearl Harbor.

There would be Japanese ships in the area, accompanied by destroyers, and there would be at least reconnaissance aircraft, if not bombers. This meant he would have to spend the next sixteen hours or so submerged. Since full speed submerged on batteries was eight knots, he would not get far enough on available battery power to make it worthwhile; for it would not get him out of the Japanese shipping lane to the Lingayen Gulf. But he had to hide.

"Dive," Commander MacGregor ordered.

"Dive! Dive! Dive!" the talker repeated.

The lookouts, then the officer of the deck, then the chief of the boat, dropped quickly through the hatch.

The captain took one last look through his binoculars as water began to break over the bow, and then dropped through the hatch himself.

The roar of the diesels had died; now there was the whine of the electric motors.

MacGregor issued the necessary orders. They were to maintain headway, that was all; as little battery energy as possible was to be expended. They might need the batteries to run if they were spotted by a Japanese destroyer. He was to be called immediately if Sonar heard anything at all, and in any event fifteen minutes before daylight. Then he made his way to his cabin.

Captain Banning was sitting on a Navy-gray metal chair before the fold-down desk. MacGregor was a little surprised that the Marine officer was not in a bunk.

"Good morning," MacGregor said. "You heard? We're submerged."

"And you want to hit the sack," Banning said. "If you'll point me in the direction of where you want me, I'll get out of your way."

"Coffee keeps most people awake," MacGregor said. "Perverse bastard that I am, I always have a cup before I go to bed. You're not keeping me up."

"I'm not sleepy," Banning said. "I've been cat-napping. I did that all the time ashore, but I thought that was because it was quiet. I thought the noises on here would keep me awake, but they haven't."

"I think it would be easier for both of us if you used my bunk," MacGregor said. "Whenever you're ready . . ."

"I could use a cup of coffee," Banning said. "Yours is first rate. And it's in short supply ashore."

"I'll get us a pitcher," MacGregor said. "Cream and sugar?"

"Black, please," Banning said.

When he returned with the stainless steel pitcher of coffee, MacGregor filled Banning's cup three-quarters full.

"There's your coffee, Captain," he said.

"I heard," Banning said. "Thank you."

He moved his hand across the table until his hand touched the mug.

"I issued, earlier on tonight, an interesting order for a Marine officer," Banning said. " 'Piss like a woman.' "

"Excuse me?" MacGregor said.

"I went to the head," Banning said. "Ashore, you learn to piss by locating the target with your knees, then direct fire by sound. I learned that won't work with your toilet, and, to keep your head from being awash with blind men's piss, went and passed the word to the others."

He's bitter, MacGregor thought. Then, *Why the hell not?*

"How did it happen?" MacGregor blurted.

"The U.S. Army done it to me," Banning said, bitterly. "The one thing they did right over here was lay in adequate stocks of artillery ammunition."

"I don't quite follow you, Captain Banning," Commander MacGregor said.

Banning very carefully raised his coffee mug to his lips and took a swallow before replying.

"I was at Lingayen Gulf, when the Japs landed," he said. "I got the arm there"—he raised his arm-in-a-sling—"and took some shrapnel in the legs. Naval artillery from their destroyers. The kid with me . . . I shouldn't call him a kid, I suppose, a mustang second lieutenant, and one hell of a Marine . . ." (A mustang is an officer commissioned from the ranks.) "Anyway, he got me to a school, where a Filipino nurse took care of me and hid me from the Japanese until I was mobile. Then she arranged to get me through the Japanese lines. We'd almost made it when the U.S. Army artillery let fly."

"Shrapnel again?" MacGregor asked gently.

"No. Concussion," Banning said. " *'There is no detectable damage to the optic nerves,'* " he went on, obviously quoting a doctor. " *'There is no reason to believe the loss of sight is permanent.'* "

"Well, that's good news," MacGregor said.

"On the other hand," Banning said bitterly, "there's no reason to believe it isn't. Permanent, I mean." His hand was tight around the cup, like a vise.

"When will you find out?" MacGregor asked.

Banning shrugged. "If they really thought it was temporary, I would not have been sent home with you," Banning said. "The official reason seemed a little flimsy."

"What was the official reason?"

"I was the Intelligence Officer for the Fourth Marines," Banning said. "They said they were under orders to do whatever they could do to keep intelligence officers from falling into Japanese hands."

"That makes sense," MacGregor said.

"Not if most of my knowledge is about China, and the Japanese have already taken Shanghai. And not if your regiment has been just about wiped out, as mine was. I think they wanted us out of the Philippines because we were just too much trouble to care for. The real pain in the ass about being blind is that people are very gentle with you, as if a harsh word, or the truth, will make you break into tears."

He raised his coffee cup and took another careful sip.

"You piss on the deck in my head, Banning," Commander MacGregor said, "and I'll have your ass."

Banning smiled.

"Aye, aye, sir," he said, lightly, and then seriously: "Thank you, Captain."

(TWO)
The Foster Peachtree Hotel
Atlanta, Georgia
1630 Hours, 6 January 1942

Flagship Dallas, a twenty-one-passenger Douglas DC-3 of Eastern Airlines' Great Silver Fleet, touched down at Atlanta on time, after a 775-mile, four-hour-and-twenty-five-minute flight from New York's LaGuardia Field.

Second Lieutenant Malcolm Pickering, USMCR, was no stranger to aerial transportation. He could not remember—even after some thought—when he had made his first flight, only that he had been a little boy. He could also recall several odd details about that airplane: The seats had been wicker, like lawn furniture, and the skin of the fuselage had been corrugated like a cardboard box.

There had been God only knew how many flights since then.

His grandfather, Andrew Foster, had leapt happily into the aviation age, for it permitted him to move between his hotels far faster than traveling by rail. He crisscrossed the country in commercial airliners, and there was even a company aircraft, a six-passenger, stagger-wing single-engine Beechcraft, which the Old Man had christened *Room Service.*

Once the Old Man had led the way, Fleming Pickering, Pick's father, had been an easy convert to aerial travel. Pacific & Far East Shipping, Inc., used ports all up and down the West Coast, from Vancouver, British Columbia, to San Diego. It made a lot more sense to hop aboard a Northwest DC-3 in San Francisco and fly the eight hundred–odd miles to Vancouver at three miles a minute than it did to take the train which traveled at a third of that speed. Very often his father and grandfather had taken him with them.

And Pick and his parents had been aboard one of the very first Pan American flights from San Francisco to Honolulu, an enormous, four-engined Sikorsky seaplane, the *China Clipper.*

But airplanes had just been there, part of the scenery, like the yellow locomotives of the Southern Pacific Railroad and the white steamships of Pacific & Far East Shipping, Inc. It had never entered his mind that he would personally fly an airplane, any more than he would have thought about climbing into the cab of a locomotive, or marching onto the bridge of the *Pacific Conqueror* and giving orders.

There were people who did that sort of thing, highly respected, well-paid professionals. But he wasn't going to be one of them. He had known from the time he had first thought of things like that that he was going to follow in the Old Man's footsteps into the hotel business, rather than in his father's into the shipping business.

By the time he was in his third year at Harvard, he got around to wondering if he hadn't hurt his father's feelings, perhaps deeply, by avoiding the shipping business. But then it had been too late. He'd gone to work for Foster Hotels at twelve, in a starched white jacket stripping tables for thirty-five cents an hour and whatever the waiter had chosen to pay him (usually a nickel a table for a party of four) out of his tips.

Before he was a junior at Harvard, Pickering had been a salad chef, a fry cook, a bellman, an elevator operator, a bartender, a broiler chef, a storekeeper, a night bookkeeper, a waiter, and an assistant manager. He had spent the summer between his junior and senior years in six different Foster Hotels, filling in for vacationing bell captains.

His motive for that had been pure and simple avarice. A bell captain took home a hell of a lot more money than everybody in a hotel hierarchy but the top executives. It was not corporate benevolence; bell captains earned every nickel they made. And it was a position of prestige within the hierarchy, especially within Foster Hotels Corporation, where the Old Man devoutly believed that bell captains made more of an impression on guests than any other individual on the staff, impressions that would either draw them back again or send them to Hilton or Sheraton.

He had been proud that the Old Man had okayed his working as a bell captain . . . and he had driven to Cambridge that fall in an all-paid-for black 1941 Cadillac convertible.

That had been the last of the easy money. From the day of his graduation until he'd gone off to the Marine Corps, Pick Pickering had been carried on the payroll of the Andrew Foster Hotel, San Francisco, as a supernumerary assistant manager. And he'd been paid accordingly, which came out to a hell of a lot less than he'd made as a bell captain. What he'd really been doing was learning what it was like to run a chain of luxury hotels from the executive suite.

He's spent a lot of time traveling with the Old Man, and a lot of that in airliners or the *Room Service,* but he had paid no more attention to the way those airplanes had worked than he had to what made the wheels go around on a locomotive.

That was now all changed. A Marine brigadier general, a pilot, who had been in the trenches in France as an enlisted man with Corporal Fleming Pickering, USMC, had saved his old buddy's son from a Marine Corps career as a club officer by arranging to have him sent to flight school.

As the passengers were escorted from the terminal at LaGuardia Field to board *Flagship Dallas,* Second Lieutenant Malcolm Pickering, USMCR, stepped out of the line and took a good close look upward at the engine mounted on the wing, then studied the wing itself. For the first time he noticed that the front of the wing was made out of rubber (and he wondered what that was for), and that the thin back part of the wing was movable, and that on the back part of the part that moved there was another part that moved. And that there were little lengths of what looked like clothesline attached to the wing.

A stewardess finally went to him, took his arm, and loaded him aboard, eyeing him suspiciously.

He did not have his usual scotch and soda when they were airborne. The stewardess seemed relieved. He sat in his single aisle seat and watched the movable parts of the wing move, and tried to reason what function they performed.

They flew above the clouds. His previous reaction to a cloud cover, viewed from above, had been *"How pretty! It looks like cotton wool."*

He now wondered for the first time how the pilot knew when it was time to fly back down through the cloud cover; how he knew, specifically, when Atlanta was going to be down there, since obviously he couldn't see it.

Before today, before he was en route to Florida to learn how to fly airplanes himself, he would have superficially reasoned that pilots flew airplanes the way masters of ships navigated across the seas. They used a compass to give them the direction, and clocks (chronometers) to let them know how long they had been moving. If they knew how fast they were going, how much time they were taking, and in what direction, they could compute where they were.

Now he saw the differences, and they were enormous and baffling. The most significant of these was that a ship moved only across the surface of the water, whereas an airplane moved up and down in the air as well as horizontally. And if things were going well, a ship moved at about fifteen miles an hour; but an airplane—the airplane he was now on—moved something like twelve times that fast. And if it was lost, an airplane could not simply stop where it was, drop its anchor, sound its foghorn, and wait for the fog to clear.

When the *Flagship Dallas* touched down at Atlanta, Pick Pickering waited until all the other passengers had made their way down the steeply slanting cabin floor and debarked, and then he went forward to the cockpit.

The door was open, and the pilot and copilot were still in their seats, filling out forms before a baffling array of instruments and controls—what looked like ten times as many instruments and controls as there were on the *Room Service.*

"Excuse me," Pickering said, and the pilot turned around, a look of mild annoyance on his face. The annoyance vanished when he saw that Pickering was in uniform.

"What can I do for you, Lieutenant?"

"You can tell me how you knew Atlanta was going to be down here when you started down through the clouds."

The pilot chuckled and looked at his watch. The watch caught Pickering's attention. It was stainless steel and had all sorts of dials and buttons.

A pilot's watch! Pickering thought.

"We just took a chance," the pilot said. "We knew it had to be down here somewhere."

"So could a mountain have been," Pickering replied.

The pilot saw that he was serious.

"We fly a radio beam," he said, pointing to one of the dials on the control panel. "There's a radio transmitter on the field. The needle on the dial points to it. When you pass it, the needle points in the other direction, and you know you've gone too far."

"Fascinating!" Pickering said. "And the altimeter tells you when you're getting close to the ground, right?"

The pilot suppressed a smile.

"Right," he said. "What the altimeter actually does is tell you how far you are above sea level. We have charts—maps—that give the altitude above sea level of the airports."

"Uh-huh," Pickering grunted his comprehension.

"There is a small problem," the pilot said. 'The altimeter tells you how high you were seven seconds ago. Seven seconds is sometimes a long time when you're letting down."

"Uh-huh," Pickering grunted again.

"Let me ask you a question," the pilot said. "This isn't just idle curiosity on your part, is it."

"I'm on my way to Pensacola," Pickering said. "To become a Marine aviator."

"Are you really?" the pilot said. "Watch out for Pensacola, Lieutenant. Dangerous place."

"Why do you say that?"

"They call it the mother-in-law of Naval aviation," the pilot said. "Blink your eyes, and you'll find yourself standing before an altar with some Southern belle on your arm."

"You sound as if you speak from experience," Pickering said.

"I do," the pilot said. "I went to Pensacola in 'thirty-five, a happy bachelor. I left with wings of gold and a mother-in-law."

"I suppose I sound pretty stupid," Pickering said.

"Not at all," the pilot said. "You seem to have already learned the most important lesson."

"Excuse me?"

"If you don't know something, don't be embarrassed to ask questions."

He smiled at Pickering and offered his hand.

"Happy landings, Lieutenant," he said. "And give my regards to the bar in the San Carlos hotel."

Pickering walked down the cabin aisle and got off the plane. The stewardess was standing on the tarmac, again looking at him with concern and suspicion in her eyes.

"I noticed that the Jensen Dynamometer was leaking oil," Pickering said, very seriously, to explain his visit to the cockpit. "I thought the pilot should know before he took off again."

He saw in her eyes that she believed him. With a little bit of luck, he thought, she would ask the pilot about the Jensen Dynamometer, and the pilot would conclude his stewardess had a screw loose.

The airlines limousine, a Checker cab that had been cut in half and extended nine feet, was loaded and about to drive away without him when he got to the terminal.

Thirty minutes later, it deposited him before the Foster Peachtree Hotel in downtown Atlanta. It was one of the smaller Foster hotels, an eight-story brick building shaped like an "E" lying on its side. The Old Man had bought it from the original owners when Pickering was in prep school, retired the general manager, built a new kitchen, installed a new air-conditioning system, and replaced the carpets and mattresses. Aside from that, he'd left it virtually untouched.

"People don't like change, Pick," the Old Man had explained to him seven or eight months ago, when they had been here on one of the Old Man's unannounced visits. "The trick to get repeat customers is to make them think, subconsciously, of the inn as another home. You start throwing things they're used to away, they start feeling like intruders."

A very large, elderly black man, in the starched white jacket of Peachtree bellmen, recognized him as he got out of the Checker limousine.

"Well, nice to see you again, Mr. Pickering," he said. "We been expecting you. You just go on inside, I'll take care of your bags."

The Old Man is right, Pickering thought as he walked up to a door being opened by another white-jacketed black man, *if we dressed the bellmen in red uniforms with brass buttons, people would wonder what else was changed in the hotel, and start looking for things to complain about.*

The resident manager spotted him as he walked down the aisle of shops toward the lobby, and moved to greet him. He was a plump, middle-aged man, who wore what hair he had left parted in the middle and slicked down against his scalp. Pickering knew him. L. Edward Locke had been resident manager of the Foster Biscayne in Miami when Pick had worked a spring vacation waiting tables around the pool during the day and tending bar in the golf course clubhouse at night.

"Hello, Mr. Pickering," Locke said. "It's good to see you."

"When did I become 'Mr. Pickering'?" Pick said, as he shook his hand.

"Maybe when you became a Marine?" Locke said, smiling.

"I'd rather, in deference to my exalted status as a Marine officer, prefer that you stop calling me 'Hey, you!' " Pick said. "But aside from that, 'Pick' will do fine."

"You look like you were born in that uniform," Locke said. "Very spiffy."

"It's supposed to attract females like moths to a flame," Pick said. "I haven't been an officer long enough to find out for sure."

"I don't think you'll have any worries about that at all," the resident manager said. "Would you like a drink? Either here"—he gestured toward the bar off the lobby—"or in your room? I've put you in the Jefferson Davis Suite." And then Locke misinterpreted the look in Pickering's eyes. "Which we cannot fill, anyway."

"I wasn't planning to stay," Pick said. "Unless my car hasn't shown up?"

"Came in two days ago," Locke said. "I had it taken to the Cadillac dealer. They serviced it and did whatever they thought it needed."

"Thank you," Pick said. "Then all I'll need is that drink and a road map."

They started toward the bar, but Pickering stopped when he glanced casually into a jewelry store. There was a display of watches laid out on velvet. One of them, in gleaming gold, band and all, had just about as many fascinating buttons and dials and sweeping bands as had the watch on the wrist of the Eastern Airlines pilot.

"Just a second," Pick said. "I have just decided that I am such a nice fellow that I am going to buy myself a present."

The price of the watch was staggering, nearly four hundred dollars. But that judgment, he decided, was a reflection of the way he had come by money—earning it himself or doing, by and large, without—until his twenty-first birthday. On his majority, he had come into the first part of the Malcolm Pickering Trust (there would be more when he turned twenty-five, and the balance when he turned thirty) established by Captain Richard Pickering, founder of Pacific & Far East Shipping, Inc., for his only grandson.

The first monthly check from the Crocker National Bank had been for four times as much money as he was getting as a supernumerary assistant manager of the Andrew Foster Hotel. He could afford the watch.

"I'll take it," he said. "If you'll take a check."

"I'll vouch for the check," Locke said quickly, as a cloud of doubt appeared on the face of the jewelry store clerk.

"That's a fascinating watch," Locke said, as Pick strapped it on his wrist. "What are all the dials for?"

"I haven't the foggiest idea," Pick said. "But the Eastern Airlines pilot had one like it. It is apparently what the well-dressed airplane pilot wears."

Locke chuckled, and then led Pickering into the lobby bar. They took stools and ordered scotch.

"I really can't offer you the hospitality of the inn for the night, Pick?"

"I want to get down there and look around," Pick said. "What we Marine officers call 'reconnoitering the area.' "

"Not even an early supper?"

"Ah understand," Pick said, in a thick, mock Southern accent, "that this inn serves South'ren fried chicken that would please Miss Scarlett O'Hara herself."

"That we do," Locke said. "Done to a turn by a native. Of Budapest, Hungary."

Pickering chuckled. He looked over his shoulder and nodded at a table in the corner of the bar.

"You serve food here?"

"Done," Locke said. He reached over the bar and picked up a telephone.

"Helen," he said. "Edward Locke. Would you have the garage bring Mr. Pickering's car around to the front? And then ask my secretary to bring the manila envelope with 'Mr. Pickering' on it to the bar? And give me the kitchen."

The manila envelope was delivered first. It contained a marked road map of the route from Atlanta to Pensacola, Florida. It had been prepared with care; there were three sections of road outlined in red, to identify them as speed traps.

"There's a rumor that at least some of the speed traps are passing servicemen through, as their contribution to the war effort," Locke said. "But I wouldn't bank on that. And on the subject of speed traps, they want cash. You all right for cash?"

"Fine, thank you," Pickering said. "What about a place to stay once I get there?"

"All taken care of," Locke said. "An inn called the San Carlos Hotel. Your grandfather tried to buy it a couple of years ago, but it's a family business and they wouldn't sell. They're friends of mine. They'll take good care of you."

"Just say I'm a friend of yours?"

"I already called them," Locke said. "They expect you."

"You're very obliging," Pick said. "Thank you."

"Good poolside waiters are hard to find," Locke said, smiling.

IV

(ONE)
Temporary Building T-2032
The Mall
Washington, D.C.
1230 Hours, 6 January 1942

There was a sign reading ABSOLUTELY NO ADMITTANCE on the door to the stairway of the two-floor frame building.

Second Lieutenant Kenneth J. McCoy pushed it open and stepped through it. Inside, there was a wall of pierced-steel netting, with a door of the same material set into it. On the far side of the wall, a Marine sergeant sat at a desk, in his khaki shirt. His blouse hung from a hanger hooked into the pierced-steel-netting wall.

The sergeant stood up and pushed a clipboard through a narrow opening in the netting. When he stood up, McCoy saw the sergeant was armed with a Colt Model 1911A1 .45 ACP pistol, worn in a leather holster hanging from a web belt. Hanging beside his blouse was a Winchester Model 1897 12-gauge trench gun.

"They've been looking for you, Lieutenant," the sergeant said.

McCoy wrote his name on the form on the clipboard and pushed it back through the opening in the pierced-metal wall.

"Who 'they'?" he asked, smiling.

"The colonel, Captain Sessions," the sergeant said.

"I was on leave," McCoy said, "but I made the mistake of letting them know where they could find me."

The sergeant chuckled and then pressed a hidden button. There was the buzzing of a solenoid. When he heard it, McCoy pushed the door in the metal wall open.

"They said it was important," McCoy said. "Since I am the only second lieutenant around here, what that means is that they need someone to inventory the paper towels and typewriter ribbons."

The sergeant smiled. "Good luck," he said.

McCoy went up the wooden stairs two at a time. Beyond a door at the top of the stairs was another pierced-steel wall. There was another desk behind it, but there was no one at the desk, so McCoy took a key from his pocket and put it to a lock in the door.

He pushed the door open and was having trouble getting his key out of the lock when a tall thin officer saw him. The officer was bent over a desk deeply absorbed with something or other. He was in his shirtsleeves (with the silver leaves of a lieutenant colonel pinned to his collar points), and he was wearing glasses. Even in uniform, and with a snub-nosed .38-caliber Smith & Wesson Chief's Special revolver in a shoulder holster, Lieutenant Colonel F. L. Rickabee, USMC, did not look much like a professional warrior.

He looked up at McCoy with an expression of patient exasperation.

"The way it works, McCoy," Lieutenant Colonel Rickabee said, as if explaining it to a child, "is that if you're unavoidably detained, you call up and tell somebody. I presume you were *unavoidably* detained?"

"Sir," McCoy said, "my orders were to report no later than oh-eight-hundred tomorrow morning."

Rickabee looked at Second Lieutenant McCoy for a moment. "Goddamn it," he said. "You're right."

"The sergeant said you were looking for me, sir," McCoy said.

"Uh-huh," Colonel Rickabee said. "I hope you haven't had lunch."

"No, sir," McCoy said.

"Good," Rickabee said. "The chancre mechanics flip their lids if you've been eating."

"I had breakfast," McCoy said.

"Don't tell them," Rickabee said.

"I had a physical when I came back, sir," McCoy said. "That was just a week ago."

"You're about to have another," Rickabee said.

He bent over the desk again, shuffled the papers he had been looking at into a neat stack, and then put them into a manila envelope stamped with large red letters SECRET. He put the envelope into a file cabinet, then locked the cabinet with a heavy padlock.

"Wait here a moment, McCoy," Lieutenant Colonel Rickabee said. "I'll fetch Captain Sessions."

He went down the corridor and into an office. A moment later, Captain Sessions, USMC, appeared. He was a tall, well-set-up young officer, whose black hair was cut in a crew cut. His brimmed officer's cap was perched on the back of his head, and he was slipping his arms into his blouse and overcoat. He had obviously removed the blouse and overcoat together.

"Hey, Killer," he said, smiling, revealing a healthy set of white teeth. "How was the leave?"

"As long as it lasted, it was fine, thanks," McCoy replied. Captain Sessions was about the only man in the Corps who could call McCoy "Killer" without offending him. Anyone else who did it seldom did it twice. It triggered in McCoy's eyes a coldness that kept it from happening again.

Captain Sessions was different. For one thing, he said it as a joke. For another, he had proved himself on several occasions to be McCoy's friend when that had been difficult. Perhaps most importantly, McCoy believed that if it had not been for Captain Sessions, he would still be a corporal somewhere—in a machine-gun section or a motor transport platoon. McCoy looked on Sessions as a friend. He didn't have many friends.

"Major Almond," Captain Sessions said as they went back down the stairs, referring to the Administrative Officer, "is looking forward to jumping your ass for reporting back in late. If he sees you before I see him, or Colonel Rickabee does, you tell him to see one of us."

"Yes, sir," McCoy said.

"With a little bit of luck, you'll be out of here before you run into him, and he won't learn that I made a fool of myself again. I really thought you were due back at oh-eight-hundred this morning."

"Yes, sir," McCoy repeated. He didn't understand the "you'll be out of here" business, but there was no time to ask. Captain Sessions was already at the foot of the stairs, reaching for the sergeant's clipboard to sign them out.

"The car's outside?" Sessions asked.

"No, sir," the sergeant said. "Major Almond took it, sir. He went over to the Lafayette Hotel, looking for Lieutenant McCoy."

"My car's in the parking lot, sir," McCoy said.

"Why not?" Sessions said, smiling. He turned to the sergeant. "When Major Almond returns, Sergeant, tell him that Lieutenant McCoy was not AWOL after all, and that I have him."

"Yes, sir," the sergeant said, then pushed the hidden switch that operated the door lock.

McCoy's car, a 1939 LaSalle convertible coupe, was covered with snow, and the windows were filmed with ice.

"I hope you can get this thing started," Captain Sessions said as he helped McCoy chip the ice loose with a key.

"It should start," McCoy said. "I just put a new battery in it."

"You didn't take it on leave?" Sessions asked.

"I went to New York City, sir," McCoy said. "You're better off without a car in New York."

"You didn't go home?" Sessions asked. He knew more about Second Lieutenant McCoy than anyone else in the Marine Corps, including the fact that he had a father and a sister in Norristown, Pennsylvania.

"No, sir," McCoy said.

Sessions found that interesting, but didn't pursue it.

The car cranked, but with difficulty.

"I hate Washington winters," McCoy said as he waited for the engine to warm up. "Freeze and thaw, freeze and thaw. Everything winds up frozen."

"You may shortly look back on Washington winters with fond remembrance," Captain Sessions said.

"Am I going somewhere, sir?"

"Right now you're going to the Bethesda Naval Hospital," Sessions said. "You know where that is?"

"Yes, sir."

The outpatient clinic at the hospital was crowded, but as soon as Sessions gave his name, the Navy yeoman at the desk summoned a chief corpsman, who took them to an X-ray room, supervised chest and torso and leg X rays, and then led them to an examining room where he ordered McCoy to remove his clothing. He weighed him, took his blood pressure, drew blood into three different vials; and then, startling McCoy, pulled off the bandage that covered his lower back with one quick and violent jerking motion.

"Jesus," McCoy said. "Next time, tell me, Chief!"

"You lost less hair the way I done it," the chief said, unrepentant, and then examined the wound.

"That's healing nicely," he said. "But there's still a little suppuration. Shrapnel?"

McCoy nodded.

"That's the first wound like that I seen since World War I," the chief said.

A younger man in a white medical smock came in the room. The silver railroad tracks of a Navy full lieutenant were on his collar points.

"I'm sure there's a good reason for doing this examination this way," he said to Sessions.

"Yes, Lieutenant, there is," Sessions replied.

The Naval surgeon examined McCoy's medical records, and while he was listening to his chest, the chief corpsman fetched the X rays. The surgeon examined them, and then pushed and prodded the line of stitches on McCoy's lower back.

"Any pain? Any loss of movement?"

"I'm a little stiff sometimes, sir," McCoy said.

"You're lucky you're alive, Lieutenant," the surgeon said, matter-of-factly. Then he grunted and prodded McCoy's upper right thigh with his finger. "Where'd you get that? That's a small-arm puncture, isn't it?"

"Yes, sir."

"Not suffered at the same time as the damage to your back? It looks older."

"No, sir," McCoy said.

"Not very talkative, is he, Captain?" the surgeon said to Sessions. "I asked him where he got it."

"In Shanghai, sir," McCoy said.

"That's a Japanese twenty-five-caliber wound?" the surgeon asked doubtfully.

"No, sir," McCoy said. "One of those little tiny Spanish automatics . . . either a twenty-five or maybe a twenty-two rimfire."

"A twenty-five?" the surgeon asked curiously, and then saw the look of impatience in Sessions's eyes. He backed down before it.

"That seems to have healed nicely," he said, cheerfully. "You don't have a history of malaria, do you, Lieutenant?"

"No, sir."

"Nor, according to this, of social disease," the surgon said. "Have you been exposed to that, lately?"

"No, sir."

"Well, presuming they don't find anything when they do his blood, Captain, he should be fit for full duty in say, thirty days. I think he should build up to any really strenuous exercise, however. There's some muscle damage, and—"

"I understand," Sessions said. "Thank you, Doctor, for squeezing him in this way."

"My pleasure," the surgeon said. "You can get dressed, Lieutenant. It'll be a couple of minutes before the form can be typed up. I presume you want to take it with you?"

"If we can," Sessions said.

When they were alone in the treatment room, McCoy put his blouse back on and fastened his Sam Browne belt in place. Then he looked at Sessions.

"Are you going to tell me what's going on?" he asked.

"Well, from here we go to my place," Captain Sessions said. "Where my bride at this very moment is preparing a sumptuous feast to honor the returned warrior, and where there is a bottle of very good scotch she has been saving for a suitable occasion."

"In other words, you're not going to tell me?"

"Not here, Ken," Sessions said. "At my place."

McCoy nodded.

"Colonel and Mrs. Rickabee will be there," Sessions said.

McCoy's eyebrows rose at that, but he didn't say anything.

(TWO)
Chevy Chase, Maryland

"The second house from the end, Ken," Captain Sessions said. "Pull into the driveway."

McCoy was surprised at the size of the house, and at the quality of the neighborhood. The houses were large, and the lots were spacious; it was not where he would have expected a Marine captain to live.

"Well, thank God that's home," Sessions said when McCoy had turned into the driveway. "Jeannie's getting a little large to have to drive me to work."

McCoy had no idea what he was talking about, but the mystery was quickly cleared up when Jean Sessions, a dark-haired, pleasant-looking young woman, came out of the kitchen door and walked over to the car. She was pregnant.

She kissed her husband, and then pointed at a 1942 Mercury convertible coupe.

"Guess what the Good Fairy finally fixed," she said. "He brought it back five minutes ago."

"I saw," Sessions said, dryly. " 'All things come to him who waits,' I suppose."

Jean Sessions went around to the driver's side as McCoy got out. She put her hands on McCoy's arms, and kissed his cheek, and then looked intently at him.

"How are you, Ken?" she asked.

It was more than a ritual remark, McCoy sensed. She was really interested.

"I'm fine, thanks," Ken said.

"You look fine," she said. "I'm so glad to see you."

She took his arm and led him to the kitchen. There was the smell of roasting beef, and a large, fat black woman in a maid's uniform was bent over a wide table wrapping small pieces of bacon around oysters.

"This is Jewel, Ken," Jean said, "whose hors d'oeuvres are legendary. And this is Lieutenant McCoy."

"You must be somebody special, Lieutenant," Jewel said, with a smile. "I heard all about you."

McCoy smiled, slightly uncomfortably, back at her.

"Colonel Rickabee called and said you were to call him when you got here," Jean Sessions said to her husband. "So you do that, and I'll fix Ken a drink."

She led him into the house to a tile-floored room, whose wall of French doors opened on a white expanse that after a moment he recognized to be a golf course.

"This is a nice house," Ken said.

"I think it is," Jean said. "It was our wedding present."

She handed him a glass dark with scotch.

"How was the leave?" she asked.

"As long as it lasted, it was fine," he said.

"I heard about that," Jean said. "You were cheated out of most of it, weren't you?"

"I made the mistake of telling them where they could find me," he said.

"How'd the physical go?" she asked. "You going to be all right?"

"It's fine," he said. "The only time it hurts is when they change the bandage. Most of the time it itches."

"Curiosity overwhelms me," Jean said. "Ed says you've got a girl. Tell me all about her."

The answer didn't come easily to McCoy's lips.

"She's nice," he said finally. "She writes advertising."

He thought: *Ernie would like Mrs. Sessions, and probably vice versa.*

Jean Sessions cocked her head and waited for amplification.

"For toothpaste and stuff like that," McCoy went on. "I met her through a guy I went through Quantico with."

"What does she look like?" Jean asked.

McCoy produced a picture. The picture surprised Jean Sessions. Not that McCoy had found a pretty girl like the one hanging on to his arm in the picture, but that he'd found one who wore an expensive full-length Persian lamb coat, and who had posed with McCoy in front of the Foster Park Hotel on Central Park South.

"She's very pretty, Ken," Jean said.

"Yeah," McCoy said. "She is."

"The colonel will be here in half an hour," Captain Ed Sessions announced from the doorway.

"So soon?" Jean asked.

"He wants to talk to Ken before his wife gets here," Sessions said. "And he asked if we could set a place for Colonel Wesley."

McCoy saw that surprised Jean Sessions.

"Certainly," she said. "It's a big roast."

"I told him we could," Sessions said.

"Ken was just showing me a picture of his girl," Jean said, changing the subject. "Show her to Ed, Ken."

Sessions said that he thought Ernestine Sage was a lovely young woman.

Lieutenant Colonel Rickabee arrived almost exactly thirty minutes later. He was followed into the room by Jewel, who carried a silver tray of bacon-wrapped oysters. Jean Sessions left after making him a drink. She explained that she had to check the roast, and she closed the door after her.

"I was sorry to have to cheat you out of the rest of your recuperative leave, McCoy," Rickabee said. "I wouldn't have done it if it wasn't necessary."

"I understand, sir," McCoy said.

"The decision had just about been made to send you over to COI, after you'd had your leave," Rickabee said.

"Sir?"

"You've never heard of it?" Rickabee asked, but it was a statement rather than a question. "You ever hear of Colonel Wild Bill Donovan?"

"No, sir."

"He won the Medal of Honor in the First World War," Rickabee explained. "He was in the Army. More important, he's a friend of the President. COI stands for 'Coordinator of Information.' It's sort of a clearinghouse for intelligence information. A filter, in other words. They get everything the Office of Naval Intelligence comes up with, and the Army's G-2 comes up with, and the State Department, us, everybody . . . and they put it all together before giving it to the President. Get the idea?"

"Yes, sir," McCoy said.

"Donovan has authority to have service personnel assigned to him," Rickabee said, "and General Forrest got a call from the Commandant himself, who told him that when he got a levy against us to furnish officers to the COI, he was not to regard it as an opportunity to get rid of the deadwood. The Commandant feels that what Donovan is doing is worthwhile, and that it is in the best interest of the Corps to send him good people. Despite your somewhat childish behavior in the Philippines, you fell into that category."

McCoy did not reply. And Rickabee waited a long moment, staring at him hard in order to make him uncomfortable—without noticeable effect.

"Let me get *that* out of the way," Rickabee said finally, with steel in his voice. "You were sent there as a courier. Couriers do *not* grab BARs and go AWOL to the infantry. In a way, you were lucky you got hit. It's difficult to rack the ass of a wounded hero, McCoy, even when you know he's done something really dumb."

"Yes, sir," McCoy said, after a moment.

"Okay, that's the last word on that subject. You get the Purple Heart for getting hit. But no Silver Star, despite the recommendation."

He reached into his briefcase and handed McCoy an oblong box. McCoy opened it and saw inside the Purple Medal.

"Thank you, sir," McCoy said. He closed the box and looked at Rickabee.

Rickabee was unfolding a sheet of paper. Then he started reading from it: ". . . ignoring his wounds, and with complete disregard for his own personal safety, carried a grievously wounded officer to safety through an intensive enemy artillery barrage, and subsequently, gathered together eighteen Marines separated from their units by enemy action, and led them safely through enemy-occupied territory to American lines. His courage, devotion to duty, and . . . et cetera, et cetera . . ."

He folded the piece of paper and then dipped into his briefcase again, and came up with another oblong box.

"*Bronze* Star," Rickabee said, handing it to him. "If the Corps had *told* you to go play Errol Flynn, you would have got the Silver. And if you hadn't forgotten to duck, you probably wouldn't have got the Bronze. But, to reiterate, it's hard to rack the ass of a wounded hero, even when he deserves it."

McCoy opened the Bronze Star box, glanced inside, and then closed it.

"For the time being, McCoy, you are not to wear either of those medals," Rickabee said.

"Sir?"

"Something has come up which may keep you from going to COI," Rickabee said. "Which is why I was forced to cancel your recuperative leave."

McCoy looked at him curiously, but said nothing.

"You're up, Ed," Rickabee said to Captain Sessions.

"When you were in China, McCoy," Sessions began, "did you ever run into Major Evans Carlson?"

"No, sir," McCoy said. "But I've seen his name." And then memory returned. "And I read his books."

"You have?" Rickabee asked, surprised.

"Yes, sir," McCoy said. "Captain Banning had them. And a lot of other stuff that Carlson wrote. Letters, too."

"And Captain Banning suggested you read the books?" Sessions asked.

"Yes, sir, and the other stuff."

"What did you think?" Rickabee asked, innocently.

McCoy considered the question, and then decided to avoid it. "About what, sir?"

"Well, for example, what Major Carlson had to say about the Communist Chinese Army?" Rickabee asked.

McCoy didn't immediately reply. He was, Sessions sensed, trying to fathom why he was being asked.

"Just off the top of your head, Ken," Sessions said.

McCoy looked at him, and shrugged. "Out of school," McCoy said. "I think he went Chink."

"Excuse me?" Rickabee said.

"It happens," McCoy explained. "People spend a lot of time over there, China gets to them. That 'thousands of years of culture' crap. They start to think that we don't know what we're doing, and that the Chinks have everything figured out. Have had it figured out for a thousand years."

"How does that apply to what Carlson thinks of the Chinese Communists?" Rickabee asked.

"That's a big question," McCoy said.

"Have a shot at it," Rickabee ordered.

"There's two kinds of Chinese," McCoy said. "Ninety-eight percent of them don't give a damn for anything but staying alive and getting their rice bowl filled for that day. And the other two percent try to push the ninety-eight percent around for what they can get out of it."

"Isn't that pretty cynical?" Rickabee asked. "You don't think that, say, Sun Yat-sen or Chiang Kai-shek—or Mao Tse-tung—have the best interests of the Chinese at heart?"

"I didn't mean that all they're interested in is beating them out of their rice bowls," McCoy said. "I think most of them want the power. They like the power."

That's simplistic, of course, Sessions thought. *But at the same time, it's a rather astute observation for a twenty-one-year-old with only a high school education.*

"Then you don't see much difference between the Nationalists and the Communists?" Rickabee asked.

"Not much. Hell, Chiang Kai-shek was a Communist. He even went to military school in Russia."

I wonder how many of his brother officers in the Marine Corps know that? Rickabee thought. *How many of the colonels, much less the second lieutenants?*

"What about the Communist notion that there should be no privileges for officers?" Rickabee went on.

"They got that from the Russians," McCoy said. "Everybody over there is 'comrade.' Chiang Kai-shek's copying the Germans. The Germans were in China a long time, and the Germans think the way to run an army is to really separate the officers from the enlisted men, make the officers look really special, so nobody even thinks of disobeying an officer."

"And the Communists? From what I've heard, they almost elect their officers."

"I heard that, too," McCoy said. "We tried that, too, in the Civil War. It didn't work. You can't run an army if you're all the time trying to win a popularity contest."

Sessions chuckled. "And you don't think it works for the Chinese Communists, either?"

"You want to know what I think the only difference between the Chinese Nationalists and the Communists is?" McCoy asked. "I mean, in how they maintain discipline?"

"I really would," Sessions said.

"It's not what Carlson says," McCoy said. "Carlson thinks the Communists are . . . hell, like they got religion. That they think they're doing something noble."

"What is it, then?" Rickabee asked.

"Somebody gets an order in the Nationalists and fails to carry it out, they form a firing squad, line up the regiment to watch, and execute him by the numbers. Some Communist doesn't do what the head comrade tells him to do, they take him behind a tree and shoot him in the ear. Same result. Do what you're told, or get shot."

"And the Japanese?"

"*That's* another ball game," McCoy said. "The Japs *really believe* their emperor is God. They do what they're told because otherwise they don't get to go to heaven. Anyway, the Japs are different than the Chinese. Most of them can read, for one thing."

"Very interesting," Rickabee said. "You really are an interesting fellow, McCoy."

"You going to tell me why all the questions?" McCoy asked, after a moment.

Rickabee dipped into his briefcase again and came up with a manila envelope stiff with eight-by-ten-inch photographs of the Roosevelt letter. He handed it to McCoy.

"Read that, McCoy," Rickabee said.

McCoy read the entire document, and then looked at Rickabee and Sessions.

"Jesus!" he said.

"If the question in your mind, McCoy," Rickabee said, "is whether the Marine Corps intends to implement that rather extraordinary proposal, the answer is yes."

McCoy's surprise and confusion registered, for just a moment, on his face.

"Unless, of course, the Commandant is able to go to the President with proof that the source of those extraordinary suggestions is unbalanced, or a Communist," Rickabee added, dryly. "The source, of course, being Evans Carlson and not the President's son. I don't know about that—about the unbalanced thing or the Communist thing—but I think there's probably more to it than simply an overenthusiastic appreciation of the way the Chinese do things."

"I'm almost afraid to ask, but why are you showing me all this stuff?" McCoy asked.

"It has been proposed to the Commandant that the one way to find out what Colonel Carlson is really up to is to arrange to have someone assigned to his Raider Battalion who would then be able to make frequent, and if I have to say so, absolutely secret reports, to confirm or refute the allegations that he is unbalanced, or a Communist, or both."

"Named McCoy," McCoy said.

"The lesser of two evils, McCoy," Rickabee said. "Either intelligence—which I hope means you—does it, or somebody else will. There's a number of people close to the Commandant who have already made up their minds about Carlson, and whoever they arranged to have sent would go out there looking for proof that he is what they are convinced he is."

"So I guess I go," McCoy said.

"There are those in the Marine Corps, McCoy," Rickabee said dryly, "who do not share your high opinion of Second Lieutenant McCoy; who in fact think that is entirely too much responsibility for a lowly lieutenant. What happens next is that a colonel named Wesley is coming to dinner. He will examine you with none of what I've been talking about entering into the conversation. He will then go home, call a general officer, and tell him that it would be absurd to entrust you with a job like this. Meanwhile, General Forrest, who is one of your admirers, will be telling the same general officer that you are clearly the man for the job. What I think will happen is that the general will want to have a look at you himself and make up his mind then."

"Sir, is there any way I can get out of this?"

"You may not hear drums and bugles in the background, McCoy," Rickabee said, "but if you will give this a little thought, I think you'll see that it's of great importance to the Corps. I don't want to rub salt in your wound, but it's a lot more important than what you were doing in the Philippines."

(THREE)
Temporary Building T-2032
The Mall
Washington, D.C.
1230 Hours, 7 January 1942

McCoy's encounter with Colonel Wesley was not what he really expected. The meeting was clearly not Wesley's idea; he had simply been ordered to have a look at the kid. Thus at dinner Wesley practically ignored him; what few questions he asked were brief and obviously intended to confirm what he had decided about McCoy before he met him.

Despite what Rickabee had said about the importance to the Corps of checking on Carlson, McCoy didn't want the job. Even the COI seemed like a better assignment. With a little bit of luck, McCoy decided, Colonel Wesley would be able to convince the unnamed general officer that McCoy was not the man for it.

He was a mustang second lieutenant. The brass would not entrust to a mustang second lieutenant a task they considered very important to the Corps.

But just before he went to sleep in a bedroom overlooking the snow-covered golf course, he had another, more practical, thought. He could get away with spying on this gone-Chink lieutenant colonel for the same reasons Colonel Wesley didn't think he could carry it off: because he *was* a mustang second lieutenant. Wesley would send some Palace Guard type out there, some Annapolis first lieutenant or captain. If Colonel Carlson was up to something he shouldn't be, he sure wouldn't do it with an Annapolis type around. Carlson would not be suspicious of a mustang second lieutenant; but if he hadn't really gone off the deep end, he would wonder why an Annapolis-type captain was so willing to go along with his Chinese bullshit.

In the morning, Captain Sessions told him to stick around the house until he was summoned, and then Sessions drove to work.

He tried to keep out of the way, but Mrs. Sessions found him reading old *National Geographic* magazines in the living room, and she wanted to talk. The conversation turned to Ernie Sage and ended with him calling her on the phone, so Mrs. Sessions could talk to her.

They had no sooner hung up than the phone rang again. It was Captain Sessions. He told McCoy to meet him outside Building T-2032 at half-past twelve.

When he got there, five minutes early, Captain Sessions was waiting for him. He was wearing civilian clothing.

"Would it be all right if we used your car again, Killer?" Sessions asked.

"Yes, sir, of course," McCoy said.

When they were in the car, McCoy looked at Sessions for directions.

"Take the Fourteenth Street Bridge," Sessions ordered.

Twenty-five minutes later, they turned off a slippery macadam road and drove through a stand of pine trees, and then between snow-covered fields to a fieldstone farmhouse on top of a hill. As they approached the house, McCoy saw that it was larger than it appeared from a distance. And when, at Sessions's orders, he drove around to the rear, he saw four cars: a Buick, a Ford, and two 1941 Plymouth sedans, all painted in Marine green.

"It figures, I suppose," Sessions said dryly, "that the junior member of this little gathering has the fanciest set of wheels."

McCoy wasn't sure whether Sessions was just cracking wise, or whether there was an implied reprimand; second lieutenants should not drive luxury convertibles. He had bought the LaSalle in Philadelphia when he had been ordered home from the 4th Marines in Shanghai. He had made a bunch of money in China, most of it playing poker, and he had paid cash money for the car. He'd bought it immediately on his return, as a corporal, before he had had any idea the Corps wanted to make him an officer.

He parked the LaSalle beside the staff cars, and they walked to the rear door of the farmhouse. A first lieutenant, wearing the insignia of an aide-de-camp, opened the door as they reached it.

"Good afternoon, sir," he said to Sessions, giving McCoy a curious look. "The general is in the living room. Through the door, straight ahead, last door on the left."

"Thank you," Sessions said, and added, "I've been here before."

In the corridor leading from the kitchen, they came across a row of Marine overcoats and caps hanging from wooden pegs. They added theirs to the row.

Then Sessions signaled for McCoy to knock on a closed sliding door.

"Yes?" a voice from inside called.

"Captain Sessions, sir," Sessions called softly.

"Come in, Ed," the voice called. McCoy slid the door open. Then Sessions walked into the room and McCoy followed him. There were five officers there: a major general and a brigadier general, neither of whom McCoy recognized; Colonel Wesley; Lieutenant Colonel Rickabee, in civilian clothing; and a captain wearing aide-de-camp's insignia. There was also an enlisted Marine wearing a starched white waiter's jacket.

The brigadier general shook Sessions's hand, and then offered his hand to McCoy.

"Hello, McCoy," he said. "Good to see you again."

McCoy was surprised. So far as he could remember, he had never seen the brigadier general before. And then he remembered that he had. *Once* before, in Philadelphia, after he had just returned from China, they had had him at the Philadelphia Navy Yard, draining his brain of everything he could recall about China and the Japanese Army. Two men in civilian clothing had come into the third-floor room where he was "interviewed." One of them, he realized, had been this brigadier general. And with that knowledge, he could put a name to him: He was Brigadier General Horace W. T. Forrest, Assistant Chief of Staff for Intelligence, USMC.

"Thank you, sir," McCoy said. *What did Rickabee mean when he said Forrest was "one of my admirers"?*

"I don't believe you know General Lesterby?" General Forrest said, gesturing to the major general.

"No, sir," McCoy said. He looked at General Lesterby and saw that the general was examining him closely, as if surprised at what he was seeing.

Then General Lesterby offered his hand.

"How are you, Lieutenant?" he said.

"How do you do, sir?" McCoy said.

"And you've met Colonel Wesley," General Forrest said.

"Yes, sir," McCoy said.

Wesley nodded, and there was a suggestion of a smile, but he did not offer his hand.

"Tommy," General Lesterby said, "make one more round for all of us. And two of whatever they're having for Captain Sessions and Lieutenant McCoy. And that will be all for now."

"Aye, aye, sir," the orderly said.

"And I think you should go keep General Forrest's aide company, Bill," General Lesterby said.

"Aye, aye, sir," General Lesterby's aide-de-camp said quickly. McCoy saw that he was surprised, and even annoyed, at being banished. But he quickly recovered. "Captain Sessions, what's your pleasure, sir?"

"Bourbon, please," Sessions said. "Neat."

"Lieutenant?" the aide asked.

"Scotch, please," McCoy said. "Soda, please."

Not another word was spoken until the drinks had been made and the aide-de-camp and the orderly had left the room.

General Lesterby picked up his glass.

"I think a toast to the Corps would be in order under the circumstances, gentlemen," he said, and raised his glass. "The Corps," he said.

The others followed suit.

"And under the circumstances," Lesterby said, "to our oath of office, especially the phrase 'against all enemies, foreign and domestic.' " He raised his glass again, and the others followed suit.

Then he looked at McCoy.

"Obviously, you're a little curious, McCoy, right? Why I sent my aide-de-camp from the room?"

"Yes, sir," McCoy admitted.

"Because if he is ever asked," General Lesterby said, "as he very well may be asked, what happened in this room today, I want him to be able to answer, in all truthfulness, that he was sent from the room, and just doesn't know."

McCoy didn't reply.

"The rest of us, McCoy," General Lesterby said, "if we are asked what was said, what transpired, in this room this afternoon, are going to lie."

"Sir?" McCoy blurted, not sure he had heard correctly.

"I said, we're going to lie," General Lesterby said. "If we can get away with it, we're going to deny this meeting ever took place. If we are faced with someone's knowing the meeting was held, we are going to announce we don't remember who was here, and none of us is going to remember what was said by anyone."

McCoy didn't know what to say.

"And we are now asking you, McCoy, without giving you any reasons to do so, to similarly violate the code of truthfulness incumbent upon anyone privileged to wear the uniform of a Marine officer," General Lesterby said, looking right into his eyes.

When McCoy didn't reply, Lesterby went on: "As perverse as it sounds—as it *is*—I am asking for your word as a Marine officer to lie. If you are unable to do that, that will be the end of this meeting. You will return to your duties under General Forrest and Colonel Rickabee, neither of whom, obviously, is going to hold it against you for living up to a code of behavior you have sworn to uphold."

McCoy didn't reply.

"Well, Sessions," General Forrest said, "you're right about that, anyway. You can't tell what he's thinking by looking at him."

"Yes, sir," McCoy said.

" 'Yes, sir,' meaning what?" General Lesterby asked.

"You have my word, sir, that . . . I'll lie, sir."

"And now I want to know, Lieutenant McCoy—and I want you to tell me the first thing that comes to your mind—why you are willing to do so."

"Colonel Rickabee and Captain Sessions, sir," McCoy said. "They're in on this. I'll go with them."

General Lesterby looked at McCoy for a moment.

"Okay," he said. "You're in. I really hope you don't later have cause—that none of us later has cause—to regret that decision."

McCoy glanced at Captain Sessions. He saw that Sessions had just nodded approvingly at him.

"I presume Colonel Rickabee has filled you in at some length, McCoy, about what this is all about?"

"Yes, sir," McCoy said.

"Just so there's no question in anyone's mind, we are all talking about a brother Marine officer, Lieutenant Colonel Evans F. Carlson, who is about to be given command of a Marine Raider battalion. We are all aware that Colonel Carlson was awarded the Navy Cross for valor in Nicaragua, and that he was formerly executive officer of the Marine detachment assigned to protect the President of the United States at Warm Springs, Georgia. We are all aware, further, that he is a close friend of the President's son, Captain James Roosevelt. Because we believe that Colonel Carlson's activities in the future may cause grievous harm to the Corps, we see it as our distasteful duty to send someone—specifically, Lieutenant McCoy here—to spy on him. This action is of questionable legality, and it is without question morally reprehensible. Nevertheless, we are proceeding because we are agreed, all of us, that the situation makes it necessary." He looked around the room and then at General Forrest. "General Forrest?"

"Sir?" Forrest replied, confused.

"Is that your understanding of what is taking place?"

Forrest came to attention. "Yes, sir."

"Colonel Wesley?"

"Yes, sir," Wesley mumbled, barely audibly.

"A little louder, Wesley, if you please," General Lesterby said. "If you are not in agreement with us, now's the time to say so."

"Yes, sir!" Colonel Wesley said, loudly.

"Rickabee?"

"Yes, sir."

"Captain Sessions?"

"Yes, sir."

General Lesterby looked at McCoy. "I understand, son," he said, "that you're very unhappy with this assignment. That speaks well for you."

Then he walked out of the room.

V

(ONE)
Pensacola, Florida
0500 Hours, 7 January 1942

Pick Pickering pulled the Cadillac convertible up before the San Carlos Hotel in Pensacola at a quarter to five in the morning. The car was filthy, covered with road grime, and Pickering himself was tired, unshaven, dirty, and starved.

From Atlanta, it had been a two-hour drive down U.S. 85 to Columbus, Georgia. Pickering saw a sign reading COLUMBUS, HOME OF THE INFANTRY, which explained why the streets of Columbus were crowded with soldiers; he was close to the Army Infantry Center at Fort Benning.

He crossed a bridge and found himself in Alabama. There he found a small town apparently dedicated to satisfying the lusts of Benning's military population. Its businesses seemed limited to saloons, dance halls, hock shops, and tourist cabins.

The next 250 miles were down a narrow, bumpy macadam road through a series of small Alabama towns and then across the border to Florida. Twenty miles inside Florida he came to U.S. 90 and turned right to Pensacola, a 125-mile, two-and-a-half-hour drive.

He had grown hungry about the time he'd passed through Columbus, Georgia, and had told himself he would stop and get something to eat, if only a hamburger, at the first place that looked even half decent. But he had found nothing open, decent or otherwise, between Columbus and Pensacola. He dined on Cokes and packages of peanut butter crackers bought at widely spaced gas stations where he took on gas.

He was grateful to find the open gas stations, and he filled up every time he came upon one. This was not the place to run out of gas.

When he opened the door of the Cadillac at the hotel, he was surprised at how cold it was. This was supposed to be sunny Florida, but it was foggy and chilly, and the palm trees on the street in front of the San Carlos Hotel looked forlorn.

The desk clerk was a surly young man in a soiled jacket and shirt who said he didn't know nothing about no reservation. When pressed, the desk clerk did discover a note saying the manager was to be notified when a Mr. Pickering showed up.

"I'm here," Pick said. "You want to notify him?"

"Don't come in until eight-thirty, Mr. Davis don't," the desk clerk informed him. "Don't none of the *assistant* managers come in till seven."

"Is there a restaurant?" Pick asked.

"Coffee shop," the desk clerk said, indicating the direction with a nod of his head.

"Thank you for all your courtesy," Pick said.

"My pleasure," the desk clerk said.

Pickering crossed the lobby and pushed open the door to the coffee shop.

It was crowded, which surprised him, for five o'clock in the morning, until he realized that nearly all the male customers were in uniform—officer's uniforms, Marine and Navy. They are beginning their day, Pick thought, as I am ending mine.

He found a table in a corner and sat down.

A couple of the officers glanced at him—with, he sensed, disapproval.

He needed a shave, he realized. But that was impossible without a room with a wash basin.

He studied the menu until a waitress appeared, and then ordered orange juice, milk, coffee, biscuits, ham, three eggs, and home fries; and a newspaper, if she had one.

The newspaper was delivered by a Marine captain in a crisp uniform.

"Keep your seat, Lieutenant," he said, as Pickering—in a Quantico Pavlovian reaction—started to stand up, "that way as few people as possible will notice a Marine officer in a mussed uniform needing a shave."

"I've been driving all night, Captain," Pick said.

"Then you should have cleaned up, Lieutenant, before you came in here, wouldn't you say?"

"Yes, sir. No excuse, sir," Pickering said.

"Reporting in, are you?"

"Yes, sir."

"Then we shall probably have the opportunity to continue this embarrassing conversation in other surroundings," the captain said. Then he walked off.

Pickering, grossly embarrassed, stared at the tableware. As he pretended rapt fascination with the newspaper, he became aware that the people in the coffee shop were leaving. He reasoned out why: Officers gathered here for breakfast before going out to the base. The duty day was about to begin, and they were leaving.

When his breakfast was served, he folded the newspaper. As he did that he glanced around the room. It was indeed nearly empty.

But at a table across the room was an attractive young woman sitting alone over a cup of coffee. She was in a sweater and skirt and wore a band over her blond hair. And she was looking at him, he thought, with mingled amusement, condescension, and maybe even a little pity.

Pick, with annoyance, turned his attention to his breakfast.

A moment later, the blonde was standing by his table. He sensed her first, and then smelled her perfume—or her cologne, or whatever it was—a crisp, clean, feminine aroma; and then as he raised his eyes, he saw there was an engagement ring and a wedding band on her hand.

"That was Captain Jim Carstairs," she said, "and as a friendly word of warning, his bite is even worse than his bark."

Pick stood up. The blonde was gorgeous. He was standing so close to her that he could see the delicate fuzz on her cheeks and chin.

"And you, no doubt, are Mrs. Captain Carstairs?" he said.

"No," she said, shaking her head. "Just a friendly Samaritan trying to be helpful. I wouldn't let him catch me needing a shave again."

"The last time he caught you needing a shave, it was rough, huh?" Pick said.

"Go to hell," she said. "I *was* trying to be helpful."

"And I'm very grateful," Pick said.

She nodded at him, smiled icily, and went back to her table.

What the hell was that all about? Pick wondered. *Obviously, she wasn't trying to pick me up. Then what? There was the wedding ring, and she knew the salty captain with the mustache. She was probably some other officer's wife, drunk with his exalted rank. Well, fuck her!*

He sat down again and picked up a biscuit and buttered it.

The blonde, whose name was Martha Sayre Culhane, returned to her table wondering what had come over her; wondering why she had gone over to the second lieutenant she had never seen before—much less met—in her life; wondering if she was drunk, or just crazy.

That he was good-looking and attractive never entered her conscious mind. What *had* entered Martha Sayre Culhane's conscious mind was that the second lieutenant looked very much like Greg, even walked like him. And *that* resemblance made her throat catch and her breathing speed up.

Greg was—had been—First Lieutenant Gregory J. Culhane, USMC (Annapolis '38), a tall, lanky, dark-haired young man of twenty-four. A navy brat, he was born in the Navy hospital in Philadelphia. His father, Lieutenant (later Vice Admiral) Andrew J. Culhane, USN (Annapolis '13), was at the time executive officer of a destroyer engaged in antisubmarine operations off the coast of Ireland. He first saw his son six months later, in December of 1917, after the War to End All Wars had been brought to a successful conclusion, and he had sailed his destroyer home to put it in long-term storage at Norfolk, Virginia.

Admiral Culhane's subsequent routine duty assignments sent him to Pearl Harbor, Hawaii; Guantanamo Bay, Cuba; San Diego, California; and to the Navy Yards at Brooklyn and Philadelphia.

Two weeks after his graduation from Philadelphia Episcopal Academy in June of 1934, Greg Culhane, who had earned letters in track and basketball at Episcopal, traveled by train to Annapolis, Maryland, where he was sworn into the United States Navy as a midshipman.

On his graduation from Annapolis in June 1938 (sixty-fifth in his class) he was commissioned at his request—and against the advice of his father—as second lieutenant, USMC, and posted to the Marine detachment aboard the battleship USS *Pennsylvania,* the flagship of the Pacific Fleet, whose home port was Pearl Harbor, Hawaii.

He immediately applied for training as a Naval aviator, which may have had something to do with his relief from the *Pennsylvania* four months later and his transfer to the Marine Detachment, Peking, China, for duty with troops.

Second Lieutenant Culhane traveled from Pearl Harbor to Tientsin, China aboard the USS *Chaumont,* one of two Navy transports that endlessly circled the world delivering and picking up Navy and Marine personnel from all corners of the globe.

In Peking, Greg Culhane served as a platoon leader for eighteen months, along with the additional duties customarily assigned to second lieutenants: He was mail officer; athletic officer; custodian of liquor, beer, and wine for the officer's mess; venereal disease control officer; and he served as recorder and secretary of various boards and committees formed for any number of official and quasi-official purposes.

In April 1939, he boarded the *Chaumont* again and returned to the United States via the Cavite Navy Base in the Philippines; Melbourne, Australia; Port Elizabeth, South Africa; Monrovia, Liberia; Rio de Janeiro and Recife, Brazil; and Guantanamo, Cuba.

Second Lieutenant Greg Culhane reported to the United States Navy Air Station, Pensacola, Florida, on June 10, 1939, nine days after the date specified on his orders. His class had already begun their thirteen-month course of instruction.

The personnel officer brought the "Culhane Case" to the attention of the deputy air station commander, Rear Admiral (lower half[1]) James B. Sayre, USN, for decision.

When he had not shown up, the training space set aside for the young Marine officer had been filled by one of the standby applicants. There were two options, the personnel officer explained. One was to go by the book and request the Marine Corps to issue orders returning Lieutenant Culhane to the Fleet Marine Force. The second option was to keep him at Pensacola and enroll him in the next flight course, which would commence 1 September.

"There's a third option, Tom," Admiral Sayre said. "For one thing, it's not this boy's fault that the *Chaumont* was, as usual, two weeks late. For another, I notice that he came here just as soon as he could after the *Chaumont* finally got to Norfolk; he didn't take the leave he was authorized. And finally, he's only nine days late. What I think is in the best interests of the Navy, as well as Lieutenant Culhane, is for me to have a word with Jim Swathley and ask him to make the extra effort to let this boy catch up with his class."

"I'll be happy to talk to Captain Swathley, sir, if you'd like," the personnel officer said.

"All right then, Tom, you talk to him. Tell him that's my suggestion."

"Aye, aye, sir."

Admiral Sayre had not considered it necessary to tell the personnel officer that he had been a year behind Greg Culhane's father at the academy, nor that in 1919–20 (before he had volunteered for aviation) he had served under Admiral Culhane with a tin-can squadron.

But as soon as the personnel officer had left his office, he had asked his chief yeoman to get Mrs. Sayre on the line, and when she came to the phone, he told her that Andy Culhane's boy had just reported aboard, and from the picture in his service jacket as well as from the efficiency reports in the record, Greg Culhane was a fine young Marine officer.

"I wonder why he went in the Marines?" Jeanne Sayre said absently, and then without waiting for a reply, she asked, "I wonder if Martha remembers him? They were just little tykes the last time . . . Well, we'll just have to have him to dinner. I'll write Margaret Culhane and tell her we're keeping an eye on him."

The engagement of Martha Ellen Sayre, the only daughter of Rear Admiral and Mrs. James B. Sayre, USN, to First Lieutenant Gregory J. Culhane, USMC, elder son of Vice Admiral and Mrs. Andrew J. Culhane, USN, was announced at the traditional Admiral's New Year's Day Reception.

It was a triple celebration, Admiral Sayre announced jovially at midnight when he was getting just a little flushed in the face: It was the new year, 1941, and that was always a good excuse for a party; he had finally managed to unload his daughter, who was getting to be at twenty-one a little long in the tooth; and her intended, even if he was a Marine, could now afford to support her, because as of midnight he had been made a first lieutenant.

Greg and Martha Culhane were married in an Episcopal service at the station chapel at Pensacola on July 1, 1941, the day after he was graduated as a Naval aviator. It was a major social event for the air station, and indeed for the Navy.

[1]The Navy rank structure provides four grades of "flag" officers corresponding to the four grades of "general" officers of the Army and Marine Corps. The lowest of these grades, corresponding to brigadier general, is rear admiral (lower half). But where brigadier generals wear only one star, rear admirals (lower half) wear two silver stars, as do rear admirals (upper half) and major generals. The result of this inconsistency is a good deal of annoyance on the part of brigadier and major generals of the Army and Marine Corps.

Seventeen flag and general officers of the Navy and Marine Corps (and of course their ladies) were in the chapel for the ceremony. And twelve of Greg's buddies (nine Marines and three swabbies) from flight school, in crisp whites, held swords aloft over the couple as they left the chapel.

Despite secret plans (carefully leaked to the enemy) that the young couple would spend their wedding night in Gainesville, they actually went no farther than a suite in Pensacola's San Carlos Hotel. And the next morning, they drove down the Florida peninsula to Opa-locka, where Greg had been ordered for final training as a flight pilot.

That lasted about two months. They had a small suite in the Hollywood Beach Hotel, which was now a quasi-official officers' hotel. Martha spent her days playing tennis and golf and swimming, and Greg spent his learning the peculiarities of the Grumman F4F-3 fighter.

In September, Greg was ordered to San Diego on orders to join Marine Fighter Squadron VMF-211. Martha drove to the West Coast with him, and she stayed until he boarded ship for Pearl Harbor. Then she left their car in storage there and returned to Florida by train. She didn't want a fight with her parents about driving all the way across the country by herself, and besides, it would be nice to have the Chevrolet Super Deluxe coupe there when Greg came back to San Diego.

Greg flew his brand-new Grumman F4F-3 Wildcat off the *Enterprise* to Wake Island on December 3, 1941. He wrote her that night, quickly, because he had to make sure the letter left aboard a Pan American *China Clipper.* Among other things, he told her that Wake had been unprepared for them, and that Marine and civilian bulldozer operations were working from first light until after dark to make revetments.

Greg also wrote that he loved her and would write again just as soon as he had the chance.

The next news she had about Greg was a letter to her father from Commander Winfield Scott Cunningham, the senior Naval officer on Wake Island. Cunningham had once worked for Admiral Sayre at Guantanamo Bay in Cuba.

Commander Cunningham wrote his old commanding officer that as soon as word of the Japanese attack on Pearl Harbor had reached Wake Island, he had ordered Major Paul Putnam, VMF-211's commanding officer, to lead a flight of four F4F-3s on a scouting mission for Japanese naval forces. The remaining eight fighter planes and the squadron itself prepared for combat.

This had posed some problems, he continued; there was more to that job than simply filling the aircraft fuel tanks and loading ammunition for the guns. Aviation fuel, presently in large tanks, had to be put into fifty-five-gallon drums and the drums dispersed. And much of the .50-caliber machine-gun ammunition had to be linked, that is to say removed from its shipping containers and fitted with metal links to make belts of ammunition.

All hands had then gone to work, officers and enlisted men alike, bulldozing revetments and taxiways; filling sandbags; pumping fuel; and working the .50-caliber linking machines.

At 0900, Putnam's four-plane patrol returned to Wake for refueling. At about 0940, immediately after the tanks of their Grumman Wildcats had been topped off, Commander Cunningham wrote, Putnam and three others took off again, taking up a course to the north and climbing to twelve thousand feet, as high as they could fly without using oxygen.

At 1158, First Lieutenant Wallace Lewis, USMC, an experienced antiaircraft artilleryman whom Major James P. S. Devereux, the senior Marine on Wake Island, had placed in charge of antiaircraft defenses, spotted a twelve-plane V of aircraft approaching Wake Island from the north at no more than two thousand feet.

The three-inch antiaircraft cannon, and the dozen .50-caliber Browning machine guns on Wake, brought the attacking formation under fire.

The pilots of the eight Grumman F4F-3 Wildcats ran for their aircraft as crew chiefs started the engines.

There were now thirty-six Japanese aircraft, three twelve-plane Vs, in sight. One-hundred-pound bombs fell from the leading V, but instead of turning away from the target once their bomb load had been released, which was the American practice, the Japanese aircraft continued on course, and began to strafe the airfield with their 20-mm machine cannon.

The projectiles were mixed explosive and incendiary. One of them, Commander Cunningham wrote Admiral Sayre, had struck Lieutenant Gregory J. Culhane, USMC, in the back of the head as he ran toward his Grumman F4F-3 Wildcat. It exploded on impact.

"I'm not even sure, Admiral," Commander Cunningham concluded, "if there will be an opportunity to get this letter out. They're supposed to be sending a Catalina in here, and we are supposed to be reinforced by a task force from Pearl, but in view of the overall situation, I'm not sure that either will be possible.

"Please offer my condolences to Martha and Mrs. Sayre."

(TWO)

Pickering had just about finished with the paper when a man came into the coffee shop, looking around, and then walked to his table.

"Lieutenant Pickering?"

Pickering looked up and nodded. The man was plump and neatly dressed in a well-cut suit. He looked to be in his early thirties.

"I understand you're an innkeeper yourself," the man said.

Pickering nodded.

"Then you'll understand that no matter how hard you try, sometimes the wrong guy gets behind the desk," the man said. He put out his hand. "I'm Chester Gayfer, the assistant manager. Much too late, let me welcome you to the San Carlos. May I join you?"

Pickering waved him into a chair. A waitress appeared with a cup of coffee.

"Put all this on my chit, Gladys," Gayfer said, and then looked at Pickering and smiled. "Unless you'd rather have a basket of fruit?"

"Breakfast is fine," Pickering said. "Unnecessary, but fine."

"We didn't expect you until later today," Gayfer said.

"I drove straight through," Pickering said.

"I think you may be able to solve one of our problems for us," Gayfer said. "If we extended a very generous innkeeper's discount, would you be interested in a penthouse suite? A large bedroom, a small bedroom, a sitting room, and a tile patio covered with an awning? There's even a butler's pantry."

"It's a little more than I had in mind," Pickering said.

"We have trouble renting something like that during the week," Gayfer said. "On weekends, however, it's in great demand by your brother officers at the air station. Two of them rent it. Eight, sometimes more, of their pals seem to extend their visits overnight. And they have an unfortunate tendency to practice their bombing—"

"Excuse me?"

"Among other youthful exuberances, your brother officers amuse themselves by filling balloon-type objects with water," Gayfer said, "which they then, cheerfully shouting 'bombs away,' drop on their friends as they pass on the sidewalk below."

Pickering chuckled.

"The management has authorized me to say that if the San Carlos could recoup just a little more by the week than it now gets for Friday and Saturday night," Gayfer said, "it would be delighted to offer the penthouse suite on a weekly basis. How does that sound to you?"

"I'm always willing to do what I can to help out a fellow hotelier," Pickering said. "That sounds fine."

They ceremoniously shook hands.

The good-looking blonde who had come to Pickering's table with the unsolicited Good Samaritan warning about Captain Carstairs stood up and walked out of the coffee shop. She had nice legs, and her skirt revealed much of the shape of her derriere. Pickering thought of himself, by and large, as a derriere man. This was one of the nicer derrieres he'd come across lately, and he gave it the careful study an object of beauty clearly deserved. Pity the owner was impressed with her role as an officer's wife.

And then he became aware that Gayfer was watching him stare.

"Some things do tend to catch one's eye, don't they?" Pick said.

There was not the understanding smile on Gayfer's face that he expected.

"I saw the wedding ring," Pick said. "No offense intended. Just a statement of appreciation."

"She's a widow," Gayfer said.

Pickering's eyebrows rose in question.

"Her name is Martha Culhane," Gayfer said. "Martha *Sayre* Culhane."

"Is that name supposed to mean something to me?" Pickering asked.

"Her father is Admiral Sayre," Gayfer said. "He's the number-three man at the Naval air station. Her husband is . . . was . . . a Marine pilot. He was killed at Wake Island."

"Oh, God!" Pickering said softly.

"She's not the only service wife around here to suddenly find herself a widow," Gayfer said. "This is a Navy town. But when she went home to her family, it was back into admiral's quarters on the base. I think that made it tougher for her. If she was back in Cedar Rapids or someplace, she wouldn't be surrounded by uniforms."

"What was she doing here this time of morning?"

"She hangs around the Marine fliers. The ones who were friends of her husband. They sort of take care of her."

Pickering would have liked an explanation of "hangs around" and "take care of her," but he suppressed the urge to ask for one.

No wonder, he thought, *that she looked at me with such amused contempt.*

"When you're through, I'll show you the suite," Gayfer said.

"I'm through," Pickering said, and stood up.

"Where's your car?" Gayfer asked as they entered the lobby.

The widow was standing, sidewards to him, by a stack of newspapers on the marble desk. *Nice legs,* Pickering thought idly, again, and then he saw how her skirt was drawn tight against her stomach, and his mind's eye was suddenly filled with a surprisingly clear image of her naked belly.

Goddamn you! You sonofabitch! She's a widow, for Christ's sake. Her husband was shot down!

"Out in front," he replied to Gayfer.

"The Cadillac with the California plates?"

Pickering nodded.

"Give me the keys," Gayfer said, and Pickering handed them to him.

There was a new clerk behind the desk. Gayfer walked over to him, gave him the keys, told him to have the bellman bring the bags in the Cadillac convertible outside up to the penthouse, and then to put the Cadillac in the parking lot.

The widow *(Martha Sayre Culhane,* Pickering remembered), who couldn't help but overhear what Gayfer said, looked at Pickering with unabashed curiosity.

Gayfer, smiling, led Pickering to the elevator. When Pickering turned and faced front, Martha Sayre Culhane was still looking at him.

(THREE)

Second Lieutenant Malcolm Pickering, USMCR, had learned from Second Lieutenant Kenneth J. McCoy, USMCR, a number of things about the United States Marine Corps that were not taught in the Platoon Leader's Course at United States Marine Corps' Schools, Quantico.

One of them was that a commissioned officer of the United States Marine Corps was not required to use rail tickets issued to move officially from one place to another. Such rail tickets, Pickering had learned from McCoy, were issued for the officer's convenience.

"There's two ways to do it, Pick," McCoy had explained. "The best way, if you know they're going to issue orders, is to request TPA—Travel by Private Auto—first. If they give you that, they also give you duty time to make the trip . . . four, five hundred miles a day. Three days, in other words, to get from Washington to Pensacola. Then they pay you so much a mile.

"But even if you don't have TPA on your orders, you can take your car. You don't get any extra travel time, all you get is what it would have taken you to make the trip by train. But when you get there, you can turn in your ticket, and tell them you traveled TPA, and they'll still pay you by the mile."

There was more: "The duty day runs from oh-oh-oh-one to twenty-four hundred."

That had required explanation, and McCoy had furnished it.

"Whether it's one minute after midnight in the morning when you leave, or half-past eleven that night, that's one day. And whether you report in after midnight or twenty-three-and-a-half hours later, so far as the Corps is concerned, it's the same day. So the trick is to leave just after midnight, and report in just before midnight."

And there had been a final sage word of advice from McCoy: "And never report in early. You report in early, they'll find something for you to do between the time you reported in and when they expected you. Something nobody else wants to do, like counting spoons, or inspecting grease pits."

Second Lieutenant Pickering's orders, transferring him from U.S. Marine Barracks, Washington, D.C., to Navy Air Station, Pensacola, Florida, for the purpose of undergoing training as a Naval aviator, had given him a ten-day delay en route leave, plus the necessary time to make the journey by rail. The schedule for rail travel called for a forty-nine-hour journey. Since forty-nine hours was one hour more than two days, he had three full days to make the rail trip.

He had flown from his Authorized Leave Destination—in other words, New York City—to Atlanta, and then driven through the night to Pensacola. He had two days of travel time left when he got to Pensacola; and taking McCoy's advice as the Gospel, he had no intention of reporting in early and finding himself counting spoons or inspecting grease pits.

He went to bed in the penthouse suite of the San Carlos and slept through the day, rising in time for the cocktail hour. He had a couple of drinks at the bar, then dinner, and then a couple of more drinks. He looked for, but did not see, the Widow Culhane, and told himself this was idle curiosity, nothing more.

Suspecting that if he stayed in the bar, he would get tanked up, which would not be a smart thing for a just-reporting-in second lieutenant to do, he left the bar and wandered around downtown Pensacola.

It was, as Chester Gayfer had told him, a Navy town. Every third male on the streets was in Navy blue. There were fewer Marines, though, and most of them seemed to be officers. There were more service people on the streets of Pensacola, Pickering decided as he saluted for the twentieth or thirtieth time, than there were in Washington.

He went into the Bijou Theatre, taking advantage of the price reduction for servicemen, and watched Ronald Reagan playing a Naval aviator in a movie called *Dive Bomber.* He was fascinated with the airplanes, and with the notion—truth being stranger than fiction—that he might soon be flying an airplane himself.

When the movie was over (he had walked in in the middle) and the lights went up, he kept his seat and stayed for the Bugs Bunny cartoon and *The March of Time,* much of which was given over to footage of the "Arsenal of Democracy" gearing up its war production.

When *Dive Bomber* started up again, he walked out of the theater and back to the San Carlos Hotel bar.

This time the Widow Culhane *(Martha Sayre Culhane,* her full name came to him) was there, in the center of a group of Marine officers and their wives and girl friends. All wore the gold wings of Navy aviators. Among them was Captain Mustache Carstairs, the one who had objected to his unshaven chin and mussed uniform the day before.

As Pickering had his drinks, both of them looked at him, the Marine captain with what Pick thought was a professional curiosity *("Has that slovenly disgrace to the Marine Corps finally taken a shave?")* and Martha Sayre Culhane with a look he could not interpret.

Pick had two drinks, and then left. He went to the penthouse suite and took off his uniform, everything but his shorts, and sat on the patio looking up at the stars and smoking a cigar until he felt himself growing sleepy. Then he went to bed.

VI

(ONE)
420 Lexington Avenue
New York City
1135 Hours, 8 January 1942

When her telephone rang, Miss Ernestine Sage was sitting pushed back in her chair with her hands—their fingers intertwined—on top of her head, looking at the preliminary artwork for a Mint-Fresh Tooth Paste advertisement, which would eventually appear in *Life, The Saturday Evening Post,* and sixteen other magazines; and on several thousand billboards across the nation.

The preliminary artwork showed a good-looking, wholesome blonde with marvelous teeth saying something. A balloon was drawn on the preliminary drawing. When Miss Sage decided exactly what Miss Mint-Fresh was going to say (and after that had been approved by her senior copywriter; her assistant account executive; her vice president and account executive; the vice president, creative; and, of course, the client) it would be put inside the balloon.

Right now the balloon was empty. The preliminary artwork gave the impression, Miss Sage had just been thinking, that someone had just whispered an obscenity in Miss Mint-Fresh's ear, and Miss Mint-Fresh had been rendered speechless.

Miss Ernestine Sage took one hand from the top of her head and reached for the telephone.

"Mint-Fresh," she said to the telephone. "Ernie Sage."

"Hello, honey," her caller said. "I'm glad I caught you."

"Hello, Daddy," Ernie Sage said. She had been expecting the call. She had, in fact, expected it yesterday.

She spun in her chair so that she could rest her feet on the windowsill. The window in Miss Ernestine Sage's closet-sized office at J. Walter Thompson Advertising, Inc. offered a splendid view of the roof of a smaller building next door, and then of the windows of the building next to that.

Miss Sage was a copywriter, which was a rank in the J. Walter Thompson hierarchy as well as a description of her function. In the Creative Division, the low man on the corporate totem pole was a "trainee." Next above that came "editorial assistant," then "junior copywriter." Above "copywriter" came "senior copywriter." Beyond that, one who kept one's nose to the grindstone could expect to move upward over the years to "assistant account executive" and "account executive" and possibly even into the "vice president and account executive" and plain "vice president" categories.

It had taken Miss Sage about three weeks to figure out that JWT, as it was known to the advertising cognoscenti, passed out titles in one or both of two ways. The first was in lieu of the substantial increase in salary, and the other was with an eye on JWT's clients. Just as JWT sold a myriad of products to the public by extolling their virtues, so it sold itself to its clients with manifestations of the degree of importance in which it held them.

A very important client, "a multimillion biller," for example, such as American Personal Pharmaceutical, Inc., who the previous year had spent "12.3 mil" in bringing its array of products before the American public, had one JWT vice president, four JWT vice presidents and account executives, eight JWT account executives, and God only knew how many JWT assistant account executives and senior copywriters devoting their full attention to American Personal Pharmaceutical's products.

Miss Sage was in the "Mint-Fresh" shop. Mint-Fresh was the third best-selling of American Personal Pharmaceutical's family of five products intended to brighten America's (and for that matter, the world's) teeth.

Miss Sage was one of three copywriters reporting to a senior copywriter, who reported to the Mint-Fresh account executive, who reported to the vice president and account executive, APP Dental Products. There were three other vice presidents and account executives, one for APP Cosmetic Products (shampoos, acne medicines, hair tonics, et cetera); one for APP Health Products (cold remedies, cough syrups, et cetera); and one for APP Personal Products (originally nostrums for feminine complaints, but now—after APP had acquired controlling interest in the companies involved in their manufacture—including three brands of sanitary napkins and eleven brands of rubber prophylactics).

Each of the vice presidents and account executives had his own empire of account executives, assistant account executives, and so on through the hierarchy, under him.

Miss Sage knew more than just about any other copywriter about the upper echelons of the "APP Family" for the same reason that she had had very little trouble getting herself hired by JWT. That was not, as the vice president, creative personnel had publicly announced, because she had proved herself to be a very bright girl, indeed, by coming out of Sarah Lawrence with a summa cum laude degree (BA, English), just the kind of person JWT was always on the lookout for. Rather it was because the grandson of the founder of American Personal Pharmaceutical (Ezekiel Handley, M.D., whose first product was "Dr. Handley's Female Elixir") was now chairman of the board and chief executive officer. His name was Ernest Sage, and he was Ernie's father.

This is not to suggest that Ernie Sage regarded her job as a sort of hobby, a socially acceptable, even chic, way to pass the time until she made a suitable marriage and took her proper place in society. She had decided in her freshman year at Sarah Lawrence that she wanted to make (as opposed to inherit) a lot of money. And after an investigation of the means to do that open to females, she had decided the way to do it was in advertising.

She had learned as much about the business as she could while in college, and she had taken courses she thought would be of value to that end. When she graduated, she had two choices. The summa cum laude would have been enough to get her a job on Madison Avenue if her name hadn't been Sage. But she decided two things about JWT. First, that they were arguably the best and biggest of all the large agencies and would thus offer her the opportunity to learn all facets of the business; and, second, with APP as their next-to-largest client, she would have certain privileges, while learning her chosen profession, that she would not have elsewhere.

It was her intention—once she felt secure, once she had learned the way things worked in the real world, once she had a portfolio of work she had done—to open her own agency. Just her, and an artist, and a secretary. She would find some small manufacturer of something who was bright enough to figure out that he wasn't getting JWT's full attention with billings under a hundred thou and convince him that she could give him more for his money than he would get elsewhere. She would build on that; she grew more and more convinced that she could.

Everything had gone according to plan, including the exercise of special privilege. She had almost bluntly told the vice president and account executive, APP Personal Products, that, substantial jump in pay or not, promotion to senior copywriter or not, she would not want to "move over into his shop" and put her now-demonstrated talents to work there.

There were a number of nice things about being rich, she told herself, and one of them was not needing a job so badly that she would have to spend her time thinking up appealing ways to sell Kotex-by-another-name and rubbers.

And then Ken McCoy had come along. And the best-laid plans of mice and men, et cetera.

The call she was taking from her father right now came about as a result of a call he had made to her the day after Thanksgiving. You were not supposed to make or receive personal calls at JWT, and rumor had it that there was official eavesdropping to make sure the rule was obeyed. No one had ever said anything to Ernie Sage about her personal calls.

"Honey, am I interrupting anything?" he'd said that Thanksgiving Friday.

"Actually, I'm flying paper airplanes out the window," she told him, truthfully. The way the air currents moved outside her window, paper airplanes would fly for astonishingly long periods of time.

"Has Pick called?"

"Any reason he should?" she'd replied. "I didn't even know he was in town."

Malcolm "Pick" Pickering had grown up calling her father "Uncle Ernie." Ernie Sage knew that sometimes her father wished she had been born a boy, since there was to be only one child. But since she *was* a girl, there was little secret that everybody concerned would be thrilled to death if Pick suddenly looked at her like Clark Gable had looked at Scarlett before carrying her up the stairs.

"He is," Ernest Sage had said. "He's at the Foster Park."

"He called you?" she had asked.

"He left a message on the bulletin board at the Harvard Club," her father had said.

"Why didn't he just call?" she had asked. "Wouldn't that have been easier?"

"He didn't leave a message for *me,*" her father had said, as realization dawned that he was having his leg pulled. "Don't be such a wise-ass. Nobody likes a wise-ass in skirts."

"Sorry," she'd laughed.

"He's having a party."

"I thought he was in Virginia playing Marine," she'd replied.

"I don't think he's *playing* Marine," her father had said, more than a little sharply.

"Sorry," she'd said again, this time meaning it.

"He's giving a party," her father had said. "Cocktails. I think you should go."

"I haven't been invited," she'd replied, simply.

"The thing on the bulletin board said 'all friends and acquaintances.' You would seem to qualify."

"If Pick wanted me, he knows my phone number," she'd said.

"I just thought you might be interested," her father had said, and from the tone in his voice and the swiftness of his getting off the line, she knew that she had hurt his feelings. Again.

Several hours later, sitting in the Oak Room of the Plaza Hotel with two girls and three young men as they debated the monumental decision where to have dinner and go afterward, she had remembered both Pick's party and her father's disappointment. And the Foster Park Hotel was only a block away.

Doing her duty, she had taken the others there. Penthouse C, overlooking Central Park, had been crowded with people, among them Ken McCoy, in a uniform like Pick's. He'd been sitting on a low brick wall on the patio, twenty-six floors above Fifty-ninth Street, looking as if he was making a valiant effort not to spit over the side.

That had turned into a very interesting evening, far more interesting than it had first promised to be. Instead of catching a cab uptown to some absolutely fascinating restaurant Billy had discovered, she'd ridden the subway downtown with Platoon Leader Candidate, McCoy, K. After he had taken her to a tiny Chinese restaurant on the third floor of a building on a Chinatown alley, she had taken him to her apartment, where she give him a drink and her virtue.

Quite willingly. This was all the more astonishing because she had ridden downtown on the subway a virgin. *More* than willingly given it to him, she subsequently considered quite often; she'd done everything but put a red ribbon on it and hand it to him on a silver platter.

And he had not been humbly grateful, either. He'd been astonished and then angry, and she'd thought for a moment that he was about to march out of the apartment in high moral outrage. He didn't in the end. He stayed.

But as he and Pick drove back to Quantico, Pick had told him about her family. Until Pick opened his fat mouth, Ken McCoy had thought she lived in the small apartment in the Village because that was all she could afford.

The result was that her letters to him had gone unanswered. And when she sent him a registered letter, it had come back marked REFUSED. At the time, she'd been firmly convinced he was ignoring her because he was a Marine officer, and Marine officers do not enter into long-term relationships with young women who enthusiastically bestow upon them their pearl of great price two hours after meeting them.

"Wham, bang, thank you, Ma'am," of course. But nothing enduring. The Marine Corps equivalent of "We must lunch sometime. I'll call you."

At first she'd been angry, then ashamed, then angry and ashamed, and then shameless. And on The Day That Will Live In Infamy, after hearing from her mother, who'd heard it from Pick's mother, that Pick had been commissioned and was in Washington, she'd gone down there to ask Pick to help.

There Pick had explained that it was not her freedom with her sexual favors that was bothering Ken McCoy; it was her money.

"What's that got to do with anything?"

"After a lot of solemn thought," Pick had replied, "I have concluded that he is afraid that you regard him as an interesting way to pass an otherwise dull evening."

"That's just not so!"

"That the minute he lets his guard down, you're going to make a fool of him. There was a woman in China who did a pretty good job on his ego."

"A Chinese woman?"

"An American. Missionary's wife. He had it pretty bad for her, the proof being that he was going to get out of the Marine Corps to marry her. For him, the supreme sacrifice."

"What happened? What did she do to him?"

"What he's afraid you're going to do to him," Pick told her. "Humiliate him."

"Goddamn her," Ernie had said. And then: "Pick, it's not that way with me. I've got to see him."

"It'll be a little difficult at the moment," Pick had said. "He's in Hawaii right now, on his way to the Philippines."

"Oh, God!" she'd wailed.

"But he'll be back," Pick had said. "He's a courier. Sort of a Marine Corps mailman."

"When?"

"A week, maybe. Ten days."

"You'll let me know when he's back?"

"I will even arrange a chance meeting under the best possible circumstances," Pick had said. "Here. He's living here with me. You can be waiting for him, soaked in perfume, wearing something transparent, with violin music on the phonograph."

"You tell me when," she said. Things were looking up.

When she'd walked through the lobby of the hotel, on her way to the station, NBC was broadcasting the bulletin that the Japanese had attacked the U.S. Naval Station at Pearl Harbor.

And a week after that, Pick had called her and told her that there had been word from the Philippines that Second Lieutenant Kenneth J. McCoy, USMCR, was missing in action and presumed dead.

Ernestine Sage's reaction to that was not what she would have thought. She had not screamed and moaned and torn her hair. She hadn't even cried. She'd just died inside. Gone completely numb.

And then, a week later, Pick had called again, his voice breaking. "I thought you might like to know that our boy just called from San Francisco. As Mark Twain said, the report of his death is somewhat exaggerated."

She's been waiting in Pick's suite at the Foster Lafayette Hotel when McCoy returned. Not soaked in My Sin, or wearing a black negligee, which had been her intention; but, because he was an hour early, she was in a cotton bathrobe with soap in her ears and her hair shower-plastered to her head.

He hadn't seemed to notice. They'd turned the Louis XIV bedroom into the Garden of Eden, and she'd wept with joy when she felt him in her. And as perverse as it sounded, with joy again when she'd changed his bandages, for it seemed proof that she was a woman who had found her mate and was caring for him.

That had been the result of her father's phone call on Thanksgiving Friday. Now he was on the line again, and there was no doubt in Miss Ernestine Sage's mind that he had on his mind now the relationship between his daughter and her Marine officer; her mother had gone to him and told him that she knew for a fact that their daughter had left her own bed in the middle of the night so that she could get in bed with Ken McCoy.

"Are you free for lunch?" Ernest Sage asked his daughter.

"Sure," she said.

"Could you come here?" he asked. "It would be better for me."

She wondered how he meant that; was his schedule tight? Or did he just want to have his little talk with her on his own ground?

He picked up on her hesitation.

"Anywhere would be fine, honey," her father said.

"Twelve-fifteen?" Ernie Sage said.

"Would you like anything in particular?" her father asked. "I think Juan's making medallions of veal."

"That'll be fine, Daddy," she said.

"Look forward to it," he said, and hung up.

The hell you do, Daddy.

At five minutes to twelve, Miss Ernestine Sage put on her overcoat and galoshes and left her office. She walked the two blocks from JWT to Madison Avenue and then the half block to the American Personal Pharmaceutical Products Building. This was a nearly new (1939) fifty-nine-story, sandstone-sheathed structure, the upper twenty floors of which housed the executive offices of APP.

She walked across the marble floor and entered an elevator.

"Fifty-six," she told the operator.

The APP building's top formed a four-sided cone, with each floor from fifty-nine down to fifty-two somewhat smaller than the floor below, from which point the walls descended straight to the street level. The fifty-sixth floor was the highest office floor, the top three floors being dedicated to various operating functions for the building itself.

Her father's office was on fifty-five. Fifty-six was the Executive Dining Room, something of a misnomer as there were actually four dining rooms on that floor, plus the kitchen and a bar. APP, like JWT, had a hierarchy. Individuals attaining certain upper levels of responsibility received with their promotions permission to take their lunch on fifty-six, on the company, or to stop by fifty-six for a little nip, also on the company, at the end of the business day.

Fully two-thirds of the floor was occupied by the Executive Dining Room itself. That establishment looked like any good restaurant in a club. And then, in addition to the Executive Dining Room, there were Dining Rooms A, B, and C. Of these, Dining Room C was the smallest, containing but one table and a small serving bar. Its use was controlled by Mrs. Zoe Fegelbinder, executive secretary to the chairman of the board of APP. And it was reserved for special occasions.

When Ernie Sage got off the elevator, the maître d'hotel spotted her right away and walked quickly to her.

"Good afternoon, Miss Sage," he said. "How nice to see you again. You're in 'C.' "

She was not surprised. This was a special occasion. The chairman of the board of APP did not want to show off his daughter in the Executive Dining Room today.

Today, the chairman of the board wanted to be alone with his daughter, so that he could talk to her about her screwing a Marine, or words to that effect.

As the maître d' ushered her across the lobby, a path was made for her and people smiled, and she heard herself being identified. She had often thought that it must be like this for Princess Elizabeth; for around here, she was sort of like royalty.

Her father was not in 'C,' but Juan was, in his chef's whites.

"Hallo, Miss Ernie," he said, smiling, apparently genuinely pleased to see her.

"Hello, Juan," she said.

She remembered now that Juan was a Filipino. As in invaded by the Japanese. As in the place where Japanese artillery had damned near killed Ken.

"Your poppa say veal medallions," Juan said. "But I think maybe you really like a little steak . . . with *marchand de vins* sauce?"

"Yes, I would," she said. "Thank you, Juan."

"Pommes frites? Haricots verts? And I find a place sells Amer'can Camembert, not bad. You try for dessert?"

"Sounds fine," she said.

"You wanna little glass wine, while you wait? Got a real nice Cal'fornia Cabernet sauvignon?"

What I really would like to have is a triple shot of cognac.

"Thank you, Juan," she said, smiling at him. "That sounds fine."

He opened the bottle and poured a glass for her.

"You wanna try?" he asked, as he gave it to her.

She took a healthy sip.

"Fine," she said. "Thank you."

"You think your poppa want a steak, too?" Juan asked.

"I thought we were having medallions of veal," Ernest Sage said, as he walked into the room.

He was a tall and heavyset man, with a full head of curly black hair, gray only at the temples. Her father, Ernie Sage often thought, looked like a chairman of the board is supposed to look, and seldom does.

"Miss Ernie," Juan said, "really wanna steak. You wanna steak, too?"

"I'll have the veal, thank you, Juan," Ernest Sage said, "with green beans and oven-roasted potatoes, if you have them. And a sliced tomato."

"Yes, sair," Juan said, and left the room.

Ernest Sage looked at his daughter as if he was going to say something, and then changed his mind. He flashed her a smile, somewhat nervously, Ernie thought, and then picked up the telephone on the table.

"No calls," he announced. "I don't care who it is."

"Said the hangman, as he began to knot the rope," Ernie Sage said.

Her father looked at her, and smiled. "Conscience bothering you?"

"Not at all," Ernie said.

"What are you drinking?" he asked.

She walked to him and handed him her glass. When he'd taken a sip and nodded his approval, she stood on her tiptoes and kissed him.

"So what's new in advertising?" he asked.

She poured him a glass of wine.

"Everyone is all agog with *'Lucky Strike Green Has Gone to War,'* " Ernie said.

"What does that mean?"

"Nothing, that's why everyone is all agog," she said.

"Not that I really give a damn, but you've aroused my curiosity."

"They changed the color on the package," she said. "It used to be predominantly green. Now it's white, with the red Lucky Strike ball in the middle. The pitch is, with appropriate trumpets and martial drums, *'Lucky Strike Green Has Gone to War.'* "

"Why'd they do that?"

"Maybe they wanted a new image. Maybe they wanted to save the price of green ink. Who knows?"

"What's that got to do with the war?"

"Nothing," she said. "That's why everyone is all agog. It's regarded as a move right up there with *'Twice as Much for a Nickel Too, Pepsi-Cola Is the Drink for You,'* which was the jingle Pepsi-Cola came onto the market with. Better even. Pure genius. It makes smoking Lucky Strike seem to be your patriotic duty."

"You sound as if you disapprove," he said.

"Only because I didn't think of it," she said. "Whoever thought that up is going to get rich."

Juan entered the room with shrimp cocktails in silver bowls on a bed of rice.

"Appetizer," he announced. "Hard as hell to get."

He walked out of the room.

Ernest Sage chuckled, and motioned for his daughter to sit down.

He ate a shrimp and took a sip of wine.

"I was sorry to have missed Pick's friend at the house. Your mother was rather taken with him."

"Was that before or after she found out I was sleeping with him?" Ernie Sage asked.

Ernest Sage nearly choked on a shrimp. "Good God, honey!" he said.

"I'm a chip—maybe a chippie?—off the old block," Ernie said, "who is frequently prone to suggest that people 'cut the crap.' "

"Whatever you are—and that probably includes a fool," Ernest Sage said, "you're not a chippie."

"Thank you, Daddy," Ernie said. "I'm sorry you missed him, too. I think you would have liked him."

"At the moment, I doubt that," he said. "I wonder what the penalty is for shooting a Marine?"

"In this case, the electric chair, plus losing your daughter," Ernie said.

"That bad, eh?" her father said, looking at her.

She nodded.

"God, you're only twenty-one."

"So's he," she said. "Which means that we're both old enough to vote, et cetera, et cetera."

"Okay, so tell me about him," Ernest Sage said.

"Mother hasn't?" Ernie asked, as she finished her last shrimp.

"I'd rather hear it from you," he said.

"He's very unsuitable," Ernie Sage said. "We have nothing in common. He has no money and no education."

"That's the debit side," her father said. "Surely there is a credit?"

"Pick likes him so much he almost calls him 'sir,' " Ernie said.

Her father nodded. "Well, that's something," he said.

"He speaks Chinese and Japanese . . . and some others."

"I'm impressed," her father said.

"No, you're not," Ernie said. "You're looking for an opening. I'm not going to give you one. Not that it would matter if I did. You're just going to have to adjust to this, Daddy."

"You're thinking of marriage, obviously?"

"I am," she said. "He's not."

"Any particular reason? Or is he against marriage on general principles?"

"He's against girls marrying Marine officers during wartime," she said. "For the obvious reasons."

"Well, there's one other point in his favor," her father said. "He's right about that. There's nothing sadder than a young widow with a fatherless child."

"Except a young widow without a child," Ernie Sage said.

"That doesn't make any sense, Ernie," he said sternly. "And you know it."

"I'm tempted to debate that," she said. "It's not as if I would have to go rooting in garbage cans to feed the little urchin. But it's a moot point. Ken agrees with you. There will be no child. Not now."

He looked at her for a long moment before he spoke again.

"You have to look down the line, honey," he said. "And you have to look at things the way they are, not the way you would wish them to be. Have you considered, really considered, what your life with this young man would be, removed from this initial flush of excitement, without the thrill . . . ?"

"I had occasion to consider what my life would be like without him," Ernie said. "He was reported missing and presumed dead. I died inside."

He looked at her with curiosity on his face.

"He's an intelligence officer," she said. "He was in the Philippines when the Japanese invaded. For a week they thought he was dead. But he wasn't, and he came home, and I came back to life."

Ernest Sage looked at his daughter, his tongue moving behind his lip as it did when he was in deep thought. "There seems to be only one thing I can do about this situation, honey," he said finally. "I go see your young man, carrying a shotgun, and demand that he do right by my daughter. Would you like me to do that?"

She got up and bent over her father and put her arms around him and kissed him. And laughed. "Thank you, Daddy," she said. "But no thanks."

"Why is that funny?" he asked.

"There is one little detail I seem to have skipped over. He didn't tell me. Pick did. They call him 'Killer' McCoy in the Marine Corps."

"Because of the Philippines? What he did there?"

"What he did in China," Ernie said. "I think I'll skip the details, but I think threatening him with a shotgun, or anything else, would be very dangerous."

"I'd love to hear the details," her father said.

"He was once attacked by four Italian Marines," Ernie said, after obviously thinking it over. "He killed two of them."

"My God!"

"And, another time, he was attacked by a gang of Chinese bandits," she went on. "He killed either twelve or fourteen of them. Nobody knows for sure."

"I think we can spare your mother those stories," her father said.

"You asked," she said simply.

"Have you considered, honey, that just maybe—considering your background—"

She interrupted him by laughing again. "That I am thrilled by close association with a killer?" she asked.

He nodded.

"I fell in love with him, Daddy," she said, "the first time I saw him. When I thought he was some friend of Pick's from Harvard. He was sitting on the patio wall of one of the penthouse suites at the Foster Park. The very first thought I had about Ken was that the Marine Corps was crazy if they thought they could take someone so gentle, so sweet, so vulnerable, and turn him into an officer."

"And when you found out what he's really like?"

"I found that out the same day," Ernie Sage said. "I didn't find out about the Italians and the Chinese until later."

Her father looked at her (she met his eyes, but her face did blush a little) until he was sure he had correctly taken her meaning, then asked, "When do I get to meet Mr. Wonderful?"

"Soon," she said. "Now that he's back in Washington, he doesn't think they'll be sending him anywhere else. Not soon, anyway."

Twenty minutes after Miss Ernestine Sage returned to her office at J. Walter Thompson, she received a telephone call from Second Lieutenant Kenneth J. McCoy, USMCR, from Washington, D.C.

Lieutenant McCoy told Miss Sage that he had been transferred to a Marine base near San Diego, California. He would write. Or call, if he had access to a phone. He was sorry, but there would be no chance for him to come to New York; he was getting in the car the moment he got off the phone.

If he was going by car, Miss Sage argued, there was no reason he couldn't go to the West Coast by way of New York. If not New York, then Philadelphia. If she left right now from New York, she could be at the Thirtieth Street Station in Philadelphia just about the time he could get there by car from Washington.

"Honey, goddamnit," Miss Sage argued. "You can't go without saying good-bye."

Lieutenant McCoy agreed to meet Miss Sage at the Thirtieth Street Station of the Pennsylvania Railroad in Philadelphia.

"But that's it, baby," Lieutenant McCoy said. "There won't be any time for anything else."

"I'll be standing on the curb," Ernie Sage said, and hung up.

VII

(ONE)
The San Carlos Hotel
Pensacola, Florida
8 January 1942

When Pick Pickering woke in the morning, he decided he would not go to the coffee shop for breakfast. It was entirely possible that Captain Mustache would be there. And Pick was not anxious to run into Carstairs again, not after the captain had eaten his ass out for being sloppy and unshaven. And there was a good chance that *Martha Sayre Culhane* would be there as well. He couldn't quite interpret them, but he saw danger flags flying in the territories occupied by the blond widow with the flat tummy and the marvelous derriere.

Discretion was obviously the better part of valor, Pick decided. *If* he decided to find some gentle breast on which to lay his weary head while he was in Pensacola, he would find one that did not belong to the widow of a Marine aviator who was not only the daughter of an admiral but who was also surrounded by noble protectors of her virtue. There was no reason at all to play with fire.

He called room service and had breakfast on his patio, surprised and disappointed that the orange juice had come from a can. This was supposed to be Sunny Florida—with orange trees. He tasted the puddle of grits beside his eggs and grimaced. There must be two Floridas, he decided, the one he knew and the one he was condemned to endure now. On Key Biscayne, which was the Florida he knew, the Biscayne Foster would not dream of serving canned orange juice or, for that matter, grits.

He called the valet and ordered them to press his uniforms, and then he dressed in the one least creased and rumpled. After that, he went down to the lobby barbershop for a haircut and a shave and a shoeshine. Then he got in the Cadillac (which, he noticed, had been washed and serviced) and put the top down.

Three blocks from the hotel, he pulled to the curb and put the top back up. Even in his green woolen blouse, he was cold. Obviously, there *were* two Floridas. This one was a thousand miles closer to the Arctic Circle.

He drove more or less aimlessly, having a look around. After a while, he found himself on a street identified as West Garden Street. And then the street signs changed, and he was on Navy Boulevard. That sounded promising, and he stayed on it, driving at the 35-MPH speed limit for five or six miles.

Here were more signs of the Navy: hock shops, Army-Navy stores, and at least two dozen bars.

Then he heard the sound of an airplane engine. Close. He leaned forward and looked up and out of the windshield.

To his right, a bright yellow, open-cockpit, single-engined biplane was taking off from a field hidden by a thick, though scraggly, stand of pine. NAVY was painted on the underside of one wing.

Pickering slowed to watch it as it sort of staggered into the air, and he was still watching when an identical plane followed it into the air. Pick pulled onto the shoulder of the road, stopped, and got out. At what seemed to be minute or minute-and-a-half intervals, more little open-cockpit airplanes flew over his head, taking off.

He was awed at the number of airplanes the Navy apparently had here, until, feeling just a little foolish, he realized he was watching the same planes over and over. After they staggered into the air, they circled back and landed, and then took off again. There were really no more than a dozen or so, he realized, and they were using two runways.

He climbed back in his car and started up again, looking for a road he could take to where he could watch the actual takeoffs and landings. But no road appeared. Instead, he came to a low bridge across some water. On the other side of the bridge was a sign, UNITED STATES NAVY AIR STATION, PENSACOLA, and immediately beyond that a guardhouse.

A Marine guard saluted crisply, waving him past the gate and onto the reservation. A few hundred yards beyond the Marine guard, he saw to his right a red, triangular flag. It bore the number "8," and its flagstaff was in the center of what looked like a very nicely tended golf green.

It had been some time since he had gone a round of golf. Much too long. He missed bashing golf balls. And then he remembered that he had found his clubs in the Cadillac's trunk when he had loaded his luggage in Atlanta. Were lowly second lieutenants permitted on Navy base golf courses? he wondered. Or was that privilege restricted to high-ranking officers? He would, he decided, find out.

He drove around the enormous base, finding barracks and headquarters and the Navy Exchange, and finally an airfield. He parked the convertible by a chain-link fence and watched small yellow airplanes endlessly take off and land, take off and land. He found this fascinating, almost hypnotic, and he lost track of time.

Eventually, his stomach told him it was time to eat; and his new wristwatch told him that it was ten minutes after twelve. Earlier he had driven past the Officers' Club. The question was, could he find it again?

The answer was yet, but it took him twenty minutes. He went inside, and for thirty-five cents was fed a cup of clam chowder, pork chops, and lima beans.

The hotelier in him told him that there was no way the Navy could afford to do this without some kind of a subsidy, and then he realized what the subsidy was. The building and the furnishings were owned by the Navy. There was no mortgage to amortize, and it was not necessary to provide for maintenance or painting. And the cooks were on the Navy payroll.

He drank a second cup of coffee and then left the dining room. Near the men's room was a map of the air station mounted on the wall. He studied it, and after a few moments he realized that with the exception of several off-the-main-base training airfields, he had covered in his aimless driving just about all of Pensacola NAS that there was to cover.

Next, he decided to leave the base, drive back into Pensacola, and ask Gayfer where he could find a good place to take a dip in the Gulf of Mexico. And then, after a swim and dinner, and maybe a couple of drinks, he would put his uniform back on and return out here and report in.

He didn't make it off the base. On the way out, he saw an arrow pointing to the officers' golf course and decided he would really rather play golf than swim. He recalled additionally that this was the arctic end of Florida and that there would probably be icebergs in the water.

He found the clubhouse without trouble. There he asked a middle-aged Navy petty officer how one arranged to play a round. Shoes and clubs were available for fifty cents in the locker room, he was told, and the greens fee was a dollar.

"And do I have to play in uniform?"

"Uniform regulations are waived while you are physically on the golf course proper, sir," the petty officer told him. "You can take off your hat and blouse and tie."

Pickering fetched his clubs and a pair of golf shoes from the trunk of the convertible and then went to the locker room and paid the fees. After that he hung his blouse, hat, Sam Browne belt, and field scarf in a locker and went outside. A lanky teenaged Negro boy detached himself from a group of his peers, offered his services as a caddy, and led him to the first tee.

A middle-aged woman was already on the tee. A woman who took her golf seriously, he saw. She was teed up, but had stepped away from the ball and was practicing her swing. He at first approved of this (his major objection to women on the links was that most of them did not take the game seriously); but his approval turned to annoyance when the middle-aged woman kept taking practice swings.

How long am I supposed to wait?

And then she saw him standing there and smiled. "Good afternoon," she said.

"Hello," he said politely.

"I didn't see you," she said. "I'm really sorry."

"Don't be silly," Pickering said.

"I was waiting for my daughter," the woman said. And then, "And here, at long last, she is."

Pickering followed her gesture and found himself looking at Martha Sayre Culhane. She was wearing a band over her blond hair, a cotton windbreaker on top of a pale blue sweater, and a tight-across-the-back khaki-colored gabardine skirt. That sight immediately urged into his mind's eye another image of her. In that one she was in her birthday suit.

Martha Sayre Culhane's eyebrows rose when she saw him; she was not pleased.

"If you don't mind playing with women," Martha Sayre Culhane's mother said. "They really discourage singles."

"I would be delighted," Pick said.

"I'm Jeanne Sayre," Martha Sayre Culhane's mother said. "And this is Martha. Martha Culhane."

In turn, they offered their hands. Martha Sayre Culhane's hand, he thought, was exquisitely soft and feminine.

"My name is Malcolm Pickering," he said. "People call me Pick."

"I thought your name was Foster," Martha Sayre Culhane said, matter-of-factly.

"Oh, you've met?" Jeanne Sayre asked.

"The desk clerk at the San Carlos, almost beside himself with awe, pointed him out to me," Martha Sayre Culhane said.

That's not true, Pickering thought, with certainty. *She asked him who I was. She was curious.*

"Oh?" her mother said, her tone making it clear that her daughter was embarrassing and annoying her.

"According to the desk clerk," Martha Sayre Culhane said, "we are about to go a round with the heir apparent to the Foster Hotel chain, now resident in the San Carlos penthouse."

"He told me about you, too," Pickering blurted.

Jeanne Sayre looked uncomfortably from one to the other. And then she looked between them, avoiding what she did not want to look at.

"But your name isn't Foster?" Martha challenged. "What about the rest of the story? How much of that is true?"

"Martha!" Jeanne Sayre snapped.

"Andrew Foster is my mother's father," Pickering said.

He saw surprise on Jeanne Sayre's face. But he didn't know what was in Martha Sayre Culhane's eyes.

"And what brought you to honor the Marine Corps with your presence?" Martha Sayre Culhane challenged.

"An old family custom," Pick snapped. "My father—my father is Fleming Pickering, as in Pacific & Far East Shipping—was a Marine in the last war. Whenever the professionals need help to pull their acorns out of the fire, we lend a hand. I am twenty-two years old. I went to Harvard, where I was the assistant business manager of the *Crimson.* I am unmarried, have a polo handicap of six, and generally can get around eighteen holes in the middle seventies. Is there anything else you would like to know?"

"Good for you, Lieutenant!" Jeanne Sayre said. "Martha, really—"

"If there's no objection," Martha Sayre Culhane interrupted her mother, "I think I'll go first."

She stepped to the tee and drove her mother's ball straight down the fairway.

Whoever had taught her to play golf, Pickering saw, had managed to impress upon her the importance of follow-through. At the end of her swing, her khaki gabardine skirt was skintight against the most fascinating derriere he had ever seen.

"If you would rather not play with us, Lieutenant," Jeanne Sayre said, "I would certainly understand."

"If it's all right with you," Pick said, "I'll play with you."

She met his eyes for a moment. Her eyes, Pick saw, were gray, and kind, and perceptive.

"You go ahead," Jeanne Sayre said. "I'll bring up the rear."

Martha Sayre Culhane hated him, Pick was aware, because *he* was here. Alive. And her husband—the late Lieutenant Whatever-his-name-had-been Culhane, USMC—had died in the futile defense of Wake Island.

Pick was ambivalent about that. Shamefully, perhaps even disgustingly ambivalent. He was sorry that Lieutenant Culhane was dead. He was sorry that Martha Sayre Culhane was a widow. *And glad that she was.*

By the time they came off the course, there was no doubt in Pick Pickering's mind that he was in love. There was simply no other explanation for the way he felt when—however briefly—their eyes had met.

(TWO)
Thirtieth Street Station
Philadelphia, Pennsylvania
1820 Hours, 8 January 1942

The weather was simply too cold and nasty for Ernie Sage to wait on the curb outside the Thirtieth Street Station as she had promised.

But she found, inside the station near one of the Market Street doors, a place where she could look out and wait for him. It was hardly more comfortable than the street: Every time the door opened, there was a blast of cold air, and she desperately needed to go to the ladies' room. But she held firmly to her spot; she was afraid she would miss him if she left.

And finally he showed up. Except for the path the wipers had cleared on the windshield, the LaSalle convertible was filthy. The bumper and grille were covered with frozen grime, and slush had packed in the fender wells.

Ernie picked up her bags and ran outside; and she was standing at the curb when he skidded to a stop.

She pulled open the door and threw her bags into the car.

"If they won't let you wait, go around the block," Ernie ordered. Then she ran back inside the Thirtieth Street Station to the ladies' room.

He wasn't there when she went back outside, but he pulled to the curb a moment later, and she got in.

She had planned to kiss him, but he didn't give her a chance. The moment she was inside, he pulled away form the curb. She slid close to him, put her hand under his arm, and nestled her head against his shoulder.

"Hi," she said.

"What's with all the luggage?" McCoy asked, levelly.

"I thought you'd probably be going through Harrisburg," Ernie said. "I thought I would ride that far with you, and then catch a train."

He looked at her for just a moment, but said nothing.

"I'm lying," Ernie Sage said. "I'm going with you. All the way."

"No you're not," he said flatly.

"I knew that was a mistake," Ernie said. "I should have waited until we were in the middle of nowhere before I told you. Somewhere you couldn't put me out."

"You can't come with me," he said.

"Why not? 'Whither thow goest . . .' Book of Ruth."

When there was no reply to that, Ernie said, "I love you."

"You think you love me," he said. "You don't really know a damn thing about me."

"I thought we'd been through all this," Ernie said, trying to keep her voice light. "As I recall, the last conclusion you came to was that I was the best thing that ever happened to you."

"Oh, Jesus Christ!"

"Well, am I or ain't I?" Ernie challenged.

"You ever wondered if . . . what happened . . . is what this is really all about?"

"You mean," she said, aware that she was frightened, that she was close to tears, "because we fucked? Because you copped my cherry?"

"Goddamn it, I hate when you talk dirty," he said furiously.

Her mouth ran away with her. "Not always," she said.

He jammed his foot on the brakes, and the LaSalle slid to the curb.

"Sorry," Ernie said, very softly.

There was something in his eyes that at first she thought was anger, but after a moment she knew it was pain.

"I love you," Ernie said. "I can't help that."

He was breathing heavily, as if he had been running hard.

Then he put the LaSalle in gear and pulled away from the curb.

"I was afraid you were going to put me out," Ernie said.

"Do me a favor," McCoy said. "Just shut up."

When she saw a U.S. 422 highway sign, Ernie thought that maybe she had won, maybe that he even would reach across the seat for her and take her hand, or put his arm around her shoulder. U.S. 422 was the Harrisburg highway. If she got that far, if they spent the night together . . .

In Norristown, ten miles or so past the western outskirts of Philadelphia, he turned off the highway and pulled into an Amoco station.

A tall, skinny, pimply-faced young man in a mackinaw and galoshes came out to the pump. McCoy opened the door and got out.

"Fill it up with high test," McCoy ordered. "Check the oil. And can you get the crap off the headlights?"

"Yes, sir," the attendant said.

"Dutch around?" McCoy asked.

"Inna station," the attendant said.

McCoy turned and looked through the windshield at Ernie, and then gestured for her to come out.

By the time she had put her feet back in her galoshes, McCoy was at the door of the service station. Ernie ran after him.

There was no one in the room where they had the cash register and displays of oil and Simoniz, but there was a man in the service bay, putting tire chains on a Buick on the lift.

"Whaddasay, Dutch?" McCoy greeted him. "What's up?"

The man looked up, first in impatience, and then with surprised recognition. He smiled, dropped the tire chains on the floor, and walked to McCoy.

"How're ya?" he asked. "Ain't that an officer's uniform?"

"Yeah," McCoy said. "Dutch, say hello to Ernie Sage."

"Hi ya, honey," Dutch said. "Pleased to meetcha."

"Hello," Ernie said.

"How's business?" McCoy asked.

"Jesus! So long as we got gas, it's fine," Dutch said. "But there's already talk about rationing. If that happens, I'll be out on my ass."

"Maybe you could get on with Budd in Philly," McCoy said. "I guess they're hiring."

"Yeah, maybe," Dutch said doubtfully. "Well, I'll think of something. What brings you to town? When'd you get to be an officer?"

"Month or so ago," McCoy said.

"Better dough, I guess?" Dutch asked.

"Yeah, but they make you buy your own meals," McCoy said.

"You didn't say what you're doing in town?"

"Just passing through," McCoy said.

"But you will come by the house? Anne-Marie would be real disappointed if you didn't."

"Just for a minute," McCoy said. "She there?"

"Where else would she be on a miserable fucking night like this?" Dutch asked. Then he remembered his manners. "Sorry, honey," he said to Ernie. "My old lady says I got a mouth like a sewer."

Ernie smiled and shook her head, accepting the apology.

She had placed Dutch. His old lady, Anne-Marie, was Ken McCoy's sister. Dutch was Ken's brother-in-law.

"Gimme a minute," Dutch said, "to lock up the cash, and then you can follow me to the house."

Anne-Marie and Dutch Schulter and their two small children lived in a row house on North Elm Street, not far from the service station. There were seven brick houses in the row, each fronted with a wooden porch. The one in front of Dutch's house sagged under his and McCoy's and Ernie's weight as they stood there while Anne-Marie came to the door.

She had one child in her arms when she opened the door, and another—with soiled diapers—was hanging on to her skirt. It looked at them with wide and somehow frightened eyes. Anne-Marie was fat, and she had lost some teeth, and she was wearing a dirty man's sweater over her dress, and her feet were in house slippers.

She was not being taken home by Ken McCoy to be shown off, Ernie Sage realized sadly, in the hope that his family would be pleased with his girl. Ken had brought her here to show her his family, sure that she would be shocked and disgusted.

Dutch went quickly into the kitchen and returned with a quart of beer.

Ernie reached for McCoy's hand, but he jerked it away.

To Dutch's embarrassment, Anne-Marie began a litany of complaints about how hard it was to make ends meet with what he could bring home from the service station. And her reaction to Ken's promotion to officer status, Ernie saw, was that it meant for her a possible source of further revenue.

In due course, Anne-Marie invited them to have something to eat—coupled with the caveat that she didn't know what was in the icebox and the implied suggestion that Ken should take them all out for dinner.

"Maybe you'd get to see Pop, if we went out to the Inn," Anne-Marie said.

"What makes you think I'd want to see Pop?" McCoy replied. "No, we gotta go. It's still snowing; they may close the roads."

"Where are you going?" Anne-Marie asked.

"Harrisburg," McCoy said. "Ernie's got to catch a train in Harrisburg."

"Going back to Philly'd be closer," Dutch said.

"Yeah, but I got to go to Harrisburg," McCoy said. He looked at Ernie, for the first time meeting her eyes. "You about ready?"

She smiled and nodded.

When they were back in the LaSalle and headed for Harrisburg, McCoy said, "A long way from Rocky Fields Farm, isn't it?"

A mental image of herself with McCoy in the bed in what her mother called the "Blue Guest Room" of Rocky Fields Farm came into Ernie's mind. The Blue Guest Room was actually an apartment, with a bedroom and sitting room about as large as Anne-Marie and Dutch Schulter's entire house.

And it didn't smell of soiled diapers and cabbage and stale beer.

"When you're trying to sell something, you should use all your arguments," Ernie said.

"What's that supposed to mean?" McCoy asked, confused.

"You asked your sister why she thought you would want to see Pop," Ernie said. "What did that mean?"

"We don't get along," McCoy said, after hesitating.

"Why not?" Ernie asked.

"Does it matter?" McCoy asked.

"Everything you do matters to me," Ernie said.

"My father is a mean sonofabitch," McCoy said. "Leave it at that."

"What about your mother?" Ernie asked.

"She's dead," McCoy said. "I thought I told you that."

"You didn't tell me what she was like," Ernie said.

"She was all right," McCoy said. "Browbeat by the Old Man is all."

"And I know about Brother Tom," Ernie said. "After he was fired by Bethlehem Steel for beating up his foreman, he joined the Marines. Is that all of the skeletons in your closet, or are we on our way to another horror show?"

There was a moment's silence, and then he chuckled. "Anyone ever tell you you're one tough lady?"

"You didn't really think I was going to say how much I liked your sister, did you?"

"I don't know," he said.

"I didn't like her," Ernie said. "There's no excuse for being dirty or having dirty children."

"That the only reason you didn't like her?"

"She was hinting that you should give her money," Ernie said. "She doesn't really like you. She just would like to use you."

"Yeah, she's always been that way," McCoy said. "I guess she gets it from Pop."

"Daughters take after their fathers," Ernie said. "I take after mine. And I think you should know that my father always gets what he goes after."

"Meaning?"

"That we're in luck. Our daughter will take after you."

There was a long moment before McCoy replied. "Ernie, I can't marry you," he said.

"There's a touch of finality to that I don't like at all," Ernie said. "What is it, another skeleton?"

"What?"

She blurted what had popped into her mind: "A wife you forgot to mention?"

He chuckled. "Christ, no," he said.

"Then what?" she asked, as a wave of relief swept through her.

"You've got a job," he said. "A career in advertising. You're going places there. What about that?"

"I'd rather be with you. You know that. And you also know that when it comes down to it, I need you more than I need a career in advertising. . . . And besides, I don't think that's what is bothering you either."

"There's a war on," McCoy said. "I'm going to be in it. It wouldn't be right to marry you."

"That's not it," Ernie said surely.

"No," he said.

"I don't give a damn about your family," Ernie said.

"That's not it, either," he said.

"Then what? What's the reason you are so evasive?"

"I can't tell you," he said. "It's got to do with the Corps."

"What's it got to do with the Corps?" she persisted.

"I can't tell you," he said.

Now, she decided, *he's telling the truth.*

"Military secret?" she asked.

"Something like that," he said.

"*What,* Ken?"

"Goddamnit, I *told* you I can't tell you!" he snapped. "Jesus, Ernie! If I could tell you I would!"

"Okay," she said, finally. "So don't tell me. But for God's sake, at least between here and Harrisburg, at least can I be your girl?"

McCoy reached across the seat and took her hand. She slid across the seat, put his arm around her shoulder, and leaned close against him.

"And when we get to Harrisburg, instead of just putting me on the train, can I be your mistress for one more night?"

"Jesus!" he said. The way he said it, she knew he meant yes.

"I'm not hard to please," Ernie said. "I'll be happy with whatever I can have, whenever I can have it."

(THREE)
Room 402
The Penn-Harris Hotel
Harrisburg, Pennsylvania
0815 Hours, 9 January 1942

Second Lieutenant Kenneth J. McCoy, USMCR, was so startled when Miss Ernestine Sage joined him behind the white cotton shower curtain that he slipped and nearly fell down.

"I hope that means you're not used to this sort of thing," Ernie said.

"I didn't mean to wake you," he said.

"I woke up the moment you ever so carefully slipped out of bed," Ernie said. "It took me a little time to work up my courage to join you."

"Oh, Jesus, Ernie, I love you," McCoy said.

"That's good," she said, and then stepped closer to him, wrapped her arms around him, and put her head against his chest. His arms tightened around her, and he kissed the top of her head. She felt his heartbeat against her ear, and then he grew erect.

She put her hand on him and pulled her face back to look up at him.

"Well," she said, "what should we do now, do you think?"

"I suppose we better dry each other off, or the sheets'll get wet," he said.

"To hell with the sheets," she said.

When she came out of the bathroom again twenty minutes later, he was nearly dressed. Everything but his uniform blouse.

When he puts the blouse on, and I put my slip and dress on, she thought, *that will be the end of it. We will close our suitcases, send for the bellboy, have breakfast, and he will put me on the train.*

"Don't look at me," Ernie said. "I'm about to cry, and I look awful when I cry."

She went to her suitcase and turned her back to him and pulled a slip over her head.

"I'm on orders to Fleet Marine Force, Pacific," McCoy said, "for further assignment as a platoon leader with one of the regiments."

She turned to look at him. "I thought you were an intelligence officer," Ernie said.

"Early next month, the Commanding General, Fleet Marine Force, Pacific," McCoy went on in a strange tone of voice, ignoring her question, "will be ordered to form the Second Separate Battalion. It will be given to Lieutenant Colonel Evans F. Carlson—"

"What's a separate battalion?" Ernie interrupted. "Honey, I don't understand these terms. . . ."

"You heard about the English Commandos?" McCoy asked. Ernie nodded. "The Corp's going to have their own. Two battalions of them."

"Oh," Ernie said, somewhat lamely. She was frightened. Her mind's eye was full of newsreels of English Commandos. There were shock troops, sent to fight against impossible odds.

"Colonel Carlson is going to recruit men from Fleet Marine Force, Pacific," McCoy went on. "He has been given authority to take anybody he wants. He's an old China Marine. I'm an old China Marine. He's probably—almost certainly—going to try to recruit me. He is not recruiting married men."

"And that's why you won't marry me?" Ernie said, suddenly furious. "So you can be a commando? And get yourself killed right away? Thanks a lot."

"Carlson's a strange man," McCoy went on, ignoring her again. "He spent some time with the Chinese Communists. There is some scuttlebutt that he's a Communist."

"Scuttlebutt?" Ernie asked.

"Gossip, rumor," McCoy explained. "And there is some more scuttlebutt that he's not playing with a full deck."

Ernie Sage had never heard the expression before, but she thought it through. Now she was confused. And still angry, she realized, when she heard her tone of voice.

"You're telling me . . . let me get this straight . . . that you're going to volunteer for the Marine commandos, which are going to be under a crazy Communist?"

"You can only volunteer after you're asked," McCoy said. "My first problem is to make sure I'm asked."

"And *then* you can go get yourself killed?"

"I didn't ask for this job," he said.

"What the *hell* are you talking about?"

"Nobody knows for sure whether Carlson is either a Communist or crazy," McCoy said.

"If there seems to be some question, why are they making him a commando?"

"When he was a captain, he was commanding officer of the Marine detachment that guards President Roosevelt at Warm Springs, Georgia. He and the President's son, who is a reserve captain, are good friends."

"Oh," Ernie said. "But what has this got to do with you? Common sense would say, stay away from all of this."

"Somebody has to find out, for sure, if he's crazy, or a Communist, or both," McCoy said.

Ernie suddenly understood. Ken McCoy had told her the military secret he wouldn't talk about in the car. But it was so incredible she needed confirmation.

"And that's you, right?"

He nodded.

"They made up a new service record for me," he said. "It says that after I graduated from Quantico, they assigned me to the Marine Barracks in Philadelphia, where I was a platoon leader in a motor transport company. There's nothing in it about me being assigned to intelligence."

"And this is what you wouldn't tell me yesterday?"

He nodded. "I'm trusting you," he said. "Even Pick doesn't know. I don't know what the hell they would do to me if they found out I told you. Or what Carlson and the nuts around him would do to me if they found out I was there to report on them."

Ernie smiled at him. "So why did you tell me?" she asked, very softly.

"I figured maybe, if you're still crazy enough to want to drive across the country with me, that is, it would be easier to put you on the train once we get there if you knew."

"That's not the answer I was looking for," Ernie said. "But it's a start."

"What answer were you looking for?" McCoy asked.

"That you love me and trust me," Ernie said.

"That, too," he said.

VIII

(ONE)
U.S. Navy Air Station
Pensacola, Florida
9 January 1942

Second Lieutenant Richard J. Stecker, USMC, was an eager-faced, slightly built young man of something less than medium height who looked even younger than his twenty-one years and who was wearing a uniform that looked every bit as fresh off the rack as it in fact was.

It was not surprising, therefore, that the Marine corporal behind the desk at the Marine Detachment, Pensacola Naval Air Station, imagined that he was dealing with your standard candy-ass second john who couldn't find his ass with both hands.

"Yes, sir?" the Marine corporal said, with exaggerated courtesy. "How may I be of assistance to the lieutenant, sir?"

"They sent me over here for billeting, Corporal," Stecker said, and laid a copy of his orders on the desk.

The corporal read the orders, and then looked at Stecker, now more convinced than ever that his original assessment was correct.

"Lieutenant," he said tolerantly, "your orders say that you are to report to Aviation Training. This is the Marine detachment. We only billet permanent party."

"An officer wearing the stripes of a full commander told me to come here," Stecker said. "Do you suppose he didn't know what he was talking about?"

The corporal looked at Stecker in surprise. It was not the sort of self-assured response he expected from a second lieutenant. The tables had been turned on him; *he* was being treated with tolerance.

And then he saw the door swing open again behind the slight, boy-faced second john, and another Marine second lieutenant walked in. Taller, larger, and older-looking than the first one, but still—very obviously—a brand-new second john.

"Excuse me, sir," the corporal said to Stecker, then: "Can I help you, Lieutenant?"

"I was sent here for billeting," Second Lieutenant Malcolm S. Pickering, USMCR, said.

"Be right with you," the corporal said, then left his desk and went into the detachment commander's officer.

"Hello," Pick said to Stecker. "My name is Pickering."

"How are you?" Stecker said, offering his hand. "Dick Stecker."

"Have you been getting the feeling that you, too, are unexpected around here?" Pickering asked. "Or, if expected, unwelcome."

"We are screwing up their system," Stecker said. "I think what's happened—"

He stopped in mid-sentence as the corporal returned with a staff sergeant, who picked up the copy of Stecker's orders and read them carefully. Then he raised his eyes to Pickering, who understood that he was being asked for a copy of his orders. He handed them over.

"You've been over to Aviation Training Reception?" the staff sergeant asked.

"And they sent us here," Stecker said.

"We only billet permanent party here, Lieutenant," the staff sergeant said.

"Far be it from me, a lowly second lieutenant," Stecker said, "aware as I am that there is nothing lower, or dumber, in the Corps, to suggest that either you or the commander who sent me here doesn't know what he's talking about, Sergeant, but that would seem to be the case, wouldn't you say?"

Pickering chuckled. Stecker looked at him and winked.

"Just a moment, please, sir," the staff sergeant said, and went back into the detachment commander's office. In a moment, a captain came out.

Pickering and Stecker came to attention. Pickering winced inwardly. He had met the captain before . . . unpleasantly, in the San Carlos Hotel. His name was Carstairs . . . Captain Mustache.

And obviously, from the way the captain looked at him, he remembered the incident, too.

"As you were," the captain said, and picked up the orders and glanced at them.

"The both of you were sent here from Aviation Reception?" the captain asked.

"Yes, sir," Pickering and Stecker said, together.

The captain looked for a number in a small, pamphlet-sized telephone book and dialed it up on the phone.

"Commander," he said, "this is Captain Carstairs at the Marine detachment. I have two second lieutenants here with orders for flight training who tell me that you sent them here for billeting."

Whatever the commander replied, it took most of a minute, after which Captain Carstairs said, "Aye, aye, sir," and hung up. Then he turned to the sergeant. "Put them somewhere, two to a room."

Finally he turned to them.

"Gentlemen," he said, "when you are settled, I would be grateful if you could spare me a few minutes of your valuable time. Say in forty-five minutes?"

"Aye, aye, sir," Stecker said, popping to attention. Pickering was a half second behind in following his lead.

Captain Carstairs walked out of the room.

The sergeant consulted a large board fixed to the wall. When Pickering looked at it, he saw it represented the assignment of rooms in the Bachelor Officers' Quarters.

"Put them in one-eleven-C," the sergeant ordered, and then he walked out of the room.

The corporal took a clipboard from a drawer in his desk and then said, "Please follow me, gentlemen."

They followed him out of the building over to what looked to be a brand-new, two-story frame barracks building. Inside he led them upstairs and down the corridor, stopping before a door.

He ceremoniously handed each of them a key.

"There is a dollar-and-a-quarter charge if you lose the key," he announced.

He waited for one of them to unlock the door; Stecker was the first to figure out what was expected of him.

Inside they found that the room was not finished; unpainted studs were exposed. Between them could be seen the tar-paper waterproofing and the electrical wiring. The floor was covered with Navy gray linoleum.

Otherwise, the place was furnished with two bunks, two desks, two upholstered armchairs, two side tables, and four lamps, one on each of the desks and side tables. A wash basin with a shelf and mirror shared one wall with a closet. A curtain, rather than a door, covered the closet entrance, but a real door led to a narrow room equipped with a water closet and a stall shower.

The corporal walked around the room, touching each piece of furniture as he announced, "One bunk, with mattress and pillow; one desk, six-drawer; one chair, wood, cloth-upholstered; one table, side, with drawer; and two lamps, reading, with bulb. There are two curtains on the closet, you each sign for one of them."

He handed Stecker the clipboard and a pencil. Stecker signed his name on the receipt for the room's furnishings and handed it back. The corporal then handed the clipboard to Pickering, who did the same.

The corporal nodded curtly at them and left them alone.

"What do you think?" Pickering asked, glancing around the room.

"I think I'm going to find someplace off base to live," Stecker said, "and leave you to wallow in all this luxury all by yourself."

"Can you do that?"

"I think I have figured out what's going on around here," Stecker said.

"Which is?"

"Let me ask you a question first," Stecker replied. "How come you're going to flight school?"

"I applied, and they sent me," Pickering said.

"You get passed over for first lieutenant?"

"Excuse me?"

"You're supposed to have two years' troop duty before they send you to flight school," Stecker said. "If you had two years' service, unless you really fucked up, you'd be a first john."

"I was commissioned just after Thanksgiving," Pickering said.

"I was commissioned second January," Stecker said.

"Last week?"

"Right."

"Quantico?"

"Actually, at West Point," Stecker said.

"I thought West Point graduated in June?"

"Not this year," Stecker said. "They needed second lieutenants, so they commissioned us right after the Christmas leave. Six months early."

"I have no idea what this conversation is all about," Pickering confessed.

"We are discussing how and where we are going to live for the next six months," Stecker said.

"That implies there is an alternative to this," Pickering said, gesturing at the bare studs and the crowded room. "One that we can *legally* take advantage of."

"I think there is," Stecker said. "Would you care to hear my assessment of the situation? I have reconnoitered the area, and carefully evaluated the enemy's probable intentions."

Pickering chuckled again. "You remind me of my buddy at Quantico," he said. "He knew his way around, too. He'd done a hitch as an enlisted man in China before they sent him to the Platoon Leader's Course."

"A China Marine," Stecker said. "I did a hitch with the Fourth Marines myself."

"Bullshit," Pickering blurted. "You're not that old."

"I was eleven when we went there," Stecker said, smugly. "I was born in the Corps. My father was the master gunnery sergeant of the Fourth Marines."

"And now he's a captain, right?" Pick demanded, suddenly. "He won the Medal of Honor in the First World War?"

"How'd you know that?" Stecker asked.

"They were sticking it to my buddy when we went through Quantico," Pick said. *"Captain Jack NMI Stecker* showed up like the avenging angel of the Lord, banged heads together, boomed, 'go and sin no more,' and left in a cloud of glory."

"That sounds like my old man," Stecker said. "He's one hell of a Marine. I'm surprised you know about the Medal, though. He never wears it."

"He wasn't wearing it," Pick said. "But I asked my buddy who he was, and he told me about him."

"How did he find out?"

"I told you, he's another China Marine," Pickering said.

"They stick together," Stecker said. "The Medal got me in the Point. Sons of guys who won it get automatic appointments to service academies if they want one. My brother went to Annapolis, but I was sick of being the little brother following him everywhere, so I went to West Point."

"How come you didn't go in the Army, then?" Pick asked.

"I will consider how recently you have been a Marine, and forgive you for asking that question," Stecker said. "The *Army?"* he added incredulously.

"You said you had reconnoitered the area?" Pickering asked, chuckling.

"Would you like the full report, or just the conclusions I have drawn?" Stecker asked.

"I think I'd better hear the full report," Pickering said. "I don't want to do anything that will get me thrown out of flight school."

"Okay," Stecker said. "It does not behoove a second lieutenant to act impulsively."

Pickering chuckled again. He liked this boy-faced character.

"The lecture begins with a history of Naval aviation," Stecker said solemnly. "Which carries us back to 1911, which was six years before my father joined the Corps, and ten years before I was born."

Pickering was aware that he was giggling.

"The flight school was established here, with two airplanes . . . and if you keep giggling, I will stop—"

"Sorry," Pickering said.

"We career Marines do not like to be giggled at by reservists," Stecker said. "Keep that in mind, Pickering."

Pickering laughed, deep in his throat.

"As I was saying," Stecker said, "flight training has continued here ever since. Pensacola is known as the Mother-in-Law of Naval Aviation."

"I heard that," Pickering said.

"You do keep interrupting, don't you?" Stecker said, in mock indignation.

Pickering threw his hands up in a gesture of surrender.

"Between wars, Pensacola trained three categories of individuals as Naval aviators," Stecker went on, seriously. "Commissioned officers of the Navy and Marines; enlisted men of the Navy and Marines; and Naval aviation cadets."

"Enlisted men? As pilots, you mean?"

"Since the question is germane, I will overlook the interruption," Stecker said. "Yes, enlisted men. There was argument at the highest levels whether or not flying airplanes required the services of splendid, well-educated, young officers such as you and me, Pickering, or whether a lot of money could be saved by having enlisted men drive them. The argument still rages. For your general fund of Naval information, there are a number of Naval aviation pilots—petty officers—in the Navy, and 'flying sergeants' in the Corps. And while we are off on this tangent, most Japanese pilots, and German pilots, and a considerable number of Royal Air Force pilots, are enlisted men."

"I didn't know that," Pickering said.

"Much as I would like to add to your obviously dismally inadequate fund of service lore by discussing the pros and cons of enlisted pilots," Stecker said, "we have to face that salty captain with the mustache in"—he looked at his watch—"thirty-two minutes, and I respectively suggest you permit me to get on with my orientation lecture."

"Please do," Pickering said, unable to contain a chuckle.

"Marine and Navy officers who applied for flight training had to have two years of service before they could come here. Since promotion to lieutenant junior grade or first lieutenant was automatic after eighteen months of service, this meant that even the junior officer flight student wore a silver bar, and there were some who were full lieutenants—or captains, USMC—and even a rare lieutenant commander or major.

"*Rank hath its privileges,* and it is presumed that anyone with two years of service as a commissioned officer does not need round-the-clock off-duty supervision. Officer flight students are given their training schedule and expected to be at the proper place at the appointed time. What they do when they are off duty is their own business."

"And that includes us?" Pickering asked.

Stecker put his index finger in front of his mouth and said, *"Ssssh!"* Then he went on: "The enlisted flight students are selected from the brightest sailors and Marines in the fleet. They pose virtually no disciplinary problems for Pensacola. And, like the officers, it is not necessary for Pensacola to teach them that a floor is a deck in the Navy, or that patting the admiral's daughter's tail is not considered nice."

A remarkably detailed image of Martha Sayre Culhane's tail popped into Pickering's mind.

"The third category, Naval aviation cadets, is a horse of an entirely different hue. In addition to teaching them how to fly, Pensacola must also teach them what will be expected of them once they graduate and are commissioned. Actually, before they come here, they have been run through an 'elimination program' at a Naval air station somewhere, during which they have been exposed to the customs and traditions of the Naval service, including close-order drill, small-arms training, and things of this nature; and, importantly, they are given enough actual flight training to determine that they were physically and intellectually capable of undergoing the complete pilot training offered at Pensacola."

"As fascinated as I am by your learned discourse," Pickering said, "so what? What has this got to with this cell they've put us in?"

"There *was* a fourth category of students," Stecker said. "Newly commissioned ensigns and second lieutenants. Such as we, Pickering. Since it came down from Mount Sinai graven on stone that ensigns and second lieutenants cannot find their ass with both hands, they were run through courses intended to teach them not to piss in the potted palms at the Officers' Club and otherwise to behave like officers and gentlemen."

" 'Was'?" Pickering asked.

"For a number of reasons, including complaints from the fleet and the Fleet Marine Force that Aviation was grabbing all the nice, bright ensigns and second lieutenants the fleet and the Fleet Marine Force needed, they stopped sending new second lieutenants here. If you want to become a Naval aviator in the future, you will have to start as an aviation cadet, or have completed two years with the fleet or with troops in the Corps."

"But *we're* here," Pickering asked, now genuinely confused.

"That's precisely the point of my lecture," Stecker said. "We have fallen somehow through the cracks; there has been a hole in the sieve. I know why I'm here . . . I qualified for aviation training last fall, before they decided to send no more second lieutenants through Pensacola. My guess is that the word didn't reach the Navy liaison officer at West Point. All he knew was that there was a note on my record jacket that I was to be sent here when I got my commission. And when I got my commission, he cut the orders. But what about you? How'd you manage to get here? You should be running around with an infantry platoon in the boondocks at Quantico, or at Camp Elliott."

Pickering decided it was the time and place to be completely truthful.

"I should be working in the Officers' Club at the Marine Barracks in Washington," he said. "That's where they sent me when I graduated from the Platoon Leader's Course at Quantico."

"Why?" Stecker asked.

"I grew up in the hotel business," Pickering said. "I worked for Foster Hotels. I know how to run a restaurant-bar operation."

"That would seem to be pretty good duty."

"I didn't join the Corps to run a bar for the brass," Pickering said.

"How'd you get out of it? And manage to get yourself sent here?"

"I had some influence," Pickering said. "With a general."

"Which general?" Stecker asked. Pickering sensed disapproval in Stecker; his eyes were no longer smiling.

"McInerney," Pickering said. "Brigadier General McInerney. You know who he is?"

"As a matter of fact, I do," Stecker said. "He and my father were in France together in the First World War. Belleau Wood."

"Then maybe my father knows your father," Pickering said. "That's where my father met McInerney. They were both corporals. McInerney got me assigned as his aide to keep me out of the Officers' Club, and then he sent me down here."

Stecker nodded absently, and Pickering sensed that he was making a decision.

"This is how I see it," Stecker said, finally. "They don't know what to do with us. The easiest thing is what they've done, nothing. Let us go to flight school, which is easier than writing letters to Headquarters, USMC, and asking what to do with us. And since there are probably just the two of us, and one of us is a regular, I don't think they're going to start up a series of 'don't piss in the potted palms' classes just for us. Because it's easier for them, they'll treat us as if we were officers sent here as first lieutenants or captains from the Fleet Marine Force."

"All of which means what?"

"Until somebody tells us we're restricted to post, as officers and gentlemen we can assume we're *not* restricted to the post. And I don't think they're going to appoint somebody to come all the way over here at midnight every night to see if we're in our bunks."

"You mean, we just go tell that corporal 'thanks but no thanks, you can keep your room'?"

"How are you fixed for money?" Stecker asked.

"All right," Pickering replied.

"If we try to check out of the BOQ," Stecker said, "Captain Mustache is likely to think it over and order us to stay here. And if he does that, it's also going to start him thinking about 'don't piss in the potted palms' lectures and sending the OD over to see if we're in bed. The whole Boy Scout routine. You follow my reasoning?"

"Yes," Pickering said.

"We'll just have to forget collecting the allowance in lieu of quarters," Stecker said.

"I understand," Pickering said.

"One other potential problem," Stecker said. "Have you got a car?"

Pickering nodded.

"Well, let's go hear what Captain Mustache has to say. He can blow this whole idea out of the water. But if he says what I think he'll say, I think we can pass the next six months in relative comfort. We started drawing flight pay the moment we reported in . . . why not spend it?"

On the walk back to the Marine detachment office, Stecker saw Pickering's Cadillac convertible.

"How'd you like to have that to use for pussy bait?" he asked.

Pickering smiled, but said nothing about the ownership of the car.

Captain Mustache put them at ease before his desk when they reported to him, but he did not offer them seats.

"I've been on the phone about you two," he said. "What you are are exceptions to the rule, pebbles that shouldn't have dropped through the sieve but did. Both of you should be running around in the boondocks at Quantico with a rifle platoon. But you're here, and it has been decided that it's easier to leave you here."

He's even using the same words that Stecker did, Pickering thought.

"When you are addressed by a superior officer," Captain Mustache said, "it is the custom to acknowledge that by saying something like 'Yes, sir.' That lets the superior officer know you're alive."

"Yes, sir," Pickering and Stecker said.

"There was a price for my curiosity," Captain Mustache said. "I presume you are familiar with the term 'in addition to his other duties'?"

"Yes, sir," Pickering and Stecker said in chorus.

"My primary duty here is as a flight instructor," Captain Mustache said. "In addition to that duty, I am the Marine detachment commander. And as of about twenty minutes ago, in addition to *that* duty, I have been given the responsibility for you two. Someone has to be responsible for your well-being and to answer for it if you misbehave. For example, if you should disturb the peace and tranquility of Pensacola by getting drunk and having yourselves thrown into jail, I will be the officer who will get you out of jail, prepare court-martial charges, and arrange to have your asses shipped out of here. Do I make my point, or will a more detailed explanation be necessary?"

"Yes, sir," they chorused.

"Which, gentlemen? Do you understand me? Or would you like a more detailed explanation?"

"I understand you, sir," Stecker said.

"You make your point, sir," Pickering said.

"Splendid," Captain Mustache said. "Getting through this course is going to be hard," he went on. "A year ago it was thirteen months. We're going to try in six months to teach you everything that was taught in that course. And what that means is that you'll have to work your asses off. And what that means is that there will be very little time for you to carouse and make whoopee. Do I make my point?"

"Yes, sir," Pickering and Stecker said in chorus.

"Splendid! I will not belabor the point," Captain Mustache said. "Take the rest of the day getting settled. If you have personal automobiles, get them registered. Take a ride around the base and orient yourselves. Report at oh-six-thirty tomorrow at Aviation Reception; the uniform is greens."

"Yes, sir," they chorused.

"That will be all, gentlemen," Captain Mustache said.

"Yes, sir, thank you, sir," the two of them said, did an about-face, and marched out of the room.

"We're home free," Stecker said. "And we have all day to find us someplace decent to live."

"I've already got a place," Pickering said, as he headed toward his car.

"Big enough for the both of us?" Stecker asked.

"Two bedrooms, a living room, a patio," Pickering said.

"On Pensacola's world-famous snow-white beaches, no doubt?"

"Actually, it's on the roof of the San Carlos Hotel," Pick said. "The penthouse."

Stecker's eyebrows rose, but he said nothing. He walked to the Cadillac, bent over, and looked inside.

"And this, it would follow, is yours?"

"Yeah," Pickering said.

"I don't suppose that it's run through your mind that a second lieutenant driving a new Cadillac convertible and living in a penthouse is going to stand out like a syphilitic pecker at a short-arm inspection?" Stecker asked.

"Seven months from now, if I don't kill myself between now and then, I will be living in a tent on some Pacific Island. At that time some people will be trying to kill me. A phrase from classic literature occurs to me: 'Live today, for tomorrow we die.' "

"You're a man after my own heart, Pickering," Stecker said. "Let's go register our cars and then go have a look at our penthouse."

"I told you, I was in the hotel business," Pickering said. "I've got a deal on the penthouse . . . a professional discount. It doesn't cost as much as you might think."

"I don't give a damn what it costs," Stecker said. "I recently came into some money."

Pickering didn't reply.

Stecker took out his wallet, and from it a folded sheet of paper. He unfolded the paper and handed it to Pickering. It was a short, typewritten note.

> *Dear Twerp,*
>
> *If at some time in the future, you should get a large check from Uncle Sam, I would be highly pissed if you did anything foolish with it . . . like putting it in the bank. Drink all the whiskey and screw all the girls while you have the chance.*
>
> *Love,*
> *Jack.*

Pickering read the short note and then looked at Stecker.

"That's from my big brother," Stecker said. "Ensign Jack NMI Stecker, Jr. Annapolis '40. He went down with the *Arizona.*"

"I'm sorry," Pickering said, very softly.

"Yeah," Stecker said. "Me, too. He was one of the good guys."

Their eyes met for a moment.

"You did say our penthouse has *two* bedrooms, didn't you?" Stecker asked. "Plus a living room? And a patio? What about a bar?"

"Two bars," Pickering said. "One in the living room, and another one, a wet bar, on the patio."

"I think that's just the sort of thing Jack had in mind," Stecker said.

IX

(ONE)
Headquarters, 2nd Joint Training Force
Camp Elliott, California
0815 Hours, 9 January 1942

Captain Jack NMI (No Middle Initial) Stecker, USMCR, was a large man, tall and erect. His uniform was perfectly tailored and sharply creased. It bore the insignia of his grade, the double silver bars of a captain, both on the epaulets of the blouse and on his shirt collar. His high-topped dress shoes were highly polished. But there were no ribbons pinned to the breast of the blouse. For what he considered good reason, Captain Stecker had put his ribbons in one of the bellows pockets of his blouse.

Captain Stecker was quite surprised that the technical sergeant functioning as Colonel Lewis T. Harris's sergeant major apparently had no idea who he was. Equally surprising was that he could not recall having ever seen the technical sergeant before.

The technical sergeant wore the diagonal hash marks of sixteen years of satisfactory enlisted service on the sleeve of his blouse. Captain Jack NMI Stecker had worn a Marine uniform since 1917. It bordered on the incredible that they had never run into each other before someplace. The Marine Corps, between major wars, was a small outfit. By the time someone had put in a couple hitches, he knew practically everybody else in the Corps.

There was supposed to be an exception to every rule, Stecker decided, and this was apparently it.

"The colonel will see you now, sir," the technical sergeant said.

"Thank you, Sergeant," Stecker said, and rose up out of his chair. He tugged on the skirt of his blouse and walked to the door with a red sign on it, lettered, "LEWIS T. HARRIS, COL, USMC, COMMANDING."

He rapped his knuckles on the jamb of Colonel Harris's door.

"Come!" Colonel Harris ordered.

Stecker marched into the office, stopped three feet from the desk, came to attention, and, looking six inches over Colonel Harris's head, barked, "Sir, Captain Stecker reporting for duty, sir."

Colonel Lewis T. Harris, a stocky, bald-headed, barrel-chested officer, looked up at Stecker without smiling. Then he stood up, walked to his office door and closed it, and returned to his desk.

"Well, you old sonofabitch, how the hell are you?" Colonel Harris asked.

"Very well, thank you, sir," Captain Stecker said.

"I'm always right, Jack," Colonel Harris said. "Some people don't understand that, but I hope this proves that to you."

"Sir?"

"If you had taken a commission when I wanted you to, you'd be sitting here with a chicken pinned to *your* collar, and I'd be reporting to you."

For the first time, Stecker met Colonel Harris's eyes.

"I'm still a little uncomfortable with the railroad tracks," he said.

"Shit!" Colonel Harris said. "Where the hell are your ribbons, Jack?"

"In my pocket," Stecker said.

"I figured," Colonel Harris said. "The Medal's something to be ashamed of, like some bare-teated dame in a hula skirt tattooed on your arm?"

"It makes people uncomfortable," Stecker said.

"Suit yourself, Jack, you can stand there at attention like some second lieutenant fresh out of Quantico, or you can sit down over there while I pour you a drink."

Stecker walked to the small couch and sat down.

"I didn't know how to handle this, Lew," he said. "So I did it by the book."

"And that's why you didn't call when you got in last night, right?" Colonel Harris said. "And spent the night on a cot in a BOQ, instead of with Marge and me?"

Captain Stecker did not reply. Colonel Harris went to a metal wall locker and took a bottle of scotch and two glasses from a shelf. He handed the glasses to Stecker and then poured an inch and a half of scotch in each glass.

He took one of the glasses and touched it against Stecker's.

"I'm glad to see you, Jack," he said. "Personally and professionally."

"Thank you," Stecker said. He started to add something, stopped, and then went on: "I was about to say, 'like old times,' but it's not, is it?"

"It never is," Harris said.

They solemnly sipped at the whiskey.

"*I* don't know how to handle this, Jack," Harris said. "I'm sorry about your boy."

"Thank you," Stecker said.

"He passed through here on his way to Pearl," Harris said. "He looked like a fine young man."

"He was," Stecker said. "Sixteenth in his class."

"I didn't hear how it happened," Harris said. "Just that it had."

"He was in the Marine detachment on the *Arizona,*" Stecker said. "I understand they got at least one of the Marine-manned antiaircraft cannon into operation before she went down. I hope Jack at least got a chance to shoot back."

"How's Elly?" Colonel Harris said.

Stecker shrugged. There was no way to put the reaction of his wife to the loss of their oldest son into words.

"And the other boy? Richard? He's in the class of 'forty-two at West Point, right?"

"He was supposed to be," Stecker said.

"Supposed to be?" Harris asked.

"They commissioned them early," Stecker said. "Dick reported to Pensacola today. Or he reports tomorrow. For aviation training."

"You don't sound pleased."

"I don't know if I am or not," Stecker said. "Elly's afraid of airplanes."

"Hell, so am I," Harris said.

Stecker looked at him and smiled. "The only thing in the world you're afraid of is your wife," he said.

"And airplanes," Harris said. "I went to Pensacola in 'thirty, when I came back from Haiti. I did fine until they actually put me in the front seat of an airplane and told me to drive. I broke out in a cold sweat and was so scared I couldn't find my ass with both hands. Once I tilted the wings, I really didn't know which way was up. Somewhere in my jacket is a remark that says 'this officer is wholly unsuited for aviation duty.' "

"I didn't know you tried it," Stecker said.

"I was afraid when I went," Harris said. "I knew I was no Charles Lindbergh. But I was a brand-new captain with three kids, and I needed the flight pay. If your boy can't hack it, Jack, he'll find out in a hurry. Nothing to be embarrassed about if he can't. Some people are meant to soar like birds, and others, like you and me, to muck around in the mud."

Stecker chuckled.

"You know Evans Carlson, Jack?" Colonel Harris asked.

The question was asked lightly, but Stecker sensed that Harris was not playing auld lang syne.

"Sure," Stecker replied.

"China?" Harris pursued.

"I was on the rifle team with him," Stecker said.

"I forgot about that," Harris said. "You're one of those who thinks the Garand's the answer to a maiden's prayer."

The U.S. Rifle, Caliber .30, M1, a self-loading weapon fed by an eight-round en bloc clip, was invented by John C. Garand, a civilian employee of the Springfield Arsenal. It was adopted as standard for the U.S. military in 1937 to replace the U.S. Rifle, Caliber .30, M1903, the Springfield, a bolt-operated rifle with an integral five-shot magazine.

"I don't know about a 'maiden's prayer,' " Stecker said. "But it's a fine weapon. It's a better weapon than the Springfield."

"I'm surprised to hear you say that," Harris said.

"You ever fire it?" Stecker asked.

"Familiarization," Harris said. "I had trouble keeping it on the target. I rarely got close to the black." (The eight, nine, and ten scoring rings of the standard rifle target are printed in black; the "bull's-eye.")

"I was on the troop test at Benning," Stecker said. (The U.S. Army Infantry Center was at Fort Benning, Georgia.) "And I had an issue piece out of the box. I had no trouble making expert with it. More important, neither did twelve kids fresh from Parris Island."

Harris grunted. A lesser man, he thought, would have quickly detected his disapproval of the Garand rifle and deferred, as is appropriate for a captain, to the judgment of a colonel. But Jack NMI Stecker, until recently Master Gunnery Sergeant Stecker, was not a lesser man. He spoke his mind.

"I've got one," Stecker went on, "that was worked over by an Army ordnance sergeant at Benning. It shoots into an inch and a half at two hundred yards."

"I've got a Springfield that'll do that," Harris argued.

"Your Springfield won't put eight shots in the black at three hundred yards as fast as you can pull the trigger," Stecker said.

"You're like a reformed drunk, Jack," Harris said. "Nothing worse than a reformed drunk. They have seen the goddamn light."

"Sorry," Stecker said.

"Maybe I'm wrong," Harris said. "I've been wrong before."

"The last time was May 13, 1937, right?" Stecker said.

Harris laughed, heartily, deep in his chest. "Moot point, anyway," he said. "This war'll be over long before the goddamned Army gets around to giving your wonderful Garand to the Corps."

"Probably," Stecker agreed, chuckling. The Marine Corps received all of its small arms through the Ordnance Corps of the U.S. Army. It was accepted as a fact of life that the Army supplied the Corps only after its own needs, real and perceived, were satisfied.

"We were talking about Evans Carlson," Harris said. "You get along with him all right, Jack?"

"Isn't *that* a moot point? I heard he resigned a couple of years ago. Actually, what I heard is that he was asked to resign. I heard he went Asiatic and annoyed some very important people."

"I don't know about that, but he's back. He applied for a reserve commission as a major, and they gave it to him. And then they promoted him. He knows some very important people."

"I hadn't heard that," Stecker said, thoughtfully. "Well, hell, why not? He's a good Marine. And here I sit wearing captain's bars."

"You didn't answer my question, Jack," Colonel Harris said.

"Do I get along with him? Sure. Is he here?"

Colonel Harris did not reply to the question directly.

"From this point, what I tell you is between us girls, Jack. I don't want it repeated."

"Yes, sir," Stecker said.

"Within the next couple of weeks, maybe the next month, the Corps is going to establish two separate battalions. One of them here. The one here will be commanded by Lieutenant Colonel Carlson."

"What do you mean, separate battalions? To do what?"

"Commando battalions," Harris said.

"I'm lost," Stecker confessed.

"A reserve captain wrote a Commandant a letter," Harris said, "in which he recommended the establishment of Marine units to do what the English Commandos do. Raids by sea on hostile shores."

"A reserve *captain* wrote the Commandant?" Stecker asked, incredulously.

"And the Commandant has decided to go along," Harris said.

Stecker didn't reply, but there was wonderment and disbelief all over his face.

"The captain who wrote the letter has friends in high places," Harris said.

"He must," Stecker said.

"His name is Roosevelt," Colonel Harris said.

"*Captain* Roosevelt," Stecker said, suddenly understanding.

"You know him?"

"I saw him a couple of times at Quantico," Stecker said. "I don't know him."

"Captain James Roosevelt will be the executive officer of the Second Separate Battalion, under Lieutenant Colonel Carlson, when it is activated," Harris said.

Stecker's eyebrows rose but he said nothing.

"I have been directed to do whatever can be done to grease the ways for Colonel Carlson and his separate battalion. He will have the authority to recruit for his battalion anywhere within the Corps. And simultaneously he will be able to transfer out from his battalion anybody he doesn't want. He will have the authority to equip and arm his battalion as he sees fit, and funds will be provided to purchase whatever he wants that can't be found in the warehouse. If there is a conflict between Carlson's battalion and some other unit for equipment, or the use of training facilities, Carlson will get what he thinks he needs. You getting the picture, Jack?"

"Yes, sir."

"Good, because as of this minute, it's your job to take care of Colonel Carlson and his separate battalion for me."

"I had hoped to get a company," Stecker said.

"No way, Jack," Harris said. "Even without Carlson, there would be no company for you. We have company commanders. We're damned short of people like you. Once you get Carlson formed and trained and he's gone from here, I've got a spot for you in S-Three. If you handle Carlson right, there'll probably be a major's leaf to go with it."

"And if not?"

"Carlson has to be handled right, period," Colonel Harris said. "Or you and me will both be doing things we won't like."

Stecker frowned thoughtfully. Finally he said, "Aye, aye, sir."

"There's more, Jack," Colonel Harris said. "And if this goes outside the walls of this room, we're both in trouble."

"I understand," Stecker said.

"Carlson not only wants to have a commando outfit, he has some very strange ideas about how it should be run."

"That I don't understand," Stecker said. "How do you mean, 'run'?"

"Well, for one thing, the original proposal would do away with the rank structure. Instead of officers and noncoms and privates, there would be 'leaders' and 'fighters.' There would be no officers' mess. Everybody would 'cooperate.' "

"You're serious," Stecker said, after a moment. "That's crazy."

"Odd that you should use that word," Harris said, dryly. "There are some very important people who think that Carlson is crazy."

"You mean *really* crazy, don't you?"

Harris nodded. "And the same people think that he may have been turned into a Communist," he added.

"Then why are they giving him a battalion?"

"Because the President of the United States has got a commando bee up his ass, and he thinks Carlson is the man to come up with American commandos," Harris said.

He waited for that to sink in, and then went on: "The Commandant is worried about three things, Jack. First and foremost, that Carlson has gone off the deep end, and after he's picked the cream of the crop for his Raiders, he'll get a bunch of them wiped out on some crazy operation. Or worse: that he'll be successful on a mission, and the entire Corps will be converted to the U.S. Commandos."

"What's wrong with that?" Stecker asked, thoughtfully. "We do what I understand the commandos do, invest hostile enemy shores."

"The British Commandos have neither aviation nor artillery," Harris said. "If the Marine Corps is turned into the U.S. Commandos, there would be no need for the Corps to have either aviation or artillery either. And after the war, Jack? What would the Corps become? A regiment, maybe two, of Commandos."

"I hadn't thought about that," Stecker admitted.

"The Commandant has had this commando idea shoved down his throat," Harris said. "And like the good Marine he is, he has said 'aye, aye, sir,' and will do his best to carry out his orders. There are some other people, close to the Commandant, who are not so sure they should go along with it."

"I don't understand that," Stecker said. "What do you mean, not go along with it?"

"There's some interesting scuttlebutt that Intelligence is going to get an officer assigned to Carlson with the job of coming up with proof that he is a Communist, or crazy, or preferably both. Proof that they could hand the Commandant, proof that he could take to the President."

"Jesus!"

"Jack," Harris said carefully. "If something out of the ordinary, something you believe would be really harmful to the Corps, comes to your attention when you are dealing with Colonel Carlson, I expect you to bring it to my attention. But don't misunderstand me. I want you to do the best job you can in supporting him."

Stecker met his eyes. After a moment, he said, almost sadly, "Aye, aye, sir."

(TWO)
The USS *Pickerel*
178 Degrees 35 Minutes West Longitude
21 Degrees 20 Minutes North Latitude
0405 Hours, 14 January 1942

Captain Edward J. Banning, USMC, awake in his bunk in the captain's cabin of the *Pickerel,* knew that it was a few minutes after 0400. He had heard the sounds of the watch changing, and that happened at precisely 0400.

He also knew that it was Wednesday, 14 January.

Not quite six hours before, the *Pickerel* had crossed the international date line; and Thursday, 15 January, had become Wednesday, 14 January, once again. From 180 degrees (which was both west and east longitude, exactly halfway around the world from Greenwich, England, which was at 0 degrees, east and west longitude), it was 22 degrees and some seconds—say 675 nautical miles—to the U.S. Navy Base at Pearl Harbor, on the Island of Oahu, Territory of Hawaii.

Captain Edward T. Banning, USMC, was aware that there was a very good chance that this Wednesday, 14 January 1942, would be the last day in his life. After a good deal of what he believed was careful, unemotional thought, he had decided that he did not want to continue living if that meant he had to live blind. And after reaching that decision, he had calmly concluded that today was the day he should do what had to be done.

He would remove the bandages from his eyes, open his lids, and if he saw nothing but black, he would use the .45 on himself.

With a little luck and a lot of careful planning, this could be accomplished with a minimum of disruption to anyone else's life. And that was important—not to make a spectacle of himself. It would be much better to go out here and now with a bullet fired through the roof of the mouth into the brain and to be buried immediately at sea than it would be, say, to jump out of a window in a VA hospital somewhere, or to swallow a handful of pills. A .45 pistol was the answer, and today was the day.

The *Pickerel* was sailing on the surface now, making sixteen or seventeen knots, and it would thus arrive at Pearl Harbor sometime between thirty-nine and forty-two hours from the time it had crossed the international date line.

Captain Banning had done the arithmetic in his head. Not without effort, for without seeming unduly curious, it was necessary to acquire the data on which to base his calculations from Captain Red MacGregor and others. And then he had to do the work in his head. There was plenty of time to do it, of course, which was fortunate, for Banning had learned that he was far less apt with mental arithmetic than he would have believed.

But he was reasonably sure that the *Pickerel* would be off Pearl Harbor waiting for the antisubmarine nets across the mouth of the harbor to be opened sometime between 1900 and 2200 hours on 16 January 1942. In other words, less than two full days from now. The antisubmarine nets would probably not be opened at night, which meant that the *Pickerel* would not actually be able to sail into Pearl until first light on 17 January.

From his observations of Captain Red MacGregor (Banning was aware of the incongruity of a blind man making observations, but he could think of no more accurate word), he had concluded that the closer the *Pickerel* came to Pearl, the more according to the book MacGregor would run his command.

Earlier, after Banning had very carefully asked if it would be possible for the blind men aboard to be given some fresh air, MacGregor had had no problem breaking the rules for him. This meant allowing them up on the conning tower, where there was really no room for them, and where they would not only be in the way, but would pose a hazard if a crash dive was necessary.

When Banning asked him, shortly after they had entered the Philippine Sea at the upper tip of Luzon, MacGregor had considered the request and denied it.

"A little later, Ed," he said then. "Maybe when we get past the Marianas."

MacGregor had meant what he said. Two days later, when Banning had still been wondering if the time was ripe to ask again, the chief of the boat had come to him, and with rather touching formality said, "The captain's compliments, sir, and will you join him on the bridge?"

Getting up the ladders to the conning tower hadn't been as difficult as Banning had thought it would be.

And the smell of the fresh salt water had been delightful after breathing nothing but the smell of unwashed bodies, paint, and diesel fuel.

Thereafter, the blind men aboard were permitted to get a little air on the conning tower once a day, for half-hour periods. And even though the time they spent on the conning tower cut into the time set aside for that for the crew of the *Pickerel,* there were no complaints. Only a real sonofabitch would deny blind men whatever pleasure they could find.

After this had been going on awhile, Captain Red MacGregor noticed (as Banning hoped that he would; the manipulation shamed him, but he considered it necessary) that Banning himself never came to the conning tower, and he asked him about it.

"I think my 'troops' need it more than I do," Banning said.

MacGregor snorted at the time, but said nothing. At that evening's meal, however, he announced, "Henceforth, Captain Banning has the privilege of the bridge."

What that meant was that Banning could go to the conning tower whenever he wished. He could then ask for permission to "come onto the bridge." If there was no good reason for him not to, permission was more or less automatic.

In practice, others with the "privilege of the bridge" (the officers and chief petty officers) quickly left the bridge to make room for Banning when he put his head through the hatch and asked for permission.

Banning was careful not to abuse his privilege. He went to the conning tower often, but never stayed long. His intent (and he was sure he succeeded) was to make his presence there routine. The officers and crew thus grew used to him coming to the bridge at all hours. And once there he kept out of the way, cleared his lungs, sometimes accepted a cigarette, and then went quickly below again.

Banning was sure, however, that as the *Pickerel* came closer to Pearl, MacGregor would tighten his command, and conning-tower privileges would be revoked. Maybe not for him, but he couldn't take the chance.

Now was the time. Twenty-four hours later the opportunity would more than likely be gone.

Banning's "observation" of Captain Red MacGregor had taught him that MacGregor woke up whenever the watch was changed. Just for a minute or two, but he was awake.

And he had awakened when the watch had changed to 0400. He hadn't moved or gotten out of his bunk, but his breathing pattern had changed, and Banning knew that he was awake and waiting to see if something would require his attention. Only when he was satisfied things were going as they should would he go back to sleep.

Banning had acquired a good deal of admiration for Red MacGregor. He was a fine officer. He hoped that what he had in mind would not appear as a derogatory remark in MacGregor's service jacket. That had been an important consideration while he was making his plans. It was unfortunate that he could not think of anything that would get MacGregor completely off the hook. He could only hope that in the circumstances it would not be a really important black mark against him.

Banning, as stealthily as he could, slipped down from the narrow upper bunk and lowered himself carefully to the deck.

He sensed that he had not been as stealthy as he had hoped, even before MacGregor spoke.

"You all right, Ed?"

"I'm going to take a piss and then get a breath of air," Banning replied, hoping that there was nothing in his voice that would betray him to MacGregor. Banning had "observed" that MacGregor, like most good commanders, was both sensitive and intuitive.

"We crossed the date line just after twenty-two-hundred," MacGregor said. "It's yesterday."

"The chief of the boat told me," Banning replied, as he felt around for the drawer in which he knew he could find freshly washed khakis.

"I had a hell of a time with that at the academy," MacGregor said. "My mind just doesn't accept that you can lose, or gain, a day just because somebody drew a line on a chart."

Banning chuckled.

He heard sounds he interpreted as the kinds MacGregor would make as he rolled over in his bunk.

Banning put on his shirt, and then his trousers, and finally socks and shoes. He did so slowly, both because he wanted to make sure that he had the right button in the right hole, and because he wanted to give MacGregor time to go back to sleep.

When he had finished tying his shoes, he felt behind him on the bulkhead for the gray metal locker MacGregor had turned over to him. He opened it as quietly as he could and then took from it a khaki-colored rubber-lined canvas foul-weather jacket. Sometimes the wind carried spray as high as the conning tower, even in relatively calm seas.

When he had the jacket on and had finished closing its metal hooks, Banning took something else from his closet where it had been concealed under a stack of skivvy shirts. He jammed it quickly in his waistband, and then pulled the foul-weather jacket down over it.

He went to the hatch and felt his way through it, and then he moved down the passageway to the head. He sensed that two crew members had flattened themselves against the sides of the passageway to make room for him to pass, but neither of them spoke to him.

He found the door to the head, and then the doorknob. He pushed down on it, and it moved. This meant the head was unoccupied. If the head was in use, the door handle would not move.

He went inside and threw the latch, and then sat down on the head. He pulled the foul-weather jacket out of the way, and then took the Colt .45 automatic from his waistband.

Banning had thought this through, too, very carefully, going over it again and again in his mind. If he actually had to do the thing, he had to do it right. That meant very quickly pulling the pistol out from under the jacket and placing the muzzle into his mouth, so that even if someone on the conning tower bridge did happen to be looking in his direction, they wouldn't have time to stop him. He thought that even if someone did happen to be looking at him when he took the Colt out, they would be so astonished that there would be a couple of seconds' delay before they would try to take it away from him. A couple of seconds would be all he needed.

That was presuming there was a cartridge in the chamber when he pulled the trigger. If the firing pin flew forward into an empty chamber, there would be no time to take the pistol out of his mouth and work the action again. If it didn't fire the first time, that would be it. They would take the pistol away from him with whatever force was necessary, and they'd never take their eyes off him until they docked at Pearl. After that he would be turned over to the men in white coats from the psychiatric ward at the Naval hospital.

There weren't that many ways to end your life aboard a submarine at sea. You couldn't just jump over the side, for example. The bulkheads on the conning tower were almost shoulder high and would be difficult to climb over even if you could see. And even if he managed to jump off the conning tower without being stopped, then what? He would probably break his leg on the fall to the deck, or else knock himself out. The best he could hope for in that circumstance would be to be able to scurry across the deck like a crippled crab and bounce off the hull into the sea, then try to swim away from the hull before the suction of the propellers sucked him down to where the blades could slice him up.

It would also be a dirty trick on Red MacGregor to blow his brains all over his cabin. Or to do it in the head where, every time one of the *Pickerel*'s crew took a leak, he would remind himself that this was where that poor, blind jarhead captain blew his brains out.

The place to do it was on the conning tower. His brains would be blown off the conning tower, and there would only be a little blood on the conning-tower deck when the body fell, easily washed away.

After Banning did it, the captain would be called to the bridge. He would probably be thoroughly pissed at the officer of the deck for not seeing what the poor, crazy, blind jarhead captain had been up to, and for not stopping it. But once that passed, MacGregor would start to think clearly, like the good commander he was. There would be no point in getting the crew upset. Then someone would be sent below for a mattress cover and some line, and something heavy (probably a couple of shells for the five-inch cannon), and the body would be tied into the mattress cover with the shells, and then lowered to the deck.

MacGregor would probably even go so far as ordering a flag placed over the mattress cover (it would be tied to the deck so it wouldn't be lost). And more than likely, he would read the Episcopal service for the burial of the dead at sea.

And then he would order the *Pickerel* submerged.

There would be a note in the log, *Captain Edward J. Banning, USMC, buried at sea 0500, 14 January 1942,* and the coordinates.

There was a school of thought, of course, that felt that suicide was the coward's way out of a tough situation. Banning had spent much time pondering that line of reasoning, and he had come to the conclusion that in his case, it just didn't wash.

The main pain in the ass for him in being blind had not turned out to be the inconvenience. The inconveniences—the difficulties of just living without sight: spilling food all over his chin, not knowing if he had been able to properly wipe his ass, the constant bumping painfully into things—he could probably get used to, in time.

What was wrong with being blind was that it gave you so much time to think. That was really driving him crazy.

Thinking about Ludmilla, for instance.

Ludmilla, "Milla," was the only woman he had ever loved in his life. And he had left her on the wharf in Shanghai when he'd been flown to Cavite with the advance party of the 4th Marines. The Japs were in Shanghai now, and it was entirely possible that Milla had already done to herself what he was going to do if it was black when he took the bandages off.

He knew that she had thought about it. Once in bed, she had told him that she had been close to it before she met him, that she just didn't think she had it in her to become a whore, and that death wasn't all that frightening to her. Certainly, she would have thought of that again when the Japanese drove down the Bund. There weren't very many options open to a White Russian woman in Shanghai besides turning herself into a whore for some Japanese officer. Milla still thought seriously about such things as honor and pride and shame, and she was very likely to have concluded that death was far preferable to the dishonor of being a Japanese whore.

And Milla had been around the block. She'd already gone through one revolution, and what she had told him about what she had experienced in St. Petersburg—the complete breakdown of society as she had known it—couldn't have been much different from what the breakdown of society in Shanghai must have been once the Japanese had come in.

Milla was practical. She would have understood that the chances of her ever again getting to be with her husband of eighteen hours—her American, Marine officer husband, gone off to fight what looked to be a losing war—were practically nil.

And she would have concluded that the eleven good months that they had had together before they had made it legal had been a brief happy interval in a miserable, frightening life.

And she didn't know, of course, that he was blind.

"The trauma to your optical nerves, Captain, is one of those things, I'm afraid, we don't know a hell of a lot about. Obviously, the trauma was of such severity to cause loss of sight, but on the other hand, it isn't as if anything in there had been severed or destroyed, in which case there would be no hope. I really can't offer an opinion whether your impaired condition will in time pass, or whether the damage is permanent. We just don't have the experience in this area. I would not be surprised, either way. In any event, we should have some indication in two or three weeks."

If the sonofabitch thought there was any real chance the "impaired condition" would "in time pass," they would not have sent him out on the *Pickerel*. The 4th Marines had been given the responsibility for defending Fortress Corregidor. They needed the regimental intelligence officer, presuming of course that he could see.

He had been sent out, with the colonel's permission, on the *Pickerel*. Q.E.D.

Banning knew what would come next. They would get him stateside, most likely to the Naval hospital at San Diego. And there they would do whatever was humanly possible for him. Following which he would be handed a white cane, his retirement orders, and a one-hundred-percent disability pension. They would then turn him over to the Veterans Administration until he learned how to maneuver with the white cane, or maybe with a seeing-eye dog.

He could handle that, too, if he didn't have all this time to think about Milla and wonder what she was doing.

The final conclusion he had drawn was that he could live without Milla, or the Corps, or his sight; but he could not give up all three at once.

If he could see when he went to the conning tower and took the bandage off, then there was something. He wouldn't be with the regiment, but he would be what he had trained all of his adult life to be, a serving Marine officer in a war. Which meant he could do *something* about Milla, too—though he had no idea how.

Banning pressed the checkered round steel magazine-release button on the Colt .45 automatic. The magazine slipped out of the butt into his hand. He laid the pistol carefully on his lap, then thumped the cartridges from the magazine, putting them one at time into the side pocket of the canvas foul-weather jacket. There were seven.

He loaded one cartridge back into the magazine, slipped the magazine into the pistol until he felt it click in place, and then worked the action. He pulled the slide back all the way, and then, still hanging on to it, let the spring move it forward into the battery.

He didn't think it had completely chambered the cartridge. He ran his thumb over the rear of the pistol where the slide mated with the frame. It was uneven. He pushed on the slide and it clicked into place.

He put the safety on and then stood up and put the pistol back in his waistband and pulled the foul-weather jacket to cover it.

Banning made his way very carefully from the head to the conning-tower ladder. When his hand found it, he gripped it firmly. He had learned that if there was someone on the ladder, there would be vibrations on the steel framework.

There were none, and he climbed the ladder into the upper compartment.

"Good morning, sir," someone said to him.

"Morning," Banning replied, smiling, as he felt for the ladder to the conning-tower bridge.

This time, there were vibrations in the steel frame. Banning stood to one side of the ladder.

"Sorry, Captain," a voice tinged with embarrassment said in his ear. "I would have—" The kid's breath smelled of peppermint chewing gum.

"It's all right, son," Banning said, reassuringly. He had recognized the voice as one of the enlisted men.

He moved in front of the ladder and went up it, until his head was through the hatch and he could smell the fresh salt air.

"Permission to come on the bridge, sir?" he asked.

"Come ahead, Captain," a voice he recognized as belonging to one of the young JG's said.

Banning went through the hatch, got to his feet, and put his hand out in search of the after bulkhead. When his fingers touched it, he went to it, turned and rested his back against it, and took a deep breath of the fresh, clean air.

"Good morning," Banning said.

Three voices replied. They were in front of him. With a little bit of luck, they would be looking forward, too, when the time came.

Banning took off his fore-and-aft cap and put it in the pocket of his foul-weather jacket.

Then he took a razor blade from his trousers pocket, got a good grip on it, and moved the hand that held it to the back of his head.

Sawing through the gauze bandage and the adhesive tape that held it in place was easier than he thought it would be. He felt he gauze slip off and fall across his face. He caught it, balled it up in his hand, and then reached his hand over the bulkhead and dropped it.

There now remained two pads of gauze, liberally greased with petroleum jelly, over his closed eyelids. The idea, the surgeon had told him, was to keep all light from the optic nerves, in the hope this might facilitate natural recovery from the trauma to the nerves.

Once a day the *Pickerel*'s pharmacist mate had replaced the Vaseline-soaked pads, and then wrapped Banning's head with gauze and adhesive tape to keep them in place.

Banning put both hands to his eyes and jerked the pads away.

He felt a cold chill and heard himself grunt.

The pads were gone, and there was no light.

He was blind.

He felt faint, weak in his knees, and shivered.

All I have to do is put my hands over my face and go below and say I must have caught the bandage on something, and jerked it off.

Fuck it! Don't turn chicken at the last minute. You took a chance and you lost.

He put his hand under the foul-weather jacket and found the butt of the .45 Colt automatic. Following the U.S. Marine Corps' near-sacred tradition that one does not put one's finger on the trigger of a loaded firearm until one is prepared to fire, he took it in his hand, the trigger finger extended along the slide rather than on the trigger, and flicked the safety off.

Then he put his finger on the trigger.

Our Father Who art in Heaven, give me the balls to go through with this . . .

Banning became aware that his eyelids were squinted closed, as they were habitually whenever the Vaseline-soaked pads were removed.

He forced them open.

Shit! Nothing. Nothing more, anyway, than a glow to one side. If I'm not blind, I'm the next fucking thing to it.

Our Father Who art in—

That's the fucking luminous dial of a wristwatch! That's what that glow is!

Captain Banning removed his finger from the trigger of his pistol.

Captain Banning could now make out the upper edge of the forward bulkhead, and rising above that three vague but unmistakable silhouettes: the officer of the deck, the talker, and somebody else, another officer, with binoculars to his eyes.

Captain Banning snapped the safety of the Colt back on, took his hand from under the foul-weather jacket, and then leaned, weak and faint, against the bulkhead.

He had a sudden terrible necessity to void his bladder.

"Permission to leave the bridge, sir?"

"Granted," the officer of the deck said automatically, and then, remembering that Banning had only minutes before come onto the bridge, asked, "Is there something wrong, Captain Banning?"

"No, thank you," Banning said. "Everything's just fine."

The light inside the conning tower hurt his eyes. He felt tears, and he closed them. He knew how to get down the ladder with his eyes closed.

With a little luck, he would go down both ladders and get to the head before his bladder let go and he pissed his pants. And then he would go to the captain's cabin and wake Red MacGregor and tell him. With a little more luck, he would be able to get the pistol back into the cabinet before MacGregor woke up.

(ONE)
San Francisco, California
0915 Hours, 14 January 1942

The office of the chairman of the board of Pacific & Far East Shipping, Inc., occupied the southwest corner of the top (tenth) floor of the P&FE Building. Its tinted plate-glass windows overlooked the harbor and the bridge; and an eight-by-twelve-foot map of the world was mounted on one wall. Every morning at six A.M., just before he went off duty, the night operations manager came up from the third floor and laid a copy of the more important overnight communications on the huge, near-antique (which is to say post-1800) mahogany desk of the chairman of the board. Then he went to the map and moved small devices on it.

The devices, mounted on magnets, were models of the vessels of Pacific & Far East Shipping. They represented tankers, bulk carriers, passenger liners, and freighters of all sizes. There were seventy-two of them, and they were arranged on the map to correspond with their last-reported position around the world. Just over a month before, there had been eighty-one ship models scattered around the map.

Now nine models—representing six small interisland freighters ranging in size from 11,600 to 23,500 tons, two identical 39,400-ton freighters, and one 35,000-ton tanker—were arranged in the lower left-hand corner of the map as if anchored together in the Indian Ocean off Australia. Eight of them had been lost to Japanese submarines. The ninth, the tanker *Pacific Virtue,* had been offloading aviation gasoline at Pearl Harbor when the Japanese struck.

In a mahogany gimbal mount near Fleming Pickering's desk, there was a globe, five feet in diameter, crafted in the 1860s. And two glass cases holding large, exquisitely detailed ship models had been placed against the wall behind the desk. One of the models was of the clipper ship *Pacific Princess* (Hezikiah Fleming, Master), which had held the San Francisco–Shanghai speed record in her day; and the second was of the 51,000-ton *Pacific Princess,* a sleek passenger ship that was the present speed-record holder for the same run.

According to the wall map, the *Pacific Princess* was sailing alone somewhere between Brisbane and San Francisco, trusting in her maximum speed of 33.5 knots to escape Japanese torpedos.

Fleming Pickering looked up from his desk with mingled annoyance and curiosity when he heard the sound of high heels on the small patches of parquet floor exposed here and there beneath fine antique (seventeenth-century) Oriental rugs. He knew it was not his secretary, the only person permitted to come into his office unannounced when he was there. Mrs. Florian wore rubber heels. All the facts considered, his visitor had to be either his wife or a very brazen total stranger.

It was his wife.

After twenty-four years of marriage, Fleming Pickering was still of the belief that he was married to one of the world's most beautiful women. And she was one of the smartest, too. Smart enough to avoid waging a losing battle against growing older than thirty. Her hair was silver, and if she was wearing makeup (which seemed likely), it didn't appear to be layered on her face with a shovel.

She sat down in one of the chairs facing his desk and crossed her legs, giving him a quick glance of thigh and black petticoat.

" 'Come into my parlor,' the spider leered at the fly," Fleming Pickering said. "To what do I owe the honor?"

"God!" Patricia Foster Pickering groaned.

"Really?" Flem Pickering joked. "The clouds opened, and a suitably divine voice boomed, *'Go to thy husband!'?"*

She shook her head, but had to chuckle, even though she didn't want to under the circumstances.

"I hate to bother you," Patricia Pickering said. "You know I wouldn't come here unless—"

"Don't be silly," he said. "Would you like some coffee?"

"I would really like a double martini," she said.

"That bad, huh?" he said.

"I'll settle for the coffee," Patricia Pickering said.

Fleming Pickering tapped three times with his toe on a switch under his desk. It was a code message to Mrs. Florian. One tap summoned her. Two taps meant *"get this idiot out of here by whatever means necessary,"* and three meant *"deliver coffee."*

"I just had a call from Ernie Sage," Patricia Pickering said.

"And? What did he want?"

"Little Ernie," she corrected him.

"And what did *she* want?"

"She's out here. In San Diego."

He looked at her curiously, waiting for her to go on.

"She wanted me to get a check cashed for her," Patricia said. "And to see if I knew someone in Diego who could find her someplace to stay."

"I hate to tell you this, honey," he said. "But the way you're presenting this, it's not coming across as a serious problem."

"She's out here with McCoy," Patricia said. "You remember him? Pick's friend from Quantico? You met him."

"I remember him very well," Flem said. "What did they do, elope?"

"That's part of the problem," she said. "No. They are not married."

"A real Marine, that boy," Flem said. "I could tell the moment I saw him."

"Flem, this is not funny," Patricia said.

"Well, it's not the end of the world, either," he said. "She is not the first nice young woman in history to go to bed with a Marine before their union was solemnized before God and the world."

She glared at him. And her face colored. "That was a cheap shot, damn you!" she said. But she smiled.

"There's something about a Marine, you know," Flem Pickering went on. "My response to this situation is that I hope whatever it is Marines have will work for Pick, too. That he gets somebody as nice as Ernie. Let her who is without sin cast the first stone."

"Well, thanks a lot," she snapped.

"Honey, this is none of our business," Flem said.

Mrs. Florian came into the office, pushing a serving cart with a silver coffee service on it.

"I like your dress, Mrs. Pickering," she said.

"I will not tell you it's an old rag I found in the back of my closet," Patricia said. "I bought it yesterday, and made them alter it right away. Surprising absolutely no one, Guess Who hasn't seemed to notice."

"The way to catch my attention is to come in here not wearing a dress," Flem said.

"I'd sock him for that," Mrs. Florian said, and left the office.

"It *is* our business, Flem," Patricia said.

"How do you figure that?"

"Elaine is my best friend," Patricia said. "And Ernie's the closest thing I have to a daughter."

"Does Elaine know about this?" he asked.

"No. I asked Ernie, and she told me she was going to call her. And she went on to ask me to please not say anything until she works up the courage to do it."

"Then don't say anything," he said.

"I think I'm going to go to Diego and talk like a Dutch aunt to her," Patricia said.

"All that would do would be to piss her off," Flem said.

"I love your language," Patricia snapped.

"It caught your attention, didn't it?" he replied, unrepentant.

She met his eyes, raised her eyebrows, and then shifted her gaze and sat up in the chair to pour coffee. She handed him a cup and then slumped back in her chair, holding her cup with both hands.

"I think it's entirely possible that Ernie may need a friend," Flem said. "If she thinks you're going to say exactly the same thing her mother would say, she won't come to you."

She looked at him again but said nothing.

"I seem to recall when I was a handsome young Marine just home from France, that your own mother had a long talk with you about not letting me get you alone—in case I tried to kiss you. I gather she was afraid I'd give you trench mouth."

"I never should have told you that," Patricia said.

"You remember where you told me?" he asked.

"Damn you!" she said.

"In a ne'er-to-be-forgotten bed in the Coronado Beach Hotel in San Diego."

"All right," she said, just a little sharply.

"Never did get trench mouth, did you?" he asked. "And neither will Ernie. And you can no more talk her out of what she has decided to do than your mother could talk you out of seducing me."

"You bastard!" she said. "*Me* seducing you!"

But their eyes met and she smiled.

"So what do we do, Flem?" she asked after a moment.

"That will depend on what you've already done," he said.

"I told her to go to the San Diego office, and we'd arrange for her to cash a check."

"That's all?"

"That's all," she said.

Fleming Pickering picked up one of the three telephones on his desk and told the operator to patch him through to San Diego.

When J. Charles Ansley, General Manager, San Diego Operations, Pacific & Far East Shipping, Inc., came on the line, Fleming Pickering told him that a Miss

Ernestine Sage was on her way to see him. She needed a check cashed. He should cash it; and then he should arrange something with the Bank of America branch in San Diego so that she could cash checks whenever she wanted in the future.

"The second thing I need from you, Charley," Fleming Pickering went on, "is to find someplace for her to live. A little house, preferably on the beach, or at least with a view of it."

"Jesus, Flem," the general manager protested. "That's going to be hard. This town is full of sailors and Marines, and most of them, the officers anyway, brought their wives and their families."

"A little house on the beach, or with a view of it, and someplace where the lady can entertain an overnight guest on a regular basis without any embarrassing questions being asked."

"It's a good thing I know you're a straight arrow, Flem," the general manager said. "Or otherwise—"

"The young lady, you dirty-minded old man, you, is the closest thing Patricia and I have to a daughter. She is visiting a young Marine officer. I don't know for how long."

"It's going to be hard finding a place."

"Do whatever has to be done, Charley," Fleming Pickering said. "And with your well-known tact and finesse. And get back to me."

When he put the phone back in its cradle, he looked at his wife. She was sitting back in the chair, tapping the balls of her extended fingers together.

"Done," he said.

"I hope we know what we are doing," Patricia Pickering said.

"Me, too," he said.

She shrugged and rose out of the chair.

"Where are you going to be at, say, one?"

"Here, probably," he said.

"I've got a few things to do," she said. "After which I thought I would drop by the apartment. Say about one?"

"Oh," he said.

"I would hate to drag you away from something important," she said.

He picked up another of the telephones on his desk.

"Mrs. Florian," he said. "If I have anything scheduled between one and three, reschedule it."

He put the phone back in its cradle.

"There was a time," Patricia Pickering said, "when you would have taken the whole afternoon off."

"I can always call back," he said.

"Braggart," Patricia Pickering said, and went through the door.

(TWO)
Pensacola Navy Air Station
18 January 1942

If they are asked, aviators will tell you there is no such thing as a "natural" or "born" pilot. The human animal, they will explain, is designed to move back and forth and sideways with one foot planted on something firm. But aircraft move in a medium that is more like an ocean than solid ground; and they move more like a fish swimming than a man walking. Controlling an aircraft, consequently, does not come naturally; a pilot has to be *taught* how to move around in the sea of air.

Aviators will also modestly point out that while it is not really much more difficult than riding a bicycle, flying requires a certain degree of hand-eye coordination. And this must be taught and learned. It is for instance often necessary for one hand to do one thing, while the other does something else. And meanwhile, the feet might be doing still another thing.

Making a climbing turn, for example, requires both rearward and sideward pressure on the control stick (or as the originally scatological term, now grown respectable, has it, the "joystick") between the legs, while the feet apply the appropriate pressure to the rudder pedals. And while he makes these movements, the pilot's eyes must take into consideration where the aircraft is relative to the horizon; and at the same time he must monitor the airspeed, vertical speed, and all the gauges indicating engine function and condition.

Almost without exception, pilots will relate that the first time they were given the controls by their instructor pilot (IP), they were all over the sky.

They will often add by way of explanation that fledgling birdmen usually "overcontrol," which is to say that they apply far more pressure to the controls than should be applied. What results is that the plane goes into a steep dive, or a steep climb, or veers sharply off to one side or the other. . . . It goes all over the sky.

This condition is made worse by the fledgling birdman's lack of experience operating with his body on its side, and/or tipped steeply upward or downward.

One's first flight at the controls, aviators will all agree, is a traumatic experience. But over a period of time—long or short, depending almost always on the skill of the instructor pilot—those student pilots who ultimately make it (there are many who simply cannot learn) gradually pick up the finesse that permits them to smoothly control their aircraft. And their bodies. They no longer are quite so dizzy, or disoriented, or nauseous.

Like riding a bicycle, aviators will affirm, piloting an aircraft is something you have to be *taught* to do—*always* under the watchful eye of a skilled instructor pilot. The way you learn to do it well is with a great deal of practice, slowly growing a little better.

And then, after they have gone through all this explanation, a puzzled look will very often come onto their faces, and there will be a caveat:

"Yeah, but I remember a guy at Pensacola [or Randolph Field, or wherever] *. . . the IP just didn't believe him. He thought he'd come to basic with at least a couple of hundred hours and was being a smart ass . . . who just got in the sonofabitch and could fly it like he really had three, four hours in it. No problem at all, not even when the IP did his best to disorient him. Looped it, whatever. When he gave him the controls, he just straightened it out. And he knew where he was.*

"Just that one guy, though. Little [or Great big, or Perfectly ordinary] *guy. I forget his name. But he just knew how to fly. All they had to do was explain to him what the propeller was doing, spinning around like that."*

Captain James L. Carstairs, USMC, had heard all the stories himself, of course, about that one character in ten thousand—or a hundred thousand—whom Mother Nature in her infinite wisdom had elected to equip naturally with a feeling for the air that others could acquire only after much time and great effort.

But until he took Second Lieutenant Malcolm S. Pickering, USMC, up for his orientation flight in an N2S[1] he had never personally met one.

Captain Carstairs had been annoyed, but not surprised, when he learned from the records of Lieutenants Pickering and Stecker that neither had been afforded the opportunity of an "orientation flight" before they had been ordered to Pensacola.

The "orientation flight" was something of a misnomer. It was designed primarily to disqualify would-be Naval aviators from the training program. If the SOP (Standing Operating Procedure) had been followed, the two second johns whom a cruel fate had placed in his hands would have been given their "orientation flights" before they came to Pensacola. And they'd have passed them; otherwise they would not have been sent to Pensacola at all.

It made much more sense to take would-be birdmen up for a ride—a ride in which the IP would do his very best to frighten and/or sicken his passenger—to determine before the kid was actually sent to Pensacola that he *really* wanted to be a pilot and was physically able to endure the physical and mental stresses of flight. They would thus eliminate before they began training those who had second thoughts about becoming aviators, or who proved unfit for flight. In that way time and money were saved.

His two second johns had slipped through that hole in the sieve, too. Neither of them should have been sent to Pensacola in the first place, so it made a certain perverted sense that they had been sent without having taken the required orientation flight. Captain Carstairs realized there were two ways the omission could be rectified. He could write a memorandum outlining the facts and requesting that the two officers named above be scheduled for an orientation flight. He could then have a clerk type it up and send it over to Mainside and let it work its way through the bureaucracy. This would take at least a week, and probably two. Or he could load his second johns in his Pontiac coupe and drive them so Saufley Field right then and take them for a ride in a Yellow Peril himself.

Second Lieutenant Stecker went first. Captain Carstairs loaded him into the backseat, carefully adjusted his mirror so that he could see Stecker's face, and then took off. He left the traffic pattern at Saufley and flew up to U.S. 98 in the vicinity of the Florida-Alabama border. There, climbing to eight thousand feet, he put the Yellow Peril through various aerobatic maneuvers, frequently glancing in his mirror to examine the effect on Second Lieutenant Stecker.

Stecker was a picture of grim determination. From time to time, his face grew deathly pale, and he frequently swallowed and licked his lips. He otherwise stared grimly ahead, as if afraid of what he would see if he looked over the side of the cockpit.

But he neither closed his eyes to shut out the horror, nor did he get sick to his stomach. Just about the reaction he expected, Captain Carstairs realized when he thought about it. Stecker was young and in superb physical condition. And, significantly, he was a West Pointer. Himself an Annapolis graduate, Carstairs was willing to grant that the U.S. Military Academy probably did nearly as good a job as the U.S. Naval Academy to instill self-discipline in its students. That meant that by pure willpower, Stecker was able to keep his eyes open and stop himself from being sick.

Forty minutes into the flight, after just about half an hour of violent aerobatics,

[1]The Stearman N2S, an open, twin-cockpit training biplane, painted yellow for visibility, was officially called the 'Cadet.' But like the other basic training aircraft, the Navy-manufactured N3N, it was rarely called anything but the "Yellow Peril."

Captain Carstairs put the Yellow Peril into straight and level flight. He then conveyed via the speaker tube that Second Lieutenant Stecker was to put his feet on the rudder pedals and his hand on the joystick and "follow through" as Carstairs maneuvered the airplane, so that he would acquire some sense of what control motions were required to go up and down and side to side.

Second Lieutenant Stecker's orientation flight lasted one minute less than an hour. When Carstairs taxied the Yellow Peril to the place where Second Lieutenant Pickering was waiting for his turn, he saw that Pickering was eating.

Enterprising merchants from Pensacola had been given permission to roam the edges of the parking aprons at Saufley, Correy, and Chevalier fields, selling box lunches to civilian mechanics and service personnel. Pickering had obviously bought himself a snack.

When he came closer, Captain Carstairs saw that what Pickering was eating was an oyster loaf. This consisted of maybe eight fried-in-batter oysters in a highly Tabasco-flavored barbecue sauce on a long, soft roll. It was not the sort of thing someone about to experience violent aerobatic maneuvers in an airplane should put in his stomach. And Pickering, he saw, was about to make a bad situation worse. He was washing the oyster loaf down with a pint bottle of chocolate milk.

There was no question whatever in Captain Carstairs's mind that Second Lieutenant Pickering was going to throw up all over the Yellow Peril. But there was a silver lining in that black cloud, Carstairs decided. For one thing, the student rode aft of the instructor. None of what erupted from Pickering's stomach would reach Carstairs.

Getting sick, moreover, would teach Pickering the important lesson that an aviator must consider what he eats or drinks before flight. And cleaning up what he threw up from the aircraft would serve two additional purposes. It would emphasize the importance of lesson one, and it would serve as a test of Pickering's determination to become a Naval aviator.

"If you have finished your snack, Pickering, get in," Captain Carstairs said.

Second Lieutenant Pickering stuffed the rest of his oyster loaf in his mouth, then washed it down with the rest of his chocolate milk, after which he climbed into the rear seat of the Yellow Peril.

Captain Carstairs flew the same course he had flown with Stecker. And once he was near the Florida-Alabama border, to start things off, he rocked the Yellow Peril from side to side. In his mirror, he saw Lieutenant Pickering's eyebrows raise in surprised delight.

Next Carstairs pulled back on the joystick and put the Yellow Peril in a climb. Eventually inertia overcame velocity and the airspeed fell below that necessary to provide lift. The Yellow Peril stalled, which is to say, it suddenly started falling toward the earth.

In his mirror, Captain Carstairs saw that Pickering's face now reflected happy surprise at this new sensation.

Carstairs recovered from the stall by pushing the nose forward until sufficient airspeed had been regained to permit flight. He pulled it straight and level for a moment, and then peeled off into a steep dive to the left.

Pickering's stomach was stronger than Carstairs would have believed. But there would be an eruption soon, either when he pulled out of the dive, or when he rolled the Yellow Peril: The aircraft would turn upside down as he reached the apex of his climbing maneuver.

When, in inverted flight, Captain Carstairs looked in his mirror at his passenger, his passenger's face bore the enchanted look of a little boy finding an unexpected wealth of presents under the Christmas tree. He was smiling from ear to ear and gazing in pure, excited rapture all around this strange and wonderful inverted world he was seeing for the first time.

An additional fifteen minutes of intricate aerobatics not only failed to make Second Lieutenant Pickering sick to his stomach, but it failed to wipe the smile of joyous discovery off his face. Indeed, if possible, each more exotic maneuver seemed to widen proportionally his ecstatic grin of delight.

Captain Carstairs was willing to admit that he was capable of making an error in judgment, and fair was fair. He put the Yellow Peril into straight and level flight and conveyed the order that Pickering was to follow him through on the controls. In a moment he felt a slight resistance to both joystick and rudder movement. This told him that Pickering had his feet on the pedals and his hand on the joystick.

Carstairs moved the aircraft up and down, and from side to side, and then made a sweeping turn. Then his own very sensitive hand on the controls told him that Pickering had let go of the controls. There was no longer any resistance when he moved them.

The arrogant sonofabitch if bored; he's taken his hands off the controls. He thinks I'm up here to take him for a ride!

He set the Yellow Peril up in a steep climbing turn to the left, and then took his own feet off the rudder pedals and his hand off the joystick.

The Yellow Peril would continue in the attitude that he had placed it in until it ran out of airspeed, whereupon it would stall. And since it would be moving leftward when it stalled, it would not fall straight through, but would slide in a sickening skid to the left. With just a little bit of luck, it would enter a spin.

That would catch Second Lieutenant Pickering's attention.

He watched the airspeed indicator as it moved downward toward stall speed, so that he would be prepared. And he frequently glanced at Second Lieutenant Pickering's face for the first glimmer of concern. This would be shortly followed by bewilderment, and then terror.

When the airspeed indicator needle showed about five miles above stall speed, Captain Carstairs sensed first that the angle of climb was diminishing, and then that the aircraft was coming out of its turn. He looked at the joystick between his legs. It was moving. And when he looked at the rudder pedals, so were they.

In a moment, the airspeed indicator began to rise again, and shortly after it did that, the control stick moved again, returning the aircraft to its turn and to a climbing attitude. But in a more shallow climb than before, one that it could maintain more or less indefinitely.

This wiseass sonofabitch is a pilot, and not too bad a pilot. That was the natural, practiced reflex action of somebody who feels in the seat of his pants that he's about to stall. He did what had to be done to recover.

Captain Carstairs put his mouth to the speaking tube. "Okay, Pickering, take us back to the field and land it," he ordered.

For the first time, a look of confusion and concern appeared on Second Lieutenant Pickering's face.

"When I give you a command, you say 'Aye, aye, sir,' " Carstairs ordered.

"Aye, aye, sir," Lieutenant Pickering responded.

The Yellow Peril entered a 180-degree turn.

Steep, Carstairs thought, *but smooth.*

Ten minutes later, after an arrow-straight flight, the traffic pattern over Saufley Field came into view. Eight or nine other Yellow Perils were waiting their turn to make their approach to the runway.

"Sir," Pickering's voice came over the tube to Carstairs's ears, "what do I do now?"

"Sit it down, Pickering."

There was a moment's pause, then, "Aye, aye, sir."

Pickering moved the Yellow Peril to a position behind the last Yellow Peril in the stack.

Carstairs finally found something to fault in Pickering's flying technique. They were a little too close to the Yellow Peril before them before Pickering retarded the throttle.

And then it was their turn to land.

"Sir," Pickering's voice came over the tube, "I've never landed an airplane before."

"Do the best you can, Lieutenant," Carstairs replied.

Pickering aimed the Yellow Peril at the runway.

When he was over the threshold, he chopped the throttle and skewed the Yellow Peril from side to side as he tried to line it up with the runway.

Carstairs made a quick decision. While it was entirely possible that Pickering was going to be able to get it safely on the ground the way he was doing it, he was coming in way too high.

"I've got it," Carstairs said over the speaking tube. He shoved the throttle forward and put his hands and feet on the controls, and they went around.

Carstairs put the Yellow Peril at the tail of the stack of Yellow Perils, and then spoke again.

"The way this is supposed to be done," he said, "is that you run out of lift the moment you level the wings. We like you to do that about ten feet off the runway, not one hundred."

Pickering shook his head to signal his understanding.

On his next attempt to land, Pickering greased the Yellow Peril in two hundred feet from the threshold. The Yellow Peril's main gear touched, and then a moment later, it settled gently onto its tail wheel.

And then, for the first time, there was terror in Pickering's voice. "I can't see to steer!"

"I've got it," Captain Carstairs responded. He braked, turned onto a taxiway, and taxied the Yellow Peril back to where Second Lieutenant Stecker waited for them.

Captain Carstairs hoisted himself out of his cockpit ahead of Pickering, and then he stood on the wing root in a position where he could look directly into Second Lieutenant Pickering's face.

"Am I to believe, Pickering, that this has been your first opportunity to attempt to fly aircraft?"

"Yes, sir," Pickering said. "Captain, I realize I screwed up. But I really think I can learn how to do it."

Carstairs looked directly into Pickering's eyes for a long moment before he spoke.

"Actually, Pickering, you didn't do too badly," he said, and a smile of relief appeared on Pickering's face. "I would, in fact, go so far as to say I saw a suggestion—faint, but a suggestion—that you may have a natural talent for flying."

The smile of relief turned into one of joy.

"Thank you, sir."

"You're going to have to work a little harder than your friend Stecker," Captain Carstairs said. "But if you apply yourself, there's really no reason why you can't get through the course."

"Thank you, sir," Pickering said, absolutely seriously. "I'll really try to do my best, sir."

Carstairs nodded at Pickering and then jumped off the wing root.

Second Lieutenant Malcolm Pickering surprised Captain James L. Carstairs a second time that same day.

At half-past six, Captain Carstairs was at the bar of the San Carlos Hotel in the company of Captain and Mrs. Lowell B. Howard, USMC, and Mrs. Martha Sayre Culhane. They were waiting for a table in the dining room; they had reserved a table for eight.

There were two empty stools beside them at the bar.

Second Lieutenant Pickering, trailed by Second Lieutenant Stecker, obviously freshly showered and shaved, crossed the room to them.

"Good evening, sir," Pickering said.

"Pickering."

"Sir, are these stools occupied?"

"No. Help yourself. We're about to leave."

"Thank you, sir," Pickering said. "Hello, Martha."

"Hello, Pick," Martha Sayre Culhane said.

"May I present Lieutenant Dick Stecker?" Pickering said.

"Hello," Martha Sayre Culhane said, and gave him her hand.

"I'm a little surprised that you know Mrs. Culhane, Pickering," Captain Carstairs said.

"My mother introduced us on the golf course," Martha said.

Captain and Mrs. Howard were introduced.

"You two here to have dinner?" Carstairs asked, to make conversation.

"Yes, sir," Pickering said.

The headwaiter appeared, and beckoned to Carstairs.

"There's our table," Carstairs said. And then he gave in to a generous impulse. "Listen, we've reserved a larger table than it looks like we're going to need. Would you like to have dinner with us? It's sometimes hard to get a table. . . ."

"Thank you, sir, but no," Second Lieutenant Stecker said.

"Shut up," Pickering said. "Yes, sir. Thank you very much."

The invitation did not seem to please Martha Sayre Culhane.

"They can probably get a table of their own without too much trouble," she said. "They live here. In the penthouse."

It was a rude thing for Martha to say, Carstairs thought. He wondered how long she had been waiting in the bar; how much she'd had to drink.

"Well, it must be nice to have a rich father," Carstairs joked.

"No, sir, we're just a pair of payday-rich second johns," Dick Stecker said. "My father's a captain at Camp Elliott."

"But *his* father," Martha Sayre Culhane said, inclining her head toward Pickering, "owns Pacific and Far East Shipping."

Martha really doesn't like Pickering, Carstairs thought. *I wonder why. I wonder what happened on the golf course.*

"I think," Pickering said, "that on reconsideration, we had best decline with thanks your kind invitation, Captain."

Carstairs could think of no other way to get out of what had become an awkward situation.

He nodded at Pickering and Stecker and, taking Martha's arm, led her away from the bar.

But at the entrance to the dining room, she shook loose from his hand and walked back to the bar. Carstairs, now sure that she was in fact drunk and about to make a scene, hurried after her.

Martha put her hand on Pickering's arm, and he turned to look at her.

"For some reason," she said, "you bring out the bitch in me. I'm sorry. Come and have dinner."

Pickering hesitated.

"Please, Pick," Martha said. "I said I'm sorry."

Carstairs saw the look on Pickering's face and knew that he was absolutely incapable of refusing anything Martha Sayre Culhane asked. And then he had a sure, sudden insight why Pickering brought out the bitch in Martha. She was attracted to him, strongly attracted to him, and under the circumstances she didn't know how to handle it.

As Captain Carstairs had recently come to realize, he himself didn't know how to handle Martha Sayre Culhane.

Carstairs had known Greg Culhane at Annapolis, where Greg had been three years behind him. They had become closer when Greg had come to Pensacola. And Carstairs had been at Admiral Sayre's quarters when Greg's engagement to Martha had been announced, and he had been the best man at their wedding.

And he had been considered part of the family after the telegram from the Secretary of the Navy had made official what Admiral Sayre had been told personally over the phone days before the Deputy Chief of Naval Operations. And he had sat with the family during the memorial service in the chapel where she and Greg had been married.

And then Martha had started to hang around with him and his friends. The polite fiction was that Martha took comfort from the company of the other officers' wives. That wasn't true. Martha took comfort from the officers, and from Captain James L. Carstairs, USMC, in particular.

This had not escaped the attention of Admiral Sayre, who had spoken to Carstairs about it: *"Mrs. Sayre and I appreciate the time and consideration you're giving Martha. She needs a friend right now, someone she can trust when she is so vulnerable, emotionally."*

Carstairs was aware then that the admiral might well mean exactly what he said. But he also thought that the admiral might well be saying, *"It would not especially displease Mrs. Sayre and myself if something developed between the two of you,"* or the reverse of that: *"I'm sure that a bright young man like you, having received a word to the wise, knows what somebody like me could and would do to you if I ever found out you had taken advantage of my widowed daughter's emotional vulnerability to get into her pants."*

Carstairs had not laid a hand on Martha Sayre Culhane. At first it had been unthinkable. He was, after all, a Marine officer, and she was the widow of a brother officer. But lately he had become very much aware of the significant difference between the words *wife* and *widow,* and he had been equally aware of her beauty. It was too soon, of course, for him to make any kind of a move. But eventually, inevitably, he had concluded (wondering if it made him some kind of a sonofabitch), time would put a scar on her wound, and nature would take over again, and there would be room in her life for a man.

Martha's behavior toward Lieutenant Pickering—that handsome, rich sonofabitch—made him now realize that even if she didn't know it, there was already a thick layer of scar tissue covering her wound.

Pickering slid off his bar stool. For a moment Martha held his hand, and then, as if she realized what she was doing, quickly let go of it.

Captain Carstairs stepped out of the way, and then followed the two of them into the dining room.

XI

(ONE)
Machine Gun Range #2
Camp Elliott, California
1030 Hours, 19 January 1942

The pickup truck was a prewar Chevrolet. It had a glossy paint job, and on each door a representation of the Marine Corps insignia was painted above the neatly painted letters "USMC." It even had chrome hubcaps.

The pickup trucks issued currently (and for several months before the war started) were painted with a flat Marine-green paint; and none of these had chrome hubcaps or the Marine emblem on the door. They did have USMC on the door, but that had been applied with a stencil, using black paint.

The driver of the pickup, seen up close, was even more unusual than the truck. He was a thin—even gaunt—man not quite forty-two years old. He was dressed in dungarees; and the letters USMC and a crude representation of the Marine Corps insignia had been stenciled in black paint on the dungaree jacket. The jacket was unpressed, and the silver oak leaves of a lieutenant colonel were half-hidden in the folds of the collar.

The lieutenant colonel parked the Chevrolet in line with the other vehicles—an ambulance, two other pickups, and two of the recently issued and still not yet common trucks, 1/4-ton, 4 × 4, General Purpose, called "Jeeps"—and got out. There were a captain, several lieutenants, and four noncoms standing in the shade of a small frame building, an obviously newly erected range house.

It was two story. The second story was an observation platform, only half framed-in. A primitive flagpole of two-by-fours rose above the observation platform. Flying from this was a red "firing in progress" pennant.

There were what the lieutenant colonel judged to be two companies of infantry (somewhere in the neighborhood of four hundred men) sitting on the ground twenty-five yards away from the firing line. It was already getting hot, and the sun was shining brightly. Shortly, the lieutenant colonel decided, they would grow uncomfortable.

The captain glanced at the newcomer and looked away. He had seen the man's face, and guessed his age, and concluded that he was probably a gunnery sergeant. It did not enter the captain's mind that the newcomer might be an officer, much less a lieutenant colonel. Officers were provided with drivers, and field-grade officers were customarily provided with Ford or Chevrolet staff cars.

The captain's ignorance was not surprising. This was the first time the lieutenant colonel had come to Machine Gun Range #2. He walked to the front of the pickup, leaned casually against the hood, studied the setup carefully.

He saw that there were twelve machine-gun positions, each constructed more or less as a machine-gun position would be set up in a tactical situation. That is to say, a low semicircle of sandbags had been erected at each position, in the center of which sat a Browning machine gun, placed so that it would fire over the sandbags.

Three different types of machine gun had been set up. Each of the four sandbag positions on the right of the firing line held a Browning Model 1919A4 .30-caliber weapon. This version of the Browning was "air cooled," with a perforated jacket on the outside of its barrel intended to dissipate the heat generated by bullets passing through the barrel. The gun was mounted on a low tripod, a single, short leg forward, and two longer legs, forming a V, to the rear. There was a steel rod between the two rearward legs. Elevation of the weapon was controlled by a threaded rod connected to and rising upward from the steel rod to the rear action of the weapon. Traverse of the weapon was limited by the length of the steel rod connecting the two rear legs of the tripod.

Four M1917A1 .30-caliber "water-cooled" Brownings had been set up in the center four firing positions. A jacket through which water was passed encased the barrel of the '17A1s. And the mounting, otherwise identical to that of the '19A4s, was different in one important respect: Traverse of the weapon was restricted only by the length of the hose connecting the water jacket to the water reservoir. In theory, the '17A1 could be fired through 360 degrees. Elevation was controlled by curved steel plates connected to the machine gun itself and the top of the tripod.

The four firing positions on the left of the firing line each held an M2 Browning. This was the .50-caliber[1] version of the Browning. And it was essentially an enlargement of the .30-caliber '19A4. The perforated steel cooling device on the barrel, however, ran only a short distance out from the receiver. The quick-replaceable barrel was fitted with a handle, for ease in handling; the cocking lever was enlarged and fitted with a wooden handle; and the "pistol grip" behind the trigger of the '19A4 was replaced with a dual wooden-handled trigger mechanism.

The lieutenant colonel found nothing wrong with the placement of the machine guns. And he saw why the weapons were silent; there was some sort of trouble with one of the 1917A1s. He saw an armorer on his knees with the '17A1 in pieces before him. He was being watched by its fascinated two-man crew.

The range was new, and consequently primitive. There was neither a target pit (a below-ground trench at the targets) or a berm (a mound of earth used as a bullet trap) behind the targets. The targets were constructed of two-by-fours, with target cloth stretched between them. The targets themselves were approximately life-size silhouettes of the human torso, rather than the expected bull's-eye targets.

The bullets fired from the machine guns impacted on low, sandy hills the lieutenant colonel judged to be a mile and a half from the firing line. He presumed that whoever had laid out the range was perfectly familiar with the ballistics of .30- and .50-caliber machine-gun projectiles and that a large area behind the hills had been declared an impact area and thus *Off Limits.*

When he had seen what he wanted to see (and he was not here to judge machine-gun training; only professionally curious) the lieutenant colonel pushed himself off the hood of the pickup and walked toward the officers gathered in the shade of the range office.

He was almost on them, as they chatted quietly together before one of the noncoms, when a staff sergeant glanced in his direction and saw the glitter of silver on his dungaree jacket collar points. He inclined his head toward the captain, who looked quickly in his direction.

[1]Caliber is expressed in decimal portions of an inch. For example, the .50-caliber machine gun projectile has a diameter of one-half inch.

When the lieutenant colonel drew close, the officers and the noncoms came to attention, and the captain saluted and smiled.

"Good morning, sir," the captain said.

"Good morning," the lieutenant colonel said, with a salute that was far short of parade-ground perfect. "Are you in charge here, Captain?"

"I'm the senior officer, sir," the captain said.

"That's what I asked," the lieutenant colonel said, reasonably, with a smile. He examined the lieutenants and picked one out. "Are you Lieutenant McCoy?"

The lieutenant came to attention. "No, sir," he said.

"I was told I could find Lieutenant McCoy here," the lieutenant colonel said.

"He's on the line, sir," the captain said. "There's a stoppage on one of the weapons." He gestured in the direction of the pit where the lieutenant colonel had seen the armorer working on the machine gun.

The lieutenant colonel started to walk toward it. The captain followed him. When they were out of hearing of the group in the shade of the range house, the lieutenant colonel stopped and turned to the captain.

"I think I can find Lieutenant McCoy myself, Captain," he said softly. "What I suggest you do is put one officer and one noncom in the observation tower, and then send the others over to the troops. If I were, say, a PFC, I would resent being ordered to sit in the sun while my sergeant stood in the shade. Much less my officers."

The captain came to attention, with surprise on his face.

"Aye, aye, sir," he said.

The lieutenant colonel walked to the machine-gin pit where there was a malfunctioning weapon.

One of the two troops saw him coming and said something to the third man, who was, the lieutenant colonel saw, just about finished reassembling the weapon. The man started to straighten up. The lieutenant colonel saw the gold bars of the second lieutenant on his dungaree shirt. The two Marines came to attention.

"Finish what you're doing," the lieutenant colonel said, in Chinese.

"Yes, sir," McCoy replied in English, and went on with his work.

"You two can stand at ease," the lieutenant colonel ordered, and then switched to Chinese: "What was wrong with it?"

"Dirt," McCoy replied, again in English. "We just drew these guns. They've been in storage since the First World War. What stopped this one was petrified Cosmoline. It was too hard to wash out with gasoline, but then firing shook it loose. It jammed the bolt as it tried to feed."

"Your record, Lieutenant, says that you are fluent in Cantonese," the lieutenant colonel said in Chinese.

"I don't speak it as well as you do, sir," McCoy said, in Cantonese. He got the machine gun back together, opened the action, and stood up. "Is there something I can do for you, sir?"

The lieutenant colonel ignored the question.

"Isn't there an armorer out here?" he asked.

"Yes, sir," McCoy said. "But I like to explain what went wrong, instead of just fix it."

"Where did you learn about machine guns?"

"I was in a heavy-weapons company with the Fourth Marines in Shanghai, sir," McCoy said.

The lieutenant colonel was pleased with what he had found. The service record of Second Lieutenant McCoy had said that he was an Expert with a .30- and a

.50-caliber Browning machine gun and that he was fluent in Cantonese. He was now satisfied that both were the case.

"You're the range officer, I understand?" the lieutenant colonel said.

"Yes, sir."

"If you would feel comfortable in turning over that responsibility to one of the other officers, I'd like to talk to you for a few minutes."

"I'll ask one of the other officers to take over for me, sir," McCoy said.

"I'll wait for you in the pickup," the lieutenant colonel said, smiling and pointing toward the Chevrolet.

When McCoy got to the pickup truck, the lieutenant colonel was inside. He signaled for McCoy to get in. After McCoy was inside, he put out his hand. His grip was firm.

"My name is Carlson, McCoy," he said. "I'm pleased to meet you. I'm an old China Marine myself."

"Yes, sir," McCoy said.

"How'd you get your commission, McCoy?" Carlson asked.

"When I came home from China, I applied for officer school and they sent me," McCoy said.

"You like being an officer?"

"It pays better," McCoy said.

Carlson chuckled.

"Most second lieutenants, faced with a malfunctioning Browning, would get a an armorer to fix it," Carlson said. "Not dirty their hands on it themselves."

"Most second lieutenants wouldn't have known what was wrong with it," McCoy said.

"I was hoping you would say you don't mind getting your hands dirty if that's the quickest solution to a problem."

"Yes, sir," McCoy said. "That, too."

"I've been given command of a special battalion, McCoy," Carlson said. "What we'll be doing is something like the British Commandos. Amphibious raids on Japanese-held islands; probably, later, working behind Japanese lines. I'm recruiting officers for it."

"I heard something about that, sir," McCoy said.

"What did you hear?"

"I heard suicide troops, Colonel," McCoy said. "That you didn't want married men."

"Well, let me correct that," Carlson said. "*Not* suicide troops. Only a fool would volunteer to commit suicide, and the one thing I *don't* want is fools. I don't want married men because I don't want people thinking about wives and children . . . because that would raise their chances of getting killed. I want them to think of nothing but the mission. If they do that, they stand a much better chance of staying alive. You follow the reasoning?"

"Yes, sir," McCoy said.

"And the training is going to be tough, and there's going to be a lot of it, and a married man would get trouble from his wife because he didn't come home at night and on weekends. My philosophy is that well-trained men stand a better chance of staying alive. You follow me?"

"Yes, sir."

McCoy had seen enough of Lieutenant Colonel Evans F. Carlson to make a fast judgment, but one he was sure of. He judged that Carlson was a good officer. McCoy had noticed, for instance, that the officers and noncoms were now doing what they were supposed to be doing, instead of standing around bullshitting in the shade of the range building; and he was sure that Carlson had straightened them out. And McCoy was impressed with Carlson, the man. There was a quiet authority about him. He didn't have to wave his silver lieutenant colonel's leaf in somebody's face to command respect.

His eyes were soft, but intelligent. He certainly didn't look crazy. Or even like he'd gone Chink. McCoy had no idea what a Communist looked like.

McCoy was worried about the intelligent eyes. They made him think that there was very little that got by Lieutenant Colonel Carlson. He wondered how long it would be before Carlson began to suspect—if he didn't already suspect—that the big brass would send somebody to keep an eye on him, to see if he was crazy, or a Communist, or whatever. And once he figured that out, it wouldn't be a hell of a jump for him to figure out that the spy was Second Lieutenant McCoy.

Shit! Why didn't they send somebody else? I like this guy.

(TWO)
Pearl Harbor, Hawaii
17 January 1942

The blind men evacuated from Corregidor aboard the *Pickerel* were taken from the wharf to the Naval hospital by ambulance.

There they were given thorough physical examinations to determine if they had any medical condition that required immediate attention. None did. One of them—who had for some unaccountable reason regained his sight—even demanded immediate return to duty, but that was out of the question. He was told that because his shrapnel wounds had not completely healed, he would be evacuated to the United States with the others.

Actually, it had been decided that this man's case indicated the necessity of a psychiatric examination. His temporary blindness was psychosomatic in nature, and that was sometimes an indication of psychiatric problems. But telling him that was obviously not the thing to do; it might even aggravate the problem.

The nine blind men and the one who had regained his sight were placed in the medical holding detachment for transport (when available) to the United States for further medical evaluation and treatment.

The first available shipping space turned out to be aboard a civilian freighter under contract to the Navy. When this came to the attention of a senior medical officer, a Navy captain, he found the time to examine the ship, and he saw that its berthing space was temporary. Its number-two and number-three holds had been temporarily rigged with bunks consisting of sheets of canvas stretched between iron pipe. The head available to the sightless men was primitive, the ladders steep, and there were many places where a blind man could smash against sharp objects.

The Navy doctor then went to see the personnel shipment officer on the staff of the Commander in Chief, Pacific Fleet, to ask him if they couldn't do a little better for the blind men in the way of accommodation.

The personnel shipment officer was also a Navy captain. Aware that the doctor might actually outrank him, he didn't stand him tall as he would have liked to do, but rather contented himself with a lecture, which touched on the fact that he was a busy man, that there was a war on, and that medical officers should really stick to medicine and leave the conduct of the Navy to line officers.

This encounter was followed, as soon as the doctor could find a telephone, by a call to the Chief of Staff to the Commander in Chief, Pacific Fleet. The doctor had a little trouble getting the Commander in Chief onto the phone, but eventually he heard the familiar voice.

"Did you really tell my aide," the admiral asked, "that you'd boot his ass from here to Diego if he didn't get me on the horn?"

"Or words to that effect," the doctor said.

"What's the problem, Charley?" the admiral said, suppressing a chuckle. The admiral had known the doctor for twenty years; they had once shared a cabin as lieutenants on the *Minneapolis.*

"One of your chickenshit part-time sailors wants to send those poor bastards, the blind guys the *Pickerel* brought here from Corregidor, to the States on a cargo ship. The pasty-faced, candy-ass sonofabitch told me with a straight face there's a war on and everyone has to make sacrifices."

"I gather you are referring to my personnel shipping officer?" the admiral asked, dryly.

"I think his name is Young," Paweley said. "Tall, thin sonofabitch. Came in the Navy the day before yesterday, and thinks he's Bull Halsey, Junior."

"I'll take care of it, Charley," the admiral said. "How many of them are there?"

"Ten."

"I'll take care of it, Charley," the admiral repeated. "Now you calm down."

"Sorry to bother you with this, Tom. I know you're busy—"

"Never too busy for something like this," the admiral said.

The next afternoon, the departure of the regularly scheduled courier flight to the United States was delayed for almost an hour. Already loaded and in the water, the Martin PBM-1 was ordered back to the seaplane ramp, where its seven passengers and six hundred pounds of priority cargo were offloaded.

Nine blind men were loaded aboard under the supervision of a Marine captain. All of the seven passengers removed from their seats were senior in grade to the captain, and all had urgent business in the United States, and protest was made to the personnel shipment officer.

It was to no avail. The personnel shipment officer, the previous afternoon, had had a brief chat with the Chief of Staff to the Commander in Chief, Pacific Fleet. No one had ever talked to him like that before in his life.

(THREE)
USMC Recruit Training Depot
Parris Island, South Carolina
0845 Hours, 19 January 1942

The motor transport officer, the officer charged with operating the fleet of trucks and automobiles for the recruit depot, was First Lieutenant Vincent S. Osadchy. A lithe, deeply tanned twenty-eight-year-old, he was a mustang with eleven years in the Corps. He had been an officer three months, and the motor transport officer nine days. The previous transport officer, a major, as the TO&E (Table of Organization & Equipment) called for, had been transferred. He knew what he was doing. Osadchy, who didn't, had been given the job until such time as an officer of suitable grade and experience could be found.

Lieutenant Osadchy drove himself in a jeep from the motor pool to the brick headquarters building, not sure of his best plan of attack. Should he make a display of anger? Or should he get down on his knees before the personel officer and weep?

The personnel officer was a major, a portly, natty man completely filling his stiffly starched khaki shirt. He wasn't bulging out of it, nor really straining the buttons; but, Osadchy thought, there would not be room inside the shirt for the major and, say, a hand scratching an itch.

"Hello, Vince," the major said, smiling. "Can I offer you some coffee?"

"Yes, sir," Osadchy said. "Thank you. And if you have one, how about a weeping towel?"

The major chuckled. He poured coffee from a thermos into a china cup and handed it to Osadchy.

"I thought maybe you'd drop by," he said.

"Can I deliver a lecture on what it takes to operate a motor pool?"

"By all means," the major said.

"Aside from vehicles," Osadchy said, pronouncing the word "*vee*-hic-els," "and tools and POL [petrol, oil and lubricants], it requires five or six good noncoms, corporals, or sergeants who know the difference between a spark plug and a transmission, and at least one, but preferably two or three, officers who know at least half as much as the noncoms."

"That sounds reasonable," the major said, smiling warmly at him.

"A month ago, our motor pool had both," Osadchy went on. "And then the Corps transferred out all—not some, all—the noncoms who could find their ass with both hands without a map."

"Very colorful," the major said, chuckling.

"And then the Corps, in its wisdom, sent us *one* sergeant who had previously seen a truck with the wheels off. Actually a pretty good man, even if he just got out of the hospital. But then—the Corps giveth and the Corps taketh away—the Corps transferred the motor transport officer out."

"The Corps is having a few little personnel problems, Vince," the major said. "It's supposed to have something to do with there being a war on."

Osadchy had to smile, although he didn't want to. He was afraid this would happen, that the major would hear him out, be as pleasant as hell, and give him no help whatsoever.

"Which left the motor pool in the hands of an officer who knows as much about operating a motor pool as he does about deep-sea fishing. And of course the one sergeant who does know what he's doing."

"And now the Corps says promote the sergeant to gunnery sergeant and transfer him, right? Is that the source of your unhappiness, Vince?"

"Yes, sir," Osadchy said. "Sir, don't misunderstand me. Sergeant Zimmerman is a good man. I'd like to see him as a staff sergeant, or a technical sergeant. But gunny? I was a gunny. Zimmerman is not the gunny type."

"In other words, if you could have your way, Zimmerman would be promoted, but not to gunnery sergeant, and kept here?"

"Yes, sir."

"I know, Vince," the major said, "that you really believe that what I do here all day is think up ways to torment people like you—"

"No, sir," Osadchy protested.

"So, you will doubtless be surprised to hear that when the TWX"—a message transmitted by teletype—"came down, and I received both your situation and Sergeant Zimmerman's record jacket, I came to the same conclusion. I TWX-ed back the day before yesterday, asked for reconsideration of the transfer. I said Zimmerman is critical here."

"And?" Osadchy asked.

"And when there was no reply, I got the Old Man's permission to call up and ask."

"And?" Osadchy asked.

"Pay attention, Lieutenant," the major said. "See for yourself how field-grade officers at the upper echelons of command are willing to grovel before the feet of their betters for the good of the command."

He picked up his telephone.

"Sergeant Asher," he said, "get a control number and then put in a call for me to Enlisted Assignment, G-One, Headquarters, Marine Corps. I want to speak to the officer in charge."

He put the telephone back in its cradle.

"Sometimes, Vince," he said, "it works. And sometimes it doesn't. I haven't called lately. Maybe we'll get lucky."

It took a minute or two to put the call through. The conversation itself took just over a minute.

"I understand, sir. Thank you very much," the major said, then hung up and turned to Lieutenant Osadchy.

"This time we weren't lucky," he said. "Both the decision to make Zimmerman a gunnery sergeant and to transfer him came from 'higher authority.' Since he carefully avoided saying *what* higher authority, I'm pretty sure he meant Intelligence. That make any sense to you?"

"No, sir," Lieutenant Osadchy said. "Zimmerman . . . Zimmerman's *not* an *intelligence* type. He's just a good China Marine motor sergeant."

"Well, that's it, Vince," the major said. "There's nothing else I can do. I'm sorry."

"Thanks for the try, sir."

The major called in his clerk and told him to cut orders promoting Sergeant Zimmerman to gunnery sergeant with date of rank 31 December 1941, and then to cut orders transferring Gunnery Sergeant Zimmerman to the 2nd Separate Battalion, USMC, at Quantico, Virginia; effective immediately.

(FOUR)
San Diego, California
0830 Hours, 19 January 1942

The Martin PBM-1 flying boat made its approach to San Diego harbor straight in from the Pacific Ocean. Her twin sixteen-hundred-horsepower Wright R-2600-6 engines had been droning steadily for nearly eighteen hours. It was three thousand miles from Pearl to Diego, a long way in an airplane that cruised at 170 knots.

When she was down to two thousand feet, and her speed retarded, her pilot ordered "floats down," and the copilot operated the lever that caused wing-tip floats to be lowered from the high, gull-shaped wings.

"Navy Four Two Four," the tower called, "be on the lookout for one or more small civilian vessels east end landing area."

"Roger," the copilot said. "We have them in sight. Four Two Four on final."

The Martin came in low and slow, touched down in a massive splash, bounced airborne, and then touched down again in an even larger splash and stayed down.

"Four Two Four down at three-one past the hour," the copilot reported.

"Four Two Four, steer zero-thirty degrees, a follow-me boat will meet you and direct you to the seaplane ramp."

"Roger."

A gray Navy staff car and two ambulances, one a glistening Packard with chrome-plated flashing lights and siren on the roof, and the other a Dodge 3/4-ton, painted olive drab and with large red crosses painted on the sides and roof, waited for the PBM to taxi across the bay to the seaplane ramp.

The PBM got as close to the seaplane ramp as her pilot intended to take her under her own power. He cut the engines. A sailor walked down the ramp into the water until it was chest high. He reached over his head and hooked a cable to a ring in the nose of the PBM. An aircraft tractor at the end of the ramp pulled the PBM out of the water by the cable far enough up the ramp so that it could back up to the PBM and hook up a rigid tow bar. Then it pulled it into the parking area.

The doors of the ambulances opened, and doctors and corpsmen went to the hatch on the side of the flying boat's fuselage. A doctor and two corpsmen entered the fuselage. And then Captain Ed Banning climbed out.

A technical sergeant, a stocky man in his thirties, got out of the staff car and walked to him, saluted, and asked, "Captain Banning?"

Baning returned the salute.

"I'll go with the men in the ambulances," Banning said.

The technical sergeant handed him a sheet of teletype paper.

PRIORITY

SECRET

HQ USMC WASH DC X 16 JANUARY 1942 X COMMANDING GENERAL X MARINE BARRACKS PEARL HARBOR HAWAII X INFO COMMANDING GENERAL MARINE BARRACKS SAN DIEGO X

REFERENCE YOUR TWX SUBJECT ARRIVAL PEARL HARBOR CAPT EDWARD J BANNING USMC X PHYSICAL CONDITION PERMITTING SUBJECT OFFICER WILL PROCEED HQ USMC BY FIRST AVAILABLE AIR TRANSPORTATION X PRIORITY AAA2 AUTHORIZED X COMMGEN MARBAR PEARL WILL ADVISE COMMGEN MARBAR DIEGO AND HQ USMC ATTN G2 ETA CONUS AND ETA WASH X

BY DIRECTION X

H W T FORREST BRIG GEN USMC

"How'd you know it was me, Sergeant?" Banning asked.

"They called—a Captain Sessions called—this morning, after they heard you'd left Pearl, sir. Captain Sessions described you. And he said to tell you 'Welcome home,' sir."

Banning nodded.

"We've got you a seat on the two thirty-five Western flight to Los Angeles, sir, connecting at five oh-five with a United flight to Washington. That's if you feel up to it."

Banning nodded again, but didn't reply. He didn't trust his voice to speak.

"It's up to you, sir. We can reschedule you later, if you're tired. My orders are to stick with you and do whatever has to be done."

Banning looked at the sergeant for a long moment, until he was reasonably sure that when he spoke he would display no more emotion than is appropriate for a Marine officer.

"What has to be done, Sergeant," he said, "if I am to get on civilian airplanes without disgracing the Corps, is to acquire a decent-looking uniform. And to do that, I'm going to have to get some money. How do I do that?"

"That's all laid on, sir," the technical sergeant said. "Captain Sessions suggested that there might be a problem with your pay and luggage."

XII

(ONE)
San Diego, California
0830 Hours, 19 January 1942

The first time Miss Ernestine Sage noticed the young woman was when she drove the LaSalle into the parking lot of the Bay-Vue Super Discount Super Market. The young woman was attractive, if harried-looking, and in what appeared to be the eighth month of her pregnancy. The pregnant young woman seemed to be examining her, or maybe the car, with more than ordinary interest.

But then, as she got out of the car, Ernie's attention was distracted by a Navy airplane, an enormous, twin-engine seaplane, coming in over the ocean and then landing in the bay with two enormous splashes. The sun was shining (it shined just about all the time here), and the bay was blue, and the airplane landing, Ernie thought, was beautiful. It made her think of Pick Pickering, who was learning to fly.

The pregnant young woman was standing in front of the plate-glass windows of the supermarket when Ernie grabbed a shopping cart and headed for the door. She smiled—shyly—at Ernie, and Ernie returned the smile.

Inside the supermarket, Ernie took her shopping list from her purse and went first to the dairy cooler for eggs and milk and butter. As they were driving across the country, and since they had arrived here, she had been astonished at Ken's enormous breakfast appetite. He regularly wolfed down four eggs and as much bacon or ham as she put before him. Once, for the hell of it, she had cooked a whole pound of bacon, and, with the exception of her own three slices, Ken had eaten all of it.

Next she went to the meat cooler and bought bacon and ham and sausage. And then she had the most extraordinary feeling that she was being followed by the pregnant young woman.

Ernie moved from the bacon and sausage display case into one of the aisles. Halfway down it, the pregnant young woman appeared, coming the other way.

Without doing anything that would suggest she was trying to lose the pregnant young woman, Ernie tried to do just that. Fixing an *"ooops, I forgot paprika"* look on her face, she twice reversed direction, and pushed her shopping cart into another aisle.

And both times the pregnant young woman, whose shopping cart held a loaf of bread and a quart bottle of ginger ale and nothing else, appeared behind her in the same aisle. The second time Ernie reversed direction she moved three aisles away, to the beef section, where she bought a half a dozen T-bone steaks; but that move didn't shake loose the pregnant woman either.

Ken never tired of steak. Which was a good thing, for her culinary skills were just about limited to frying eggs and bacon and broiling steak.

As she maneuvered her cart, Ernie had managed to glance at the young woman (even to study her for a long moment in a curved mirror apparently installed to discourage shoplifters). And by now she was convinced that she had never seen the young woman before. But she was also convinced that whatever the young woman was—and she looked like a nice young woman—she was not a threat.

But she unnerved Ernie. And feeling a little foolish, Ernie cut short her shopping trip. She had steaks for dinner and stuff for breakfast in the shopping cart. She could pick up bread and toilet tissue on the way to the checkout counter. What else she needed she would get tomorrow. Or maybe even later today, if Ken called up and said he would be a little late again.

Ernie didn't see the young woman as she went through the checkout line, but when she pushed the shopping cart out of the supermarket, the young woman was in the parking lot, between Ernie and the LaSalle.

Ernie pushed the shopping cart off the concrete sidewalk onto the macadam and toward the car. The pregnant young woman was now looking at her. Ernie put on a faint smile (the only explanation for her behavior, she suddenly concluded, was that the young woman mistakenly believed that she knew her) and headed for the car.

"Excuse me," the pregnant young woman said, "you're an officer's wife, aren't you?"

Ernie hesitated.

"I saw the Camp Elliott sticker," the pregnant young woman said, making a vague gesture toward a sticker on the LaSalle's windshield. It identified the car as having been registered on the post by a Marine officer.

"The car belongs to a friend," Ernie said.

"Oh," the pregnant young woman said, obviously disappointed, and then added, "I am. A Marine officer's wife, I mean."

"Right now," Ernie blurted, "that's the great ambition of my life. To be a Marine officer's wife."

The young woman smiled. It was a nice smile, Ernie thought, and the young woman was obviously a nice young woman.

"Is there something I can do for you?" Ernie asked.

The pregnant young woman dipped into her purse and came up with a wallet. She took from it a dependent's identification card, which she thrust at Ernie. There was a photograph on it, which made the pregnant young woman look all of sixteen years old. Her name was Dorothy Burnes and she was the dependent wife of Martin J. Burnes, 1st Lt., USMCR.

"Can I talk to you?" Dorothy Burnes said.

"Sure," Ernie said. "Mine is a second lieutenant."

"I've been following you around the supermarket," Dorothy said.

"I noticed," Ernie said. A look of embarrassment crossed Dorothy Burnes's face. "Why don't you sit in the car?" Ernie added.

"Thank you," Dorothy said. She got in the passenger seat. Then Ernie unloaded the groceries from the shopping cart into the LaSalle and pushed the basket to a steel-pipe enclosure. When that was done she walked back to the convertible. The roof was down and the boot snapped in place. The car glistened. Ernie had waxed it, with Simoniz, partly because she had come to understand how important the car was to Ken, and partly because there wasn't much to do with him gone all day.

Ernie got behind the wheel, pulled the door closed, and turned to Dorothy Burnes.

"I'm desperate," Dorothy said. "They put me out of the motel today, and unless I find someplace to stay between now and half-past five, my husband's going to put me on the Lark at half-past six."

"The Lark?"

"The train to Los Angeles," Dorothy explained. "Where you can connect with trains to Kansas City. We're from Kansas City."

"Oh," Ernie said.

"I really thought if I offered them twice as much money, they'd let me stay," Dorothy said. "But the lady said that wouldn't be 'fair to the other girls,' and that I would have to check out."

"Oh, hell," Ernie said.

"So," Dorothy said, trying and failing to sound amusing, "I got this clever idea that maybe if I asked some other officer's wife, who looked like she had some place to stay, maybe she'd know of something. And then I decided the best place to find some officer's wife who had a place to stay was at a supermarket. If she was buying groceries, she would have a place to cook them. So I came here and you came in."

"Good thinking, anyway," Ernie said.

She's just like me. Or, there but for the grace of God and Pick's father, go I.

"But I suppose you're living with your folks," Dorothy said, "and have no idea where I could find a place . . . anyplace out of rain?"

"I'm living on a boat," Ernie said. "And I don't, I'm afraid, know of any place for rent."

"A boat?" Dorothy asked.

Ernie nodded. "One of those things that goes up and down in the water," she said.

"And you don't have any idea—" Dorothy said.

Ernie shook her head.

"Damn," Dorothy said, and then started to sniffle.

The tears, Ernie knew, were genuine, not a pitch for sympathy. Dorothy Burnes was at the end of her rope. She was pregnant and didn't have a place to stay, and her Marine was about to send her home.

"Sorry," Dorothy Burnes said, wiping her nose with a Kleenex.

"If they threw you out, where's your luggage?" Ernie asked.

"In the motel office," Dorothy said.

"Well, you can stay with us tonight," Ernie said. "And in the morning, you and I will start looking for a place for you."

"Have you got room?"

Ernie nodded.

"I've got money," Dorothy said. "I can pay. I really thought if I offered them twice as much money . . . I wired my father for money, and I wasn't going to tell Marty—"

"Where's the motel?" Ernie interrupted, as she pushed the LaSalle's starter button.

"I don't know how to thank you," Dorothy said.

"I guess we camp followers have to stick together," Ernie said.

That made Dorothy Burnes giggle. She smiled shyly at Ernie. Ernie was pleased.

Twenty minutes later, Ernie stopped the LaSalle near Pier Four of the San Diego Yacht Club. A hundred yards out on the pier, the *Last Time* bobbed gently up and down. It was separated from the wharf by five white rubber bumpers the size of wastebaskets, and connected to it by a teak gangplank and electric service and telephone cables.

The *Last Time,* the property of a San Diego attorney whose firm did a good deal of business with Pacific & Far East Shipping, Inc., was fifty-three feet long, sixteen feet in the beam, and drew six feet. She was powered with twin General Motors Detroit diesels.

Her owner had been delighted, when approached, to offer it, via the chairman of the board of Pacific & Far East Shipping, to the daughter of the chairman of the board of the American Personal Pharmaceutical Corporation for as long as she wanted it. Not only for the obvious reasons, but also because her normal three-man crew, carried away on a wave of patriotism, had enlisted in the Coast Guard, leaving the *Last Time* untended.

"Oh, my God!" Dorothy Burnes said when she stepped down into the lounge. "I've never been on one this big. What is it, a Bertram?"

Which question indicates, Ernie decided, *that you are not entirely unfamiliar with yachts. And it follows from that, and from other things you have said, that while you obviously are a homeless and pregnant waif, you are probably not a poor homeless waif.*

"No," she said. "It's a Mitchell. It was made in Florida and sailed here."

"It's yours?"

"It belongs to a friend of a friend," Ernie said. "We're boat-sitting. The crew went off to the Coast Guard."

"I just hope I'm not dreaming," Dorothy said. "I can't tell you how grateful I am."

"I'm glad to have the company," Ernie said. And she realized then that although they would certainly look around the next day, and diligently, for some place for Dorothy Burnes and her husband to live, they almost certainly were not going to find one.

Which means they will stay here. Which, on balance, may be a pretty good idea. It'll give me company. And we are, in a sense, sisters.

"Maybe I should have told you this before," Ernie said. "I think the phrase for what my Marine and I are doing on here is 'shacking up.' "

There was a look of embarrassment in Dorothy Burnes's eyes. "You didn't have to tell me that," she said, softly. "That's none of my business."

"Ken doesn't think that Marine officers, about to be sent overseas, should be married," Ernie said.

"Do you love him?"

"Oh, yes," Ernie said.

"Isn't that all that's important? I mean, really?"

"So my reasoning goes," Ernie said.

"Maybe, when he sees Marty and me, it will be contagious," Dorothy said.

"That's a nice thought," Ernie said. "Come on, I'll show you your room . . . cabin."

By four o'clock, Ernie Page and Dorothy Burnes had become friends. They were of an age, and of roughly comparable background. Dorothy's father operated a large condiment-bottling business (pickles, relish, horseradish, et cetera) founded by his grandfather. She had gone to Emma Willard, and then on to Vanderbilt College, where, as a junior, she had married Marty, then a senior. Marty had gone to Quantico for the Platoon Leader's Course when he graduated.

"Ken went through Quantico," Ernie offered, "with my childhood sweetheart. That's how we met. And my childhood sweetheart's parents fixed it for us to live on the boat."

"They know?" Dorothy asked. The rest of the sentence, "that you and Ken are living together on this boat?" went unsaid.

"They know," Ernie said. "My parents know, too, but they pretend not to. I mean, they know I'm out here with Ken. They don't know about the boat."

"Where did Ken go to school?" Dorothy asked.

"He didn't," Ernie replied, with a sense of misgiving. "He's what they call a mustang. He came up from the ranks."

"Oh?"

"He's very bright," Ernie said. "And the Marine Corps saw it, and they sent him to officer's school."

"He must be," Dorothy readily agreed.

A clock chimed four times.

"Time to get him," Ernie said, and then, "What do we do about yours? What will he do, go to the motel?"

Dorothy nodded.

"Well, then, I'll drop you off there and go fetch Ken," Ernie said. "You bring him here."

Ken, who was wearing dungarees, looked tired when Ernie picked him up behind the orderly room at Camp Elliott. When he was tired, he looked older. Sometimes, she thought, he looked like a boy. And in his dungarees, he did not much resemble the Marine officer in the recruiting posters.

She pushed the door open and then slid halfway across the seat to let him get behind the wheel.

"Been waiting long?" she asked.

"No," he said simply.

"Don't I get a kiss?"

He graciously offered the side of his face. It wasn't what she had had in mind, but she knew that it was all she was going to get. The official excuse was that there was a Marine Corps regulation—yet another regulation—that proscribed the public display of affection by officers and gentlemen. The real reason was that *Ken* was made uncomfortable by public displays of affection; the regulation just gave him the excuse he needed to treat her, when in public, like a sister.

Sometimes, as now, this annoyed Ernie.

She moved her hand and quickly groped him.

"Jesus Christ!" Ken said, knocking her hand away.

"There's a time and place, right?" she teased. "And this isn't it?"

He looked at her and shook his head.

"You're something," he said.

"Uh-*huh,*" she agreed.

For just a moment, he touched her cheek very gently with the back of his hand.

"Watch out!" she said in mock horror. "Someone will see, and they will cut your buttons off and drum you out of the Corps in disgrace!"

He laughed softly and smiled at her.

"How was your day?"

"Noisy," he said. He dug in his shirt pocket and handed her a brass cartridge case.

"What's this?"

"Look at the stamp," he said. "On the bottom."

"I'm looking," she said. "What do I see?"

"See where it says 'FA 15'?" She nodded. "That means it was made by the Frankfurt Arsenal in 1915; before the First World War."

They were at the gate then. A Marine MP saluted crisply as he waved them through.

"Do you think he'd do that if he suspected that you and I are carrying on?" Ernie said innocently after Ken had returned the salute. "Or do you think he'd turn you in? *'Sir, I saw an officer today I just know is carrying on with a female civilian.'* "

He laughed again and smiled at her.

"You just don't give up, do you?"

"Does it still work?"

"Does what still work?"

"Bullets made before the First World War," Ernie said.

"The bullet is the pointed thing that comes out the barrel," Ken said. "The round consists of the case, the powder, the primer—*and* the bullet."

"Sorry," she said, mockingly.

"And the answer is most of the time," he said. "It's really surprising."

"What happens if it doesn't work?" she asked.

"Colonel Carlson came to see me today," McCoy said, changing the subject.

"What?" she asked, confused. It wasn't the answer she expected.

"Colonel Carlson came out to the machine-gun range," McCoy said. "Looking for me."

"What did he want?"

"He spoke to me in Cantonese," McCoy said, and smiled. "You should have seen the looks on the kids' faces when he did that."

"What did he want?" Ernie repeated.

"Well, I guess he wanted to have a look at me, and to see if I really spoke Chinese."

"And?" she asked, impatiently.

"He wanted to know if I had heard of the Chinese Route Army, and if so, what I thought about them."

"What did you tell him?"

"What I thought he wanted to hear," McCoy said. "That they do a pretty good job."

"That's all?"

"Oh, he asked me the usual questions; he was feeling me out," McCoy said. "And then he told me he was forming a battalion, and asked if I was interested in joining it."

"And you, of course, said yes," Ernie said.

"That's why they sent me out here," McCoy said. "You know that. The whole idea was to get him to recruit me."

He suddenly pulled out of the line of traffic and stopped before a commercial laundry. He went in and came out a minute or two later carrying two enormous bundles of paper-wrapped laundry. He threw them in the back and got behind the wheel.

"What's for supper?" he asked.

"Steak, for a change," she said.

He nodded his approval.

"Well, are you going to tell me, or not?"

"Tell you what?"

"Did he 'recruit' you, or not?"

"He fed me a line about how he wanted to compare me against other volunteers," McCoy said. "But that was just bullshit. He'll take me. I'm a young old China Marine."

"What does that mean?"

"He wants old China Marines, people who may think like Orientals. And he wants young officers and men. He'll take either. I'm both."

"Well, is he crazy, or not?"

"I liked him," McCoy said. "Ain't that a kick in the ass?"

"He's not crazy?"

"No, he's not crazy, and he struck me as a damned good officer. He's obviously smarter than hell, and his ideas abut making raids with highly trained people make sense."

"What about the other thing, his being a Communist?"

"He didn't talk politics," McCoy said. "And I could hardly ask him."

"So what happens now?"

"I call Captain Sessions and tell him," McCoy said.

"I mean, to you?"

"In a couple of days, maybe a week, I think they'll transfer me," McCoy said.

He turned off the highway through the gates of the San Diego Yacht Club and drove to the water's edge.

A Pontiac coupe with Missouri license plates was parked with its nose against the Pier Four sign. There was a Marine officer, in greens, sitting behind the wheel, and Ernie could see the back of Dorothy Burnes's head.

"Oh, good," Ernie said. "They're here."

" 'Oh, good,' " Ken McCoy parroted, *"who's* here?"

Oh, my God! I should have told him before we got here!

"We have houseguests," Ernie said, as she opened the door of the LaSalle and got out.

The door of the Pontiac opened and Dorothy Burnes, grunting, pushed herself out of the car. She smiled warmly and gratefully at Ernie. Her husband got out from behind the wheel, looking a little uneasy.

Then he saluted. Ernie wondered why he had done that, and then realized he was returning Ken's salute. And then she understood why. There were silver bars on Martin J. Burnes's epaulets; he outranked Ken, and Ken had saluted him.

"Well, I see you found each other all right," Ernie said. She turned and saw Ken walking up. "This is Ken," she said. "Ken, this is Marty Burnes."

"How do you do, sir," Ken McCoy said formally. Ernie did not like the look on Ken McCoy's face.

"And this is Dorothy," Ernie plunged ahead.

"Hi," Dorothy said.

"Dorothy and I are old pals, and she's having a hard time finding a place to stay, so they'll be staying with us for a couple of days."

"I hope we're not going to put you out too much," Marty Burnes said to McCoy.

"It's her boat," Ken said simply.

Oh, God! He doesn't like this at all. Why not? What's wrong with him? He could easily be in Marty Burnes's place. And then she understood. *He's not here as just one more lieutenant; he's going to spy on that Colonel Whatsisname, and he's afraid that the Burneses being on the boat will get in the way of that. And, damnit, maybe he's right.*

"Well, let's go aboard," Ernie said, trying to be bright and cheerful. "Dorothy and I have spent the afternoon making hors d'oeuvres."

"And then there'll be steaks," Dorothy chimed in.

"And I'm sure you both could use a drink," Ernie said. She stole a glance at Ken. His eyes were cold. But not angry, she thought. Disappointed, resigned, as if he had expected her to do something dumb like this.

McCoy forced a polite smile on his face.

"I could use a drink," he said. "After you, Lieutenant."

"Can't we forget the Marine Corps?" Ernie said. "Just for an hour or two? What I mean is can't you two use your *names?"*

"Sure," Marty Burnes said. He smiled and put out his hand to McCoy. "I'm Marty."

McCoy took the hand and forced another brief smile. "Ken," he said.

"You two unload the cars," Ernie ordered. "By the time you're finished, we'll have drinks made."

When the drinks were made, Ernie proposed a toast. "I think, for the Burneses, that this is the proverbial any old port in a storm," she said. "Welcome aboard, Burneses."

McCoy chuckled and raised his glass, and this time his smile was genuine.

"Welcome aboard," he said.

He sat slumped in the largest of the four upholstered chairs in the cabin. He was still in dungarees with his rough-side-out field shoes stretched out in front of him. And for the first time (probably because Marty Burnes was in a green uniform, she thought) she noticed how incongruous a Marine dressed that way looked in the plush cabin.

Ernie and Dorothy passed the tray of hors d'oeuvres. McCoy helped himself to several chunks of cheddar, and then gulped down his drink.

"Now that I am refueled," he said, "I think I'll scrape off some of the barnacles."

He went down the passageway to the master cabin.

In a minute, they could hear the shower start, and a moment after that, faintly, the sound of McCoy singing.

Thank God, he's over the mad.

"He does that, too," Dorothy Burnes said, nodding fondly at her husband.

Ernie made Marty Burnes another drink.

When the sound of the shower stopped and McCoy did not appear in a reasonable time, she excused herself and went to their cabin.

If there's going to be a fight, I might as well get it over with.

She got to the cabin as Ken, naked, lay back on the bed with the telephone in his hand.

He looked at her but said nothing, and he did not react to the way she raised her eyebrows approvingly at his nakedness.

"Collect for anyone, operator, from Lieutenant McCoy to Liberty seven, oh nine five six in Washington, D.C. I'll hold."

"Ken, she had no place to stay. He was going to send her home," Ernie said.

He held the telephone away from his head as if to explain why he couldn't talk to her, and then he put it back. Although she knew that it was not his intention, Ernie chose to interpret the gesture as an invitation to lie down beside him and listen to the conversation. For a moment he stiffened, and she was afraid he would roll away from her, or get up. But then he relaxed.

"Liberty seven, oh nine five six," a none-too-friendly male voice came on the line.

"I have a collect call for anyone from a Lieutenant McCoy," the operator said. "Will you accept charges?"

"We'll accept," the male voice said.

"Go ahead, sir," the operator said. "Your party is on the line."

"How are you, Sergeant?" McCoy said to the telephone. "Is Captain Sessions around?"

"I'll buzz for him. I know he wants to talk to you. How's things in the boondocks?"

"I'm looking for a sergeant who knows how to take a 'Seventeen A-Four apart," McCoy said.

The sergeant chuckled, and then another voice came on the line.

"Captain Sessions."

"Lieutenant McCoy is on the line, sir," the sergeant said.

"Oh, good. Ken?"

"Yes, sir."

"I was about to call you. I was going to wait until I was sure you were home. What's on your mind?"

"Colonel Carlson looked me up today," McCoy said. "I was on the machine-gun range, and he found me there."

"And?"

"He checked to see if I really speak Cantonese, and then pumped me for what he could get."

"What did he get?"

"He wanted to know what I thought of the Mao Tse-tung tribe of slopeheads," McCoy said. "So I told him what he wanted to hear."

"Anything about the Raiders?"

" 'Raiders'? Is that what they're going to call them?"

"Yeah, it looks that way. The Commandant is going to order the formation as of four February, of the Second Separate Battalion, there at Elliott. The same day, a reinforced company—about two hundred fifty people—is going to be transferred from the First Separate Battalion at Quantico to the Second at Elliott. Our friend Zimmerman, who is now a gunnery sergeant, will be one of them. On nineteen February, the Second will be redesignated as the Second Raider Battalion. That's one of the reasons I wanted to talk to you, to tell you that."

"Maybe you better not spread this around, sir," McCoy said. "But I think he's got a good idea."

"He talked to you about it?"

"Yes, sir. And what he said made sense."

"Did he say anything about you joining up? The reason I ask, is that unless you can get into the Second Battalion out there, Colonal Rickabee's going to transfer you back to Quantico, assign you to the First Separate Battalion, and then send you back out to Carlson when they transfer the company from the First Battalion out there."

"He gave me the usual bullshit about comparing me against other volunteers, but I would be damned surprised if he didn't have me transferred."

"Good. Then we'll leave it that way. If you're wrong, if he doesn't pick you . . . any suggestion that he questioned your neatly doctored service record?"

"No, sir."

"If he doesn't pick you, we'll worry about that then."

"Captain, can I talk to you man to man?"

"Of course not, said the officer to the officer who saved his life," Sessions said. "What's on your mind, Ken?"

"I don't like this job," McCoy said. "I feel like a real slimy sonofabitch, spying on Colonal Carlson. I like him. He's a good officer, and I think the commandos are a good idea."

"Raiders," Sessions corrected him automatically, and then fell silent.

"I went too far, huh?" McCoy said, after a long moment.

"No, no," Sessions said. "I was trying to frame my reply. I think I know how you feel, Ken. The only thing I can really say is that it has to be done, and you're the fellow to do it. I don't think anyone is going to be happy if you find out he is either unbalanced or a Communist."

"I do. I've had a chance to think about this a lot. It looks to me that a lot of the brass want to stick it to Carlson because he's got a direct line to the President."

"There's some of that, sure," Sessions said. "But I also think that if he actually goes off the deep end, he could do the Corps a lot of damage. More damage, Ken, than I think you can fully appreciate."

"Aye, aye, sir," McCoy said.

"Excuse me, Ken?" Sessions asked.

"That means I understand the order and will carry it out," McCoy said. "Didn't you ever hear that before, Captain, sir?"

"Don't be a wiseass, you're only a second lieutenant," Sessions said, and then his voice grew serious. "For what it's worth, Ken, I think what you're doing has to be done.

"I knew that," McCoy said. "It's the main reason I'm doing it."

"I just had another patriotic, flag-waving, hurrah-for-the-Corps thought," Sessions said. "You want to hear it?"

"Sure."

"When they get both of the Raider battalions up to strength and trained, Ken, I don't think there will be fifty people in them, officer or enlisted, who have ever heard the sound of a shot fired in anger. Even though nobody will know about it, with your doctored service record, you'll be one of the most experienced officers around. Certainly the most experienced lieutenant. The only test that counts for an officer is how he behaves when people are shooting at him. And you've passed that test twice, Killer, and with flying colors."

"Shit," McCoy said.

"No shit, Ken. I'm a living witness to how well you conduct yourself under stress. If you do nothing else with the Raiders, you'll probably be able to keep some of the kids alive."

Ernie had moved on the bed, so that she could rest her head on McCoy's shoulder while she listened to the conversation. Now she raised her head so that she could see Ken's eyes.

He shrugged his shoulders, as if embarrassed by what Captain Sessions had said.

"You said you had a couple of things to tell me," McCoy said.

"Oh, yeah. I'm glad you reminded me. One of them was about Zimmerman."

"He doesn't know what I'm doing out here, does he?"

"No, and don't tell him," Sessions said. "Let him think it's because you both speak Chinese, or because Carlson likes China Marines."

"Yes, sir," McCoy said. "What else?"

"You didn't happen to see Captain Banning, did you?"

"Captain *Banning? Our* Captain Banning?"

"Banning was evacuated from Corregidor by submarine. He passed through Diego today on his way here. There was a chance he might have bumped into you. I had to ask. The worst possible case would have been for him to greet you like a long-lost brother within Carlson's hearing. Even worse, to have him thank you for saving his life. That would have blown your new service record out of the water, and told Carlson that he's being watched."

"I didn't see him," McCoy said. "What's going to happen to him?"

"Well, for one thing, he's going to be told that he never heard of you in his life, and aside from that, I can't tell you."

"Can you give him my regards?"

"Sure, Ken," Sessions said.

"I guess that's about it," McCoy said.

"How's your love life, Ken?" Sessions asked.

"None of your business."

"I was just going to say to give her my regards."

McCoy didn't reply.

"You better check in every day from now on, either with me or Colonel Rickabee."

"Aye, aye, sir."

McCoy sat up, taking Ernie with him, and put the phone back in its cradle on the bulkhead behind him.

"He knows about us?" Ernie asked. McCoy nodded. "What did you tell him?"

McCoy smiled. "That you're the best piece of ass I ever had in my life," he said, and then put his arms up to defend himself from the blows he was sure would follow.

They did not. Ernie waited for him to put his arms down, and then said, "Well, I'm glad you told him the truth."

Then she got out of the bed and went back to the main cabin.

McCoy put on a pair of khaki trousers and a T-shirt, then went out and made himself another drink.

"I understand," Lieutenant Marty Burnes said, "that you're in a heavy-weapons company."

"That's right," McCoy said. "What do they have you doing?"

"At the moment I'm assigned to S-Three," Burnes said.

"At the moment?" McCoy asked.

"You've heard about the Raiders?" Burnes asked.

"A little," McCoy replied. He was aware that Ernie had picked up on the conversation and was watching them.

"Well, I've applied, and I think I'm going to be accepted," Burnes said. "I talked to Captain Roosevelt—the President's son?—and he said I would probably qualify."

"It's a very good way to get your ass blown away," McCoy said.

"Ken!" Ernie said.

"Sorry," McCoy said. "I shouldn't have said that."

XIII

(ONE)
Saufley Field
Pensacola Navy Air Station
20 February 1942

There was no doubt in the mind of Lieutenant Junior Grade Allen W. Minter, USNR, that Second Lieutenant Malcolm S. Pickering, USMCR, had a good deal more time in aircraft cockpits than his record showed; or, off the record, than he was willing to admit.

That made Pickering a liar. Not only a liar, but a good liar. Of course it was possible to put that more kindly, to say that he was a good role player. One could possibly maintain—or at least imagine—that Pickering was playing the role of someone who knew nothing about flying or aircraft, but who was eager to learn, and was a very quick learner.

From the moment Minter first took him out to the flight line, Pickering asked both the natural and the dumb questions Minter expected of a student whose flight records had "NONE" written in the "PREVIOUS FLYING EXPERIENCE" block. And he appeared to listen with rapt attention—as if he was hearing it all for the first time—while Minter pointed out the parts of the N3N Yellow Peril and explained their function.

And Minter was perfectly willing to accept that Pickering was learning for the first time that the thing that sat upright at the back of the Yellow Peril was the vertical stabilizer, and that the back part of it moved when the rudder pedals were pressed; that in the sea of air it served the same function that the rudder of a boat served in the water.

And Pickering seemed absolutely fascinated to learn that while the altimeter did indeed indicate the height of the aircraft above sea level, it did so seven seconds late. In other words, because it took some time for the change in air pressure to work upon the membrane of the barometric altimeter, the altimeter reported what the altitude had been seven seconds ago, not what it was at the moment.

It was only when he took Pickering up for the first time that Minter began to smell a rat.

Instructor pilots were given some latitude in teaching their students. Lieutenant Minter did not believe the way to turn an eager young man into a pilot was to take him up and scare the shit out of him, and/or make him sick to his stomach.

He believed that it was best to start out very simply, to show the student that a very slight rearward pressure on the stick would cause the nose of the Yellow Peril to rise, and that a very slight downward pressure would put the Yellow Peril in a nosedown attitude.

As the student understood and became familiar with one movement, he could be taught another. Eventually, he would reach the point where he would understand what coordinated control movement was necessary to make the aircraft perform any maneuver it was capable of.

Slow and easy was better, in Lieutenant Minter's professional judgment, than throwing things at a student too fast and scaring hell out of him. He would have the hell scared out of him soon enough.

On the first flight, Minter demonstrated climbing and descending, and then gentle turns to the left and right, pointing out to his new student that what one tried for was to make the turn without either gaining or losing altitude. In order to do that, one tried to keep one's eye on the vertical speed indicator, which indicated (faster than the altimeter responded) the deviation, and the rate of deviation (in thousands of feet per minute, up or down) from the altitude where the aircraft started when its needle was in the center of the instrument.

As he was demonstrating, Minter cautioned Pickering that not much movement of the controls was required to move the airplane around, and that most student pilots tended to overcontrol, to move the controls farther and more violently than was necessary.

And then when Minter turned the controls over to Pickering and told him to go up, and then down, the first thing he thought was that he had a student who paid attention to what he was told. He did not overcontrol. And he had a gentle, sure touch on the joystick and rudder pedals.

The first time Pickering tried to make a 360-degree turn to the right, for instance, the needle on the vertical speed indicator didn't even flicker. And when he came out of the turn and straightened up, he wasn't more than two degrees off the course he had been on before he began to make the turn. The whole maneuver was smooth as silk.

Much too smooth for somebody trying it for the first time. Q.E.D., Pickering knew how to fly. Ergo, Pickering was a liar, for he had told the U.S. Navy that his PREVIOUS FLIGHT EXPERIENCE was "NONE."

Viewed one way, it was an innocent little joke that Lieutenant Pickering was playing on the Navy and Lieutenant Junior Grade Allen W. Minter. Viewed another way, it was a serious breach of discipline. Pickering was a commissioned officer, and the code was quite clear: Officers told the truth. An officer's word was his bond. An officer who knowingly affixed his signature to a document he knew contained an untruth was subject to court-martial and dismissal from the service.

In the beginning, Lieutenant Minter decided that he would give Lieutenant Pickering the benefit of the doubt. Pickering seemed to be a nice enough guy, and he hadn't been in the service for very long, and he was young; and maybe he didn't understand that what he probably thought of as a little joke was something that could get his ass kicked out of Pensacola. Minter had heard that officers dismissed for cause from the service no longer got to go home, but were immediately pressed into service in the ranks. Unless it was really necessary, he didn't want to be responsible for sending Second Lieutenant Pickering to the Marine boot camp at Parris Island as a private.

When they landed, he conversed pleasantly with Pickering, told him that he had done remarkably well (which caused Pickering to beam), and gave him every opportunity to admit that he'd had at least a little pilot training before today. Pickering responded that Captain Carstairs had taken him for a ride when he'd first come to Pensacola, but that was it.

Minter then went over Pickering's records very carefully. He could have made a mistake, he told himself. But he had not. The record said "NONE" in the "PREVIOUS FLIGHT EXPERIENCE" block. And Pickering had signed the form.

Minter next sought out Captain James L. Carstairs, who had the administrative responsibility for Pickering, as well as for the other Marine second john, Stecker. Minter did not like Carstairs, which was his natural reaction to the fact that Carstairs did not like him. Carstairs was a Marine. Not only a Marine but a regular, out of Annapolis. Carstairs was tall, good-looking, and mustachioed. A regular fucking recruiting-poster marine.

As a class, officers like Carstairs did not particularly like people like Minter, who joined the Navy right out of the University of Ohio to get flight training, and who planned to get out of the service just as soon as possible to take a job with an airline. And who were, moreover, just a little plump, and who did not look like the tall, erect, blue-eyed Naval aviators in the recruiting posters.

But he made a point of finding Captain Carstairs at the bar of the officers' club during happy hour.

"Hello, Captain," he said.

"Well, if it isn't Lieutenant Dumpling," Carstairs said.

Minter let that ride. "I took your two second lieutenants up for the first time this morning," he said, signaling the bartender to bring two beers.

"Did you really?"

"One of them, Pickering, seems to have a really unusual flair."

"Does he really?"

"Either that or he's got time, bootleg or otherwise," Minter said.

"What does his record say?"

"It says no previous flight experience," Minter said.

"Then we must presume, mustn't we, that he has none," Carstairs said.

"He tells me you had him up," Minter pursued. "What did you think?"

"Nothing special," Carstairs said. "He struck me as your typical red-blooded American boy burning with ambition to earn his wings of gold," Carstairs said.

"You don't know anything about him, expect what's in his records?" Minter asked.

Carstairs looked at Minter, and then over his shoulders, as if to make sure no one could overhear him.

"I have heard," Carstairs said, confidently, "that when Henry Ford runs a little short of cash, the first person he thinks of for a loan is Pickering. Is that what you mean?"

"Oh, come on, Carstairs, I'm serious," Minter said impatiently.

For a moment, Minter thought that Carstairs was going to jump his ass for calling him by his last name. But instead, Carstairs flashed him a broad smile.

"But my dear Dumpling, I am serious," Carstairs said. "You *do* know he lives in the penthouse of the San Carlos Hotel?"

"No, I didn't," Minter confessed, wondering if Carstairs was pulling his leg about that, too.

Carstairs shook his head in confirmation.

"If that's so," Minter blurted, "what's he doing in the Marine Corps?"

"Why, Dumpling, he's doing the same thing as you and me. Remembering Pearl Harbor, avenging Wake Island, and making the world safe for democracy. I'm really surprised that you had to ask."

Minter, not without effort, kept his temper and his mouth shut, finished his beer, and left.

The next morning, when it was time to take Pickering up again, he was just about ready to call Pickering on lying about and concealing his previous flying experience. And then he decided, fuck it.

He still wasn't sure whether or not Carstairs had been telling the truth in the officers' club bar about Pickering being rich and living in the San Carlos penthouse. It was equally credible that Carstairs was pulling his leg, making a fool of him.

What really counted was that Pickering seemed like a nice kid; and the Marines needed good pilots. Despite the black-and-white code of conduct expected of officers, what was really important was what he had been ordered to do, which was to turn Pickering into a pilot of sufficient skill to be promoted to Squadron-2. Minter told himself that he was an instructor pilot, not an FBI agent, and that saying you had no previous flying experience when you did was not a sin of the first magnitude.

He flew with Pickering for two hours, and then with Stecker for two hours. When he dismissed them to have lunch before going to ground school during the afternoon, he thought that he had proof that he was teaching Stecker, but that Pickering was just going through the motions of learning something he already knew. But it didn't seem important.

The next day, the two of them had ground school in the morning and flight training during the afternoon. Minter took Stecker up first, and spent two hours having him practice the skills necessary to get an aircraft off the ground, to make turns, and then to get it back on the ground again. He spent the last half hour with Stecker shooting touch-and-go landings, with Stecker following him through on the controls.

He did essentially the same thing when he gave Pickering his two hours, except that he devoted the last hour to touch-and-goes, and the last fifteen minutes of that to having Pickering actually make the landings and takeoffs.

But when the two hours were up, and he had permitted Pickering to taxi the Yellow Peril from the runway to the parking ramp himself, instead of ordering him to shut it down, he climbed out of the forward cockpit, knelt on the wing root beside the rear cockpit, and looked intently into Pickering's face.

"I can't think of any reason why you shouldn't take it up yourself, Pickering, can you?"

Pickering smiled. "No, sir," he said.

"Then do so, Lieutenant," Minter ordered, and got off the wing root.

Pickering had some trouble, Minter saw, taxiing the Yellow Peril back to the runway. And for a moment he really thought Pickering was about to collide with another Yellow Peril on the center line of the runway.

Just enough trouble to give Minter pause to consider that maybe he had done the wrong thing, that just maybe Pickering really didn't have any experience, and that he should not be sending him up to solo with the absolute minimum of five hours' instruction.

But then the tower flashed the green lamp at Pickering's Yellow Peril, giving him permission to take off. The Yellow Peril began to move down the runway. The tail wheel came off the ground smoothly and when it should have, and a moment later, very smoothly, the Yellow Peril was airborne.

And Pickering followed the orders he had been given for his first solo flight: Take off, enter the landing pattern, and land. That's all.

Except when he was in the line of Yellow Perils waiting for their turn to land, he swung the Yellow Peril from side to side. Just once. It was a gesture of joy and exuberance. Minter decided that he would not mention it once Pickering was back on the ground, as he was now ninety-five percent sure he soon would safely be.

The landing was as smooth as Minter expected it to be. But what surprised him was the look on Pickering's face when he taxied to the parking ramp and shut the Yellow Peril down. It was the same look—mingled awe, relief, pride, and even a little disbelief—that Minter had learned to expect from other young men who had really just made their first solo flight.

And when he'd climbed down from the Yellow Peril he looked at Minter and said, "Jesus Christ, that's something, isn't it?"

"That really was your first time, wasn't it?" Minter blurted.

"Yes, sir," Pickering said. The question obviously confused him.

"Don't let it go to your head, Pickering," Minter said. "The University of California did a study that proved conclusively that any high-level moron can be taught to fly."

(TWO)
Gayfer's Department Store
Pensacola, Florida
20 February 1942

Second Lieutenant Malcolm S. Pickering, USMCR, could see Martha Sayre Culhane two aisles away. She was standing before triple full-length mirrors as she held a black dress to her body and examined her reflection thoughtfully.

Martha wore a light brown sweater and a brown tweed skirt. A single coil of pearls around her neck had shifted so that it curled around her left breast. And she was wearing loafers and bobby socks.

She was, Pick thought, the most exquisitely feminine creature he had ever seen. Just looking at her made his throat tight and dry, and his heart change its beat.

She was across a two-aisle no-man's-land of ladies' lingerie—glass counters stacked high with underpants and brassieres and girdles and slips. Headless-torso dummies had been placed here and there on the counters, dressed in more or less translucent brassieres and pants.

The intimate feminine apparel made Pick uncomfortable. And so did being where he was, and why. Without being aware that he was doing it, he closed his eyes and shook his head.

Martha nodded, as if making a decision, and then stepped away from the triple mirror and out of Pick's sight.

He moved an aisle away and saw her enter a dressing room and close its curtain. "May I help you, Lieutenant?" a female voice said, behind him, startling him.

"No," he said. "No, thank you. Just browsing."

He looked at the counters immediately around him. He had moved to the expectant-mother section. The dummies here displayed nursing brassieres.

She must think I'm crazy! Obviously, I am.

The hem of the curtain over Martha's dressing room was eighteen inches off the floor. He saw Martha's tweed skirt drop to the floor. Then she stepped out of it and scooped it up. And then, over the top of the curtain, he could see her hands and arms as she pulled the sweater off over her head.

He could imagine her now, in his mind's eye, standing behind the curtain wearing nothing but her string of pearls and her brassiere and her underpants.

He closed his eyes and shook his head again, and when he opened them he could see her hands as she stepped into the black dress and pulled it up.

And then a moment later, she came out and went back to the triple mirrors and looked at herself again. She had not zipped up the black dress, and he could see the strap of her brassiere stretched taut over her back.

And then he walked toward her, taking long, purposeful strides that shortened and grew hesitant as he came close.

"Surprise, surprise," he said, as jovially as he could manage. "Fancy running into you here!"

"I don't know why you're surprised, Pick," Martha said, looking directly at him. "You followed me from the air station."

He felt his face color.

"I soloed today," he blurted. "A couple of hours ago."

"Good for you," she said.

"Christ!" he said, furious and humiliated.

"I didn't mean that the way it sounded," Martha said. "Congratulations, Pick. Really. I know what it means, and I'm happy for you."

"I want to celebrate," Pick said.

"You should," Martha said. "It's a bona fide cause for celebration."

"I mean, with you," Pick blurted.

"I was afraid of that," she said.

"I thought maybe dinner, and then . . ."

She shook her head, and held up her left hand with her wedding and engagement rings on it.

"It sometimes may not look like it, Pick, but I'm in mourning."

"You go out with Captain Mustache," Pick blurted.

She laughed a delightful peal of laughter.

"Is that what you call him?" Martha said. "Marvelous! You better pray he doesn't hear you. Jimmy is very proud of his mustache."

"You go out with him," Pick persisted.

"That's different," Martha said. "He's a friend."

"And I can't be your friend?"

"You know what I mean," Martha said. "Jimmy was *our* friend. He was best man at the wedding."

"I'll settle for being your friend," Pick said.

"You don't take no for an answer, do you?" Martha said.

"Usually, I take anything less than 'oh, how wonderful' for no," Pick said.

"Well, Mr. Pickering," Martha said, "I'm truly sorry to disappoint you, but not only will I not go out with you, but I would consider it a personal favor if you would stop following me around and staring at me like a lovesick calf."

"Jesus!"

"I'm a *widow,* for God's sake," Martha went on furiously. "I'm just not interested, understand? I don't know what you're thinking—"

She stopped in mid-sentence, for Second Lieutenant Pickering had turned and fled down the aisle.

Martha told herself that there was really no reason for her to be ashamed of herself for jumping on him that way, or to be sorry that she had so obviously and so deeply hurt his feelings.

She *was* a widow, for God's sake.

Greg, my wonderful Greg, was killed only two months and twelve days ago. Only a real bitch and a slut would start thinking about another man only two months and twelve days after her husband, whom she had loved as much as life itself, had been killed. And if that handsome, arrogant sonofabitch was any kind of a gentleman he would understand that.

Martha Sayre Culhane vowed that she would never again think of the terrible hurt look in Pick's eyes when she told him off. It would not bother her, she swore, for she would simply not think about it.

Let him look at some other girl, some other woman, with those eyes. That would get him laid, and that, certainly, was all he was really after anyway. He had probably stood in front of a mirror and practiced that look.

Goddamn him, anyway! What did he think she was?

She went back in the dressing room and took the black dress off. She did not buy it.

She went from Gayfer's Department Store to the bar at the San Carlos. She waited for Jimmy Carstairs to come in. By the time he came in, she was feeling pretty good.

When she woke up the next morning, she remembered two things about the night before. She'd had a scrap with Jimmy Carstairs, who had refused to let her drive herself home. And that once—or was it twice?—she had tried to call Pick on the house phone. He had had no right to walk away from her like that before she had finished telling him off, and she had been determined to finish what she had started.

There had been no answer in the penthouse, even though Martha remembered letting the telephone ring and ring and ring.

(THREE)
San Diego Navy Base, California
21 February 1942

Although it was surrounded by a double line of barbed-wire-topped hurricane fencing, the brig at Diego was not from a distance very forbidding. It looked like any other well-cared-for Naval facility.

But inside, Lieutenant Commander Michael J. Grotski, USNR, thought as he waited to be admitted to the office of the commanding officer, it was undeniably a prison. Cleaner, maybe, but still a prison. Until November 1941, Lieutenant Commander Grotski had been engaged in the practice of criminal law in his native Chicago, Illinois. He had spent a good deal of time visiting clients in prison.

"You can go in, Commander," the natty, crew-cutted young Marine corporal in a tailored, stiffly starched khaki uniform said as he rose from his desk and opened a polished wooden door. Above the door was a red sign on which was a representation of the Marine insignia and the legend "C. F. KAMNIK, CAPT. USMC BRIG COMMANDER."

The "C," Commander Grotski knew, stood for "Casimir." He had come to know Captain Kamnik pretty well. They were not only two good Chicago Polack boys in uniform, but they had both once served as altar boys to the Reverend Monsignor Taddeus Wiznewski at Saint Teresa's. Monsignor Wiznewski had installed a proper respect for what they were doing in his altar boys by punching them in the mouth when Mass was over whenever their behavior fell below his expectations.

They had not been altar boys at the same time. Captain Kamnik was six years older than Lieutenant Commander Grotski. And he had enlisted in the Marine Corps when Grotski was still in the sixth grade at St. Teresa's parochial school. But it had been a pleasant experience for the both of them to recall their common experience, and to find somebody else from the old neighborhood who was a fellow commissioned officer and gentleman.

"Good morning, Commander," Captain Kamnik said as he rose up behind his desk and grinned at Grotski. "How can the Marine Corps serve the Navy?"

"Oh, I just happened to be in the neighborhood and I thought I would drop in and ruin your day."

"Let me guess," Kamnik said, first closing the office door and then going to a file cabinet. From this he took out a bottle of Seagram's Seven Crown. Then he continued, "You are about to rush to the defense of some innocent boy out there, who has been unjustly accused."

"Close, but not quite," Grotski said, taking a pull from the offered bottle and handing it back. Kamnik took a pull himself, and then put the bottle back in the filing cabinet. Technically, it was drinking on duty, one of many court-martial offenses described in some detail in the *Rules for the Governance of the Navy Service.* But it was also a pleasant custom redolent of home for two Polack former altar boys from the same neighborhood.

Kamnik looked at Grotski with his eyes raised in question.

"You have a fine young Marine out there named McCoy, Thomas Michael," Grotski said.

It was evident from the look on Kamnik's face that he had searched his memory and come up with nothing.

"McCoy?" he asked, as he went to his desk and ran his finger down one typewritten roster, and then another. "Here it is," he said. "*Ex*-Marine. He's on his way to do five-to-ten at Portsmouth." Portsmouth was the U.S. Naval Prison.

"Not anymore, he's not," Grotski. "You have his file?"

"Somewhere, I'm sure. Why?"

"You're going to need it," Grotski said, simply.

Captain Kamnik walked to the door and pulled it open.

"Scott, fetch me the jacket on a prisoner named McCoy. He's one of those general prisoners who came in from Pearl. On his way to Portsmouth."

"Aye, aye, sir," the corporal said.

Kamnik turned to Grotski.

"You going to tell me what this is all about?"

"After you read the file," Grotski said. "Or at least glance at it. I'll throw you a bone, though: I have the feeling the commanding general of the joint training force in Diego is more than a little pissed at me."

"Really? You don't mind if I'm happy about that?"

"I'm flattered," Grotski said.

Corporal Scott entered the office a minute later, carrying a seven-inch-thick package wrapped in water-resistant paper and sealed with tape. On it was crudely lettered, "McCoy, Thomas Michael."

The package contained a complete copy of the general court-martial convened in the case of PFC Thomas M. McCoy, USMC, 1st Defense Battalion, Marine Barracks, Pearl Harbor, Hawaii, to try him on charges that on the twenty-fourth day of December 1941, he had committed the offense of assault upon the person of a commissioned officer of the U.S. Navy in the execution of his office by striking him with his fists upon the face and on other parts of his body.

The record showed that PFC McCoy was also charged with having committed an assault upon a petty officer of the United States Navy in the execution of his office by striking him with his fists upon the face and on other parts of his body, and by kicking him in the general area of his genital region with his feet.

The record showed that PFC McCoy was additionally accused of having been absent without leave from his assigned place of duty at the time of the alleged offenses described in specifications 1 and 2.

The record showed that in secret session, two-thirds of the members present and voting, a general court-martial convened under the authority of the general officer commanding Marine Barracks, Pearl Harbor, T.H., had found PFC McCoy guilty of each of the charges and specifications; and finally that, in secret session, two-thirds of the members present and voting, the court-martial had pronounced sentence.

As to specification and charge number 1, PFC McCoy was to be reduced to the lowest enlisted grade, suffer loss of all pay and allowances, and be confined at hard labor for a period of five to ten years at Portsmouth or such other Naval prison as the Secretary of the Navy may designate, and at the completion of his term of imprisonment, be dishonorably discharged from the Naval service.

As to specification and charge number 2, PFC McCoy was to be reduced to the lowest enlisted grade, suffer loss of all pay and allowances, and be confined at hard labor for a period of three to five years at Portsmouth or such other Naval prison as the Secretary of the Navy may designate, and at the completion of his term of imprisonment, be dishonorably discharged from the Naval Service.

As to specification and charge number 3, PFC McCoy was to be reduced to the lowest enlisted grade, suffer loss of all pay and allowance, and be confined at hard labor for a period of six months in the U.S. Navy brig at Pearl Harbor, or such other place of confinement as the Commanding General, Marine Barracks, Pearl Harbor, T.H., may designate.

"Another of your innocent lambs, I see, Commander," Captain Kamnik said.

"Lovely fellow, obviously," Grotski said.

"So what about him?"

Grotski handed a single sheet of paper to Kamnik.

OP-29-BC3
L21-[5]-5
SERIAL 0002

FROM: THE COMMANDER IN CHIEF, PACIFIC FLEET
TO: GENERAL OFFICER COMMANDING,
MARINE BARRACKS, PEARL HARBOR
REFERENCE: RECORD OF TRIAL, MCCOY, PFC THOMAS MICHAEL, USMC

1. THE REVIEW REQUIRED BY LAW OF THE TRIAL, CONVICTION, AND SENTENCING OF PFC MCCOY HAS BEEN COMPLETED BY THE UNDERSIGNED.

2. THE REVIEW REVEALED THAT THE COMPOSITION OF THE GENERAL COURT-MARTIAL WAS NOT IN KEEPING WITH APPLICABLE REGULATIONS AND LAW. (SEE ATTACHMENT 1 HERETO.)

3. IT IS THEREFORE ORDERED THAT THE FINDINGS AND SENTENCE IN THE AFOREMENTIONED CASE BE, AND THEY HEREBY ARE, SET ASIDE.

E. J. KING
ADMIRAL, USN

"You mean we're going to have to try this character again?" Captain Kamnik asked. "What about the 'composition' of the court-martial?"

"The law requires that 'all parties to the trial,' " Grotski said, "be present for all sessions of the court. They weren't. The trial lasted three days. Three times, one officer or another was called away. The court reporter, apparently a very thorough individual, put it in the record every time somebody left, and when they came back."

"I can't imagine why they would be called away," Kamnik said, sarcastically. "It's not as if there's a war on, or anything important like that."

"CINCPAC really doesn't review these cases himself," Grotski said. "He gives them to a lawyer on the judge advocate's staff to review, and he generally goes by his recommendations. Whoever reviewed this saw that members of the board kept wandering in and out."

"You're not telling me we have to go through the whole goddamned trial again?" Kamnik said.

"No," Grotski said. "You remember I said the general is pissed at me?"

"What about?"

"Well, by the time the case was reviewed, McCoy was already on his way to Portsmouth . . . here, in other words. So this was sent here for action. And the general called me in and said that somebody had fucked up in Hawaii, and that we were going to have to try Brother McCoy all over again, and would I please see that it was done very quickly and efficiently, and that I was to personally make sure that no member of the board left the room for any purpose while the trial was on.

"So I said, 'Aye, aye, sir,' and read the file. Then I went back to see the general and told him that in my professional judgment, we could not retry Brother McCoy. For two reasons: The first was double jeopardy. He'd already been tried. The government had its shot at him. They should not have gone on with the trial with any member of the court missing, but they did. That was not McCoy's fault. He was there. And I told the general that it was not the responsibility of his defense counsel to object; that he was almost obliged to take advantage of mistakes the prosecution made. And then I told him that even if they sort of swept that under the rug and tried him again here, McCoy was entitled to face his accusers. The Navy would have to bring here from Pearl (or from wherever they are now) the officer he punched out, and the shore patrolman, plus all of McCoy's buddies who had previously testified that McCoy was just sitting there innocently in the whorehouse when the shore patrol lieutenant came in and viciously attacked him for no reason that they could see."

"You mean this sonofabitch is going to get away with punching out an officer? A shore patrol officer?" Captain Kamnik asked incredulously.

"Think of it this way, Casimir," Commander Grotski said dryly, " 'it is better that one thousand guilty men go free than one innocent man be convicted.' "

"But the sonofabitch is guilty as hell! Innocent, my ass!"

"He was entitled to a fair trial, and he didn't get one," Grotski said. "I must say the general took this better than you are."

"I thought you said he was pissed," Kamnik said.

"At me. As the bearer of bad news. He doesn't seem to be annoyed with Brother McCoy nearly as much. As a matter of fact, he even had a thought about where PFC McCoy can make a contribution to the Marine Corps and the war effort in the future."

"What does that mean?"

"I'm here to 'counsel' McCoy," Grotski said. "You're welcome to watch, but only if you can keep your mouth shut."

"I wouldn't miss this for the world," Kamnik said. "You want him brought here?"

"That would be very nice, Captain Kamnik," Grotski said. "I appreciate your spirit of cooperation."

"Scott!" Captain Kamnik called. The natty corporal stuck his head in the door. "Do you know where to find the sergeant of the guard?"

"He's out here, sir. He's waiting to see you."

"Ask him to come in, please."

The sergeant of the guard was the meanest-looking sonofabitch Commander Grotski had seen in some time, a bald, stocky staff sergeant of thirty or so, with an acne-pocked face. Grotski searched for the word, and came up with "porcine." The sergeant of the guard was porcine, piglike, a mean boar pig.

The sergeant of the guard came to attention before Kamnik's desk.

"What's on your mind, Sergeant?" Kamnik asked.

"I didn't know that the captain was busy, sir."

"Don't mind me, Sergeant," Grotski said amiably.

The sergeant still hesitated.

"Go one Sergeant," Captain Kamnik said.

"The captain said he wanted to hear," the sergeant of the guard reluctantly began, "of an 'incident.' "

"Yes, I did."

"We had a little trouble with one of the transits, sir," the sergeant of the guard said.

"Oh?"

"He gave one of the guards some lip, sir," the sergeant of the guard said. "And then he assaulted two guards. The point of it is, sir, before we could restrain him, he busted PFC Tober's nose."

"The situation is now under control?"

"Oh, yes, sir," the sergeant of the guard said. "But I thought you'd want to hear right away about PFC Tober. I sent him over to the dispensary."

"And the transient?"

"We have him restrained, sir. I was going to ask the captain's permission to keep him in the box until we can ship him out of here."

"The 'box,' Sergeant?" Commander Grotski asked, innocently.

"That's what we call our 'solitary detention facility,' " Captain Kamnik explained.

"Oh, I see," Grotski said. "And just out of idle curiosity, what's the name of the prisoner who broke the guard's nose?"

The sergeant of the guard looked at Captain Kamnik for permission to reply. Kamnik nodded.

"McCoy, sir," the sergeant of the guard said. "He's a mean sonofabitch, a general prisoner on his way to Portsmouth. He's gonna do five-to-ten. Assault on an officer and some other stuff."

"Curiosity overwhelms me," Commander Grotski said. "I would like to see this villain."

The sergeant of the guard looked distantly uncomfortable. He looked to Captain Kamnik for help and got none.

"Do you suppose you could bring him here, Sergeant?" Commander Grotski asked.

"Commander," the sergeant of the guard said, "you don't really want to see to this character, do you?"

"Oh, but I do. Go get him, Sergeant."

The sergeant of the guard again looked in vain for Captain Kamnik's help.

When he had gone, Commander Grotski asked, "Are you a betting man, Casimir?"

"Sometimes," Kamnik said.

"How about three will get you five that this McCoy will fall down the stairs on his way here?"

"It happens, Commander," Kamnik said. "I do my best to stop it, but sometimes it happens."

Five minutes later General Prisoner Thomas Michael McCoy was led into the brig commander's office. He was dressed in dungarees. A ten-inch-high letter "P" had been stenciled to the thighs of his trousers and onto the rear of his jacket. He was in handcuffs, and the handcuffs were chained to a thick leather belt around his waist. His ankles were encircled with heavy iron rings, and the rings were chained together, restricting his movement to a shuffle.

His hands were swollen, and red with iodine. There was more iodine on his face, on his mouth, and above his eyes. His face was swollen, and in a few hours both of his eyes would be dark.

They must have been really pissed at him, which was not surprising, since he broke a guard's nose, Commander Grotski thought. *Otherwise the marks of his beating would not be so visible.*

"What happened to your face?" Commander Grotski asked.

General Prisoner McCoy thought about his reply for a moment before he gave it.

"I fell down in the shower," he said.

"I fell down in the shower, *sir,*" Grotski corrected him.

"I fell down in the shower, sir," McCoy dutifully parroted.

"That will be all, Sergeant," Commander Grotski said. "When we need you, we'll call for you."

The sergeant is worried that the moment he's out of the room, Grotski thought, *McCoy will tell us that three, four, maybe five guards got him in the box and had at him with billy clubs, or saps, or whatever they thought would cause the most pain. That's against the* Regulations for the Governance of the Naval Service.

"You really fell down in the shower, McCoy?" Grotski asked, when the sergeant of the guard had gone, closing the door after him.

"Yes, sir," McCoy said, after thinking it over.

"Tough guy, are you?" Grotski asked.

McCoy didn't answer.

"I asked you a question, McCoy," Grotski said.

"I guess I'm as tough as most," McCoy said, and remembered finally to add, "sir."

"You don't know what tough is, you dumb Mick sonofabitch," Grotski said. "And you're the dumbest sonofabitch I've seen in a long time. You don't even know what you're facing, do you? It hasn't penetrated that thick Mick head of yours, has it? You're really so dumb you think you can take on Portsmouth, don't you?"

McCoy didn't reply.

"That sergeant isn't even very good at what he did," Grotski said. "He's nowhere near good enough to get himself assigned to Portsmouth. At Portsmouth, he would be a rookie. When they beat you at Portsmouth, they got it down to a fine art. No marks. It just hurts. And how long are you going to be in Portsmouth, McCoy?"

"They gave me five-to-ten, sir," McCoy said.

"Let me tell you how it works. The first time you look cockeyed at somebody at Portsmouth, you dumb Mick, they'll give you a working over that'll make the one you just had feel like your mother kissed you. And then they'll add six months on your sentence for 'silent insolence.' And every time you look cockeyed at a guard there, you'll get another working over, and another six months, until one of two things happens. You won't look cockeyed at anyone, or you will fall down the stairs and break your neck. Then they'll bury you in the prison cemetery. You don't really understand that, do you?"

"I'm going to keep my nose clean, sir," McCoy said.

"Bullshit! You're not smart enough to keep your nose clean," Grotski said, nastily.

He let that sink in.

"You wouldn't even know what to do, would you, you stupid sonofabitch, if I told you I can get you out of Portsmouth?"

McCoy looked at him uncomprehendingly.

Finally, he said, "Sir?"

"If I was in your shoes, you miserable asshole, and somebody told me he could get me out of Portsmouth, I would get on my knees and ask him what I had to do, and pray to the Blessed Virgin that he would believe me when I said I would do it."

McCoy looked at him, his eyes widening.

And then he dropped to his knees. He tried to raise his hands together before him in an attitude of prayer, but his handcuffed wrists were chained to the leather belt around his waist, and he could move them only slightly above his waist.

"You tell me what I have to do, sir, and I'll do it. I swear on my mother's grave!"

"And now you pray, you miserable bastard," Grotski ordered. "And out loud!"

McCoy looked at him, frightened and confused.

"What do I pray?"

"Say your Hail Marys, you pimple on the ass of the Marine Corps," Grotski ordered icily.

"Hail Mary, full of grace," McCoy began, "the Lord is with thee. Blessed art thou amongst women and blessed is the fruit of thy womb, Jesus. Holy Mary, Mother of God, pray for us sinners now and at the hour of our death. Amen."

Grotski looked at Captain Kamnik, then nodded his head in an order for him to leave the room.

He closed the door to the office after them.

"He's pretty good at that, Casimir," he said. "Do you think maybe he was an altar boy, too?"

"Jesus!" Kamnik said, and then spotted the sergeant of the guard. "Wait outside please, Sergeant," he ordered.

When he looked at Grotski, Grotski was grinning broadly.

"Now what?"

"It's what is known as psychological warfare," he said. "I'll let him keep it up awhile until I'm sure he is in the right state of mind, and then I'll offer him a chance to redeem himself."

"How?" Kamnik ordered.

"You ever hear of a Lieutenant Colonel Carlson?" he asked.

Kamnik shook his head. "No."

"Well, he's apparently on the general's shitlist, too. Some kind of a nut. He's being given some kind of commando outfit. The general said when I got McCoy out of here, he thought it would be nice if McCoy volunteered for it. I had the feeling he wouldn't be all that unhappy if McCoy got himself blown away as one of Carlson's commandos."

"And you think he'll volunteer?"

"I'm not going to let him off his knees until he does," Commander Grotski said.

XIV

(ONE)
The San Diego Yacht Club
1400 Hours, 28 February 1942

The Yellow Cab dropped Second Lieutenant Kenneth J. McCoy, USMCR, wearing dungarees, at the end of Pier Four at the yacht club. The driver was not accustomed to carrying dungaree-clad Marines—for that matter Marines period—to the yacht club. And he watched curiously as McCoy walked down the pier and finally crossed the gangplank onto the *Last Time.* Then he shrugged his shoulders and drove off.

McCoy slid open the varnished teak door to the lounge and stepped inside.

Ernie Sage and Dorothy Burnes were there, listening to the radio. Dorothy was sitting uncomfortably in one of the armchairs, draped in a tentlike cotton dress. Ernie Sage, wearing very brief shorts and a T-shirt, jumped up from one of the couches when she saw him.

"What are you doing home so early?" she asked as she crossed the room to him. She grabbed his ears, pulled his face to hers, and kissed him wetly and noisily on the mouth. "Not that I'm not glad to see you, as you can see."

Dorothy laughed.

"They gave me the afternoon off," McCoy said.

"You should have called me, I would have come for you," Ernie said. She put her arm around him and pressed against him, confirming his suspicion that there was nothing but Ernie under the T-shirt.

"It was quicker catching the bus," he said.

"And how did you get here?"

"In a cab."

"And what did that cost?"

"Buck and a half, with the tip."

"Mr. Moneybags," Ernie said.

Ernie's attitude toward money—she was a real cheapskate—was another of the things about her that continually surprised him. With the exception, maybe, of Pick Pickering, she was the richest person he had ever known, but she was really tight about some things, like his taking a taxicab. It really bothered her.

He reached down and pinched her tail under the shorts, confirming that there was nothing but her under there, either.

She yelped in mock protest and jumped away from him.

"You want something to eat? A beer? A drink? Anything?"

"I thought you would never ask," McCoy said. "About anything."

"You better watch him." Dorothy laughed. "You would be amazed the kind of trouble that sort of thing can get you into."

"How goes it, Dorothy?" McCoy asked.

"How do you think?" Dorothy replied, patting her stomach. "I'm beginning to think it has to be triplets."

"Well?" Ernie asked.

"Well, what?"

"You want something to eat? Or to drink?"

"That wasn't the original offer," McCoy said.

"It must be something the Corps puts in their food," Dorothy laughed.

"Well?" Ernie pursued.

"What I need now is a shower," McCoy said, and started across the lounge to the passageway to the cabins.

"Why did they give you the afternoon off?" Ernie said. "I thought you were supposed to get transferred today?"

"I was," he said. "And tomorrow they're sending me to Northern California." He saw the look on her face, and quickly added, "Just for a couple of days."

Then he entered the passageway to avoid further explanation.

Ernie was in their cabin when he came naked out of the bathroom. She had a plate in one hand and a bottle of Schlitz in the other.

"Sardines on saltines," she said. "And Schlitz. And I could be talked into anything, too, if that was a bona fide offer."

And then she looked at him, and her face colored, and she laughed, deep in her throat.

"And I see it was," she said.

"You do that to me," he said. "I think it's something you put in the sardines."

"I wish I knew what it was," she said as she put the tray and the beer down on the bedside table. "We could give the formula to my father on a royalty basis and get rich."

She pushed the shorts down off her hips and then pulled the T-shirt over her head.

"Oh, baby," McCoy said huskily as she walked to him and put her arms around him.

"Are you going to tell me what you're going to do in Northern California?" Ernie asked, her face against his chest.

"I've got to call," he said. "You can listen."

"Before, or after?"

"After," he said.

"You don't know how lucky you are you gave the right answer," Ernie said as she pulled him backward onto the bed.

"Colonel Rickabee." The voice came over the telephone flat and metallic.

"Sir, I'm sorry, I asked for Captain Sessions," McCoy said.

"What's the matter, McCoy?" Rickabee replied. "You don't like me?"

Ernie, who was lying half on top of McCoy, giggled, and then she moved higher up so that she could hear better.

When there was no reply from McCoy, Colonel Rickabee said, "What is it exactly that you feel you can tell Sessions and can't tell me?"

"Nothing, sir," McCoy said.

"Good!" Rickabee said, gently sarcastic.

"I went over to the Second Raider Battalion today, sir."

"How did it go?"

"It went smoothly, sir. I was further assigned to Baker Company, as a platoon leader, but that's not what they're going to have me doing."

"What *happened,* McCoy? Take it from the beginning. Tell me about the red flags, and the a cappella choir singing the *Internationale.*"

"Nothing like that, sir," McCoy said, chuckling.

"Did you see Colonel Carlson?"

"Yes, sir."

"And Captain Roosevelt?"

"Yes, sir."

"Was either of them howling at the moon?"

Ernie giggled so loudly that Rickabee heard her.

"Is there someone with you?" he asked, now deadly serious. "I presume you are using a secure line?"

"The line is secure, sir," McCoy said.

"Okay, once again. Take it from the beginning."

"The adjutant was waiting for me when I showed up to take the reveille formation, sir. He said he had my orders transferring me to the Raiders, and there was no sense complaining about them, because the battalion commander had already gone to the Second Joint Training Force personnel officer trying to keep me."

"Another of many ways Colonel Carlson is endearing himself to the rest of the Corps," Rickabee said dryly, "is by kidnapping their best people. Go on."

"So they sent me over to the Second Raider Battalion in a truck," McCoy said. "And I reported to the adjutant. And he sent me in to report to Colonel Carlson."

"Roosevelt?"

"I didn't see him until later, sir."

"Go on."

"Colonel, it was just like my reporting in to the Third Battalion," McCoy said. "Colonel Carlson shook my hand and welcomed me aboard. Told me I was joining the best outfit in the Corps, and that it was a great opportunity for me, a great challenge . . . the usual bullshit."

"I hope Carlson didn't sense your cynicism," Rickabee said. "You are supposed to be bright-eyed and eager, McCoy."

"Colonel, he makes sense," McCoy said. "I wasn't making fun of him. What I was trying to say was that it was like reporting in anywhere else."

"As opposed to what?"

"I read that letter, sir, the one Roosevelt wrote, where he wanted to have 'leaders' and 'fighters' and the rest of that Red Army stuff."

"And there was none of that?" Rickabee asked.

"Not what I expected, sir."

"Explain."

"First, he talked about what the Raiders were supposed to do. I mean, the raid business, shaking the Japs up by hitting them where they didn't expect to get hit. The *Commando* business. And then he said that the mission was so important that the Corps had given him top priority for personnel and equipment, and that meant the personnel—"

"Let me interrupt," Rickabee said. "Do you think he believes the Corps thinks the Raider mission is so important that he has carte blanche?"

"Sir?"

"That he can have anything, do anything, he wants?"

"He sure sounded like he did. But on the other hand, you could hardly expect him to say anything else."

Rickabee snorted. "Go on."

McCoy mimed wanting a cigarette. Ernie leaned across him to the bedside table and picked up his Lucky Strike package and Zippo. In the process, she rubbed her breast across his face. McCoy wondered if it had been an accident, and realized, pleased with the realization, that it had not been.

"Then he said because he had such high-class enlisted men, it would be possible to treat them differently."

"How differently?" Rickabee asked softly.

"I want to say 'better,' " McCoy said. "But that's not quite it. He said they can be given greater responsibility. . . . Colonel, what I think he was saying is that he thinks you can get more out of the men if they're making the decisions. Or some of the decisions. Or if they *think* they're making the decisions."

"You sound as if you're a convert," Rickabee said, dryly.

"When Colonel Carlson says it, it doesn't sound so nutty as when I try to tell you about it," McCoy said.

"Anything specific?" Rickabee asked.

"He said that he's been both an enlisted man and an officer, and that what really pissed him off as an enlisted man was when the officers had special privileges and rubbed them in the enlisted men's faces, and that he wasn't going to let that happen in the Raiders."

"Interesting," Rickabee said.

"I think I know what he means, Colonel," McCoy said. "He doesn't want to burn down the officers' club. All he's saying is that if you're in the field, and the men are sleeping on the ground, the officers should not have bunks and sheets."

"Neither do I," Rickabee said. "That doesn't sound like the revolution."

"I'm beginning to think, Colonel, that if Roosevelt hadn't written that nutty 'fighters' and 'leaders' letter—"

"But he did," Rickabee interrupted. "And if he hadn't, there probably would be no Raider battalions."

"Yes, sir."

"Did Colonel Carlson say anything else out of the ordinary? Anything unusual?"

"No, sir."

"How long were you with him?"

"About fifteen minutes, sir. Then he sent me down to the company."

"Baker Company, you said?"

"Yes, sir. Captain Coyte, Ralph H."

"What about him?"

"Looked like a real Marine to me. Seemed to know what he was doing. And like a nice guy."

"And he gave you a platoon?"

"Yes, sir, but I never got there. He was still feeling me out. I hadn't been there ten minutes, when Captain Roosevelt showed up."

"What did he want?"

"He told Captain Coyte that he was going to borrow me. He told him I used to be in a heavy-weapons company in the Fourth Marines and knew about weapons, so he was going to send me up to some Army ordnance depot near San Francisco to make sure the Army didn't give us all junk when we drew weapons."

"Okay," Colonel Rickabee said. "That makes sense."

"And then he gave me the rest of the day off."

"What did you think of Roosevelt?"

"I liked him, too," McCoy said. "He acts like a Marine."

"And he wasn't walking around with a copy of the Communist Manifesto in his pocket?"

"No, sir." McCoy chuckled.

"Well, it looks like you're in, and nobody's suspicious," Rickabee said. "So all you have to do is keep your mouth shut and your eyes open."

"Yes, sir."

"I want to make the point, McCoy, that we want to hear about anything unusual, *anything* unusual."

"Yes, sir," McCoy replied. "The weapons are a little unusual, sir."

"What do you mean by that?"

"Well, what I'm going to draw—*try* to draw—from the Army, are shotguns and carbines."

The U.S. Carbine, Caliber .30, M1 was an autoloading shoulder arm with a fifteen-round magazine. It fired a pistol-sized cartridge, and was intended to replace the .45 Colt automatic pistol. The later M2 version was fully automatic, and there was later a thirty-round magazine.

"That's just the sort of thing I mean," Rickabee said. "By shotguns, I presume you mean twelve-gauge trench guns?"

"Yes, sir. From the First World War. And carbines. I've never even seen a carbine."

"Well, then, if you're the weapons expert, it will be a case of the blind leading the blind, won't it?" Rickabee said.

"I guess so," McCoy said.

"Anything else?"

"Roosevelt told me that they're going to give everyone a knife and a pistol," McCoy said.

"I heard about that," Rickabee said. "Anything else?"

"I ran into Gunnery Sergeant Zimmerman."

"You knew he was being sent out there, didn't you?"

"Yes, sir. Captain Sessions told me."

"Sessions felt," Colonel Rickabee said, "and I agreed, that it might be handy for you to have somebody out there you could trust. Another set of eyes."

"Zimmerman thinks that the Raiders are a great idea," McCoy said.

"You didn't tell him what you're doing out there, did you?"

"No, sir, of course not."

"Then leave it that way, McCoy. Zimmerman can be an extra set of eyes and ears in the ranks for you."

"I understand, sir," McCoy said. "He wouldn't understand that. I'm not so sure I do."

"And that's all?"

"Yes, sir."

"I relay herewith the best wishes of Captain Ed Banning," Rickabee said.

"Thank you, sir," McCoy said. "He's with you in Washington?"

"Actually, he's in the Naval hospital in Brooklyn," Rickabee said.

"What's wrong with him?" McCoy asked quietly.

"He was blind for a while," Rickabee said. "You didn't know that?"

"No, sir," McCoy said, shocked.

"Well, it was apparently psychosomatic," Rickabee said. "Which means no evident physical damage. He can see now, but the medics want to check him out carefully."

"Yes, sir."

"Okay, that seems to be it. Check in with me when you come back from San Francisco. Let me know how you made out with the Army. And anything else that comes to mind."

"Aye, aye, sir."

"So long, McCoy," Colonel Rickabee said. "Keep up the good work."

The line went dead.

McCoy put the handset back in its cradle, and then looked at Ernie.

"Any questions?" he asked.

"Sergeant Zimmerman's here?" Ernie asked.

"Uh-huh."

"Why don't you have him to dinner?" Ernie said.

"It doesn't work that way," McCoy said. "Officers don't socialize with enlisted men."

"You're a snob," she said. "Who would ever know?"

"What would Marty Burnes think?" McCoy said, teasingly.

"Fuck him, it's our boat," Ernie said.

McCoy chuckled. *"Fuck him?"* he parroted. "When I met you, you didn't use words like that."

"When I met you, I was a virgin," Ernie said. "Cussing like a Marine is not the only bad habit I learned from you."

She lowered her head to his chest and nipped his nipple, and then she jumped out of bed and went into the bathroom.

McCoy picked up the telephone again and called Camp Elliott and spoke with the sergeant major of the Second Raider Battalion. He told him that if it were possible, he would like to have Gunnery Sergeant Zimmerman go with him to Northern California.

"We were in the Fourth Marines together, Sergeant Major, and he knows about weapons," McCoy said.

"And, with respect, sir," the sergeant major said, chuckling, "you old China Marines stick together, don't you?"

"Let me tell you, sometime, Sergeant Major, how it was in the Old Corps."

"Do that," the sergeant major, who was twice McCoy's age, said, laughing. "I'll have Zimmerman at the motor pool when you get there, Lieutenant."

(TWO)
U.S. Navy Hospital
Brooklyn Navy Yard
2 March 1942

The headshrinker was wearing a white medical smock with an embroidered medical insignia on the breast, but there was no name tag with his rank on it. And since the Navy did not wear rank insignia on the collar points of their white shirts, Banning could not tell what rank he was. He could have been anything, to go by his age, from a junior grade lieutenant to a lieutenant commander.

"Come in, Captain Banning," the headshrinker said, when he saw Banning in the outer office.

Banning was in pajamas and a blue bathrobe, his bare feet in cloth hospital slippers.

"Good morning, sir," Banning said. "I was told to report to you."

"I'm Dr. Toland," the headshrinker said. "I've been looking forward to this."

"Why?" Banning challenged. It sounded like a bullshit remark.

The headshrinker looked at him intently for a moment, and then smiled.

"Actually, because I thought you would be more interesting than my general run of patients. These go from bed-wetting sailors trying to get out of the service to full commanders experiencing what we call the 'midlife crisis.' You're my first battle-scarred veteran."

Banning had to chuckle. "And you're the one who decides whether or not I'm crazy, right?"

"If I were in your shoes, Captain, that would annoy me too," Dr. Toland said. "So let me get that out of the way. I find you to be remarkably stable, psychologically speaking, considering what you've gone through."

"I just walked in here," Banning said. "Can you decide that quickly?"

"Sit down, Banning," Dr. Toland said. "I'll get us some coffee, and we can go through the motions."

Banning expected a corpsman, or a clerk, to bring coffee, but instead Toland walked out of the office and returned with two china mugs.

"You take cream and sugar?" he asked.

"No, black's fine," Banning said, taking the cup. "Thank you."

"The way it works," Toland said, "unless somebody walks in here wild-eyed and talking to God, is that I consider the reason an examination was requested; the aberrations, if any, that the patient has manifested; and the stress to which he has been subjected. Taking those one at a time, I'm a little surprised that you're surprised that they wanted you examined."

"I don't quite follow that," Banning said.

"According to General Forrest," Dr. Toland said, "the duties they have in mind for you are such that they just can't take the chance that you will either get sick, physically as opposed to mentally; or that you will suddenly decide you're Napoleon."

Banning looked at him sharply. He had not expected to hear General Forrest's name. He wondered if Toland was telling him the truth or whether this was some kind of a headshrinker's game. After a moment he concluded that Toland was telling the truth and that he had been discussed by this headshrinker and the Deputy Chief of Staff for Intelligence, USMC. Then he wondered why that had happened. Why was he important enough for Forrest to spend time talking about him to a headshrinker?

"That seems to surprise you," Toland said, and Banning knew that *was* a headshrinker's question.

"I'm just a captain," Banning said.

"Not for long," Toland said. "One of the questions on General Forrest's mind was whether or not it was safe to make you a major."

Banning was surprised at that, too, but when he looked at Dr. Toland for an explanation, Toland was going through a stack of papers on his desk. He found what he was looking for, took a pen from a holder, and signed his name on each of four copies. Then he handed one to Banning.

"The significant part is on the back side," Toland said.

It was a Report of Physical Examination. In the "Comments" block on the reverse side there was a single typewritten line and a signature block:

> "Captain Edward J. Banning, USMC, is physically qualified without exception to perform the duties of the office (Major, USMC) to which he has been selected for promotion.
>
> "Jack B. Toland, Captain, Medical Corps, USNR"

Banning looked at Toland with mixed surprise and relief. Toland didn't look old enough to be a captain. (A Naval captain is equivalent to a colonel, USMC.) And he was surprised to learn—in this way—that he was being promoted. But mostly, he was enormously relieved to read the words *physically qualified without exception.*

Toland smiled at him.

"We watched you while we were running you through the examinations," Toland said. "What I was afraid we might find was a tumor. That's sometimes the case when there is an unexplained loss of sight."

"What was it, then?"

"I think it falls into the general medical category we refer to as, *'we don't know what the hell it is,'* " Toland said. "If I had to make a guess, I'd say it was probably either a brain concussion or that the nerves to the eyes were somehow bruised, so to speak, by concussion. I understand you were shelled twice, and pretty badly."

"Yes, sir," Banning said.

"Well, whatever it was, *Major* Banning, I think you can stop worrying about it."

"I'm astonished at my relief," Banning blurted. "I suddenly feel—hell, I don't know—like a wet towel."

"That's to be expected," Toland said. "What's unusual is that someone like you would admit it."

Banning looked at him, but didn't reply.

"You could do me a service, Banning, if you would," Toland said.

"Sir?"

"Other men are going to be blinded," Toland said. "Some of them are already coming back. It would help me if you could tell me what it's like."

"Frightening," Banning said. "Very frightening."

Toland made a gesture, asking him to go on.

"And then I got mad," Banning said. "Furious. Why me? Why hadn't I been killed?"

Toland nodded, and then when Banning said nothing else, he asked, "Suicide? Any thoughts of suicide?"

Banning met Toland's eyes for a long moment before he replied. "Yes," he said.

"Why didn't you?" Toland asked.

"I had a cocked pistol in my belt when I took the bandages off," Banning asked.

"And do you think you would have—could have—gone through with it?"

"Yes," Banning said, simply.

"Because you didn't want to face life without sight?"

"Because I was useless," Banning said. "I'm a Marine officer."

"And didn't want to be a burden to your family?"

"The only family I have, aside from the Corps, is a wife. And I left her on the wharf in Shanghai. God knows where she is now."

"I knew you were married," Dr. Toland said. "I didn't know the circumstances. That makes it a little awkward."

"Sir?"

"My next line was going to be 'Well, now that we're through with you, you're entitled to a thirty-day convalescent leave. A second honeymoon at government expense.' "

"Christ!" Banning said.

"What's worse is that it's not 'do you want a convalescent leave?', but 'you *will* take a thirty-day convalescent leave,' " Toland said. "That's out of my hands. No family anywhere? Cousin, uncle . . . ?"

"None that I want to see," Banning said. "I'd really rather go back to duty."

Toland shook his head, meaning "that's out of the question."

"The BOQ rooms here are supposed to be the cheapest hotel rooms in New York City," Toland said. "Dollar and a half a day. Be a tourist for a month."

Banning looked at him doubtfully.

"You'd be able to get a lot of the paperwork out of the way," Toland pursued. "And get yourself some new uniforms."

"Sir?"

"Our benevolent government, Major Banning," Dr. Toland said dryly, "is not only going to finally pay you, once they get your service records up to date, but is going to compensate you for the loss of whatever you were forced to leave behind in the Far East. Household goods, car, everything. And I understand the only uniform you have is the one you were wearing when you came in here. You'll have to make up a list of what you lost, and swear to it."

"I hadn't thought about that," Banning admitted.

"You'll have a good deal of money coming to you," Toland said. "And a newly promoted major should have some decent uniforms. Hell, you'll be able to afford going to Brooks Brothers for them."

"Brooks Brothers?" Banning parroted, and then laughed.

"Is that funny?"

Banning cocked his head and chuckled.

"The day the Japanese came ashore in the Philippines," he said, "I was on a bluff overlooking the beach. There's a couple of companies of Marines, Fourth Marines, on the beach, with nothing but machine guns. The artillery we were supposed to have, and the bombers, just didn't show up. There's half a dozen Japanese destroyers and as many troopships offshore. And just before the invasion started, a mustang second lieutenant, a kid named McCoy, joined me. He worked for me as a corporal in China, and he was in the Philippines as a courier. So he came running, like the cavalry, with a BAR and loaded down with magazines." (The Browning Automatic Rifle is a fully automatic, caliber-.30–06 weapon, utilizing 20-round magazines.) "The Japanese started their landing barges for the beach, and the destroyers started to fire ranging rounds. And then McCoy, absolute horror in his voice, says 'Oh, my God!' and I looked at him to see what else could possibly be wrong. And he says, 'My pants! My pants! They're going to be ruined, and you wouldn't believe what I paid for them. I bought them in *Brooks Brothers!*"

Toland laughed, and then asked, "What happened to him?"

"They dropped a five-inch round on us a couple of minutes later, and the next thing I knew I was in the basement of a church. McCoy had carried me there."

"Well, when he gets back, the government will replace his pants, too," Toland said.

"He's back," Banning said. "He was a courier, and he got out." He chuckled. "And he probably got off the plane with the form for the loss of his trousers already filled out. McCoy is a very bright young man."

"If he's a friend of yours," Toland said, "you could use part of your leave to go see him."

"That's not possible," Banning said, shortly.

Toland's eyebrows rose but he didn't respond.

"If you're going to be here—and this is a request, Major—I really would like to talk to you some more about your feelings when you thought you were blind."

"Sure," Banning said. "If you think it would be helpful."

"It would," Toland said. "I'd be grateful."

Banning nodded.

"There's one final thing, Banning," Toland said. "A little delicate. One of the reasons they give convalescent leave is because of the therapeutic value of sexual intercourse."

Banning's eyebrows rose.

"Seriously," Toland said. "And while I am not *prescribing* a therapeutic visit to a whorehouse . . ."

"I take the captain's point," Banning said.

"Good," Toland said.

XV

(ONE)
Camp Elliott, California
3 March 1942

At the regular morning officer's call, Colonel Carlson reported the arrival of the 240 carbines from the Army Ordnance Depot, and then turned toward McCoy and called his name.

McCoy rose to his feet.

"Sir?"

"For those of you who haven't had a chance to meet him," Carlson said, "this is Lieutenant Ken McCoy. He's fresh from Quantico, but don't prejudge him by that. Before he went through Quantico, he was a noncom with the Fourth Marines in Shanghai."

McCoy was uncomfortable; and then he was made even more so by First Lieutenant Martin J. Burnes, who turned around to beam his approval of the attention McCoy was being paid by Colonel Carlson. But Carlson was not through.

"I sent McCoy, rather than someone from S-Four, to get the carbines from the Army," Carlson said, "because, of all the people around here, I thought he and Gunnery Sergeant Zimmerman, another old China Marine, would do the best job of bringing back what I sent them to get—despite the roadblocks I was sure the Army would put in their path. I didn't think they'd take either 'no' or 'come back in two weeks' for an answer. If it got down to it, I was sure that they were coming back with the carbines if they had to requisition them at midnight when the Army was asleep."

Carlson waited for the expected chuckles, and then went on: "There's a moral in that, and for those who might miss it, I'll spell it out: *The right men for the job, no matter what the Table of Organization and Equipment says they should be doing.* What everybody has to keep in mind is the mission. The rule is to do what has to be done in the most efficient way. Without regard to rank, gentlemen. An officer loses no prestige getting his hands dirty doing what has to be done, so long as what he's doing helps the Raider mission."

McCoy sat down.

"I'm not through with you, McCoy," Colonel Carlson said. McCoy stood up again.

"McCoy, if you had to make sure everybody in the battalion got a quick but thorough familiarization course in the carbine—say, firing a hundred rounds—how would you go about it?"

The question momentarily floored McCoy, not because he didn't have a good idea how it should be done, but because lieutenant colonels do not habitually ask second lieutenants for suggestions.

But he explained what he thought should be done.

Carlson considered McCoy's suggestions for a moment, and then asked: "What about an armorer?"

"Gunny Zimmerman, sir, until he can train somebody to take over," McCoy said.

"Okay, Lieutenant, do it." He then addressed the other officers. "McCoy was in the heavy weapons with the Fourth Marines in China. Until somebody better equipped comes along, he's our new-and-special-weapons training officer; and until armorers can be trained, Sergeant Zimmerman will handle that."

McCoy sat down again, now convinced that Carlson was through with him. He was pleased with what had happened. He agreed that Carlson was making it official that the Raiders were to assign the best-qualified man to the job no matter what his billet was, and it was sort of flattering to have his recommendations about how to set up a familiarization program accepted without change.

"What do I have to do, McCoy? To keep you on your feet? Put a grenade on your chair?" Carlson said, amused rather than angry.

"Sorry, sir," McCoy said, jumping to his feet in embarrassment.

"We have another problem that McCoy is going to help us solve. Man's third-oldest weapon, the first two being the rock and the stick, is the knife. From what I've noticed, most of our people think that the primary function of a knife is to open beer cans. But actually, in the hands of somebody who knows what he's doing, a knife is a very efficient tool to kill people. For one thing, it doesn't make any noise when it's used. There are a lot of self-appointed experts in knife fighting around. The problem with them is that by and large they are theoreticians rather than practitioners. Very few of them have ever used a knife to take a life."

McCoy sensed what was coming, and winced.

"In addition to that, people being trained in the lethal use of a knife seem to sense that their instructors don't *really* know much more about using a knife on another individual than they do; and consequently, they don't pay a lot of attention to what the instructor's saying."

There were more agreeable chuckles, and Carlson waited for them to subside before he went on.

"When McCoy was in Shanghai, they called him *'Killer,'* " Carlson said. "And with just cause. One night he was ambushed by four Italian Marines who wanted to rearrange his facial features and turn him into a soprano. They picked on the wrong guy. He had a knife, and before that little discussion was over, two of the Italian Marines were dead, and one other was seriously wounded."

There was silence in the room now, and all faces were turned to McCoy. Marty Burnes's face mirrored his amazement.

"McCoy was trained in knife fighting by a real expert," Carlson went on. "Captain Bruce Fairbairn of the Shanghai Municipal Police. Fairbairn designed a fighting knife—called, for some reason, the Fairbairn. McCoy carries his up his left sleeve strapped hilt down to his wrist so he can get at it in a hurry. Maybe, if you ask him very nicely, he'll show it to you. But in any event, we're going to teach our people how to use a knife for something besides opening beer cans, and I announce herewith the appointment of Lieutenant *'Killer'* McCoy as instructor in knife fighting . . . in addition to his other duties, of course."

Lieutenant Marty Burnes applauded, and after a moment's hesitation, the others joined in.

When it had died down, Carlson said, *"Now* you can sit down, Killer."

When the officer's call was over, McCoy ran after Colonel Carlson, who was walking with Captain Roosevelt toward battalion headquarters.

"Sir, may I see you a moment?"

"Sure, Killer," Carlson said. "But first, why don't you show Captain Roosevelt your fighting knife?"

"Sir, I'm not carrying a knife," McCoy said.

"If I had the reputation for being a world-class knife fighter, Killer," Carlson said, "I don't think anyone would ever catch me without my knife."

"Sir," McCoy blurted, "I'm not a knife fighter."

"Ab esse ad posse valet elatio, McCoy," Carlson said.

"Sir?"

"That means, in a very rough rendering, that the facts stand for themselves," Carlson said.

"Well, the facts are that I'm not a knife fighter," McCoy said, firmly.

Carlson switched to Cantonese.

"I know that, and you know that," he said. "But it *is* true that you did have to kill those Italians with a knife, and that they called you *'Killer'* in Shanghai. That story will be all over the battalion by noon. And when you start to teach knife fighting, you will have a very attentive audience."

"Sir," McCoy replied in Cantonese, "I don't know how to teach knife fighting. I only saw Captain Fairbairn once, at a regimental review. He doesn't know I exist, and he certainly never taught me anything."

"He did write a very good book on the subject," Carlson said. "I happen to have a copy of it. I'll get it to you in plenty of time for you to read it and adapt it to your purposes before your first class."

McCoy didn't reply.

"Were you listening in officer's call, Killer? When I talked about getting the best man for the job?"

"Yes, sir," McCoy said.

"You're it," Carlson said. "You're a clever young man, McCoy. Much more clever than people at first believe. You know what I want you to do, and I expect you to give it your best shot."

"Aye, aye, sir," McCoy said, in English.

"May I ask what that was all about?" Roosevelt asked.

"Killer was telling me that he doesn't have his knife today," Carlson said, "but that he will carry it with him in the future, and the next time he sees you, he'd be happy to show it to you."

"Fine." Roosevelt beamed.

"Anything else on your mind, Killer?" Colonel Carlson asked.

"No, sir," McCoy said, and then blurted, "Sir, I would really appreciate it if you didn't call me 'Killer.' "

Carlson smiled sympathetically. "I'm afraid that falls under the category of public relations, McCoy. We could hardly call our world-class knife fighting expert anything else, could we? Not and get the same reaction from the Raiders."

McCoy didn't reply.

"If there's nothing else, Killer," Carlson said, "you may return to your duties."

McCoy saluted.

"Aye, aye, sir."

"I'd really like to see your knife, Killer," Captain Roosevelt said.

(TWO)
Camp Elliott, California
7 March 1942

Second Lieutenant Kenneth J. McCoy, Gunnery Sergeant Ernst Zimmerman, and a detail of twelve Marines from Able Company had come to the range in two Chevrolet half-ton pickups and a GMC 6×6[1] at dawn.

The 6×6 dragged a water trailer, and all the trucks were heavily laden and full. There were stacks of fifty-five-gallon garbage cans; stacks of buckets; bundles of rags; stacks of oblong wooden crates with rope handles; stacks of olive drab oblong ammunition cans; five-gallon water cans; five-gallon gasoline cans; and an assortment of other equipment, including eight gasoline-powered water heaters.

The detail from Able Company had come under a sergeant and a corporal; and Gunnery Sergeant Zimmerman—with a confidence that surprised McCoy, who remembered Zimmerman as a mild-mannered motor sergeant in the 4th Marines—quickly and efficiently put them to work.

All but one of the garbage cans were filled with water from the trailer and then placed twenty yards apart in a line.

Zimmerman watched as the sergeant set up one of the water heaters in one of the garbage cans and then fired it off. Satisfied that he could do the same thing with the other heaters (these were normally used to boil water in garbage cans set up at field kitchens to sterilize mess kits), he turned to what else had to be done.

He ordered the cans of ammunition removed from the Chevrolet pickup that had brought McCoy to the range and stacked inside the range house. On each olive drab can was lettered, in yellow:

CALIBER .30 US CARBINE
110 GRAIN BALL AMMUNITION
480 ROUNDS PACKED
4 BANDOLIERS OF 12 10-ROUND STRIPPER CLIPS

He next ordered that one of the garbage cans, four of the five-gallon cans of gasoline, and a bundle of rags be loaded in the back of the pickup.

Then he went to one of the heavy oblong wooden crates with rope handles removed from the 6×6. These crates were also stenciled in yellow:

10 US CARBINES CAL .30 M1
PACKED FOR OVERSEAS SHIPMENT IN COSMOLINE
DO NOT DESTROY CONTAINER INTEGRITY WITHOUT SPECIFIC AUTHORIZATION

There was a good deal of container integrity. The cases were wrapped with stout wire. When Zimmerman had cut the wire loose, he saw the lid to the case was held down by eight thumbscrews. When these were off, he looked around and

[1]A two-and-one-half-ton-capacity, canvas-bodied truck, called "6×6" (pronounced "six-by-six") because all of its six wheels could be driven. Six-by-six was something of a misnomer, because the double axles at the rear usually held eight wheels.

borrowed a ferocious-looking hunting knife from the nearest Raider, who looked about eighteen years old and as ferocious as a Boy Scout.

When he pried the lid of the case loose, there was a piece of heavy, tarred paper over the contents. Zimmerman cut it free. Inside the case were ten heavy paper-and-metal envelopes. Zimmerman took two of them out and handed them to the Raider from whom he had borrowed the hunting knife.

"Put these in the back of the lieutenant's pickup," he ordered.

Zimmerman then sought out the detail sergeant.

"Twenty-four cases," he said. "Ten carbines per case. Two hundred forty carbines, less two the lieutenant has. I want to see two hundred and thirty-eight carbines out of their cases when I get back here. And I want to see twelve people busy boiling the Cosmoline off twelve carbines."

"Where you going, Gunny?" the buck sergeant asked.

"To inspect the range with the lieutenant," Zimmerman said, gesturing down range.

He then walked to the pickup, got behind the wheel, and drove the truck past the one-hundred-, two-hundred-, and three-hundred-yard ranges to a dip in the ground fifty yards from the five-hundred-yard target line. When the pickup went into the dip, it was invisible to the people on the firing line.

McCoy and Zimmerman got out of the cab of the truck.

"How are we going to do this?" Zimmerman asked.

"Carefully," McCoy said.

He climbed into the bed of the truck, picked up the garbage can, and lowered it to the ground. Zimmerman took one of the five-gallon cans of gasoline, opened it, and poured it into the garbage can. And then, as McCoy picked up one of the metal-foil envelopes from the bed of the truck and carefully tore the top off, Zimmerman poured the gas from the other three cans into the garbage can.

Inside the envelope was a very small rifle, not more than three feet long, with its stock curved into a pistol grip behind the trigger. It was covered with a dark brown sticky substance. McCoy delicately lowered the small rifle into the gasoline in the garbage can, and then repeated the process with the second metal foil envelope.

Then the two of them began, carefully, to slosh the weapons around in the gasoline.

The removal of Cosmoline from weapons by the use of gasoline or other volatile substance was strictly forbidden by USMC regulations. It was also the most effective way to get the Cosmoline off—far more effective than boiling water.

The sharp outlines of the small rifle began to appear as the Cosmoline began to dissolve.

"Don't breathe the fumes," McCoy cautioned.

Zimmerman passed the barrel of the carbine he was holding to McCoy.

"I got a can," he said.

He went to the truck and took from it an empty No. 10 can. He took a beer-can opener from his pocket and punched small drain holes around the bottom rim. Then he set the can down, unfolded a piece of scrap canvas on the bed of the truck, and then took one of the small rifles from McCoy.

He disassembled the small rifle into the stock and action, handed the stock and the forestock (a smaller piece of wood, which sat atop the barrel) to McCoy, sloshed the now-exposed action in the gasoline again, and then took it to the piece of canvas, where he took it down into small pieces and put them into the No. 10 can.

McCoy, meanwhile, using a rag and a toothbrush, stripped the stock and forestock of Cosmoline. When he was satisfied, he took the wooden pieces to the truck and laid them down. Zimmerman sloshed the parts in the No. 10 can around, then wiped them with a rag and scrubbed them with a toothbrush.

They worked quickly, but without haste. Soon, both of the rifles were on the scrap of canvas, free of Cosmoline. Except for the trigger group, they were stripped down to their smallest part.

"You think we have to take these down?" McCoy asked, looking doubtfully at the complex arrangement of small parts and springs.

Zimmerman picked up the second trigger group assembly and studied it carefully. "No," he said, issuing a professional judgment, "I don't think so."

"I don't suppose you've got a book?" McCoy asked. "So we can figure out how to put it back together?"

Zimmerman produced a small, paperbound manual, the U.S. Army Technical Manual for the U.S. Carbine, Caliber .30, M1, from the breast pocket of his dungarees, and displayed it triumphantly.

"You may turn into a passable gunny yet," McCoy said.

"Fuck you, McCoy," Zimmerman said, as he thumbed through the book looking for the disassembly instructions. When he found it, he opened the small book wide, breaking its spine so that it would lie flat.

Then, after carefully oiling each part and consulting the drawings in the book, they put the small rifles back together.

They worked the actions and dry-fired the weapons to make sure they were operable.

"What do we do about the gas?" Zimmerman asked.

"Dump it out, leave the can here until later," McCoy ordered. He took Zimmerman's carbine from him and climbed back into the pickup. Zimmerman tipped the garbage can on its side, watched for a moment as the sandy soil soaked up the gasoline, and then got behind the wheel.

They were gone no more than fifteen minutes. Steam was now rising from the water-filled garbage cans, and the men they had left were sloshing carbines around in it. It would be a long and dirty job using boiling water, McCoy thought, but there was no other way for these guys to do it. Doing it with gasoline was something only old Marines could handle safely; these kids, and that included their sergeant, would just blow themselves up using gas.

It did not occur to him that both the sergeant and the corporal, and at least two of the Raiders, were as old as, or older than, he was. He and Zimmerman had done a hitch with the 4th Marines. They were Marines, China Marines, and the others were kids.

As McCoy walked down the line of steaming garbage cans, Zimmerman went to the 6×6, pulled out a large flat cardboard carton, and took from it two large two-hundred-yard bull's-eye targets. Then he looked around and saw a tall, good-looking kid who didn't seem to have much to do.

He snapped his fingers, and when he had the kid's attention, beckoned to him with his finger.

"You might as well learn how to do this," Zimmerman said, and demonstrated the technique of making glue from flour and water in a No. 10 can.

When the glue had been mixed, Zimmerman led the kid to the one-hundred-yard line. There, target frames, constructed of two-by-fours with cotton "target cloth" stretched over them, were placed on the ground. He showed the kid how to brush the flour-and-water paste onto the target cloth, and then how to rub the targets smooth against it. Then they hoisted the target frames erect, put their legs into terra cotta pipes in the ground, and walked back to the firing line.

Zimmerman saw that a red (firing in progress) pennant had been hoisted on the flagpole, and that McCoy, with the sergeant, the corporal, and several kids watching him, had found the carbine magazines and other missing parts, and was trying to finish the assembly process.

"Gunny," Lieutenant McCoy said sternly, "do you know how to put the sling on this piece?"

"Yes, sir," Gunnery Sergeant Zimmerman said, confidently, even though he had absolutely no idea how to do it.

The carbine sling was a piece of canvas. Unlike the Springfield and Garand rifles, which had sling swivels top and bottom, however, the carbine sling fitted into a sling swivel mounted on the front side of the weapon with a "lift-the-dot" fastener. McCoy had figured out that much for himself.

He was having a problem fastening the rear end of the sling. Zimmerman took the carbine from McCoy. The right side of the stock of the carbine had, near the butt, a three-inch-long slot cut into it. In the center of the slot, there was a hole cut all the way through the stock. The left side of the stock had been inlet, the cut obviously designed to accommodate the sling.

There was a metal tube intended to fit into the slot of the right side of the stock. And the sling was intended to go through the stock from the left side, loop around the metal tube, and then pass through the stock again, holding the sling in place.

The problem Lieutenant McCoy was having, Gunnery Sergeant Zimmerman saw, was that when he looped the sling around the tube, it wouldn't fit it in the hole. And it obviously had to, for otherwise the metal tube would fall off.

Zimmerman took the metal tube in his hands.

"This, sir," he announced, "is the sling keeper."

At that moment, he noticed that one end of the tube was knurled. He unscrewed it. There was a piece of wire, flattened at one end, under the cap.

"Which, as you can see," Zimmerman said, "also contains the oiler."

He screwed the cap back in place, and wondered what the hell he was going to do now. And then inspiration struck. He knew how the goddamned thing worked.

"To insert the sling, sir," he pontificated, "*first* you insert the sling keeper/oiler—I'm not exactly sure of the nomenclature, sir—into the stock, and *then* you feed the sling around it."

It was only a theory, but it was all he had to go on; so he tried it, and it worked. The metal tube was securely inside the slot in the stock, and the sling was in place.

"In that manner, sir," Gunnery Sergeant Zimmerman said.

"Very good, Gunny," Lieutenant McCoy said.

"It's really very simple, sir," Gunnery Sergeant Zimmerman said.

"Sergeant," McCoy said, "the gunny and I are going to test-fire these weapons. Pass the word to your men, and make sure they keep well back of the firing line."

"Aye, aye, sir," the sergeant said. "Sir, are we going to get to fire them?"

"You'll be the first to fire when the company shows up," McCoy said.

Zimmerman opened an ammunition can and took from it an olive drab cotton bandolier. It had six pockets, each of which held two ten-round stripper clips separated by a strip of paperboard. He freed one of the small, shiny cartridges and looked at the base. It was stamped FC 42.

He showed it to McCoy.

"Brand-new, sir," he said, obviously impressed.

"That's the first brand-new ammo I've ever seen," McCoy said.

Zimmerman examined a stripper clip and a carbine magazine carefully, and he saw where one end of the stripper clip was obviously designed to fit over the lips of the magazine. He put it in place and shoved down with his thumb. The cartridges slipped into the magazine.

He looked at McCoy and saw that McCoy had been watching him. McCoy loaded a stripper clip into each of two magazines.

Then they walked to the firing line. McCoy sat down, and Zimmerman followed his example. He made as much of a sling as he could from the canvas strap, then shifted himself around until he was in what he considered to be a satisfactory shooting position.

Then he looked over his shoulder and around the range to make sure none of the kids had wandered into a dangerous position. Just to be sure, he counted heads. They were all in sight. He raised his voice.

"Ready on the right, ready on the left. Ready on the firing line. The flag is up, the flag is waving, the flag is down, commence firing!"

He lined up the sights on the bull's-eye and let off a round as well as he could. The trigger was stiff, heavy as hell, he thought. Probably because it was brand new. There was very little recoil; and the muzzle blast, while sharp, was less than he expected.

They fired slowly and carefully. Zimmerman was finished before McCoy took the carbine from his shoulder.

"Both clips?" Zimmerman asked.

"Might as well," McCoy said, and exchanged clips and resumed firing.

When they had finished, and McCoy had issued the formal commands to clear all weapons and leave the firing line, they handed the carbines to the sergeant and walked to the targets at the one-hundred-yard line.

There were twenty holes in each target. Zimmerman's were scattered around the bull's-eye, and McCoy's were at the lower left of the target. What counted, however, was not the location of the holes, but the size of the group. Sight adjustment would move the group.

"Piece of shit," Zimmerman said, disgustedly, reaching up and laying his extended hand with the thumb on one hole and the little finger on another. "That's eight fucking inches, for Christ sake, at a hundred yards."

"Some of them were fliers," McCoy said. "And some were from a fouled barrel, and the triggers are stiff because they're new."

"Bullshit, McCoy," Zimmerman said. "It's a piece of shit, and you know it."

"Get some rounds through them," McCoy insisted. "Let the sears wear in a little and you can cut those groups in half."

"Down to five inches?" Zimmerman said, sarcastically.

"Ernie, this thing is not supposed to be a rifle. It's to replace the pistol," McCoy said. "I don't know about you, but I can't put ten rounds from a forty-five into five inches at a hundred yards rapid fire."

Zimmerman looked at him.

"I'm not sure I could do it with a Thompson, either," McCoy insisted. "This thing fires fifteen rounds, and with the recoil, you're right back on the target as fast as you call pull the trigger. It's not a piece of shit, Ernie."

"Well, maybe to *replace* the pistol," Zimmerman grudgingly agreed.

"That's what it's for," McCoy said.

"Here they come," Zimmerman said, jerking his head toward the firing line.

A column of men, four abreast and fifty deep, was double-timing up the range road. They were in dungarees and wearing field gear, except for rifles and helmets. It was Company B, 2nd Ranger Battalion, which McCoy expected. But he had not expected it to be led by the company commander, or to be accompanied by its officers. He thought the Baker Company gunny would probably bring them out.

"Issue and familiarization firing of the US Carbine, Caliber .30, M1, 16 Hours," as the training schedule called it, was really the gunny's business; but the Old Man was at the head of the column, and all the other officers except the executive officer were in the column behind him.

Zimmerman reached up, worked his fingers under the target, and jerked it free of the target cloth.

"What did you do that for?"

"I don't want anybody to see me all over a hundred-yard target that way," Zimmerman said, as he balled the target up in his hands.

McCoy laughed, and then started trotting to the firing line so he would be there when the column double-timed up.

Captain Coyte turned the company over to the gunny, and walked toward McCoy.

McCoy saluted.

"Good morning, sir," he said. "I didn't expect to see the captain out here."

"I've never seen a carbine," Captain Coyte said. "Just include me in, Killer. It's your show."

"Aye, aye, sir," McCoy said.

"I thought I heard firing," Captain Coyte said.

"Yes, sir, Gunny Zimmerman and I test-fired two of them."

"Is that a couple of them on the table?" Coyte asked, nodding toward one of the four rough wooden tables behind the firing line. Without waiting for an answer, he walked toward the table, gesturing to the other officers to join him.

When he got to the table, he picked up one of the carbines, looked into the open action to confirm that it was not loaded, and then released the operating rod, threw it to his shoulder, drew a bead on the one target remaining, and dry snapped it. He tried, and failed, to get the bolt to remain open, and then looked at McCoy for help.

"There's a little pin on the rear operating-rod lever, Captain," McCoy explained. "Hold it back, push the pin in."

Captain Coyte succeeded in keeping the action open.

"I suppose this is the wrong word to use on a weapon," he said. "But it's kind of cute, isn't it?"

"If you think of it as a replacement for the pistol, sir," McCoy said, "it's not bad."

"Accuracy?"

"We managed to get ten shots into about eight inches at one hundred yards," McCoy said.

Captain Coyte's eyebrows went up. "There are a couple of reasons that might have happened," he said.

"I think, from a clear bore, with maybe a hundred or two hundred rounds to smooth it up, we can tighten those groups, sir."

"If you could cut them in half, that would still give you four inches," Captain Coyte said thoughtfully. "I now understand, I think, your reference to thinking of it as a replacement for the pistol."

"Captain, why don't you let me put up some targets and let you and the other officers fire?" McCoy asked. "The way I had planned to run this was to have the men clean their pieces—"

Coyte looked around. "McCoy, it's your range, and your class," he said. "If that could be done without fouling up your schedule . . ."

"Yes, sir."

"Well, then," Captain Coyte said, "in the interest of efficiency, not because I dare think that rank has its privileges, let's do it, Killer."

There was a smile in his eyes, and McCoy knew that he was mocking Colonel Carlson's "no special privileges" philosophy. He was surprised that a captain would mock the battalion commander, but especially that he would do so for the amusement of the junior second lieutenant in his company.

It took no more than fifteen minutes for McCoy to paste the holes in his target and then to give Captain Coyte enough quick instruction to understand what he was doing, and for Coyte to fire twenty rounds at the target.

By the time they were finished, Baker Company's gunny had broken the company down into four groups, and one group was gathered around each of the tables. At the first table, Zimmerman was demonstrating to a group of NCOs the disassembly technique on one of the two carbines they had cleaned with gasoline. The idea was that the NCOs would then go to the other tables and try disassembling the partially cleaned weapons themselves.

The system McCoy had dreamed up out of his head, and then modified after suggestions from Zimmerman, seemed to be working. The bottleneck was going to be getting the carbines free of Cosmoline, but nothing could be done about that. The safety precautions were in place. There would be inspections by platoon sergeants of weapons before they were shown to the gunnys, and finally Zimmerman would inspect them himself.

He saw that Zimmerman had also just about selected the armorer for the carbines. One of the kids. He had seen him mixing paste and pasting targets.

McCoy glanced at the tables and the faces. They were mostly kids, he thought, some of them as young as seventeen. And some he suspected were seventeen using somebody else's birth certificate.

And then he did a quick double take. There was a familiar face at the next-to-the-last table. At first it seemed incredible, but then there was no question about it at all. One of the Raiders struggling to get a good look at a sergeant taking a carbine to pieces was Tommy. Thomas Michael McCoy. PFC Thomas Michael McCoy, USMC, was Second Lieutenant Kenneth J. McCoy's little brother.

Younger brother, McCoy thought. *The sonofabitch is even bigger than I remembered. And meaner looking.*

"You look stunned, McCoy," Captain Coyte said. "Was my marksmanship that bad?" McCoy was startled, and it showed on his face when he looked up at Coyte.

"McCoy?"

"Sir, I just spotted my kid brother. The PFC with the broken nose, by Table Three?"

"I saw the similarity in name when he reported in," he said. "He reported in from Pearl. They must have lost his records, for he has a brand-new service record."

"They give you a new service record when they throw out a court-martial sentence, too," McCoy said.

"But we don't know that, do we, McCoy?" Coyte said. "So far as I'm concerned, so far as the Raiders are concerned, he has a clear record."

Their eyes met for a moment, and then Coyte went on, "If this is going to be a problem, McCoy, I can try to have him transferred."

"No problem, sir," McCoy said. "I can handle the sonofabitch."

"I'm sure you can, Killer," Captain Coyte said.

XVI

(ONE)
Annex #2, Staff NCO Club
Camp Elliott, California
10 March 1942

Gunnery Sergeant Ernst Zimmerman, USMC, sat alone on a wooden folding chair at one of the small, four-man tables of the club. He was freshly showered and shaved, and in freshly washed dungarees. His feet were on a folding chair.

Annex #2 of the staff NCO club was a Quonset building. It was intended to provide a place for the staff noncommissioned officers—the three senior pay grades—to go for a beer when they came off duty tired, hot, and dirty. The wearing of the green uniform was prescribed for the main staff NCO club.

Annex #2 was simple, in fact crude. The bar, for instance, ran a third of the length of the building and was made of plywood. After it was built, someone had gone over the surface with a blow torch, which brought out the grain of the wood. Then it had been varnished. There were fifteen stools at the bar, and a dozen of the small tables. There was a jukebox and four slot machines. Two took nickels, one took dimes, and one quarters.

Zimmerman never played the slot machines. He would play acey-deucey for money, or poker, and he had been known to bet on his own skill with the Springfield rifle, but he thought that playing the slots was stupid, fixed as they were to return to the staff NCO club twenty-five percent of the coins fed to them.

And he had never been in the main staff NCO club. He thought it was stupid to get all dressed up in greens, just to sit around with a bunch of other noncoms and tell sea stories. Green uniforms had to be cleaned and pressed, and that cost money. You could get hamburgers and hot dogs and bacon, lettuce, and tomato sandwiches and french fries at the main club, but Zimmerman thought it was stupid to buy your food when the Corps was providing three squares a day.

If you really wanted a good meal, Zimmerman reasoned, take liberty off the base and go to some civilian restaurant and get a steak.

There was a row of whiskey bottles behind the bar, but Zimmerman rarely had a drink. He had nothing against the hard stuff, just against buying it by the drink at thirty cents a shot. For the price of ten drinks, you could get a bottle, and there were a lot more than ten shots in a bottle.

Annex #2 offered a two-quart pitcher of draft beer for forty cents. They also offered little bags of Planter's peanuts for a nickel. Zimmerman liked peanuts, but he didn't like to pay a nickel for half a handful, so he bought them in cans in the PX for twenty-nine cents, two or three cans at a time, when he bought his weekly carton of Camel cigarettes. He kept them in his room. When he was going to Annex #2 for a pitcher of beer, he dumped half a canful of peanuts on a piece of paper, folded it up, and carried it with him. He figured that way he could eat twice as many peanuts with his beer for the same money.

All things considered, Zimmerman was satisfied with his present assignment. He sort of missed being around a motor pool, but you couldn't work in a motor pool if you were a gunnery sergeant, and it was nice being a gunny. He had never expected to become a gunny. Probably a staff sergeant, or maybe even a technical sergeant. But not a gunny. It was either the building of the Corps for the war, or else there had been a fuck-up at Headquarters, USMC, and some clerk was told to make him a staff sergeant and he hadn't been paying attention and had made a gunny instead. But he wasn't going to ask, or complain, about it. If there was a fuck-up, it would be straightened out.

He had liked being a gunny in the 1st Separate Battalion at Quantico. He had liked it better before they had transferred the company from Quantico to the 2nd Separate Battalion out here, and he had been a little worried when they had renamed the outfit the 2nd Raider Battalion.

It was supposed to be all volunteer. That wasn't so. Nobody had asked him when they'd transferred him from the motor pool at Parris Island whether he wanted to volunteer, and nobody had said anything about volunteering for anything since he'd been out here, either.

They were running the asses off the volunteers, a lot of time at night; but since he had been working for McCoy, he had been relieved from all other duties. That didn't mean it wasn't hard work, but the work McCoy had him doing made more sense than what everybody else was doing, especially the running around in the dark and the "close personal combat" training.

He didn't say anything about it, of course, but there was a lot of bullshit in the Raider training. They all thought they were going to be John Wayne, once they got to the Pacific, cutting Japanese throats. They seemed to have the idea that the Japs were obligingly going to stand still and raise their chins so they could get their throats cut.

Zimmerman knew that aside from McCoy, and maybe Colonel Carlson, he was one of the few people who had even seen a Japanese soldier up close. And the ones he had seen looked like pretty good soldiers to him. Some of the Japs he had seen were as big and heavy as he was. Most of the Raiders, especially the kids (which meant most of the Raiders; Zimmerman had heard that eighty-two percent of the enlisted men were under twenty years old), had the idea that Japs were buckteethed midgets who wore thick glasses.

Colonel Carlson was trying to make them understand that wasn't so, that the Japs were tough, smart, and well trained. But the kids thought he was just saying that to key them up. They wouldn't change their minds until some Jap started to stick one of those long Jap bayonets in them.

There were some things the Raiders were doing that made sense to Zimmerman. Everybody was getting, or was supposed to get, a .45 in addition to whatever weapon he would be issued. In the Old Corps, that didn't happen. Only people in crew-served weapons, plus some senior noncoms, and officers, got .45s. Most people couldn't hit the broad side of a barn with a pistol, but still it made sense to give people one in case something went wrong with their basic weapon.

Except, Zimmerman thought, that the Raiders were going apeshit over Thompsons and carbines, trying to get them issued instead of what they should have, these new eight-shot self-loading, .30–06 Garands.

In all his time in the Corps, Zimmerman had known only two people who could handle a Thompson properly. Major Chesty Puller, who was a short, stocky, muscular sonofabitch (in Zimmerman's mind, Puller, not Gunnery Sergeant Lou Diamond, was the Perfect Marine) and could handle the recoil with brute strength; and McCoy. McCoy, compared to Puller, was a little fucker, but he had learned how to control the recoil of a Thompson by controlling the trigger. He got off two-round bursts that went where he pointed them, and he could get off so many two- and three-round bursts that he could empty the magazine, even a fifty-round magazine, just about as fast as Major Puller, who just pulled the trigger and held it back and used muscles to keep ten-, fifteen-, even twenty-round bursts where he wanted them to go.

Aside from McCoy and Puller and, he now remembered, a gunnery sergeant with the Peking Horse Marines, everybody else he had ever seen trying to deliver accurate rapid fire from a Thompson had wound up shooting at the horizon. Or the moon.

But it was classy, *salty,* to have a Thompson, and everybody was breaking their ass to get one. In the Old Corps, you took what the book said, period. But Colonel Carlson, McCoy had told him, had been given permission to arm the Raiders just about any way he wanted to. If a Raider, officer or enlisted, could come up with almost any half-assed reason why he should have a Thompson, more often than not, they let him have one.

Zimmerman had personally stripped down and inspected ninety-six of the fuckers—half of them brand new, and half of them worn-out junk—that they'd got from the Army and that McCoy had sent him after.

But most of the officers loved the Thompsons. Though if they couldn't talk themselves into one of those, they wanted carbines. Maybe there was something to what McCoy had said, that the carbine was intended to replace the pistol. But he was about the only one that ever said that. Everybody else wanted it because they thought it would be a lot easier to haul around than a Springfield or a Garand.

And then there were the knives. Every sonofabitch and his brother in the Raiders was running around with a knife, like they were all Daniel Boones and they were going to go out and scalp the Japs, for Christ sake.

McCoy was the only Marine Zimmerman ever knew who had ever used a knife on anybody. There had been some guys in Shanghai who'd gotten into it with the Italian Marines during the riots with Springfield bayonets, but that was different. Bayonets weren't sharp, and they had been used almost like clubs, or maybe small, dull swords. And so far as Zimmerman remembered hearing, none of those Italian Marines had died.

Two of the four Italian Marines who had jumped McCoy in Shanghai had died. McCoy had opened them up with his Fairbairn, which was a knife invented by a Limey captain on the Shanghai Municipal Police. It was a sort of dagger, razor sharp on both edges, and built so that the point wouldn't snap off if it hit a bone. McCoy's wasn't a *real* Fairbairn, but a smaller copy of one run up by some Chinese out of an old car spring. It was about two-thirds as long as the real one. The real Fairbairn was too big to hide inside your sleeve above your wrist and below your elbow; McCoy's Baby Fairbairn was.

McCoy was now carrying his Fairbairn. When Zimmerman had asked him why, McCoy had first said, *"Because Carlson told me to."* And then he jumped all over his ass, saying he had a big mouth and that he should have kept it shut about what happened in Shanghai. Zimmerman had told him, truthfully, that he hadn't said a goddamned word about that, but he wasn't sure McCoy believed him.

Well, everybody in the goddamned Raiders knew about it now, and was calling him "Killer," the officers to his face, and the others behind his back. Until they stopped it, a lot of the kids were even trying to go around with their knives strapped to their wrists. That didn't work, but they thought it was salty as hell.

All this salty knife and submachine-gun bullshit was fine in training,

Zimmerman thought; but if the Raiders ever got to do what everybody thought they were going to do—sneak ashore in little rubber boats from destroyers-converted-to-transports onto some Jap-held island and start, like John Wayne and Alan Ladd in some bullshit movie, to cut throats and shoot up the place—they were going to find out it was a hell of a lot different from what they thought.

Only once in his life had Gunnery Sergeant Ernst Zimmerman found himself in a situation where armed men were really trying to kill him. Forty or fifty Chinese "bandits," who were working for the Japs, had ambushed him and a Marine officer named Sessions when they had become separated from the rest of a motor supply convoy.

He hadn't shit his pants or tried to hide or run or anything like that. He'd just stood there with a .45 in a hip holster and just absolutely forgot he had a weapon, until McCoy had come charging up like the goddamned cavalry taking Chinese down with a Thompson. Even *then* he hadn't done anything. McCoy had had to scream at him, *"Shoot, for Christ's sake!"* before he took the .45 out and started to use it to save his own ass.

Zimmerman didn't think that would happen again—after he had "woken up," he had done what had to be done—but he wondered how these Raiders who were swaggering around Camp Elliott with their knives and carbines and Thompsons were going to react when they found themselves facing some Jap who was as big as they were, and who wasn't wearing thick glasses and didn't have buck teeth and was about to shoot them or run them through with a bayonet.

Baker Company's gunnery sergeant, Danny Esposito, appeared at the table with a pitcher of beer in one hand and a mug in the other. He was a large, heavy, leather-skinned man of thirty (either a Spaniard or an Italian, Zimmerman wasn't sure which), and he was wearing greens.

"You saving this table?" he asked.

"Sit down," Zimmerman said.

"You ready?" Gunnery Sergeant Esposito asked, holding his pitcher of beer over Zimmerman's mug.

"Why not?"

Esposito topped off Zimmerman's mug, and then sat down. Zimmerman pushed the piece of waxed paper with the peanuts over to him. Esposito scooped some up, tossed them in his mouth, and nodded his thanks.

"Scuttlebutt says that if somebody's got a worn-out Thompson and wants one of the new ones," Gunnery Sergeant Esposito said, "you're the man to see."

"You want a Thompson?" Zimmerman asked evenly.

"One of my lieutenants," Esposito said. "I put a hundred rounds through a Garand, and I sort of like it. It ain't no Springfield, of course, but I'm getting two-, two-and-a-half-inch groups."

"The Garand is a pretty good weapon," Zimmerman said. "People don't like it 'cause it's new, that's all."

"What about the Thompson? Can you help me out?"

"I'll see what I can do," Zimmerman said. "That why you come looking for me?"

"What makes you think I come looking for you?"

"You're all dressed up," Zimmerman said.

Esposito shrugged and drained his beer mug and refilled it before he replied. "I was hoping maybe I'd run into you, Zimmerman," he confessed.

"You did," Zimmerman said.

"Out of school?" Esposito asked.

Zimmerman nodded.

"You're pretty tight with Lieutenant McCoy," Esposito said.

"We was in the Fourth Marines together," Zimmerman said. "He's all right."

"Scuttlebutt says he had you to dinner," Esposito said. "On some yacht, where he's shacked up."

"That's what the scuttlebutt says?" Zimmerman replied.

"What do you know about his brother?"

"Not much," Zimmerman said.

"I got an old pal at the Diego brig," Esposito said.

"What'd he do?" Zimmerman said.

"I said 'at,' not 'in,' " Esposito said, before he realized that Zimmerman was pulling his leg. *"Shit,* Zimmerman!"

"What about your pal at the brig?"

"He says McCoy—*PFC* McCoy was in there," Esposito said. "You know anything about that?"

Zimmerman shook his head. "No."

"He was supposed to be on his way to Portsmouth to do five-to-ten for belting an officer."

"That's what you heard, huh?" Zimmerman said.

"I also found out when he reported in here, he had just had full issue of new uniforms, and he's got a brand-new service record."

"What does that mean?"

"It means I got the straight poop from my friend at the brig," Esposito said. "If they vacate a general court-martial sentence and turn somebody loose, they give him a new service record. And since general prisoners don't have uniforms, except for dungarees with a 'P' painted on them, they give them a new issue."

"If I was you, Esposito," Zimmerman said, "I wouldn't be running off at the mouth about this."

"Because of Lieutenant McCoy, you mean?"

"Because if the Corps gave him a new service record, it means the Corps wants him to have a clean slate. Don't go turning over some rock."

"How would your friend Lieutenant McCoy react if I kicked the shit out of his little brother?"

"Why would you want to do that?" Zimmerman asked.

"For one thing, he's a wisenheimer," Esposito said. "For another, he thinks he's a real tough guy. He beat the shit out of two of my kids. No reason, either, that I can get out of anybody, except that he wanted to show people how tough he is. And he's running off at the mouth, too. About his brother, I mean. What's with the shack job on the yacht? Is that true? And while I'm asking questions, what's the real poop about Lieutenant McCoy?"

Zimmerman lit a Camel with his Zippo, and then took a deep pull at his beer mug.

"What do you mean, real poop?"

"He really kill a bunch of Italian Marines with that little knife of his?"

"Two Italians," Zimmerman said. "He killed *two* Italians. Stories get bigger and better every time they get told."

"You was there?"

"I was there," Zimmerman said.

"Mean little fucker, isn't he?" Gunnery Sergeant Esposito said, approvingly. "I heard fifteen, twenty Italians. I knew that was bullshit."

"It was twenty *Chinamen,"* Zimmerman said. "Not Italians, *Chinamen."*

"No shit?"

"Okay, we're out of school, right?" Zimmerman said. He waited for Esposito to nod his agreement and then went on. "McCoy and I were buddies in the Fourth. We had a pretty good rice bowl going. We ran truck supply convoys from Shanghai to Peking. We got pretty close. One time the convoy got ambushed. Chinese bandits, supposed to be. Actually the Japs were behind it. McCoy killed a bunch of them—twenty, anyway, maybe more—with a Thompson."

"No shit?" Esposito said, much impressed.

"You don't want to get him mad at you, Esposito," Zimmerman said. "You was asking about the boat—"

"*Yacht,* is what the brother says," Esposito said. "And the rich broad who lets him drive her LaSalle convertible."

"One thing at a time . . . Christ, what do you guys do, spend all your time gossiping about your officers like a bunch of fucking women?"

Esposito gave Zimmerman a dirty look, but didn't say anything.

"First of all," Zimmerman went on, "the LaSalle is McCoy's. He come home from China with a bunch of money—"

"Where'd he get it?"

"He's a goddamned good poker player," Zimmerman said. "And on top of that, he was lucky, real lucky, a couple of times."

Esposito nodded his acceptance of that.

"So he bought the LaSalle; that's his," Zimmerman said. "And so we both wound up here. And like I said, we were buddies. But he's now an officer, so he can't come in here, and I can't go to the officers' club. So he has a girl friend. A *real nice* girl, Esposito, you understand? I personally don't like it when you say 'shack job.' And she lives on a boat, not a yacht, a boat. And McCoy tells her about me and his kid brother, and she says bring us to dinner. So we go. And that's it. We had dinner and drank some beer, and then McCoy drove us back out here."

"I figured it was probably something like that," Esposito said. "His brother's got a real big mouth."

"I saw that myself," Zimmerman agreed.

"And he's a mean sonofabitch, too," Esposito said. "I told you; he really beat the shit out of a couple of my kids."

"I don't want to put my nose in where it ain't welcome," Zimmerman said. "But, maybe, if you would like, I could talk to the brother."

"I don't kow," Esposito said, doubtfully. "You think he'd listen to you? He sure as shit don't listen to me when I try to talk to him."

"You start beating up on him, you're liable to lose your stripes," Zimmerman said.

"Well, shit, Zimmerman, if you think you could do any good," Esposito said.

"It couldn't hurt none to try," Zimmerman said.

"What the hell," Esposito said. "Why not? And what about the Thompson?"

"You take the old one to the armory, tomorrow," Zimmerman said. "And tell the armorer I said to swap it for you."

"You want to split another pitcher of beer?"

"Nah, hell, I got to get up in the wee hours. But thanks anyway."

Ten minutes later, Gunnery Sergeant Ernst Zimmerman was outside the enlisted beer hall, known as the Slop Chute.

There was a cedar pole ten feet from the entrance. Seventy-five or so knives were stuck into it. Zimmerman had heard about the cedar pole, but it was the first time he had seen it. There was a regulation that the Raiders could not enter the Slop Chute with their knives. So rather than going to his barrack or tent to leave his knife there, some ferocious Raider had stuck it in the cedar pole and reclaimed it when he left the Slop Chute. The idea had quickly caught on.

"Dodge fucking City," Zimmerman muttered under his breath, disgustedly.

He pushed the door open and walked inside, grimacing at the smell of sour beer, a dense cloud of cigarette smoke, and the acrid fumes of beer-laden urine.

"Hey, Mac, no knives," a voice behind him said. Zimmerman turned and saw there was a corporal on duty at the entrance. Zimmerman didn't reply. Finally, the corporal recognized him. "Sorry, Gunny," the corporal added. "Didn't recognize you at first."

Zimmerman looked around the crowded room until he spotted PFC Thomas McCoy, who was sitting with half a dozen others at a crude table drinking beer out of a canteen cup.

He walked across the room to him.

"Hey, whaddasay, Gunny!" one of the others greeted him, cheerfully. "You want a beer?"

"I want to see McCoy for a minute, thanks anyway," Zimmerman said.

"What the hell for?" PFC McCoy replied. He was a little drunk, Zimmerman saw.

Zimmerman, on the edge of snapping, "Because I said so, asshole! On your feet!", stopped himself and smiled. "Colonel Carlson's got a little problem he wants you to solve for him."

The others laughed, and a faint smile appeared on McCoy's face. He got to his feet.

"This going to take long?" he asked.

"I don't think so," Zimmerman said.

He motioned for McCoy to go ahead of him, and then followed him across the room and out of the building. McCoy went to the cedar post, jerked one of the knives from it, and slipped it into the sheath on his belt.

"Where we going?" he asked.

"Right over this way," Zimmerman said, "it's not far."

Behind the Slop Chute building was a mixed collection of other buildings, some frame with tar-paper roofs, some Quonsets, and some tents. Here and there a dim bulb provided a little light.

Zimmerman went to the door of one of the small frame buildings, took off his dungaree jacket and his hat, and hung them on the doorknob.

"What's this, Gunny?" McCoy asked, suspiciously.

"You know what it means, you fucking brig bunny," Zimmerman said. "It means that right now you can call me 'Zimmerman,' 'cause right now, I ain't a gunny. I just hung my chevrons on the doorknob."

"What the hell is wrong with you?" McCoy asked.

"Nothing's wrong with me," Zimmerman said. "What's wrong is wrong with you, asshole."

"I don't know what the fuck you're talking about, Gunny, but if you think I'm going to get in it with you and wind up back in the brig, you have another think coming."

"You're not going back to the brig," Zimmerman said, moving close to him. "Having his brother in the brig would embarrass Lieutenant McCoy, and you've embarrassed him enough already, brig bunny."

"I wish I believed that," McCoy said. "I would like nothing better than to shove your teeth down your throat."

"Have a shot," Zimmerman said. "Look around, there's nobody here. And your brother's an officer. He wouldn't let them put you in the brig on a bum rap."

"Fuck you," McCoy said.

"I thought that you were supposed to be a tough guy," Zimmerman said. "I guess that's only when you're picking on kids, right?"

McCoy balled his fists, but kept them at his side.

"Come on, tough guy," Zimmerman said. "What's the matter, no balls?"

McCoy threw a punch, a right, with all his weight behind it.

Zimmerman deflected the punch with his left arm and kicked McCoy in the crotch.

McCoy made an animal sound, half scream and half moan, and fell to the ground with his hands at his crotch and his knees pulled up.

"You *cocksucker,"* he said indignantly, a moment later. "You *kicked* me."

Zimmerman kicked him again, in the stomach.

"That's for calling your brother's lady friend a 'shack job,' " Zimmerman said, conversationally. He kicked him again. "And that's for calling me a 'cocksucker.' You got to learn to watch your mouth, brig bunny."

McCoy was writhing around on the ground, gasping for breath, moaning as he held his scrotum.

Zimmerman, his arms folded on his chest, watched silently. After several minutes, McCoy managed to sit up.

"Are you getting the message, tough guy? Or do you want some more?"

"You don't fight fair," McCoy said, righteously indignant. "You kicked me, for Christ's sake!"

"Get up then, Joe Louis," Zimmerman said. "Try it with your fists."

McCoy took several deep breaths, and then got nimbly to his feet, balled his fists, and took up a crouched fighting posture.

"I must have missed," Zimmerman said, almost wonderingly. "Usually when I kick people, they stay down."

"You cocksucker!" McCoy said, and charged him. He threw a punch. Zimmerman caught the arm, spun around, and threw McCoy over his back. McCoy landed flat on his back. The air was knocked out of him.

Zimmerman walked to him and kicked him in the side.

"I *told* you," he said. *"Don't* call me a cocksucker."

With a massive effort, McCoy got his wind back and struggled to his knees. And then he heaved himself upright.

Zimmerman slapped him twice with the back of his left hand across the face, and then with the heel of his right hand across the throat. The first blow was hard enough to make McCoy reel, and the second sent him flying backward, his hands to his throat, gasping for breath. And then he fell heavily onto his backside.

Zimmerman stepped up to him and kicked him in the side again. McCoy bent double and threw up.

"I hit you with my open hand," Zimmerman said, conversationally. "If I had hit you with the side of it,"—he demonstrated with his left hand—"you would have a broken nose, and you wouldn't be able to talk for a week. If I had hit you hard enough, I would have crushed your Adam's apple and you would choke. The only reason I didn't do that is because your brother is a friend of mine, and he might feel bad about it."

"Jesus Christ!" McCoy said, barely audibly.

"The next time, McCoy, that I hear that you said one fucking word out of line, or that you took a poke at anybody, I'm going to be back and give you a real working over. Tough guy, my ass!"

He walked over to McCoy and raised his foot to kick him again.

McCoy scurried away as best as he could.

Zimmerman lowered his foot and laughed.

"Shit!" he said, contemptuously. And then he walked to the small building, put his dungaree jacket on, and walked off.

PFC Thomas McCoy waited until he was really sure that he was gone, and then he got to his feet. His balls hurt, and his sides, and inside, and it hurt him to breathe.

He took a handkerchief from his pocket and wiped at the vomitus on his jacket and trousers and boots. Then, gagging, he staggered off toward his barrack.

(TWO)
The Foster Peachtree Hotel
Atlanta, Georgia
14 March 1942

Second Lieutenant Richard J. Stecker, USMC, stood with a glass of Dickel's 100-proof twelve-year-old Kentucky sour mash bourbon whiskey in his hand, looking out the window of his bedroom in the General J. E. B. Stuart suite. It was raining—it looked as if it couldn't make up its mind to snow or rain—and the wind had blown the rain against the windowpane. Stecker idly traced a raindrop as it slid down.

He was more than a little pissed with his buddy, Second Lieutenant Malcolm S. Pickering, USMCR, for a number of reasons, all attributable to Pick's infatuation with the female Stecker thought of alternately as "the Admiral's Daughter" and "the Widow."

Stecker was either sorry for the poor sonofabitch—who really had a bad case of puppy love for Martha Sayre Culhane, or unrequited love, or the hots, or whatever the hell it was—or pissed off with him about it.

At the moment, the latter condition prevailed.

From yesterday at noon until fifteen minutes ago, there had come a ray of hope:

At noon yesterday, using a concrete beam foundation of one of the hangars at Saufley Field for a table, they had been having their lunch (a barbecue sandwich and a pint container of milk) when Pick, out of the blue, spoke up. "How would you like to get laid?"

"Are you seeking to increase your general fund of knowledge, Pickering, or do you have some specific course of action in mind?"

"I was thinking we might drive to Atlanta," Pick said, "and take in the historical sights. They have a panorama of the Battle of Atlanta, which should be fascinating to a professional warrior such as yourself. There are also a number of statues of heroes on horseback, which I'm sure you would find inspirational."

"I thought you said something about getting laid?"

"That too," Pick said.

"You realize, of course, that if we go to Atlanta, you won't be able to hang around the lobby of the San Carlos panting for a glimpse of the fair Martha?"

"Fuck fair Martha," Pick said, just a little bitterly, and then quickly recovered. "Which might be a good idea, come to think of it."

"I heard it takes two," Dick said.

"Do you want to go to Atlanta, or not?"

It was necessary to get permission to travel more than a hundred miles from the

Pensacola Navy Air Station. And before they could run down Captain Mustache and obtain his approval, it was after six. As a result they got to the Foster Peachtree Hotel after midnight. The bar wasn't closed, but there were no females dewy-eyed with the thought of consorting with two handsome and dashing young Marine officers.

That didn't seem to bother Pick. He was interested in drinking, and the two of them closed the bar long after everyone else had left. Stecker wondered why the bartender hadn't thrown them out, until he remembered that Pick's grandfather owned the hotel.

And Pick of course waxed drunkenly philosophic about his inability to get together with the Admiral's Daughter. Dick Stecker had heard it all before, and he was bored with it.

"I'll make a deal with you, Pick," he said. "You won't mention Whatshername's name all weekend, and I will not pour lighter fluid on your pubic region and set it on fire while you sleep."

In the morning, Pick slept soundly, snoring loudly until long after ten.

Then, determinedly bright and cheerful, he went into Stecker's room, ordered an enormous breakfast from room service, and then explained that they really shouldn't eat too much, for they were meeting his Aunt Ramona for lunch at quarter to one."

"Your *Aunt Ramona?"* Dick asked, disgustedly.

"My Aunt Ramona loves me," Pick said. "And I always try to see her when I am in Atlanta. Only the cynical would suggest I do this because dear Aunt Ramona usually is accompanied by two or more delightful young belles, straight from *Gone with the Wind."*

"No shit?"

"You will have to watch your foul mouth, Stecker," Pick said. "There is nothing that will chase away a well-reared South'ren lady quicker than a foul-mouthed Marine. And if you talk dirty, my Aunt Ramona will rap you over the head with her cane."

Aunt Ramona was not what Dick Stecker had been led to expect. She turned out to be a good-looking redhead, wearing a silver fox hat to match her knee-length silver fox coat. She was in her thirties, Stecker judged, as he watched her give her cheek to Pick to kiss.

"Aunt Ramona," Pick said, on his very good manners, "may I present my good friend, Lieutenant Richard Stecker? Dick, this is Mrs. Heath."

"I'm very pleased to meet you, Lieutenant," she said, extending a diamond-heavy hand with a gesture that would have done credit to the Queen of England.

"My pleasure, ma'am," Stecker said.

"If I had known you were coming, before ten o'clock this morning, Pick," Aunt Ramona said, "I would have set something up."

"I realize this has inconvenienced you," Pick said politely.

"You have always been an imp," Aunt Ramona said. "But I am glad to see you."

And then the girls appeared.

One was a blonde, and the other was a redhead, and they were gorgeous.

The first thing Dick Stecker thought was that they were not going to get laid. Not the same day they met these gorgeous creatures. Probably not until after they had walked down an aisle with them to be joined together in holy matrimony. Then he thought, *That doesn't matter. Just being with them is enough. You just don't often get to meet girls like this.*

They had thick Southern accents, which Dick Stecker found absolutely enchanting, and names to match. The blonde's name was Catherine-Anne, and the redhead's Melanie. Melanie had light blue eyes and a most enchanting way of licking at her lips with the tip of her delicate red tongue. And she, even more than Catherine-Anne, seemed to be fascinated to meet a West Point graduate who had gone into the Marines and was learning to be a Naval aviator.

They had lunch in the high-ceilinged main dining room—an elegant, delicious lunch, which Dick Stecker thought was very appropriate for the circumstances. There had even been champagne.

"This is a celebration," Aunt Ramona said. "And—as wicked as this might make me sound—I'd just *love* to have some champagne."

When the champagne was delivered and poured, and they all touched their glasses, Melanie had met Dick Stecker's eyes over the rim of her glass.

And three times, by accident of course, her knee had brushed against his under the table. The last two times she had pulled it away, of course, but she had also looked into his eyes.

Everything had at first gone swimmingly. They had had a second bottle of champagne. There was a string quartet, and they had danced. Both of them danced with Aunt Ramona first, of course, and then with the girls. When he had finally gotten his arms around Melanie, her perfume made him a little dizzy, and she seemed oblivious to her breasts pressing against his abdomen.

Pick seemed interested in Catherine-Anne, and she in him; and that all by itself seemed to be a blessing. All that had to be done now was to ask to take them to dinner. And get rid of Aunt Ramona, of course.

And then Aunt Ramona looked at her diamond-encrusted watch and cried in her ladylike way, "I had absolutely no *idea* it was so late! Girls, we have to go this *minute!*"

Pick jumped to his feet, and Dick had been sure that what he was going to do was make his move. He was a smooth sonofabitch, and there was no question that he would say precisely the right thing, and in precisely the right way, and that the result would be that they would get to take Catherine-Anne and Melanie to dinner. Maybe starting with early cocktails.

But he didn't. He kissed his goddamned aunt on the cheek and told her it had been nice to see her. And then he smiled at the girls and told them it had been a pleasure to make their acquaintance and that he hoped sometime to see them again.

And that was it. Melanie gave Dick one of those looks, and her hand; but then she was gone, following the other two out of the dining room.

"Jesus Christ, you blew that!" Dick snapped.

"Blew what?"

"They're *gone!* Goddamnit! Didn't you *notice?*"

"As opposed to what?" Pick had asked, innocently.

"I thought we were here to get laid," Dick whispered furiously and a little too loudly. Heads turned.

"You really didn't think . . . Aunt Ramona's friends?"

"I thought maybe dinner."

"They just met you, Dick," Pick explained. "Things just aren't done that way in Atlanta."

"Why not?"

"Well, if we get back here, maybe the next time I could get Aunt Ramona to give me their phone numbers, and maybe we could get them to meet us somewhere for a drink."

"What about now, for Christ's sake? What's wrong with now?"

"Can I say something to you without offending your feelings?" Pick said.

"I don't know," Dick said. "Right now, you're on pretty thin ice."

"You don't know much about girls like that," Pick said, seriously. "That's not a criticism; it's a simple statement of fact."

"So what? I can learn."

"You sort of liked the redhead, didn't you?" Pick asked.

"Melanie, her name is Melanie," Dick said. "Yeah, I did."

"Well, like I said, the next time we're here, if we come back, *maybe* I can get Aunt Ramona to put a good word in for you."

"But not now, huh?" Dick said, resignedly.

"Did you really think that something would happen?"

"Ah, hell, I guess not."

"I really feel bad about this," Pick said, as he signed his name to the bill and got up. "I really feel that I gave you the wrong impression about girls like that."

"Forget it," Dick said.

He followed Pickering out of the dining room and to the bank of elevators.

"Where are we going now?"

"Nature calls," Pick said.

"Yeah, me too," Dick said.

When they were in the suite, Pick touched Dick's arm.

"Hey, buddy," he said, "I've got an important phone call to make. Would you mind staying in your room until I yell?"

"You mean we drove seven hours just so we can't get laid and you can call your fucking widow?" Dick exploded.

Pick looked as if he had been about to say something but had changed his mind. Dick Stecker was instantly ashamed of himself.

"I'm a horse's ass," he said. "Good luck when you call her."

"Take the bar with you, why don't you?" Pick said.

"What?"

Pick pointed. There was something in the suite now that hadn't been in it when they had gone downstairs to meet Aunt Ramona, a cart mounted on huge brass wheels and holding an assortment of bottles, an ice bucket, and even two bottles of champagne.

"I'm liable to be some time," Pick said.

"In that case, I will take it," Dick said.

"Gimme one of the champagne bottles," Pick said, and took one from the cooler.

Then he turned his back on Stecker and started to open the champagne.

Stecker pushed the cart into his bedroom. He didn't want any champagne. For one thing, there didn't seem to be any point in drinking something romantic if you were alone in a hotel room. And for another, it tasted to him like carbonated vinegar.

He examined the bottles, selected the bourbon, made himself a drink, and then went to look out the window.

Always look for the bright side, he told himself. *At least you're here, in the fanciest hotel room you have ever seen. And you at least met her, and maybe you can come back. And the day isn't over. There is always hope.*

Dick had been looking out the window for perhaps five minutes when there was a knock at his door.

"I'm here by the window," he said, "contemplating jumping."

"Oh, don't do that," a soft Southern female voice said. "There's all sorts of interesting ways to spend a rainy afternoon."

Dick Stecker did not, literally, believe what he saw when he turned from the window to face the door.

Melanie was there. She had a smile on her face, and a champagne glass in her hand, and she was stark naked.

"Holy Christ!" Dick said.

Melanie walked slowly across the room to him. Her boobs, he thought, were absolutely gorgeous. And she was a real redhead.

"Can you handle that all right, Lieutenant?" Pickering called. "Or should I make you up a flight plan?"

Dick's eyes snapped to the open door. Pickering was standing there, one hand holding a bottle of champagne, the other wrapped around Catherine-Anne's waist. Catherine-Anne was wearing nothing but a smile and a garter-belt. She was not a real blonde.

Melanie walked up to Dick and started to unbuckle his Sam Browne belt. When Dick looked at the door again, it was closing. He heard Pickering laugh. And then he turned his attention to Melanie.

On the way back to Pensacola the next day, Pick furnished Dick with an explanation. Ramona Heath was a madam, not his aunt. He had known her for years—since he had been a sixteen-year-old bellhop. She had a stable of girls with which she traveled all over the country. Her girls were expensive, because they were the best. Most of her middle-aged clients were perfectly willing to close their eyes to the fact that the fees were paid by the people trying to sell their product and to allow themselves to think their charm and good looks were responsible for their being in bed with beautiful young women.

"I'm surprised," Jack said.

"Surprised? We went to get laid; we got laid."

"I mean, in good hotels," Stecker said. "Does that make me seem naive?"

"My grandfather once said," Pick said, "not to me, of course, but I heard about it, that the only thing he had against a paying guest coupling with an elephant in his room was that it was sometimes hard to clean the carpet."

"What did that little joke of yours cost you?" Stecker asked.

"Nothing. I tried to pay her—we danced, remember?—but she said no. She said I should think of it as her contribution to the war effort."

"Jesus Christ, Pickering, you're amazing."

"Yeah, I am," Pickering said, and there was something rueful in his tone of voice that made Dick Stecker look at him.

"Now what's wrong?"

"Well, I went to get laid. And I got laid. Getting it to stand up took all the skill at the command of the hooker, which I must say was most imaginative and thorough. And when it was over, I felt like a piece of dog shit. *How could I be unfaithful to good old Whatshername?"*

"Oh Jesus, Pick, I'm sorry," Stecker said.

"What the fuck am I going to do, Dick?" Pick asked plaintively.

Stecker said the only thing he could think of. "Hang in there, buddy," he said. "Just hang in there."

XVII

(ONE)
The New York Public Library
1215 Hours, 25 March 1942

Carolyn Spencer Howell was thirty-two years old. She was tall, chic, and much better dressed than most of the other librarians in the Central Reading Room of the New York Public Library on Forty-second Street, and she wore her black hair parted in the middle, and long enough to reach her shoulder blades. She had begun—not without feeling a little foolish and wondering what her real motives were—what she thought of as her special "research project" four days before.

Although one saw more and more men in uniform on the streets these days, one did not encounter many in the library, except in the lobby waiting out the rain. But there was one who was spending considerable time in the Central Reading Room, and Carolyn Spencer Howell found him very interesting. She had no way of knowing, of course, how long he had been coming into the Central Reading Room before she noticed him; but since she had noticed him ten days earlier, he had come in every day.

He was a Marine, and an officer. She knew that much about the military services. Marines wore a fouled anchor superimposed on a representation of the world as their branch-of-service insignia. Officers wore pins representing their rank on the epaulets of their tunics and overcoats, and in the case of this man, on his collar points. Carolyn had to go to the Britannica to find out that a golden oak leaf was the insignia of a major.

From the time she had first noticed him, the Marine major had followed the same schedule. He arrived a few minutes after nine in the morning and went to the periodicals, where he read that day's *New York Times,* and then the most recent copies available of the *Baltimore Sun* and the San Diego *Union Leader*. He could have just been killing time, which of itself would be interesting, but he seemed to be looking for something particular in the newspapers.

When he came into the library every day, the Marine major had with him an obviously new leather briefcase, in which he carried two large green fabric-bound looseleaf notebooks, a supply of pencils, two fountain pens, cigarettes, and a Zippo lighter and a can of lighter fluid. She had once watched while he refilled his lighter. It was unusual to carry a supply of lighter fluid around with you, but it seemed to make sense if you thought about it.

He would make notes in one of the two notebooks, writing in pencil in one of them and in ink in the other. When he had finished reading the newspapers, he would come to the counter—sometimes to Carolyn Spencer Howell, and sometimes to one of the other girls—and fill out the little chits necessary to call up material from the stacks.

The first words he ever said to Carolyn Spencer Howell were "Would it be possible to get the *New York Times* from November fifteenth, nineteen forty-one, through, say, December thirty-first?"

"Of course," she said, "but it would make quite an armful. How about four days at a time? Starting with November fifteenth, nineteen forty-one?"

"That would be fine," the major said. "Thank you very much."

He had a nice, deep, masculine voice, she thought, and spoke with a regional accent that told her only that he was not a New Yorker. And there was something a little unhealthy about him, she thought. He didn't look quite as robust and outdoorsy as she expected a Marine major to look.

On the plus side, he had nice, warm, experienced eyes.

The second time he spoke to her, the major asked if by any chance the library had copies of the *Shanghai Post.*

"Well, yes, of course," she said. "Up to when the war started, of course."

"Could I have them from November first, nineteen forty-one . . . up to the last?"

"Certainly."

While he was reading the *Shanghai Post,* Carolyn noticed something strange. The major was just sort of staring off into space. There was a strange, profoundly sad look on his face. And in his eyes.

Some of the other requests he made of Carolyn Spencer Howell were of a military or politico-military nature. For instance, she got for him the text of the Geneva Conventions on Warfare, and several volumes on stateless persons. He was especially interested in Nansen passports.[1]

Most of his requests concerned the Japanese, which was understandable, but what in the world was a major of Marines doing spending all day, every day, in the public library? Didn't the military services have more information on the enemy than a public library could provide?

An even more disturbing thought came to Carolyn Spencer Howell. Was he *really* a Marine officer? Or some character who had simply elected to put on a service uniform? This was New York City, and anything was possible in New York, even in the main reading room of the public library. This unpleasant thought was fertilized when Carolyn realized that the major's uniforms were brand new. There was even a little tag that he had apparently missed stitched below one of the pockets on one of his blouses.

Yet he wore decorations, or at least the little colored ribbons that represented decorations, on the breast of his uniform. And for some reason she came to believe that these were the real thing—which made *him* the real thing. Finding out what they represented became important to Carolyn. She thought of it as her "research project."

He had four ribbons. And when he came to the counter, she looked at them carefully and later made notes describing their colors. She checked her notes for accuracy when she had reason to walk through the reading room.

One had a narrow white stripe at each end, then two broader red stripes, and a medium-sized blue stripe in the middle. Next to it was one that was all purple, except for narrow white stripes at each end. And there was a little gold pin on this one, an oak leaf maybe. Another one was all yellow, with two narrow red-white-and-blue bands through it. And there was another yellow one, this one with two white-red-white bands *and* a blue-white-red band. This one had a star on it.

Carolyn was, after all, a librarian; she was trained to do research. Thus it wasn't

[1]In 1920, the League of Nations authorized an identity/travel document to be issued to displaced persons, in particular Russians who did not wish to return to what had become the Soviet Union. It came to be called the "Nansen passport" after Fridtjof Nansen, League of Nations High Commissioner for Refugee Affairs.

hard to find out what the ribbons represented. The one that sat on top of the other three was the Bronze Star Medal, awarded for valor in action. The purple one was the Purple Heart, awarded for wounds received in action. The little pin (officially, according to *United States Navy Medals and Decorations, Navy Department, Washington D.C., January 1942, 21 pp., unbound,* an *oak leaf cluster)* signified the second award. Or, in other words, it said he had been wounded twice. The mostly yellow one with the star on it was awarded for service in the Asiatic-Pacific Theater of Operations; the star meant participation in a campaign. The other mostly yellow one was the American Defense Medal, whatever that meant.

That meant that the somewhat pale and hollow-eyed major was a bona fide hero. Either that or that he was a psychotic subway motorman who was enduring his forced retirement by vicariously experiencing the war—dressing up in a Marine officer's uniform and spending his days reading about the war in the public library.

Today, the Marine officer, with an armload of books, came directly to Carolyn Spencer Howell's position behind the counter.

"I wonder if you could just keep these handy?" he asked, "while I go have my lunch."

"Certainly," Carolyn said, and then she blurted, "I see you've seen service in the Pacific."

For the first time he looked at her, really looked at her as an individual, rather than as part of the furnishings.

"I was in the Pacific," he said, and then, "I'm surprised you know the ribbons. Few civilians do."

"I know them," Carolyn heard herself plunge on. "And you've been wounded twice. According to the ribbons."

"Correct," he said. "You have just won the cement bicycle. Would you care to try for an all-expense-paid trip to Coney Island?"

And then his smile vanished. He looked at her intently, then shook his head and started to laugh.

"What were you about to do?" he asked. "Call the military police?"

She felt like a fool, but she was swept along with the insanity.

"I was just a little curious how you could have served in the Pacific and be back already," she said.

"Would you believe a submarine?" he asked, chuckling. He reached in his pocket and took his identity card from his wallet and handed it to her.

It had a photograph of him on it, and his name: BANNING, EDWARD J. MAJOR USMC.

"Now will you guard my books for me while I have lunch?" he asked.

"I'm sorry," Carolyn Spencer Howell said, flushing. Then she lowered her head and spoke very softly.

There was no reply, and when she looked up, he was gone.

Carolyn Spencer Howell shook her head.

"Oh, damn!" she said so loudly that heads turned.

Fifteen minutes later, she walked into a luncheonette on East Forty-first Street and headed for an empty stool. A buxom Italian woman with her hair piled high on her head beat her to it, and Carolyn turned in frustration and found herself looking directly at Major Edward J. Banning, USMC, who was seated at a small table against the wall.

"You wouldn't be following me, would you?" he asked.

Carolyn flushed, and started to flee.

Banning stood up quickly and caught her arm.

"Now, I'm sorry," he said. "Please sit down. I'm about finished anyway."

She sat down.

"I have made an utter fool of myself," she said. "But I wasn't really following you. I often come here for lunch."

"I know," Banning said. "I've seen you. I hoped maybe you'd come here for lunch today."

She looked at him.

"I've been thinking," he said. "Under the circumstances, I would have thought I was suspicious, too."

"Would you settle for 'curious'?" Carolyn asked.

"You were suspicious," he said. "Why should that embarrass you?"

A waitress appeared, saving her from having to frame a reply. She ordered a sandwich and coffee, and the waitress turned to Banning.

"If the lady doesn't mind me sharing her table, I'll have some more coffee," he said.

"Please," Carolyn said quickly.

She looked at him. Their eyes met.

"You remember me asking for stuff on Nansen passports?" Banning asked. She nodded. "The reason I wanted to find out as much as I can is that my wife, whom I left behind in Shanghai, is traveling on a Nansen."

"I see," she said.

"I wanted that out in front," Banning said.

"Yes," Carolyn Spencer Howell said. And then she said, "I was married for fifteen years. My husband turned me in on a younger model. It cost him a good deal of money. I had to find a way to pass the time, so I went back to work in the library."

He nodded.

We both know, she thought. *And he knew before I did. I wonder why that doesn't embarrass me? And what happens now?*

They walked back to the library together. Just before she was to go off shift, he walked to the counter and asked her how she would respond to an invitation to have a drink before he got on the subway to go back to Brooklyn. She said she would meet him for a drink in the Biltmore Hotel. She would meet him under the clock . . . he couldn't miss the clock.

And so after work they had a drink, and then another. When the waiter appeared again, she said that she didn't want another just now. Then he asked her if she was free for dinner, and she told him she was, but she would have to stop by her apartment for a moment.

In the elevator, she looked at him.

"I can't remember one thing we talked about in the Biltmore," she said.

"We were just making noise," he said.

"I don't routinely do this sort of thing," Carolyn Spencer Howell said softly, as they moved closer together.

"I know," he said.

Afterward, she went to the Chinese restaurant on Third Avenue, and returned with two large bags full of small, white cardboard containers that Ed Banning said looked like they held goldfish.

Then she took off her clothes again, and they ate their dinner where she had left him, naked, in the bed.

(TWO)
Bachelor Officers' Quarters
U. S. Navy Hospital
Brooklyn, New York
0930 Hours, 26 March 1942

The spartan impersonality of the bachelor officers' quarters struck Major Edward J. Banning the moment he pushed open the plate-glass door and walked into the lobby. It was in some ways like a small hotel.

There was a reception desk, usually manned by a petty officer third. But he wasn't there. And the lobby and the two corridors that ran off it were deserted.

The lobby held a chrome-and-plastic two-seater couch; a chrome-and-plastic coffee table in front of the couch; and two chrome-and-plastic chairs on the other side of the coffee table. There was a simple glass ashtray on the coffee table, and nothing else.

The floor was polished linoleum, bearing the geometric scars of a fresh waxing. There were no rugs. Two photographs were hanging on the walls, one of the Battleship *Arizona,* the other of a for-once-not-grinning-brightly Franklin Delano Roosevelt. There was a cork bulletin board, onto which had been thumbtacked an array of mimeographed notices for the inhabitants.

A concrete stairway led to the upper floors. Its railings were steep pipe, and its stair-tread edges were reinforced with steel.

Banning went to the desk and checked for messages by leaning over the counter for a look at the row of mailboxes where a message would be kept. There was no message, no letter. This was not surprising, for he expected none.

Banning went up the concrete stairs to the second floor. It was identical to the first, except there was no receptionist's desk. That space was occupied by a couch-and-chairs-and-table ensemble identical to the one in the lobby, which left the center of the second floor foyer empty. There was an identical photograph of President Roosevelt hanging on the wall, next to a photograph of two now-long-obsolete Navy biplane fighters in the clouds.

Halfway down the right corridor, his back to Banning, the petty officer who usually could be found at the reception desk was slowly swinging a large electric floor polisher across the linoleum. Banning walked down the left corridor to his room.

The reason he noticed the spartan simplicity of the BOQ, he realized, was that forty-five minutes earlier, he had walked down a carpeted corridor illuminated by crystal chandeliers to an elevator paneled in what for some strange reason he had recognized as fumed oak, and then across carpets laid on a marble floor past genuine antiques to a gleaming brass-and-glass revolving door spun by a doorman in what looked to be the uniform of an admiral in the Imperial Russian Navy.

"Good morning, Mrs. Howell," the doorman had politely greeted Carolyn. "It's a little nippy. Shall I call a cab?"

"No, thank you," Carolyn had said. "I'll walk."

The doorman's face had been expressionless. Or at least his eyebrows had not risen when he recognized Mrs. Carolyn Howell coming out of the building with a Marine. Nevertheless, Carolyn's face had colored, and Banning had seen that she was embarrassed.

She had quickly recovered, however, and almost defiantly took his arm before they walked down the street.

The sex had been precisely what the doctor had ordered. From the moment he had kissed her in the elevator on the way up, there had been no false modesty, no pushing him away, no questions about what kind of a woman did he think she was. She wanted him—or at least a man—just about as bad as he had wanted her—or at least a woman.

She had told him later, and he had believed her, that it had been the first time for her since the trouble with her husband.

"It *is* like riding a bicycle, isn't it?" she had asked, with a delightfully naughty—and pleased—smile as she forked a shrimp from one of the little cardboard Chinese take-out containers. "You don't forget how. Except that I feel, with you, like you've just won the Tour de France."

And it had been, aside from the sex, a very interesting (or perverse?) experience to lie naked in Carolyn's bed and tell her about Milla, while she, with genuine sympathy in her eyes, was kneeling naked beside him. To think that Milla would like Carolyn, and Carolyn would like Milla. And to wonder if he was really a sonofabitch for feeling that somehow Milla, if she knew about Carolyn, would not be all that hurt, or pissed off. That she might even be happy for him.

He reached his room, found the key, and pushed the gray metal door open.

The BOQ room was furnished with a bed; a straight-backed chair; a chest of drawers; a chrome-and-plastic armchair; a small wooden desk; and a framed photograph of a broadly smiling Franklin Delano Roosevelt.

Lieutenant Colonel F. L. Rickabee, USMC, in uniform, was sitting in the straight-backed chair, his feet on the bed, reading the *New York Times*. He had removed his uniform blouse, revealing that he used suspenders to hold up his trousers. There were outer straps around his torso, which only after a moment Banning recognized as the kind that belonged to a shoulder holster.

"Ah, Banning," Rickabee said, "there you are. All things come to him who waits."

"Good morning, sir."

"I feel constrained to tell you that I caught the four A.M. milk train from Sodom on the Potomac in the naive belief that by so doing I could catch you before you went out."

"If you had called, sir . . ." Banning said.

Rickabee swung his feet off the bed, refolded the newspaper carefully, and tossed it on the bed. When he faced Banning, Banning saw the butt of what he thought was probably a Smith & Wesson Chief's Special in the shoulder holster.

"No problem," Rickabee said. "It gave me a chance to talk with Captain Toland about you, which was also on my agenda. And it also gave me my very first chance to play secret agent."

"Sir?"

"I asked the white hat on duty downstairs to let me into your room. He told me it was absolutely against regulations." He bent over the bed, took what looked like a wallet from his blouse, and tossed it to Banning. "So I got to show him that. He was awed."

Banning caught it and opened it. Inside was a gold badge and a sealed-in-plastic identification card. The card, which carried the seal of the Navy Department, held a photograph of Rickabee, and identified him as a special agent of the Secretary of the Navy, all questions about whom were to be referred to the Director of Naval Intelligence.

Banning looked at Rickabee.

"I think I could have ordered him to set the building afire," Rickabee said. "It had an amazing effect on him. You could almost hear the trumpets." He held his hand out for Banning to return the identification.

Banning chuckled and tossed the small folder back to him.

"Very impressive, sir," he said.

"In the wrong hands, a card like that could be a dangerous thing," Rickabee said.

"Yes, sir, I can see that," Banning said.

A leather folder came flying across the room. Banning just managed to catch it.

"That's yours," Rickabee said. "You're a field-grade officer now, so I suppose it won't be necessary to tell you to be careful with it."

Close to astonishment, Banning opened the folder. It held the same badge and card, except that his photograph peered at him from it.

"You also get a pistol," Rickabee said, pointing to a large, apparently full, leather briefcase. "Since I didn't think you'd have to repel boarders between here and San Diego, I took the liberty of getting you a little Smith & Wesson like mine."

A dozen questions popped into Banning's mind.

"Sir—" he began.

"Let me talk first, Ed," Lieutenant Colonel Rickabee interrupted him. "It will probably save time."

"Yes, sir," Banning said.

"General Forrest sent me here," Rickabee said. "My first priority was to settle to my own satisfaction the question of your mental stability. Dr. Toland's diagnosis—that there is nothing wrong with you that a good piece of ass wouldn't cure—confirmed my own. Toland told me that the way you handled yourself when you thought you were blind was as tough a test of your stability as he could think of."

Banning waited for Rickabee to go on.

"So you are now officially certified as an officer who, because of the extraordinary faith placed in his ability and trustworthiness by both the Assistant Chief of Staff for Intelligence of the Marine Corps, and the Commandant, can be entrusted with the highest-level secrets of the Corps, and with some extraordinary authority," Rickabee said.

"Jesus Christ," Banning said. "What the hell does that mean?"

"Just what I said," Rickabee said. "Secret one is that General Forrest at this time yesterday morning was cleaning out his desk and wondering how he was going to tell his wife that he was being retired from the Corps in disgrace—a disgrace that was no less shameful because the reasons were secret."

"Forrest? Christ, he's a good man. What the hell—"

"At two yesterday afternoon, the Commandant summoned General Forrest to his office and told him that he had reconsidered; that the needs of the Corps right now—there being no one available with his qualifications and experience to replace him—were such that he would not be retired."

"Colonel," Banning said, "I don't have any idea—"

"Major General Paul H. Lesterby was retired from the Corps as of oh-oh-oh-one hours this morning," Rickabee went on. "Colonel Thomas C. Wesley—"

"Used to be with Fleet Marine Force Atlantic?" Banning interrupted.

Rickabee nodded. "And more recently, he was Plans and Projects in the Commandant's office. Wesley is now on a train for California, where he will function as special assistant to the commanding officer of the supply depot there until the Commandant makes up his mind whether he will be retired, or court-martialed. The Commandant was honest enough to tell Wesley that he would prefer to court-martial him, and the only thing that was stopping him was the good of the Corps."

"What the *hell* did he do?"

"You know Evans Carlson, I understand?"

"Yes, sir."

"From this point, Ed, as you will see, we are getting into an even more sensitive area," Rickabee said, and went into his briefcase. First he took out a small revolver in a shoulder holster and laid it on the bed. Then he handed Banning a thick stack of papers. "These documents were given to the Commandant the day before yesterday. I can't let them out of my hands. You'll have to read them now. When I get back to Washington, the whole file will be burned, and I am to personally report to the Commandant that it has been burned."

The first document in the stack was stamped SECRET. It was entitled, "Report of the Activities of Evans Carlson, late Major, USMC, during the period April 1939–April 1941."

Halfway down the stack was Captain James Roosevelt's letter to the Major General Commandant of the Marine Corps. At the bottom of the stack, also stamped SECRET, were transcripts of telephone conversations between Lieutenant Colonel Rickabee or Captain Edward Sessions and Second Lieutenant K. J. McCoy.

"I wondered what McCoy was doing at Elliott," Banning said when he had finished reading everything and was tapping the stack on his chest of drawers to get it in order.

"Any other questions?" Rickabee asked.

"You want an honest response to that?" Banning asked.

"Please," Rickabee said.

"This is a despicable thing to do to Carlson," Banning said.

"Yes, it was," Rickabee said. "And that was one of the more printable terms used by the Commandant to describe it."

"Was?"

"Was," Rickabee confirmed. "Just as soon as the Commandant saw it, it was over. Except for cleaning up the mess, of course."

"How did it happen?" Banning said. "How did it get started in the first place?"

"The goddamned Palace Guard got carried away with its own importance," Rickabee said. "Wesley took it upon himself to save the Corps from Carlson. He enlisted General Lesterby in that noble cause, and then the two of them went to Forrest with their little idea. When Forrest balked, they led him to believe they were acting for the Commandant."

"Jesus Christ!"

"And that goddamned Wesley suckered me, too," Rickabee said. "There was no question in my mind that he was working for the Commandant. Otherwise—"

"It's hard to believe," Banning said. But when he heard what he had said, he offered a quick clarification. "I mean, a colonel and a major general. Jesus Christ!"

"I think the real reason the Commandant's mad at Forrest is that Forrest was apparently willing to believe the Commandant was capable of something like that. Fortunately, I'm only a lieutenant colonel, and lieutenant colonels are supposed to be stupid. The Commandant treated me with condescending contempt, and spelled out very slowly and carefully what he wants me to do about cleaning up the mess."

"That involves me? You said something about Diego," Banning asked.

"The Commandant told me—this was during the eighteen-hour period General Forrest thought he was being retired in disgrace, and there was nobody to deal with but me—that the worst thing you can do to a commander is let him know his superiors question his ability. If necessary, the Commandant is prepared to go to California and apologize to Carlson and assure him of his personal confidence in him. But he hopes that Carlson doesn't know we sent an officer out there to spy on him, and that an apology won't be necessary."

"Apologies being beneath the dignity of the Commandant?" Banning asked, sarcastically. "You don't suppose he could be worried that President Roosevelt will find out about this half-cocked spying operation?"

Rickabee hesitated a moment before he replied. "I'm sure he is," he said finally. "And the damage to the Corps if that happens is something I don't even like to think about. If the President found out, the Commandant would have to go. And that would be bad for the Corps, for all the reasons that come quickly to mind."

Banning grunted.

"But having granted that, Ed, no, I don't think apologizing would bother the Commandant at all. But *making* the apology would be an admission that there was doubt in Carlson's loyalty and ability—doubt high enough within the Corps to have the Commandant personally involved. What the Commandant wants to know is whether Carlson knows, or strongly suspects, what's been going on. That's where you come in."

"How?"

"The forward element of the First Raider Battalion will leave Quantico one April for Diego, and sail for Hawaii as soon as shipping can be found for them. The Second Battalion, Evans Carlson's, is supposed to complete their training at Camp Elliott on fifteen April. There will be an inspection of the Second Raider Battalion by officers from Headquarters, USMC. You will be part of that delegation, charged, as an experienced regimental S-Two, with having a look at Carlson's intelligence section. Not, if I have to say it, as somebody assigned to us. You'll prepare the usual report, which will make its normal passage through channels. You will also be prepared, immediately on your return, to tell the Commandant personally whether or not you think Carlson suspects anything."

"Lovely job," Banning said, dryly.

"Check with McCoy, of course. And there's somebody else out there you probably should talk to. You remember Master Gunnery Sergeant Stecker?"

"Did a hitch with the Fourth? Has the Medal of Honor?"

"He's a captain, now, in Diego. At Second Joint Training Force headquarters. He works for Colonel Lou Harris, and Harris has had him greasing Carlson's ways. If approached discreetly, you might ask him if Carlson has smelled a rat."

"I don't know if he would talk to me. He's a starchy sonofabitch."

"He's a good Marine," Rickabee said. "Use your judgment, Ed."

"I get the picture, sir," Banning said. "When do I go?"

"Your leave is over two April," Rickabee said. "I've got orders for you. You are assigned to the office of the Inspector General, Headquarters, USMC, on that date, and to the inspection team for the Second Raiders. They will have left Washington one April. You've got a rail priority, and Sergeant Gregg—you remember him?"

Banning shook his head. "No."

"Gregg got you a compartment on the Twentieth-Century Limited to Chicago, and then on whatever they call that train with the observation cars—"

"I know what you mean," Banning said. "I can't think of the name."

"Well, anyway, after you cruise through the Rockies in luxury to Los Angeles, you take a train called the Lark to San Diego. The inspection team will return to Washington by air. You'll travel with them."

"Aye, aye, sir," Banning said.

"By the time you get to Washington, have your mind made up," Rickabee said. "The Commandant has a tough call to make, and he'll have to make it pretty much on what you decide."

Banning grunted, and nodded his head thoughtfully.

"I knew the good life was too good to last," he said.

XVIII

(ONE)
Company B, 2nd Raider Battalion
Camp Elliott, California
26 March 1942

The men of Baker Company were spread out on both sides of the dirt road—hardly more than a path—in the hills above Camp Elliott when the jeep drove up. The platoon leader and Gunnery Sergeant Esposito were standing up. And a few of the men were sitting up, but most of them were flat on their backs, still breathing heavily. Gunny Esposito had elected to have them pass the last five minutes before the break at double-time. After forty-five minutes of marching at quick time with full field gear, including a basic load of ammo, five minutes of double-time feels like five hours.

The jeep was driven by the company clerk. Unlike the stereotype of most company clerks, Baker Company's company clerk looked like the fullback he had been on the Marion (Ohio) High School "Tigers" before he had enlisted in the Corps three days after Pearl Harbor. You had to have a "C" average to remain eligible for varsity football, and since Rocky Rockham wasn't too comfortable with geometry or English, the coach had suggested that if he wanted to play football, he better take something he could do well in, something that would bring his grade average up, like typing.

At Parris Island the personnel clerk had asked Rocky Rockham if he had any skills, like typing. And Rocky told him that he could type pretty good, forty-five words a minute. Naturally the personnel clerk hadn't believed him, and made him take a test. Rocky Rockham didn't look like somebody who could type, but he passed the test, and he left Parris Island for the Joint Training Force at Diego as a clerk/typist.

Rocky quickly realized that telling the personnel clerk that he could type had been a mistake. He had joined the Corps to kill Japanese, to pay the buckteethed bastards back for Pearl Harbor and Wake Island, not to sit at a fucking typewriter in a fucking office, filling out fucking requisition forms.

At the reveille formation one day, there had been a call for volunteers to serve in something called the 2nd Separate Battalion. The first sergeant told them the 2nd Separate Battalion was going overseas as soon as they finished their training. So Rocky volunteered. That was what he wanted, getting overseas, and out from behind the typewriter.

"Well, lad," the first sergeant of Baker Company said, smiling at him the day he reported aboard, "I'm damned glad to see you. You can really type forty-five words a minute?"

A minute after that, not smiling, the first sergeant of Baker Company pointed out to PFC Rockham that he was in the Marine Corps, and the Marine Corps didn't give a flying fuck what *he* wanted to do. He would do what the Corps told him to do, and if he was smart, he would do it wearing a fucking smile. He was now Baker Company's company clerk, and that was fucking *it.*

When Rocky wrote home that he had been made a corporal, he didn't add that he was the company clerk of Baker Company, 2nd Raider Battalion, USMC; just that he was in the Raiders and hoped to soon be killing Japs.

Rocky stopped the jeep, and walked over to the lieutenant who was taking the march for the Old Man. He saluted and delivered his message.

"Go get him, Gunny," the lieutenant ordered.

Gunny Esposito turned around.

"McCoy!" he bellowed. "Up here! On the double!"

PFC Thomas M. McCoy, still breathing heavily, still red-faced, pushed himself off the ground and trotted to where Gunny Esposito stood with the lieutenant and Rocky Rockham.

"Throw your gear in the vee-hicle," Gunny Esposito said, "and go with Corporal Rockham."

"Where'm I going, Gunny?"

"In the vee-hicle with Corporal Rockham," Gunny Esposito explained.

When they were bouncing back down the hill, McCoy asked Rockham where he was going.

"Able Company," Rockham said. "You been transferred."

"What the fuck for?"

"Who the fuck knows?" Rockham asked rhetorically. "First sergeant give me your service record, told me to collect you and your gear and take you over to Able Company."

PFC McCoy naturally concluded that Zimmerman, that fat, mean cocksucker, was responsible. He had seen Zimmerman three, four times since the night Zimmerman had taken him from the Slop Chute and worked him over. And it was always the same thing. Zimmerman would motion for him to come over to wherever he was standing.

"I hear you been keeping your mouth shut and your nose clean," Zimmerman had said. "Maybe you aren't as dumb as you look, brig bunny."

When Rockham dropped him off at the Able Company orderly room, with his sea bag, his records, and all his gear, McCoy put the bag and his field gear by the side of the door, and then he complied with the order painted on the door to "KNOCK, REMOVE HEADGEAR, WAIT FOR PERMISSION TO ENTER."

"Come!" a voice called.

McCoy stepped inside.

"You're McCoy," the company clerk announced. The company clerk was a little fucker with glasses.

"I was told to report here," McCoy said.

The first sergeant looked up from his desk. He was a mean-looking sonofabitch, a tall, skinny Texan.

"You got your gear, I hope?" the first sergeant asked. When McCoy nodded, he motioned to McCoy to hand him his service record.

He opened the envelope, took out all the records it contained, and picked out the service record itself, leaving the clothing forms and the shot records and all the other documents on the table. Then he stood up and walked through a door under a sign reading "MERWYN C. PLUMLEY, 1ST LT, USMC, COMMANDING," carrying the service record with him.

He was inside maybe two minutes before he opened the door and stuck his head out.

"McCoy, report to the commanding officer."

McCoy walked to the open door and followed the protocol. He rapped twice on the doorjamb with his knuckles, waited until he was told to come in, and then he marched in. He stopped eighteen inches from Lieutenant Plumley's desk, coming to attention; and then, looking six inches over the officer's head, he barked, "Sir, PFC McCoy reporting to the company commander as ordered, sir."

"Stand at ease, McCoy," Lieutenant Plumley said. McCoy spread his feet and put his hands in the small of his back. Now he could look at Lieutenant Plumley. When he did, he saw that Plumley was examining him very carefully.

"Gunnery Sergeant Zimmerman has been talking to me and to First Sergeant Lowery about you, McCoy," Lieutenant Plumley said.

Well, that fucking figures!

"When the lieutenant talks to you, McCoy, you say 'Yes, sir,' " First Sergeant Lowery snapped.

"Sorry, sir," PFC McCoy said.

"Tell me, McCoy," Lieutenant Plumley said, "why you did so badly with the BAR in Baker Company?"

What the fuck is that all about?

"Sir, I qualified with the BAR," McCoy said.

"Marksman," Lieutenant Plumley said. "Only Marksman."

Record firing scores qualified a marine as Marksman, Sharpshooter, or Expert. Marksman was the lowest qualifying score, and extra pay was given those qualifying as Expert.

"Sir," McCoy blurted, "the BAR I had was a piece of shit, one of them worn-out ones we got from the Army."

"And you think you could do better if you had a better weapon?"

"Yes, sir," McCoy said.

"So does Gunnery Sergeant Zimmerman," Lieutenant Plumley said.

"He's sure big enough," First Sergeant Lowery said. There was a faint hint of approval in his voice. McCoy looked at him in surprise.

"Gunnery Sergeant Zimmerman, as you know, McCoy," Lieutenant Plumley said, "has been temporarily assigned other duties. But when we deploy, he will come back to the company. He is naturally interested in what he will find here when he comes back."

"Yes, sir," McCoy said.

"We're short a couple of squad leaders," Lieutenant Plumley said. "And when the first sergeant and I discussed this with Gunnery Sergeant Zimmerman, he recommended that you be transferred from Baker Company and be given one of those billets."

"Sir?" McCoy was now completely baffled. He was sure he hadn't heard right.

"Gunny Zimmerman has recommended that you be given one of the squad-leader billets. It carries with it a promotion to corporal," Lieutenant Plumley said. "That's why I was curious when I saw that you'd only made Marksman when you fired for record."

"Yes, sir," McCoy said.

"If the first sergeant could arrange for you to requalify, with a weapon in first-class condition, do you think you could do better than Marksman?"

"Yes, sir."

"Well, then, we'll do it this way. We will assign you temporarily as a BAR fire-team leader," Lieutenant Plumley said. "Sergeant Lowery will arrange for you to requalify. If you make Sharpshooter—I would hope Expert—I'll give you your corporal's stripes. Fair enough?"

"Yes, sir."

"Do you have anything else, First Sergeant?"

"No, sir."

"Then that will be all for now, Sergeant," Lieutenant Plumley said. "I would like a word with McCoy alone."

"Aye, aye, sir," First Sergeant Lowery said, and walked out of the office, closing the door behind him.

Plumley looked at McCoy.

"There's something about me I think I should tell you, McCoy," he said. "I don't listen to scuttlebutt. I don't like scuttlebutt."

"Yes, sir."

"If someone comes to me with a clean service record, so far as I am concerned, he has a clean record. So far as I am concerned, you have reported aboard with a clean record. Do you take my point?"

"Yes, sir," McCoy said.

Lieutenant Plumley smiled and reached across the desk with his hand extended.

"Welcome aboard, McCoy," he said. "You come recommended by Gunny Zimmerman, and therefore I expect good things of you."

"Thank you, sir."

"You're dismissed, McCoy," Lieutenant Plumley said.

McCoy came to attention, did an about-face, and marched out of the office.

First Sergeant Lowery was waiting for him in the outer office.

"Come on, I'll show you where you'll bunk," he said. Outside the orderly room, he picked up McCoy's field gear and carried it for him.

Halfway to the barrack, he laid a hand on McCoy's arm.

"I understand you're pretty good with your fists, McCoy."

"I guess I'm all right," McCoy said.

"You use your fists in Able Company, McCoy, and I'll work you over myself. And compared to me, what Zimmerman did to you will be like being brushed with a feather duster."

McCoy looked at him.

"You understand me?" First Sergeant Lowery asked.

"Yeah, I understand you."

First Sergeant Lowery smiled, and patted McCoy, a very friendly pat, on the shoulder.

"Good," First Sergeant Lowery said. "Good."

(THREE)
The New York Public Library
1415 Hours, 26 March 1942

Carolyn Spencer Howell had expected Major Edward Banning to join her for lunch. But when he hadn't been there, and after she had finally given up on him and gone to eat, she knew she had to come to terms with the reality of what had happened.

The conclusion she drew was that she had made a grand and glorious ass of herself. That, for reasons probably involving the moon, but certainly including the fact that she was a healthy female with normal needs, as well as the fact that Ed

Banning was a good-looking healthy male, she had played the bitch in heat. And she'd done everything a bitch in heat does but back up to the male, rub her behind against him, and look over her shoulder to see what was keeping him from doing what she wanted done.

She had even performed the human version of that. Before they kissed in the elevator, she had with conscious and lascivious aforethought pressed her breasts against him.

All this morning Carolyn relived with surprise and embarrassment her shamelessly lewd behavior with him in her apartment. The reason she thought of nothing else all morning was that until the reality dawned on her, she had wondered how she would behave when he returned from Brooklyn.

The last thing he said to her when she left him at the subway entrance was that he would go change his uniform and come back. He even kissed her. Rather distantly, she thought even at the time, but a kiss was a kiss. Once she reached the library, there had been time to consider what she had done: She had allowed one of the patrons to buy her a drink, following which she had taken him directly to bed.

Her worrying started when she began to imagine how she was going to be able to look him in the eye when he came back from Brooklyn. But after he hadn't returned by eleven (when she thought she would take him into the staff lounge, which you could do for a "friend," and give him a cup of coffee and maybe a Danish), she began to worry, to give her imagination free rein.

By noon, one theory of the several that had occurred to her seemed to stand the test of critical examination. The point of this one was that he was *not* entirely a sonofabitch. He had at least been decent enough to tell her he was married. And she was now convinced that he was indeed a Marine officer.

Yet he had been very vague about what exactly he did as a Marine officer, and where he did it. And in fact, now that she had time to think about it, it no longer seemed entirely credible that he was in New York on leave simply because his family was gone and he had no place else to go, and New York seemed as good a place as any to take a holiday.

If he was so bored with his leave, why was he on leave?

And viewed with the cold and dispassionate attitude that she believed she had reached by one o'clock—when it was apparent that he was not going to come—his melodramatic story of the White Russian wife left on the pier in Shanghai clearly served two purposes. First, it told her he was married, so don't get any ideas. And second, it clearly infected the heart of the librarian with terminal nymphomania and inspired her to perform sexual feats right out of the Kama Sutra. He had probably enormously embellished the original tale as soon as he had realized how much of it she was so gullibly willing to swallow.

Over lunch (preceding which she had a Manhattan to steady her nerves and keep her from throwing the ashtray across the room), she remembered what her father told her when she told him she was going to divorce Charley: "Everybody, sooner or later, stubs their toe. When that happens, the thing to do is swallow hard and go on to what happens next."

And so, by the time she walked back in the library, Carolyn was at peace with herself. She accepted the situation for what it was, and she was already beginning to see small shafts of sunlight breaking through the black cloud. All she had done was make a fool of herself, and thank God, no one knew about it. Except, of course, Henry the Doorman; and he was just the doorman. In her state of temporary insanity, she could have introduced Banning to her colleagues in the library. With her state of rut in high gear, it would have been clear to any of her colleagues that she had more of an interest in Major Ed Banning than as a fellow lover of books.

And being absolutely brutally honest about it, she hadn't come out of the encounter entirely empty-handed. Obviously, she had wanted to be taken to bed, and Ed had certainly done that with great skill and finesse. She would not need such servicing again any time soon.

Now she would simply put Major Ed Banning out of her mind.

And then, *there* he was, in the Central Reading Room. He was sitting at a table close to the counter. He quickly rose up, with a worried look on his face, when he saw her approach him.

"Hello," he said.

"Hello," Carolyn said.

"I thought you would be interested to know that you don't work here," he said.

"I beg your pardon?"

"I called up and asked to speak to you—"

"You did?"

He's obviously lying. After some thought, he has decided to come back for another drink at the well.

"And a woman said there was no one here by that name," Ed Banning said.

"Oh, really?"

"So I called back, thinking I would get somebody else, and I got the same woman, and she said, in righteous indignation, 'I told you there is no Mrs. Powell on the staff.' "

My God, he doesn't even know my name!

"It's *Howell,"* Carolyn said. "With an 'H.' "

"Well, that explains that, doesn't it?" Ed Banning said. And then he looked at her and blurted, "I was afraid that maybe you had told her to say that, that you just wished I would go away."

"No," Carolyn said, very simply.

"I got my orders," Ed said. "That's why I was delayed. That's what I was trying to tell you on the telephone."

"Where are you going?" she asked.

"The West Coast," he said.

"When are you going?"

"Two April," Ed said. "That's a week from today."

"Oh," she said.

"Are you free for dinner?" Ed asked.

"Dinner?"

"I don't want to intrude in your life, Carolyn," Ed Banning said. "But I had hoped that we could spend some time together."

"Oh," she said.

"Dinner?" he asked again, and when there was no immediate reply, "Maybe tomorrow night?"

My God, he's afraid I'll say no.

"What are your plans for this afternoon?" Carolyn asked.

"I have to go to Brooks Brothers," Banning replied.

"Brooks Brothers?" She wasn't sure she had heard correctly.

"When I replaced my uniforms, I didn't buy as much for the tropics as I should have," he said.

"Meaning you're headed for the tropics . . . the Pacific?"

"Meaning that I realized this morning that I don't have enough uniforms," he said.

Is that the truth? Or does he know he's on his way to the Pacific and doesn't want to tell me?

"That's all you have planned?" Carolyn asked.

"That's it."

"For this afternoon, or for the rest of the week?"

"For the week," Ed Banning said.

"I thought maybe you'd be going home or something," she said.

"I thought I told you," he said. "Like a lot of Marines, the Corps's home."

Carolyn looked into his eyes.

"Wait for me in the lobby," she said. "It'll take me about five minutes to tell my boss I'm going, and to get my coat."

When she went outside, he was at the bottom of the stairs, standing by one of the concrete lions that seem to be studying the traffic on Fifth Avenue passing the library. It was snowing, and there was snow on the shoulders of his overcoat and on his hat.

She went quickly down the stairs and put her hand under his arm, and then she absolutely shocked herself by blurting, "Hi, sailor, looking for a good time?"

He touched her gloved hand for a moment and smiled at her.

"Have any trouble getting the afternoon off?" he asked.

"I told my boss I was just struck with some kind of flu," Carolyn said, "that'll keep me from work for a week."

"Can you get away with it?" he asked.

"Sure," she said. "Now, aside from Brooks Brothers, what would you like to do?"

His eyebrows rose. She nudged him with her shoulder.

"Aside from that, I mean," she said.

He shrugged.

"Is there some reason you have to stay in the city?" Carolyn asked, as they started to walk across Fifth Avenue to Forty-first Street.

"No," he said. "The only thing I have to do is get on the Twentieth-Century Limited on two April at seven fifty-five in the evening. Why do you ask?"

"How do you feel about snow?" she asked.

"I hate it," he cheerfully admitted.

"How about snow outside?" Carolyn pursued. "On fields. Unmarked, except maybe by deer tracks?"

"Better," he said.

"With a fireplace inside? Glowing embers?"

"A loaf of bread, a glowing ember, and thou?"

"Beside you in the wilderness," Carolyn said. "I have a place in Bucks County. Overlooking the Delaware. An old fieldstone canal house."

"And you want to go there?"

"I want to go there with you," she said.

"Christ, and I was afraid you were trying to get rid of me," Banning said.

Carolyn squeezed his arm. She didn't trust her voice to speak.

(FOUR)
Battalion Arms Room
2nd Raider Battalion
Camp Elliott, California
1300 Hours, 9 April 1942

There are few things that frighten the United States Marine Corps. One of them is the acronymn "IG," for "Inspector General," which usually means not only the officer bearing that title but his entire staff. This ranges from senior noncommissioned officers upward, and what they do is visit a unit and compile long lists of the unit's shortcomings in all areas of military endeavor.

When a visit from the IG is scheduled, the unit to be inspected instantly begins a frenzied preparation for the inspection, so that the IG will find as little wrong as possible. The IG *will* find something wrong, or else the IG (including the staff) would not be doing the job properly. No IG report has ever said that the unit inspected was perfect in every detail of its organization, personnel, and equipment. The best a unit can hope for is that the shortcomings the IG will detect will be of a minor, easily correctable nature.

The fear, and the resultant near-hysteria, is compounded when the phrase "from Washington" is appended to "IG." Colonels who could with complete calm order a regimental attack across heavily mined terrain into the mouths of cannon, and master gunnery sergeants who would smilingly lead the attack with a fixed bayonet, break into cold sweats and suffer stomach distress when informed their outfit is about to be inspected by "the IG from Washington." There is a reason for this concern. An IG evaluation of "Unsatisfactory" is tantamount to the announcement before God and the Corps that they have been weighed in the balance and found not to be Good Marines.

The 2nd Raider Battalion was not immune to IG hysteria. There were several "preinspections" before the "IG from Washington's" inspection, during which the staff examined the equipment and personnel of the Raiders and searched for things the IG would likely find fault with. And there were twice as many pre-preinspections, in which platoon leaders and gunnery sergeants sought to detect faults that would likely be uncovered by the battalion brass during their preinspections.

Depending on the individual, experience with IG inspections tends to lessen the degree of hysteria. Inasmuch as Second Lieutenant Kenneth J. McCoy had gone through four annual IG inspections while an enlisted man with the 4th Marines, he had not been nearly as concerned with the preinspections—or even with the "IG from Washington" inspection itself—as had been First Lieutenant Martin Burnes (whose permanent presence, and that of his wife, aboard the *Last Time* was now an accepted fact of life).

McCoy was so experienced with IG inspections, in fact, that he knew the rules of the game, and took several precautionary steps in his own area of responsibility (weaponry) to keep the IG inspectors happy. He was aware that IG inspectors would keep inspecting things until they found something wrong. So he gave them something to find.

After details of Raiders who'd been sent up from the companies to the armory had cleaned the crew-served and special (shotguns, et cetera) weapons to Gunnery Sergeant Zimmerman's highly critical satisfaction, and after they had all been laid out for the IG's inspection, Second Lieutenant McCoy and Gunnery Sergeant Zimmerman had gone through them and fucked things up a little here and there. While Zimmerman partially unfastened a sling on a Thompson, for example, McCoy would rub a finger coated with grease over the bolt of a Browning Automatic Rifle, or on the barrel of one of the Winchester Model 1897 12-gauge trench guns.

When it came, the inspection went as McCoy thought it would. The inspecting officer was a captain who took a quick look around and then turned over the actual inspection to a chief warrant officer, a tall, leathery-faced man named Ripley who looked as if he had been in the Marine Corps since the Corps had gone ashore at Tripoli. Gunnery Sergeant Zimmerman had subtly, if quickly, let Chief Warrant Officer Ripley know that Second Lieutenant McCoy had been in the heavy-weapons section of the 4th Marines in Shanghai. This had disabused Mr. Ripley of the notion that, for some inexplicable reason, the Raiders had turned their armory over to a baby-faced candy-ass second john fresh from Quantico—which is what he had thought when he first set eyes on Lieutenant McCoy.

Chief Warrant Officer Ripley then, for a couple of minutes, searched for discrepancies of the type to be expected in any repository of arms, such as dirt and fire hazards and inadequate records. Then he looked for such things as malfunctioning weapons not properly tagged, so they could be repaired. And then he detail-stripped several weapons selected at random, searching for specks of dirt or rust. Finding none, he then compiled his list of minor discrepancies: *"excess lubricant on three (3) Browning Automatic Rifle bolts; improperly fastened slings on two (2) Thompson submachine guns; and grease on barrels of two (2) shotguns, trench M1897."*

By then it was evident to him that the baby-faced second john knew how to play the game. What the hell, he was an old China Marine, too.

Then he grew serious.

"Out of school, Lieutenant, where'd you and the gunny hide the junk weapons?" Ripley asked. His voice sounded like gravel.

"No junk weapons," McCoy said. "That's them."

"The Army liked you, right, Lieutenant?" Ripley asked, dryly sarcastic. "And gave you all good stuff and none of their junk?"

"After the third, or fourth, or fifth time we gave them their junk back," McCoy replied, "they got tired. Or maybe they ran out of junk. But these weapons are all ours, and there is no junk."

Ripley believed him. His rule of thumb about judging officers, especially junior lieutenants, was to believe what their gunnys thought of them. And this gunny obviously thought highly of this second lieutenant.

The inspection of the armament and armory had taken the full afternoon allotted to it on the plan of inspection, but three and a half of the four hours were spent by McCoy and Zimmerman showing the warrant officer the exotic, nonstandard weapons Colonel Carlson had obtained using his special authority to arm the Raiders as he saw fit, and then listening to the warrant officer's sea stories about what it had been like in the 4th Marines in the old days, when he'd been there in '33–35.

Chief Warrant Officer Ripley had never before had the chance to closely examine three of the special weapons Carlson had acquired for the Raiders. One of them was the Reising caliber .45 ACP submachine gun. Invented by Eugene G. Reising, the closed-breech, 550-round-per-minute weapon had gone into production in December 1941. McCoy had learned the Army had received several hundred of them, and had told Colonel Carlson, and Carlson had promptly signed a requisition for two hundred of them.

"If we don't like them, we can always give them back, can't we, McCoy?"

Ripley had never even heard of the Reising before he found it in McCoy's special-weapons arms room. But he had heard a lot about the other two, though he'd never actually seen them: These were the brainchild of a Marine, Captain Melvin Johnson, USMCR, who (as a civilian) had submitted the first models to the Army Ordnance Corps in 1938.

The Johnson rifle was a self-loading .30-06 rifle with a unique rotary ten-shot magazine and an unusual eight-radial-lug-bolt locking system. Barrels could be replaced in a matter of seconds.

The Johnson light machine gun was a fully automatic version of the rifle, with a magazine feeding from the side; a heavier stock with a pistol grip; and a bipod attached to the barrel near the muzzle.

Warrant Officer Ripley was fascinated with them. And after a solemn examination, he pronounced the Reising to be *"a piece of shit";* the Johnson rifle to be *"twice as good as that fucking Garand";* and the Johnson machine gun *"probably just as good as the Browning automatic rifle."* Lieutenant McCoy agreed with Ripley about the Reising; and he too thought that the Johnson rifle was probably going to be a good combat weapon (because its partially empty magazine could be reloaded easily; the en bloc eight-round clip of the Garand could not be reloaded in the rifle); and he thought the BAR was a far better weapon than the Johnson. But he kept his opinions to himself, deciding that he was in no position to argue with a chief Warrant officer, whose judgment was certainly colored by the fact that the Johnsons were invented by a Marine.

Second Lieutenant McCoy and Gunnery Sergeant Zimmerman were relieved, but not really surprised, when Warrant Officer Ripley showed them the clipboard on which was the pencil copy of his report. (A neatly typewritten report in many copies would be prepared later.) He had found their armory "Excellent" overall (one step down from the theoretical, never—in McCoy's experience—awarded "Superior"); and aside from "minor, readily correctable discrepancies noted hereon" there was no facet of their operation that would require a reinspection to insure that it had been corrected.

Gunnery Sergeant Zimmerman then produced a jug he just happened to come across where someone had hidden it behind a ceiling rafter, and they had a little nip.

"The brass'll keep at it for a while," Ripley said. "Between us China Marines, most of 'em got a real hard-on for Carlson. What the fuck is that all about?"

"I think it's because he got out of the Corps and then came back in," McCoy said. "And then got promoted."

"Carlson got out of the Corps?" Ripley said, obviously surprised. "I didn't know that. How come?"

McCoy shrugged his shoulders.

"I was with him in Nicaragua when he got the Navy Cross," Ripley said with a touch of pride in his voice. "The last I heard, he had the Marine detachment at Warm Springs. What'd he do, piss off the President?"

"I don't think so," McCoy said. "Otherwise the President's son wouldn't be the exec."

"No shit?" Chief Warrant Officer Ripley said. "That tall drink of water is really the President's son? I thought they were pulling my chain."

"That's him," McCoy said.

"I'll be goddamned," Ripley said.

"Is the brass going to fuck with your report? So they can stick it in Carlson?" McCoy asked.

"I call things like I see them," Ripley said indignantly. "You guys are more shipshape than most. And nobody fucks with my reports. Shit!"

"Well, this isn't the first time I heard that they're trying to stick it to Carlson," McCoy said. "And there are some real sonsofbitches around."

"When they handed me this shitty assignment—I'd rather be with the First Division; hell, I'd rather be *here*—the Commandant himself told me if anybody tried to lay any crap on me, I was to come to him personal."

XIX

(ONE)
Aboard the Yacht *Last Time*
San Diego Yacht Club
1900 Hours, 9 April 1942

Major Edward J. Banning, Captain Jack NMI Stecker, and Lieutenants McCoy and Burnes were sitting on teak-and-canvas deck chairs with their feet on the polished mahogany rail at the deck. Music and the smell of something frying came up from the portholes of the galley.

"You look deep in thought, Jack," Banning said.

"You really want to know what I'm thinking?" Stecker replied. "That there are two kinds of Marines. There is the one kind, the ordinary kind, the *Campbell's Baked Beans with Ham Fat* kind; and then there's the *steak* kind. That one"—he pointed at McCoy—"is the steak kind. I don't know how they do it, but they always wind up living better than other people."

He smiled at McCoy. "No criticism, McCoy. I'm jealous. Christ, this is real nice."

Banning chuckled. "I know what you mean, Jack," he said. "When all the other PFCs in the Fourth were playing acey-deucey for dimes with each other in the barracks, McCoy was playing poker for big money in the Cathay Mansions Hotel with an ex–Czarist Russian general, and he was living in a whorehouse the General owned."

"Jesus!" McCoy said. "Be quiet, Ernie'll hear you."

Stecker and Banning laughed.

"I didn't know you knew about that," McCoy said to Banning.

"I know a good deal about you that you don't know I know," Banning said, a little smugly.

"The first time I saw him, he was a corporal; but he was driving that big LaSalle," Stecker said, pointing down the wharf. "I was a *technical sergeant* before I drove anything fancier than a used Model A Ford."

"This seems to have developed a leak, Ken," Banning said, examining his bottle of Schlitz. "It's all gone."

"I'll get you another, sir," First Lieutenant Martin J. Burnes, USMCR, said quickly, taking the bottle from Banning's hand and scurrying down the ladder to the aft cockpit.

"There's another proof of your theory, Jack," Banning said. "When *I* was a second lieutenant, *I* did the running and fetching for first lieutenants."

Stecker chuckled.

"He's all right, Major," McCoy said. "Eager as hell. *Gung ho!*"

Marty Burnes returned almost immediately with four bottles of Schlitz.

"Here you are, sir," he said, respectfully, handing one of the bottles to Banning, and then passing the others around.

"Burnes," Jack Stecker said, "McCoy just accused you of being *'gung ho!'* I keep hearing that phrase around here. What's that all about?"

"You never heard it in China?" Banning asked, and then before Stecker could reply, he went on. "Oh, that's right. You had your family with you. No sleeping dictionary. You weren't *really* a China Marine then, were you, Jack? *No speakee Chinaman."*

McCoy snorted.

"It's a Chinese phrase, sir," Burnes said, almost eagerly. "It means 'all pull together.' "

"What's that got to do with the Raiders?" Stecker pursued.

"Cooperate, sir, for the common good. Do something that has to be done, even if it's not your responsibility."

"Give me a for-example," Banning asked, politely.

"Oh, for example, sir," Burnes said, "suppose an officer is walking around the area, and he sees that a garbage can is knocked over. Instead of finding somebody, an enlisted man, to set it up, he would do it himself. Because it should be set straight, sir, for the common good of the unit."

Banning looked at McCoy and saw that his eyes were smiling.

Burnes sensed that the example he had given was not a very good one. "You can explain it better than I can, Ken," Burnes said. "You tell the major."

"First of all," McCoy said, in Cantonese, "it doesn't mean 'all pull together.' It means something like 'strive for harmony.' And while it strikes me, and probably strikes you, as the night soil of a very large and well-fed male ox, you can see from this child that the children have adopted it as holy writ. What's wrong with it?"

Burnes's eyes widened, first at the flow of Chinese, and then as Major Banning choked on his beer. He went to Banning and vigorously pounded his back until Banning waved him off.

"You all right, sir?" Burnes asked, genuinely concerned.

"I'm fine," Banning said. "It went down the wrong pipe."

"Well, Burnes," Stecker said. "We know who had those dictionaries, don't we? Nobody likes a wiseass second lieutenant, McCoy."

Ernie Sage came onto the forward deck skillfully balancing a tray in her hands. The tray held two plates of hors d'oeuvres, one with bacon-wrapped chicken livers, the other with boiled shrimp and a bowl of cocktail sauce. She was wearing a T-shirt and shorts. The front of her T-shirt was emblazoned with a large, red Marine Corps insignia.

"Steak," Stecker said. "See my point?"

Ernie smiled nervously, wondering if that meant disapproval of the T-shirt.

Banning laughed.

"I'm not so sure all these hors d'ouevres are a good idea," Ernie said. "The steaks are enormous. Ken ran into some China Marine he knew working in the commissary."

Stecker laughed out loud in delight, and Banning shook his head.

Ernie smiled with relief; they did not disapprove of her shorts and T-shirt. But now that she thought about it, she did. It was a dumb idea, something she had done in hurt and anger. Her mother had called the day before, and they had gotten into it. The conversation had started out politely enough, but that hadn't lasted long. And her mother had played her ace: *"I just hope you know how you're hurting your father's feelings, how it hurts him to have his friends seeing his daughter acting like . . . like nothing more than a camp follower."*

"Nice to talk to you, Mother," Ernie said. "Call again sometime next year," and then she'd hung up.

But it had hurt, and she'd cried a little, and then she'd stopped that nonsense. But then she had been downtown, and she'd seen a half dozen real camp followers, the girls who—either professionally or otherwise—plied their trade in San Diego bars patronized by Marines. They had been wearing Marine Corps T-shirts, and Ernie had wondered if she was really like them, and then she'd decided it didn't matter whether she was or not, her mother thought she was.

And she'd gone into a store and bought the T-shirt.

"I'm glad that the steaks are enormous, because so is my appetite," Banning said.

"Good," she said, smiling.

"Ernie, take these two with you, will you, please?" Banning said. "I've got to have a quiet word with Jack Stecker."

When McCoy and Burnes had followed Ernie off the deck, Banning nodded after them.

"Very nice," he said.

"The hors d'oeuvres, or McCoy's lady friend?" Stecker asked.

"Both," Banning said. "But especially her. She's all right, Jack."

"Yes, she is," Stecker said.

"I understand you've been greasing Evans Carlson's ways," Banning said.

"Oh, so that's what this all about," Stecker said.

Banning didn't reply directly.

"See a lot of him, do you?"

"Every other day," Stecker said.

"I've got a couple of questions I'd like to ask," Banning said.

"Let me save you some time, Major," Stecker said. "No, I don't think he's either crazy or a Communist."

"Why did you say that, Jack?" Banning asked.

"Isn't that what you wanted me to say? That he is? So they can relieve him and put these Raider battalions out of business?"

"No," Banning said. "As a matter of fact, it's not. I have it on the highest authority—relayed from General Holcomb himself—that Carlson is none of the unpleasant things he's being accused of."

Stecker met his eyes. "I'm really relieved to hear you say that," he said.

"There's some scuttlebutt that an officer has been sent out here to spy on Carlson," Banning said. "You pick up any of that?"

"Yeah, I've heard that," Stecker said.

"Do you think Carlson has?"

"Oh, I'm sure he has," Stecker said. "But I don't think he knows it's McCoy."

"McCoy?" Banning said.

"Come on, Ed, we've known each other too long to be cute," Stecker said.

"Please respond to the question," Banning said, formally. "What gave you the idea McCoy is in any way involved in this?"

"All right," Stecker said after a moment. "Because I happen to know that McCoy went from the Platoon Leader's Course at Quantico to work for Rickabee in Washington, and I took the trouble to find out that's not on his service record; his record says he was a platoon leader at Quantico until he came out here."

"You mention any of those theories of yours to Carlson?"

"No," Stecker said. "Frankly, I was tempted."

"Why didn't you?"

"Because I have been around the Corps long enough to know the shit's going to hit the fan sooner or later, and I didn't want to get splattered," Stecker said. "And also because I like McCoy, and I knew this wasn't his idea."

"The shit has already hit the fan," Banning said. "General Paul H. Lesterby was retired; Colonel Thomas C. Wesley's been assigned to the supply depot at Murdoch, while the Commandant makes up his mind whether or not to court-martial him."

Stecker's face grew thoughtful. His eyebrows rose, he pursed his lips, and he cocked his head to one side. "The scuttlebutt I got on that," he said, "was that Lesterby had a mild heart attack and that Wesley finally was recognized for the horse's ass he's always been."

"Do you think Carlson believes that?"

"I suppose he does," Stecker said. "Why that line of questions?"

"Although he will do so if necessary," Banning said, "which is to say if he thinks—which means I tell him—that Carlson knows about the officer Lesterby sent out here, the Commandant would really rather not come out and formally apologize to Carlson."

"Carlson? He better worry about having to apologize to the President," Stecker said.

"If he thought it would be the best thing for the Corps, I think the Commandant would resign in the morning," Banning said. "*I* don't think that would be good for the Corps."

"Neither do I," Stecker said. "How the *hell* did you get involved in this? You used to be a good, simple, honest Marine."

"Well, Jack, I didn't volunteer for it," Banning said, a little coldly.

"I'm sorry, I shouldn't have said that," Stecker said. "I can't imagine why the hell I did. I'm sorry."

"Forget it," Banning said.

"To answer your question, Ed," Stecker said, "if Carlson is worried about having a spy in his outfit, he doesn't seem concerned. I think he would have said something to me if he did. Or, probably, now that I think about it, suspected that it was me. I don't think he thinks it's one of his officers, and I'm almost positive he doesn't suspect McCoy of anything."

Banning nodded.

"But if you want, I can ask him," Stecker said. "Discreetly, of course. I'm going to see him tomorrow at eleven hundred."

"No, this is it," Banning said. "I'm flying back to Washington at oh-nine-hundred. To report to the Commandant as soon as I get there."

"I really wish I could be more helpful," Stecker said.

"You've been very helpful," Banning said.

"So what happens to McCoy?" Stecker said.

"It would raise questions if he were suddenly relieved from the Raiders," Banning said.

"So who really pays for this idiocy is a nice young kid—a fine young officer," Stecker said bitterly. "Lesterby gets to draw his pension, and Wesley, too, and McCoy gets his ass blown away playing commando on some unimportant little island in the South Pacific."

"I thought you were all for Carlson and his Raiders," Banning said, surprised.

"I think the whole idea of Raiders is stupid from start to finish," Stecker said. "You didn't ask me that."

The smell of charring beef began to float up to the flying bridge.

Stecker sniffed. "Are we about finished?" he asked. "Oddly enough, after this conversation of ours, I still have an appetite."

Banning set his beer bottle down and stood up. "Thank you, Jack," he said.

When they went into the main cabin, they saw that the women had changed. Ernie Sage was now wearing a pale yellow cotton dress, which she wore with a single strand of pearls that Banning knew were real, and had cost what a Marine second lieutenant made in three months.

The table had been very elegantly set in the main lounge of the *Last Time.* There was gold-rimmed bone china, crystal glasses, and heavy sterling. There were two bottles of wine on the table, and a reserve supply, plus a bottle of brandy, on a sideboard.

Banning reflected that Ernie Sage seemed to have grasped what was expected of the wife of a junior officer when entertaining in their quarters a field-grade officer. Except she wasn't married to Killer McCoy, and this yacht was not exactly what came to mind when you thought of the quarters of a second lieutenant living off the post.

McCoy seemed to have read his mind.

In Chinese, he asked, softly, "It's a long way from that one-room apartment of mine over the whorehouse in Shanghai, isn't it?"

Banning laughed. McCoy started to pour the wine. He did it naturally, Banning thought. He was perfectly at ease with it, and even with this elaborate arrangement of crystal, china, and silver. He wondered if McCoy himself knew how much he had changed since Shanghai.

"You know, I knew that Ken spoke Chinese—" Marty Burnes gushed.

"Two kinds, plus Japanese, and God only knows what else," Banning interrupted.

"But I didn't really *believe* it until I heard the two of you talking," Burnes concluded.

"The day I met him," Ernie said, "he took me to a Chinese restaurant in Chinatown in New York City. And spoke Chinese to them. I was awed."

"Knowing all those languages," Jack Stecker said innocently, "I wonder if the greatest contribution he can make to the Marine Corps is in the armory of the Second Raider Battalion."

Banning looked toward Stecker and found Stecker's eyes on his. He did not reply, but he had already made up his mind that one of the first things he was going to do when he got back to Washington was try to justify getting McCoy out of the Raiders. Stecker was of course right. Second Lieutenants who spoke Japanese and two kinds of Chinese were in very short supply and should not be expended while they were trying to paddle up to some obscure Japanese-held island in a rubber boat.

He looked away from Stecker and found Ernie Sage's eyes on him. She had nice eyes, he thought. Perceptive eyes. But what he saw in them now was sad disappointment that he had not responded to Stecker. And that meant, Banning decided, that Ernie Sage knew what McCoy was doing here.

The dumb, lovesick sonofabitch told her! He knew that was expressly forbidden. He isn't even married to her, for Christ's sake!

And then he was forced to face the shameful fact that Major Edward J. Banning, that professional intelligence officer of the U.S. Marine Corps, that absolute paragon of military virtue, had only a week before shown his credentials to a civilian female for no better reason than that he wanted to look good in her eyes.

Banning decided that if McCoy had told Ernie at least some of what he was really doing with the 2nd Raider Battalion at Camp Elliott, he had done so with a reason, and only after thinking it over. The cold truth to face was that McCoy had almost certainly had a better reason for telling Ernie than he had for showing Carolyn his credentials.

Banning spent the night aboard the *Last Time;* and in the morning, McCoy drove him to the airfield, where a Navy Douglas R4D was waiting to fly the "IG from Washington" team back to Washington.

As he gave McCoy his hand, there was time to tell him what he had decided.

"You've done a good job here, Ken, in a rotten situation," Banning said. "I'm going to try to talk Rickabee into getting you out of here. I'm not sure he will, but I'm going to try."

(TWO)
Headquarters, 2nd Raider Battalion
Camp Elliott, California
23 April 1942

Though it appeared loose and informal—everyone sat on the ground in the shade—and Colonel Carlson pointedly did not use the official term, there was a 2nd Raider Battalion officers' call in everything but name. Colonel Carlson probably did not like the official term, McCoy thought, because there was an implied exclusion of enlisted men from an official officers' call. But with the exception of a very few enlisted men (the sergeant major; the S-3 [Plans & Training] and S-4 [Supply] sergeants; two of the first sergeants; and three gunnery sergeants, including Zimmerman), everybody at the meeting was an officer, and most of the battalion officers had been summoned and were present.

A week or so before, Captain Roosevelt gave a lecture on the Rules of Land Warfare, a subject that McCoy was more than casually familiar with. Because of the situation in China at the time, there had been frequent lectures on the Rules of Land Warfare in the 4th Marines. And as he listened to Roosevelt, McCoy reflected that he had been lectured on the Rules of Land Warfare so often that he knew most of them by heart. But McCoy did learn one thing during Roosevelt's lecture: Roosevelt used two terms McCoy had never heard before. Since he did not have an appetite to stand up and confess his ignorance, McCoy wrote the terms down, intending to look them up in a dictionary.

As it happened, the dictionary did not turn out to be necessary. When he asked Ernie about it, she questioned him about what he wanted to look up, and then she explained the meaning of *de facto* and *de jure.*

And now he realized that those terms fit this case: Carlson's meeting, with everybody sitting on the ground in the shade of the battalion headquarters building, was a *de facto* officers' call, even if Carlson was reluctant to make it a *de jure* officers' call.

The first item on the agenda was significant. Carlson told his officers and senior noncoms that, as of that day, the 2nd Raider Battalion had officially completed its stateside training, and that Admiral Nimitz (Commander in Chief, Pacific Fleet) had so officially informed Admiral King, and had requested transportation for the battalion to Hawaii, where they would be trained in rubber-boat techniques and in making landings from submarines.

Additionally, Carlson continued, the advance element of the "competition" (which everyone knew meant the 1st Raider Battalion) had sailed from San Diego aboard the USS *Zeilin* 11 April, more than likely for Samoa, although that was just a guess, and in any event should not be talked about.

Then he told them that a report from Major Sam Griffith[1] had "somehow come into hand."

"Griffith thinks our organization of the 2nd Raider Battalion is the way the entire Corps should go," Carlson said, with just a hint of smugness in his dry voice. "That is to say, six line companies and a headquarters company, as opposed to the competition's four line companies, a heavy-weapons company, and a headquarters company. And he has made that a formal recommendation to the Commandant."

There was a round of applause, and Carlson grinned at his men.

"And he agrees, more or less, with our organization[2] of the companies as well," Carlson went on. "He agrees more than he disagrees."

There was another round of applause.

And then, on the subject of mortars, Carlson told them that the decision by the brass had not been made, but that he hoped it would "go our way."

There were two mortars available, a 60-mm and an 81-mm. The 81-mm was the more lethal weapon. It was capable of throwing a nearly seven-pound projectile 3,000 yards (1.7 miles). It was standard issue in the heavy-weapons company of a Marine infantry battalion. On the other hand, the 60-mm's range, with a three-pound projectile, was just about a mile.

For a number of reasons (with which McCoy, who fancied himself a decent man with either weapon, agreed completely), Carlson was opposed to the Raiders carrying the 81-mm mortar into combat. For one thing, the kind of combat the Raiders anticipated would be close range, and the 60-mm was better for that purpose. More importantly, considering that the Raiders planned to enter combat by paddling ashore in rubber boats, a ready-for-action 81-mm mortar weighed 136 pounds. It would of course be broken down for movement, but the individual components—the tube itself, and especially the base plate—were heavy as hell, and were going to be damned hard to get into and out of a rubber boat. As would the ammunition, at seven pounds per round.

It was not, furthermore, a question of choosing *either* the 60-mm *or* the 81-mm. The TO&E provided for *both* 81-mm *and* 60-mm mortars in each company; and that meant that if they did things by the book and took the 81-mm too, they would have to wrestle two kinds of mortars and two kinds of ammunition into and out of the rubber boats.

But Carlson told him that he thought he had come up with a convincing argument against the Raiders following standard Marine Corps practice requiring an 81-mm mortar platoon in each company: Such a platoon would exceed the carrying capacity of the APDs.[3] If the 81-mm mortar platoon went along on the APDs,

[1]As a captain, Griffith had been sent with Captain Wally Greene to observe and undergo British Commando training. He was regarded within the Marine Corps as an expert on commando, or Raider, operations.

[2]Each company consisted of two rifle platoons, plus a company headquarters. Each platoon, under a lieutenant, consisted of three squads. Each squad consisted of a squad leader, and a three-man fire-team, armed with a BAR, an M1 Garand, and a Thompson submachine gun.

[3]Grandly known as High Speed Transports, the APDs, which were supposed to transport Raiders on missions, were in fact modified World War I–era "four-stacker" destroyers. Two of their four boilers and their exhaust stacks had been removed, and the space reclaimed converted to primitive troop berthing. They were "high speed" only when compared to freighters and other slow-moving vessels.

it would be necessary to split the companies between several ships. That obviously was a bad idea.

"But there are those," Carlson said, "close to the Deity in Marine Corps heaven who devoutly believe the Corps cannot do without the eighty-one-millimeters. So I have proposed that we drag them along with us—without personnel—in case we need them. In which case, they would be fired by the sixty-millimeter crews."

McCoy thought Carlson was absolutely right about the mortars, and he hoped that the brass would let him have his way. But he wondered if they actually would. He had not forgotten Chief Warrant Officer Ripley's disturbing remark about the "brass really having a hard-on for Carlson." He knew they hadn't changed that attitude because the Commandant had blown his stack about spying on Carlson. A lot of the brass, and even people like Captain Jack Stecker, thought the whole idea of Raiders was a lousy one. Which meant that a lot of people were still going to be fighting Carlson at every step. If Carlson said the moon was made of Camembert, they would insist it was cheddar.

"That will be all, gentlemen," Colonel Carlson said, a few minutes and a few minor items later. "Thank you. If there are no questions . . ."

There were questions. There was always some dumb sonofabitch who didn't understand something. But finally the questions had been asked and answered, and Carlson waved his hand in a gesture of dismissal. In a regular unit, the exec would have called attention and then dismissed them after the commanding officer had walked away. Doing it Carlson's way, McCoy thought, made more sense.

Colonel Carlson called out to him as McCoy started to get to his feet.

"McCoy, stick around, please. I'd like a word with you."

"Aye, aye, sir," McCoy said.

Carlson went into the building, after motioning for McCoy to follow. When he went inside, the sergeant major waved him into Carlson's office. Captain Roosevelt was there.

"Stand at ease, McCoy," Carlson said, and searched through papers on his desk. Finally he found what he was looking for and handed it to McCoy. It was a TWX.

ROUTINE

HEADQUARTERS USMC WASH DC 1545 21APR1942

COMMANDING OFFICER

2ND RAIDER BN

CAMP ELLIOTT CALIF

THERE EXISTS THROUGHOUT THE MARINE CORPS A CRITICAL SHORTAGE OF OFFICER PERSONNEL FLUENT IN FOREIGN LANGUAGES. RECORDS INDICATE THAT 2ND LT KENNETH R MCCOY PRESENTLY ASSIGNED COMPANY B 2ND RAIDER BN IS FLUENT IN CHINESE JAPANESE AND OTHER FOREIGN LANGUAGES. UNLESS HIS PRESENT DUTIES ARE CRITICAL TO THE 2ND RAIDER BATTALION IT IS INTENDED TO REASSIGN HIM TO DUTIES COMMENSURATE WITH HIS LANGUAGE SKILLS.

YOU WILL REPLY BY THE MOST EXPEDITIOUS MEANS WHETHER OR NOT SUBJECT OFFICER IS CRITICAL TO THE MISSION OF YOUR COMMAND.

BY DIRECTION

STANLEY F. WATT COLONEL USMC OFFICE OF THE ASSISTANT CHIEF OF STAFF FOR PERSONNEL

"You don't seem especially surprised, McCoy," Colonel Carlson said in Cantonese.

"No, sir," McCoy answered, in the same language. "Major Banning told me there was a shortage of people who could speak Chinese and Japanese."

Carlson smiled, and nodded at Roosevelt. "The Big Nose doesn't know what we're talking about, does he?"

Chinese often referred to Caucasians as "Big Noses."

"No, sir," McCoy said, now in English.

"Then in English," Carlson said.

"Thank you, gentlemen," Captain Roosevelt said.

"Well, McCoy, are you critical to the Raiders?" Carlson asked.

"I don't know, sir," McCoy said.

"Well, let me put it this way, then, Lieutenant," Carlson said. "In your opinion, can you make a greater contribution to the Corps doing what you're doing with the Raiders, or doing whatever Major Banning has in mind for you to do? And I don't think there is any more question in your mind than there is in mine that Ed Banning is behind that TWX."

"Straight answer, sir?"

"I certainly hope so," Carlson said.

"I think I can do more here, sir," McCoy said.

"Huh," Carlson snorted. "Go buy yourself a bigger hat, Lieutenant McCoy. I am about to designate you as Critical to the Second Raiders."

"Thank you, sir."

"Not even the Big Nose is critical," Carlson said, in Cantonese, and smiled benignly at Captain Roosevelt, who smiled back. "Only you and me, McCoy."

McCoy grinned back.

Still in Cantonese, Carlson went on: "I don't think you need to know the name of the island, yet, McCoy, so I won't give it to you. But for our first mission, we are going to conduct a raid on a *certain* island. That's subject to change, of course, but I have a hunch it won't. The reason I'm telling you this much is that it is currently projected that we will be transported in submarines, rather than the converted destroyers. That will limit the force to no more than two hundred people. I want you—alone, don't confer with anyone else—to start thinking how we'll have to structure that force, and equip it."

"Aye, aye, sir," McCoy said, in English. "Does that mean I will go with the assault force, sir?"

"Uh-huh," Carlson said. "I thought you'd want to go."

"Oh, yes, sir," McCoy said.

And then he thought, *Oh, shit! What the hell have I done?*

ONE
The San Carlos Hotel
Pensacola, Florida
8 August 1942

Second Lieutenant Richard J. Stecker, USMC, was in direct violation of the uniform regulations of the U.S. Navy Air Station, Pensacola, which, in addition to specifying in finite detail what a properly dressed officer would wear when leaving the post, took pains to specifically proscribe the wearing of flight gear except immediately before, while participating in, and immediately after aerial flight.

He was wearing a gray cotton coverall, equipped with a number of zippered pockets. This was known to the Naval Service as "Suit, flight, aviator's, cotton, tropical," and to Stecker, who had copied Pick Pickering's description, as "Birdman's rompers." Sewn to the breast of the rompers was a leather patch, stamped in gold with Naval aviator's wings and the words "STECKER, R.J. 2ND LT USMC." Pick said they did that so that professional Marines could look down and see who the Marine Corps said they were.

The flight suit was dark with sweat. Enormous patches of it spreading from the back and the armpits and the seat nearly overwhelmed the dry areas. The patches were ringed with white, remnants of the salt taken aboard in the form of salt pills and then sweated out.

Stecker was aware that he was learning bad habits from Pick Pickering. Or, phrased more kindly, that Pickering had given him insight into the functioning of the Naval establishment that had not previously occurred to him. Previously, he had obeyed regulations, no matter how petty, because they were regulations and Marine officers obeyed regulations. He had in fact cautioned Lieutenant Pickering (a friendly word of advice from a professional Naval establishment person to a temporary officer and gentleman): "You're gonna get your ass in a crack if they catch you driving home in your flight suit," he'd told him.

Lieutenant Pickering had not only been unrepentant, but had patiently pointed out to Lieutenant Stecker the flaws in his logic.

"First of all, I don't intend to get caught. I drive through the woods, not past the Marine guard at the gate. Secondly, I think the MPs have better things to do than establish roadblocks to catch people wearing flight suits. And I come into the hotel through the basement, not the lobby. I think the chances of my getting caught run from slim to none. But, for the sake of argument, what if I'm caught? So what?"

"You'll find yourself replying by endorsement,"[1] Stecker argued.

[1]When an officer was caught doing something he should not be doing, such as being out of uniform, he would receive a letter from his commanding officer specifying the offense and directing him to "reply by endorsement hereto" his reasons for committing the offense.

"And I will reply by endorsement that since officers who live in quarters on the post can go from the flight line to their quarters in their rompers, I thought I could go directly to my quarters so attired. And that if I have sinned, I am prepared to weep, beat my breast, pull out my hair, and in other ways manifest my shame and regret."

"You can get kicked out of here."

"Oh, bullshit! We're nearly through this fucking course. They might throw us out for showing up on the flight line drunk, or something else serious like that. But so much time and money has been invested in us, and they need pilots so bad, they're not going to throw anybody out for wearing rompers off base."

And he was right, of course.

Lieutenant Stecker had spent three hours that afternoon between six and ten thousand feet over Foley, Alabama. He had been at the controls of a Grumman F4F-3 wildcat, engaged in mock aerial combat with an instructor pilot.

The Wildcat had been rigged with a motion picture camera. The camera was actuated when he activated the trigger that would normally have fired the six .50-caliber Browning machine guns with which the Wildcat was armed.

The film was now being souped, and they would look at it in the morning. Dick Stecker knew that in at least four of the engagements, the film from the gun camera would show that he had successfully eluded his IP and then gotten on his IP's tail and "shot him down."

It had been almost—not quite, but almost—pleasant tooling around at six, seven thousand feet with the twelve hundred horsepower of the Wright XR-1830-76 moving the Wildcat at better than three hundred knots. And, although he had consciously fought getting cocky about it, it had been satisfying to realize that he had acquired a certain proficiency in the Wildcat. The odds were that in about two months, certainly within three, he would be flying a Wildcat against the Japanese.

When the training flight was over, however, it was not at all pleasant. He opened the canopy before he had completed his landing roll at Chevalier Field. By the time he had taxied to the parking ramp, the skin of the aircraft was too hot to touch, and he was sweat-soaked. The temperature had been over one hundred degrees for three days, and the humidity never dropped out of the high nineties.

He actually felt a little faint as he walked to the hangar, carrying a parachute that now seemed to weigh at least one hundred pounds. His IP came into the hangar red-faced and sweat-soaked, and went directly to the water cooler, where he first drenched his face in the stream, and then filled a paper cup and poured it over his head.

The post-flight critique was made as brief as possible. Then the IP had walked to his car in his rompers and drove off. That left Stecker with a choice: He could be a good little second lieutenant who obeyed all the rules. Or he could do what he ended up doing. What he did was get in his car and drive through the woods to the Foley Highway and then to the hotel.

He parked the car behind the hotel and entered through the basement. He planned to use the service elevator, but it wouldn't answer his ring, so he had to summon a passenger elevator.

With my luck, he thought, *the elevator will stop in the lobby, answering the button-push of the base commander, who will be accompanied by the senior Marine Corps officer assigned to Pensacola.*

But the elevator rose without stopping to the top floor, and there was no one in the small foyer when the door opened. Stecker crossed quickly to the penthouse door, put his key in, and opened it. A wave of cold air swept over him. The basement of the building was not air-conditioned, and the allegedly air-conditioned elevators seldom were.

Stecker emitted a deep, guttural groan of relief.

Then he worked the full-length zipper on the rompers to its lower limit and spread the sweaty material wide. When the cold air struck his lower chest, he groaned appreciatively again.

Then he walked into the penthouse and found it was occupied.

The occupant was a female. The female was clothed in brief shorts and a T-shirt decorated with a red Marine Corps insignia. And she was smiling at him. Not a friendly smile, Stecker quickly realized, but a "see the funny man, ha ha" smile.

"What am I expected to say in reply to your groans?" Ernie Sage asked. "You Tarzan, me Jane?"

"Not that I really give a damn," Dick Stecker said, "but how did you get in here?"

"I told them I was Pick's sister," Ernie said. "Where is he?"

"I'm Dick Stecker," Dick said.

"How about this to start a conversation, Dick Stecker?" Ernie said. " 'Your fly's open.' "

"Oh, Jesus," he groaned and dived for it.

"To quickly change the subject, you were telling me where Pick is," she said.

"He took off about an hour after we did," Stecker said. "He should be here in about an hour."

"Took off for where?"

"Local," Stecker said. "Training flight. Mock dogfights."

She turned and went to the bar, returned with a bottle of beer, and handed it to him.

"You look like you could use this," she said. When she saw the surprise on his face, she added, "Yes, I did make myself right at home, didn't I?"

"You didn't say who you were?"

"Just another Marine camp-follower," she said. "Mine has gone overseas, so I figured I'd better latch on to another."

"Ah, come on," Stecker said.

"I'm Ernie Sage," she said. "I'm the closest thing Pick has to a sister."

"Oh, sure. The one he's always talking to on the phone. In California."

"Used to," she said. "My second lieutenant's gone. Now I'm back in New York."

"I'm Dick Stecker," Stecker repeated.

"I know," she said. "I know your father. I like him; Pick likes you. Our acquaintance is off to a flying start."

"What brings you here?" Stecker asked.

"I have been holding Pick's hand about the Sainted Widow for months. Now it's his turn to hold mine for a while."

"Is there anything I can do?"

"Can you miraculously transport me to Camp Catlin?"

"I never even heard of it," Stecker said.

"That's surprising," Ernie said. "According to Pick, you're a walking encyclopedia of military lore."

"Where is it?"

"It's in—on?—Hawaii. And if you can't miraculously transport me there, why don't you take a shower? I can smell you all the way over here."

"Do you always talk like that?" Stecker asked, shocked but not offended.

"Only to friends," Ernie said. "And any son of Captain Jack NMI Stecker, any friend of Pick's, et cetera et cetera . . ."

"I'm flattered," Stecker said.

"And well you should be," Ernie said. "Go bathe; and when you come out, you can give me a somewhat more accurate picture of the Sainted Widow than the one I got from Pick."

"How do you know the one you got from Pick isn't accurate?"

"No one, not even me, is that perfect," Ernie said. She pointed toward one of the bedrooms. "Go shower."

Stecker took a shower, and put on a khaki uniform. When he came out, Ernie Sage was leaning on the glass door leading to the patio.

"How much further along are you than Pick?" she asked, smiling at him.

"I beg your pardon?"

"You're wearing wings," Ernie said. "I thought you got those only when you're finished training."

"When you finish the school," he said. "We got rated the first of the month."

"Then you're finished?"

"Yes, we are. Now we're getting trained in F4F-3s."

"I thought—Pick told me—they were going to send you to Opa-something for that?"

"Opa-locka," Stecker said. "Farther down in Florida. They usually do. But they have some F4F-3s, and qualified IPs here . . . and Pick and I make up a class of two, so we stayed here."

"Congratulations," Ernie said.

"Excuse me?"

"On being a Naval aviator," she said.

"Oh," Stecker said. "Thank you."

"Now tell me about the Sainted Widow," Ernie said.

"I'm not sure I should," Stecker said.

"Think of me as a kindly old aunt," Ernie said.

"That would be hard," Stecker said. "You don't look anything like a kindly old aunt."

"I think I should tell you that my boyfriend is a Raider," Ernie said. "Their idea of a good time is chewing glass. I have no way of knowing what he would do if he thought someone was paying me an unsolicited compliment."

"That would be 'Killer' McCoy," Stecker said. "Pick's told me all about him."

"Did he tell you that Killer McCoy and I were sharing living accommodations, without benefit of marriage, at what I have now learned to call Diego?" Ernie asked.

"Yeah," Stecker said. "As a matter of fact, he did."

"Well, now that he's told you my shameful secret, you tell me his. What's this Sainted Widow done to him?"

"I don't think she's done anything to him," Stecker said. "That's what you could call the root of the problem."

By the time Pick walked in the door (in a crisp tropical worsted uniform, without a drop of sweat on him, which sorely tempted Stecker to spill the beer he handed him into his lap), Stecker had covered the dead-in-the-water romance between Pick and Martha Sayre Culhane in some detail.

He had explained to Ernie that he believed, or at least hoped, that the romance was beginning to pass. Since the Navy had kept them busy flying, Pick simply didn't have time to moon over his unrequited love. And when they did have a Sunday off, Pick drank—but not too much, for he knew he would have to fly the next day.

Stecker went on to tell her that he thought it was a shame they hadn't gone to Opa-locka for fighter training. That would have gotten Pick out of Pensacola. And once he was out of Pensacola, he believed that Martha Sayre Culhane would, however slowly, begin to fade. In his opinion, absence did not make the heart grow fonder.

And then, after Pick arrived, his role and Ernie's were reversed. Ernie, with a couple of drinks in her, revealed how much she missed Ken McCoy and how worried she was about him. Pick and Stecker tried to comfort her, after their peculiar fashion: Pick told her, for instance, that it was her romance she should be worried about, not Ken McCoy's life. He told her that she was responsible for teaching McCoy bad habits. Which meant that at this very moment, he was probably on some sunny, wave-swept Hawaiian beach with some dame wearing a grass skirt.

In time, Pick and Ernie got more than a little smashed. And Stecker found himself making the decisions and driving. They went to Carpenter's Restaurant, where he made them eat deviled crabs and huge mounds of french-fried potatoes, to counter the alcohol.

That didn't seem to work with Pick, who slipped into a sort of maudlin stupor, but it seemed to sober up Ernie. Consequently, she was acutely aware of the look on Dick Stecker's face when Martha Sayre Culhane walked into Carpenter's with Captain Mustache and two other couples. And she followed his eyes and turned to him with a question on her face.

Dick Stecker nodded as he put his finger quickly before his lips, and he then glanced at Pick, begging her not to let him know.

She nodded her understanding of the situation.

But there was nothing Dick Stecker could do when Ernie Sage saw Martha Sayre Culhane go into the ladies' room. Ernie suddenly jumped to her feet and went in after her.

When Martha Sayre Culhane came out of the stall, a young woman wearing a T-shirt with a large red Marine Corps emblem on it was sitting on the makeup counter. The young woman examined her shamelessly, and said "Hi!"

"Hello," Martha said, a little uncomfortably. She took her comb from her purse and ran it through her hair. Then she took out her lipstick and started to touch up her lips.

"Funny," Ernie said. "You really are nearly as beautiful as Pick thinks you are."

"I beg your pardon?"

"You don't look like a selfish bitch, either," Ernie went on. "More like what Dick Stecker says, 'the Sainted Widow.' I guess you work on that, huh?"

"Who the hell are you?"

"Just one more Marine Corps camp-follower," Ernie said.

"I don't know what this is all about, but I don't like it," Martha said.

"We have something in common, believe it or not," Ernie said.

"I can't imagine what that would be," Martha said.

"I got one of those telegrams," Ernie said. "From good ol Frank Knox. He regretted that my man was 'missing in action and presumed dead.' "

Martha looked at Ernie.

"I'm sorry," she said.

"As things turned out, he wasn't dead," Ernie said. "I told you that to explain what we had in common. I know what it's like."

Martha started to say something, but stopped.

"At the moment, I'm crossing my fingers again," Ernie said. "No, I'm not. I'm *praying.* Mine's back in the Pacific. He's an officer in the Second Raider Battalion."

"What is it you want from me?" Martha said.

"I want to talk to you about Pick," Ernie said. "He's in love with you."

"I don't really think that's true," Martha said.

"It's true," Ernie said. "Take it from me. I've known Pick since we used to play doctor. I know about him and women. He's *in love* with you."

"Well, I don't happen to be in love with him, not that it's any of your business," Martha snapped.

"So what?" Ernie said. "Lie about it. You're going to have to stop playing the sainted widow sooner or later. Give it up now. Give that poor, frightened, wonderful sonofabitch a couple of weeks, a couple of months, however long he's got before they ship him off to the Pacific. It won't cost you anything. You might even like it. I've never heard any complaints. And if you don't, Martha, and he gets killed, too, you'll regret it the rest of your life."

"You're crazy," Martha said. "My husband—"

"Is dead," Ernie said. "And he's not coming back. I told you, I know what that feels like. Pick is alive. *He's in love with you.* Stop being so goddamned selfish!"

Ernie pushed herself off the counter and walked out of the room.

When the Sainted Widow came out of the ladies' room two minutes later, she looked as if she had been crying. She gazed around the room, found Pick, and stared at him for almost a minute before turning and rushing out of the restaurant.

And a moment after that, Captain Mustache crossed the room, obviously in pursuit of the Sainted Widow. They did not return to the restaurant.

Stecker would have really liked to ask what had gone on in the ladies' room. He couldn't ask, of course, with Pick sitting right there.

(TWO)
Pearl Harbor, Territory of Hawaii
8 August 1942

In compliance with Operations Order (Classified SECRET) No. 71-42, from Commander in Chief, United States Pacific Fleet, Task Group 7.15 (Commander John M. Haines, USN) got underway at 0900 hours, Hawaiian time.

Task Group 7.15 consisted of the submarines USS *Argonaut* (Lt. Commander William H. Brockman, Jr., USN) and USS *Nautilus* (Lt. Commander J. H. Pierce, USN); and Companies A and B, 2nd Raider Battalion, USMC (Lt. Colonel Evans F. Carlson, USMCR).

The mission of Task Group 7.15 was to land a force of Marines on Makin Island, where they were to engage and destroy the enemy; to destroy any enemy matériel stocks they found; to destroy any buildings, radio facilities, and anything else of military or naval value; and then to withdraw.

There was never any consideration given to holding Makin Island once it had been taken. It would have been impossible to supply, much less reinforce. And there was nothing the Americans wanted with the island anyway.

It was a *raid,* the purpose of which was to force the Japanese to reinforce *all* of their islands, in order to attempt to prevent subsequent Raider raids. To do so, it was reasoned, would force the Japanese to assign troops and matériel to protect all their islands, and that the troops and matériel so assigned would therefore not be available for use elsewhere.

There would also be some positive public relations aspects of a successful raid; the American ego was still smarting from Pearl Harbor and the fall of the Philippine Islands. In that sense, it would be the Navy's answer to the Air Corps's bombing of the Japanese homelands by a flight of B-25 aircraft commanded by Lieutenant Colonel Jimmy Doolittle.

There were some cynics. They claimed it made absolutely no sense to spend so much time and effort putting several hundred Marines ashore on an island of little importance—and which we did not intend to keep, anyway. Such a raid would indeed force the Japanese to station men on all of their islands, but doing so would pose fewer problems for the Japs than it would, in the future, for the United States. After the Makin Raid, they believed, we would have to fight our way ashore on every island we wished to take and keep. And *that* would cost lives.

There were even those who said that the whole Raider concept was a Chinese fire drill, because the President's son was involved and because the Commandant didn't have the balls to tell the President the whole idea was a drain on manpower and resources that could be better used elsewhere.

The dissent was heard, duly noted, and ignored.

The *Argonaut*[2] was a one-of-a-kind submarine. She was designed in 1919 to be something of a copy of the German U-Cruiser class, and she was intended for use for both long-distance cruising and underwater mine laying. She was launched at Portsmouth on November 10, 1927, and commissioned on April 2, 1928. Powered by two German-made MAN diesel engines developing 3,175 horsepower, she was capable of making fifteen knots on the surface. And her electric motors would move her at eight knots submerged. She was armed with two six-inch cannon, three .30-caliber machine guns, and four 21-inch torpedo tubes. Immediately after Pearl Harbor, she had gone through a refit at Mare Island Navy Yard, converting her to a transport submarine.

The *Nautilus* was one of two submarines in the Narwhal class. Generally similar to the *Argonaut,* she did not have a mine-laying capability. When she was launched at Mare Island in March 1930, she had MAN diesels, but these were replaced by Fairbanks Morse engines just before World War II. She had two aft-firing torpedo tubes plus four forward firing and was armed, like the *Argonaut,* with two 6-inch Naval cannon.

Both vessels were considerably larger than "fleet" submarines of the period, and for this reason had been chosen to transport the elements of the 2nd Raider Battalion charged with making an attack upon the Japanese-held Makin atoll, which lay 2,029 nautical miles to the southwest, roughly halfway between Hawaii and Australia.

The *Argonaut* and the *Nautilus* were led through the antisubmarine cables and other defenses of Pearl Harbor, and for some distance at sea by a patrol craft (PC 46), which stood by while (at 1500 hours) the submarines dived to test hull integrity and to determine trim. At 2015 hours, the *Argonaut* left the formation, under orders to visually reconnoiter the Makin atoll before the arrival of the *Nautilus.*

At 2100 hours the patrol craft was released as escort and the *Nautilus* got underway to rendezvous with the *Argonaut* off Makin Atoll.

[2]She was to be sunk by Japanese destroyers between Lae and New Guinea on 10 January 1943.

(THREE)
Makin Island
0530 Hours, 17 August 1942

Not surprising Second Lieutenant Kenneth J. McCoy one little bit, the landing was all fucked up.

The faithful Gunnery Sergeant Zimmerman, leading a couple of squads, was at his side as they lay in the sand fifteen yards off the beach. The trouble with the situation was that Zimmerman was with Able Company, and Lieutenant McCoy was performing his duties as a platoon leader with Baker Company. He didn't know where Zimmerman was supposed to be, except that it wasn't here.

A large Raider came running up and dropped on his belly beside McCoy. "How's it going?" he asked cheerfully.

Under the circumstances, McCoy decided, since they were where they were, and since the large Raider was his little brother, he would not deliver a lecture on the proper manner for a corporal to address a commissioned officer and gentleman. Then he noticed the awesome weapon, a Boys antitank rifle,[3] with which Tom was armed.

"Where'd you get that, Tommy?" McCoy asked.

"I gave it to him," Zimmerman said, softly. "We got orders to bring the sonofabitch and he's the only one big enough to carry it, much less shoot it."

McCoy chuckled.

"I'm going to blow some Jap general a new asshole," Tommy said confidently. "A *big* new asshole."

McCoy looked up at the sky. It was lighter than it had been; dawn was obviously breaking, but it was still dark. Too dark, he decided, to order Zimmerman to go look for his officers and find out where he was supposed to be. That would just add Zimmerman and his bunch to those already milling around in the dark.

"Stay here," McCoy said, and crawled back to the beach. Then he stood up, because he couldn't see lying down.

The force had been loaded into eighteen rubber boats. And they had planned to land at several points along the seaside shore of Butaritari Island. But at the last minute (when, in McCoy's private opinion, Colonel Carlson had seen how fucked up the offloading from the subs into the boats had gone), Carlson had the word passed that everybody was to land at Beach "Z," which was across the island from Government House.

What everybody called "Makin *Island*" was correctly "Makin *Atoll,*" a collection of tiny islands forming a small hollow triangle around a deep-water lagoon. The base of the triangle, shaped like a long, low-sided "U," was Butaritari Island, the largest of the islands. Off its northern point was Little Makin Island. When they had finished here, the Raiders were scheduled to attack and to destroy what personnel and matériel might be found there.

What civilization there was on Butaritari Island was all on the lagoon side—wharves running out from warehouses and building to the deep water of the la-

[3]A British weapon, essentially an oversize bolt-action rifle. Loaded, on its monopod, it weighed almost forty pounds. Fed with a top-mounted clip, the .55-caliber weapon fired a tungsten-cored bullet larger than the U.S. .50-caliber machine-gun round. It had proved ineffective against German tanks, but it was believed it would be effective against lighter armored Japanese vehicles.

goon. To the north of the built-up area were Government Wharf and Government House, now the Japanese headquarters. That was where the vast bulk of the Japanese forces were supposed to be.

McCoy counted rubber boats. He counted fifteen; that meant three were missing.

On the beach somewhere out of sight? Or swamped?

A trio of Raiders came running down the beach in a crouch, their weapons (Thompsons and Garands) at the ready.

"Whoa!" McCoy ordered.

Somewhat sheepishly they stopped, stood erect, and looked at him. Privately hoping it would set an example, McCoy had elected to arm himself with a Garand rather than with any of the array of gung ho automatic weapons in the arms room. He thought that the planned operation called for rifles . . . and not submachine guns that most people couldn't shoot well anyway, or carbines, whose effectiveness as a substitute for a rifle he questioned.

Their faces were streaked with black grease, and they were wearing what looked like, and in fact were, khaki uniforms that had been dyed black. There was no more India ink in the drafting offices at Camp Catlin, but the Raiders had the black uniforms Carlson couldn't find in quartermaster warehouses anywhere.

"We've been looking for you, Lieutenant," the corporal said, somewhat defensively.

"Where are you?" McCoy asked, clearly meaning the rest of the platoon.

The corporal gestured down the beach behind him. "About a hundred yards, sir."

"You run into anybody from Able Company?" McCoy asked.

"Yes, sir, there's a bunch of them down there, sir," the corporal said.

"You two stay here," McCoy ordered the two Raiders. Then he pointed at the corporal. "You go get the others," he said, and pointed inland. "I'm about fifteen yards in there."

"Aye, aye, sir," the corporal said, and started down the beach.

Colonel Carlson appeared, coming up the beach.

McCoy saluted.

"Oh, it's you, McCoy," Carlson said. "Getting your people sorted out?"

"Yes, sir," McCoy said. "I've got at least a platoon of Able Company with me. I'm about to send them down the beach."

"Good," Carlson said. "But despite the confusion, so far so good."

"Yes, sir," McCoy said.

The unmistakable crack of a .30-06 cartridge broke the stillness, clearly audible above the hiss of the surf.

"Oh, *shit!*" McCoy said, bitterly.

There was no following sound of gunfire. Just the one shot.

"What was that?" one of the Raiders asked, when neither Colonel Carlson nor McCoy spoke.

"That was some dumb sonofabitch walking around with his finger on the trigger," McCoy said furiously. "He might as well have blown a fucking bugle."

"I think this might be a good time for you to join your men, McCoy," Colonel Carlson said, conversationally, and then walked back down the beach.

XXI

(ONE)
Butaritari Island, Makin Atoll
0700 Hours, 17 August 1942

At a quarter to six, a runner from Lieutenant Plumley's Able Company had reported to Colonel Carlson that his point (that is, the leading elements of Plumley's troops) was at Government Wharf and that he had captured Government House without resistance. Carlson sent the runner back with orders for Plumley to move down the island in the direction of the other installations, that is to say, southeast, or to the left.

Carlson had expected the bulk of Japanese forces to be in the vicinity of Government House, and had made his plans accordingly. Now it seemed clear to him that the Japanese were in fact centered around On Chong's Wharf, about two miles away. If he had known that, he could have ordered Plumley to move quickly down the island, so that he could get as far as possible before he encountered resistance.

But once the presence of the Raiders on Butaritari became known to the Japanese—and the goddamned fool who had fired his Garand had taken care of that—the situation would change rapidly. If *he* were the Japanese commander, Carlson reasoned, he would move up Butaritari's one road as fast as he could, until he ran into the enemy.

Carlson's prediction was quickly confirmed. Another runner appeared, saluted, and, still heaving from the exertion of his run, announced, "We got Japs, Colonel."

Carlson extended his map.

"Show me where, son," he said, calmly.

When the runner pointed to the Native Hospital, Carlson nodded. His professional judgment was that the Japanese commander had established his line at the best possible place; the island was only about eleven hundred feet wide at that point.

He turned to his radio operator and told him to try to raise either of the submarines. So far Carlson's radio communication with the submarines had been just about a complete failure, but this time, he was lucky.

"I got the *Argonaut,* sir," the radio operator reported.

Carlson snatched the microphone and requested Naval gunfire on both the island (to shell Japanese reinforcement routes) and the lagoon, where two small ships were at anchor.

"We do not, repeat not," the *Argonaut* replied, "have contact with our spotter."

"Then fire without him," Carlson snapped, and tossed the microphone to the radio operator.

There came almost immediately the boom of the cannon firing, and then the whistle of the projectile in the air. Then there was the sound of a shell landing on the island, and almost simultaneously an enormous plume of water in the lagoon.

"Get them again, if you can," Carlson ordered the radio operator. "Tell them to keep it up."

Without thinking about it, without realizing he was doing it, Carlson counted the rounds fired by the cannon on the submarines, just as a competitive pistol shooter teaches you to habitually count shots. When the booming stopped, he was up to sixty-five, and both of the ships in the lagoon were in flames.

And then the *Nautilus* called him, and before the voice faded, Carlson heard that the Japanese-language linguist aboard the *Nautilus* had heard the Japanese send a message in the clear reporting the Raider attack and asking for reinforcements. Carlson asked if there had been a reply, but the radio was out again.

That made Carlson think of McCoy, and to wonder if it would not have been smarter to leave him aboard the *Nautilus* or not even bring him along at all. Japanese-speaking Americans were in short supply.

A moment later, McCoy showed up in person.

"I thought you would want to know what we're facing, sir," he said, and pointed out on Carlson's map the locations of four Japanese water-cooled machine guns, two grenade launchers, and a flame thrower.

"They got riflemen, a bunch of them, filling in the blanks in the line," McCoy said, pointing, "and snipers in the tops of most of the coconut trees along here."

"You didn't want to send a runner?"

"I didn't have one handy that I trusted with a map, sir," McCoy said.

"Well, then, Lieutenant, you can just keep running. Go find the Baker Company commander and tell him I said to get moving, down the island."

"Aye, aye, sir," McCoy said, and ran off.

In the next four hours, a procession of runners reported that Baker Company was making slow but steady progress down the island.

At 1130, two Japanese Navy Type 95 reconnaissance planes appeared over the island, flew back and forth for fifteen minutes, dropped two bombs, and then flew away. Carlson knew that meant the *Argonaut* and the *Nautilus,* essentially defenseless against aircraft, had dived, and there was no longer any reason even to try to raise them on the radio.

The *Nautilus* surfaced against at 1255, but immediately dived again after the radar detected a flight of twelve aircraft approaching the island. The submarines would remain submerged until 1830 hours.

At 1330, the Japanese aircraft arrived over Butaritari Island. It was quite an armada: two four-engined Kawanishi flying boats (bombers); four Zero fighters; four Type 94 reconnaissance bombers; and two Type 95 seaplanes. They promptly began to bomb and strafe the Raiders, and they kept it up for an hour and a half, but without doing much real damage.

Then, apparently convinced they had wiped out whatever antiaircraft capability the Raiders might have had, one of the four-engined Kawanishis and one of the Type 95s landed in the lagoon. They were promptly engaged by .30-caliber Raider machine-gun fire. The Type 95 caught fire. And the Kawanishi hurriedly taxied out of .30-caliber range and began to discharge its passengers—thirty-five Japanese soldiers intended to reinforce the Butaritari garrison—apparently oblivious to the fact that a slow but steady fire from a Boys .55-caliber antitank rifle was being delivered.

When the Kawanishi made its takeoff, it almost immediately entered into a series of violent circling maneuvers. The last of these sent it, with an enormous splash, into the lagoon.

The Japanese aircraft that remained over Butaritari then left, but more Zeros returned at 1630 and bombed and strafed the island for another thirty minutes. From the way they were flying and choosing to drop their bombs, it was evident to Carlson that there was little if any communication between the Japanese defenders of Butaritari and the aircraft that came to their assistance: The Zeros were attacking a portion of the island he had ordered the Raiders out of (to better counter Japanese sniper fire). And the Japanese had promptly moved into this position. The Zeros were consequently attacking Japanese positions and troops.

By 1700, Carlson understood that he had an important decision to make. He had two options. His mission was to destroy enemy forces and vital installations, and to capture prisoners and documents. So far, the Raiders had killed a number of Japanese, but there were no prisoners, no documents, and no serious damage to installations.

Choice One was to continue his advance.

But the operations plan called for the Raiders to evacuate Butaritari at some time between 1930 and 2100. And it also called for attacking Little Makin Island the next morning.

Choice Two was to hold his present position and make a very orderly withdrawal by stages to the beaches, the boats, and ultimately the submarines. If he did that, he would be in a position to attack Little Makin on schedule. After some thought, he decided that made the most sense.

By 1900, Carlson had established (under his own command; he felt it his duty to be the last Marine off the beach) a covering force for the disengagement, and the bulk of the Raiders were on the beach, loading the rubber boats for the return to the submarines, which had surfaced at 1845, and were now prepared to cover the withdrawal with Naval gunfire in addition to taking the Raiders aboard.

But now he was facing another enemy, the sea. The surf, which had posed no serious problems as they landed, now wouldn't let them off the island. This came as a surprise; for the waves were not especially large. And until he actually got in them, he didn't see what the problem was. They were moving very fast, and succeeding waves piled in very quickly. The trouble was that the waves were crowded too close together for the boats to operate.

Raiders walked their boats into the surf, and they generally managed to get past the first four waves without trouble. But then the agony started. Only a few of the outboard engines could be made to start, and those that they did get running were quickly drowned as waves crashed over the bows of the rubber boats and soaked coils and points.

After that, the Raiders tried paddling.

But paddling rhythmically and furiously for all they were worth, the Raiders could not make it past the rollers coming into the beach; they would make it over one roller only to be hit and thrown back by the next before they could gain momentum.

Boats filled to the gunwales. The Raiders bailed furiously. Then they loosened the outboard motors and dropped them over the side. And then they got out and pulled the boats by their own efforts, by swimming.

Surf turned boats over, which sent the Raiders' weapons, ammunition, and equipment to the bottom. But even empty, it was impossible to get the boats past the wave line.

After an hour, Carlson ordered back to the beach everybody that had not made it through the close-packed waves. When he got there, he found that less than half of the boats had made it through the surf. Thus more than half of the Raiders were still on the beach, and they were exhausted. Most of them had lost their weapons and equipment and rations. And there were a few wounded men, including four stretcher cases. These men were in pain, and obviously in no condition to keep trying to get off the beach.

So Carlson ordered all the boats pulled well up on the shore. He collected what weapons there were, set up a perimeter defense, and did what he could for the wounded. Then he formed teams to keep trying (it was possible that the surf was a freak condition, which would pass) to get through the surf, one boat at a time.

Carlson conducted a nose count. There were 120 Raiders still on the beach. And then, as if to suggest that God was displeased, it began to rain.

As soon as daylight made it possible, the Raiders tried Carlson's idea of forcing their boats through the surf one at a time. When one boat made it, another tried, and when it made it, then another tried. The wounded, Carlson knew, could not be extracted this way, and he would not leave them. He therefore ordered Captain Roosevelt into one of the boats so he could assume command of the Marines on the submarines. When he was sure Roosevelt had made it, he ran another nose count. Now there were seventy men on the beach.

At 0740, five Raiders aboard the *Nautilus* volunteered to take a boat with a working motor as close to shore as it could manage. Then one of the Raiders swam ashore from it with a message from Commander Haines that the subs would lay off the island as long as necessary to get the Raiders off the beach.

Then Japanese Zeros appeared. And the subs made emergency dives. The Japanese strafed the beach, and then turned their attention to the rubber boat with its volunteer crew. Nothing more was ever seen of it—or of them.

When Roosevelt, whose rubber boat had been the fourth and last to make its way through the rollers, started counting noses aboard the *Nautilus,* he came across Lieutenant Peatross and the remaining eight of the men who had been with him in his rubber boat during the initial landing.

He was convinced that Peatross and his men had been swamped. But they hadn't. The current had taken them a mile farther down the beach than any of the others, where they had made it safely ashore. When they heard the firing, they had literally marched toward the sound of gunfire. And then he and his men had spent the day harassing the Japanese rear. They had burned down his buildings, blown up a radio station, and burned a truck.

And in compliance with orders, still not having made their way through Japanese lines to the others, they had at 1930 gotten back in their rubber boat and made it through the surf to the waiting submarine.

During the afternoon of August 18, Carlson moved what was left of his forces to Government House on the lagoon side of the island. There they found a sloop. And for a short while (until it was determined that the sloop was unseaworthy), there was a spurt of hope that they could use it to get off the island.

Meanwhile, a radio was made to work long enough to establish a brief tie with the *Nautilus.* Evacuation would be attempted from the lagoon side of the island at nightfall.

Carlson sent men to manhandle the boats from the seaside beaches across the narrow island to the lagoon. Then he led a patrol toward the Japanese positions. He stripped the deserted office of the Japanese commander of what he had left behind (including his lieutenant general's flag, which the Raiders forwarded to Marine Commandant Holcomb). And then they burned and blew up one thousand barrels of Japanese aviation gasoline.

The fire was still burning at 2308 hours, when Colonel Carlson, believing himself to be the last man off the beach, went aboard the *Nautilus.*

There was no question of attacking Little Makin Island. For one thing, they would be expected. And the men not only had no weapons, they were exhausted.

The Raid on Makin Island was over. The *Nautilus* and the *Argonaut* got underway for Pearl Harbor.

(TWO)
Pearl Harbor Navy Base, Territory of Hawaii
26 August 1942

It is a tradition within the submarine service for the crew to stand on deck as the boat eases up to its wharf on return from a patrol. In keeping with this tradition, men were standing on the deck of the *Nautilus.* In fact, the deck was crowded; for in addition to the crew, the Marine Raiders who'd been "passengers" on the boat were on the deck, too.

The Raiders would have failed an inspection at Parris Island (or anywhere else in the Marine Corps). And they would have brought tears to the eyes of the gunnery sergeant of a Marine detachment aboard a battleship, a cruiser, or an aircraft carrier.

They were not at attention, for one thing. For another, no two of them seemed to be wearing the same uniform. Some were in dungarees, some in dyed-black khaki, some wore a mixture of both uniforms, and some wore parts of uniforms scrounged from the *Nautilus*'s crew. Some wore steel helmets, some fore-and-aft caps, and some were hatless.

There was a Navy band on the wharf, and it played "Anchors Aweigh" and the "Marines' Hymn," and the Raiders watched with their arms folded on their chests, wearing what were either smiles of pleasure or amused tolerance.

The Pearl Harbor brass came aboard after that. And on their heels corpsmen started to offload the stretcher cases and ambulatory wounded. A line of ambulances, their doors already open, waited on the wharf behind the gray staff cars of the brass and the buses that would carry the Raiders.

Lieutenant W. B. McCracken, Medical Corps, USNR, was wearing, proudly, dyed-black trousers and an unbuttoned Marine Corps dungaree jacket—as if to leave no question that he had been the doc of Baker Company, survivor of the Makin Raid, as opposed to your typical natty, run-of-the-mill chancre mechanic. McCracken walked up to Second Lieutenant Kenneth J. McCoy, USMC, grabbed his dungaree jacket, and looped a casualty tag string through a button hole.

"Go get in an ambulance, Killer," he said.

"I don't need it," McCoy said.

It was neither bravado nor modesty. He had not, in his mind, been wounded. A wound was an incapacitating hole in the body, usually accompanied by great pain. He had been *zinged* twice, *lightly* zinged. The first time had been right after they'd started moving down the island. A Japanese sniper in a coconut tree had almost got him, or almost missed. A slug had whipped through his trousers, six inches above his knee, grazed his leg, and kept going. It had scared hell out of him, but it hadn't even knocked him down.

Almost immediately, he had seen another muzzle flash and fired four shots from his Garand into the coconut tree. The Jap's rifle had then come tumbling down, and a moment later the sniper followed it—at least to the length of the rope he'd used to tie himself up there.

After that McCoy had pulled his pants leg up, then opened his first aid packet and put a compress on the hole, which was a groove about as wide as his pinky finger and about as long as a bandage. And then he'd really forgotten about it. Or rather, the wound hadn't been painful until that night, when he'd waded into the surf and the salt water had gotten to it and made it sting like hell.

And he had been *zinged* again the next morning, when he'd led a squad down the island to see what the Japs were up to. He had been looking around what had been a concrete-block wall when a Japanese machine gun had opened up on them. A slug had hit the blocks about two feet from him, and a chunk of concrete had clipped him on the forehead. It had left a jagged tear about three inches long, and it had given him a hell of a headache, but it hadn't even bled very much. And it was not a real *wound.*

The doc on the *Nautilus* had put a couple of fresh bandages, hardly more than Band-Aids, on him; and until now, that had been the end of it. He had spent the return trip trying to come up with a casualty list: who had been killed; who was missing from the fucked-up landing and the even more fucked-up withdrawal from the beach; and who, if anybody, was still unaccounted for. He hadn't thought of much else after it had become apparent to him that they had left as many as eight people on the beach.

"Hot showers," Doc McCracken said, pushing him toward the gangplank, "sheets, mattresses, good chow, and firm-breasted sweet-smelling nurses. Trust me, Killer."

Doc McCracken was smiling at him.

"What the hell," McCoy said. "Why not?"

It took about two hours before he had gone through the drill and was in a room in the Naval hospital with something to eat. A couple of doctors had painfully removed the scabs and dug around in there as if they hoped to find gold. Then they'd given him a complete physical. And of course the paper pushers were there, filling in their forms.

McCoy was just finishing his second shower—simply because it was there, all that limitless fresh hot water—and putting on a robe over his pajamas, and getting ready to lie on his bed and read *Life* magazine, when Colonel Carlson pushed open the door and walked into the room. He was still in mussed and soiled dungarees. McCoy supposed he'd come to the hospital to check on the wounded. The *real* wounded.

"Go on with what you were doing," Carlson said, as McCoy started to straighten up to attention. "Go on, get on the bed. It's permitted. Then tell me how you feel."

"I don't think I really belong here, Colonel," McCoy said, climbing onto the bed.

"Clean sheets and a hot meal," Carlson said, smiling.

"That's what the doc said, sir," McCoy said.

"I'm about to go out to Camp Catlin," Colonel Carlson said. "I thought I'd drop by and say 'so long.' "

"Sir?"

Carlson dipped into the cavernous pocket of his dungaree jacket and came out with a sheet of teletype paper, which he handed to McCoy.

PRIORITY

HEADQUARTERS USMC WASH DC 8AUG42

COMMANDING OFFICER
2ND RAIDER BN
FLEET MARINE FORCE PACIFIC
YOU WILL ON RECEIPT ISSUE APPROPRIATE ORDERS DETACHING SECOND LIEUTENANT KENNETH J. MCCOY USMCR FROM COMPANY B 2ND RAIDER BN AND TRANSFERRING HIM TO HEADQUARTERS USMC.
TRAVEL FROM HAWAII TO WASHINGTON BY AIR IS DIRECTED PRIORITY AA2.
BY DIRECTION
STANLEY F. WATT COLONEL USMC OFFICE OF THE ASSISTANT CHIEF OF STAFF FOR PERSONNEL

McCoy looked at Carlson.

"Well, you'll be in here for forty-eight hours," Carlson said. "That'll give us time to get your gear from Catlin to you."

"I guess they really need linguists, sir," McCoy said.

"Certainly, they do. Linguists are valuable people, McCoy. There's far too few of them—you did notice that TWX was dated 8 August—for the Corps to risk losing one of them storming some unimportant beach."

Their eyes met.

"When you get to Washington, McCoy, say hello to Colonel Rickabee for me."

McCoy saw that Carlson was smiling.

"You've known all along, then, sir?"

"Not everyone in the Corps thinks I'm a crazy Communist, McCoy," Carlson said. "I've still got a few friends left who try to let me know what's going on."

"Oh, shit!" McCoy said.

"Nothing for you to be embarrassed about, McCoy," Carlson said. "You're a Marine officer. A *good* Marine officer. And good Marine officers do what they're told to do, to the best of their ability."

He stepped to the bed and put out his hand.

"Take care of yourself, son," he said. "I was glad you were along on this operation."

And then he turned and walked out of the room.

(THREE)
Navy Air Station
Pensacola, Florida
29 August 1942

Second Lieutenant Malcolm S. Pickering's first response to the knock at the penthouse door was to simply ignore it. Either it would go away or Dick Stecker would get up and answer it.

It was Saturday morning, and they had drunk their Friday supper.

They were finished at Pensacola. Orders would be cut on Monday, 31 August, certifying that Second Lieutenants Pickering and Stecker were rated as fully qualified in F4F-3 aircraft, and placing them on a ten-day-delay-en-route leave to wherever the hell the Marine Corps was sending them.

It was occasion to celebrate, and they had celebrated until the wee hours.

The knocking became more persistent, and Pickering finally gave in. Wrapping a sheet around his middle, calling out "Keep your pants on!" he walked to the door and jerked it open.

It was Captain James L. Carstairs, USMC, *Captain Mustache,* in his usual impeccable uniform.

"Good morning, sir," Pickering said.

"May I come in?" Captain Carstairs asked. "You alone?"

"I'm alone," Pickering said. "But . . . Captain Carstairs, Stecker has a guest."

"The one with her hair piled two feet over her head?" Captain Carstairs said. "And the enormous bazooms?"

"Uh . . ."

"We saw you last night," Captain Carstairs said. "I rather doubt that in your condition you saw us, but we saw you."

"I saw you, sir," Pickering said. "I didn't know you had seen us."

"You should have come over and said hello," Captain Carstairs said. "I had the feeling Mrs. Culhane rather wished you would."

Pickering looked at him in surprise, and blurted what popped into his mind.

"Is that why you're here? To tell me that?"

"Unfortunately, no," Captain Carstairs said, and handed Pickering a yellow Western Union envelope.

"What's this?"

"Keep in mind the other possibility," Carstairs said. "The word is they left a lot of people on the beach."

Pickering ripped the envelope open.

> GOVERNMENT
> WASHINGTON DC
> 5PM AUGUST 28 1942
> SECOND LIEUTENANT M. S. PICKERING, USMCR
> NAVY AIR STATION PENSACOLA FLORIDA
> THE SECRETARY OF THE NAVY REGRETS TO INFORM YOU THAT YOUR FRIEND SECOND LIEUTENANT KENNETH J. MCCOY USMCR 2ND RAIDER BATTALION WAS WOUNDED IN ACTION AGAINST THE JAPANESE ON MAKIN ISLAND 17 AUGUST 1942. HE HAS BEEN REMOVED TO A NAVAL HOSPITAL AND IS EXPECTED TO FULLY RECOVER. FURTHER DETAILS WILL BE FURNISHED AS AVAILABLE.
> FRANK KNOX JR SECRETARY OF THE NAVY

"There's another word in the lexicon," Captain Carstairs said, "one they did not use. The adjective 'seriously,' as in 'seriously wounded.' And they included the phrase 'fully recover.' "

"Yeah," Pickering said, and then looked at Carstairs. "Thank you."

"My curiosity is aroused," Carstairs said. "Doesn't he have a family?"

"Not one he gives much of a damn about," Pickering said. "He's got a brother, but he's in the Raiders, too."

"He came through it, that's what counts," Carstairs said. "That's all that counts."

"Oh, Christ!" Pickering said, having just then thought of it. "Ernie!"

"Who's Ernie?"

"His girl friend," Pick said. "I'll have to tell her."

"Why?" Carstairs said, practically. "If he's not seriously hurt, he'll write her and tell her. Why worry her?"

"Because she would want to know," Pick flared. "Jesus Christ!"

"Keep your cool, Pickering," Carstairs said. "Think it over. What would be gained?"

"Yeah," Pick said. 'This is not the first telegram from the Secretary of the Navy—" He stopped. "I am about to have a drink. Would you like one?"

"I thought you would never ask," Captain Carstairs said.

Pick made drinks, and then told Captain Mustache about the first telegram from the Secretary of the Navy about Ken McCoy when he had been in the Philippines, the one that said he was "missing in action and presumed dead." They made enough noise to raise Dick Stecker and his guest from their bed.

They had another couple of drinks, and then ordered room service breakfast, and in the end Pick decided he would not call Ernie, not now. It made more sense to wait and see what happened. There was no sense getting Ernie all upset when there was nothing at all that she could do.

Captain Mustache stayed with them. He even got a little smashed, and it had all the beginnings of a good party. Now that they were about to be certified as fully qualified brother Naval aviators, it was fitting and proper for him to associate with two lowly second lieutenants as social equals.

Sometime during the evening, Captain Mustache told him that he had just about given up on Martha Sayre Culhane. It had become clear to him that she was just not interested.

Pickering recalled that the next morning (now Sunday) when some other sonofabitch was knocking at the door.

As Pick staggered to open it, he remembered telling Captain Mustache that he knew just how he felt. And then Captain Mustache had said something else: He thought it wasn't absolutely hopeless for Pick, and that it was a shame Pick was about to ship out.

Pick jerked the door open. It was Captain Mustache again.

"Why didn't you just crap out on the couch?" Pick asked, somewhat snappishly.

"I took the brunette in the glasses home, remember?" Captain Mustache said, and then added, demonstrating, "You've got another one," and handed him a yellow Western Union envelope.

"Oh, shit, now what?" Pick asked.

The second telegram, to his relief and confusion, appeared to be identical to the first. He was afraid that it would be one expressing the condolences of the Secretary of the Navy.

"What the hell is this?" he asked. "A duplicate? In case I didn't get the first one?"

"I don't know," Carstairs answered. And then they saw that the two telegrams were not identical. The second said McCoy had been wounded on August 18; the first had said August 17.

"I guess he got shot twice," Carstairs said, "and the paperwork just got caught up."

"I'm going to have to call Ernie," Pick said, firmly. "She has a right to know."

"Can I have a hair of the dog?" Captain Mustache asked.

"Make me one, will you? I think I'm going to need it."

It took Ernie so long to answer her phone that he was afraid she wasn't at her apartment, but finally, she came on the line.

"What is it?" she snapped.

"This is Pick, Ernie," he said.

"What do you want at this time of the morning?" she snapped.

"I've got a little bad news," Pick said, gently.

"About what?" she asked, now with concern in her voice.

"About Ken," Pick said. "Ernie, did you read in the paper or hear on the radio about the Marine Raiders and Makin Island?"

"Yes," she said. "What the *hell* are you talking about?"

"I'm talking about Ken," Pick said.

"Just a minute," Ernie said, and went off the line. And stayed off.

"Hello?" Pick said, finally.

"Hello, yourself," Ken McCoy's voice came over the wire. "You have a lousy sense of timing, asshole. Did I ever tell you that?"

"When did you get back?"

"I got into Washington about ten last night," McCoy said. "And I caught the four A.M. train into New York. I've been here about an hour and a half. Get the picture?"

"Sorry to have bothered you, sir," Pick said, and hung up.

Captain Mustache handed him a drink. Pick looked at it and set it down.

"Our twice-wounded hero is in New York," he said. "I don't know how the hell he worked that, but I'm not really surprised."

"Well, there's our excuse to celebrate again," Carstairs said.

"No," Pick said.

"No?" Carstairs asked.

"Actually, I think I'll go to church," Pick said.

"Well, sure," Carstairs said, uncomfortably, forcing a smile.

(FOUR)
Navy Air Station Chapel
Pensacola, Florida
30 August 1942

Chaplain (Lieutenant Commander) J. Bartwell Kaine, USNR, who until three months before had been rector of the Incarnation Episcopal Church of Baltimore, Maryland, was pleased to see the two Marine second lieutenants at his morning prayer service.

It had been his experience since coming to Pensacola that few, too few, of the officer aviation students attended worship services of any kind, and that those who did went to the nondenominational Protestant services at 1100. He was interested in keeping, so to speak, Episcopalian personnel within the fold, and there was no question in his practiced eye that the two handsome young Marines in the rear pew were Episcopal. They knew the service well enough to recite the prayers and doxology from memory, and they knew when and how to kneel.

Chaplain Kaine made a special effort, when the service was over, to speak to them, to let them know they were more than welcome, and to invite them to participate in the activities of what he referred to as "the air station Episcopal community."

They informed him that while they appreciated the offer of hospitality, they had finished their training and were about to leave Pensacola.

Then Second Lieutenants Pick Pickering and Dick Stecker walked to Pickering's car and got in. As Pickering pushed the starter button and got the Cadillac running, Stecker spoke:

"Even though I'm aware of the scriptural admonition to 'judge not, lest ye be judged,' why is it that I have the feeling that you dragged me over here more in the interests of your sinful lusts of the flesh than to offer thanks for your buddy coming through all right?"

"Fuck you, Dick," Pickering said, cheerfully.

"What made you think she'd be there? And if she had been, what makes you think she would have rushed into your arms?"

"I saw the picture of her father in the base newspaper. He's a vestryman. It was worth a shot."

"You're desperate, aren't you?" Stecker replied, half mockingly, half sympathetically.

"You're goddamn right I am. We're leaving here Tuesday."

"You're nuts, Pick," Stecker said, not unkindly.

"I'm in love, all right? People in love are allowed to be a little crazy."

"What you need is a piece of ass," Stecker said. "It has amazing curative power for crazy people. Let's go back to the hotel and commit every sin—except worshipping graven images."

"Let's go sailing," Pickering said.

"Let's do what?"

"Sailing. Boats, sails. You *have* been on a boat?"

"How are we going to do that?"

"Trust me, my son," Pickering said solemnly. "Put thy faith in me, and I will work miracles."

Five minutes after they passed the Marine guard on the Pensacola Navy Air Station, Pickering turned off Navy Boulevard. Five hundred yards beyond he passed between two sandstone pillars.

"You *did* notice the sign?" Stecker asked, dryly.

"The one that said 'Pensacola Yacht Club'?"

"The one that said 'Members Only.' "

"Oh, ye of little faith," Pickering said.

"You really think she's going to be in here?"

"There was another story about her father," Pickering said, "in the Pensacola newspaper. In addition to being an admiral, he's the vice commodore here."

"Jesus, you are desperate."

"It also said they serve a buffet brunch, starting at ten," Pickering said. "Admirals have to eat, just like human beings. Maybe he brought his daughter with him."

"And what if he did? Presuming we don't get thrown out on our asses, what are you going to do, just walk up and say, 'Hi, there'?"

"Why not?" Pickering said, smiling at Stecker as he parked the car and pulled the emergency brake on.

A portly, suntanned man in a blue blazer with an embroidered patch on the pocket walked up to them as they entered the lobby of the yacht club.

"Good morning, gentlemen," he said. "Meeting someone?"

"Gee," Stecker said, under his breath, "we lasted a whole ten seconds before we got caught."

"No, we thought we'd try the buffet," Pickering said.

The man in the blazer looked uncomfortable, making Stecker think that he disliked throwing servicemen out of his yacht club, even if that was precisely what he was about to do.

"Gentlemen," he said, "I'm afraid this is a private club—"

"But you are affiliated with the American Yachting Association?" Pickering asked, as he took out his wallet.

"Yes, of course," the man said.

Pickering searched through the wallet and came up with a battered card and handed it over.

"Welcome to the Pensacola Yacht Club, Mr. Pickering," the man said, smiling, and handing him back the card. "I won't have to ask, will I, what brings you into our waters?"

"Our Uncle Samuel," Pickering said.

"Well, let me show you to the dining room," the man said. "If you don't think it's too early, the first drink is traditionally on the club."

"How nice," Pickering said.

The corridor from the lobby to the dining room was lined with trophy cases and framed photographs.

"Well, there's a familiar face," Pickering said, pleased, pointing to a photograph of a large sailboat with its crew. They were standing along the port side, hanging on to the rigging, and they were obviously delighted with themselves.

A thin strip of typewritten legend on the photograph said, "FAT CHANCE, 1st Place, Wilson Cup, San Francisco-Hawaii 1939."

"That was the 'thirty-nine Wilson Cup," the man from the yacht club said. "Jack Glenn, one of our members, was on her."

"Fat Jack," Pickering said. "But please note that splendid sailor about to fall off the bowsprit."

Stecker looked. It was Pickering, as obviously drunk as he was delighted with himself, holding on firmly to the bowsprit rigging.

"That's you," Stecker accused.

"Indeed," Pickering said.

From the look on the man from the yacht club, Stecker decided, the Pensacola Yacht Club was theirs.

"God is in his heaven," Pickering said solemnly. "Prayer pays. All is right with the world."

"What the hell?" Stecker asked, and then looked where Pickering was looking.

A rear admiral, a woman obviously his wife, and Martha Sayre Culhane were coming down the corridor.

"Well, hello, there," Mrs. Sayre said, offering her hand to Pickering. "It's nice to see you again, Lieutenant. You're a sailor, too?"

"Quite a sailor, Mrs. Sayre," the man from the yacht club said. He pointed to the photograph. "He was on the *Fat Chance* with Jack Glenn."

"Good morning, Martha," Pickering said.

"Hello, Pick," Martha said.

She did not seem nearly as glad to see Pickering as Pick was to see her.

"Since no one seems to be about to introduce us, gentlemen," Admiral Sayre said, "I'll introduce myself. I'm Admiral Sayre."

"How do you do, sir?" Pickering said politely.

"Jim, this is Lieutenant Pickering," Mrs. Sayre said. "I'm afraid I don't know this—"

"Stecker, ma'am," Stecker said. "Dick Stecker."

"We're here for the brunch," Mrs. Sayre said. "Why don't you join us?"

"We wouldn't want to intrude," Stecker said.

"That's very kind, thank you very much, we'd love to," Pickering said.

"I'd like to thank you for doing this, Dick," Mrs. Jeanne Sayre said to Stecker.

"Ma'am?" Stecker asked.

They were in the cabin of the *Martha III,* a twenty-eight-foot cruising sailer, now two miles offshore, and heeled twenty degrees from the vertical in nasty choppy seas. Jeanne Sayre had boiled water for tea on a small stove. Stecker had welcomed the opportunity to get out of the spray by helping her. When he had come below, Martha was with her father in the cockpit, and Pick was way up front, just behind what Stecker had earlier learned (looking at the photo in the yacht club) was the "bowsprit."

"I'm sure you and Pick had other plans for this afternoon," Jeanne Sayre said.

"This is fine," he said. "I'm glad to be here."

"Even though you're going to have to have your uniform cleaned, if it's not ruined, not to mention buying shoes, which have already been ruined?" she asked, smiling tolerantly.

"I've never had a chance to do something like this before," Stecker said.

"My husband too rarely gets the chance to do anything like this," Jeanne Sayre said. "He really works too hard, and he's reluctant—he's really a nice guy—to ask his aides to 'volunteer.' I saw his eyes light up when he heard Pick was a real sailor. I didn't have the heart to kick him under the table when he asked if anybody would like a little sail."

"Pick's having a fine time," Stecker said, smiling.

He'd be having a much better time, of course, if it wasn't for you, the admiral, and me; and it was just him and your well-stacked daughter sailing off into the sunset on this goddamned little boat.

The boat at the moment started to change direction. Stecker's eyes reflected his concern.

"We're turning," she said. "I guess my husband decided we're far enough offshore."

The *Martha III* came to a vertical position, and then started heeling in the other direction.

"Man overboard!" a male voice, obviously the admiral's, cried.

For a moment, Stecker thought it was some sort of joke in bad taste, but then he saw the look on Mrs. Sayre's face, and knew it was no joke. Obviously, Pick, playing Viking up front, had lost his footing and gone into the water. There was a quick sense of amusement—serves the bastard right—quickly replaced by a feeling of concern. The water out there was choppy. People drowned when they fell off boats, particularly into choppy water.

He followed Jeanne Sayre as she went quickly to the cockpit. He looked forward. Pick hadn't gone overboard. He was halfway between the bow and the cockpit. And he had taken his blouse off.

Pick ripped a circular life preserver free and threw it over the side; and then, in almost a continuous motion, he made a quick running dive over the side. He still had his socks on, Stecker saw, but he had removed his shoes.

Stecker looked over the stern. Surprisingly far behind the boat, he saw Martha Sayre Culhane's head bobbing in the water, held up by an orange life preserver.

Mrs. Sayre had taken her husband's position at the wheel, and while she watched both her husband (who was lowering the mainsail) and her daughter behind her in the water, she was trying to start the gasoline auxiliary engine.

The moment it burst into life, Admiral Sayre lowered the sail all the way.

"Bring her around!" he ordered, and then pushed past Stecker to get a boat hook from the cabin.

Stecker felt both useless and absurd.

He searched the water and found first Martha and then Pickering. Pickering was swimming with sure, powerful strokes to Martha, towing the life ring behind him on its line.

It seemed to take a very long time for the *Martha III* to turn, but once she was through the turn, she seemed to pick up speed. When Stecker saw Martha again, Pick was beside her in the water.

It took three minutes before the *Martha III* reached them. Mrs. Sayre expertly stopped the boat beside them, and then Stecker and Admiral Sayre hauled them in, first Martha, and then Pickering. They were blue-lipped and shivering.

"Take them below, and get them out of their clothes," Admiral Sayre said. "There's still some blankets aboard?"

"Yes," his wife said.

The admiral looked around the surface of the water, located a channel marker, and pointed it out to Stecker.

"Make for that," he ordered. "I'll relieve you in a minute."

"Aye, aye, sir," Stecker said, obediently. And for the first time in his life he took the conn of a vessel underway.

When he went to the cabin, Admiral Sayre—seeing that his wife had already stripped their daughter of her dress and was working on her slip—faced Pickering aft before he ordered him out of his wet clothing. Pick stripped to his underwear, and then Admiral Sayre wrapped a blanket around his shoulders.

"I'll hang your pants and shirt from the rigging. You'll look like hell, but it will at least be dry," the admiral said.

"Thank you, sir," Pick said.

"Why the hell did you go over the side?" the admiral demanded.

"I thought maybe she was hurt," Pick said.

"Well, I'm grateful," the admiral said. He looked down the cabin. "You all right, honey?" he asked.

"A little wet," Martha said.

"I'll do what I can to dry your clothes," her father said. "Jeanne, you go topside and take the helm."

"Aye, aye, Admiral, sir," his wife replied, dryly sarcastic.

Now wrapped, Martha and Pick looked at each other across the cabin.

And then Pick crossed the cabin to her.

"You want to tell me what that was all about?" Martha asked.

"If I had a bicycle, I would have ridden it no hands," Pick said.

She walked past him to the ladder to the cockpit, and turned and walked in the other direction.

"It was a dumb thing to do," Martha said. "You weren't even wearing a life jacket. You could have drowned, you damn fool."

"So could you have," Pick said slowly. "And if you were going to drown, I wanted to drown with you."

"Jesus," she said. And she looked at him. "You're crazy."

"Just in love," he said.

"My God, you are crazy," she said.

"Maybe," Pick said. "But that's the way it is. And this was my last chance. We're leaving Tuesday."

"Jim Carstairs told me," Martha said, and then: "Oh, Pick, what are you doing to me?" she asked, very softly.

"Nothing," he said. "What I would like to do is put my arms around you and never let you go."

Her hand came out from under her blanket and touched his face. His hand came out and touched hers, and then his arms went around her, as he buried his face in her neck.

This served to dislodge the blankets covering the upper portions of their bodies.

Martha had removed her brassiere, and was wearing only her underpants. As if with a mind of its own, Pick's hand found her breast and closed over it.

"My God!" she whispered, taking her mouth from his a long, long moment later. "My parents!"

They retrieved their blankets.

When Admiral Sayre came into the cabin no more than a minute later, they were on opposite sides of the cabin, Martha sitting down, Pick leaning against a locker.

But maybe it wasn't necessary. They had color in their faces again. Martha's face, in fact, was so red that she could have been blushing.

"You two all right?"

"Yes," Martha said.

"Couldn't be better, sir," Pick Pickering said.

POSTSCRIPT

Kwajalein Island
16 October 1942

The following is factual. It is taken from *"Record of Proceedings of a Military Commission convened on April 16, 1946, at United States Fleet, Commander Marianas, Guam, Marianas Islands," under the authority of Rear Admiral C. A. Pownall, USN, the Commander, Marianas Area, to deal with the cases of Vice Admiral Koso Abe, Captain Yoshio Obara, and Lieutenant Commander Hisakichi Naiki, all of the Imperial Japanese Navy:*

Early in October, a Lieutenant Commander Okada, who was a staff officer of the Central Japanese Headquarters, visited Kwajalein in connection with an inspection of Japanese defense fortifications. While he was there, Vice Admiral Abe, Kwajalein commander, solicited Commander Okada's assistance in securing transportation to Japan of nine prisoners of war, Marine enlisted men who had been captured following the Makin Island operation and brought to Kwajalein. The Imperial Japanese Navy had been unable, or unwilling, so far to divert a vessel to transport the prisoners.

Commander Okada replied to Vice Admiral Abe that *"from now on, it would not be necessary to transport prisoners to Japan; from now on, they would be disposed of on the island* [*Kwajalein*]*"* or words to that effect.

On October 11, 1942, Vice Admiral Abe delegated the responsibility of disposing of the prisoners to the Commanding Officer, 61st Naval Guard Unit, Imperial Japanese Navy, Captain Yoshio Obara, IJN, a career naval officer and a 1915 graduate of the Imperial Japanese Naval Academy. The Marine prisoners of war were then being held by the 61st Naval Guard unit.

Vice Admiral Abe's orders to Captain Obara specified that the executioners, as a matter of courtesy to the prisoners of war, hold the grade of warrant officer or above.

There was a pool of approximately forty warrant officers (in addition to officers of senior grade), none of whom was initially willing to volunteer for the duty. When prevailed upon by Captain Obara and Lieutenant Commander Naiki, however, three warrant officers stepped forward, as did an enlisted man, who would serve as "pistoleer."

Lieutenant Commander Naiki proposed to dispose of the Marine prisoners on October 16, which was the Yasakuni Shrine Festival, a Japanese holiday honoring departed heroes. This proposal received the concurrence of Captain Obara and Vice Admiral Abe.

A site was selected and prepared on the southwestern part of the island.

Captain Obara ordered that the evening meal of October 15, 1942 for the prisoners include beer and sweet cakes.

On October 16, the Marine prisoners were blindfolded and had their hands tied behind them. They were moved from their place of confinement to a holding area near the disposal site and held there until Vice Admiral Abe and Captain Obara arrived, in full dress uniform, by car from activities in connection with the Yasakuni Shrine Festival.

The Marine prisoners were then led one at a time to the edge of a pit dug for the purpose, and placed in a kneeling position. Then they were beheaded by one or another of the three warrant officers—using swords, according to Japanese Naval tradition. The services of the pistoleer, who would have fired a bullet into their heads should there not be a complete severance of head from torso, were not required.

A prayer for the souls of the departed was offered, under the direction of Vice Admiral Abe, who then left.

A woven fiber mat was placed over the bodies, and the pit filled in. Additional prayers were offered, and then the disposal party was marched off.

On 19 June 1947, Lieutenant Colonel George W. Newton, USMC, Provost Marshal of Guam, reported to the Commandant of the Marine Corps that, in accordance with the sentence handed down by the Military Commission, Vice Admiral Abe, Captain Obara, and Lieutenant Commander Naiki, late of the Imperial Japanese Navy, had that day been, by First Lieutenant Charles C. Rexroad, USA, hanged by the neck until they were dead.

COUNTERATTACK

I

(ONE)
Pearl Harbor
Oahu Island, Territory of Hawaii
7 December 1941

The Japanese Carrier Task Force charged with the destruction of the United States Pacific Fleet began launching aircraft approximately 305 nautical miles north of Pearl Harbor.

These aircraft proceeded in a single stream until they were about 125 miles from Pearl Harbor, where the stream split in two. Fifty miles from Oahu, the left column of the attacking force divided again into three more streams.

The first two streams of the left column turned right and headed for Pearl Harbor, across the island. The third stream continued on course until it had flown beyond the tip of Oahu, then turned toward the center of the island and made its approach to Pearl Harbor from the sea. It began its attack at 0755 hours.

Meanwhile, the right stream of Japanese aircraft had divided in two as it approached Oahu. One stream crossed the coastline and made for Pearl Harbor, on the other side of the island. The second continued on course past the island, and then turned back to attack Pearl Harbor from the open sea. Its attack began at 0900.

All of these attacks went off smoothly and as planned. And at 1030, the Task Force radioed a coded message to Imperial Japanese Naval Headquarters. The code was *"Tora, Tora, Tora."* It signified success.

Fortunately for the Americans, the Japanese success was not unqualified. The surprise attack had found all of the battleships of the United States Pacific Fleet at anchor, and had sunk or severely damaged most of them. But two U.S. aircraft carriers, seven cruisers, and their screening vessels were at sea, in three task forces, and were not harmed.

When the first Japanese bombs fell at Pearl Harbor, Staff Sergeant Joseph L. Howard, USMC, of Headquarters Company, 1st Marine Defense Battalion, was asleep. He shared a room with a mess sergeant, who was on duty, and who could be counted on to bring a thermos of coffee and some doughnuts back to their room when the mess had finished serving breakfast.

Staff Sergeant Howard was twenty-four, young for his rank. He was six feet one inches tall, weighed 185 pounds, and was broad-shouldered and slim-waisted. He had sharp features, intelligent eyes, and wore his light brown hair just long enough to part. At one time it had been seriously proposed that Staff Sergeant Howard be used as a model for the photographs in a new edition of the *Handbook for Marines.*

The *Handbook for Marines* was issued to every enlisted Marine; many officers—including most company-grade officers—also had copies. Among its many illustrations were photographs of a Marine modeling the various service uniforms. A Good Marine was supposed to look like that. Similarly, there were photographs showing the correct way to execute the manual of arms and the various movements in close-order drill.

Staff Sergeant Joe Howard, in one of his perfectly fitting uniforms, with his erect carriage and broad shoulders, looked *exactly* like the Perfect Marine.

Joe Howard had been a Marine for seven years and six months.

He had enlisted right out of high school, on what was called a "baby cruise," a term of enlistment which extended to his twenty-first birthday; the regular term of enlistment was four years. At that point (he turned twenty-one on August 14, 1937), he was given the choice of being transferred to the Fleet Reserve—in effect discharged—or shipping over for a regular, four-year enlistment.

For most of his "baby cruise," Howard served with the Marine detachment on board the battleship *Arizona,* and he won promotion to private first class at the recommendation of her captain, who had been impressed with his bearing and appearance when Howard had served as his orderly. After leaving *Arizona,* he was assigned to the Philadelphia Navy Yard.

At the Navy Yard, a salty old gunnery sergeant took a liking to him, had him assigned to the arms locker as an armorer, and taught him how to shoot. *Really* shoot. Not only well enough to qualify for the extra pay that went with the Expert Rifleman qualification badge, but well enough to shoot competitively. He almost made it onto the East Coast Rifle Team (one step down from the U.S. Marine Corps Rifle Team), and he was fairly confident that he could make it the next time around.

Gunny MacFarland also got him a job as an off-duty bartender in the officers' club, working Friday and Saturday nights and for the luncheon buffet on Sunday. That thirty cents an hour added enough to his PFC's thirty dollars a month, supplemented by his five-dollar-a-month Expert Rifleman's pay, to permit him to buy a Ford Model A.

In August of 1937 he had to choose between getting out of the Corps and taking his chances on civvy street, where jobs were hard to come by, particularly if you didn't have a trade, or shipping over, which meant a dollar and a dime a day, plus uniforms, three square meals a day, and a place to sleep out of the rain. That's what Joe had told his mother.

But there was more to it than that. Not only were there other material advantages, like being paid to do something you liked to do—shooting, and the opportunities for travel that went with being a competitive rifle shooter, and things like that—but there was also the chance to make something of himself. And just *being* a Marine.

Gunny MacFarland told him that with his record, and providing he kept his nose clean, it was almost a sure thing that he would make corporal before his second hitch was up, maybe even sooner than that, say in two years.

Joe Howard knew that Gunny MacFarland was bullshitting him to get him to ship over. In two years he would be twenty-three. There were very few twenty-three-year-old corporals in the Marines. In 1937 the Corps had an authorized strength of only twenty-five thousand officers and men, which meant that nobody moved up in rank very fast. His chances of making corporal on his second hitch were almost nonexistent.

But it was more than a little flattering to have MacFarland bullshit him in order to get him to ship over and stay in the Corps. MacFarland was one hell of a Marine, and to know that MacFarland wanted him to stay in the Corps meant that MacFarland thought he had at least the potential to be a good Marine.

Besides, if Howard shipped over, there was nothing in it for MacFarland, either. He wasn't a recruiting sergeant. And nothing made MacFarland ask Joe over to his quarters for Sunday-night supper, sort of taking him into the family. Mrs. MacFarland even made him a birthday cake with candles when Joe turned twenty.

There really had not been much of a choice between going back to Birmingham, Alabama, and maybe getting lucky and getting a job in a steel mill, or shipping over in the Corps, even if MacFarland *was* bullshitting him about making corporal.

The same month he shipped over, PFC Howard met the Major General Commandant of the Marine Corps, Thomas Holcomb. More or less for the hell of it, thinking that it was at least practice, Joe Howard got into his civilian clothes one Sunday, drove his Model A across New Jersey to a place called Sea Girt, and entered a civilian rifle match run by the National Rifle Association on the New Jersey National Guard's rifle range.

You had to pay three dollars and fifty cents to enter, plus, he found out when he got there, another five dollars to join the NRA if you were competing as a civilian, as he was. So he was out eight-fifty, plus the cost of gas and wear and tear on the Model A, plus the loss of the dollar and a half he would have made working the Sunday brunch at the officers' club.

He'd just about decided that coming to Sea Girt was one of the dumber things he'd done lately, when he checked the scoreboard and saw that he was leading in the one-hundred- and three-hundred-yard matches. All that was left was the twenty-round timed fire at five hundred yards. If he took that, they'd give him a loving cup. He wasn't sure if it was silver, or just silver-plated, but he could probably get at least five dollars for it in a hockshop. And if it really was silver, he might even make a couple of bucks over his expenses.

When he fired the five-hundred-yard timed fire, Joe Howard tried very hard. It was some of the best shooting he had ever done, and luck was with him. The wind was light, and right down the range. He took the match by fifteen points, and he put eleven of the twenty rounds in the X-ring.

The only picture he had ever seen of Thomas Holcomb, Major General Commandant of the Marine Corps, was the photograph of the General in full uniform, medals and all, which hung at various places in every Marine Corps installation. He hadn't paid much attention to it.

So Joe did not recognize the civilian big shot who handed him the loving cup, a more or less chubby guy, sweating in his vested cord suit and flat-brimmed straw hat. For that matter, he didn't even look closely at the man until he made an odd remark:

"That was fine shooting, son. Congratulations. If you don't have any other plans, the Marine Corps always has a place for someone who can shoot like that."

The comment brought laughter from the other big shots.

The confusion on Joe Howard's face as Major General Commandant Holcomb shook his hand and simultaneously handed him the loving cup was evident. One of the big shots thought an explanation was in order.

"General Holcomb is Commandant of the Marine Corps, son. He was kind enough to come down here from Spring Lake to make the presentation of the awards."

For three years, Joe Howard, as a Pavlovian reflex, had come to attention when greeting any officer, from second lieutenant up. At that instant he popped to attention. Because the handle of the eighteen-inch-tall silver loving cup was in his left hand, however, this proved a little difficult.

His movement caught Commandant Holcomb's eye, and he turned to look at the young man.

"Sir," PFC Howard boomed in the manner he had been taught, "PFC Howard, Joseph L., Marine Barracks, Philadelphia."

"Carry on," General Holcomb said, and then added, with a smile, to the other big shots, "Why am I not surprised?"

He then walked off with the other big shots, but Joe Howard saw him say something behind his hand to a young man with him, who was also in civilian clothing. The young man nodded, took a notebook from his pocket, and wrote in it.

There was no doubt whatever in Joe's mind that his name had been taken down. He had had his name taken down before—always in connection with something he had done wrong, or for something he had omitted. So he decided that it was probably against some regulation for him to enter a civilian NRA match.

When he thought more about it, he decided his particular sin had been to go to the armory and take his rifle, a 1903 Springfield .30-06 with a Star Gauge barrel, and use it to compete in a civilian match.

Star Gauge Springfields were capable of extraordinary accuracy, far beyond that of standard-issue Springfields. They were so called because the Army's Frankford Arsenal, after checking their dimensions ("gauging them") and determining that they met a set of very strict standards, had stamped their barrels near the muzzle with a star.

With a sinking feeling in his stomach, Joe realized that if some other Marine came to his armory and asked to check out one of the Star Gauge Springfields so he could fire it in a civilian match, there was no way he would let him do it without written permission from some officer.

And he hadn't been caught using a Star Gauge Springfield in a civilian match by just some officer, but by the Major General Commandant of the Marine Corps!

On the way back to Philadelphia, Joe considered confessing his sins right off to Gunny MacFarland, but chickened out. The Gunny would really be pissed; the one thing he could not stand was stupidity. And it was also likely that the Gunny, being the Gunny, would try to accept the responsibility for his stupidity himself.

That wouldn't be right. Taking the Star Gauge Springfield had been his idea, Joe decided, and he would take whatever came his way because of it.

Nothing happened on Monday. Or on Tuesday, or Wednesday. And by Thursday Joe began to think that just maybe nothing would happen. Maybe he would get away with it, even though the officer in civvies had taken down his name.

On Friday, just before lunch, he was summoned by the Sergeant Major and told to report to the Commanding Officer.

"Sir, PFC Howard reporting as ordered to the commanding officer!"

"Stand at ease, Howard," said the Commanding Officer, a paunchy, middle-aged major, and then handed him a sheet of teletype machine paper.

HEADQUARTERS US MARINE CORPS WASH DC
27 AUGUST 1937
TO: COMMANDING OFFICER
US MARINE BARRACKS
US NAVY YARD PHILA PENNA
INFO: COMMANDING OFFICER

US MARINE CORPS RECRUIT DEPOT
PARRIS ISLAND SC

1. THE FOLLOWING IS TO BE RELAYED TO PFC JOSEPH L. HOWARD, AND SUITABLE NOTATION MADE IN HIS SERVICE RECORD: "REFERENCE YOUR WINNING 1937 NEW JERSEY STATE RIFLE MATCH. WELL DONE. THOMAS HOLCOMB MAJOR GENERAL COMMANDANT."

2. YOU ARE DIRECTED TO ISSUE NECESSARY ORDERS TRANSFERRING PFC HOWARD TO US MARINE CORPS RECRUIT DEPOT PARRIS ISLAND SC FOR DUTY AS RIFLE INSTRUCTOR. PFC HOWARD IS TO BE ENCOURAGED TO TRY OUT FOR USMC RIFLE TEAM.

BY DIRECTION OF THE MAJOR GENERAL COMMANDANT:

S. T. KRALIK, LT COL USMC

When he had graduated from Boot Camp at Parris Island, Joe Howard had devoutly hoped he would never again see the place. While he was willing to grant that he had come to Parris Island a candy-ass civilian and had left at least looking and thinking vaguely like a Marine, he had painful and bitter memories of the place and of his drill instructors.

It was different, of course, when he went back, but he still didn't like the place.

He ran into one of his drill sergeants at the gas station, and was surprisingly disappointed when the sergeant told him that he didn't remember him at all. And he was equally surprised to realize that not only did the drill sergeant not look as mean and salty as he had in his memory, but that he was in fact not nearly as sharp looking as some Marines Joe had come to know later. He was just an average Marine, doing his job.

Howard didn't get along too well, at least at first, with the other guys teaching basic marksmanship or the ones on the rifle team. He came to understand that was because he hadn't followed the established route to the Weapons Committee. They were supposed to select you; he had been thrust upon them by the Major General Commandant.

It got better after he qualified for the Marine Corps Rifle Team, and even better when he shot third overall at the National Matches at Camp Perry, Ohio, in the summer of 1938. And in September of 1938, he came out number three on the list for promotion to corporal. He had made it less than a year after shipping over, and a year before Gunny MacFarland had bullshitted him he might make it.

Almost as soon as he'd sewed his chevrons on, he started trying to think of some way to get out of Parris Island. He applied for transfer to the 4th Marines in China, and was turned down. He could, they said, enlist for the 4th Marines the next time he shipped over, but right now the Corps wanted him at Parris Island, teaching recruits how to shoot.

Then, out of the blue, he found himself at the U.S. Army Infantry Center at Fort Benning, Georgia. The Army Ordnance Corps had come up with a new rifle, the M-1, known as the Garand after the man who had invented it. It was self-loading, which meant that it was almost automatic. It used the forces of recoil to extract the fired cartridge from the chamber and then to load a fresh one from the magazine. The magazine held eight rounds. The Marines were invited to participate in the service test of the weapon, and they sent a provisional platoon to Fort Benning in charge of a master gunnery sergeant named Jack NMI (No Middle Initial) Stecker from the U.S. Marine Corps Schools base at Quantico.

A third of the platoon were taken from regular Marine units; a third came right out of boot camp; and the final third were people recognized to be outstanding marksmen. Corporal Joe Howard had been assigned to this last group.

Master Gunnery Sergeant Jack NMI Stecker had won the Medal of Honor in France in 1918, and was something of a legend in the Corps. Joe figured that probably had something to do with his being put in charge of the Fort Benning detail; it looked like a good detail, the sort of detail a man would be given who was entitled to wear the blue ribbon with the silver stars sprinkled on it.

When Corporal Joe Howard reported to Gunny Stecker, he was surprised to see that Stecker was not wearing his Medal of Honor ribbon. The only things pinned to his blouse were his marksmanship medals. Not surprisingly, he was Expert in every small-arms weapon used by the Corps. Joe later found out, not from Stecker, that Stecker had taken High Overall at Camp Perry in 1933 and 1936; he was a world-class rifleman.

But Master Gunnery Sergeant Stecker was more than just impressive. Best of all, he got Corporal Howard out of Parris Island. A couple of days before they left Fort Benning, Stecker called him in and asked him what he thought of the M-1 Garand.

It was almost holy writ in the Corps that the finest, most accurate rifle ever made was the '03 Springfield. Even among the expert riflemen who had fired the Garand at Benning, the weapon was known as a Mickey Mouse piece the Army had dreamed up; it would never come close to being as good a rifle as the '03.

But Joe Howard had come to believe that the Garand was a fine weapon even off the shelf, and that with some fine-tuning by an armorer it would be capable of greater accuracy than the '03. He told Gunny Stecker just that.

"That makes it you and me against the Marine Corps, son," Gunny Stecker replied. "You happy at Parris Island?"

Joe told him the truth about that, too: he didn't like what was generally considered to be a great berth for a brand-new, very young corporal—as opposed, say, to being in a Marine detachment on a man-of-war, or in a line company in a regiment somewhere—and he had been trying to get out of it.

"Would you be interested in coming to Quantico and working on the Garand? The basic detail would be teaching riflery to kids in the Basic Officer Course, and college kids who come for training in the summer. But when you're not doing that, there would be time to work on the Garand."

"I'd love it, Gunny," Joe replied. "But they won't let me go from Parris Island."

"Why not?"

Joe told him about his getting sent there by the Major General Commandant.

"I'll see what I can do," Stecker said.

Two weeks after he reported back into Parris Island, Joe was put on orders to U.S. Marine Corps Schools, Quantico, Virginia.

The next year was good duty. Aside from maybe once a month catching Corporal of the Guard, and maybe once every other month catching Junior Charge of Quarters at Headquarters, Marine Corps Schools, Joe Howard was subject to no other details.

He was either teaching brand-new officers how to fire the '03, which he liked, or running people through the Annual Rifle Firing; but that didn't take all that much time. There was plenty of time to see what could be done with the Garand.

Putting several thousand rounds through M-1s taught him what was basically wrong with the weapon, and how to fix it. The primary problem was the barrel. When it was heated up by firing, it expanded and jammed into the stock. The result was that in rapid fire the later rounds through it (the twentieth, say) would strike a couple of inches—sometimes much more—from where the first round had struck.

The fix for that was to make the barrel free-floating. You had to carefully whittle wood away from the inside of the stock so that the barrel didn't get bent by the stock when it heated up.

The sights left a little to be desired, too. Joe learned to fix that by machining from scratch a new rear sight aperture, or "peep sight hole," that was smaller than the original, and by taking a couple of thousandths of an inch off the front sight. He also did some work on the gears that moved the rear sight horizontally and vertically, smoothing them out, making them more precise. And he tinkered with the trigger group, smoothing the sear so the let-off could be better controlled, and with the action itself, smoothing it to improve functioning. In the process, he learned where and how much lubricant was required. Finally, he mated barrels which had demonstrated unusual accuracy to his specially worked-over actions and trigger groups.

There were soon a half-dozen M-1s in the Arms Room just as accurate as any Star Gauge Springfield. One of these was informally reserved for Corporal Howard, and one other for Master Gunnery Sergeant Jack NMI Stecker.

Joe Howard made a nice little piece of change that year proving to visiting riflemen during informal sessions on the range that the M-1 Garand wasn't really the Mickey Mouse Army piece of shit everybody said it was.

And three times Gunny Stecker had handed him money—once ninety dollars—which the Gunny said was his fair share of what he had taken away from visiting master gunnery sergeants and sergeants major who also had an unfounded faith in the all-around superiority of the Springfield, and who were foolish enough to put their money where their mouths were. A Garand fine-tuned by Corporal Joe Howard, in the hands of a marksman like Gunny Stecker, was hard to beat.

In the late summer of 1940, after France had fallen to the Germans and Congress had authorized the first of what were to be many expansions of the Corps, there were a flock of promotions—promotions that came to many men long before they thought they had any chance of getting them. Joe Howard became a sergeant then. Six months later, a veteran ordnance sergeant assigned to the just-formed 1st Defense Battalion at the Navy Base at Pearl Harbor, Territory of Hawaii, became terminally ill. Soon afterward, someone in personnel remembered that Master Gunnery Sergeant Jack NMI Stecker at Quantico had a really bright and competent ordnance buck sergeant working for him.

That the kid had worked for Gunny Stecker for two years, and been promoted during that time, was all-around recommendation enough; people who didn't measure up to Gunny Stecker's high standards didn't get promoted, they got themselves shipped someplace else. On the same order that Headquarters U.S. Marine Corps ordered Sergeant Joseph L. Howard to the 1st Defense Battalion at Pearl, it promoted him to staff sergeant.

When the Japanese attack began, even as he listened to the sound of exploding bombs and the roar of low-flying aircraft, it was very difficult for Joe Howard to accept that what was happening *actually* was happening.

He had been conditioned to regard Pearl Harbor as America's mighty—and impregnable—fortress in the Pacific. In his view, if war came, the Japanese would probably attack Wake Island and Guam, and some of the other islands, and maybe even (Joe thought this highly unlikely) the Philippines. But Hawaii? Never. Not with Pearl Harbor and its row of dreadnought battleships, and its cruisers and aircraft carriers. And with the Army Air Corps fighters and bombers, not to mention the Navy and Marine Corps fighters and torpedo bombers afloat and ashore.

No goddamn way!

If the Japs were really stupid enough to try, say, invading Guam, Pearl would be the fortress from which the mightiest naval force the world had ever known would sail (carrying a Marine landing force aboard, of course) to bloody the Japs' noses and send the little bastards back to their rice paddies and raw fish with a lesson they wouldn't soon forget.

But, incredibly, when he looked out his barracks window, there was smoke rising from Battleship Row, and the sound of heavy explosions, and the same thing over at the seaplane base. And finally, when he saw a dozen Japanese aircraft in perfect formation—four three-plane vees—making low-level torpedo and strafing runs against Battleship Row, he realized that the impossible was indeed happening.

He couldn't do a goddamned thing to help the battleships, but he damned sure could do something at the seaplane hangars, where there were Marine-manned .50-caliber water-cooled Browning machine guns on antiaircraft mounts.

Because access to ammunition and the fully automatic weapons was limited to commissioned officers, he wasn't supposed to have a key to the arms locker, but he did; he was a good Marine Sergeant and knew which regulations should be violated. He went to the ammo locker and opened it up. By the time the first Marines came for ammo for the .50s, and to draw Browning Automatic Rifles and air-cooled .30-caliber Browning machine guns, and ammo for them, he was ready for them—long before the first officer showed up.

When an officer finally came and saw that most of the weapons and ammo had already been issued, he didn't ask any questions about how come the locker was open. Joe Howard didn't think that he would.

With nothing to do at the ammo locker, the officer went off to make himself useful somewhere else. That left Joe there alone with nothing to do either. After thinking about it a moment, he decided he couldn't just sit this goddamned attack out in an ammo bunker; so he took the last BAR and eight twenty-round magazines for it and ran outside.

A Ford ton-and-a-half truck came racing up with a buck sergeant driving and a PFC in the cab beside him.

"Have you got any belted fifty?" the buck sergeant demanded. "I can't get in our goddamned locker!"

"Come on!" Joe said, turning back toward the locker to show him where it was.

And then he looked over his shoulder to see if the sergeant was following him.

The sergeant was still sitting behind the wheel, but the top of his head was gone, and the windshield and the inside of the truck were smeared with a mass of blood and brain tissue.

Staff Sergeant Howard threw up.

Then he ran to the truck, grabbed the handle, pulled the door open, and dragged the buck sergeant's body out onto the ground. Blood spurted from somewhere and soaked Joe Howard's T-shirt and trousers.

After that he looked into the truck cab. The PFC was slumped in the seat, his head wedged back against the cushion, his eyes wide open but unseeing, his chest ripped open, blood streaming from the wound.

Joe Howard leaned against the truck fender and threw up again and again, until there was nothing in his stomach and all that came was a foul green bile.

And then he went back into the arms locker and huddled behind the counter, shaking, curled up, with his arms around his knees. He stayed there for he didn't know how long, except that when he finally came out, the attack was over, and the Ford ton-and-a-half had somehow caught on fire and burned, and the PFC inside was nothing but a charred lump of dead meat.

(TWO)
Oahu Island, Territory of Hawaii
0845 Hours 7 December 1941

Technical Sergeant Charles M. Galloway, USMC, a good-looking, slim, deeply tanned, and brown-haired young man of twenty-five, lay naked on his back, his head propped up with pillows, in a somewhat battered but sturdy and comfortable bed in one of the two bedrooms of a hunting lodge in the mountains.

He had a Chesterfield cigarette in one hand. The other hand was wrapped around a large glass of pineapple juice, liberally laced with Gordon's London Dry Gin.

Ensign Mary Agnes O'Malley, Nurse Corps, USN, a slim, five-foot-four-inch, red-haired, pert-breasted woman, similarly undressed, knelt on the bed, about to begin another game of what she called "ice cream cone." This involved the dribbling of creme de cacao on certain portions of the body, and then removing it with the tongue. Until the previous day, Charley Galloway had never heard of—or even, in his sometimes wild fantasies, thought about—the kind of thing she was doing; but he was learning to like it.

The other bedroom of the hunting lodge, which was actually a simple, tin-roofed frame cabin, was occupied by Technical Sergeant Stefan "Big Steve" Oblensky, USMC, and Lieutenant Florence Kocharski, Nurse Corps, USN.

Big Steve, who was Polish and in his forties, was a great bull of a man. But Lieutenant Kocharski was big enough to be a match for him, which is to say that she was Valkyrie-like, in her late thirties, and also Polish. Several months before, she'd been attracted to Big Steve when she'd met him at the Naval Hospital at Pearl Harbor. He'd come in for his annual physical examination, and the examination had kind of expanded and become *more* physical.

And vice versa. So strongly that the two of them had chosen to ignore the cultural and, more important, the legal prohibition against socialization between commissioned and enlisted members of the Naval Service.

Florence Kocharski was a full lieutenant, about to make lieutenant commander; Big Steve expected to make master sergeant any day. Both of them had been around the service long enough to know about keeping indiscretions a hundred miles from the flagpole. A hundred miles was an impossibility on Oahu, but a hunting cabin in the hills was a reasonable approximation. (It was owned by an old pal of Big Steve's who had retired and gone to work for Dole.)

But to get to the cabin required an automobile. Lieutenant Florence Kocharski didn't have one, and Big Steve Oblensky was six months away from getting his driver's license back, after having been caught driving drunk. But not to worry: T/Sgt. Charley Galloway had a lovingly maintained yellow 1933 Ford V-8 convertible. Big Steve had been able to borrow Charley's car without any trouble the first time. He and Charley both knew that Big Steve would return the favor somewhere down the pike.

But the second weekend Big Steve asked to borrow the Ford, he had to tell Charley why he wanted it. And Charley Galloway asked if Big Steve's nurse had a friend.

"Jesus Christ, Charley! I can't ask her nothing like that! Be a pal."

"You ask her, she says no, then I'll be a pal. But you ask her."

To Big Steve's surprise, Flo Kocharski was neither outraged nor astonished when, with remarkable delicacy, Big Steve brought the subject up.

Ensign Mary Agnes O'Malley, Lieutenant Kocharski's roommate, had already noticed T/Sgt. Charles Galloway at the wheel of his yellow Ford convertible and asked her about him. She'd asked specifically about how he came to have pilot's wings. Ensign O'Malley had just recently entered the Navy and had not known that enlisted men could be pilots.

There was a small corps of enlisted pilots, Lieutenant Kocharski explained to her. These were officially called Naval Aviation Pilots, but more commonly "flying sergeants." T/Sgt. Charles Galloway was one of them. He was a fighter pilot of VMF-211, where her Stefan was the NCO in charge of Aircraft Maintenance.

"He's darling," Ensign O'Malley replied.

Lieutenant Kocharski didn't think "darling" was the right word, but Charley Galloway *was* a good-looking kid, and she was not surprised that Mary Agnes O'Malley found him attractive.

Lieutenant Kocharski ended the conversation on that particular note—to protect young Sergeant Galloway from Ensign O'Malley. Ensign O'Malley was not a bright-eyed innocent. She had entered the Navy late, at thirty-three, rather than right out of nursing school, which was usually the case. Florence, naturally curious, had in time wormed her history out of her.

Before she joined the Navy, Ensign Mary Agnes O'Malley had been a nun, a nursing sister of the Sisters of Mercy. She had become a postulant in the order at sixteen. And she had served faithfully and well for many years after that. First she became a registered nurse, and later she qualified as both an operating-room nurse and a nurse anesthesiologist. Later still, she was seduced by a married anesthesiologist, an M.D., while taking an advanced course at Massachusetts General Hospital.

She didn't blame the doctor, Mary Agnes told Florence. She had not been wearing her Sisters of Mercy habit at Mass General, and she had not told the doctor, ever, that she was a nun. But once she had tasted the forbidden fruit, she realized that she could no longer adhere to a vow of chastity, and petitioned the Vatican for release from her vows.

The Navy was then actively recruiting nurses, and she was highly qualified, so she signed on.

In the four months she had known her, Flo had come to understand that beneath Mary Agnes O'Malley's demure and modest façade, there lurked a predator with the morals of an alley cat. Mary Agnes frankly admitted, in confidence, that she was making up for lost time.

So when Big Steve came to her about Charley Galloway, Flo Kocharski felt a certain uneasiness about turning Mary Agnes loose on him. Charley was a really nice kid. On the other hand, if he hadn't leaned on Stefan to get himself fixed up as the price of borrowing his car, she wouldn't have had to.

What neither Flo nor Big Steve knew, or even remotely suspected, was that Charley Galloway was far less experienced in relations between the sexes than anyone who knew him would have suspected. During their first night together in the cabin, Mary Alice quickly and delightfully learned that Charley was the antithesis of jaded. Yet not even she suspected that the first time in his twenty-five years Charley had spent the whole night with a woman was that very same night.

Charley's sexual drives—and sometimes he thought he was cursed with an overgenerous issue of them—were flagrantly heterosexual. Neither was he troubled with any religious or moral restraints. His fantasies were about equally divided between the normal—meeting a well-stacked nymphomaniac whose father owned a liquor store—and meeting a nice, respectable girl and getting married.

He had encountered neither in his eight years in the Corps.

And there was something else: he didn't want to fuck up. The price would be too high. The most important thing in the world, during his first few years in the Corps, had been to work his way up to the point where the Corps would send him to Pensacola and teach him how to fly.

Catching a dose of the clap, or maybe just getting hauled in by the military police in one of their random raids on a whorehouse, would have kept him from getting promoted and getting sent to flight school. And once he'd made staff sergeant and won a berth at Pensacola and then his wings, just about the same restrictions had applied.

Naval Aviation Pilots were *non*commissioned officers, in other words, enlisted men. Since Aviation was set up with a general understanding that pilots would be commissioned officers and gentlemen, the Marine Corps had never really figured out how to deal with noncom fliers.

Enlisted pilots had crept into the system back in the 1920s. The three originals had been aircraft mechanics who had learned how to fly on the job during the Marine intervention in Santo Domingo. The criterion for selection of pilots then, as Charley had heard it, and as he believed, was "anyone who was demonstrably unlikely to crash a nonreplaceable airplane."

The Marine commander in Santo Domingo had looked at his brand-new, fresh-from-flight-school commissioned pilots and then at his experienced sergeants, and had decided that the very, very nonreplaceable airplanes at his disposal were better off being flown by the sergeants, whether they were officially rated or not.

The second reason for the existence of "flying sergeants" was money. In the years between the wars, Congress had been parsimonious toward the armed services, and especially toward the Corps. Officer manning levels were cast in concrete. This meant that every enlisted Naval Aviation Pilot freed up an officer billet for use elsewhere. And, of course, flying sergeants were paid less than officers.

Charley Galloway had started out as an aviation mechanic, right out of Parris Island, when he was seventeen. Three years later, a space for an NAP had unexpectedly opened at Pensacola, and he was the only qualified body around to fill it. On the other hand, he was an enlisted man. Most Naval Aviators (Marine pilots were all Naval Aviators) were commissioned officers and gentlemen, and many of them were graduates of the United States Naval Academy at Annapolis.

There was an enormous social chasm between commissioned officers and gentlemen and noncommissioned officers, who were, under law, *men,* and not *gentlemen.* There was also resentment from the other direction toward flying sergeants from sergeants who didn't fly and who thus didn't get extra pay for what looked to them like a cushy berth.

Charley Galloway soon learned that about the only people who didn't think Naval Aviation Pilots were an all-around pain in the ass were fellow pilots, who judged NAPs by their flying ability. As a rule of thumb, NAPs were, if anything, slightly more proficient than their commissioned counterparts. In the first place, most of them were older and more experienced than Charley. And most of them had large blocks of bootleg time before they went to Pensacola to learn how to fly officially.

Charley had developed a good relationship with the pilots of VMF-211 (Marine

Fighter Squadron 211), based on his reputation both as a pilot and a responsible noncom. That would go down the toilet in an instant if he came down with a dose of the clap, or got caught visiting a whorehouse or screwing somebody's willing wife. They would take his wings away and he wouldn't fly anymore. It looked to him like a choice between flying and fucking, and flying won hands down.

But since Friday night, when they'd picked up Big Steve's nurse and her roommate in Honolulu, there seemed to be convincing evidence that he could accomplish both.

"Ouch!" Technical Sergeant Charles M. Galloway yelped. "Jesus Christ!"

"Sorry," Ensign Mary Agnes O'Malley said contritely. "The last thing in the world I want to do is *hurt* it." She looked up at him and smiled. She kissed it. "All better!" she said.

She straddled him.

The door burst open.

Big Steve stood there in his skivvy shorts, a strange look on his face.

"Get the hell out of here!" Charley flared.

"Well, really! Don't people knock where you come from, for Christ's sake?" Mary Agnes O'Malley snapped.

"The Japs are bombing Pearl Harbor," Big Steve said. "It just come over the radio."

"I heard the engines," Charley said. "I thought it was those Air Corps B-17s."

Charley Galloway sat up, and dislodged Mary Agnes.

How the hell am I going to fly? he thought. *I've been drinking all night.*

And then he had another thought.

I'll be a sonofabitch! I should have known that the first time I ever got to have a steady piece of ass, something would come along to fuck it up.

(THREE)
Marine Airfield
Ewa, Oahu Island, Territory of Hawaii
7 December 1941

While everybody else on December 7 was running around Ewa—and for that matter, the Hawaiian Islands—like chickens with their heads cut off, Technical Sergeants Charley Galloway and Stefan "Big Steve" Oblensky had gone to Captain Leonard J. Martin, the ranking officer on the scene, and asked for permission to take a half-dozen men and try to salvage what they could from the carnage of the flight line and the mess in the hangars.

The reason they had to ask permission, rather than just doing what Captain Martin thought was the logical thing to do in the circumstances, was that some moron in CINCPAC (Commander-in-Chief, Pacific Fleet) at Pearl Harbor had issued an order that aviation units that had lost their aircraft would immediately re-form and prepare to fight as infantry.

Captain Martin had no doubt that the order applied to VMF-211. After the Japanese had bombed and strafed Ewa, VMF-211 had zero flyable aircraft. And it was possible, if not very likely, that the Japanese would invade Oahu, in which case every man who could carry a rifle would indeed be needed as an infantryman.

But it was unlikely, in Captain Martin's judgment, that infantrymen would be needed that afternoon. In the meantime, it just made good sense to salvage anything that could be salvaged. Captain Martin had been a Marine long enough to believe that replacement aircraft and spare parts—or, for that matter, replacement mess-kit spoons—would be issued to VMF-211 only after the Navy was sure that aircraft, spare parts, and mess-kit spoons were not needed anywhere else in the Navy.

It made much more sense to have Galloway and Big Steve try to salvage what they could than to have them forming as infantry. Even if he was absolutely wrong, and Japanese infantry were suddenly to appear, there was nothing Galloway and Oblensky could be taught about infantry in the next couple of days that they already didn't know. They were technical sergeants, the second-highest enlisted grade in the Corps, and you didn't get to be a tech sergeant in the Corps unless you knew all about small arms and small-unit infantry tactics.

And there was a question of morale, too. Big Steve, and especially Charley Galloway, felt guilty—more than guilty, ashamed—about what had happened to VMF-211. Their guilt was unreasonable, but Martin understood their feelings. For one thing, they hadn't been at Ewa when it happened. And by the time they got to Ewa, it was all over. *Really* all over; even the fires were out and the wounded evacuated.

Captain Martin knew, unofficially, where Big Steve and Galloway were when the Japanese struck. So he didn't have much trouble reading what was behind their eyes when they finally got back to Ewa, still accompanied by their nurse "friends," and saw the destroyed aircraft and the blanket-wrapped bodies of their buddies on the stretchers.

If we had been here, we could have done something!

Captain Martin agreed with them. And, he further reasoned, they had to do something that had meaning. Practicing to repel boarders as infantrymen would be pure bullshit to good, experienced Marine tech sergeants.

So Captain Martin told them to go ahead, and to take as many men as they could reasonably use. If they ran into any static, they were to shoot the problem up to him.

What Technical Sergeants Galloway and Oblensky had not told Captain Martin was that they had already examined the carnage and decided that they could make at least one flyable F4F-4 by salvaging the necessary parts from partially destroyed aircraft and mating them with other not completely destroyed machines.

It was a practical, professional judgment. T/Sgt. Big Steve Oblensky had been an aircraft mechanic as far back as Santo Domingo and Nicaragua, and T/Sgt. Charley Galloway had been a mechanic before he'd gone to flight school.

By sunset, Captain Martin saw that they had found tenting somewhere, erected a makeshift, reasonably lightproof work bay, and moved one of the least damaged F4F-4s into it. Over the next week they cannibalized parts from other wrecks. Then there was the sound of air compressors and the bright flame of welding torches; and finally the sound of the twelve hundred horses of a Pratt & Whitney R-1830 Twin Wasp being run up.

But Captain Martin was surprised to discover what Big Steve and Charley had salvaged. By December 15, the engine he had heard run up was attached to a patched-together but complete and flyable F4F-4 Wildcat fuselage.

"That doesn't exist, you know," Captain Martin said. "All the aircraft on the station have been surveyed and found to be destroyed."

"I want to take it out to the *Saratoga,*" Charley Galloway said.

"Sara's in 'Dago, Galloway," Captain Martin said. "What are you talking about?"

"Sara's in Pearl. Sometime today, she's going to put out to reinforce Wake. Sara, and the *Astoria* and the *Minneapolis* and the *San Francisco.* And the 4th Defense Battalion, on board the *Tangier.* They're calling it Task Force 14."

Martin hadn't heard about that, at least in such detail, but there was no doubt that Galloway and Oblensky knew what they were talking about. Old-time sergeants had their own channels of information.

"That airplane can't be flown until it's been surveyed again and taken through an inspection."

"Skipper, if we did that, the Navy would take it away from us," Oblensky argued. "The squadron is down to two planes on Wake. They need that airplane."

"If Sara is sailing today, there's just no time to get permission for something like that."

"So we do it without permission," Galloway said. "What are they going to do if I show up over her? Order me home?"

"And what if you can't find her?"

"I'll find her," Galloway said flatly.

"If you can't?" Martin repeated.

"If I have to sit her down in the ocean, the squadron's no worse off than it is now," Galloway said, with a quiet passion. "Captain, we've got to do something."

"I can't give you permission to do something like that," Martin said. "Christ, *I* would wind up in Portsmouth. It's crazy, and you know it."

"Yes, Sir," Oblensky said, and a moment later Galloway parroted him.

"But, just as a matter of general information," Captain Martin added, "I've got business at Pearl in the morning, and I won't be able to get back here before 0930 or so."

He had seen in their eyes that both had realized further argument was useless. And, more important, that they had just dismissed his objections as irrelevant. Charles Galloway was going to take that F4F-4 Wildcat off from Ewa in the morning, come hell or high water.

"Thank you, Sir."

"Good luck, Galloway," Captain Martin said, and walked away.

(FOUR)
Above USS *Saratoga* (CV.3)
Task Force 14
0620 Hours 16 December 1941

A moment after Charley Galloway spotted the *Saratoga* five thousand feet below him, she began to turn into the wind. They had spotted the Wildcat, and her captain had issued the order, "Prepare to recover aircraft."

By that time Sara knew he was coming. Ten minutes after Galloway took off from Ewa, the Navy was informed he was on the way, and was asked to relay that information to the *Saratoga.* A Navy captain, reflecting that a week before, such idiocy, such blatant disregard for standing orders and flight safety, would have seen those involved thrown out of the service—most likely via the Navy prison at Portsmouth—decided that this wasn't a week ago, it was now, after the Pacific

Fleet had suffered a disaster, and he ordered a coded message sent to the *Saratoga* to be on the lookout for a Marine F4F-4 believed attempting a rendezvous.

As the *Saratoga* turned, so did her screening force, the other ships of Task Force 14. They were the cruisers *Minneapolis, Astoria,* and *San Francisco;* nine destroyers; the *Neches,* a fleet oiler; and the USS *Tangier,* a seaplane tender pressed into service as a transport. They had put out from Pearl Harbor at 1600 the previous day.

Charley retarded his throttle, banked slightly, and pushed the nose of the Wildcat down.

He thought, *That's a bunch of ships and a lot of people making all that effort to recover just one man and one airplane.*

He dropped his eyes to the fuel quantity gauge mounted on the left of the control panel and did the mental arithmetic. He had thirty-five minutes of fuel remaining, give or take a couple of minutes. It was now academic, of course, because he had found Task Force 14 on time and where he believed it would be, but he could not completely dismiss the thought that if he hadn't found it, thirty minutes from now, give or take a few, he would have been floating around on a rubber raft all alone on the wide Pacific. Presuming he could have set it down on the water without killing himself.

By the time he was down to fifteen hundred feet over the smooth, dark blue Pacific, and headed straight for the *Saratoga*'s bow, she had completed her turn into the wind. Galloway looked down at her deck and saw that she was indeed ready to receive him. He could see faces looking up at him, and he could see that the cables had been raised. And when he glanced at her stern, he could see the Landing Control Officer, his paddles already in hand, waiting to guide him aboard.

He started to lower his landing gear.

He did not do so in strict accordance with Paragraph 19.a.(1) of AN 01-190FB-1, which was the U.S. Navy Bureau of Aeronautics *Pilot's Handbook of Flight Operating Instructions for F4F-Series Aircraft.* Paragraph 19.a.(1), which Charley Galloway knew by heart, said, "Crank down the landing gear." Then came a CAUTION: "Be sure the landing gear is fully down."

The landing gear on the Wildcat, the newest and hottest and most modern fighter aircraft in the Navy's (and thus the Marine Corps') arsenal, had to be cranked up and down by hand. There was a crank on the right side of the cockpit. It had to be turned no less than twenty-nine times either to release or retract the gear. The mechanical advantage was not great, and to turn it at all, the pilot had to take his right hand from the stick and fly with his left hand while he cranked hard, twenty-nine times, with his right hand.

Charley Galloway had learned early on—he had become a Naval Aviator three days after he turned twenty-one—that there wasn't room in the cockpit for anyone to come along and see how closely you followed regulations.

The records of VMF-211 indicated that Charles M. Galloway was currently qualified in F2A-3, F4F-4, R4D, and PBY-5 and PBY-5A aircraft.

The R4D was the Navy version of the Douglas DC-3, a twin-engined, twenty-one passenger transport, and the PBY-5 was the Consolidated Catalina, a twin-engined seaplane that had started out as sort of a bomber and was now primarily used as a long-range observation and antisubmarine aircraft. The PBY-5A was the amphibian version of the PBY-5; retractable gear had been fitted to it.

The Marine Corps had no R4D and PBY-5 aircraft assigned to it; Charley Galloway had learned to fly them when he and some other Marine pilots had been borrowed from the Corps to help the Navy test them, get them ready for service, and ferry them from the factories to their squadrons. He had picked up a lot of time in the R4D, even going through an Army Air Corps course on how to use it to drop parachutists.

He was therefore, in his judgment, a good and experienced aviator, with close to two thousand hours total time, ten times as much as some of the second lieutenants who had just joined VMF-211 as replacements. He was also, in his own somewhat immodest and so far untested opinion, one hell of a fighter pilot, who had figured out a way to get the goddamned gear down without cranking the goddamned handle until you were blue in the face.

It involved the physical principle that an object in motion tends to remain in motion, absent restricting forces.

Charley had learned that if he unlocked the landing gear, then put the Wildcat in a sharp turn, the gear would attempt to continue in the direction it had been going. Phrased simply, when he put the Wildcat in a sharp turn, the landing-gear crank would spin madly of its own volition, and when it was finished spinning, the gear would be down. All you had to do was lock it down. And, of course, remember to keep your hand and arm out of the way of the spinning crank.

He did so now. The crank spun, the gear went down, and he locked it in place.

Then, from memory, he went through the landing check-off list: he unlocked the tail wheel; he lowered and locked the arresting hook, which, if things went well, would catch one of several cables stretched across the deck of the *Saratoga* and bring him to a safe but abrupt halt.

He pulled his goggles down from where they had been resting on the leather helmet, and then slid open and locked the over-the-cockpit canopy.

He pushed the carburetor air control all the way in to the Direct position, retarded the throttle, and set the propeller governor for 2100 rpm. He set the mixture control into Auto Rich, opened the cowl flaps, and lowered the wing flaps.

All the time he was doing this, he was turning on his final approach, that is to say, lining himself up with the deck of the *Saratoga.*

The Landing Control Officer was ready for him. Using his paddles, he signaled to Charley Galloway that he was just a hair to the right of a desirable landing path. Then, at the last moment, he made his decision, and signaled Charley to bring it in and set it down.

Charley's arresting hook caught the first cable, and the Wildcat was jerked to a sudden halt with a force that was always astonishing. Whenever he made a carrier landing, Charley Galloway felt an enormous sense of relief, and then, despite a genuine effort to restrain it, a feeling of smug accomplishment. Ships and airplanes were different creatures. They were not intended to mate on the high seas. But he had just done exactly that. Again. This made Carrier Landing Number Two Hundred and Six.

And there weren't very many people in the whole wide world who could do that even once.

As the white hats rushed up to disengage the cable, he quickly went through the "Stopping the Engine" checklist, again from memory.

By the time the propeller stopped turning and he had shut off the ignition, battery, and fuel selector switches, a plane captain was there to help him get out of the cockpit. And he saw Major Verne J. McCaul, USMC, Commanding Officer of VMF-221, standing on the deck, smiling at him. VMF-221, equipped with fourteen F2A-3 Brewster Buffalos, was stationed aboard the *Saratoga.* Galloway had known him for some time, liked him, and was glad to see him.

Charley jumped off the wing root and walked to him.

"I am delighted," said Major McCaul, who was thirty-five and looked younger, "nay, *overjoyed* to see you."

Galloway looked at him suspiciously.

"The odds were four to one you'd never make it out here," McCaul said. "I took a hundred bucks' worth at those odds, twenty-five of them for you."

"You knew I was coming?"

"There was a radio from Pearl about an hour ago," McCaul said.

Apparently it didn't say "arrest on sight," or there would be a Marine with irons waiting for me.

"Well, that certainly was very nice of you, Sir," Galloway said, not absolutely sure that McCaul wasn't pulling his leg. Proof that he was not came when McCaul handed him five twenty-dollar bills.

It then occurred to him that he had, literally, jumped from the frying pan into the fire. He had made it this far. But the next stop was Wake Island. The odds, bullshit aside, that Wake could be held against the Japanese seemed pretty remote. He had no good reason to presume that he would be any better a pilot, or any luckier, than the pilots of VFM-211 on Wake who had already been shot down.

Then he remembered what Big Steve Oblensky had once told him. The function of Marines was to stop bullets for civilians; that's what they were really paying you for.

"The Captain wants to see you after you're cleaned up," Major McCaul said. "In the meantime, I'm sorry to have to tell you, you're to consider yourself under arrest."

"Am I in trouble that deep, Major?"

"I'm afraid so, Charley. The Navy's really pissed," Major McCaul said. "I'll do what I can for you, but . . . they're *really* pissed."

"Oh, hell," Charley said. And then, not too convincingly, he smiled. "Well, what the hell, Major. What can they do to me? Send me to Wake Island?"

II

(ONE)
Washington, D.C.
19 December 1941

As his taxi drove past the White House, Fleming Pickering, a tall, handsome, superbly tailored man in his early forties, noticed steel-helmeted soldiers, armed with rifles, bayonets fixed, guarding the gates.

He wondered if they were really necessary. Was there a real threat to the security of either the President or the building itself? Or were these guards being used for a little domestic propaganda, a symbol that the nation had been at war for not quite two weeks, and that the White House was now the headquarters of the Commander in Chief?

Certainly, he reasoned, even before what the President had so eloquently dubbed "a day that will live in infamy," the Secret Service and the White House police must have had contingency plans to protect the President in case of war. These would have called for more sophisticated measures than the posting of a corporal's guard of riflemen at the White House gates.

Fleming Pickering, Chairman of the Board of the Pacific & Far Eastern Shipping Corporation, was not an admirer of Franklin Delano Roosevelt, President of the United States. This was not to say that he did not respect him. Roosevelt was, he acknowledged, both a brilliant man and a consummate master of the art of molding public opinion.

Roosevelt had managed to garner public support for policies—Lend-Lease in particular—that were, in Pickering's judgment, not only disastrous and probably illegal, but which had, in the end, on the day of infamy, brought the United States into a war it probably could have stayed out of, and which it was pathetically ill-prepared to fight.

Fleming Pickering was considerably more aware than most Americans of what an absolute disaster Pearl Harbor had been. He and his wife had been in Honolulu when the Japanese struck. They had witnessed the burning and sinking battleships at the Navy Base, and the twisted, smoldering carnage at Hickam Field.

Despite his personal misgivings about Roosevelt, less than an hour after the last Japanese aircraft had left, as he watched the rescue and salvage operations, he had understood that the time to protest and oppose the President had passed, that it was clearly his—and everyone's—duty to rally around the Commander in Chief and make what contribution he could to the war effort.

Fleming Pickering had come to Washington to offer his services.

He had two additional thoughts as the taxi drove down Pennsylvania Avenue past the White House.

First, a feeling of sympathy for the soldiers standing there in the freezing cold in their steel helmets. A tin pot is a miserable sonofabitch to have to wear when it's cold and snowing and the wind is blowing. He knew that from experience.

Corporal Fleming Pickering, USMC, had worn one in the trenches in France in 1918.

And second, that with a little bit of luck, when the American people learned the hard way what that sonofabitch in the White House had gotten them into, he could be voted out of office in 1944. If there was still something called the United States of America in 1944.

The taxi, a DeSoto sedan painted yellow, turned off Pennsylvania Avenue, made a sharp U-turn, and pulled to the curb before the marquee of the Foster Lafayette Hotel. A doorman in a heavy overcoat liberally adorned with golden cords trotted out from the protection of his glass-walled guard post and pulled open the door.

"Well, hello, Mr. Pickering," he said, with a genuine smile. "It's nice to see you, Sir."

"Hello, Ken," Pickering said, offering his hand. "What do you think of the weather?"

Once out of the cab, he turned and handed the driver several dollar bills, indicating with his hand that he didn't want any change, and then walked quickly into the hotel and across the lobby to the reception desk.

There was a line, and he took his place in it. Four people were ahead of him. Finally it was his turn.

"May I help you, Sir?" the desk clerk asked, making it immediately plain to Fleming Pickering that the clerk had no idea who he was.

"My name is Fleming Pickering," he said. "I need a place to stay for a couple of days, maybe a week."

"Have you a reservation, Sir?"

Pickering shook his head. The desk clerk raised his hands in a gesture of helplessness.

"Without a reservation, Sir . . ."

"Is Mr. Telford in the house?"

"Why, yes, Sir, I believe he is."

"I wonder if you could tell him I'm here, please?"

Max Telford, resident manager of the Foster Lafayette Hotel, a short, pudgy, balding man wearing a frock coat, striped trousers, and a wing collar, appeared a moment later.

"We didn't expect you, Mr. Pickering," he said, offering his hand. "But you're very welcome, nonetheless."

"How are you, Max?" Pickering said, smiling. "I gather the house is full."

"Yes, indeed."

"What am I to do?" Pickering said. "I need a place to stay. Is there some Democrat we can evict?"

Telford chuckled. "I don't think we'll have to go that far. There's always room for you here, Mr. Pickering."

"Is Mrs. Fowler in town?"

"No, Sir. I believe she's in Florida."

"Then why don't I impose on the Senator?"

"I'm sure the Senator would be delighted," Telford said. He turned and took a key from the rack of cubbyholes. "I'll take you up."

"I know how to find it. Come up in a while, and we'll have a little liquid cheer."

"Why don't I send up a tray of hors d'oeuvres?"

"That would be nice. Give me fifteen minutes to take a shower. Thank you, Max."

Pickering took the key and walked to the bank of elevators.

Max Telford turned to the desk clerk.

"I know you haven't been with us long, Mr. Denny, but you *do* know, don't you, who owns this inn?"

"Yes, Sir. Mr. Foster. Mr. Andrew Foster."

"And you know that there are forty-one other Foster Hotels?"

"Yes, Sir."

"Well, for your general information, as you begin what we both hope will be a long and happy career with Foster Hotels, I think I should tell you that Mr. Andrew Foster has one child, a daughter, and that she is married to the chairman of the board of the Pacific & Far Eastern Shipping Corporation."

"The gentleman to whom you just gave the key to Senator Fowler's suite?" Mr. Denny asked, but it was more of a pained realization than a question.

"Correct. Mr. Fleming Pickering. Mr. Pickering and Senator Fowler are very close."

"I'm sorry, Mr. Telford, I just didn't know."

"That's why I'm telling you. There is one more thing. Until last week, we had a young Marine officer, a second lieutenant, in the house. His name is Malcolm Pickering. If he should ever appear at the desk here, looking for a room, which is a good possibility, I suggest that it would behoove you to treat him with the same consideration with which you would treat Mr. Foster himself; he is Mr. Foster's grandson, his only grandchild, and the heir apparent to the throne."

"I take your point, Sir," Mr. Denny said.

"Don't look so stricken," Telford said. "They're all very nice people. The boy, they call him "Pick,' worked two summers for me. Once as a sous-chef at the Foster Park in New York, and the other time as the bell captain at the Andrew Foster in San Francisco."

(TWO)
Washington, D.C.
1735 Hours 19 December 1941

When Senator Richardson S. Fowler walked in, Fleming Pickering was sitting on the wide, leather-upholstered sill of a window in the Senator's sitting room. A glass of whiskey was in Pickering's hand.

Senator Fowler's suite was six rooms on the corner of the eighth floor of the Foster Lafayette, overlooking the White House, which was almost directly across Pennsylvania Avenue from the hotel.

"I had them let me in," Fleming Pickering said. "I hope you don't mind. The house is full."

"Oh, don't be silly," Senator Fowler said automatically, and then, with real feeling, "Jesus, Flem, it's good to see you!"

Senator Fowler was more than a decade older than Fleming Pickering. He was getting portly, and his jowls were starting to grow rosy and to sag.

He looks more and more like a politician, Flem Pickering thought, aware that it was unkind. Years ago, as a very young man, Pickering had heard and immediately adopted as part of his personal philosophy an old and probably banal observation that to have friends, one must permit them to have one serious flaw. So far as Pickering was concerned, Richardson Fowler's flaw was that he was a politician, the Junior Senator from the Great State of California.

Flem Pickering had a habit of picking up trite and banal phrases and adopting them as his own, ofttimes verbatim, sometimes revising them. So far as he was concerned, Richardson Fowler was the exception to a phrase he had lifted from Will Rogers and altered. Will Rogers said he had never met a man he didn't like. Pickering's version was that—Richardson Fowler excepted—he had never met a politician he had liked.

He had tried and failed to understand what drove Fowler to seek public office. It certainly wasn't that he needed the work. Richardson Fowler had inherited from his father the *San Francisco Courier-Herald,* nine smaller newspapers, and six radio stations. His wife and her brother owned, it was said, more or less accurately, two square blocks of downtown San Francisco, plus several million acres of timberland in Washington and Oregon.

If Fowler was consumed by some desire to do good, to lead people in this direction or that, it seemed to Pickering that the newspapers and the radio stations gave Fowler the means to accomplish it. He didn't have to run for office—with all that meant—for the privilege of coming east to the hot, muggy, provincial, small Southern town that was the nation's capital, to consort with a depressing collection of failed lawyers and other scoundrels.

But, oh, Flem Pickering, he thought, *what a hypocrite you are! Right now you are delighted to have access to a man with the political clout you pretend to scorn.*

Senator Fowler dropped his heavy, battered, well-filled briefcase at his feet and crossed the room to Pickering. They shook hands, and then the Senator put his arm around the younger man's shoulders and hugged him.

"I was worried about you, you bastard," he said. "You and Patricia. She here with you?"

"She's in San Francisco," Pickering said. "She's fine."

"And Pick?"

"He's at Pensacola, learning how to fly," Pickering said. "I thought you knew."

"I knew he was going down there," the Senator said. "I had dinner with him, oh, six days, a week ago. But he never came to say good-bye to me."

There was disappointment, perhaps even a little resentment, in his voice. Senator Fowler had known Pick Pickering from the day he was born.

"If you were a second lieutenant and they gave you two days off, would you spend them seeing an aging uncle-politician, or trying to get laid?" Pickering asked with a smile.

The Senator snorted a laugh. "Well, he could have tried to squeeze in fifteen minutes for me between jumps," he said. He turned and walked to an antique sideboard loaded with whiskey bottles. "I have been thinking about having one of these for the last two hours. You all right?"

Flem Pickering raised his nearly full glass to show that he was.

Senator Fowler half-filled a glass with Johnnie Walker Black Label Scotch, added one ice cube, and then sprayed soda into it from a wire-wrapped soda bottle.

"This stuff," the Senator said, raising his glass, "is already getting in short supply. God*damn* German submarines."

"I have four hundred and eleven cases," Fleming Pickering said. "If you treat me right, I might put a case or two aside for you."

Fowler, smiling, looked at him curiously.

"Off the *Princess,* the *Destiny,* and the *Enterprise,"* Pickering explained.

The *Pacific Princess,* 51,000 tons, a sleek, fast passenger liner, was the flagship of the Pacific & Far Eastern Shipping Corporation. The *Pacific Destiny* and the *Pacific Enterprise,* 44,500 tons each, were sister ships, slightly smaller and slower, but, some said, more luxurious.

"Is that why you're here?" Senator Fowler asked. "The Navy after them again? Flem . . ."

Pickering held up his hand to shut him off.

"I sold them," he said.

"When rape is inevitable, et cetera, et cetera?" Fowler asked.

"No," Pickering said. "I think I could have won that one in the courts. The Navy could have commandeered them, but they couldn't have forced me to sell them."

Senator Fowler did not agree, but he didn't say so.

"And it wasn't patriotism, either," Pickering said. "More like enlightened self-interest."

"Oh?"

"Or a vision of the future," Pickering said.

"Now you've lost me," Senator Fowler confessed.

"We came home from Hawaii via Seattle," Pickering said, pausing to sip at his drink. "On the *Destiny.* We averaged twenty-seven knots for the trip. It took us one hundred twenty hours—"

"Fast crossing," Fowler interrupted, doing some quick, rough arithmetic. "Five and a half days."

"Uh-huh," Pickering said, "testing the notion that a fast passenger liner can run away from submarines."

"Not proving the theory? You made it."

"The theory presumes that submarines are not sitting ahead of you, waiting for you to come into range," Pickering said. "And there may not have been any Japanese submarines around."

"OK," Senator Fowler agreed. *"Theory."*

"While we were in Seattle, I drove past the Boeing plant. Long lines of huge, four-engine airplanes, B-17s, capable of making it nonstop to Hawaii in eleven, twelve hours."

"Uh-huh," Fowler agreed. He had flown in the B-17 and was impressed with it. "That airplane may just get our chestnuts out of the fire in this war."

Pickering went off at a tangent.

"You heard, Dick, that some military moron had all the B-17s in Hawaii lined up in rows for the convenience of the Japanese?"

Fowler shook his head in disbelief or disgust or both. "There, and in the Philippines," he said. "Christ, they really caught us with our pants down."

"I talked to an Army Air Corps pilot in the bar of the hotel," Pickering said. "He said a flight of B-17s from the States arrived while the raid was going on. And with no ammunition for their machine guns."

"I heard that, too."

"Anyway," Pickering said, "looking at those B-17s in Seattle, it occurred to me that they could more or less easily be modified to carry passengers, and that, presuming we win this war, that's the way the public is going to want to cross oceans in the future. Twelve hours to Hawaii beats five or six days all to hell."

"Out of school—this is classified—Howard Hughes proposes to build an airplane—out of plywood, no less—that will carry four hundred soldiers across the Atlantic."

"Then you understand what I'm saying. The day of the passenger liner, I'm afraid, is over. And since the Navy was making a decent offer for my ships, I decided to take it."

"A decent offer?"

"They're spending the taxpayers' money, not their own. A *very* decent offer."

"All of them?"

"Just the liners. I'm keeping the cargo ships, and I will *not* sell them to the Navy. If the Navy tries to make me sell them, I'll take them to the Supreme Court, and win. Anyway, that's where I got all the Scotch. I can also make you a very good deal on some monogrammed sterling silver flatware from the first-class dining rooms."

Fowler chuckled. "I'm surprised the Navy let you keep that."

"So am I," Pickering said.

"What are you going to do with all that money?" Fowler asked.

"Get rid of it, quickly, before that sonofabitch across the street thinks of some way to tax me out of it," Pickering said.

"You are speaking, Sir," Fowler said, mockingly sonorous, "of your President and the Commander in Chief."

"You bet I am," Pickering said. "I told my broker to buy into Boeing, Douglas, and whatever airlines he can find. I think I'd like to own an airline."

"And when Pick comes home from the war, he can run it?"

Pickering met his eyes. "Sure. Why not? I don't intend to dwell on the other possibility."

"I don't know why I feel awkward saying this," Senator Fowler said, "but I pray for him, Flem."

"Thank you," Pickering said. "So do I."

"So what are you doing in Washington?" Fowler said, to change the subject.

"You know a lawyer named Bill Donovan? Wall Street?"

"Sure."

"You know what he's doing these days?"

"Where did you think he's getting the money to do it?" He examined his now-empty glass. "I'm going to build another one of these. You want one?"

"Please, Dick."

"You think you'd make a good spy?" Senator Fowler asked.

"No."

"Then why are you going to see Donovan?"

"He called me. Once before December seventh, and twice since. Once when Patricia and I were still in Honolulu, and the second the day before yesterday, in Frisco. He got me the priority to fly in here."

"Do you know what he's doing?"

"I figured you would."

Fowler grunted as he refilled their glasses. He handed Pickering his drink, and then went on, "Right now, he's the Coordinator of Information. For a dollar a year. It was Franklin Roosevelt's idea."

"That sounds like a propaganda outfit."

"I think maybe it's supposed to. He's got Robert Sherwood, the playwright, and some other people like that, who will do propaganda. They've moved into the National Institutes of Health building. But there's another angle to it, an intelligence angle. He's gathered together a group of experts—he's got nine or ten, and he's shooting for a dozen, and this is probably what he has in mind for you—who are going to collect all the information generated by all the intelligence services, you know, the Army's G-2, the Office of Naval Intelligence, the FBI, the State Department, everybody, and try to make some overall, global sense out of it. For presentation to the President."

"I don't think I understand," Pickering confessed.

"Donovan makes the point, and I think he's right, that the service intelligence operations are too parochial, that they have blinders on them like a carriage horse. They see the war only from the viewpoint of the Navy or the Army or whatever."

The Senator looked at Pickering to see if he was getting through. Pickering made a "come on, tell me more" gesture with his hand.

"OK. Let's say the Navy finds out, as they did, that the Germans had established a weather station and aerial navigation facilities in Greenland. The Navy solution to the problem would be to send a battleship to blow it up—"

"Where would they get one? The Navy's fresh out of battleships. The Japanese used them for target practice."

"You want to hear this or not?"

"Sorry."

"You're going to have to learn to curb your lip, Flem, if you're going to go to work for Bill Donovan. Or anywhere else in the government."

"What happened to free speech?"

"It went out the same window with Franklin Roosevelt's pledge that our boys would never fight on foreign soil," the Senator said.

"I'm not working for him yet," Pickering said.

Smiling, Senator Fowler shook his head, and then went on, "As I was saying, if Navy Intelligence finds something, they propose a Navy solution. If the Army Air Corps had found out about the Germans on Greenland, they would have proposed sending bombers to eliminate them. Am I getting through to you?"

Pickering nodded.

"The idea is that Donovan's people—his 'twelve disciples,' as they're called—will get intelligence information from every source, evaluate it, and make a strategic recommendation. In other words, after the Navy found the Greenland Germans, Donovan's people might have recommended sending Army Air Corps bombers."

"That sounds like a good idea."

"It is, but I don't think it will work."

"Why not?"

"Interservice rivalry, primarily. And that now includes J. Edgar Hoover and the FBI. Until Bill Donovan showed up, Edgar thought that if war came, the FBI would be in charge of intelligence, period. Edgar is a very dangerous man if crossed."

"The story I got was that Donovan got Hoover his job, running the FBI."

"That was yesterday. In Washington, the question is, 'What have you done for me today, and what can you do for me tomorrow?' Anyway, the facts are that everybody has drawn their knives to cut Donovan's throat. I'm betting on Donovan, but I've been wrong before."

"Really?" Pickering teased.

"That's what you'd be getting into if you went to work for him, Flem. When do you see him?"

"He wanted me to have dinner with him tonight, but I wasn't in the mood. I told him I would come to his office in the morning."

"Boy, have you got a lot to learn!" Fowler said.

"Meaning I should have shown up, grateful for the privilege of a free meal from the great man?"

"Yeah. Exactly."

"Fuck him," Fleming Pickering said. "So far as I'm concerned, Bill Donovan is just one more overpaid ambulance chaser."

"You'd better hope he doesn't know you think that."

"He already does. I already told him."

"You did?" Senator Fowler asked, deciding as he spoke that it was probably true.

"He represented us before the International Maritime Court when a Pacific & Orient tanker rammed our *Hawaiian Trader.* You wouldn't believe the bill that sonofabitch sent me."

"I hope you paid it," Fowler said wryly.

"I did," Pickering said, "but not before I called him up and told him what I thought of it. And him."

"Oh, Christ, Flem, you're something!" Fowler said, laughing.

"I couldn't get near the club car, much less the dining car, on the train from New York," Pickering said. "All I've had to eat all day is a roll on the airplane and some hors d'oeuvres. I'm starving. You have any plans for dinner?"

Fowler shook his head no.

"Until you graced me with your presence, I was going to take my shoes off, collapse on the couch, and get something from room service."

There was a knock at the door. It was Max Telford.

"Come on in, Max," Pickering called. "The Senator was just extolling the virtues of your room service."

"I've got someone with me," Telford said, and a very large, very black man, in the traditional chef's uniform of starched white hat and jacket and striped gray trousers, pushed a rolling cart loaded with silver food warmers into the room.

"Hello, Jefferson," Pickering said, as he crossed the room to him and offered his hand. "How the hell are you? I thought you were in New York."

"No, Sir. I've been here about three months," the chef said. "I heard you were in the house, and thought maybe you'd like something more than crackers and cheese to munch on."

"Great, I'm starving. Do you know the Senator?"

"I know who the Senator is," Jefferson Dittler said.

"Dick, Jefferson Dittler. Jefferson succeeded where Patricia failed; he got Pick to wash dishes."

"Lots of dishes," Dittler laughed. "Then I taught him a little about cooking."

"Oh, I've heard about you," Senator Fowler said, shaking hands. "You're the fellow who taught Pick how to make hollandaise in a Waring Blender."

"That was supposed to be a professional secret," Dittler said.

"Well, Pick betrayed your confidence," Fowler said. "He taught that trick to my wife."

"He's a nice boy," Dittler said.

Pickering turned from the array of bottles and handed Dittler a glass dark with whiskey. "That's that awful fermented corn you like, distilled in a moldy old barrel in some Kentucky holler."

"That's why it's so good," Dittler said. "The moldy old barrel's the secret." He raised his glass. "To Pick. May God be with him."

"Here, here," Senator Fowler said.

Fleming Pickering started lifting the silver food covers.

"Very nice," he said. "One more proof that someone of my superior intelligence knows how to raise children for fun and profit. Jefferson never did this sort of thing for me before Pick worked for him."

"He's a nice boy," Jefferson Dittler repeated, and then, his tone suggesting it was something he desperately wanted to believe, "Smart as a whip. He'll be all right in the Marines."

(THREE)
Building "F"
Anacostia Naval Air Station
Washington, D.C.
20 December 1941

The interview between Mr. Fleming Pickering, Chairman of the Board of the Pacific & Far Eastern Shipping Corporation, and Colonel William J. Donovan, the Coordinator of Information to the President of the United States, did not go well.

For one thing, when Mr. Pickering was not in Colonel Donovan's outer office at the agreed-upon time, 9:45 A.M., Colonel Donovan went to his next appointment. This required Mr. Pickering, who arrived at 9:51 A.M., to cool his heels for more than an hour with an old copy of *Time* magazine. Mr. Pickering was not used to cooling his heels in anyone's office, and he was more than a little annoyed.

More importantly, Mr. Pickering quickly learned that Colonel Donovan did not intend for him to become one of the twelve disciples that Senator Fowler had mentioned, but rather that he would be an adviser to one of the disciples—should he "come aboard."

That disciple was named. Mr. Pickering knew him, both personally and professionally. He was a banker, and Pickering was willing to acknowledge that Donovan's man had a certain degree of expertise in international finance, which was certainly closely connected with international maritime commerce.

But the United States was not about to consider opening new and profitable shipping channels. Victory, in Fleming Pickering's judgment, was going to go to whichever of the warring powers could transport previously undreamed of tonnages of military equipment, damn the cost, to any number of obscure ports, under the most difficult conditions. In that connection there were two problems, as Pickering saw the situation.

First, there was the actual safe passage of the vessels—getting them past enemy surface and submersible warships. That was obviously going to be the Navy's problem. The second problem, equally important to the execution of a war, was cargo handling and refueling facilities at the destination ports. A ship's cargo was useless unless it could be unloaded. A ship itself was useless if its fuel bunkers were dry.

Carrying the war to the enemy, Pickering knew, meant the interdiction of the enemy's sea passages, and denying to him ports through which his land and air forces had to be supplied.

If the President was going to get evaluations of the maritime situation, it seemed perfectly clear to Fleming Pickering that it should come from someone expert in the nuts and bolts, someone who could make judgments based on his own experience with ships and ports, not someone whose experience was limited to the bottom line on a profit-and-loss statement, or whose sea experience was limited to crossing the Atlantic in a first-class cabin on the *Queen Mary* or some other luxury liner.

Someone like him, for example.

This was not overwhelmingly modest, he realized, but neither was it a manifestation of a runaway ego. When Fleming Pickering stepped aboard a P&FE ship—or, for that matter, ships of a dozen other lines—he was addressed as "Captain" and given the privilege of the bridge.

It was not simply a courtesy given to a wealthy shipowner. When Fleming Pickering had come home from France in 1918, he had almost immediately married. Then, to the horror of his new in-laws, he'd shipped out as an apprentice seaman aboard a P&FE freighter. As his father and grandfather had done before him, he had worked his way up in the deck department, ultimately sitting for his master's ticket, any tonnage, any ocean, a week before his twenty-sixth birthday.

He had been relief master on board the *Pacific Vagabond,* five days out of Auckland for Manila, when the radio operator had brought to the bridge the message that his father had suffered a coronary thrombosis and that in a special session of the stockholders (that is to say, his mother), he had been elected Chairman of the Board of the Pacific & Far Eastern Shipping Corporation.

Pickering tried to make this point to Colonel Donovan and failed. He was not particularly surprised when Donovan politely told him, in effect, to take the offer of a job as adviser to the disciple or go fuck himself. The disciple was one of Donovan's Wall Street cronies; Pickering would have been surprised if Donovan had accepted the wisdom of his arguments.

And, he was honest enough to admit, he would have been disappointed if he had. He didn't want to fight the war from behind a goddamned desk in Sodom on Potomac.

"General McInerney will see you now, Mr. Pickering," the impeccably shorn, shined, and erect Marine lieutenant said. "Will you come with me, please, Sir?"

Brigadier General D. G. McInerney, USMC, got to his feet and came around from behind his desk as Fleming Pickering was shown into his office. He was a stocky, barrel-chested man wearing Naval Aviator's wings on the breast of his heavily beribboned uniform tunic.

"Why, Corporal Pickering," he said. "My, how you've aged!"

"Hello, you baldheaded old bastard," Pickering replied. "How the hell are you?"

General McInerney's intended handshake degenerated into an affectionate hug. The two men, who had become friends in their teens, beamed happily at each other.

"It's a little early, but what the hell," General McInerney said. "Charlie, get a bottle of the good booze and a couple of glasses."

"Aye, aye, Sir," his aide-de-camp replied. Although he was a little taken aback by the unaccustomed display of affection, and it was the first time he had ever heard anyone refer to General McInerney as a "baldheaded old bastard," he was not totally surprised. Until a week ago, General McInerney's "temporary junior aide" had been a second lieutenant fresh from Quantico, whom General McInerney had arranged to get in the flight-training program at Pensacola.

His name was Malcolm Pickering, and this was obviously his father. The General had told him that they had served together in France in the First World War.

"Pick's a nice boy, Flem," General McInerney said, as he waved Pickering into one end of a rather battered couch and sat down on the other end. "I was tempted to keep him."

"I'm grateful to you for all you did for him, Doc," Pickering said.

"Hell," McInerney said, depreciatingly, "the Corps needs pilots more than it needs club officers, and that's what those paper pushers in personnel were going to do with him."

"Well, I'm grateful nonetheless," Pickering said.

"I got one for you," McInerney said. "I called down there to make sure they weren't going to make him a club officer down there, and you know who his roommate is? Jack Stecker's boy. He just graduated from West Point."

Fleming Pickering had no idea what McInerney was talking about, and it showed on his face.

"Jack Stecker?" McInerney went on. "Buck sergeant? Got the Medal at Belleau Wood?"

The Medal was the Medal of Honor, often erroneously called the Congressional Medal of Honor, the nation's highest award for valor in action.

"Oh, yeah, the skinny guy. Pennsylvania Dutchman. No middle name," Pickering remembered.

"Right," McInerney chuckled, "Jack NMI Stecker."

"I always wondered what had happened to him," Pickering said. "He was one hard-nosed sonofabitch."

The description was a compliment.

The aide handed each of them a glass of whiskey.

"Mud in your eye," McInerney said, raising his glass and then draining it.

"Belleau Wood," Pickering said dryly, before he emptied his glass.

"Jack stayed in the Corps," McInerney went on. "They wanted to send him to Annapolis. Christ, he wasn't any older than we were, he could have graduated with a regular commission when he was twenty-three or twenty-four, but he wanted to get married, so he turned it down. Until last summer he was a master gunnery sergeant at Quantico."

"Was?"

"They made him a captain; he's at Diego."

"And now our kids are second lieutenants! Christ, we're getting old, Doc."

"Jack had two boys. The older one went to Annapolis. He was an ensign on the *Arizona*. He was KIA on December 7."

"Oh, Christ!"

The two men looked at each other a moment, eyes locked, and then McInerney shrugged and Pickering threw up his hands helplessly.

"So what brings you to Washington, Flem?" McInerney asked, changing the subject. "I thought you hated the place."

"I do. And with rare exceptions, everyone in it. I'm looking for a job."

"Oh?"

"I just saw Colonel William J. Donovan," Pickering said. "He sent for me."

"Then I guess you know what he's up to."

"I've got a pretty good idea."

"Out of school, he's giving the Commandant a fit."

"Oh? How so?"

"The scuttlebutt going around is that Roosevelt wants to commission Donovan a brigadier general in the Corps."

"But he was in the Army," Pickering protested.

"Yeah, I know. The President is very impressed, or so I hear, with the British commandos. You know, hit-and-run raids. He wants American commandos, and he thinks they belong in the Corps. I hope to hell it's not true."

"It sounds idiotic to me," Pickering said.

"Tell your important friends. Senator Fowler, for example."

"I will."

"Just don't quote me."

"Don't be silly, Doc."

"You were about to tell me, I think, what you're going to do for Donovan."

"Nothing. I decided I didn't want to work for him. Or maybe vice versa. Anyway, I'm not going to work for him."

"Won't you have enough to do running your company? Hell, transportation is going to win—or lose—this war."

"I sold the passenger ships, at least the larger ones, to the Navy," Pickering replied. "And the freighters and tankers will probably go on long-term charter to either the Navy or the Maritime Administration—the ones that aren't already, that is. There's not a hell of a lot for me to do."

"So what are you going to do?"

"Strange, *General,* that you should ask that question," Pickering said.

"What's on your mind, Flem?" McInerney asked, a hint of suspicion in his voice.

"How about 'Once a Marine, always a Marine'?"

McInerney looked at him with disbelief and uneasiness in his eyes.

"Flem, you're not talking about you coming back in the Corps, are you? Are you serious?"

"Yes, I am, and yes, I am," Pickering said. "Why is that so—to judge from the look in your eyes and your tone of voice—incredible?"

"Come on, Flem," McInerney said. "You've been out of the Corps since 1919—and then, forgive me, you were a corporal."

"There should be some job where I could be useful," Pickering said. "Christ, I've been running eighty-one ships. And their crews. And all the shore facilities."

"I'm sure the Navy would love to commission someone with your kind of experience. Or, for that matter, the Transportation Corps of the Army."

"I don't want to be a goddamn sailor."

"Think it through," McInerney said. "Flem, I'm telling you the way it is."

"So tell me. I'm apparently a little dense."

"Your experience, your shipping business experience, is in what I think of as Base Logistics. Moving large amounts of heavy cargo by sea from one place to another. The Navy does that for the Marine Corps."

"It occurred to me that I could be one hell of a division supply officer, division quartermaster, whatever they call it."

"That calls for a lieutenant colonel, maybe a full colonel. If there was strong resistance among the palace guard to commissioning people—Marines, like Jack Stecker, a master gunnery sergeant—as captains, what makes you think they'd commission a civilian, a former corporal, as a lieutenant colonel?"

"I'm willing to start at the bottom. I don't have to be a lieutenant colonel."

McInerney laughed. "I think you really believe that."

"Yes, I do."

"As a major? A captain? That your idea of starting at the bottom?"

"Why not?"

"Flem, when was the last time someone told you what to do, gave you an order?"

"Well, just for the sake of argument, I think I can still take orders, but I have the feeling that I'm just wasting my breath."

"You want the truth from me, old buddy, or bullshit from some paper pusher?"

"That would depend on what the bullshit was."

" 'Why, we would love to have you, Mr. Pickering,' followed by an assignment as, say, a major, and deputy assistant maintenance officer for mess-kit rehabilitation at Barstow, or some other supply depot. Where you would do a hell of a job rehabilitating mess kits, and be an all-around pain in the ass the rest of the time. You want to march off to war again, Flem, and that's just not going to happen. Unless, of course, you go to the Navy. They really would love to have you."

"Fuck the Navy," Fleming Pickering said.

He stood up. General McInerney eyed him warily.

"I suppose I've made a real fool of myself, haven't I, Doc?" Pickering said calmly.

"No, not at all. I'm just sorry things are . . . the way things are."

"Well, I've kept my master's ticket up. And I still own some ships. Taking a ship to sea is better than being . . . what did you say, a 'deputy assistant mess-kit-repair officer'?"

"Yes, of course it is. But I keep saying, and you keep ignoring, that the Navy would love to have you."

"And I keep saying, and you keep ignoring, 'Fuck the Navy.' "

McInerney laughed.

"Have it your way, Flem. But they *are* on our side in this war."

"Well, then, God help us. I was at Pearl Harbor."

"Is it fair to blame Pearl Harbor on the Navy?"

"On who, then?" Fleming Pickering said, and put out his hand. "Thank you for seeing me, Doc. And for doing what you did for Pick."

"If you were twenty-one, I'd get you in flight school, too. No thanks required. Keep in touch, Flem."

(FOUR)
The Foster Lafayette Hotel
Washington, D.C.
20 December 1941

"Thank you very much," Fleming Pickering said politely, then took the receiver from his ear and placed it, with elaborate care, in its base. It was one of two telephones on the coffee table in the sitting room of Senator Richardson Fowler's suite.

Then he said, quite clearly, "Well, I'll be a sonofabitch!"

Transcontinental and Western Airlines had just told him that even though he already had his ticket for a flight between New York and San Francisco, with intermediate stops at Chicago and Denver, he could not be boarded without a priority. He had explained to them that he had come from San Francisco with a priority and was simply trying to get home, and that he had presumed that the priority which had brought him to Washington also applied to his return trip. TWA had told him that was not the case; he would need another priority to do so.

Fleming Pickering considered his predicament and swore again.

"That goddamned sonofabitch!"

He was referring to Colonel William J. Donovan, Coordinator of Information to the President of the United States. This was his fault. Donovan should have arranged for him to get home, gotten him a priority to do so. While he didn't think it was likely the ambulance-chasing sonofabitch was vindictive enough to have canceled his return-trip priority after their unpleasant encounter that morning, it *was* possible. And whether he had canceled the priority or simply neglected to arrange for one, what this meant for Fleming Pickering was that unless he wanted to spend four days crossing the country by train—and they probably passed out compartments on the train to people with priorities, which might well mean sitting up in a coach all the way across the country—he was going to have to call the bastard up and politely beg him to get him a priority to go home.

There was no question in Pickering's mind that Donovan would get him a priority, and no question either that Donovan would take the opportunity to remind Pickering that priorities were intended for people who were making a contribution to the war effort, not for people who placed their own desires and ambitions above the common good, by, for example, declining to serve with the Office of the Coordinator of Information.

Then Fleming Pickering had another thought: Richardson Fowler could probably get him a priority. Dick was a politician. Whatever law the politicians wrote, or whatever they authorized some agency of the government to implement—such as setting up an air-travel priority system—those bastards would take care of themselves first.

The thought passed through his mind, and was quickly dismissed, that perhaps he was being a horse's ass, that he was not working for the government and therefore had no right to a priority, and that getting one through Fowler's political influence would deprive of a seat some brave soldier en route to battle the Treacherous Jap. He was not going to California to lie on the beach. He still had a shipping company to run; coming here had taken him away from that.

There came a knock at the door. Pickering looked at it, and then at his watch. It was probably Dick Fowler. But why would Fowler knock?

"Come!"

It was Max Telford.

"Hello, Max, what's up?"

"I have a somewhat delicate matter I thought I should bring to your attention," Telford said.

"Will it wait until I pour us a drink? I've had a bad day and desperately need one."

"I could use a little taste myself," Telford said. "Thank you."

"Scotch?"

"Please."

When Pickering handed him his drink, Telford handed him a woman's red leather wallet.

"What's this?"

"It belongs to Miss Ernestine Sage," Telford said.

Ernestine "Ernie" Sage was the daughter of Patricia Pickering's college roommate.

"Where'd you get it?" Pickering asked.

"Miss Sage left it behind when she left the inn. The wallet and some other things."

"I don't quite follow you."

"She was not registered, Mr. Pickering," Telford said carefully.

"She was here with Pick?" Fleming Pickering's eyes lit up. He liked Ernie Sage, and there had been more than a tiny seed of hope in the jokes over the years, as Ernie and Pick had been growing up, that they could be paired off permanently. Still, it was a dumb thing for Pick to do. Ernest Sage, Ernie's father, was Chairman of the Board of American Personal Pharmaceuticals. And he routinely stayed in the Foster Lafayette. Pick should have known she would be recognized.

"With Pick's friend," Telford said. "Lieutenant McCoy."

"I know him," Pickering said, without thinking. "He's a nice kid."

Pick and McCoy had gone through the Officer Candidate School at the Marine base at Quantico together. They had nothing in common. McCoy had been a corporal in the peacetime Marine Corps, and what he had, he had earned himself. But Pickering had not been surprised when he'd met McCoy and seen the affection between him and his son. Doc McInerney and Flem Pickering had become lifelong friends in the Corps in France, despite a wide disparity in backgrounds.

"Then you know he was wounded," Telford said.

"No. I hadn't heard about that."

"I don't have all the details," Telford said. "I didn't want to pry, but McCoy is apparently some sort of officer courier. He was in the Pacific when the war started, and Pick got one of those 'missing and presumed dead' telegrams. He was pretty shook up about it. And then McCoy called from the West Coast and said he was back. Anyway, Pick came to me and said that McCoy was on his way to Washington, and if there was ever a time a Foster hotel should offer its very best, it was now, to McCoy. And his lady friend. And that all charges should be put on his account."

"And the lady friend turned out to be Ernestine Sage?"

"Yes, Sir. I recognized her immediately, but I don't know if she knows I knew who she is."

"And they were here for a while? Lots of room service?"

"Yes. That's a nice way to put it."

"Andrew Foster once told me that so far as he's concerned, he's prepared to offer accommodations to two female elephants in heat, plus a bull elephant, just as long as they pay the bill and don't soil the carpets," Pickering said. "So what's the problem?"

Telford laughed. "He told me a variant of that philosophy. It was two swans in heat, so long as they paid the bill and didn't flap their wings and lay eggs in the elevators."

Pickering chuckled, and then repeated, "So what's the problem? I'd rather my wife didn't hear about this, but so far as I'm concerned, whatever Ernie Sage did in here with Lieutenant McCoy is their business and no one else's."

"The problem is how to return Miss Sage's property to her," Telford said. "The only address I have for either of them is the one on her driver's license. That's in Bernardsville, New Jersey. Her parents' home, I think."

"Telford, your discretion is in keeping with the highest traditions of the innkeeping trade," Pickering said, meaning it. "If Ernest Sage found out—or even suspected—that his only child, his precious little Ernie, was shacked up with a Marine officer in a hotel in Washington, there would be hell to pay. Let me think."

He did just that, as he took a deep pull at his drink.

"Ernie works for an advertising agency in New York," he said, after a moment. "J. Walter Thompson. It's on Madison Avenue. Check the phone book.

Send it to her there, special delivery, and put Pick's address on it as the return address."

"All I have for that would be 'Pensacola, Florida.' "

"Add 'Student, Flight Training Program, U.S. Navy Air Station,' " Pickering said.

"I'm glad I brought this to your attention," Telford said.

"So am I. You about ready for another of these?"

"No, thank you."

The door opened and Senator Richardson Fowler walked in. There was someone with him, a stocky, well-dressed man in his sixties. He stopped inside the door, took gold-rimmed pince-nez from a vest pocket, polished them quickly with a handkerchief, and then put them on his nose.

"Good evening, Mr. Secretary," Telford said. "It's nice to see you, Sir."

"Hello, Telford, how are you?" said Secretary of the Navy Frank W. Knox.

"Fine, and on my out, Sir," Telford said. "Is there anything I can send up?"

"All we want right now is a drink, Max, thanks," Fowler said. He waited until Telford had left, closing the door behind him, and then went on, "Frank told me at lunch, to my surprise, that you two don't know each other."

"Only by reputation," Pickering said, crossing the room to Knox and giving him his hand.

"I was about to say just that," Knox said. "How do you do, Pickering?"

The two examined each other with unabashed curiosity.

"Scotch for you, Frank?" Senator Fowler asked, looking over his shoulder from the array of bottles.

"Please," Knox said absently, and then, "Dick tells me you're going to work for Bill Donovan."

"That didn't work out," Pickering said.

"I'm sorry to hear that," Knox said.

"Why should you be sorry?"

"It takes away an argument I was going to use on you."

"What argument was that?"

Senator Fowler knew Frank Knox almost as well as he knew Fleming Pickering. Sensing that their first meeting already showed signs of becoming confrontational, he hurried over with the drinks.

"You all right, Flem?"

"Oh, I think I might have another. You can't fly on six or seven wings, you know." He walked to the array of liquor.

"I gather your meeting with Bill Donovan was not entirely successful?" Fowler asked.

"No, it wasn't," Pickering replied.

"You want to tell me why?"

"Well, aside from the fact that we don't like each other, which is always a problem if you're going to work for somebody, you were wrong about his wanting to make me one of his twelve disciples. What he had in mind was my being a minor saint—Saint Fleming the Humble—to one of his Wall Street moneymen."

"You have been at the sauce, haven't you?"

"It is a blow to the masculine ego, especially in these times of near-hysterical patriotism, for an ex-Marine to be told, 'No, thanks, the Corps can't use you.' I have had a drink or five. Guilty, Your Senatorship."

"I don't think I understand you," Fowler said.

"After I saw Donovan, I tried to enlist, and was turned down."

"You were a Marine?" Knox asked.

"I was," Pickering said, "but, as the General reminded me, only a corporal."

"Both Napoleon and Hitler were only corporals," said Frank Knox. "I, on the other hand, was a sergeant."

Pickering looked at the dignified Secretary of the Navy, saw the twinkle in his eyes, and smiled.

"Were you really?"

"First United States Volunteer Cavalry, Sir," Knox said. "I charged up Kettle Hill with Lieutenant Colonel Theodore Roosevelt."

"The *good* cousin," Pickering said.

"Oh, I wouldn't put it quite that way," Knox said. "Franklin grows on you."

"I will refrain from saying, Mr. Secretary, how that man grows on me."

Knox chuckled. "The Marine Corps turned you down, did they?"

"Politely, but firmly."

"The Marine Corps is part of the Navy. I'm Secretary of the Navy. Are you a bartering man, Pickering?"

"I'll always listen to an offer."

Knox nodded, and paused thoughtfully before going on.

"The reason I was sorry to hear that you're not going to be working for Bill Donovan, Pickering, is that I came here with the intention of making this argument to you: Since you will be working for Donovan, you will not be able to run the Pacific & Far Eastern Shipping fleet, so you might as well sell it to the Navy."

"Since Fowler apparently has been doing a lot of talking about me," Pickering replied, not pleasantly, "I'm surprised he didn't tell you I told him I have no intention of selling any more of my ships. To the Navy, or anyone else."

"Oh, he told me that," Knox said. "I came here to try to get you to change your mind."

"Then I'm afraid you're on a wild-goose chase."

"You haven't even heard my arguments."

Pickering shrugged.

"We're desperate for shipping," Knox said.

"My ships will haul anything the Navy wants hauled, anywhere the Navy wants it hauled."

"There are those who believe the maritime unions may cause trouble when there are inevitable losses to submarines and surface raiders."

"My crews will sail my ships anywhere I tell them to sail them," Pickering said.

"There are those who believe the solution to that problem, which I consider more real than you do, is to send them to sea with Navy crews."

"Then they're fools," Pickering said.

"Indeed?" Knox asked icily.

"Pacific & Far Eastern doesn't have a third mate, or a second assistant engineer, who is not qualified to sail as master, or chief engineer," Pickering said. "Which is good for the country. My junior officers are going to be the masters and chief engineers of the ships—the vast fleets of cargo ships—we're going to have to build for this war, and my ordinary and able-bodied seamen and my engine room wipers are going to be the junior officers and assistant engineers. You can't teach real, as opposed to Navy, seamanship in ten or twelve weeks at the Great Lakes Naval Training Center. If somebody is telling you that you can, you had better get a new adviser."

"What's the difference between Navy seamanship, Flem, and 'real' seamanship?" Fowler asked.

"It takes three or four Navy sailors to do what one able-bodied seaman is expected to do on a merchantman," Pickering replied. "A merchant seaman does what he sees has to be done, based on a good deal of time at sea. A Navy sailor is trained not to blow his nose until someone tells him to. And then they send a chief petty officer to make sure he blows it in the prescribed manner."

"You don't seem to have a very high opinion of the U.S. Navy," Knox said sharply.

"Not if what happened at Pearl Harbor is any indication of the way they think. I was there, Mr. Knox."

Knox glowered at him; Fowler saw the Secretary's jowls working.

"There are those," Knox said after a long pause, "who advise me that the Navy should stop trying to reason with you and simply seize your vessels under the President's emergency powers."

"I'll take you to the Supreme Court and win. You can force me—not that you would have to—to have my ships carry what you want, wherever you want it carried, but you can *not* seize them."

"A couple of minutes ago, the thought entered my head that I might be able to resolve this difference reasonably by offering you a commission in the Marine Corps, say, as a colonel. That now seems rather silly, doesn't it?"

"I don't think *silly* is the word," Pickering said nastily. "*Insulting* would seem to fit. To both the Corps and me."

"Flem!" Senator Fowler protested.

"It's all right, Dick," Knox said, waving his hand to shut him off. "And I don't suppose saying to you, Pickering, that your country needs your vessels would have much effect on you, would it?"

"My ships are at my country's disposal," Pickering said evenly. "But what I am not going to do is turn them over to the Navy so the Navy can do to them what it did to the Pacific Fleet at Pearl Harbor."

"*That's* an insult," Knox said, "to the courageous men at Pearl Harbor, many of whom gave their lives."

"No, it's not," Pickering said. "I'm not talking about courage. I'm talking about stupidity. If I had your job, Mr. Secretary, I would fire every admiral who was anywhere near Pearl Harbor. Fire them, hell, stand them in front of a firing squad for gross dereliction of duty. Pearl Harbor should not have happened. That's a fact, and you can't hide it behind a chorus of patriotic outrage that someone would dare sink our fleet."

"I'm ultimately responsible for whatever happens to the Navy," Knox said.

"If you really believe that, then maybe you should consider resigning to set an example."

"Now goddamn it, Flem!" Senator Fowler exploded. "That's going too goddamned far. You owe Frank an apology!"

"Not if he really believes that, he doesn't," Knox said. He leaned over and set his glass on the coffee table. "Thank you for the drink, Dick. And for the chance to meet Mr. Pickering."

"Frank!"

"It's been very interesting," the Secretary of the Navy said. "If not very fruitful."

"Frank, Flem's had a couple too many," Senator Fowler said.

"He looks like the kind of man who can handle his liquor," Knox said. "Anyway, *in vino veritas.*" He walked to the door and opened it, and then half-turned around. "Mr. Pickering, I offered my resignation to the President on December seventh. He put it to me that his accepting it would not be in the best interests of the country, and he therefore declined to do so."

And then he went through the door and closed it after him.

Fleming Pickering and Richardson Fowler looked at each other. Pickering saw anger in his old friend's eyes.

There was a momentary urge to apologize, but then Fleming Pickering decided against it. He had, he realized, said nothing that he had not meant.

III

(ONE)
On Board USS *Tangier*
Task Force 14
1820 Hours 22 December 1941

"Now hear this," the loudspeakers throughout the ship blared, harshly and metallically. "The smoking lamp is out. The smoking lamp is out."

Staff Sergeant Joseph L. Howard, USMC, was on the bow of the *Tangier* when the announcement came. He was smoking a cigarette, looking out across the wide, gentle swells of the Pacific at the other ships of Task Force 14.

The USS *Tangier,* a seaplane tender pressed into duty as a troop transport, with the 4th Marine Defense Battalion on board, was in line behind the aircraft carrier USS *Saratoga,* which flew the flag of Rear Admiral Frank Fletcher, Commander of Task Force 14.

Behind the *Tangier* was the *Neches,* a fleet oiler, riding low in the water. The three ships considered most vulnerable to attack formed the center of Task Force 14. Sailing ahead of the *Saratoga* were the cruisers USS *Astoria* and USS *Minneapolis.* The cruiser USS *San Francisco* brought up the rear. The cruisers themselves were screened by nine destroyers.

Task Force 14 had put out from Pearl Harbor five days before, six days after the Japanese had attacked Pearl, under orders from Admiral Husband E. Kimmel, the U.S. Pacific Fleet Commander, to reinforce Wake Island.

Wake Island desperately needed reinforcement. Already there were what the Corps euphemistically referred to as "elements" of the 1st Marine Defense Battalion. These amounted to less than four hundred Marines, commanded by Major James P. S. Devereux. Devereux had two five-inch naval cannon, obsolete weapons removed from men-of-war; four three-inch antiaircraft cannon, only one of which had the necessary fire-control gear; twenty-four .50-caliber Browning machine guns; and maybe a hundred .30-caliber Brownings, mixed air- and water-cooled. That, plus individual small arms, was it.

Staff Sergeant Joe Howard knew what weaponry had been given to Major Devereux's "elements" because he'd talked to the battalion's ordnance sergeant. It had been decided, literally at the last minute, that the ordnance sergeant would be of more value to the Corps left behind at Pearl, doing what he could to get the newly formed 4th Defense Battalion's weaponry up and running.

And he knew what Task Force 14 was carrying to reinforce Wake Island. In addition to the 4th Defense Battalion, at near full strength, and the Brewster Buffalos of VMF-211 that would fly off *Saratoga* and join what was left of the dozen Wildcats already on Wake, there were, aboard *Tangier* and in the holds of other ships, nine thousand rounds of five-inch ammunition; twelve thousand rounds of three-inch shells for the antiaircraft cannon; and three million rounds of .50-caliber machine-gun ammunition.

After the devastating, humiliating whipping they had taken at Pearl on December 7, the Navy and the Marine Corps were finally coming out to fight.

Howard took a final, deep drag on his Camel, then flicked the glowing coal from its end with his thumbnail. He carefully tore the cigarette paper down its length and let the wind scatter the tobacco away. Then he crumbled the paper into a tiny ball between his thumb and index fingers and let the wind take that away, too.

Howard was "under arms." That is, he was wearing his steel helmet and a web belt from whose eyelets hung a canteen, a first-aid pouch, a magazine pouch for two pistol magazines, and a Model 1911A1 .45-caliber Colt pistol in a leather holster. The canteen was empty, as were the magazine pouch and the magazine in the .45. Ammunition had not been authorized for issue to the guard, much less to the troops, although there was a metal box in the guardroom with a couple of dozen five-round stripper clips of .30-06 ammunition for Springfield '03 rifles and a half-dozen loaded seven-round .45 magazines.

Joe Howard had seen the Officer of the Guard slip one of the loaded magazines into his .45 just before guard mount. The Officer of the Guard was a second lieutenant, a twenty-one-year-old, six months out of Annapolis. Joe had wondered whom he thought he was going to have to shoot.

He hadn't said anything, of course. Staff sergeants in the Marine Corps don't question anything officers do, even twenty-one-year-old second lieutenants, unless it is really stupid and likely to hurt somebody. If Lieutenant Ellsworth Gripley felt that it was necessary to carry a loaded pistol in the performance of his duties as officer of the guard, that was his business.

Howard set his steel helmet at the appropriately jaunty angle for a sergeant of the guard and set out to find the Officer of the Guard. He was a little worried about Second Lieutenant Ellsworth Gripley, USMC. It had finally sunk in on the young officer that this wasn't a maneuver; within forty-eight hours the 4th Defense Battalion would be ashore on Wake Island and engaging the Japanese, and he would be expected to perform like a Marine officer.

Lieutenant Gripley wasn't *afraid,* Joe Howard thought. More like nervous. That was understandable. And he saw it as his duty to do what he could to make Gripley feel a little more sure of himself.

The ships making up Task Force 14 were, of course, blacked out to avoid detection by the enemy. One of the functions of the guard detail—in S/Sgt. Joe Howard's opinion, the most important function—was to make sure that no one sneaked on deck after dark for a quick smoke. The glow of a cigarette coal was visible for incredibly long distances on a black night. Even so, there seemed to be a large number of people, including officers, who seemed unwilling, or unable, to believe that *their* cigarette was *really* going to put anyone in danger.

They seemed to think that maybe if three or four hundred people lined the ship's rails, merrily puffing away, a Japanese submarine skipper could see this through a submarine periscope, but one little ol' cigarette, carefully concealed in the hand? Not goddamned likely.

Because of his zealous enforcement of the no-smoking regulations, Howard had already earned a reputation among some of the officers as a rather insolent noncom. Marine officers are not accustomed to being firmly corrected by staff sergeants. Or to being threatened by them:

"Sir, if you don't put that out right now, I'll have to call the officer of the guard."

When he had said that, the cigarettes were immediately put out. But in half a dozen instances, the officer had asked for his name and billet. He didn't think the information had been requested so the officers could seek out the Headquarters Company commander to tell him what a fine job S/Sgt. Howard had been doing.

He had had less trouble with the enlisted men, although there were about ten times as many of them as there were officers. The lower-ranking Marines were either afraid of defying orders or of Japanese submarines—or probably of both. And Joe Howard was aware that most of the senior noncoms probably knew, as he did, just how far a cigarette coal could be seen at night and did not wish to end their war by drowning after being torpedoed.

And, besides, they would be in a shooting war soon enough. The word had leaked out of Officer's Country, via a PFC orderly whom Joe had known at Quantico, that at 1800 hours they were about 550 miles from Wake Island. The Task Force was making about fifteen knots, which translated to mean they were then thirty-six hours steaming time from Wake. In other words, they should be at Wake at daybreak the day after tomorrow.

The ships in the center of the Task Force, the *Saratoga,* the *Tangier,* and the oiler, had been making course changes regularly, zigzagging across the Pacific so as to present as difficult a target as possible for any enemy submarine that might be stalking the Task Force. The cruisers and destroyers had been making course changes that were more frequent and of greater magnitude than those of the carrier and the ships following in its wake. The destroyers had been weaving in and out between the larger ships like sheepdogs guarding their flock.

Joe Howard had grown used to changes in course—the slight tilting of the deck, the slight change in the dull rumble of the engine, the change in the pitching and rolling of the *Tangier*—to the point where he paid almost no conscious attention to them.

But now, as he made his way aft along the portside boat deck, looking for Lieutenant Gripley, he slowly came to realize that *this* course change was somehow different. He stopped, putting his hand on the damp inboard bulkhead to steady himself.

For one thing, he thought, *it's taking a lot longer than they normally do.*

And then he understood. The *Tangier,* and thus all of Task Force 14, was not changing course, but reversing course.

What the hell is that all about?

The *Tangier*'s public-address system, which never seemed to shut up, was now absolutely silent. If something was up, it certainly would have gone off, accompanied by harshly clanging bells, calling General Quarters.

He decided that nothing had happened, except that his imagination was running away with him.

He began moving aft again, telling himself that after he found Lieutenant Gripley, he would go to the guardroom and have a ham sandwich and a cup of coffee.

When he reached the rear of the boat deck, there was someone leaning on the railing beside the ladder to the main deck. At first he thought it was the guard posted there, and that he had deserted his post at least to the point of taking off his steel pot and assuming an unmilitary position. He was considering how badly to ream him when he saw the guard, steel pot in place, standing at parade rest.

Whoever was leaning on the rail was an officer—not Lieutenant Gripley, but somebody else.

When he got close, he saw that it was the Executive Officer of the 4th Defense Battalion. And when he heard Joe's footsteps, he first turned his head, and then stood erect.

"Sergeant Howard, Sir. Sergeant of the Guard."

"Yes," the Exec said absently. "How are you tonight, Sergeant?"

It was not the expected response.

"Just getting a little air, Sergeant," the Exec continued. "Stuffy in my cabin."

"Yes, Sir," Joe said.

"Trying to get my thoughts in order, actually," the Exec said.

"Sir?" Joe asked, now wholly confused.

The Exec straightened.

"Sergeant," he said. "At 2100 tonight, there was a radio from Pearl Harbor. Task Force 14 is to return to Pearl."

"Sir?"

"Task Force 14 is ordered to return to Pearl. We have already reversed course."

"But what about Wake Island?"

"It would appear, Sergeant," the Exec said throatily, huskily, speaking with difficulty, "that Major Devereux and his men are going to have to make do with what they have."

"Jesus Christ," S/Sgt. Howard blurted. He knew, perhaps as well as anyone, what few arms and how little ammunition, and how few Marines, were at Major James P. S. Devereux's command.

"Orders are orders, Sergeant," the Exec said, and pushed his way past Joe Howard. There was not much light, but there was enough for Joe to see that tears were running down the Exec's cheeks.

Goddamn them! Staff Sergeant Howard thought. *How the hell can they turn around, knowing that unless we can reinforce Wake, the Japs will take it, and all those guys will be either dead or prisoners? Who the hell could be responsible for such a chickenshit order?*

And then he thought: *Who the fuck are you kidding? If we'd gone to Wake, when the first shot was fired, you'd be hiding behind the nearest rock, curled up like a fucking baby, and crying, the way you behaved on December seventh.*

(TWO)
Lakehurst Naval Air Station
Lakehurst, New Jersey
1605 Hours 1 January 1942

PFC Stephen M. Koffler, USMC, heard his relief coming, the crunch of their field shoes on the crusty snow, the corporal quietly counting cadence, long before he saw them. Koffler was eighteen years and two months old, weighed 145 pounds, and stood five feet seven inches tall.

The relief was marching across the front of the enormous airship hangar; and Koffler's post, Number Four, was a marching post, back and forth, along the side of the hangar.

Permission had been granted to the guard to carry their Springfield 1903 caliber .30-06 rifles at sling arms, muzzle down. The idea was to keep snow out of the muzzle.

PFC Koffler unslung his piece and brought it to port arms. The moment he saw the corporal turn the corner, he issued his challenge: "Halt, who goes there?"

He had learned how to do this and a number of other things peculiar to the profession of arms generally, and to the United States Marine Corps specifically, at the United States Marine Corps Recruit Depot, Parris Island, South Carolina, during the months of October and November and in the first weeks of December, but the first time he had done it for real was here in Lakehurst.

There were five rounds in the magazine of his rifle, and a total of forty more in the pockets of the "Belt, Web, Cartridge" he was wearing around his waist. His bayonet was fixed to the muzzle of his rifle. Sometimes, walking back and forth alongside the dirigible hangar, he had forgotten it was there and bumped into it with his lower leg.

"Corporal of the Guard," the corporal called.

"Advance, Corporal of the Guard, to be recognized."

The Corporal of the Guard ordered the guard detail to halt. When they had done that, he took another half-dozen steps toward PFC Koffler.

"Giblet," PFC Koffler challenged.

"Gravy," the Corporal of the Guard replied, giving the countersign.

When he had first been told the night's challenge and countersign, PFC Koffler had been more than a little surprised. Somebody around here apparently had a sense of humor. There had been none of that at Parris Island, not with something as important as guard duty.

Not that what he was doing here at Lakehurst wasn't serious. The hangar had been built to house dirigibles before PFC Stephen Koffler was born, back when the Navy had thought that enormous rigid airships were the wave of the future. It now held half a dozen Navy blimps, used to patrol the waters off New York harbor for German submarines. A blimp was a nonrigid airship, like a balloon. Last night in the guardhouse, PFC Koffler had heard that the first Navy nonrigid airship had been called the "A-Limp," and the second model the "B-Limp." That's where the name had come from.

There were German submarines out there, and it was quite possible that German saboteurs would attempt to destroy the blimps in their hangar. There were a whole lot of Nazi sympathizers in New York's Yorktown district. Before the war, they used to hire Madison Square Garden for their meetings.

Guarding the dirigible hangar and its blimps was not like guarding the recruit barracks at Parris Island. PFC Koffler had taken his responsibilities seriously.

"PFC Koffler, Post Four, Corporal," Koffler said. "All is well."

They went through the formalized ritual of changing the guard. The first Marine in the line behind the corporal marched up and held his Springfield at port arms while Koffler recited his Special Orders, then the Corporal of the Guard barked "Post," and PFC Koffler marched away from his post and took up a position at the rear of the relief guard.

This was his last tour. He'd gone on duty, "stood guard mount," at 1600 yesterday afternoon, and been assigned to the First Relief. He'd gone on guard at 1600, walked his post for two hours, and been relieved at 1800. Four hours later, at 2200, he had gone on again and walked his post until midnight, which was New Year's. Then he'd had another four hours off, going back on at 0400 until 0600. Another four hours off until ten, then two hours more until noon, then four hours off, and then this, the final tour, two hours from 1400 to 1600.

It had not entered his mind to feel sorry for himself for having to walk around in below-zero weather on New Year's Day, any more than it had entered his mind on Monday, when he'd gotten off the Sea Coast Limited train that had carried him from Parris Island, South Carolina, to Newark, that if he got on the subway, he could be home in thirty minutes.

It had been instilled in him at Parris Island that he no longer had any personal life that the Corps did not elect to grant him. He was not a candy-ass civilian anymore, he was a Marine. He could go home only when, and if, the Corps told him he could. You were supposed to get a leave home when you graduated from Parris Island, but that hadn't happened. There was a war on.

Maybe he could get a leave, or at least a weekend liberty, while he was going to school at Lakehurst. Or when he graduated. If he graduated. He wasn't holding his breath. For one thing, the sergeant major on Mainside at Parris Island, where he'd been transferred after graduating from Boot Camp, had really been pissed at him. They had gone through the records looking for people with drafting experience, and they'd found him and transferred him to Mainside to execute architectural drawings for new barracks. He hadn't joined the Corps to be a draftsman. If he'd wanted to be a draftsman, he would have stayed with the Public Service Corporation of New Jersey, where he had been a draftsman trainee in the Bus & Trolley Division.

There'd been an interesting notice on the bulletin board. Regulations said you had to read the bulletin board at least twice a day, so it wasn't his fault he'd seen the notice. The notice had said that volunteers were being accepted for parachute duty. And that those volunteers who successfully completed the course of instruction at Lakehurst would receive an extra fifty dollars a month in pay. That was a lot of money. As a PFC, his total pay was forty-one dollars a month, thirty-six dollars plus five dollars for having qualified as Expert on the firing range with the Springfield.

So he had applied, which immediately pissed off the Sergeant Major, who needed a draftsman. "Let some other asshole jump out of goddamned airplanes," the Sergeant Major yelled at him. The Sergeant Major was so pissed and he made so much noise that one of the officers came out to see what was going on.

"Well, you'll have to let him apply, Sergeant Major," the officer said, "if he wants to. Put on his application we need him here, but let him apply."

Stephen Koffler felt sure that was the last he would ever hear of parachute school, but three days later the Sergeant Major called him into his office to tell him to pack his fucking gear and get his ass on the train, and he personally hoped Koffler would break his fucking neck the first time he jumped.

He never even left Pennsylvania Station when he got off the Sea Coast Limited at Newark. He just went downstairs from the tracks to ask Information about when the New Jersey Central train left for Lakehurst. They told him it would be another two and a half hours. While he was waiting, he got asked three times for his orders, twice by sailors wearing Shore Patrol brassards, and once even by fucking doggie MPs. Steve Koffler was already Marine enough to be convinced that the goddamned Army had no right to let their goddamned MPs ask a *Marine* anything.

When he got to Lakehurst, a truck carried him out to the Naval Air Station. And then the Charge of Quarters, a lean and mean-looking sergeant, told him where he could find a bunk, but that he'd have to do without a mattress cover, a pillow, and sheets because the supply room was locked up. He might even have to wait until after New Year's.

In the morning, he had a brief encounter with the First Sergeant, who was lanky and mean-looking like the Charge of Quarters, just older. The First Sergeant said that he really hadn't expected him, and that he thought the new class would trickle in over the next couple of days, but now that he had reported in, he should get his gear shipshape and be ready to stand guard mount at 1600.

Koffler spent the day getting ready for guard, pressing his green blouse and trousers and a khaki shirt and necktie, which he now knew was not a necktie but a "field scarf." He restored the spit-shine on his better pair (of two pairs) of field shoes, and cleaned and lightly oiled his 1903 Springfield .30-06 rifle.

It had been pretty goddamned cold, walking up and down alongside the dirigible hangar, but there was hot coffee in the guardhouse when you'd done your two hours; and the Sergeant of the Guard had even come out twice with a thermos of coffee and fried-egg sandwiches, an act that really surprised Koffler, based on his previous experience with both sergeants and guard duty at Parris Island.

After the guard that was just relieved marched back to the guardhouse and turned in their ammunition, every round carefully counted and accounted for, Steve Koffler took a chance and asked the Sergeant of the Guard a question. He seemed like a pretty nice guy.

"What happens now? I mean, what am I supposed to do?"

"If I was you, kid, I'd make myself scarce around the billet. There's always some sonofabitch looking for a work detail."

"You mean we're not restricted to the barracks?"

"No. Why should you be? You just get out of Parris Island?"

"Yeah."

"It shows," the Sergeant said.

"Where should I go to get away from the barracks?"

"You can go anyplace you can afford to go. It's about an hour on the train to New York City, but you better be loaded, you want to go there."

"How about Newark?"

"Why the hell would you want to go to Newark?"

"I live just outside, a town called East Orange."

"You just came off Boot Camp leave, right?"

"No."

"What do you mean, 'No'?"

"I mean I didn't get any leave. When we graduated, they sent me to Mainside, and then they sent me here."

"No shit? You're supposed to get a leave, ten days at least."

"Well, I didn't get one."

"I find out you've been shitting me, kid," the Sergeant said, "I'll have your ass."

Then he picked up the telephone.

"I hope you're really hung over, you old sonofabitch," he said to whoever answered the phone.

There was a reply, and the Sergeant laughed.

"Hey, I just been talking to one of the kids who's reporting in. I don't know what happened, but they didn't give him a leave out of Parris Island. He lives in Newark, or near it. Would it be OK with you if I told the CQ to give him a seventy-two-hour pass?"

There was a pause.

"He already pulled guard. We just got off."

Something else was said that Koffler couldn't hear.

"OK, Top, thanks," the Sergeant of the Guard said, and hung up. "He was in a good mood. You get an *extended* seventy-two-hour pass."

"I don't know what that means," Steve Koffler confessed.

"Well, you get one pass that runs from 1700 today until 1700 Sunday. That's seventy-two hours. Then you tear that one up and throw it away, and go on the second one, which lasts until 0500 Monday. The First Sergeant says that nothing's going on around here until then, anyway."

"Jesus Christ!"

"Now for Christsake, don't do nothing like getting shitfaced and arrested."

"I won't."

An hour later, PFC Stephen Koffler passed through the Marine guard at the gate and started walking toward the Lakehurst train station. He hadn't gone more than a hundred yards when a Chrysler convertible pulled to the side of the road ahead of him, and the door swung open. The driver was a naval officer, a young one.

"I'm going into New York City if that would be any help, son," he said.

On the way to Newark, where the officer went out of his way to drive him into the city and drop him off at Pennsylvania Station, he told Koffler that he was a navigator on one of the blimps and had spent New Year's Eve freezing his tail ten miles off the Jersey coast, down by Cape May, at the mouth of the Delaware River.

Steve told him he had just arrived to go to the parachute school. And the officer replied that Steve had more balls than he did. There was no way anybody could get him to jump out of an airplane unless it was gloriously in flames.

Steve caught the Bloomfield Avenue trolley in the basement of Penn Station and rode it up to the Park Avenue stop by Branch Brook Park in Newark. Then he got off, walked up to street level, and caught the Number 21 Park Avenue bus and took it twenty blocks west across the city line into East Orange. He got off at Nineteenth Street, right across from his apartment building.

Steve's mother and her husband lived on the top floor of the four-story building, on the right side, in the apartment that overlooked the entranceway in the center of the U-shaped building. There were no lights on in the apartment, which meant they were out someplace; but there were lights on in the Marshall apartment, which was on the same side of the building, and a floor down.

He wondered if Bernice Marshall was home. He had known Bernice since the sixth grade, when his mother had married Ernie and they had moved into the apartment building at 121 Park Avenue. Bernice Marshall wasn't his girlfriend or anything like that. What she was was a girl with a big set of knockers and dark hair, and she was built like somebody who would probably get fat when she got older. But she was a girl. And as Steve looked up at her apartment now, his mind's eye was full of Bernice taking a sunbath on the roof of the building, with her boobs spilling out of her bathing suit.

Whenever the Marshall girls, Bernice and her sister Dianne, took sunbaths on the roof of the apartment, the males in the building usually found some excuse to go up there and smoke a cigarette and have a look. Dianne was a long-legged, long-haired blonde four years older than Bernice. She had run away to get married when she was a senior in East Orange High. And then she had had some kind of trouble and moved back home with her baby.

Dianne had gotten a job in the Ampere Branch of the Essex County Bank & Trust, right next door to where Mr. Marshall ran the Ampere One-Hour Martinizing Dry Cleaning & Laundry. Steve didn't know what Bernice was doing. She'd tried to go to college, at Upsala, in East Orange, but just before he had joined the Marines, Steve remembered now, he'd heard that hadn't worked out and that Bernice was going to try to get some kind of job.

It then occurred to him that he didn't have a key to get in. His keys and every other thing he had owned as a civilian had been put into a box and shipped home from Parris Island the very first morning he was there, right after they'd given him a haircut and a set of utilities and a pair of boots. Even before the Corps had issued him the rest of his gear.

Jesus Christ!

There was a door on either side of the lobby of 121 Park Avenue, which could be opened if you had a key, or if someone in one of the apartments pushed a button. Or if you gave the brass plate on it a swift kick. That's what Steve did next, giving him access to the first-floor foyer and stairwell.

He went up the stairs two at time. When he passed the third-floor landing, he could hear female laughter from the Marshall apartment, but couldn't tell if it was Bernice or Dianne, or maybe even Mrs. Marshall.

More or less for the hell of it, he tried the door to his apartment. It was locked, as he thought it would be. Then he went up to the roof. With a lot of effort he pushed the door open against the snow that had accumulated up there.

What they called "the deck"—the place where Bernice and Dianne took their sunbaths—was a platform of boards with inch-wide spaces between them. Now it was covered with ice and snow, and it was slippery under his feet as he made his way across it to the fire escape.

There was a ladder down from the roof to the top level of the fire escape, which was right outside his room. He climbed down it and tried his windows. They were locked.

Just beyond the railing of the fire escape was the bathroom window. If that was locked, he didn't know what the fuck he would do. He leaned over and pushed up on it, and it slid upward.

But to get through it meant you had to stand on the fire escape railing and support yourself on the bricks of the building, while you leaned far enough over until you could put your head and shoulders into the window without falling off. Then you gave a shove. After that, you could wiggle through and end up head-down in the bathtub.

Steve realized there was no way he could do that wearing his overcoat and brimmed cap and gloves. After he considered that, he decided he couldn't make it wearing his blouse either; so he took all of them off and laid them on the steel-strap floor of the fire escape.

Then he was so goddamned cold he started to shiver.

When he stood up on the railing of the fire escape, he thought there was a very good chance that he was not going to make it, and that when his mother and her husband came home, they would find him smashed and bloody on the concrete of the entranceway four floors down, dead.

Sixty seconds later, he was in the bathtub, head down.

He pushed out of the way his mother's underwear and stockings, hanging to dry over the tub, and found the light switch and flicked it on.

He saw himself in the mirror. He didn't look familiar. There was no fat on his face anymore, and his eyes looked like they had sunk inward. But the big difference, he realized, was the hair. Before he'd enlisted, he had had long hair, worn in a pompadour, with sideburns. What he had now was hair not half an inch long, and no sideburns.

He went into his bedroom, opened the window, and reclaimed the rest of his uniform from the fire escape. He opened his closet and put the cap on the shelf, then found a heavy hanger for the overcoat and hung that on the pipe. It really looked strange in there, he thought, beside his red and white Mustangs Athletic Club jacket.

His "rig" was on the shelf. He had been interested in amateur radio since he was a high school freshman and had joined the Radio Club. By the time he was a sophomore, he had learned Morse code and joined the American Amateur Radio Relay League. He had built his first receiver when he was still a sophomore, and his first really good receiver when he was a junior. He had passed the Federal

Communications Commission examination for his ham ticket and had then gone on and gotten his second-class radio telephone license when he was a senior.

Getting the money to build his first transmitter and the antenna that it needed had meant giving up a lot of nights out with the Mustangs, but finally he had it up and running in the early spring of his senior year. That had lasted a week, until the neighbors in the building found out what was causing all the static when they tried to listen to "Lowell Thomas and the News" and Fred Allen and "The Kate Smith Hour." They'd bitched to the superintendent, and the super had made him take the antenna down from the roof.

His mother's husband had acted as if he had done something criminal. He'd even bitched at him for just *listening* to the traffic on the twenty-meter band, refusing to understand that receivers don't cause interference. The fights they had over that had been one of the reasons he had joined The Corps.

He took his Mustangs jacket off its hanger and slipped it on. It had a red velveteen body and white sleeves and red knit cuffs and collar. *Mustangs Athletic Club* was spelled out in flowing script on the back, and *Mustang AC* and *Steve* in smaller block letters on the front.

He closed the bedroom door to examine himself in the full-length, somewhat wavy mirror mounted on it. The Mustangs jacket didn't look right; either it had shrunk or he had grown. It was tight across his shoulders and chest, and the cuffs seemed to ride too high on his arms. He took it off and noticed something else. It looked cheap. It looked like a cheap piece of shit.

That made him feel disloyal and sad.

He hung the jacket back up and put on his uniform blouse, then looked at himself again in the mirror. He looked right, and the PFC stripe and the glistening silver marksman badges didn't look bad either. He had two, an Expert Medal with little medals reading RIFLE and PISTOL hanging under it, and a Sharpshooter medal with BAR hanging under it. He hadn't made Expert with the Browning Automatic Rifle, but Sharpshooter was nothing to be ashamed of. He'd only made Marksman with the .30-caliber machine gun and mortar. They had a medal for that too, but he had elected not to wear it. Everybody who qualified—and you didn't get to graduate from Parris Island if you didn't qualify—was a Marksman, so why the fuck bother?

He went into the foyer, where the mystery of his missing mother and her husband was solved. There was a brochure on the table. *Three Days and Three Nights, Including New Year's Eve, at the Luxurious Beach Hotel, Asbury Park, N.J. Only $99.95 (Double Occupancy).*

That's where they were, not thirty miles from Lakehurst.

Christ, didn't they know there was a war on? That the Japs had taken Wake Island two days before Christmas? That the Japs had invaded the Philippine Islands? That while they were sipping their fucking Seven-and-Seven in the Beach Hotel, there were German submarines right offshore, waiting to put torpedoes into American ships?

(THREE)
121 Park Avenue
East Orange, New Jersey
2105 Hours 1 January 1942

What I'll do, thought PFC Stephen Koffler, USMC, *is get together with the guys, maybe get a couple of drinks.*

He went to the telephone mounted on the wall in the kitchen and dialed from memory the number of his best buddy.

Mrs. Danielli told him Vinny was out someplace, she didn't know where. She would tell him Steve had called, she said, and asked him to wish his mom and dad a happy New Year.

He started to call Toddy Feller, but remembered that his mother had written that Toddy had enlisted in the Navy right after Pearl Harbor Day.

He thought, unkindly, that at this very moment Toddy was probably on his hands and knees, his fat ass in the air, scrubbing a deck at the Great Lakes Naval Training Center with a toothbrush.

He went back into his bedroom, where he now remembered seeing the package from Parris Island, unopened, on the closet shelf. He took it down, tore the paper off, and dug through it. There was dirty underwear and dirty socks, and the pants and shirt and shoes and toilet kit (a brand-new one) he'd taken to the post office when he'd enlisted.

And his keys. To the lobby door, to the mailbox in the lobby, to the apartment door, and to his locker in East Orange High School. He'd kept that one for a souvenir, even though it meant paying the bastards two-fifty for a key you could have made in Woolworth's Five & Ten for a quarter.

He put the keys in his pocket and went out the front door and down the stairs to the Marshall apartment, on the floor below.

He heard conversation inside when the doorbell sounded, and then he heard someone who was probably Bernice say, "I wonder who that can be?" and then the door was opened.

Mr. Marshall looked at him a minute without recognition, until Steve spoke.

"Hello, Mr. Marshall, is Bernice around?"

"I'll be damned!" Mr. Marshall said. "I didn't recognize you. Hazel, you'll never guess who it is!"

"So tell me," Mrs. Hazel Marshall said.

"Come on in," Mr. Marshall said, taking Steve's arm, then putting his arm around his shoulder, as he led him into the living room.

"Recognize this United States Marine, anybody?" Mr. Marshall said.

"Why, my God, it's Stevie," Mrs. Marshall said. "Stevie, your mother and father are in Asbury Park!"

"Yeah, I know."

"Oh, she'll be heartbroken she missed you!" Mrs. Marshall said as she came to him and kissed him. Then she held him by both arms and looked at him intently. "You've changed."

"Hello, Stevie," Dianne Marshall said. "Remember me?"

"Yeah, sure. Hello, Dianne."

"And this is Leonard," Mrs. Marshall said. "Leonard Walters. He and Dianne are sort of keeping company."

Leonard Walters looked like a candy-ass, Steve decided. Dianne looked good. She didn't have big boobs like Bernice, but the ones she had pressed attractively against her sweater.

"I'm very pleased to meet you, I'm sure," Leonard said as he shook Steve's hand. "You're a Marine, huh?"

"That's right."

"How about a little something against the cold, Steve?" Mr. Marshall said.

"Charlie, he's only seventeen."

"Eighteen," Steve corrected her. "I was hoping Bernice would be home."

"She had a date," Dianne said. "She'll be sorry she missed you."

"No big deal," Steve said.

"Seven-and-Seven OK, Steve?"

Seven-and-Seven was Seagram's Seven Crown Blended Whiskey and 7-Up. Steve hated it.

"No, thank you," Steve said.

"See, I told you," Mrs. Marshall said.

"How about a little Scotch, then? That's what I'm having."

"Scotch would be fine," Steve said. He wasn't even sure what it was, only that he had never had any before.

"Water or soda?"

"Soda, please."

Dianne walked across the room to him.

"What are those things on your uniform, medals?"

"Marksmanship medals."

She stood close to him and bent over and examined them carefully. He could see her scalp where she parted her hair; and he could smell her; and he could see the outline of her brassiere strap.

"I'm impressed," she said, straightening, still so close he could feel the warmth of her breath and smell the Sen-Sen she had been chewing.

Mr. Marshall handed him a glass and Steve took a sip. It tasted like medicine.

"That's all right, son?"

"Just fine," Steve said.

Dianne walked away. He could see her rear end quiver; she was wearing calf-high boots. Steve thought that calf-high boots were highly erotic, ranking right up there with pictures he had seen in *The Police Gazette* in the barbershop, of women in brassieres and underpants and garter belts.

"So how do you like it in the Marines, Steve?" Mr. Marshall asked.

"I like it fine," Steve said. That wasn't the truth, the whole truth, and nothing but the truth, but he understood that he couldn't say anything else.

"What have they got you doing?"

"Monday I start parachute school," Steve said.

"I don't know what that means," Mr. Marshall said.

"The Corps is organizing parachute battalions," Steve explained. "I volunteered for it."

"You mean you'll be jumping out of airplanes?" Mrs. Marshall asked.

"Yes, Ma'am."

"Really?" Dianne asked. When he looked at her and nodded, she added, "I'll be damned."

"Dianne!" her mother said. "Try to remember you're a lady."

Steve sensed that Leonard wished he would leave, and while Steve thought Leonard was a candy-ass, fair was fair. If he had a date with some girl, he'd want to get her alone and away from her family and neighbors, too.

He refused Mr. Marshall's offer to freshen his drink, and then left.

He called the Danielli house again, thinking that maybe Vinny had come back; but Mrs. Danielli said she hadn't heard from him and didn't expect to, as late as it was. He apologized for calling so late and turned the radio on.

He quickly grew bored with that. From his living room window he could see the candy store on the corner of Eighteenth Street and Park Avenue but it was closed. So there was no place he could go without a car.

He had a damned good idea where Vinny was. He was up at The Lodge, on the mountain in West Orange, where you could get a drink even if you weren't twenty-one. But getting one around here was an impossibility. They all knew who you were and how old you were. And you needed a car to get to The Lodge.

But then he remembered hearing that if you were in uniform you could get a drink, period. The idea began to grow on him. There was a bar by the Ampere station. His mother and her husband never went there, so the people there wouldn't connect him with them.

It was worth a try. It was a shame to waste a seventy-two-hour pass sitting around listening to the radio all by yourself. If they wouldn't serve him, he'd just leave. He'd turn red in the face, too; but that wouldn't be too bad.

He put on his overcoat and his brimmed cap, turned the overcoat collar up against the cold wind, and walked to the bar by the Ampere station.

It was crowded and noisy. He pushed his cap back on his head, unbuttoned his overcoat, and found an empty seat at the bar.

"What'll it be?" the bartender asked.

"Scotch and soda," Steve said.

The bartender said, "You got it," and went to make it. Steve took a five-dollar bill from his wallet and laid it on the bar.

When the bartender delivered the drink, he pushed the five-dollar bill back across the bar. "On the house," he said.

Steve took a sip of the whiskey. It still tasted like medicine. Not as bad as the first one, but still bad. It was probably, he decided, another brand.

The bartender set another drink on the bar in front of Steve.

"From the lady and the gentleman at the end," the bartender said. Steve looked down the bar to where a middle-aged couple had their glasses raised to him.

"My privilege," the man called.

"God bless you!" the woman called.

Steve felt his face flush, and desperately hoped he wasn't blushing to the point where it could be seen.

"Thank you," he called.

It was the first time in his life that anyone had bought him a drink in a bar.

"You meeting somebody?" a male voice asked in his ear. He turned and saw that it was Leonard.

"No," Steve said. "I just came in for a drink."

"Whyn'tcha come sit with us?" Leonard asked, with a nod toward the wall. There was a wall-length padded seat there and tiny tables, eight or ten of them, in front of it. Dianne Marshall was sitting on the bench, smiling and waving at him.

"Wouldn't I be in the way?"

"Don't be silly," Leonard said. "If we knew you were coming here, you could have come with us."

Steve picked up his five-dollar bill and followed Leonard over. Dianne patted the seat next to her.

"You should have said something, Steve," Dianne said, "about coming here. You could have come with us. What did you do, walk?"

"Yeah."

"I guess you get a lot of that, walking, in the Marines, huh?" Leonard asked.

"Try a thirty-mile hike with full field equipment," Steve said.

"Thirty *miles?*" Dianne asked.

"Right. It toughens you up."

"I'll bet it does," Dianne said, and squeezed his leg over the knee.

She wasn't, he saw, looking for any reaction from him. She was looking at Leonard, smiling. She relaxed her fingers, but didn't take them from his leg.

She doesn't mean anything by that, he decided solemnly. *She has a boyfriend and I'm just the kid friend of her little sister. I mean, Jesus, she was* married, *and has a* kid!

He was not used to drinking liquor; he started to feel it.

"It's been a long day," he announced. "I'm going to tuck it in."

"You haven't even danced with me yet!" Dianne protested.

"To tell you the truth, I'm a lousy dancer," he said, getting up.

"Ah, I bet you're not," Dianne said.

"You better dance with her, kid, or she won't let you go," Leonard said.

"Don't call me 'kid,' " Steve said, nastily.

Jesus Christ, I am getting drunk. I better leave that fucking Scotch alone!

"Sorry, no offense," Leonard said.

"What's the matter with you, Lenny?" Dianne snapped. She got up and took Steve's hand. "I'll decide whether you're a lousy dancer."

She led him to the dance floor and turned around and opened her arms for him to hold her. And he danced with her. He was an awkward dancer, and he was wearing field shoes. And he got an erection.

"I think we better call this off," he said, aware that his face felt really flushed now, and that it was probably visible, even in the dim light.

"Yes, I think maybe we should."

He didn't sit down again with them, just claimed his overcoat and brimmed cap and put them on. After that he shook hands with Leonard and left.

It was a ten-minute walk back to the apartment. Snow had started again, but it was still cold enough for him to feel that he was sobering up. He told himself he had made a mistake leaving, that maybe Dianne *had* meant something when she didn't take her hand off his leg. And then came the really thrilling thought that she *had* felt his erection, and it hadn't made her mad.

By the time he got to the apartment, however, and was shaking the snow off his overcoat and wiping it off the leather brim of his cap, he had changed his mind again. Dianne was twenty-what? Twenty-two at least, probably twenty-three. She was an ex–married woman, for Christsake. She had a boyfriend. His imagination was running wild, more than likely because he had had all those medicine-tasting Scotch-and-sodas.

The telephone rang.

It had to be Vinny Danielli. The sonofabitch had finally come home, and his mother had told him he had called.

"Hello, asshole, how the hell are you, you guinea bastard?"

"Steve?"

"Jesus!"

"It's Dianne."

"I know. I thought it was somebody else."

"I sure hope so," she said.

"I'm sorry about that."

"What are you doing?"

"Nothing."

"We left right after you did. Leonard lives in Verona and was worried about getting home in the snow."

"Oh."

"Your parents get home?"

"They won't be home until tomorrow sometime."

"Mine are in bed," she said. "And so's Joey."

Joey, Steve now recalled, was her little boy.

There was a long, awkward pause.

"You want to come up?" he heard himself asking.

Oh, my God, what did I say?

"To tell you the God's honest truth, Steve, I'd love to," Dianne said. "But what if anybody found out?"

"Who would find out?"

"I wouldn't want Bernice to find out, for example. Not to mention my parents."

"She wouldn't get it from me," Steve said, firmly. "Nobody would."

"But, Jesus, if we got caught!" Dianne said, and then the phone clicked and went dead.

He felt his heart jump.

She wouldn't come up. She's had a couple of drinks, a couple of drinks too many, and it's a crazy idea. Once she actually went so far as calling up, she realized that, and hung up. She absolutely would not come up.

The doorbell rang.

He ran and opened it, and she pushed past him, closing the door behind her and leaning on it. She was wearing a chenille bathrobe and slippers that looked like rabbits. She had a bottle of Scotch in her hand.

"I saw that you liked this," she said, holding it up.

"Yeah," he said. "I'm glad you came."

"Can I trust you? If one word of this got out, oh, Jesus!"

"Sure," Steve said.

She leaned forward quickly and kissed him on the mouth.

"Leonard is a good man," she said.

"Huh?"

"Leonard is a good man. I mean that. He's really a good man, and he wants to marry me, and I probably will. But . . . can I tell you this?"

"Sure."

"He thinks you should wait until you're married," she said. "I mean, maybe that's all right if you're a virgin. But I was married, you know what I mean?"

"Sure."

"If I hadn't come up here, were you going to do it to yourself?"

"What?"

"You know what I mean," she said.

"Yeah, probably," he said. He had never confessed something like that to anyone before, not even to one of the guys.

"You didn't, did you?" she asked, and then decided to seek, with her fingers, the answer to her own question.

"I think I would have killed you if you had," she said a moment later, pleased with the firm proof she had found that he had not, at least recently, committed the sin of casting his seed upon the ground. "After I took a chance like this."

"You want to come in my room?"

"There, and in the living room, and in every other place we can think of." She pulled his head down to hers and kissed him again, and this time her tongue sought his.

It took him a moment to take her meaning. It excited him. He wondered if she would be able to tell, her having been married and all, that he was a virgin.

Jesus, I'm really going to get laid.

(FOUR)
121 Park Avenue
East Orange, New Jersey
0830 Hours 2 January 1942

Dianne Marshall Norman woke up sick with the memory of what had happened between her and the kid upstairs. She knew why she had done it, but that didn't excuse it, or make it right. She had done it because she was drunk. And she knew why she had gotten drunk; but that didn't excuse it, or make getting drunk right, either.

Maybe she really was a slut, she thought, lying there in her bed with her eyes closed, hung over. A whore. That's what Joe had called her when he'd caught her with Roddie Norman in the house at the shore. She'd been drunk then, too, and that had been the beginning of the end for her and Joe. He had moved out of their apartment two weeks later and gone to a lawyer about a divorce. And been a real sonofabitch about it, too.

His lawyer had told her father's lawyer that Joe would pay child support, but that was it. He would keep the car and all the furniture and everything else, and he wouldn't give her a dime. He would pay for her to go to Nevada for six weeks to get a divorce. If she didn't agree to that, he would take her to Essex County Court in Newark and charge her with adultery with Roddie Norman, and it would be all over the papers.

Dianne didn't think doing it with just one man (two, actually, but Joe didn't know about Ed Bitter) really made her a whore or a slut. And there was no question in her mind that Joe had been fooling around himself. She'd even caught him at the Christmas office party feeling up the peroxide blonde, Angie Palmeri, who worked in the office of his father's liquor store. And there had been a lot of times when he'd had to "work late" at the store and couldn't come home, and she had driven by and he hadn't been there.

What had happened with Roddie Norman wouldn't have happened if everybody hadn't been sitting around drinking Orange Blossoms all afternoon; it had been raining and they couldn't go to the beach. And the real truth of the matter, not that anybody cared, was that she had been mad with Joe because he had been making eyes at Esther Norman all day and looking down her dress.

And then, because Roddie was taking a nap on the couch and Joey was asleep, Joe and Esther had gone to get Chinese take-out at the Peking Palace in Belmar. God only knew what those two had been up to when they were gone, but that's when it had happened. Roddie had awakened and the phonograph had been playing and they'd started to dance, and the first thing she knew they had both been on the couch and he had her shorts off, and Joe had walked in.

Dianne sometimes thought that if Joe had been able to beat Roddie up, it wouldn't have gone so far as the divorce. What actually happened was that Roddie knocked Joe on his backside with a punch that bloodied Joe's nose. Getting beaten up by Roddie was the straw that broke the camel's back, so to speak.

So she'd gone to the Lazy Q Dude Ranch, twenty miles outside of Reno, Nevada, for the six weeks it took to establish legal residence. Then she'd gotten the divorce and moved back home, where her parents treated her as though she had an "A" for "Adultery" painted on her forehead.

And then her father brought Leonard Walters home. Leonard sold dry cleaner's supplies, everything from wire hangers and mothproof bags to the chemicals they used in the dry-cleaning process itself. She had seen him around, seen him looking at her, and knew that he was interested. That was really one way to get her life fixed up, she thought. But Leonard was the single most boring male human being Dianne had ever met.

Dianne's father brought him home to a potluck supper. That was so much bull you-know-what. They just *happened* to have a pot roast for supper, and Bernice just happened not to be there, and they ate at the dining room table off the good china and a tablecloth, all usually reserved for Sunday dinner, if then.

It had been carefully planned, including a little dialogue between her mother and her father to explain Dianne's situation. The story they fed Leonard used the phrase "Dianne's mistake" a lot. But "Dianne's mistake," the way they told it, was not getting caught letting Roddie Norman in her pants, but in "foolishly running off to get married."

In her parents' version, Joe Norman had stolen her out of her cradle. And then, once he got her to elope with him—in the process throwing away her plans for college and a career—he started to abuse her and drink and run around with a wild crowd who drank and gambled and did other things that could not be discussed around a family dining table.

Leonard Walters not only swallowed the tale whole, but embarked on what he called "our courtship." The courtship had not moved very rapidly, though. The reason was that Leonard's name had been Waldowski before his parents changed it when they were naturalized. The Waldowskis were Polish and Roman Catholic, and Leonard's mother was a large and formidable woman who did not believe Roman Catholics should marry outside The One True Faith. She knew that Dianne was a Methodist, but Leonard hadn't told her about Dianne's marriage, and she didn't know about Little Joey either.

It was not now the time to tell her about it, Leonard said. "Let her learn to know you and love you."

Leonard was pretty devout himself, and he did not believe in premarital or extramarital sex. In his view, the thing to do about sex and everything else was "wait until things straighten themselves out."

On the day that PFC Stephen Koffler, USMC, entered her life, Dianne and Leonard had dinner, served precisely at noon, at the Walters' house in Verona. It was a strain, relieved somewhat by several large glasses of wine.

Then they went to East Orange, where Dianne's mother had promptly dragged her into the bedroom to deliver a recitation about how badly Joey had behaved while she was gone. After that she demanded a play-by-play account of all that was said at the Walters' dinner. When Dianne explained that Leonard had not yet told his mother about Dianne and Joe, and, more important, about Joey, there followed a two-minute lecture about why Dianne should make him do that.

Once her mother let her go, Dianne went from the bedroom to the kitchen and made a fresh pot of coffee. She laced her cup with a hooker of gin. By the time Steve Koffler marched in, looking really good in his Marine Corps uniform, she was on her fourth cup.

At first he remained the way she always had remembered him—"the kid upstairs," a peer of Bernice's, one of the mob of dirty-minded little boys who always came up to the deck on the roof to smirk and snicker behind their hands whenever she and Bernice tried to take a sunbath.

It was difficult for her to believe that he was really a *Marine.* Marines were men. Stevie Koffler, she thought, probably still played with himself.

That risqué thought, which just popped into her mind out of the blue, was obviously the seed for everything else that happened. A seed, she realized after it was over, more than adequately fertilized by the gin in her coffee.

It was immediately followed by the thought—not original to the moment—that playing with himself was what good old Leonard must be doing. Either that or he just didn't care about women, another possibility that had occurred to her. She had tried to arouse Leonard more than once; and she'd worked at that as hard as she could without destroying his image of her as the innocent child bride snatched from her cradle by dirty old Joe Norman. But she'd had no luck with him at all.

Maybe Steve doesn't play with himself. Marines are supposed to have women falling all over them.

When Steve Koffler walked into the Ampere Lounge & Grill an hour after that, there was proof of that theory. Dianne saw several women—all of them older than she was—look with interest at the Marine who walked up to the bar in that good-looking uniform, his hat cocked arrogantly on the back of his head.

And then, if you wanted to look at it that way, Leonard himself was responsible for what had happened. If he hadn't gone to Steve at the bar and practically dragged him back to the table, Steve would have had a couple of drinks and gone home. Maybe with one of the women who had been looking at him.

But Leonard dragged him back to their table. And then she felt his leg. And it was all muscle. The couple of times she had squeezed Leonard's leg, playfully, of course, it had been soft and flabby. Steve Koffler's leg was muscular, even more muscular than Joe's, and Joe had played football.

And then, when she danced with him, and *that* happened to him, and she knew that he wanted her, too . . .

She tried to talk herself out of it. She even went so far as to put on her nightgown after Leonard took her home and gave her the standard we-can-wait-until-we're-married goodnight kiss. But then she decided to have a nightcap, so she could sleep. And when she stood in the kitchen drinking it, the telephone was right there, on the wall, in front of her nose.

Things, she told herself, always looked different in the morning. They did this morning. What they looked like this morning was that she'd gotten drunk and gone to bed with the kid upstairs. Marine or not, that's what he was, the kid upstairs.

Christ, he can't be any older than eighteen!

And what they'd done! What she'd done, right from the start, right after the first time, when it had been all over for him before she even got really started.

Joe had taught her that, and from the way Steve acted, she had taught him. That, and some other things she knew he had never done before.

Jesus, what if he starts telling people?

She had another unsettling thought: Sure as Christ made little apples, Steve Koffler is going to show up at my door.

She got out of bed and took a shower. When she came out, her father was in the kitchen.

"I promised Joe's mother that I would take Joey over there," she said. "Can I borrow the car?"

"Sure, honey," her father said. "But be back by five, huh?"

"Sure."

When she got back, a few minutes after five, she met Steve coming out of the apartment with his mother and his mother's husband.

Steve's mother didn't like her. Dianne supposed, correctly, that Steve's mother knew what had really happened with Joe Norman. So, as they passed each other, all Dianne got was a cold nod from Steve's mother, and a grunt from the husband.

Steve didn't know what to do. But then he turned around and ran back to her.

Dianne told him that she had to do things with her family that night and the next day. And she managed to avoid him the rest of the time he was home.

IV

(ONE)
Office of the Chairman of the Board
Pacific & Far Eastern Shipping Corporation
San Francisco, California
16 January 1942

The ten-story Pacific & Far Eastern Shipping Corporation Building had been completed in March of 1934, six months before the death of Captain Ezekiel Pickering, who was then Chairman of the Board. There were a number of reasons why Captain Pickering had two years before, in 1932, ordered its construction, including, of course, the irrefutable argument that the corporation needed the office space.

But it was also Captain Pickering's response to Black Tuesday, the stock market crash of October 1929, and the Depression that followed. Pacific & Far Eastern—which was to say Captain Pickering personally, for the corporation was privately held—was not hurt by the stock market crash. Captain Ezekiel Pickering was not in the market.

He had dabbled in stocks over the years, whenever there was cash he didn't know what else to do with for the moment. But in late 1928 he had gotten out, against the best advice of his broker. He had had a gut feeling that there was something wrong with the market when, for example, he heard elevator operators and newsstand operators solemnly discussing the killings they had made.

The *idea* of the stock market was a good one. In his mind it was sort of a grocery store where one could go to shop around for small pieces of all sorts of companies, or to offer for sale your small shares of companies. Companies that you knew—and you knew who ran them, too. But the market had stopped being that. In Ezekiel Pickering's mind, it had become a socially sanctioned crap game where the bettors put their money on companies they knew literally nothing about, except that the shares had gone up so many points in the last six months.

The people playing the market—and he thought "playing" was both an accurate description of what they were doing and symbolic—often had no idea what the company they were buying into made, or how well they did so. And they didn't really understand that a thousand shares at thirty-three-and-a-quarter really meant thirty-three thousand two hundred fifty real dollars.

And it was worse than that: they weren't even really playing craps with real money, they were buying on the margin, putting up a small fraction of the thirty-three thousand two hundred fifty and borrowing the rest.

Ezekiel Pickering had nothing against gambling. When he had been twenty-nine and First Mate of the tanker *Pacific Courier,* he had once walked out of a gaming house in Hong Kong with fifty thousand pounds sterling when the cards had come up right at chemin de fer. But he had walked into the Fitzhugh Club with four thousand dollars American that was his, not borrowed, and that he was prepared—

indeed, almost expected—to lose. To his way of looking at it, the vast difference between his playing chemin de fer with his own cash money at the Fitzhugh Club and the elevator man in the Andrew Foster Hotel playing the New York stock market with mostly borrowed Monopoly money was one more proof that most people were fools.

The stock market was a house of cards about to collapse, and he got out early. And he took with him his friend Andrew Foster. So that when Black Tuesday struck, and people were literally jumping out of hotel-room windows, both the Pacific & Far Eastern Shipping Corporation and Foster Hotels, Inc., remained solvent.

Of course, the Depression which followed the crash affected both corporations. Business was down. But retrenchment with cash in the bank is quite a different matter from retrenchment with a heavy debt service. Other shipping companies and hotels and hotel chains went into receivership and onto the auctioneer's block, which gave both Ezekiel Pickering and Andrew Foster the opportunity to buy desirable properties, ships and hotels, at a fraction of their real value.

There never had been any doubt in Ezekiel's mind that the domestic and international economies would in time recover. In fact, he agreed with President Franklin Delano Roosevelt's 1932 inaugural declaration that the nation had "nothing to fear but fear itself," and he said so publicly. Thus, when a suitable piece of real estate went on the auction block, he put his money where his mouth was and bought it.

The Pacific & Far Eastern Shipping Corporation Building was both a structural and an architectural marvel. It was designed not only to remain standing after what the engineers called a "hundred-year earthquake," but to reflect the dominant position of the corporation in Pacific Ocean shipping.

An oil portrait of Ezekiel Pickering, completed after his death, was hanging in the office of the current Chairman of the Board. It showed him standing with his hand resting on a five-foot globe of the earth. The globe in turn rested in a mahogany gimbal. There were the traditional four gold stripes of a ship's master around his jacket cuff, and a uniform cap with the gold-embroidered P&FE insignia was tucked under his arm.

His lips were curled in a small smile. In his widow's view, that smile caught her late husband's steely determination. But Fleming Pickering had a somewhat different take on it: while the artist had indeed captured a familiar smile of his father, based on Fleming's own personal experience with it, that smile meant, *Fuck you. I was right and you were wrong; now suffer the cost of your stupidity.*

He had once told this to his wife, Patricia, and it had made her absolutely furious. But when he had told the same thing to old Andrew Foster, the hotelman had laughingly agreed.

It was a quarter past two on a Friday afternoon, and Fleming Pickering was alone in his office. There was a glass of Old Grouse Scotch whiskey in his hand. He drank his Scotch with just a dash of water and one ice cube. His father had taught him that, too. Good whiskey has a distinct taste; it is stupidity to chill it with ice to the point where that taste is smothered.

While there was always whiskey available in the office—kept in a handsomely carved teak cabinet removed from the Master's cabin of the *Pacific Messenger* when she was retired from service and sent to the ship breakers—Fleming Pickering almost never drank alone. But the glass in his hand was the third today, and he was about to pour a fourth, when a light illuminated on one of the three telephones on the huge mahogany desk.

Since Pearl Harbor, Pacific & Far Eastern had lost nine of its fleet, eight to Japanese submarines and one, the tanker *Pacific Virtue,* at Pearl. It had been caught by Japanese bombers while it was unloading aviation gasoline. Three other P&FE ships were now overdue. Fleming Pickering thought it reasonable to presume that at least one of them would never make port.

He knew every officer on every crew, as well as a good many of the seamen, the black gang, and the stewards. He was not ashamed to have taken a couple of drinks.

Pickering reached over and picked up the handset of the telephone.

"Yes?"

"A Captain Haughton for you," said Mrs. Helen Florian, his secretary, adding: "A Navy captain."

I know what this sonofabitch is going to say, Pickering thought, as he punched the button that would put him on the line. *"I'm afraid I have some bad news to report, Mr. Pickering."*

"This is Fleming Pickering," he said to the telephone.

"Good afternoon, Sir. I'm Captain Haughton, of the Secretary's staff."

"How may I help you, Captain?"

"Sir, I'm calling for Secretary Knox. The Secretary is in San Francisco and wonders if you could spare him an hour or so of your time."

Well, no news is good news, I suppose.

"What does he want?"

I know goddamn well what he wants. He wants my ships. He's a tenacious bastard, I'll say that for him.

"I'm afraid the Secretary didn't confide that to me, Sir," Captain Haughton said. "At the moment, the Secretary is on the Navy Station at Treasure Island. From there he's going to the Alameda Naval Air Station to board his aircraft. Whichever would be most convenient for you, Sir."

"No," Fleming Pickering said.

"Excuse me, Sir?"

Obviously, Pickering thought, *Captain Haughton, wrapped in the prestige of the Secretary of the Navy, is not used to hearing "no" when he asks for something.*

"I said no. I'm afraid I don't have the time to go to either Treasure Island or Alameda."

"We'd be happy to send a car for you, Sir."

"I have a car. What I don't have is time. I can't leave my office. But you can tell Mr. Knox that I will be in the office for the next several hours."

"Mr. Pickering, you do understand that the Secretary is on a very tight schedule himself," Captain Haughton said, and then added something he instantly regretted. "Sir, we're talking about the Secretary of the Navy."

"I know who he is. That's why I'm willing to see him if he wants to come here. But you might save his time and mine, Captain, if you were to tell him that I have not changed my mind, and I will fight any attempt by the Navy to take over my ships."

"Yes, Sir," Captain Haughton said. "I will relay that to the Secretary. Good afternoon, Sir."

Pickering put the handset back in its cradle.

If I wasn't on my third drink, would I have been less difficult? Well, fuck him! I told him in plain English that if the Navy tries to seize my ships, I'll take it to the Supreme Court. He should have listened to me.

He stood up from behind his desk, walked to the liquor cabinet, and made himself another Old Grouse and water. Then he walked to an eight-by-twelve-foot map of the world that hung on an interior wall. Behind it was a sheet of light steel. Models of the ships of the P&FE fleet, each containing a small magnet, were placed on it so as to show their current positions.

After he checked the last known positions of the *Pacific Endeavor,* the *Pacific Volition,* and the *Pacific Venture,* he mentally plotted their probable courses. Then he wondered—for what might have been the seven hundredth time—whether it was an exercise in futility, whether he should move the three models down to the lower left-hand corner of the map to join the models of the P&FE ships he knew for sure were lost.

Almost exactly an hour later, the bulb on one of his telephones lit up. When he picked it up, Mrs. Florian said, "Mr. Frank Knox is here, Mr. Pickering. He says you expect him."

Well, I'll be goddamned. He really is a tenacious sonofabitch!

"Please show Mr. Knox in," Fleming Pickering said. He opened the upper right drawer of his desk, intending to put his Old Grouse and water out of sight.

Then he changed his mind. As the door opened, he stood up, holding the glass in his hand. The Hon. Frank Knox walked in, trailed by a slim, sharp-featured, intelligent-looking Navy officer with golden scrambled eggs on the brim of his uniform cap. He had to be Captain Haughton.

(TWO)

Before speaking, the Hon. Frank Knox, Secretary of the Navy, stared for a moment at Fleming Pickering, Chairman of the Board of Pacific & Far Eastern Shipping. There was no expression on his face, but Pickering saw that his Old Grouse and water had not gone unnoticed.

Christ, he'll think I'm a boozer; I was half in the bag the last time, too.

"Thank you for seeing me on such short notice," Knox said. "I know you're a busy man."

"I have three overdue ships," Pickering replied. "It's the reason I didn't come to meet you. I didn't want to get far from a telephone."

Knox nodded, as if he understood.

"Mr. Pickering, may I present Captain David Haughton, my administrative officer?"

The two shook hands. Pickering said, "We spoke on the telephone."

"I'd like to talk to Mr. Pickering alone, David, if you don't mind," Knox said.

"Yes, Sir."

"Mrs. Florian," Pickering said, "would you make the Captain comfortable? Start with a cup of coffee. Something stronger, if he'd like."

"Coffee will be fine," Haughton said, as he followed Mrs. Florian out of the office.

"May I offer you something?" Pickering asked.

"That looks good," Knox said, nodding at Pickering's glass. "Dick Fowler told me you had cornered the Scotch market."

Is he indulging me? Or does he really want a drink?

"It's Old Grouse," Pickering said, as he walked to the liquor cabinet to make Knox a drink. "And I'm glad you'll have one. I'm a little uneasy violating my own rule about drinking, especially alone, during office hours."

Knox ignored that. He waited until Pickering had handed him the glass, then he nodded his thanks and said, "Haughton doesn't like you."

"I'm sorry. I suppose I was a little abrupt on the telephone."

"He doesn't think you hold the Secretary of the Navy in what he considers to be the proper degree of awe."

"I meant no disrespect," Pickering said.

"But you aren't awed," Knox insisted. "And that's what I find attractive."

"I beg your pardon?"

"There was a movie—or was it a book?—about one of those people who runs a motion-picture studio. He was surrounded by a staff whose primary function was to say 'Right, J.B.,' or 'You're absolutely right, J.B.,' whenever the great man paused for breath. After our interesting encounter in Dick Fowler's apartment, when I calmed down a little, I realized that sort of thing was happening to me."

"I don't think I quite follow you," Pickering said.

"This is good stuff," Knox said, looking down at his glass.

"I'll give you a case to take with you," Pickering said. "I have a room full of it downstairs."

"Because I'm the Secretary of the Navy?"

"Because I would like to make amends for my behavior in Fowler's apartment. I had no right to say what I said."

"The important thing, I realized, was that you said it," Knox said. "And you might have been feeling good, but you weren't drunk. I think you would have said what you said if you hadn't been near a bottle."

"Probably," Pickering said. "That doesn't excuse it, of course; but, as my wife frequently points out, when silence is called for, I too often say exactly the wrong thing."

"Are you withdrawing what you said?" Knox asked evenly.

"I'm apologizing for saying it," Pickering said. "I had no right to do so, and I'm sure that I embarrassed Richardson Fowler."

"But you believe what you said, right?"

"Yes, I'm afraid I do."

"You had me worried there for a moment," Knox said. "I was afraid I had misjudged you."

"It may be the Scotch, but I have no idea what we're talking about," Pickering said.

Knox chuckled.

"We're talking about you coming to work for me."

My God, he's serious!

"Doing what?"

"Let me explain the problem, and then you tell me if you think you could be helpful," Knox said. "I mentioned a moment before that David Haughton doesn't like you because you're not sufficiently awed by the Secretary of the Navy. That attitude—not only on Dave Haughton's part, but on the part of practically everybody else—keeps me from hearing what I should be hearing."

"You mean what's wrong with the Navy?"

"Precisely. Hell, I can't blame Haughton. From the moment he entered Annapolis, he's been taught as an article of faith that the Secretary of the Navy is two steps removed from God. The President sits at the right hand of God, and at his feet the Secretary of the Navy."

"I suppose that's so," Pickering said, chuckling.

"To Haughton's way of thinking, and to others like him, the Secretary of the Navy controls the very fate of the Navy. That being so, the information that is presented to him has to be carefully processed. And above all, the Navy must appear in the best possible light."

"I think I understand," Pickering said. "And I can see where that might be a problem."

Knox removed his pince-nez, took a handkerchief from the sleeve of his heavy woolen suit—now that he noticed it, Pickering was sure the suit was English—and polished the lenses. He put them back on his nose, stuffed the handkerchief back up his jacket cuff, and looked directly at Pickering.

"That might be an overstatement, but it's close," he said. "And to that problem is added what I think of as the Navy's institutional mind-set. From the very beginning, from the first Secretary of the Navy, the men in blue have been certain that the major cross they have to bear is that the man with the authority is a political appointee who really doesn't know—is incapable of knowing—what the Navy is *really* all about."

"Huh," Pickering grunted.

"Their quite understandable desire is—and I suppose always has been—to attempt to manage the Secretary of the Navy. To see that he hears what they want him to hear, and that he does not hear—or at least is presented with in the best possible light—what they'd rather he didn't hear at all."

"One doesn't think of the Navy as an institution," Pickering said, "but of course that's what it is."

"On October 13, 1775, Congress voted to equip seven ships to support George Washington," Knox said. "Less than a month later, on November 10, 1775, the Congress authorized the Marine Corps. And before that, there were states' navies—Rhode Island's in particular. In July 1775, Washington sent a frigate of the Rhode Island navy to Bermuda to get gunpowder for the Continental Army. In 167 years, a certain institutional mind-set is bound to occur."

Pickering chuckled. There was something professorial in the way Knox had precisely recounted the origin of the Navy, and about the man himself, with his pince-nez and superbly tailored English suit. It was difficult to imagine him during the Spanish-American War, a Rough Rider sergeant charging up Kettle Hill with Lieutenant Colonel Teddy Roosevelt's 1st United States Volunteer Cavalry.

As it is difficult for me to accept that I once actually fixed a bayonet onto my '03 Springfield, and that when the whistle blew, I went over the top and into no-man's-land in Belleau Wood.

"They had an interesting tradition, early on," Pickering said. "Privateers. I don't suppose I could talk you out of a Letter of Marque, could I?"

Knox looked at him with annoyance, and then smiled. "You really think there's a place in this war for a pirate?"

"A pirate is an outlaw," Pickering said. "A privateer was authorized by his government—and our government issued a hell of a lot of Letters of Marque—to prey on the enemy's shipping. There's a substantial difference."

"You sound as if you're serious."

"Maybe I am," Pickering said.

Knox looked at him for a moment, his demeanor making it clear he was not amused that Pickering was proposing, even half-jokingly, an absurd idea. Then he went on, "I understand why you felt you couldn't work for Bill Donovan, but I think you'll have to grant that he has the right idea."

That was pretty stupid of me, Pickering thought. *He's going to think I'm a fool or a drunk. Or both.*

"Excuse me? What idea?"

"The country will be better off—if the Army and the Navy let him get away with it, which is open to some doubt—if, that is to say, intelligence from all sources *can* be filtered through Donovan's twelve disciples . . . and if they will use it as the basis for recommending to the President action that is in the best interests of the United States, as opposed to action recommended on the basis of the parochial mind-set of the Army or Navy."

"I agree," Pickering said. "I'm a little surprised—maybe 'disturbed' is the word—to hear you doubt the Army and Navy will 'let him get away with it.' "

"I try to see things as they are," Knox said. "And I'm fully aware that in addition to being at war with the Germans, the Italians, and the Japanese, the Army and Navy are at war with each other."

Pickering chuckled again.

"I laugh, too," Knox said. "Even knowing that it's not funny."

"Why do I think that the Navy is having a hard time managing you?" Pickering said.

"Well, they're trying," Knox said. "And the odds would seem to be in their favor. Franklin Roosevelt is partial to the Navy. He was once an Undersecretary, for one thing. For another, he has a lamentable habit of calling in Ernie King—"

"Admiral King?" Pickering interrupted.

Knox nodded. "King replaced Admiral Stark as Chief of Naval Operations on December 31. Stark was a good man, but after Pearl Harbor he had to go. Anyway, Roosevelt has already started giving Admiral King marching orders without asking or telling me about it. And he's about to throw Admiral Bill Leahy into the equation."

"*That* you'll have to explain," Pickering said.

"Leahy—and understand, Pickering, that I admire all the people I'm talking about—is functioning as sort of chief of military staff to Roosevelt, a position that does not exist in the law. They're about to organize a committee, comprised of the Chief of Staff of the Army, the head of the Army Air Corps, the Chief of Naval Operations, and the Commandant of the Marine Corps. They're going to call it the Joint Chiefs of Staff, or something like that. And Leahy will preside over that. Without any legal authority to do so, except a verbal one from Roosevelt."

"Huh," Pickering snorted, and added, "You seem to be outnumbered, Mr. Secretary. But I don't see what any of this could possibly have to do with me."

"My responsibility to the President, as I see it, is to present him with the most accurate picture that I can of the Navy's strengths . . . and, more importantly, its weaknesses. His decisions have to be based on the uncolored facts, not facts seen through parochial, rose-colored glasses. I cannot, in other words, let myself be managed by Ernie King, or Bill Leahy, or the Association of Annapolis Graduates."

Knox looked at Pickering, as if waiting for his reaction. When there was none, he went on, "I've come to the conclusion that I need some—more than that, several—people like Bill Donovan's disciples."

"And that's where I come in? As one of them?"

Knox nodded. "Interested?"

"I don't know what you're really asking of me."

"I want you to be my eyes and ears in the Pacific," Knox said. "You know as much about maritime affairs in the Pacific as anyone I know, including all of my admirals."

"I'm not sure that's true," Pickering said.

"I'm not talking about Naval *tactics,* about which I am prepared to defer to the admirals, but about *logistics,* by which I mean tonnages and harbors and stevedoring and time/distance factors. I don't want my admirals to bite off more than they can chew as they try to redeem themselves in the public—and their own—eye after Pearl Harbor. Logistics affects strategy, and advising the President on strategy is my business. I want the facts. I think you're the man who can get them for me."

"Yeah," Pickering said thoughtfully. "I could do that, all right."

"My original thought was to offer you an assistant secretaryship, but I don't think that would work."

Pickering looked at him curiously.

"You'd be political. *Both* the political appointees and the Navy would hate you and try to manage you. And they'd probably succeed. If you were in uniform, however, the political appointees would not see you as a threat. As a naval officer, as a captain on the staff of the Secretary of the Navy . . ."

"A Navy captain?"

"Yes."

"How's the Navy going to react to an instant captain?"

"We're commissioning a lot of 'instant captains.' Civil engineers, doctors, lawyers, all sorts of professionals. Even a few people who are already entitled to be called 'captain,' like yourself." Knox paused and smiled at Pickering. "Since you already know the front of the ship is the bow and the floor is the deck, you'll be way ahead of most of them."

Pickering chuckled.

"Does this interest you, Pickering?"

"You think I could do something worthwhile?"

"Yes, I do. I really do."

"Then I'm at your service, Mr. Knox," Pickering said.

Knox walked up to him and offered his hand. "I'd like to have you as soon as possible. When do you think . . . ?"

"Tomorrow morning be all right?" Pickering replied.

Now it was Knox's turn to chuckle.

"Things don't move quite that quickly, even for the Secretary of the Navy," he said. "Could you call Captain Haughton back in here, please?"

Pickering picked up one of the telephones.

"Would you ask Captain Haughton to come in here, please, Mrs. Florian?"

The slim Navy officer, his eyes wary, appeared a moment later.

"David, Mr. Pickering has kindly offered me a case of this excellent Scotch. Would you see that it gets on the plane?"

"Yes, of course, Mr. Secretary."

"And before we get on the plane, I want you to find out who handles officer procurement out here. Then call them and tell them I want a suitable officer assigned to walk Mr.—*Captain*—Pickering through the processing. Make it clear to them that this is important to me. As soon as we can get him sworn in, Captain Pickering will be joining my staff."

"Aye, aye, Sir," Haughton said. He looked at Pickering, briefly but intently. He was obviously surprised at what he had just heard.

"And stay on top of it when we get back to Washington," Knox ordered. "I don't want the process delayed by bureaucratic niceties. Tell them they are to assume that if any waivers are required, I will approve them. And while I'm thinking about it, tell the Office of Naval Intelligence that while we'll go through the normal security-clearance process with Captain Pickering, I have—based on my own knowledge of Captain Pickering, and on the unqualified recommendation of Senator Fowler—already granted him an interim top-secret clearance. Have that typed up. Make it official."

"Aye, aye, Sir."

Knox turned to Pickering. "That should get the ball rolling. Haughton will be in touch. Thank you, Pickering. Not only for the Scotch. And now I have to get out of here. They're waiting for me at Alameda."

"May I send someone for the Scotch, Captain Pickering?" Haughton asked.

"It won't take a minute to get it. You can take it with you."

"Whatever you say. I'll get the driver."

"It doesn't weigh all that much," Pickering said, without thinking. "I'll get it."

Haughton gave him a quick, dirty look.

Well, here you go, Fleming Pickering, not five minutes into your naval career, and you're already pissing people off.

"Let's get it now," Knox said. "Before he has a chance to change his mind."

Pickering led them to the storeroom on the ground floor that held the greater part of the whiskey removed from the sold Pacific passenger liners. He pulled a case of Old Grouse off a stack. When he started to carry it out, he saw that Haughton was uncomfortable, visibly unable to make up his mind whether he should volunteer to carry the case of whiskey himself—or to insist on it.

A sailor who had been leaning against the front fender of a 1941 Navy gray Chrysler quickly stood erect when he saw them coming out of the building. He opened the rear door, then quickly moved to take the case of whiskey from Pickering.

At least he *knows what he's doing,* Pickering thought.

Knox nodded to Pickering and got in the car. Houghton, at first hesitantly, and then enthusiastically, offered his hand to Pickering.

"Welcome aboard, Captain," he said.

"Thank you," Pickering said. He did not like the feel of Haughton's hand.

He watched the Chrysler move down Nob Hill, and then went back to his office.

He made himself another drink, and drank it looking out his window at San Francisco bay. Then he looked for a moment at his father's picture. He wondered what the Old Man would have said: *Hooray for you for enlisting!* or, *You damned fool!* Then he sat on the edge of his desk and called his home.

"Hi!" he said, when Patricia's cheerful voice came on the line.

"You've heard, haven't you?" Patricia Pickering said.

"What?" he replied, only afterwards remembering that she was talking about the overdue *Endeavor, Volition,* and *Venture.* They had, shaming him, slipped from his immediate attention.

"What's on your mind, Flem?" Patricia asked.

"Frank Knox, the Secretary of the Navy, was just in to see me."

"About the ships? Oh God, that sounds ominous!"

"He wants me to go into the Navy," Pickering said.

There was a pause before Patricia replied, "If you had turned him down, you would have said 'wanted.' "

"Yes, that's right."

He heard her inhale deeply; it was a moment before she spoke.

"When do you go? What are you going to do?"

"Soon. Work for him. He's arranging for me to be commissioned as a captain."

"Oh, goddamn him!"

"I suppose I should have discussed this with you," Pickering said.

"Why should you start now, after all these years?" It was a failed attempt at lightness; a genuine bitterness came through.

"I'm sorry, Pat," he said, meaning it.

"My father would say, 'Never be sorry for doing something you want to do.' And you do want to go, Flem, don't you?"

"Yes. I suppose I do."

"Don't come home now. I'd say things I would later regret."

"OK."

"Give me an hour. Make it an hour and a half. Then come."

He heard the click as she hung up.

(THREE)
Building "F"
Anacostia Naval Air Station
Washington, D.C.
30 January 1942

First Lieutenant Charles E. Orfutt, aide-de-camp to Brigadier General D. G. McInerney, stepped inside McInerney's office, closed the door quietly behind him, and waited until the General raised his eyes from the paperwork on his desk.

"Sergeant Galloway is outside, Sir."

That the news did not please General McInerney was evident on his face. He shrugged, exhaled audibly, and said, "Give me two minutes, Charlie, and then send him in."

"Aye, aye, Sir," Orfutt said, and quietly left the office.

Precisely two minutes later, there was a polite knock at McInerney's door.

"Come!"

Technical Sergeant Charles M. Galloway, USMC, in greens, marched into the office, stopped precisely eighteen inches from McInerney's desk, and came to attention. Then, gazing twelve inches over McInerney's head, he said, "Technical Sergeant Galloway reporting to the General as ordered, Sir."

General McInerney pushed himself backward in his chair, locked his fingers together, and stared at Galloway for a full thirty seconds before he spoke.

"Look at me," he said.

Oh, shit. Here it comes, Charley Galloway thought. He dropped his eyes to meet McInerney's.

"Do you have any idea how much goddamned trouble you've caused?"

"Yes, Sir. I think so."

"You don't look especially penitent, Sergeant."

"Sir, I'm sorry about the trouble I caused."

"But you think it was *really* caused by a bunch of chickenshit swabbies, and in your heart of hearts you don't think you did anything wrong, do you?"

The old bastard can read my mind.

Galloway's face went pale, but he didn't reply.

"You're thinking that you were almost a Marine Corps legend, is that it? That you'd be remembered as the guy who fixed up a shot-up fighter with his own hands, flew it without orders onto the *Saratoga,* and then on to Wake, and died gloriously in a battle that will live forever in the memory of man?"

Again, Galloway's face paled momentarily, but he didn't say anything.

That's not true. I wasn't trying to be a fucking hero. All I was trying to do was get that Wildcat to Wake, where it was needed.

"What the hell were you thinking, Galloway? Can you at least tell me that?"

"I was thinking they needed that Wildcat on Wake, Sir."

"Did it occur to you that in the shape that Wildcat was, you could have done some real damage, crashing it onto the deck of the *Saratoga?"*

"Sir, the aircraft was in good shape," Galloway said.

"It had been surveyed, for Christ's sake, by skilled BUAIR engineering personnel and declared a total loss." He was referring to the U.S. Navy Bureau of Aeronautics.

"Sir, the aircraft was OK," Galloway insisted doggedly. "Sir, I made the landing."

General McInerney believed everything Galloway was telling him. He also believed that if he were a younger man, given the same circumstances, he would—he hoped—have done precisely what Galloway had done. That meant doing what you could to help your squadron mates, even if that meant putting your ass in a potentially lethal crack. It had taken a large set of balls to take off the way Galloway had. If he hadn't found Sara, he would have been shark food.

The general also found it hard to fault a young man who, fully aware of what he was going to find when he got there, had ridden—OK, *flown*—toward the sound of the guns. Purposely sailed, to put it poetically, into harm's way.

And he also believed that Galloway had actually come very close to becoming a Marine Corps legend. Professionally—as opposed to parochially, as a Marine—General McInerney believed that it had been a mistake to recall Task Force 14 before, at the very least, it had flown its aircraft off to reinforce the Wake Island garrison.

That move came as the result of a change of command. Things almost always got fucked up during a change of command, at least initially. How much Admiral Husband E. Kimmel, the former Commander in Chief, Pacific Fleet, was responsible for the disaster at Pearl Harbor was open to debate. But since he *was* CINCPAC, he *was* responsible for whatever happened to the ships of his command. And after the Japanese had wiped out Battleship Row, he had to go.

McInerney privately believed—from his admittedly parochial viewpoint as an aviator—that the loss of most of the battleship fleet was probably a blessing in disguise. There were two schools in the upper echelons of the Navy, the Battleship Admirals and the Carrier Admirals. There was no way that the Battleship Admirals could any longer maintain that their dreadnoughts were impregnable to airplanes; most of their battleships were on the bottom at Pearl.

Conversely, the Carrier Admirals could now argue that battleships were vulnerable to carrier-borne aircraft, using the same carnage on Battleship Row at Pearl Harbor as proof of their argument. That just might give command of the naval war in the Pacific to the Carrier Admirals.

McInerney knew that it wouldn't be an all-out victory for the Carrier Admirals over the Battleship Admirals. The battleships that could be repaired would be repaired and sent into action; those still under construction would be completed. But if it came to choosing between a new battleship and a new carrier, the Navy would get a new carrier. And the really senior Navy brass would no longer be able to push Carrier Admirals subtly aside in favor of Battleship Admirals.

No aircraft carriers had been sunk at Pearl. It might have been just dumb luck that they were all at sea, but the point was that *none* of them had been sunk. And since there were no longer sufficient battleships to do it, it would be the aircraft carriers that would have to carry the battle to the enemy. And when the discussions were held about *how* to take the battle to the enemy, the opinions of the Carrier Admirals would carry much more weight than they had on December 6, 1941.

Admiral Husband E. Kimmel had to go, and he knew it, and so did everybody else in CINCPAC Headquarters. From 1100 on December 7, Kimmel had had to consider himself only the caretaker of the Pacific Fleet, holding the authority of CINCPAC only until his replacement could get to Hawaii. As it actually turned out, he wasn't even given that. He was relieved, and an interim commander appointed, while Admiral King and the rest of the brass in Washington made up their minds who would replace him.

They had settled on Admiral Chester W. Nimitz. McInerney personally knew Nimitz slightly, and liked him. Professionally, he knew him better and admired him. But Nimitz hadn't even been chosen to be CINCPAC when the decision had been made to send three carrier groups to sea, two to make diversionary strikes, and the third, Task Force 14, to reinforce Wake.

The decision to recall it had come after the humiliated Kimmel had been relieved, and before Nimitz could get to Hawaii and raise his flag as CINCPAC.

McInerney believed the recall order did not take into consideration what a bloody nose the Americans on Wake had given the Japanese with the pitifully few men, weapons, and aircraft at their disposal. Commander Winfield Scott Cunningham, the overall commander on Wake, and the Marines under Majors Devereux and Putnam, had practically worked miracles with what they had.

The decision to recall Task Force 14 had obviously been made because it was not wise to risk Sara and the three cruisers. McInerney was willing to admit that probably made sense, given the overall strength of the battered Pacific Fleet; but there was no reason for not making a greater effort to reinforce Wake.

Another twelve hours' steaming would have put them within easy range to fly VFM-221's F2A-3 Buffalo fighters (and Galloway's lone F4F-4 Wildcat) off Sara onto Wake. It seemed likely to McInerney that risking the *Tangier,* with her Marine Defense Battalion and all that ammunition aboard, by sending her onto Wake would have been justified. Tangier could probably have been given air cover by VFM-221 and, for a while at least, as Sara steamed in the opposite direction, by Navy fighters aboard Sara.

Instead, *Tangier* had turned around with the others and gone back to Pearl Harbor . . . and at the moment she turned, she was almost at the point where the carriers could have launched aircraft to protect her.

McInerney was not willing to go so far as to assert that the presence of the additional aircraft (he was painfully aware of the inadequacies of the Buffalo) and the reinforcement Defense Battalion would have kept the Japanese from taking Wake, but there was no doubt in his mind that the planes and the men—and, more important, the five-inch shells—would have made it a very costly operation for them.

If that had happened, and if T/Sgt. Charley Galloway had managed to get his Wildcat onto Wake and into the battle, he *would* have become a Marine Corps legend.

But it hadn't happened. Sara and the rest of Task Force 14 had returned to Pearl with Galloway and his F4F-4 aboard.

There was a good deal of frustration aboard Sara when that happened. McInerney had learned that a number of senior officers had actually recommended to the Task Force Commander that he ignore the recall order from Pearl and go on with the original mission. In the end, of course, they had obeyed their orders.

Meanwhile, McInerney guessed—very sure he was close to the truth—that some chickenshit sonofabitch, probably a swabbie, had pointed out that what that damned Marine flying sergeant had done was in clear violation of any number of regulations.

Since that sort of thing couldn't be tolerated, charges were drawn up. And since people were looking for something, or someone, on whom to vent their frustration, Galloway had wound up being charged with everything but unlawful carnal knowledge.

General court-martial charges had actually been drawn up against him. But when it came to convening the court, they had found out that general court-martial authority was not vested in CINCPAC, but in the Commanding General of the 2nd Marine Aircraft Wing, back in San Diego, because VFM-211 was under its command.

So they had put T/Sgt. Galloway under arrest, on a transport bound for San Diego. And they'd air-mailed all the charges and specifications to the Commanding General, 2nd Marine Air Wing, "for appropriate action."

The Commanding General of the 2nd Marine Air Wing, realizing a hot potato had dropped in his lap, had quickly tossed it upstairs and into the lap of Major General D. G. McInerney, at Headquarters, USMC.

A court-martial was now out of the question, as a practical matter. It would be impossible to gather the witnesses necessary for a successful prosecution in Washington. They were all over the Pacific. And some of them were dead. There was, besides, the question of the press. It would look to the press—as it looked to McInerney—as though the Marine Corps was about to try to punish somebody for trying to fight for his country.

"But we have to do something, Mac," the Major General Commandant had said when McInerney reluctantly brought the matter to his attention. "Even Ernie King has heard about your Sergeant Galloway. Use your best judgment; I'll back you up, whatever you decide."

McInerney knew what would satisfy the Navy, short of a court-martial: a letter saying that Galloway had been relieved of flying duties and assigned elsewhere.

"I'm really furious with you, Galloway, about this," McInerney said. "You've cost me a fine fighter pilot and what I'm sure would have been a superior squadron commander."

"Sir?"

"You! You dumb sonofabitch!" McInerney said, with a fury that started out as an act, but became genuine as he realized that he was speaking the truth.

"I'm sorry, Sir, I don't understand."

"If you could have restrained your Alan Ladd–Errol Flynn–Ronald Reagan movie-star heroics for a couple of weeks, there would have been bars on your collar points and a squadron to command. You could more than likely have done some real damage to the enemy, a lot more than you could have caused even if you had managed to get that jury-rigged wreck to Wake. And probably taught some of these kids things that just might have kept them alive."

"I never even thought about a commission," Galloway replied, so surprised, McInerney noticed, that he did not append "Sir" to his reply.

"That's your goddamn trouble! You don't think!"

"Yes, Sir."

"The Corps spent a lot of time and money training you, Galloway, and now that's all going to be wasted."

"Sir?"

"It will be a cold day in hell, Galloway, before you get in a cockpit again."

"Yes, Sir," Galloway said.

McInerney saw in Galloway's eyes that that had gotten to him. The worst punishment that could be meted out to someone like Galloway was to take flying, any kind of flying, but especially flying a fighter plane, away from him.

I wonder why I said that? I don't mean it. For a number of reasons, including both that the Corps needs pilots like Galloway, and that I have no intention of punishing him for doing something I would have done myself.

"It has not been decided whether to proceed with your court-martial, Galloway. Until that decision has been made, you will report to MAG-11 at Quantico. You will work in maintenance. But you will not get in the cockpit of a Texan, or any other aircraft, to so much as taxi it down a taxiway."

"Aye, aye, Sir."

"That's all, Sergeant. You may go."

"Yes, Sir. Thank you, Sir," T/Sgt. Charley Galloway said. He did an about-face and marched out of General McInerney's office.

Lieutenant Orfutt came into General McInerney's office a moment later.

"Have a memo typed up to General Holcomb," McInerney said, "saying that I have temporarily assigned Sergeant Galloway to Quantico for duty as an aircraft maintenance supervisor. And then do a letter to CINCPAC saying that appropriate action in the case of Sergeant Galloway is being implemented."

"Aye, aye, Sir," Orfutt said. "Damned shame to lose his experience."

"You're not listening carefully, again, Charlie," McInerney said. "The operative word is *temporarily.*"

"Oh," Orfutt said, and smiled. "Yes, Sir."

"And I said something in the heat of anger that might make some sense. Get a teletype out to the 1st and 2nd Aircraft wings, telling them to review the records of the Naval Aviation Pilots and submit to me within seven days a list of those they can recommend for commissions. Put in there somewhere that the lack of a college degree is not to be considered disqualifying."

"Aye, aye, Sir."

"Is there anything else, Charlie?"

"Sir, you're having lunch at the Army-Navy Club with Admiral Ward."

"Oh, Christ! Can I get out of it?"

"This would be the third time you've canceled, Sir."

McInerney looked at his watch.

"Order up the car."

"I've done that, Sir. It's outside."

"Sometimes you're just too goddamn efficient, Charlie. With a little bit of luck, maybe it would have had an accident on the way here from the motor pool."

"Sorry, Sir," Orfutt said, and went to the clothes tree and took General McInerney's overcoat from it and held it up for him.

Fifteen minutes later, as the Marine-green 1941 Ford was moving down Pennsylvania Avenue near the White House, General McInerney suddenly sat up. He had been glancing casually out the side window, but now he stared intently, then turned and stared out the back.

"Stop the car!" he ordered.

"Sir?" the driver, a young corporal, asked, confused.

"That was English, son," McInerney snapped. "Pull to the curb and stop!"

"Aye, aye, Sir," the Corporal replied, and complied with his orders.

"There's a Navy officer coming up behind us on the sidewalk. Intercept him and tell him I would be grateful for a moment of his time," McInerney said. Then he slumped low in the seat.

The driver got quickly out of the car, found the Navy officer, and relayed General McInerney's desires to him. He walked just behind him to the car, then quickly stepped ahead of him to pull the door open.

The Navy officer, a captain, saluted.

"Good afternoon, General," he said.

"Get in," General McInerney ordered.

"Aye, aye, Sir," the Captain said.

The Captain complied with his orders.

General McInerney examined him carefully.

" 'Fuck the Navy!' Isn't that what I remember you saying, Captain?"

"Yes, Sir, I seem to recall having said something along those lines."

"And how long now have you been wearing Navy blue?"

"Three days, Sir. How do I look?"

"If people didn't know any better, they'd think you were a Navy captain. The look of confusion in your eyes, for example."

"Thank you, Sir."

"I've got a lunch date I can't get out of," General McInerney said. "But I can give you a ride. Where are you headed?"

"Just down the block, Sir."

"To the hotel your father-in-law owns?"

"Actually, General, to the White House. Secretary Knox wants me to meet the President. I've been invited to lunch."

"Oh, Flem, you sonofabitch! Why am I not surprised?"

(FOUR)
The White House
Washington, D.C.
30 January 1942

"My name is Pickering," Fleming Pickering said to the civilian guard at the White House gate. The civilian had come out of a small, presumably heated guardhouse at his approach. The two soldiers on guard, their ears and noses reddened by the cold, apparently were required to stay outside and freeze.

"Let me see your identification," the guard said curtly, even rudely.

Fleming produced his new Navy identification card. The guard examined it carefully, comparing the photograph on it to Pickering's face.

"Wait here," the guard said, and went back into the guardhouse. Pickering saw him pick up a telephone and speak with someone. He did not come back out of the guardhouse.

A minute later, a Marine sergeant in greens came down the driveway. He saluted.

"Would you come with me, please, Captain Pickering?" he said politely, crisply.

Pickering marched after him up the curving drive toward the White House. There was a crust of ice on the drive. It had been sanded, but the road was slippery.

The Marine led him to a side entrance, toward the building that had been built at the turn of the century to house the State, War, and Navy departments of the U.S. Government, and then up a rather ordinary staircase to the second floor.

Pickering found himself in a wide corridor. A clean-cut man in his early thirties sat at a small desk facing the wall, and two other men cut from the same bolt of cloth were standing nearby. Pickering was sure they were Secret Service agents.

"This is Captain Pickering," the Marine sergeant said. The man at the desk nodded, glanced at his wristwatch, and made a notation in a small, wire-bound ledger.

"This way, please, Captain," the Marine said, and led Pickering halfway down the corridor to a double door. He knocked. The door was opened by a very large, very black man in a starched white jacket.

"Captain Pickering," the Marine sergeant said.

The black man opened the door fully. "Please come in, Sir," he said. "The President's expecting you."

This was, Pickering realized, the President's private suite, the Presidential apartments, or whatever it was called. He was surprised. He had expected to be fed in some sort of official dining room.

A tall, well-built, bespectacled man in the uniform of a Marine captain came out of an inner room. In the moment, Pickering recognized him as one of Roosevelt's sons, he had no idea which one. The Captain said, "Good afternoon, Sir. Let me help you with your coat. Dad and Mr. Knox are right inside."

Pickering handed him his uniform cap and then took off his topcoat and handed that over. Captain Roosevelt handed both to the steward, then motioned Pickering ahead of him through a door.

The President of the United States, in a wheelchair, rolled across the room to him, his hand extended. Pickering knew, of course, that Franklin Delano Roosevelt had been crippled by polio, but the wheelchair surprised him. He was almost never photographed sitting in it.

"We've been talking about you, Captain," Roosevelt said as he shook Pickering's hand in a very firm grip. "Have your ears been burning?"

"Good afternoon, Mr. President," Pickering said.

He heard his father-in-law Andrew Foster's dry voice in his mind: "The sonofabitch is obviously a socialist, but giving the devil his due, he probably saved this country from going communist."

"Naval officers are forbidden to drink on duty," the President said, smiling warmly, "except, of course, when the Commander in Chief doesn't want to drink alone."

Another steward appeared at that moment with a glass of whiskey on a small silver tray.

"Thank you," Pickering said, and raised the glass. "Your health, Sir," he said, then took a sip. It was Scotch, good Scotch.

"That all right?" Roosevelt asked. "Frank said you're a Scotch drinker."

"This is fine, Sir."

"He also told me that you'd much rather be wearing a uniform like Jimmy's," the President went on, "but that he'd convinced you you would be of greater use in the Navy."

"I was a Marine, Sir," Pickering said. "Once a Marine, always a Marine."

Roosevelt laughed.

"Frank also told me to watch out for you—that if I let my guard down, you'd probably ask me for a Letter of Marque."

Pickering glanced at Frank Knox, who smiled and shook his head.

"May I have one, Sir?" Pickering said.

Roosevelt laughed heartily.

"No, you may not," he said. "I admire your spirit, Pickering, but I'm afraid you're going to have to fight this war like everybody else—including me—the way someone tells you to."

"Aye, aye, Sir," Pickering said, smiling.

I am being charmed. I wonder why.

"Why don't we go to the table and sit down?" Roosevelt said, gesturing toward a small table near windows overlooking the White House lawn. Pickering saw there were only four places set.

Stewards immediately began placing small plates of hors d'oeuvres before them.

Roosevelt began to talk about the British commandos. Pickering quickly saw that he was very impressed with them—as much for the public's perception of them as for any bona fide military capability.

"When Britain was reeling across Europe from the Nazi Blitzkrieg," Roosevelt announced, as if making a speech before a large audience, "when they were literally bloody and on their knees, and morale was completely collapsing, a few small commando operations, militarily insignificant in themselves, did wonders to restore civilian morale and faith in their government."

"I had really never thought of it in that context," Pickering said honestly. "But I can see your point."

Roosevelt, Pickering was perfectly willing to grant, was a genius at understanding—and molding—public opinion.

"A very few brave and resourceful men can change the path of history, Pickering," the President said sonorously. "And fortunately, right now we have two such men. You know Colonel Jim Doolittle, don't you?"

"If you mean, Mr. President, the Jim Doolittle who used to be vice-president of Shell Oil, yes, Sir. I know him."

"I thought you might," the President said. "Two of a kind, you know, you two. Not thinking of the cut in pay that putting on a uniform meant, but rather rushing to answer the call of the trumpet."

I really am being charmed, Fleming Pickering decided. *He wants something from me. I wonder what. Not the damned ships again!*

"Frank, have you told Captain Pickering what Jim Doolittle's up to?"

"It's top secret, Mr. President," Secretary Knox replied.

"Well, I think we can trust Captain Pickering. . . . Captain Pickering, would you be offended if I called you by your Christian name?"

"Not at all, Mr. President."

"Well, Frank, if Flem's going to be working for you, he'll find out soon enough anyway. Wouldn't you say?"

"Probably, Mr. President."

"Jim Doolittle, Flem, came to me with the idea that he can take B-25 Mitchell bombers off from the deck of an aircraft carrier."

"Sir?" Pickering asked, not understanding.

"The Japanese Emperor is sitting in his palace in Tokyo, convinced that he's absolutely safe from American bombing. Colonel Doolittle and his brave men are about to disabuse him of that notion," Roosevelt said, cocking his cigarette holder almost vertically in his mouth as he smiled with pleasure.

"The idea, Pickering," Secretary Knox said, "is that we will carry Doolittle on a carrier within striking distance of Tokyo; they will launch from the carrier, bomb Tokyo, and then fly on to China."

"Fascinating," Pickering said, and then blurted, "but can Doolittle do it? Can you fly airplanes that large from aircraft carriers?"

"Doolittle thinks so. They're down in Florida now, in the Panhandle, learning how," Knox said. "Yes, I think it can be done."

"Christ, that's good news!" Pickering said excitedly. "So far, all we've done is take a licking."

"And there will be other reverses in the near future, I am very much afraid," Roosevelt said.

"The Philippines, you mean?" Pickering asked.

"You don't believe that Douglas MacArthur will be able to hold the Philippines?" Roosevelt asked. He was still smiling, but there was a hint of coldness in his voice.

Jesus Christ, my mouth has run away with me again!

"Mr. President, I don't pretend to know anything about our forces in the Philippines, but I do know that they will require supplies. I do know something about shipping. I know that there are not enough bottoms to supply a large military force, and even if there were, there are not enough warships after Pearl Harbor to protect the sea lanes to the Philippines."

"Aren't you concerned, talking like that," Roosevelt asked, carefully, "that someone who doesn't know you might think you're a defeatist?"

"If I have spoken out of turn, Mr. President . . ."

Roosevelt looked at him thoughtfully for a long moment before he spoke again.

"I said, a while ago, we have two brave and resourceful men," he said. "Jimmy here is allied with the other one. And don't tell me this is top secret, too, Frank. I know."

"Yes, Mr. President," Knox replied.

"The commander of the Marine Guard at White Sulphur Springs a few years back," Roosevelt said, "was a man named Evans Carlson. You happen to know him?"

"No, Sir."

"Major Carlson is now out in San Diego, starting up a unit I think of as American Commandos. But I don't want it to appear as if we're slavishly copying our British cousins, so we're calling them Raiders. All volunteers, highly trained, who will hit the Japanese and then run."

"Sounds very interesting," Pickering said.

I wonder how he's going to move them around? It's thirty, forty miles from the English coast to the French. Distances in the Pacific are measured in multiple hundreds, multiple thousands, of miles.

"Frank had the Navy yards convert some old four-stacker destroyers to high-speed transports," Roosevelt said.

He's reading my mind, Pickering thought.

"The idea, Flem," Captain Roosevelt said, "is that by striking the Japanese where they don't expect it, in addition to what damage we do there, we will force the Japanese to put forces they could use elsewhere to work guarding all of their islands."

"I see," Pickering said.

"And, Flem," the President said passionately, "think of what it will do for morale! As you just said, all we've done so far in this war is take a licking and lick our wounds!"

"Yes, Sir. I understand."

"Well, I'm sorry to tell you that my enthusiasm is not shared by either the Navy *or* the Marine Corps," the President said.

"Now, Frank," Secretary Knox said, "that's not true."

"They are dancing with Evans Carlson with all the enthusiasm of a fourteen-year-old in dancing school paired off with a fat girl," Roosevelt said, and everyone laughed. "They have to do it, but they don't have to like it."

"Frank," Secretary Knox said, "if you really think that's the case, I'll send Captain Pickering out there to see what needs straightening out."

Roosevelt looked as if he had just heard a startlingly brilliant suggestion for the first time.

You fraudulent old sonofabitch, Pickering thought, *that's what this whole thing with your boy here for a private lunch is all about. Knox brought me here to let you know what he intended to do with me, and you'll let him, providing I take care of this Major Evans Carlson. Tit for tat. I haven't been here a week, and I'm already in politics.*

"That might not be a bad idea, Frank," Roosevelt said thoughtfully, and then added, "Now that I think about it, if you can spare Fleming, he's probably just the right man for the job. You *were* a Marine, Flem, after all."

"Yes, Sir, I was."

"I'll send him out there tomorrow, Mr. President," Knox said.

"Good idea, Frank!"

When they left the White House, Knox waited until they were in his limousine and then said, "I have a Commander Kramer who has all the background material on Major Carlson, the Raiders, and their target. An island called Makin. I'll have him bring it around to your hotel tomorrow. And then you get on the Monday-morning courier plane to San Diego. I'm not really sure how I feel about the whole idea. . . . I understand why people may be dragging their feet; they think it's both a waste of time and materiel and an idea that may go away. . . . But now I know that it's important to Roosevelt. Given that, it's important to you and me that you go out there and light a fire under people."

"I'm sympathetic to the notion that a victory, any kind of a victory, even a small one, is important right now."

"And it will be even more important when the Philippines fall," Knox said. "So it's important, for a number of reasons, that you go out there right away. We can get you an office and a secretary when you come back."

V

(ONE)
Security Intelligence Section
U.S. Naval Communications
Washington, D.C.
0730 Hours 31 January 1942

When Mrs. Glen T. (Ellen) Feller passed through the security gate on her way to work, the civilian guard smiled at her and handed her a note. It read, "Ellen, please see me at 0800." It was initialed "AFK." Commander A. F. Kramer was the officer-in-charge.

Ellen Feller, who was tall and thirty, with pale skin and long, light brown hair which she normally wore in a bun, glanced at the note for a second. It sparked her curiosity, but it did not cause her any real concern. She often found essentially identical notes waiting for her as she came to work.

"Thank you," she said, smiling at the guard; then she entered the restricted area. She either nodded and smiled or said good morning to a dozen people as she made her way to her desk at the far end of the long and narrow room. People smiled back at her, some of them a little warily. Ellen was aware that her co-workers thought of her as devoutly religious. She had several times heard herself referred to as a "Christer."

Personnel records, and especially reports of what were known as Complete Background Investigations, are classified Confidential, the security classification a step below Secret. They were thus theoretically *really* confidential, and their contents were made available only to those with a "need to know," who had been granted the appropriate security clearances.

In practice, however, personnel records and reports, "interim" and "final," of Complete Background Investigations of new or potential employees were available to anyone who was curious—even secretaries. This was especially the case in the Security Intelligence Section, where even the clerk-typists held Top Secret security clearances. There the Confidential classification was considered something of a joke.

Before Mrs. Feller had reported for duty, some time ago, as an Oriental Languages Linguist, all the girls in the office knew that their new co-worker was married to the Reverend Glen T. Feller of the Christian & Missionary Alliance; that she had perfected her language skills in the Orient; and that until the previous May, she and her husband had operated a C&MA missionary school in China.

They also knew that the Fellers had no children and that Reverend Feller was off doing the Lord's work among the American Indians on a reservation in Arizona. Meanwhile, Mrs. Feller had noticed a classified advertisement placed by the U.S. Government seeking U.S. citizens with fluency in foreign languages, and she'd answered it.

Soon after that, the Navy offered her a job as an Oriental Languages Linguist.

It wasn't known whether she accepted the job as a patriotic citizen; or because the Fellers needed the money; or because she didn't want to live in the Arizona desert. Her application for employment stated simply that she "wanted to serve."

In fact, although the job paid her more than she'd expected, she had taken it for the very simple reason that she really didn't want to go to Arizona. And that meant she had to find work.

The actual fact was that Ellen Feller had absolutely no interest in doing the Lord's work or, for that matter, in saving her immortal soul. And even more to the point, she loathed the Reverend Feller. She didn't want to live with him in Arizona or anywhere else.

Were it not for her father, who was rich and elderly—approaching the end of his time on earth—and a religious zealot, she would have divorced her husband. But a divorce would almost certainly inspire him to cut Ellen out of his will and leave all of his money to the Christian & Missionary Alliance. The way it stood now, he intended to leave half of his worldly goods to his daughter and her husband.

With that understanding, and of course after days of prayerful consideration, the Reverend Feller had announced to the hierarchy of his denomination that it was God's will for him to go alone to bring the Gospel of the Lord Jesus Christ to the Navajos. His beloved wife would meanwhile make what contribution she could to the war effort in Washington, D.C. This move would cause them both a huge personal sacrifice, but they had prayerfully and tearfully decided to endure it.

The Reverend Feller had been honestly unhappy to leave Ellen behind in Washington. Not because he particularly liked her, or even because he would be denied his connubial privileges, but because the old man was in a nursing home in Baltimore, forty miles from Washington. The Reverend was afraid that while he was off in Arizona, Ellen would attempt to poison her father against him with reports of his misbehavior, sexual and otherwise, in China.

In the end, he had acquiesced to the move solely because Ellen had threatened to go to the authorities, both governmental and ecclesiastical, and inform them of some of the lesser-known facts about her husband's activities in China. From the day they had entered that country, for example, he had been involved in the illegal export to the United States of Chinese archeological treasures looted from tombs.

The Reverend Feller had gone to great lengths to conceal what he called his "personal pension plan" from his wife. He had therefore been astonished to learn that she knew about it. He incorrectly suspected that one of the Chinese had told her. She had actually learned about it from an American Marine. As one of their last missions before being transferred to the Philippines, the 4th Marines had provided a guard detachment for the convoy of missionary vehicles as they left for home.

Ellen Feller had had a brief fling in those days with one of the young Marines. She now realized the affair had been both foolish and stupid; but at the time she had endured a long abstinence from men, the Marine himself was extraordinarily fascinating, and she'd imagined that the odds were very much against her ever seeing him again.

When she first saw him staring with interest at her body, she presumed he was a simple Marine in charge of the Marine trucks. It was only after they'd made the beast with two backs half a dozen times that she learned that Corporal Kenneth R. "Killer" McCoy, USMC, wasn't anything of the kind.

He was, in fact, on an intelligence-gathering mission for the 4th Marines. His mission was concerned both with the location of Japanese army units in the area he was passing through—and with reports that missionaries were smuggling out of China valuable Chinese artifacts: jade, pottery, and other items.

Until she was actually aboard the ship that brought her home, Ellen Feller managed to convince Ken McCoy that she was fonder of him than was the case. Largely because of that, she was reasonably assured that he did not report to his superiors that some of the shipping containers the Marines had obligingly transported for them to Tientsin contained material having nothing to do with the work of the Christian & Missionary Alliance.

But of course, she couldn't be sure.

Her concern diminished with time, and especially when she learned that the 4th Marines had indeed been transferred from China to the Philippines as scheduled. It was about that time that she entered the Navy's employ.

Just before Pearl Harbor, however, she was instructed to deliver to the office of the officer in charge, Commander A. F. Kramer, a packet of classified documents that were to be transported to the Far East by officer courier. The officer courier turned out to be Killer McCoy, now wearing the uniform of a Marine lieutenant.

Since McCoy was driven directly from the office to meet his airplane, there was no time then for Ellen Feller to do anything but make it plain to him that she was perfectly willing—even anxious—to resume their intimate relationship. There was enough time, nevertheless, for her to reassure herself that McCoy had still not informed anyone about the material her husband had illegally brought into the United States.

Not long after that, there was a cable reporting that Lieutenant McCoy was missing in action in the Philippines and presumed dead—news that for a few days flooded Ellen Feller with considerable relief. The matter was finally over and done with, she told herself.

But then McCoy dropped out of the blue alive and well, and that put her back on square one. Beyond that, McCoy showed no interest whatever in resuming their relationship. And soon after that, McCoy disappeared from Washington. There was a credible rumor (which she now thought of as "scuttlebutt") that McCoy was on a confidential, undercover mission in California.

Ellen Feller was nothing if not resourceful. A short time later—though after a good deal of thought—she came up with a reasonable plan in the event McCoy reported the crates. First of all, there was a good chance that he would not report them at all. If he did, the question would naturally arise as to why he hadn't made his report to the proper authorities in China; his failure to do so would constitute, almost by definition, dereliction of duty.

And even if he did report them, it would come down to his word against hers and the Reverend Feller's. Besides, Ellen Feller had so far been unable to locate the crates, although she'd tried very hard to find them. Her husband had obviously hidden them well. Under the present circumstances, she doubted that anyone in the government would spend a lot of time looking for them—or that they could find them if they did. Glen Feller might be a miserable sonofabitch, but he was not stupid.

And even if the crates did show up, she could profess to know nothing whatever about them; or alternatively, she could claim that she had reported the matter to McCoy. What was important, she concluded, was to earn the reputation of being a simple, loyal, hardworking employee, who was so devoutly religious that she could not possibly be involved in anything dishonest.

It was not difficult for her to play this role. In China she had successfully played the role of a pious, hardworking, good Christian woman for years.

Playing it in Washington turned out to be even easier. In fact, partially because of the mushrooming of the Intelligence staff, it produced unexpected benefits. Other linguists came aboard after she did, and many of them, like her, were former missionaries. Soon she was given greater responsibility: since there was neither time nor need to translate every Chinese or Japanese document that came into their hands, Ellen Feller became sort of an editor. She separated those documents that would be of interest to the Navy from the others, which were discarded, and then she assigned the job of translating the important ones to someone or other. She rarely made the actual translations herself. Because she had taken on greater responsibility, her official job description was changed, and this resulted in a promotion.

At precisely five minutes before eight, Ellen Feller rose from her desk and visited the ladies' room to inspect her hair and general appearance. She was generally pleased with what she saw in the mirror, yet she wished, as she almost always did, that she could wear lipstick without destroying the image she was forced to convey. Without it, she thought, she looked like a drab.

She checked very carefully to make sure that no part of her lingerie was visible. She took what she was perfectly willing to admit was a perverse pleasure in wearing black, lacy lingerie. It made her feel like a woman. But of course she didn't want anyone, especially Commander Kramer, to see it.

When she finished, she went to Commander Kramer's office, stood in the open doorway, and knocked on the jamb.

"Come in, Ellen," Commander Kramer said, smiling. "Good morning."

"Good morning, Sir," she said, and stepped inside.

There was a captain in the office, who rose as she entered.

"Ellen, this is Captain Haughton, of Secretary Knox's office. Captain, Mrs. Ellen Feller."

Haughton, Ellen saw, was examining her carefully. There was a moment's concern *(What does someone from the office of the Secretary of the Navy want with me?)* but it passed immediately. She sensed that Captain Haughton liked what he saw.

"Good morning, Sir," Ellen Feller said politely. "I'm very pleased to meet you."

(TWO)
The Foster Lafayette Hotel
Washington, D.C.
31 January 1942

Captain Fleming Pickering, USNR, had been talking with his wife in San Francisco. Just after he put the telephone handset back in its cradle, the telephone rang again.

The ring disturbed him. During the last few minutes of his call he had said some unflattering things about the President of the United States, and he'd performed a rather credible mimicry of both the President's and Mrs. Eleanor Roosevelt's voices. As he did that, it occurred to him that his telephone might be tapped, and that Roosevelt would shortly hear what Fleming Pickering thought of him.

The possibility that his telephone might indeed be tapped was no longer a paranoid fantasy. Telephones *were* being tapped. The nation was at war. J. Edgar Hoover and the FBI had been given extraordinary authority. And so, certainly, had the counterintelligence services of the Army and Navy. The Constitution was now being selective in whose rights it protected.

The great proof of that was just then happening in Pickering's home state. A hysterical Army lieutenant general in California had decided that no one of Japanese ancestry could be trusted. And he had been joined in this hysteria by California's Attorney General, a Republican named Earl Warren. Warren was more than just an acquaintance of Fleming Pickering's. Pickering had played golf with him—and actually voted for him.

"To protect the nation," the Army lieutenant general and the California Attorney General had decided to scoop up all the West Coast Japanese, enemy alien and native-born American alike, and put them in "relocation camps."

Just the West Coast Japanese. Not Japanese elsewhere in the United States. Or, for that matter, Japanese in Hawaii. And not Germans or Italians either . . . even though it wasn't many months earlier that the German-American Bund was marching around Madison Square Garden in New York, wearing swastika-bedecked uniforms, singing *"Deutschland Über Alles,"* and saluting with the straight-armed Nazi salute.

It was governmental insanity, and it was frightening.

Pickering had already concluded that if he were J. Edgar Hoover—or one of his counterintelligence underlings (or for that matter, some captain in Naval Intelligence)—and had learned that Fleming Pickering, Esq., had appeared out of nowhere, been commissioned as a captain directly and personally by the Secretary of the Navy, and was obviously about to move around the upper echelons of the defense establishment with a Top Secret clearance, he would want to learn instantly as much as he could about Pickering and his thoughts and opinions. The easy way to do that was to tap his telephone.

Among the many opinions Pickering had broadcast over the phone moments earlier, he'd said that "the President of the United States is either the salvation of the nation, or he's quite as mad as Adolph Hitler, and I don't know which." And "if he goes ahead with this so-called relocation of the Japanese, especially the ones who are citizens, and isn't stopped, I can't see a hell of a lot of difference between him and Hitler. The law is going to be what he says it is."

Fortunately, he'd sensed that he was upsetting Patricia, so he'd switched to mimicking Roosevelt's and Eleanor's quirks of speech. He knew that always made her laugh.

Of course, he had not informed Patricia of the subjects discussed over lunch in the Presidential Apartments. Without giving it much solemn thought, he'd decided that anything the Commander in Chief had said to the Secretary of the Navy and a Navy Reserve captain was none of the captain's wife's business.

"Hello," he said, picking up the telephone.

"Captain Pickering, please."

"This is Captain Pickering."

"Sir, this is Commander Kramer. I'm in the lobby."

Oh, Christ. I should have answered the telephone in The Navy Manner. This isn't the Adams Suite in the Lafayette. This is the quarters of Captain F. Pickering, USNR, and I should have answered the phone by saying "Captain Pickering."

"Please come up, Commander."

"Aye, aye, Sir."

Pickering pushed himself out of the upholstered chair in the sitting room and went into the bedroom to put on his uniform. Commander Kramer had probably already decided he had been selected by ill fortune to baby-sit another goddamned civilian in uniform. Opening the door to him while wearing a Sulka's silk dressing robe would confirm that opinion beyond redemption.

The door chimes went off while Pickering was still tying his tie. He muttered, "Damn," then went to the door and pulled it open.

Commander Kramer, a tall, thin man with a pencil-line mustache, was not alone. He had with him a lieutenant junior grade and a woman. The JG was a muscular young man who was carrying a well-stuffed leather briefcase. Fleming would have given odds that he'd not only gone to Annapolis, but that he'd played football there.

The woman, smooth-skinned, wearing little or no makeup, was in her middle thirties. She was wearing a hat—a real hat, not a decorative one—against the snow and cold. She had unbuttoned her overcoat, and Fleming Pickering noticed, *en passant,* that she had long, shapely calves and a nice set of breastworks.

"I was just tying my tie," Pickering said. "Come in."

"Yes, Sir," Commander Kramer said, then thrust a small package at Pickering. "Sir, this is for you."

"Oh? What is it?"

"The Secretary asked me to get those for you, Sir. They're your ribbons. The Secretary said to tell you he noticed you weren't wearing any."

"Would you say, Commander, that that's in the order of a pointed suggestion?"

"Actually, Sir," Kramer said, "it's probably more in the nature of a regal command."

Pickering chuckled. At least Kramer wasn't afraid of him. Frank Knox had described Kramer as "the brightest of the lot," and Pickering had jumped to the conclusion that Knox meant Kramer was sort of an academic egghead. He obviously wasn't.

"Captain, may I introduce Mrs. Ellen Feller? And Mr. Satterly?"

"How do you do?"

Mrs. Feller gave him her hand. He found it to be soft and warm. Lieutenant Satterly's grip was conspicuously firm and masculine. Pickering suspected he would love to try a squeeze contest.

"Let me finish, and I'll be right with you," Pickering said, and started to the bedroom.

"Captain, may I have a word with you alone, Sir?" Kramer asked.

"Come along."

He held the door to the bedroom open for Kramer, and closed it after he'd followed him through it.

"Mrs. Feller is a candidate nominee, maybe, for your secretary, Captain," Kramer said.

"I wondered who she was."

"The Secretary said I should get you someone a little out of the ordinary," Kramer said. "I took that to mean I should not offer you one of the career civil-service ladies."

"How did you get stuck with me, Kramer?"

"I'm flattered that I did, Sir."

"Really?"

"It's always interesting to work with somebody who doesn't have to clear his decisions with three levels of command above him."

"So it is," Fleming said. "Tell me about Mrs. . . . what did you say?"

"Feller, Captain. Ellen Feller. She's been with us about six months."

" 'Us' is who?" Pickering interrupted.

"Naval Intelligence, Sir."

"OK." He had figured as much.

"She and her husband were missionaries in China before the war. She speaks two brands of Chinese, plus some Japanese."

"Now that you think about it, she does sort of smell of missionary."

"She doesn't bring it to work, Sir. I can tell you that. She's been working for me."

"Why are you so willing to give her up?" Pickering challenged, looking directly at Kramer.

There was visible hesitation.

"The lady has character traits you forgot to mention? She likes her gin, maybe?"

"No, Sir. There's an answer, Captain. But it sounds a bit trite."

"Let's hear it."

"If I understand correctly what your role is going to be, you need her more than I do."

"Oh," Pickering replied. "That's very nice of you. I thought perhaps you might be giving her to me so she could tell you everything you wanted to know about me. And about what I'm doing."

"No, Sir," Kramer smiled. "That's not it."

"How do I know that?"

"Well, for one thing, Sir, I don't need her for that purpose. The back-line cables will be full of reports on you."

"What's a back-line cable?"

"Non-official messages. Personal messages. What the admirals send to each other when they want to find out, or report, what's really going on."

"OK," Fleming said. "You're a very interesting man, Commander."

"I don't know about that. But I like what I'm doing, and I'm smart enough to know that if I got caught spying on you—as opposed to getting my hands on back-line cables—I would spend this war at someplace like Great Lakes, giving inspirational talks to boots."

"Did you ever consider selling life insurance?" Pickering asked. "You're very convincing. People would trust you."

"Some people can. People I admire can trust me completely."

"How do I rate on your scale of admiration?"

"Way at the top."

"Is that what the Navy calls soft-soap?"

"I really admire the Secretary," Kramer said. "He admires you, or you wouldn't be here. Call it 'admiration by association.' And then there are these."

He walked to the dresser where Pickering had laid the small package Kramer had given him. He opened it and took out two rows of multicolored ribbons.

"These are very impressive, Captain. You didn't get these behind a desk."

Pickering went to him and took them, then looked at them with interest.

"I don't even know what they all are," he said.

"Turn them the other way around," Kramer said, chuckling. "They're upside down. And then, from the left, we have the Silver Star, the Navy and Marine Corps Medal, the Purple Heart with two oak leaf clusters. . . ."

"I never got a medal called the Purple Heart," Pickering interrupted.

"It's for wounds received in action," Kramer said. "It was originally a medal for valor conceived by General Washington himself in 1782. In 1932, on the two-hundredth anniversary of his birth, it was revived. It is now awarded, as I said, for wounds received in action."

"We had wound stripes," Pickering said softly, and pointed at his jacket cuff. "Embroidered pieces of cloth. Worn down here."

"Yes, Sir. I know. You had three. Now you have a Purple Heart with two oak leaf clusters. On the left of the lower row, Captain, is your World War I Victory Medal, and then your French medals, the Legion d'Honneur in the grade of Chevalier, and finally the Croix de Guerre. A very impressive display, Sir."

"Kramer, I was an eighteen-year-old kid. . . ."

"Yes, Sir. I know. But I suspect the Secretary feels, and I agree, that someone who has never heard a shot fired in anger—and we have many senior officers in that category, Sir—will not automatically categorize as a goddamn civilian in uniform a man who was wounded three times while earning three medals for valor."

Pickering met Kramer's eyes, but didn't respond.

"You've noticed, Sir, that the Secretary wears his Purple Heart ribbon in his buttonhole?"

"No, I didn't. I saw it. I didn't know what the hell it was."

"The Secretary got that, Sir, as a sergeant in the Rough Riders in Cuba in 1899."

"OK. You and the secretary have made your point. Now what about the young officer?"

"He's carrying the bag. I didn't know what you were interested in, so I brought everything you might be. It's a heavy bag. You pick out what you want, and he'll return the rest. Do you have a weapon, Sir?"

"I beg your pardon?"

"Are you armed? Do you have a gun?"

"As a matter of fact, I do. Am I going to need one?"

"Much of that material is top secret, Captain. It either has to be in a secure facility or charged to someone who has the appropriate security clearance and is armed."

"My pistol is stolen," Fleming Pickering said.

"Sir?"

"I brought it home from France in 1919," Pickering said. "It's stamped 'U.S. Property.' "

Kramer chuckled and smiled. "I'm sure the Statute of Limitations would apply, Sir. A Colt .45?"

"Yeah," Pickering said. He went to a chest of drawers, opened it, and held up a Colt Model 1911 pistol.

"Well, we'll get you another one, Captain. But that should do for the time being."

"Is there any reason I can't just read this stuff here and give it all back?"

"None that I can think of, Sir. May I make a suggestion?"

"Sure."

"Make a quick survey, select what you want, and then we'll send Mr. Satterly back to the office with the rest. For that matter, I could go with him. And then—presuming you find Mrs. Feller at least temporarily satisfactory—she could stay here until you're finished, then bring the rest back."

"What would Mrs. Feller do about a gun?" Pickering asked drily.

"She carries one in her purse, Sir."

"I'll be damned!"

Pickering put the Colt automatic back in the drawer and closed it. Then he examined his tie, straightened it, and shrugged into his uniform jacket.

"Let me help you with your ribbons," Kramer said.

He pinned them on for Pickering, then they went into the sitting room.

"Mrs. Feller," Pickering said, "Commander Kramer speaks very highly of you. If you think it's worth trying, I'd be grateful if you would come on board to help me."

"If you're not pleased with how I work out, Captain Pickering," she said, "I'll understand."

"Well, we'll give it our best shot," Pickering said. "Mr. Satterly, you want to hand me that briefcase?"

"Aye, aye, Sir," Lieutenant Satterly said. For the first time, Pickering saw that the briefcase was attached to Satterly's wrist with a length of stainless steel cable and a handcuff.

"Mrs. Feller," Pickering said, "why don't you call room service and order some coffee?"

"Just for the two of you," Kramer explained. "Ellen, you'll stay and see what Captain Pickering decides to send back with you to the office."

She nodded. As Pickering dipped into the briefcase, he heard her ask the operator for room service.

A moment or two later, he glanced around for Commander Kramer to ask him a question. Before he found Kramer, however, his eyes went up Ellen Feller's dress. Quite innocently, he was sure, she was sitting in such a way that he could see that her lingerie was lace and black.

I'll be damned, a missionary lady who wears black lace underwear and carries a gun in her purse.

"Commander, would you tell me what the hell this is, please?" he said, turning his attention to the business at hand.

(THREE)
Headquarters, 2nd Joint Training Force
Camp Elliott, California
1005 Hours 2 February 1942

Offices in Marine headquarters are usually well equipped with signs identifying the various functions performed therein. And often the signs identify the name of the functionary as well. That didn't seem to be true of Headquarters, 2nd Joint Training Force. There were sign brackets mounted over the doors, but no signs hung from them.

Second Joint Training Force, whatever the hell that was, was either moving in or moving out, Staff Sergeant Joe Howard decided. He was not surprised. The whole Corps seemed to be in a state of upheaval.

Though Staff Sergeant Joe Howard normally took a great deal of professional pride in his appearance, he looked slovenly now, and he knew it. He needed a shave, for one thing, and his greens were mussed and bore the stain of a spilled cup of coffee.

Howard had just flown into San Diego from Pearl Harbor on a Martin PBM-3R

Mariner. The Mariner was a "flying boat," a seaplane. Most of the twin-engined, gull-winged aircraft had a crew of seven. They were armed with one .30- and five .50-caliber machine guns and had provision to carry and drop a ton of ordnance, either bombs or depth charges.

The one Howard had flown from Pearl Harbor, however, was the unarmed transport version, the "Dash-Three-R." But this one wasn't a standard Dash-Three-R. It had been fitted up inside for Navy brass. For admirals or better, Joe judged from the comfortable leather seats, the steward, and even an airborne crapper. There were sixteen passengers aboard, including a rear admiral, a half-dozen Navy captains, three Marine and one Army full colonels, and some lesser brass. And two enlisted men. The other one was a gold-stripe Navy Chief Radioman who had made it plain even before they were taken out to the airplane at Pearl that he was not interested in conversation.

Rank didn't get you on the Mariner, the priority on your orders did. They left a roomful of brass behind them at Pearl, including a highly pissed Marine lieutenant colonel who had strongly asserted that there was something seriously wrong with a system that made him give up his seat to a lowly staff sergeant.

It had been Joe Howard's first ride on an airplane of any kind. As a consequence, he had not been aware that aircraft have a tendency to make sudden rapid ascents and descents while proceeding in level flight. The price he paid to gain such an awareness was a nearly full cup of coffee spilled on his chest, soiling his shirt, field scarf, and blouse, and painfully scalding his skin. All this took place while the gold-stripe Chief Radioman watched him scornfully.

A heavyset, middle-aged master gunnery sergeant came down the deserted, signless corridor.

"Gunny, excuse me, I'm looking for Captain Stecker in Special Planning," Staff Sergeant Joe Howard said to him.

The Gunny examined him carefully, critically. There was no way he could miss the stubble on Howard's face or the brown stains on his field scarf and khaki shirt.

I am now going to get my ass eaten out, and this sonofabitch looks like he's had a lot of practice.

"You're Howard, right?" the Gunny said.

"That's right," Joe said, and then blurted, "They just flew me in from Pearl, Gunny. That's when I spilled coffee on me."

"Captain Stecker's the third door on the right, Howard," the Gunny said, turning and pointing. "You bring your records jacket with you?"

"Yeah," Howard said, surprised. An enlisted man's records were not ordinarily put into his hands when he was transferred. They either found some officer going to the same place and gave them to him, or they sent them by registered mail. But Howard had been handed his along with the set of orders transferring him to 2nd Joint Training Force.

"Good," the Gunny said, and walked down the corridor.

How the hell does he know about my records? Or my name?

Joe went to the third door on the right and knocked.

"Come!"

It was Jack NMI Stecker's familiar voice. But it was no longer Gunny Stecker, his friend from Benning and Quantico. It was now Captain Jack NMI Stecker.

Joe opened the door, marched in, and reported to Stecker as a Marine sergeant is supposed to report to a Marine captain.

"Jesus, you're a mess," Stecker said. It was an observation, not a criticism; and there was gentle laughter in his voice when Stecker added, "You may stand at ease, Sergeant."

Howard dropped his eyes to Stecker's, and saw that he was smiling at him.

"What did you spill on yourself, Joe?" Stecker asked.

"A whole goddamned cup of coffee," Joe said, and remembered to add, "Sir."

"Well, come on," Stecker said, "we'll get you cleaned up. You look like something the cat dragged in."

"I'm sorry," Joe said.

"You *look* sorry," Stecker chuckled.

He led him out of the building, opened the trunk of a 1939 Ford coupe, and motioned for him to put his bag in the back. At Quantico, Joe remembered, Stecker had driven an enormous black Packard Phaeton.

"I left Elly the Packard," Stecker said, as if reading his mind. Elly was his wife. "She went to Pennsylvania for a while. I bought this when I got here."

"How's she doing?" Howard asked uneasily. He knew that the Steckers' son, Ensign Jack NMI Stecker, Jr., USN, had been killed on the *Arizona.*

"All right," Stecker said evenly. "I suppose it's tougher on a mother than the father."

That's bullshit, Howard thought.

"How are you doing?" Joe asked.

"Well, I seem to be getting used to it," Stecker said. "At least I don't salute lieutenants anymore."

Joe chuckled, as he knew he was expected to. And he knew that Jack NMI Stecker had purposefully misunderstood him, in order to change the subject from the death of his son.

It doesn't matter, Howard thought. *I had to ask, and I asked, and he knows I'm sorry as hell about his kid. That's enough.*

"How was the flight? Aside from the coffee?" Stecker asked.

"It was a fancied-up Mariner. Real nice. They put a lieutenant colonel off it to put me on."

"Is that so?"

"What's going on?"

"That airplane used to belong to the Rear Admiral at Guantanamo," Stecker said. "They took it away from him to use it as a courier plane between here and Pearl."

"That's not what I was asking," Howard said.

"I know," Stecker chuckled. "Well, here we are. Home sweet home."

Howard saw that they were pulling into a dirt parking lot beside three newly built frame two-story buildings. There was a plywood sign reading, BACHELOR OFFICERS' QUARTERS.

It was the first time Joe Howard had ever been in Officers' Country for any purpose. For what he understood was good reason, these were off limits to enlisted men. If it had been anyone but Captain Jack NMI Stecker, he would have asked what he was doing here now.

Stecker's quarters inside were not fancy—the opposite, in fact. The studs in the wall were exposed. There were no doors on the closets, but just a piece of cloth hung on a wire. There was a bed, an upholstered chair, a folding metal chair, and a chest of drawers. In a small alcove there was a desk and another folding metal chair.

Only a few things in the room had not been issued. There were graduation pictures of Stecker's sons: one of Jack Junior in his brand-new ensign's uniform, taken at Annapolis; and another of Second Lieutenant Richard S. Stecker, USMC, his dress blue uniform making him stand out from his fellow graduates at the Military Academy at West Point. There was also a picture of Stecker and Elly and the boys when they were just kids. It was taken on a beach somewhere, and everybody was in bathing suits.

There was a radio, a hot plate with a coffeepot, and a small refrigerator. And that was it.

"You better take a shower," Stecker said. "You got a towel?"

"Yeah."

"And your other greens?" Stecker asked. "They going to be pressed?" He nodded toward Howard's bag.

"They should be all right," Joe said.

"I've got an iron if they're mussed."

Howard took his carefully folded greens from the bag. They would be all right, even up to Jack NMI Stecker's high standards.

"You going to tell me what's going on?" Howard asked.

"Take a shower and a shave," Stecker said. "Right now, you're probably the sloppiest sergeant on the base."

"In other words, you're not going to tell me."

"When you're shipshape," Stecker replied.

When Joe Howard came out of the shower, a tin-lined cubicle shared with the next BOQ room, Stecker was sitting slumped in the one upholstered chair, holding a beer in his hands.

Joe's eyebrows rose.

"You can have one later," Stecker said. "First let me tell you about Colonel Lewis T. Harris."

"Lucky Lew? He's here? I thought he was in Iceland."

"He's here. Scuttlebutt—I believe it—says he's about to make general. But right now he's Chief of Staff of the 2nd Joint Training Force."

"What's that got to do with me?"

"Well, among other things, he's the president of the Officer Selection Board for the West Coast."

"I don't even know what that is," Howard confessed.

"The Corps is pretty hard up for officers. We don't have enough right now, and the way they're building the Corps up, that situation will get worse."

"So?"

"When you're finished dressing—you better take a brush to your shoes, while you're at it—you're going to go up before him. We're desperately short of officers who know anything about small arms beyond what we taught them in Basic School at Quantico. I've recommended you for a direct commission as a first lieutenant."

"Jesus Christ!"

"You may not get it. You may have to settle for being a second lieutenant, but that's not so bad. Scuttlebutt has it again that from here on in, promotion will be automatic after six months."

How the hell can I be an officer? You can't be a Marine officer if you get hysterical and hide behind a counter when you see somebody get killed.

"I don't know what to say," Howard said.

"When you're in there with Colonel Harris, what you say is 'Yes, Sir,' 'No, Sir,' 'Thank you, Sir,' and 'Aye, aye, Sir.' "

"I meant about becoming an officer."

"Don't you, of all people, start handing me that crap," Stecker said.

"What crap?"

"Why do you think I had you brought here from Hawaii, for Christ's sake, so that you could go work in a battalion small-arms locker someplace? Goddamn you, don't you dare tell me, 'Thanks, but no thanks.' "

"A year ago, I was a corporal. I don't how to be an officer. Captain, I just don't think I could handle it."

"If I handed you a list with the names of every officer you know on it, you could go down it and say, 'This one is a good Marine officer,' and 'That one is a feather merchant.' Do what you've seen the good officers do."

"And what if I fuck up? What if I can't?"

"Then we'll give you your stripes back," Stecker said. "For Christ's sake, do you think I would have recommended you if I didn't think you could pass muster? And anyway, you'll be an ordnance officer; you won't have to worry about running a platoon."

"It just never entered my mind, is all. . . ." He stopped, then started to tell Stecker about what had happened at Pearl, but realized he couldn't. He added lamely, "I almost said 'Gunny.' "

"I get into something sometimes and answer the phone that way," Stecker said. "Usually with some real asshole calling." He laughed. "You know those indelible pens with the soft tip you use to write on celluloid overlays?"

Howard nodded.

"Harris came in my office when I first got here, told me to give him my hand, and when I did he wrote *C-A-P-T* on the palm. Then he said, 'Every time you answer your phone, *Captain* Stecker, read your hand before you speak.' He said he was getting tired of explaining to people that I was retarded."

"Really?"

"Yeah. Harris is one of the good guys. We were in France together. In Domingo, too. Nicaragua. We go back a long way. I had a hell of a time getting that stuff off my hand. It's *really* indelible."

"You sure you're doing this because you think I'd make a passable officer?"

"Or what?"

"Because we're friends."

"That pisses me off," Stecker snapped.

"Sorry, I didn't mean it that way. But, Jesus, this came right out of the goddamned blue!"

"You'll be able to handle it, Joe," Stecker said.

Maybe as an ordnance officer. Just maybe. Maybe they'll assign me here, or at Quantico. Someplace in the States, some rear area. I know weapons, at least. I could earn my keep that way.

"When is all this going to happen?"

"We'll go back to the office. You'll see Harris. If you don't fuck that up, you'll go into 'Diego to the Navy Hospital and take what they call a 'pre-commissioning physical.' That'll take the rest of the day. In the meantime, we'll get all the paperwork typed up, there's a lot of it. Jesus . . . you *do* have your records?"

"In the bag."

"OK. Come back to the office tomorrow morning, we'll get you discharged. And then you go over to the Officers' Sales Store and get your uniforms. Colonel Harris can swear you in after lunch."

"That quick?"

"That quick."

"Where will I be assigned?"

"Here. To work for me, stupid. Why do you think I went to all this trouble?"

"What will I be doing?"

"You ever hear of the Raiders?"

"No. What the hell is that?"

"American commandos. Long story. Nutty story. No time to tell you all about them now. But they've been authorized to arm themselves any way they want to. I need somebody to handle that for me, to get them whatever they want. You."

(FOUR)
Headquarters, 2nd Joint Training Force
Camp Elliott, California
1205 Hours 2 February 1942

One of the two telephones on Captain Jack NMI Stecker's desk rang, and he answered it on the second ring, and correctly:

"G-3 Special Planning, Captain Stecker speaking, Sir."

"Stecker, this is Captain Kelso."

There was a certain tone of superiority in Captain Kelso's voice. Stecker knew what was behind that. Although Captain Kelso was in fact outranked by Captain Stecker, by date of rank, he could not put out of his mind that Captain Stecker was a Mustang, an officer commissioned from the ranks. As an Annapolis man himself, Kelso considered that he was socially superior to a man who had served in the ranks. This opinion was buttressed by his duty assignment: he was aide-de-camp to the Commanding General, 2nd Joint Training Force.

What Captain Kelso did not know was that the Commanding General of the 2nd Joint Training Force had discussed him with Captain Stecker over a beer in the General's kitchen when Captain Stecker had first reported aboard.

"My aide may give you some trouble, Jack," the General had said. He and Stecker had been in Santo Domingo, Nicaragua, and France together. "He's an arrogant little prick, thinks he's salty as hell. Efficient as hell, too, to give the devil his due, which is why I keep him. But he's capable of being a flaming pain in the ass. If he does give you any trouble, let me know, and I'll walk all over him."

"General, I've had some experience with young captains who thought they were salty," Stecker had replied dryly, "going *way* back."

"Your commanding general, Captain, is sure you are not referring to anyone in this kitchen," the General replied, laughing.

"Don't be too sure, General," Stecker chuckled.

"I have never known a master gunnery sergeant who couldn't handle a captain," the General said. "I don't know why I brought that up."

"I appreciate it," Stecker said. "But don't worry about it."

"And how may I be of service to the General's aide-de-camp, Captain Kelso?" Stecker said, oozing enough sarcastically insincere charm to penetrate even Captain Kelso's self-assurance and cause him to become just a little wary. Kelso recalled at that moment that the General habitually addressed Captain Stecker by his first name.

"There's a Navy captain, from the Secretary of the Navy's office, on his way to see you . . ." He paused just perceptibly, and added, "Jack."

"Oh? Who is he? What's he want?"

"His name is Pickering, and I don't know what he wants. He just walked in out of the blue and asked for the General; and when I told him the General wasn't available, he asked for you. I've never seen a set of orders like his."

Now Stecker was curious.

"What about his orders?"

"They say that he is authorized to proceed, on a Four-A priority, wherever he deems necessary to travel in order to perform the mission assigned to him by the Secretary of the Navy, and that all questions concerning his duties will be referred to the office of the Secretary of the Navy."

"That's *goddamned* unusual," Jack Stecker thought aloud. "I wonder what the hell he wants with me?"

"I have no idea. But I'm sure the General would be interested in knowing, too."

"What did you say his name was?"

"Pickering."

Stecker's office door opened and his sergeant stuck his head inside.

"Sir, there's a Captain Pickering to see you, a *Navy* captain."

"He's here," Stecker said, and hung the telephone up. He got to his feet, checked the knot of his field scarf as an automatic reflex action, and then said, "Ask the Captain to come in, please."

Captain Fleming Pickering, USNR, walked into the office.

"Good afternoon, Sir," Stecker said. "Sir, I'm Captain Stecker, G-3 Special Planning."

Pickering looked at him, smiled, and then turned and closed the door in the Sergeant's face. Then he turned again and faced Stecker.

"Hello, Dutch," he said. "How the hell are you?"

"Sir, the Captain has the advantage on me."

"I always have had, Dutch. Smarter, better looking . . . You really don't recognize me, do you?" Pickering laughed.

"No, Sir."

"I would have recognized you. You're a little balder, and a little heavier, but I would known you. The name Pickering means nothing to you?"

"No, Sir."

"I'm crushed," Pickering said. "Try Belleau Wood."

After a moment, Stecker said, "I'll be damned. Flem Pickering, right? California? Corporal? You took two eight-millimeter rounds, one in each leg, and all they did was scratch you?"

"I don't think 'scratch' is the right word," Pickering protested. "I spent two weeks in the hospital when that happened."

"You went into the Navy? Back to college, and then into the Navy? Is that what happened?"

"I just came into the Navy," Pickering said.

"Am I allowed to ask what's going on? You awed the general's aide with your orders, but they didn't explain much."

Pickering reached into his uniform jacket pocket and handed Stecker a copy of his orders.

"*I'm* awed, too," Stecker said, after he read them.

"You don't have to be awed, but I thought I should show them to you."

"What do you want with me?" Stecker asked, as he handed the orders back. "You didn't come from Washington to see me?"

"To tell you the truth, it wasn't until that self-important young man told me that General Davies was not available that I remembered that Doc McInerney told me you were out here someplace."

"You've seen Doc?"

"Sure have. And I got another interesting bit of information from him. Our boys are roommates at Pensacola."

"I'll be damned!" Stecker said. "How about that?"

"It would seem, Dutch, that we're getting to be a pair of old men, old enough to have kids who rate salutes."

"I don't know about you, Captain," Stecker said dryly, "but *I* still feel pretty spry. Too spry to be sitting behind a desk."

"They don't want us for anything else, Dutch," Pickering said. "Mac made that painfully clear to me. We're relics from another time, another war."

"How'd you wind up in the Navy? Or is that one of those questions I'm not supposed to ask?"

"I tried to come back in the Corps. I went to see Mac. He made it pretty plain that I would be of no use to the Corps. Then Frank Knox offered me a job working for him, as sort of a glorified gofer, and I took it. I jumped at it."

"*Frank* Knox? The one I think of nearly reverently as *Secretary* Knox?"

"You'd like him, Dutch. He was a sergeant in the Rough Riders. Good man."

"And you're out here for him?"

"Yeah. I'll tell you about it over lunch. Let's go over to the Coronado Beach Hotel. They generally have nice lunches."

"They generally have *great* lunches, and everybody knows about them, and you need a reservation. I don't think we could get in. We could eat at the club here."

"Indulge me, Dutch," Pickering said. "It isn't only the food I'm thinking of."

"You want to see somebody else?"

"I'm about to appoint you—I'd really rather have gotten into all this over lunch—the Secretary of the Navy's Special Representative to See that Carlson's Raiders Get What They Want. You know about the Raiders?"

"I'm already the General's man who does that," Stecker said. "Is that why you're here?"

Pickering nodded. "So much the better, then. The Navy brass are as curious as a bunch of old maids about what I'm doing here. It will get back to them that I had lunch in the Coronado with you. It might come in handy for them to remember you have friends in very high places when you're asking for something outrageous for the Raiders."

Stecker looked at Pickering for a moment, until he concluded that Pickering was both serious and right.

"OK. But first we have to get from here to the hotel, and my car may not start. Bad battery, I think. I had to push it off this morning."

"The Admiral's aide met my plane and graciously gave me the use of the Admiral's car for as long as I need it," Pickering said.

"And *then* we have to get in the dining room."

"I think I can handle that," Pickering said. "Can I have your sergeant make a call for me?"

"Sure," Stecker said, and called the sergeant into the office.

"Yes, Sir?"

"Sergeant," Pickering said, "would you call the dining room at the Coronado Beach for me, please? Tell the maitre d' that Captain Stecker and myself are on the way over there, and that I would like a private table overlooking the pool. My name is Fleming Pickering."

"Aye, aye, Sir," the sergeant said. "A *private* table, Sir?"

"They'll know what I mean, Sergeant," Pickering said. "They'll move other tables away from mine, so that other people won't be able to hear what Captain Stecker and I are talking about."

"Why is this making me nervous?" Stecker asked.

"I have no idea," Pickering said. "Maybe because you're getting old, Dutch."

"If there are any calls for me, Sergeant, tell them that I went off with Captain Pickering of Secretary Knox's office, and you have no idea where I went or when I'll be back."

Pickering chuckled. "You're a quick learner, Dutch, aren't you?"

"For an old man," Stecker said.

(FIVE)
United States Naval Hospital
San Diego, California
1515 Hours 2 February 1942

"Tell me, Sergeant," the Navy doctor, a full commander, said to Staff Sergeant Joseph L. Howard, "do you suffer from syphilis?"

"No, Sir."

"How about gonorrhea?" Commander Nettleton asked.

"No, Sir."

Commander K. J. Nettleton, MC, USN, was a career naval officer. In his fifteen years of service, he had discussed venereal disease with maybe fifteen thousand Navy and Marine Corps enlisted men. In his experience, it was seldom possible to judge from an enlisted man's appearance whether he had been diving the salami into seas of spirochetes or not.

He had treated angelic-looking boys who—as their advanced state of social disease clearly proved—had been sowing their seed in any cavity that could be induced to hold still for twenty seconds. And he'd treated leather-skinned chief bosun's mates and mastery gunnery sergeants who had not strayed from the marital bed in twenty years, yet were hysterically convinced that a little urethral drip was God finally making them pay for a single indiscretion two decades ago in Gitmo or Shanghai or Newport.

But it was also Dr. Nettleton's experience that when regular sailors and Marines—sergeants and petty officers on their second or third or fourth hitch—contracted a venereal disease somewhere along the line, they tried to get their hands on their medical records so they could remove and destroy that portion dealing with their venereal history. They had learned how the services subtly and cruelly treated men with social diseases.

His experience told him that's what he had at hand, in the person of Staff Sergeant Joseph Howard, USMC. Sergeant Howard was taking a pre-commissioning physical. That meant he had applied for a commission. An Officer Selection Board was likely to turn down an applicant who had a history of VD, even one who was obviously a good Marine. You didn't get to wear staff sergeant's chevrons as young as this kid was without being one hell of a Marine—and one who looked like he belonged on a recruiting poster.

"Sergeant," he said, "if anyone was to hear what I am about to say, I would deny it."

"Sir?" Howard asked, confused.

"There are ways to handle difficult *situations,*" Commander Nettleton said.

"But destroying your records is not one of them. Now, what did you have, and when did you have it?"

"Sir, if you mean syphilis or the clap, I never did."

Nettleton fixed Howard with an icy glare.

You dumb sonofabitch, I just told you I'd fix it!

"Never?"

"No, Sir," Howard replied, both confused and righteously indignant.

I'll be damned, I think he's telling the truth!

"Then how do you explain the absence of the results of your Wassermann test in this otherwise complete stack of reports?"

Staff Sergeant Howard did not reply.

"Well?"

"Sir, I don't know what—what did you say, Wasser Test?—is."

"Wassermann," Doctor Nettleton corrected him idly. "It's an integral part of your physical."

"Sir, I don't know. I went everywhere they sent me."

Commander Nettleton looked at him intently, and decided he didn't really know if he was looking at Innocence Personified or a skilled liar.

He reached for the telephone, found the number he was looking for on a typewritten sheet of paper under the glass on his desk, and dialed it quickly.

"Venereal, Lieutenant Gower."

"This is Commander Nettleton, Gower. How are you?"

"No complaints, Sir. How about you?"

"You don't want to hear them, Lieutenant. I need a favor. How are you fixed for favors?"

"If I've got it, Commander, you've got it."

"You got somebody around there who can draw blood for a Wassermann for me? And then do it in a hurry?"

"Yes, Sir. I'll take it to the lab myself. They owe me a couple of favors up there."

"It has to be official. I need the form and an MD to sign off on it."

"No problem."

"I'm sending a Staff Sergeant Howard to see you. Make him wait. If it comes back negative, send him and the report back to me. If it's positive, put him in a bathrobe and find something unpleasant for him to do. Call me and I'll see that he's admitted."

"Aye, aye, Sir," Lieutenant Gower said.

"Appreciate it, Gower," Commander Nettleton said, hung up, and turned to Staff Sergeant Howard. "You heard that, Sergeant. The Venereal Disease Ward is on the third floor. Report to Lieutenant Gower."

"Aye, aye, Sir," Staff Sergeant Howard said.

Like Commander Nettleton, Lieutenant Gower was a career naval officer, with nearly as much commissioned service as he had. She had entered the Naval Service immediately upon graduation from Nursing School, and, in the fourteen years since, had served at naval hospitals in Philadelphia; Cavite (in the Philippines); Pearl Harbor; and San Diego. She had just learned that she was to be promoted to lieutenant commander, Nurse Corps, USN.

While on the one hand Lieutenant Hazel Gower did not consider herself above the mundane routine of the VD ward, of which she was Nurse-in-Charge, on the other hand, Rank Did Have Its Privileges.

She rapped on the plate-glass window surrounding the Nurse's Station with her Saint Anthony's High School graduation ring, and caught the attention of Ensign

Barbara T. Cotter, NC, USNR. Ensign Cotter had just reported aboard, fresh from the Nurse's Orientation Course at Philadelphia.

Lieutenant Gower gestured to Ensign Cotter to come into the nurses' station.

"Yes?" Ensign Cotter asked.

"The way we do that in the Navy, Miss Cotter," Lieutenant Gower said, "is 'Yes, Ma'am?' "

"Yes, Ma'am," Ensign Cotter said, her face tightening.

"This is not the University of Pennsylvania, you know."

"Yes, Ma'am," Ensign Cotter said, just a little bitchily.

That remark made reference to Ensign Cotter's nursing education. Ensign Cotter, unlike most of her peers, had a college degree. She had graduated with a bachelor of science degree in psychology from the University of Pennsylvania Medical School, and had earned, from the same institution, the right to append "RN" to her name. She'd been trained as a psychiatric nurse. And she had been lied to by the recruiter, who told her the Navy really had need of her special skills. In fact, the Navy used medical doctors with psychiatric training and large male medical corpsmen to deal with its mentally ill.

When Ensign Cotter reported aboard Naval Hospital, San Diego, the Chief of Nursing Services told her that since they had no need for a female psychiatric nurse, she wondered how she would feel about working in obstetrics. An unpleasant scene followed, during which it was pointed out to Ensign Cotter that she was now in the Navy, and that the Navy decided where its people could make the greatest contribution. Following that, Lieutenant Gower in Venereal received a telephone call from the Chief of Nursing Services, a longtime friend, telling her she was getting a new ensign who was an uppity little bitch who thought her college degree made her better than other people. The little bitch needed to be put in her place.

"There's a syphilitic Marine sergeant on his way up here," Lieutenant Gower said to Ensign Cotter. "Draw some blood for a Wassermann."

"He's not on the ward?"

"I'm getting tired of telling you this, Cotter. When you speak to a superior female officer, you use 'ma'am.' "

Ensign Cotter exhaled audibly.

"He's not on the ward, *Ma'am?"*

"No."

"Then how, *Ma'am,* do we know he's syphilitic?"

"The Wassermann will tell us that, won't it, Miss Cotter?"

"Only if he *is* syphilitic, *Ma'am,"* Ensign Cotter said.

"Commander Nettleton wouldn't have sent him up here unless he was," Lieutenant Gower flared. And then she remembered that Nettleton had said to send the sergeant back if the Wassermann was negative. She was going to look like a horse's ass in front of this uppity little bitch if it did come back negative.

"Just do what you're ordered to do, Miss Cotter," she said icily.

"Yes, *Ma'am."*

Barbara Cotter saw Staff Sergeant Joseph L. Howard the moment she walked out of the glass-walled nurses' station, and she reacted to him precisely the same way most other men and women did when they first saw him. *God, that fellow looks like what a Marine should look like!*

"Excuse me, Ma'am," Joe Howard said, "I'm looking for Lieutenant Gower."

"You're here for a Wassermann, Sergeant?" Barbara asked, telling herself that she had sounded professionally distant.

This beautiful man has syphilis?

"Yes, Ma'am. I was told to report to Lieutenant Gower."

"I'll take care of you, Sergeant. Come with me, please."

"Yes, Ma'am."

She led him to an examination room.

"Take off your jacket, please, and roll up your shirt sleeve."

When he took his uniform jacket off, Barbara saw that his shirt was tailored; it fit his body like a thin glove, which allowed her to clearly make out the firm muscles of his chest and upper arms inside it.

What's going on with me? He's not only an enlisted man—and there is a regulation against involvement between officers and enlisted men—but he's syphilitic*!*

She wrapped a length of red rubber tubing around his upper arm, drew it tight, and told him to pump his hand open and closed. He winced when she slipped the needle into his vein.

"Have you had any symptoms?" she heard herself asking, as his blood began to fill the chamber.

"Ma'am?"

"Lesions . . . sores? Anything like that."

"No, Ma'am."

"Then what makes you think you've contracted . . . ?"

"I don't think I've contracted anything," Joe Howard said, unable to take his eyes from Ensign Cotter's white brassiere, which had come into view when she had leaned over his arm to stick him with the needle.

"Then why are we giving you a Wassermann?" Barbara blurted, looking up at him and noticing that he quickly averted his eyes. *God, he's been looking down my dress!* "You know what a Wassermann is for, don't you?"

"For syphilis," he said. "I just figured that out."

"Why has somebody ordered the test?" she asked. "If you don't think you've—"

"They put me in for a commission," Joe said. "Some asshole—oh, shit! Sorry, Ma'am."

He's going to be an officer? Is that what he means?

"Some asshole *what,* Sergeant?" Barbara said.

"Somebody forgot to send me for the test," Joe said. "And now that Commander . . . he thinks I've got it."

"And you don't?"

"I *know* I don't," Joe said.

Barbara pulled the needle from his vein, dabbed at the puncture with an alcohol swab, and told him to bend his arm.

"Well, we'll soon know for sure, won't we?" she said.

It will come back negative, she thought. *I* know *it will come back negative. Up yours, Lieutenant Gower, Ma'am!*

(SIX)
Officers' Sales Store
U.S. Naval Base
San Diego, California
1100 Hours 3 February 1942

To Joe Howard, the Officers' Sales Store looked like a cross between a supply room and a civilian clothing store. There were glass-topped counters, and shelves loaded with shirts and skivvies, and racks containing jackets and trousers. There were even mannequins showing what the well-dressed Naval or Marine Corps officer should wear. Even two mannequins of Navy nurses, one wearing blues and the other summer whites.

He had a semi-erotic thought: Here there were no female mannequins in underwear, as there were in civilian department stores. That was just as well; those always made him feel a little uncomfortable. It didn't take him long to guess why that thought popped into his mind: the nurse at the hospital yesterday. It would be a long time before the image of her brassiere and the soft, swelling flesh above it faded from his mind.

Jesus, she was a looker!

"Can I help you, Sergeant?"

It was a plump and middle-aged Storekeeper First Class, obviously the man in charge. He looked ridiculous in his bell-bottomed pants and blouse, Joe thought. The Navy's enlisted men's uniform was worn by everybody but chief petty officers. It didn't look bad on young guys. But on middle-aged guys like this one, with a paunch and damned little hair, it looked silly.

"I need some uniforms," Joe said, and handed the Storekeeper First a copy of his brand-new orders.

Paragraph One said that Staff Sergeant Joseph L. Howard, USMC, was honorably discharged from the Naval Service for the convenience of the government.

Paragraph Two said that First Lieutenant Joseph L. Howard, USMCR, was ordered to active duty, for the duration of the war plus six months, with duty station 2nd Joint Training Command, San Diego, Cal.

"Well, you came to the right place," the Storekeeper First said. "It's going to cost you."

"I figured," Joe said.

He had a lot of money in his pocket, so it didn't matter. They had brought his pay up to date for his discharge. And they had returned to him the savings money they had been taking out of his pay every month; the government had been paying him three percent on it. He had been saving money since he'd come in the Corps, redepositing it when he shipped over. Now it had all been returned to him. Officers were expected to manage their own money, not have their hands held by the Corps to encourage them to put a little aside.

There was even more. He had been paid for his unused accrued leave, and for what it would have cost him to go to his Home of Record. And Captain Stecker had told him that when he drew his first pay as an officer, he would be paid for what it took to come from Birmingham out here. And finally, there was a one-time payment of three hundred dollars for uniforms.

The Storekeeper First was far more helpful than Joe had expected him to be.

And in a remarkably short time, one of the glass counters was stacked high with the uniforms Joe would need as an officer.

The three-hundred-dollar uniform allowance didn't come close to covering the cost of the uniforms. The officer's brimmed cap alone, for example, with just one cover—and he needed four more covers—came to $19.65. The covers were expensive, because Marine officers' covers—unlike Army and Navy officers' covers—had woven loops sewn to their tops. These were now purely decorative, but they went back to the days of sailing ships, Joe remembered hearing somewhere. Marine sharpshooters in the rigging could distinguish their officers on deck below because of woven line loops sewn on top of their caps.

Aside from the Sam Browne leather belt ($24.35), there wasn't much outward difference between officers' and enlisted men's greens. Officers' trousers had hip pockets, and enlisted men's trousers did not. The quality of the material was better.

The only alteration Joe required was the hemming of the trousers. The chubby little Storekeeper First said he would have a seamstress hem one pair immediately, and Joe could pick up the rest the next afternoon. Joe suspected he was getting a little better service than most people. The Storekeeper First was probably one of the enlisted men who was pleased when a peer became an officer. A lot of people resented Mustangs.

When the Storekeeper First helped Joe into his blouse, expertly buttoning the epaulet over the crosspiece of the Sam Browne belt, the reason why he was being so obliging came out.

"I can offer you a little something for your enlisted stuff," he said. "Not much, because it's nowhere near new, but as much as you'd get hocking it off the base."

Joe had not considered getting rid of his old uniforms; still, all of them were in a duffel bag in the trunk of Captain Stecker's Ford, which he had borrowed.

"Make me an offer," he said. "I've got a duffel bag full."

"Here?"

"Outside. In the trunk of a car."

"Let's go look at it, maybe we can do a little business."

"I'm not sure I'm allowed to wear this yet," Joe said, staring at the image of First Lieutenant Joseph Howard, USMCR, in a three-way mirror. He found what he saw very pleasing—yet unreal enough to make him feel uncomfortable.

"Why not?"

"I don't get sworn in until half past two."

"You're supposed to get sworn in in uniform," the Storekeeper First said, *"Officer's* uniform. Nobody's going to say anything."

"You're sure?"

"You aren't the first Mustang to come through here."

"OK," Joe said. "When they throw me in the brig, I can quote you, right?"

"Absolutely," the Storekeeper First said. "Pay for this, and then we'll go see what you've got in the car."

The price the Storekeeper First offered for all of Joe's enlisted men's uniforms was insulting. He was being raped, but he could think of nothing to do about it. He could, of course, tell him to go fuck himself, in which case when he returned to The Officers' Sales Store for the rest of his new uniforms tomorrow, they wouldn't be ready. Or worse.

He managed to get the total price up to $52.50, but beyond that the Storekeeper First not only wouldn't budge, he showed signs of getting nasty.

"Sold to the man in the bell-bottom pants," Joe said, forcing a smile.

"A pleasure doing business with you, Lieutenant," the Storekeeper First said as he hoisted Joe's duffel bag onto his shoulder.

"Don't forget my fifty-two-fifty," Joe said.

"I'll have it for you tomorrow."

"You can have the stuff tomorrow, then," Joe said.

"You don't trust me?"

"Not as far as I could throw you," Joe said. "I show up there tomorrow and you're not there, then what would I do?"

The Storekeeper First heaved the duffel bag back into the trunk, and then shrugged. He dipped his hand behind the thirteen-button fly of his bell-bottoms and came out with two twenties and a ten.

"That's all I got," he said. "I'll have to owe you the two-fifty."

"Either look in your sock or somewhere, or put two of the wool shirts back."

The Storekeeper First looked carefully at Howard, then shrugged and dipped into his thirteen-button fly again. He came out with a wad of singles and counted off three of them. Joe put them in his pocket and gave the man two quarters in change. They exchanged dry little smiles, and the Storekeeper First, grunting, hoisted the duffel bag to his shoulder again and marched off.

That fat old sonofabitch has got a nice little racket going, he thought. *He paid me less than half of what that stuff is worth in any hockshop. And there's probably one or two guys like me going through there every day. Christ, not only Marines! The Navy must be commissioning Mustangs too.*

"I'll be a sonofabitch," he said aloud, more out of admiration than anger, as he considered that the Storekeeper First must be taking in probably as much as a hundred fifty dollars a day.

"I'm almost afraid to ask what all that was about," a voice, a female voice, said behind him. Surprised, he turned quickly to see who it was. It was an officer, a female officer, a Navy nurse, and specifically the one who had drawn his blood for the Wassermann test the day before.

Joe saluted crisply, without thinking about it, a Pavlovian reflex: an officer had spoken to him; therefore he saluted.

"I think I was supposed to do that," the nurse said. She was carrying a paper sack from the Commissary.

"Excuse me?" Joe said.

"Those are silver bars you're wearing? Mine, you'll notice, are gold. I think I was supposed to salute first."

"Jesus Christ!" Joe said.

She smiled. "What *was* going on?"

"I sold him my old uniforms," Joe said.

"You look very nice in your new one," Barbara Cotter said, smiling. "Are congratulations in order?"

"I haven't been sworn in yet," he said.

"But you did pass the Wassermann," Barbara said. She had suspected this Adonis could blush when she had told him he looked nice in his uniform; now there was inarguable proof. His face was flushed.

This isn't the first time, she thought. *He blushed when I caught him looking down my whites. Adonis is actually shy!*

"Yeah, I did that, all right," Joe said. And then he took the chance: "Can I offer you a ride? I've got a borrowed car."

Ensign Barbara Cotter hesitated, not about taking the ride, but because she had her own car.

I don't want to start off lying to this man. Isn't that strange?

"I've got a car," she said. "I'm on my way to lunch. Have you eaten?"

"No."

"Follow me over to the hospital, then," she said. "The food's not bad."

Joe looked at his watch. There was time.

"Sure," he said.

"The blue Plymouth coupe," she said, and pointed down the line of cars.

With a little bit of luck, Lieutenant Hazel Gower, USN, will be having her lunch when I walk into the officer's section of the hospital mess with this Wassermann-negative Adonis. Is that why I went up to him in the parking lot? To get at dear old Hazel?

As she put her key in the ignition of her Plymouth, she understood that while zinging Lieutenant Gower might be nice, it was *not* the reason her heart had jumped when she saw Joe Howard standing by the open trunk of the Ford.

"Oh, *God!*" she muttered, as she pushed the starter button. "What is this?"

(SEVEN)
Office of the Chief of Staff
Headquarters, 2nd Joint Training Force
San Diego, California
1445 Hours 3 February 1942

"Congratulations, Lieutenant Howard," Colonel Lewis T. "Lucky Lew" Harris said, offering his hand to Joe Howard. "You are now a Marine officer. I have every confidence that you will bring credit to the uniform you're wearing, and to the Corps. Good luck to you!"

"Thank you, Sir," Joe said.

"Will you wait outside a moment, please?" Harris said. "I'd like a word with Captain Stecker."

"Yes, Sir," Joe said, and did an about-face and marched out of Harris's office.

"That one, I think, will do all right," Harris said to Stecker. "But, frankly, I'm a little uncomfortable about not sending him to Quantico for Basic School."

"Sir, he's not going to get a platoon, or even go to the Division—"

"Not today, anyway," Harris said, dryly. "I've already read today's teletypes from Washington reassigning our officers. But what about tomorrow?"

"Until he appears on a list of officers who have completed Basic School, he's not eligible for assignment with troops," Stecker said. "And as long as we 'forget' to request a space for him at Quantico, he won't be ordered there. In the meantime, we can put him to work."

"And if some zealous paper pusher sends a TWX asking why we haven't requested a Basic School slot for Lieutenant Howard, what do we say?"

"When all else fails, tell the truth," Stecker said. "We tell them that Howard, a small-arms expert, has been charged with getting the 2nd Raider Battalion the weaponry they want. And, that since this is a matter of the highest priority, according not only to the Commandant, but to the Secretary of the Navy as well, we thought this assignment was more in the best interests of the Corps than sending him to Quantico."

Lucky Lew Harris still looked doubtful.

"Colonel," Stecker said, "I talked to Captain Pickering about him. He said if anybody gave us any trouble, to call him. He made it pretty plain to me that what the Secretary of the Navy wants is to give the Raider Battalions what the President wants them to have . . . which is anything they want."

"Just between you and me, Jack, I don't like the whole idea of these so-called Raider Battalions a damn bit."

"I don't really know how I feel," Stecker said. "Evans Carlson is a hell of a Marine."

"He *used* to be, anyway," Harris said. "But it's a moot point, Jack, isn't it?"

"Yes, Sir, it is."

"And your pal Captain Pickering makes me nervous, frankly. Can he be trusted?"

There was a moment's hesitation before Stecker answered. "He can be trusted to do what the Secretary tells him to do. And beyond that, I think he still thinks like a Marine."

"What did he tell you about me? About the General?" Harris asked.

"Sir?"

"I suppose what I'm asking is whether he wants reports from you directly."

"Sir, he told me to feel free to call him if I saw any problems coming up. But I wouldn't do that without checking with you."

"No, of course you wouldn't," Harris said. "No offense intended. Christ, Jack, why do things get so complicated?"

"It wouldn't be the Corps, Sir, if there wasn't some moron putting his two cents in and getting in the way of simple riflemen trying to do their job," Stecker said.

Harris chuckled.

"Keep Carlson happy, Jack," he said. "Let me know if I can help."

"Yes, Sir. Thank you, Sir."

Lieutenant Joe Howard was sitting on a battered, chrome-framed, plastic-upholstered couch in Colonel Harris's outer office, thumbing through a copy of *Collier's*. He got to his feet when Stecker came out of Harris's office.

"What we'll do now, *Lieutenant,*" Stecker said, "is take you out to the 2nd Raider Battalion and introduce you to Colonel Carlson, his S-4, and Captain Roosevelt. Then we'll get you settled in a BOQ. And then, I thought, tonight we'll celebrate your bar, wash it down, and maybe get a steak, at the officers' club."

Howard looked a little uncomfortable.

"Something wrong with that?"

"Sir, I've got sort of a date tonight."

"Oh?"

"I met a nurse at the hospital," Joe said. "I asked her to supper."

"Well, hell, I wouldn't want to interfere with that," Stecker said. Then he smiled, dug in his pocket, and came out with a key. "Here," he said, handing it to Howard.

"What is this, Captain?" Joe asked, confused. Stecker had handed him a hotel key from the Coronado Beach Hotel.

"We Mustangs have to stick together," Stecker said, as they walked down the corridor toward the front door. "Captain Fleming Pickering, USNR, gave that to me. We served together in France in the first war. I was a buck sergeant, and he was a corporal. He just came in the Navy, as a captain."

Howard was visibly confused.

"Between wars, Pickering is in the shipping business. Specifically, Pacific & Far Eastern Shipping. He owns it. And they keep a suite at the Coronado Beach Hotel, permanently, to put up their officers who are in port. If you want to impress the nurse, take her out there. Just show that key to the maitre d', and he'll give you a table. Without a reservation, I mean."

"And I can use it?"

"I think Captain Pickering would be delighted to have you use it, under the circumstances," Stecker said. "And who knows, Joe, you might get lucky. The suite has four bedrooms. Odds are, one of them ought to be empty."

"She's not that kind of a girl," Joe Howard said.

"The one thing I've learned about women, Joe, over the years," Stecker laughed, "is that you never can tell about women."

"I said she's a nice girl," Joe Howard said sharply. "From Philadelphia. She's even got a college degree."

"I'm sure she is," Stecker said.

(EIGHT)
The Coronado Beach Hotel
San Diego, California
1930 Hours 3 February 1942

There was a long line of people waiting to get into the main dining room. The line overflowed the bank of upholstered benches intended for those waiting for a table.

"We're never going to get in here," Ensign Barbara Cotter said to Lieutenant Joe Howard.

"Trust me," Joe said, with far more confidence than he felt. He put his hand on her arm and marched her past the sitting and standing people waiting to get in. Some of them, senior officers, many with their wives, looked at them either curiously or unpleasantly.

The maitre d', in his good time, raised his eyes from his list of reservations.

"Your name, Sir?"

Joe showed him the hotel key.

The maitre d's eyebrows rose.

"Certainly, Sir, will you come with me, please?"

The enormous, old fashioned, high-ceilinged dining room was almost full, but here and there there were empty tables with Reserved signs mounted on brass stands. The maitre d' led them to a table by a wide window overlooking the water. The window was now covered by a heavy black curtain.

"Your waiter will be here shortly, Sir," the maitre d' said, as he held Barbara's chair for her. "Enjoy your meal."

"What did you show him?" Barbara asked.

He handed her the key.

"I don't know what you think I am, or who you are—" Barbara flared, and started to get to her feet. She saw the horrified look on his face, and stopped.

"Captain Stecker loaned me that," Joe said. "He said to show it to the headwaiter, and it would get us a table."

"Who is Captain Stecker?" Barbara asked, partially mollified.

Why am I so furious? So far, he hasn't even looked directly at me, much less tried to put his hands on me.

"He's my boss, the one that got me the commission," Joe said, and then blurted, "I'm not trying to get you into a hotel room or anything like that."

"I certainly hope not," she said.

"All the key is for is so we could get a table," Joe said.

"You said that," she said. "He lives here, or something?"

"No. The key . . . this is an involved story. . . ."

"I'm fascinated," she said.

He told her what Stecker had told him. Their eyes met, and in them she saw that he was telling the truth.

And now that's over, she sighed inwardly. *The key has been explained, and I believe he did not get himself a room here, confident that I would jump in bed with him. So why do I feel a little let down? He almost sounds as if he doesn't want to go to bed with me. My God, this is an insane situation!*

"I'm sorry," he concluded.

"Why should you be sorry?"

"Because you thought—"

"Let's just let it drop, OK?"

"OK," he said, with enormous relief. "What would you like to drink? I mean, do you drink?"

"Scotch," she said.

"Scotch?" he asked, in disbelief.

"Something wrong with Scotch?"

"I didn't think girls drank Scotch."

"Girls drink gin fizzes and brandy Alexanders, right? Things like that? And then they get sick to their stomachs. Well, this girl learned that in college, and this girl drinks Scotch. If that's all right with you."

My God, why did I snap at him like that? What the hell is wrong with me?

"Sorry," he said.

"Stop saying you're sorry!"

"Good evening," a waiter said. "May I get you something from the bar?"

"Scotch," Joe said. "Scotch and soda. Two of them."

"I'm very sorry, Sir, we're out of Scotch."

Barbara looked at Joe, and she saw that he was looking at her, and that his lips and his eyes were curled in laughter he was afraid to let out.

"That figures," Barbara said, and then she laughed; then, without thinking about it, she reached out and touched his hand with hers. But instantly withdrew it.

"What now?" Joe asked.

"Do you have any rye whiskey?" Barbara asked the waiter.

"Yes, Ma'am."

"Rye and ginger ale, please," Barbara said.

"Two, please," Joe said.

He handed them menus and left.

They read the menu. Joe was astonished at the prices; Barbara was horrified.

He's only a first lieutenant. He can't afford this. I wonder how he would react if I suggested we go Dutch treat?

"I'm not really very hungry," she said. "I think I'll just have a salad."

"I know what you're thinking," he said.

"I certainly hope not," she said. "What am I thinking?"

"You're thinking the prices are crazy."

"They are," she said.

"Two big things have happened in my life in the last forty-eight hours. And I happen to have a lot of money. Let me splurge. Please."

"What two big things?"

"Look at my shoulders," Joe said. "A year ago, I was a buck sergeant."

"Being an officer is important to you, isn't it?"

"I'm not sure I'll be able to hack it," he said.

"Why not?"

He shrugged. "I'm just not sure, is all."

As if with a mind of its own, her hand touched his again, and was again instantly withdrawn.

"What was the other thing?" she asked, idly curious.

"You," he said.

Her eyes moved to his, and then away.

My God, he means that. And I'm blushing!

"I wish you hadn't said that," she said.

"Why?"

"It makes me uncomfortable."

"Sorry."

"Stop saying you're sorry!"

The waiter appeared with a silver ice bucket on a stand. There was a towel-wrapped bottle in the cooler.

"We didn't order any wine," Joe said.

The waiter disappeared without a word.

"What's that all about?" Barbara asked.

Joe shrugged.

The waiter reappeared, this time carrying a silver ice bucket, tongs, two glasses, and a soda-water siphon.

"What's all this?" Barbara demanded.

"I wasn't aware before, Sir, that you're Pacific & Far Eastern," the waiter said, almost in a whisper. "The cooler contains Scotch, Sir. From the P&FE cellar. You won't mind mixing your own? And please keep the towel in place. Because of the other guests."

And he disappeared again.

"Do you understand what he said?" Barbara asked.

Joe shook his head, then took the bottle from the cooler. He unwrapped the towel, then closed it again.

"Scotch," he said. "Something called Old Grouse."

"Let me see," Barbara said, and he handed her the towel-wrapped bottle.

"It's Scotch, all right," she said. "*Good* Scotch."

"Where did it come from?" Joe asked.

"You ever hear the expression 'Don't look a gift horse in the mouth'?"

He took the bottle from her, and made a drink for her. It was, to judge by the color, far stronger than Barbara would have preferred, but she didn't want to make a fuss.

After the first couple of sips, I'll dilute it with more soda.

She waited until he had fixed his own drink, then touched her glass to his.

"Congratulations on your promotion," she said.

"To you and me," he said.

She met his eyes for a moment, then echoed him.

"To you and me," she said.

The waiter took his sweet time coming back for their order. She had just about finished her second drink by the time he did. She had really only wanted one, and that to be sociable. The second drink was as dark as the first, but it didn't seem to taste as strong.

She indulged him and gave up the idea of having just a salad, telling herself that she would make it up to him somehow. She ordered a shrimp cocktail, a New York strip, and asparagus.

"And for a wine, may I suggest a very nice Cabernet Sauvignon? It's Mr. and Mrs. Pickering's favorite, I might add."

"Well, if it's good enough for them . . ."

"I think you'll like it, Sir. It's made right here in California."

I will have just one sip of the wine. The last thing I can afford to do is get tight.

She looked down at her glass and saw that he had refilled it.

I don't need that. I just won't drink it.

"What's a New York strip?" Joe asked. "I don't think I've ever had one."

The admission took Barbara by surprise.

He really doesn't know, which is not surprising. Since the day before yesterday he was a Marine sergeant, a prewar *Marine sergeant, someone my father would claim was in the Marines because he couldn't find a job, and because the Marines offered three square meals a day and a place to sleep. Regular Marine enlisted men have few of what my father would call the social graces. And no social graces came to Joe miraculously when he put on that officer's uniform. Ordinarily, God forgive me, I am uncomfortable around the enlisted men. Why is it different with this man?*

"You know a T-bone?" she asked, and he nodded. "The big piece. They cut the bone out of T-bone. The little piece is a filet mignon, and the big piece is a New York strip."

"I came in the Corps when I was seventeen," Joe said, and she took his meaning: that she had a social background and he didn't; and that was why he didn't know what a New York strip was. New York strip was not common fare for Marine enlisted men.

My God, is he reading my mind?

She felt a wave of compassion for him as her mind's eye filled with a picture of Joe Howard at seventeen, looking like the kids she saw in the Marine Recruit Depot here. Frightened little boys in uniform.

That's all he is now. The only difference is that he's twenty-four or twenty-five and wearing an officer's uniform. But he's still alone and more than a little frightened.

She finished her drink before the meal was served. And she had three glasses of the Cabernet Sauvignon with the steak. The steak was delicious. While they ate, a band started to play. When they were finished eating, he asked her to dance.

She could smell his after-shave when they were close, and she remembered the firm muscles of his chest and arms.

What I'm going to do now, when we finish dancing, is go back to the table and have a cup of coffee, and then I'm going to tell him I have an early day tomorrow and have to go home.

He spun her about, and her eyes moved across the people at the tables around the dance floor.

And fell on Lieutenant Hazel Gower, NC, USN, who was staring at her. She was with another nurse, the skinny little old bitch who had sent her to the Venereal Diseases Ward after Barbara told her she didn't want to work in Obstetrics.

"Let's quit," Barbara said to Joe. "I'm a little dizzy."

When they returned to the table, the wine was gone, and so was the Scotch in the wine cooler. These had been replaced by a tray of cheese and two brandy snifters.

I don't want that, either. But it's his party and I don't want to appear bitchy.

"Did you order that?" she asked.

He shook his head.

"If you don't want it, don't drink it," he said.

"It would be a shame to waste it," she said.

A short time later, Joe said, "I don't think I've ever had a better time in my life. I hate for it to end."

"It has to. I've got a busy day tomorrow."

"Sure. I understand. I didn't mean . . ."

Her hand reached for his again, and touched it, and this time she did not immediately withdraw it.

"I've had a fine time, too. Really. I'm glad we came here."

His hand closed on hers, and they held hands for a moment, and then he pulled his away.

"I'll get the check," he said, and started looking for the waiter. It took him some time to find him. After the waiter noticed Joe waving and started moving toward their table, she caught Joe glancing at her, and then averting his eyes.

"Will there be something else, Sir? A pastry, perhaps?"

"You want a piece of cake?" Joe asked, and she shook her head. "Just the check, please."

"Excuse me, Sir?"

"Can I have the check, please?"

"Sir, that'll go on the Pacific & Far East house ledger."

"I'd like to pay for it," Joe said.

"Sir, that would be . . . difficult."

"Let it go, Joe," Barbara said. "Don't look a gift horse in the mouth."

"OK," he said, hesitantly. "Thank you."

"I hope you enjoyed your meal, Sir."

He took her arm again as he led her from the room. They walked within ten feet of Lieutenant Gower and her friend. When Barbara smiled at her, Gower stared right through her.

In the lobby just outside the dining room entrance, Barbara stopped.

"Where's the room the key goes to?"

"I don't know. It says 418."

"Then it would seem reasonable to assume it is on the fourth floor, wouldn't you say?"

"I suppose."

"And I think it would also be reasonable to assume that it would have a bathroom, wouldn't you say?"

"Sure. I'm sure it would."

"Nature calls," she said. "And there, lucky me, are the elevators."

"Would you like me to wait here?"

"No."

She walked ahead of him and got on the elevator.

"Four, please," she said to the elevator operator.

She didn't look at him on the way up. He followed her into the corridor.

She stopped and turned to him, and looked into his eyes.

"If you don't kiss me right now, I'm going to lose my nerve," she said.

He didn't move. He looked paralyzed.

"Didn't anybody ever tell you not to look a gift horse in the mouth?" Barbara said.

He kissed her.

And then they walked, arms around each other, down the corridor until they found suite 418. He had a little trouble fitting the key to the lock, but once they were inside, and after he kissed her again, everything went off without a hitch.

VI

(ONE)
Building "F"
Anacostia Naval Air Station
Washington, D.C.
0845 Hours 13 February 1942

"General McInerney," Brigadier General D. G. McInerney answered his telephone, not taking his eyes off the thick stack of paper before him.

"Colonel Hershberger, Sir."

"Hello, Bobby, how are you? What can I do for you?"

Colonel Robert T. Hershberger was Chief of Staff, 1st Marine Air Wing, Quantico, Virginia.

"General, the General is gone. He's at New River. I'm minding the store."

The General was Brigadier General Roy S. Geiger, Commanding, 1st Marine Air Wing.

"Got something you can't handle, Bobby?"

"General, I can handle this. What I would like is your advice on *how* to handle it."

"Shoot. Advice is cheap."

"I have a requirement to send one R4D, rigged for parachutists, to Lakehurst, to arrive NLT 0600, 14 February. That's tomorrow."

"I know. I laid that requirement on you."

"And your Major made it pretty plain that this is a must-do."

"It is."

"And thirty minutes ago, I got a call from the Director of Public Relations, just checking to see that the aircraft was scheduled, and asking me if I could take particular care to see that the crew was 'photogenic.' "

"The sonofabitch called me just a few minutes ago," General McInerney said. "He told me that the Commandant had 'expressed enthusiastic interest in the project.' You know what it is?"

"*Life* magazine is sending a photographer. Photographers. Plural. To watch the parachute trainees jump out of the airplane."

"Right. The idea, apparently, is that when the red-blooded youth of our nation see these heroic daredevils, they will rush to the nearest recruiting office to join up," General McInerney said dryly.

"That being the case, I figured there was no way I could get out of sending my only R4D up there," Colonel Hershberger said.

"If that's why you called, Bobby, save your breath. I don't know if General Holcomb really knows about whatever this public-relations operation is, but that requirement came down here from the Throne Room."

"There are four people here qualified in the R4D," Hershberger said.

"That's all?" McInerney asked, surprised.

"General, you may not have noticed, but people have been sending my pilots overseas."

"I can do without the sarcasm, thank you very much, Bobby," McInerney said. "And you may not have noticed, but there's a war on."

Colonel Hershberger did not reply.

"What's the problem, Bobby?" McInerney said, more cordially. "It only takes two pilots to fly one of those things, doesn't it?"

"Two of the four pilots don't look old enough to vote; and they have just finished the checkout. The check pilot, aware of the pilot shortage, was not as critical as he should have been."

"How do you know that?" McInerney snapped.

"I was the check pilot," Hershberger said. "Primarily because I am the only R4D Instructor Pilot here."

"You said four pilots."

"Well, *he* has two hundred–odd hours in the aircraft, and he went through the parachute-dropping course at Fort Benning."

"Well, then, what the hell is the problem? Send him. And send the two kids with him to see how it's done."

"Aye, aye, Sir. I hoped the General would say that. The name of the only fully qualified pilot for this mission is Technical Sergeant Charles Galloway."

General McInerney exhaled audibly.

"Oh, you sonofabitch, Bobby," he said. "You sandbagged me."

"The options, General, as I see them, are to send the two kids and pray they don't dump the airplane, or drop the parachutists in the Atlantic or over Central Park, while *Life*'s cameras are clicking. Or fly it myself. I've never dropped parachutists. I can probably find Lakehurst all right, but it occurred to me that it would look a little odd to have a full bird colonel flying a mission like this. Or send Charley Galloway."

"I told you about Galloway."

"Yes, Sir, I know that he embarrassed the U.S. Navy by getting repaired an airplane that BUAIR said was beyond repair. And then he further embarrassed the U.S. Navy's security procedures by finding out where a Task Force was, and then flying the unrepairable airplane out to it. And I know the only excuse he offered for this outrageous behavior was that he thought Marines were supposed to fight the enemy."

"It's a damned good thing we've been friends for twenty-odd years, Bobby," McInerney said. "Otherwise, I'd have your ass for talking to me that way."

"Doc, for God's sake, I'm bleeding for pilots. Not only for this stupid public-relations nonsense, but all over. It makes absolutely no sense to have a pilot like Galloway sitting on the goddamned ground with a wrench in his hand when he could be, for example, teaching the kids how to fly the goddamned R4D."

McInerney didn't reply.

"And if we hadn't been friends for twenty years, Doc, and somebody else was sitting at your desk, I would have just sent him without asking, and said, 'Fuck you, court-martial me,' if anybody said anything about it."

There was a long silence.

Finally, McInerney said, "Got your mouth under control now, Bobby?"

"Yes, Sir. Sorry, Sir."

"Colonel Hershberger, you have my permission to restore Sergeant Galloway to flight status. You have my permission to have Sergeant Galloway fly this public-relations mission to Lakehurst. And you may utilize Sergeant Galloway in such other flying roles as you deem appropriate for someone of his skill and experience, except that he will not leave the Quantico local area without my express permission."

"Aye, aye, Sir. Thank you, Sir."

"And you tell that sonofabitch, Bobby, that if he so much as farts and embarrasses you, me, or Marine Aviation in any way, I personally guarantee that he will spend the rest of this war as a private in a rifle company."

"Aye, aye, Sir."

General McInerney slammed the handset into its cradle and returned his attention to the thick stack of papers on his desk.

(TWO)
Lakehurst Naval Air Station
Lakehurst, New Jersey
14 February 1942

Lieutenant Colonel Franklin G. Neville, USMC, who was thirty-seven years old, balding, barrel-chested, and carried 212 pounds on a six-foot-two-inch body, had seen the future and it was Vertical Envelopment.

In 1937, as a very senior (and nearly overage-in-grade) captain, Neville was appointed Assistant Naval Attaché, United States Embassy, Helsinki, Finland. His previous assignment had been as an infantry company commander.

When he was not selected to attend the U.S. Army Command and General Staff College at Fort Leavenworth, Kansas, and was then asked if he would accept the Helsinki embassy assignment, Neville understood that his Marine Corps career was drawing to a close.

If he was lucky, he might be promoted major while on the four-year embassy assignment. But promoted or not, he knew—in fact, he'd been unofficially informed—that in the spring of 1941, when his Helsinki tour was over, he would be retired.

He'd also been told—and he believed—that he himself was in no way personally responsible for his coming retirement. He had, in other words, not been found wanting. He was a good officer who performed his assigned duties well. There was no record, official or whispered, that he was too fond of the bottle or of the ladies, or of any other sport inappropriate for a Marine officer.

The bottom line was that there were only so many billets available for majors in the peacetime Marine Corps, either in the serving Corps or in the professional schools. And others competing for these spots were *better* qualified than he was. The rule was "up or out"—meaning that if an officer was not selected for promotion, he was either separated from the Corps or retired. Retirement was the fate of officers like Captain Neville, who had enough years of service to qualify for it.

He'd understood the rules of the game when he'd accepted a regular Marine commission in 1919; and he had no complaints now—although, naturally, he was disappointed.

Franklin G. Neville had entered the Marine Corps as a second lieutenant in June of 1916, on his graduation from Purdue University. He had come home from France a wounded, decorated captain, who had taken over command of his company when its commander had been killed at Belleau Wood.

The Corps, and the war, had changed him. He no longer wanted to become a lawyer specializing in banking law, like his father. He now knew that any personal satisfaction he might find in the practice of law could not compare with the satisfaction he had known leading men in battle.

His father never understood that. Worse, he shared with most of his peers the notion that a man served in the peacetime military only if he could do nothing else. And he was simply incapable of understanding why anyone would want to settle for the pittance paid regular officers when a financially rewarding career right there in St. Louis was available.

Available, hell, it's being handed to you on a silver platter, you damned fool!

Estelle Wachenberg Neville, whom he had married five days before shipping out to France, *had* understood. And she had also brought into the marriage a substantial trust fund established for her by her maternal grandfather, who had been one of the original investors in the Greater St. Louis Electric Power Generation & Street Railway Company.

So money was never a problem, except in the perverse sense that he and Estelle had had to be very careful not to let their relative affluence offend anyone. In fact, this did not turn out to be much of a drawback. Franklin didn't think that a young lawyer in Saint Louis could drive a Harmon or a Pierce Arrow, or even a Cadillac, without offending someone senior to him. Not many in that hierarchy had a quarterly check from a trust fund.

By the time the Helsinki assignment—his "tailgate" assignment—came along, there was no longer a requirement to be "discreet" about their affluence. So he and Estelle decided to go out in style. They left the boys behind in the States, at Phillips-Exeter, to join them in the summers. And in Finland, Estelle found a furnished villa in Helsinki's most aristocratic section, Vartio Island, about five miles from the embassy.

The waters of Kallahden Bay were solidly frozen from February to April, permitting the Neville's Packard 280 sedan (Estelle's) and Auto-Union roadster (Franklin's) to drive directly from the mainland to the front door. In the warmer months, a varnished speedboat carried them back and forth from the island to the shore.

His Excellency the Ambassador was a political appointee, a deserving St. Louis Democrat who professed a closer friendship with both Estelle's and Franklin's parents at home than was the case. In point of fact, a letter from Estelle's father indicated that so far as he was concerned, the Ambassador was a traitor to his class for supporting that socialist sonofabitch in the White House.

Nevertheless, the polite fiction served both to keep the Naval and Army attachés off Franklin's back and to open social doors that permitted Estelle to enjoy a role as hostess that she had been denied all those years.

Between Franklin's social contacts within the diplomatic-military community and Estelle's with the diplomatic people and their neighbors on Vartio Island, it was a rare evening indeed when their butler served dinner to them alone at home.

When the boys arrived in the summer (they spent the Christmas holidays with their grandparents in St. Louis), they were, as Estelle wrote home, "received by the best young people in Finland." They fished and sailed, and they danced and kept close company with a number of splendidly beautiful and astonishingly blond Finnish girls. In due course, Franklin found it necessary to have a serious man-to-man talk with them about how they would embarrass not just their mother but the United States of America if one of the young ladies should find herself in the family way. He then counseled them on the absolute necessity of faithful use of rubber contraceptives.

In October of 1939, Captain Franklin G. Neville was promoted major. The promotion came as a surprise. He could not imagine that his immediate superior, Lieutenant Commander H. Raymond Fawcett, USN, the Naval Attaché, had been writing glowing efficiency reports on him. Fawcett's disapproval (and/or jealousy) of the Nevilles' lifestyle was nearly visible. But still, it would be nice, when they went back to St. Louis, to be able to call themselves "Major and Mrs. Neville."

In November of 1939, the Union of Soviet Socialist Republics attacked Finland across the southeastern province of Karelia. Before the 1917 Revolution, Finland had been part of Tsarist Russia; specifically, it was a Grand Duchy thereof. When Finland declared its independence, the military forces of the Soviet Union were in no position to do anything about it.

Now they were. They regarded Finland as part of Russia, and they wanted it back.

Major Franklin Neville immediately went to the war zone as an observer. It was clearly his duty, perhaps the most important duty a military attaché can perform, to observe the combatants at war, to report on their relative efficiency and capabilities, and to learn what he could.

Neville, along with an officer from the Finnish High Command and Lieutenant Colonel Graf Friedrich von Kallenberg-Mattau, an assistant military attaché at the German Embassy with whom Neville played golf and tennis in the summer and hunted and skied in the winter, drove to Karelia in Freddy von K's Mercedes. Freddy argued that the Mercedes had a better heater and more luggage space than either Neville's Auto-Union roadster or the official, smaller Mercedes sedan the Finnish General Staff officer had been given.

As they drove off, there was little question in Franklin Neville's mind that soon, perhaps within the day, he would be in the hands of the Russians. They outnumbered the Finns by a factor of better than twenty to one. As courageous as the Finns might prove to be, that sort of a disbalance of opposing forces could result in only one end: the Finns would be overrun and wiped out.

He wondered if the Russians would honor his diplomatic status, or whether he would be shot out of hand, or whether he would perhaps simply disappear.

It didn't matter. It was his duty to go; and without any false heroics whatever, he could no more not have gone than he could have flapped his wings and flown.

What he found in Karelia Province was not in any way what he expected.

He could not believe that the military forces of a major, contemporary world power would be committed to combat with such poor planning, or with such an absolute ignorance of the kind of warfare they would have to wage.

Though the wintertime temperature in Karelia regularly dropped to below minus forty degrees Fahrenheit, eighty or ninety percent of the attacking Russian forces were not clothed or otherwise equipped to fight in such conditions.

The apparent Russian plan to penetrate and overrun the Finns swiftly, through sheer numbers and massive artillery barrages, was an absolute disaster. The Russian artillery, for instance, was almost useless in the bitter cold. And when the pieces could be coaxed into firing, most of the projectiles simply buried themselves deep in the snow before exploding. Rarely did they do any real harm.

The Finns, on the other hand, were not only superbly equipped to deal with the weather (they even had stoves and facilities to build "warming areas" where troops were routinely returned to be fed and warmed), but were able to wage war effectively in it. Their infantry was equipped with skis and snowshoes, permitting rapid movement over deep snow. They had snow-colored parkas, glasses to prevent snow blindness, and even white sleeves to place over their rifles to camouflage them.

And they were superbly led and disciplined.

The result was that the Finns were able to cause severe personnel and materiel losses to Russian forces at little cost to themselves. Finnish forces would suddenly appear when and where the Russians did not expect them. When the Russians marshaled forces sufficient to repel the Finnish attackers, the Finns simply disappeared in the vast snowy terrain, where the Russians were unable to pursue them.

Any other army but the Red Army, Neville cabled Washington, would have called off the offensive after suffering such terrible losses. Yet even their apparent total willingness to disregard personnel losses was not going to permit them to accomplish their objective of a quick and decisive victory.

But the Russians did have one military capability that deeply impressed Major Neville, even if they used it improperly—they literally threw it away. The Russians had massed a large fleet of transport aircraft, from which they parachuted infantry, plus some supplies, to the ground.

In practice, the Russians generally dropped their parachute troops in the wrong places, where Finnish forces quickly wiped them out; and Russian planning made little or no provision for reinforcing or resupplying the parachutists once they were on the ground, which meant that they ended up, in effect, dying on the vine. In Neville's professional opinion, however, these failings did not detract in any way from the obvious fact that the use of parachute troops—the Theory of Vertical Envelopment—was an idea whose time had come.

This theory was not new. Neville recalled that in the notoriety surrounding his court-martial for insubordination, it was often forgotten that U.S. Army Air Corps Brigadier General "Billy" Mitchell had written as long ago as the World War that parachute troops would play an important—perhaps a dominant—role on the battlefields of the future.

As for poor little Finland, in the end, of course, Goliath prevailed against David. Courage, discipline, and skill in the techniques of warfare cannot stand up forever against an enemy who possesses both overwhelming logistical superiority and manpower, and who is not responsible to his people for the loss of their sons in battlefield slaughter. The Finns sued for armistice in early 1940.

In February 1940, shortly after the armistice was put into effect, Major Franklin G. Neville was ordered home—but *not* to retire, as he had anticipated. Instead, he was ordered to Headquarters, USMC, in Washington. There he was given a desk in a crowded office and asked to expand on the reports he had cabled from Helsinki of the Russo-Finnish conflict. He was to make such observations and recommendations as he thought would be of value for planning for possible Marine Corps operations in the future.

It was temporary duty, and government quarters were not authorized in Washington. He was, however, paid a per diem allowance. Quarters at his next duty station, USMC Schools, Quantico, Virginia, *were* authorized; but Estelle had no intention of going to Quantico alone and hibernating there while her husband was in Washington. And he had no quarrel with her on that.

So the Nevilles moved into a suite at the Wardman Park Hotel. After Helsinki, Estelle argued, she was not about to return to that idiotic business of living as if they didn't know where their next nickel was coming from.

It was generally agreed among those who counted that Major Neville's reports on the Russo-Finnish conflict were outstanding. Indeed, his paper on Finnish command relationships and discipline earned him a "well done" on a buck slip from the Major General Commandant himself.

But Major Franklin G. Neville was now a *much* changed man. Retirement from the Corps no longer loomed before him. No more did he have to face a suitable job arranged by his family in Saint Louis, with lunch at the Athletic Club and drinks at the Country Club. Instead, he could now look forward to further service as a Marine officer.

There was a new war coming, he felt sure of it. And he—prophetically—had a vision of a new cutting edge for the Marine Sword. He saw properly trained and equipped and properly utilized Marine parachutists changing the face of Marine warfare.

No longer would Marines assault an enemy beach from the sea, he wrote in a paper he titled "Hostile Shore Assault by Vertical Envelopment." They would no longer be left vulnerable to murderous fire from shore batteries as their landing barges brought them to the beach. Aerial reconnaissance would show where the enemy was *not.* And in *that* place a fleet of transports would drop, by parachute, companies, battalions, and possibly even full regiments. Initially, these forces would be resupplied from the air, until, attacking from the rear, they could secure the beach.

And, of course, he saw Franklin G. Neville, appropriately promoted, leading this invulnerable force of elite Marine parachutists. He had led men in combat well as a young captain. It was not arrogant to presume he could do so even better as a colonel. Or as a brigadier general.

After completing his Headquarters assignment, Major Neville asked for and was granted a thirty-day leave. He went to Fort Benning, Georgia, where he met like-minded Army parachute enthusiasts. They received him cordially; not only had he seen the light, but he had actually witnessed vertical assaults in combat. He gave several little seminars on Russian parachute operations and techniques, pointing out in these talks his perceptions of Russian strengths and weaknesses.

The Army obligingly arranged for him to go through their experimental parachute-jumping program. He made nine jumps, and, in a quasi-official ceremony at the Benning Officers' Club, was given a set of silver Army parachutist's wings and named an Honorary U.S. Army Paratrooper.

When Major Neville reported to Quantico, he was assigned to the G-2 Section, where his duties were to examine French, English, and German military publications, extracting therefrom material he believed should be made available to the Corps.

He did not find this difficult. He was fluent in German, primarily because of his long friendship and association in Helsinki with Lieutenant Colonel Graf Friedrich von Kallenberg-Mattau; and he had no trouble reading the German material made available to him. Equally important, he had two sergeants of foreign extraction who could make the actual translations into English.

Major Neville therefore had the time to gather all his thoughts, distill them, and express them clearly. The result of this was, "Vertical Envelopment in the U.S. Marine Corps: A Study of the Potential Uses of Parachute Troops in Future Warfare, by Major Franklin G. Neville, USMC, based on his observations during the Russo-Finnish War," which he submitted for publication in *The Marine Corps Gazette.*

It was duly decided that Neville's article was "not appropriate" for publication, and it was returned to him with the thanks of the editors.

But it wasn't long before the article took on a life of its own—especially after scuttlebutt had it that the piece had been killed by someone far superior to the Major who edited the *Gazette.* Copies of it were run off on mimeograph machines and made their way around the Marine Corps.

Despite the resulting wide distribution, Major Neville's concept of the Theory of Vertical Envelopment as it could apply to the Marine Corps met a mixed to negative reception. There were those who genuinely believed Major Neville was just one more of those harmless Marine Corps characters who were doomed to play the game of life with less than a full deck:

Marines going into combat by jumping out of airplanes? Jesus H. Christ! Do you remember that loony who actually proposed building troop-carrying submarines, so we could sneak *up to the enemy's beach?*

And there were those who read Neville's arguments with a more open mind and decided that whatever merits the theory might contain, for the time being at least, it was an idea whose time had not come.

Parachute warfare would require large numbers of large airplanes, but these were not available, nor were they likely to be. And even if an aircraft fleet were miraculously to materialize, it would require an enormous logistical tail, which the Navy certainly would not want to provide:

You could do the arithmetic for that in your head. There are roughly two hundred men in a company. With, say, twenty men per airplane, that would mean ten airplanes to drop one company. There aren't that many R4-Ds, the only airplane that will carry that many people, in the whole Marine Corps. Using the rule of thumb of 1.5 pilots per cockpit seat, ten airplanes would require thirty pilots per parachute company, plus a like number of mechanics and crew chiefs.

And Neville makes the doubtless valid point that the reason the Russian parachute troops couldn't get the job done was that the Russians made no provision to resupply them. So, since a reasonable ballpark figure for resupply of ammunition and food is a couple of hundred pounds per man, and since a couple of hundred pounds is what a man weighs, that means you would need ten airplanes to drop the infantry, and another ten airplanes to resupply them.

That's twenty airplanes, sixty pilots, sixty mechanics, and twenty crew chiefs for one company. Not to mention things like people driving the gas trucks, and extra cooks to feed the pilots and mechanics and truckdrivers.

And what good could one lousy company do? You'd need a battalion. A battalion is five companies. Multiply the above by five, and you get one hundred airplanes, and three hundred pilots. . . .

Major Neville, the poor bastard, obviously got carried away with the romance of it all. As a practical matter, there's just no way the Corps could do it. No wonder the brass killed his article.

But, as a result of Major Franklin G. Neville's rejected *Marine Corps Gazette* article, there were those in the senior hierarchy of the Marine Corps who were forced to consider, for the first time, that the U.S. Army was indeed going ahead with Vertical Envelopment. If the Army was successful in fielding a regimental-size airborne force—and there was already scuttlebutt that the Army intended to redesignate the 82nd Infantry Division as the 82nd *Airborne* Division—this would constitute a threat to the Marine Corps' perception of itself, and, more important, to the Congress's perception of the Marine Corps, as the assault element of United States military forces.

The Marine Corps believed—as, for that matter, did many soldiers and sailors—that the function of the Marine Corps was to storm enemy beaches, holding them only long enough for the Army to follow up with its heavy artillery and logistical elements.

If the Army developed its own capability to land regiments or divisions on hostile shores—in other words, if they could field an airborne division—the question would naturally be raised, "So why do we need the Marines?"

On the other hand, if the Marine Corps had—in place—its own experts in Vertical Envelopment, or possibly even its own small force of parachutists, say a battalion, together with plans to apply their techniques to larger forces, up to a division, then the Marine Corps could reasonably argue that the Army was treading on its turf and should back off.

While no one really thought that the Army's parachutists posed a deadly threat to the very existence of the Marine Corps, neither was any senior Marine officer prepared to state that they posed no threat at all.

And money, as 1941 passed, became less and less an issue than it had been in previous years. There was little doubt in Congress's mind that war was on the horizon and that the American military establishment was ill-prepared to wage it. And Congress devoutly believes the solution to any problem is to throw money at it.

The Marine solution to the problem posed by the Army's parachutists proved to be simple. In a supplemental appropriation, Congress provided funds for USMC Schools, Quantico, to conduct such tests as the Major General Commandant of the Marine Corps thought pertinent regarding the use of parachute forces in future Marine Corps operations.

Marine Corps Headquarters delegated overall responsibility for Marine Parachutists to Marine Aviation, following the German practice of subordinating their *Falschirmjaeger* to the Luftwaffe rather than to the Wehrmacht. And they decreed that Major Franklin G. Neville would be action officer for the program.

In August 1941, Major Neville submitted a report to Headquarters, USMC, of the original tests at Quantico, together with a list of recommendations. Surprising no one, he reported that the tests proved beyond any doubt that Vertical Envelopment offered great advantages to the Marine Corps. He recommended also:

(1) That a provisional battalion of parachute troops be formed, and that a suitably experienced officer be named as its commander. Neville listed desirable qualifications for such an officer. These surprised no one: With the exception that the recommended commanding officer should be a lieutenant colonel, these qualifications matched those of Major Franklin G. Neville and no one else anyone could think of in the Marine Corps.

(2) That Marine parachutists should be removed from subordination to Marine Aviation.

(3) That the Marine Corps establish a formal parachutist's school, preferably at some location other than Quantico, whose training facilities were already overloaded.

The report was submitted through Marine Aviation channels to Headquarters, USMC. The endorsement stated that the Director of Marine Aviation did not feel qualified either to recommend or recommend against the incorporation of parachutists into the Marine Corps. But, clearly, parachutists were now a practical matter.

If, however, it was decided to establish Marine parachutists, Marine Aviation was in complete agreement with Major Neville's recommendations that such a force be withdrawn from subordination to Marine Aviation. And Marine Aviation strongly endorsed the recommendation that any further Marine parachutist training be conducted elsewhere than Quantico. For example, the U.S. Naval Lighter Than Air Station at Lakehurst, New Jersey, which was currently underutilized, might well prove to be a suitable location.

There were those who regarded the Marine Aviation endorsement as another example that there was really no intraservice rivalry between the air and ground components of the Marine Corps. But cynics maintained that Marine Aviation actually wanted to distance itself as far as possible from paratroops generally and from Major Franklin G. Neville specifically. That Neville was now known popularly as "Fearless Frank" was not taken as an auspicious omen for the future development of Marine Vertical Envelopment. Almost to a man, Marine Aviation personnel believed that anyone who willingly jumped out of a perfectly functioning aircraft was, kindly, a little strange.

Action on the Neville report and its recommendations came unusually quickly, within a month. All the recommendations were approved:

Marine Aviation was relieved of responsibility for airborne forces.

A Provisional Parachute Battalion was authorized, to be subordinate to Fleet Marine Force, Atlantic.

The Director, Marine Corps Parachute Forces, was authorized to seek volunteers for parachute duty from Marine units within the continental limits of the United States.

Marine Corps Schools, Quantico, was ordered to establish a subordinate facility to train parachutists at Naval Lighter Than Air Station, Lakehurst, New Jersey.

Major Franklin G. Neville was appointed Director of Marine Corps Parachute Forces.

Franklin G. Neville was promoted lieutenant colonel the day he first visited Lakehurst to determine how its facilities (which is to say those not needed to support the Navy's blimps) could be quickly adapted to train parachutists.

With the exception of not being named Commanding Officer of the Parachute Battalion (and it could be argued that there was no point in naming a commanding officer of a battalion that did not yet exist), Neville had gotten everything he'd asked for.

He understood, however, that the greatest test was yet before him: turning the theory into reality. And he had a plan for that, too. And high on the plan was getting rid of every last damned one of the Marine Aviation people. Especially the enlisted men. The only Marine Aviation people he wanted to see in the future would be the ones flying the aircraft.

Based both upon his experience as a company commander in France, and on what he had observed in the Russo-Finnish War, Colonel Neville knew that the keys to military success were esprit de corps and impeccable discipline. The two went hand in hand. The former, Neville believed, was a result of the latter.

In his early planning phases, he had been foolish enough to believe that because he was starting with Marines, he would have a leg up. All Marines, in his opinion, had the kind of esprit de corps and impeccable discipline that the Finns he so admired in combat had possessed. The only thing he had to worry about, then, was how to actually instruct them in the skill of parachuting.

His experience at Quantico with Marine Aviation, and especially with the enlisted men there, quickly showed him how wrong he was about that. Not only were the enlisted men a long-haired, slovenly bunch, who slouched around with their ties pulled down and their blouses unbuttoned, but their officers let them get away with it.

At the officers' club in Quantico, he actually came as close to losing his temper in public as he ever had as a Marine. He sought out a Marine Aviation major to have a word with him, out of school, about a situation he found intolerable. He had come across a Marine lieutenant, an aviator, a staff sergeant, some sort of aircraft mechanic, and a PFC, whose function he did not really know, leaning on the wall of hangar, laughing and joking together as if they were civilians in a pool hall.

When he relayed what he had seen to the Major, telling him that while he didn't want to bring charges, he felt sure the Major would agree that sort of behavior was intolerable and had to be nipped in the bud, the Major actually said to him, "You have to understand, Neville, that Aviation is different."

"We are all Marines," Neville argued.

"Yeah, of course we are," the Major replied. "But that doesn't mean everybody has to walk around as if he has a broomstick shoved up his ass like you do."

"I can't believe I'm hearing what I'm hearing," Major Neville said indignantly.

The Aviation Major beckoned Major Neville closer with a wiggle of his index finger. Then he whispered in Neville's ear, "Go fuck yourself, Fearless. Leave my people alone." Then he leaned back on his barstool, grinned cordially, and asked, "Do we understand each other, Fearless?"

Neville realized at the time that reporting the incident to Colonel Hershberger, the Marine Aviation Major's immediate superior, would have been fruitless. Those goddamned aviators stuck together. And, furthermore, it would have been necessary to report that "Fearless" business, too, a matter he didn't want to get into.

The solution to the problem was to get rid of the Marine Aviation people. He went from Lakehurst (now that he was Director of Marine Corps Parachute Forces, he no longer had to justify official travel) to Quantico, where he asked for volunteers. One of them he knew: a handsome, charming lieutenant named R. B. Macklin, who shared his enthusiasm for Vertical Envelopment. Macklin had served with the 4th Marines in China and, for reasons Neville did not understand, had been wasting his talents as a mess officer at Marine Corps Schools. He also recruited six second lieutenants from a group about to graduate from Officer's Basic Course.

He actually had eleven volunteer second lieutenants. But some sonofabitch from the 1st Division, to which the young officers were supposed to be assigned on graduation, complained to Personnel that the 1st Division had a more critical need for them than Neville did. And after a rather bitter discussion, he was allowed to take only six.

From Quantico he went to Parris Island and recruited from boots about to be graduated and from the cadre of drill instructors. He argued to them that if making Marines out of civilians was important, making Para-Marines out of ordinary Marines was even more so. And besides, once they became parachutists, it would increase their pay by fifty dollars a month. Over protests from both the 1st Division and Parris Island itself, he was allowed to take nine drill instructors and no more than three volunteers from each graduating platoon of recruits, up to a maximum of 1,200 men.

He then went to Fort Benning, Georgia, where he received permission for the nine ex–drill instructors and forty-one others (to be named when they became available) to go through the Army's Jump School en route to the Marine Parachute Training School at Lakehurst.

As the drill instructors reported aboard Lakehurst from Fort Benning, the Marine Aviation parachutists would be returned, on a one-to-one basis, to Marine Aviation. He couldn't get rid of all of them, of course; he had to keep some around—parachute riggers, for example. But by the first of the year, Major Neville's broom would otherwise have swept a new and clean path through Lakehurst.

PFC Steven M. Koffler, USMC, of course knew nothing about any of this. All he knew was that he was being carried as AWOL when he returned from the "extended" three-day pass the Sergeant of the Guard had arranged with the First Sergeant for him to have when he had first reported aboard Lakehurst.

There is legally no such thing as an "extended" three-day pass. Absences of less than seventy-two hours are not chargeable as leave. Absences over seventy-two hours are. Consequently, someone who is absent over seventy-two hours and is not on leave orders (which will charge the time against his accrued leave) is absent without leave, or AWOL.

Steve Koffler, who did not understand this technicality, told his First Sergeant what had happened. The First Sergeant, who had had a number of "extended" three-day passes himself over the years, decided to buck the problem up to the Company Commander. So Steve Koffler repeated his story to the Company Commander, First Lieutenant R. B. Macklin.

Lieutenant Macklin, who was a graduate of the United States Naval Academy at Annapolis, was very concerned with his professional reputation. He was a very senior lieutenant whose promotion to captain was long overdue.

Before the war, he had been stationed in Shanghai, China, with the 4th Marines. There, for reasons he had never been able to fathom fully, he had earned the dislike of the Regimental Intelligence Officer, a captain named Banning. Banning, for still more reasons Macklin simply couldn't understand, was held in the high regard of the Regimental Commander, even though, in Macklin's professional judgment, Banning's performance of duty left a good deal to be desired, and his off-duty conduct was inexcusable.

Among other things, Banning maintained a White Russian mistress, and didn't particularly care who knew it. If that wasn't conduct unbecoming an officer and a gentleman, Ed Macklin couldn't imagine what would be.

Banning had entered the Corps from the Citadel, a civilian trade school, which of course was not the same thing as coming out of Annapolis. That probably explained some of the trouble such people had. It was well known that men from places like the Citadel, Norwich, and VMI were not only jealous of Annapolis graduates, but went out of their way to get them, whenever and however they could.

What happened in Shanghai was that Banning, demonstrating a clear lack of good judgment, had assigned a corporal—a corporal!—to gather intelligence data on Japanese troop dispositions, while he was ostensibly serving as a truckdriver in a motor convoy under Macklin's command.

Predictably, even though Macklin tried to help him, the Corporal was unable to perform his mission in the best interests of the command. Not only that, but he managed to touch off a confrontation with Chinese bandits that saw more than twenty Chinese killed.

Macklin wrote a report about the failure of the intelligence-gathering mission and the causes of the shooting incident. The report made clear that the whole thing could have been avoided if a low-ranking enlisted man had not been placed in a position he could not be expected to handle. Instead of accepting the report for what it was, namely constructive criticism, Banning wrote a wildly imaginative, wholly dishonest reply in which he placed on Macklin the blame for both the failure of the mission and the shooting incident.

It was difficult to believe, but the Colonel (who had gone into the Corps from Princeton, of all places!) took Banning's side. And an efficiency report was placed in Macklin's personnel file that questioned his judgment, his honesty, and his potential for command.

At the time, Macklin was so upset by this gross injustice that he did not demand, as was his right, a court-martial to determine the truth of the accusations against him. It was his intention to just leave the Corps. After the way he had been treated, he no longer could serve in good conscience.

But with war on the horizon, resignations were no longer being accepted. He was consequently assigned to the Marine Corps Base at Quantico, Virginia, as a mess officer at Marine Corps Schools. He was prepared, of course, to carry out to the best of his ability that and any other assigned duty.

Several months later, he was shocked but not especially surprised, when he later thought about it, to see Banning's corporal from Shanghai enrolled as a candidate for a commission as an officer. The man had no education beyond high school, and was, literally, a murderer.

Corporal Kenneth R. "Killer" McCoy was so called because he had stabbed three Italian Marines to death on the streets of Shanghai. And here he was, about to become a Marine officer!

While he realized that he had no proof of any allegations he could make about McCoy, he was sure it was his obligation to the Corps to see that a man like that never became an officer. Macklin therefore had had a quiet word with several of the noncommissioned officers in the school. If McCoy could be terminated from the school for failure to meet its high standards, that would be the end of the matter. He would be no worse off than he had been; he would be assigned as a corporal.

It was then that Macklin learned just how much the Corps was infiltrated and corrupted by secret alliances, and how much power they had. Corporal McCoy must have gotten the word out that he was in trouble; for the next thing Macklin knew, a master gunnery sergeant named Stecker (he was the senior enlisted man at Quantico, and presumably had more important things to do) was nosing around the rifle range. And the day after that, Ed Macklin was standing in front of his Colonel, accused of improper interference with the officer candidate class.

"Find yourself a new home, Macklin," the Colonel told him then. "Or I'll find one for you!"

It was at that point that Macklin volunteered for and was accepted in the Marine Corps parachute program.

He and Lieutenant Colonel Franklin G. Neville saw eye-to-eye from the first. And after a period of time, he was able to tell Neville how unfairly he had been treated in Shanghai and at Quantico. Neville understood and was instantly sympathetic.

"You do a good job with my parachute school," Neville said, "and I'll write you an efficiency report that will take care of any problems you had in Shanghai. You should be a captain, and if you do a good job for me, you will be."

Macklin knew all about "extended" three-day passes: he considered them an affront to his perception of good order and discipline. So armed, he concluded he had in PFC Koffler a fine opportunity to make his position on "extended" three-day passes known to his new command.

He announced to Koffler that he didn't believe a word of his story; that no Marine NCO worthy of the name would tell a PFC not to worry about the seventy-two-hour limitation. He went on to explain that absence without leave was nearly as heinous an offense as cowardice in the face of the enemy, and that he really deserved to be brought before a court-martial.

But since the former First Sergeant and the Sergeant of the Guard had been transferred to Quantico, and since it would be inconvenient to bring them all the way back to Lakehurst to testify, and since Koffler was new to the Corps and probably didn't realize the seriousness of his offense, Macklin told Koffler he would graciously give him a second chance.

He would thus be permitted to begin parachute training. But the first time he stepped half an inch out of line would prove he was unworthy of a second chance.

In that event, the whole business would be brought up again, and he could expect a court-martial and confinement at the Portsmouth Naval Prison.

If he managed to get through the course, there would be a clean slate.

And, of course, it went without saying that he could forget any liberty or other privileges while he was in parachute training. He would, in fact, consider himself confined to barracks when off-duty.

(THREE)
Marine Air Station
Quantico, Virginia
1030 Hours 13 February 1942

First Lieutenant James G. Ward, USMCR, and First Lieutenant David F. Schneider, USMC, marched into the office of Colonel Robert T. Hershberger and came to attention before his desk.

"Sir," Lieutenant Ward barked, "Lieutenants Ward and Schneider reporting as ordered."

Lieutenant Ward, a tall, brown-haired, loose-framed twenty-two-year-old, had come into Marine Aviation via Princeton, Officer Candidate School at Quantico, and Pensacola. Lieutenant Schneider, who was stocky, broad-shouldered, and wore his blond hair in a closely cropped crewcut, was also twenty-two, and had received his commission upon graduation from the U.S. Naval Academy at Annapolis.

With war on the horizon, and because he had the necessary credit hours, Lieutenant Ward had been permitted to graduate from Princeton (B.A., with a major in history) halfway through his senior year. He was graduated from Officer Candidate School at Quantico and commissioned five days before Lieutenant Schneider got to throw his midshipman's cap into the air at Annapolis. He had similarly been promoted to first lieutenant five days before Schneider was given that promotion.

Although he was personally fond of Lieutenant Ward, Lieutenant Schneider regarded himself as a member of the professional officer corps of the Naval Service of the United States; he did not like being outranked by a goddamned reservist from Princeton.

There was an enlisted man sitting in Colonel Hershberger's office. He stood up when the two lieutenants marched in. Colonel Hershberger promptly introduced him.

"This is Sergeant Galloway."

Sergeant Galloway was wearing utilities. Both Ward and Schneider had seen him on the flight line, working as a mechanic. They had also heard scuttlebutt that the sergeant had stolen an airplane somewhere and taken it for a joyride, and had been sent to Quantico to await court-martial.

Schneider nodded uncomfortably at the Sergeant. Because Lieutenant Ward was a reservist and couldn't be expected to know the subtleties of dealing with an enlisted man over his ass in trouble, he graciously offered Galloway his hand.

"You will be taking our R4D to Lakehurst tomorrow," Colonel Hershberger said to them. "Headquarters USMC has arranged for *Life* magazine to do a story on the Marine parachutists being trained there. This operation, I am reliably informed, has the approval of the highest authority within the Marine Corps. In other words, if you screw up, you will embarrass not only yourselves, but me, Brigadier General McInerney, Marine Aviation, and the Corps itself as well. I want you to understand that very clearly."

"Yes, Sir," they parroted.

"Sergeant Galloway has kindly offered to go along on this little jaunt," Colonel Hershberger said, smiling wryly, "and I have accepted his offer."

Both young officers looked between the Colonel and the Sergeant with mingled curiosity and surprise.

"Sergeant Galloway will function as pilot-in-command," Hershberger said, startling them, "and the reason I called you all in here is to make sure you know what that means."

"Sir," Lieutenant Schneider said, "I'm a little confused."

"I thought you might be, Mr. Schneider," Hershberger said. "So I will explain it to you. What it means is that senior authority—in this case, me—has reviewed the qualifications of the pilots available to fly this mission and has chosen the best-qualified pilot—in this case, Sergeant Galloway—to serve as pilot-in-command. And *that* means just what it says. He is in command of the aircraft and is responsible for the accomplishment of the mission. So long as it has to do with the airplane and the mission, he speaks with my authority. Clear?"

"Yes, Sir," Lieutenant Schneider replied.

Colonel Hershberger looked at Lieutenant Ward until it occurred to Ward that a response was expected from him.

"Yes, of course," he said.

Hershberger went on, apparently not concerned that Ward had not appended the expected "Sir" to his answer, "If, in Sergeant Galloway's judgment, there is time and opportunity on this mission, he can give you instruction in the operation of the aircraft and on dropping parachutists from it. Galloway is both an R4D IP and a graduate of the Army Air Corps course on parachutist dropping. He has also been flying since you two were in high school. Any questions so far?"

"No, Sir."

"On the other hand, we all of course are in the Marine Corps, and are therefore subject to all the rules and the customs of the Service. Sergeant Galloway is required to treat you with the military courtesy to which your rank entitles you. The flip side of the coin is that as officers you are as responsible for Sergeant Galloway's well-being—his rations and quarters, so to speak—and his conduct, as you would be for any enlisted man you found yourselves associated with on a mission. In other words, if it should come to my attention that Sergeant Galloway got drunk and punched out a shore patrolman while you are all off doing this public-relations nonsense, it will be your ass as well as his. Questions?"

"No, Sir," Lieutenants Ward and Schneider said in unison.

"Charley?"

"Colonel, what I've been thinking of doing is shooting some touch-and-goes here—I haven't flown one of these for a while—and then fueling up and going up there this afternoon."

"Sure, why not? Just don't bend the goddamned bird."

"Sirs," Sergeant Galloway said, looking at Lieutenants Ward and Schneider, "would it be possible for you to pack your gear and meet me at Base Ops in an hour?"

"Certainly," Lieutenant Schneider said.

"Yes, Sir," Lieutenant Ward said, which earned him a look of amazed disgust from Lieutenant Schneider and a chuckle from Colonel Hershberger.

"Charley," Colonel Hershberger said, "am I going to have to remind you that you're on thin ice?"

"No, Sir, you don't," Sergeant Galloway said.

"That will be all, gentlemen, thank you," Colonel Hershberger said, dismissing them.

While they packed their bags in the bachelor officers' quarters, and as they drove to Base Operations, Lieutenants Ward and Schneider discussed Sergeant Galloway and the situation they found themselves in.

Lieutenant Schneider could not restrain himself from reminding Lieutenant Ward that officers should not say "Yes, Sir" to sergeants. After that, they considered all the possibilities of the scuttlebutt concerning Sergeant Galloway, the significance of Colonel Hershberger's remarks about Sergeant Galloway being on thin ice, and the Colonel's pronouncement that if Sergeant Galloway got drunk and punched out a shore patrolman, they would be held responsible.

Once they arrived at Base Operations, however, Sergeant Galloway's behavior and appearance made them a little less nervous. He was wearing green trousers and a fur-collared leather flight jacket when they joined him. There were golden, somewhat wear-faded, Naval Aviator's wings just like their own stamped on a leather patch on the breast of the flight jacket; and the real thing was pinned to the breast of his uniform blouse, which he carried on a hanger. The hash marks on the blouse cuff, signifying eight years of Marine service, were also reassuring.

And there was something about his calm competency as he laid out the flight plan, went through the weather briefing, and dealt with the crew chief and the preflight inspection of the aircraft that reminded them of their IPs at Pensacola. Since flight instructors, like drill sergeants, are always remembered by their former students as individuals of vast knowledge and awesome competence, both Ward and Schneider were able to tell themselves that whatever else Sergeant Galloway was, he was an extraordinarily qualified aviator. And this too was reassuring.

They even found his little joke with the crew chief, himself a technical sergeant, somehow comforting: "Well, let's wind up the rubber bands and see if we can get this thing in the air."

Galloway climbed up the door ladder and walked through the fuselage to the cockpit. Then he turned and found Lieutenant Ward behind him. He pointed to the copilot's seat.

"Why don't you crawl in there, Lieutenant?" he suggested. But it was an order, and both lieutenants knew it. Sergeant Galloway was now functioning as pilot-in-command.

Lieutenant Schneider stood between the seats and watched critically as Galloway went through the checklist and fired up the engines. He could find nothing to fault, even when he was summarily ordered to the cabin: "You can go strap yourself in now, Lieutenant."

That was simply following established safety regulations, Schneider told himself, actually a little chagrined that he had to be told by a sergeant to do something he knew he should do, and hadn't done.

Galloway then took the R4D off, got in the pattern, and shot four touch-and-go landings. All of them, Schneider was forced to admit, were as smooth as glass. Then he shot another five. The first of these was pretty rough and sloppy, Schneider was pleased to judge—until it occurred to him that *Ward,* not Sergeant Galloway, was now at the controls.

And then Ward came into the cabin, sat down beside Schneider, and said, "Your turn."

When Schneider went to the cockpit, Galloway was in the copilot's seat and obviously functioning as an IP. Schneider made five touch-and-goes, more than a little annoyed that not only was his performance being judged by this damned sergeant, but that he had found it wanting.

"Go around again," Galloway ordered, shoving the throttles forward. "Try to set up your approach so that you touch down closer to the threshold."

Dave Schneider's next landing was better, but still apparently not up to Sergeant Galloway's standard. He told him to go around again.

They refueled then, rechecked the weather, and got back into the R4D. This time Galloway told Dave Schneider to get into the copilot's seat. Schneider, chagrined, correctly interpreted this to mean that Galloway thought he required more of his instructional attention than Ward did.

While they were climbing to their ten-thousand-foot cruising altitude, Galloway summoned Ward from the cabin and installed him on the jump seat in the cockpit. When Ward had his headset on, Galloway explained that they were going to fly the airways, first to the east of Washington, about twenty-five miles from Quantico, and then over Baltimore, and then Wilmington, Delaware, 120 miles and forty-five minutes from their departure point.

Galloway didn't touch the controls, letting Schneider fly and make the en route radio calls. When nothing was happening, he delivered, conversationally, what Lieutenant Ward genuinely believed was a truly learned discourse on the peculiarities of R4D aircraft and instrument flight techniques generally.

The sun had come out, and the day was clear, and the flight very pleasant.

And then Sergeant Galloway's voice came over the earphones.

"There's a little roughness in the port engine," he announced.

Neither Ward nor Schneider had detected any roughness in the port engine. Both quickly scanned the instrument panel for any signs of mechanical irregularity, but found none. Lieutenant Ward was perfectly willing to defer to Sergeant Galloway's expert judgment, but Lieutenant Schneider was not.

"Sergeant," Lieutenant Schneider said, "I don't hear anything in either of the engines."

"You really don't have all that much time in one of these things, do you, Lieutenant?" Galloway asked tolerantly.

Schneider's face flushed.

"I think we better sit down and have a look at it," Galloway went on. He picked up the microphone: "Philadelphia, this is Marine Two-Six-Two. I am diverting to Willow Grove at this time. Estimate Willow Grove in five minutes. Please close me out to Willow Grove."

The Willow Grove Naval Air Station, just north of Philadelphia, was not far from Lieutenant Ward's home in Jenkintown, Pennsylvania, an affluent Philadelphia suburb. He looked out the cockpit window and saw that they were approaching South Philadelphia. He could see the Navy Yard.

"Marine Two-Six-Two, Philadelphia," the Philadelphia controller replied, "understand diverting to Willow Grove at this time, ETA five minutes."

"Roger, Philadelphia, thank you," Galloway said, and then switched to the Willow Grove tower's radio frequency: "Willow Grove, Marine Two-Six-Two, an R4D aircraft, fifteen miles south of your station. Approach and landing, please."

Curiosity overwhelmed Lieutenant Dave Schneider.

"What's going on?"

"I told you. The port engine sounds a little rough. I'm going to sit down and have a look at it."

"I don't hear anything wrong with the engine," Schneider said.

"I could be wrong, of course," Sergeant Galloway said. "But you can never be too careful, can you?"

"Willow Grove clears Marine Two-Six-Two as number one to land on Runway One-Niner. The winds are from the north at five miles. Visibility and ceiling unlimited. The time is ten past the hour."

"Roger, Willow Grove, we have the field in sight," Galloway said, and then added, to Schneider, "I've got it, Lieutenant."

Schneider took his hands and feet off the controls, turning control over to Galloway, who began to make the descent.

"We probably could have made it into Lakehurst," Schneider said. "It's only forty miles, maybe not that far."

"That's very good, Lieutenant," Galloway said dryly. "A copilot should always be prepared to give the pilot their location, and the location of an alternative airfield."

Schneider had the feeling Galloway was making a fool of him, but he couldn't figure out exactly how.

"I really would like to know why are we landing here," Lieutenant Schneider said.

"Lieutenant, do you know what they have at Lakehurst in February?" Galloway asked. "One of the world's biggest buildings, maybe a dozen blimps, and a lot of snow. Period." Then he picked up the microphone and said, "Willow Grove, Marine Two-Six-Two turning on final," and began to line the airplane up with the runway.

Lieutenant Schneider was now sure what Sergeant Galloway was up to. It fit in with everything he had heard. There was nothing wrong with the engine. Galloway did not want to go to Lakehurst because there was nothing, in his own words, at Lakehurst in February but one of the world's largest buildings, a dozen blimps, and a lot of snow. Period.

What was outside of Willow Grove Naval Air Station was the city of Philadelphia. And in Philadelphia there were a lot of bars where Galloway could get drunk and punch out a shore patrolman, for which, Colonel Hershberger had made it absolutely clear, they would be held responsible.

Schneider motioned to Ward to come close, covered his mouth with his hand, and said, "We have to talk."

Galloway greased the R4D onto the runway, then reached for the microphone again.

"Willow Grove, Two-Six-Two. We'll need some gas, and I'd like a mechanic to check out one of my engines, please."

"Two-Six-Two, take taxiway C, and taxi to the transient area by the tower. A fuel truck and a maintenance crew will meet you there."

"Thank you very much, Willow Grove."

"We flew right over my house," Lieutenant Ward said.

"We did?" Galloway said.

"I live in Jenkintown," Lieutenant Ward said.

"Well, I guess that means you can go home for supper, huh?" Galloway said.

"Sergeant Galloway," Lieutenant Schneider said, with what he hoped was the appropriate combination of courtesy and firmness, "if the engine checks out all right, I think we should go on to Lakehurst."

"Jesus, Dave, why?" Lieutenant Ward said. "I don't live fifteen minutes from here."

Schneider gave him a look of mingled disgust and fury.

"In fact, Sergeant," Schneider said, "I'm afraid I must insist that we do so."

"You don't have the right to insist on anything, Dave," Lieutenant Ward said furiously. "You heard what Colonel Hershberger said. So far as the airplane and the mission are concerned, Sergeant Galloway's in charge."

"Goddamn it! Can't you see what's going on?" Schneider flared. "He doesn't want to go to Lakehurst! You heard what he said about Lakehurst! What he wants is a night on the town. That's why he landed here. There's nothing wrong with that engine."

"Let's hope not," Sergeant Galloway said innocently.

"Then we're going to fly on to Lakehurst?" Schneider snapped.

"If we could, and I say *if,* then Lieutenant Ward wouldn't get to go home," Galloway said reasonably.

"So what?" Schneider snapped.

"That engine sounded a little rough to me, too," Lieutenant Ward said solemnly. "I think we better have it checked out pretty carefully."

The two Navy mechanics who came out to the R4D were accompanied by a gold-stripe Chief Naval Aviation Pilot. He saluted Lieutenants Ward and Schneider and shook hands cordially with Sergeant Galloway.

"What seems to be the trouble?"

"The port engine sounded a little rough," Galloway said. "I thought it best to sit down and have an expert look at it."

"Good thinking!" the Chief said. "I'll have a look at it myself."

That sonofabitch did everything but wink at Galloway, Dave Schneider thought furiously. *He knows exactly what's going on! Two goddamn birds of a feather flocking together!*

The mechanics backed their pickup truck under the wing and started to remove nacelle panels.

Schneider took Ward's arm and led him out of hearing.

"You know damned well what's going on here, Jim," he said. "Galloway wants a night on the town. There's nothing wrong with that engine."

"I'd like to go home," Ward said.

"And let him go out on the town? You heard Hershberger. We're responsible for his conduct."

"We can take him with us," Ward said.

"What do you mean?"

"We all go to my house. We have dinner, a couple of drinks, and then we all come back here together. I'd like to see my girl. And I'm sure she has a friend."

"We can't go out in public with him. To a restaurant or a bar, you know that. Officers cannot socialize with enlisted men."

"So we don't go to a restaurant or a bar," Ward said. "We go to my house. I repeat, we don't let him out of our sight."

Dave Schneider grunted.

The Chief Aviation Pilot, surprising Lieutenant Dave Schneider not at all, returned from his mechanic's initial inspection of the port engine to report that they could find nothing wrong with it, but that in the interests of safety, he thought it would be a good idea if they drained the engine oil and had a look at it. That way they would know for sure. That would take an hour or an hour and a half; so why didn't they just RON here and take off first thing in the morning? The initials were short for "remain overnight."

The Chief said he could put Sergeant Galloway up in the Chief's quarters, and there was room in the transient BOQ for the officers.

"That's very kind of you, Chief," Lieutenant Schneider said, "but Lieutenant

Ward lives near here, and we'll just go to his house. We'll leave you the number, and when you find out about the engine, you call me. All right?"

The Chief Aviation Pilot shrugged and said, "Aye, aye, Sir."

Tough luck, Chief! You did your best for Sergeant Galloway, but I outsmarted you.

Thirty minutes later, a wooden-sided Mercury station wagon with a VISITOR placard stuck against the dashboard pulled up in front of Base Operations.

"That your mother?" Dave Schneider asked.

Ward looked.

"No. It's my Aunt Caroline," he said, and pushed open the door.

Caroline Ward McNamara, who was thirty-two, blond, long-haired, long-legged, and three months divorced, kissed her nephew and shook hands with Lieutenant Schneider and Sergeant Galloway. Charley Galloway thought that Mrs. McNamara was as beautiful and elegant as a movie star. Like Greer Garson, except with long blond hair.

"I was at the house," she said. "Your mother wanted to go to the Acme to get steaks, so I volunteered to come get you."

Any woman that beautiful has to be married. Or engaged. And even if she wasn't, she's a lady. She wouldn't want to have anything to do with a Marine Sergeant.

Lieutenant Schneider and Sergeant Galloway got in the backseat of the Mercury, and Jim Ward got in front beside his aunt.

"Which airplane is yours?" she asked.

"The third one," Jim Ward said. "The one with 'Marines' painted on the fuselage."

"I'm impressed," Aunt Caroline said. "I didn't know you were flying something that large."

"I'm just learning how, to tell you the truth," Jim Ward said.

"And you're the teacher, Lieutenant Schneider? Is that it? Is Jim a good student?"

"Actually, Caroline," Jim Ward said, "Sergeant Galloway is the IP. Instructor Pilot."

Aunt Caroline shifted her head so that she could see Sergeant Galloway in the rearview mirror.

Their eyes met. Charley Galloway felt his heart jump.

"Isn't that a little unusual?" she asked.

"No, Ma'am," Charley Galloway said.

The hell it isn't, Aunt Caroline thought. *And that isn't all that's interesting about that young man!*

"Have you been flying airplanes like that long, Sergeant?"

"No, Ma'am," Charley Galloway said.

"What do you ordinarily fly? And stop calling me 'Ma'am,' it makes me feel ancient."

"Until recently, I was a fighter pilot," Charley Galloway said. "I usually fly Wildcats."

"I didn't know that, Charley," Jim Ward said, impressed. Aunt Caroline picked up on that, too.

"Why aren't you flying them now? And for that matter, what's a Wildcat?"

"The hottest fighter in the world," Jim Ward said firmly, almost with awe.

"We lost all of our planes on December seventh," Charley Galloway said. "At Pearl."

"You were at Pearl Harbor?"

"Yes, Ma'am."

"If we're going to be friends, Charley," Aunt Caroline said, "you're really going to have to stop calling me 'Ma'am.' "

How the hell could we possibly get to be friends?

Charley saw, in the rearview mirror, that Aunt Caroline was smiling at him. He had a momentary, insane thought: *She's smiling at me the same way Ensign Mary Agnes O'Malley smiled at me just before she grabbed my joint in the Ford on the way up to the cabin in the mountains.*

Immediately, he had more sensible thoughts:

Jesus Christ, I'm letting my imagination run wild. Lieutenant Ward's Aunt Caroline is a lady, for Christ's sake! Probably a married one. Not a slut in a Navy uniform. Ward's Aunt Caroline is not about to grab the joint of a Marine sergeant! And you better watch your fucking step, pal. You're out of your depth around these people. Schneider, that starchy little prick, would love to tell Hershberger I got out of line here. And Hershberger told me what General McInerney said would happen to me if I so much as farted and embarrassed Marine Aviation. You know the rules. It's always been the same choice, fucking or flying. They're giving you a second chance to fly. Don't fuck it up!

Charley Galloway smiled politely at Ward's Aunt Caroline's reflection in the rearview mirror.

"Yes, Ma'am," he said.

Lieutenant Ward laughed.

Charley took the chance. He winked at her reflection in the mirror.

Aunt Caroline stuck her tongue out at Charley's reflection in the rearview mirror. Charley's heart jumped again.

(FOUR)
2307 Watterson Avenue
Jenkintown, Pennsylvania
2140 Hours 13 February 1942

Because Lieutenant Jim Ward's mother and dad really went out of their way to make Sergeant Charley Galloway feel welcome and comfortable, they severely undermined his determination to stay off the sauce in the process. Mr. Ward, who'd been in the Army in World War I, made a pitcher of martinis soon after they came in the house. Charley didn't like martinis, but he had two—the first to be polite and the second because he saw that Lieutenant Schneider didn't like to see him drinking at all.

There was red wine during dinner to go with the steaks; and cognac after dinner, when they went down to the basement game room. Mr. Ward poured generously, and whenever Charley lowered the level in his glass a quarter-inch, he "topped it off."

Jim Ward's girlfriend and a friend of hers for Lieutenant Schneider were both good looking, but Charley thought that neither of them was as classy or as good looking as Aunt Caroline. Wearing a soft, pale blue cashmere sweater and a pleated skirt, she was even more beautiful than he had thought the first moment he saw her. With absolute innocence, they had been sort of paired off, as the only unattached people who would make up a couple.

They sat beside each other at dinner, and several times their knees brushed under the table. Charley didn't think it was his fault. He didn't have much room for his knees, squeezed as he was between Ward's mother and Aunt Caroline.

Aunt Caroline was wearing a perfume he had never smelled before. He had a wild fantasy of burying his face between Aunt Caroline's breasts and inhaling to his heart's content.

He smelled the perfume again in the basement game room when Aunt Caroline bent over, at Mr. Ward's order, to "touch off" his cognac snifter.

"No more for me, please, Ma'am," Charley said.

"I don't think you're having a very good time, Charley Galloway," Aunt Caroline said.

"I'm having a fine time, thank you," Charley said.

"Why don't you dance with Sergeant Galloway, Caroline?" Lieutenant Ward's mother said.

"Would you like to dance with me, Charley?" Aunt Caroline asked.

I'd cut off my left nut for the chance to put my arms around you.

"I'm not a very good dancer," he said.

He saw Lieutenant Schneider looking at him uneasily.

He's afraid I'm going to grab her on the ass, or say something dirty in her ear.

Aunt Caroline spread her arms for him, and Charley stood up.

He put his arms around her and felt the warmth of her back, and then the soft pressure of her breasts against his chest; and the smell of her filled his nostrils; and the primary indicator of his gender popped to attention the moment that Aunt Caroline elected to move a little closer to him.

She was startled; but he was literally immobilized with humiliation. They stopped dancing. When he glanced nervously around to see if anyone was watching, he saw that they were alone in a small corner of the game room. He wondered how they had gotten here.

"I'm sorry," Charley said.

"I'm not," Aunt Caroline said matter-of-factly, not withdrawing her midsection at all. "I was beginning to think you were a faggot."

"Do I look like a faggot?" Charley asked, shocked, after a moment.

"Not at all, but neither did my husband, and he was—is—as queer as a three-dollar bill," Aunt Caroline said.

"Your husband's queer?"

"My *ex*-husband is," she said.

Her hand had been brushing his neck. She dropped it, caught his hand, and led him back to the main area of the game room. She let go of his hand.

"Charley's too polite to say so," Aunt Caroline said. "But he's bushed and wants to go back to the base."

Very quickly, Lieutenant Schneider said, "Galloway, we'll all be leaving shortly. We can leave together."

"Oh, I know how Charley feels," Aunt Caroline said. "Four's company and five is a crowd, right, Charley?"

"Something like that," Charley said.

"And I've got a busy day tomorrow, too," Aunt Caroline said. "And I drive right past Willow Grove, so I'll take Charley back to the base."

"That's very good of you, Caroline," Charley's dad said. "Then I'll take the boys back later."

"Oh, I can drive them, Mr. Ward," Jim Ward's girlfriend said. "You won't have to."

They were almost at the gate to Willow Grove before Aunt Caroline spoke.

"I'm sorry you didn't have a good time tonight."

"I had a good time."

"You were uncomfortable," she argued. "Because Jim and his friends are officers, and you're not?"

"That didn't bother me," Charley said.

"Then it was me," she said. It was not a question. "You don't have to be afraid of me, Charley."

He didn't reply.

"How old are you, Charley?"

"Twenty-five."

"I'm thirty-three," she said. "Is that what's been bothering you? God, that never happened to me before, the older woman."

"I don't give a damn how old you are," Charley blurted. "You're the most beautiful woman I've ever seen."

Startling him, she pulled the station wagon to the curb and slammed on the brakes. She switched the interior lights on and looked at him intently, into his eyes. After a long moment, her hand came up and lightly stroked his face.

Then she turned from him, switched off the interior lights, and pulled away from the curb. When they reached the gate to the Willow Grove Naval Air Station, she drove right past.

(FIVE)
Willow Grove Naval Air Station
Philadelphia, Pennsylvania
0205 Hours 14 February 1942

When Lieutenant Schneider and Ward and their dates returned to Willow Grove Naval Air Station, Dave Schneider asked the MP at the gate how to find the Chief Petty Officer's Quarters. He had the girls drop them off there.

But then he wanted to be absolutely sure that Sergeant Galloway was there and not drunk in some saloon, about to punch out a shore patrolman. After Colonel Hershberger's little speech, Lieutenant Schneider regarded the likelihood of that happenstance as probable.

Technical Sergeant Galloway was not in the Chief Petty Officer's quarters. A chief petty officer, visibly annoyed to be wakened by a pair of damned jarhead lieutenants, gave Schneider directions to the transient enlisted quarters. Technical Sergeant Galloway was not there, either.

The crew chief was. He reported that he had not seen Sergeant Galloway since he had "driven off with you and that knockout blond lady," and that he had no idea where he might be.

"He'll show up," Lieutenant Jim Ward said, without much real conviction. Sergeant Galloway had left the Ward home with Aunt Caroline Ward McNamara at about ten minutes to ten.

"He goddamed well better!" Dave Schneider replied angrily. "I knew damned well we shouldn't have left him out of our sight!"

When Sergeant Galloway did not appear by half past three, Schneider began preparing to make the flight to Lakehurst without Technical Sergeant Galloway. He checked the aircraft books. The red-line "engine roughness" comment had been written off: "Sparkplug replaced. Running smoothly."

They made up the flight plan, which was pretty simple. Direct, VFR, off the airways. It was about forty miles from Willow Grove to Lakehurst. They got a weather briefing, and made sure that the aircraft had been fueled and that a ground auxiliary power unit and a fire extinguisher would be in place. And then they waited.

"Absence without leave," Lieutenant David Schneider declared five minutes later, "is defined as 'failure to repair at the properly appointed time at the proper place in the properly appointed uniform.' If Galloway's absence does not meet those criteria, I'd like to know why not."

"Come on, Dave," Jim Ward said uncomfortably. "What's the 'properly appointed time'? Did you tell him to be here at any specific time? *I* didn't."

"I think," Dave Schneider said, "that the courts will hold that 'the properly appointed time' in this case would be when Sergeant Galloway knew he had to be here in time to fly to Lakehurst, in order to arrive there at the scheduled time. In other words, 0600, less the time to prepare to fly there, and make the flight. Zero four-thirty hours. I'm going to give him until 0430, and then we're going, Jim, without him; and I will report him AWOL when we get there. It might also be called 'missing a scheduled military movement.' The Judge Advocate will have to decide that."

There was no reply from Jim Ward. And Dave Schneider, who was nearly as annoyed with Jim Ward as he was with Sergeant Galloway, looked at him angrily.

"Here he comes, I think," Jim Ward said, pointing out the door.

A wooden-sided Mercury station wagon was pulling into the Base Operations parking lot. Technical Sergeant Galloway was driving. It looked to Dave Schneider as if he was driving with his arm around Aunt Caroline, but he couldn't be absolutely sure.

But he *was* sure that they walked from the station wagon almost to the door of Base Operations with their arms around each other.

And then Sergeant Charley Galloway came through the door, touched his hand to his forehead in a gesture that might just barely be considered a salute, smiled brightly, and said, "Good morning, gentlemen."

"Where have you been, Galloway?" Dave Schneider demanded.

"With me," Aunt Caroline said. "Good morning. Jim, I wanted to talk to you about that."

"About what?"

"Well, on the way here from your house last night, it occurred to me that it was pretty late. And then I got to thinking about all the empty bedrooms in my house, just a few minutes away from here; and then that it hardly made sense for Charley—Sergeant Galloway—to go through the bother of checking into a hotel, or whatever you call it, here on the base. So we went to my house."

"Oh," Jim Ward said lamely.

"So we sat around there for a while, and had a cup of coffee and whatever, and then Charley got a couple of hours' sleep in one of the bedrooms."

"Oh," Jim Ward repeated.

"But then it occurred to me that maybe your mother wouldn't understand," Aunt Caroline went on. "So maybe it would be better if you didn't mention it to her. OK?"

"Sure," Jim Ward said.

While Lieutenant Dave Schneider, in all modesty, did not regard himself as an infallible expert in sexual matters, he did have enough experience to recognize the signs on the female of having just had her bones jumped upon—almost certainly more than once; and the signs of sexual satiation, plus a hickey on the neck, on the male.

Either Jim Ward is too stupid to realize what happened, or he knows that this goddamned sergeant has been screwing his Aunt Caroline and doesn't give a damn.

He realized that whatever he said would be likely to exacerbate the situation, so he said nothing. But at that moment, his fondness for the reserve and enlisted components of the U.S. Marine Corps was at a low ebb.

The crew chief appeared.

"They changed a plug on number-five cylinder," he reported to Galloway, "and she's fueled."

"We filed a flight plan," Jim Ward said, "and weather says nothing significant until tonight, if then."

"Let me see the flight plan," Galloway said, and Schneider handed it to him, aware that by so doing, Galloway had again put on the mantle and authority of pilot-in-command.

Galloway read it carefully.

"OK," he said finally, handing it back to Schneider. "Then let's go. You want to drive, Lieutenant Ward?"

"Yes . . ." Ward replied, thrilled—stopping himself, it was clear to everyone, a split second before adding, "Sir."

"OK. Then you do the preflight," Galloway said. He turned to Aunt Caroline. "Thanks for all the hospitality," he said.

"Oh, don't be silly," she said. "It was my pleasure."

I'll bet it was, Dave Schneider thought bitterly. His sexual status was exactly the opposite of Charley Galloway's. Jim Ward's girlfriend's girlfriend had roused him to exquisite heights of sexual anticipation, allowing him, among other things, to explore the soft wonders of her naked bosom. She had then made it clear that she was not the sort of girl who did *that* on the first date.

His attitude was improved not at all when he noticed that Aunt Caroline was running her fingers between Charley Galloway's legs while she kissed him chastely on the cheek.

"Jimmy," she then said, "if I drove over to Lakehurst, could I watch you drop the paratroopers?"

"I don't know," Jim Ward said. "What about it, Charley?"

"Why not?" Galloway replied. "Just tell the guard at the gate that you're there to meet the plane from Quantico."

He set that up, too, Dave Schneider realized furiously. *What has that sonofabitch got planned for tonight?*

As they were climbing out of Willow Grove, on a due-east course for Lakehurst, the crew chief, who was wearing a headset, got out of his seat and leaned over Dave Schneider.

"He wants you up forward, Sir," he said.

Schneider walked through the cabin into the cockpit. Jim Ward was in the pilot's seat. Galloway mimed for Dave to put on a headset.

"You still plugged in back there, Nesbit?"

"Yes, Sir."

"OK. Now, since the weather isn't going to be a problem, we will discuss what is going to probably be the problem at Lakehurst. His name is Neville. He's a lieutenant colonel. Just made it. Starchy sonofabitch."

Dave Schneider was about to speak, to point out to Galloway that, aircraft commander or not, he was a sergeant, and sergeants did not refer to a Marine Corps lieutenant colonel as a "starchy sonofabitch." But then Galloway went on, "Colonel Hershberger warned me about him and gave me the game plan. If he proposes something idiotic for us to do—this is a public-relations job, and there's no telling what nutty ideas they'll come up with—I will take the heat for refusing to do it. All you have to say to him is that Hershberger told you I'm the aircraft commander, and the only person who can change that is Hershberger himself. Clear?"

"What makes you so sure, Sergeant Galloway," Schneider asked icily, "that Colonel Neville will propose something . . . idiotic, as you put it?"

"Well, for one thing, they call him 'Fearless,' " Galloway said. "What does that tell you? And for another, Colonel Hershberger wouldn't have given me the game plan if he didn't think it would be necessary. He's dealt with this sonofabitch before."

"I am deeply offended, Galloway, by your repeated references to a senior officer as a sonofabitch!" Dave Schneider said icily.

"Oh, for Christ's sake, Dave!" Jim Ward said, turning to look at Schneider in disgust.

Galloway met Schneider's eyes.

"Lieutenant," he said politely, "you want to go back in the cabin now and strap yourself in? It's getting a little turbulent, and I wouldn't want you to bang your head on a bulkhead or anything."

"This conversation is not over, Sergeant," Dave Schneider said before he took off the headset and went back in the cabin.

VII

(ONE)
Lakehurst Naval Air Station
Lakehurst, New Jersey
0515 Hours 14 February 1942

Lieutenant Colonel Franklin G. Neville had driven up from Washington in his Auto-Union roadster the day before. He would have preferred to take the train, which was quicker and more comfortable, but he might need the car at Lakehurst because of the press people. It even entered his mind that the press people might want a photograph of him in his Auto-Union. Fast sports cars and parachutists, that sort of thing.

Actually he had hoped to travel to Lakehurst in the R4D from Quantico; it had even occurred to him that he might arrive at Lakehurst by jumping from the R4D just before it landed, to give the press people a sample of what they could expect. But when he'd asked Hershberger whether the R4D could pick him up at Anacostia, Hershberger told him it was already en route to Lakehurst.

When he got to Lakehurst, of course, the airplane wasn't there. And it was only after frantic telephone calls to Colonel Hershberger and Willow Grove that he was able to put his worries about that to rest. Hershberger told him the plane had made a precautionary landing at Willow Grove. And then Willow Grove told him there was nothing wrong with the airplane, and that it was on The Board for an 0430 takeoff.

It was vital for the R4D to arrive. It *had* to be a *Marine* airplane doing the dropping for the press people's cameras—*not* a Navy airplane. Neville would not lie about it, but he had no intention of *volunteering* the information to the press people that Navy pilots, flying Navy R4Ds, actually had done all the dropping of Marine parachutists at Lakehurst so far.

Colonel Neville was convinced that if things went well today, their future would be secure—presuming, of course, that it all resulted in *Life* magazine doing one of their spreads on Marine parachutists, and that the spread showed Marine parachutists in a good light. On the other hand, if things did not go well, it could be a fatal blow to Vertical Envelopment within the Marine Corps.

Consequently, a lot of thought and planning and effort had gone into preparing everything and everybody for the visit of the *Life* photojournalists to Lakehurst. The public-relations people at Marine Corps headquarters had been enthusiastic and cooperative, which was more than could be said for some other people in the head shed.

The Deputy Chief of Public Relations, Headquarters USMC, a full colonel named Lenihan, had told him that he had assigned the task of publicizing the demonstration jump to Major Jake Dillon, who would head a team of nine public-relations specialists.

"You've heard of Dillon, of course, haven't you, Neville?" Colonel Lenihan asked.

Neville searched his mind, but could come up with no recollection of a major or a captain named Dillon.

"No, Sir, I don't think so."

"Metro-Magnum Pictures," Colonel Lenihan said, significantly.

Metro-Magnum Pictures was a major Hollywood studio.

"Sir?"

"Dillon was Chief of Publicity for Metro-Magnum," Colonel Lenihan said. "He just came on active duty. Amazing fellow. Knows all the movie stars. He introduced me to Bette Davis at the Willard Hotel last night."

"Is that so?" Neville replied. He wondered if this Major Dillon could arrange for a movie star to be present at Lakehurst. Bringing somebody like Bette Davis there, or even Lana Turner or Betty Grable, would get his Para-Marines in the newsreels.

Major Dillon's public relations team had come to Lakehurst two days before. The team had two staff cars, two station wagons, and a jeep. The tiny vehicle, officially called a "Truck, ¼ Ton 4X4," had just entered the service. Neville had seen one in the newsreels—it was actually flying through the air—but this was the first one he had ever seen in person. The team also included four photographers, two still and two motion-picture.

When Colonel Neville mentioned his notion of asking some beauty like Lana Turner to the demonstration, Major Dillon, a stocky, crewcut man in his middle thirties, explained that he didn't think that publicizing the Marine parachutists was the sort of job that required teats and thighs to get good coverage.

"I really don't want to sound as if I'm trying to tell you your job—" Colonel Neville began, convinced that the presence of a gorgeous star would insure a public-relations coup.

"Then don't," Dillon interrupted.

"I'm not sure I like your tone of voice, Major."

"Colonel, I think you're going to have to trust me to do my job. If you don't like the way I'm doing things, you get on the horn and tell Colonel Lenihan. He's the only one I take orders from."

Franklin G. Neville considered the situation quickly, and forced a smile.

"No offense, Major. I was just trying to be helpful."

Later, Major Dillon explained to Neville that the still photographers would back up the *Life* photographers; they'd make the pictures they took available to the magazine in case it missed something. After a seven-day "embargo," the pictures *Life* didn't want would be made available to the press generally.

The motion-picture film would be taken to Washington, processed, reviewed, and after the same seven-day embargo to preserve *Life*'s exclusivity, it would be made available to the various newsreel companies.

Dillon brought with him three Marine "correspondents," two corporals and a sergeant, supervised by a lieutenant. They had prepared a "press background packet," which included a history of parachuting generally, and of Marine parachuting in some detail. There were short biographies of Lieutenant Colonel Neville and Lieutenant Macklin, together with eight-by-ten-inch official glossy photographs of them.

All of this served to impress Colonel Neville with Major Dillon's expertise. It even caused Neville to realize that he would best forget the little flare-up he'd had with the Major over inviting a Hollywood star to the demonstration.

Besides, Colonel Neville was feeling pretty pleased with himself in general. Everything was going well. And everything at the school itself was shipshape. In a remarkably short time, the ex–Parris Island drill instructors had done marvels in establishing standards of discipline and dress that were appropriate for the men Neville considered "the elite of the elite." In Neville's view, if Marines were by definition disciplined military men, Marine parachutists had to strive to reach even higher standards.

The Major, of course, wanted to go a bit further in helping the press than Major Dillon was prepared to go; and the Major had to caution him that in his experience, it was possible to "direct" the attention of the press, especially high-class places like *Life,* only so far.

"If they begin to feel they're getting a snow job," Major Dillon said, "they start looking for what's hidden under the rocks. The best way to deal with them is to make yourself useful but not pushy, and to somehow convince them that what you want publicized is something they discovered themselves."

Major Dillon, his lieutenant, and Lieutenant Macklin were going to meet the press people at the Lakehurst gate when they drove over from New York City. Colonel Neville decided that it would be beneath his dignity as Director of Marine Corps Parachuting to be at the gate himself.

The press people would then be taken to his office, where coffee and doughnuts would be served. Following that, Lieutenant Macklin would brief them. Neville attended a rehearsal briefing, made a few small suggestions, and then approved it.

The press would then be taken on a tour of the school's facilities. The tour would demonstrate how the school was turning Marines into Para-Marines. Neville intended to use that term, even though he had specific directions not to do so. He thought it was honestly descriptive and had a certain flair to it—and he was convinced that once it had appeared in *Life,* it would become part of the language.

Then there would be luncheon in the enlisted men's mess. Neville would have preferred to feed the press people in the officers' club, but Major Jake Dillon argued that the press liked to eat with the troops. In the event, that really posed no problems. Lieutenant Macklin directed the mess sergeant to move up the stuffed-pork chop, mashed-potato, and apple-cobbler supper to the noon meal. The troops could eat the bologna sandwiches originally scheduled for the noon meal at supper, after the press people had gone.

At 1245 hours, the press would be taken to the far side of the airfield to witness their first parachute drop. Chairs, a table, and a coffee thermos would be set up for their convenience. The Marine R4D from Quantico would have been dropping parachutists, four times, during the morning. It would probably have been better to show the press people a jump before they toured the school facilities, so that then they'd know the object of the whole thing; but Neville had insisted on scheduling the demonstration drop for 1245, so that the R4D crew would have a chance to practice.

The drop was all-important. If that didn't go well, nothing else would matter.

Actually, there was to be more than one drop for the press. At 1245, the first drop would show them how it was done. Then the R4D would land, taxi up to the press people, and take on another load of parachutists there. That would give the press people the opportunity to see how quickly and efficiently that was done.

Then the plane would take off, wait for the press people to move over to the actual drop zone, and then drop the second load of parachutists. This would give the press people a chance to see the parachutists landing.

Neville had earlier persuaded the Commanding Officer of Willow Grove Naval Air Station to let him have a pair of SJ6 Texans, which were low-winged, single-engined, two-seat trainers. While the R4D landed to take on still another load of parachutists, one of the two Texans would have taxied to where it could take aboard a *Life* photographer. The second Texan, carrying a Marine photographer equipped with a motion-picture camera, would by then already be in the air.

He would capture on film the Para-Marines exiting the door of the R4D. Individual prints made from that motion-picture film would be offered to *Life,* if they wanted them. After that the film would be made available to the newsreel companies.

So far as Lieutenant Colonel Neville could see, he and Lieutenant Macklin had covered all the bases.

When, as he asked them to, the Lakehurst Control Tower telephoned to report that a Marine R4D out of Willow Grove had just requested landing permission, he felt the situation was well in hand.

And then things, of course, promptly began to go wrong.

He went out to watch the R4D land. He liked the sight of it, gleaming in the sun of the crisp winter day, with MARINES lettered along the fuselage. He wondered, for the future—it was too late to do anything about it now, of course—if he could arrange to have an aircraft lettered PARA-MARINES. But then, as the aircraft turned off the runway and started to taxi toward the dirigible hangar, he saw that the port engine nacelle and the wing behind it were filthy. Absolutely filthy!

He started walking toward the spot where Lieutenant Macklin had marked out the parking space for the aircraft. He reached it moments after the airplane arrived, and he waited while the pilot turned it around. In order to do that, the pilot had to gun the starboard engine; when he did so, the prop blast caught some snow in its path and blew it all over Neville.

It wasn't clean snow; it was mixed with dirt and parking-area debris, and it soiled Lieutenant Colonel Neville's fresh green uniform. He was not in a very good mood when he stood by the door of the aircraft, waiting for the door to open.

A sergeant in coveralls looked at him curiously, and then dropped a ladder from holes in the bottom of the doorframe. Only then did he finally remember rudimentary military courtesy. Still not wearing suitable headgear, he saluted and said, "Good morning, Colonel."

"Inform the pilot that I would like to see him. I'm Colonel Neville."

"Aye, aye, Sir," the crew chief said, and disappeared inside the aircraft.

In a moment, a good-looking young man appeared; he was wearing a fur-collared jacket with Naval Aviator's wings. Hatless. But he at least looked like a Marine, Neville thought, and acted like one.

"Good morning, Sir," he said, saluting crisply; he held it until Neville returned it. Only then did he start climbing down the ladder. "Are you Colonel Neville, Sir?" Neville nodded. "I was told to report to you, Sir."

"Your airplane is dirty," Colonel Neville said.

"Sir?"

"The port engine nacelle and wing. They're filthy!"

The pilot looked surprised and went to look.

"Don't you have a uniform cap?" Neville called after him.

"Yes, Sir. Sorry, Sir," the pilot said. He took a fore-and-aft cap from the pocket of his leather jacket and put it on.

An enlisted man's cap! That goddamned Hershberger knows how important a mission this is to me and to the Para-Marines, and he's sent me a goddamned Flying Sergeant!

Neville walked to the wing.

"Sir, they drained the oil at Willow Grove. I guess they spilled a little, and it picked up crud from the taxiway and runway," Charley Galloway said.

"Well, have it cleaned up," Neville said. "We don't want *Life*'s readers to think the Marine Corps tolerates filthy aircraft, do we?"

"Aye, aye, Sir."

"Tell me, Sergeant, does Colonel Hershberger routinely send noncoms on missions of this importance?"

"I don't think, Sir, that the Colonel had any qualified officer pilots to send."

That's so much bullshit and we both know it. Goddamn *Hershberger!*

"Colonel, I have two lieutenants on board," Galloway said, adding, "pilots, I mean."

"Then where are they? I told your crew chief I wanted to speak to the pilot."

"Sir, I'm pilot-in-command."

"How can that be, Sergeant?" Neville said, making what he recognized to be a valiant effort not to jump all over the sergeant. He was a sergeant; he was just doing what he was told. "With officer pilots, how can you be in command?"

"Colonel Hershberger set it up that way, Sir."

"Would you tell the officers I would like a word with them, Sergeant, please?"

"Aye, aye, Sir."

Lieutenants Ward and Schneider were standing on the ground beside the rear door when Charley Galloway went to fetch them.

"Colonel Neville would like to see you, gentlemen," he said loudly, and added softly, "Watch yourselves. He's got his balls in an uproar about something."

Lieutenant Schneider gave Galloway a withering look, and then saluted Colonel Neville as he appeared.

"Which of you is senior?" Neville asked.

"I believe I am, Sir," Jim Ward said.

"Jack," Galloway said to the crew chief, "will you get the crud off the port nacelle and wing?"

"What the hell for?" the crew chief replied. "The minute we start to taxi through this shit, it'll get dirty again."

"Do me a favor, Jack," Galloway said, nodding his head toward Neville. "Do what you can to clean it up."

Neville felt his temper rise. An order had been given. Instead of carrying it out, the recipient had replied "What the hell for?" And instead of immediately correcting the man on the spot, the response was "Do me a favor." And all of this with two commissioned officers watching and doing or saying nothing.

These people, none of them, are Marines. They're goddamned civilians wearing Marine uniforms!

"Then, Lieutenant, may I presume you're in charge of this aircraft?"

"No, Sir."

" 'No, Sir'?" Neville echoed incredulously. "Are you qualified to fly this aircraft or not?"

"I'm checked out in the R4D, Sir. Yes, Sir."

"Then, according to the Customs of the Service, since you are the senior officer present," Neville pursued icily, "doesn't it then follow that you are in charge of this aircraft?"

"Sir, Colonel Hershberger, the Chief of Staff, 1st Marine Air Wing—"

"I know who Colonel Hershberger is, Mr. Ward," Neville interrupted him.

"Sir, Colonel Hershberger appointed Sergeant Galloway as pilot-in-command," Ward said uncomfortably.

"I never heard of such a thing!" Neville exploded.

"Sir," Galloway said, "I've got more experience in the R4D than either of these officers. I believe, considering the importance of this mission, that that's what Colonel Hershberger had in mind."

"Are you in the habit of offering your opinions before they're solicited, Sergeant?" Neville flared.

"No, Sir, sorry, Sir."

There was the sound of aircraft engines. Charley Galloway's eyes rose involuntarily toward the sky and confirmed what his ears had told him: *Pratt & Whitney Wasp, probably the six-hundred-horse R1340-49. More than one.*

There were two North American Texans in the landing pattern.

"There are my other aircraft," Colonel Neville announced. "Mr. Ward, will you give my compliments to their pilots, and ask them to join me in my office as soon as possible? And bring this officer and the sergeant with you."

(TWO)

The shit, thought Technical Sergeant Charles Galloway, *is about to hit the fan.*

He rose, very reluctantly, to his feet.

"You have a question, Sergeant?" Lieutenant Richard B. Macklin asked. He had just finished explaining, with the help of a blackboard and a pointer, where the Texans would fly relative to the R4D, so that the still and motion-picture photographers could capture the Para-Marines jumping from the R4D's door.

"Sir, that would be dangerous," Charley said.

"Would it, now?" Macklin asked, smiling but sarcastic.

"Sir, one aircraft flying close to the R4D is dangerous enough. Two are too dangerous."

"Would you care to explain your position?"

"Yes, Sir. I'll be flying the R4D—"

"That hasn't been decided yet," Lieutenant Colonel Neville said.

"Sir, *whoever* is flying the R4D will have enough trouble keeping his eye on one Texan. It would be impossible to keep an eye on both of them, if they were flying close enough to take pictures."

"And?" Macklin asked, now clearly sarcastic. "Are you suggesting that they would fly into you, Sergeant?" He looked at the two Texan pilots, both lieutenants junior grade, and smiled at them. "I'm sure these officers are skilled enough not to do that."

"I'm more concerned about dropping the paratroops—"

"Para-*Marines,*" Colonel Neville said.

"—into the flight path of one of the Texans," Charley finished.

"That's our concern, Sergeant, isn't it?"

"No, Sir, with respect, it's mine," Charley said.

"Galloway," one of the Naval Aviators said, "believe me, I intend to stay as far away from you as I can."

Galloway smiled at him, but didn't reply.

"I presume your concerns have been put to rest, Sergeant?" Lieutenant Macklin said.

"No, Sir," Charley said. "With respect, they haven't."

"What exactly are you saying, Sergeant?" Colonel Neville asked.

"Sir . . . Sir, if you put two Texans near my aircraft at the same time, I won't drop your paratroops."

"Then we won't burden you with that responsibility, Sergeant. Lieutenant Schneider will pilot the R4D. I can see no necessity for you even to be aboard."

"Sir, Lieutenant Schneider is not qualified to drop parachutists. I won't authorize him to do so."

"Well, we'll just see about that, Sergeant," Neville flared. "We'll see who's authorized to give—or refuse—orders around here. Will you all wait outside, please? Macklin, get Colonel Hershberger on the telephone. Make it a priority call."

Four minutes later, Lieutenant Macklin appeared in the door to Lieutenant Colonel Neville's office and beckoned for Galloway to come inside.

"Colonel Hershberger wishes to speak with you, Sergeant," he said.

Galloway picked up the telephone that was lying on its side on Neville's desk. As he did so, he saw Neville pick up an extension and cover the mouthpiece with his hand.

"Sergeant Galloway, Sir."

"You didn't waste any time stirring things up, did you, Charley?"

"I'm sorry about this, Sir."

"Tell me about the filthy airplane."

"They drained the oil from the port engine at Willow Grove, Sir. They spilled some. It got on the nacelle and wing and picked up crud when I moved the aircraft."

"Tell me about Willow Grove," Hershberger said. "Was that necessary?"

"I was attempting to avoid a storm I had reason to think might be in the Lakehurst area, Sir," Charley said. He stole a quick look at Neville, and saw that he hadn't picked up on that.

"OK," Colonel Hershberger said, after a barely perceptible pause which told Charley that Hershberger had correctly interpreted his reply. "So tell me about the Texans."

"I don't want two of them off my tail when I'm dropping parachutists, Colonel."

"Neville says you refused to fly with *any* Texans around you."

"No, Sir. I can keep my eye on one of them. Two are too dangerous."

"Anything else you want to say?"

"No, Sir."

"Get Colonel Neville back on the line, please, Charley."

"Sir," Charley heard his mouth run away with him, "the Colonel has been on an extension all the time."

"Hang your phone up, then, Charley," Colonel Hershberger said, pleasantly enough, after a moment. "I want a private word with Colonel Neville."

Charley put the telephone back in its cradle and started to leave the office. But Lieutenant Macklin hissed at him that he had not been dismissed. So Charley assumed the at-ease position facing Lieutenant Colonel Neville's desk, and was thus witness to the conversation between Hershberger and Neville. Both sides were audible, because Colonel Hershberger seemed to be talking considerably louder to Colonel Neville than he had to Charley.

Both Lieutenant Macklin and Sergeant Galloway pretended, however, not to hear what Colonel Hershberger said. They both knew that it was an embarrassment for a senior officer to be referred to as a "pompous asshole" by an even more senior officer in the hearing of his subordinates. And it got worse: Colonel

Hershberger went on to say—actually shout—that Neville was not only unfit to wear a lieutenant colonel's silver leaf, but the Marine uniform, period. Any officer who calculatedly lied in order to get in trouble a good Marine sergeant who was just obeying his orders was worse than contemptible.

Lieutenant Colonel Neville's replies to Colonel Hershberger were a number of brief and muted "Yes, Sirs."

When Lieutenant Colonel Neville finally hung up, Charley shifted from "at ease" to "parade rest" (head erect, eyes looking six inches above Colonel Neville, hands folded smartly together in the small of the back), and stayed that way for a very long sixty seconds.

Finally, Lieutenant Colonel Neville said, "That will be all, Sergeant. Thank you."

Charley Galloway popped to attention, did a smart about-face, and marched out of Neville's office.

(THREE)

PFC Stephen M. Koffler, USMC, participated in three parachute jumps on the day everybody involved was to remember for a very long time as "the day it happened."

They were his eighth, ninth, and tenth parachute jumps. His first five jumps had been performed as a student. Four of these had been during daylight, and the fifth at night, all onto what Lieutenant Colonel Franklin G. Neville had named Drop Zone Wake, in memory of the heroic Marine defense of Wake Island.

Drop Zone Wake was in fact an area between the runways in the center of the Lakehurst airfield. It was marked out with white tape and little flags on stakes.

According to what he had been told when he began the course, he would be rated as a Marine Parachutist after he had successfully completed his fifth jump, a night drop. That hadn't happened. Lieutenant R. B. Macklin, who was the Deputy Commandant of the Marine Parachute School, had announced that Colonel Neville had decided to postpone the ceremony during which Parachutists' wings would be awarded until 14 February. On that day, a team of civilian (from *Life* magazine) and Marine Corps journalists would be at Lakehurst, Lieutenant Macklin told them; Colonel Neville thought the journalists might want to photograph the ceremony.

Meanwhile, PFC Steve Koffler had changed his mind about wanting to be a Para-Marine. He was now convinced that volunteering for parachute duty was about the dumbest thing he had ever done in his life. *Really* dumb: there was a very good chance that he was going to get killed long before he got near a Japanese soldier.

He had begun to form that opinion long before he made his first jump. For starters, the physical training the trainees had gone through made the physical training at Parris Island look like a walk through a park.

Beginning right after reveille, the trainees had been led on a run around the airfield fence. Somebody said that the distance was 5.2 miles, and he believed it. And they made you run until you literally dropped. As often as Steve Koffler had run around the fence, he had never made it all the way without collapsing, and usually throwing up, too.

The running, he had been told, was to develop the muscles of the lower body. The muscles of the upper body were developed in several ways, primarily by doing push-ups. Steve Koffler had come out of Parris Island proud that he could do forty push-ups. During parachute training, he had once made it to eighty-six before his arms gave out and he collapsed on his face onto the frozen ground.

But there were other upper-body conditioning exercises. Ten trainees at once picked up a log, about ten inches in diameter, and performed various exercises with it. Most of these involved holding the log at arm's length above the head. And there was a device that consisted of pipes inserted through large pieces of wood, sort of a ladder mounted parallel to the ground. One moved along this like Tarzan, swinging by hand from one end to the other. The difference being that all Tarzan wore was sort of a little skirt over sort of a jockstrap; but the Para-Marine trainees wore all their field gear, including helmets, full canteens, and Springfield rifles.

There had also been a lot of classroom work. Steve and the others had a good deal of trouble staying awake in classes. Not only were they pretty worn out from all the upper- and lower-body-developing exercises, but the lesson material was pretty dull, too.

When you fell asleep, the penalty was for one of the sergeants to kick the folding chair out from under you; then you had to run around the building with your Springfield held at arm's length over your head and shout at the top of your lungs, "I will not sleep in class." You did that until the sergeant finally decided you had enough—or you crashed to the frozen earth, unconscious or nauseated.

Steve Koffler would thus remember for the rest of his life a large amount of esoteric military data. For example, he now knew that his parachutes were manufactured by the Switlick Company of the finest silk that money could buy; that his main 'chute was thirty-five feet in diameter and had twenty-eight panels (each of which was made up of a number of smaller pieces, so that if a rip developed, it would spread no farther than the piece where it started); and that his main 'chute would cause him to fall through the air at a speed of approximately twenty feet per second. This meant he would strike the ground at approximately 13.5 miles per hour.

The main 'chute was worn on the back. It was opened upon exiting the airplane by a static line connected to the airplane. This pulled the canopy from its container, and then ripped free. The canopy would then fill with air, with the parachutist suspended beneath it.

If something happened, and the main 'chute did not deploy, there was a second parachute, worn on the chest. This 'chute, which had twenty-four panels of the best silk money could buy, was approximately twenty-four feet in diameter. It would slow the descent of a falling body to approximately twenty-five feet per second, which worked out to approximately seventeen miles per hour. This emergency chute was deployed by pulling a D-ring on the front of the emergency 'chute pack.

If both 'chutes failed, the sergeants told them, there was no problem. Just bring them to the supply sergeant, and he would exchange them for new 'chutes.

Since the human body was not designed to encounter the earth in a sudden stop at thirteen and a half miles per hour (or seventeen, if the emergency 'chute was utilized), the Marine Corps, ever mindful of the welfare of its men, had developed special techniques which permitted the human body to survive under such circumstances.

These were demonstrated; and then, until the correct procedures were automatic, the trainees were permitted to practice them: first they jumped from the back of a moving truck, and later from tall towers, from which they were permitted to leap wearing a parachute harness connected to a cable.

A parachutist's troubles didn't stop once he touched the ground.

Once he touched down, he might encounter another hazard. The parachute canopy, which had safely floated him onto the earth at 13.5—or seventeen—miles per hour, had an unhappy tendency to fill up again if a sudden gust of wind took hold of it. The 'chute would then drag the parachutist along the ground, often on his face, until the gust died down—or the parachutist encountered an immovable object, such as a truck, or possibly a tree.

Because of that hazard, the techniques of "spilling the air from the canopy" had been demonstrated to the trainees, who were then permitted to practice them. This was accomplished by placing the trainee on his back behind the engine of a Navy R4D aircraft. He was strapped into a parachute harness with the parachute canopy stretched out on the ground behind him. The engine of the R4D was then revved up so that prop blast could fill the canopy (held up by an obliging sergeant to facilitate filling). The prop blast dragged the canopy and the Para-Marine trainee across the ground, until he managed to spill the air from it by pulling on the "risers" that connected the harness to the canopy.

Inasmuch as every Para-Marine trainee was a volunteer, it was theoretically possible to un-volunteer—to quit. But PFC Steve Koffler believed that option had been taken away from him as a result of the "extended three-day pass" that had already gotten him in so much trouble with Lieutenant Macklin. If he quit, he would be brought before a court-martial and sentenced to the Naval Prison at Portsmouth.

Several times during his training, he'd actually wondered if Portsmouth—as bad as everybody said it was—could really be worse than Jump School. In fact, on several occasions he'd come close to standing up and screaming at one instructor or another, "Fuck it! I quit! Send me to Portsmouth!"

But for several reasons he had not done that: he believed, for instance, all the horrible things he'd heard about Portsmouth. It was logical that Portsmouth had to be worse than Parris Island and the Jump School; otherwise it would be full of refugees from both places.

The most important reason, however, was Mrs. Dianne Marshall Norman. He went to bed every night thinking of Dianne and all they had done to each other in his bed and on the living room couch, and even on the kitchen table. And he woke up thinking of very much the same thing.

He even called her to mind in the R4D just before he made his first jump. He credited thinking about Dianne not only with keeping him from getting sick to his stomach but from quitting the Para-Marines right there.

He was in love with Dianne. He could not bear the thought of having her learn that he was a craven coward who had not only quit Jump School but had been sentenced to the Naval Prison at Portsmouth. He would rather die—say, from a "cigarette roll." That was what they called it when your 'chute canopy failed to fill with air, and instead twisted around itself until it looked like a cigarette instead of a big mushroom. When that happened, the parachute hardly slowed you down at all, and you went down like a rock, ultimately hitting the ground at something like 125 miles per hour.

And furthermore, once he had won his wings as a Para-Marine, that AWOL business would be forgotten (if he could believe Lieutenant Macklin), and he would have a clean slate. When that happened, he would be eligible for another pass—and maybe even the leave he never got when he graduated from Parris Island. And he could go and be with her.

He had managed to establish communication with her only once since he had started Jump School. On his fourth attempt to call her, he'd gotten her on the phone. The first three times, Bernice or her mother had answered the phone, and he'd just hung up. Dianne seemed glad enough to hear from him, but she told him that her parents and Bernice would not understand his calling her—her having her Leonard and being older and everything—so it would be better if he waited until he got home again, and then maybe they could get together and talk or something, if it could be arranged without making anybody suspicious.

He didn't want to say it on the telephone, but in addition to all those things that went through his mind the last thing at night and the first thing in the morning, he did want to just talk to her. He would tell her that he wasn't just an ordinary PFC anymore but a Para-Marine, which meant that with his jump pay he was making almost twice as much money as a regular PFC. And it also meant that he stood a better chance of making corporal, and maybe even sergeant. And then there was an allowance, called an allotment or something, that he could get if he was married. And he intended to tell her that he would be honored to raise little Joey just as if he was really his kid.

So a great deal hinged on his getting through Jump School, and having his slate wiped clean, and getting at least a pass so that he could go see her.

But then they didn't hold the graduation ceremony because of the people coming from *Life* magazine. And when he went to the First Sergeant and reminded him about what Lieutenant Macklin had said about getting the slate wiped clean if he kept his nose clean and got through Jump School, the First Sergeant told him that so far as he was concerned, his slate was wiped clean. But when Steve asked about a pass, the First Sergeant said that would have to wait until the *Life* magazine people had come and gone. In the meantime there would be no free time.

Over the days before they arrived, there were several pre-inspections; and then the last inspection itself, conducted by Lieutenant Macklin, to make sure everything would be shipshape.

On the morning of 14 February, they were marched out to a Marine R4D. It was the first one Steve had ever seen; he didn't even know the Marines had R4Ds. Then they 'chuted up and took off just as usual. But this time, instead of just making a swing around the field and then dropping the parachutists, the pilot flew the airplane out to the ocean, and then over the beach from Asbury Park down to Point Pleasant, and then back and forth several times, until he apparently got the word on the radio and flew back to Lakehurst. Then they jumped.

That was Jump Six.

The Marine R4D landed while Steve was still folding up his parachute; and he watched it take on another load of Para-Marines while he was walking back to the staging area after the truck had come and taken up the 'chutes.

As he and the others were 'chuting up again, he saw that stick of Para-Marines jump. The R4D landed immediately, and they loaded aboard and jumped almost immediately.

Steve decided that what they were doing was showing the people from *Life* magazine how it was done.

That was Jump Seven. It was just like Jump Six, except that the guy leading the stick, a corporal, sprained his ankle because he landed on the concrete runway instead of on the grassy area. So he was not going to be able to jump again for a while.

That made Steve lead man in the stick for Jump Eight. He wasn't sure if he would have the balls to jump first. If you were anywhere but lead man in the stick, it was automatic, and you didn't have to think about it. But in the end he decided that if he hesitated, the jumpmaster would just shove him out the door.

Another trainee was added to the stick at the end. He would jump last.

And then, after the pilot had already restarted the left-hand engine on the R4D, something very unusual happened. A face in a helmet appeared at the door and ordered the crew chief to put the ladder down. And then Lieutenant Colonel Franklin G. Neville himself climbed into the airplane, wearing a set of coveralls. And his parachutes. And all of his field gear—except that he had a Thompson submachine gun instead of a Springfield rifle.

And then they took off.

Colonel Neville pulled Steve's head close to him and shouted in his ear.

"I'm going to jump with you," he said. "You just carry on as usual."

"Aye, aye, Sir!" Steve shouted back.

This time, instead of just circling the field and jumping the Para-Marines, the R4D flew south. From where Steve was sitting, he couldn't see much, but he became aware that there was a little airplane out there, too, flying close to the R4D.

During one of the brief glimpses he got of it, he saw that there was a man in the backseat with a camera.

Colonel Neville apparently knew all about it. He was standing in the door, hanging on to the jamb, making what looked like "come closer" signs to the pilot.

And then they were making their approach to Landing Zone Wake.

The commands now came quickly.

"Stand up."

"Hook up."

"Check your equipment."

"Stand in the door."

There were two little lights mounted on the aircraft bulkhead by the door. One was red and the other was green. The red one came on when you started getting ready to jump. The green one came on when the pilot told the jumpmaster to start the jumping.

Steve stood by the door, watching the red light.

"One minute!" the jumpmaster shouted in his ear.

Steve nodded his understanding.

He thought of Dianne Marshall Norman's breasts, and how their nipples stood up.

The light turned green.

Somebody pushed him out of the way and dove out the door. Steve saw that the little airplane was really close, and that the man in the backseat had what looked like a movie camera in his hands. The jumpmaster shouted "Go!" in his ear and pushed him out the door.

It all happened pretty quickly, maybe in two seconds, no more. As Steve went out the door he saw that something was bent around what he thought of as "the little wing on the back" of the R4D.

And then, as he fell beneath it to the end of the static line and he could hear the main 'chute slither out, and as he steeled himself for the opening shock, he realized that what he had seen wrapped around the little wing on the back of the R4D was a man. And then, as his canopy filled and the harness knocked the breath out of him, he realized that the man must be Lieutenant Colonel Neville.

And then he looked below him.

And saw a man's body falling, just falling, toward the earth. There was no main 'chute, and no emergency chest 'chute. The body just fell to the ground and seemed to bounce a little, and then just lay there.

PFC Stephen M. Koffler, USMC, lost control of his bowels.

And then the ground was there, and he prepared to land as he had been taught; and he landed, and rolled as he had been taught. And then he got to his feet. He was immediately knocked onto his face as the canopy filled with a gust of wind and dragged him across the hard, snow-encrusted earth.

He had been taught how to deal with the situation, and dealt with it. He spilled the air from the canopy by manipulating the risers, and then he slipped out of the harness.

He stood up and rather numbly began to gather the parachute to him. He knew the truck would appear to pick it up.

And then he saw the body of Lieutenant Colonel Franklin G. Neville, not fifteen feet away. It looked distorted, like a half-melted wax doll.

He was drawn to it. Still clutching his parachute harness to his chest, he walked over to it and looked down at it.

A photographer, one of the civilians, came running up, and a flashbulb went off.

Oh, shit! PFC Steve Koffler thought. *What are they going to do to me when they find out I've shit my pants?*

Another flashbulb went off, and Steve gave the photographer a dirty look. It didn't seem to bother him.

"What's your name, kid?" he asked.

"Fuck you," Steve said.

"That's PFC Koffler, Stephen M.," a familiar voice said. Steve turned his head and saw that it was Lieutenant Macklin. "He is, understandably I think, a little upset."

"I wonder why," the photographer said, and took Steve's picture again.

(FOUR)
Lakehurst Naval Air Station
Lakehurst, New Jersey
1425 Hours 14 February 1942

Major Jake Dillon had returned to active duty with the U.S. Marine Corps sixty days previously. The last time he had worn a Marine uniform was in Shanghai, China, with the 4th Marines in 1934. Major Dillon had then been a sergeant.

In 1933, while watching an adapted-from-a-novel adventure motion picture in Shanghai, it had occurred to Sergeant Dillon that it was a bullshit story and that he could easily write a better one. Blissfully unaware of the difficulties facing a first-time novelist, he set out to do so. It was a melodrama; its hero, a Marine sergeant, rescued a lovely Chinese maiden from a fate worse than death in a Shanghai brothel. Dillon had no trouble calling forth from memory the description of that establishment.

Next, Dillon's hero slaughtered Chinese evildoers left and right; there was a chase sequence on horseback; and the book ended with the sergeant turning the girl back over to her grateful family and then returning to his Marine duties. Dillon wrote the novel at night on the company clerk's typewriter. It took him two months. He mailed it off, and was not at all surprised two months after that when a contract, offering an advance of five hundred dollars, arrived in Shanghai.

The book was published, and it sold less than two thousand copies. But it was optioned, and then purchased, by a major motion-picture studio in Los Angeles. The studio saw in it a vehicle for a very handsome but none-too-bright actor they had under contract. With all the fight and chase scenes, plus a lot of attention devoted to the Chinese girl having her clothing ripped off, it was believed they could get the handsome actor through the production without him appearing to be as dull-witted as he was.

It was necessary to find a suitable vehicle for the handsome young man because he was a very close friend of a very successful producer. More precisely, he was sharing the producer's bed in an antebellum-style mansion in Holmby Hills.

Sergeant Dillon was paid five thousand dollars for the motion-picture rights to his novel, an enormous sum in 1934. And he had, he thought, discovered the goose that laid the golden eggs. If he could write one novel in two months, he could write six novels a year. And at $5,500 per, that was as much money as the Major General Commandant of the Marine Corps made.

He did not ship over when his enlistment ran out. Instead, he was returned to the United States aboard the naval transport USS *Chaumont,* and honorably discharged in San Diego.

Since he was so close to Los Angeles, and his film was in production there, he went to Hollywood.

When he visited the set, the Handsome Young Actor greeted him warmly, expressed great admiration for his literary talent, and invited him for dinner at his little place in Malibu.

That night, in the beachfront cottage, as Dillon was wondering if he could gracefully reject the pansy's advances (and if he could not, how that might affect his literary career), the Producer appeared.

Words were exchanged between the Producer and the Handsome Young Actor, primarily allegations of infidelity. The exchange quickly accelerated out of control, ending when the Producer slapped the Handsome Young Actor and the Handsome Young Actor shoved the Producer through a plate-glass door opening on a balcony over the beach.

A shard of heavy plate glass fell from the top of the doorframe, severely cutting the Producer's right arm. Dillon noted with horror the pulsing flow of arterial blood. And then he saw the Handsome Young Actor, his face contorted with rage, advancing on the fallen, bleeding Producer with a fireplace poker in his hand, showing every intention of finishing him off with it.

Without really thinking about it, Dillon took the Handsome Young Actor out of action, by kicking him repeatedly in the testicles. (The story, when it later, inevitably, made the rounds in Hollywood, was that ex-Marine Dillon had floored him with a single, well-placed blow of his fist.) Then he put a tourniquet on the Producer's arm and announced that they needed an ambulance.

The Producer told him they couldn't do that. The police would become involved. The story would get out. He would lose his job.

Dillon was even then not unaccustomed to developing credible story lines to explain awkward or even illegal circumstances on short notice, prior to the imminent arrival of the authorities.

"We were fixing the door. It was out of the track, and it slipped," he said.

"But what was I doing here, *with him?*" the Producer asked somewhat hysterically, obviously more concerned with his public image than with losing his arm, or even his life.

"You brought me out here to introduce me to the star of my movie," Dillon replied, reaching for the telephone. "Where do I tell the cops we are?"

Two days later, at the Producer's request, Dillon called upon him at Cedars of Lebanon Hospital.

The Producer was no longer hysterical. And he was grateful. His doctor had told him that if Dillon hadn't applied the tourniquet when he did, he would almost certainly have bled to death before the police arrived.

"I am very grateful to you, Mr. Dillon," the Producer said.

"Call me Jake," Dillon said. "That's my middle name. Jacob."

"Jake, then. And I want to repay you in some small way . . ."

"Forget it."

"Please hear me out."

"Shoot."

"What are your plans, now that you've left the Marine Corps? Do you mind my asking?"

"Well, I thought I'd do another couple of quick novels, put a little money in the bank for a rainy day . . ."

"And if you can't sell your next novel?"

The Producer had had a copy of *Malloy and the Maiden* by H. J. Dillon, sent to his hospital room. It was arguably the worst novel he had ever read; and as a major film producer, he had more experience with really bad novels than most people. He couldn't imagine why a publisher had ever acquired it, except possibly that it had been bought by an editor who knew he was about to be fired and wanted to stick it to his employers.

Dillon had not considered that possibility. But looking at the Producer now, he saw that it was not just possible but probable.

"I don't know."

"Are you open to suggestion?"

"Shoot."

"You obviously have a way with words, and you have proven your ability to deal with potentially awkward situations. In my mind, that adds up to public relations."

"Excuse me?"

"Public relations," the Producer explained. "Making the studio, and our actors, and our films, look as good to the public as they possibly can."

"Oh."

"The man who runs our studio public relations is a friend of mine. I'm sure that he would be interested in having someone of your demonstrated talents."

Dillon thought it over for a moment.

"How much would something like that pay?"

"About five hundred to start, I'd say. And there would be time, I'm sure, for you to continue with your writing."

"Everything seems so expensive here. After China, I mean. Can you make do around here on five hundred a month?"

"You can, but I'm talking about five hundred a week, Jake."

Jake Dillon then looked at the Producer very carefully.

"No strings?"

The Producer, after a moment, caught Jake's meaning. "No, Jake, no strings. I would really much rather have you as a friend than a lover."

Jake Dillon found his natural home in motion-picture public relations. He quickly became known as the only man who was ever able to get "the world's most famous actor" out of the teenaged Mexican girls on his sailboat, and then off the sailboat and back to Hollywood sober—and to get him there on time to start shooting—and in a relatively cooperative mood. A half-dozen of his more experienced peers had tried to do all of that, and had failed to pull him off even one of the chiquitas.

Actresses trusted him. If Jake showed up at some party and told you there was an early call tomorrow and it was time to drink up and tuck it in, you knew he had your interests at heart and not just the fucking studio's. So you went home. Sometimes with Jake.

And the Producer, who found that Jake offered a comforting shoulder to weep on when his romances went sour, made it known among those of similar persuasion, a powerful group in Hollywood, that Jake was his best "straight" friend.

And he gradually came to be known as a man with a rare insight into how a motion picture or an actor should be publicized. In other words, his nerve endings told him what he could get printed in newspapers, or broadcast over the radio, and what would be thrown away.

Within two years, his pay tripled. And he began to run around not only with stuntmen and grips but also with a small group of the big-time actors. He fished with Duke Wayne, hunted with Clark Gable, played poker with David Niven, and with all three of them he drank and jumped on the bones of an astonishing number of ladies.

And he could often be found—puffing on his cigar and sipping at a cool beer—in screening rooms when daily rushes and rough cuts were screened. The stars of these opera invited him there. And they solicited his opinions, and he gave them. Sometimes his judgments were not flattering.

But, as the head of the studio said, "Jake is a walking public-opinion poll. He knows what the ticket buyers will like, and what they won't."

Jake Dillon's opinions of a story, a treatment, a screenplay, rushes, rough cuts, and final cuts were solicited and respected.

The only thing he failed to do, because he refused to do it, was talk some sense to David Niven. Niven was clearly on the way to superstardom. Which meant that very few people in Hollywood could understand why he was about to throw his career down the toilet. He was returning to England and again putting on the uniform of an officer of His Britannic Majesty's Royal Army.

"You guys don't understand," Dillon told the head of Niven's studio. "David went to Sandhurst—that's like our West Point. He's an old soldier, and somebody blew the fucking bugle. He had to go."

With Europe at war, Hollywood's attention turned to making war movies. One of them dealt with the United States Marine Corps, specifically with Marine fighter pilots. Headquarters USMC sent a full colonel to Los Angeles to serve as technical adviser. Ex-Marine Dillon was charged with keeping the Colonel happy.

Their relationship was a little awkward at first, for both of them were aware that the last time they'd met, Jake Dillon had been in Shanghai wearing sergeant's stripes and standing at attention for the Colonel's inspection. But the relationship quickly grew into a genuine friendship. This was based in large part on the Colonel's realization that Jake was as determined as he was that the motion picture would reflect well on the Corps.

There was an element of masculine camaraderie in it, too. The Colonel took aboard a load one night at Jake's house in Malibu and confessed that he couldn't get it up anymore—not after his wife of twenty-two years had left him for a doctor at Johns Hopkins. Dillon was more than sympathetic; he arranged for the Colonel to meet a lady the Colonel had previously seen only on the Silver Screen. The lady owed Jake Dillon a great big favor, and she was more than happy to discharge it the way Dillon had in mind. She did wonders vis-à-vis restoring the Colonel's lost virility.

And Jake took a load aboard and confessed to the Colonel that he'd felt like a feather merchant when he'd put David Niven on the Broadway Limited on his way to England. He was as much a Marine as Niven was a soldier. And Niven had gone back in. And here he was, sitting with his thumb up his ass in Malibu, with the country about to go to war.

When the Colonel returned to Washington, he wrote a Memorandum for the Record to the Director of Personnel, stating his belief that in the event of war, the Corps was going to require the services of highly qualified public-relations officers; that he had recently, in the course of his duties, encountered a man who more than met the highest criteria for such service; that he could be induced to accept a reserve commission as a captain; and that he believed a commission as a reserve captain should be offered to him, notwithstanding the fact that the man did not meet the standard educational and other criteria for such a commission.

The Colonel was two weeks later summoned to the office of the Deputy Commandant, USMC, who tossed his Memorandum for the Record at him.

"I know you and Colonel Limell don't get along," the Deputy Commandant said. "I think that's why he sent this to me—to make you look like a fool. Can you really justify giving this ex-sergeant a captain's commission, or did you lose your marbles out in Hollywood?"

The Colonel made his points. Though he wasn't sure how well they were being received, he did see the Deputy Commandant's eyes widen when he told him how much money Jake Dillon was paid (it was more than twice as much as the Major General Commandant got); and he took some small comfort that he was neither interrupted nor dismissed.

When he was finished, the Deputy Commandant looked at the Colonel thoughtfully for a very long thirty seconds. Then he grunted and reached for his telephone.

"Colonel Limell, about this Hollywood press agent, the one who was a sergeant with the 4th Marines? Offer him a majority."

Then, surprising the Colonel yet again, Jake Dillon was not overwhelmed with gratitude when he was offered a Marine Majority.

"I'm not qualified to be a major. Jesus Christ! I was thinking about maybe a staff sergeant. Maybe even a gunnery sergeant. But a major? No way."

The Colonel argued unsuccessfully for thirty minutes that the greatest contribution Jake Dillon could make to the Corps was as a public-relations officer, and that to do that well, he had to carry the rank of a field-grade officer on his collar points. The best he was able to do was to get Jake to agree to come to Washington and talk it over.

"I'll put you up, Jake."

"That's nice, but we keep a suite in the Willard," Jake said. "I'll stay there. I'll catch a plane this afternoon, and call you when I get there."

Jake called two days later, at three in the afternoon, as soon as he got into the studio's suite in the Willard. The Colonel, who had a certain sense of public relations himself, immediately called the Deputy Commandant.

"Sir, Mr. Dillon is in Washington."

"That's the press-agent sergeant?"

"Yes, Sir."

"I want to talk to him."

"Yes, Sir, I thought you might want to. Sir, I understand you're taking the retreat ceremony at Eighth and Eye today?"

"Splendid," the Deputy Commandant said, taking the Colonel's meaning. "I'll have my aide arrange two seats for you in the reviewing stand."

The Formal Retreat Ceremony (the lowering of the colors at sunset) is held at the Marine Barracks at Eighth and Eye Streets, Southeast, in the District of Columbia. The Marine Band, in dress blues, plays the Marine Hymn, while impeccably uniformed Marines march with incredible precision past the reviewing stand. The ceremony has brought tears to the eyes of thousands of pacifists and cynics.

Its effect on a former 4th Marines sergeant was predictable: When the Color Guard marched past, Jake Dillon was standing at attention with his hand on his heart. And tears formed in his eyes.

When the ceremony was over, and the Marine Band was marching off the field to the tic-tic of drum sticks on drum rims, a first lieutenant in dress blues walked up to him.

"Sir, the Deputy Commandant would like a word with you."

"Dillon?" the Deputy Commandant of the U.S. Marine Corps, in his dress blues, said to former Sergeant Dillon, offering him his hand.

"Yes, Sir."

"Once a Marine, always a Marine. Welcome back aboard, Major."

"Thank you, Sir."

"When you get settled, call my aide. I want a long talk with you."

"Aye, aye, Sir."

Jake Dillon never again raised the question of his lack of qualifications to be a major. If the Deputy Commandant of the Corps thought he could hack it, who was he to ask questions?

In the Corps, you say, "Aye, aye, Sir," and do what you're told to the best of your ability.

When Major Dillon reported two weeks later for duty at Headquarters USMC, he was assigned as Officer-in-Charge, Special Projects, Public Affairs Office.

The visit of the team of *Life* photojournalists to the Parachute School at Lakehurst Naval Air Station was a Special Project. And from the moment Major Jake Dillon met Lieutenant Colonel Franklin G. Neville, he knew in his bones that something or someone was going to fuck it up.

He couldn't understand the feeling, but he trusted it. He anticipated no trouble with the people from *Life.* He knew a couple of them; and more important, he knew their bosses. And the story itself looked like a natural. Marines were always good copy, and parachutists were always good copy, and here he had both. The confirmation of that came when he called a guy he knew at *Life* and learned that unless something else came along of greater importance, and providing that the pictures worked out, they were scheduling the Para-Marines as the cover story, two issues down the pike.

"Bill, do me a favor, forget you ever heard the phrase 'Para-Marines.' I don't know why, but it pisses off a lot of the important brass."

The Managing Editor of *Life* chuckled.

"OK. So what do I call them?"

"Marine Parachutists, please."

"Marine Parachutists it is. You going to be at Lakehurst?"

"Sure."

"What I sort of have in mind, Jake, is a nice clean-cut kid hanging from a parachute. For the cover, I mean."

"You got him. I'll have a dozen for you to choose from."

"Excuse me, Major," Lieutenant R. B. Macklin said to Major Homer J. Dillon, "may I have a word with you, Sir?"

Jake Dillon gave Lieutenant Macklin an impatient look, shrugged his shoulders, and jerked his thumb toward the door.

God only knows what this horse's ass wants.

"This is far enough," Major Jake Dillon said to Lieutenant R. B. Macklin, once they were out of earshot of the people from *Life*. "What's on your mind?"

"Sir, I thought I had best bring you up to date on PFC Koffler."

"OK. What about him?"

"I have confined him to barracks. My adjutant is drawing up the court-martial charges. He believes that 'conduct prejudicial to good order and discipline' is the appropriate charge."

"What the *hell* are you talking about?"

"The Major is aware that Koffler . . . that Koffler said 'Fuck you' to the gentleman from *Life* when he asked him what his name was?"

"I wasn't, but so what?"

"Right there on the Landing Zone, as he stood over Colonel Neville's body. I was there, Sir."

"I repeat, so what?"

"Well, Sir, we just can't let something like that pass."

"Jesus H. Christ!" Jake Dillon flared. "Now listen to me, Macklin. What you're going to do, Lieutenant, is tell your adjutant to take his goddamned court-martial charges out of his goddamned typewriter and put in a fresh sheet of paper. And on that sheet of paper, backdated to day before yesterday, he will type out an order promoting PFC Koffler to corporal."

"Sir, I don't understand."

"That doesn't surprise me at all, Lieutenant. Just do it. I want to see that kid here in thirty minutes. Showered and shaved, in a fresh uniform, with his parachute wings on his chest and corporal's stripes on his sleeves. Those parachutists' boots, too. I just talked to AP. They saw the picture of him that *Life* took, and they're coming down here to interview him. And that Flying Sergeant who was flying the airplane. If AP's coming, UP and INS won't be far behind. Get the picture?"

"Sir, technically," Macklin said, uneasily but doggedly, "he's not entitled to wear either boots or wings. We haven't had the graduation ceremony. Colonel Neville delayed it for the *Life* people, and after . . . what happened . . . I postponed it indefinitely."

"Parachute boots, wings, and corporal's stripes, Lieutenant," Jake Dillon said icily. "Here. In thirty minutes."

"Aye, aye, Sir," Lieutenant Macklin said.

(FIVE)

"I think that's about enough, fellas," Major Jake Dillon said, rising to his feet. "Sergeant Galloway and Corporal Koffler have had a rough day. I think we ought to let them go."

There were the expected mumbles of discontent from the press, but they started to fold up their notebooks and get to their feet. The interview was over.

Jake Dillon was pleased that he had thought about putting Sergeant Galloway in the press conference. Galloway had handled himself well, even better than

Dillon had hoped for. And Corporal Koffler, bless his little heart, was dumber than dog shit; if Galloway hadn't been there, that would have come out.

And the press seemed to have bought the story line that it was a tragic accident, something that just happened to a fine officer who was undergoing training with his men.

But Jake Dillon knew that when two or three are gathered together in the name of honest journalism, one of them will be a sonofabitch determined to find the maggots under the rock, even if he has to put them there himself. In this case, he wouldn't have to look far.

Jake Dillon had formed his own unvarnished version of the truth vis-à-vis the tragic death of Lieutenant Colonel Franklin G. Neville, USMC, based on what he had heard from the jumpmaster, from Corporal Steve Koffler, and on his own previous observations of Lieutenant Colonel Franklin G. Neville.

Neville had been bitten by the publicity bug. When the guys from *Life* had shown very little interest in Neville himself, preferring instead to devote their attention to young enlisted men, it had really gotten to him. The whole thing was his idea, and nobody gave a damn.

And so he flipped. He was determined to have his picture in *Life,* and that meant he had to put himself in a position where the photographers could not ignore him. And he figured out that would be when they were shooting the parachutists exiting the aircraft. If he was first man out the door, they would have to take his picture, and they couldn't edit him out.

So he pushed out of the way the kid Koffler, who was supposed to be first man out, and jumped. And something went wrong. Instead of being in center frame, he found himself wrapped around the horizontal stabilizer. That either killed him straight off, or it left him unconscious. Either way, he couldn't pull the D-ring on his emergency 'chute.

Jake Dillon didn't want that story to come out. It would hurt the widow, and would hurt the Corps.

"I would like a word with you, Sergeant, please," Jake Dillon called after Galloway as Galloway and Koffler left the room. "You and Corporal Koffler."

When he had them alone and out of earshot, he said, "OK. Where are you two headed?"

"Sir," Sergeant Galloway said, "I understand that General McInerney's coming up here in the morning. I've been told to make myself available to him for that."

"I mean now, tonight. I know about the General."

"Well, Sir, I thought I would like to get off the base. Find a room somewhere."

"Good. Go now, and take Corporal Koffler with you. The one thing I don't want you to do is talk to the press. Period. Under any circumstances. Consider that an order."

"Aye, aye, Sir," Charley Galloway said. A split second later, Steve parroted him.

"I've talked to General McInerney," Major Dillon went on. "Here's what's happening. Colonel Neville's body is to be taken to the Brooklyn Navy Yard for an autopsy. Then it will be put in a casket and brought back here. After the inquiry tomorrow morning, you and Koffler will take it to Washington. You will travel with General McInerney and an honor guard of the parachutists. Colonel Neville will be buried in Arlington. You and Koffler will be pallbearers."

"Yes, Sir," Sergeant Galloway said.

Jake Dillon thought he could bleed the story for a little more, with pictures of the honor guard and the flag-draped casket. And if they were still burying people in Arlington with the horse-drawn artillery caisson, maybe a shot of that and the firing squad, too. With a little bit of luck, he could get a two-, three-minute film sequence tied together for the newsreels. But that was none of Galloway's or Koffler's business, so he didn't mention it.

"I don't care where you guys go, or what you do. But I will have your ass if you either talk to the press or get shit-faced and make asses of yourselves. Do I have to make it plainer than that?"

"No, Sir," they said, together.

Jake Dillon put his hand in his pocket.

"You need some money, either of you?"

"No, Sir," they replied.

"OK. I want you back here at seven in the morning."

"Get in the backseat," Technical Sergeant Charles Galloway ordered Corporal Stephen Koffler as they approached the Mercury station wagon.

Galloway got in the front beside Mrs. Caroline Ward McNamara.

"Now what?" Aunt Caroline said, touching Charley's hand.

"I'm sorry you had to wait like this," Charley said. "Caroline, this is Corporal Steve Koffler. Koffler, this is Mrs. McNamara."

"Hello," Aunt Caroline said, looking at Steve. "I repeat, now what?"

"I have been ordered to keep an eye on Corporal Koffler overnight, and to bring him back here at 0700 in the morning."

"Oh," Aunt Caroline said.

"We are going to find a hotel room—rooms—someplace," Charley said. "I wondered how that would fit in with your plans."

"Well, it's already dark, and I hate to drive at night, with the snow and all. Maybe I should think about getting a hotel room myself. Where's Jim and the other lieutenant?"

"I understand Major Dillon sent for them. Maybe it would be better if we got off the base before he's finished with them. I'm a little afraid that Major Dillon will tell one of them to keep an eye on me and Koffler."

"Oh, I see what you mean," Aunt Caroline said. She started the engine and headed for the gate.

"Just how close an eye do you have to keep on the corporal?" Aunt Caroline asked.

"I think an adjacent room would be close enough."

"Adjacent but not adjoining, you mean?" Aunt Caroline said.

"Exactly."

"Excuse me, Sergeant?" Corporal Koffler said.

"What, Koffler?"

"Sergeant, I live in East Orange. Do you suppose it would be all right if I went home?"

"You live where?"

"East Orange. It's right next to Newark."

"Oh, really?" Aunt Caroline said. "Maybe you could find a hotel in Newark for yourself, and Corporal Koffler could spend the night with his family."

"The Essex House Hotel's in Newark," Steve offered helpfully. "I never stayed there, but I hear it's real nice. You both probably could get rooms there."

"Now there's a thought," Aunt Caroline said innocently.

"But I'm supposed to keep an eye on him," Charley Galloway said. "If he went home alone, and Major Dillon or Lieutenant Ward or Lieutenant Schneider ever heard about it, we'd all be in trouble."

"Well, we don't have to tell them, do we?" Steve asked shrewdly.

"No, I guess we wouldn't really have to," Charley Galloway said. "Could I trust you to stay out of trouble, Koffler, and be waiting for me at, say, 0530, outside your house in the morning?"

"It's an apartment house," Steve said. "Sure, you could trust me, Sergeant. I'd really like to see my girl, Sergeant."

"You'd better be careful about that, Koffler. Women have been known to suffer uncontrollable sexual frenzies at the mere sight of a Marine in uniform. That could lead to trouble."

Aunt Caroline giggled, and Charley Galloway yelped in pain, as if someone had dug fingernails into the soft flesh of his upper thigh.

"My girl won't get me in trouble, Sergeant," Steve said.

"OK. Then we'll do it. You give Mrs. McNamara directions to your house."

On the outskirts of Newark, Aunt Caroline pulled into a gasoline station. As the attendant filled the tank and she visited the rest room, Charley Galloway saw a rack of newspapers.

"I'll be damned," he said, and went to the rack and bought two copies of the *Newark Evening News.*

He walked back to the station wagon and handed one to Steve Koffler.

"You're a famous man now, Koffler," he said. "Try not to let it go to your head."

There was a three-column picture in the center of the front page. It showed Steve Koffler holding the risers and shroud lines of his parachute against his chest; he was looking down at the body of Lieutenant Colonel Franklin G. Neville. Tears were visible on his cheeks.

Over the picture was a headline, EVEN THE TOUGH CAN WEEP, and below it was a caption: "Cpl. Stephen Koffler, of East Orange, a member of the elite U.S. Marine Corps Parachute Force, weeps as he looks at the body of his commanding officer, Lt. Col. F. G. Neville, who fell to his death moments before when his parachute failed to open during training exercises at the Lakehurst Naval Air Station this morning. Koffler was second man in the 'stick' jumping from the Marine airplane, behind Col. Neville. [Associated Press Photograph from *Life*]"

On the way from the gasoline station to 121 Park Avenue, East Orange, Corporal Stephen Koffler of the "elite U.S. Marine Corps Parachute Force" (*Jesus Christ, that sounds* great!) ran over several times in his mind the sequence of events that would occur once he got home.

Dianne would have seen the *Newark Evening News.* Everybody read it. She would see his picture. She would wonder, naturally, when she would see him again. And she would more than likely realize that the reason he had been unable to come to see her was that he was busy with his duties with the Elite Marine Corps Parachute Force.

He would appear at her door. She would answer it. Her family would be gone somewhere. She would look into his eyes. They would embrace. Her tongue would slip into his mouth. She would break away.

"I saw your picture in the paper," she would say. "Was it just awful?"

And he would say, "No. Not really. You have to expect that sort of thing."

And they would kiss again, and she would slip her tongue in his mouth again. And this time he would put his hand up under her sweater, or maybe down the back of her skirt.

And she would say, "Not here," but she wouldn't mean it, and he would take her into her living room and do it to her on the couch. Or maybe even into her bedroom—and do it to her in her own bed.

Just by way of saying hello.

"Let's get out of here," he would say. "Where we can really be alone."

"But where could we go?" she would ask.

"How about the Essex House?"

And she would say, "The Essex House? Could we get a room in the *Essex House?"*

And he would say, "Sure, we can. I'm a corporal on jump pay."

He wasn't born yesterday. Sergeant Galloway and the blond lady in the station wagon were going to shack up in the Essex House. That was just so much bullshit about getting two rooms. And if Sergeant Galloway was going to screw this blond lady in the Essex House, why shouldn't he screw Dianne there?

And Dianne would say, "But what about Leonard?"

And he would say, "Fuck Leonard. You're through with that candy-ass civilian."

No. He didn't want to talk like that around Dianne. He would say, "To hell with Leonard. You're through with that civilian."

And once he got her into the Essex House and they'd done it a couple of times more, he would tell her that it didn't matter that she was a couple of years older than he was, he was psychologically older than the age on his birth certificate. He was a Marine, for Christ's sake, a member of the Elite Marine Corps Parachute Force. What he had done, and what he had seen, made him at least as old as Leonard, psychologically speaking.

It did not work out quite the way Steve envisioned it.

The first thing that went wrong was that his mother was not only home but looking out the window when Sergeant Galloway stopped to let him out of the blond lady's station wagon.

By the time he got to the foyer, she had run downstairs and was waiting for him. She threw her arms around him and started crying, for Christ's sake.

Steve hadn't even thought of his mother. As she gave him the weepy bear hug, he was conscious that if she hadn't been looking out the window, he could have gone straight to Dianne's and started things off the way he planned.

But he was caught now. He was only too aware that he would have to spend a little time with her before going to see Dianne.

His mother's husband appeared and shook his hand and, for the first time ever, seemed glad to see him. The sonofabitch even worked up a smile and said, "Come on up, I'll make us a little Seven-and-Seven."

As they were going up the stairs, Dianne came down them. Dianne and Leonard.

"Hi!" Steve said.

"Hey, kid," Leonard said. "I saw your picture in the paper."

"Hello, Steve," Dianne said. "Nice to see you."

"Great to see you."

That was it. The next second, Dianne and Leonard were down the stairs and gone.

The phone was ringing when they got in the apartment. It was Mrs. Danielli. She had probably seen his picture in the *Newark Evening News,* because his mother said to her, "Yeah, sure, we seen it. He's *here,* Anna, he just this minute walked in the door."

And then Mrs. Danielli must have told Vinny that he was home, because his mother handed him the telephone and said, "Say hello to Vinny, Stevie."

"Ask them if they want to go out with us and get some spaghetti or something, why don't you?" Steve's mother's husband chimed in. Steve pretended not to hear him. If he got involved with the Daniellis, he would never get loose to go look for Dianne.

His mother jerked the phone out of his hand.

"Vinny, tell your mother Stanley asked do you and your mother and father want to go out with us and get some spaghetti."

It was agreed they would meet the Daniellis at the Naples Restaurant on Orange Street by Branch Brook Park in half an hour.

His mother hung up the telephone and turned to him.

"What were you so nice to that tramp about?"

"What are you talking about?"

"I'm talking about Dianne Marshall whatever-her-married-name-is, is what tramp I'm talking about—the one whose husband threw her out because she was fooling around."

"You don't know what you're talking about!"

"Don't you ever dare talk to me like that!"

"You don't know what the hell you're talking about, Ma!"

She slapped him.

"Don't think you're a big shot, Mr. Big Shot, who can swear at his mother!"

"What the hell is going on out there?" his mother's husband called from the kitchen.

"Nothing, dear."

They had to wait for a table at the Naples Restaurant. The Daniellis—Mr. and Mrs., and Maria and Beryl, Vinny's little sisters, and Vinny—showed up just before they finally got one.

When they got inside, Dianne and Leonard were there, sitting at a table for two with a candle in a Chianti bottle. The table was over against the wall-sized mural of what was supposed to be, Steve guessed, Naples and some volcano with smoke coming out of it.

They were just finishing up their meal. Leonard hadn't seen them, and Steve wasn't sure whether Dianne had or not. She wasn't looking in their direction, anyhow. And then she got up to go to the john.

She saw me. She pretended she didn't see me. She must know what my mother thinks about her, so she wanted to avoid trouble. And she doesn't really have to go to the toilet; she knows I'll see her go in there and will meet her outside, in that little corridor or whatever the hell it is.

"Excuse me, please, I have to visit the little boys' room."

"Again?" his mother said. "You just went before we left the apartment!"

He prayed his mother had not seen Dianne.

He had to wait a long time in the little corridor between the door that said REST ROOMS and the doors to the men's and ladies' johns, but finally Dianne came out.

"Hi!"

"What the hell are doing here?"

"Waiting for you."

"You crazy, or what? Christ!"

Steve tried to kiss her. She averted her face. When he tried harder, and started putting his arms around her, she kneed him in the balls.

"Jesus Christ," Dianne said, as he leaned against the wall, faint and in agony. "Can't you take the hint? Stay the hell away from me. You come near me again, I'll tell my father, and he'll beat the shit out of you!"

VIII

(ONE)
The Foster Lafayette Hotel
Washington, D.C.
17 February 1942

Captain Fleming Pickering, USNR, got out from behind the wheel of the black Buick Roadmaster two-door sedan and tiptoed through the slush to the marquee. He had purchased the Buick, used, three days before, from a classified advertisement in the *Washington Post.*

"You should have slid out the driver's side, Captain Pickering," the doorman said, chuckling.

"But that would have been the intelligent thing to do," Pickering said. "I won't need it anymore today. But presuming you can make it run, can you have it out here at half past seven in the morning?"

"It'll start. The garage told me all it needed was a battery."

"We'll see," Pickering said. "I would be very surprised."

"Senator Fowler came in a couple of minutes ago, Captain," the doorman said. "Asked if I'd seen you."

"As soon as I thaw my frozen feet, I'll call him," Pickering said. "Thank you."

He checked at the desk for mail, but his slot was empty. Then he remembered that it would of course be empty. If they hadn't sent it up with a bellboy, the ever-efficient Mrs. Ellen Feller would have picked it up when she came to the apartment.

Pickering and Mrs. Feller had been assigned office space in the Navy Department. He thought of it as "the closet," but it was just outside Secretary Knox's suite. Since there was really no reason for him to spend much time there, he had had Max Telford, the hotel manager, install a desk and a typewriter in his suite for Mrs. Feller. She brought whatever papers needed his attention to the hotel, and he went to his official office as seldom as possible.

Am I getting old? Or am I just tired?

The junior United States Senator from California, the Hon. Richardson S. Fowler, was in the sitting room of Pickering's suite when Pickering let himself in.

"Senator, finding a politician sitting in my chair tossing down my booze is not an entirely unexpected cap to an all-around lousy day," Pickering greeted him.

Fowler swung his feet off the footstool of a high-backed leather overstuffed chair, and started to get up.

"Oh, for Christ's sake, stay there. I was only kidding."

"I never know with you."

"Whenever I call you 'Senator,' I'm kidding," Pickering said. "OK?"

He took off his uniform overcoat, tossed it on the back of one of the two couches facing a coffee table before the fireplace, laid his gold-encrusted uniform cap on top, sat down on the left couch, and started taking off his shoes and socks.

"My God," Ellen Feller said, coming into the room from the small bedroom that was now more or less converted into an office for her, "you're all wet!"

She wore a dark green silk dress with an unbuttoned cardigan over it. Her hair was combed upward from the base of her neck.

"I've noticed," he said.

"You look frozen. Can I get you a cup of coffee?" she asked. "Or a drink?"

"I don't suppose that's in your official job description, Ellen, but yes, thank you, both."

"Sir?"

"Put a generous hooker of cognac in a cup of black coffee, please."

"Where the hell have you been?" Senator Fowler asked.

"At Arlington. At a funeral. Standing in a snowdrift."

"You'd better change your trousers, too," Ellen said, as she poured coffee into a cup.

"A funeral? Anybody I know?" Senator Fowler asked.

"The last time I counted, I owned three pairs of trousers. I refuse to believe that the other two are already back from the cleaners."

"Count again," Ellen chuckled. "There was an enormous package from Brooks Brothers. *I* counted three blue jackets and *six* pairs of blue trousers when I hung it all up."

"Thank God! Finally!" Pickering said, and picked up his shoes and socks and went into the master bedroom.

Senator Fowler went to Mrs. Feller, took the brandy-laced coffee from her with a smile, and carried it into the bedroom. Pickering was in his shorts, buttoning braces to a pair of uniform trousers.

He took the coffee, nodded his thanks, and took a sip.

"Thank you," he said.

"Who were you burying?"

"A Marine lieutenant colonel. Fellow named Neville. His parachute didn't open."

"I saw that in the paper," Fowler said. "You knew him?"

"I was there representing Frank Knox. Frank knew him. He said he would have preferred to go himself, but if he did, it would be setting a precedent; he would be expected to show up every time they buried a lieutenant colonel or a commander."

"You didn't seem grief-stricken," Fowler said dryly.

"From what I hear, he did it to himself," Pickering said.

"Suicide?"

"Jake Dillon told me 'he got so carried away with his role that he got run over by the camera,' " Pickering said, chuckling.

"Jake Dillon? The press agent?"

"Yeah. He's a major in the Corps."

"I didn't know, and I didn't know you knew him."

"Oh, sure. Jake shoots skeet with Bob Stack. That's how I met him. Interesting man. He stayed at the house in '39, he and the Stacks, when we had the state championships in San Francisco. Anyway, Jake was sort of running the burial ceremony. Newsreel cameras, three buglers, an honor guard of Marine parachutists, a firing squad, and a cast of thousands. Look for me at your local movie. I will be the handsome Naval person saluting solemnly as I stand there up to my ass in snow."

"I thought you said this man committed suicide?"

"No. Not the way that sounded. What Jake said was that when he found out

Life wasn't going to take his picture, he flipped. He figured if he was the first man out of the airplane when they jumped, they'd have to take his picture. So he pushed the kid who was supposed to be first out of the way, and jumped himself. The wind, or the prop blast, caught him the wrong way and threw him into the horizontal stabilizer. The autopsy showed that hitting the horizontal stabilizer killed him. Not the sudden stop when he hit the ground."

"You sound pretty goddamned coldblooded, Flem, do you realize that?" Senator Fowler said.

Pickering, who was pulling on his trousers, didn't reply until he had the braces in place, the shirttail tucked in, and the zipper closed.

"Before I went out to Arlington," he said in an even voice, "I was reading a pretty reliable report that the Japs just executed two-hundred-odd American civilians—the labor force we took out to Wake Island to fortify it and then permitted to get captured when we didn't reinforce Wake. They shot them out of hand. I find it a trifle difficult to get worked up over a light colonel here who did it to himself."

"Jesus Christ!" Fowler said, shocked.

"And an hour before that," Pickering went on dryly, "I had a telephone call from my wife, who is finding it difficult to understand why I didn't telephone her when I was on the West Coast. I was seen having lunch at the Coronado Beach Hotel, but I didn't have time for her. . . ."

"Tell me about the civilians on Wake."

"No. I shouldn't have said that much."

"Why not?"

"Senator, you just don't have the right to know," Pickering said.

"The operative word in that sentence, Flem, is 'Senator,' " Fowler said flatly.

Pickering looked at him with his eyebrows raised.

"As in 'United States Senator, representing the people,' " Fowler went on. "If a United States Senator doesn't have 'the right to know,' who does?"

"Interesting point," Pickering said. "Fortunately, I am not at what is known as the policy-making level, and don't have to make judgments like that. I just do what I'm told."

"How much do you know that I don't?" Fowler asked.

"Probably a hell of a lot," Pickering said.

"I want to know about the civilians on Wake Island," Fowler said. "I won't let anyone know where I got it, if that's bothering you."

"About ten people, including the cryptographers, know about it. If Frank Knox finds out you know about it, he'll know damned well where you got it."

"You wouldn't be a captain in the Navy, Flem, working for Knox, if I hadn't brought him here," Fowler said. "And it seems to me that the American people have a right to know if the Japanese are committing atrocities against civilian prisoners."

"They do, but they can't be told," Pickering said.

"Why not?"

"Because . . . do you realize what a goddamned spot you're putting me on, you sonofabitch?"

"Yes, I do," Fowler said.

"Oh, goddamn it!"

"I am rapidly getting the idea that you don't think I can be trusted with something like this," Senator Fowler said. "I can tolerate your contempt for Congress, generally. But this is getting personal. I don't think you question my patriotism, so it has to be my judgment you question."

"Shit!" Pickering said in frustration. He picked up and drained the brandy-laced cup of coffee, then turned to face Fowler. "We have broken the Japanese naval code. The information about the Japs shooting the civilians came from what they call an 'intercept.' If the Japanese find out we know about them shooting the civilians, they'll know we broke their code. And I can't tell you how valuable reading their radio traffic is to us."

"Thank you," Fowler said, seriously. "That will, of course, go no further than these walls."

Pickering nodded.

"Unless, of course, Mrs. Feller, in her role as oh-so-efficient secretary, has been eavesdropping at the door," Fowler added.

"I don't think she has," Pickering said. "But she knows."

"They really shot two hundred civilians?"

"Made them dig their graves, twenty at a time, and then shot them. Too much trouble to feed, you understand."

"God*damn* them!"

"I wonder what Frank'll do with me now?" Pickering said, as he pulled fresh stockings on his feet. "Let me out of the Navy, in which case I could go back to running Pacific & Far East, or send me to Iceland, someplace like that, as an example?"

"What are you talking about?"

"Obviously, I'm going to have to tell Knox that I told you about what happened on Wake. And about our having broken the Japanese code."

"Why?" Fowler asked.

"I realize the concept is seldom mentioned around Washington, but, ethically, I have to. He made me privy to this—"

"Flem," Fowler interrupted him. "Christ, you're naïve!"

"I haven't been accused of that in a long time."

"I know Frank Knox pretty well, too, you know," Fowler said. "Much better than you do, as a matter of fact. And he knows that we're very good friends. It hasn't occurred to you that he told you about Wake, and probably about some other things, pretty sure that you would tell me? *Hoping* you would?"

Pickering raised his eyes to Fowler. After a moment he said, "I am having trouble following that convoluted line of reasoning."

"I think Frank Knox wants me to know about Wake Island. And about a lot of other things the Secretary of the Navy cannot conveniently—or maybe even legally—tell the Junior Senator from California. And now I do, and Frank can lay his hand on a Bible and swear he didn't tell me."

"You really believe that?" Pickering asked doubtfully.

"Yeah, Flem, I do. And if you rush over there crying, 'Father, I cannot tell a lie. I chopped down the cherry tree,' you'll put the system out of kilter. It would not, Flem, be in the best interests of the country."

"My God!"

"Welcome to the real world, Captain Fleming," Fowler said dryly.

"You're suggesting that's the reason he got me this commission," Pickering said.

"It's certainly one of them. I'm on his side, Flem. He knows that. I really should know what the hell is really going on."

"Then why doesn't he just call you in and tell you? Brief you, as they say?"

"The Senate is full of monstrous egos. If he briefed me, he would have to brief a dozen other people. Two dozen. Some of whom, I'm sorry to say, should not be trusted with this kind of information."

"You're right, I'm naïve. Until just now, I thought what I was doing was lending my shipping expertise."

"That too," Fowler said. "But think about it. What does this Wake Island atrocity have to do with that? You don't really have that 'need to know' you threw in my face."

Pickering put on a fresh pair of shoes, tied them, and stood up, holding the wet pair in his hand.

"I think I'm going to have a stiff drink," he said. "Interested?"

"Fascinated," Fowler said, touching his arm. "But one final comment, Flem. Knox has paid you one hell of a compliment. Since he can't tell anyone what material should be passed to me, he had to have someone in whose intelligence and judgment he felt safe. He picked you."

"You didn't get into that?"

"No. For obvious reasons."

"I feel like Alice must have felt when she walked through the looking glass," Pickering said.

He went back into the sitting room, opened the door to the corridor, and put the wet shoes outside. Then he went to the bar and poured an inch of Scotch into a large-mouthed glass.

"I would have made that for you," Ellen Feller said.

"Ellen, would you get Secretary Knox on the phone for me?" Pickering said.

"What are you doing, Flem?" Fowler asked, concern in his voice.

"Why don't you just listen? And see if everybody has guessed right about my judgment and intelligence?"

He walked to where Ellen was dialing a telephone on a small, narrow table against the wall.

"Captain Pickering for Secretary Knox," she said when someone answered the phone. Pickering wondered how she knew where Knox would be at this time of day.

Knox came on the line. "Yes, Pickering?"

"I thought I had best report on the funeral of Colonel Neville, Sir."

"Well, thank you. But it wasn't really necessary. I trust you."

"It went well, Sir."

"Good."

"If you have nothing more for me tonight, Sir, I think I'm going to just get in bed. I got chilled out at Arlington."

"Well, we can't have you coming down with a cold. I need you. But why don't you put off actually going to bed for a while? I ran into Senator Fowler, and he said he was going to drop in on you for a drink. We can't afford to disappoint him. We have very few Republican friends on the Hill, you know."

"I understand, Sir."

"Yes," Knox said. "Good night, Captain."

Pickering hung the telephone up and turned to look at Fowler, who met his eyes.

"Ellen," Pickering said, "you might as well run along. Senator Fowler and I are going to sit here and communicate with John Barleycorn. I'll see you in the morning."

"There are some things in here you should read, Captain," she said.

"Leave them. I'll read them when I get up in the morning."

"There's a couple of 'eyes only' in there," she said, nodding toward a leather briefcase, "which should go back in the vault. I could either wait, or arrange for a courier."

"I'll call for a courier when I'm through with them," Pickering said. "Thank you, Ellen."

"Yes, Sir."

When she had gone, Fowler said, "Very nice. Speaking of naïve, does Patricia know about her?"

"What the hell do you mean by that?"

"Now I know that Patricia has the understanding of a saint, but there are some women whose active imaginations would jump into high gear if they learned their husbands were spending a lot of time in a hotel suite with an attractive—very attractive—female like that."

"Dick . . . Jesus! *A,* I don't run around on Patricia, never have, and you know it. *B,* she's some kind of a missionary."

"Oh, a *missionary!* I *forgot.* Missionaries are neutered when they take their vows. They don't have whoopee urges. The reason your missionary lady looks at you the way she does is because she sees in you a saint who would *never* even *think* of slipping it to her."

"You're a dirty old man, Dick," Pickering said. He walked to the briefcase, picked it up, worked the combination lock, and opened it. He spent a full minute looking at the folders it contained without removing them, and then he handed the briefcase to Senator Fowler.

"In for a penny, in for a pound," he said. "Read what's in there, and then I'll answer any questions."

Fowler handed the briefcase back to him.

"You still don't understand the rules of the game, do you?" he said.

"I guess not."

"Right now I can put my hand on the Bible and swear that you never showed me one classified document, and you can swear that you never showed me one. I want to keep it that way."

"So what do you want?"

"I want a briefing," Fowler said. "I want *your opinion* of what's going on."

"With a map and a pointer?" Pickering asked sarcastically.

"A map would be nice," Senator Fowler said. "You probably won't need a pointer. Have you got a map?"

Pickering saw that Fowler was serious.

"Yeah," he said. "I've got a map. It's in the safe. I had a safe installed in here to make sure people who don't have the need to know don't get to look at my map."

"Why don't you get it, Flem?" Senator Fowler said, ignoring the sarcasm. "Maybe thumbtack it to the wall?"

Fleming went into his bedroom, and returned a moment later with several maps.

"I don't have any thumbtacks," he said seriously. "I'll lay these on the floor."

"Fine."

"OK, what do you want to know?"

"I know a little bit about what's going on in Europe," Fowler said. "And your area of expertise is the Pacific. So let's start with that."

I have a counterpart, maybe in the Army, who's doing this for him for Europe. I'll be damned!

"Where should I start?"

"December seventh," Fowler said. "I know you're not prepared for this, Flem. Would it help if you went on the premise that I know nothing about it?"

"OK," Pickering said, getting on his knees beside the large map. "Here's the way the pieces were on the board on December seventh. The U.S. Pacific Fleet was here, at Oahu, in the Hawaiian Islands. That's about three thousand nautical miles from San Francisco, and four thousand from Tokyo. It's as far from San Francisco to Hawaii as it is to New York. And it's about as far from San Francisco to Hawaii as it is from New York to London.

"Wake Island is here, 2,200 miles from Tokyo and 2,500 from Pearl Harbor. Guam, here, is two thousand miles from Tokyo, and four thousand from Pearl, and it's about two thousand miles from Tokyo to Luzon, in the Philippines, and 8,500 from the West Coast to Luzon."

Pickering sat back and rested on his heels.

"So, Factor One is that distances in the Pacific favor the Japanese."

"Obviously," Fowler said.

"Factor Two is protection of the sea lanes. We lost most of our battleships at Pearl Harbor. How *well* they could have protected the sea lanes is a moot point, but they're gone. And, obviously, their loss had a large part to do with the decision to pull back Task Force 14 to Pearl, and not to reinforce Wake Island."

"Should we have taken the chance with the aircraft carriers and reinforced Wake?" Fowler asked.

"I think so. We could, in any event, have made taking it far more costly. The Japanese do not have a really good capability to land on a hostile beach. They managed it at Wake because there was not an effective array of artillery on Wake. They only had one working rangefinder, for one thing. And not much ammunition. And no planes. All were aboard Task Force 14. I think they should have been put ashore."

Fowler grunted.

"Again, now a moot point, Wake is gone. So is Guam. On December tenth, the Japanese landed two divisions on Luzon. Three weeks later they were in Manila. We are now being pushed down the Bataan Peninsula. It will fall, and eventually so will Corregidor."

"It can't be reinforced?"

"There is a shortage of materiel to load on ships; a shortage of ships; and the Japanese have been doing a very creditable job of interdicting our shipping."

"And how much damage are we doing to them?"

"MacArthur has slowed down their advance. From our intercepts, we know that the Japanese General—Homma is his name; interesting guy, went to school in California, speaks fluent English, and did not, *did not,* want to start this war—anyway, Homma is under a lot of pressure to end resistance in the Philippines. It's a tough nut to crack. After they finally get rid of Luzon and Corregidor, they have to take Mindanao, the island to the south. We have about thirty thousand troops there, and supplies, under a general named Sharp."

"Why don't they use his forces to reinforce Luzon?"

"Transportation. If they put out to sea, the Japanese have superiority: submarines, other vessels. It would be a slaughter."

"And what are we doing to the Japanese?"

"Very little. They're naturally husbanding what's left of the fleet: aircraft carriers, cruisers. . . ."

"What about our submarines?"

"Our torpedoes don't work," Pickering said simply.

"What do you mean, they don't work?"

"They don't work. They either don't reach the target, or they do and don't explode."

"I'd never heard that," Fowler said, shocked. "Not *all* of them?"

"No, of course, not all of them. But apparently many. A hell of a lot, maybe half, maybe even more. The submarine brass, obviously, are not talking about it much. The story goes that submarine captains returning to Pearl Harbor who complained have been ordered to keep their mouths shut. I'm going out there to see for myself."

"I can't understand that," Fowler said. "Didn't they have any idea they wouldn't work?"

"I don't know. I understand it has something to do with the detonators. And since the detonators are the brainchildren of some highly placed admirals, obviously the submarine captains, not the detonators, are at fault."

"How can you hide something like that? In training, I mean. A torpedo that doesn't explode?"

"They didn't fire many of them in training, apparently. I asked that question. It cost too much," Pickering said. "The admiral I asked also made it rather clear that he objected to a civilian, even one wearing a captain's uniform, asking questions like that of a professional sailor."

"How did that go down?" Fowler asked.

"I told him I had been master of a ship when he was still a midshipman."

"You didn't!"

"No, I didn't. I was tempted, Christ, how I was tempted. But I kept my mouth shut."

"I'm impressed, Flem," Senator Fowler said.

"OK. Let's get on with this. The Japanese were already in French Indochina. The French—I don't suppose they had much choice, with the Germans occupying France—permitted them to station troops and aircraft in Hanoi, Saigon, and other places, and there was a naval presence as well. From French Indochina, the Japs moved into Thailand. The Japanese have been in Korea for years.

"They landed in Malaya and conquered Singapore, our British allies having cleverly installed their artillery pointing in the wrong direction. The British surrendered seventy thousand men. That's the largest Allied surrender so far—Frank Knox told me it was the worst defeat the English had suffered since Burgoyne surrendered at Saratoga—but it will lose its place in the history books when the Philippines fall."

"There's no way we can hang on to the Philippines? Not even Mindanao? What about General Sharp and his thirty thousand men?"

"We probably could—hang on to Mindanao, I mean. But Roosevelt has decided the first stage of the war has to concentrate on Europe. That means no reinforcement for the Philippines."

"You sound as if you disagree."

"So far as I'm concerned, we should let the Germans and the Russians bleed each other to death," Pickering said. "But my theories of how the war should be fought have so far not been solicited."

"So what happens now?" Fowler asked.

"Well, we try to keep the Japanese from taking both Australia and New Zealand, which are obviously on their schedule. And we try to establish bases in Australia and New Zealand from which we can eventually start taking things back. It's six thousand five hundred miles from San Francisco to Brisbane. At the moment that sea lane is open. MacArthur has already been asked, politely, to leave the Philippines and go to Australia."

"What do you mean, 'asked'?"

"I mean *asked.* If he doesn't go, I suppose Roosevelt will eventually make it an order. General Marshall's been urging him to do it right away. MacArthur and Marshall hate each other, did you know that?"

"I'd heard rumors."

"When George Marshall was a colonel at Fort Benning, MacArthur was Army Chief of Staff. He wrote an efficiency report on Marshall, saying he should never be given command of anything larger than a regiment. MacArthur thinks Marshall—who's now in MacArthur's former position, of course—was returning the compliment when he recalled MacArthur as a lieutenant general."

"I don't understand."

"MacArthur retired as a general, a full four-star general, when he was Chief of Staff. Then he got himself appointed Marshal of the Philippine Armed Forces. When Roosevelt called MacArthur back from retirement to assume command in the Philippines, he called him back as a lieutenant general, with three stars—junior to a full general, in other words. MacArthur thinks Marshall was behind that. I frankly wouldn't be surprised if he was. Anyway, their relationship is pretty delicate.

"So the idea is that MacArthur will go to Australia. And that we will stage out of Australia and New Zealand. That's presuming we can hang on to New Zealand and Australia. There are no troops there to speak of. They're all off in Africa and England defending the Empire.

"And the Japanese know they can take it unless we can maintain a reasonably safe sea route to Australia and New Zealand, and they have already made their first move. On January twenty-third—which is what, three weeks ago?—they occupied Rabaul. Here."

He pointed at the map, at the Bismarck Archipelago, east of New Guinea.

"They've already established forces on New Guinea, and if they can build an air base at Rabaul, they can bomb our ships en route to Australia and New Zealand. And, of course, they can bomb New Zealand and Australia."

"And we're doing nothing about that, either?"

"In that briefcase you won't look at—"

"I told you why."

"—there is just about the final draft of an operations order from Admiral King. Unless somebody finds something seriously wrong with it, and I don't think they will, he'll make it official in the next couple of days. It orders the soonest possible recapture of Rabaul. To do that, we'll have to set up a base on Éfaté Island, in the New Hebrides."

"Where the hell is that?"

Pickering pointed to the map. Fowler saw that Éfaté was a tiny speck in the South Pacific, northwest of New Caledonia, which itself was an only slightly larger speck of land east of the Australian continent.

"Why there?"

"It's on the shipping lanes. Once they get an airfield built, they can bomb Rabaul from it. And again, once the airfield is built, they can use it to protect the shipping lanes."

"Have we got any troops to send there? And ships to send them in?"

"Army Task Force 6814, which isn't much—it's much less than a division—is already on the high seas, bound for Éfaté," Pickering said.

"Not even a division? That's not much."

"It's all we've got, and it's something."

"What about the Marines?"

"What about them?"

"Where are they? What are they doing?"

"The day the Japanese landed at Rabaul, the 2nd Marine Brigade landed on Samoa, reinforcing the 7th Defense Battalion. The 4th Marines, who used to be in China, are on Bataan. They're forming Marine divisions on both coasts, but they won't be ready for combat until early 1943."

"This is all worse than I thought. Or are you being pessimistic?"

"I don't think so. I think . . . if we can keep them from taking Australia, or rendering it impotent, we may even have bottomed out. But right now, our ass is in a crack."

"I heard . . . I can't tell you where . . ."

"Can't, or won't?"

"Won't. I heard that Roosevelt has authorized the launching of B-26 bombers from an aircraft carrier to bomb Japan."

"B-twenty-*fives,*" Pickering corrected him. "The ones they named after General Billy Mitchell. They're training right now on the Florida Panhandle."

"What do you think about that?"

"I think it's a good idea. It may not do much real damage, but it will hurt the Japanese ego, and probably make them keep a much larger home defense force than they have at home; and it's probably going to do wonders for civilian morale here. That's probably worth the cost."

"What cost?"

"I talked to Jimmy Doolittle. He used to be vice-president of Shell. Very good guy. He left me with the impression he doesn't really expect to come back."

"Jesus!"

"There are lieutenant colonels and then there are lieutenant colonels," Pickering said.

"You're talking about the one you buried?"

"You accused me of being cold-blooded."

"OK. I apologize."

"I wish I was," Pickering said. "Cold-blooded, I mean."

"I was going to use my knowledge of Jimmy Doolittle and the B-25s to dazzle you, and get you to tell me about the Marine Raiders."

"Same sort of thing, I think. Roosevelt is dazzled by all things British, and thinks we should have our own commandos. We have to have some kind of military triumph or the public's morale will go to hell."

"You think that's all it is? A public-relations stunt, for public morale?"

"I think there's more, but I don't find anything wrong with doing something to buttress public morale. And Roosevelt's at least putting his money where his mouth his. His son Jimmy is executive officer of one of the Raider battalions, the 2nd, now forming at San Diego."

"Tell me about it," Senator Fowler said. "You say you were out in San Diego?"

"After dinner. I didn't have any lunch."

"You buying?"

"Why not?"

They ate in the hotel's Grill Room, lamb chops and oven-roast potatoes and a tomato salad, with two bottles of Cabernet Sauvignon.

"Did I tell you," Pickering said, as he selected a Wisconsin Camembert from the display of cheeses, "that the 26th Cavalry in the Philippines just shot their horses? They needed them for food."

"Jesus Christ, Flem!" the Senator protested.

"Why don't I feel guilty about eating all this? Maybe you're right, Dick. Maybe I really am cold-blooded."

"I don't know whether you are or not, but that's the last you get to drink. I know you well enough to know there are times when you should not be drinking, and this is one of those times."

After dinner, Captain Fleming Pickering, USNR, returned to his suite, took a shower, had a nightcap—a large brandy—and went to bed.

Something happened to him that had not happened to him in years. He had an erotic dream; it was so vivid that he remembered it in the morning. He blamed it then on everything that had happened the day before, plus the Camembert, the wine, and the cognac.

He dreamed that Mrs. Ellen Feller, the missionary's wife, had come into his bedroom wearing nothing but the black lace underwear she had been wearing the day he met her, and then she had taken that off, and then he had done what men do in such circumstances.

(TWO)
Office of the Chief of Staff
Headquarters, 2nd Joint Training Force
San Diego, California
21 February 1942

Captain Jack NMI Stecker, USMCR, knocked at the open door of Colonel Lewis T. "Lucky Lew" Harris's office and waited for permission to enter.

"Come," Colonel Harris said, throwing a pencil down with disgust on his desk. "Why the hell is it, Jack, that whenever you tell somebody to put some simple idea on paper, he uses every big word he ever heard of? And uses them wrong?"

"I don't know, Sir," Stecker smiled. "Am I the guilty party?"

"No. This piece of crap comes from our beloved adjutant. They're worse than anybody, which I suppose is why we make them adjutants." He raised his voice: "Sergeant Major!"

The Sergeant Major, a very thin, very tall, leather-skinned man in his late thirties, quickly appeared at the office door.

"Sir?"

"Sergeant Major, would you please give this to the Adjutant? Tell him I don't understand half of it and that it needs rewriting. Tell him I said he is forbidden to use words of more than two syllables."

"Aye, aye, Sir," the Sergeant Major said, chuckling, winking at Stecker, and taking the clipped-together sheaf of papers from Colonel Harris's desk. "Sir, I presume the Colonel knows he's about to break the Adjutant's heart? He really is proud of this."

"Good," Harris said. "Better than good. Splendid! Tell him I want it in the morning. Anybody who writes crap like that doesn't deserve any sleep."

"Aye, aye, Sir," the Sergeant Major said, smiling broadly, and left the office.

"Close the door, Jack," Colonel Harris said. Stecker did so. When he turned around, there was a bottle of Jack Daniel's bourbon and two glasses on Harris's desk. "A little something to cut the dust of the trail, Jack?"

"It's a little early for me, Sir."

"We're wetting down a promotion," Harris said. "And now that I am about to be a general officer, I will decide whether or not it's a little early for you."

"In that case, General, I would be honored," Stecker said.

"I said '*about to be* a general.' Not 'am.' You listen about as closely as that goddamned Adjutant. You're going to have to watch that, Jack, now that you're a field-grade officer."

"Sir?"

"Now I've got your attention, don't I?" Harris said, pleased with himself. He handed Stecker an ex–Kraft Cheese glass, half-full of whiskey.

"Yes, Sir."

"Mud in your eye, Major Stecker," Colonel Harris said.

"I'm a little confused, Sir," Stecker said, as he raised the glass to his mouth and tossed the whiskey down.

"General Riley was on the horn just now," Harris said. He drained his glass and returned the bottle to the drawer before going on. "He said that my name has gone to the Senate for B.G., and presumably, as soon as they can—*if* they can—gather enough of them, sober enough to vote, for a quorum, the orders will be cut."

"It's well deserved," Stecker said sincerely.

"I'm glad you think so," Harris said softly. "Thank you, Jack."

Harris touched Stecker's arm in what was, for him, a gesture of deep affection.

Then the tone of his voice changed.

"But we were talking about *your* promotion, weren't we, *Major* Stecker? You owe me a big one for this, Major."

"I didn't realize that I was even being considered," Stecker said.

"Let me tell you what happened," Harris said. "You ever know a guy named Neville? Franklin G. Neville?"

"Yeah. The last I heard, he was on a tailgate assignment as a Naval attaché somewhere."

"In Finland. Well, he came back, got involved with parachute troops of all things, and made lieutenant colonel. A couple of days ago, he jumped out of an airplane at Lakehurst without a parachute, or at least with one that didn't work, and killed himself."

"I'm sorry to hear that."

"Well, they need a replacement for him. I remain to be convinced that paratroops have any place in the Corps, but we have them. I think if the Army came up with an archery corps, some wild-eyed sonofabitch in Headquarters would start buying bows and arrows and claiming it was our idea in the first place."

He looked at Stecker for a little appreciation of his wit, and found instead concern—perhaps even alarm—in his eyes.

"No, Major Stecker," he said, chuckling. "You are not going to the Para-Marines, or whatever the hell they call them. You are going to the 1st Division at New River, North Carolina, to replace the guy who is going to jump into—pun intended—the shoes of the late Colonel Neville."

"You had me worried for a moment," Stecker confessed.

"I could see that," Harris said. "Here's what happened: General Riley asked me if I had a major I could recommend to take this guy's place in the 5th Marines. He's the Exec of Second Battalion. I told him no, but that I did have a captain I knew for a fact could find his ass with either hand . . ."

"Battalion Exec? Christ, I don't know . . ."

"Come on, Jack. When I was a battalion commander, I had a master gunnery sergeant who made it pretty clear that he thought he could run the battalion at least as well as I could. His name was Jack Stecker."

"That attitude goes with being a gunny," Stecker said. "I'm not sure how it really works."

"Well, you're about to find out," Harris said. "The original idea . . . Riley is one of your admirers, Jack, did you know that?"

Stecker shook his head.

"Well, he is. The original idea was to send you there as a captain. But then, genius that I am, it occurred to me that, *A,* you're junior as hell, and that, *B,* if I had the battalion, I would assign an ex–master gunnery sergeant, now a captain, as a company commander."

"I'd like to have a company," Stecker said. "You know that."

"Yeah, well, we have nice young first lieutenants who can be trained to do that. By a battalion exec who knows what it's like in a battalion. So I told this to the General, and he said, 'Well, I guess we'll have to make him a major before we cut the orders sending him to New River.' "

"How's the Battalion Commander, and, for that matter, the Regimental Commander, going to like having somebody shoving Jack Stecker down their throats? They're bound to have somebody in mind."

"Well, they'll probably hate it at first, to tell you the truth. But after they are *counseled* by the Assistant Division Commander, I'm sure they will come to understand the wisdom of the decision."

"Why should he do that? I don't even know, off the top of my head, who the 1st Division ADC is."

"As soon as they can sober up enough senators for a quorum, his name will be Brigadier General Lewis T. Harris," Harris said.

Stecker, smiling, shook his head.

(THREE)
Office of the Chief of Nursing Services
United States Naval Hospital
San Diego, California
27 February 1942

"You wanted to see me, Commander?" Ensign Barbara Cotter, NC, USNR, asked, sticking her head into the office of Lieutenant Commander Jane P. Marwood, NC, USN.

"Come in, Cotter," Commander Marwood said. Commander Marwood, whom Barbara Cotter thought of as "that skinny old bitch," was in blues. She was a very small woman, and thin. With the three and a half gold stripes of a lieutenant commander on her jacket cuffs, and several ribbons over her breast, Barbara Cotter thought she looked like a caricature of a Naval officer, almost like a woman dressed up for a costume party.

Barbara saw that Lieutenant Commander Hazel Gower, NC, USN, her newly promoted immediate supervisor, was also in the office, standing up and looking out the window.

I'm in some kind of trouble, otherwise good ol' Hazel wouldn't be here. I wonder what I'm supposed to have done?

And then she had an even more discomfiting thought: *I wonder how long this is going to take?*

She was supposed to meet Joe Howard in forty-five minutes. She would be pressed for time as it was, going through the controlled-drug inventory with the nurse who would come on duty, and then getting out of her whites, grabbing a quick shower, dressing, and then meeting him at the main entrance.

She had been thinking about Joe—and about herself and Joe—when she'd been summoned to Commander Marwood's office. She had come to the conclusion that she was in love with him. *In love,* as opposed to *infatuated with,* sexually or otherwise. The emotion was new to her. She had been infatuated before. This was different.

Viewed clinically, of course, Barbara Cotter knew it was probably just sex alone, and nothing more than that. He was a healthy young male, and she was a healthy young female. There was nothing Mother Nature liked better than to turn on the chemical transmitters and receptors of a well-matched pair. She had a way of convincing both parties that the other was a perfect specimen, in all respects, of the opposite sex, and of turning off that portion of the brain that might question the notion that the two of them were experiencing an emotion never felt by anyone before.

What Mother Nature was after was propagation of the species, and Mother was totally unconcerned with the problems that might cause. Such as her family's reaction to someone like Joe, and that there was a war on, and that she was in the United States Naval Service.

But none of that really mattered to Barbara. The only thing that mattered was that when she was with Joe, in bed or out of it, she felt complete and content, and that when they were separated, she felt incomplete and miserable.

She had felt incomplete and miserable all week. Joe had gone somewhere in northern California with an officer and a sergeant from the 2nd Raider Battalion at Camp Elliott. They'd gone to some Army depot to get weapons for the Raiders.

She had been unpatriotically overjoyed with the realization that Joe was what he called an "armchair commando," a Marine officer who commanded only a desk, and was not about to be sent off to fight the Japanese. And that when he was in San Diego, he was free just about every night and every weekend, and not running around in the boondocks day and night, practicing war.

And in forty minutes he would meet her at the main entrance, and they would get in her car and drive over to the Coronado Beach Hotel, and because the bar looked so crowded, they would go upstairs and have a drink before dinner in the Pacific & Far Eastern Suite, which translated to mean that half an hour after she met Joe, forty-five minutes from now, they would be in one of the wide and comfortable beds in their birthday suits.

And now this, whatever the hell this is all about!

Barbara walked over and stood before Commander Marwood's desk.

I don't care what she thinks I've done, what good ol' Hazel has told her I've done. I will plead guilty, swear I will never do it again, and beg forgiveness. Just so I can meet Joe!

"Yes, Ma'am?"

"Apparently, Cotter," Commander Marwood said, "the Navy has decided there is a slot where you may practice your special skills."

What the hell is she talking about?

"Ma'am?"

"There has been a TWX from the Surgeon General's office," Marwood said. "Actually, two of them. The first of them requested a list of the nurses in San Diego with experience, or special training, in psychiatric service. I provided your name. The second TWX put you on orders."

"Excuse me?"

"This is your formal notification, Miss Cotter, of your selection for overseas service. Do you understand what I'm telling you?"

"No, Ma'am."

"I didn't think you would," Marwood said. "When a member of the Naval Service is officially notified that he, or she, is about to be sent to sea, or overseas, as I have just notified you, the officer making the notification is required to advise the person being sent overseas that failure to make the shipment—missing the ship or the airplane, or failing to report to the departure point as scheduled—is a more serious offense than simple absence without leave. Specifically, that offense is called 'absence without leave for the purpose of avoiding hazardous service.' Severe court-martial penalties are provided."

Barbara felt rage flow through her; Joe Howard was immediately forgotten.

"Are you implying that I would go AWOL?" she flared.

"Not at all," Commander Marwood replied.

"It sounded like it!"

"I don't like your tone of voice, Ensign Cotter," Commander Marwood said, angrily.

Barbara glared at Commander Marwood, but said nothing. Commander Marwood glared back.

Finally, Commander Marwood said, "Cotter, there was nothing personal in this. Regulations require that an individual being sent overseas be informed of the penalties provided for AWOL with the intent of avoiding hazardous service."

"Then I'm sorry," Barbara said.

"I'm really getting sick and tired of telling you, Cotter," Lieutenant Commander Hazel Gower said, "that a junior appends 'Ma'am' to whatever she says to a superior officer."

"I'm sorry, Ma'am," Barbara said.

Commander Marwood waved her hand in a sign that meant, *OK, forget it.*

"Where am I going?" Barbara asked, remembering just in time to append "Ma'am."

"I don't know," Commander Marwood said. "Possibly to Hawaii. Possibly elsewhere. If they were going to station you aboard one of the hospital ships, I think your orders would have spelled that out. All your orders say is that you are to report to the Personnel Center, San Diego Navy Yard, for overseas service."

"When?" Barbara asked.

"There's some processing to go through. A physical. Shots, that sort of thing. Getting your pay up to date. Getting your personal affairs in order. Making sure you have the necessary uniforms and equipment. That'll take a couple of days. Then you will be given a delay en route leave, up to fourteen days, which should give you time to go home. So, as a specific answer to your question, you will report to the Navy Yard two weeks from the day your processing is over and you begin your leave. When you will leave there depends on the availability of shipping."

"I see."

"Now, regulations also require that I ask you if there is any reason you wish to apply for relief from your orders on humanitarian grounds."

Joe Howard reappeared in Barbara's thinking.

"Sick parents, that sort of thing?" Commander Marwood pursued.

"No, Ma'am," Barbara said. "Nothing like that."

"I've scheduled your last day of duty for Sunday," Lieutenant Commander Gower said. "You can start your out-processing on Monday morning."

"I'd sort of planned on having the weekend off," Barbara said, adding, again, just in time, "Ma'am."

"Your shipping out has left me short of people," Commander Gower said. "I had to rearrange the shifts. That requires that you pull a shift on Sunday. Sorry."

Barbara nodded her understanding.

"That will be all then, Cotter," Commander Marwood said. "Good luck. I'll try to see you before you ship out."

"Thank you," Barbara said.

She had not appended "Ma'am" to her reply, but neither Commander Gower nor Commander Marwood called her on it.

When she was gone, Commander Gower said, "Well, there goes the romance of the century, down the toilet."

"That's a pretty goddamned bitchy thing to say, Hazel!" Commander Marwood snapped.

Ensign Barbara Cotter was twenty-five minutes late meeting First Lieutenant Joseph L. Howard. Her replacement was late, and taking the goddamned drug inventory took longer than it usually did, and then she caught herself just standing in the shower, washing the same shoulder over and over again, lost in thought, and with no idea whatever how long she'd been doing that.

And then when she finally got to the main entrance, he wasn't there.

He was here, and left.

Or he couldn't get off, and won't be here.

Oh, Jesus, now what?

A LaSalle convertible pulled up before the main entrance and tapped its horn. She saw a Marine officer in it.

No, goddamn you, I don't want a goddamned ride!

Where the hell can he be?

The Marine officer in the shiny LaSalle convertible blew the horn again. Barbara glowered at him, working up what she hoped was a magnificent look of contempt. The Marine officer waved at her.

Oh, my God, it's Joe!

She ran to the car as he opened the door.

"Hi!" he said, as she got in.

She kissed him. Hard. On the lips.

"They frown on public displays of affection," Joe said.

"Fuck 'em," Barbara said.

"Ooooh! I'll have to wash out your mouth with soap."

She slid next to him on the seat.

I'll have to tell him. But not just yet.

"Where did you get this?"

"Nice, huh?" he said.

"Where'd you get it?"

"It belongs to the guy from the 2nd Raiders," Joe said. "We're going to have dinner with him and his girlfriend."

"Do we have to?"

"I told him we would," he said. "Any reason you don't want to?"

"I wanted to be alone."

"He's a nice guy. A Mustang, like me. Out of the 4th Marines. But he went through officer candidate school. Killer McCoy."

"*Killer* McCoy?"

"Yeah. They call him that because he killed a bunch of Chinese and a couple of Italian Marines in China," Joe said admiringly. "He carries a knife in his sleeve."

He pointed to his left sleeve to demonstrate.

"You're kidding, right?"

"No, I'm not. Everybody in the Corps knows about Killer McCoy."

"I know," she said, aware that she was acting the bitch, "you and your friend the Killer and me, we're going to go down to the waterfront and see if we can pick a fight, right?"

"Hey!" he said. "What's the matter with you?"

"Sorry," Barbara said.

"Actually, we're going to the San Diego Yacht Club," Joe said. "How's that for class?"

"Where?"

"The Yacht Club. Killer lives there. On a yacht."

"I don't believe any of this conversation," she said.

"You'll see."

Twenty minutes later, they passed through the gates of the San Diego Yacht Club. And five minutes after that, they stepped from a floating pier onto the aft deck of a fifty-three-foot, twin-diesel-powered Mitchell yacht named *Last Time.*

"Hi!" a very good-looking young woman greeted Barbara. She wore her black hair in a pageboy, and was wearing shorts and a T-shirt. "Welcome aboard! I'm Ernie Sage."

"Hello," Barbara said.

A trim, brown-haired young man in shorts and a Hawaiian shirt appeared at the door to the interior. He was even younger than Joe.

"I was getting a little worried," he said. "And you're right, she's gorgeous!"

"I'm very glad to meet you," Barbara said. "I'm Barbara."

"I'm Ken McCoy," he said. "Romeo here has been bending my ear all week about you."

"He was just pulling your leg. He does that," Barbara replied. "He told me on the way over here that we were going to meet somebody who carries a knife in his sleeve, and is called 'Killer' because he kills people. Chinese and Italians, Joe said."

"Thanks a lot, asshole," Ken McCoy said furiously, and went back inside the cabin of the boat.

"Ken!" the girl called Ernie Sage said, and, after giving Joe a withering look, went into the cabin after him.

"What did I say?"

"I'm the asshole, not you. I should have warned you, getting called 'Killer' pisses him off."

"You mean it's true? He *has* killed people?"

Joe nodded.

Ernie Sage reappeared, holding Second Lieutenant Kenneth R. McCoy, USMCR, by the ear.

"Ken has something to say," she said.

"Ouch!" he said, as she twisted the ear. He looked at Barbara. "I apologize for my language." Ernie Sage let go of his ear, whereupon McCoy added, "I'm sorry I called your asshole of a boyfriend an asshole."

"You *bastard!*" Ernie Sage said, and jabbed him in the ribs.

"Hey, Ken," Joe said. "I'm sorry."

"Ah, forget it," McCoy said. "I never thought you were very bright."

"What we're going to do," Ernie Sage said brightly, "is do this all over again. Hello, my name is Ernestine Sage. This gentlemen is Lieutenant Kenneth R. McCoy. I know that you're Lieutenant Howard, but I don't believe I know this young lady."

"How do you do," Barbara said, going along, and deciding she liked both this young woman and her boyfriend. "I'm Barbara Cotter."

"How do you do," Ernie Sage said. "Welcome aboard the *Last Time.*"

"Miss Cotter?" Ken McCoy asked politely. "May I call you Barbara?"

"Yes, of course."

"Anybody ever tell you, Barbara, that your boyfriend is an asshole?"

"That did it," Ernie Sage said, and struck McCoy with both hands, palms open, on the chest—which action caused him to stagger backward, encounter the low rail of the aft cockpit, and do a backward flip into the water.

Joe Howard laughed deep in his stomach, went to the rail, looked over the side, and waved.

Whereupon Ensign Barbara Cotter struck Lieutenant Howard in the small of his back with both hands, palms open, which caused Lieutenant Howard to go over the side and into the water, face first.

Ernie Sage looked at Barbara Cotter.

"Why do I have this feeling that what we're witnessing here is the beginning of a long, close, rewarding friendship?"

"Oh, God!" Barbara wailed, and tears formed in her eyes.

"Did I say something wrong?" Ernie asked.

Barbara did not trust her voice to speak; she shook her head.

"I'm sorry, really sorry, if this upset you," Ernie said.

Barbara shook her head and made a gesture with her hand meaning that it didn't matter.

"Can I get you a drink?" Ernie asked.

"I got my orders today," Barbara blurted. "I haven't told him yet."

Ken McCoy's head appeared at the rail.

"If you're wearing anything that will melt in water, I respectfully suggest you have ten seconds to take it off."

"Barbara got her orders today," Ernie said evenly. "Joe doesn't know."

"Oh, Christ!" McCoy said. He hoisted himself into the boat. Then he turned and gave his hand to Joe Howard and hauled him aboard.

Joe stood there, dripping water onto the deck.

"Which of these two goes in first?" he asked.

"Barbara got her orders today," Ernie said.

"Oh, Jesus!" Joe said. "When?"

"I start processing Monday," Barbara said softly.

"When did you find out?"

"Just before I met you."

He took a couple of steps toward her, and then, remembering he was soaking wet, stopped.

And then she took several steps to him and threw herself in his arms.

(FOUR)
Pensacola Naval Air Station
Pensacola, Florida
1525 Hours 28 February 1942

The pilot of the Army Air Corps twin-engine "Mitchell" bomber was slight and balding. There were the silver leaves of a lieutenant colonel on his collar points. He picked up his microphone, then put it back in its hanger, adjusted the frequency of his transceiver, and then picked up the microphone again.

"Pensacola, Army Six-Four-Two, a B-25 aircraft, twenty miles east of your station, for approach and landing."

"Army Six-Four-Two, Pensacola, say again?"

"Six-Four-Two, a B-25 aircraft, twenty miles east of your station, for approach and landing."

"Army Six-Four-Two, be advised that Pensacola is closed to transient traffic without prior approval. Suggest you try Eglin Army Air Corps Field."

"Pensacola, Six-Four-Two has a Navy captain aboard who wishes to deplane at Pensacola. We will require no ground services."

"Army Six-Four-Two, advise Naval officer's name and purpose of his visit to Pensacola."

"Pensacola, the Navy Captain's Pickering. I spell: Peter Item Charley King Easy Roger Item Nan George. Be advised that any questions regarding him are to be directed to the Office of the Secretary of the Navy."

"Army Six-Four-Two, stand by."

There was a ninety-second pause.

"Army Six-Four-Two, Pensacola. You are cleared for a straight-in approach to runway two-seven. The winds are from the west at fifteen. The altimeter is two-nine-niner-eight. The time is two-five past the hour. Report over Pensacola Bay."

"Army Six-Four-Two, Pensacola. Thank you very much."

As the B-25 Mitchell, a light bomber, dropped low over Pensacola Bay, a telephone call was placed from the office of Base Commander, Pensacola Naval Air Station, to the office of the Secretary of the Navy:

"Office of the Secretary, Captain Haughton."

"Captain, this is Captain Summers. At Pensacola. I'm calling for the Admiral."

"What can I do for you?"

"Does the name Pickering mean anything to you, Captain?"

"Is Captain Pickering at Pensacola?"

"He's about to land here."

"Great! The Secretary's been wondering where he was. Would you ask him to call me just as soon as he can, please, Captain?"

"Yes, of course. Be glad to. Captain, we could probably be of greater usefulness to Captain Pickering if we knew what it is he's after at Pensacola."

Captain Haughton chuckled.

"I have no idea, I'm afraid, but I'm sure he'll tell you when he lands. When did you say that will be?"

"He should be landing right now. I'll relay the message."

Captain Summers first called the Officer of the Day.

"I don't know who this captain the B-25 wants to drop off—Pickering—is, Jack," Captain Summers said, "or what he wants. But pass the word to him to call

Captain Haughton in the Secretary of the Navy's office, as soon as he can. And then ask what we can do for him."

He then called Rear Admiral Richard B. Sayre, who stood third in the chain of command at Pensacola, and was, at the moment, the senior officer aboard. He reported what little he knew about Captain Pickering, and what steps he had taken. Admiral Sayre grunted, and then told Summers to keep him posted.

Less than a minute later, Admiral Sayre called back.

"Pickering, you said? The VIP from Washington?"

"Yes, Sir."

"Present my compliments to Captain Pickering, please, and inform him I would be pleased to receive him at my office at his earliest convenience."

"Aye, aye, Sir."

Captain Fleming Pickering was driven directly to Admiral Sayre's office from the airfield. The Admiral's aide was waiting on the sidewalk when the staff car pulled up, and escorted him directly to the Admiral's office.

"Welcome to Pensacola, Captain," Admiral Sayre said. "May I offer you a cup of coffee, or something a little stronger?"

"Admiral, I feel like a kid caught with his hand in the cookie jar," Fleming Pickering said. "I'm not here officially . . ."

"You did get the message to call Captain Haughton?"

"Yes, Sir. I did. Thank you. Sir, I was about to say that I'm not here officially, and that what I hoped to do was get off and back on the base with no one noticing."

"Oh?"

"Sir, I've been over at Eglin Field on duty. I've got a seat on the courier plane to Washington from here tomorrow morning. I have some personal business in Pensacola."

"I thought that might be it," Admiral Sayre said.

"Sir?" Pickering asked, surprised.

"He's a nice boy, according to both my wife and Doc McInerney," the Admiral said. "And actually, he's the reason I asked you to come to see me."

Pickering's surprise was evident on his face.

"Doc and I went through flight school here together," Admiral Sayre said. "We're still pretty close. When your boy was sent here, Doc called me and told me about him. And you. I frankly found it comforting."

"Sir?"

"He spoke highly of your boy—Pick, they call him, don't they?"

"Yes, Sir."

"And he said that the only favor you asked of him was that the Marine Corps didn't make him a club officer. I thought that spoke well of you, Captain. And, as I said, I found that rather comforting."

"Comforting, Sir?"

"Your son is in hot pursuit of my daughter," Admiral Sayre said. "I'm not supposed to know that, but I do."

Pickering didn't reply.

"You don't seem surprised to hear that," the Admiral said.

Pickering knew more than his son thought he knew about the boy's romantic affairs. There had been an astonishing number of them, and they could more accurately be described as "carnal" than "romantic."

"Pick is attracted to the ladies, Admiral," Pickering replied. "And vice versa. Actually, from what I've seen, more the latter than the former. I can only presume your daughter is not only extraordinarily good looking, but something special. Pick is seldom reported 'in pursuit'; usually the phrase is 'in flight from.' "

The Admiral chuckled.

"I have *seen* him," he said. "Good-looking young Marine officers driving Cadillac convertible automobiles do seem to attract the ladies, don't they?"

"I've noticed," Pickering said, chuckling.

"Once Martha told him, rather forcefully, that she's not interested, I would have thought that he would have looked elsewhere."

What is this? Did he call me in here to tell me to keep my son away from his precious daughter?

"Pick's not her type? Has he been making an ass of himself?"

"No. He's been a perfect gentleman," Admiral Sayre said. "And I have the feeling that Martha is more attracted to him than she's willing to admit to herself or anyone else."

"Admiral—"

"My daughter's a widow," Admiral Sayre interrupted. "Her husband, Admiral Culhane's boy, an aviator, was killed at Wake Island."

"Oh," Fleming Pickering said, and then added, "I'm sorry to hear that."

"He was a really nice kid," Admiral Sayre said. "It's a damned shame."

"Are you saying this . . . relationship . . . between Pick and your daughter is serious?" Pickering asked.

Hell, of course it's serious. Chasing after a widow, especially a widow whose husband has been dead only a couple of months, and especially after she told him to get lost, is simply not Pick's style.

"I don't know," Admiral Sayre said. "But since Colonel Doolittle was kind enough to drop you in my lap, I thought I should introduce myself and mention it."

"Colonel Doolittle?" Pickering asked, trying to sound confused.

"Oh, come on, Pickering. Doc and Jimmy and I used to race airplanes together. And I thought that, doing what you're doing, you would have learned by now that whenever two people know something, it's no longer a secret. I know what's going on at Eglin, and my Officer of the Day recognizes Jimmy Doolittle when he sees him in a cockpit window."

"I think, Admiral, if that invitation is still open, I will have a drink."

(FIVE)
The San Carlos Hotel
Pensacola, Florida
1725 Hours 28 February 1942

"Good afternoon, Sir," Second Lieutenant Richard J. Stecker, USMC, said to the Navy Captain. "May I help you, Sir?" The Captain was in the act of hanging up the telephone in the penthouse suite of the San Carlos Hotel.

Dick Stecker, a good-looking, trim young man wearing a fur-collared leather jacket over a flight suit, was torn between surprise, anger, and alarm at finding a fucking four-striper nosing around the suite. But he was a graduate of the United States Military Academy at West Point and a regular officer of the United States

Marine Corps, and West Pointers and regular Marine officers do not demand of U.S. Navy captains, *Who the fuck are you, and what are you doing in my hotel room?*

"You must be Lieutenant Stecker," Captain Pickering said.

"Yes, Sir."

"It has been reported to me that these quarters are not only infested with females of notorious reputation, but awash, as well, in cheap whiskey," Pickering said sternly.

Lieutenant Stecker looked stunned.

Another Marine second lieutenant, similarly dressed, stepped around Lieutenant Stecker to see what the hell was going on, and then yelped in delight:

"Dad! God, am I glad to see you! What are you doing here?"

He ran across the room and wrapped his father in a bear hug.

"I'm catching a plane out of here in the morning," Pickering said.

"You've been on the base?" Pick asked uneasily.

He does not want anyone to know that his father is a Navy captain. Good boy!

"Just to get off an airplane," Pickering said. "I was hoping I could bunk with you tonight."

"Hell, yes! But what are you doing down here?"

"I was over with the Army Air Corps at Eglin Air Force Base," Pickering said. "It's right down the coast."

"Doing what?"

"None of your business, Lieutenant."

"You're involved with the B-25s," Pick Pickering challenged.

"What B-25s?" Pickering asked innocently.

"As if you didn't know," Pick said. "They've got an airfield over there with the dimensions of an aircraft-carrier deck painted on it. And they're trying to get B-25s off it."

"I have no idea what you're talking about," Pickering said. "But if I were you, I'd watch my mouth. You haven't seen those posters, 'Loose Lips Sink Ships'?"

Pick's look was both hurt and wary.

"That sounded pretty official," he said after a moment. "You're my *father,* for Christ's sake!"

"Pick, you and I are officers," Pickering said.

"See, wiseass?" Dick Stecker said. "Learn to keep your mouth shut."

"I'd still like to know what the hell they think they're doing over there," Pick Pickering said.

"You keep wondering out loud about it, you can read all about it in the newspapers. In your cell at Portsmouth. I'm serious, Pick."

Their eyes met.

"I didn't mean to put you on the spot, Dad," he said. "Sorry."

"Forget it," Pickering said.

"Don't forget it," Dick Stecker said. "Write it on your goddamned forehead."

"Well, the both of you can go to hell," Pick said cheerfully. "You can stand here and feel self-righteous. I need a shower."

"Can I make you a drink, Captain Pickering?" Dick Stecker asked. "You name it, we've got it."

"At least one of the occupants of this rooftop brothel is an officer and a gentleman," Pickering said. "Scotch, please. With soda, if you have it."

"Yes, Sir. Coming right up."

"I saw your dad a while back. In San Diego."

"Yes, Sir. Dad wrote me that he'd seen you; that you were in the Corps in War One together."

"Is that what you call it now? 'War One'?"

"Yes, Sir. Isn't that what it was, the First World War?"

"At the time, it was called 'the war to end all wars,' " Pickering said.

Dick Stecker handed him a drink.

"Thank you," Pickering said. "Is my being here going to interfere with any serious romantic plans you two had for tonight?"

"No, Sir. Not at all."

"When I had them let me in here, I was a little surprised not to find an assortment of local lovelies," Pickering said.

"Yes, Sir," Stecker said uncomfortably, then blurted, "You're asking about Martha Culhane, aren't you, Captain?"

"I am. But I would rather Pick didn't know I knew about her. Something about her. If this puts you on a spot, the subject never came up."

Dick Stecker made a circling motion with his index finger at his temple.

"He's nuts about her," he said. "She's a widow. Did you know?"

Pickering nodded.

"He's really got it bad for her. And she won't give him the time of day."

"You think that's maybe what it is? That she's not interested? That his Don Juan ego is involved?"

"No. I wish it was."

"What do you think of her?"

"I don't know what to think," Stecker said. "Maybe it'll pass when we graduate and get the hell out of here. But I don't know."

"OK. Thank you. Subject closed."

They ate in the hotel dining room, which was crowded with men in Navy and Marine Corps uniforms.

Over their shrimp cocktail, Fleming Pickering told them he was headed, via Washington and the West Coast, for Hawaii.

"When are you coming back?"

"I don't know," Pickering said. "Captains, like second lieutenants, go when and where they're told to go."

That was not true. Although he was still traveling on the vague orders that Captain Jack NMI Stecker had described as "awesome," permitting him to go where and when he pleased, no questions asked, he now had specific orders from the Secretary of the Navy:

Stay at Pearl Harbor as long as you want, Flem; learn what you can. But the President is going to order MacArthur out of the Philippines and to Australia. I want you there when he gets there. I want to know what he's up to. Haughton will message you wherever you are when Roosevelt orders him to leave, if you're not already in Australia by then.

Lieutenants Pickering and Stecker laughed dutifully.

There was a stir in the room while they were eating their broiled flounder. Pickering followed the point of attention to the door. Rear Admiral Richard Sayre, a woman almost certainly his wife, and a beautiful young blond woman almost certainly the widowed daughter, followed the headwaiter to a table across the room. Moments later, a Marine captain, a Naval Aviator, walked quickly to join them.

"That's Admiral Sayre, Captain," Dick Stecker said. "He's number three at Pensacola. And his wife and daughter."

Fleming Pickering was aware that his son was looking intently, perhaps angrily, at Stecker.

"And Captain Mustache," Stecker added.

"Captain 'Mustache'?" Pickering asked.

"He's one of our IPs . . . Instructor Pilots," Pick said.

"Oh," Pickering said.

"And like a lot of people around here, he's got a crush on the Admiral's daughter," Stecker said.

"She's a beautiful young woman," Pickering said.

"Yeah," Pick said. "She is."

That was all he had to say about Martha Sayre Culhane. But he kept looking over at her. And when Fleming Pickering looked in that direction, more often than not, Martha Sayre Culhane was surreptitiously looking in their direction.

IX

(ONE)
Aboard the Motor Yacht *Last Time*
The San Diego Yacht Club
San Diego, California
7 March 1942

Ensign Barbara Cotter, USNR, and Miss Ernestine Sage were alone aboard the *Last Time*. Ensign Cotter was barefoot; she wore the briefest of white shorts, and her bosom was only barely concealed beneath a thin, orange kerchief bandeau. Miss Sage was wearing the briefest of pale blue shorts and a T-shirt, beneath which it was obvious she wore nothing else.

Although it was nearly noon, they were just finishing the breakfast dishes. They had been up pretty late the night before; there had been a certain amount of physical activity once they had gone to bed. After breakfast, they'd waved bye-bye to Lieutenants Joseph L. Howard, USMCR, and Kenneth R. McCoy, USMCR, as they departed for duty. Then Miss Sage had suggested to Ensign Cotter, "To hell with the dishes, let's go back to bed," and they had done just that, rising again only a few moments ago.

Barbara Cotter did not go home to Philadelphia on her overseas leave. She had called her parents and told them she was being shipped out; and no, she didn't know where she was going, and no, she wouldn't be able to get home before she left.

It was the first time she had ever lied to her parents about anything important, and it bothered her. But the choice had been between going home, alone, and staying in San Diego with Joe for the period of her leave. She was perfectly willing to admit that she was being a real shit for not going home, and then lying about it, but she wasn't sorry.

And in Ernie Sage she had found both a friend and a kindred soul; it was no time before Ernie offered Barbara and Joe the starboard stateroom for as long as they wanted it—just because they felt so close so quickly. Both of them were nice, Protestant, middle-class (in Ernie's case, maybe upper-class) girls who had gone to college and had bright futures. And both of them were shacked up with a couple of Marines.

And were completely unashamed about it.

In no time they were both sharing deep, mutual confidences:

The first time they had laid eyes on Joe and Ken, they had known in their hearts that if they wanted to do *that,* and they hoped they would want to do *that,* they were going to let them.

It was the first time either of them had *really* felt that way, although in Ernie's case there had been a poet from Dartmouth, and in Barbara's case a gastroenterologist, who had made them feel *almost* that way.

And they talked, seriously, about why those things were going on. Barbara's theory was that Mother Nature caused the transmitters and receptors to be turned on in the interests of propagation. And Ernie's tangential theory was that Nature wanted to increase pregnancies in time of war.

And they talked of getting pregnant, and/or of getting married. They both reached the same conclusion: they weren't going to get married, not right away, anyhow. Because Joe and Ken thought they were probably going to get killed—or worse, crippled—in battle, both men refused to consider marriage. Yet Barbara and Ernie both agreed that what they really wanted, maybe most in the world, was to make babies with Joe and Ken. If they did, Joe and Ken would be furious—for the same reason they didn't want to get married. And further, since it was really better to have a baby when the baby was wanted, it was probably really better to wait until The Boys Came Home.

And in the meantime, they played housewife, and they loved it. They either prepared elaborate meals in the *Last Time*'s galley, or they went out for dinner to the Coronado Beach Hotel dining room, or to some hole-in-the-wall Mexican or Chinese restaurant. They carried their men's uniforms to the laundry, sewed their buttons on, and bought them razor blades and boxer shorts and Vitalis For The Hair. And loved them at night. And refused to think that it couldn't last forever—or, in Barbara and Joe's case, not later than the time her orders gave her, 2300 hours 16 March 1942. She was supposed to report to the Overseas Movement Officer, San Diego Naval Yard; and for her the *Last Time* would turn into a pumpkin.

Ernie told Barbara that after she was gone, and after Ken McCoy had shipped out, she was going back to New York City and back to work. She promised to visit Barbara's family in Philadelphia then, and tell them about Joe. She would confirm what Barbara was going to write them about him once she was on the ship headed nobody would tell her where.

The telephone rang, and Ernie Page answered it, then held up the phone to Barbara.

"It's somebody from the Navy Yard," she said.

Lieutenant Joe Howard, ever the dedicated officer, had advised her that if she wasn't going home, she was required to let "the receiving station" (by which he meant the Navy Yard) know where she was and how she could be reached.

"Ensign Cotter," Barbara said to the telephone.

"Ma'am, this is Chief Venwell, of Officer Movement, at the Navy Yard."

"What can I do for you, Chief?"

"Ma'am, you're to report here, with all your gear, for outshipment by 0630 tomorrow."

"What are you talking about? I'm on leave until the sixteenth."

"No, Ma'am. That's why I'm calling. Your orders have been changed. You're to report in by 0630 tomorrow."

"Why?"

"Ma'am, I guess they found a space for you to outship."

"But what if I was in Philadelphia?"

"Ma'am?"

"I was authorized a leave to Philadelphia. You couldn't do this to me if I was in Philadelphia," Barbara said. "I couldn't get from Philadelphia to San Diego by six o'clock tomorrow morning."

"Ma'am, you're in San Diego," Chief Venwell said. "Ma'am, I'm sorry about this, but I can't do a thing for you."

(TWO)
The Coronado Beach Hotel
San Diego, California
8 March 1942

"It's been a long time since I came here with a man in uniform," Patricia Foster Pickering said to her husband as they approached the hotel entrance.

Fleming Pickering was at the wheel of a 1939 Cadillac Sixty-Two Special he had borrowed from J. Charles Ansley, General Manager, San Diego Operations, Pacific & Far Eastern Shipping. He looked at his wife in some confusion until he took her meaning.

"Oh," he said wickedly, "that stuck in your mind, did it?"

It was a reference to their rendezvous in San Diego in 1919. Corporal Fleming Pickering, USMC, was going through the separation process at the San Diego Marine Barracks when, unannounced, Miss Patricia Foster of San Francisco had shown up at the gate to announce that she just happened to be in the neighborhood and thought she would just drop by.

She had had a suite in the Coronado Beach, a complimentary courtesy rendered by the management to the only daughter of Andrew Foster, Chairman of the Board of the Foster Hotel Corporation. There she had presented him with a welcome-home present of a nature he had not really expected to receive until after their relationship was officially sanctioned by the Protestant Episcopal Church.

"From time to time, I think of it," she admitted.

Throughout their marriage, Patricia had often surprised him. She had surprised him at two-fifteen that morning by slipping, naked, into his bed at Charley Ansley's house on a bluff overlooking the Pacific.

He had called her from Oklahoma City to tell her that he was en route in a Navy plane to San Diego, where he had some business with the Navy. He also intended to see his secretary—soon his ex-secretary—aboard the U.S. Navy transport *President Millard G. Fillmore,* ex–*Pacific Princess.* He would then, he told her, see about catching a plane home.

She could expect him late that night, or early the following morning. They would have four or five days home before he had to take the San Francisco–Pearl Harbor courier plane. She should think of something interesting for them to do.

He had wrapped his arms around her in Charley Ansley's bedroom and somewhat sleepily asked, "What brings you here, honey?"

"You said I should think of something interesting for us to do," Patricia had said, gently touching a sensitive part of his anatomy. "How does this strike you?"

She had come to join him by plane to Los Angeles, and then on the damned Greyhound bus to San Diego. Over breakfast, she told him she thought it would be fun to borrow a car from Charley Ansley, drive to Los Angeles, have dinner with friends there, and then drive leisurely on to San Francisco, perhaps spending another night on the way.

He told her he had to make a quick call on the Admiral commanding the San Diego Naval Yard, prepare a quick memorandum for Frank Knox reporting what the Admiral had told him, and then find an officer courier to take it to Washington. He also told her that Ellen Feller had arrived a couple of days before and was in the Pacific & Far East suite at the Coronado Beach.

"She's going to work at CINCPAC," Pickering said. There was an implication that she was going to become secretary to someone else. That was not actually the case. Officially, Ellen was going to work with the highly secret cryptographic unit at Pearl Harbor, putting her knowledge of Japanese and Chinese to work. And she had a second mission, to serve as a conduit for Fleming Pickering's confidential reports to the Secretary of the Navy. He would prepare the reports himself and send them to her at Pearl Harbor, sealed, via an officer courier. At Pearl Harbor, Ellen Feller would encrypt them with a special code and send them to Washington, either by cable or radio, classified TOP SECRET, EYES ONLY, THE SECRETARY OF THE NAVY.

That way, only Pickering, Ellen Feller, a cryptographer who worked solely for Captain Dave Haughton, Haughton himself, and the Secretary of the Navy would ever see Pickering's reports. Knox knew that if more people were brought into the link, or if standard Navy encryption-decryption procedures were followed, the Navy brass would be reading Pickering's reports before they got to him. Since the reports made considerable reference to the Navy brass, including, for instance, Pickering's opinion of their ability and performance, it would not have been clever to offer them to the brass on a silver platter, as it were.

None of that, obviously, was any of Patricia's business.

"Aren't you going to miss her?" Patricia asked, poker-faced. He wasn't sure whether she was serious or teasing, or even if there was a touch of jealousy in the question.

"There's a war on, Madam. We must all make what sacrifices are necessary in the common good," Pickering replied sonorously.

After Pickering stopped the Cadillac in front of the door, he opened the car door and started to get out. As he did that, the doorman rushed over and said, "I'm sorry, Sir, we no longer offer valet parking . . ." And then he recognized Pickering. "I'll take care of it, Mr. Pickering. You going to be long?"

"We're going to have lunch."

"Then I'll leave it right over there, Sir. Nice to see you, Mrs. Pickering. It's been some time."

"Hello, Dick. How are you?" Patricia said.

Pickering called the Pacific & Far East suite from a house phone in the lobby.

"I'm not quite packed," Ellen Feller said. "Could you come up for a minute?"

"Sure," Pickering said. "The ship sails at two-forty-five, so I've been told."

"Then we have plenty of time."

Pickering put the phone down.

"She's not quite ready," he said.

"I thought she was Miss Efficiency of 1942?" Patricia said.

"We're not running late," Pickering said loyally.

"You go up," Patricia said. "I'll get her a box of candy or a basket of fruit. For Bon Voyage."

"I'll go with you."

"No, you won't. You know how I hate it when you breathe impatiently over my shoulder in a shop. And I know where the suite is."

(THREE)

Ellen Feller spent a good deal of time considering very carefully the pluses and minuses of her new assignment. Some of the pluses were inarguable. She'd been promoted from Oriental Languages Linguist to Intelligence Analyst. And after her name on her travel orders now appeared the parenthesized phrase "(Assimilated Grade of Lt. Commander)." That meant she was entitled to the privileges the armed forces gave to an officer of that rank; and that she was earning just about as much money as a Lieutenant Commander made.

Back in Washington, Commander Kramer had informed her that when she reached Hawaii, she would be provided with bachelor women officer's quarters on the Navy Base at Pearl Harbor. ("The last time I was there, lieutenant commander nurses had nice little bungalows; they'll probably assign you one of those.") And she would be entitled to membership in the officers' club, where she would take her meals, and have access to everything else—the base exchange and the golf course, that sort of thing—that a lieutenant commander would have.

A remarkably short time after starting as a temporary civilian employee brought in to help with foreign-language translation (really a sort of multilingual clerk), she had risen to the upper echelons of Navy intelligence. The proof was that she was privy to, and would be working with, the Big Secret: that the Navy had cracked the Imperial Japanese Navy code. And she would continue to work—though remotely—with Captain Fleming Pickering, who answered to nobody but the Secretary of the Navy.

It now seemed very unlikely that there would be any difficulty about the crates shipped home from China. And since she was going to Hawaii, it would no longer be necessary for her to make the weekly trips to the nursing home in Baltimore to see her father. Or to endure the hour-long sermon he always delivered.

There were just a few minuses to her promotion and transfer; and they were all spelled Captain Fleming Pickering, USNR.

She had been attracted to him from the very first moment she had met him in his suite in the Foster Lafayette Hotel. The expensively furnished suite itself represented a style of living that she had previously believed existed only in the movies. And as she had learned more about him, her fascination with him grew: He *owned* steamships, a *fleet* of them! His wife's father *owned* a chain of hotels, including the Foster Lafayette! He personally knew a large number of *very important* people, people like Senator Fowler and Henry Ford, and even the President of the United States!

There was a physical attraction, too. From that first day, she had wondered what it would be like to be in bed with him. He was tall, good looking, and in splendid physical shape. She loved the deep timbre of his voice. But just about as immediately, she also recognized that any notions of getting him into her bed were dangerous.

Since a rich and handsome man like Fleming Pickering must have had any number of women to choose from, she was convinced that he must have grown very selective. It was entirely possible that he would not be interested in her at all, and that any overtures from her would see her returned to her old job. It didn't especially surprise her to learn that he was faithful to his wife, and that they apparently had had a long and successful marriage . . . but it disappointed her, all the same.

After a while, as he grew to rely on her faithful services, she realized that he was taking her under his wing. She was protected by his authority and influence. If questions about the crates from China now came up, she was sure that she could convince him of her innocence, and that he would defend her—with all of his influence—against any accusations.

Of course, with her in Hawaii and Fleming Pickering in Australia—or God knew where else—that would no longer be the case. She would be an ex-employee, no longer his faithful right hand. She could probably call on him for help, but the situation would be changed. She might be an "assimilated lieutenant commander" in Hawaii, but she would no longer be Captain Fleming Pickering's assistant.

On the train to California, she wondered whether she had made a mistake in playing out her perfectly platonic half of their entirely platonic relationship. More than once she had seen him looking at her as a man looks at a desirable woman.

But it would now be in her interest for Fleming Pickering to remember her as a woman he had bedded, and who had asked for nothing from him. There had been several occasions in the Foster Layfayette suite when he might well have responded to an overture. More than once he had been at his Old Grouse beyond the point where his judgment was affected.

But she had let those opportunities pass, and there was nothing that would bring them back. That was really a pity, she thought ruefully. It almost certainly would have been a very pleasant experience to have Fleming Pickering in her bed. Or, for that matter, on the floor. Anywhere.

And then he had sent word that he would come to the hotel and see her aboard the ship.

(FOUR)

When Ellen Feller answered Pickering's knock at the door, she was wearing a dressing gown. It was flowing—and translucent. Not missionary-lady style, he thought, recalling the black lace underwear she had worn the day he met her. And in that grossly embarrassing erotic dream.

"Hi!" she said. "Come in. I'm almost ready. I just stopped to make myself a drink. Nerves."

"I didn't know you drank," Pickering said.

"There's a lot about me you don't know," Ellen said. She walked across the room to the bar. The light behind her revealed the outline of her body beneath the thin dressing gown. And certain anatomical details.

"Old Grouse," she said, reaching for a bottle. "I know how you like it."

She made a drink, and then held it out to him. Her upper leg parted the dressing gown as he, uncomfortably, walked to her to take the drink.

"I don't mind if you look," Ellen said.

"I beg your pardon?"

"I said, I don't mind if you look," she repeated. "I was beginning to think there was something wrong with me. The most fascinating man I've ever met, and he appears totally immune."

"Ellen . . ."

"Have a good look," she said. She tugged at the dressing-gown cord and it fell open. "Do I pass inspection?"

"My wife is on her way up here," Pickering said.

Oh, Goddamn it! What have I done now?

"I'm sorry," she said evenly, after a moment.

"You'd better get your clothes on."

"Pity," she said, then put his glass of Scotch down and walked into one of the bedrooms. She stopped at the door and looked at him. The dressing gown was still open.

"Fleming," she said, using his first name for the first time ever, "the last thing in the world I want is to cause you trouble with your wife."

He nodded.

"Thank you."

She walked into the bedroom, took the dressing gown off, and tossed it toward the bed. Then she walked, naked, to the door and closed it.

Jesus Christ! She must be drunk. I wonder if we can get through the next couple of hours without a major disaster.

Fantastic teats!

(FIVE)
United States Navy Yard
San Diego, California
8 March 1942

"Sir, I can pass you in, but not with these ladies," the Marine sergeant at the gate said, handing the identification card back to Captain Fleming Pickering, USNR.

"Sergeant, this lady is on orders," Pickering said. "Ellen, show him your damned orders."

Mrs. Ellen Feller took from her purse a thin stack of mimeographed orders and her identification card and handed them over the seatback to Pickering, who then passed them to the sergeant. The sergeant read the orders, looked at the ID card, compared the photograph on it with her face, and then handed it all back.

"Sir, this lady can pass. But the other one—"

" 'The other one' is my wife!" Pickering flared.

"Sir, she doesn't have any ID."

"Flem," Patricia Foster Pickering said, aware that her husband was about to lose his temper, "I'll just wait here. You put Ellen on the ship and come back and pick me up."

"Patricia, please butt out of this," Pickering said sharply.

They had managed to get through lunch without a disaster. When Ellen came out of the bedroom to meet Patricia, she was modestly dressed, her hair was done up in a simple bun, and she wore no makeup.

She thanked Patricia for the basket of fruit, apologized for not having been ready, and never again called him Fleming. She was a perfect lady at lunch. But he didn't want to set the stage for something happening aboard the ship by being alone with her there.

"Sergeant, please call the Officer of the Guard," Captain Pickering ordered.

"Aye, aye, Sir."

It took the Officer of the Guard three minutes to reach the gate in a Navy-gray Ford pickup. He found a Navy captain at the wheel of a glistening 1939 Cadillac Sixty-Two Special sedan, which did *not* have San Diego Navy Base identification. A civilian woman was next to him, a nice-looking lady wearing a diamond engagement ring that looked like it weighed a pound. Another woman was sitting in the back of the Cadillac. She was a little younger than the other one, but somewhat plain—not at all bad-looking, though. She had a Navy Department ID card and a set of orders giving her AAA travel priority to CINCPAC Headquarters in Hawaii.

The Officer of the Guard was a first lieutenant; Pickering thought he looked like a regular. The Officer of the Guard saluted.

"Good afternoon, Sir. May I help you?"

"My name is Pickering, Lieutenant. This lady is my wife. The other lady is Mrs. Feller, who is to board the . . . the *President Fillmore.* I don't want to leave my wife here at the gate while I take Mrs. Feller aboard."

"No problem at all, Sir," the Lieutenant said. "If you'll just follow me in the pickup."

Pickering looked at the sergeant who had denied him access.

"Sergeant, when I was a Marine corporal, there was a saying that 'a Marine on guard duty has no friends.' Do they still say that?"

"Yes, Sir, they do."

"Your sergeant, Lieutenant, was the soul of tact," Pickering said.

"I'm glad to hear that, Sir. If you'll just follow me, Sir?"

The little convoy moved out.

In the Cadillac, Patricia Foster Pickering said, "What was that all about?"

"That sergeant was just doing his duty. I didn't want to get him in trouble."

"Why should he?"

"The Lieutenant obviously knows who I am," Pickering said.

"Who you are? What a monumental ego! Am I missing something? Who *are* you?"

"I mean that I work for Frank Knox. We're in, aren't we? And what does ego have to do with it?"

In the cab of the pickup, the Marine Lieutenant said to the driver, "Take us down to the *Millard Fillmore.*"

"That's that great big civilian liner, Sir?"

"Yeah. They used to call it the *Pacific Princess.* As soon as I take that Captain up the gangplank, you find a telephone, call the Officer of the Day, and tell him that Captain Pickering just came into the yard, and that I'm escorting him aboard the *Millard Fillmore.* You get that name?"

"Yes, Sir. Pickering. Who is he?"

"He works for the Secretary of the Navy. He's got the brass scared shitless. He showed up here yesterday for a private conference with the Admiral, after which the Admiral thought Pickering was going back to Washington. But he didn't. He wasn't on the courier plane. They passed the word that the Admiral was to be notified the moment anybody saw him anywhere."

The pickup truck driver drove as close as he could to the great ship, and then stopped. The Lieutenant got out and walked to the Cadillac.

"This is as close as we can get, Sir. If you'll wait a moment, I'll get someone to carry the lady's luggage."

"I'm not too old to carry a couple of suitcases," Pickering said.

"Sir, they frown on officers, particular senior ones, carrying luggage."

"Oh, hell. OK. Go get someone, then."

"Aye, aye, Sir."

Pickering got out from behind the wheel, walked to the edge of the wharf, and looked up at the stern of the ship. Her once-glistening white hull was now a flat Navy gray. PRESIDENT MILLARD G. FILLMORE was painted in enormous letters across her stern. But if you looked closely, you could see where the raised lettering PACIFIC PRINCESS SAN FRANCISCO had been painted over.

Her superstructure was still mostly white, although her funnels were also in Navy gray, probably so that the Pacific & Far Eastern logo on them could be obliterated. Pickering had learned from the Admiral the day before that they were carrying a work crew aboard in order to finish the painting and to make other modifications under way. Shipping space was so tight they could not afford to take her out of service for modifications any longer than was absolutely necessary.

What I should be doing is standing on her bridge, preparing to take her to sea, not functioning as a make-believe Naval officer and high-class errand boy for Frank Knox.

"It's sad, seeing her in gray," Patricia said softly, at his elbow.

"It has to be done, I suppose," he said. "Anyway, she's now the Navy's. Not ours."

(SIX)

One by one, the umbilicals that tied the *President Millard G. Fillmore* to the dock were cut. Finally, only one gangplank remained, and there seemed to be no activity on that.

From the boat deck, Ensign Barbara Cotter, NC, USNR, looked down at the small crowd of people on the dock. Ernie Sage was there, and her Ken McCoy, and Joe. They had waved excitedly at each other when Barbara had found a place for herself at the rail. But that was forty-five minutes ago; now they just forced smiles and made little waves at each other.

Finally, three people appeared on the single remaining gangway, a Marine officer, a Navy captain, and a civilian woman.

"Oh, my God!" Ernie Sage said. "Ken, that's Pick's father and mother."

"Where?" McCoy asked.

"The Navy guy and the woman coming down the gangway."

"You want me to get their attention, or what?"

"No!"

"I know them. I met them when we graduated from Quantico."

"If they see me here, Aunt Pat would feel obliged to tell my mother," Ernie said.

"Just where do you think your mother thinks you are? She doesn't know what you're doing?" McCoy said.

"Will you just leave it, please?"

Right in front of them, two sailors pulled an enormous hawser free of a hawser stand, and it began to rise up along the steep side of the ship.

Joe Howard looked down the dock. Nothing now held the *President Millard G. Fillmore* to the shore.

"It's moving," Ernie said.

A rather small Navy band began to play "Anchors Aweigh."

The *President Millard G. Fillmore* was an enormous ship and difficult to get into motion. When the band finished "Anchors Aweigh" and segued into "The Marine Hymn" there were only a few feet of water between the ship and the dock. Then, in deference to a battalion of U.S. Army Engineers aboard, the band played "The Caissons Go Rolling Along." By the time that was finished, twenty feet of water separated the shore and the ship.

Then the ship added the power of her engines to that of the tugs; there was a swirl of water at her stern, and her stern moved farther away from the dock.

The band began to play "Auld Lang Syne."

Barbara Cotter and Joe Howard waved bravely at each other.

"You OK, Joe?" Ken McCoy asked.

"This is not the way it's supposed to be," Joe Howard said. "I'm the goddamned Marine, and here I am on the goddamned shore, waving good-bye as my girlfriend goes overseas."

The band stopped playing; and to the ticking of drumsticks on drum rims, they marched off toward a Navy-gray bus.

First Lieutenant Joe Howard walked to the end of the dock and stood there watching until the *President Millard G. Fillmore* sailed out of sight.

(SEVEN)

Eyes Only—The Secretary of the Navy

DUPLICATION FORBIDDEN
ORIGINAL TO BE DESTROYED AFTER ENCRYPTION AND TRANSMITTAL TO SECNAVY

Melbourne, Australia
Saturday, 21 March 1942

Dear Frank:

Despite a nearly overwhelming feeling that this should be addressed "Dear Mr. Secretary," I am complying with your orders to write this in the form of a personal letter; to include my opinions as well as the facts as I understand them; and to presume that I am your sole source of information regarding what is going on in this area of the world.

This is written in my apartment in the Menzies Hotel, Melbourne, which I was able to get through the good offices of our (Pacific & Far East) agent here. It is my intention to deliver it, triply sealed, into the hands of the Captain of the USS John B. Lester, a destroyer which put in here for emergency repairs (now just about completed), and that is bound directly for Pearl Harbor. Using my letter of authority from you, I will direct Captain (Lt. Commander) K. L. White to deliver it into the hands of Mrs. Feller, or, if for some reason that is impossible, to burn it.

TOP SECRET

His willingness to comply with those orders, it seems to me, depends on whether he accepts your letter of authority at face value. The whipping we have taken so far seems to me to have produced a lack of confidence here—perhaps even an aura of defeatism. What I'm suggesting is that he may decide either to throw this whole thing away or to open it, or to do something other than what I am ordering him to do. Ellen Feller—if she gets this—will be able to determine whether or not it has been opened. I would very much appreciate your advising me of the receipt of this, including when, and to tell me if this is the sort of thing you would like to have me continue to do.

Obviously, I did not get into the Philippines. Haughton's message that MacArthur had been ordered to leave Corregidor was waiting for me when I arrived in San Francisco from San Diego on March 10. I left the next morning for Hawaii aboard a Navy Martin Mariner. At CINCPAC, I was told that the only way into the Philippines, either Corregidor or Mindanao, would be by submarine. I had just missed the Permit, which was scheduled to be at Corregidor on the 13th, and another "courier" submarine was not scheduled.

I could not have reached Corregidor, in other words, until after MacArthur was gone. And it was made clear to me that it would be very difficult to leave the Philippines once I got there. Under those circumstances, I decided not to go. I visited the Special Detachment and told the commanding officer of your special orders to Mrs. Feller. He was very cooperative, and I feel there will be no problems with him.

The next morning, I left Hickam Field, TH, aboard an Army Air Corps B-17, one of a flight of four en route from Seattle to Vice Admiral Herbert F. Leary's command in Australia. We arrived without incident early on March 13.

I presented myself to Admiral Leary and showed him my letter of authority from you. He was obviously torn between annoyance at having someone from Washington looking over his shoulder and a hope that perhaps I could convince "those people in Washington" of the terrible shape things are in here.

The only bright light in the whole area, he said, was that elements of Task Force 6814, including some Engineer troops, had the day before landed on Efate Island. If Admiral King's order to recapture Rabaul as soon as possible can be carried out at all, it is essential for them to construct an air base on the island. I sensed that Leary is not overly confident that the Army can build such a field in a short time.

Leary also told me that a radio message had come from Corregidor reporting that MacArthur, his wife, and small son, together with President Quezon and some others, had left Corregidor at sunset, March 11, bound for Mindanao. They were aboard four PT boats; and there had been no report on them since then. Leary said he was not yet concerned; the boats were under the command of a

Lieutenant Buckley, whom he knows, and considers an extraordinarily competent officer.

He was far more concerned to learn that the Japanese have occupied the island of Buka, 170 miles southeast of Rabaul, and that aerial reconnaissance has shown them unloading the engineer equipment for building an airfield.

While I was in his office, he and I learned that MacArthur and his people had turned up safe. A radio came from General Sharp's headquarters on Mindanao reporting that "the shipment was received" but that it would "require some maintenance." Leary and I decided (correctly, it turned out) that this meant the trip had been rough on MacArthur and/or Quezon and/or the others. MacArthur is, after all, sixty-two, Quezon is even older, and they had just completed a long voyage in small boats across rough seas.

At this point Major General George S. Brett, the senior Army Air Corps officer here, entered the picture. Brett wanted Leary to dispatch four B-17s to Mindanao to pick up the MacArthur party and bring them here. Leary refused, citing as his reasons that the four planes had just flown from the United States and required maintenance; and that in any event, he needed them for operational use. He had just learned that the 20,000-odd Dutch troops on Java had surrendered, and in his opinion that had removed the last obstacle the Japanese had to overcome before invading Australia. He could not spare heavy bombers to carry passengers, no matter how important the passengers.

I was privy to this conversation. I think Leary knew what Brett wanted of him, and wanted me to hear it so that it would be reported to you.

Brett was highly upset. Part of it, I think, was that he placed more importance on getting the MacArthur party out of Mindanao than Leary does; and part of it was the humiliation an Air Corps officer felt about asking a Navy officer for Army Air Corps airplanes, and then getting refused. Anyway, Brett stormed out, promising that the President would hear about this and make it right. Leary said he did not see the need for immediate action; Sharp has 30,000 effective troops, and Mindanao is not in immediate danger of being overrun. The MacArthur party, he feels, can be safely taken off by submarine. I was prone to agree with Leary.

Brett came back shortly afterward, saying that he had learned of a B-17 that was available. Leary was already aware of it; it was an early model, old and worn, and he could not guarantee how safe it was. Brett insisted, and Leary gave in.

The plan was for MacArthur and party to be flown in the B-17 from Mindanao to Darwin, which is on the northern coast of Australia. There they would transfer to two civilian DC-3s Brett chartered from the Australian airlines and fly across the continent to Melbourne. General Brett graciously allowed me to fly to Darwin on one of the civilian airplanes.

We expected to find the MacArthur party waiting for us at Darwin. But on landing we learned that MacArthur had inspected the B-17 sent to pick him up, and had refused to fly in it. The airplane then returned to Australia without passengers.

Brett shortly afterward learned that Leary had changed his mind about the newer B-17s, and three of the four took off to get MacArthur. One of them had to turn back when it developed engine trouble over the Australian desert; the other two made it to Mindanao just before midnight on Monday (March 16). (These details from Lt. Frank Bostrom, Army Air Corps, who was the senior pilot, and who flew MacA's airplane.)

An engine supercharger on one of Bostrom's engines went out en route. He could have made it back without having it repaired, but it would have lowered his weight-carrying ability and caused other problems I don't really understand. He managed to get it repaired, however, which meant that he and the other B-17 could carry all of the MacArthur party (but none of their luggage).

But then another of Bostrom's engines acted up during takeoff, and he was really afraid he couldn't get the airplane off the ground. In the end, though, he managed it. After that, it was a five-hour flight to Darwin—about the same distance as from New Orleans to Boston—and there was violent turbulence en route. Nothing had been done to convert the airplanes from their bombing role. Mrs. MacArthur and the boy had the only "upholstery," a mattress laid on the cabin floor. MacArthur rode in the radio operator's seat.

Along with his immediate family, the general brought his staff out with him, none of whom, frankly, I care for—although MacArthur feels they are to a man superb officers. To me they're more like the dukes who used to surround a king.

As soon as they were able to establish radio contact with Darwin, they were informed that Darwin was under Japanese air attack and that they should divert to Batchelor Field, which is about fifty miles away. I was already there with the two Air Australia DC-3s, when they landed about nine in the morning (Tues., Mar 17). A good deal of what follows may well be unimportant—certainly, some of it is petty—but you wanted my opinion of MacArthur, his thinking, and the people around him.

He seemed very disturbed to find on hand to greet him only Brigadier Royce (who had been on the Air Australia plane with me), representing General Brett. For good cause, certainly, he looked exhausted.

I told his aide, a man named Huff, that I was your personal representative, and that I wished to pay my respects to MacArthur and ask him for his evaluation of the situation so that I could pass it on to you. Huff made it plain that MacArthur was entitled to a far more senior Navy officer than a lowly captain. He also felt that I had seriously violated military protocol by not presenting myself to Admiral Rockwell before daring to approach the throne of King Douglas.

Rockwell was the former senior Navy officer in the Philippines, and he came in on the second B-17.

Admiral Rockwell was displeased with me, too, and you may hear about that. There was a scene that in other circumstances would have been humorous, during which he kept demanding to know who was my immediate superior, to which I kept answering "Secretary Knox," to which he kept replying, ad infinitum, "You're not listening to me. I mean your *immediate* superior." During all this, he simply refused to look at my letter of authority from you until I answered the simple question of who was my immediate superior.

This little farce came to an end when Mrs. MacArthur recognized me. Not as a Naval officer, but as my wife's husband. Apparently, they had met in Manila, and Mrs. MacA. regards Patricia as a friend. Or at least a social peer. She told her husband of my connection with Pacific & Far East, and I was permitted to approach the throne.

I had met MacArthur only briefly once or twice before, and I am sure he did not remember those occasions; but he greeted me warmly and told me he was anxious to learn (these are his words as closely as I can remember them) "details of the buildup in Australia; troop and naval dispositions; and the tentative timetable for the recapture of Luzon."

I explained to him that there was no buildup; that there were only about 34,000 troops of any description in Australia; that the only unit of any size was the understrength 1st Brigade of the 6th Australian Division; and that the strategic problem as I understood it was to attempt to keep the Japanese from taking Australia—which might not be possible—and that, consequently, nothing whatever had yet been done about attempting to take Luzon back from the Japanese.

His eyes glazed over. He turned to another of his aides, a brigadier general named Sutherland, and said, "Surely he is mistaken." Then he marched off to a small shack where breakfast (baked beans and canned peaches) was served.

Brigadier Royce, who is a nice fellow, followed him into the shack. And later he emerged from it looking dazed. Mrs. MacArthur did not wish to fly anymore, perhaps ever again, and General MacArthur had therefore ordered Royce to immediately form a motorcade to transport the party to the nearest railhead. Royce had informed MacArthur that the nearest railhead was in Alice Springs, about as far away across the desert (1,000 miles or so) as Chicago is from New Orleans, and that, among other things, there were no vehicles available to form a motorcade.

MacArthur's response was, "You have your orders; put them into execution."

This apparently impossible situation was resolved by Major Charles H. Morehouse, an Army doctor who had come out of the Philippines with them. He told Royce that such a trip would proba-

bly kill the MacArthur boy, Arthur, who is five or six, and who was ill. Morehouse was feeding him intravenously. Morehouse also said that he could not guarantee whether MacArthur himself would live through a 1,000-mile automobile trip across the desert.

Royce somewhat forcefully suggested to Dr. Morehouse that he make this point emphatically to MacArthur. So Morehouse went into the shack. After several minutes MacArthur came out and announced, "We are prepared to board the aircraft." It was the royal "we," Frank.

We got on the airplanes. As the engines were being started, the air-raid sirens went off; several of the Japanese bombers attacking Darwin had broken off their attack and were headed for Batchelor Field. Whether or not they knew the MacArthur party was there, I don't know.

All the same, we got off safely, and made the trip to Alice Springs without incident. Alice Springs looks like a town in a cowboy movie, and it's the northern terminus of the Central Australian Railway . . . and it lies a good deal beyond the range of the Japanese Mitsubishi bombers.

Alice Springs, MacArthur announced, was as far as he intended to fly. He could not be moved from this position even after he was told that the next train would not come for six days. And then Ambassador Hurley[1] flew in to tell MacArthur that MacA. had been named Supreme Commander, Allied Forces, Southwest Pacific, by Prime Minister Curtin and President Roosevelt. He also tried to get MacA. to take a plane to Melbourne, but he had no more luck than anybody else.

So a special train was ordered up. We still had the Air Australia DC-3s. So Hurley and most of MacA.'s staff—except Huff, Sutherland, and Dr. Morehouse, the intimate guardians of the throne—flew off to Melbourne. I was sorely tempted to fly with them, and I might have gone—until General Sutherland imperiously ordered me to do it.

I guess I'm learning the Machiavellian rules of the game: I did not think the Personal Representative of the Secretary of the Navy should place himself under the orders of an Army officer.

The train arrived the next morning. It too looked like something from a cowboy movie: a tiny locomotive, two third-class coaches, and a caboose. The tracks there—between Alice Springs and Adelaide, a thousand-odd miles—are three feet between the rails. Should the Japanese invade Australia, this single-track, narrow-gauge railroad, with rolling stock to match, will simply not be adequate to supply, much less to transport, anything close to an infantry division. Which doesn't matter, I guess: we don't have an infantry division to transport; and if we did, one division would obviously not be adequate to repel a Japanese invasion.

[1]Patrick Jay Hurley, formerly Secretary of War and then Ambassador to New Zealand.

The first coach of the train had wooden seats; and the second held an Australian Army nurse, a couple of Australian Army sergeants, an army field stove, and a supply of food. It was a three-day trip. For the first twenty-four hours, no one spoke to me but the sergeants.

Then MacArthur sent for me. He ran Sutherland and Huff off and began a nonstop lecture that lasted several hours. Obviously, he was playing to you, vicariously, through me. He began with Japanese economics and politics and how these made the war in the Pacific inevitable. Then he discussed Japanese strategy generally and in the Philippines specifically. He had at his fingertips a literally incredible encyclopedia of dates, names, and figures (tonnages, distances, etcetera).

By the time it was over, I was dazed. Using the word very carefully, the man is clearly a genius. I shall never think of him again as just one more general. It seems to me now that he fits in the same category as Roosevelt and Churchill. I also believe that, like Roosevelt and Churchill, he sees himself as a latter-day Moses, divinely inspired to lead his people out of the desert. In this connection, he feels a personal obligation to the Filipinos.

MacA. seems to understand that Roosevelt's decision to aid Britain (and the Russians) first is irrevocable and that, as a good soldier, he will of course support it. But he also makes it plain that he believes the decision was the wrong one, made because (a) Churchill can play Roosevelt like a violin (and I rather agree with that), and (b) George Marshall, who has Roosevelt's ear, is determined that MacArthur shall not be allowed to demonstrate his military genius (which, of course, is absurd).

General Marshall (MacA.'s Deputy C/S; not the other one, obviously) boarded the train at a small station several hours before we got to Adelaide the next afternoon. I started to leave, but MacA. motioned for me to stay. Marshall then confirmed what I had told MacA. in Darwin; that there were no troops to speak of in all of Australia; and that there was doubt that Australia itself could be held.

Marshall said something to MacA. about creating a "Brisbane Line"; the Australian General Staff was planning to abandon the northern ports, including Darwin, to the Japanese, and attempt to hold the population centers along the southern and eastern coasts.

"They can just forget that," MacArthur said. "We shall hold Australia."

Logic told me, Frank, that that was highly improbable. But my heart told me that we would indeed hold Australia. MacArthur had just said so.

Marshall also reported that two companies of the 182nd Infantry and a company of Army Engineers had landed on Efate with orders to build an airfield, "whatever the hell that means."

Without reference to a map, <u>and more important, without my having told him that Admiral King had ordered the recapture of</u>

Rabaul—and if I hadn't told him, who else had this knowledge and could have?—MacArthur explained that Efate was an island in the New Hebrides, about 700 miles southeast of Tulagi, and that "someone with a knowledge of strategy" had seen the establishment of an air base there as essential to the recapture of Rabaul, which was itself essential to deny the Japanese a chance to make a successful landing on the Australian continent.

Marshall also told him that there would be reporters waiting for him in Adelaide, and that some sort of a statement would be expected.

The two of them started to work on that, and were still working on it when he arrived at Adelaide. This is, essentially verbatim, what he said there:

"The President of the United States ordered me to break through the Japanese lines for the purpose, as I understand it, of organizing the American offensive against Japan, a primary object of which is the relief of the Philippines. I came through, and I shall return."

If you want to know what he's thinking, Frank, I suggest you study that short speech carefully. It was not off the cuff.

The Commissioner of Railroads had sent his own private car to Adelaide, where it was attached to the Melbourne Express. From Adelaide to Melbourne, the track is standard width. I scurried around getting a sleeper on the train, and had just succeeded when Huff found me. I was, so I was informed, to have one of the staterooms in the private car. I don't know who was more surprised, Huff or me.

We got to Spencer Street Station, Melbourne, just before ten a.m. the next day. We backed in, with MacA. standing like a politician on the rear platform of the private car. There were half a hundred reporters in the station, and even an honor guard.

MacA. delivered another speech, which I am sure was as carefully prepared as the "I shall return" speech in Adelaide. In it, again just about verbatim, he said, "success in modern war means the furnishing of sufficient troops and materiel to meet the known strength of the enemy. No general can make something out of nothing. My success or failure will depend primarily upon the resources which the respective governments place at my disposal."

He cold-shouldered General Brett and General Royce at the station, rather cruelly I thought; and I think he's going to hold a grudge about the B-17s. There is no excuse for it that I can see. Nor—as I just learned from Huff—is there any excuse for recommending the award of a Presidential Unit Citation to every unit on Corregidor except the 4th Marines. His reason for not giving it to the Marines, again quoting Huff, is that "they have enough publicity as it is."

He also, politely, refused the offer of several mansions and moved into the Menzies. I can only wonder what will happen when he finds out that lowly Captain Pickering, USNR, occupies an identical apartment directly above him.

I don't think he has made up his mind what to do about me, and for the moment, at least, I am considered a member pro tem of the palace guard.

One final thing: I learned from the Australians that they have left behind, on various islands now (or about to be) occupied by the Japs, former colonial officers, planters, missionaries, etcetera. They are calling these people "Coastwatchers," and they feel they will be able to provide very valuable intelligence. They have commissioned them into the Royal Australian Navy Reserve, so they'll be under the Geneva Convention. I suspect that they are just whistling in the wind about that.

Admiral Leary does not seem to be impressed with their potential. I am. If we have anybody who speaks Japanese, and who can be spared, I suggest you send them over here now to establish a relationship with the Coastwatchers.

I really hope this is what you were hoping to get from me.

Respectfully,

Fleming Pickering, Capt., USNR.

(EIGHT)
Walker Hasslinger's Restaurant
Baltimore, Maryland
1 April 1942

The basic principles of both leadership and organization have evolved over many centuries. Among the most important of these principles is the chain of command. The military services, and for that matter any organization, may be thought of as a pyramid. Authority and responsibility flow downward from the pinnacle, passing through progressively junior levels of command. Simplistically, if the first sergeant of an infantry company, for example, wants a PFC to load a truck with sandbags, he does not stop the first PFC he encounters and tell him to do so. Instead, he tells a platoon sergeant, who tells a section leader, who tells a corporal, and the corporal selects the PFC who gets the sandbags loaded.

To do otherwise would create chaos. The corporal would wonder where his PFC had gone without orders. The man in charge of the sandbags would question the PFC's right to take them away. The truckdriver would not know why sandbags were being loaded on his truck.

The chain of command is even more important at the highest echelons of military and naval service. Although in law the Secretary of the Navy has the authority, he does not issue direct orders to captains of ships, or even to commanders-in-chief of the various fleets.

He tells the Chief of Naval Operations what he wants done, in general terms: "I think we should reinforce the Pacific Fleet." The Chief of Naval Operations decides how the Pacific Fleet should be reinforced, again in rather general terms: "Add a battleship, two cruisers, and a half-dozen destroyers." As the order moves down through the pyramid, other officers make more specific decisions and issue more specific orders: which battleship, which cruisers, and which destroyers; in other words, which commands will lose assets to reinforce the Pacific Fleet, and when.

Only six or seven levels down in the chain of command will the captain of a destroyer finally order the officer of the deck to make all preparations to get under way, and then to set course for the Hawaiian Islands. And he will not associate the movement of his vessel with a vague suggestion given to the Chief of Naval Operations by the Secretary of the Navy.

The chain of command is so important that it is almost never violated. People at the top, civilian or military, very rarely issue orders to anyone not in the level of command immediately subordinate to them.

But there are exceptions to every rule.

Captain David Haughton, USN, Administrative Assistant to the Secretary of the Navy, got off the Congressional Limited of the Pennsylvania Railroad and climbed the stairs to the Baltimore Pennsylvania Station. He walked across the waiting room, left the station, and turned right. He was in uniform, and he was carrying a black briefcase.

A block away, he entered the bar of Walker Hasslinger's Restaurant, a Baltimore landmark that justly enjoyed the reputation of serving the finest seafood in town. Captain Haughton had been coming to Walker Hasslinger's since he was a midshipman at Annapolis. He looked up and down the bar for the man he was here to meet, but didn't find him.

He took a stool at the bar, and reached for a bowl of oyster crackers.

"The free lunch went out when the New Deal came in," a large, red-faced man in chef's whites said, sliding the bowl out of his reach. "Now it's cash on the bar."

But Eckley Walker, the proprietor, was smiling and extending his hand.

"How are you, Dave?" he said. "It's been some time."

"You still serving those condemned oysters?" Haughton said.

"Only to sailors who can't tell the difference," Walker said. He snapped his fingers and a bartender appeared. He said only one word, "Rye," but made certain gestures with his head and hand that conveyed to the waiter that he wanted a dozen oysters and two drinks, the latter from his private bottle of rye whiskey, which was kept out of sight.

The bartender poured stiff drinks, added a dash of ginger ale, and slid them across the bar.

"Mud in your eye," Walker Hasslinger said. "Good to see you, Dave."

"Bottoms up," Haughton said.

They smiled at each other.

A slight, tall, balding man in civilian clothing, holding a beer glass, slipped onto the stool next to Haughton.

"Amazing, the strange people you run into in obscure, out-of-the-way restaurants," he said.

"Eckley," Haughton said, "have you got a little room someplace where this guy can make his life-insurance pitch without disturbing the paying guests?"

"We've already got one," the slight man said.

"I'll have them take the oysters there, if you like," Eckley Walker said.

"Please," Haughton said.

Walker nodded. "Enjoy your lunch."

As they walked to the rear of the bar, the slight man turned and said, "I suppose I should warn you. I've got my boss with me."

"Is there a reason for that?"

"He asked me where I was going, and when I told him, he said he thought he would come along. If you don't like that, tell him."

There was a door at the end of the barroom, opening on a flight of stairs. At the top of stairs was a corridor. The tall, slight man opened a door and gestured for Haughton to precede him.

A trim man, his gray hair shorn in a crewcut, sat at the table. A napkin was tucked into his collar to protect his pin-striped, double-breasted blue suit from dripping butter as he attacked a steaming pile of crab and shrimp.

"You look unhappy to see me, Haughton," he said. "Now I'm glad I came."

"Good afternoon, General," Haughton said. "I am a little surprised, Sir."

"Consider your hand shaken, Captain," said Brigadier General Horace W. T. Forrest, Assistant Chief of Staff G-2 (Intelligence), USMC. "My fingers are dirty."

"Thank you, Sir," Haughton said.

"I could tell you I came here because this is the best seafood on the East Coast, but that would be a lie. What the hell are you up to, Haughton?"

"I'm acting for the Secretary, Sir," Haughton said.

"Clever fellow that I am, I already had that figured out," General Forrest said, "but the question was, 'What the hell are you up to?' "

There was a knock at the door, and the waiter appeared with a battered oblong tray holding what looked like two dozen oysters.

"Why don't you order while he's here?" General Forrest said. "Then we can talk without being disturbed every two minutes."

"Can I get a lobster?" Haughton asked. The waiter nodded. "A cup of clam chowder and a lobster, then, please," Haughton said.

"Twice," the slight man said. He was Lieutenant Colonel F. L. Rickabee, USMC. Rickabee was carried on the organizational chart of Headquarters USMC as being assigned to the Office of Congressional Liaison. That had absolutely nothing to do with what he really did.

"And to drink? A bottle of wine?" the waiter asked.

"I don't want a whole bottle," Haughton said.

"We'll help you, Haughton," General Forrest said. "Yes, please. A dry white."

"And a lobster for you, too, Sir?"

General Forrest looked at the shrimp and oysters before him.

"What the hell, why not? I just won't eat again for the next couple of weeks. But hold the clam chowder."

The waiter left.

"You were saying, Haughton?" General Forrest said, the moment the door closed.

Haughton hesitated just perceptibly. He had decided that Rickabee had told him the truth, which was that General Forrest had asked where he was going, and Rickabee had told him. He knew Rickabee well enough to know that while he often would do a great many things without telling General Forrest, he would not evade a question from him. And Forrest was naturally curious as to why the Secretary of the Navy's alter ego wanted to meet Rickabee in a restaurant in Baltimore, rather than somewhere in Washington. That implied an unusual degree of secrecy, and that had fired his curiosity.

"I have a project for Colonel Rickabee, General," Haughton said. "One which we will fund from the Secretary's Confidential Fund."

General Forrest, who had just popped a large shrimp in his mouth, gestured for Haughton to continue.

"Do you know Captain Fleming Pickering, Sir?" Haughton asked.

"I don't *know* him. I know who he is. I *don't* know what he's doing."

"He's in Australia, Sir, as the Secretary's personal liaison officer to General MacArthur."

"The admirals must love that," Forrest said dryly.

"Captain Pickering has learned from the Australians of a special force they have. Coastwatchers. They have arranged for people who lived on the islands in that area—plantation managers, civil servants, even some missionaries—to remain behind when the islands were lost to the Japanese—"

"I've heard about that," Forrest cut him off.

"Captain Pickering feels that these people have an enormous intelligence potential," Haughton went on. "His opinion is apparently not shared by senior Navy officers in the area."

"I can understand that," Forrest said. "I mean, hell, everybody knows that if you didn't go to Annapolis, you're stupid, right?"

Haughton smiled at General Forrest, but did not rise to the challenge. "The Secretary feels that Captain Pickering is right, and that these people could be of great use to us," he said. "He is, however, understandably reluctant to intervene personally and override the officers in question."

Forrest grunted.

"What I wanted to discuss with Colonel Rickabee was the formation of a special Marine unit to establish contact with the Coastwatcher organization, see what, if anything, we can do to assist them, and ensure that their intelligence is readily available to us when we commence operations in that area. In the interests of efficiency, and considering the time element, the Secretary feels that setting up such an organization under Colonel Rickabee is the way to go."

"And with a little bit of luck, maybe the admirals won't find out what's going on, right, until it's too late to do anything about it?"

"That's just about it, Sir."

"Now drop the other shoe, Haughton," Forrest said. "You couldn't hide an operation like that from the admirals, and both you and I know it."

Did I handle that badly? Or is he that clever? You don't get to be head of Marine Corps intelligence by being dull, and it's a sure thing he and Rickabee played "What's Haughton up to?" for an hour, as they drove over here from Washington.

"In addition to his liaison duties with General MacArthur's headquarters, Captain Fleming is performing other, classified, duties for the Secretary," Haughton said.

"Spying on the admirals, you mean," Forrest said. "And, of course, MacArthur."

"I don't think I'd use those words, Sir."

"I'll bet those are the words the admirals are using."

"If they are, Sir, they're wrong," Haughton said.

Forrest met his eyes. "They are?" he asked softly.

"The Secretary feels that he needs a set of eyes on the scene. Expert eyes. Dispassionate. Perhaps *nonparochial* would be a better word. Captain Pickering has been charged with reporting to the Secretary on matters he feels will be of interest to the Secretary. If the Secretary feels that's necessary, I don't think it appropriate for me to categorize it as 'spying.' "

"You don't?"

"I think Captain Pickering's role is analogous to that of an aide-de-camp in the nineteenth century. Or the eighteenth. He has no command function. All he is, as aides on horseback were, is an extra set of eyes for the commander."

Captain David Haughton had originally been offended both by the way Fleming Pickering had entered the Navy—commissioned from civilian life as a captain, a rank Haughton had taken eighteen years to reach—and by the role intended for him. It had taken him a long time and a lot of thought to come up with the aide-de-camp analogy. But once he had reached it, he knew it to be the truth.

"You dropped the other shoe, Haughton," General Forrest said, "but so far I haven't heard it."

"The Secretary feels that Captain Pickering can better perform his duties if he has some help," Haughton said carefully. "What I had hoped to get from Colonel Rickabee is an officer who could, covertly, provide that help, in addition to his intelligence duties. With the Coastwatchers, I mean."

"A *junior* aide-de-camp on a horse, huh?" Forrest said dryly. He looked at Colonel Rickabee.

"Banning," Rickabee said.

Forrest grunted.

"Excuse me?" Haughton asked.

"We have an officer," Forrest said, "who just might fit the ticket. He used to be the 4th Marines' intelligence officer in Shanghai. In the Philippines, too. He went blind over there—temporarily, apparently some sort of concussion from a Japanese artillery round—and they evacuated him by submarine. He regained his sight. Just made major. Bright, tough officer. His name is Ed Banning."

"There would be few raised eyebrows in the Corps," Rickabee said, "or in the Navy, if Banning was sent to Australia with an intelligence detachment."

"You seem pretty willing to go along with Haughton," Forrest said.

"I want to get in with the Coastwatchers," Rickabee said. "I think that's important. And this way, we get the Confidential Fund to pay for it."

"And, just incidentally, you'd like to know what Pickering is reporting to the Secretary, right?" Haughton said.

"You're a pretty bright fellow, Haughton," General Rickabee said. "Why aren't you a Marine?"

Haughton laughed.

"You seem rather unconcerned about the possibility that Banning would report to me what your man Pickering is up to, and that I would promptly tell the Navy," General Forrest said.

"I've always thought you were a pretty bright fellow yourself, General," Haughton said. "Certainly bright enough to know that would not be in your best interests."

General Forrest glared icily at Haughton for a long moment. Finally he looked at Rickabee. "You're right, Rickabee," he said. "He *is* a Machiavellian sonofabitch. I like him."

The door banged open, and the waiter returned with an enormous tray heaped high with steaming lobsters.

X

(ONE)
Headquarters
U.S. Marine Corps Parachute School
Lakehurst Naval Air Station
Lakehurst, New Jersey
8 April 1942

First Lieutenant R. B. Macklin, USMC, (Acting) Commanding Officer, USMC Parachute School, had a problem. He had been directed by TWX from Headquarters USMC to furnish by TWX the names of volunteers for a special mission. The volunteers must be enlisted men of his command who met certain criteria. He was to furnish these names within twenty-four hours.

That special mission was officially described as "immediate foreign service of undetermined length; of a classified nature; and involving extraordinary hazards. Volunteers will be advised that the risk of loss of life will be high."

The criteria set forth in the TWX directed that "volunteers should be at least corporals but not higher in rank than staff sergeants; and have no physical limitations whatever.

"The ideal volunteer for this mission will be an unmarried sergeant with at least three years of service who has, in addition to demonstrated small-arms and other infantry skills, experience in a special skill such as radio communications, demolitions, rubber-boat handling, and parachuting.

"Especially desirable are volunteers with French and Japanese language fluency, oral or written. Individuals who are now performing, or in the past have performed, cryptographic duties are not eligible."

In compliance with his orders, Lieutenant Macklin had his First Sergeant gather together all the corporals, sergeants, and staff sergeants of his command in the brand-new service club, where, after warning them that the subject of the meeting was classified and was not to be discussed outside the room where they had gathered, he read them the pertinent portions of the TWX.

There were twenty-one men present. Nineteen of them lined up before the First Sergeant, and he wrote their names down on a lined pad on his clipboard.

Viewed in one way, nineteen of twenty-one eligibles volunteering for an undefined mission where "the risk of loss of life will be high," could be interpreted as one more proof that young Marine noncoms were courageous, red-blooded American patriots, eager for an opportunity to serve their country, regardless of the risk to their very lives.

Viewed in another, more realistic, way, Lieutenant Macklin was very much afraid that if he forwarded the names of all nineteen, as he had been directed, questions would be asked as to why ninety percent of his junior noncoms were willing to take such a chance. It suggested, at the very least, that they didn't like their present assignment and would take a hell of a chance to get out of it.

And that would tend to reflect adversely on the professional reputation of First Lieutenant R. B. Macklin, USMC.

And of course, if he sent the names forward and only half of them wound up on orders, that would play havoc with the parachute training program. And if the program collapsed, that too would reflect adversely on his professional reputation.

Lieutenant Macklin was very concerned with his professional reputation, especially since Colonel Neville had jumped to his death before there had been time for him to write an efficiency report on Macklin. Macklin didn't even know who was going to write his efficiency report, now that Neville was dead.

But he did know that unless he handled this volunteer business the right way, he was in trouble.

He flipped through the stack of service records on his desk.

Every one but two of those ungrateful, disloyal sonsofbitches volunteered! Goddamn them! Willing to leave me in a lurch like this, making me look like some Captain Bligh with a mutiny on his hands! The ungrateful bastards, after all I've done for them!

He wondered who the two loyal Marines were. He compared the names of the volunteers against the roster.

Staff Sergeant James P. Cumings, the mess sergeant, was one of those who had not volunteered. Cumings was in his middle thirties, a career Marine, married and with a flock of kids.

Nor had Corporal Stephen M. Koffler. He was the little sonofabitch who went AWOL and then turned out to be the first one to reach Colonel Neville's body on The Day That It Happened.

And then he had been painted as some sort of hero and given an unjustified promotion to corporal—just because he happened to be next out of the airplane when the Colonel jumped to his death.

He was practically useless around here, too. The first sergeant had him driving a truck.

Christ, you'd just know that the one sonofabitch you would like to get rid of would be the only one that doesn't want to go!

Lieutenant R. B. Macklin, USMC, tapped his pencil absently against his white china coffee cup as he thought the problem through.

The basic question, he thought, is what is *best for the Corps?*

While it's probably true that whatever these volunteers are needed for is important, I don't know *that. What I* do *know is that parachutists are the wave of the future, and ergo, that the parachute school is very important, perhaps even critical, for future Marine operations in the Pacific and elsewhere. It follows logically from that that if I lose all, many, or even* any *of my middle-ranking noncommissioned officers to whatever it is they have volunteered for, I am setting parachute training back for however long it would take to train their replacements. I don't think I have the right to do that to the Marine Corps.*

I do know *that Corporal Stephen M. Koffler is* not *needed around here. Truckdrivers are a dime a dozen.*

First Lieutenant R. B. Macklin made his decision.

"First Sergeant!" he called.

(TWO)

First Sergeant George J. Hammersmith, having determined that Corporal Koffler had not been given a pass and that he was not in his barracks, looked for him first in the slop chute, and finally located him in the service club.

The service club was a new building that had been put up in a remarkably short time not far from the huge dirigible hangar. It was a large building, two stories tall in the center, and with one-floor wings on either side. It had been furnished with upholstered chairs and couches, tables, magazine racks, and pool and Ping-Pong tables. Somewhere down the pike there was supposed to be a snack bar and a small stage for USO shows and for a band, for dances.

With the exception of Corporal Koffler and two hostesses in gray uniforms, it was now empty. Lieutenant Macklin thought that parachutist trainees had more important things to do in their off-duty hours than loll around on their asses, and had placed the service club off limits to trainees except on weekends.

The permanent party did not patronize the club very much. There was a club, with hard liquor, for noncommissioned officers, and a slop chute, beer only, for corporals and down. Furthermore, the permanent party was well aware that the First Sergeant and other senior noncoms held the belief that only candy-asses would go someplace where you couldn't get anything to drink or do anything more than smile at the hostesses.

Corporal Koffler was sitting in an upholstered armchair, a can of peanuts at his side, reading the *Newark Evening News,* on which there was a banner headline: BATAAN FALLS; WAINWRIGHT'S FORCES WITHDRAW TO FORTRESS CORREGIDOR.

That news had been on the radio all day, and it had bothered George Hammersmith. He had a lot of buddies with the 4th Marines, and the last he'd heard, they'd taken a real whipping. And he'd done his time in the Far East. There was no way that Corregidor could hold out for long. The fortress had been built on an island in Manila Bay to protect Manila; and Manila was already in the hands of the Japanese.

That little shit probably doesn't have the faintest fucking idea where the Philippines are, much less Corregidor. Sonofabitch probably never even looked at the front page, just turned right to "Blondie and Dagwood" in the comic section.

First Sergeant Hammersmith restrained a surprisingly strong urge to knock the paper out of Koffler's hands, but at the last moment he just put his fingers on it and jerked it, to get Koffler's attention.

"Jesus!" Koffler said. He was, Hammersmith saw, surprised but not afraid. So far as he knew, there was nothing wrong with Koffler except that Macklin had a hard-on for him. He had never explained why, and Hammersmith had never asked.

"Got a minute, Koffler?"

"Sure."

"You was at the formation when they asked for volunteers, wasn't you?"

"I was there."

"I was sort of wondering why you didn't volunteer."

Because I'm not a fucking fool, that's why. "Volunteers will be advised that the risk of loss of life will be high." I learned my lesson about volunteering when I volunteered for jump duty. So I didn't volunteer for whatever the fuck this new thing is.

"I didn't think I was qualified," Steve said.

"Why not?"

"They want people with special skills. I don't have any. I don't speak Japanese or French, or anything."

"You're a Marine parachutist," Hammersmith said.

"I just made corporal," Steve said. "I ain't been in the Corps a year."

"You're yellow, is that it?"

"I'm not yellow."

"You didn't volunteer."

"That don't mean I'm yellow; that just means I don't want to volunteer."

"What's Lieutenant Macklin got on you?"

"I don't know."

"He doesn't like you."

"Maybe because they promoted me."

"Maybe. But I do know he doesn't like you. He thinks you're a worthless shit."

"I didn't know that."

"I don't like you, either," Hammersmith said. "You're supposed to be a Marine, and you're yellow."

"I'm not yellow."

"You were given a chance to volunteer for an important assignment, and you didn't. In my book that makes you yellow."

"They said 'volunteer.' "

"And you didn't."

"What do you want from me, Sergeant?"

"I don't want anything from you."

"Then I don't understand what this is all about."

"Just a little chat between Marines," First Sergeant Hammersmith said, "is all."

"You want me to volunteer, that's what this is all about."

"If I made you volunteer, then you wouldn't be a volunteer, would you?" Hammersmith asked. "Don't do nothing you don't want to do. But you know what I would do if I was you?"

"No."

"If *I* was in an outfit where *my* company commander thought *I* was a worthless shit, and *my* first sergeant thought I was yellow, *I* would start thinking about finding myself a new home."

(THREE)
San Diego, California
17 April 1942

Major Edward J. Banning, USMC, arrived in San Diego carrying all of his worldly possessions in two canvas Valv-Paks.

That fact—that he had with him all he owned—had occurred to him on the Lark, the train on which he had made the last leg of his trip from Los Angeles. He had flown from Washington to Los Angeles.

He had once had a good many personal possessions, ranging from books and phonograph records to furniture, dress uniforms, civilian clothing, a brand-new Pontiac automobile, and a wife.

Of all the things he'd owned in Shanghai six months before, only one was left, a Model 1911A1 Colt .45 pistol; and that, technically, was the property of the U.S. Government. The 4th Marines were now on Corregidor. Banning sometimes mused wryly that in one of the lateral tunnels off the Main Malinta tunnel under the rock, there was probably, in some filing cabinet, an official record that the pistol had been issued to him and never turned in. The record—if not Major Ed Banning or the 4th Marines—would more than likely survive the war. And his estate would receive a form letter from the Marine Corps demanding payment.

His household goods had been stored in a godown in Shanghai "for later shipment." It was entirely credible to think that some Japanese officer was now occupying his apartment, sitting on his chairs, eating supper off his plates on his carved teak table, listening to his Benny Goodman records on his phonograph, and riding around Shanghai in his Pontiac.

He did not like to think about Mrs. Edward J. (Ludmilla) Banning. Milla was a White Russian, a refugee from the Bolshevik Revolution. He had gone to Milla for Japanese and Russian language instruction, taken her as his mistress, and fallen in love with her. He had married her just before he flew out of Shanghai with the advance party when the 4th Marines were ordered to the Philippines.

There were a number of scenarios about what had happened to Milla after the Japanese came to Shanghai, and none of them were pleasant. They ranged from her being shot out of hand to being placed in a brothel for Japanese enlisted men.

It was also possible that Milla, who was a truly beautiful woman, might have elected to survive the Japanese occupation by becoming the mistress of a Japanese officer. Practically speaking, that would be a better thing for Milla than getting herself shot, or becoming a seminal sewer in a Japanese Army comfort house.

Ed Banning believed in God, but he rarely prayed to Him. Yet he prayed often and passionately that God would take mercy on Milla.

He was profoundly ashamed that he could no longer remember the details of Milla's face, the color of her eyes, the softness of her skin; she was fading away in his mind's eye. Very likely this was because he had taken another woman into his bed and, for as long as the affair had lasted, into his life. He was profoundly ashamed about that, too. No matter how hard he tried to rationalize it away, in the end it was a betrayal of the vow he had made in the Anglican Cathedral in Shanghai to cleave himself only to Milla until death should them part.

He had met Carolyn Spencer Howell in the New York Public Library. He had been sent to the Navy Hospital in Brooklyn, ostensibly for a detailed medical examination relating to his lost and then recovered sight. But he was actually there for a psychiatric examination. During his time in Brooklyn he was free—indeed, encouraged—to get off the base and go into Manhattan. (There'd also been strong hints that female companionship wouldn't hurt, either.)

Carolyn was a librarian at the big public library on 42nd Street in Manhattan. He went to her to ask for copies of the *Shanghai Post* covering the months between the time he had left Milla in Shanghai and the start of the war. He also wanted whatever she had on Nansen Passports. As a stateless person, Milla had been issued what was known as a Nansen Passport. He had a faint, desperate hope that perhaps the Japanese would recognize it, and that she could leave Shanghai somehow for a neutral country. Because Banning had given her all the cash he could lay his hands on, just over three thousand dollars, Milla didn't lack for the resources she'd need to get away. Would that do her any good? Probably not, he realized in his darkest moments.

He did not set out to pursue Carolyn as a romantic conquest. It just happened.

Carolyn was a tall, graceful divorcee. Her husband of fifteen years, whom Banning now thought of as a colossal fool, had, as she put it, "turned her in for a later model, without wrinkles."

They met outside the library in a small restaurant on 43rd Street, where he'd gone for lunch. And they wound up in her bed in her apartment. Banning and Carolyn were very good in bed together, and not only because being there ended long periods of celibacy for each of them. They both had a lot of important things they needed to share with someone who was sensitive enough to listen and understand. He told her about Milla, for instance, and she told him about her fool of a husband.

It was nice while it lasted, but now it was over. He could see in her eyes that she knew he was lying when he said good-bye to her and told her he would write. And she actually seemed to understand, which made him feel even more like a miserable sonofabitch.

Since Carolyn knew about Milla from the beginning, they managed to convince themselves for a while that they were nothing more than two sophisticated adults who enjoyed companionship with the other, in bed and out of it. They both told themselves that it was a temporary arrangement, with no possibility of a lasting emotional involvement—much less some kind of future with a vine-covered cottage by the side of the road. They thought of themselves as friends with bed privileges, and nothing more.

But it became more than that. Otherwise, why would a sophisticated, mature woman be unable to keep from hugging her friend so tightly, not quite able to hold back her sobs, while a Marine major tried, not successfully, to keep his eyes from watering?

The bottom line seemed to be that he was in love with two women, and he was in no position to do anything for either of them.

Major Jack NMI Stecker, USMC, was waiting on the platform when Major Ed Banning threw his Valv-Paks down from the club car. There was nothing fragile in the bags except a small framed photograph of Carolyn Howell she had slipped into his luggage. He had found it while rooting for clean socks when the plane had been grounded for the night in St. Louis.

They shook hands.

"How'd you know I'd be on the train?" Banning asked.

"Colonel Rickabee called and told me what plane you were on. And I knew you couldn't get a plane further than L.A. And I didn't think you would take the bus."

"Well, I'm grateful. When did you put the leaf on, Major?"

"Day before yesterday. I just cleared the post. *You* can put *me* on the train in the morning."

"You didn't stick around because of me, I hope?"

"Well, sort of. I got you an office, sort of, in a Quonset hut at Camp Elliott, and I thought I should show you where it is. You've already got eight people who reported in. I put the senior sergeant in charge and told him you would be out there in the morning."

"Thank you," Banning said, simply.

They walked to Stecker's Ford coupe. When Stecker opened the trunk, there were two identical Valv-Paks in it. There was not enough room for two more, so one of Banning's was put in the backseat.

Stecker got behind the wheel and then handed Banning a sheet of teletype paper.

HEADQUARTERS US MARINE CORPS
WASHINGTON DC 1345 9APR42

COMMANDING GENERAL
2ND JOINT TRAINING FORCE
SAN DIEGO, CAL

1. SPECIAL DETACHMENT 14 USMC IS ACTIVATED 9APR42 AT CAMP ELLIOTT CAL. DETACHMENT IS SUBORDINATE TO ASSISTANT CHIEF OF STAFF FOR INTELLIGENCE, HEADQUARTERS USMC.

2. INTERIM TABLE OF ORGANIZATION & EQUIPMENT ESTABLISHED MANNING TABLE OF ONE (1) MAJOR; TWO (2) CAPTAINS (OR LIEUTENANTS); AND SIXTEEN (16) ENLISTED MEN.

3. COMMANDING GENERAL 2ND JOINT TRAINING FORCE IS DIRECTED TO PROVIDE LOGISTICAL AND ADMINISTRATIVE SUPPORT AS REQUIRED.

BY DIRECTION OF THE COMMANDANT:
HORACE W. T. FORREST, BRIG GEN USMC

Stecker started the car. After Banning had read the teletype message, he said, "That came in day before yesterday. The G-2 here is very curious."

"I'll bet he is," Banning said. "Do I get to keep this?"

"Yeah, sure."

Banning looked out the window and saw they were not headed toward Camp Elliott.

"Where are we going?"

"Coronado Beach Hotel," Stecker said. "I figured before you begin your rigorous training program, you're entitled to one night on a soft mattress."

"What training program? My orders are to collect these people and get them on a plane to Australia."

"You just can't do that," Stecker said. "There's a program to follow. You have to draw your equipment—typewriters, field equipment, a guidon, field stoves, organizational weapons, training films and a projector to show them—all that sort of thing. Then you start the training program. If there's no already published training program, you have to write one and submit it for approval."

Banning looked at Stecker with shock in his eyes, and then saw the mischief in Stecker's eyes.

"Jack?"

"Well, that's what I'm going to have to do the minute I get to New River and start to organize a battalion," he said. "And I figured that if I have to do it, you should."

"You had me worried."

"You *are* going to have to do some of that stuff. You're going to have to turn in a morning report every day, which means you will need a typewriter and somebody who knows how to use it. There's all kinds of paperwork, Ed, that you just won't be able to avoid—payrolls, allotments, requisitions."

"That never entered my mind."

"That's why I brought it up," Stecker said. "Maybe one of the people you've recruited can handle the paperwork, but just in case, I had a word with the G-1 about getting you a volunteer who can do it for you."

"Jesus!" Banning said.

"The Marine Corps, Major," Jack Stecker said solemnly, "floats upon a sea of paper."

"I'd forgotten."

"Your manning chart calls for two company-grade officers," Stecker said. "You got them?"

"No. I asked for McCoy—and not only because he speaks Japanese. But I got turned down flat."

"You know what McCoy is up to. That didn't surprise you, did it?"

"I guess not."

"I know a guy—Mustang first lieutenant—named Howard. He doesn't speak Japanese. Before the war, he was on the rifle team. He's been seeing that the 2nd Raider Battalion got all the weapons they thought they wanted. That's about over. Good man."

"How come you don't want him for your battalion?"

"I do. I offered him a company."

"And?"

"He told me he wasn't sure he could handle it. He was at Pearl on December seventh. He panicked. He found himself a hole—actually a basement arms room—and stayed there. *After* he saw that the arms were passed out."

"That doesn't sound so terrible."

"He thinks it makes him unfit to take a command."

"You don't, I gather?"

"No. And I told him so. I think he would be useful to you, Ed."

"Would he volunteer?"

"I don't know. All you could do is ask him, I suppose."

"Where would I find him?"

"You'll see him tomorrow. I told him to keep an eye on your people."

"All this and the Coronado Beach Hotel, too? Or are you pulling my leg about that, too?"

"No," Stecker chuckled. "That's where we're going. Truth being stranger than fiction, I've got the keys to the Pacific & Far Eastern Shipping Company suite there. They keep it year round for the officers of their ships who are in port."

"How the hell did you work that?"

"The guy that owns the company and I were in France together."

"His name is Fleming Pickering, and he's a captain in the Navy reserve."

"How'd you know?"

"He's the man I'm to report to in Melbourne," Banning said. "I didn't know about you and him. Or that he'd been a Marine."

"Somehow, I don't think you were supposed to tell me that."

"I'm sure I wasn't."

"Then I won't ask why you did. But at least that solves the problem of where you sleep while you're out here."

"You mean in the hotel?"

"Sure. Why not? I'm sure Pickering would want me to give you the keys. And speaking of keys, I'm going to leave you the Ford, too."

"I don't understand that."

"Well, cars are getting harder and harder to come by. They've stopped making them, you know, and people are buying up all the good used cars. I figure that I'll be out here again, or my boy will, or else friends who need wheels. So why sell it? I've got two cars on the East Coast."

"Jesus, Jack, I don't know . . ."

"I've already arranged to park it in the hotel garage. Just leave the keys with the manager when you're through with it."

"Things are going too smoothly. A lot of that, obviously, is thanks to you. But I always worry when that happens."

"You know what the distilled essence of my Marine Corps experience is?" Stecker said.

"No," Banning chuckled.

"You don't have to practice being uncomfortable; when it's time for you to be uncomfortable, the Corps will arrange for it in spades. In the meantime, live as well as you can. I'm surprised you didn't learn that from McCoy."

Stecker pulled up in front of the Coronado Beach Hotel.

"Here we are," he said. "Of course, if you'd rather, I can still drive you out to Elliott, and the Corps will give you an iron bunk and a thin mattress in a Quonset hut."

"This will do very nicely, Major Stecker, thank you very much."

"My pleasure, Major Banning."

(FOUR)
Headquarters Motor Pool
2nd Joint Training Force
Camp Elliott, California
18 April 1942

When First Lieutenant Joseph L. Howard, USMCR, walked up to the small shack that housed the motor pool dispatcher, he gave in to the temptation to add a little excitement to the lives of the dispatcher and the motor sergeant. Both of them, he saw, were engrossed in the *San Diego Times.*

He squatted and carefully tugged loose from the ground a large weed and its dirt-encrusted root structure. Then he spun it around several times to pick up speed, and let it fly. It rose high in the air.

"Good morning," Lieutenant Howard said loudly, marching up to the dispatch shack.

The weed reached the apogee of its trajectory, and then began its descent.

The motor sergeant looked up from his newspaper and got to his feet.

"Good morning, Sir," he said, a second before the weed struck somewhere near the center of the tin roof of the dispatch shack. There was a booming noise, as if an out-of-tune bass drum had been struck.

"Holy fucking Christ!" the motor sergeant said, "what the fuck was that?"

"Excuse me?" Lieutenant Howard said. "Were you speaking to me, Sergeant?"

The motor sergeant, still wholly confused, looked at Lieutenant Howard suspiciously.

"If the chaplain," Joe Howard said, still straight-faced, "heard a fine noncommissioned officer such as yourself using such language, Sergeant, he would be very disappointed."

The sergeant's wits returned.

"What the fuck did you do, Lieutenant?" he asked. "You scared the shit out of me."

"You're not really suggesting that an officer and gentleman, such as myself, would do anything to disturb your peace and quiet, are you, Sergeant?"

"No, Sir, I'm sure the Lieutenant wouldn't do nothing like that," the motor sergeant said, "but I used to know a wiseass armorer corporal at Quantico who had a sick sense of humor."

Howard laughed. "Les, you looked like you were coming out of your skin."

"You shouldn't do things like that to an old man like me."

"I'm trying to keep you young, Les."

"Christ, you got a letter," the motor sergeant said.

"Huh?"

"Mail clerk brought it over," the motor sergeant said. "He called over here yesterday, looking for you. Said the letter had been there three days. I told him you would be here this morning. Wait till I get it."

He rooted in a drawer and came out with a small envelope and handed it to Howard. There was no stamp on the envelope, just a signature. As a member of the armed forces of the United States serving overseas, the sender was given the franking privilege.

Howard's heart jumped when he saw the return address. He tore the envelope open and resisted the temptation to sniff the stationery; he thought he detected a faint odor of perfume.

He was afraid to read the letter. He hadn't heard from Barbara since she'd sailed, and was beginning to wonder if he ever would. His fear grew when he saw how short the letter was, and how it began:

Special Naval Medical Unit
Fleet Post Office 8203
San Francisco, California

My Dearest Joe,

Well, here I am. I can't tell you where.

We have been told that, because we are officers and can be trusted not to write home things that would interest the enemy, our mail will not be censored. It will be, however, subject to "random scrutiny." What that means, I think, is that the senior nurses here will open outgoing letters they think will be interesting, in terms of intimacy. Consequently, I will not write the things I would like to write. I don't consider what we have to be a spectator sport, and I don't want a bunch of dried-up old maids giggling over my correspondence.

On the way over here, I had a lot of time to think about us, and you are constantly in my thoughts here "somewhere in the South Pacific." There is not much for us to do, except prepare for what we all know is going to happen.

I have carefully considered what happened between us, and I've given a lot of thought to our different backgrounds. I am fully aware that the both of us behaved very foolishly, and that any marriage counselor worthy of hanging out his shingle would have to conclude that the odds against us getting married in the first place, much less making a success of it, are very long indeed.

Having said that, I have concluded that meeting you was the best thing that's happened to me in my life. Until you, I really had no idea what being a woman really meant. I will not be alive until I feel your arms around me again.

I love you. Today. Tomorrow. Forever.

May God protect you,
Barbara

PS: Picture enclosed, so you don't forget what I look like.

Joe Howard had trouble focusing his eyes on Barbara's picture; they seemed to be full of tears.

He put the letter back into its envelope and carefully put it into his pocket.

"Thanks very much, Les," he said.

"Ah, hell, Lieutenant," the motor sergeant said. Then he raised his voice, and the tenor changed. "Well, get off your ass, asshole," he said to the dispatcher, "and go get the Lieutenant's truck."

(FIVE)
Headquarters
Special Detachment 14
Camp Elliott, California
18 April 1942

The Quonset hut was so called because it had been invented at the Quonset Point Naval Station. It was originally envisioned as an easy-to-erect shelter—sort of a portable warehouse—not as barracks. The huts were built out of curved sheets of corrugated steel, which formed the sides and roof in a half-circle. And there was a wooden floor, the framework of which visibly traced its design to forklift pallets.

When they were to be transported, the curved sheets of corrugated steel could be nestled together. Then they, and the framework which supported them, could be steel-banded together on top of the plywood floor and its underpinning. So packed, they took up little cubic footage, and could be erected quickly at their destination by unskilled labor using simple tools.

Quonset huts had sprouted like mushrooms over the rolling hills of Camp Elliott. Many of these had been put to use as barracks in lieu of tents, "until adequate barracks could be erected."

Major Edward J. Banning followed Major Jack NMI Stecker up to one of them and stepped through the door behind him in time to hear someone call "Ten-*hut.*"

The hut was furnished with two folding metal chairs, two small folding wooden tables, on one of which sat a U.S. Army field desk, and a telephone. There were eight Marines in the forty-foot-long room. They were now all standing erect, at attention; but most of them, obviously, had a moment earlier been sprawled on mattresses on the floor. Their duffel bags, some of them open, were scattered around the floor. Their stacked '03 Springfield rifles were at the far end of the room.

Banning wondered idly why Jack Stecker didn't put them at rest, and then he belatedly realized that Jack was deferring to him, as the commanding officer.

"At ease," Banning said. He smiled. "My name is Banning. I have the honor to command this splendid, if brand-new, military organization."

There were a couple of chuckles, but most of them looked at him warily. That was understandable. Reporting aboard an ordinary rifle company was bad enough. The unknown is always frightening; and you naturally wonder what the new company commander and first sergeant will be like, how you will be treated, where you will be going, and what you will be doing. Reporting in here posed all those questions, plus those raised by the words "classified"; "involving extraordinary hazards"; and "the risk of loss of life will be high."

And there wasn't much he could do to put their minds at rest. This was one of those (in Banning's judgment, rare) situations where the necessity for secrecy was quite clear. It was even possible that the Japanese didn't know of the very existence of the Coastwatchers. Sometimes, not often, the Japanese were quite stupid about things like that; this might be one of them. If the Japanese did not yet know about the Coastwatchers, then every effort, clearly, should be made to keep them from finding out, as long as possible. They inevitably would, of course. When that happened, the less they learned the better.

All I can do is try to get these people to trust me. I can't even tell them where we're going, much less what we're going to be doing, until we're on the ship. Or maybe not even then. Not until we get to Australia. If we go over there on a troopship, I can't afford to have everybody else on the ship talking, and talk they would, about that strange little detachment with the strange mission.

Banning had long ago learned that enlisted Marines trust their officers on a few occasions only: first, when the officer knows more about what's expected of them than they do; second, when he will not ask them to do something he will not do himself; and, third, perhaps most important, when he is genuinely concerned with their welfare.

There were two staff sergeants, five buck sergeants, and a corporal. Banning went to each man in turn and shook his hand. He asked each man his name, what he had been doing up to now in the Corps, and where he was from.

"Who's senior?" Banning asked, after he'd met them all.

One of the staff sergeants took a step forward.

"Richardson, right?"

"Yes, Sir."

"Well, for the time being, Sergeant, you'll act as First Sergeant. Your first orders are to get some bunks and bedding to go with those mattresses."

Staff Sergeant Richardson looked uncomfortable.

"Problem with that, Sergeant?"

"Sir, the warehouse is a hell of a ways from here, and we don't have any motor transport."

"You seem to have managed to draw mattresses and get them here without transport," Banning said.

That made Sergeant Richardson look even more uncomfortable. Banning glanced at Major Stecker, whose eyes looked mischievous again. And then Banning understood: somewhere on the post, much closer than the issue point for bedding, another Marine Corps unit was dealing with the problem of eight missing mattresses.

That was clearly theft, or at least unauthorized diversion of government property—in either case a manifestation of a lack of discipline. On the other hand, getting mattresses to sleep on when the Corps didn't provide any could be considered a manifestation of initiative, which was a desirable military quality.

"Well, I'll look into the problem of transportation, Sergeant. What I would like to do, right now, is have a look at everybody's service record, and then I'd like to talk to you one at a time."

"Yes, Sir," Staff Sergeant Richardson said, visibly relieved that the subject of the source of the mattresses seemed to have been passed over.

"Sergeant, has Lieutenant Howard been over here today?" Jack Stecker asked.

"Yes, Sir. He was here about oh-six-hundred to make sure we were going to get breakfast. He said he would be back"—he raised his wrist to look at his watch—"about now, Sir. He said he would be back before you got here, Sir."

As if on cue, there came the sound of tires crunching and an engine dying. A moment later, Lieutenant Joe Howard came through the door.

"Good morning, Sir," he said to Stecker. "Sorry to be late. I had a little trouble getting wheels from the motor officer."

"Major Banning," Stecker said. "This is Lieutenant Joe Howard."

"How do you do, Sir?" Howard said.

Banning liked what he saw. Like others before him, he thought that Joe Howard looked like everything a clean-cut, red-blooded, physically fit young Marine officer should look like. And then he remembered what Jack Stecker had said about Howard having found, and stayed in, a safe hole during the attack at Pearl Harbor.

I'm in no position to be self-righteous about that. When the Jap barrages began, I would have swapped my soul for a safe hole to hide in.

"I'm happy to meet you, Howard," Banning said, putting out his hand and raising his voice just enough to make sure everyone in the hut heard him. "Major Stecker speaks very highly of you. I've known him a long time, and he doesn't often do that."

Lieutenant Howard looked as uncomfortable as Staff Sergeant Richardson had a moment before.

"I've got to get out of here," Stecker said. "I can't miss that plane. Howard can drive me."

He put out his hand to Banning. "Good luck, Ed. Send a postcard."

"Take care of yourself," Banning said. "Say hello to Elly."

"I will," Stecker said, and then turned to the men watching curiously. "Listen up," he said. "You guys have fallen in the you-know-what and come up smelling like roses. Major Banning is one hell of Marine. He probably wouldn't tell you, so I will: He's already been in this war, wounded and evacuated from the 4th Marines in the Philippines. Before that, he was with the 4th Marines in China. When he tells you something, it's not coming out of a book, it's from experience. So pay attention and do what he says, and you'll probably come out of what you're going to do alive. Good luck. Semper Fi."

And then, without looking at Banning again, Stecker quickly walked out of the Quonset hut. Banning found himself alone with his new command; they were now looking at him almost with fascination.

That was a hell of a nice thing for Jack Stecker to do, Banning thought.

"Well, Sergeant Richardson," he said, "now that we have wheels, we can get bedding. Take half the men and the truck and go get it."

"Aye, aye, Sir."

"And when you've finished, take the mattresses here back where you got them."

"Aye, aye, Sir."

"Try not to get caught," Banning said.

"Yes, Sir."

"I want to talk to each of you alone," Banning said, after Richardson and the men he took were gone. "I'll start with you, Sergeant. The rest of you wait outside."

The first man, the other staff sergeant, a thirty-year-old named Hazleton, was a disappointment. By the time he finished talking with him, Banning was sure he had volunteered for a mission "where the risk of loss of life will be high" because he was unwelcome where he was. That he had, in other words, been "volunteered" by his first sergeant or company commander. For all of his last hitch before the war, he had been the assistant NCO club manager at Quantico. Rather obviously, he had been swept out of that soft berth when the brass was desperately looking for noncoms to train the swelling Corps.

And at 2nd Joint Training Force, where the broom had swept him, Hazleton had been found unable to cut the mustard. When the TWX soliciting volunteers had arrived, his company commander had decided it was a good, and easy, way to get rid of him.

Banning was not surprised. That was the way things went. No company commander wanted to lose his best men. Lieutenant Colonel Rickabee had warned Banning that was going to happen, and he had made provision to deal with it. The staff sergeant's name would be TWXed to Rickabee, and shortly afterward there would be a TWX from Headquarters USMC, transferring the staff sergeant out of Special Detachment 14.

Banning wondered how many of the others would be like the staff sergeant. With one exception, however, none were. To Banning's surprise, the others were just what he had hoped to get. They were bright—in some cases, very bright—young noncoms who were either looking for excitement or a chance for rapid promotion, or both.

Unfortunately, none of them spoke Japanese, although four of them had apparently managed to utter enough Japanese-sounding noises to convince their first sergeants that they did. That wasn't surprising either. Japanese linguists were in very short supply. Officers who had them would fight losing them as hard as possible. Nevertheless, Rickabee had promised to pry loose as many as he could (maybe four), and send them directly to Melbourne.

The last man Banning interviewed, the only corporal who had so far arrived, was the second disappointment. Corporal Stephen Koffler had come to Special Detachment 14 from the Marine Corps Parachute School at Lakehurst Naval Air Station. It didn't take more than a couple of minutes for Banning to extract from him the admission that he had "been volunteered." The kid's first sergeant had made what could kindly be called a pointed suggestion that he volunteer.

"Why do you think he did that, Koffler?"

"I don't know, Sir. So far as I know, I didn't do nothing wrong. But right from the first, Lieutenant Macklin seemed to have it in for me."

"What was that name? Who 'had it in' for you?"

"Lieutenant Macklin, Sir."

"Tall, thin officer? An Annapolis graduate?"

"Yes, Sir. Lieutenant R. B. Macklin. He told us he went to Annapolis. And he said that he had learned about the Japs from when he was in China."

I'll be damned. So that's where that sonofabitch wound up! Doesn't sound like him. You could hurt yourself jumping out of airplanes. But maybe that pimple on the ass of the Corps was "volunteered" for parachute duty by somebody else who found out what a despicable prick he is, and hoped his parachute wouldn't open.

"I believe I know the gentleman," Banning said. "Tell me, Koffler, what were you doing at the Parachute School? Some kind of an instructor?"

Even if this kid is no Corporal Killer McCoy, if he's rubbed Macklin the wrong way, he probably has a number of splendid traits of character I just haven't noticed so far. "The enemies of my enemies are my friends."

"No, Sir. They had me driving a truck."

"I don't suppose you can type, can you, Koffler?"

There was a discernible pause before Corporal Koffler reluctantly said, "Yes, Sir. I can type."

"You sound like you're ashamed of it."

"Sir, I don't want to be a fucking clerk-typist."

"Corporal Koffler," Banning said sternly, suppressing a smile, "in case you haven't heard this before, the Marine Corps is not at all interested in what you would like, or not like, to do. Where did you learn to type?"

That question obviously made Corporal Koffler just as uncomfortable as he'd been when he was asked if he could type at all.

"Where did you learn to type, Corporal? More important, how fast a typist are you?"

"About forty words a minute, Sir," Koffler said. "I got a book out of the library."

"A typing book, you mean? You taught yourself how to type?"

"Yes, Sir."

"Why?"

"I needed to know how to type to pass the FCC exam. You have to copy twenty words a minute to get your ticket, and I couldn't write that fast."

"You're a radio operator?" Banning asked, pleased.

"No, Sir. I'm a draftsman."

"A draftsman?" Banning asked, confused.

"Yes, Sir. That's why I volunteered for parachuting."

"Excuse me?"

"Sir, they wanted to keep me at Parris Island as a draftsman, painting signs. The only way I could get out of it was to volunteer for parachute training."

"In other words, Corporal Koffler," Banning said, now keeping a straight face only with a massive effort, "it could be fairly said that you concealed your skill as a radio operator from the personnel people . . ."

"I didn't *conceal* it, Sir," Koffler said. "They didn't ask me, and I didn't tell them."

"And then, since the personnel people were unaware of your very valuable skill as a radio operator, they elected to classify you as a draftsman?"

"That's about it, Sir."

"And then you volunteered for the Para-Marines because you didn't want to be a draftsman, and then you volunteered for the 14th Special Detachment because you didn't want to be a Para-Marine?"

Koffler looked stricken.

"It wasn't exactly that way, Sir."

"Then you tell me exactly how it was."

There was a knock at the door of the Quonset hut.

"Come!" Banning said, and Lieutenant Joe Howard entered the hut.

"Major Stecker got off all right, Sir. I've got the keys to his car for you."

"Stick around, Lieutenant. I'll be with you in a minute," Banning said. "Corporal Koffler and I are just about finished. Go on, Corporal."

"I don't know what to say, Sir," Steve Koffler said unhappily.

Banning glowered at him for a moment.

"I will spell it out for you, Koffler. This is the end of the line for you. There's no place else you can volunteer for so you can get out of doing things you don't like to do. From here on in, you are going to do what the Marine Corps wants you to do. You are herewith appointed the detachment clerk of the 14th Special Detachment, U.S. Marine Corps. And if there are any signs to be painted around here, you will paint them. Am I getting through to you?"

"Yes, Sir."

"Any questions?"

"No, Sir."

"Then report to Sergeant Richardson, tell him I have appointed you detachment clerk, and tell him I said he should see about getting you a typewriter. Do you understand all that?"

"Yes, Sir."

"I don't want to hear that you are even thinking of volunteering for anything else, Koffler!"

"No, Sir."

"That will be all, Corporal," Banning said solemnly.

"Aye, aye, Sir. Thank you, Sir," Steve Koffler said, did an about-face, and marched to the door of the hut. When the door had closed, Banning pushed himself back on the legs of his folding chair and laughed.

"Oh, God," he said, finally.

"What was that all about, Sir?" Howard asked, smiling.

"I'd forgotten what fun it is sometimes to be a unit commander," Banning said. "That's a good kid; but, my God, how wet behind the ears! Anyway, I need a clerk, and he can type. He can also paint signs. The square peg in the square hole."

"He really isn't what you think of when somebody says, 'Para-Marine Corporal,' is he?"

"Until I started talking to him and somebody said, 'Corporal,' I usually thought of one I had in the 4th. I used to send him snooping around the Japanese for weeks at a time and never thought a thing about it. I'm not sure that kid could be trusted to go downtown in 'Diego and get back by himself."

"He might surprise you, Sir. He *is* wearing parachutist's wings. He had the balls to jump out of an airplane. I'm not sure I would."

Banning's smile vanished as he looked at Howard.

"Talking about balls, Lieutenant. The 14th Special Detachment is accepting company-grade volunteers."

"Are you asking me to volunteer, Sir?"

"No. I'm just telling you I need a couple of lieutenants. Whether you would care to volunteer is up to you."

"Sir, there's something about me I don't think you know," Joe Howard said.

"Major Stecker told me all about that. We're old friends, and we both think you're wrong about what happened at Pearl Harbor."

"Sir, with respect, you weren't there."

"For Christ's sake, Howard, anybody with the brains to pour piss out of his boots gets scared when shells start falling. Or sick to his stomach when he sees somebody blown up, torn up, whatever. What the hell made you think you would be different?"

"Sir—"

"You have two options, Lieutenant. Of your own free will, you volunteer for this outfit, or a week from now you'll report to New River, North Carolina, where you'll be given a company in the 2nd Battalion, 5th Marines."

Howard's face worked for a moment. He did not need Banning to remind him of his options. He had been thinking of them carefully. And since getting Barbara's letter this morning, he had been thinking of little else.

"Actually, Sir, there's a third option. Colonel Carlson said he would like to have me in the 2nd Raider Battalion."

"That's right, you've been working with them, haven't you? You tell Colonel Carlson about this low opinion you have of yourself?"

"Yes, Sir. I mean, I told him about what happened to me at Pearl."

"And he still wants you?"

"Yes, Sir. He said . . . just about the same thing that you and Major Stecker said, Sir."

"Well, make up your mind, Howard. If you don't want in here, I've got to find somebody else."

"Sir, I'd like to go with you, if that would be all right. But I've already told Colonel Carlson I'd volunteer for the Raiders."

"Don't worry about that. I'll handle Colonel Carlson. You're in. Your first job is to teach our new detachment clerk to fill out the appropriate forms to send a TWX to Washington. As soon as he knows how, send one. Here's the address. The message is to transfer Staff Sergeant Hazleton out and you in."

"Aye, aye, Sir."

"You may first have to get Corporal Koffler a typewriter," Banning said.

"Yes, Sir. I thought about that. I know where I can get one. Actually, two, an office Underwood and a Royal portable. And some other stuff we're going to need."

"Aren't they going to miss you where you're working?"

"No, Sir. Major Stecker arranged with 2nd Training Force for me to work for you for a week. By the time the week is over, I suppose I'll have orders transferring me here."

"Did Major Stecker tell you what they're going to have us doing?"

"No, Sir. I don't think he knows."

"I'd like to tell you, but I don't think I'd better until we get you officially transferred."

"I understand, Sir."

"We won't be able to tell the men what we're going to do, or even where we're going, until we get there. That may be a problem."

There was no question in Howard's mind where they were going. They were going to the Pacific. Anywhere in the Pacific would be closer to Barbara than New River, N.C.

"I understand, Sir."

"OK, Howard. Go get our new detachment clerk a typewriter. As a wise old Marine once told me, the Marine Corps floats on a sea of paper."

"Aye, aye, Sir."

(SIX)

TOP SECRET

Eyes Only—The Secretary of the Navy

DUPLICATION FORBIDDEN
ORIGINAL TO BE DESTROYED AFTER ENCRYPTION AND TRANSMITTAL TO SECNAVY

Melbourne, Australia
Tuesday, 21 April 1942

Dear Frank:
I suspect that you have been expecting more frequent reports than you have been getting. This is my second, and it was exactly a month ago that I sent the first. So, feeling much like a boy at boarding school explaining why his essay has not been turned in when expected, let me offer the following in extenuation:

Your radio of 1 April, in addition to relieving me of my enormous concern that I was not providing what you hoped to get, also told me that it is going to take 7–9 days for these reports to reach you, if they have to travel from here to Hawaii by sea for encryption and radio transmission from there. I see no solution to shortening this time frame, other than hoping that some sort of scheduled air courier service between here and Pearl Harbor will be established. Encryption here, for radio transmission via either Navy or MacA.'s facilities, would mean using their codes and cryptographers, and the problems with that are self-evident.

The only way I see to do it is the way I am preparing this report, all at once, to be turned over to an officer bound for Pearl. This one is being given to Lt. Col. H. B. Newcombe, U.S. Army Air Corps, who has been here visiting General Brett, and is returning to the United States. He is flying as far as Pearl on a converted B-17A Brett has placed into service as a long-range transport.

Let me go off tangentially on that: The service range of the newer B-17s is 925 miles. That is to say, they can strike a target 925 miles from their base and return to their takeoff field. That limitation is going to have a serious effect on their employment here, where there are few targets within a 925-mile range of our bases.

The B-17A on which this will travel has had auxiliary fuel tanks installed; these significantly add to its range, but eliminate its bomb-carrying capacity. This one, which everyone calls the "Swoose," never even had a tail turret; and it was built up from parts salvaged off the B-17s lost in the early assaults on the Philippines. The Air Corps phrase for this is "cannibalization," and it applies to much that we are doing here.

In addition to the difficulty of transmission, the week-to-nine-day transmission time seems to me to render useless any "early warning" value my reports might have. By the time my reports reach Washington, you will have already learned through other channels most of what I have to say.

So what these letters are going to be, essentially, are after-action reports, narrating what has happened here from my perspective, together with what few thoughts I feel comfortable offering about the future.

MacA. and his wife and son are still occupying the suite immediately below this one in the Menzies Hotel. That I am upstairs doesn't seem to bother the Generalissimo, in fact quite the contrary seems true; but it does greatly annoy what has become known as "The Bataan Gang," that is, those people who were with him in the Philippines.

I have resisted pointed suggestions from Sutherland, Huff, and several others that I vacate these premises in order to make them available to the more deserving (and, of course, senior) members of the MacA. entourage. I have been difficult about this, for two major reasons. First, being where I am, close to MacA., permits me to do what I believe you want me to do. Second, giving in to the suggestion (in the case of Huff, an order: "I have arranged other quarters for you, Captain Pickering.") that I move out would grant the point that I am subject to their orders. I don't think that the Special Representative of the Secretary of the Navy should make himself subordinate even to MacA. himself, and certainly not to members of his staff.

I do actually believe the above, but I must in candor tell you that I took great pleasure in telling them, especially Huff, to go to hell. I know I probably should not have taken pleasure in that, but I don't like them. And they don't like me. I'm convinced that their hostility mostly arises from MacA.'s growing tendency to have me around, often alone with him. And I'm sure it is constantly exacerbated by that. Huff, in particular, sees himself as Saint Peter, guarding access to the throne of God. He simply cannot understand MacA. waiving the rules of protocol for anyone, and especially for a civilian/sailor.

I have spent a good deal of time wondering why MacA. <u>does</u> want me around, and have come up with some possible reasons, listed below, <u>not</u> in order of importance.

It began shortly after he was given office space for his headquarters. The Australians turned over to him a bank building at 401 Collins Street. He now occupies what was the Managing Director's office. The old board room is now the map room.

There was—is—a critical shortage of maps. I was able to help somewhat here when I learned about it.

Going off tangentially again: I learned about the map shortage at dinner, shortly after we arrived in Melbourne. My telephone rang, and in the Best British Manner, one of the Australian sergeants they gave him as orderlies announced to me, "General MacArthur's compliments, Sir. The General and Mrs. MacArthur would be pleased to have you join them for dinner in half an hour."

I went downstairs to the restaurant half an hour later and found the Bataan Gang and an assortment of Australians having their dinner. But not MacA. I asked one of the entourage where MacA. was, and was informed that the General dines alone. When I went to the MacA. apartment, I was perfectly prepared to find myself the butt of a practical joke. But I was expected. We dined en famille; in addition to MacA. and his wife, there were little Arthur and his Chinese nurse/governess.

Dinner was small talk—about people Mrs. MacA. knew in Manila, Honolulu, and San Francisco. The war wasn't mentioned until after dinner. Brandy and a cigar were produced for me, and Mrs. MacA. left us alone. I had the feeling (I realize how absurd this sounds; and please believe me, I gave it a lot of thought before putting it down on paper) that MacA. regards me as a fellow nobleman, the visiting Duke of Pickering, so to speak—with himself, of course, as the Emperor. The rules that apply to common folk—everybody around here but us—naturally do not apply to the nobility. The common folk don't get to eat, for example, with the Emperor, en famille.

Some of this, I am quite sure, is because I think I am one of the few really well-off individuals he has been close to. I think Mrs. MacA. told him that Pacific & Far East is privately held, and that Patricia is Andrew Foster's only child, and this has made an extraordinary impression on him. In support of that thesis, I offer this: On 6 April, the Pacific Duchess was part of the convoy that brought the 41st Infantry Division into Adelaide. MacA. informed me of this by saying, "Your ship, the PD, has arrived in Adelaide." I responded that she was no longer mine, that she now belonged to the Navy. He asked me how much I had been paid for it, and what the taxes were on a transaction like that. I told him. The numbers obviously fascinated him.

On the other hand, most of the special treatment I am getting, I'm sure, is because I am your special representative. MacA.'s clever. More than clever, brilliant. He knows how useful a direct line to your ear will be.

In any event, over my cigar and his cigarette, he discussed his intention to immediately return to the Philippines, and how he planned to do so. In the course of the conversation, he explained how very much aware he is of the vast distances involved, and of the problems that is going to pose. In that connection, he bitterly complained about the lack of maps. He is convinced that the Navy

has better maps than he has, and that for petty reasons they are refusing to make them available to him.

I volunteered to look into that. The next day I spoke with Admiral Leary, and then with his intelligence and planning people. And it turned out that MacA. was wrong about the reason he didn't have decent maps. The Navy was not being petty. The Navy doesn't have decent maps either. I was astonished to see the poor quality of the charts they had, and equally astonished to see how few charts are available, period.

I don't pretend to have solved the problem, only to have made a dent in it: but I did manage to gather together charts from the various ship chandlers around (a thought that apparently did not occur to the Navy). The charts I picked up, anyhow, were superior to any the Navy had. I then went to the P&FE agent here and borrowed, on a semipermanent basis, several of his people. They are going to all the masters of ships plying the Southwest Pacific trade, down to the smallest coaster, as they make port; and they'll get them to update charts, especially for the small islands, based on the mariners' own observations.

The P&FE agent here has arranged to have the updated charts printed. I offered to make them available to Admiral Leary, but he made it clear that (a) he is not interested: not having come from the appropriate Navy bureaucracy, they cannot be considered reliable; and that (b) therefore it is an effrontery on my part to ask that I be reimbursed for expenses incurred.

MacA., on the other hand, was really grateful for the maps. I think that was the reason I was invited to go with him on March 25, when he was invested with the Medal of Honor. His acceptance speech was brilliant; my eyes watered.

And the next day, for the first time, MacA. met John Curtin, the Prime Minister. Now, in case you don't know it, Curtin is so far left that he makes Roosevelt look like Louis XIV. All the same, he and MacA. immediately began to act like long-lost brothers. I know for a fact (the P&FE agent here sits in the Australian parliament) that Curtin was flatly opposed to (a) abolishing the Australian Military Board and (b) transferring all of its powers to MacA.

Apparently, neither Willoughby (his G-2) nor our State Department explained to MacA. just who Curtin is or what he'd done. Indeed, MacA. seems to believe exactly the opposite, i.e., that Curtin was responsible for his being named commander-in-chief and given all the powers of the former Military Board. Or else MacA. was told, and regally decided to ignore the implications. With a massive effort, I have obeyed your orders not to involve myself in something like this.

Or—an equally credible scenario—he knows all about Curtin and his politics, and his publicly professed camaraderie and admiration for Curtin is a sham intended for public consumption—to bolster the

very much sagging Australian morale. The people believe, with good reason, that they are next on the Japanese schedule. Curtin has complained bitterly that Australian (and New Zealand) troops are off in Africa fighting for England when they are needed to defend their homeland. He consequently stands high in the public esteem, even of those who think he is a dangerous socialist.

Into this situation comes MacArthur, promising to defend the Australian continent. The words he used in his Medal of Honor acceptance speech—"we shall win or we shall die; I pledge the full resources of all the mighty power of my country, and all the blood of my countrymen"—were reported in every newspaper, and over the radio . . . again and again. There was hope once more.

And right on top of that came word of Colonel Doolittle's raid on Tokyo. From my perspective here, I think it's impossible to overestimate the importance of that raid. Militarily, MacA. told me, it will require the Japanese to pull back naval and aerial forces, as well as antiaircraft artillery forces, to protect the homeland. Politically, it is certain to have caused havoc within the Japanese Imperial Staff. Their senior officers are humiliated. And it will inevitably have an effect on Japanese civilian morale.

Since MacArthur, not surprising me at all, immediately concluded that the attack had been launched from an aircraft carrier, I decided that the Commander-in-Chief SWPAC was entitled to hear other information the Japanese probably already knew. I therefore provided him with the specific details of the attack as I knew them. An hour or so later, when Willoughby came to the office and provided MacA. with what few details he had about the raid, MacA. delivered a concise lecture to him and to several others, based on what I had told him. It was of course obvious where he'd gotten his facts. The unfortunate result is I am now regarded as a more formidable adversary than before.

But Doolittle's bombing of Tokyo, added to MacArthur's presence here and his being named Commander-in-Chief, and his (apparently) roaring friendship with Curtin, gave Australian morale a really big boost just when one was needed. And that surge of confidence would have been destroyed if MacA. had started fighting with Curtin—or even if there was any suggestion that they were not great mutual admirers or were not in complete agreement.

The more I think about it, I think this latter is the case. MacArthur understands things like this.

Turning to the important question "Can we hold Australia?" MacArthur believes, supported to some degree by the intelligence (not much) available to us, that the following is the grand Japanese strategy: While Admiral Yamamoto is taking Midway away from us, as a stepping-stone to taking the Hawaiian Islands, the forces under Admiral Takeo Takagi will occupy Australia's perimeter islands, north and west of the continent.

We have some pretty good intelligence that Takagi intends to put "Operation Mo" into execution as soon as he can. That is the capture of Port Moresby, on New Guinea. Moresby is currently manned, I should say undermanned, by Australian militiamen with little artillery, etcetera. They could not resist a large-scale Japanese assault. Once Moresby falls, all the Japanese have to do is build it up somewhat and then use it as the base for an invasion across the Coral Sea to Australia. It's about 300 miles across the Coral Sea from Port Moresby to Australia.

Both to repel an invasion and to prevent the Japanese from marching across Australia, MacA. has two divisions (the U.S. 32nd Infantry, arrived at Adelaide April 15); one brigade of the 6th Australian Division; and one (or two, depending on whom one chooses to believe) Australian divisions being returned "soon" from Africa. He has sixty-two B-17 bombers, six of which (including the "Swoose," which carries no bombs) are airworthy. Some fighter planes have begun to arrive, but these are generally acknowledged to be inferior to the Japanese Zero.

MacA. believes further that the Japanese intend to install fighter airplane bases in the Solomon Islands. We have some unconfirmed (and probably unconfirmable) intelligence that major fighter bases are planned for Guadalkennel (sp?) and Bougainville. Fighters on such strips could escort Japanese Betty and Zeke bombers to interdict our ships bound for Australia, cutting the pipeline. We don't have the men or materiel to go after them at either place.

On top of this, we have had what MacA. feels is an unconscionable delay in reaching an interservice agreement about who is in charge of what. I found myself wondering too, frankly, just who the hell was in charge in Washington. MacA. was not named CIC SWPA until April 18. And even when that happened, it violated a rule of warfare even Fleming Pickering understands: that it is idiocy to split a command. Which is exactly what appointing Admiral Nimitz as CIC Pacific Ocean Areas does.

It means that from this point on, we have started another war. In addition to fighting the Japanese, the Army and the Navy are going to be at each other's throats. A sailor, or a soldier, MacArthur or Nimitz, should have been put in charge. Somebody has to be in charge.

Under these circumstances, I was not at all surprised, the day Bataan fell, when MacA. radioed Marshall asking for permission to return to the Philippines to fight as a guerrilla. I could hear the snickers when that radio arrived in Sodom-on-Potomac.

He showed me the cable before he sent it. I told him what I thought the reaction would be. He said he understood that, but thought there was a slight chance his "enemies" (George Marshall, Ernie King, and the U.S. Navy) would see that he was given permission as a way to get rid of him.

I think I should confess, Frank, that if he had been given permission, I think I would have gone with him.

Colonel Newcombe just called from the lobby. I have to seal this up and give it to him.

Respectfully,

Fleming Pickering, Captain, USNR

XI

(ONE)
The Willard Hotel
Washington, D.C.
30 April 1942

"General," Congressman Emilio L. DiFranco (D., 8th N.J. Congressional District) said to Brigadier General D. G. McInerney, USMC, "I so very much appreciate your finding time for me in your busy schedule."

The Congressman waited expectantly for the General to notice him; but General McInerney was listening to Congressman DiFranco with only half an ear. The rest of his attention was smitten by a hard rush of curiosity. It was the group sitting three tables away from him in the upstairs cocktail lounge of the Willard Hotel that had caught his eye, indeed his fascination. He had not in fact seen the Congressman making his way across the room to him.

"The Marine Corps always has time for you, Congressman," General McInerney said, rising to his feet and with some effort working up a small smile. He cordially detested Congressman DiFranco, whom he had met a half-dozen times before.

Doc McInerney wasn't *sure* that the tall, remarkably thin blond woman at the table was *really* Monique Pond, the motion-picture actress, but she sure as hell looked like her. A photograph of the actress wearing a silver lamé dress open damned near to her navel hung on every other vertical surface in the military establishment.

Two other people were at the table with Miss Pond, if indeed it was Miss Pond. One was another long-legged, long-haired blond female. McInerney wouldn't have been surprised if that one was also a star of stage, screen, and radio. She was pretty enough. He didn't recognize her, but he wasn't all that familiar with movie stars.

Nor, for that matter, was he all that familiar with the upstairs cocktail lounge of the Willard Hotel. The Willard was an expensive hostelry, catering to high government officials and members of Congress—and, more important, to those individuals who wished to influence government policy and Congressional votes, and who did their drinking on an expense account.

The word *lobbyist* was coined around the time of the Civil War to describe those who hung around the lobby of the Willard Hotel, waiting for Congressmen whose vote they hoped to influence. Not much had changed since then.

The prices in the Willard were of such magnitude that few members of the military establishment, including general officers, could afford them. McInerney came here rarely—only when, as today, there was no way he could get out of it. He had been invited for a drink by the Hon. Mr. DiFranco; it does not behoove officers of the regular Marine Corps to turn down such invitations.

McInerney knew what the Congressman wanted. When the invitation had come, he had checked with the Congressional Liaison Office and learned that Congressman DiFranco had been in touch with them regarding the son of one of his more important constituents. After an initial burst of patriotic fervor that had led to his enlisting in the Marine Corps, this splendid young gentleman now found that he didn't like the life of a Marine rifleman. He wanted instead to be assigned to duties that were more to his liking; specifically, he wanted to be an aircraft mechanic. He had apparently communicated this desire to his daddy, and his father had gotten in touch with Mr. DiFranco.

With all the courtesy due a Congressman, the Congressional Liaison Office had in effect told the Congressman to go fuck himself. At that point, Congressman DiFranco had apparently remembered meeting Brigadier General McInerney a number of times. He decided then to take his constituent's problem directly to the second senior man in Marine Aviation, unofficially, socially, over a drink at the Willard.

It was not the first time this sort of thing had happened to Doc McInerney, nor even the first time with the Hon. Mr. DiFranco. Getting someone special treatment in the Corps because his father happened to know a Congressman rubbed McInerney the wrong way.

Congressman DiFranco sat down and started looking for a waiter. General McInerney looked again at the table where maybe Monique Pond sat with another good-looking blonde who might also be a movie star. Both ladies were with a young man about whose identity Doc McInerney had no doubts at all. His name was Charles M. Galloway, and he was a technical sergeant in the United States Marine Corps.

"I'll have a dry martini with an onion," Congressman DiFranco said to a waiter. "And you, General?"

"The same," McInerney said, raising his glass. He was about through with his second Jack Daniel's and water.

Congressman DiFranco handed General McInerney a slip of paper. On it was written the name of PFC Joseph J. Bianello, his serial number, and his unit, Company A, Fifth Marines, New River, North Carolina.

"What's this?" McInerney asked, innocently.

"He's the young man I want to talk to you about."

McInerney saw that the waiter was busy at the other table. He delivered three fresh drinks and a small silver platter of hors d'oeuvres.

I hope you're having a good time, Galloway. When the bill comes, you'll probably faint.

"Oh?" McInerney said to Congressman DiFranco.

"I've known him all his life. He's a really fine young man. His father owns a trucking firm, Bianello Brothers."

"Is that so?"

The other blonde, the one who was not (maybe) Monique Pond, lovingly fed Technical Sergeant Galloway a bacon-wrapped oyster on a toothpick. He chewed, looked thoughtful, and then nodded his head approvingly, which obviously thrilled the blonde.

"What he did was act impetuously," Congressman DiFranco said. "He's young."

"How do you mean, impetuously?"

"Without thinking before he leaped, so to speak."

"You mean he now regrets having joined the Marine Corps?"

"No, not at all," the Congressman said firmly.

The blonde who was maybe Monique Pond now fed Technical Sergeant Galloway something on a toothpick that Doc McInerney couldn't identify. Galloway chewed, made a face, and valiantly swallowed. The blonde who was maybe Monique Pond leaned over and kissed him on the cheek. Galloway drank deeply from his glass.

"I'm afraid I don't understand," Doc McInerney said.

Squirm, you bastard.

"His father wants to get him out of the infantry," Congressman DiFranco said.

The Congressman's unexpected candor surprised McInerney. He met DiFranco's eyes.

"The kid complained to Daddy, and Daddy came to you. Is that it?"

"The boy knows nothing about this," DiFranco said.

McInerney decided he was being told the truth.

"I'm glad to hear that," he said.

"The boy is eighteen years old, General."

"I saw some statistics last week that said the average age of enlisted men in the First Marine Division—the Fifth Marines are part of the First Division—is eighteen-point-six years," McInerney said. "He won't be lonely."

"Well, I asked," DiFranco said.

"His father is important to you, huh?"

DiFranco shrugged, acknowledging that.

"OK. I'll tell you what I'll do—" McInerney said, and then stopped abruptly. Another Marine had entered the cocktail lounge and was making his way to the table where Technical Sergeant Galloway sat with maybe Monique Pond. This one was a major. He looked familiar, but Doc McInerney could not put a name to the face.

The Major shook Galloway's hand, kissed maybe Monique Pond, then looked around for the waiter. When he had caught his eye, he mimed signing the check.

"General?" Congressman DiFranco said, puzzled by McInerney's pause.

"You can tell this kid's father that you talked to me; that I was difficult about special treatment, but in the end, as a special favor to you, I told you I would arrange to have him transferred into a battalion in the Fifth Marines which is commanded by a friend of mine, who happens to be one of the finest officers in the Marine Corps. That much is for the father. For you, I will add that I will do it in such a way that my friend will not learn why he is getting this boy, and will see that his records don't get flagged as someone who has Congressional influence."

Congressman DiFranco looked at General McInerney carefully.

"I really can't ask for more than that, can I?" he said, finally.

"No, I don't think you can," Doc McInerney replied. "This way, everybody stays honest."

"Then I'm grateful to you, General," Congressman DiFranco said, putting out his hand.

"Any time, Congressman," McInerney said, shaking it.

The waiter delivered a check to the Marine major, who scrawled his name on it, and then walked out of the cocktail lounge.

What the hell is that all about?

"Would you be offended if I cut this short?" DiFranco said. "I really have a busy schedule."

"Not at all," McInerney said. "So do I."

DiFranco fished money from his pocket and dropped a ten-dollar bill on the table.

"Thank you again, General," he said, and walked out of the room.

McInerney drained his glass and then stood up. He started to leave, but as he did, the waiter delivered the drinks Congressman DiFranco had ordered.

"Let me settle up now," he said to the waiter. The four drinks and a ten-percent tip ate up most of the Congressman's ten dollars; McInerney waved the rest of the change away, thinking, *This has to be the most expensive booze in town!*

Then he picked up the fresh drink and walked to Galloway's table.

"Hello, Sergeant Galloway," he said. "How are you?"

Galloway stood up.

"Good evening, Sir."

"Keep your seat. What brings you to town?"

"I've got a VIP flight back and forth to New River in the morning, Sir. Miss Pond and some other people. Oh, excuse me, Sir. General McInerney, this is Miss Pond and Mrs. McNamara."

So it is her. Of course! Now I know who that major is! Jake Dillon, the ex–Hollywood press agent. I met him when Colonel Whatsisname's parachute didn't open.

"I thought I recognized you, Miss Pond. And of course, you too, Mrs. McNamara. I'm very pleased to meet you."

"You recognized me?" Mrs. Caroline Ward McNamara asked, surprised. "Have we met?"

"Well, aren't you an actress, too? Or should I say 'the actress'?"

"No," Caroline McNamara said, laughing throatily. "But thank you. I love your mistake. I'm just a friend of Charley's." She patted Charley's hand fondly, possessively.

McInerney saw on her hand several thousand dollars' worth of rubies set in gold.

Galloway didn't meet this woman in the staff NCO mess at Quantico.

"Well, I just wanted to say hello," McInerney said. "It's nice to meet you."

He walked back to his table and sat down.

Less than a minute later, Galloway and the two women got up and left the lounge. McInerney followed them. They walked across the lobby and got into an elevator.

This is really none of my business, McInerney decided, only to amend that decision a moment later: *Fuck it! Watching out for the welfare of his Marines is always an officer's responsibility.*

He went to the desk and inquired whether Miss Monique Pond was registered in the Willard. The desk clerk took a moment to decide that a man in the uniform of a brigadier general of the United States Marine Corps was probably not a fan intent on bothering a movie star.

"I believe that Miss Pond is part of the party staying with Mr. Dillon, Sir."

"You mean *Major* Dillon? And the rest of the party being the other Marine and the other lady?"

"Yes, Sir. They're in the Abraham Lincoln suite."

"Thank you," McInerney said, and walked to the house phones and asked the operator to connect him with the Abraham Lincoln suite.

"Hello?"

"Major Dillon, please."

"This is Jake Dillon."

"Major, this is General McInerney. I'm in the lobby, and I'd like a moment of your time."

There was a perceptible pause before Dillon asked, "Would you like to come up, General?"

"I think it would better if you came down. I'll wait for you in the bar. The one on the second floor."

"I'll be right there, Sir."

A waiter did not appear to serve General McInerney until after Major Dillon walked in the room. Then one appeared almost immediately, carrying on a tray a drink McInerney knew Dillon hadn't had time to order.

"They do that," Dillon said. "They know what I like. Should I just let it sit there?"

He had used neither of the words "Sir" nor "General," McInerney noticed.

"This is not official," McInerney said. "Bring me a Jack Daniel's and water, please."

Dillon pushed his glass across the table to him.

"Please," he said. "Help yourself."

"I'll wait."

"Please take it. I'm trying to be ingratiating."

"Why would you want to do that?"

"Because I think this has to do with Charley Galloway, not with me. He told me you'd come up to him in here."

"It has to do with both of you," McInerney said.

"What's the problem, General?"

"I don't know if there is one. I am curious what one of my sergeants is doing in here, sharing an expensive suite with a movie star, a field-grade officer, and a woman with rubies on her hand worth more money than he makes in a year."

"She's good for him. I wouldn't be surprised if she's in love with him. She keeps him on the straight and narrow."

"What about the field-grade officer?" McInerney said.

"I thought that's what this was about," Dillon said. "I didn't just come into the Corps, General. I just *came back* in the Corps. I know all about not crossing the line between officers and enlisted men."

"Then why are you crossing it?"

"You did say, General, that this conversation isn't official?"

"Not yet. I'm trying to keep Charley Galloway out of trouble. You too, if that can be arranged."

"Well, if there's going to be trouble about this, dump it on me. I invited Charley here, and when he said that might cause trouble, I told him we'd be careful, and that if something—like this—happened, I'd take the rap."

"What's your interest in Galloway?"

"I like him. We're pals."

"He's a sergeant and you're an officer."

"I'm not really a major, I'm a flack wearing a Marine uniform."

"A what?"

"A press agent. My contribution to the war effort is getting people like Monique Pond to go to New River so she can flash her boobs at the cameramen and get the Marine Corps in the newsreels. Charley, on the other hand, is one hell of a Marine. He told me about flying the Wildcat out to the carrier off Pearl Harbor. But instead of commanding a fighter squadron, the Corps has him flying a bunch of brass hats and feather merchants around in a VIP transport airplane. So what we have here is an officer who should be an enlisted man, and a sergeant who should be an officer. So we hang around together. My idea, not his."

"What you're doing, both of you," General McInerney said, "is important."

Why did I say that? I don't believe it.

"General, I told Charley I would take the heat if something like this came up. I really would be grateful if you let me do that."

"Major Dillon," General McInerney said, after a long moment during which a few connections went *click* in his mind, "I really have no idea what you're talking about. The reason I asked to have a word with you, when I saw you come in here alone, was that I know you are in charge of the public-relations activities marking the bringing of the 1st Marine Division to wartime strength at New River tomorrow. I want to know if there is anything, anything at all, that Marine Corps Aviation can do to insure that the ceremonies are a rousing public-relations success."

Dillon's eyebrows rose thoughtfully.

"I can't think of a thing, Sir," he said.

"And to make sure there is absolutely no problem at all flying the VIPs back and forth to New River, I wanted to tell you that I have personally assigned one of our finest enlisted pilots, Technical Sergeant Galloway, to the mission. If he has not reported to you yet, I am sure he will do so momentarily. I remind you that, as an officer, you are responsible for seeing that the Sergeant is properly quartered and rationed. If there are questions regarding how and where, in the necessarily extraordinary circumstances, you elect to do that, refer whoever raises them to me."

"Aye, aye, Sir."

"That will be all, Major Dillon. Thank you."

"Yes, Sir."

Dillon stood up and started to leave. He had taken three steps when McInerney called his name.

"Yes, Sir?"

"Just between a couple of old Marines, Dillon, I don't like flying my goddamned desk, either."

(TWO)
The Commandant's House
United States Marine Corps Barracks
Eighth and "I" Streets, S.E.
Washington, D.C.
2230 Hours 9 May 1942

A glistening black 1939 Packard 180 automobile pulled into the driveway and stopped before the Victorian mansion. Mounted above its front and rear bumpers it had the three silver stars on a red plate identifying the occupant as a lieutenant general of the United States Marine Corps.

The driver, a lean, impeccably turned-out Marine staff sergeant, got quickly out from behind the wheel, but he was not quick enough to open the rear door before Thomas Holcomb, the first Marine ever promoted to lieutenant general, opened it himself. The Commandant was home.

"*Early* tomorrow, Chet," General Holcomb said to his driver. "Five o'clock."

"Aye, aye, Sir."

The general's senior aide-de-camp, a very thin lieutenant colonel, slid across the seat and got out.

"Goodnight, Chet," General Holcomb said.

"Goodnight, Sir."

"I don't see any need for you to come in, Bob," General Holcomb said to his aide. "I'm for bed."

The porch lights came on. General Holcomb's orderlies had seen the headlights.

"General," the aide said, "I took the liberty of telling Captain Steward to be prepared to brief you on the Coral Sea battle. He's probably inside, Sir."

"OK," Holcomb said wearily. He was tired. It had been a long day, ending with a long and tiring automobile ride back to Washington from Norfolk, where there had been an interservice conference at Fortress Monroe. Whatever had happened in the Coral Sea had already happened; he didn't have to learn all the details tonight. But young Captain Steward had apparently worked long and hard preparing the briefing, and it would not do right now to tell him it wasn't considered important.

Besides, I'll have to take the briefing sooner or later anyway, why not now and get it over with?

The Commandant raised his eyes to the porch, intending to order, as cheerfully as he could manage, that the orderly put on the coffeepot. There was someone on the porch he didn't expect to see, and really would rather not have seen.

"Hello, Doc," he called to Brigadier General D. G. McInerney. "Did I send for you?"

"No, Sir. I took the chance that you might have a minute to spare for me."

Good God, a long day of the problems of Navy Ordnance and the Army's Coast Artillery Corps is enough. And here comes Marine Aviation wanting something!

"Sure. Come on in the house. I was about to order up some coffee, but now that you're here, I expect Tommy had better break out the bourbon."

"Coffee would be fine, Sir."

"Don't be noble, Doc. God hates a hypocrite."

"A little bourbon would go down very nicely, Sir."

"I'm about to be briefed on a battle in the Coral Sea. You familiar with it?"

"Only that we lost the *Lexington,* Sir."

"Yeah. Well, you can sit in on the briefing," Holcomb said. He led the small procession into the house, handed his uniform cap to an orderly, and then went into the parlor.

"Good evening, Sir," Captain Steward said. Holcomb saw that Steward had come with all the trappings: an easel, covered now with a sheet of oilcloth bearing the Marine Corps insignia; a large round leather map case containing a detailed map; and a dozen folders covered with TOP SECRET cover sheets—probably the immediate, radioed after-action reports themselves.

"Hello, Stew," he said. "Sorry to keep you up this late. You know General McInerney."

"Yes, Sir. Good evening, General."

"Is there anything in there General McInerney is not supposed to hear?"

"No, Sir. General McInerney is on the Albatross list."

The Albatross list was a short list of those officers who were privy to the fact that the Navy codebreakers at Pearl had broken several of the most important Japanese naval codes.

That's a pretty short list, General Holcomb remembered now, *a* goddamned *short list, and for very good reason. If the Japanese don't find out we're reading their mail, it's hard to overestimate the importance of the broken codes. But the more people who know a secret, the greater the risk it won't stay a secret long.*

"How is that, Doc?" Holcomb asked evenly. "Why are you cleared for Albatross?"

"General Forrest brought me in on that, Sir."

The Commandant considered that for a moment, and decided to give Brigadier General Horace W. T. Forrest, Assistant Chief of Staff for Intelligence, the benefit of the doubt.

If Forrest told Doc, he must have had his reasons.

The Commandant turned to one of the orderlies. "Coffee ready?"

"Yes, Sir."

"Well, bring it in, please. And a bottle of bourbon. And then see that we're not disturbed."

"Aye, aye, Sir."

"While we're waiting, Stew, why don't you pass around those after-actions. That's what they are, right?"

"Yes, Sir."

Captain Steward divided the half-dozen documents with the TOP SECRET cover sheets between Generals Holcomb and McInerney. Before they had a chance to read more than a few lines, the orderly pushed in a cart with a coffee service, a bottle of bourbon, glasses, and a silver ice bucket. It had obviously been set up beforehand.

"Tommy must have been a Boy Scout," Holcomb said. "He's always prepared. We'll take care of ourselves, Tommy. Thank you."

The orderly left the room, closing the sliding doors from outside.

Holcomb closed his folder.

"Let's have it, Stew. I can probably get by without reading all that."

"Yes, Sir."

Captain Steward went to the easel and raised the oilskin cover. Beneath it was a simple map of the Coral Sea area. A slim strip of northern Australia was visible, as was the southern tip of New Guinea. Above New Guinea lay the southern tip of New Ireland and all of New Britain. Rabaul, which was situated at the northern tip of New Britain, was prominently labeled; it had fallen to the Japanese and was being rapidly built up as a major port for them.

To the east were the Solomon Islands. The major ones were labeled: Bougainville was the most northerly; then they went south through Choiseul, New Georgia, Santa Isabel, Tulagi, Guadalcanal, Florida, and Malaita, to San Cristobal, the most southerly.

"Keep it simple, Stew, but start at the beginning," the Commandant ordered.

"Aye, aye, Sir," Captain Steward said. "In late April, Sir, we learned, from Albatross intercepts, details of Japanese plans to take Midway Island, and from there to threaten Hawaii, with the ultimate ambition of taking Hawaii, which would both deny us that forward port and logistic facility and permit them to threaten the West Coast of the United States and the Aleutian Islands.

"Secondly, they planned to invest Port Moresby, on the tip of Eastern New Guinea. From Port Moresby they could threaten the Australian continent and extend their area of influence into the Solomon Islands. If they succeed in this intention, land-based aircraft in the Solomons could effectively interdict our supply lines to Australia and New Zealand."

I've heard all this before, and I'm tired. But I'm not going to jump on this hard-working kid because I'm grouchy when I'm tired.

"Via Albatross intercepts we learned that there would be two Japanese naval forces. Vice-Admiral Takeo Takagi sailed from the Japanese naval base at Truk in command of the carrier striking force, the carriers *Zuikaku* and *Shokaku,* which represented a total of 125 aircraft, and its screening force.

"The second Japanese force, under the overall command of Vice-Admiral

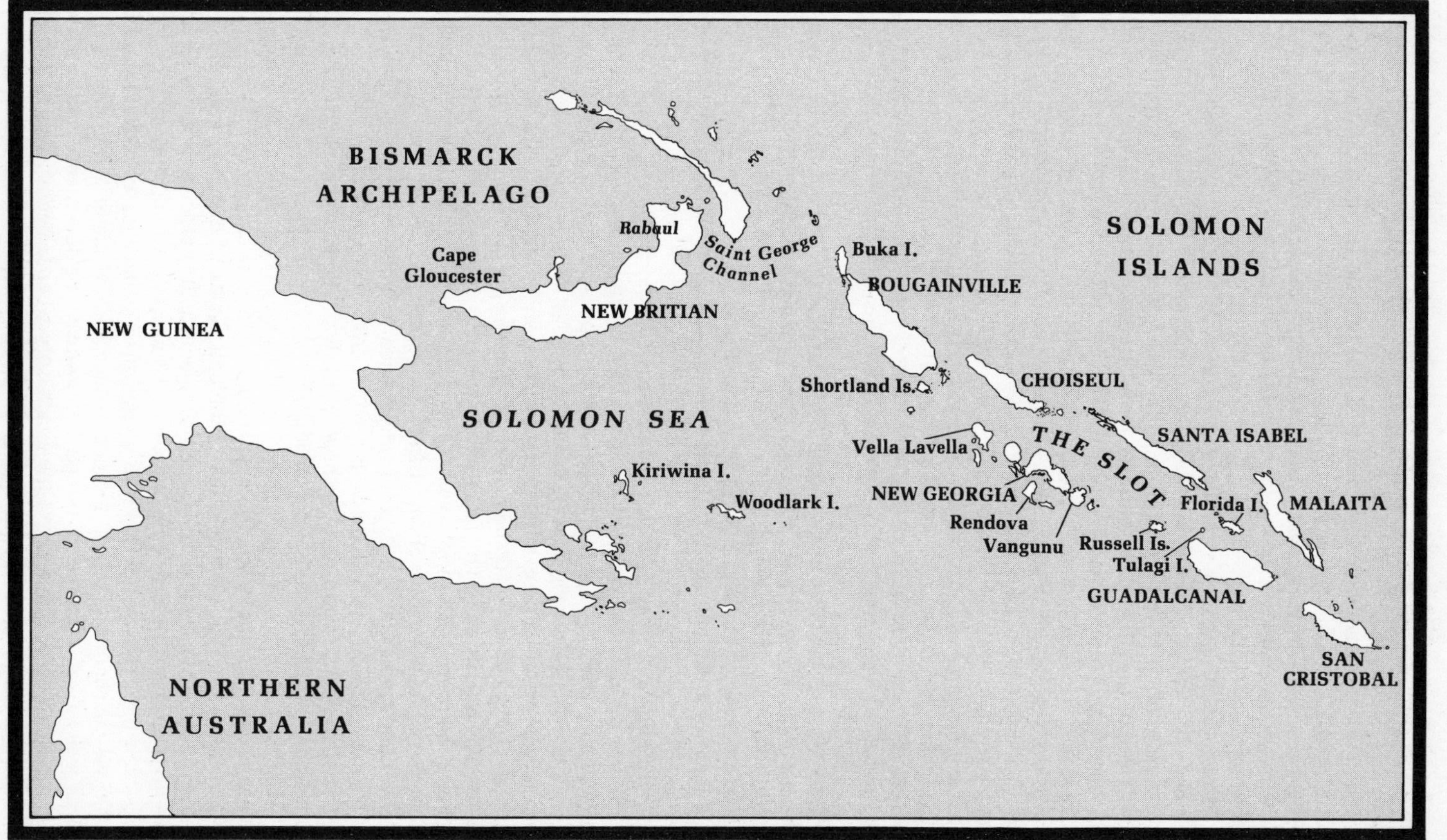
BISMARCK
ARCHIPELAGO
Rabaul
Cape
Gloucester
Saint George
Channel
NEW BRITIAN
NEW GUINEA
Buka I.
BOUGAINVILLE
SOLOMON
ISLANDS
Shortland Is.
CHOISEUL
SOLOMON SEA
Vella Lavella
THE SLOT
SANTA ISABEL
Kiriwina I.
Woodlark I.
NEW GEORGIA
Rendova
Vangunu
Florida I.
MALAITA
Russell Is.
Tulagi I.
GUADALCANAL
SAN
CRISTOBAL
NORTHERN
AUSTRALIA

Shigeyoshi Inouye, and sailing from their base at Rabaul on New Britain, included the carrier *Shoho* and several cruisers, transports, and oilers.

"On 3 May, elements of this second force, which had apparently sailed from Rabaul several days earlier, landed on Tulagi, a small island here in the Solomons"—Steward pointed with what looked like an orchestra leader's baton—"approximately equidistant between the three larger islands of Santa Isabela, Malaita, and Guadalcanal. They immediately began to construct a seaplane base.

"Based on the Albatross intercepts, Admiral Nimitz ordered Task Force 17, with Admiral Fletcher flying his flag aboard the carrier *Yorktown,* into the area. At the same time, Admiral Nimitz ordered Task Force 11, with Admiral Fitch flying his flag aboard the carrier *Lexington,* and Task Force 44, a mixed force of U.S. and Australian cruisers, under Admiral Crace, to join up with Task Force 11.

"Admiral Fletcher ordered a strike on the Japanese invasion force on Tulagi, which was carried out at 0630 hours 6 May. The after-action reports on the success of that attack, which are in the folder marked 'Tulagi,' have had to be revised."

"What the hell does that mean?" the Commandant asked sharply.

"Sir, there are Australian Coastwatchers on Tulagi. Their radioed reports of the damage inflicted differed from that of the personnel involved in the attack. Admiral Nimitz feels that inasmuch as the Coastwatchers are on Tulagi, theirs are the more credible reports."

"In other words," the Commandant said angrily, "the flyboys let their imaginations run wild again, but the Coastwatchers produced the facts."

"Yes, Sir," Captain Steward said uncomfortably.

"Nothing personal, Doc," the Commandant said.

"I know why it happens, Sir," McInerney said evenly. "But that doesn't excuse it."

"Why does it happen? I'm really curious, Doc."

"I think it has to do with movement, Sir. Perspective. Two, or three, or four pilots report, honestly, what they have seen. But because they are looking at what they all see from different places, both in terms of altitude and direction, no two descriptions match. For example, one aircraft shot down, or one seaplane destroyed in the water, becomes three airplanes shot down, or four seaplanes destroyed, because there are four different reports from people who are, in fact, reporting honestly what they saw. You need a pretty good G-2 debriefing team to separate the facts. Or consolidate them."

The Commandant grunted. "Bad intelligence is worse than no intelligence."

"I agree, Sir," McInerney said.

"We sent a special unit over there to work with the Coastwatchers," the Commandant said. "Did you know about that?"

"Yes, Sir."

"Is that going to help this, do you think?"

"Sir, I don't think it's possible to overstate the value of the Coastwatchers. They will get us, quickly, valid intelligence from the islands, particularly about Japanese air activity, but also of course about ship movement. If we know as soon as it happens what the Japanese are launching against us, what type of aircraft, and how many, we can launch our own aircraft in time to have them in the air when and where it is to our advantage. As opposed to detecting the enemy with patrolling aircraft, or worse, learning about the attack only when it begins, which catches us on the ground. Or when we're in the air almost out of fuel."

The Commandant grunted.

"I recommended to General Forrest," McInerney went on, "that he—we—

should do whatever it takes, whatever it costs, to get our people tied in to the Coastwatchers. And I want some of our own people as quickly as possible to get onto the islands as Coastwatchers. I think I was preaching to the convinced, but he said he intended to do just that. But if you were asking, Sir, whether it will do anything about the confusing reports we get from pilots, I don't think so. We're just going to have to work on that. It's inexperience, Sir, rather than dishonesty."

"I didn't mean to insult your people, Doc. You know that."

"Yes, Sir."

"OK, Stew. Pardon the interruption."

"After the attack on Tulagi, Sir, Task Force 17 moved south to join up with Task Forces 11 and 14. They did so at 0930 6 May, and together steamed westward to intercept the Port Moresby invasion force.

"At 1030 hours, 6 May, Army Air Force B-17 aircraft from Australia bombed the carrier *Shoho* and her covering force, apparently without effect.

"The next day, 7 May, at 1135 hours, aircraft from the *Lexington* spotted the *Shoho* again. They attacked and sank her. Three of Lady Lex's aircraft were lost in the attack."

"But they got the Jap carrier? That wasn't one of these perception problems General McInerney is talking about?"

"No, Sir. In addition to the pilot's after-action reports, there has been confirmation of the loss via Albatross intercepts."

"OK. Go on."

"At noon, 7 May, Japanese bombers and torpedo bombers flying off Admiral Takagi's carriers, the *Zuikaku* and *Shokaku*, found the fleet oiler *Neosho,* escorted by the destroyer *Sims.* The *Sims* was sunk and the *Neosho* damaged. The last word on that is that she will probably have to be scuttled.

"Just before noon the next day, Japanese aircraft from Admiral Tagaki's carriers attacked the combined Task Force. Both *Yorktown* and *Lexington* were damaged. Yorktown's damage was minimal, but Lexington was badly damaged, and she was scuttled at 1956 hours 8 May."

"Damn!" the Commandant said.

"At that point, Admiral Nimitz ordered Task Forces 11 and 17 to withdraw to the south. Task Force 44, the cruiser force, steamed westward to intercept the Port Moresby invasion force.

"By that time, Albatross intercepts indicated that Admiral Inouye had called off 'Operation Mo,' which was the Port Moresby invasion, but inasmuch as this information could not be made available to Admiral Crace, his Task Force patrolled the Coral Sea south of New Guinea until word from the Coastwatchers confirmed the withdrawal of the Japanese invasion force."

"That's it, then, Stew?" the Commandant asked.

"Sir, the radio messages are in the folders, and I have precise maps—"

"No, thank you. That was first-class, Stew. I know how hard you had to work to get that up in the time you had. I appreciate it."

Captain Steward beamed.

"My pleasure, Sir," he said.

"Now go get some sleep," the Commandant said. "And you too, Bob," he added to his aide. "I'm going to have a quick drink with General McInerney and then hit the sheets myself."

The Commandant waited until Captain Steward and his aide had gathered up all the briefing material before speaking.

"Was it worth it, Doc? One of our carriers for one of theirs?"

"Probably not," McInerney said, after a moment's thought. "They have more carriers to lose than we do. But if it—and it looks like it did—if it called off, or even delayed for any appreciable time, their invasion of Port Moresby, then it was. If they had taken Moresby, I don't think we could have held Australia."

"You don't think they'll be back?"

"I think they will. But we've bought some time. What worries me is that seaplane base on that island—what was it?—Tulagi. If they get a decent air base going in that area, we're in deep trouble as far as our shipping lanes are concerned. We're going to have to do something about that."

"Such as?"

"Maybe take one of the other islands and put a dirt-strip fighter base on it."

"With what? We don't have anything over there. My God, we couldn't even hang on to Corregidor."

Three days earlier, on May 6, Lieutenant General Jonathan M. Wainwright, USA, had surrendered the fortress of Corregidor, in Manila Bay, to the Japanese.

"I know."

"That's the first time a Marine regiment ever had to surrender," the Commandant said. *"Ever!"*

"They were ordered to surrender, Sir, by the Army."

"That's a lot of consolation, isn't it?"

The Commandant walked to the whiskey tray and poured himself a drink. He held up the bottle to McInerney, who shook his head no and said, "No, thank you, Sir."

"What's on your mind, Doc?" the Commandant asked.

"General, I'm really desperate for qualified fighter squadron commanders."

"I'll bet if Al Vandergrift was here, he would say, 'I'm really desperate for qualified company commanders.' "

Major General Alexander Vandergrift commanded the 1st Marine Division, which consisted of the 1st and 5th Marines, plus the 11th Marines, Artillery, and which had just been brought up to war strength on May 1 at New River, North Carolina.

"Sir, I have one Naval Aviation Pilot, Technical Sergeant Galloway, who is qualified by both experience and temperament to command a fighter squadron. I would like to commission him and give him one."

The Commandant flashed him an icy stare.

"Galloway? That's the young buck who flew the Wildcat onto the carrier off Pearl and enraged the Navy? I'm still hearing about that. Whenever the Navy wants an example of irrational Marine behavior, they bring up Sergeant Galloway's flight onto the *Saratoga."*

"Yes, Sir."

"You ever hear the story, Doc, of General Jubal T. Early in the Civil War? Somebody sent him a plan he turned down. So this staff officer sent it back, respectfully requesting that the commanding general reconsider his previous decision. Early sent that back, too, after he wrote on it, 'Goddammit, I already told you "no." I ain't gonna tell you again.' "

"Yes, Sir."

The Commandant looked at him thoughtfully, even disbelievingly.

"That's the *only* reason you came here tonight? You sat out there on the porch for hours, waiting for me to come home just to ask me to do something you knew damned well I wouldn't do?"

"Sergeant Galloway got a raw deal, Sir. And I need squadron commanders."

"Loyalty to your men is commendable, General," the Commandant said, "but there is a point beyond which it becomes counterproductive."

"Yes, Sir."

"And goddammit, Doc," the Commandant said, warming to his subject, "I'm disappointed that you don't know what that point is."

Well, I tried, McInerney thought. *And really pissed him off. I wonder what that's going to cost Marine Aviation somewhere down the pike?*

He set his glass on the table.

"With your permission, Sir, I'll take my leave."

The Commandant glowered at him.

"Keep your seat, and finish your drink, you hard-headed Scotchman," he said. "I can't afford to lose any more old friends."

(THREE)
Headquarters, U.S. Marine Corps Parachute School
Lakehurst Naval Air Station
Lakehurst, New Jersey
15 May 1942

First Lieutenant Richard B. Macklin, USMC, heard the knock at the jamb of his open office door, and then his peripheral vision picked up First Sergeant George J. Hammersmith standing there with a sheet of teletype paper in his hand.

Macklin did not raise his eyes from the papers on his desk. First Things First made sense. If you interrupted your work every time someone appeared at your door, you never got anything done. And he certainly didn't want Sergeant Hammersmith to form the opinion, as so many old Marines did, that a commanding officer had nothing to do but sit behind a desk and wait for payday while the sergeants ran the Corps.

He finished what he was doing, which was to consider a request from the Navy Commander of Lakehurst that he permanently detail two enlisted men a day to work with the Base Engineer on roads and grounds. He decided against it; Para-Marines had more important things to do than pick up trash and cut weeds. Then he raised his head.

"You wish something, First Sergeant?"

"Got a TWX here, Sir, I thought you'd want to see right away."

Macklin made an impatient gesture for Hammersmith to give him the sheet of teletype paper. He judged in advance that the message would probably be of little genuine importance and could just as easily have been sent by mail. In his view, ninety-five percent of TWXs were a waste of time.

He was wrong.

HEADQUARTERS USMC
WASHDC 0755 15MAY42
ROUTINE

COMMANDING OFFICER
USMC PARACHUTE SCHOOL
LAKEHURST NAVAL AIR STATION
LAKEHURST NJ

1. ON RECEIPT, ISSUE NECESSARY ORDERS DETACHING 1ST LT RICHARD B. MACKLIN, USMC, FROM HEADQUARTERS AND HEAD-

QUARTERS COMPANY USMC PARASCHOOL LAKEHURST NAS NJ FOR TRANSFER TO HQ & HQ COMPANY 1ST USMC PARA BN, FLEET MARINE FORCE PACIFIC.

2. LT MACKLIN WILL REPORT TO US NAVAL BASE SAN DIEGO CAL NOT LATER THAN 2400 HOURS 30 MAY 1942 FOR FURTHER SHIPMENT TO FINAL DESTINATION. TRAVEL BY FIRST AVAILABLE MIL AND/OR CIV RAIL, AIR, OR MOTOR TRANSPORTATION TO SAN DIEGO IS AUTHORIZED. TRAVEL BEYOND SAN DIEGO WILL BE BY US GOVT SEA OR AIR TRANSPORT, PRIORITY BBBB2B.

3. TIME PERMITTING LT MACKLIN IS AUTHORIZED NO MORE THAN SEVEN (7) DAYS DELAY EN ROUTE OVERSEAS LEAVE.

4. LT MACKLIN WILL COMPLY WITH ALL APPLICABLE REGULATIONS CONCERNING OVERSEAS TRANSFER BEFORE DEPARTING LAKEHURST. STORAGE OF PERSONAL AND HOUSEHOLD GOODS AND ONE (1) PRIVATELY OWNED AUTOMOBILE AT GOVT EXPENSE IS AUTHORIZED.

5. HEADQUARTERS USMC (ATTN: PERS/23/A/11) WILL BE NOTIFIED BY TWX OF DATE OF LT MACKLIN'S DEPARTURE.

BY DIRECTION:

FRANK J. BOEHM, CAPT, USMCR

The first thing that occurred to Lieutenant Macklin was that it was sort of funny that as the Commanding Officer of the Parachute School, he would be ordering himself overseas.

Then it no longer seemed amusing at all.

His promotion had not come through.

He was supposed to be in San Diego two weeks from tomorrow, and from there he was going to the Pacific—in other words, to war.

It didn't seem fair. Just as he was getting the Parachute School shipshape, they were taking it away from him.

It seemed to him that he could make a far greater contribution to the Marine Corps where he was—as an expert in place, so to speak—than in a routine assignment in the 1st Parachute Battalion.

After some thought, he picked up the telephone and called Captain Boehm, who had signed the TWX and had presumably made the decision to send him overseas. He outlined to Boehm the reasons it would be to the greater benefit of the Marine Corps if the TWX was rescinded.

Captain Boehm was not at all receptive. He was, in fact, downright insulting:

"I heard you were a scumbag, Macklin. But I never thought I would personally hear a Marine officer trying to weasel out of going overseas."

(FOUR)
The Officers' Club
U.S. Marine Corps Base
Quantico, Virginia
1730 Hours 17 May 1942

When he entered the club, First Lieutenant David F. Schneider, USMC, was not exactly *pleased* to bump into First Lieutenant James G. Ward, USMCR, and Lieutenant Ward's aunt, Mrs. Caroline Ward McNamara. But neither was he exactly unhappy. He reacted like a man for whom fate has made a decision he would rather not have made himself.

Now that he had accidentally bumped into them, so to speak, as opposed to having gone looking for them, he could begin to rectify an unpleasant situation that it was his duty, as a regular Marine officer, to rectify for the good of the Corps.

Schneider had learned of Mrs. McNamara's presence on the base the day before: He was looking for Lieutenant Ward; so he walked into the squadron office and asked the sergeant on duty if he had seen him.

"He took the lady over to the Officers' Guest House, Lieutenant."

The Guest House was a facility provided to temporarily house (there was a seventy-two-hour limit) dependents and friends of Quantico officers.

"What lady?"

"Didn't get her name. Nice looking. First, she asked for Sergeant Galloway; and when I told her he wasn't back yet, she asked for Lieutenant Ward, so I got him on the phone, and he came over and fetched her and told me he was taking her over to the Guest House." There was a perceptible pause before the sergeant added, "Sir."

There was little question that the lady was Mrs. Caroline Ward McNamara, but Schneider was a careful, methodical man. He called the Guest House later that day to inquire if there was a Mrs. McNamara registered. And, of course, there was.

Technical Sergeant Charles M. Galloway had gone to Washington in response to a telephone call from General McInerney's office. But Washington was to be only his first stop. Schneider suspected that Major Jake Dillon, the Public Affairs Officer, was behind the mysterious call from General McInerney's office. If that was the case, there was no telling where Galloway had gone after he left Washington.

"Hey, Dave," Ward called to him. "I thought you would show up here."

"Good evening," Schneider said.

"You remember my Aunt Caroline, don't you?"

"Of course. How nice to see you again, Mrs. McNamara."

"Oh, call me Caroline!"

Dave Schneider smiled at her, but did not respond.

"Let's go in the bar," Jim Ward suggested. Schneider smiled again, and again did not reply.

The bar was crowded with young officers. With varying degrees of discretion, they all made it clear that they considered Mrs. Caroline Ward McNamara one of the better specimens of the gentle gender.

Dave Schneider wondered if they would register so much approval of the "lady" if they were aware that Mrs. McNamara was not only shacked up with an enlisted man but apparently didn't much care who knew about it.

They found a small table across from the bar.

"Dave, do you have any idea where Charley Galloway is?" Jim Ward asked, as soon as the waiter had taken their order.

"I believe he's in Washington," Schneider said. "Specifically, with Major Dillon."

"No, he's not," Caroline said. "We just called Jake. Jake said he hadn't heard from him since Tuesday morning, when he left the Willard. He spent Monday night there with Jake."

Reserve officer or not, Mustang or not, Lieutenant Schneider thought angrily, *Major Jake Dillon should know better than to offer an enlisted man the freedom of his hotel suite.*

"He called Caroline from Pensacola—" Jim Ward said.

"Pensacola?" Schneider interrupted.

"Pensacola. He called on Wednesday. He told Caroline he was going to the West Coast," Jim Ward said.

"Actually, he said he had a week to get out there," Caroline McNamara said, "and suggested we could drive out there together."

Jim Ward looked a little uncomfortable when she said that, Schneider noticed.

And well he should. There is absolutely no suggestion that his aunt finds anything wrong with the idea that she has been asked to drive cross-country alone with a man to whom she's not married. Having a shameless aunt like that should embarrass anybody.

"That sounds like he's on orders," Jim Ward said. "But when Caroline showed up here, and no Charley Galloway, I checked. No orders have come down on him that anyone knows about."

"I can't imagine what's going on," Schneider said. "Did anyone in the squadron office know he was in Pensacola?"

"All the squadron knows is that he went to Washington on the verbal orders of Colonel Hershberger. That was eight, nine days ago," Jim Ward said.

"Is there a Lieutenant Jim Ward in here?" the bartender called, holding up a telephone.

Jim Ward got up and walked to the bar and took the telephone. Less than a minute later he was back at the table, smiling.

"Our wandering boy has been heard from," he said. "That was Jerry O'Malloy. He's the duty officer. I asked him to let me know the minute he heard anything about Galloway."

"And?" Caroline McNamara asked excitedly.

"Charley just called the tower. He's twenty minutes out," Ward said, then turned to look at Schneider and added, "In an F4F."

"In a what?" Caroline asked.

"A Wildcat," Jim Ward said. "A fighter plane. I wonder where he got that, and what he's doing with it?"

"Well, I intend to find out," Lieutenant David Schneider said, and started to get up.

"Sit down, Dave. I told O'Malloy to have Charley call me here the minute he gets in."

"I'm going to be at Base Operations when he lands," Schneider said.

"What the hell is the matter with you?"

"You know damned well what's the matter with me. For one thing, and you know it as well as I do, he is absolutely forbidden to fly fighters."

"And for another?" Ward asked coldly.

"I would prefer to discuss that privately with you, if you don't mind."

"Sit down, Dave," Jim Ward said.

Schneider looked at him in surprise.

"You heard me, sit down," Jim Ward repeated firmly. "I don't know what Charley is doing with an F4F, but I do know that it's none of your business or mine. That's between him and the squadron commander."

Schneider sat down.

"When he calls, I'll ask him what's going on," Jim Ward said. "In the meantime, we'll pursue the legal principle that you're innocent until proven guilty."

"I don't like the way this sounds," Caroline said. "What's going on? What's wrong?"

"Never worry about things you can't control," Jim Ward said. "So far as we *know,* nothing is wrong."

Charley Galloway did not telephone. Half an hour later, he walked up to the table, leaned down, said, "Hi, baby," to Mrs. McNamara, and kissed her on the lips.

He was wearing his fur-collared leather flight jacket over tropical worsteds. He had jammed a fore-and-aft cap in one pocket of the flight jacket, and thin leather flying gloves in the other. He almost needed a shave, and there was a light band around his eyes where his flying goggles had protected the skin from the oily mist that often filled a Wildcat cockpit. It was obvious that he had come to the club directly from the flight line.

"Where have you been, honey?" Caroline asked. "I was getting really worried."

"That's a long story," he said.

"Charley," Jim Ward asked uncomfortably, "should you be in here?"

"He knows damn well he shouldn't," Dave Schneider flared. "What the *hell* do you think you're doing, Galloway?"

"Are you talking to me, Lieutenant?" Charley asked pleasantly. He shrugged out of the leather jacket and dropped it on the floor.

"Yes, I am."

"Then please use the words 'Captain,' and 'Sir,' " Charley said. He faced Dave Schneider, smiled broadly, and pointed to the twin silver bars on each of his collar points.

"Jesus!" Jim Ward said. "Are they for real?"

"I got them from the Commandant himself, believe it or not," Charley said. "Together with a brief, but memorable, lecture on the conduct expected of me now that I was going to be an officer and a gentleman."

"What about the West Coast?" Caroline asked softly.

"I'm going to be given a fighter squadron, baby," Charley Galloway said. "As soon as I can get out to the Pacific and organize one. They're going to fly me at least as far as Pearl. I've got six days to get to San Diego."

"Oh, God!"

"Can I go with you?" Jim Ward asked softly.

"With Aunt Caroline and me? Hell, no," Charley Galloway said indignantly. "Didn't you ever hear that three's a crowd?"

"That's not what I meant, Captain, Sir."

"If, in the next three weeks or a month, you can scare up an IP here who is willing to check you out in that Wildcat I just brought up here, you can come along later. I've got authorization to steal five pilots from here," Galloway said. Then he faced Dave Schneider. "That's an invitation to you too, Dave. You're a real horse's ass sometimes, but you're not too bad an airplane driver."

(FIVE)
Melbourne, Australia
19 May 1942

The Martin PBM-3R Mariner made landfall on the Australian continent near Moruya, in New South Wales, seventy-five miles southeast of the Australian capital at Canberra. The PBM-3R Mariner was the unarmed transport version of the standard PBM Mariner, a deep-hulled, twin-engined gull-winged monoplane.

Aboard were a crew of six, nineteen passengers, and eight hundred pounds of priority cargo, including a half-dozen mail bags.

When the excitement of finally making landfall had died down—for most aboard, it was their first view of Australia—Captain D. B. Toller, Civil Engineer Corps, USN, permitted his curiosity to take charge. He walked to the forward part of the cabin, just below the ladder leading to the cockpit, and sat down beside a Marine Corps major.

"All right if I sit here?"

"Certainly, Sir."

"I'm Captain Dick Toller, Major," he said, offering his hand.

"Ed Banning, Sir."

"Well, we're finally here. Or almost. This has been a long flight."

"Yes, Sir, it has. I'll be glad to get off this thing and stretch my legs."

"Now, if I'm asking something I shouldn't, just tell me to mind my own business," Captain Toller said. "But I'm really curious about something."

"Yes, Sir?"

"Him," Captain Toller said, nodding his head to a small area to the left of the ladder of the cockpit, where Corporal Stephen M. Koffler was curled up asleep, under blankets he had removed from his duffel bag. Koffler had rolled around in his sleep and wound up with his arm around his Springfield 1903 rifle. It looked as if he was holding it protectively, affectionately, as a child holds a teddy bear.

Banning chuckled.

"Corporal Koffler. He's got the right idea. He slept from 'Diego to Hawaii; and except to eat, he's been asleep most of the way here."

"I saw you get on the plane at Pearl," Captain Toller said. "I mean to say, I saw a very annoyed lieutenant commander and an even more annoyed captain being told to give up their seats in favor of passengers with higher priorities. And then you two came aboard."

Banning didn't reply. He was not particularly surprised by the question. The bumped-from-the-flight captain and lieutenant commander had glowered at him with barely contained indignation when they climbed down from the airplane into the launch and he and Koffler climbed aboard. Getting bumped by a Marine major was bad enough; but to be bumped by a Marine corporal with a higher priority was a little too much of a blow to a senior officer's dignity.

It *was* a question of priorities. Lieutenant Colonel F. L. Rickabee had set up their travel; and he apparently had easy—and probably unquestioned—access to the higher priorities. Special Detachment 14 had occupied most of the seats on the Mariner from San Diego to Pearl. The Air Shipment Officer at Pearl had been almost apologetic when he explained that seats were in even shorter supply from Pearl onward, and that all he could provide on this flight were two seats. The others in Special Detachment 14 would have to follow later. A lot of people with high priorities had to get to Australia.

Banning had decided to take one of the two available seats himself, not as a privilege of rank, but because he was hand-carrying a letter from the Secretary of the Navy himself to Captain Fleming Pickering, and because he thought that, as commanding officer, he should get there as soon as possible. He had taken Koffler with him because he suspected that his most important personnel requirement immediately on reaching Australia would be for a typist. Koffler had boarded the Mariner carrying his portable typewriter as well as his rifle.

Banning had no intention of satisfying Captain Toller's curiosity about Corporal Koffler's presence on the Mariner. For one thing, it was none of Captain Toller's business why Koffler was aboard the Mariner. And for another, it would only exacerbate the Captain's annoyance if he told him the unvarnished truth.

"It's a strange war, isn't it?" Captain Toller went on, "when getting a major and his corporal to the theater of operations is of more importance to the war effort than getting a lieutenant commander and a captain there."

Banning resisted the temptation to, politely of course, tell the Captain to go fuck himself.

"Our orders are classified, Sir," Banning said. "But out of school, apropos of nothing at all, may I observe that there are very few people in the Naval Service, commissioned or enlisted, who were raised in Yokohama and speak Japanese fluently?"

Captain Toller nodded solemmly.

"I thought it might be something like that," he said. "I wasn't trying to pry, Major, you understand. Just curious."

"Your curiosity is certainly understandable, Sir. But I think I've said more than I should already."

Captain Toller put his finger in front of his lips in the gesture of silence, and winked.

"Thank you, Sir," Banning said politely.

There was now a range of mountains off the right wing tip. When there was a break in their tops, Banning could see what was obviously a near-desert area on the far side. Below them, the terrain was either green or showed signs of fall cultivation.

I should have remembered that the seasons here are the reverse of those in America.

The plane began to let down an hour or so later. When the pilot corrected his course, Banning for a moment could see they were approaching a populated area. And then an enclosed body of water appeared.

Port Phillip Bay, Banning decided, pleased that he had taken the trouble to look at some maps.

He went to Koffler and pushed at him with the toe of his shoe. And then pushed twice more, harder, before Koffler sat up.

"Yes, Sir?"

"We're here," Banning said.

"Already?" Koffler asked.

The Mariner touched down several minutes later with an enormous splash, bounced airborne again; and then, with an even larger splash, it made final contact with the waters of Port Phillip Bay and slowed abruptly.

A launch carried them from the Mariner to a wharf. U.S. NAVY was stenciled on the wharf's sides. There was a bus, an English bus, now painted Navy gray. But when Banning started toward it, someone called his name.

"Major Banning?"

A tall, handsome, distinguished-looking man in a Navy captain's uniform was smiling at him.

"Yes, Sir."

"I'm Fleming Pickering," the Captain said, offering his hand. "Welcome to Australia."

Steve Koffler came up to them, staggering under the weight of his duffel bag, rifle, and typewriter.

"I'll get your bags, Sir," he said, and walked back toward the launch.

"He's with you?"

"Yes, Sir. I thought I was probably going to need a typist."

"Good thinking," Pickering chuckled. "But I didn't know you would have him with you, so that's one problem I hadn't thought of."

"Sir?"

"Putting him up," Pickering said. "You'll be staying with me. But having a corporal there would be a little awkward."

"I understand, Sir."

"Don't misunderstand me, Major," Pickering said. "I have nothing whatever against Marine corporals. In fact, I used to *be* a Marine corporal; and therefore I am well acquainted with what splendid all-around fellows they are. But you and I are in the Menzies Hotel, in an apartment directly over MacArthur and his family. We'll have to get him into another hotel for the time being."

"Sir, I have a letter for you from Secretary Knox."

"Wait till we get in the car," Pickering said, and gestured toward a 1939 Jaguar drop-head coupe.

"Nice car."

"Yes, it is. I hate like hell having to give it back. It belongs to a friend of mine here. It annoys the hell out of MacArthur's palace guard."

Major Ed Banning decided he was going to like Captain Fleming Pickering, and his snap judgment was immediately confirmed when Pickering picked up Steve Koffler's duffel bag and Springfield and started toward the Jaguar.

"It's been a long time since I had a duffel bag in one hand and a Springfield in the other," Pickering said, smiling. "You go help the Corporal with your bags, while I put these in the car."

"Your tax dollars at work," Captain Pickering said, chuckling, to Major Banning, when Banning came out of the bathroom in a bathrobe. He handed Banning a green slip of paper.

It was a check drawn on the Treasurer of the United States. It was payable to the bearer, and was in the amount of $250,000.

They were in Pickering's suite in the Menzies Hotel. First they'd installed Corporal Koffler in a businessmen's hotel (Pickering had handed him some money and told him to get something to eat, and to try to stay out of trouble). Then they'd come to the Menzies, where Pickering had made him a drink, then called the valet to have Banning's uniforms pressed.

"The Commander-in-Chief dresses in worn thin khakis, no tie, and wears a cap I think he brought home from World War I. Naturally, if you know MacArthur, he consequently expects everyone else around him to look like a page from *The Officer's Guide.*"

"Sir, what is this?" Banning asked, pointing to the check.

"Your expense money. Or *our* expense money. It's from the Secretary's Confidential Fund. It was in the letter you brought. Knox says that it's unaccountable, but I think it would be wise for us to keep some sort of a record of where we spend it. Koffler's hotel bill, for example. In the morning we'll go around to the Bank of Victoria, deposit it, and arrange for you to be able to write checks against it. And you'd better take some cash, too. Six thousand–odd dollars of that is mine."

"Sir?"

"I bought some maps that neither the Army nor the Navy could come up with on their own. I was happy to do it, but I want my money back. Whiskey all right?"

"I'm overwhelmed by your hospitality, Sir."

"I'm delighted that you're here. I sometimes feel very much the lonely soul. At least I won't have to watch what I say to you after I've had a couple of drinks."

"I'm carrying a message for you from Mrs. Feller, Sir, too."

"Oh. She was my secretary in Washington when I first came in the Navy. And, of course, you know what she's doing in Hawaii."

"Yes, Sir. When I saw her there, she said to give you her best regards, and to tell you that she hopes you'll soon have a chance to resume your interrupted conversation."

"What?"

"She sends her regards and says she hopes you'll soon have a chance to resume your interrupted conversation."

"Oh. Yes, of course. Private joke."

My God, she's not only not embarrassed about what happened in the Coronado Beach Hotel, but wants me to know she meant what she said. Thank Christ she's in Hawaii!

A bellman delivered a crisply pressed uniform and a pair of highly polished shoes.

Pickering followed Banning into the bedroom as Banning started to get dressed.

"Tomorrow, I'm going to take you around to meet Admiral Brewer," he said. "Australian. Deputy chief of their naval intelligence. I want you to meet him and see if we can't get a letter of introduction for you to the man who runs the Coastwatcher operation. They're working out of a little town called Townesville, on the northeastern coast. The man in charge is a guy named Eric Feldt, Lieutenant Commander, Australian Navy. Nice guy. Until I met you, I was a little worried. He is not overly fond of the U.S. Navy officers he's met. But I think he'll get along with you."

"That's flattering, Sir, but why?"

"Just a feeling. I think you're two of a kind."

"Captain, I don't know how soon, but probably within the next couple of days, the rest of my people will be coming in from Hawaii, probably in dribs and drabs. Should I make arrangements to put them into that hotel with Koffler?"

"How many?"

"One officer, a first lieutenant, and fifteen enlisted men."

"I'm not trying to tell you how to run your operation, but presumably you'll be moving them, or at least most of them, to Townesville?"

"If that's where the Coastwatchers are, yes, Sir."

"Open to suggestion?"

"Yes, Sir, of course."

"I think you'd better go up there alone at first. If things work out, you can rent a house for them up there."

" 'If things work out,' Sir?"

"Commander Feldt can be difficult," Pickering said. "Both the Army and the Navy have sent people up there. He told both groups to 'sod off.' Can you guess what that means?"

"I think so, Sir," Banning said, smiling.

"I'm hoping that he will see you as someone who has come to be of help, not take charge. If he does, then you can rent a house for your people up there. In the meantime, it might get a little crowded, so we'll put them up in my house, here."

"Your house, Sir?"

"Against what I suppose is the inevitable—my being told to vacate these quarters—I rented a house." He saw the confusion on Banning's face. "A number, a large number, of MacArthur's Palace Guard want me out of here; I am too close to the Divine Throne."

"I understand, Sir," Banning said, turning from the mirror where he was tying his field scarf to smile at Pickering.

"I'll call. Right now, as a matter of fact, and have the house activated. If I had known you would have that kid with you, I would already have done it."

"Activated, Sir?"

"It comes with a small staff. Housekeeper, maids, a cook. Since I'm not in it, I put them on vacation."

"That sounds fine, but who pays for it? I'm not sure I'm authorized to put my people on per diem."

"Frank Knox's Confidential Fund will pay for it," Pickering said, "but let me make it clear to you, Banning, that you're authorized to do about anything you damned well please. You answer only to me."

He went to a telephone and gave the operator a number.

"Mrs. Mannshow, this is Fleming Pickering. I'm glad I caught you in. Do you think you could get those people to come off Ninety Mile Beach and start running the house starting tomorrow?"

He looked at Banning and smiled, and gestured for Banning to make himself another drink.

(SIX)

Eyes Only—The Secretary of the Navy

DUPLICATION FORBIDDEN

ORIGINAL TO BE DESTROYED AFTER ENCRYPTION AND TRANSMITTAL TO SECNAVY

Menzies Hotel
Melbourne, Australia
Wednesday, 20 May 1942

Dear Frank:

I thought it appropriate to report on the status quo here, especially

the thinking of the General, insofar as the Battle of the Coral Sea and other events seem to have affected it.

But before I get to that, let me report the arrival of my own reinforcements. Major Ed Banning arrived yesterday, together with his advance party, one ferocious Marine paratrooper who must be all of seventeen. The balance of his command is still in Hawaii, trying to get on an airplane for the trip here. If it could be arranged to get them a higher priority without causing undue attention, I suggest that it be provided to them. In my judgment, it is more important to get Banning's people here and integrated with the Australian Coastwatchers than it is to send more Army and Marine colonels and Navy captains here so they can start setting up their empires.

Banning, of course, carried your letter, for which I thank you (and the check, for which I thank you even more; if Banning has to start chartering fishing boats, etc., his operation can become very expensive, very soon). And he brought me up to date on Albatross operations in Hawaii, in particular their effectiveness vis-a-vis what happened in the Coral Sea.

I am very impressed with Banning, but fear that he is less than pleased with me. He made it clear that he considers himself to be under my orders, which I immediately made use of by forbidding him even to think about going behind Japanese lines himself. Because of his Japanese language skills and understanding of their minds, for one thing, and for another, because I think he knows too much about Albatross, he is too valuable to risk being captured.

Now to the General:

Until he learned that the Japanese had occupied Tulagi, I really didn't think he paid much attention to the fact that the border between his area and Nimitz's had been moved from 160 degrees east longitude, where the Joint Chiefs originally established it, to where it is now. But after the Japs took Tulagi, he became painfully aware that Nimitz now had responsibility for both Tulagi and Guadalcanal, the much larger island to the south.

He is now convinced that the new division of responsibility was established—the line changed—by his cabal of enemies, Marshall and King again, to deny him authority over territory he considers essential to his mission of defending Australia. I am finding it harder and harder to fault his logic and support that of the JCS.

The argument, I know, is that it is the Navy's responsibility to maintain the sea lanes, and that was the argument for putting the border at 160 EL. MacArthur counters that this would hold water only if the Navy were occupying the land in question and using it for that purpose. And, of course, they are not, and have shown no indication that they intend to.

All of this was exacerbated when he learned that the day after he had surrendered Corregidor, General Wainwright went on the radio in Manila and ordered all forces in the Philippines to lay down their

arms. This enraged him for several reasons, not necessarily in proportion to their importance to the war.

He seemed most enraged (and found it another proof that George Marshall stays awake nights thinking up new evil things to do to him) by the fact that Wainwright, apparently encouraged by Washington, no longer considered himself subordinate to MacArthur, and thus surrendered Corregidor on his own—without, in other words, MacA.'s authority to do so.

Second, he is absolutely convinced that Wainwright, again encouraged by Washington, went even further than that, by assuming authority for all U.S./Filipino Forces in the Philippines, an authority MacA., with reason, believed he still retained, having never been formally relieved of it.

General Sharp, on Mindanao, was specifically ordered to surrender by Wainwright. According to MacA., Sharp had 30,000 U.S./Filipino troops, armed, and in far better shape insofar as ammunition, rations, etcetera, than any others in the islands. It is hard to understand why they were ordered to surrender. As it turns out, MacA. has learned that Sharp paid only lip service to Wainwright's orders and encouraged his men to go to the hills and organize as guerrillas. He himself and most of his immediate staff felt obliged to follow orders, and they surrendered.

MacArthur feels a sense of shame (wholly unjustified, I think) for the loss of the Philippines. And he has an at least partially justified feeling that he is being treated unfairly by Washington in his present command.

Two days after Corregidor fell, he cabled General Marshall (ignoring the implication that Marshall couldn't figure this out himself) that the Japanese victory in the Philippines will free two infantry divisions and a large number of aircraft that they will probably use to take New Guinea, and then the Solomons. They will then cut his supply routes to the United States, which would mean the loss of Australia.

MacA. proposed to go on the counterattack, starting with the recapture of Tulagi, and then establishing our own presence on Guadalcanal. In his mind (and in mine) he tried to be a good soldier and to "coordinate" this with South Pacific Area Headquarters. But he was (a) reminded that Guadalcanal and Tulagi are not "within his sphere of influence" and that (b) under those circumstances it was really rather presumptuous of him to ask for Navy aircraft carriers, etcetera, to conduct an operation in their sphere of influence, but that (c) he was not to worry, because Admiral Nimitz was already making plans to recapture Tulagi with a Marine Raider battalion.

There is no way that one small battalion can take Tulagi; but even if they could, they cannot hold it long—if the Japanese establish bases, which seems a given, on either Guadalcanal or Malaita.

What MacArthur wants to do makes more sense to me than what the Navy proposes to do, unless, as MacA. believes, the Navy's pri-

mary purpose is to render him impotent and humiliated, so that the war here will be a Navy war.

I fight against accepting this latter theory. But what I saw at—and especially after—Pearl Harbor, with the admirals pulling their wagons into a circle to avoid accepting the blame, keeps popping into my head.

Respectfully,

Fleming Pickering, Captain, USNR

XII

(ONE)
The Elms
Dandenong, Victoria, Australia
22 May 1942

"Oh, good morning! We didn't expect you to be up so early," Mrs. Hortense Cavendish said, with a smile, to Corporal Stephen M. Koffler, USMC, when she saw him coming down the stairway. "Why don't you just go into the breakfast room, and I'll get you a nice hot cup of tea?"

"Good morning, thank you," Steve said, smiling, but not really comfortable.

Mrs. Cavendish was as old as his mother, and looked something like her, too. She was the housekeeper at The Elms, a three-story, twelve-room, red brick house set in what looked to Steve like its own private park fifteen miles or so outside Melbourne. It was called The Elms, Major Banning had told him, because of the century-old elm trees which lined the driveway from the "motorway" to the house.

He also told him *(You've come up smelling like a rose again, Koffler.)* that the whole place had been rented by Captain Pickering, and, for the time being at least, he and the other members of Special Detachment 14 would be living there. He explained that the housekeeper was something like the manager of a hotel, in charge of the whole place, and was to be treated with the appropriate respect.

At the moment, Corporal Koffler was the only member of Special Detachment 14 in residence. The day before, Major Banning had driven him out here in a brand-new Studebaker President, then had him installed in a huge room with a private bathroom. After that, Captain Pickering had come out and taken Major Banning to the railroad station in Melbourne. Banning was going "up north" to some place called Townesville, Queensland, where the Coastwatchers had their headquarters. He told Steve he had no idea when he would be back, but that he would keep in touch.

Steve now understood that Queensland, New South Wales, and Victoria were something like the states in America, but that was really about all he understood about Australia.

From what Major Banning had told him, and from what he'd heard from the other guys, the Japs were probably going to take Australia. He had heard Major Banning talking to Lieutenant Howard back in 'Diego about it. Steve had long ago decided that if *anybody* would have the straight poop about *anything,* Major Banning would. Major Banning had told Lieutenant Howard that he didn't see how anything could keep the Japs from taking Australia, as long as they took some island named New Guinea first. And he really didn't see how the Japs could be kept from taking New Guinea.

To tell the truth, the closer they got to Australia, the more nervous Koffler had become. More than nervous. Scared. He tried hard not to let it show, of course, in front of all the Army and Navy officers on the airplane (he was, after all, not only a Marine, but a Marine parachutist, and Marines aren't supposed to be nervous or scared). But when the airplane landed, he would not really have been surprised if the Japs had been shelling or maybe bombing the place. That would have meant they'd have started fighting right away. He had cleaned and oiled his Springfield before they left Hawaii, just to be double sure.

But it hadn't been that way at all. There was no more sign of war, or Japs, in Melbourne than there was in Newark. Melbourne was like Newark, maybe as big, and certainly a hell of a lot cleaner. Except for the funny-looking trucks and cars, which the Australians drove on the wrong side of the road, and the funny way the Australians talked, sort of through their noses, you'd never even know you were *in* Australia.

He'd spent his first night in a real nice hotel, and Captain Pickering had given him money, and he had had a real nice meal in a real nice restaurant. The steak was a little tough, but he had no call to bitch about the size of it—it just about covered the plate—and he had trouble getting it all down. Then he went to the movies, and they were playing an American movie. It starred Betty Grable, and he remembered seeing it in the Ampere Theatre in East Orange just before he joined the Corps. And that started him off remembering Dianne Marshall and what had happened between them. And between the movie and the memories, he got a little homesick . . . until he talked himself out of that by reminding himself that he was a Marine *parachutist,* for Christ's sake, and not supposed to start crying in his goddamned beer because he was away from his mommy or because some old whore had made a goddamned fool out of him.

The table in the breakfast room was big, and the wood sort of glowed. There was a bowl of flowers in the middle of it. When he sat down at it, he looked out through windows running from the ceiling to the floor; outside he could see a man raking leaves out of a flower garden. There was a concrete statue of a nearly naked woman in the garden, in the middle of a what looked like a little pond, except there wasn't any water in the pond.

Mrs. Cavendish followed him in in a moment, and laid a newspaper on the table. Right behind her was a maid, a plain woman maybe thirty years old, wearing a black dress with a little white apron in front. She smiled at Steve, then went to one of the cabinets in the room, and took out a woven place mat and silver and set it up in front of him.

"What would you like for breakfast?" Mrs. Cavendish asked. "Ham and eggs? There's kippers."

Steve had no idea what a kipper was.

"Ham and eggs would be fine," he said. "Over easy."

"We have tomato and pineapple juice."

"Tomato juice would be fine," Steve said.

"The tea's brewing," Mrs. Cavendish said. "It'll just be a moment."

She and the maid left the room. Steve unfolded the newspaper. It was *The Times of Victoria.* The pages were bigger than those of the *Newark Evening News,* but there weren't very many of them. He flipped through it, looking in vain for comics, and then returned to the first page.

There were two big headlines: ROMMEL NEARS TOBRUK and NAZI TANKS APPROACH LENINGRAD. There was a picture of a burning German tank, and a map of North Africa with wide, curving arrows drawn on it.

Steve wondered why there wasn't anything in the newspaper about the Japs being about to invade Australia.

He went through the newspaper, mostly reading the advertisements for strange brands of toothpaste, used motorcars, and something called Bovril. He wondered what Bovril was, whether you ate it, or drank it, or washed your mouth out with it, or what.

The maid delivered his ham and eggs, cold toast in a little rack, tomato juice, and a tub of sour orange marmalade. He had just about finished eating when the maid came in the breakfast room.

"Telephone for you, Sir," she said, and pointed to a telephone sitting on a sideboard.

The telephone was strange. There was sort of a cup over the mouthpiece, and the wire that ran from the base to the handset was much thinner than the one on American phones; it looked more like a couple of pieces of string twisted together than like a regular wire.

"Corporal Koffler, Sir," Steve said.

"Good morning, Corporal," a cheerful voice said. "Lieutenant Donnelly here." He pronounced it "leftenant," so Steve knew he was an Australian.

"Yes, Sir?"

"I'm the Air Transport Officer, Naval Station, Melbourne. We have two things for you. Actually, I mean to say, two shipments. There's several crates, priority air shipment, and we've been alerted that several of your people are scheduled to arrive about noon."

"Yes, Sir."

"Your Captain Pickering said to send the crates out there by lorry, and that you'll meet the aircraft. Any problems with that?"

"No, Sir," Steve said, an automatic reflex. Then he blurted, "Sir, I'm not sure if I can find . . . where the plane will be. Or how to get back out here."

Lieutenant Donnelly chuckled. "Well, you'll be able to find your way about soon enough, I'm sure. In the meantime, I'll just send a map, with the route marked, out there with the lorry driver. Do you think that will handle it?"

"Yes, Sir. Thank you."

"The lorry should be there within the hour. Thank you, Corporal."

"Thank you, Sir."

Steve hung up and went looking for Mrs. Cavendish. He was going to need some place to store the crates, whatever they contained. She showed him a three-car garage behind the house, now empty, that was just what he was looking for. There were sturdy metal doors which could be locked, and there were no windows.

The truck arrived forty-five minutes later. Steve, who had been looking out his bedroom window for it, saw that it said "Ford" on the radiator, but it was unlike any Ford Steve had ever seen. There were three people in the cab, all in uniform, and all female.

They all wore the same kind of caps, something like a Marine cap, except the visor wasn't leather. They wore the caps perched straight on top of their hair, and Steve thought they all looked kind of cute, like girls dressed up in men's uniforms. Two of them wore gray coveralls. The third, who looked like she was in charge, wore a tunic and a shirt and tie and a skirt, with really ugly stockings.

"Corporal Koffler?" she said, smiling at him and offering her hand. "I'm Petty Officer Farnsworth."

"Hi," Steve said. She was, he guessed, in her early twenties. He couldn't really tell what the rest of her looked like in the nearly shapeless uniform and those ugly cotton stockings, but her face was fine. She had light hazel eyes and freckles.

"Good day," the other two women said. In Australia that came out something like "G'die," which took some getting used to. One of them looked like she was about seventeen, and the other one looked old enough to be the first one's mother.

Neither of them, Steve immediately decided, had the class of Petty Officer Farnsworth.

"How are you?" Steve said, and walked over and shook hands with them.

"After we unload your crates," Petty Officer Farnsworth said, "Lieutenant Donnelly said I was to ask if you would like me to wait around and drive into Melbourne with you, to show you the way."

"Great!" Steve said.

"Where would you like the crates?"

"Let's see what they are," Steve said, and walked to the back of the truck. He saw three wooden crates, none of them as large as a footlocker. He couldn't tell what they contained, and there was nothing stenciled on them to identify them.

Petty Officer Farnsworth, who had followed him, handed him a manila envelope. "The shipping documents," she said.

He tore the envelope open. The U.S. Army Signal Center, Fort Monmouth, New Jersey, had shipped, on AAAA Air Priority, by authority of the Chief Signal Officer, U.S. Army, to the Commanding Officer, USMC Special Detachment 14, Melbourne, Australia:

1 EA SET, TRANSCEIVER, RADIO, HALLICRAFTERS MODEL 23C, W/48 CRYSTALS
1 EA ANTENNA SET, RADIO TRANSMISSION, PORTABLE, 55-FOOT W/ CABLES & GUY WIRES
1 EA GENERATOR, ELECTRICAL, FOOT AND HAND POWERED, 6 AND 12 VOLT DC

"Wow!" Steve said. He knew all about the Hallicrafters 23C, had studied carefully all of its specifications in the American Amateur Radio Relay League magazine, but he'd never seen one before.

"Am I permitted to ask what they are?" Petty Officer Farnsworth asked.

"Just about the best shortwave radio there is," Steve said.

"Lieutenant Donnelly said that I wasn't to ask questions," Petty Officer Farnsworth said, "about what you're doing out here."

"You didn't. You just asked what was in the boxes. There's nothing secret about that."

She smiled at him.

Nice teeth. Nice smile.

"Where would you like them?"

"Around in back," Steve said. "I'll show you."

When the crates had been unloaded, Petty Officer Farnsworth sent the truck back into Melbourne.

"It will take us no more than forty-five minutes to get to the quay," she said. "Which means we should leave here at eleven-fifteen. It's now quarter past nine. Where can I pass two hours out of your way, where I will see nothing I'm not supposed to see?"

"I don't have anything to do. And there's nothing out here for you to see. Would you like a cup of coffee?"

"Tea?"

"Oh, sure."

"That would be very nice, Corporal," Petty Officer Farnsworth said.

Steve took her into the breakfast room, sat her down, and then went into the kitchen and asked for tea. They waited for several minutes in an awkward silence until one of the maids delivered a tea tray, complete to toast and cookies.

"Where are you from in America?" Petty Officer Farnsworth asked.

"Where the radios come from. New Jersey. How about you?"

"I'm from Wagga Wagga, in New South Wales."

"Wagga Wagga?" he asked, smiling.

"I think that's an Aborigine name."

"That's what you call your colored people?"

"Yes, but as I understand it, they're not like yours."

"How come?"

"Well, yours were taken from Africa and sent to America, as I understand it, and the Aborigines were here when we English arrived."

"Sort of Australian Indians, in other words?"

"I suppose. New South Wales, of course, is named after South Wales, in England."

"So is New Jersey," he said. "Jersey is in England."

"I thought it was an island."

"Well, it could be. I never really paid much attention."

Petty Officer Farnsworth had an unkind thought. Corporal Koffler was a nice enough young man, and not unattractive, but obviously bloody goddamned stupid.

Petty Officer Farnsworth was twenty-three years old, and she had been married for five years to John Andrew Farnsworth, now a sergeant with the Royal Australian Signals Corps somewhere in North Africa.

Before the war, she and John had lived in a newly built house on his family's sheep ranch. When John had rushed to the sound of the British trumpet—a move that had baffled and enraged her—his family had decided that she would simply shoulder his responsibilities at the ranch in addition to her own. After all, John's father, brothers, and amazingly fecund sisters reasoned, she had no children to worry about, and One Must Do One's Part While the Family Hero Is Off Defending King and Country.

Petty Officer Farnsworth, whose Christian name was Daphne, had no intention of becoming a worn-out woman before her time, as the other women of the family either had or were about to. She used the same excuse to get off the ranch as John had: patriotism. When the advertisements for women to join the Royal Australian Navy Women's Volunteer Reserve had come out, she had announced that enlisting was her duty. Since John was already off fighting for King and Country, she could do no less, especially considering, as everyone kept pointing out, that she had no children to worry about.

The RANWVR had trained her as a typist and assigned her to the Naval Station in Melbourne. She had a job now that she liked, working for Lieutenant Donnelly. There was something different every day. And unlike some of the other officers she had worked for, Lieutenant kept his hands to himself.

Every once in a while she wondered if Donnelly's gentlemanly behavior was a mixed blessing. Lately she had been wondering about that more and more often, and it bothered her.

"Do all Marines wear boots like that?" she asked.

"No. Just parachutists."

"You're a parachutist?"

He pointed to his wings.

"Our parachutists wear berets," she said. "Red berets."

"You mean like women?"

My God, how can one young man be so stupid?

"Well, I suppose, yes. But I wouldn't say that where they could hear me, if I were you."

"I didn't mean nothing wrong by it, I just wanted to be sure we were talking about the same thing."

"Quite. So you're a wireless operator?"

"Yes and no."

"Yes and no?"

"Well, I am, but the Marine Corps doesn't know anything about it."

"Why not?"

"I didn't tell them, and then when they gave everybody the Morse code test, I made sure I flunked it."

"Why?" Now Daphne Farnsworth was fascinated. John had written a half-dozen times that the worst mistake he'd made in the Army was letting it be known that he could key forty words a minute. From the moment he'd gotten through basic training, the Army had him putting in long days, day after day, as a high-speed wireless telegrapher. He hated it.

"Well, I figured out if they was so short of guys who could copy fifty, sixty words a minute—you don't learn to do that overnight—they would be working the ass off those who could. Ooops. Sorry about the language."

"That's all right," Daphne said.

Well, Daphne, you bitchy little lady, you were wrong about this boy. Not only is he smart enough to take Morse faster than John, but he's smart enough not to let the service hear about it.

"My husband's a wireless operator," Daphne said. "With the British Eighth Army in Africa. He's a sergeant, but he hates being a wireless operator."

"I figured somebody as pretty as you would be married," Steve Koffler replied.

Is that the distilled essence of your observations of life, or are you making a pass at me, Corporal Koffler?

"For five years."

"You don't look that old."

"Thank you."

"You know what I'd really like to do before we go into town?"

Rip my clothes off, and throw me on the floor?

"No."

"I'd like to unpack that Hallicrafters. I've never really seen one. Could you read the newspaper, or something?"

"I think I'd rather go with you and see the radio. Or is it classified?"

"What we're doing is classified. Not the radio."

And now I am curious. What the bloody hell is going on around here? Marine parachutists? Villas in the country? "World's best wireless" shipped by priority air?

(TWO)
Townesville Station
Royal Australian Navy
Townesville, Queensland
24 May 1942

The office of the Commanding Officer, Coastwatcher Service, Royal Australian Navy (code name FERDINAND) was simple, even Spartan. The small room with whitewashed block walls in a tin-roofed building was furnished with a battered desk, several well-worn upholstered chairs, and some battered filing cabinets. A prewar recruiting poster for the Royal Australian Navy was stapled to one wall. On the wall behind the desk was an unpainted sheet of plywood, crudely hinged on top, that Major Ed Banning, USMC, immediately decided covered a map, or maps.

The Officer Commanding, Lieutenant Commander Eric A. Feldt, Royal Australian Navy, was a tall, thin, dark-eyed, and dark-haired man. He was not at all glad to see Banning, or the letter he'd brought from Admiral Brewer; and he was making absolutely no attempt to conceal this.

"Nothing personal, Major," he said finally, looking up at Banning from behind the desk. "I should have bloody well known this would be the next step."

"Sir?" Banning replied. He was standing with his hands locked behind him, more or less in the at-ease position.

"This," Feldt said, waving Admiral Brewer's letter. "You're not the first American to show up here. I ran the others off. I should have known somebody would sooner or later go over my head."

"Sir," Banning said, "let me make it clear that all I want to do here is help you in any way I can."

"Help me? How the hell could you possibly help me?"

"You would have to tell me that, Sir."

"What do you know about this area of the world?"

Banning took a chance: "I noticed you drive on the wrong side of the road, Sir."

It was not the reply Commander Feldt expected. He looked carefully at Banning; and after a very long moment, there was the hint of a smile.

"I was making reference, Major, to the waters in the area of the Bismarck Archipelago."

"Absolutely nothing, Sir."

"Well, that's an improvement over the last one. He told me with a straight face that he had studied the charts."

"Sir, my lack of knowledge is so overwhelming that I don't even know what's wrong with studying the charts."

"Well, for your general information, Major, there are very few charts, and the ones that do exist are notoriously inaccurate."

"Thank you, Sir."

"I don't suppose that you're any kind of an expert concerning shortwave wireless, either, are you, Major?"

"No, Sir. I know a little less about shortwave radios than I do about the Bismarck Archipelago."

There was again a vague hint of a smile.

"I know about your game baseball, Major. I know that the rule is three strikes and you're out. You now have two strikes against you."

"I'm sorry to hear that, Sir."

"Here's the final throw—"

"I believe the correct phrase is 'pitch,' Sir."

"The final *pitch,* then. What do you know of our enemy, the Jap?"

In Japanese, Banning said, "I read and write the language, Sir, and I learned enough about them in China to come to believe that no Westerner can ever know them well."

"I will be damned," Commander Feldt said. "That was Japanese? I don't speak a bloody word of it myself."

"That was Japanese, Sir," Banning said, and then translated what he had said a moment before.

"What were you doing in China?"

"I was the Intelligence Officer of the 4th Marines, Sir."

"And you went home to America before they were sent to the Philippines?"

"No, Sir, afterward."

"Are we splitting a hair here, Major? You went home before the war started?"

"No, Sir. After."

"You were considered too valuable, as an intelligence officer who speaks Japanese, to be captured?"

"No, Sir. I was medically evacuated. I was blinded by concussion."

"How?"

"They think probably concussion from artillery, Sir. My sight returned on the submarine that took me off Corregidor."

"Are you a married man, Major?"

"Yes, Sir."

"How would your wife react to the news—actually, there wouldn't be any news, she just wouldn't hear from you—that you were behind the Japanese lines?"

"That's a moot point, Sir. The one thing I have been forbidden to do is serve as a Coastwatcher myself."

Feldt grunted. "Me too," he said.

"My wife is still in China, Commander," Banning said.

Feldt met his eyes.

"I'm sorry," he said.

Feldt grunted as he heaved himself to his feet. He raised the sheet of plywood with another grunt, and shoved a heavy bolt through an eyebolt so that it would stay up. A map, covered with a sheet of celluloid, was exposed.

"This is our area of operation, Major," Commander Feldt said. "From the Admiralty Islands here, across the Pacific to the other side of New Ireland, and down to Vitiaz Strait between New Guinea and New Britain, and then down into the Solomon Sea in this area. The little marks are where we have people. The ones that are crossed out are places we haven't heard from in some time, or know for sure that the Japs have taken out."

Banning walked around the desk and studied the map for several minutes without speaking. He saw there were a number of Xs marking locations which were no longer operational.

"The people manning these stations," Feldt explained, "have been commissioned as junior officers, or warrant officers, in the Royal Australian Navy Volunteer Reserve. The idea is to try to have the Japs treat them as prisoners of war if they are captured. There's sort of a fuzzy area there. On one hand, if someone is in uniform, he is supposed to be treated as a POW if captured. On the other hand, what these people are doing, quite simply, is spying. One may shoot spies. The Japanese do. Or actually, they either torture our people to death; or, if they're paying attention to the code of Bushido, they have a formal little ceremony, the culmination of which is the beheading of our people by an officer of suitable rank."

Banning now grunted.

"My people," Feldt went on, "are primarily former civil servants or plantation managers and, in a few cases, missionaries. Most of them have spent years in their area. They speak the native languages and dialects, and in some cases—not all—are protected by the natives. They are undisciplined, irreverent, and contemptuous of military and naval organizations—and in particular of officers of the regular establishment. They are people of incredible courage and, for the obvious reasons, of infinite value to military or naval operations in this area."

"I heard something about this," Banning said. "I didn't realize how many of them there are."

"Supporting them logistically is very difficult," Feldt went on, as if he had not heard Banning, "for several reasons. For one thing, the distances. For another, the nonavailability, except in the most extreme circumstances, of submarines and aircraft. And when aircraft and submarines are available, they are of course limited to operation on the shorelines; and my people are most often in the mountains and jungle, some distance from the shore. Landing aircraft in the interior of the islands is ninety percent of the time impossible, and in any case it would give the Japs a pretty good idea where my people are. The result is that my people are eating the food they carried with them into the jungle (if any remains), and native food, which will not support health under the circumstances they have to live under. If illness strikes, or if they accidentally break an ankle, their chances of survival are minimal."

"Christ!" Banning said.

"In addition, the humidity and other conditions tend to render wireless equipment inoperable unless it is properly and constantly cared for. And these people are not technicians."

Banning shook his head.

"And now, Major, be good enough to tell me how you intend to help me."

"In addition to what you tell me to do," Banning said, after a moment, "money, parachutists, and radios. I might also be able to do something about aircraft priorities."

"Do you Americans really believe that money can solve any problem? I noticed you mentioned that first."

"I'm not sure about *any,*" Banning replied. "But *many?* Yes, Sir, I believe that. I've got a quarter of a million dollars in a bank in Melbourne that can be used to support you, and I can get more if I need more."

"That sounds very generous."

"The Marine Corps wants access to your intelligence," Banning said.

"You would have it anyway, wouldn't you, via your Navy?"

"We would like it direct," Banning said.

Feldt grunted.

"You said "parachutists'? Have you got parachutists?"

"I have one, Sir, already in Australia," Banning replied. He did not say, of course, *The notion of sending Koffler off on a mission like these is absurd on its face.* Then he added, "I can get more in a short period of time."

"What about wireless sets? I thought you said you didn't know anything about that."

"Sir, I don't," Banning said. "But some are on the way."

"What kind?"

"Sir, I don't know. I was told 'the best there is.' "

"I would like to know what kind."

"I'll find out for you," Banning said. "Just as soon as they show up. So far, the only asset I have in Australia is the money."

"And, of course, you."

"Yes, Sir. And my clerk," Banning said, and added, "He's the parachutist I mentioned. He's eighteen years old. I can't imagine sending him off to parachute onto some island. But, Sir, he knows about parachuting. He could tell us what we need, and probably what's available in the States."

Feldt either grunted or snorted, Banning wasn't sure which. Then he turned and pulled the bolt out of the eyebolt and lowered the sheet of raw plywood so that it again covered the map.

"Tell me, Major Banning," he said, "do you have a Christian name?"

"Yes, Sir. Edward."

"And your friends call you that? Or 'Ed'?"

"Ed, Sir."

"And do you drink, Ed? Wine, beer, spirits?"

"Yes, Sir. Wine, beer and spirits."

"Good. Having a Yank around here will be bad enough without him being a sodding teetotaler."

"May I interpret that to mean, Sir, that I may stay?"

"On condition that you break yourself of the habit of using the word 'Sir.' Are you aware, Ed, that you use 'Sir' in place of a comma?"

"I suppose I do."

"My Christian name is Eric," Feldt said. "But to keep things in their proper perspective around here, Ed, I think you had better call me 'Commander.' "

They smiled at each other.

"Let's go drink our lunch," Feldt said. "When we've done that, we'll see what can be done about getting you and your savages a place to live."

(THREE)
Townesville Station
Townesville, Queensland
31 May 1942

Major Edward Banning, USMC, was on hand when his command, less the rear echelon (Corporal Koffler), disembarked from the Melbourne train. USMC Special Detachment 14 debarked after the last of the civilian and a half-dozen Australian military passengers had come down from the train to the platform.

The first Marine off the train was Staff Sergeant Richardson, the senior NCO, who either didn't see Major Banning or pretended not to. He took up a position on the platform facing the sleeper car. Then, one by one, quickly, the others filed off and formed two ranks facing Staff Sergeant Richardson. They were carrying their weapons at sling arms. Most of them had Springfields, but here and there was a Thompson submachine gun.

They were not, however, wearing any of their web field equipment, Major Banning noticed. They were freshly turned out, in sharply creased greens, their fore-and-aft caps at a proper salty angle. Two or three of them seemed a bit flushed, as if, for example, they had recently imbibed some sort of alcoholic beverage.

Staff Sergeant Richardson fell them in, put them through the dress-right-dress maneuver, and did a snappy, precise, about-face. At that point, First Lieutenant Joseph L. Howard descended the sleeping-car steps.

He too either did not see Major Banning or pretended not to. He marched before Staff Sergeant Richardson, who saluted him crisply.

"Sir," Staff Sergeant Richardson barked, "the detachment is formed and all present or accounted for."

Lieutenant Howard returned the salute crisply.

"Take your post, Sergeant," he ordered.

Salutes were again exchanged. Then Staff Sergeant Richardson did a precise right-face movement, followed by several others that ultimately placed him in line with, and to the right of, the troop formation. At the same time, Lieutenant Howard did an equally precise about-face movement and stood erectly at attention.

Major Banning understood his role in the ceremony. He dropped his cigarette to the ground, ground his toe on it, and then marched erectly until he faced Lieutenant Howard.

Howard saluted.

"Sir," he barked, "Special Detachment 14, less the rear echelon, reporting for duty, Sir."

Banning returned the salute.

He looked at his men, who stood there stone-faced, even the two or three who he suspected had been at the sauce.

"At ease!"

The detachment assumed the position.

"Welcome to Townesville," Banning said. "And let me say the good news: your drill sergeants would be proud of you. You would be a credit to any parade ground."

There were smiles and chuckles.

"The bad news is that it's about a mile and a half from here to our billets, and there are no wheels."

Now there were grins on all their faces.

"May I respectfully suggest that the Major underestimates his command, Sir?" Joe Howard said.

"What's that supposed to mean?" Banning asked.

"If the Major would be good enough to accompany me, Sir?" Howard asked.

"Where?"

"To the rear of the train, Sir," Howard said.

"All right," Banning said.

"First Sergeant," Lieutenant Howard ordered formally, "take the detachment."

Staff Sergeant Richardson marched up in front again, and a final salute was exchanged.

Banning and Howard walked to the end of the train, where he stopped at a flatcar. Whatever it carried was covered with a canvas tarpaulin.

"They call these things 'open goods wagons' over here, Sir," he said. "That caused a little confusion for a while. We kept asking for flatcars, and they didn't know what the hell we were talking about."

"What's in here? The radios?"

"I think the radios are in the last car, Sir," Howard said.

He put his fingers in his mouth and whistled shrilly, then gestured. Half a dozen Marines handed their weapons to the others and came trotting down the platform.

An officer and a gentleman is not supposed to whistle like that, Banning thought, *so it's a good thing there's nobody here but me to see it.*

The Marines clambered up on the flatcar and started to remove the tarpaulin. Large wheels were revealed.

"You stole a truck," Banning accused Howard.

"No, Sir. That truck was issued to us. It's perfectly legal."

The tarpaulin was now almost off, revealing a Studebaker stake-bodied truck. In the bed of the truck was a 1941 Studebaker automobile. On the doors of both the truck and the car were neatly stenciled the Marine Corps emblem and the letters USMC.

"Is that the car from The Elms?" Banning asked, and then, without giving Howard a chance to reply, continued, "You sure that's not stolen, Joe?"

"I checked on it myself, Sir, when Richardson showed up with them."

"Them?"

"We have two trucks and three cars, Sir. I mean, counting the one you already had. I left that in Melbourne with Koffler. I figured you'd need it when you went back there."

Banning saw that the automobile was stuffed with duffel bags.

Well, that explains why they weren't carrying them over their shoulders when they got off the train.

"How do you propose to get that truck off the flatcar?" Banning asked.

"No problem, Sir," Lieutenant Howard said.

The Marines now pulled thick planks from under the truck and placed them against the flatcar, forming a ramp. As two of the Marines loosened chains holding the truck chassis to the railroad car, a third got behind the wheel and started the engine.

Moments later, the truck was on the platform. The planks were now moved to form a ramp so that the car could be driven off the truck. The duffel bags were taken from the car and thrown onto the truck.

As the entire process was being repeated for the second flatcar, Major Banning said to Lieutenant Howard, "Why do I have this uncomfortable feeling that I am going to end my career in Portsmouth?"

"This is all perfectly legal, Sir," Howard said. "Trust me."

"God, it better be!"

When the tarpaulin covering a third flatcar was removed, Banning walked down to see what it held. There were wooden crates, containing Hallicrafters radios, portable antennas, and generators.

Well, they're here. I hope to hell they work. I'm going to look like a fool in front of Eric Feldt if they don't.

"Let's hope at least one of them works," Banning said to Howard.

"They all work, Sir," Howard said. "Sergeant Haley and Corporal Koffler checked them out."

Sergeant Haley, Banning remembered, was a pudgy-faced buck sergeant, one of his three radio operators. But he also remembered that Haley had told him he was an operator, not a technician. And *Koffler?*

"Haley and Koffler?"

"Yes, Sir. When I got to The Elms, I saw Koffler had set up one of the radios and an antenna and some batteries and was listening to KYW in Honolulu. I had them check out the others as they came in to make sure they worked. I figured if they didn't, it would be easier to get them fixed in Melbourne than here. A couple of them needed a little work, but they're all working now."

"Haley fixed them?"

"No. Koffler. Haley had never seen one of them before."

"And Koffler had?"

"No. But . . . it took me a while to figure this out, Major. Haley went to Radio School. He knows about Marine and Navy radios. Koffler was a radio amateur, what they call a ham."

"He told me," Banning interrupted. "So what?"

"So he can apparently make a radio from parts. He understands what makes them work. Even Haley was impressed. There's more to Koffler than meets the eye."

"That wouldn't be hard," Banning said dryly, then asked, "How many radio sets are there?"

"Eight, Sir. I brought seven of them up here. Koffler rigged one of them so we can talk to Melbourne as soon as we get one set up here."

Another sergeant, whose name, after a moment, Banning remembered was Solinski, marched happily up and saluted.

"Sir, the convoy is formed. If the Major would care to enter his staff car?"

"Thank you, Sergeant," Banning said. "Nice work, getting this all organized so quickly."

"Thank you, Sir," Sergeant Solinski said, pleased.

Lieutenant Commander Feldt had arranged for USMC Special Detachment 14 to take over a two-story, tin-roofed frame building that had belonged to the now-defunct Townesville Young Men's Christian Association. In addition to a small suite of offices, there was a room with a billiards table, as well as six small bedrooms, a small gymnasium with a rusty collection of weightlifting machines, and a reception room with a soft-drink bar that Banning suspected was about to be converted to a saloon.

Banning had prepared notes for the little speech he intended to deliver to his men, but he decided that would have to wait until he got the full story of the cars and trucks. The speech mostly dealt with the importance of getting along with the Aussies, and included the details of their rationing (with the Aussies) and other housekeeping information. The story of the cars and trucks was obviously more important.

He called Lieutenant Howard and Staff Sergeant Richardson into what would serve as the detachment office and told Howard to close the door.

"I want to know about the trucks and cars," he said. "And I want the truth, the whole truth, and nothing but the truth."

"Yes, Sir," Staff Sergeant Richardson said. "Well, Sir, Lieutenant Howard sent me and Sergeant Jenkins on the next plane. After yours and Koffler's. Koffler met us on the dock, with the Studebaker, and drove us out to The Elms. I asked him where he got the car. He said he didn't know where it had come from."

"Captain Pickering arranged for it. He got it from a Navy depot."

"Yes, Sir. But Koffler didn't know that. So I told him to ask somebody. He asked an Aussie lady sailor he'd met, and she told him there was a Navy depot. A U.S. Navy depot. So I went down there. It's not a regular depot. What I found out is that it's a place they store stuff that was supposed to go China, but didn't make it."

"Go over that again?"

"Well, Sir. There was a lot of stuff being shipped to China. What they call Lend-Lease. When they couldn't get in there, they went on to Australia and just unloaded the stuff. The only Americans around was a small Corps of Civil Engineers depot, and they suddenly had all this stuffed dumped in their laps. They didn't know what the hell to do with it all. One of the ships was full of Studebakers, cars and trucks."

"I see. And you stole the ones you brought with you?"

"No, Sir. I didn't have to. I just had Koffler drive me down there, and I told an officer I found that I had come for the rest of our vehicles. He said he couldn't issue any of what he had without authority, and I told him we had the authority, and there was our Studebaker, to prove it. He asked me who we worked for, and since you weren't in Melbourne, I told him this Captain Pickering. Lieutenant Howard gave me his name in Hawaii, in case we needed it."

"And this officer called Captain Pickering?"

"Yes, Sir. And Captain Pickering, I guess, told him it was all right. He asked me how many trucks I wanted, and how many cars, and I said two, and he said,

'All right, but you're going to have to get them running yourself, I don't have anybody to help you.' I think I could have gotten a dozen of each, if I had been smart enough to ask for them."

"I think you've done very well, Sergeant Richardson," Banning said. "Thank you."

(FOUR)
Air Transport Office
Royal Naval Station, Melbourne
1 June 1942

Lieutenant Vincent F. Donnelly, RAN, said, "Yes, Sir. Right away," and put the telephone handset back in its cradle.

He looked across the crowded office to where Yeoman Third Class Daphne Farnsworth, her lower lip clipped under her teeth in concentration, was filling out one more sodding form on her typewriter.

"Daphne!" he called. He had to call again before he broke through her concentration.

"Yes, Sir?"

"We've been summoned to the Captain's office," Donnelly said.

"I don't suppose we could ask him to wait thirty minutes, could we?" Daphne asked, smiling. "I'm finally *almost* finished with this."

"He wants us right away."

"Should I bring my pad?"

"No, I don't think so."

Lieutenant Junior Grade Eleanor McKee, Royal Australian Navy Women's Volunteer Reserve, commanding officer of all the women aboard RA Naval Station, Melbourne, was in the Captain's office when they got there.

She looks as if she's been sucking a lemon again, Daphne thought. *I wonder what the hell this is all about. I haven't done a damned thing, so far as I know.*

The Captain stood up.

"Yeoman Farnsworth," he said, "it is my sad duty to inform you that your husband, Sergeant John Andrew Farnsworth, Royal Australian Signals, has been killed in action in North Africa."

"Oh, God!"

"You will, I am sure, be able to find some solace in knowing he died for king and country," the Captain said.

"Oh, shit!" Daphne said.

"I'm very sorry, my dear," the Captain said.

(FIVE)
Townesville, Queensland
5 June 1942

"I'm only saying this, you two must understand, because I have been drinking," Lieutenant Commander Eric A. Feldt, RAN, said to Major Edward J. Banning, USMC, and Lieutenant Joe Howard, USMCR, "but I am far more impressed with your band of innocents than I ever thought would be the case."

They were in Commander Feldt's quarters, sitting on folding steel chairs, facing one another across a rickety wooden table on which sat a half-filled bottle of Dewar's Scotch and the empty hulk of another. A rusting bucket on the floor held a half-dozen bottles of beer and a soda siphon in a pool of melting ice.

"You're only saying that," Major Banning responded, "because you found out I outrank you."

"That's beneath you, Banning," Feldt said, "bringing up a sodding six days' difference in the dates of our promotions."

"And we gave you a truck," Joe Howard said, somewhat thickly. "We have a saying in America, 'Never look a gift truck in the mouth.' "

"You didn't *give* me the truck, you only *loaned* it to me. And anyway, the steering wheel is on the wrong side."

"The steering wheel is in the right place," Howard said. "You people insist on driving on the wrong side of the road."

Feldt stood up and walked, not too steadily, to a chest of drawers. He returned with a box of cigars, which he displayed with an elaborate gesture.

"I mean it," he said. "Have a cigar."

"Thank you, I don't mind if I do," Banning said. He took one and passed the box to Howard.

"I got them from a Dutchman, master of an inter-island tramp," Feldt said, sitting down again, and helping himself to a little more of the Dewar's. "He swore they were rolled between the thighs of fourteen-year-old Cuban virgins."

Banning raised his glass. "Here's to fourteen-year-old Cuban virgins."

"Here, here," Howard said.

"And here's to Captain Vandenhooven," Feldt said. "He gave me those cigars just in time."

"Just in time?" Banning asked.

"The next time he went out for me, the Japs got him. One of their sodding destroyers. They caught him off Wuvulu Island."

"Shit," Howard said.

Banning raised his glass again. "To the Captain," he said.

He lit the cigar and exhaled slowly through pursed lips.

"That's all right," he said approvingly.

"Virginal thighs'll do it every time," Feldt pronounced solemnly.

There was a polite knock at the door.

"Come," Feldt called.

A young, thick-spectacled young man in the uniform of a Leading Aircraftsman, Royal Australian Air Force, came into the room and, in the British manner, quick-marched to the rickety table and saluted with the palm outward as he stamped his foot.

"Sir!" he barked.

Feldt made a vague gesture with his right hand in the direction of his forehead; it could only charitably be called a salute.

"What have you there, son?"

"Group Captain Deane's compliments, Sir. He said he thought you should see these straight off."

He handed Feldt a large manila envelope. Feldt tore it open. It contained a slightly smaller envelope, this one stamped MOST SECRET. Feldt opened this one and took out a half-dozen eight-inch-square photographs. Banning guessed they were aerials.

"These are from where?" Feldt asked after a moment. Banning heard no suggestion in his voice now that Feldt had been drinking.

"Buka Island, Sir," the RAAF man said.

"That will be all, thank you. Please convey to Group Captain Deane my deep appreciation."

"Sir!" the RAAF man barked again, saluted and stamped his foot, and quick-marched out of the room.

Feldt shoved the thin stack of photographs across the table to Banning and then stood up.

Banning saw a man in a field, holding his arms above his head. There were three views of this, each differing slightly, as if they had been taken within seconds of each other. Matching each view were blow-ups, showing just the man and a small area around him.

Feldt reappeared with a large magnifying glass with a handle. He dropped to his knees and examined each of the photographs with great care.

"Well, at least he was still alive when these were taken," Feldt said.

"What am I looking at?" Banning asked. He enunciated the words very carefully; for he now very much regretted helping himself so liberally to the Scotch, and he wanted at least to sound as sober as possible.

"Can I look?" Joe Howard asked.

"Sure," Feldt said, and then went on, "Sub-Lieutenant Jacob Reeves. From whom we haven't heard in the last ten days or so. He's on Buka. Important spot. I was afraid the Nips had nipped him. But it's just that his wireless is out."

Banning looked at him. There had been no intent on Feldt's part, he saw, to play with words. Feldt was perfectly serious when he said nipped by the Nips. He was now icily serious.

"How do you know his radio is out?" Howard asked.

"What the bloody hell else do you think 'RA' could mean?" Feldt asked impatiently, almost contemptuously. He pointed, and Banning saw what he had missed. The tall grass, or whatever the hell it was, in the field had been cut down so it spelled out, in letters twenty-five or thirty feet tall, the letters *RA*.

More gently now, as if he regretted his abruptness, Feldt said, "Interesting man, Jacob Reeves. He's the far side of forty. Been in the islands since he was a boy. Been on Buka for fifteen years. Never married. Has a harem of native girls. I don't think he's been off the island more than three times since he's been there. We had a hell of a time teaching him Morse code, at first. And of course, he doesn't know a sodding thing about how a wireless works."

Banning raised his eyebrows at that.

"It could be anything from a loose wire," Feldt explained, "through a complete failure. Or his generator has gone out—he has a small gasoline-powered generator . . . God only knows."

"Where does he get gas for the generator?" Howard asked.

"There were supplies of it on Buka," Feldt said. "He took a truckload of supplies, presumably including fuel, when he went up into the hills. If he was out of petrol, I think he would have cut PET in the grass."

"Where did the pictures come from?" Banning asked.

"I asked Group Captain Deane to send an aircraft over there. He has a couple of Lockheed Hudsons."

Banning nodded. The twin-engine, low-winged monoplane with a twin tail obviously traced its heritage to the famous airplane in which Amelia Earhart had been lost trying to set an around-the-world speed record.

"I think we had better send Sub-Lieutenant Reeves one of your Hallicrafters sets, Major Banning," Feldt said. "I'm glad you mentioned the petrol. I have no idea how much he has left. If any. That bicycle generator is what he needs."

"They're yours," Banning said immediately.

"That poses several questions. First, how we get it to him. He's in the hills, so that eliminates either a submarine—even if I could get the use of one—or a ship."

"By parachute, then," Banning said. "Would your Group Captain Deane be able to do that?"

Feldt nodded, meaning that he could get an aircraft. "The question then becomes, can a Hallicrafters set be dropped by parachute?"

"I'm sure our Corporal Koffler could answer that," Banning said. "Off the top of my head, I can't think of a reason why not."

"The question then becomes, would your Corporal Koffler be willing to go in with it?"

"Why would that be necessary?" Banning asked.

He immediately saw on Feldt's face that his simple question had been misinterpreted; Feldt suspected that Banning was reluctant to send one of his men behind the Japanese lines.

"I'm afraid it really would be necessary, Banning," Feldt said. "Otherwise dropping the Hallicrafters would be useless; Reeves would have no idea how to operate it. And I don't think he could work from a set of directions; his mind doesn't work that way."

"How soon would you like Koffler to jump in?" Banning asked.

"Today's Friday. How long would it take your man to prepare the Hallicrafters to be rigged for a parachute drop?"

"Again, I'll have to ask him. But again, off the top of my head, I can't imagine why it would take more than a couple of hours. I presume we can get parachutes from the RAAF?"

Feldt nodded. "I'll ring Deane and ask him to arrange for your man to be flown up here tomorrow."

"Am I allowed to say something?" Howard asked.

Banning looked at him curiously, even impatiently.

"Sure," Feldt said.

"If I understand this correctly," Howard said, "what we have here is a very important Coastwatcher station—"

"Arguably, *the* most important station," Feldt agreed. "Certainly one of the most important."

"Staffed by one man who apparently knows very little or nothing about radios."

"That's why we're going to jump Koffler in to join him."

"Koffler doesn't know a Zero from a Packard," Howard said. "If something happens to your man Reeves, Commander, what you're going to have is a perfectly functioning radio station from which we'll get no intelligence because Koffler won't know what to send."

"Granted," Feldt said. "So what?"

"So what you need is a team. Send two people in. The other one should be someone who can identify Japanese aircraft and ships as well as your man Reeves. If something should happen to Reeves, that man could possibly keep the station operating. At least better than someone who was in high school this time last year."

"I don't have anybody to spare at the moment," Feldt said. "I grant your point. Reeves should have a replacement. I'll work on it."

"The time to send him in is now," Howard argued. "You said that getting planes is difficult. You might not be able to get another; and even if you could, it seems to me the Japanese would sense that something important was going on in that area."

"Commander Feldt says he doesn't have anyone to send," Banning said curtly.

"I was in the First Defense Battalion at Pearl," Howard said. "In addition to my other duties, I taught Japanese aircraft and vessel recognition."

"Fascinating," Commander Feldt said, softly.

"You're not a parachutist," Banning said.

"Neither was Steve Koffler, this time last year," Howard argued.

"Ed," Feldt said softly, "I was given a briefing on agent infiltration by an insufferably smug British Special Operations Executive officer. He told me, among other things, that their experience parachuting people into France has been that they lost more people training them to use parachutes than they did jumping virtually untrained people on actual operations. Consequently, as a rule of thumb, they no longer subject agents going in to the risks of injury parachute training raises."

Banning looked between the two of them, but said nothing.

"What worries me about this is why Joe wants to go," Feldt said. He looked directly at Howard. "Why do you want to do this?"

"I *don't* want to do it," Howard said after a moment. "I think somebody has to do it. Of the people available to us, I seem to have the best qualifications."

"Are you married? Children?" Feldt asked.

"I have a . . . fiancée," Joe said. It was, he realized, the first time he had ever used the word.

"The decision, of course, is Major Banning's," Commander Feldt said formally.

Banning met Howard's eyes for a moment.

"I think it might be better if Joe and I went to Melbourne," Banning said finally, evenly. "I don't know, but maybe Joe and Koffler will need some equipment I don't know about. If there is, it would more likely be available in Melbourne to a major than to a lieutenant."

"Your other ranks seem to do remarkably well getting things from depots," Feldt said. "But of course you're right. I'll arrange with Deane to have you two flown down there in the morning."

He reached for the Scotch bottle and topped off everyone's glass.

"And of course, Melbourne's the best place to get the shots."

"Shots?"

"Immunizations."

"The Marine Corps has given me shots against every disease known to Western man," Howard said.

"I don't really think, Joe, that your medical people have a hell of a lot of experience with the sort of thing you're going to find on Buka," Feldt said. "And since Major Banning and I have decided to indulge you in this little escapade, it behooves you to take your shots like a good little boy."

"Aye, aye, Sir," Howard said.
"Cheers," Feldt said, raising his glass.

(SIX)
Two Creeks Station
Wagga Wagga, New South Wales
6 June 1942

It had been called a memorial service, but what it really had been, Daphne Farnsworth realized, was a regular funeral missing only the body. There had even been an empty, flag-covered casket in the aisle of St. Paul's Church. The Reverend Mr. Bartholomew Frederick, his World War I Australian–New Zealand Army Corps ribbons pinned to his vestments, had delivered a eulogy that had been at least as much a recitation of the virtues of Australian military prowess and courage generally as it had been a recounting of the virtues of the late Sergeant John Andrew Farnsworth.

And before and after, before even she had gotten home, the neighbors had gone through the ritual of visiting the bereaved. In the event, Daphne Farnsworth only barely counted as one of the bereaved. The visitors had "called on" John's parents at the big house, instead of at John's and her house. Their house had been more or less closed up, of course, and his parents' house was larger; but she suspected that the roasts and the casseroles and the clove-studded hams and potato salad would have been delivered to the big house even if she hadn't joined the Navy.

She was both shamed and confused by her reaction to the offerings of sympathy. They annoyed her. And she resented all the people, too. She was either being a genuine bitch, she decided, or—as she had heard at least a half-dozen people whisper softly to her in-laws—she was still in shock and had not really accepted her loss. That would come later.

She had been annoyed at that, too. They didn't know what the hell they were talking about. She had accepted her loss. She knew that John was never coming back, even, for Christ's sake, in a casket when the war was over. She knew, with a horrible empty feeling in her heart and belly, that she would never again feel John's muscular arms around her, or have him inside her.

She was angry with him, too—the decisive proof that she was a cold-hearted bitch. He didn't have to go. He had gotten himself killed over there for the sole reason that he had *wanted* to go over there, answering some obscene and ludicrous male hunger to go off and kill something . . . without considering at all the price she was going to have to pay.

And their childlessness—a question John had decided for all time by enlisting and getting himself killed—had been a subject of some conversation by those who had come to call to express their sympathy. The males, gathered in the sitting room, drinking, and the women in the kitchen, fussing with all the food, seemed to be divided more or less equally into two groups: those who thought it a pity there wasn't a baby, preferably a male baby, to carry on the name; and those who considered it a manifestation of God's wise compassion that he had not left poor Daphne with a fatherless child to add to her burden.

Daphne had started drinking early in the morning, when she awoke in their bed and cried with the knowledge that John would never again share it with her.

She had tossed down a shot of straight gin before she'd left their bed for her bath.

And she'd had another little taste just before they'd gotten in the cars to go to St. Paul's for the service. And she had had three since they had returned from church, timing them carefully. John had once told her that if you took only one drink an hour, you could never get drunk; the body burned off spirits at the rate of a drink an hour. She believed that.

As if she needed another one! There was one more proof that she was a bitch, because she knew that what she really wanted to do was get really drunk. She had been really drunk only three times in her life, the last time the day after she had returned here after watching John's ship move away from the pier in Melbourne.

She could not do that today, of course. It would disgrace her—not that that seemed important. But it would hurt her family, especially her mother and John's mother, if she let the side down by doing something like that, when she was expected to be the grieving, virtuous young widow.

She left the crowd of people in the big house to walk to her own house. She did that because she had to visit the loo, and there was actually a line before the loo in the big house.

She just happened to notice the car coming across the bridge over the Murrumbidgee River. It made the sharp right onto their property.

Still somebody else coming? I really *don't want one more expression of sympathy, one more man to tell me, "Steady on, girl," or one more woman to tell me, "The Lord works in mysterious ways. You must now put your trust in the Lord."*

There's no one behind the wheel.

Of course not. It's an American car, a Studebaker like the Americans at The Elms have.

What is an American car doing coming here?

Oh, my God, it's him. It can't be. But it is.

What in the name of God is Steve Koffler doing here?

She cut across the field and got to the Studebaker a moment after Steve Koffler had parked it at the end of a long row of cars, got out, and opened the rear door.

The first thought she had was unkind. When she saw his glistening paratrooper boots, sharply creased trousers, and the tightly woven fabric of his tunic and compared it with the rough, blanketlike material John's uniform had been cut from, and his rough, hobnailed boots, she was annoyed: *Bloody American Marines, they all look like officers.*

He got whatever he was looking for from the backseat of the Studebaker, then stood erect and turned around and saw her.

"Hello," he said, startled, and somewhat shy.

"What are you doing here?"

"Lieutenant Donnelly told me about your husband," Steve said, holding out what he had taken from the backseat: a bouquet of flowers, a tissue-wrapped square box, and a brown sack, obviously containing a bottle.

"What are you doing here?" Daphne repeated.

"I didn't know what you're supposed to do in Australia," he said, "to show you're sorry."

"What is all that?"

"Flowers, candy, and whiskey," Steve said. "Is that all right?"

"It's unnecessary," Daphne snapped, and was sorry. "*What* are you *doing* here?"

"I came to tell you how sorry I am about your husband getting killed," Steve said.

"And you drove all the way out here to do that?"

"It's only two hundred and eighty-six miles," he said. "I just checked. And that includes me getting lost twice."

It never even entered his stupid American mind that he might be intruding here; he wanted to come, so he just got in his sodding car and came!

"I really don't know what to say to you," she said.

"You don't have to say anything," he said. "I just wanted you to know I'm sorry."

Is that it? Or did you maybe think that now that I'm a widow, you could just jump into my bed?

What the hell is the matter with me? He's just stupid and sweet. Except that I know he's not really as stupid as I first thought. Naïve and sweet, rather than stupid.

"That's very kind of you, Steve, I'm sure. Thank you very much."

Steve Koffler relaxed visibly.

"It's OK. I wanted to do it."

But my mother is not going to understand this. Or John's mother. Or anybody. They're going to suspect that this boy and I are . . . what? Something we shouldn't be. That that is absurd won't matter. That's what they're going to think.

And I can't just send him packing, either. Not only would that be cruel of me, but by now everyone has seen the car and will be wondering who it is. What the hell *am I going to do?*

"I suppose you must think I'm terrible," Daphne Farnsworth said to Steve Koffler as the Studebaker turned onto the bridge over the Murrumbidgee River, "lying to my family like that."

"No. I understand," he replied, turning his head to look at her.

"Well, I feel rotten about it," she said. "But I just couldn't take any more. I was going to scream."

After quickly but carefully coaching Steve in the story, she had led him up to the big house and introduced him to her family. She had told them that her officer, Lieutenant Donnelly, had learned that the American Marines were sending a car to the Wagga Wagga airfield. The lieutenant had arranged with a Marine officer to have Steve, the driver, whom she referred to as "Corporal Koffler," stop by the station and offer her a ride back to Melbourne. Her "death leave" was up the next day anyway. It would save her catching a very early train, and a long and uncomfortable ride.

It sounded credible, and she was reasonably sure that no one had questioned the story. They had been effusive in their thanks to Steve for doing her a good turn. All of which, of course, had made her feel even worse.

"I'm just glad I decided to come," Steve Koffler said.

They rode in silence for a long time, while Daphne wallowed in her new perception of herself as someone with a previously unsuspected capacity for lying and all-around deceit, the proof of which was that she felt an enormous sense of relief at being able to get away from people who shared her grief and would, quite literally, do anything in the world for her.

Steve Koffler broke the silence as they reached the outskirts of Wangaratta, fifty miles back into Victoria.

"Would it be all right if I looked for someplace I could get something to eat? I could eat a horse."

"You mean you haven't eaten?"

He nodded.

"You should have said something at the station," she said. "There was all kinds of food . . ."

He shrugged.

"On condition that you let me pay," Daphne said. "I really do appreciate the ride."

"I've got money," he said.

"I pay, or you go hungry."

He smiled at her shyly.

As he wolfed down an enormous meal of steak and eggs, Daphne asked, "Tell me about your family, Steve. And your girl."

"There's not much to tell about my family. My mother and father are divorced. I live with her and her husband. And I don't have a girl."

"I thought Marines were supposed to have a girl in every port."

"That's what they say," he said. "I know a *bunch* of girls, of course, but there's no one special. I've been too busy, I suppose, to have a steady girl."

He's lying. That was bravado. He's afraid of women. Then why did he drive all the way out to Wagga Wagga? For the reason he gave. He felt really sorry for me. Whatever this boy is, he is no Don Juan. He's just a sweet kid.

When they were back on the road, she found herself pursuing the subject, wondering why it was important.

"There must have been one girl that . . . stood out . . . from all the others?"

From his reaction to the question, she sensed that there had not only been a girl in Steve Koffler's life, but that it had not been a satisfactory relationship.

"Who was she, Steve?"

Why am I doing this? What do I really care?

Over the next hour and a half, Daphne drew from Steve, one small detail after another, the story of Dianne Marshall Norman. By the time she was sure she had separated fact from fantasy and had assembled what she felt was probably the true sequence of events, she had worked up what she told herself was a big-sister-like dislike for Diane Marshall Norman and a genuine feeling of sympathy for Steve.

Women can be such bitches, she thought, *getting what they want and not caring a whit how much they hurt a nice kid like Steve Koffler.*

(SEVEN)
U.S. Navy Element
U.S. Army General Hospital
Melbourne, Australia
1705 Hours 6 June 1942

Soon after they met, Commander Charles E. Whaley, M.D., USNR, told Ensign Barbara T. Cotter, NC, USNR, that he had given up a lucrative practice of psychiatry in Grosse Point Hills, Michigan, and entered the Naval Service in order to treat the mental disorders of servicemen who had been unable to cope with the stress of the battlefield. He was happy to do so.

But he had not entered the Naval Service, he went on to tell Ensign Cotter, to administer to the minor aches and pains of the Naval brass gathered around the headquarters of the Commander-in-Chief, Southwest Pacific, General Douglas

MacArthur, and especially not to cater to their grossly overdeveloped sense of medical self-protection. And he had absolutely no intention of doing so.

He specifically told Ensign Cotter, who was in his eyes an unusually nice and bright kid, that he had no intention of making a goddamned house call to the "residence" of some Navy brass hat named Pickering. This guy had apparently heard somewhere of a battery of rare tropical diseases. Since, for some half-assed reason, he felt threatened by those diseases, he wanted himself immunized against them. At his quarters.

"I think I know where this goddamn thing started, Barbara," Dr. Whaley said. "I have never even *seen* a case of any of these things—and I interned and did my residency in Los Angeles, where you see all sorts of strange things—but this morning there was a Marine officer in here, armed with a buck slip from an admiral on MacArthur's staff, ordering that he be immediately immunized against them. They had to get the stuff from the Australians to give it to him.

"Then I get a message—if I'd been here to take the call, I would have told him what I thought—from this Captain Pickering, ordering me to come to his residence prepared to give the same series of shots to at least one other person. What I think happened is that this sonofabitch Pickering heard about the Marine and decided he wasn't going to take the risk of coming down with something like this himself. No, Sir. I mean, why should he? I mean, after all, here he is, far from the Army-Navy Club in Washington, risking his life as a member of MacArthur's palace guard."

Barbara chuckled.

"What would you like me to do, Doctor?"

"If I go over there, Barbara, I'm liable to forget that I'm an officer and a gentleman and tell this Pickering character what I think of him specifically and the Naval Service generally. So, by the power vested in me by the Naval Service, Ensign Cotter, I order you to proceed forthwith to"—he handed her an interoffice memorandum—"the address hereon, and immunize this officer by injection. See if you can find a dull needle. A large one. And it is my professional medical judgment that you should inject the patient in his gluteus maximus."

"Aye, aye, Sir," Ensign Cotter replied.

"And go by ambulance," Commander Charles E. Whaley, M.D., USNR, added.

"Ambulance?"

"With a little bit of luck, Captain Pickering will inquire about the ambulance. Then you will tell him that the immunizations sometimes produce terrible side effects," Dr. Whaley said, pleased with himself. "And that the ambulance is just a precaution."

"You're serious?" Barbara chuckled.

"You bet your ass I am," Commander Whaley said.

(EIGHT)
The Elms
Dandenong, Victoria, Australia
1755 Hours 6 June 1942

When Barbara Cotter saw The Elms, she was glad that Dr. Whaley had sent her and not come himself. This Captain Pickering, whoever he was, seemed one more proof that Karl Marx might have been onto something when he denounced the overaccumulation of capital in the hands of the privileged few. Navy captains, for rank hath its privileges, lived well. But not this well. Dr. Whaley could have gotten himself in deep trouble, letting his Irish temper loose at this Navy brass hat.

A middle-aged woman opened the door.

"Hello," Mrs. Hortense Cavendish said with a smile. "May I help you?"

"I'm Ensign Cotter, to see Captain Pickering. I'm from the hospital."

"Are you a doctor?"

"I'm a nurse," Barbara said.

"I think he was expecting a doctor," Mrs. Cavendish said. "But please come in, I'll tell him you're here."

She left Barbara waiting in the foyer and disappeared down a corridor. A moment later a man appeared and walked up to her. He was in his shirtsleeves and wearing suspenders. And his collar was open and his tie pulled down. He held a drink in his hand.

Barbara was prepared to despise him as a palace-guard brass hat with an exaggerated opinion of his own importance—and with what Dr. Whaley had so cleverly described as "an overdeveloped sense of medical self-protection."

"Hello," Pickering said. "I'm Fleming Pickering. I was rather expecting Commander Whaley, but you're much prettier."

"Sir, I'm Ensign Cotter."

"I'm very pleased to meet you," he said. "We saw the ambulance. What's that all about? Is the Navy again suffering from crossed signals?"

"Sir, I'm here to administer certain injections," Barbara said. "There is a chance of a reaction to them. The ambulance is a precaution."

"Well, the first stickee seems to be doing fine," Pickering said. "We're hoping that your intended target will show up momentarily. I'm afraid you're going to have to wait until he does."

"Sir?"

"You're here to immunize Corporal Koffler," Pickering said. "At the moment, we don't know where he is. You'll have to wait until he shows up. If that's going to pose a problem for you at the hospital, I'll call and explain the situation. This is rather important."

"I was under the impression the immunizations were intended for you, Captain."

"Oh, no," Pickering said, and smiled. "I suspected crossed signals. Shall I call the hospital and straighten things out?"

"If I'm going to have to stay, I'd better call, Sir," Barbara said.

"The phone's right over there," Pickering said, pointing to a narrow table against the foyer wall. "If you run into any trouble, let me know. Sometimes the Regular Navy is a bit dense between the ears."

She looked at him in shock.

"Between us amateurs, of course," Pickering smiled. "I presume you're a fellow amateur?"

"I'm a reservist, Sir, if that's what you mean."

"I was sure of it," Pickering said. "When you're through on the phone, please come in the sitting room." He pointed to it.

"Yes, Sir," Barbara said.

"Oh, Barbara," Dr. Whaley said when she called him at his quarters. "I hope you're calling because you're lost."

"Excuse me?"

"You found The Elms without any trouble?"

"Yes, Sir. I'm here now. I've just met Captain Pickering."

"How did that go?"

"It's not what you thought, Doctor."

"I already found that out. The men to be immunized, the Marine officer who was here at the hospital, and the one you're there to see, are about to go on some hush-hush mission behind the lines. High-level stuff. And I learned five minutes after you left that Pickering is not what I led you to believe he was."

"He's really nice," Barbara said.

"He's also General MacArthur's personal pal," Dr. Whaley said. *"And* Frank Knox's personal representative over here. *Not* the sort of man to jab with a dull needle."

"No, Sir," Barbara chuckled. "The other man to be immunized isn't here yet. Captain Pickering said I'll have to stay here until he shows up. That's why I'm calling."

"You stay as long as you're needed," Dr. Whaley said, "and be as charming as possible, knowing that you have our Naval careers in your hands."

"Yes, Sir."

"You better send the ambulance back, Barbara. When you're finished, I'll send a staff car for you."

"Yes, Sir."

Barbara hung up, walked out of The Elms, sent the ambulance back to the hospital, and then reentered the house.

"Everything go all right?" Captain Pickering asked her when she reached the room he'd directed her to. "Come in."

"Everything's fine, Sir," Barbara said.

"Gentlemen, this is Ensign Cotter," Pickering said. "Ensign Cotter, this is Major Ed Banning, Lieutenant Vince Donnelly, and Lieutenant Joe Howard."

Lieutenant Joe Howard, who had been mixing a drink at the bar, turned, looked at Barbara, dropped the glass, and said, "Oh, my God!"

"Joe!" Barbara wailed.

"Why do I suspect that these two splendid young junior officers have met?" Banning asked dryly.

"Lieutenant Howard," Captain Pickering said, "Ensign Cotter was just telling me that sometimes these shots have adverse effects. Why don't you take her someplace where she can examine you?"

He hardly had time to congratulate himself on having produced—snatching it from out of the blue—a Solomon-like solution to the problem of how to handle two young lovers who were embarrassed to manifest a display of affection before senior officers. For, unfortunately, his brilliance was wasted; Ensign Cotter, forgetting that she was an officer and a gentlewoman, ran to Howard and threw herself in his arms, and cried, "Oh, my darling!"

After a moment, Captain Pickering spoke again.

"Joe, why don't you take your girl and show her the grounds?"

Howard, not trusting his voice, nodded his thanks and, with his arms around Barbara, led her out of the sitting room and started down the corridor.

All of a sudden, she stopped, spun out of his arms, and faced him.

"You're on this mission, aren't you?" she challenged.

He nodded.

"Oh, my God!"

"It'll be all right," he said.

"They don't send people on missions like that unless they volunteer," she said, adding angrily, "You volunteered, didn't you?"

He nodded.

"Goddamn you!"

He didn't reply.

"Why? Can you tell me why?"

"It's important," he said.

"When do you go?"

"Tomorrow."

"Tomorrow?" she wailed. He nodded.

"What are we going to do now?" she asked.

He shrugged helplessly.

"We could go to my room," Joe blurted.

She met his eyes.

"They'd know," she said.

"Do you care?" he asked.

She reached out and touched his face and shook her head.

He took her hand from his face and held it as he led her the rest of the way down the stairs and then up the broad staircase to his room.

XIII

(ONE)
The Elms
Dandenong, Victoria, Australia
2105 Hours 6 June 1942

As Corporal Stephen M. Koffler and Petty Officer Daphne Farnsworth approached Melbourne, they came up to a road sign indicating a turnoff to Dandenong. It occurred to Corporal Koffler then that he'd better check in before he took Petty Officer Farnsworth home.

"Would you mind sitting in the car for a minute while I tell Mrs. Cavendish I'm back?" Steve asked as he made the turn. "Maybe there's a message for me, or something."

"Of course not."

He drove down the long line of ancient elms that lined the driveway. When they reached the house, there were two cars parked in front of it. One was a drop-head Jaguar coupe and the other a Morris with Royal Australian Navy plates. After a moment, to her surprise, Daphne recognized it as Lieutenant Donnelly's car.

She wondered what he was doing out here, and then she wondered what he was going to think when he saw her with Corporal Steve Koffler of the United States Marines; she was supposed to be still at home, grief-stricken.

"Oh, shit!" Steve Koffler said, when he saw the cars.

When Major Edward J. Banning, USMC, noticed the glow of the headlights flash across the front of The Elms, he rose to his feet and went to one of the French windows in the library. As he pushed the curtain aside, the Studebaker pulled up beside the Jaguar and the Morris.

It has to be Corporal Steven Koffler, goddamn the horny little AWOL sonofabitch!

I am not going to eat his ass out. It is not in keeping with the principles of good leadership to eat the ass out of an enlisted man just before you ask him to parachute onto an enemy-held island. If he doesn't kill himself in the jump, there is a very good chance he will be killed by the Japanese, probably in some very imaginative way.

If I were a corporal, and they left me all alone with the keys to a car, would I take the car and go out and try to get laid? Never having been a corporal, I can't really say. But probably.

Banning couldn't help recalling Kenneth R. "Killer" McCoy, late Corporal, 4th Marines, Shanghai.

If I had set up the Killer in a house like this in China, and told him he would be left alone for a week or ten days minimum, he would have had a nonstop poker game going here in the library, a craps table operating in the foyer, half a dozen ladies of the evening plying their trade upstairs; and he'd be using the Studebaker to ferry customers back and forth to town.

It was not the first time Banning had thought of Corporal Killer McCoy during the past twenty-four hours. He started remembering McCoy just after he and Captain Pickering arrived at The Elms; they were informed then by Mrs. Cavendish that Corporal Koffler had taken the Studebaker at five the previous afternoon, and that he hadn't been seen since. And no, she had no idea where he might have gone. That sounded like something McCoy would have done.

Which did not mean that Corporals McCoy and Koffler were not stamped out of the same mold—far from it. Banning would have been nervous about sending Killer McCoy to jump on Buka, but he wouldn't have had this sick feeling in his stomach. Killer was probably capable of carrying off something like this with a good chance of coming through it alive. Banning did not think that would be the case with Joe Howard and Steve Koffler. The words had come into his mind a half-dozen times: *I am about to send two of my men to their deaths.*

It was not a pleasant feeling, and his rationalizations, although inarguably true, sounded hollow and irrelevant: *I am asking him to risk, and perhaps even give, his life so that other men may live.* And: *He's a volunteer, nobody pushed him into this at the point of a bayonet.* And even: *He's a Marine, and Marines do what they are ordered to do.*

There was really no point whatever in wishing that the Killer was here. For one thing, Killer was no longer a corporal. He was now an officer and a gentleman and would soon find himself ordering some enlisted Marine to do something that would probably get him killed.

And there was no other enlisted man in Special Detachment 14 who could be sent. No one else, not even the Commanding Officer, knew how to jump out of an airplane without getting killed. And *that,* as applied to Joe Howard, violated a principle of leadership that Banning devoutly believed, that an officer should not order—or ask—someone to do something he would not do himself.

"I think that's him," Banning said, turning from the window to Captain Pickering and Lieutenant Donnelly. He kept his voice as close to a conversational tone as he could muster as he continued, "Maybe I'd better go find Howard and his nurse." They had not been seen, which surprised no one, since they had left the sitting room.

"I'll get him, Major," Lieutenant Donnelly said.

"Good evening, Sir," Corporal Koffler said, coming into the library. Nervously, he looked at Pickering and Banning in turn, and said, "Sir," to each of them.

"Welcome home," Banning said.

"Sir, I didn't expect to see you."

"Well, you're here. Have you been drinking?"

"No, Sir."

Lieutenant Donnelly came into the room.

"They'll be here in a minute," he said.

"You know Captain Pickering," Banning said to Koffler, "and I understand you've met Lieutenant Donnelly."

"No, Sir. I talked to him a couple of times on the phone."

"How are you, Corporal?" Donnelly said.

"How do you do, Sir?"

Banning saw in Donnelly's eyes that he had expected Corporal Koffler to be somewhat older. Say, old enough to vote.

"Something pretty important has come up," Banning said.

"Yes, Sir?"

"There's several *ifs*," Banning continued. "Let me ask a couple of questions. First, would it be possible to drop one of the Hallicrafters sets by parachute? Or would it get smashed up?"

"I thought about that, Sir."

"You did?" Banning replied, surprised.

The door opened again, and Ensign Barbara Cotter and Lieutenant Joe Howard came into the room.

Barbara Cotter averted her eyes and looked embarrassed, confirming Fleming Pickering's early judgment of her as a nice girl. Then he had a thought that made him feel like a dirty old man: *Christ, I could use a little sex myself.*

"How goes it, Steve?" Joe Howard asked. "We were getting a little worried about you."

"Hello, Sir."

"The lady is Ensign Cotter, Koffler," Banning said. "Lieutenant Howard's fiancée."

"Hello," Barbara said.

"Ma'am," Koffler replied uneasily.

"Should I be in here?" Barbara asked.

"You don't look like a Japanese spy to me," Pickering said. "And it seems to me you have an interest in what's going on."

"Sir . . ." Banning started to protest. Ensign Barbara Cotter, whatever her relationship with Joe Howard, had no "need to know."

"Ensign Cotter is a Naval officer," Pickering said formally, "who is well aware of the need to keep her mouth shut about this operation."

Banning had called Pickering as soon as he arrived at the airport in Melbourne. He thought he should know that USMC Special Detachment 14 was about to drop two of its men behind Japanese lines. Pickering had been more than idly interested. In fact, he promptly announced that if he "wouldn't be in the way," he would pick Banning up and drive him out to The Elms while the operation was being set up. Banning had wondered then if Pickering was in fact going to get in the way, and now it looked as if he was.

For a moment, Banning looked as if he was on the edge of protesting further, but then reminded himself that Special Detachment 14 wouldn't even exist if it weren't for Pickering.

"Yes, Sir," Banning said finally.

"Corporal Koffler was telling us how he would drop one of the Hallicrafters by parachute," Pickering said. "Go on, please, Koffler."

"You'd need a parachute," Koffler said. "I mean," he went on quickly, having detected the inanity of his own words, "I mean, I think you'd have to modify a regular C-3 'chute. All the cargo 'chutes I've ever seen would be too big."

"I don't understand," Fleming Pickering confessed.

"Sir, the whole set, when you get it out of the crates," Steve Koffler explained, "doesn't weigh more than maybe a hundred and fifty pounds. Cargo 'chutes, the ones I've seen, are designed to drop a lot more weight—"

"The question is moot," Lieutenant Donnelly said. "There are no cargo 'chutes available. Period. You're talking about modifying a standard Switlick C-3 'chute, Corporal?" Steve nodded. "How?" Donnelly pursued.

"Do you think I might be able to get you the parachute, parachutes, you need, Banning?" Pickering asked.

"Sir," Donnelly replied for Banning, "I don't think there's a cargo parachute in Australia."

"OK," Pickering said. "You were saying, Corporal Koffler?"

"Sir, I think you could make up some special rigging to replace the harness. Make straps to go around the mattresses."

"Mattress?" Banning asked.

"Mattress*es,*" Steve said. "What I would do is make one package of the antenna and the generator. I think you could just roll them up in a mattress and strap it tight. And then add sandbags, or something, so that it weighed about a hundred seventy-five pounds. Where do you want to drop the radio, Sir?"

"Why sandbags? Why a hundred seventy-five pounds?"

"That's the best weight for a standard 'chute. Any more and you hit too hard. Any lighter and it floats forever. You couldn't count on hitting the drop zone," Koffler said, explaining what he evidently thought should be self-evident to someone who was not too bright.

He obviously knows what he's talking about. Why does that surprise me?

"And then do the same thing with the transceiver itself," Koffler went on. "Wrap it in mattresses, and then weight it up to a hundred seventy-five pounds. It would probably make sense to wrap some radio tubes—I mean spare tubes—in cotton or something, and put them with the transceiver. They're pretty fragile."

"I have some parachute riggers, Corporal," Lieutenant Donnelly said. "Civilian women. They have some heavy sewing machines. Could you show them, do you think, how to make such a replacement for the harness?"

"Yes, Sir," Koffler said. "I think so."

He looked uncomfortable.

"Speaking of civilian women, Sir, I've got a lady outside in the car. Could I take a minute to talk to her? I was about to take her home."

"Sure," Banning said. "Go ahead."

When he was gone, Fleming Pickering said, "Well, what do you think, Ed?"

"I don't know what to think, Sir. He doesn't seem to think there will be much of a problem. More important, he seems to know what he's talking about."

"I was thinking, for a moment, that he seems so young for something like this. But then I remembered that I was a Corporal of Marines when I was his age; it's probably not that he's so young, but that I'm so old."

Steve Koffler didn't have to go out to the Studebaker to find Yeoman Daphne Farnsworth; she was standing in the foyer, just outside the corridor to the library.

"I had to go to the ladies'," she said.

"You found it all right, I hope?"

"Yes, thank you."

"Something's come up," Steve said.

"I heard, I went looking for you."

"I don't know how long this will take," Steve said. "I'm sorry, I should have taken you home first."

"Are you in some kind of trouble? About taking the car, maybe?"

"No, I don't think so. I thought I would be when I saw that Captain Pickering was here, but I think they want me to jump in with the radio. Otherwise, I think my ass would have been in a crack."

"You're sure?"

He nodded. "I'm sorry you have to wait. I was going to tell you to wait in there," he said, pointing toward the sitting room. "There's couches and chairs and a radio."

"All right," Daphne said. "You're sure you didn't get in trouble coming out to see me?"

"I'm fine," he said, smiling. "No trouble. Things couldn't be better."

He turned and went back down the corridor. Daphne walked into the sitting room. She sat down on a couch and picked up a magazine, and then threw it down angrily.

That American Navy captain and Steve's major and lieutenant and Donnelly didn't come here on a Saturday evening to discuss a training mission. I know what the Marines are doing here with the Coastwatchers. If they're going to parachute him anywhere, it will be onto some island in Japanese hands. And the only reason they would do that is because there's some sort of trouble with the Australian already there.

She looked impatiently around the room. Her eyes fell on several bottles, one of them of Gilbey's gin. She walked over to it, looked over her shoulder nervously, and then took a healthy pull at the neck of the bottle.

" *'Otherwise,'* " she quoted bitterly, " "I think my ass would have been in a crack! Oh, Steve, you bloody ass!"

Then she capped the Gilbey's bottle and walked down the corridor to the library door, where she could hear what was being said.

"I'll try to get to the airfield to see you off, Steve," Captain Fleming Pickering said, "but if something comes up . . . good luck, son."

"Thank you, Sir," Steve said.

They were standing on the porch of The Elms. All that could be done tonight had been done. The officers, except Lieutenant Howard and his girlfriend, were leaving.

"You've been taking some kidding, I'm sure, about being a corporal, as young as you are," Pickering went on.

"Yes, Sir. Some."

"Well, it's going to get worse," Pickering said. "As of this moment, you're a sergeant."

"Sir?"

"I think, Ed," Pickering said to Banning, "that between us we should have the authority to make that promotion, shouldn't we? I'm not going to have to trouble the Secretary of the Navy with an administrative problem like that, am I?"

"No, Sir," Banning chuckled. "I don't see any problem with that."

"Then good luck again, Sergeant Koffler," Pickering said, and patted Steve, a paternal gesture, on the arm. He went down the stairs and got in the Drop-Head Jaguar.

"I will see you and Lieutenant Howard at half past six, *Sergeant,* right?" Lieutenant Donnelly said. "At the airfield."

"Aye, aye, Sir."

"Don't get carried away with your girlfriend tonight, *Sergeant,*" Banning said softly. "Have fun, but be at the airport at 0630."

"She's not my girlfriend, Sir," Steve said.

"Oh?"

"I wish she was, but all she is . . . is a very nice lady."

"I see."

"I'll be at the airport on time, Sir."

"Goodnight, Steve," Banning said.

He got in Pickering's Jaguar. Steve stood on the porch until both cars had disappeared down the driveway, then went looking for Daphne. He suspected that she would probably be sort of hiding in the sitting room. It would have been very embarrassing for her if Lieutenant Donnelly had seen her. He would have gotten the wrong idea.

Daphne Farnsworth was not in the sitting room. Nor in the toilet off the corridor. Nor in the kitchen, Nor anyplace.

Jesus! What she did was walk all the way to the goddamned road, so that she can try to catch a ride!

He ran to the Studebaker. Daphne's bag was not in the backseat.

She's even carrying her goddamned suitcase!

He got behind the wheel, squealed the tires backing out and turning around, and raced down the drive between the ancient elms. She was not in sight when he reached the highway. He swore, and then drove toward Melbourne. Once he thought he saw her, but when he got close it was not Daphne sitting on her suitcase, but a pile of paving stones, neatly stacked by the side of the road.

Finally, swearing, he gave up, and drove back to The Elms.

At least she didn't have to carry that heavy goddamned suitcase; I would have carried it to her in the morning.

And that would have at least given me the chance to say "so long."

When he got back to The Elms, he saw there was only one light on, on the second floor. That meant Lieutenant Howard and his girlfriend had gone to bed. Together.

Jesus, talk about good luck! Having your girlfriend right here. But then he considered that. *Maybe it would be better if she wasn't here, especially since she knows what's going to happen tomorrow. The minute they were alone, she probably started crying or something, and that would be hard to deal with.* And then he considered that again. *At least they could put their arms around each other and not feel so fucking alone.*

Steve went into the library. He thought he would write his mother. But when he was sitting at the little writing table with a sheet of paper in front of him, he realized that was a lousy idea.

What the hell can I write? "Dear Mom, I'm fine. How are you? I've been wondering when I'm going to get a letter from you. Nothing much is happening here, except that I'm living in a mansion outside Melbourne; and tomorrow or the next day they're going to jump me onto an island called Buka. I don't even know where it is."

I can't even write that. This whole thing is a military secret.

He thought about going into the kitchen and maybe making himself an egg sandwich, but decided against it; the last time he'd done that, he'd awakened Mrs. Cavendish, and he didn't want to do that tonight.

He went up the broad staircase to the second floor, and down the corridor to his room.

Tomorrow night, or maybe the night after that, I'll be sleeping in the goddamned jungle with bugs and snakes and Christ knows what else. I should have known a good deal like this couldn't last—a room of my own, with a great big bed all for myself.

He pushed open the door to his room and turned on the light.

Yeoman Daphne Farnsworth was in his bed, with the sheet pulled up around her chin.

"Jesus Christ!" Steve said.

"I saw you drive off in the car," Daphne said. "I didn't know when, or if, you would be back, so I decided to go to bed and worry about getting into Melbourne in the morning."

"I was looking for you," he said. "When I couldn't find you downstairs, I thought you had probably tried to hitch a ride into Melbourne."

"Oh," she said.

"I'm going to jump onto some island called Buka."

"I know. I heard."

"How come you took your bag out of the car?" Steve blurted. "I mean, you must have—"

"I know what you mean," she said, very softly.

"Jesus!"

"I didn't want you to be alone tonight," Daphne said. "If that makes you think I'm some kind of a wh—"

"Shut up!" he said sharply. "Don't talk like that!"

"And I didn't want to be alone, either," she said.

"Once, in the car," Steve said, "we were talking about something, and you leaned close to me and put your hand on my leg, and I could smell your breath and feel it on my face, and I thought my heart was going to stop. . . ."

They looked into each other's eyes for a long moment.

Finally, softly, reasonably, Daphne said, "Steve, since you have to be at the airfield at half past six, don't you think you should come to bed?"

(TWO)
Port Moresby, New Guinea
0405 Hours 8 June 1942

When Flight Sergeant Michael Keyes, RAAF, went to the tin-roofed Transient Other Ranks hut to wake him, Sergeant Steve Koffler, USMC, was awake and nearly dressed, in greens that still carried the stripes of a corporal.

Lieutenant Howard had tried to fix it so they could be together overnight, but the Aussies hadn't let them. Steve had told Howard not to worry about it. He thought Howard had enough to worry about, like making his first jump, without having to worry about him having to sleep by himself.

"Briefing time, lad," Sergeant Keyes said.

"OK."

"First, breakfast, of course. The food here is ordinarily bloody awful, which explains the stuff we brought with us."

"I'm not really very hungry."

"Well, have a go at it anyway. It's likely to be some time before steak and eggs will be on your ration again."

"Some time," shit. By tonight I'm probably going to be dead.

"I guess I better put this on now, huh?" Steve said, holding up an RAAF flight suit, a quilted cotton coverall.

"Yes, I think you might as well," Keyes said.

Steve put his legs into the garment and shrugged into it. There were the chevrons of a sergeant of the United States Marine Corps on the sleeves, and the metal lapel insignia of the Corps on the collar points. Staff Sergeant Richardson had taken care of that yesterday in Townesville, when Steve and the crew of the Lockheed Hudson were packing the Hallicrafters set and loading it into the airplane.

He had also given Steve a Colt Model 1911A1 .45 pistol. Steve suspected that

Staff Sergeant Richardson had given him his own pistol; only the officers and a couple of the staff sergeants had been authorized pistols. He thought that had been a very nice thing for Staff Sergeant Richardson to do.

Steve had decided the best—really the only—way to take his Springfield along was to drop it with the antenna set; it and his web cartridge belt and two extra bandoliers of .30-06 ammunition and a half-dozen fragmentation grenades had been wrapped in cotton padding, and then that bundle had been strapped to the antenna parts.

Now that Richardson had given him the pistol, at least when he got on the ground he would have a weapon right away. There was no telling how quickly he could get the Springfield out of the antenna bundle. If he could find it at all.

Steve took a couple of foil-wrapped Trojans from a knee pocket in the flight suit, ripped one of them open with his teeth, unrolled it, and then tied it around the top of his boots. Then he bloused the left leg of the flight suit under it.

As he repeated the process for the right leg, Flight Sergeant Keyes said rather admiringly, "I wondered how the hell you did that to your trousers."

"They call it 'blousing,' " Steve said.

He strapped Staff Sergeant Richardson's pistol belt around his waist, and then tied the thong lace around his leg through an eyelet at the bottom of the holster.

"Ready," he said.

"Good lad," Keyes said. "We have to get hopping."

They left the tin-roofed hut and walked across the airfield to the mess. Based on his previous experience—in the movies—with what war should look like, Port Moresby was what Steve had expected to find when he got off the Martin Mariner in Melbourne. The people here went around armed, and they wore steel helmets. There were sandbags all over the place, at the entrances to bomb shelters, and around buildings, and to protect machine-gun positions. This place had been bombed.

Their airplane, the Lockheed, had been pushed into a revetment with sandbag walls. There were other airplanes, none of which was very impressive. There were three bi-wing English fighter planes, for instance, that looked as if they were left over from the First World War.

In the mess hut, Sergeant Keyes took his arm and guided him into an anteroom under a sign that said, OFFICERS. Lieutenant Howard and the rest of the airplane crew were there: the pilot, who was a "flying officer," and the navigator, who was a sergeant, and the gunner, who was a corporal. Steve decided that in the RAAF, if you were a flyer, you got to eat with the officers.

But he quickly learned that wasn't the reason Sergeant Keyes had taken him in the Officers' Room.

"Good morning, Sergeant," a voice said behind him. "About ready to get this show started?"

Startled, Steve looked over his shoulder. There was another RAAF officer, an older one, with a bunch of stripes on his sleeve, standing by the door.

He's at least a major, or whatever the hell they call a major in the RAAF.

"Yes, Sir," Steve said.

"We're running a bit behind schedule, so I'll just run through this while you eat, all right?"

"That'll be fine, Sir," Lieutenant Howard said.

The officer gestured to the navigator, who picked up a four-by-four sheet of plywood and set it down on the table.

"Sit here, Sergeant," the navigator said, indicating a chair at the table beside Howard. Steve saw that Howard had already been served his breakfast, but hadn't eaten much of it.

Steve sat down. The old RAAF officer went to the map.

"Here we are, in Port Moresby," the RAAF officer said, pointing. "And here's where you're going.

"Buka is an island approximately thirty miles long and no greater than five or six miles wide. It is the northernmost island in the Solomons chain, just north of Bougainville, which is much larger. Where you are going, here, is 146 nautical miles from the Japanese base at Rabaul on New Britain. There is a Japanese fighter base on Buka, another on Bougainville, and of course there are fighters based at Rabaul, along with bombers, seaplanes, and other larger aircraft. From his base, Sub-Lieutenant Reeves has in the past been able to advise us of Japanese aerial movements as they have occurred. These reports have obviously been of great value both tactically and for planning purposes, and now that they have been interrupted, getting Reeves's station up and running again is obviously of great importance."

A heavy china plate was put in front of Steve. On it was a T-bone steak covered with three fried eggs, sunny side up. This was followed by a smaller plate with three pieces of toast and a tub of orange marmalade, and finally by a cup of tea.

I don't like tea, hate orange marmalade, and, anyway, I'm not hungry. But unless I start eating that crap, they're going to think I'm scared. I am, of course, but I can't let these Aussies see that I am. And maybe if I eat mine, Lieutenant Howard will eat his.

He unrolled a heavy paper napkin, took stainless-steel cutlery from it, and sawed off a piece of the steak and dipped it in the yolk of one of the eggs.

When he looked up again, he saw the RAAF officer was waiting for him to give him his attention again.

"On leaving Port Moresby, the Hudson will climb to maximum altitude, which we estimate will be about twenty thousand feet, and will maintain this altitude, passing to the west of Kiriwina Island, until it nears Buka itself. There is nothing in the Solomon Sea, except, of course, the to-be-expected Japanese Navy vessels, and possibly some Japanese naval reconnaissance aircraft. The thinking is that at high altitude our chances of being spotted—or, if spotted, identified—by Japanese surface vessels will be minimal. Further, we expect that if Japanese reconnaissance aircraft are encountered, they will be at ten thousand feet or so, and will be directing their attention downward. And again, the chances of detection are minimal. Finally, if we *are* spotted by Japanese reconnaissance aircraft, the odds are they will be seaplanes or amphibians, which will have neither the speed nor the agility to pursue the Lockheed. In the worst-case scenario, detection and/or interception by Japanese fighter aircraft, we have the twin .303 Brownings on the Lockheed to protect ourselves. Are you following me, Son?"

"Protect ourselves*"? Bullshit!* You're *not going.*

"Yes, Sir."

"As I say, I think that on the way in, our chances of detection are minimal."

"Yes, Sir."

The navigator replaced the map of the whole area with a map of Buka itself. This one was drawn on white-coated cardboard.

"You've seen the photographs, I understand, of Sub-Lieutenant Reeves, and the message he cut out in the grass?"

"Yes, Sir."

"They were taken here," the RAAF officer said, pointing. "There is a natural field, a plateau, so to the speak, in the hills. It is at 2,100 feet above sea level. It is approximately twelve hundred feet long and, at its widest, about seven hundred feet wide, narrowing to about five hundred feet near this end."

Jesus Christ! We're going to wind up in the fucking trees!

"Once the Lockheed nears the target area, it will make a rapid descent to 3,500 feet and approach the drop zone from the north. From the time the descent begins, of course, the chance of detection increases. We believe, however, that it will not be possible for the Japanese to launch fighter aircraft in time to interfere with the drop."

"What happens afterward?" Steve blurted.

"Well, you'll be gone, won't you?" the RAAF officer said.

"We'll hide in the clouds, Sergeant Koffler," Flight Sergeant Keyes said. "With a little luck, we'll have some at ten to fifteen thousand. Once we're in them, finding us will require a bit of luck on the part of the Nip."

"You will exit the aircraft at 3,300 feet, and the aircraft will have established an indicated airspeed of ninety miles per hour. If there are the expected prevailing winds, that will produce a speed over the ground of approximately seventy-five to eighty-five miles per hour."

"You can't get any lower than that? Thirty-three hundred feet will be twelve hundred feet over the drop zone. You can get yourself blown a long way if you jump at twelve hundred feet," Steve said.

"I'll put you in at any altitude you want," the pilot said.

"Eight hundred feet," Steve said.

"Done."

"Will there be enough time, if you jump at eight hundred feet, to activate your reserve parachute?" the RAAF asked.

"No," Steve said. "But I don't want us to get blown into the trees. We won't take the reserve."

The RAAF officer looked at him with his eyebrows raised for a moment.

"Is that all right with you, Lieutenant Howard?"

"Steve's the expert," Howard replied. "Whatever he says."

"Well," the RAAF officer said, after a moment's thought, "unless there are any other questions, I think that wraps it up."

Steve looked down at his steak and eggs.

He was suddenly ravenously hungry.

"Can I finish my breakfast?" he asked.

"Yes, certainly," the RAAF officer said.

(THREE)
Buka Island
0725 Hours 8 June 1942

The pitch of the Lockheed's two Pratt & Whitney 1,050-horsepower Twin Wasp radial engines suddenly changed, bringing Sergeant Steve Koffler back to the tail section of the Hudson. He had been in the neat little bungalow he was sharing with Mrs. Koffler, the former Yeoman Daphne Farnsworth, in postwar Melbourne, Australia.

He'd seen such a bungalow, a whole section of them, on curving little streets on a hill. From the top of the hill you could see the water in Port Phillip Bay. On the way from Port Moresby, he had picked the exact house and furnished it, paying a lot of attention to the bedroom and the bathroom. In the final version of the bathroom, there was a shower—not just a tub with a shower head and a curtain, but a *pure* shower, with a door with frosty glass, so you could see somebody taking a shower inside.

When the sound of the engines changed, slowed down, he had just come home from work. He didn't know exactly what kind of job he had, but it had something to do with importing things from the States to Australia, and it was a pretty good job. He wasn't rich, but there was enough money for the bungalow and a car, and the steaks and stuff he'd brought home from the grocery store. Daphne wasn't in the kitchen or the living room. When he looked in the bedroom he heard the sound of the shower, so he stuck his head in the bathroom, and just stood there *admiring,* just that, *admiring,* nothing dirty or anything. Daphne was just standing there on the other side of the frosty glass, and she was letting the shower hit her on the face and a little lower.

Then he went to the shower and opened it just a crack and said, "I'm home, honey. I got some steaks."

And she covered her bosom and down below with her hands, because she was modest, even if they were married and had done it several hundred times, not just three the way they really had.

And Daphne smiled and said, "Steaks are fine, but I'm really not hungry right now. Don't you need a shower?"

And he knew what she meant. He put the steaks down and started to get undressed so he could get in the shower with her; and then the fucking engines changed pitch, the way they do when the pilot is slowing it down and lining it up with the drop zone. And he was back in the rear of the Lockheed, wearing an oxygen mask and fifty pounds of sheepskin jackets and pants and boots and hat and still freezing his ass.

He felt like crying.

He pushed himself to his feet so he could look out the window, and at that moment the Lockheed began a steep, descending turn to the left. He slipped and fell against one of the aluminum fuselage ribs, and pulled the oxygen tube loose from the bottle.

He had a hell of a time trying to plug the damned thing in again, with the heavy gloves on, holding his breath until he did; Sergeant Keyes had told him he would lose consciousness in ninety seconds without oxygen.

He took several deep breaths when he had it back on, and then tried to look out the window again. All he could see was clouds and far below, water.

The Flight Sergeant navigator came back, carefully making his way past the bomb bay. He was wearing a walk-around oxygen bottle. When he got close to Steve, he pulled it away from his face.

"You all right?"

Steve decided if the Flight Sergeant could take his mask off, he could too.

"Fine."

"We're over Buka, making our descent."

Steve nodded.

"It won't be long now. You'd better 'chute up."

Steve looked around until he saw the parachutes, then made his way to them. Lieutenant Howard came up; and following Steve's lead, he started to take off his sheepskin flying clothes.

It was still so cold that Steve started to shiver as, with difficulty, he worked into the harness. The Flight Sergeant gave the straps a couple of good jerks, drawing them tight around his legs.

If they weren't tight, they slapped and burned the shit out of your legs when the canopy opened, and Steve had heard stories of what happened to guys who got their balls between the harness strap and their legs when the canopy opened.

If the straps were tight enough, they were too tight, and your legs started to go to sleep, like now.

Steve motioned for Lieutenant Howard to stand with his hands holding on to the fuselage frame above him, and then he checked Howard's harness, tugging the straps very tight.

He felt very sorry for Howard. Making your first jump was bad enough. Steve clearly remembered his. But when that had happened, he had had a lot of training, and a reserve parachute, and there had been medics on the ground in case something went wrong.

Lieutenant Howard must be scared shitless. Poor bastard.

It seemed like it took forever to make the descent. Steve remembered a Clark Gable movie where a test pilot had torn the wings off an airplane by making it dive too fast.

Then the plane started to level out. Steve looked out the window again, and all he could see was green. Trees. Not even a lousy little dirt road. He wondered how the hell the pilot knew where they were.

The moment the plane was level, the bomb-bay doors started to open, and there was a hell of a rush of air and the surprisingly loud sound of the slipstream.

Steve made his way to the bomb bay. The bombardier was on the far side of it, wearing a set of earphones. He had secured the two bundles on either side of the open bomb bay, their static lines already tied to a hole in one of the aluminum fuselage ribs.

The Flight Sergeant touched Steve's shoulder and, when Steve turned to look at him, gestured for Steve to get in position. Very carefully, Steve lowered himself to the aircraft floor, and then scooted forward so that his feet hung over the edge.

He looked over his shoulder again, and saw the Flight Sergeant giving a good jerk to the static line he had tied to a fuselage rib.

Steve looked across the open bomb bay, where Lieutenant Howard was getting into position. He smiled at him, to show that he wasn't scared.

I am, after all, a member of the elite of the elite, a Marine Paratrooper.

Howard smiled at him, and gave him a thumbs-up sign.

What he's doing, Steve realized with surprise and admiration, *is trying to make me feel good!*

There was immediate confirmation. Howard cupped his hands and shouted. Steve could hear him, even over the roar of the engines and the whistling slipstream.

"How you doing, Koffler?"

Steve cupped his hands over his mouth, and shouted back, "Semper-fucking-Fi, Lieutenant!"

Lieutenant Howard smiled and shook his head.

Steve smiled back, and then looked over his shoulder to smile at the Flight Sergeant.

The Flight Sergeant was doing something weird. He had his hands in holes in the fuselage ribs, and was hanging from them, with both of his feet in the air.

And, in the moment Steve understood what was going on, the Flight Sergeant really did it. Steve felt an irresistible force on his back.

That sonofabitch really kicked me out!

Arms flailing, face downward, Steve fell through the bomb bay. He felt the rush of air from the slipstream, and then a slight tug. He didn't hear, or sense, the pilot chute being pulled loose. Just all of a sudden, the canopy opened, and there came the shock, the sensation of being jerked upward.

He looked up and saw the other parachutes. Lieutenant Howard's canopy filled with air as he watched, and then, almost together, the canopies of the cargo chutes opened. The load in one of them began to swing wildly back and forth. The second load was hanging just about straight down. Both were going to land on the field.

Steve looked down between his legs. He had three or four seconds to realize that he was going into the fucking trees, and to realize that there was not one fucking thing he could do about it.

"Oh, shit!" he said.

He pulled his elbows against his side and covered his face with his hands and waited to hit.

There was a brief sensation of his feet touching something, and then of passing through something, and then something was lashing against his legs and body and the hands he had against his face. And then he felt another jerk, even harder than the opening shock, and he stopped.

He opened his eyes. Everything was fuzzy at first, but then came into focus. It was dark, and he wondered if something had happened to his eyes, but then he saw bright spots, with rays of light coming through them, and understood that the reason it was dark was because the branches and leaves of the trees came together, forming a roof.

He was swinging gently back and forth, forty or fifty feet in the air. When he looked up, he could see the canopy, torn and collapsed, with tree branches holding it. Above the canopy, the branches of the trees had closed up again.

I've got to get the fuck out of here before the canopy starts ripping and lets me fall the rest of the way.

He started to make himself swing, by jerking his legs, with ever increasing force. Twice the canopy ripped and he felt himself falling, once about six feet. But both times other branches caught part of the canopy and stopped his fall.

Eventually he was able to reach a branch with his hand, and then, carefully, to pull himself onto a substantial limb. He straddled it, holding it tightly between his legs, pulled the safety from the quick-release, and shoved on it. The harness came free and moved upward with surprising and frightening speed, propelled by the elasticity of the branches on which the canopy was caught. One of the metal ends slashed across his forehead, hurting him like getting hit in the head with a rock. When he put his hand to it, it came away covered with blood.

He probed his face with his fingers and they all came away bloody.

"Shit!" he said softly.

After a moment his heart stopped pounding so quickly, so he moved his extremities and limbs enough to know that while he was sore all over, nothing was broken. Then he started, very carefully, to climb down the tree.

Twenty feet off the ground, he ran out of branches to stand or hang from. He wrapped his arms around the trunk, putting his fingers in ridges in the bark. They were more like ribs in the tree than bark.

Like handles! I can even wedge my toes in them!

He started to very carefully climb the rest of the way down. He had gone perhaps two feet when, at the same moment, the bark his left hand was holding and the bark his left toe was jammed into gave way.

He fell to the right, on his back. He felt himself hit something squishy and then everything went black.

* * *

Someone was slapping his face. He opened his eyes.

A man was looking at him, so close that Steve could smell garlic on his breath. He was sharp-featured and had a bushy black mustache. Steve started to try to get up.

He felt strong hands pushing him back.

"See if you can move your legs," the man ordered. Steve moved his legs. "And your arms." Steve moved his arms.

The hands that had been pushing him down now pulled him into a sitting position.

"I'm Jacob Reeves," he said. "Who are you?"

"I'm Corp—*Sergeant* Koffler, United States Marine Corps."

"*United States* Marine Corps? Well, I *will* be goddamned. A sodding American!"

"Yes, Sir," Steve said.

Steve felt a sting, and slapped at his face, and then looked at his hand. It was the largest mosquito he had ever seen, if it was a mosquito. He also became aware of a stench, something rotten.

"What smells?" he asked.

"At the moment, old boy, I'd say that's you. The jungle stinks, but not quite that much."

Oh, my God, I shit my pants! he thought in horror. And then he had another horrifying thought: *Lieutenant Howard! Where the fuck is he? Did he go into the trees, too?*

"Sir, there's somebody else. And two cargo parachutes . . ."

"We have the mattresses," Reeves said. "Your other man landed in the trees."

"Is he all right?"

"I don't know. We're still looking for him. The girls are already carrying the packages to the village. Are you all right to walk?"

"I think so," Steve said.

"Good," Reeves said. "The sodding Jap chose to send another of his sodding patrols looking for us. We're going to have to do something about that."

"You think they're going to find us?"

"*We* have to find *them,*" Reeves said. "They must have seen the aircraft and the sodding parachutes, so they know there's something going on up here except some unfriendly natives."

"I don't understand, Sir."

"The Japs are now headed down the hill," Reeves explained, "to report what they saw. We have to make sure they don't make it. Otherwise, the Jap will send troops up here and keep them here until they do find us."

Steve got to his feet. He had to steady himself for a moment against a tree trunk, but then he was all right.

He slapped at another mosquito.

"What about Lieutenant Howard?" he asked.

"I told my head boy he has five minutes to find him," Reeves said.

"And if he doesn't find him in five minutes, then what?"

"Then we'll have to stop looking, I'm afraid. What has to be done is stop the sodding Japs from reporting what they saw."

"Fuck you," Steve said. "I'm not going anywhere without Lieutenant Howard."

"I've explained the situation, lad," Reeves said evenly.

"So have I," Steve said. "I'm a fucking Marine. We just don't take off and leave our people behind."

"That's a very commendable philosophy, I'm sure, but—"

"I don't give a shit what you think of it," Steve interrupted. "That's the way it's going to be."

The discussion proved to be moot.

A brown-skinned, fuzzy-haired man appeared out of nowhere. He was wearing a loincloth, a bone in his nose, and a web cartridge belt around his neck, and he was carrying a British Lee-Enfield MK III .303 rifle. He announced, in understandable English, "We have the other bloke, Mr. Reeves. He was hanging from the trees. He has broken his arm."

At least he's alive, Steve thought. *Thank God!* Then he thought, *What's he going to think when he finds out I shit my pants? My God, I can't believe I really did that!*

A moment later, there was the sound of something moving through the muck on the forest floor. And then Lieutenant Howard appeared. His left arm was folded and strapped across his chest with his cartridge belt; his right arm was around the shoulder of a short, plump, brown-skinned, fuzzy-headed, bare-breasted woman. She was wearing what looked like a dirty towel, and carrying Howard's Thompson .45-caliber submachine gun.

"Jesus, I was worried about you," he said to Koffler.

"I'm Jacob Reeves," Reeves said.

"Lieutenant Howard, U.S. Marine Corps," Howard said.

"Cecilia," Reeves said to the bare-breasted woman, "I want you to take this gentleman to the village. You think you can do that?"

Cecilia smiled, revealing that her teeth were stained almost black.

"Of course," she said. "I think one or two of the other girls are about to help, if need be."

Christ, she sounds just like Daphne!

"Make him as comfortable as you can. Give him some of the whiskey. When we get there, we'll tend to his arm."

"You better take that tommy gun, Sergeant," Reeves said to Steve Koffler, adding to Howard, "We'll see you a bit later, then."

"Where are you going?" Howard asked.

Reeves didn't answer. He started trotting off into the jungle. Steve Koffler took the Thompson and two extra twenty-round magazines from Howard's pocket, and ran after him.

(FOUR)

Steve became aware as they moved through the forest that others were with them besides Jacob Reeves and the guy with the bone through his nose, although he had trouble getting a clear look at any of them.

They were going downhill. Although it wasn't like the sticky muck where they had landed, the ground was still wet and slippery. He had to watch his footing and to keep his eye on Reeves. His chest hurt from the exertion. There seemed to be a cloud of insects around his face, crawling into his ears and nostrils and mouth.

What seemed like hours later, they stopped. According to his watch, it was only thirty-five minutes. Steve stood there, sweat-soaked, breathing hard, looking with mingled amazement and horror at his hands and arms, which were covered with insect stings.

Reeves came up to him.

"Do you know how to use that tommy gun?"

"I fired it in boot camp," Steve said.

"In other words, you don't."

"I qualified," Steve said sharply.

"The way we're going to do this," Reeves said, "the Japs will be coming down a path this way. What I would like you to do is make sure that none of them gets past you. This will be successful only if we take all of them. If one of them gets away . . . You understand?"

Steve nodded.

"We'll have our go at them about fifty yards up the footpath," Reeves said. "It then passes just a few yards from here. You go have a look at it, and then find yourself a place. Clear?"

"OK," Steve said.

"It shouldn't take them long to get down here, so be quick," Reeves ordered.

"OK," Steve repeated. He swung the Thompson off his shoulder. When he looked up again, Reeves was nowhere in sight.

Steve made his way through the thick undergrowth until he found the path. He walked ten yards up it, and then ten yards in the other direction, and then backed off into the underbrush again and leaned against a tree.

After a moment, he allowed himself to slip to the ground. This action reminded him that his shorts, and now his trouser legs, were full of shit.

He started to think about his and Daphne's bungalow in postwar Melbourne again.

Shit, if I do that, I'm liable to doze off and get my fucking throat cut!

All he could hear was the buzzing of the insects.

And then there was noise.

He worked the action of the Thompson and then looked down inside at the shiny brass cartridge. When he pulled the trigger, the cartridge would be stripped from the magazine by the bolt, driven into the chamber, and fired. Then, so long as he held the trigger and the magazine held cartridges, the bolt would be driven backward by recoil, hit a spring, and then fly forward again, stripping another cartridge from the magazine.

He heard something on the trail.

What the fuck is that? It can't be a Jap. If it was a Jap, Reeves and the others would have been shooting by now.

But, curious, he slowly pulled himself to his feet.

It was a Jap. He was wearing a silly little brimmed cap on his head; and he was carrying a rifle slung over his shoulder that looked much too big for him. He was coming down the trail as if he were taking a walk through the fucking woods.

Shit!

The one thing he had learned at Parris Island was that you couldn't hit a fucking thing with a Thompson the way Alan Ladd shot one in the movies, from the hip. You had to put it to your shoulder like a rifle, get a sight picture, and just *caress* the trigger.

He did so.

Nothing happened. He really pulled hard on the trigger. Nothing happened.

The safety! The fucking safety!

He snapped it off, pulled on the trigger, and the Thompson jumped in his hands.

The Jap dropped right there.

There was no other sound for a moment, and that too was scary.

And then there was fire. Different weapons. A burp-burp noise, probably from that funny-looking little submachine gun Reeves had; and booming cracks like from a Springfield, and sharper cracks. Probably from the Japs' rifles.

Now he could see figures moving through the trees. Not well. Not enough to tell if they were Reeves's Fuzzy-Wuzzies, or whatever the fuck they were, or Japs.

Jesus Christ!

There's a Jap!

The Thompson burped again and suddenly stopped.

Oh, shit! Twenty rounds already?

He slammed another magazine in and saw another Jap and fired again, and seemed to be missing.

Another figure appeared.

One of the fucking Fuzzy-Wuzzies.

And then Jacob Reeves.

"I think that's all of them," Reeves said. "We counted. There were eight. They usually run eight-man patrols."

Steve came out of the underbrush onto the trail.

"You all right, son?" Reeves asked.

"I'm all right," Steve said.

There was a body on the trail. Steve walked up to look at it. It was the first one he'd shot.

He looked at the face of the first man he had killed.

The first man he had killed looked back at him with terror in his eyes.

"This one's still alive!" Steve said.

"We can't have that, I'm afraid," Reeves said, walking up.

Steve pointed the Thompson muzzle at the Jap's forehead and pulled the trigger.

I already shit my pants and now I think I'm going to throw up.

The village looked like something out of *National Geographic* magazine. It was much larger, too, than Steve had expected, although when he thought about that, he couldn't understand why he thought it would be any particular size at all.

Brown-skinned, flat-nosed people watched as he marched after Reeves into the village. Some of them had teeth that looked like they had been dyed blue and then filed to a point. Most of the women weren't going around in nothing but dirty towels with their boobs hanging out, like Cecilia. They were wearing dirty cotton skirts and loose blouses, some of which opened in the front to expose breasts that were anything but lust inciting.

There were chickens running loose, and pigs with one leg tied to a stake. There were fires burning. And he saw women beating something with a rock against another rock.

A clear stream, about five feet wide and two feet deep, meandered through the center of the collection of grass-walled huts.

"I'll go see about your lieutenant's arm," Reeves said.

"What can you do about it?" Steve asked.

"Set it, of course," Reeves said.

"Can you do that? I mean, really do it right?"

"I'm not a sodding doctor, if that's what you mean," Reeves snapped.

"No offense," Steve said lamely.

"I'll have them put up a hut for you, while you're having your bath," Jacob Reeves said after a moment. "Just leave your clothing there. The girls will take care of it for you. And I'll send you down a shirt and some shorts to wear."

He pointed to a muddy area by the stream, at the end of the village. It was apparently the community bath and wash house.

I think he actually expects me to just take off my clothes in front of everybody and sit in that stream and take a bath.

"That water's safe for bathing," Reeves said, as if reading Steve's mind. "But don't drink it. I've been here since Christ was a babe, and I still haven't built up an immunity to the sodding water. There's boiled water and beer."

Steve looked at him in surprise.

"Well, it's not really beer," Reeves admitted. "We make it out of rice and coconuts. But it's not all that bad."

Reeves walked off. And after a moment, Steve Koffler walked to the edge of the stream and started to take his clothing off.

(FIVE)

Eyes Only—The Secretary of the Navy

DUPLICATION FORBIDDEN
ORIGINAL TO BE DESTROYED AFTER ENCRYPTION AND TRANSMITTAL TO SECNAVY

Melbourne, Australia
Monday, 8 June 1942

Dear Frank:

This will deal with the Battle of Midway, from MacArthur's perception of it here, and the implications of it for the conduct of the war, short- and long-term, as he sees them.

But before I get into that: Willoughby somehow found out, I have no idea how, that I am on the Albatross list; and he promptly ran to tell MacA. MacA., of course, knew; like everyone else on it, he had been furnished with the list itself. I am quite sure that MacA. brings Willoughby in on anything that would remotely interest him whenever he (MacA.) receives Magic intelligence. But Willoughby is not on the Albatross list himself, and as a matter of personal prestige (he is, after all, a major general and MacA.'s G-2), he found this grossly humiliating even before he learned that lowly Captain Pickering was on it.

The result of this is that MacA. fired off a cable demanding that Willoughby be added to the Albatross list. Then he made a point of mentioning to me that he understands how critical it is that Magic not be compromised, and the necessity for keeping the Albatross list as short as possible. The implication I took was that he really would be happier if Willoughby were kept off the list and rather hoped that I would pass this on to you.

I'm not sure what his motive is (motives are), but I don't think they have anything to do with making sure Magic isn't compromised. Quite possibly, MacA. regards the Albatross list as a prerogative of the emperor, not to be shared with the lesser nobility. He may also be hoping that if you ("Those bastards in Washington") refuse to add Willoughby to the Albatross list, it will ensure that Willoughby hates you as much as the emperor himself does.

Personally, I <u>hope</u> that Willoughby is added to the list. It would certainly improve my relationship with him and make my life here in the palace a little easier. But that's <u>not</u> a recommendation. Magic is so important that I refuse to recommend anything that might pose any risk whatever that would compromise it.

Tangentially, I do <u>not</u> receive copies of Magic messages reaching here. I don't have any place to store them, for one thing. I don't even have an office, much less a secretary with the appropriate security clearances to log classified material in and out. There are four people here (in addition to MacA. and me) on the Albatross list. They are all Army Signal Corps people: the Chief of Cryptographic Services, a captain; and two cryptographers, both sergeants. There is also a Lieutenant Hon, a Korean (U.S. citizen, MIT '38) who speaks fluent Japanese. He is often able to make subtle changes in interpretation of the translations made at Pearl.

When a Magic comes in, the captain calls me. I go to the crypto room and read it there. Lieutenant Hon hand-carries the Magics to MacA., together with his interpretation of any portion of them that differs from what we get from Pearl. MacA. stops whatever else he is doing and reads them—or, I should say, commits them to his really incredible memory. The paper itself is then returned to the crypto safe. Only twice to my knowledge has MacA. ever sent for one of them to look at again.

On the subject of the Albatross/Magic list: I would like permission to make Major Ed Banning privy to Magic messages. He has managed to establish himself with the Australian Coastwatchers. He speaks Japanese, and has, I think, an insight into the way the Japanese military think. I have the feeling that with input both from the Australians and the Magic intercepts, he could come up with analyses that might elude other people—of whom I'm certainly one. He already knows a good deal about Albatross/Magic, and I can't see where my giving him access to the intercepts themselves increases the risk of compromising Magic much—if at all. I would appreciate a radio reply to this: "yes" or "no" would suffice.

Finally, turning to the Battle of Midway: We had been getting some rather strong indications of the Japanese intentions throughout May—not only from Magic—and MacA. had decided that it was the Japanese plan to attack Midway, as a stepping-stone to Hawaii.

I asked MacA. what he thought the American reaction to the loss of Hawaii would be. He said that it might wake the American people up to the idea that basic American interests are in the Pacific, not

in Europe; but that if it fell, which he couldn't imagine, American influence in the Pacific would be lost in our lifetimes, perhaps forever. Then he added that a year ago he would have been unable to accept the thought that the American people would stand for the reinforcement of England, knowing that it would mean the loss of the Philippines.

MacA. expected that Admiral Yamamoto, for whom he has great professional admiration, would launch either a two-pronged attack, with one element attacking Midway, or a diversionary feint coinciding with an attack on Midway. He would not have been surprised if there had been a second attack (or a feint) at Port Moresby.

MacA. reasoned that the Japanese loss of the carrier *Shoho* and the turning of the Port Moresby invasion force in early May had been the first time we'd actually been able to give the Japanese a bloody nose. For the first time, they had been kept from doing what they had started out to do. Their admirals had lost face. But now they'd had a month to regroup, lick their wounds, and prepare to strike again. They could regain face by taking Port Moresby, and that would have put their Isolate Australia plan back on track.

He was surprised when the Magic messages began to suggest an attack on the Aleutians. He grilled me at length about the Aleutians, whether there was something there he hadn't heard about. He simply cannot believe the Japanese want to invade Alaska. What could they get out of Alaska that would be worth the logistical cost of landing there? MacA. asks. Their supply lines would not only be painfully long, but would be set up like a shooting gallery for interdiction from the United States and Canada.

He therefore concluded that the attack on the Aleutians, which came on June 3, was a feint intended to draw our Naval forces off; that the Japs believe that the Americans would place a greater emotional value on the Aleutians than was the case; and that we would rise to the bait. MacA. predicted this would be a miscalculation on their part.

"Nimitz is no fool," he said. "He doesn't care about the Aleutians."

Events, of course, proved him right. We learned from Magic intercepts that Admiral Nagumo (and thus the entire Japanese fleet) was very surprised on 4 June, when his reconnaissance aircraft reported seeing a large American Naval force to the northeast of Midway.

We later learned—from Magic!—that these were the aircraft carriers Yorktown, Enterprise, and Hornet, under Admirals Spruance and Fletcher. We were getting our information about the movements of our own fleet from Japanese intercepts, via Hawaii, before we were getting reports from the Navy. MacA. is convinced, in the absence of any other reason to the contrary, that the Navy believes that the war in the Pacific is a Navy war, and consequently they have no obligation to tell him what's happening.

I have a recommendation here: I strongly recommend that you direct Nimitz (or have King direct Nimitz) to assign one commander or captain the sole duty of keeping MacA. posted on what's going on while it's happening—not just when the Navy finds it convenient to tell him.

We learned (again via Magic intercepts) that the Japanese came under attack by torpedo bombers at 0930 4 June. The aircraft carriers Hiryu, Kaga, Soryu, and Akagi all reported to Yamamoto that they were relatively unhurt, and that the American losses were severe. Then came a report from Hiryu, saying she had been severely damaged by American dive bombers. Nothing was intercepted from any of the others.

Then there were Magic intercepts of Yamamoto's orders to the fleet to withdraw.

And then, many hours later, we heard from the Navy, and learned that the carriers Soryu, Kaga, and Akagi had been sunk, and that we had lost the carrier Yorktown. It was a day later that we learned that the Hiryu was sunk that next morning, and about the terrible losses and incredible courage of the Navy torpedo bomber pilots who had attacked the Japanese carriers. And that Marine Fighter Squadron VMF-211, land-based on Midway, had lost fifteen of its twenty-five pilots; in effect it had been wiped out.

The Japanese seem to have suffered more than just their first beating; it was also a very bad mauling. And MacA. sent what I thought were rather touching messages to Nimitz, Spruance, and Fletcher, expressing his admiration and congratulations.

And today he sent a long cable to Marshall, asking permission to attack New Britain and New Ireland (in other words, to take out the Japanese base at Rabaul) with the U.S. 32nd and 41st Divisions and the Australian 7th Division. To do so would mean that the Navy would have to provide him both with vessels capable of making and supporting an amphibious invasion, and with aircraft carriers. I don't think he really expects the Navy to give him what he asks for. But not to ask for the operation—indeed fight for it, and the necessary support for it from the Navy—would be tantamount to giving in to the notion that the Navy owns the war over here.

I won't presume to suggest who is right, but I frankly think it is a tragedy that the Army and the Navy should be at each other's throats like this.

I mentioned earlier on in this report that Banning has developed a good relationship with the Australian Coastwatchers. Early this morning, the RAAF parachuted two Marines, a lieutenant and a sergeant, and a replacement radio, onto Buka Island, north of Bougainville, where the Coastwatcher's radio had gone out. Loss of reports from the observation post was so critical that great risks to get it up and running again were considered justified. The only qualified (radio operator, parachutist) Marine was eighteen years

old. And that is all he can do. He can't tell one Japanese aircraft from another, or a destroyer from a battleship. So one of Banning's lieutenants, Joe Howard, a Mustang, who had taught aircraft/ship recognition, volunteered to parachute in, too, although he had never jumped before. Banning confided to me that he thought he had one chance in four or five of making a successful landing.

The Lockheed Hudson that was to drop them was never heard from. We took the worst-possible-case scenario, and decided it had been shot down by Japanese fighters on the way in and that everyone was lost. Banning immediately asked for volunteers to try it again. All of his men volunteered.

As I was writing this, Banning came in with the news that Buka was back on the air. The Lockheed had been shot down on the way home. With contact reestablished, the RAN people here had routinely asked for "traffic." This is what they got, verbatim: "Please pass Ensign Barbara Cotter, USNR, and Yeoman Daphne Farnsworth, RAN. We love you and hope to see you soon. Joe and Steve."

Those boys obviously think we're going to win the war. Maybe, Frank, if we can get the admirals and the generals to stop acting like adolescents, we can.

Respectfully,
Fleming Pickering, Captain USNR

(SIX)
Menzies Hotel
Melbourne, Victoria
16 June 1942

Lieutenant Hon Song Do, Signal Corps, Army of the United States, was sitting in one of the chairs lining the hotel corridor when Captain Fleming Pickering, USNR, stepped off the elevator. Captain Pickering had just finished dining, *en famille,* with the Commander-in-Chief and Mrs. Douglas MacArthur. Over cognac afterward, General MacArthur had talked at some length about the German campaign in Russia. The dissertation had again impressed Captain Pickering with the incredible scope of MacArthur's mind; and the four snifters of Rémy Martin had left him feeling just a little bit tight.

"Well, hello, Lieutenant," Pickering said when he saw Lieutenant Hon. Hon sometimes made him feel slightly ill at ease. For one thing, he didn't know what to call him. Something in his mind told him that "Hon" was, in the American sense, his last name. He could not, in other words, do what he had long ago learned how to do with other junior officers; he couldn't put him at ease by calling him by his first name, or even better, by his nickname. He simply didn't know what it was.

And Lieutenant Hon was not what ordinarily came to Pickering's mind when "Asian-American" or "Korean-American" was mentioned. For one thing, he was a very large man, nearly as tall and heavy as Pickering; and for another, he had a deep voice with a thick Boston accent. And on top of this, he was what Pickering thought of as an egghead. He was a theoretical mathematician. He had been commissioned as a mathematician, and he'd originally been assigned to Signal Intelligence as a mathematician. Only afterward had the Army learned that he was a Japanese linguist.

"Good evening, Sir," Lieutenant Hon said, rising to his feet. "I have a rather interesting decrypt for you, Sir."

"Why didn't you bring it downstairs?"

"I didn't think it was quite important enough for me to have to intrude on the Commander-in-Chief's dinner."

Pickering looked at him. There was a smile in Lieutenant Hon's eyes.

"Well, come on in, and I'll buy you a drink," Pickering said, then added, "Lieutenant, I think I know you well enough to call you by your first name."

"I wouldn't do that, Sir," Lieutenant Hon said dryly. " 'Do' doesn't lend itself to English as a first name. Why don't you call me Pluto?"

"Pluto?"

"Yes, Sir. That's what I've been called for years. After Mickey Mouse's friend, the dog with the sad face?"

"OK," Pickering chuckled. "Pluto it is."

He snapped the lights on.

"What will you have to drink, Pluto?"

"Is there any of that Old Grouse Scotch, Sir?"

"Should be several bottles of it. Why don't you give me the decrypt and make us both one? I think there's a can of peanuts in the drawer under the bar, too. Why don't you open that?"

"Thank you, Sir," Pluto Hon said, and handed Pickering a sealed manila envelope.

Pickering tore it open. Inside was a TOP SECRET cover sheet, and below that a sheet of typewriter paper.

NOT LOGGED
ONE COPY ONLY
DUPLICATION FORBIDDEN
FOLLOWING IS DECRYPTION OF MSG 234545 RECEIVED 061742
OFFICE SECNAVY WASHDC 061642 1300 GREENWICH
COMMANDER-IN-CHIEF SOUTHWEST PACIFIC
EYES ONLY CAPTAIN FLEMING PICKERING USNR
REF YOUR 8 JUNE 1942 REPORT
SECNAVY REPLIES QUOTE
PART ONE YES
PART TWO YOUR FRIEND BEING INVITED HAWAIIAN PARTY
PART THREE BEST PERSONAL REGARDS SIGNATURE FRANK
END QUOTE
HAUGHTON CAPT USN ADMIN OFF TO SECNAVY

Pickering walked to the bar. Pluto was just about finished making the drinks.

"A little cryptic, even decrypted, isn't it?" he said to Pluto, taking the extended drink.

Pluto chuckled. "I don't think it's likely, but even if the Japs have broken the Blue Code, their analysts are going to have a hell of a time making anything out of that."

"Would you care to guess, Pluto?"

"There was a message from the JCS adding General Willoughby to the Albatross list. Am I getting warm?" Banning smiled and nodded. "I have no idea what 'Yes' means," Pluto Hon said.

"I asked for permission to give Major Banning access to Magic intercepts," Pickering said. "What I decide to show him. I didn't ask that he be put on the Albatross list."

Pluto nodded. "Are you going to want that logged, Sir?"

Pickering shook his head, then took out his cigarette lighter and burned the sheet of typewriter paper, holding it over a wastebasket until it was consumed.

Lieutenant Pluto Hon refused a second drink and left. Pickering went to bed.

In the morning, at breakfast, Major General Willoughby walked over to Captain Pickering's table in the Menzies Hotel dining room and sat down with him. A large smile was on his face.

"Have you had a chance to read the overnight Magics yet, Pickering?"

"No, Sir," Captain Pickering said.

"You should have a look. Very interesting."

General Willoughby looked very pleased with himself.

(SEVEN)
The Elms
Dandenong, Victoria, Australia
1825 Hours 1 July 1942

It was windy; and there was a cold and unpleasant rain. As Captain Fleming Pickering drove the drop-head Jaguar coupe under the arch of winter-denuded elms toward the house, he was thinking unkind thoughts about the British.

As cold as it gets in England, and as much as this car must have cost, it would seem reasonable to expect that the windshield wipers would work, and the heater, and that the goddamned top wouldn't leak.

As he neared the house and saw Banning's Studebaker, his mind turned to unkind thoughts about Major Ed Banning, USMC.

He didn't know what he was doing here, except that he would be meeting "a friend" and somebody else Banning wanted to introduce him to. Banning, on the telephone, acted as if he was sure the line was tapped by the Japanese, even if all he was discussing was goddamned dinner. No details. Just cryptic euphemisms.

And I will bet ten dollars to a doughnut that both "a friend" and "somebody else" are going to be people I would rather not see.

He got out of the car and ran through the drizzle up onto the porch.

Mrs. Cavendish answered his ring with a warm smile.

"Oh, good evening, Captain," she said. "How are you tonight?"

"Wet and miserable, Mrs. Cavendish, how about you?"

She laughed. "A little nip will fix you right up," she said. "The other gentlemen are in the library."

I had no right to snap at her, and no reason to be annoyed with Banning. For all I know the goddamned phone is *tapped. Maybe by Willoughby. And it is absurd to fault an intelligence officer for having a closed mouth. You are acting like a curmudgeonly old man. Or perhaps a younger man, suffering from sexual deprivation.*

The latter thought, he realized, had been triggered by the perversity of his recent erotic dreams. He had had four of them over not too many more nights than that. Only one had involved the female he was joined with in holy matrimony. A second had involved a complete stranger who had, in his dream, exposed her breasts to him in a Menzies Hotel elevator, then made her desires known with a lewd wink. The other two had been nearly identical: Ellen Feller had stood at the side of his bed, undressed slowly, and then mounted him.

"I didn't mean to snap at you, Mrs. Cavendish," Pickering said.

"I didn't know that you had," she said, smiling, as she took his coat.

He walked down the corridor to the library and pushed the door open.

"I will be damned," he said, smiling. It really was a friend. "How are you, Jake?"

Major Jake Dillon, USMC, crossed the room to him, smiling, shook his hand, and then hugged him.

"You should be ashamed of yourself," Dillon said. "Patricia's sitting at home knitting scarfs and gloves for you, imagining you living in some leaking tent; and here you are, living like the landed gentry—even including a Jaguar."

"If I detect a broad suggestion of jealousy, I'm glad," Pickering said. "I see you're already into my booze."

"Banning took care of that, after I told him how dry it was all the way from the States to Wellington, New Zealand."

"That was probably good for you. I'm sure you hadn't been sober that long in years. You came with the 1st Division?" Headquarters, 1st Marine Division, and the entire 5th Marines had debarked at Wellington, New Zealand, on June 14, 1942.

"All the way. And it was a *very* long way. The ship was *not* the *Pacific Princess.* The cuisine and accommodations left a good deal to be desired."

"What are you doing here? And where did you meet Ed Banning?"

"Here. Tonight. He's a friend of Colonel Goettge."

"Who's Colonel Goettge?"

"I am, Sir," a voice said, and Pickering turned. Banning and a tall, muscular Marine colonel had come into the library from the kitchen. "I suspect that I may be imposing."

"Nonsense," Pickering said, crossing to him and offering his hand. "Any friend of Banning's, et cetera et cetera."

"Very kind of you, Captain," Goettge said.

"Also of Jack Stecker's," Jake Dillon said. "It was Jack's idea that I come along. He sends his regards."

"So far, Colonel," Pickering said, "that's two good guys out of three. But how did you get hung up with this character?"

"Watch it, Flem. I'll arrange to have you photographed being wetly kissed by a bare-breasted aborigine maiden, and send eight-by-ten glossies to Patricia."

"He would, too," Pickering said, laughing. "Colonel, you're in dangerous company."

"Colonel Goettge is the 1st Division G-2, Captain Pickering," Banning said. "He was sent here to gather intelligence on certain islands in the Solomons."

Pickering met Banning's eye for a moment. They both knew more about pending operations in the Solomon Islands than Colonel Goettge was supposed to know, even though he was G-2 of the 1st Marine Division.

Pickering was worried, however, about how much Goettge actually knew.

On Friday, June 19, twelve days before, Vice-Admiral Robert L. Ghormley, USN, had activated his headquarters at Auckland, New Zealand, and become Commander, South Pacific, subordinate to Admiral Nimitz at Pearl Harbor.

Pickering immediately flew down to meet him, not sure in his own mind if he was doing so in his official role as observer for Frank Knox, or as a member (if unofficial) of MacArthur's palace guard.

Once he saw Pickering's orders, Admiral Ghormley had no choice but to brief him on his concept of the war, and on his planning. But he went further than paying appropriate respect to an officer wrapped in the aura of a personal representative of the Secretary of the Navy required.

There were several reasons for this. For one, they immediately liked each other. Over lunch, Ghormley drew out of Pickering the story of how he had worked his way up from apprentice seaman in the deck department to his "Any Ocean, Any Tonnage" master's ticket. And it quickly became clear that the two of them were not an admiral and a civilian in a captain's uniform, but that they were two men who had known the responsibility of the bridge in a storm.

And, too, Ghormley had come to the South Pacific almost directly from London. Thus he had not spent enough time in either Washington or Pearl Harbor to become infected with the parochial virus that caused others of his rank to feel that the war in the Pacific had to be fought and won by the Navy alone—perhaps as the only way to overcome the shame of Pearl Harbor.

And to Pickering's pleased surprise, Ghormley had independently come up with a strategy that was very much like MacArthur's. He saw the Japanese base at Rabaul on New Britain as a likely and logical target for the immediate future. He thought it would be a very reasonable expenditure of assets to assault New Britain amphibiously with the 1st Marine Division, and, once the beachhead was secure, to turn the battle over to the Army's 32nd and 41st Infantry Divisions.

Pickering then informed Admiral Ghormley that he was privy to General MacArthur's thinking, and that the two of them were in essential agreement. He made this admission after briefly considering that not only was it none of Ghormley's business, but that telling Ghormley such things would enrage both Frank Knox and Douglas MacArthur if they learned of it, as they almost certainly would.

Which was to say, of course, that MacArthur and Ghormley both disagreed with Admiral Ernest King's proposed plans for immediate action: These called for a Navy attack under Admiral Nimitz on both the Santa Cruz and Solomon Islands, while MacArthur launched a diversionary attack on the East Indies.

When Pickering returned to Brisbane, he dropped the other shoe (after one of MacArthur's private dinners) and informed MacArthur of Ghormley's ideas for the most efficient prosecution of the war. Lengthy "independent" cables then went from Ghormley (to Admiral King, Chief of Naval Operations) and MacArthur (to General Marshall, Chief of Staff of the Army). These strenuously urged an attack to retake Rabaul as the first major counterattack of the war.

General Marshall cabled MacArthur that he fully agreed Rabaul should be the first target, and that he would make the case for that before the Joint Chiefs of Staff.

Admiral King, however, not only flatly disagreed with that, but was so sure that his position would prevail when the final decision was made by the Joint Chiefs of Staff that he "unofficially" alerted Nimitz, who in turn "unofficially" alerted Ghormley, that a Navy force, with or without MacArthur's support, would attack the Solomons as soon as possible—probably within a month or six weeks.

"Presuming" that Nimitz certainly would have told MacArthur of the Navy's plans, Ghormley discussed (by memoranda, hand-carried by officer courier) Nimitz's alert with MacArthur. This, of course, resulted in more emphatic cables from MacArthur to Marshall. It was still possible that the Joint Chiefs of Staff would decide against King and in favor of striking at Rabaul first.

The decision of the Joint Chiefs of Staff was not yet made, although it was clear that it would have to be made in the next few days.

Pickering had briefed Banning on his meetings with Ghormley and all that had happened after that. He now wondered if that had been a serious mistake. Had Banning told his old friend, Goettge, the First Division G-2, any—or all—of what Pickering had told him in confidence?

"Captain Pickering," Colonel Goettge said, "it's been my experience that when you have something delicate to say, you almost always get yourself in deeper trouble when you pussyfoot around it."

"Mine, too," Pickering replied. "What's on your mind?"

"I can only hope this won't leave this room—"

"You're pussyfooting," Pickering interrupted.

"The word in the 1st Division is that General MacArthur's attitude toward the Navy generally, and the Marine Corps in particular, is 'Fuck you,' " Goettge said.

"That's unfortunate," Pickering said.

"There's a story going around that he wouldn't give the 4th Marines a Presidential Unit Citation in the Philippines because 'the Marines already get enough publicity,' " Goettge said.

"I'm afraid that's true," Pickering said. "But I'm also sure that he made that decision under a hell of a strain, and that he now regrets it. MacArthur is a very complex character."

"General Vandergrift thinks we will invade the Solomons. Or at least two of the Solomon Islands, Tulagi and Guadalcanal," Goettge said.

"Where did he get that?" Pickering said.

"I don't know, Sir."

Pickering looked at Banning. Banning just perceptibly shook his head, meaning *I didn't tell him.*

I should have known that, Pickering thought. *Why the hell did I question Banning's integrity?*

"My job, therefore," Colonel Goettge said, "is to gather as much intelligence about Guadalcanal and Tulagi as I possibly can. Phrased as delicately as I can, there is some doubt in General Vandergrift's mind—and in mine—that, without a friend in court, so to speak, I won't be able to get much from General Willoughby when I go to see him tomorrow."

My God, Pickering thought, sad and disgusted, *has it gone that far?*

"And you think I could be your 'friend at court'?"

"Yes, Sir, that's about it."

"It's all over Washington, Flem," Jake Dillon said, "that you and Dugout Doug have become asshole buddies."

A wave of rage swept through Fleming Pickering. It was a long moment before he trusted himself to speak.

"Jake, old friends or not," he said finally, calmly, "if you ever refer to

MacArthur in those terms again, I'll bring you up on charges myself." But then his tone turned furious as anger overwhelmed him: "God*damn* you, you ignorant sonofabitch! General Willoughby—who is a fine officer despite the contempt in which you, Goettge, and others seem to hold him—told me that on Bataan, MacArthur was often so close to the lines that there was genuine concern that he would be captured by Japanese infantry patrols. And on Corregidor they couldn't get him to go into the goddamned tunnel when the Japs were shelling! Who the *fuck* do you think *you* are to call *him* 'Dugout Doug'?"

"Sorry," Dillon said.

"You fucking well should be sorry!" Pickering flared. "Stick to being a goddamned press agent, you miserable pimple on a Marine's ass, and keep your fucking mouth shut when you don't know what the fuck you're talking about!"

There was silence in the room.

Pickering looked at them, the rage finally subsiding. Jake Dillon looked crushed. Colonel Goettge looked painfully uncomfortable. Ed Banning was . . .

The sonofabitch is smiling!

"You are amused, Major Banning?" Pickering asked icily.

"Sir, I think Major Dillon was way out of line," Banning said. "But, Sir, I was amused. I was thinking, 'You can take the boy out of the Marines, but you can't take the Marines out of the boy.' I was thinking, Sir, that you sounded much more like a Marine corporal than like the personal representative of the Secretary of the Navy. You did that splendidly, Sir."

"Christ, Flem," Jake Dillon said. "I just didn't know . . . If I knew what you thought of him . . ."

"Jake," Pickering said. "Just shut up."

"Yes, Sir," Dillon said.

"Do something useful. Make us a drink."

"Would it be better if I just left, Sir?" Colonel Goettge asked.

"No. Of course not. I'm going to get on the phone and ask General Willoughby out here for dinner. I'm going to tell him that you're an old friend of mine. If he comes, fine. If he doesn't, at least he'll know who you are when I take you in tomorrow morning to see him."

"Sir," Banning said, "I thought it would be a good idea to put Colonel Goettge in touch with the Coastwatchers—"

"Absolutely!"

"To that end, Sir, I asked Commander Feldt—he's in town—"

"I know," Pickering interrupted.

"—and Lieutenant Donnelly to dinner."

"Good."

"He's bringing Yeoman Farnsworth with him," Banning said.

"Why?"

"It was my idea, Sir. I thought it would be nice to radio Lieutenant Howard and Sergeant Koffler that we had dinner with their girls. I asked Ensign Cotter, too."

"If General Willoughby is free to have dinner with us, Ed, I can't imagine that he would object to sharing the table with two pretty girls. God knows, there's none around the mess in the Menzies."

XIV

(ONE)

Eyes Only—The Secretary of the Navy

DUPLICATION FORBIDDEN
ORIGINAL TO BE DESTROYED AFTER ENCRYPTION AND TRANSMITTAL TO SECNAVY

Water Lily Cottage
Manchester Avenue
Brisbane, Australia
Tuesday, 21 July 1942

Dear Frank:
I'm not sure if it was really necessary, but the emperor decided to move the court; and so here, after an enormous logistical effort, we are. It is (MacA.'s stated reason for the move) "1,185 miles closer to the front lines."

El Supremo's Headquarters are in a modern office building, formerly occupied by an insurance company. MacA. has a rather elegant office on the eighth floor (of nine). I am down the corridor, and was surprised to learn that General Sutherland himself assigned me my office. I would have wagered he would put me in the basement, or left me in Melbourne.

MacA. and family, and the senior officers, are living in Lennon's Hotel, which is a rambling, graceful old Victorian hostelry that reminds me of the place the Southern Pacific railroad used to operate in Yellowstone Park. This time I was assigned quarters appropriate to my rank: that is to say, sharing a two-room suite with an Army Ordnance Corps colonel. Because the Colonel is portly, mustached, and almost certainly snores, and because I wanted a place affording some privacy, and because I didn't think I should permit anyone in Supreme Headquarters to tell me to do anything, I have taken a small cottage near the (unfortunately closed for the duration) Doomben Race Track, where this is written.

It should go without saying that I think the JCS decision of 2 July to invade the Solomons was wrong. I have the somewhat nasty suspicion that it was based on Roosevelt's awe of King, and his dislike of MacA., rather than for any strategic purpose.

The night before (1 July) I had dinner with a colonel named Goettge, who is the First Marine Division G-2. There was no question in his mind how the JCS was going to decide the issue. I found that rather disturbing, as theoretically it was still under consideration. He was in with MacA.'s intelligence people, getting what they had on Tulagi and Guadalcanal when the JCS cable ordering Operation PESTILENCE came in.

He tells me—and I believe—that it is going to be one hell of a job getting the 1st Marines ready to make an amphibious landing in five weeks, including, of course, the rehearsal operation in the Fiji Islands.

Ghormley has requested that the 2nd Marines, of the 2nd Marine Division, be combat-loaded at San Diego. The 5th Marines were <u>not</u> combat-loaded, which means that they had to unload everything onto the docks, Aotea Quay, at Wellington, sort it out, and then reload it, so that it meets the needs of an amphibious landing force. That's what they are now doing; and according to a friend of mine in the 5th Marines, it is an indescribable mess, with cans spilling out of ordinary cardboard boxes, and so on.

The problem is compounded by the dock workers, a surly socialist bunch who, I suspect, would rather see the Japs in New Zealand than work overtime or over a weekend. I'm sure that the Marines and Navy people here have been raising hell about it with port people in America, but if you could add your weight to getting something <u>done</u> about it, your effort would be worthwhile.

On the Fourth of July, we learned from Coastwatchers that the Japanese have started construction of an airfield on Guadalcanal. That's frightening. Both MacA. and Ghormley are fully aware of the implications of an air base there, but they both, separately, insist that the Guadalcanal operation should not be launched until we are prepared to do it properly. It is not pleasant to consider the ramifications of a failed amphibious invasion.

That opinion is obviously not shared by the JCS. I don't know how Ghormley took it in Auckland, but I was with MacA. when a copy of the JCS cable of 10 July ordering Ghormley to "seize Guadalcanal and Tulagi at once" reached here. He thinks, to put it kindly, it was a serious error in judgment.

It wasn't until the next day (11 July) that the other infantry regiment (the 1st Marines) and the artillery (11th) of the 1st Marine Division reached Wellington, N.Z. Now they are expected to unload, sort, and combat-load their equipment and otherwise get set for an amphibious landing in twenty days.

The same day, as you know, we learned that Imperial Japanese Headquarters has called off its plans to seize Midway, New Caledonia, and Samoa. Under those circumstances, no one here can see the need for "immediately" landing at Guadalcanal.

Last Thursday (16 July), a courier brought a copy of Ghormley's operation plan (OPPLAN 1-42). There are three phases: a rehearsal

in the Fiji Islands; the invasion of Guadalcanal and Tulagi; and the occupation of Ndeni Island in the Santa Cruz Islands. MacA.'s reaction to it was that it is as good as it could be expected to be, given the circumstances.

MacA. made B-17 aircraft available to the 1st Marine Division for reconnaissance, and they flew over both Guadalcanal and Tulagi on Friday. On Saturday we learned that the aerial photographs taken differ greatly from the maps already issued—and there is simply no time to print and issue corrected ones.

I'm going to leave here first thing in the morning for New Zealand, and from there will join the rehearsal in the Fijis. I don't know what good, if any at all, I can do anyone. But obviously I am doing no one any good here.

Respectfully,

Fleming Pickering, Captain, USNR

(TWO)
Supreme Headquarters
Southwest Pacific Area
Brisbane, Australia
1705 Hours 21 July 1942

It was the first time Pickering had been to the Cryptology Room in Brisbane. He found it in the basement, installed in a vault that had held the important records of the evicted insurance company. There was a new security system, too, now run by military policemen wearing white puttees, pistol belts, and shiny steel helmets. The security in Melbourne had been a couple of noncoms armed with Thompson submachine guns, slouched on chairs. They had come to know Captain Fleming Pickering and had habitually waved him inside. But the MPs here not only didn't know who he was, but somewhat smugly told him that he was not on the "authorized-access list."

Finally, reluctantly, they summoned Lieutenant Pluto Hon to the steel door, and he arranged, not easily, to have Pickering passed inside.

Hon waved Pickering into a chair, and then typed Pickering's letter to Navy Secretary Frank Knox onto a machine that looked much like (and was a derivative of) a teletype machine. It produced a narrow tape, like a stock-market ticker tape, spitting it out of the left side of the machine. Hon ripped it off, and then fed the end of the tape into the cryptographic machine itself. Wheels began to whir and click, and there was the sound of keys hitting paper. Finally, out of the other end of the machine came another long strip of tape.

When that process was done, Lieutenant Hon took that strip of paper and fed it into the first machine. There was the sound of more typewriter keys, and the now-encrypted message appeared at the top of the machine, the way a teletype message would. But there were no words there, only a series of five-character blocks.

Hon gave his original letter and both strips of tape to Pickering; then, carrying the encrypted message, he left the vault for the radio room across the basement. Pickering followed him.

"Urgent," Hon said to the sergeant in charge. "For Navy Hawaii. Log it as my number"—he paused to consult the encrypted message—"six-six-oh-six."

Pickering and Hon watched as a radio operator, using a telegrapher's key, sent the message to Hawaii. A few moments later there came an acknowledgment of receipt. Then Hon took the encoded message from the radio operator and handed it to Pickering.

In a couple of minutes, Pickering thought, that will be in the hands of Ellen Feller. He wondered if her receiving a message from him triggered any erotic thoughts in her.

He followed Hon back to the Cryptology Room. Hon turned a switch, and there was the sound of a fan. Pickering dropped his letter, the two tapes, and the encrypted printout into a galvanized bucket, and then stopped and set it all afire with his cigarette lighter. He waited until it had been consumed, and then reached in the bucket and broke up the ashes with a pencil.

It wasn't that he distrusted Hon, or any of the others who encrypted his letters to the Secretary of the Navy. It was just that if he personally saw to it that all traces of it had been burned, there was no way it could wind up on Willoughby's, MacArthur's, or anyone else's desk.

"I wish I was going with you," Pluto Hon said.

Pickering was surprised. It was the first time Pluto had even suggested he was familiar with the contents of one of Pickering's messages. He was, of course—you read what you type—but the rules of the little game were that everyone pretended the cryptographer didn't know.

"Why?"

"It's liable to be as dull here as it was in Melbourne," Pluto said.

"I could probably arrange to have you dropped onto some island behind Japanese lines," Pickering joked. "They're short of people, I know."

"I already asked Major Banning," Pluto replied, seriously. "He said I could go the day after you let him go. 'We also serve who sit in dark basements shuffling paper.' "

"It's more than that, Pluto, and you know it," Pickering said, and touched his shoulder.

"Good night, Sir," Lieutenant Hon said.

Pickering walked back through the basement, then up to the lobby and to the security desk, where, after duty hours, it was necessary to produce identification and sign in and out.

"There he is," a female voice said as he scrawled his name on the register.

I am losing my mind. That sounded exactly like Ellen Feller.

He straightened and turned around.

"Good evening, Captain Pickering," Ellen Feller said.

"I hope you have some influence around here, Captain," Captain David Haughton said, as he offered Pickering his hand, smiling at his surprise. "We have just been told there is absolutely no room in the inn."

"Haughton, what the hell are you doing here?" Pickering asked. He looked at Ellen Feller. "And you, Ellen?"

"I'm on my way to Admiral Ghormley in Auckland. They're servicing the plane. Ellen's for duty."

"For duty?" Pickering asked her. "What do you mean?"

"I was asked if I would be willing to come here," Ellen Feller said. "I was."

Jesus Christ, what the hell is this all about?

"The boss arranged it," Haughton said. "In one of your letters you said something about not having a secretary. So he sent you one. Yours."

"You don't seem very pleased to see me, Captain Pickering," Ellen said.

"Don't be silly. Of course I am," Pickering said.

"Your billeting people are being difficult," Haughton said. "I tried to get Ellen a room in the hotel . . . Lennon's?"

"Lennon's," Pickering confirmed.

"And they say she's not on their staff, and no room."

"I can take care of that," Pickering said.

"I tried to invoke your name, and they gave me a room number. But the door was opened by a fat Army officer who said he hadn't seen you since Melbourne."

"I've got a cottage just outside of town. We can stay there tonight, and I'll get this all sorted out in the morning. Christ, no I won't either. I'm leaving first thing in the morning. But I'll make some phone calls tonight."

"Where are you going?"

"To the rehearsal," Pickering said. "I just sent Knox a letter . . ."

Ellen Feller read his mind.

"I've taken care of everything in Hawaii. If it's in Hawaii now, it will be on his desk, decrypted, in three hours."

"Have you got a car?" Haughton asked.

Pickering nodded. "Why?"

"Well, Ellen's luggage is still at the airfield. If you've got a car, you could pick that up; and at the same time, I can check in about the plane."

Pickering pointed out the door, where the drop-head Jaguar was parked in front of a sign reading GENERAL AND FLAG OFFICERS ONLY.

"That's beautiful," Ellen said. "What is it?"

"It's an old Jaguar. The roof leaks."

Haughton chuckled. "I see you are still scrupulously refusing to obey the Customs of the Service."

Pickering was surprised at how furious the remark made him, but he forced a smile.

"Shall we go?"

Ellen Feller sat between them on the way to the airport. Whether by intent or accident, her thigh pressed against his. That warm softness and the smell of her perfume produced the physiological manifestation of sexual excitement in the male animal.

An inspection of the aircraft had revealed nothing seriously wrong, Haughton was told. They would be leaving in an hour.

There was a small officers' club. They had three drinks, during which time Ellen Feller's leg brushed, accidentally or otherwise, against Pickering's. Then they called Haughton's flight. They watched him board the Mariner for New Zealand.

Fleming Pickering would not have been surprised at anything Ellen did now that they were alone. She did nothing, sitting ladylike against the far door, all the way out to the cottage.

"What's this?" she asked.

"It's a cottage I rented. I told you—"

"I would have bet you were taking me to an officers' hotel!" she said.

Why the hell didn't I? I could have gotten her a room if I had to call General Sutherland himself.

"No."

"Fleming, don't look so guilt-stricken," Ellen said. "We both know you wouldn't do this if Mrs. Pickering were around."

He didn't reply for a moment. Then he pulled up on the parking brake, took the key from the ignition, got out of the car, and walked up to the house and unlocked the door.

The telephone rang. He walked across the living room to it.

"Pickering."

"Captain Pickering?"

"Yes."

"Sir, this is Major Tourtillott, Billeting Officer at the Lennon."

"Yes, Major."

"Sir, there was a Naval officer, a Captain Haughton, looking for you."

"Yes, I know, he found me."

"Sir, he was trying to arrange quarters for a Navy Department civilian, a lady, an assimilated Oh-Four."

"A what?"

"An assimilated Oh-Four, Sir. Someone entitled to the privileges of an Oh-Four, Sir."

"What the hell is an Oh-Four?"

"An Army or Marine Corps major, Sir, or a Navy Lieutenant Commander."

"The lady has made other arrangements for tonight, Major. I'll get this all sorted out in the morning. She is a member of my staff, and quarters will be required."

"Yes, Sir. I'll take care of it. Thank you, Sir."

Pickering hung the telephone up and turned to see what had happened to Ellen Feller.

She wasn't in the small living room. He found her in the bedroom, in bed.

"I've been flying for eighteen hours," she said. "I'm probably a little gamey. Will that bother you? Should I shower?"

Fleming Pickering shook his head.

(THREE)
Aboard USS *Lowell Hutchins*
Transport Group Y
17 degrees 48 minutes south latitude, 150 degrees west longitude
4 August 1942

Just about everyone on board knew that five months ago the USS *Lowell Hutchins* had been the Pacific & Far East passenger liner *Pacific Enchantress;* no one had any idea who Lowell Hutchins was, or, since Naval ships were customarily named only after the dead, who he had been.

She had been rapidly pressed into service, but the conversion from a plush civilian passenger liner to a Naval transport was by no means complete. Before she had sailed from the States with elements of the 1st Marine Division aboard, she had been given a coat of Navy gray paint. It had been hastily applied, and here and there it had already begun to flake off, revealing the pristine white for which Pacific & Far East vessels were well known.

The furniture and carpeting from the first-class and tourist dining rooms had been removed. Narrow, linoleum-covered, chest-high steel tables had been welded in place in the former tourist dining room. Enlisted men and junior officers now took their meals from steel trays, and they ate standing up.

Not-much-more-elegant steel tables, with attached steel benches, had been installed in the ex-first-class dining room. Generally, captains and above got to eat there, sitting down, from plates bearing the P&FE insignia.

Most of the former first-class suites and cabins, plus the former first- and tourist-class bars, libraries, lounges, and exercise rooms, had been converted to troop berthing areas. It had been relatively easy to remove their beds, cabinets, tables, and other furniture and equipment and replace them with bunks. The bunks were sheets of canvas, suspended between iron pipe, stacked four high.

The bathrooms were still identified by porcelain BATH plates over their doors, although they had now become, of course, Navy "heads." It would have taken too much time to remove the plates. And it would also have taken too much time to expand them. So a "bath" designed for the use of a couple en route to Hawaii now served as many as thirty-two men en route to a place none of them had ever heard of a month before, islands in the Solomon chain called Guadalcanal, Tulagi, and Florida.

There was not, of course, sufficient water-distilling capability aboard to permit showers at will. Showers, and indeed drinking water, were stringently rationed.

The former tourist-class cabins had proved even more of a problem for conversion. To efficiently utilize space, the beds there had usually been mattresses laid upon steel frameworks, with shelves built under them. These could not be readily moved. These rooms had become officers' staterooms for captains and above, sometimes with the addition of several other bunks. Because they afforded that most rare privilege of military service, privacy, the few single staterooms now became the private staterooms of senior majors, lieutenant colonels, and even a few junior full colonels.

The most luxurious accommodations on the upper deck had been left virtually unchanged. Even the carpets were still there, and the oil paintings on the paneled bulkheads, and the inlaid tables, and the soft, comfortable couches and armchairs. These became the accommodations of the most senior of the Marine officers aboard, the one general officer and the senior full colonels. These men took their meals with the ship's officers on tables set with snowy linen, glistening crystal, and sterling tableware.

It was almost taken as gospel by those on the lower decks that this was one more case of the brass, those sonsofbitches, taking care of themselves. But the decision to leave the upper-deck cabins unchanged had actually been based less on the principle that rank hath its privileges than on the practical consideration that to convert them to troop berthing would have required two hundred or so men to make their way at least twice a day from the upper deck to the mess deck through narrow passageways. That many men on that deck might actually interfere with the efficient running of the ship.

Brigadier General Lewis T. Harris, Deputy Commander, 1st Marine Division, and the senior Marine embarked, actually had a strong feeling of uneasiness every time he took his seat in the ship's officers' mess.

Because he often went twice a day to see it, he knew what was being served in the troop messes. The troop mess—jammed full of men, some of them seasick, standing at tables with food slopped around steel mess trays—offered a vivid contrast to the neatly set table at the officers' mess, with its baskets of freshly baked rolls and bread, and white-jacketed stewards hovering at his shoulder to make sure the levels in his delicate china coffee cup and crystal water glass never dropped more than an inch, or to inquire How the General Would Like His Lamb Chop.

General Harris tried to live the old adage that an officer's first duty was the welfare of the men placed under his command. If it had been within his power, Marines on the way to battle would all be seated at a linen-covered table, eating steaks to order. That was obviously out of the question, a fantasy. He had done the next best thing, however. He told his officers that he expected the men to be fed as well as humanly possible under the circumstances, and then he repeatedly went to see for himself how well that order was being carried out. He was convinced that the mess officers and sergeants were indeed doing the best they could.

He could, he knew, take his meals with the troops in that foul-smelling mess; and if he did, his officers would follow his example. But the only thing he would accomplish—aside from being seen there, implying that he was concerned about the chow—would be to strain the facilities that much more.

The ship's officers—and why not?—would go on eating well, no matter where he and his officers ate. The officers' mess cooks and stewards were not being strained by feeding the Marine senior officers. And every meal they fed to a senior Marine officer was one less to be prepared down below.

So, in the end, after making sure the senior officers knew he expected them to check on the troop mess regularly and personally, General Harris continued to eat off bone china and a linen tablecloth; and he continued to feel uneasy about it.

There was a table by the door to the ship's officers' mess, on which sat a coffee machine and three or four insulated coffee pitchers and a stack of mugs. Between mealtimes, it was used by the stewards to take coffee to the bridge and to the cabins on the upper deck.

When General Harris left the mess, he stopped by the table, filled a pitcher a little more than half-full of coffee, and picked up two of the china mugs.

"General," one of the stewards said, "can I carry that somewhere for you?"

"I can manage, thank you," Harris said with a smile. He left the mess and went to his cabin.

In one of the drawers of a mahogany chest, there were a dozen small, olive-drab cans. Each was neatly labeled BORE CLEANER, 8 OZ. They looked like tiny paint cans, and there was a neat line of red candle wax sealing the line where the top had been forced tight on the body of the can. Anyone seeing the cans would understand that General Harris did not want the bore cleaner to leak.

He took a penknife from his pocket and carefully scraped the wax seal from one of the cans, and then switched to the screwdriver blade. He pried the lid carefully off, then poured the brown fluid the can held into the coffee pitcher.

After that, he left his cabin, headed aft, and passed through a door opening onto the open deck. This deck had previously been a promenade where the affluent could take a constitutional or sit on deck chairs in an environment denied to the less affluent down below. Now he had trouble making his way past the bulky life rafts that had been lashed on the deck to provide at least a shot at survival, should the USS *Lowell Hutchins* be torpedoed.

There was still enough light to see several of the ships of the Amphibious Force. There were eighty-two ships in all, sailing in three concentric circles. The twelve transports, including the USS *Lowell Hutchins,* formed the inner circle. Next came a circle of cruisers and, outside that, the screening force of destroyers.

General Harris stared at the ships long enough to reflect (again) that although it appeared to be a considerable armada, it was not large enough to accomplish their mission with a reasonable chance of success. He then made his way down three ladders to what had once been the second of the tourist decks, and through a passageway to cabin D-123, where he knocked at the door.

When there was no response, he put his mouth to the slats in the door and called, "Stecker!"

"Come!"

He pushed the door open. Major Jack NMI Stecker, Commanding Officer, 2nd Battalion, 5th Marines, wearing only his skivvies, was sitting on the deck of the tiny cabin beside the narrow single bunk that formed part of the bulkhead.

"Jack, what the hell are you doing?" Harris asked.

Stecker turned and, seeing the General, jumped to his feet.

"At ease, Major," Harris said, just a trifle sarcastically. "What the hell were you doing down there?"

"I was cleaning my piece, Sir," Stecker said, gesturing at the bunk.

Harris went to look. There was a rifle, in pieces, spread out on the bunk.

Harris snorted, and then extended the coffee pitcher.

"I thought you might like some coffee, Jack," he said.

"I'm pretty well coffeed out, Sir."

"Jack. Trust me. You need a cup of coffee."

"Yes, Sir," Stecker said.

Harris set the cups down on a steel shelf, filled each half-full of the mixture of "bore cleaner" and coffee, and handed one to Stecker.

Stecker sipped his suspiciously, smiled, and said, "Yes, Sir, the General is right. This is just what I needed."

Harris smiled back. "We generals are always right, Jack. You should try to remember that. What are you doing with the Garand? And now that I think about it, where the hell did you get it?"

"I found it on post at Quantico, General," Stecker said. "And just as soon as I can find time, I will turn it in to the proper authorities."

Harris snorted. He walked to the bunk and picked up the stripped receiver. His expert eye picked out the signs of accurizing.

"I forgot," he said. "You think this a pretty good weapon, don't you?"

"It's a superb weapon," Stecker said. "I've shot inch-and-a-half groups at two hundred yards with that one."

"Bullshit."

"No bullshit. And the kid—I shouldn't call him a kid—Joe Howard. He took a commission, and is now off doing something hush-hush for G-2—the *man* who did the accuracy job on that one had one that was more accurate than this one."

"You realize that ninety-five percent of the people in the Corps think the Garand is a piece of shit that can never compare to the Springfield?"

"Then ninety-five percent of the people in the Corps are wrong."

"Ninety-five percent of the people in this Amphibious Force think that Guadalcanal is going to be a cakewalk, a live-fire exercise with a secondary benefit of taking some Japanese territory."

"Ninety-five percent of the people in this Amphibious Force have never heard a shot fired in anger," Stecker said.

"Is that the same thing as saying they're wrong, too?" Harris asked.

"You're putting me on the spot," Stecker said uncomfortably.

"That's why I'm sharing my bore cleaner with you," Harris said. "I want to get you drunk, so you'll give me a straight answer."

Stecker looked at him without replying.

"Come on, Jack," Harris said. "We go back a long way. I want to know what you're thinking."

Stecker shrugged, and then asked, "You ever give any thought to why the brass are going ahead with this, when they damned well know we're not ready?"

"You're talking about the drill?" Harris asked.

The "drill," the practice landings in the Fiji Islands that the convoy carrying the Amphibious Force had just come from, had been an unqualified disaster. Nothing had gone as it was supposed to.

"That's part of it, but that's not what I meant," Stecker said. "The brass knew before the Fiji drill that the LCP(L)s were no fucking good."

There were 408 landing craft in the Amphibious Force. Of these, 308 were designated LCP(L), a thirty-six-foot landing craft with a fixed bow. In other words, when the craft touched shore, personnel aboard would have to exit *over* the bow and sides, rather than across a droppable ramp. Similarly, supplies would have to be manhandled over the sides. And, of course, LCP(L)s could not discharge vehicles or other heavy cargo onto the beach.

"They're all we have, Jack. We can't wait to re-equip with LCP(R)s or LCMs."

Both the thirty-six-foot LCP(R) and the forty-five-foot LCM had droppable ramps. The LCP(R) could discharge over its ramp 75mm and 105mm howitzers and one-ton trucks. The LCM could handle 90mm and five-inch guns and heavier trucks.

"Ever wonder why we can't?" Stecker asked softly.

"Because the Japanese are almost finished with their air base on Guadalcanal. We can't afford to let them do that. We have to grab that air base before they make it operational."

"That's what I mean. The Japanese know how important that air base is. To them. And to us—if we take it away from them and start operating out of it ourselves. So they're going to fight like hell to keep us from taking it; and if we do, they're going to fight like hell to take it back."

"That's what we're paid to do."

"No cakewalk. No live-fire exercise. An important objective. If it's important to them, they're going to be prepared to defend it. We're going to have three-fourths of our landing barges exposed as the troops try to get over the sides and onto the beach. And once we start manhandling cargo out of those damned boats . . . Jesus, if they have any artillery at all, or decent mortar men, or, for that matter, just some well-emplaced machine guns, we're going to lose those boats! No boats, no reinforcements, no ammunition, no rations."

"You don't sound as if you're sure we can carry it off," Harris said. "Is that what you think?"

"I wouldn't say this to anyone but you, but I don't know. I've got some awful good kids, and they'll try, but balls—courage, if you like—sometimes isn't enough."

Brigadier General Lewis T. Harris and Major Jack NMI Stecker had known each other for most of their adult lives. They had been in combat all over the Caribbean basin together. Harris didn't have to recall Stecker's Medal of Honor for proof of his personal courage. Stecker was no coward. He was calling the upcoming battle for Guadalcanal as he saw it.

Harris was afraid Stecker's analysis was in the X-ring.

"Have some more coffee, Jack," Harris said.

"No, thank you, Sir."

" 'No, thank you'? You getting old, Jack? Taken up religion?"

"Yes, Sir, I'm getting old," Stecker replied. He pulled a canvas rucksack from under the mattress of his bunk, and took from it a large pink bottle which bore a label from the Pharmacy, Naval Dispensary, Quantico, Virginia. Under a skull and crossbones, it read, CAUTION!! HIGHLY TOXIC!! FOR TREATMENT OF ATHLETE'S FOOT ONLY. IF FLUID TOUCHES EYES OR MOUTH, FLOOD COPIOUSLY WITH WATER AND SEEK IMMEDIATE MEDICAL ATTENTION!!

He put the bottle to his mouth and took a healthy pull, then exhaled in appreciation.

Harris chuckled.

"I'm giving some serious thought to religion, General, but I haven't said anything to the chaplain yet," Stecker said. "Do you have to go, or can we sit around and drink coffee, cure my athlete's feet, and tell sea stories?"

"I'm not going anywhere, Jack," Harris chuckled. "But you better put that Garand back together before you take another pull at that pink bottle and forget how."

(FOUR)
Off Cape Esperance
Guadalcanal, Solomon Islands
0240 Hours 7 August 1942

At 0200, Transport Groups X and Y, the Amphibious Force of Operation PESTILENCE, reached Savo Island, which lay between the islands of Guadalcanal and Florida. The skies were clear, and there was some light from a quarter moon, enough to make out the land masses and the other ships.

The fifteen transports of Transport Group X turned and entered Sealark Channel, between Savo and Guadalcanal. They carried aboard the major elements of the 1st Marine Division and were headed for the beaches of Guadalcanal.

Transport Group Y sailed on the other side of Savo Island, between it and Florida Island, and headed toward their destination, Florida, Tulagi, and Gavutu islands. Group Y consisted of four transports carrying 2nd Battalion, 5th Marines, and other troops, and four destroyer transports. These were World War I destroyers that had been converted for use by Marine Raiders by removing two of their four engines and converting the reclaimed space to troop berthing. These carried the 1st Raider Battalion.

The Guadalcanal Invasion Force was headed for what the Operations Plan called "Beach Red." This was about six thousand yards east of Lunga Point, more or less directly across Sealark Channel from where the Tulagi/Gavutu landings were to take place. The distance across Sealark Channel was approximately twenty-five miles.

The Guadalcanal Fire Support Group (three cruisers and four destroyers) began to bombard assigned targets on Guadalcanal at 0614, adding their destructive power to the aerial bombing by U.S. Army Air Corps B-17s which had been going on for a week. At 0616, the Tulagi Fire Support Group (one cruiser and two destroyers) opened fire on Tulagi and Gavutu.

By 0651 the transports of both groups dropped anchor nine thousand yards off their respective landing beaches. Landing boats were put over the side into the calm water, and nets woven of heavy rope were put in place along the sides of the transports. Marines began to climb down the ropes into the landing boats.

Minesweepers began to sweep the water between the ships of both transport groups and their landing beaches. No mines were found.

The only enemy vessel encountered was a small gasoline-carrying schooner in Sealark Channel. It burned and then exploded under both Naval gunfire and machine-gun fire from Navy fighter aircraft and dive bombers. These were operating from carriers maneuvering seventy-five miles from the invasion beaches.

The Navy sent forty-three carrier aircraft to attack Guadalcanal, and nearly as many—forty-one—to attack Tulagi and Gavutu. The aircraft attacking Tulagi either sank or set on fire eighteen Japanese seaplanes.

Zero-Hour for Operation PESTILENCE, when Marines were to hit Beach Red on Guadalcanal, was 0910. H-Hour, when Marines would go ashore on Tulagi, was an hour and ten minutes earlier, at 0800. But the first Marine landing in the Solomons took place across the beaches of Florida Island. That operation, however, did not rate having its own Hour in the Operations Order.

At 0740, B Company, 1st Battalion, 2nd Marines, went ashore near the small village of Haleta, on Florida Island. Their mission was to secure an elevated area from which the Japanese could bring Beach Blue on Tulagi under fire. They encountered no resistance; there were no Japanese in the area.

At 0800, the first wave of the Tulagi force—landing craft carrying Baker and Dog Companies of the 1st Raider Battalion—touched ashore on Blue Beach. There was one casualty. A Marine was instantly killed by a single rifle shot. But there was no other resistance; the enemy had not elected to defend Tulagi on the beach, but from caves and earthen bunkers in the hills inland and to the south.

The landing craft returned to the transports and loaded the second wave (Able and Charley Companies, 1st Raiders) and put them ashore. Then a steady stream of landing craft made their way between the transports and the beach and put the 2nd Battalion, 5th Marines, on shore.

Once on Tulagi, the 2nd Battalion, 5th Marines, crossed the narrow island to their left (northwest) to clear out the enemy, while the Raiders turned to their right (southeast) and headed toward the southern tip of the island. About 3,500 yards separates the southern tip of Tulagi from the tiny island of Gavutu (515 by 255 yards) and the even smaller (290 by 310 yards) island of Tanambogo, which was connected to Gavutu by a concrete causeway.

Operation PESTILENCE called for the invasion of Gavutu by the 1st Parachute Battalion at 1200 hours. The parachutists, once they had secured Gavutu, were to cross the causeway and secure Tanambogo.

The Raiders encountered no serious opposition until after noon. And 2nd Battalion, 5th Marines, encountered no serious opposition moving in the opposite direction until about the same time.

Off Guadalcanal, at 0840, the destroyers of the Guadalcanal Fire Support Group took up positions to mark the line of departure for the landing craft, five thousand yards north of Beach Red.

Almost immediately, small liaison aircraft appeared over Beach Red and marked its 3,200-yard width with smoke grenades.

Immediately after that, at exactly 0900, all the cruisers and destroyers of the Guadalcanal Fire Support Group began to bombard Beach Red and the area extending two hundred yards inshore.

The landing craft carrying the first wave of the Beach Red invasion force (the 5th Marines, less their 2nd Battalion, which was on Tulagi) left the departure line on schedule. When the Landing Craft were 1,300 yards off Beach Red, the covering bombardment was lifted.

At 0910, on a 1,600-yard front, the 5th Marines began to land on the beach, the

1st Battalion on the right (west), and the 3rd Battalion on the left (east). Regimental Headquarters came ashore at 0938. Minutes later they were joined by the Heavy Weapons elements of the regiment.

Again, there was virtually no resistance on the beach.

As the landing craft returned to the transports to bring the 1st Marines ashore, the 5th Marines moved inland, setting up a defense perimeter six hundred yards off Beach Red, along the Tenaru River on the west, the Tenavatu River on the east, and a branch of the Tenaru on the south.

Once it had become apparent that they would not be in danger from Japanese artillery on or near the beach, the transports began to move closer to the beach, dropping anchor again seven thousand yards away.

At about this point, serious problems began with the offloading process on the beach. In many ways these duplicated the disastrous trial run in the Fiji Islands.

The small and relatively easy-to-manhandle 75mm pack howitzers (originally designed to be carried by mules) of the 11th Marines (the artillery regiment) had come ashore with the assault elements of the 5th Marines.

The 105mm howitzers now came ashore. But because there were not enough drop-ramp landing craft to handle them, they did not bring their "prime movers." The prime mover intended to tow the 105mm howitzer was the "Truck, 2½ Ton, 6×6," commonly called the "six-by-six." Six-by-six refers to the number of driving wheels. The standard six-by-six actually had eight wheels in the rear, for a total of ten powered wheels. So equipped, the six-by-six became legendary in its ability to carry or tow enormous loads anywhere.

But the 11th Marines were not equipped with six-by-sixes. Instead, they had been issued a truck commonly referred to as a "one-ton." It was rated as having a cargo capacity of one ton (as opposed to the two-and-a-half-ton capacity of the six-by-six), and it had only four powered wheels with which to move itself through mud, sand, or slippery terrain.

Since there were insufficient drop-bow landing craft to move this "prime mover" immediately onto Beach Red, when the 105mm howitzers arrived on the beach, there was no vehicle capable of towing them inland to firing positions—except for a few overworked amphibious tractors, which had a tanklike track and could negotiate sand and mud.

These were pressed into service to move the 105mm howitzers. But in so doing, their metal tracks chewed up the primitive roads—as well as whatever field telephone wires they crossed. That effectively cut communication between the advanced positions and the beach and the several headquarters.

Within an hour or so of landing on the beach, moreover, the Marines were physically exhausted. For one thing, the long periods of time they'd spent aboard the troop transports had caused them to lose much of the physical toughness they'd acquired in training.

For another, Guadalcanal's temperature and high humidity quickly sapped what strength they had. And the effects of the temperature and humidity were magnified because they were slogging through sand and jungle and up hills carrying heavy loads of rifles, machine guns, mortars, and the ammunition for them.

And there was not enough water. Although medical officers had strongly insisted that each man be provided with two canteens (two quarts) of drinking water, there were not enough canteens in the Pacific to issue a second canteen to each man.

The Navy had been asked, and had refused, to provide beach labor details of sailors to assist with the unloading of freight coming ashore from the landing craft, and then to move the freight off the beach to make room for more supplies.

It was presumed by Naval planners that the Marines could provide their own labor details to offload supplies from landing craft, and that trucks would be available to move the offloaded supplies from the beach inland.

Marines exhausted by the very act of getting ashore managed slowly to unload supplies from landing craft, further exhausting themselves in the process. But then, at first, there were no trucks to move the supplies off the beach; and when the one-ton trucks finally began to come ashore, they proved incapable of negotiating the sand and roads chewed up by amphibious tractors.

The result was a mess. Landing craft loaded with supplies were stacked up three rows deep off the beach. They were unable even to reach the beach, much less rapidly discharge their cargoes.

(FIVE)
Aboard LCP(L) 36
Off Gavutu Island
1225 Hours 7 August 1942

First Lieutenant Richard B. Macklin, USMC, was unhappy with Operation PESTILENCE for a number of reasons, and specifically with his role in the operation.

He had arrived at the 1st Parachute Battalion three weeks earlier after long and uncomfortable voyages, first aboard a destroyer from San Diego, and then a mine sweeper from Pearl Harbor. When he had finally reached the 1st Parachute Batallion, the commanding officer, Major Robert Williams, had promptly told him that he hadn't expected him and frankly didn't know what the hell to do with him.

"I had rather hoped, Sir, that in view of my experience, I might be given a company."

Macklin felt sure service as a company commander would get him his long-overdue promotion.

"Company commanders are captains, Macklin," Williams replied.

"Company 'C' is commanded by a lieutenant," Macklin politely argued, "one who is junior in rank to me."

"I'm not going to turn over a company to you at this late date. They're a team now, and I don't intend to screw that up by throwing in a new quarterback just before the kickoff," Williams said. "Sorry."

Not only was what they were about to do not a football game, Macklin fumed privately, but refusing to give him the command was a clear violation of regulations, which clearly stated that the senior officer present for duty was entitled to command.

Williams seemed to be one of those officers who obeyed only those orders it was convenient to obey. In this regard he had obviously been influenced by the Army paratroopers with whom he had trained. Macklin had seen enough of that collection of clowns to know that any resemblance between Army paratroop officers and professional officers was purely coincidental.

They thought the war *was* a football game, and acted like it. Macklin had actually witnessed Army paratroop officers drinking, and probably whoring, if the truth were known, with their enlisted men in Phoenix City, Alabama, across the river from Fort Benning. If the Army's 82nd Airborne Division was ever sent into combat, there was no question in Macklin's mind that it would fail, miserably, to accomplish its mission. Discipline was the key to military success, and Army paratroop discipline was a disgrace.

But insisting on his legal rights would not have been wise, Macklin concluded. There was no doubt in his mind that if he appealed to the proper authorities, Williams would be ordered to place him in command of "C" Company. But if he did that, Major Williams would from that moment just be looking for an excuse to relieve him. And being relieved of command was worse than not being given a command at all.

So here he was, in a landing craft, about to assault an enemy-held beach, having been officially designated a "supernumerary officer." *Supernumerary* was a euphemism for "replacement"—an officer with no duties, waiting to replace someone wounded or killed.

Meanwhile, the First Parachute Battalion, the "Chutes," was obviously being improperly employed, that is to say as regular infantry. The rationale for that was that there were no aircraft to drop them.

Macklin personally doubted that. He had seen ships in San Diego loaded with partially disassembled R4Ds, for instance. Perhaps they were Air Corps C-47s, destined for China or Australia, as he had been told; but the planes were identical, only the nomenclature was different. If the senior officers had wanted to use Para-Marines, they could have gotten the aircraft somewhere.

And if aircraft were truly not available, then the obvious thing to do was not commit the Para-Marines. It made no military sense to waste superbly trained men, the elite of the elite, as common infantry, sacrificing them in assaulting a beach on an island that had no real military importance that Macklin could see. It was only five hundred yards long and half that wide!

What they should have done, if they really thought the island was a threat, was to shell or bomb it level. Not send Marines to throw away their lives and all their superb training to occupy it. All the Japanese were using it for was a seaplane base. By definition, seaplanes could be used anywhere there was enough water for them to land and take off.

Probably the whole thing was regarded by the brass as a live-fire exercise, to give the Para-Marines a blooding and Naval Aviation some practice. Navy SBD dive-bombers had attacked Gavutu for forty minutes, starting at 1145.

Ten minutes after the dive-bombers started their attack, the Navy started shelling the island, a barrage that lasted five minutes, causing huge clouds of smoke and dust to rise from Gavutu.

Macklin reminded himself of what he knew of the explosive force of one-hundred-pound bombs and Naval artillery. It was awesome. It was reasonable to assume that, on an island only five hundred yards long, very few Japanese soldiers, much less their armament, could survive forty minutes of dive-bombing and an intense five-minute Naval barrage.

Macklin was close enough in the landing barge to hear the Coxswain when he muttered, with concern and resignation, "Oh, shit!"

"What's the matter?"

The Coxswain took his hand from his wheel long enough to point ahead, at the beach. Macklin was reluctant to raise his head high enough over the bow to look—doing so would make his head a target—but curiosity, after a moment, got the best of him. He raised his head, kept it up long enough to look around, and then ducked again.

Either bombs from the dive-bombers or shells from the Naval artillery, or maybe some of each, had struck the concrete landing ramps used by the Japanese to get their seaplanes in and out of the water. Huge blocks of concrete had been displaced.

The Operations Order called for this landing craft and the landing craft to each side to run aground on the concrete ramps. But that would not be possible.

Aware that his heart was beating rapidly and that his mouth was dry, Macklin considered the alternatives. The Coxswain could continue on his prescribed course until the landing craft ran into one of the huge blocks of concrete and had to stop. There was no telling how deep the water would be at that point; it was even possible they would be in water over their heads when they went over the side of the landing craft. If he had to jump into water over his head with all the equipment he was carrying, he would drown.

There was a concrete pier extending maybe two hundred yards from shore. The Coxswain could run the landing craft against that, and the Marines could then climb onto the pier and run down the pier to shore.

But, he realized with alarm, if the Naval artillery had hit the concrete ramps, it probably had hit the concrete pier as well. There was a good possibility that at least a portion of the pier was destroyed, and that it would be impossible to run all the way ashore.

And in the moment it occurred to him that even if the pier was intact, anyone running down its length would be like a target in a shooting gallery for riflemen and machine-gunners defending the beach, the Coxswain throttled back his engine. A moment later, the landing craft grated against the concrete pier.

Now it was quiet enough for the Coxswain to shout to the senior officer in the boat, the Captain commanding Able Company, "There's debris in the water by the landing ramps; this is as close as I can take you!"

Macklin could tell by the look on the Captain's face what he thought of this news.

"Everybody out of the boat!" the Captain shouted. "Follow me! Let's go! Get the lead out!"

He clambered up onto the side of the landing craft and from there onto the concrete pier, and vanished from sight.

Lieutenant Macklin decided that in the absence of orders to do something specific (his orders had been, "Macklin, you go in with Boat Nine.") it behooved him to remain aboard the landing craft to make sure that everyone else got off.

He did so.

Then he climbed onto the pier, on his stomach, with his Thompson submachine gun at the ready. He heard the engine of the landing craft rev, and knew that the boat was backing away from the pier to return to the transport for the second wave.

When he looked down the pier, the last of the Marines reached the end of it, turned to the left, and disappeared.

There was the sound of small-arms fire, but it was, as far as Macklin could tell, the familiar crack of .30-06 rifles and the deeper-pitched boom of .45-caliber submachine-gun and pistol ammo. He had been told that the sound of the smaller-caliber Japanese small arms would be different.

That means we're not under fire!

He got to his feet and began to trot down the pier toward the shore. Once erect, he could see Marines on the beach, moving inland through the vegetation and around the burned and shattered buildings of the Japanese seaplane base.

He started to run, to catch up.

Near the shore, he saw that his initial assessment of probable damage from the bombing and shellfire had been correct. A bomb, or a shell, had struck the pier about fifteen yards from shore, taking out all but a narrow strip of concrete no more than three feet wide.

As he made his way carefully across this narrow strip, he felt as if, in the same moment, someone had struck his leg with a baseball bat and slapped him, very hard, in the face.

And then he felt himself flying through the air. There was a splash, and he went under water. There was a moment of abject terror, and then his flailing hand encountered a barnacle-encrusted piling. He clung to it desperately, to keep himself from slipping off and drowning.

Then he became aware that his foot was touching bottom. He straightened his bent leg, and found that he was in water about chest-deep.

Where the hell is my weapon?

I dropped it. It's in the water. I'll never be able to find it. Now what the hell am I going to do?

What the hell did I fall over? I must have slipped. No. I was struck by something!

He put his hand to his face. His fingers came away sticky with blood.

My God, I've been shot in the face! I'll be disfigured for life!

And then he remembered the blow to his leg. He felt faint and nauseous, but finally gathered the courage to try to find some damage to his leg. He became aware of a stinging sensation. Salt water, he realized, was making an open sore—a *wound!*—sting.

He couldn't bend far enough over to reach the sting without putting his face into the water. Gingerly, he raised the stinging leg. He couldn't feel anything at first, and only after a moment detected a swelling in the calf.

But then he saw a faint cloud of red oozing out of his trouser leg.

I've been shot in the leg! But why doesn't it hurt?

Shock! It doesn't hurt because I'm in shock!

I'm going to pass out and then drown!

A glob of blood dropped off his cheek into the water and began to dissolve as it sank.

I'm going to bleed to death!

Our Father which art in heaven, hallowed by Thy Name . . .

What the hell is the rest of it?

Dear God, please don't let me die!

Yea, though I walk through the valley of the shadow of death . . .

"Move your ass! Run!Run!Run!Run!Run!Run!"

It's the second wave!

Now there was small-arms fire, single shots and automatic, and it didn't sound like .30-06s or Thompsons, and then there was a whistling sound followed by a *crump* and then a dull explosion, and he felt a shock wave and then another and another in the water.

"Get your dumb ass up and off the pier, or die here, you dumb sonofabitch!"

He saw, vaguely, figures running across the pier above him.

He found his voice.

"Medic! Medic! Medic!"

There was no response, and there didn't seem to be any more movement on the pier above him. The strange-sounding—the *Japanese*—smalls-arms fire continued, and there were more mortar rounds landing in the water.

"Medic! Medic! For Christ's sake, somebody help me!"

Now the leg started to ache, and his cheek. He put his hand to his face again, and the fingers came away this time with a clot of blood.

"For the love of Christ, will somebody help me? Medic! Medic!"

There was splashing in the water from the direction of the shore.

It's a Jap! It has to be a Jap! The invasion failed, and now I'm going to die here under this fucking pier!

"What happened to you, Mac?"

"I've been wounded, you ignorant sonofabitch! And it's 'Lieutenant'!"

Fingers probed his face.

"That's not bad," the medic said, professionally. "Another half an inch and you would have lost your teeth, maybe worse. But you just got grazed. Is that all that's wrong with you?"

"My leg, I've been wounded in the leg."

Fingers probed his leg.

"That hurts, goddamn you!"

"I'll tell you what I'm going to do. I'm going to get you ashore. Let go of that piling and wrap your arms around my neck."

"Ashore?"

"Lieutenant, I've got badly wounded people ashore. Please don't give me any trouble."

"I'm badly wounded," Macklin said indignantly.

"No, you're not. Your leg ain't broke. You got one of them half-million-dollar wounds. Some muscle damage. Keep you out of the war for maybe three months. In ten days you'll be in the hospital in Melbourne, looking up nurses' dresses. Now come on, put your arms around me and I'll get you ashore, and somebody will be along in a while to take you back to the ship."

Lieutenant Macklin did as he was told. The medic carried him on his back to the shore, and a few yards inland. Then he lowered him gently onto the sand, cut his trouser leg open, and applied a compress bandage.

"My leg," Macklin said, with as much dignity as he could muster, "is beginning to cause me a great deal of pain."

"Well, we have just the thing for that," the medic said, taking out a morphine hypodermic. "Next stop, Cloud Nine."

Macklin felt a prick in his buttocks, and then a sensation of cold.

"I gotta go," the medic said, patting him comfortably on the shoulder. "You're going to be all right, Lieutenant. Believe me."

A warm sensation began to ooze through Macklin's body.

I'm going to be all right, he thought. *I'm going to live. They're going to send me to the hospital in Melbourne. It will probably take longer than three months for my leg to heal. I will receive the Purple Heart.* Two *Purple Hearts, one for the leg and one for the face. There will probably be a small scar on my face. People will ask about that. "Lieutenant Macklin was wounded while attacking Gavutu—*twice *wounded when assaulting the beach at Gavutu with the first wave of the Para-Marines."*

I'll be a captain for sure, now. And for the rest of my Marine Corps career, the scar on my face will be there to remind people of my combat service.

(SIX)
Command Post, Tulagi Force
1530 Hours 8 August 1942

The headquarters of Brigadier General Lewis T. Harris, Commanding General of the Tulagi/Gavutu/Tanambogo Force, were now in the somewhat seedy white frame building that had before the war housed the Colonial Administrator of Tulagi, and was somewhat grandly known as "the Residence."

Thirty minutes before, the building had been the forward command post of Lieutenant Colonel "Red Mike" Edson, commanding the 1st Raider Battalion. When the Commanding Officer, 2nd Battalion, 5th Marines, drove up to attend a commanders' conference called by General Harris, the small detachment of Raiders charged with protecting the Raider command post were still in place, close to but not actually manning their weapons (rifles, BARs, and light .30-caliber machine guns).

Thirty minutes before, the island of Tulagi had been officially reported "secure."

There was a moment's hesitation before a sergeant called, "Atten-*hut!*" and saluted the 2nd Battalion Commander. For one thing, he was hatless, riding a captured Japanese motorcycle, and was carrying a rifle slung over his back, which was not the sort of thing the Raiders expected of a Marine major.

But the salute was enthusiastic and respectful. The reputation of the 2nd Battalion Commander had preceded him. It had been reliably reported that during the mopping-up phase of the invasion, the 2nd Battalion Commander had been seen standing in the open, shooting a particularly determined Japanese sniper who had until then been firing with impunity through a one-foot-square hole in his coral bunker. The Commanding Officer of the 2nd Battalion had fired at him twice; and when they pulled his body from the cave, they learned the sniper had taken two hits in the head.

The story had been of particular interest, and thus had quickly spread, both because that wasn't usually the sort of thing majors and battalion commanders did personally, and also because he had done it with an M-1 Garand rifle. The Garand was supposed to be the new standard rifle, although none had yet been issued to the Marine Corps; and it was supposed to be a piece of shit, incapable of hitting a barn door at fifty yards.

But there was no denying the story. A dozen people had seen Major Jack NMI Stecker stand up, as calmly as if he had been on the rifle range at Parris Island or 'Diego, and let off two shots and put both of them, so to speak, in the X-ring.

There was also scuttlebutt going around that Major Stecker had won the Big One, the Medal of Honor, as a buck sergeant in the First World War in France. No one could remember ever having seen a real, honest-to-Christ hero like that. And as Major Stecker walked up the shallow steps to the Residence, two dozen sets of eyes watched him with something close to awe.

General Harris was in his office, the Sergeant Major told Major Stecker, and he was to go right in.

There were no enlisted men in General Harris's office, but only the other two commanding officers he had summoned to the commanders' conference, Major Robert Williams of the 1st Parachute Battalion and Lieutenant Colonels Red Mike Edson and Sam Griffith, CO and Exec of the 1st Raider Battalion.

They were all holding canteens, presumably full of coffee. There were two cans of bore cleaner on the shelf of the field desk.

"Forgive me for saying so, Major," General Harris greeted Major Stecker, "but aren't you a little long in the tooth for a motorcycle?"

"With respect, General," Major Stecker said, "I am not too old for a motorcycle. I *am* too old, and much too tired, to walk up here."

"May I then offer you coffee, to restore your vitality? Or did you bring your own athlete's-foot lotion?"

"I gave that to my company commanders," Stecker said.

General Harris handed him a canteen cup.

"That's the good news," he said.

"Thank you, Sir," Stecker said. "What's the bad?"

"You're about to go report to General Vandergrift," Harris said.

"Why me?"

"You're junior to these three," Harris said.

"I couldn't plead old age?" Stecker asked.

"No," Harris said simply.

"Aye, aye, Sir," Stecker said. "Sir, before I go, I want to put in one of my officers for a Silver Star. I'd like to be able to tell General Vandergrift that you approve."

"Who?"

"Captain Sutton, Sir."

"What did he do?"

"We were having a hell of a time getting pockets of Nips out of their caves," Lieutenant Colonel Griffith answered for him. "We couldn't shoot them out, and when we threw grenades and explosives in, they just threw it right back out. Sutton—I saw this, and agree with Jack that he should be decorated—Sutton tied explosives to a piece of timber—"

"Where'd he get the timber?" Harris asked curiously.

"From the blown-up buildings on the beach," Griffith went on. "As I was saying, he tied explosives to a plank, a board, and then under covering fire ran to the mouth of the cave—*caves;* I saw him do it half a dozen times—and put it inside."

"Why didn't the Japs just throw it back out?" Harris asked. "Am I missing something?"

"He hung on to the board, General," Griffith said. "Wedged it against the inside of the cave until it blew."

"Oh," Harris said.

"If any of the Japs had figured out what was going on, they'd have come a little further toward the mouth of the cave and shot him. He was really exposed, doing what he was doing, and he saved a lot of lives."

"OK," Harris said. "You can tell the General that I approve of the award of the Silver Star to your Captain Sutton, Jack."

"Thank you, Sir."

"Now that that's decided," Red Mike Edson said, laughing, "I will tell you something else Captain Sutton did."

"Something funny?" Harris said, as he poured more bore cleaner in their canteen cups.

"He got carried away. He found some gasoline somewhere, and added a can of that to the explosives."

"That didn't work?"

"It worked. It blew his clothes off and damn near fried him."

"Was he hurt?" Harris asked.

"No, not seriously. But he was down to his skivvy shorts, and they were singed, and there's not a hair on his body."

There were chuckles all around.

"And speaking of people who really exposed themselves," Edson said, "I heard of an officer—and I think Sam saw this, too—who stood out in the open, really exposed, with a Mickey Mouse rifle he got somewhere, and put two rounds into the head of a Jap sniper at a hundred, maybe a hundred and fifty yards. How about a medal for him?"

"No," Jack Stecker said firmly. "Absolutely not."

"The motorcycle kid here?" General Harris asked.

"Sir, I did what any Marine private is supposed to do. Engage the enemy with accurate rifle fire. That's all. Nobody should get a medal for doing his duty."

"I'm not sure I can disagree with that," Harris said, after a moment. "And what the hell, Red, Jack's already got enough medals."

"He sure inspired a lot of kids out there," Edson said.

"I'm sure he did, but that's something else we have to expect from a Marine officer," Harris said, his tone of voice making it clear that he did not wish to entertain any further discussion of the matter.

"Before Jack goes over there, I want from each of you, starting with Jack as the junior commander, a one-word description of the Japanese we just fought."

"What for?"

"I want it, and I want Jack to give it to General Vandergrift, something we're thinking before the adrenaline goes away. Jack?"

" 'Courageous.' Maybe 'tenacious.' "

"One word."

"Then 'courageous,' " Stecker said.

General Harris wrote that down, then said, "Williams?"

"I'll agree with 'tenacious,' " Major Williams said after a moment's thought.

"Griffith?"

"Fanatical," Lieutenant Colonel Griffith said.

"Red?"

"I was going to say 'fanatical,' " Edson said.

"Say something else, anything but 'zealous,' " Harris said.

"OK. How about 'suicidal'?" Edson said.

"If that's what you think, fine," Harris said, as he wrote it down.

"Just out of idle curiosity, why couldn't I have said 'zealous'?"

"Because that's my word," Harris said.

" 'Zealous'?" Edson asked incredulously. "As in 'He was zealous in his pursuit of the busty virgin'?"

"The word comes from *zealot,*" Harris explained. "They were a band of Jews in biblical times who jumped off a mountain rather than surrender—after a hell of a fight—to the Romans."

"I wonder how well versed General Vandergrift is in biblical lore?" Edson replied dryly.

"They're not really small, bucktoothed people needing thick glasses, that we can whip with one hand tied behind us, are they?" Major Stecker asked softly.

"It doesn't look that way, does it, Jack?" Harris replied, then added, "But so far things seem to be going pretty well on Guadalcanal."

"I've been on the radio to the 5th Marines," Stecker said. "That's not the case. So far, all we have is a beach. We're about to lose the equipment that's still aboard the transports, including rations and ammunition; and we're going to lose the Marines that are there, too. The Japanese have not yet counterattacked. They will, and I think they will in force. If not today or tomorrow, then soon. They want that airfield as much as we do, maybe more. And they're in a much better position to reinforce than we are. That's going to be a long and bloody fight, and I wouldn't give odds who's ultimately going to win it."

"Jesus Christ, Jack," Griffith protested. "When I was in England I heard the Germans shoot their officers out of hand for talking like that. They call it 'defeatism.' You're a goddamned Marine. I don't like hearing something like that from a Marine."

"That's enough, Sam!" General Harris flared. "I think Jack put the situation very succinctly." He raised his voice, "Sergeant Major!"

When the Sergeant Major appeared at the door, General Harris said, "Find some wheels to drive Major Stecker to the beach. I don't want him having an accident on his motorcycle between here and there."

(SEVEN)

Eyes Only—The Secretary of the Navy

DUPLICATION FORBIDDEN
ORIGINAL TO BE DESTROYED AFTER ENCRYPTION AND TRANSMITTAL TO SECNAVY

Aboard USS McCawley
Off Guadalcanal
1430 Hours 9 August 1942

Dear Frank:
This is written rather in haste; and it will be brief because I know of the volume of radio traffic that's being sent, most of it unnecessarily.

As far as I am concerned, the battle of Guadalcanal began on 31 July, when the first Army Air Corps B-17 raid was conducted. They have bombed steadily for a week. I mention this because I suspect the Navy might forget the bombing in their reports. They were MacA.'s B-17s, and he supplied them willingly. That might be forgotten, too.

The same day, 31 July, the Amphibious Force left Koro in the Fijis, after the rehearsal. On 2 August, the long-awaited and desperately needed Marine Observation Squadron (VMO-251, sixteen F4F3 photo-recon versions of the Wildcat) landed on the new airbase at Espiritu Santo. Without the required wing tanks. They are essentially useless until they get wing tanks. A head should roll over that one.

The day before yesterday, Friday, 7 Aug., the invasion began. The Amphibious Force was off Savo Island on schedule at 0200.

The 1st Marine Raider Bn under Lt. Col. Red Mike Edson landed on Tulagi and have done well.

The 1st Parachute Bn (fighting as infantrymen) landed on Gavutu, a tiny island two miles away. So far they have been decimated and will almost certainly suffer worse losses than this before it's over for them.

The 1st and 3rd Bns, 5th Marines, landed on the northern coast of Guadalcanal, west of Lunga Point, to not very much initial resistance. They were attacked at half past eleven by Japanese bombers from Rabaul, twenty-five to thirty twin-engine ones.

I can't really tell you what happened the first afternoon and through the first night, except to say the Marines were on the beach and more were landing.

Just before eleven in the morning yesterday (8 Aug.), we were alerted (by the Coastwatcher on Buka, where Banning sent the radio) to a 45-bomber force launched from Kavieng, New Ireland (across the channel from Rabaul). They arrived just before noon and caused some damage. Our carriers of course sent fighters aloft to attack them, and some of our fighters were shot down.

At six o'clock last night, Admiral Fletcher radioed Ghormley that he had lost 21 of 99 planes, was low on fuel, and wants to leave.

I am so angry I don't dare write what I would like to write. Let me say that in my humble opinion the Admiral's estimates of his losses are overgenerous, and his estimates of his fuel supply rather miserly.

Ghormley, not knowing of this departure from the facts, gave him the necessary permission. General Vandergrift came aboard the McCawley a little before midnight last night and was informed by Admiral Fletcher that the Navy is turning chicken and pulling out.

This is before—I want you to understand, in case this becomes a bit obfuscated in the official Navy reports—before we took such a whipping this morning at Savo Island. As I understand it, we lost two U.S. cruisers (Vincennes and Quincy) within an hour, and the Australian cruiser Canberra was set on fire. The Astoria was sunk about two hours ago, just after noon.

In thirty minutes, most of the invasion fleet is pulling out. Ten transports, four destroyers, and a cruiser are going to run first, and what's left will be gone by 1830.

The ships are taking with them rations, food, ammunition, and Marines desperately needed on the beach at Guadalcanal. There is no telling what the Marines will use to fight with. And there's not even a promise from Fletcher about a date when he will feel safe to resupply the Marines. If the decision to return is left up to Admiral Fletcher, I suppose that we can expect resupply by sometime in 1945 or 1950.

I say "we" because I find it impossible to sail off into the sunset on a Navy ship, leaving Marines stranded on the beach.

I remember what I said to you about the admirals when we first met. I was right, Frank.

Best Personal Regards,

Fleming Pickering, Captain, USNR

(EIGHT)
Headquarters, 1st
U.S. Marine Division
Guadalcanal, Solomon Islands
1705 Hours 9 August 1942

"I don't believe I know you, Colonel, do I?" Major General A. M. Vandergrift, Commanding, said to the tall man in Marine utilities with silver eagles pinned to his collar. The Colonel was sitting on a sandbag in the command post.

"No, Sir," the man said, rising to his feet and coming to attention. "I don't have the privilege. And it's 'Captain,' Sir. I borrowed the utilities."

"Are you waiting to see me, Captain?"

"I'd hoped to, Sir. I'd hoped to make myself useful somehow."

"You have about fifteen minutes to get to the beach in time to board your ship before they pull out, Captain."

"With your permission, Sir, I'm staying."

"We don't really need the services of a Naval captain right now, Captain, but I appreciate the thought."

"How about those of a Marine corporal, Sir?"

"What?"

"Once a Marine, always a Marine, Sir. I served in France."

"Oh, now I know who you are. You're Jack NMI Stecker's friend, right? Pickleberry? Something like that. Frank Knox's spy?"

"Pickering, Sir," he corrected.

"Isn't Admiral Fletcher going to wonder why you're not on the *McCawley?"*

"Fuck Admiral Fletcher, General."

Vandergrift flashed him an icy look.

"My hearing goes out from to time, Captain," he said. "I didn't hear that. But I rather liked the sound of it." He raised his voice. "Sergeant Major!"

That luminary appeared at just about the same moment that Major Jack NMI Stecker came into the command post.

"Get Captain Pickering some sort of a weapon," Vandergrift said. "And then take him down to Colonel Goettge."

"Get him an '03, Sergeant Major," Major Stecker said.

The Sergeant Major, who had been told that a Navy captain was outside waiting to see General Vandergrift, looked at this senior Naval personage and then back at Major Stecker, whom he knew and admired, and asked, dubiously, "A *rifle,* Sir?"

"It's all right, Sergeant Major. Captain Pickering is a Marine; he knows what a rifle is for," Major Stecker said.

"You heard the Major, Sergeant Major," General Vandergrift said. "Get him a Springfield."

"Aye, aye, Sir."